BIRDS OF PREY

Also by Wilbur Smith

THE COURTNEYS
When the Lion Feeds
The Sound of Thunder
A Sparrow Falls

THE COURTNEYS OF AFRICA
The Burning Shore
Power of the Sword
Rage
A Time to Die
Golden Fox

THE BALLANTYNE NOVELS
A Falcon Flies
Men of Men
The Angels Weep
The Leopard Hunts in Darkness

also
The Dark of the Sun
Shout at the Devil
Gold Mine
The Diamond Hunters
The Sunbird
Eagle in the Sky
The Eye of the Tiger
Cry Wolf
Hungry as the Sea
Wild Justice
Elephant Song
River God
The Seventh Scroll

WILBUR SMITH

BIRDS OF PREY

MACMILLAN

First published 1997 by Macmillan

an imprint of Macmillan Publishers Ltd
25 Eccleston Place, London SW1W 9NF
and Basingstoke

Associated companies throughout the world

ISBN 0 333 65330 0 (Hardback)
ISBN 0 333 711637 (Trade Paperback)

19 18 17 16 15 14 13 12 11 10

A CIP catalogue record for this book is available from the British Library

Typeset by CentraCet, Cambridge
Printed by Mackays of Chatham plc, Chatham, Kent

This book is for Danielle Antoinette.
For thirty years your love has been my shield;
your strength and courage have been my sword.

Author's Note

Although this story is set in the mid-seventeenth century, the galleons and caravels in which my characters find themselves are more usually associated with the sixteenth century. Seventeenth-century ships often bore a strong resemblance to those of the sixteenth century, but as their names may be unfamiliar to the general reader, I have used the better-known, if anachronistic, terms to convey an accessible impression of their appearance. Also, for the sake of clarity, I have simplified terminology in respect of firearms and, as it exists as such in common idiom, I have occasionally used the word 'cannon' as a generic.

The boy clutched at the rim of the canvas bucket in which he crouched sixty feet above the deck as the ship went about. The mast canted over sharply as she thrust her head through the wind. The ship was a caravel named the *Lady Edwina*, after the mother whom the boy could barely remember.

Far below in the pre-dawn darkness he heard the great bronze culverins slat against their blocks and come up with a thump against their straining tackle. The hull throbbed and resonated to a different impulse as she swung round and went plunging away back into the west. With the south-east wind now astern she was transformed, lighter and more limber, even with sails reefed and with three feet of water in her bilges.

It was all so familiar to Hal Courtney. He had greeted the last five and sixty dawns from the masthead in this manner. His young eyes, the keenest in the ship, had been posted there to catch the first gleam of distant sail in the rose of the new day.

Even the cold was familiar. He pulled the thick woollen Monmouth cap down over his ears. The wind sliced through his leather jerkin but he was inured to such mild discomfort. He gave it no heed and strained his eyes out into the darkness. 'Today the Dutchmen will come,' he said aloud, and felt the excitement and dread throb beneath his ribs.

High above him the splendour of the stars began to pale and fade, and the firmament was filled with the pearly promise of new day. Now, far below him, he could make out the figures on the deck. He could recognize Ned Tyler, the helmsman, bowed over the whipstaff, holding the ship true; and his own father stooping over the binnacle to read the new course, the lantern lighting his lean dark features and his long locks tangling and whipping in the wind.

With a start of guilt Hal looked out into the darkness; he should not be mooning down at the deck in these vital minutes when, at any moment, the enemy might loom close at hand out of the night.

By now it was light enough to make out the surface of the sea rushing by the hull. It had the hard iridescent shine of new-cut coal. By now he knew this southern sea so well; this broad highway of the ocean that flowed eternally down the eastern coast of Africa, blue and warm and swarming with life. Under his father's tutelage he had studied it so that he knew the colour, the taste and run of it, each eddy and surge.

One day he also would glory in the title of Nautonnier Knight of the Temple of the Order of St George and the Holy Grail. He would be, as his father was, a Navigator of the Order. His father was as determined as Hal himself to bring that about, and, at seventeen years of age, his goal was no longer merely a dream.

This current was the highway upon which the Dutchmen must sail to make their westings and their landfall on the mysterious coast that still lay veiled out there in the night. This was the gateway through which all must pass who sought to round that wild cape that divided the Ocean of the Indies from the Southern Atlantic.

This was why Sir Francis Courtney, Hal's father, the Navigator, had chosen this position, at 34 degrees 25 minutes south latitude, in which to wait for them. Already they had waited sixty-five tedious days, beating monotonously back and forth, but today the Dutchmen might come, and Hal stared out into the gathering day with parted lips and straining green eyes.

A cable's length off the starboard bow he saw the flash of wings high enough in the sky to catch the first rays of the sun, a long flight of gannets coming out from the land, snowy chests and heads of black and yellow. He watched the leading bird dip and turn, breaking the pattern, and twist its head to peer down into the dark waters. He saw the disturbance below it, the shimmer of scales and the seething of the surface as a shoal came up to the light. He watched the bird fold its wings and plunge downwards, and each bird that followed began its dive at the same point in the air, to strike the dark water in a burst of lacy foam.

Soon the surface was thrashed white by the diving birds and the struggling silver anchovies on which they gorged. Hal turned away his gaze and swept the opening horizon.

His heart tripped as he caught the gleam of a sail, a tall ship square-rigged, only a league to the eastward. He had filled his lungs and opened his mouth to hail the quarterdeck before he recognized her. It was the *Gull of Moray*, a frigate, not a Dutch East Indiaman. She was far out of position, which had tricked Hal.

The *Gull of Moray* was the other principal vessel in the blockading squadron. The Buzzard, her captain, should be lying out of sight below the eastern horizon. Hal leaned out over the edge of the canvas crow's nest and looked down at the deck. His father, fists on his hips, was staring up at him.

Hal called down the sighting to the quarterdeck, 'The *Gull* hull up to windward!' and his father swung away to gaze out to the east. Sir Francis picked out the shape of the Buzzard's ship, black against the darkling sky, and raised the slender brass tube of the telescope to his eye. Hal could sense anger in the set of his shoulders and the way in which he slammed the instrument shut and tossed his mane of black hair. Before this day was out words would be exchanged between the two commanders. Hal grinned to himself. With his iron will and spiked tongue, his fists and blade, Sir Francis struck terror into those upon whom he turned them – even his brother Knights of the Order held him in awe. Hal was thankful that this day his father's temper would be directed elsewhere than at him.

He looked beyond the *Gull of Moray*, sweeping the horizon as it extended swiftly with the coming of day. Hal needed no telescope to aid his bright young eyes – besides, only one of these costly instruments was aboard. He made out the others' sails then exactly where they should be, tiny pale flecks against the dark sea. The two pinnaces maintaining their formation, beads in the necklace, were spread out fifteen leagues on each side of the *Lady Edwina*, part of the net his father had cast wide to ensnare the Dutchmen.

The pinnaces were open vessels, with a dozen heavily armed men crowded into each. When not needed they could be broken down and stowed in the *Lady Edwina*'s hold. Sir Francis changed their crews regularly, for neither the tough West Country men nor the Welsh nor the even hardier ex-slaves that made up most of his crew could endure the conditions aboard those little ships for long and still be fit for a fight at the end of it.

At last the full steely light of day struck as the sun rose from the eastern ocean. Hal gazed down the fiery path it threw across the waters. He felt his spirits slide as he found the ocean empty of a strange sail. Just as on the sixty-five preceding dawns, there was no Dutchman in sight.

Then he looked northwards to the land mass that crouched like a great rock sphinx, dark and inscrutable, upon the horizon. This was the Agulhas Cape, the southernmost tip of the African continent.

'Africa!' The sound of that mysterious name on his own lips raised goose pimples along his arms and made the thick dark hair prickle on the back of his neck.

'Africa!' The uncharted land of dragons and other dreadful creatures, who ate the flesh of men, and of dark-skinned savages who also ate men's flesh and wore their bones as decoration.

'Africa!' The land of gold and ivory and slaves and other treasures, all waiting for a man bold enough to seek them out, and, perhaps, to perish in the endeavour. Hal felt daunted yet fascinated by the sound and promise of that name, its menace and challenge.

Long hours he had pored over the charts in his father's cabin when he should have been learning by rote the tables of celestial passages, or declining his Latin verbs. He had studied the great interior spaces, filled with drawings of elephants and lions and monsters, traced the outlines of the Mountains of the Moon, and of lakes and mighty rivers confidently emblazoned with names such as 'Khoikhoi', and 'Camdeboo', 'Sofala' and 'the Kingdom of Prester John'. But Hal knew from his father that no civilized man had ever travelled into that awesome interior and wondered, as he had so many times before, what it would be like to be the first to venture there. Prester John particularly intrigued him. This legendary ruler of a vast and powerful Christian empire in the depths of the African continent had existed in the European mythology for hundreds of years. Was he one man, or a line of emperors? Hal wondered.

Hal's reverie was interrupted by shouted orders from the quarterdeck, faint on the wind, and the feel of the ship as she changed course. Looking down, he saw that his father intended to intercept the *Gull of Moray*. Under top sails only, and with all else reefed, the two ships were now converging, both running westward towards the Cape of Good Hope and the Atlantic. They moved sluggishly – they had been too long in these warm southern waters, and their timbers were infested with the Toredo worm. No vessel could survive long out here. The dreaded shipworms grew as thick as a man's finger and as long as his arm, and they bored so close to each other through the planks as to honeycomb them. Even from his seat at the masthead Hal could hear the pumps labouring in both vessels to lower the bilges. The sound never ceased: it was like the beating of a heart that kept the ship afloat. It was yet another reason why they must seek out the Dutchmen: they needed to change ships. The *Lady Edwina* was being eaten away beneath their feet.

As the two ships came within hailing distance the crews swarmed into the rigging and lined the bulwarks to shout ribald banter across the water.

The numbers of men packed into each vessel never failed to amaze Hal when he saw them in a mass like this. The *Lady Edwina* was a ship of 170 tons burden, with an overall length of little more than 70 feet, but she carried a crew of a hundred and thirty men if you included those now manning the two pinnaces. The *Gull* was not much larger, but with half as many men again aboard.

Every one of those fighting men would be needed if they were to overwhelm one of the huge Dutch East India galleons. Sir Francis had gathered intelligence from all the corners of the southern ocean from other Knights of the Order, and knew that at least five of these great ships were still at sea. So far this season twenty-one of the Company's galleons had made the passage and had called at the tiny victualling station below the towering Tafelberg, as the Dutch called it, or Table Mountain at the foot of the southern continent before turning northwards and voyaging up the Atlantic towards Amsterdam.

Those five tardy ships, still straggling across the Ocean of the Indies, must round the Cape before the south-easterly trades fell away and the wind turned foul into the north-west. That would be soon.

When the *Gull of Moray* was not cruising in the *guerre de course*, which was a euphemism for privateering, Angus Cochran, Earl of Cumbrae, rounded out his purse by trading for slaves in the markets of Zanzibar. Once they had been shackled to the ringbolts in the deck of the long narrow slave hold, they could not be released until the ship docked at the end of her voyage in the ports of the Orient. This meant that even those poor creatures who succumbed during the dreadful tropical passage of the Ocean of the Indies must lie rotting with the living in the confined spaces of the 'tween decks. The effluvium of decaying corpses, mingled with the waste odour of the living, gave the slave ships a distinctive stench that identified them for many leagues down wind. No amount of scouring with even the strongest lyes could ever rid a slaver of her characteristic smell.

As the *Gull* crossed upwind, there were howls of exaggerated disgust from the crew of the *Lady Edwina*. 'By God, she stinks like a dung-heap.'

'Did you not wipe your backsides, you poxy vermin? We can smell you from here!' one yelled across at the pretty little frigate. The language bawled back from the *Gull* made Hal grin. Of course, the human bowels held no mysteries for him, but he did not understand much of the rest of it, for he had never seen those parts of a woman to which the seamen in both ships referred in such graphic detail, nor knew of the uses to which they could be put, but it excited his imagination to hear them so described. His amusement was enhanced when he imagined his father's fury at hearing it.

Sir Francis was a devout man who believed that the fortunes of war could be influenced by the god-fearing behaviour of every man aboard.

He forbade gambling, blasphemy and the drinking of strong spirits. He led prayers twice a day and exhorted his seamen to gentle and dignified behaviour when they put into port – although Hal knew that this advice was seldom followed. Now Sir Francis frowned darkly as he listened to his men exchange insults with those of the Buzzard but, as he could not have half the ship's company flogged to signal his disapproval, he held his tongue until he was in easy hail of the frigate.

In the meantime he sent his servant to his cabin to fetch his cloak. What he had to say to the Buzzard was official and he should be in regalia. When the man returned, Sir Francis slipped the magnificent velvet cloak over his shoulders before he lifted his speaking trumpet to his lips. 'Good morrow, my lord!'

The Buzzard came to his rail and lifted one hand in salute. Above his plaid he wore half-armour, which gleamed in the fresh morning light, but his head was bare, his red hair and beard bushed together like a haystack, the curls dancing on the wind as though his head was on fire. 'Jesus love you, Franky!' he bellowed back, his great voice easily transcending the wind.

'Your station is on the eastern flank!' The wind and his anger made Sir Francis short. 'Why have you deserted it?'

The Buzzard spread his hands in an expressive gesture of apology. 'I have little water and am completely out of patience. Sixty-five days are enough for me and my brave fellows. There are slaves and gold for the taking along the Sofala coast.' His accent was like a Scottish gale.

'Your commission does not allow you to attack Portuguese shipping.'

'Dutch, Portuguese or Spanish,' Cumbrae shouted back. 'Their gold shines as prettily. You know well that there is no peace beyond the Line.'

'You are well named the Buzzard,' Sir Francis roared in frustration, 'for you have the same appetite as that carrion bird!' Yet what Cumbrae had said was true. There was no peace beyond the Line.

A century and a half ago, by Papal Bull *Inter Caetera* of 25 September 1493, the Line had been drawn down the mid-Atlantic, north to south, by Pope Alexander VI to divide the world between Portugal and Spain. What hope was there that the excluded Christian nations, in their envy and resentment, would honour this declaration? Spontaneously, another doctrine was born: 'No peace beyond the Line!' It became the watchword of the privateer and the corsair. And its meaning extended in their minds to encompass all the unexplored regions of the oceans.

Within the waters of the northern continent, acts of piracy, rapine and murder – whose perpetrator previously would have been hunted down by the combined navies of Christian Europe and hanged from his own yard-arm – were condoned and even applauded when committed beyond the Line. Every embattled monarch signed Letters of Marque that, at a stroke, converted his merchantmen into privateers, ships of war, and sent them out marauding on the newly discovered oceans of the expanding globe.

Sir Francis Courtney's own letter had been signed by Edward Hyde, Earl of Clarendon, the Lord Chancellor of England, in the name of His Majesty King Charles II. It sanctioned him to hunt down the ships of the Dutch Republic, with which England was at war.

'Once you desert your station, you forfeit your rights to claim a share of any prize!' Sir Francis called across the narrow strip of water between the ships, but the Buzzard turned away to issue orders to his helmsman.

He shouted to his piper, who stood at the ready, 'Give Sir Francis a tune to remember us by!' The stirring strains of 'Farewell to the Isles' carried across the water to the *Lady Edwina*, as the Buzzard's topmast men clambered like monkeys high into the rigging, and loosed the reefs. The *Gull*'s top-hamper billowed out. The main sail filled with a boom like the discharge of cannon, she heeled eagerly to the south-easter and pressed her shoulder into the next blue swell, bursting it asunder.

As the Buzzard pulled away rapidly he came back to the stern rail, and his voice lifted above the skirling of the pipes and the whimper of the wind. 'May the peace of our Lord Jesus Christ shield you, my revered brother Knight.' But on the Buzzard's lips it sounded like blasphemy.

With his cloak, which was quartered by the crimson *croix patté* of the Order, billowing and flapping from his wide shoulders, Sir Francis watched him go.

Slowly the ironic cheering and heavy banter of the men died away. A sombre new mood began to infect the ship as the company realized that their forces, puny before, had been more than halved in a single stroke. They had been left alone to meet the Dutchmen in whatever force they might appear. The seamen that crowded the *Lady Edwina*'s deck and rigging were silent now, unable to meet each other's eyes.

Then Sir Francis threw back his head and laughed. 'All the more for us to share!' he cried, and they laughed with him and cheered as he made his way to his cabin below the poop deck.

For another hour Hal stayed at the masthead. He wondered how long the men's buoyant mood could last, for they were down to a mug of water twice a day. Although the land and its sweet rivers lay less than half a day's sailing away, Sir Francis had not dared detach even one of the pinnaces to fill the casks. The Dutchmen might come at any hour, and when they did he would need every man.

At last a man came aloft to relieve Hal at the lookout. 'What is there to see, lad?' he asked, as he slipped into the canvas crow's nest beside Hal.

'Precious little,' Hal admitted, and pointed out the tiny sails of the two pinnaces on the distant horizon. 'Neither carry any signals,' Hal told him. 'Watch for the red flag – it'll mean they have the chase in sight.'

The sailor grunted. 'You'll be teaching me to fart next.' But he smiled at Hal in avuncular fashion – the boy was the ship's favourite.

Hal grinned back at him. 'God's truth, but you need no teaching, Master Simon. I've heard you at the bucket in the heads. I'd rather face a Dutch broadside. You nigh crack every timber in the hull.'

Simon let out an explosive guffaw, and punched Hal's shoulder. 'Down with you, lad, before I teach you to fly like an albatross.'

Hal began to scramble down the shrouds. At first he moved stiffly, his muscles cramped and chilled after the long vigil, but he soon warmed up and swung down lithely.

Some of the men on the deck paused at their labours on the pumps, or with palm and needle as they repaired wind-ripped canvas, and watched him. He was as robust and broad-shouldered as a lad three years older, and long in limb – he already stood as tall as his father. Yet he still retained the fresh smooth skin, the unlined face and sunny expression of boyhood. His hair, tied with a thong behind his head, spilled from under his cap and glistened blue-black in the early sunlight. At this age his beauty was still almost feminine, and after more than four months at sea – six since they had laid eyes on a woman – some, whose fancy lay in that direction, watched him lasciviously.

Hal reached the main yard and left the security of the mast. He ran out along it, balancing with the ease of an acrobat forty feet above the curling rush of the bow wave and the planks of the main deck. Now every eye was on him: it was a feat that few aboard would care to emulate.

'For that you have to be young and stupid,' Ned Tyler growled, but shook his head fondly as he leaned against the whipstaff and stared up. 'Best the little fool does not let his father catch him playing that trick.'

Hal reached the end of the yard and without pause swung out onto the brace and slid down it until he was ten feet above the deck. From there he dropped to land lightly on his hard bare feet, flexing his knees to absorb the impact on the scrubbed white planks.

He bounced up, turned towards the stern – and froze at the sound of an inhuman cry. It was a primordial bellow, the menacing challenge of some great predatory animal.

Hal remained pinned to the spot for only an instant then instinctively spun away as a tall figure charged down upon him. He heard the fluting sound in the air before he saw the blade and ducked under it. The silver steel flashed over his head and his attacker roared again, a screech of fury.

Hal had a glimpse of his adversary's face, black and glistening, a cave of a mouth lined with huge square white teeth, the tongue as pink and curled as a leopard's as he screamed.

Hal danced and swayed as the silver blade came arcing back. He felt a tug at the sleeve of his jerkin as the sword point split the leather, and fell back.

'Ned, a blade!' he yelled wildly at the helmsman behind him, never taking his eyes off those of his assailant. The pupils were black and bright as obsidian, the iris opaque with fury, the whites engorged with blood.

Hal leaped aside at the next wild charge, and felt on his cheek the draught of the blow. Behind him he heard the scrape of a cutlass drawn from the boatswain's scabbard, and the weapon slide across the deck towards him. He stooped smoothly and gathered it up, the hilt coming naturally to his hand, as he went into the guard stance and aimed the point at the eyes of his attacker.

In the face of Hal's menacing blade, the tall man checked his next rush and when, with his left hand, Hal drew from his belt his ten-inch dirk and offered that point also, the mad light in his eyes turned cold and appraising. They circled each other on the open deck below the mainmast, their blades weaving, touching and tapping lightly, as each sought an opening.

The seamen on the deck left their tasks – even those on the handles of the pumps – and came running to form a ring around the swordsmen as though they watched a cockfight, their faces alight with the prospect of seeing blood spurt. They growled and hooted at each thrust and parry, and urged on their favourites.

'Hack out his big black balls, young Hal!'

'Pluck the cockerel's saucy tail feathers for him, Aboli.'

Aboli stood five inches taller than Hal, and there was no fat on his lean, supple frame. He was from the eastern coast of Africa, of a warrior tribe highly prized by the slavers. Every hair had been carefully plucked from his pate, which gleamed like polished black marble, and his cheeks were adorned with ritual tattoos, whorls of raised cicatrices that gave him a terrifying appearance. He moved with a peculiar grace, on those long muscular legs, swaying from the waist like some huge black cobra. He wore only a petticoat of tattered canvas, and his chest was bare. Each muscle in his torso and upper arms seemed to have a life of its own, serpents slithering and coiling beneath the oiled skin.

He lunged suddenly, and with a desperate effort Hal turned the blade, but almost in the same instant Aboli reversed the blow, aiming once more at his head. There was such power in his stroke that Hal knew he could not block it with cutlass alone. He threw up both blades, crossing them, and trapped the Negro's high above his head. Steel rang and thrilled on steel, and the crowd howled at the skill and grace of the parry.

But at the fury of the attack Hal gave a pace, and another then another as Aboli pressed him again and again, giving him no respite, using his greater height and superior strength to counter the boy's natural ability.

Hal's face mirrored his desperation. He gave more readily now and his movements were uncoordinated: he was tired and fear dulled his responses. The cruel watchers turned against him, yelling for blood, urging on his implacable opponent.

'Mark his pretty face, Aboli!'

'Give us a look at his guts!'

Sweat greased Hal's cheeks and his expression crumpled as Aboli drove him back against the mast. He seemed much younger suddenly, and on the point of tears, his lips quivering with terror and exhaustion. He was no longer counter-attacking. Now it was all defence. He was fighting for his life.

Relentlessly Aboli launched a fresh attack, swinging at Hal's body, then changing the angle to cut at his legs. Hal was near the limit of his strength, only just managing to fend off each blow.

Then Aboli changed his attack once more: he forced Hal to overreach by feinting low to the left hip, then shifted his weight and lunged with a long right arm. The shining blade flew straight through Hal's guard and the watchers roared as at last they had the blood they craved.

Hal reeled sideways off the mast and stood panting in the sunlight, blinded by his own sweat. Blood dripped slowly onto his jerkin – but from a nick only, made with a surgeon's skill.

'Another scar for you each time you fight like a woman!' Aboli scolded him.

With an expression of exhausted disbelief, Hal raised his left hand, which still held the dirk, and with the back of his fist wiped the blood from his chin. The tip of his earlobe was neatly split and the quantity of blood exaggerated the severity of the wound.

The spectators bellowed with derision and mirth.

'By Satan's teeth!' one of the coxswains laughed. 'The pretty boy has more blood than he has guts!'

At the gibe, a swift transformation came over Hal. He lowered his dirk and extended the point in the guard position, ignoring the blood that still dripped from his chin. His face was blank, like that of a statue, and his lips set and blanched frosty white. From his throat issued a low growl, and he launched himself at the Negro.

He exploded across the deck with such speed that Aboli was taken by surprise and driven back. When they locked blades he felt the new power in the boy's arm, and his eyes narrowed. Then Hal was upon him like a wounded wild-cat bursting from a trap.

Pain and rage put wings on his feet. His eyes were pitiless and his clenched jaws tightened the muscles of his face into a mask that retained no trace of boyishness. Yet his fury had not robbed him of reason and cunning. All the skill that the lad had accumulated, over hundreds of hours and days upon the practice deck, suddenly coalesced.

The watchers bayed as this miracle took place before their eyes. It seemed that, in that instant, the boy had become a man, had grown in stature so that he stood chin to chin and eye to eye with his dark adversary.

It cannot last, Aboli told himself, as he met the attack. His strength cannot hold out. But this was a new man he confronted, and he had not yet recognized him.

Suddenly he found himself giving ground – He will tire soon – but the twin blades that danced before his eyes seemed dazzling and ethereal, like the dread spirits of the dark forests that had once been his home.

He looked into the pale face and burning eyes and did not know them. He felt a superstitious awe assail him, which slowed his right arm. This was a demon, with a demon's unnatural strength. He knew that he was in danger of his life.

The next coup sped at his chest, glancing through his guard like a sunbeam. He twisted aside his upper body, but the thrust raked under his raised left arm. He felt no pain but heard the rasp of the razor edge against his ribs, and the warm flood of blood down his flank. And he had ignored the weapon in Hal's left fist and the boy used either hand with equal ease.

At the edge of his vision he saw the shorter, stiffer blade speed towards his heart and threw himself back to avoid it. His heel caught in the tail of the yard brace, coiled on the deck, and he went sprawling. The elbow of his sword arm slammed into the gunwale, numbing it to the fingertips, and the cutlass flew from his fingers.

On his back, Aboli looked up helplessly and saw death above him in those terrifying green eyes. This was not the face of the child who had been his ward and special charge for the last decade, the boy he had cherished and trained and loved over ten long years. This was a man who would kill him. The bright point of the cutlass started down, aimed at his throat, with the full weight of the lithe young body behind it.

'Henry!' A stern, authoritative voice rang across the deck, cutting through the hubbub of the blood-crazed spectators.

Hal started, and stood still with the point against Aboli's throat. A bemused expression spread across his face, like that of an awakening dreamer, and he looked up at his father on the break of the poop.

'Avast that tomfoolery. Get you down to my cabin at once.'

Hal glanced around the deck, at the flushed, excited faces surrounding him. He shook his head in puzzlement, and looked down at the cutlass in his hand. He opened his fingers and let it drop to the planks. His legs turned to water under him and he sank down on top of Aboli and hugged him as a child hugs his father.

'Aboli!' he whispered, in the language of the forests that the black man had taught him and which was a secret no other white man on the ship shared with them. 'I have hurt you sorely. The blood! By my life, I could have killed you.'

Aboli chuckled softly and answered in the same language, 'It was past time. At last you have tapped the well of warrior blood. I thought you would never find it. I had to drive you hard to it.'

He sat up and pushed Hal away, but there was a new light in his eyes as he looked at the boy, who was a boy no longer. 'Go now and do your father's bidding!'

Hal stood up shakily and looked again round the circle of faces, seeing an expression in them that he did not recognize: it was respect mingled with more than a little fear.

'What are you gawking at?' bellowed Ned Tyler. 'The play is over. Do you have no work to do? Man those pumps. Those topgallants are luffing. I can find mastheads for all idle hands.' There was the thump of bare feet across the deck as the crew rushed guiltily to their duties.

Hal stooped, picked up the cutlass, and handed it back to the boatswain, hilt first.

'Thank you, Ned. I had need of it.'

'And you put it to good use. I have never seen that heathen bested, except by your father before you.'

Hal tore a handful of rag from the tattered hem of his canvas pantaloons, held it to his ear to staunch the bleeding, and went down to the stern cabin.

Sir Francis looked up from his log-book, his goose quill poised over the page. 'Do not look so smug, puppy,' he grunted at Hal. 'Aboli toyed with you, as he always does. He could have spitted you a dozen times before you turned it with that lucky coup at the end.'

When Sir Francis stood up there was hardly room for them both in the tiny cabin. The bulkheads were lined from deck to deck with books, more were stacked about their feet and leather-bound volumes were crammed into the cubby-hole that served his father as a bunk. Hal wondered where he found place to sleep.

His father addressed him in Latin. When they were alone he insisted on speaking the language of the educated and cultivated man. 'You will die before you ever make a swordsman, unless you find steel in your heart as well as in your hand. Some hulking Dutchman will cleave you to the teeth at your first encounter.' Sir Francis scowled at his son, 'Recite the law of the sword.'

'An eye for his eyes,' Hal mumbled in Latin.

'Speak up, boy!' Sir Francis's hearing had been dulled by the blast of culverins – over the years a thousand broadsides had burst around his head. At the end of an engagement, blood would be seen dripping from the ears of the seamen beside the guns and for days after even the officers on the poop heard heavenly bells ring in their heads.

'An eye for his eyes,' Hal repeated roundly, and his father nodded.

'His eyes are the window to his mind. Learn to read in them his intentions before the act. See there the stroke before it is delivered. What else?'

'The other eye for his feet,' Hal recited.

'Good.' Sir Francis nodded. 'His feet will move before his hand. What else?'

'Keep the point high.'

'The cardinal rule. Never lower the point. Keep it aimed at his eyes.'

Sir Francis led Hal through the catechism, as he had countless times before. At the end, he said, 'Here is one more rule for you. Fight from the first stroke, not just when you are hurt or angry, or you might not survive that first wound.'

He glanced up at the hourglass hanging from the deck above his head. 'There is yet time for your reading before ship's prayers.' He spoke in Latin still. 'Take up your Livy and translate from the top of page twenty-six.'

For an hour Hal read aloud the history of Rome in the original, translating each verse into English as he went. Then, at last, Sir Francis closed his Livy with a snap. 'There is improvement. Now, decline the verb *durare*.'

That his father should choose this one was a mark of his approval. Hal recited it in a breathless rush, slowing when he came to the future indicative. '*Durabo*. I shall endure.'

That word formed the motto of the Courtney coat-of-arms, and Sir Francis smiled frostily as Hal voiced it.

'May the Lord grant you that grace.' He stood up. 'You may go now but do not be late for prayers.'

Rejoicing to be free, Hal fled from the cabin and went bounding up the companionway.

Aboli was squatting in the lee of one of the hulking bronze culverins near the bows. Hal knelt beside him. 'I wounded you.'

Aboli made an eloquent dismissive gesture. 'A chicken scratching in the dust wounds the earth more gravely.'

Hal pulled the tarpaulin cloak off Aboli's shoulders, seized the elbow and lifted the thickly muscled arm high to peer at the deep slash across the ribs. 'None the less, this little chicken gave you a good pecking,' he observed drily, and grinned as Aboli opened his hand and showed him the needle already threaded with sailmaker's yarn. He reached for it, but Aboli checked him.

'Wash the cut, as I taught you.'

'With that long black python of yours you could reach it yourself,' Hal suggested, and Aboli emitted his long, rolling laugh, soft and low as distant thunder.

'We will have to make do with a small white worm.'

Hal stood and loosed the cord that held up his pantaloons. He let them drop to his knees, and with his right hand drew back his foreskin.

'I christen you Aboli, lord of the chickens!' He imitated his own father's preaching tone faithfully, and directed a stream of yellow urine into the open wound.

Although Hal knew how it stung, for Aboli had done the same many times for him, the black features remained impassive. Hal irrigated the wound with the very last drop and then hoisted his breeches. He knew how efficacious this tribal remedy of Aboli's was. The first time it had been used on him he had been repelled by it, but in all the years since then he had never seen a wound so treated mortify.

He took up the needle and twine, and while Aboli held the lips of the wound together with his left hand, Hal laid neat sailmaker's stitches across it, digging the needle point through the elastic skin and pulling his knots up tight. When he was done, he reached for the pot of hot tar that Aboli had ready. He smeared the sewn wound thickly and nodded with satisfaction at his handiwork.

Aboli stood up and lifted his canvas petticoats. 'Now we will see to your ear,' he told Hal, as his own fat penis overflowed his fist by half its length.

Hal recoiled swiftly. 'It is but a little scratch,' he protested, but Aboli seized his pigtail remorselessly and twisted his face upwards.

At the stroke of the bell the company crowded into the waist of the ship, and stood silent and bare-headed in the sunlight – even the black tribesmen, who did not worship exclusively the crucified Lord but other gods also whose abode was the deep dark forests of their homes.

When Sir Francis, great leather-bound Bible in hand, intoned sonorously, 'We pray you, Almighty God, deliver the enemy of Christ into our hands that he shall not triumph . . .' his eyes were the only ones still cast heavenward. Every other eye in the company turned towards the east from where that enemy would come, laden with silver and spices.

Half-way through the long service a line squall came boring up out of the east, wind driving the clouds in a tumbling dark mass over their heads and deluging the decks with silver sheets of rain. But the elements could not conspire to keep Sir Francis from his discourse with the Almighty, so while the crew huddled in their tar-daubed canvas jackets, with hats of the same material tied beneath their chins, and the water streamed off them as off the hides of a pack of beached walrus, Sir Francis missed not a beat of his sermon. 'Lord of the storm and the wind,' he prayed, 'succour us. Lord of the battle-line, be our shield and buckler . . .'

The squall passed over them swiftly and the sun burst forth again, sparkling on the blue swells and steaming on the decks.

Sir Francis clapped his wide-brimmed cavalier hat back on his head, and the sodden white feathers that surmounted it nodded in approval. 'Master Ned, run out the guns.'

It was the proper course to take, Hal realized. The rain squall would have soaked the priming and wet the loaded powder. Rather than the lengthy business of drawing the shot and reloading, his father would give the crews some practice.

'Beat to quarters, if you please.'

The drum-roll echoed through the hull, and the crew ran grinning and joking to their stations. Hal plunged the tip of a slow-match into the charcoal brazier at the foot of the mast. When it was smouldering evenly, he leapt into the shrouds and, carrying the burning match in his teeth, clambered up to his battle station at the masthead.

On the deck he saw four men sway an empty water cask up from the hold and stagger with it to the ship's side. At the order from the poop, they tossed it over and left it bobbing in the ship's wake. Meanwhile the guncrews knocked out the wedges and, heaving at the tackles, ran out the culverins. On either side of the lower deck there were eight, each loaded with a bucketful of powder and a ball. On the upper deck were ranged ten demi-culverins, five on each side, their long barrels crammed with grape.

The *Lady Edwina* was low on iron shot after her two-year-long cruise, and some of the guns were loaded with water-rounded flint marbles hand-picked from the banks of the river mouths where the watering parties had gone ashore. Ponderously she came about, and settled on the new tack, beating back into the wind. The floating cask was still two cables' length ahead but the range narrowed slowly. The gunners strode from cannon to cannon, pushing in the elevation wedges and ordering the training tackles adjusted. This was a specialized task: only five men aboard had the skill to load and lay a gun.

In the crow's nest, Hal swung the long-barrelled falconet on its swivel and aimed down at a length of floating kelp that drifted past on the current. Then with the point of his dirk he scraped the damp, caked powder out of the pan of the weapon, and carefully repacked it with fresh powder from his flask. After ten years of instruction by his father, he was as skilled as Ned Tyler, the ship's master gunner, in the esoteric art. His rightful battle station should have been on the gundeck, and he had pleaded with his father to place him there but had been answered only with the stern retort, 'You will go where I send you.' Now he must sit up here, out of the hurly-burly, while his fierce young heart ached to be a part of it.

Suddenly he was startled by the crash of gunfire from the deck below. A long dense plume of smoke billowed out and the ship heeled slightly at the discharge. A moment later a tall fountain of foam rose dramatically from the surface of the sea fifty yards to the right and twenty beyond the floating cask. At that range it was not bad shooting, but the deck erupted in a chorus of jeers and whistles.

Ned Tyler hurried to the second culverin, and swiftly checked its lay. He gestured for the men on the tackle to train it a point left then stepped forward and held the burning match to the touch hole. A fizzling puff of smoke blew back and then, from the gaping muzzle, came a shower of sparks, half-burned powder and clods of damp, caked muck. The ball rolled down the bronze barrel and fell into the sea less than half-way to the target cask. The crew howled with derision.

The next two weapons misfired. Cursing furiously, Ned ordered the crews to draw the charges with the long iron corkscrews as he hurried on down the line.

'Great expense of powder and bullet!' Hal recited to himself the words of the great Sir Francis Drake – for whom his own father had been christened – spoken after the first day of the epic battle against the Armada of Philip II, King of Spain, led by the Duke of Medina Sidonia. All that long day, under the dun fog of gunsmoke, the two great fleets had loosed their mighty broadsides at each other, but the barrage had sent not a single ship of either fleet to the bottom.

'Fright them with cannon,' Hal's father had instructed him, 'but sweep their decks with the cutlass,' and he voiced his scorn for the rowdy but ineffectual art of naval gunnery. It was impossible to aim a ball from the plunging deck of one ship to a precise point on the hull of another: accuracy was in the hands of the Almighty rather than those of the master gunner.

As if to illustrate the point, after Ned had fired every one of the heavy guns on board six had misfired and the nearest he had come to striking the floating cask was twenty yards. Hal shook his head sadly, reflecting that each of those shots had been carefully laid and aimed. In the heat of a battle, with the range obscured by billowing smoke, the powder and shot stuffed in haste into the muzzles, the barrels heating unevenly and the match applied to pan by excited and terrified gunners, the results could not be even that satisfactory.

At last his father looked up at Hal. 'Masthead!' he roared.

Hal had feared himself forgotten. Now, with a thrill of relief, he blew on the tip of the smouldering slow-match in his hand. It glowed bright and fierce.

From the deck Sir Francis watched him, his expression stern and forbidding. He must never let show the love he bore the boy. He must be hard and critical at all times, driving him on. For the boy's own sake – nay, for his very life – he must force him to learn, to strive, to endure, to run every step of the course ahead of him with all his strength and all his heart. Yet, without making it apparent, he must also help, encourage and assist him. He must shepherd him wisely, cunningly towards his destiny. He had delayed calling upon Hal until this moment, when the cask floated close alongside.

If the boy could shatter it with the small weapon where Ned had failed with the great cannon, then his reputation with the crew would be enhanced. The men were mostly boisterous ruffians, simple illiterates, but one day Hal would be called upon to lead them, or others like them. He had made a giant stride today by besting Aboli before them all. Here was a chance to consolidate that gain. 'Guide his hand, and the flight of the shot, oh God of the battle-line!' Sir Francis prayed silently, and the ship's company craned their necks to watch the lad high above them.

Hal hummed softly to himself as he concentrated on the task, conscious of the eyes upon him. Yet he did not sense the importance of this discharge and was oblivious of his father's prayers. It was a game to him, just another chance to excel. Hal liked to win, and each time he did so he liked it better. The young eagle was beginning to rejoice in the power of his wings.

Gripping the end of the long brass monkey tail, he swivelled the falconet downwards, peering over the yard-long barrel, lining up the notch above the pan with the pip on the muzzle end.

He had learned that it was futile to aim directly at the target. There would be a delay of seconds from when he applied the slow-match, to the crash of the shot, and in the meantime ship and cask would be moving in opposite directions. There was also the moment when the discharged balls were in flight before they struck. He must gauge where the cask would be when the shot reached it and not aim for the spot where it had been when he pressed the match to the pan.

He swung the pip of the foresight smoothly over the target, and touched the glowing end of the match to the pan. He forced himself not to flinch away from the flare of burning powder nor to recoil in anticipation of the explosion but to keep the barrels swinging gently in the line he had chosen.

With a roar that stung his ear-drums the falconet bucked heavily against its swivel, and everything disappeared in a cloud of grey smoke. Desperately he craned his head left and right, trying to see around the smoke, but it was the cheers from the decks below that made his heart leap, reaching him even through his singing ears. When the wind whisked away the smoke, he could see the ribs of the shattered cask swirling and tumbling astern in the ship's wake. He hooted with glee, and waved his cap at the faces on the deck far below.

Aboli was at his place in the bows, coxswain and gun captain of the first watch. He returned Hal's beatific grin and beat his chest with one fist, while with the other he brandished the cutlass over his bald head.

The drum rolled to end the drill and stand down the crew from their battle stations. Before he dropped down the shrouds Hal reloaded the falconet carefully and bound a strip of tar-soaked canvas around the pan to protect it from dew, rain and spray.

As his feet hit the deck he looked to the poop, trying to catch his father's eye and glean his approbation. But Sir Francis was deep in conversation with one of his petty officers. A moment passed before he glanced coldly over his shoulder at Hal. 'What are you gawking at, boy? There are guns to be reloaded.'

As he turned away Hal felt the bite of disappointment, but the rowdy congratulations of the crew, the rough slaps across his back and shoulders as he passed down the gundeck, restored his smile.

When Ned Tyler saw him coming he stepped back from the breech of the culverin he was loading and handed the ramrod to Hal. 'Any oaf can shoot it, but it takes a good man to load it,' he grunted, and stood back critically to watch Hal measure a charge from the leather powder bucket. 'What weight of powder?' he asked, and Hal gave the same reply he had a hundred times before.

'The same weight as that of the round shot.'

The blackpowder comprised coarse granules. There had been a time when, shaken and agitated by the ship's way or some other repetitive movement, the three essential elements, sulphur, charcoal and saltpetre, might separate out and render it useless. Since then the process of 'corning' had evolved, whereby the fine raw powder was treated with urine or alcohol to set it into a cake, which was then crushed in a ball mill to the required size of granules. Yet the process was not perfect and a gunner must always have an eye for the condition of his powder. Damp or age could degrade it. Hal tested the grains between his fingers and tasted a dab. Ned Tyler had taught him to differentiate between good and degenerate powder in this way. Then he poured the contents of the bucket into the muzzle, and followed it with the oakum wadding.

Then he tamped it down with the long wooden-handled ramrod. This was another crucial part of the process: tamped too firmly, the flame could not pass through the charge and a misfire was inevitable, but not tamped firmly enough, and the blackpowder would burn without the power to hurl the heavy projectile clear of the barrel. Correct tamping was an art that could only be learned from prolonged practice, but Ned nodded as he watched Hal at work.

It was much later when Hal scrambled up again into the sunlight. All the culverins were loaded and secured behind their ports and Hal's bare upper body was glistening with sweat from the heat of the cramped gundeck and his labours with the ramrod. As he paused to wipe his streaming face, draw a breath and stretch his back, after crouching so long under the cramped headspace of the lower deck, his father called to him with heavy irony, 'Is the ship's position of no interest to you, Master Henry?'

With a start Hal glanced up at the sun. It was high in the heavens above them: the morning had sped away. He raced to the companionway, dropped down the ladder, burst into his father's cabin, and snatched the heavy backstaff from its case on the bulkhead. Then he turned and ran back to the poop deck.

'Pray God, I'm not too late,' he whispered to himself, and glanced up at the position of the sun. It was over the starboard yard-arm. He positioned himself with his back to it and in such a way that the shadow cast by the main sail would not screen him, yet so that he had a clear view of the horizon to the south.

Now he concentrated all his attention on the quadrant of the backstaff. He had to keep the heavy instrument steady against the ship's motion. Then he must read the angle that the sun's rays over his shoulder subtended onto the quadrant, which gave him the sun's inclination to the horizon. It was a juggling act that required strength and dexterity.

At last he could observe noon passage, and read the sun's angle with the horizon at the precise moment it reached its zenith. He lowered the backstaff with aching arms and shoulders, and hastily scribbled the reading on the traverse slate.

Then he ran down the ladder to the stern cabin, but the table of celestial angles was not on its shelf. In distress he turned to see that his father had followed him down and was watching him intently. No word was exchanged, but Hal knew that he was being challenged to provide the value from memory. Hal sat at his father's sea-chest, which served as a desk, and closed his eyes as he reviewed the tables in his mind's eye. He must remember yesterday's figures and extrapolate from them. He massaged his swollen ear-lobe, and his lips moved soundlessly.

Suddenly his face lightened, he opened his eyes and scribbled another number on the slate. He worked for a minute longer, translating the angle of the noon sun into degrees of latitude. Then he looked up triumphantly. 'Thirty-four degrees forty-two minutes south latitude.'

His father took the slate from his hand, checked his figures, then handed it back to him. He inclined his head slightly in agreement. 'Close enough, if your sun sight was true. Now what of your longitude?'

The determination of exact longitude was a puzzle that no man had ever solved. There was no timepiece, hourglass or clock that could be carried aboard a ship and still be sufficiently accurate to keep track of the earth's majestic revolutions. Only the traverse board, which hung beside the compass binnacle, could guide Hal's calculation. Now he studied the pegs that the helmsman had placed in the holes about the rose of the compass each time he had altered his heading during the previous watch. Hal added and averaged these values, then plotted them on the chart in his father's cabin. It was only a crude approximation of longitude and, predictably, his father demurred. 'I would have given it a touch more of east, for with the weed on her bottom and the water in her bilges she pays off heavily to leeward – but mark her so in the log.'

Hal looked up in astonishment. This was a momentous day indeed.

No other hand but his father's had ever written in the leather-bound log that sat beside the Bible on the lid of the sea-chest.

While his father watched, he opened the log and, for a minute, stared at the pages filled with his father's elegant, flowing script, and the beautiful drawings of men, ships and landfalls that adorned the margins. His father was a gifted artist. With trepidation Hal dipped the quill in the gold inkwell that had once belonged to the captain of the *Heerlycke Nacht*, one of the Dutch East India Company's galleons that his father had seized. He wiped the superfluous drops from the nib, lest they splatter the sacred page. Then he trapped the tip of his tongue between his teeth and wrote with infinite care: 'One bell in the afternoon watch, this 3rd day of September in the year of our Lord Jesus Christ 1667. Position 34 degrees 42 minutes South, 20 degrees 5 minutes East. African mainland in sight from the masthead bearing due North.' Not daring to add more, and relieved that he had not marred the page with scratchings or splutterings, he set aside the quill and sanded his well-formed letters with pride. He knew his hand was fair – though perhaps not as fair as his father's, he conceded as he compared them.

Sir Francis took up the pen he had laid aside and leaning over his shoulder wrote: 'This forenoon Ensign Henry Courtney severely wounded in an unseemly brawl.' Then, beside the entry he swiftly sketched a telling caricature of Hal with his swollen ear sticking out lopsidedly and the knot of the stitch like a bow in a maiden's hair.

Hal gagged on his own suppressed laughter, but when he looked up he saw the twinkle in his father's green eyes. Sir Francis laid one hand on the boy's shoulder, which was as close as he would ever come to an embrace, and squeezed it as he said, 'Ned Tyler will be waiting to instruct you in the lore of rigging and sail trimming. Do not keep him waiting.'

Though it was late when Hal made his way forward along the upper deck, it was still light enough for him to pick his way with ease over the sleeping bodies of the off-duty watch. The night sky was filled with stars, such an array as must dazzle the eyes of any northerner. This night Hal had no eyes for them. He was exhausted to the point where he reeled on his feet.

Aboli had kept a place for him in the bows, under the lee of the forward cannon where they were out of the wind. He had spread a straw-filled pallet on the deck and Hal tumbled gratefully onto it. There were no quarters set aside for the crew, and the men slept wherever they could find a space on the open deck. In these warm southern nights they all preferred the topsides to the stuffy lower deck. They lay in rows, shoulder to shoulder, but the proximity of so much stinking humanity was natural to Hal, and even their snoring and mutterings could not keep him long from sleep. He moved a little closer to Aboli. This was how he had slept each night for the last ten years and there was comfort in the huge figure beside him.

'Your father is a great chief amongst lesser chieftains,' Aboli murmured. 'He is a warrior and he knows the secrets of the sea and the heavens. The stars are his children.'

'I know all this is true,' Hal answered, in the same language.

'It was he who bade me take the sword to you this day,' Aboli confessed.

Hal raised himself on one elbow, and stared at the dark figure beside him. 'My father wanted you to cut me?' he asked incredulously.

'You are not as other lads. If your life is hard now, it will be harder still. You are chosen. One day you must take from his shoulders the great cloak of the red cross. You must be worthy of it.'

Hal sank back on his pallet, and stared up at the stars. 'What if I do not want this thing?' he asked.

'It is yours. You do not have a choice. The one Nautonnier Knight chooses the Knight to follow him. It has been so for almost four hundred years. Your only escape from it is death.'

Hal was silent for so long that Aboli thought sleep had overcome him, but then he whispered, 'How do you know these things?'

'From your father.'

'Are you also a Knight of our Order?'

Aboli laughed softly. 'My skin is too dark and my gods are alien. I could never be chosen.'

'Aboli, I am afraid.'

'All men are afraid. It is for those of us of the warrior blood to subdue fear.'

'You will never leave me, will you, Aboli?'

'I will stay at your side as long as you need me.'

'Then I am not so afraid.'

Hours later Aboli woke him with a hand on his shoulder from a deep and dreamless sleep. 'Eight bells in the middle watch, Gundwane.' He used Hal's nickname: in his own language it meant 'Bush Rat'. It was not meant pejoratively, but was the affectionate name he had bestowed on the four-year-old who had been placed in his care over a decade before.

Four o'clock in the morning. It would be light in an hour. Hal scrambled up and, rubbing his eyes, staggered to the stinking bucket in the heads and eased himself. Then, fully awake, he hurried down the heaving deck, avoiding the sleeping figures that cluttered it.

The cook had his fire going in the brick-lined galley and passed Hal a pewter mug of soup and a hard biscuit. Hal was ravenous and gulped the liquid, though it scalded his tongue. When he crunched the biscuit he felt the weevils in it pop between his teeth.

As he hurried to the foot of the mainmast he saw the glow of his father's pipe in the shadows of the poop and smelled a whiff of his tobacco, rank on the sweet night air. Hal did not pause but went up the shrouds noting the change of tack and the new setting of the sails that had taken place while he slept.

When he reached the masthead and had relieved the lookout there, he settled into his nest and looked about him. There was no moon and, but for the stars, all was dark. He knew every named star, from the mighty Sirius to tiny Mintaka in Orion's glittering belt. They were the ciphers of the navigator, the signposts of the sky, and he had learned their names with his alphabet. His eye went, unbidden, to pick out Regulus in the sign of the Lion. It was not the brightest star in the zodiac, but it was his own particular star and he felt a quiet pleasure at the thought that it sparkled for him alone. This was the happiest hour of his long day, the only time he could ever be alone in the crowded vessel, the only time he could let his mind dance among the stars and his imagination have full rein.

His every sense seemed heightened. Even above the whimper of the wind and the creak of the rigging he could hear his father's voice and recognize its tone if not the words, as he spoke quietly to the helmsman on the deck far below. He could see his father's beaked nose and the set of his brow in the ruddy glow from the pipe bowl as he drew in the tobacco smoke. It seemed to him that his father never slept.

He could smell the iodine of the sea, the fresh odour of kelp and salt. His nose was so keen, purged by months of sweet sea air, that he could even whiff the faint odour of the land, the warm, baked smell of Africa like biscuit hot from the oven.

Then there was another scent, so faint he thought his nostrils had played a trick on him. A minute later he caught it again, just a trace, honey-sweet on the wind. He did not recognize it and turned his head back and forth, questing for the next faint perfume, sniffing eagerly.

Suddenly it came again, so fragrant and heady that he reeled like a drunkard smelling the brandy pot, and had to stop himself crying aloud in his excitement. With an effort he kept his mouth closed and, with the aroma filling his head, tumbled from the crow's nest, and fled down the shrouds to the deck below. He ran on bare feet so silently that his father started when Hal touched his arm.

'Why have you left your post?'

'I could not hail you from the masthead – they are too close. They might have heard me also.'

'What are you babbling about, boy?' His father came angrily to his feet. 'Speak plainly.'

'Father, do you not smell it?' He shook his father's arm urgently.

'What is it?' His father took the pipe stem from his mouth. 'What is it that you smell?'

'Spice!' said Hal. 'The air is full of the perfume of spice.'

They moved swiftly down the deck, Ned Tyler, Aboli and Hal, shaking the off-duty watch awake, cautioning each man to silence as they shoved him towards his battle stations. There was no drum to beat to quarters. Their excitement was infectious. The waiting was over. The Dutchman was out there somewhere close, to windward in the darkness. They could all smell his fabulous cargo now.

Sir Francis extinguished the candle in the binnacle so that the ship showed no lights, then passed the keys of the arms chests to his boatswains. They were kept locked until the chase was in sight for the dread of mutiny was always in the back of every captain's mind. At other times only the petty officers carried cutlasses.

In haste the chests were opened and the weapons passed from hand to hand. The cutlasses were of good Sheffield steel, with plain wooden hilts and basket guards. The pikes had six-foot shafts of English oak and heavy hexagonal iron heads. Those of the crew who lacked skill with the sword chose either these robust spears or the boarding axes that could lop a man's head at a stroke from his shoulders.

The muskets were racked in the blackpowder magazine. They were brought up, and Hal helped the gunners load them with a handful of lead pellets on top of a handful of powder. They were clumsy, inaccurate weapons, with an effective range of only twenty or thirty yards. After the lock was triggered, and the burning match mechanically applied, the weapon fired in a cloud of smoke, but then had to be reloaded. This operation took two or three vital minutes, during which the musketeer was at the mercy of his foes.

Hal preferred the bow; the famous English longbow that had decimated the French knights at Agincourt. He could loose a dozen shafts in the time it took to reload a musket. The longbow carried fifty paces with the accuracy to strike a foe in the centre of the chest and with the power to spit him to the backbone, even though he wore a breastplate. He already had two bundles of arrows lashed to the sides of the crow's nest, ready to hand.

Sir Francis and some of his petty officers strapped on their half armour, light cavalry cuirasses and steel pot helmets. Sea salt had rusted them and they were dented and battered from other actions.

In short order the ship was readied for battle, and the crew armed and armoured. However, the gunports were closed and the demi-culverins were not run out. Most of the men were hustled below by Ned and the other boatswains, while the rest were ordered to lie flat on the deck concealed below the bulwarks. No slow-match was lit – the glow and smoke might alert the chase to her danger. However, charcoal braziers smouldered at the foot of each mast, and the wedges were knocked out of the gunports with muffled wooden mallets so that the sound of the blows would not carry.

Aboli pushed his way through the scurrying figures to where Hal stood at the foot of the mast. Around his bald head he wore a scarlet cloth whose tail hung down his back, and thrust into his sash was a cutlass. Under one arm he carried a rolled bundle of coloured silk. 'From your father.' He thrust the bundle into Hal's arms. 'You know what to do with them!' He gave Hal's pigtail a tug. 'Your father says that you are to remain at the masthead no matter which way the fight goes. Do you hear now?'

He turned and hurried back towards the bows. Hal grimaced rebelliously at his broad back, but climbed dutifully into the shrouds. When he reached the masthead he scanned the darkness swiftly, but as yet there was nothing to see. Even the aroma of spice had evaporated. He felt a stab of concern that he might only have imagined it. 'It is only that the chase has come out of our wind,' he reassured himself. 'She is probably abeam of us by now.'

He attached the banner Aboli had given him to the signal halyard, ready to fly it at his father's order. Then he removed the cover from the pan of the falconet. He checked the tension of the string before setting his longbow into the rack beside the bundles of yard-long arrows. Now there was nothing to do but wait. Below him the ship was unnaturally quiet, not even a bell to mark the passage of the hours, only the soft song of the sails and the muted accompaniment of the rigging.

The day came upon them with the suddenness that in these African seas he had come to know so well. Out of the dying night rose a tall bright tower, shining and translucent as an ice-covered alp – a great ship under a mass of gleaming canvas, her masts so tall they seemed to rake the last pale stars from the sky.

'Sail ho!' he pitched his voice so that it would carry to the deck below but not to the strange ship that lay, a full league away, across the dark waters. 'Fine on the larboard beam!'

His father's voice floated back to him. 'Masthead! Break out the colours!'

Hal heaved on the signal halyard, and the silken bundle soared to the masthead. There it burst open and the tricolour of the Dutch Republic streamed out on the south-easter, orange and snowy white and blue. Within moments the other banners and long pennants burst out from the head of the mizzen and the foremast, one emblazoned with the cipher of the VOC, die Verenigde Oostindische Compagnie, the United East India Company. The regalia was authentic, captured only four months previously from the *Heerlycke Nacht*. Even the standard of the Council of Seventeen was genuine. There would scarce have been time for the captain of the galleon to have learned of the capture of his sister ship and so to question the credentials of this strange caravel.

The two ships were on converging courses – even in darkness Sir Francis had judged well his interception. There was no call for him to alter course and alarm the Dutch captain. But within minutes it was clear that the *Lady Edwina*, despite her worm-riddled hull, was faster through the water than the galleon. She must soon begin to overtake the other ship, which he must avoid at all costs.

Sir Francis watched her through the lens of his telescope, and at once he saw why the galleon was so slow and ungainly: her mainmast was jury-rigged, and there was much other evidence of damage to her other masts and rigging. He realized that she must have been caught in some terrible storm in the eastern oceans – which would also account for her belated arrival off her landfall on the Agulhas Cape. He knew that he could not alter sail without alarming the Dutch captain, but he had to pass across her stern. He had prepared for this: he signed to the carpenter, at the rail, who with his mate lifted a huge canvas drogue and dropped it over the stern. Like the curb on a headstrong stallion it bit deep in the water and pulled up the *Lady Edwina* sharply. Again Sir Francis judged the disparate speeds of the two vessels, and nodded with satisfaction.

Then he looked down his own deck. The majority of the men were concealed below decks or lying under the bulwarks where they were invisible even to the lookouts at the galleon's masthead. There was no weapon in sight, all the guns hidden behind their ports. When Sir

Francis had captured this caravel she had been a Dutch trader, operating off the west African coast. In converting her to a privateer, he had been at pains to preserve her innocent air and prosaic lines. Only a dozen or so men were visible on the decks and in the rigging, which would be normal for a sluggish merchantman.

As he looked up again the banners of the Republic and the Company broke out at the Dutchman's mastheads. Only a trifle tardily she was acknowledging his salute.

'She accepts us,' Ned grunted, as he held the *Lady Edwina* stolidly on course. 'She likes our sheep's clothing.'

'Perhaps!' Sir Francis replied. 'And yet she cracks on more sail.' As they watched, the galleon's royals and top-gallants bloomed against the morning sky.

'There!' he exclaimed a moment later. 'She is altering course, sheering away from us. The Dutchman is a cautious fellow.'

'Satan's teeth! Just sniff her!' Ned whispered, almost to himself, as a trace of spices scented the air. 'Sweet as a virgin, and twice as beautiful.'

'It's the richest smell you'll ever have in your nostrils.' Sir Francis spoke loudly enough for the men on the deck below to hear him. 'There lies fifty pounds a head in prize money if you have the notion to fight for it.' Fifty pounds was ten years of an English workman's wages, and the men stirred and growled like hunting hounds on the leash.

Sir Francis went forward to the poop rail and lifted his chin to call softly up to the men in the rigging, 'Make believe that those cheese-heads over there are your brothers. Give them a cheer and a brave welcome.'

The men aloft howled with glee, and waved their bonnets at the tall ship as the *Lady Edwina* edged in under her stern.

Katinka van de Velde sat up and frowned at Zelda, her old nurse. 'Why have you woken me so early?' she demanded petulantly, and tossed the tumble of golden curls back from her face. Even so freshly aroused from sleep, it was rosy and angelic. Her eyes were of a startling violet colour, like the lustrous wings of a tropical butterfly.

'There is another ship near us. Another Company ship. The first we have seen in all these terrible stormy weeks. I had begun to think there was not another Christian soul left in all the world,' Zelda whined. 'You are always complaining of boredom. It might divert you for a while.'

Zelda was pale and wan. Her cheeks, once fat, smooth and greased with good living, were sunken. Her great belly was gone, and hung in folds of loose skin almost to her knees. Katinka could see it through the thin stuff of her nightgown.

She has puked away all her fat and half her flesh, Katinka thought, with a twinge of disgust. Zelda had been prostrated by the cyclones that had assailed the *Standvastigheid* and battered her mercilessly ever since they had left the Trincomalee coast.

Katinka threw back the satin bedclothes and swung her long legs over the edge of the gilded bunk. This cabin had been especially furnished and redecorated to accommodate her, a daughter of one of the omnipotent *Zeventien*, the seventeen directors of the Company. The décor was all gilt and velvet, silken cushions and silver vessels. A portrait of Katinka by the fashionable Amsterdam artist Pieter de Hoogh hung on the bulkhead opposite her bed, a wedding present from her doting father. The artist had captured her lascivious turn of head. He must have scoured his paint pots to reproduce so faithfully the wondrous colour of her eyes – and their expression, which was at once both innocent and corrupt.

'Do not wake my husband,' she cautioned the old woman as she flung a gold-brocade wrap over her shoulders and tied the jewelled belt around her hourglass waist. Zelda's eyelid drooped in conspiratorial agreement. At Katinka's insistence the Governor slept in the smaller, less grand cabin beyond the door that was locked from her side. Her excuse was that he snored abominably, and that she was indisposed by the *mal-de-mer*. In truth, caged in her quarters all these weeks, she was restless and bored, bursting with youthful energy and aflame with desires that the fat old man could never extinguish.

She took Zelda's hand and stepped out onto the narrow stern gallery. This was a private balcony, ornately carved with cherubs and angels, looking out over the ship's wake and hidden from the vulgar eyes of the crew.

It was a morning dazzling with sunlit magic, and as she filled her lungs with the salt tang of the sea she felt every nerve and muscle of her body quiver with the impetus of life. The wind kicked creamy feathers from the tops of the long blue swells, and played with her golden curls. It ruffled the silk over her breasts and belly with the caress of a lover's fingers. She stretched and arched her back sensuously like a sleek, golden cat.

Then she saw the other ship. It was much smaller than the galleon but with pleasing lines. The pretty flags and pennants that streamed from her masts contrasted with the pile of her white sails. She was close enough for Katinka to make out the figures of the few men that manned her rigging. They were waving a greeting, and she could see that some were young and clad only in short petticoats.

She leaned over the rail and stared across. Her husband had commanded that the crew of the galleon observe a strict dress code while she was aboard, so the figures on this strange ship fascinated her. She folded her arms over her bosom and squeezed her breasts together, feeling her nipples harden and engorge. She wanted a man. She burned for a man, any man, just as long as he was young and hard and raging for her. A man like those she had known in Amsterdam before her father had discovered her taste for strong game and sent her out to the Indies, to a safe old husband who had a high position in the Company and even higher prospects. His choice had been Petrus Jacobus van de Velde who, now that he was married to Katinka, was assured of the next vacancy on the Company's board, where he would join the pantheon of the *Zeventien*.

'Come inside, *Lieveling*.' Zelda tugged at her sleeve. 'Those ruffians over there are staring at you.'

Katinka shrugged off Zelda's hand, but it was true. They had recognized her as a female. Even at this distance their excitement was almost palpable. Their antics had become frenzied and one strapping figure in the bows took a double handful of his own crotch and thrust his hips towards her in a rhythmic and obscene gesture.

'Revolting! Come inside!' Zelda insisted. 'The Governor will be furious if he sees what that animal is doing.'

'He should be furious that he cannot perform as nimbly,' Katinka replied angelically. She pressed her thighs tightly together the better to savour the sudden moist warmth at their juncture. The caravel was much closer now, and she could see that what the seaman was offering her was bulky enough to overflow his cupped hands. The tip of her pink tongue dabbed at her pouting lips.

'Please, mistress.'

'In a while,' Katinka demurred. 'You were right, Zelda. This does amuse me.' She raised one white hand and waved back at the other ship. Instantly the men redoubled their efforts to hold her attention.

'This is so undignified,' Zelda moaned.

'But it's fun. We'll never see those creatures again, and being always dignified is so dull.' She leaned further out over the rail and let the front of her gown bulge open.

At that moment there was a heavy pounding on the door to her husband's cabin. Without further urging Katinka fled from the gallery, rushed to her bunk and threw herself upon it. She pulled the satin bedclothes up to her chin, before she nodded at Zelda, who lifted the cross bar and dropped into an ungainly curtsy as the Governor burst in. He ignored her and, belting his robe around his protruding belly, waddled to the bunk where Katinka lay. Without his wig his head was covered by sparse silver bristles.

'My dear, are you well enough to rise? The captain has sent a message. He wishes us to dress and stand to. There is a strange vessel in the offing, and it is behaving suspiciously.'

Katinka stifled a smile as she thought of the suspicious behaviour of the strange seamen. Instead she made a brave but pitiful face. 'My head is bursting, and my stomach—'

'My poor darling.' Petrus van de Velde, Governor-elect of the Cape of Good Hope, bent over her. Even on this cool morning his jowls were basted with sweat, and he reeked of last evening's dinner, Javanese curried fish, garlic and sour rum.

This time her stomach truly churned, but Katinka offered her cheek dutifully. 'I may have the strength to rise,' she whispered, 'if the captain orders it.'

Zelda rushed to the bedside and helped her sit up, and then lifted her to her feet, and with an arm around her waist, led her to the small Chinese screen in the corner of the cabin. Seated on the bench opposite, her husband was afforded only vague glimpses of shining white skin from behind the painted silk panels, even though he craned his head to see more.

'How much longer must this terrible journey last?' Katinka complained.

'The captain assures me that, with this wind holding fair, we should drop anchor in Table Bay within ten days.'

'The Lord give me strength to survive that long.'

'He has invited us to dine today with him and his officers,' replied the Governor. 'It is a pity, but I will send a message that you are indisposed.'

Katinka's head and shoulders popped up over the screen. 'You will do no such thing!' she snapped. Her breasts, round and white and smooth, quivered with agitation.

One of the officers interested her more than a little. He was Colonel Cornelius Schreuder, who, like her own husband, was *en route* to take up an appointment at the Cape of Good Hope. He had been appointed military commander of the settlement of which Petrus van de Velde would be Governor. He wore pointed moustaches and a fashionable van Dyck beard, and bowed to her most graciously each time she went on deck. His legs were well turned, and his dark eyes were eagle bright and gave her goose pimples when he looked at her. She read in them more than just respect for her position, and he had responded most gratifyingly to the sly appraisal she had given him from under her long eyelashes.

When they reached the Cape, he would be her husband's subordinate. Hers also to command – and she was sure that he could relieve the monotony of exile in the forsaken settlement at the end of the world that was to be her home for the next three years.

'I mean,' she changed her tone swiftly, 'it would be churlish of us to decline the captain's hospitality, would it not?'

'But your health is more important,' he protested.

'I will find the strength.' Zelda slipped petticoats over her head, one after another, five in all, each fluttering with ribbons.

Katinka came from behind the screen and raised her arms. Zelda lowered the blue silk dress over them and drew it down over the petticoats. Then she knelt and carefully tucked up the skirts on one side to reveal the petticoats beneath, and the slim ankles clad in white silk stockings. It was the very latest fashion. The Governor watched her, entranced. If only the other parts of your body were as big and busy as your eyeballs, Katinka thought derisively, as she turned to the long mirror and pirouetted before it.

Then she screamed wildly and clutched her bosom as, from the deck directly above them, there came the sudden deafening roar of gunfire. The Governor screamed as shrilly and flung himself from the bench onto the Oriental carpets that covered the deck.

'*De Standvastigheid*!' Through the lens of the telescope Sir Francis Courtney read the galleon's name off her high gilded transom. '*The Resolution*.' He lowered the glass and grunted, 'A name which we will soon put to the test!'

As he spoke a long bright plume of smoke spurted from the ship's upper deck, and a few seconds later the boom of the cannon carried across the wind. Half a cable's length ahead of their bows, the heavy ball plunged into the sea, making a tall white fountain. They could hear drums beating urgently in the other ship, and the gunports in her lower decks swung open. Long barrels prodded out.

'I marvel that he waited so long to give us a warning shot,' Sir Francis drawled. He closed the telescope, and looked up at the sails. 'Put up your helm, Master Ned, and lay us under his stern.' The display of false colours had won them enough time to duck in under the menace of the galleon's crushing broadside.

Sir Francis turned to the carpenter, who stood ready at the stern rail with a boarding axe in his hands. 'Cut her loose!' he ordered.

The man raised the axe above his head and swung it down. With a crunch the blade sliced into the timber of the stern rail, the drogue line parted with a whiplash crack and, free of her restraint, the *Lady Edwina* bounded forward, then heeled as Ned put up the helm.

Sir Francis's manservant, Oliver, came running with the red-quartered cloak and plumed cavalier hat. Sir Francis donned them swiftly and bellowed at the masthead, 'Down with the colours of the Republic and let's see those of England!' The crew cheered wildly as the Union flag streamed out on the wind.

They came boiling up from below decks, like ants from a broken nest, and lined the bulwarks, roaring defiance at the huge vessel that towered over them. The Dutchman's decks and rigging swarmed with frantic activity.

The cannons in the galleon's ports were training around, but few could cover the caravel as she came flying down on the wind, screened by the Dutchman's own high counter.

A ragged broadside thundered out across the narrowing gap but most of the shot fell wide by hundreds of yards or howled harmlessly overhead. Hal ducked as the blast of a passing shot lifted the cap from his head and sent it sailing away on the wind. A neat round hole had appeared miraculously in the sail six feet above him. He flicked his long hair out of his face, and peered down at the galleon.

The small company of Dutch officers on the quarterdeck were in disarray. Some were in shirtsleeves, and one was stuffing his night-shirt into his breeches as he came up the companion-ladder.

One officer caught his eye in the throng: a tall man in a steel helmet with a van Dyck beard was rallying a company of musketeers on the foredeck. He wore the gold-embroidered sash of a colonel over his shoulder, and from the way he gave his orders and the alacrity with which his men responded seemed a man to watch, one who might prove a dangerous foe.

Now at his bidding the men ran aft, each carrying a murderer, one of the small guns especially used for repelling boarders. There were slots in the galleon's stern rail into which the iron pin of the murderer would fit, allowing the deadly little weapon to be traversed and aimed at the decks of an enemy ship as it came alongside. When they had boarded the *Heerlycke Nacht* Hal had seen the execution the murderer could wreak at close range. It was more of a threat than the rest of the galleon's battery.

He swivelled the falconet, and blew on the slow-match in his hand.

To reach the stern the file of Dutch musketeers must climb the ladder from the quarterdeck to the poop. He aimed at the head of the ladder as the gap between the two ships closed swiftly. The Dutch colonel was first up the ladder, sword in hand, his gilded helmet sparkling bravely in the sunlight. Hal let him cross the deck at a run, and waited for his men to follow him up.

The first musketeer tripped at the head of the ladder and sprawled on the deck, dropping his murderer as he fell. Those following were bunched up behind him, unable to pass for the moment that it took him to recover and regain his feet. Hal peered over the crude sights of the falconet at the little knot of men. He pressed the burning tip of the match to the pan, and held his aim deliberately as the powder flared. The falconet jumped and bellowed and, as the smoke cleared he saw that five of the musketeers were down, three torn to shreds by the blast, the others screaming and splashing their blood on the white deck.

Hal felt breathless with shock as he looked down at the carnage. He had never before killed a man, and his stomach heaved with sudden nausea. This was not the same as shattering a water cask. For a moment he thought he might vomit.

The Dutch colonel at the stern rail looked up at him. He lifted his sword and pointed it at Hal's face. He shouted something up at Hal, but the wind and the continuous roll of gunfire obliterated his words. But Hal knew that he had made a mortal enemy.

This knowledge steadied him. There was no time to reload the falconet, it had done its work. He knew that that single shot had saved the lives of many of his own men. He had caught the Dutch musketeers before they could set up their murderers to scythe down the boarders. He knew he should be proud, but he was not. He was afraid of the Dutch colonel.

Hal reached for the longbow. He had to stand tall to draw it. He aimed his first arrow down at the colonel. He drew to full reach, but the Dutchman was no longer looking at him: he was commanding the survivors of his company to their positions at the galleon's stern rail. His back was turned to Hal.

Hal held off a fraction, allowing for the wind and the ship's movement. He loosed the arrow and watched it flash away, curling as the wind caught it. For a moment he thought it would find its mark in the colonel's broad back, but the wind thwarted it. It missed by a hand's breadth and thudded into the deck timbers where it stood quivering. The Dutchman glanced up at him, scorn curling his spiked moustaches. He made no attempt to seek cover, but turned back to his men.

Hal reached frantically for another arrow, but at that instant the two ships came together, and he was almost catapulted over the rim of the crow's nest.

There was a grinding, crackling uproar, timbers burst, and the windows in the galleon's stern galleries shattered at the collision. Hal looked down and saw Aboli in the bows, a black colossus as he swung a boarding grapnel around his head in long swooping revolutions then hurled it upwards, the line snaking out behind.

The iron hook skidded across the poop deck, but when Aboli jerked it back it lodged firmly in the galleon's stern rail. One of the Dutch crew ran across and lifted an axe to cut it free. Hal drew the fletchings of another arrow to his lips and loosed. This time his judgement of the windage was perfect and the arrowhead buried itself in the man's throat. He dropped the axe and clutched at the shaft as he staggered backwards and collapsed.

Aboli had seized another grapnel and sent that up onto the galleon's stern. It was followed by a score of others, from the other boatswains. In moments the two vessels were bound to each other by a spider's web of manila lines, too numerous for the galleon's defenders to sever though they scampered along the gunwale with hatchets and cutlasses.

The *Lady Edwina* had not fired her culverins. Sir Francis had held his broadside for the time when it would be most needed. The shot could do little damage to the galleon's massive planking, and it was far from his plans to mortally injure the prize. But now, with the two ships locked together, the moment had come.

'Gunners!' Sir Francis brandished his sword over his head to attract their attention. They stood over their pieces, smoking slow-match in hand, watching him. 'Now!' he roared, and slashed his blade downwards.

The line of culverins thundered in a single hellish chorus. Their muzzles were pressed hard against the galleon's stern, and the carved, gilded woodwork disintegrated in a cloud of smoke, flying white splinters and shards of stained glass from the windows.

It was the signal. No command could be heard in the uproar, no gesture seen in the dense fog that billowed over the locked vessels, but a wild chorus of warlike yells rose from the smoke and the *Lady Edwina*'s crew poured up into the galleon.

They boarded in a pack through the stern gallery, like ferrets into a rabbit warren, climbing with the nimbleness of apes and swarming over the gunwale, screened from the Dutch gunners by the rolling cloud of smoke. Others ran out along the *Lady Edwina*'s yards and dropped onto the galleon's decks.

'Franky and St George!' Their war-cries came up to Hal at the masthead. He saw only three or four shot down by the murderers at the stern before the Dutch musketeers themselves were hacked down and overwhelmed. The men who followed climbed unopposed to the galleon's poop. He saw his father go across, moving with the speed and agility of a much younger man.

Aboli stooped to boost him over the galleon's rail and the two fell in side by side, the tall Negro with the scarlet turban and the cavalier in his plumed hat, cloak swirling around the battered steel of his cuirass.

'Franky and St George!' the men howled, as they saw their captain in the thick of the fight, and followed him, sweeping the poop deck with ringing, slashing steel.

The Dutch colonel tried to rally his few remaining men, but they were beaten back remorselessly and sent tumbling down the ladders to the quarterdeck. Aboli and Sir Francis went down after them, their men clamouring behind them like a pack of hounds with the scent of fox in their nostrils.

Here they were faced with sterner opposition. The galleon's captain had formed up his men on the deck below the mainmast, and now their musketeers fired a close-range volley and charged the *Lady Edwina*'s men with bared steel. The galleon's decks were smothered with a struggling mass of fighting men.

Although Hal had reloaded the falconet, there was no target for him. Friend and foe were so intermingled that he could only watch helplessly as the fight surged back and forth across the open deck below him.

Within minutes it was apparent that the crew of the *Lady Edwina* were heavily outnumbered. There were no reserves – Sir Francis had left no one but Hal aboard the caravel. He had committed every last man, gambling all on surprise and this first wild charge. Twenty-four of his men were leagues away across the water, manning the two pinnaces, and could take no part. They were sorely needed now, but when Hal looked for the tiny scout vessels he saw that they were still miles out. Both had their gaff main sails set, but were making only snail's progress against the south-easter and the big curling swells. The fight would be decided before they could reach the two embattled ships and intervene.

He looked back at the deck of the galleon and to his consternation, realized that the fight had swung against them. His father and Aboli were being driven back towards the stern. The Dutch colonel was at the head of the counter-attack, roaring like a wounded bull and inspiring his men by his example.

From the back ranks of the boarding-party broke a small group of the *Lady Edwina*'s men, who had been hanging back from the fight. They were led by a weasel of a man, Sam Bowles, a forecastle lawyer, whose greatest talent lay in his ready tongue, his skill at arguing the division of spoils and in brewing dissension and discontent among his fellows.

Sam Bowles darted up into the galleon's stern and dropped over the rail to the *Lady Edwina*'s deck, followed by four others.

The interlocked ships had swung round ponderously before the wind, so that now the *Lady Edwina* was straining at the grappling lines that held them together. In panic and terror, the five deserters fell with axe and cutlass upon the lines. Each parted with a snap that carried clearly to Hal at the masthead.

'Avast that!' he screamed down, but not one man raised his head from his treacherous work.

'Father!' Hal shrieked towards the deck of the other ship. 'You'll be stranded! Come back! Come back!'

His voice could not carry against the wind or the noise of battle. His father was fighting three Dutch seamen, all his attention locked onto them. Hal saw him take a cut on his blade, and then riposte with a gleam of steel. One of his opponents staggered back, clutching at his arm, his sleeve suddenly sodden red.

At that moment the last grappling line parted with a crack, and the *Lady Edwina* was free. Her bows swung clear swiftly, her sails filled and she bore away, leaving the galleon wallowing, her flapping sails taken all aback, making ungainly sternway.

Hal launched himself down the shrouds, his palms scalded by the speed of the rope hissing through them. He hit the deck so hard that his teeth cracked together in his jaws and he rolled across the planks. In an instant he was on his feet, and looking desperately around him. The galleon was already a cable's length away across the blue swell, the sounds of the fighting growing faint on the wind. Then he looked to his own stern and saw Sam Bowles scurrying to take the helm.

A fallen seaman was lying in the scupper, shot down by a Dutch murderer. His musket lay beside him, still unfired, the match spluttering and smoking in the lock. Hal snatched it up and raced back along the deck to head off Sam Bowles.

He reached the whipstaff a dozen paces before the other man and rounded on him, thrusting the gun's gaping muzzle into his belly. 'Back, you craven swine! Or I'll blow your traitor's guts over the deck.'

Sam recoiled, and the other four seamen backed up behind him, staring at Hal with faces still pale and terrified from their flight.

'You can't leave your shipmates. We're going back!' Hal screamed, his eyes blazing green with wild rage and fear for his father and Aboli. He waved the musket at them, the smoke from the match swirling around his head. His forefinger was hooked around the trigger. Looking into those eyes, the deserters could not doubt his resolve and retreated down the deck.

Hal seized the whipstaff and held it over. The ship trembled under his feet as she came under his command. He looked back at the galleon, and his spirits quailed. He knew that he could never drive the *Lady Edwina* back against the wind with this set of sail: they were flying away from where his father and Aboli were fighting for their lives. At the same moment Bowles and his gang realized his predicament. 'Nobody ain't going back, and there's naught you can do about it, young Henry.' Sam cackled triumphantly. 'You'll have to get her on the other tack, to beat back to your daddy, and there's none of us will handle the sheets for you. Is there, lads? We have you strapped!'

Hal looked about him hopelessly. Then, suddenly, his jaw clenched with resolution. Sam saw the change in him and turned to follow his gaze. His own expression collapsed in consternation as he saw the pinnace only half a league ahead, crowded with armed sailors.

'Have at him, lads!' he exhorted his companions. 'He has but one shot in the musket, and then he's ours!'

'One shot and my sword!' Hal roared, and tapped the hilt of the cutlass on his hip. 'God's teeth, but I'll take half of you with me and glory in it.'

'All together!' Sam squealed. 'He'll never get the blade out of its sheath.'

'Yes! Yes!' Hal shouted. 'Come! Please, I beg you for the chance to have a look at your cowardly entrails.'

They had all watched this young wildcat at practice, had seen him fight Aboli, and none wanted to be at the front of the charge. They growled and shuffled, fingered their cutlasses and looked away.

'Come on, Sam Bowles!' Hal challenged. 'You were quick enough from the Dutchman's deck. Let's see how quick you are to come at me now.'

Sam steeled himself and then, grimly and purposefully, started forward, but when Hal poked the muzzle of the musket an inch forward, aiming at his belly, he pulled back hurriedly and tried to push one of his gang forward.

'Have at him, lad!' Sam croaked. Hal changed his aim to the second man's face, but he broke out of Sam's grip and ducked behind his neighbour.

The pinnace was close ahead now – they could hear the eager shouts of the seamen in her. Sam's expression was desperate. Suddenly he fled. Like a scared rabbit he shot down the ladder to the lower deck, and in an instant the others followed him in a panic-stricken mob.

Hal dropped the musket to the deck, and used both hands on the whipstaff. He gazed forward over the plunging bows, judging his moment carefully, then threw his weight against the lever and spun the ship's head up into the wind.

She lay there hove to. The pinnace was nearby and Hal could see Big Daniel Fisher in the bows, one of the *Lady Edwina*'s best boatswains. Big Daniel seized his opportunity, and shot the small boat alongside. His sailors latched onto the trailing grappling lines that Sam and his gang had cut, and came swarming up onto the caravel's deck.

'Daniel!' Hal shouted at him. 'I'm going to wear the ship around. Get ready to train her yards! We're going back into the fight!'

Big Daniel flashed him a grin, his teeth jagged and broken as a shark's, and led his men to the yard braces. Twelve men, fresh and eager, Hal exulted, as he prepared for the dangerous manoeuvre of bringing the wind across the ship's stern rather than over her bows. If he misjudged it, he would dismast her, but if he succeeded in bringing her round, stern first to the wind, he would save several crucial minutes in getting back to the embattled galleon.

Hal put the whipstaff hard alee, but as she struggled wildly to feel the wind come across her stern, and threatened to gybe with all standing, Daniel paid off the yard braces to take the strain. The sails filled like thunder, and suddenly she was on the other tack, clawing up into the wind, tearing back to join the fight.

Daniel hooted and lifted his cap, and they all cheered him, for it had been courageously and skilfully done. Hal hardly glanced at the others, but concentrated on holding the *Lady Edwina* close hauled, heading back for the drifting Dutchman. The fight must still be raging aboard her, for he could hear the faint shouts and the occasional pop of a musket. Then there was a flash of white off to leeward, and he saw the gaff sail of the second pinnace ahead, the crew waving wildly to gain his attention. Another dozen fighting men to join the muster, he thought. Was it worth the time to pick them up? Another twelve sharp cutlasses? He let the *Lady Edwina* drop off a point, to head straight for the tiny vessel.

Daniel had a line ready to heave across and, within seconds, the second pinnace had disgorged her men and was on tow behind the *Lady Edwina*.

'Daniel!' Hal called him. 'Keep those men quiet! No sense in warning the cheese-heads we're coming.'

'Right, Master Hal. We'll give 'em a little surprise.'

'Batten down the hatches on the lower decks! We have a cargo of cowards and traitors hiding in our holds. Keep 'em locked down there until Sir Francis can deal with them.'

Silently the *Lady Edwina* steered in under the galleon's tumblehome. Perhaps the Dutchmen were too busy to see her coming in under shortened sail for not a single head peered down from the rail above as the two hulls came together with a jarring grinding impact. Daniel and his crew hurled grappling irons over the galleon's rail, and immediately stormed up them, hand over hand.

Hal took only a moment to lash the whipstaff hard over, then raced across the deck and seized one of the straining lines. Close on Big Daniel's heels, he climbed swiftly and paused as he reached the galleon's rail. With one hand on the line and both feet planted firmly on the galleon's timbers, he drew his cutlass and clamped the blade between his teeth. Then he swung himself up and, only a second behind Daniel, dropped over the rail.

He found himself in the front rank of the fresh boarding party. With Daniel beside him, and the sword in his right fist he took a moment to glance around the deck. The fight was almost over. They had arrived with only seconds to spare for his father's men were scattered in tiny clusters across the deck, surrounded by its crew and fighting for their lives. Half their number were down, a few obviously dead. A head, hacked from its torso, leered up at Hal from the scupper where it rolled back and forth in a puddle of its own blood. With a shudder of horror, Hal recognized the *Lady Edwina*'s cook.

Others were wounded, and writhed, rolled and groaned on the deck. The planks were slick and slippery with their blood. Still others sat exhausted, disarmed and dispirited, their weapons thrown aside, their hands clasped over their heads, yielding to the enemy.

A few were still fighting. Sir Francis and Aboli stood at bay below the mainmast, surrounded by howling Dutchmen, hacking and stabbing. Apart from a gash on his left arm, his father seemed unhurt – perhaps the steel cuirass had saved him from serious injury – and he fought with all his usual fire. Beside him, Aboli was huge and indestructible, roaring a war-cry in his own tongue when he saw Hal's head pop over the rail.

Without a thought but to go to their aid, Hal started forward. 'For Franky and St George!' he screamed at the top of his lungs, and Big Daniel took up the cry, running at his left hand. The men from the pinnaces were after them, shrieking like a horde of raving madmen straight out of Bedlam.

The Dutch crew were themselves almost spent, a score were down, and of those still fighting many were wounded. They looked over their shoulders at this latest phalanx of bloodthirsty Englishmen rushing upon them. The surprise was complete. Shock and dismay was on every tired and sweat-lathered face. Most flung down their weapons and, like any defeated crew, rushed to hide below decks.

A few of the stouter souls swung about to face the charge, those around the mast led by the Dutch colonel. But the yells of Hal's boarding-party had rallied their exhausted and bleeding shipmates, who sprang forward with renewed resolve to join the attack. The Dutchmen were surrounded.

Even in the confusion and turmoil Colonel Schreuder recognized Hal, and whirled to confront him, aiming a cut, backhanded, at his head. His moustaches bristled like a lion's whiskers, and the blade hummed in his hand. He was miraculously unhurt and seemed as strong and fresh as any of the men that Hal led against him. Hal turned the blow with a twist of his wrist and went for the counter-stroke.

In order to meet Hal's charge the colonel had turned his back on Aboli, a foolhardy move. As he trapped Hal's thrust and shifted his feet to lunge, Aboli rushed at him from behind. For a moment Hal thought he would run him through the spine, but he should have guessed better. Aboli knew the value of ransom as well as any man aboard: a dead enemy officer was merely so much rotting meat to throw overboard to the sharks that followed in their wake but a captive was worth good gold guilders.

Aboli reversed his grip, and brought the steel basket of the cutlass hilt cracking into the back of the colonel's skull. The Dutchman's eyes flew wide open with shock, then his legs buckled under him and he toppled face down on the deck.

As the colonel went down, the last resistance of the galleon's crew collapsed with him. They threw down their weapons, and those of the *Lady Edwina*'s crew who had surrendered leapt to their feet, wounds and exhaustion forgotten. They snatched up the discarded weapons and turned them on the beaten Dutchmen, herding them forward, forcing them to squat in ranks with their hands clasped behind their heads, dishevelled and forlorn.

Aboli seized Hal in a bear-hug. 'When you and Sam Bowles set sail, I thought it was the last we would see of you,' he panted.

Sir Francis came striding towards his son, thrusting his way through the milling, cheering pack of his seamen. 'You deserted your post at the masthead!' He scowled at Hal as he bound a strip of cloth around the nick in his upper arm and knotted it with his teeth.

'Father,' Hal stammered, 'I thought—'

'And for once you thought wisely!' Sir Francis's dark expression cracked and his green eyes sparkled. 'We'll make a warrior of you yet, if you remember to keep your point up on the riposte. This great cheese-head,' he prodded the fallen colonel with his toe, 'was about to skewer you, until Aboli tapped his noggin.' Sir Francis slipped his sword back into its scabbard. 'The ship is not yet secure. The lower decks and holds are crawling with them. We'll have to drive them out. Stay close to Aboli and me!'

'Father, you're hurt,' Hal protested.

'And perhaps I would have been more sorely wounded had you come back to us even a minute later than you did.'

'Let me see to your wound.'

'I know the tricks Aboli has taught you – would you piss on your own father?' He laughed, and clapped Hal on the shoulder. 'Perhaps I'll give you that pleasure a little later.' He turned and bellowed across the deck, 'Big Daniel, take your men below and winkle out those cheese-heads who are hiding there. Master John, put a guard on the cargo hatches. See to it there is no looting. Fair shares for all! Master Ned, take the helm and get this ship on the wind before she flogs her canvas to rags.'

Then he roared at the others, 'I'm proud of you, you rascals! A good day's work. You'll each go home with fifty gold guineas in your pocket. But the Plymouth lassies will never love you as well I do!'

They cheered him, hysterical with the release from desperate action and the fear of defeat and death.

'Come on!' Sir Francis nodded to Aboli and started for the ladder that led down into the officers' and passengers' quarters in the stern.

Hal followed at a run as they crossed the deck, and Aboli grunted over his shoulder, 'Be on your mettle. There are those below who would be happy to stick a dirk between your ribs.'

Hal knew where his father was going, and what would be his first concern. He wanted the Dutch captain's charts, log and sailing directions. They were more valuable to him than all the fragrant spices and precious metals and bright jewels the galleon might be carrying. With those in his hands he would have the key to every Dutch harbour and fort in the Indies. He would read the sailing orders of the spice convoys and the manifest of their cargoes. To him they were worth ten thousand pounds in gold.

Sir Francis stormed down the ladder and tried the first door at the bottom. It was locked from within. He stepped back and charged. At his flying kick, the door flew open and crashed back on its hinges.

The galleon's captain was crouched over his desk, his cropped pate wigless and his clothing sweat-soaked. He looked up in dismay, blood dripping from a cut on his cheek onto his silken shirt, its wide fashionable sleeves slashed with green.

At the sight of Sir Francis, he froze in the act of stuffing the ship's books into a weighted canvas bag, then snatched it up and rushed to the stern windows. The casements and glass had been shot away by the *Lady Edwina*'s culverins, and they gaped open, the sea breaking and swirling under her counter. The Dutch captain lifted the bag to hurl it through the opening but Sir Francis seized his raised arm and flung him backwards onto his bunk. Aboli grabbed the bag, and Sir Francis made a courteous little bow. 'You speak English?' he demanded.

'No English,' the captain snarled back, and Sir Francis changed smoothly into Dutch. As a Nautonnier Knight of the Order he spoke most of the languages of the great seafaring nations, French, Spanish and Portuguese, as well as Dutch. 'You are my prisoner, Mijnheer. What is your name?'

'Limberger, captain of the first class, in the service of the VOC. And you, Mijnheer, are a corsair,' the captain retorted.

'You are mistaken, sir! I sail under Letters of Marque from His Majesty King Charles the second. Your ship is now a prize of war.'

'You flew false colours,' the Dutchman accused.

Sir Francis smiled bleakly. 'A legitimate ruse of war.' He made a dismissive gesture and went on, 'You are a brave man, Mijnheer, but the fight is over now. As soon as you give me your word, you will be treated as my honoured guest. The day your ransom is paid, you will go free.'

The captain wiped the blood and sweat from his face with his silken sleeve, and an expression of resignation dulled his features. He stood and handed his sword hilt first to Sir Francis.

'You have my word. I will not attempt to escape.'

'Nor encourage your men to resistance?' Sir Francis prompted him. The captain nodded glumly. 'I agree.'

'I will need your cabin, Mijnheer, but I will find you comfortable quarters elsewhere.' Sir Francis turned his attention eagerly to the canvas bag and dumped its contents on the desk.

Hal knew that, from now on, his father would be absorbed in his reading, and he glanced at Aboli on guard in the doorway. The Negro nodded permission at him, and Hal slipped out of the cabin. His father did not see him go.

Cutlass in hand, he moved cautiously down the narrow corridor. He could hear the shouts and clatter from the other decks as the crew of the *Lady Edwina* cleared out the defeated Dutch seamen and herded them up onto the open deck. Down here it was quiet and deserted. The first door he tried was locked. He hesitated then followed his father's earlier example. The door resisted his first onslaught, but he backed off and charged again. This time it burst open and he went flying through into the cabin beyond, off balance and skidding on the magnificent Oriental rugs that covered the deck. He sprawled on the huge bed that seemed to fill half the cabin.

As he sat up and gazed at the splendour that surrounded him, he was aware of an aroma more heady than any spice he had ever smelt. The boudoir odour of a pampered woman, not merely the precious oils of flowers, procured by the perfumer's art, but blended with these the more subtle scents of skin and hair and a healthy young female body. It was so exquisite, so moving that when he stood his legs felt strangely weak under him, and he snuffed it up rapturously. It was the most delicious smell that had ever set his nostrils a-quiver.

Sword in hand he gazed around the cabin, only vaguely aware of the rich tapestries and silver vessels filled with sweetmeats, dried fruits and pot-pourri. The dressing table against the port bulkhead was covered with an array of cut-glass cosmetic and perfume bottles with stoppers of chased silver. He moved across to it. Laid out beside the bottles was a set of silver-backed brushes and a tortoiseshell comb. Trapped between the teeth of the comb was a single strand of hair, long as his arm, fine as a silk thread.

Hal lifted the comb to his face as though it were a holy relic. There was that entrancing odour again, that giddy woman's smell. He wound the hair about his finger and freed it from the teeth of the comb, then reverently tucked it into the pocket of his stained and sweat-stinking shirt.

At that moment there came a soft but heartbreaking sob from behind the gaudy Chinese screen across one end of the cabin.

'Who's there?' Hal challenged, cutlass poised. 'Come out or I'll thrust home.'

There was another sob, more poignant than the last. 'By all the saints, I mean it!' Hal stalked towards the screen.

He slashed at the screen, slicing through one of the painted panels. At the force of the blow it toppled and crashed to the deck. There was a terrified shriek, and Hal stood gaping at the wondrous creature who knelt, cowering, in the corner of the cabin.

Her face was buried in her hands, but the mass of shining hair that tumbled to the deck glowed like freshly minted gold escudos, and the skirts spread around were the blue of a swallow's wings.

'Please, madam!' Hal whispered. 'I mean you no ill. Please do not cry.'

His words had no effect. Clearly they were not understood and, inspired by the moment, Hal switched into Latin. 'You need not fear. You are safe. I will not harm you.'

The shining head lifted. She had understood. He looked into her face, and it was as though he had received a charge of grape shot in the centre of his chest. The pain was so intense that he gasped aloud. He had never dreamed that such beauty could exist.

'Mercy!' she whispered pitifully in Latin. 'Please do not harm me.' Her eyes were liquid and brimming, but her tears served only to enhance their magnitude and intensify their iridescent violet. Her cheeks were blanched to the translucent lustre of alabaster, and the tears upon them gleamed like tiny seed pearls.

'You are beautiful,' Hal said, still in Latin. His voice sounded like that of a victim on the rack, breathless and agonized. He was tortured by emotions that he had never dreamed existed. He wanted to protect and cherish this woman, to keep her for ever for himself, to love and worship her. All the words of chivalry, which, until he looked upon her, he had read and mouthed but never truly understood, rushed to his tongue demanding utterance, but he could only stand and stare.

Then he was distracted by another soft sound from behind him. He spun round, cutlass at the ready. From under the satin sheets that trailed over the edge of the huge bed crawled a porcine figure. The back and belly were so well larded as to wobble with every movement the man made. Rolls of fat swaddled the back of his neck and hung down his pendulous jowls. 'Yield yourself!' Hal bellowed, and prodded him with the point of the blade. The Governor screamed shrilly and collapsed on the deck. He wriggled like a puppy.

'Please do not kill me. I am a rich man,' he sobbed, also in Latin. 'I will pay any ransom.'

'Get up!' Hal prodded him again, but Petrus van de Velde had only enough strength and courage to reach his knees. He knelt there, blubbering.

'Who are you?'

'I am the Governor of the Cape of Good Hope, and this lady is my wife.'

These were the most terrible words Hal had ever heard spoken. He stared at the man aghast. The wondrous lady he already loved with his very life was married – and to this grotesque burlesque of a man who knelt before him.

'My father-in-law is a director of the Company, one of the richest and most powerful merchants in Amsterdam. He will pay – he will pay anything. Please do not kill us.'

The words made little sense to Hal. His heart was breaking. Within moments he had gone from wild elation to the depths of the human spirit, from soaring love to plunging despair.

But the Governor's words meant more to Sir Francis Courtney, who stood now in the entrance to the cabin with Aboli at his back.

'Please calm yourself, Governor. You and your wife are in safe hands. I will make the arrangements for your ransom with all despatch.' He swept off his plumed cavalier hat, and bent his knee towards Katinka. Even he was not entirely proof against her beauty. 'May I introduce myself, madam? Captain Francis Courtney, at your command. Please take a while to compose yourself. At four bells – that is in an hour's time – I would be obliged if you would join me on the quarterdeck. I intend to hold a muster of the ship's company.'

Both ships were under sail, the little caravel under studding-sails and top sails only, the great galleon with her mainsail set. They sailed in close company on a north-easterly heading, away from the Cape and on a closing course with the eastern reaches of the African mainland. Sir Francis looked down paternally upon his crew in the galleon's waist.

'I promised you fifty guineas the man as your prize,' he said, and they cheered him wildly. Some were stiff and crippled with their wounds. Five were laid on pallets against the rail, too weak from loss of blood to stand but determined not to miss a word of this ceremony. The dead were already stitched in their canvas shrouds, each with a Dutch cannonball at his feet, and laid out in the bows. Sixteen Englishmen and forty-two Dutch, comrades in the truce of death. None of the living now gave them a thought.

Sir Francis held up one hand. They fell silent and crowded forward so as not to miss his next words.

'I lied to you,' he told them. There was a moment of stunned disbelief and then they groaned and muttered darkly. 'There is not a man amongst you . . .' he paused for effect '. . . but is the richer by two hundred pounds for this day's work!'

The silence persisted as they stared incredulously at him, and then they went mad with joy. They capered and howled, and whirled each other around in a delirious jig. Even the wounded sat up and crowed.

Sir Francis smiled down on them benignly for a while as he let them give vent to their joy. Then he waved a sheaf of manuscript pages over his head and they fell silent again. 'This is the extract I have made of the ship's manifest!'

'Read it!' they pleaded.

The recital went on for almost half an hour, for they cheered each item of the bill of lading that he translated from the Dutch as he read aloud. Cochineal and pepper, vanilla and saffron, cloves and cardamom with a total weight of forty-two tons. The crew knew that, weight for weight and pound for pound, those spices were as precious as bars of silver. They were hoarse with shouting, and Sir Francis held up his hand again. 'Do I weary you with this endless list? Have you had enough?'

'No!' they roared. 'Read on!'

'Well, then, there are a few sticks of timber in her holds. Balu and teak and other strange wood that has never been seen north of the equator. Over three hundred tons.' They feasted on his words with shining eyes. 'There is still more, but I see that I weary you. You want no more?'

'Read it to us!' they pleaded.

'Finest Chinese blue and white ceramic ware, and silk in bolts. That will please the ladies!' They bellowed like a herd of bull elephants in musth at the mention of women. When they reached the next port, with two hundred pounds in each purse, they could have as many women, of whatever quality and comeliness their fancies ordered.

'There is also gold and silver, but that is boarded over in sealed steel chests in the bottom of the main hold, with three hundred tons of timber on top of it. We will not get our hands on it until we reach port and unload the main cargo.'

'How much gold?' they pleaded. 'Tell us how much silver.'

'Silver in coin to the value of fifty thousand guilders. That's over ten thousand good English pounds. Three hundred ingots of gold from the mines of Kollur on the Krishna river in Kandy, and the Good Lord alone knows what those will bring in when we sell them in London.'

Hal hung in the mainmast shrouds, a vantage point from which he could look down on his father on the quarterdeck. Hardly a word of what he was saying made sense to Hal, but he realized dimly that this must be one of the greatest prizes ever taken by English sailors during the course of this war with the Dutch. He felt dazed and light-headed, unable to concentrate on anything but the greater treasure he had captured with his own sword, and which now sat demurely behind his father, attended by her maid. Chivalrously Sir Francis had placed one of the carved, cushioned chairs from the captain's cabin on the quarterdeck for the Dutch governor's wife. Now Petrus van de Velde stood behind her, splendidly dressed, wearing high rhinegraves of soft Spanish leather that reached to his thighs, bewigged and beribboned, his corpulence covered with the medallions and silken sashes of his office.

To his surprise Hal found that he hated the man bitterly, and lamented that he had not skewered him as he crawled from under the bed, and so made the angel who was his wife into a tragic widow.

He imagined devoting his life to playing Lancelot to her Guinevere. He saw himself humble and submissive to her every whim but inspired to deeds of outstanding valour by his pure love for her. At her behest, he might even undertake a knightly errand to search for the Holy Grail and place the sacred relic in her beautiful white hands. He shuddered with pleasure at the thought, and stared down longingly at her.

While Hal daydreamed in the rigging, the ceremony on the deck below him drew to its conclusion. Behind the Governor were ranked the Dutch captain and the other captured officers. Colonel Cornelius Schreuder was the only one without a hat, for a bandage swathed his head. Despite the blow Aboli had dealt him his eye was still keen and unclouded and his expression fierce as he listened to Sir Francis list the spoils.

'But that is not all, lads!' Sir Francis assured his crew. 'We are fortunate enough to have aboard, as our honoured guest, the new Governor of the Dutch settlement of the Cape of Good Hope.' With an ironic flourish he bowed to van de Velde, who glowered at him: now that his captors had realized his value and position, he felt more secure.

The Englishmen cheered, but their eyes were on Katinka, and Sir Francis obliged them by introducing her.

'We are also fortunate to have with us the Governor's lovely wife—' He broke off as the crew sounded their appreciation of her beauty.

'Coarse peasant cattle,' van de Velde growled and laid his hand protectively upon Katinka's shoulder. She gazed upon the men with wide violet eyes, and her beauty and innocence shamed them into an embarrassed silence.

'Mevrouw van de Velde is the only daughter of Burgher Hendrik Coetzee, the *stadhouder* of the City of Amsterdam, and the Chairman of the governing board of the Dutch East India Company.'

The crew stared at her in awe. Few understood the importance of such an exalted personage, but the manner in which Sir Francis had recited these titles had impressed them.

'The Governor and his wife will be held on board this ship until their ransom is paid. One of the captured Dutch officers will be despatched to the Cape of Good Hope with the ransom demand to be transmitted by the next Company ship to the Council in Amsterdam.'

The crew goggled at the couple as they considered this, then Big Daniel asked, 'How much, Sir Francis? What is the amount of the ransom you have set?'

'I have set the Governor's ransom at two hundred thousand guilders in gold coin.'

The ship's company was stunned, for such a sum surpassed their understanding.

Then Daniel bellowed again, 'Let's have a cheer for the captain, lads!' And they yelled until their voices cracked.

Sir Francis walked slowly down the ranks of captured Dutch seamen. There were forty-seven, eighteen of them wounded. He examined the face of each man as he passed: they were rough stock, coarse-featured and unintelligent of expression. It was obvious that none had any ransom value. They were, rather, a liability, for they had to be fed and guarded, and there was always the danger that they might recover their courage and attempt an insurrection.

'The sooner we are rid of them the better,' he murmured to himself, then addressed them aloud in their own language. 'You have done your duty well. You will be set free and sent back to the fort at the Cape. You may take your ditty bags with you, and I will see to it that you are paid the wages owing you before you go.' Their faces brightened. They had not expected that. That should keep them quiet and docile, he thought, as he turned away to the ladder down to his newly acquired cabin, where his more illustrious prisoners were waiting for him.

'Gentlemen!' he greeted them, as he entered and took his seat behind the mahogany desk. 'Would you care for a glass of Canary wine?'

Governor van de Velde nodded greedily. His throat was dry and although he had eaten only half an hour previously his stomach growled like a hungry dog. Oliver, Sir Francis's servant, poured the yellow wine into the long-stemmed glasses and served the sugared fruits he had found in the Dutch captain's larder. The captain made a sour face as he recognized his own fare, but took a large gulp of the Canary.

Sir Francis consulted the pile of manuscript on which he had made his notes, then glanced at one of the letters he had found in the captain's desk. It was from an eminent firm of bankers in Holland. He looked up at the captain and addressed him sternly. 'I wonder that an officer of your service and seniority with the VOC should indulge in trade for his own account. We both know it is strictly forbidden by the Seventeen.'

The captain looked as though he might protest, but when Sir Francis tapped the letter he subsided and glanced guiltily at the Governor, who sat beside him.

'It seems that you are a rich man, Mijnheer. You will hardly miss a ransom of two hundred thousand guilders.' The captain muttered and scowled darkly, but Sir Francis went on smoothly, 'If you will pen a letter to your bankers, the matter can be settled as between gentlemen, just as soon as I receive that amount in gold.' The captain inclined his head in acquiescence.

'Now, as to the ship's officers,' Sir Francis went on, 'I have examined your enlistment register.' He drew the book towards him and opened it. 'It seems that they are all men without high connections or financial substance.' He looked up at the captain. 'Is that the case?'

'That is true, Mijnheer.'

'I will send them to the Cape with the common seamen. Now it remains to decide to whom we shall entrust the ransom demand to the Council of the Company for Governor van de Velde and his good lady – and, of course, your letter to your bankers.'

Sir Francis looked up at the Governor. Van de Velde stuffed another candied fruit into his mouth and replied around it, 'Send Schreuder.'

'Schreuder?' Sir Francis riffled through the papers until he found the colonel's commission. 'Colonel Cornelius Schreuder, the newly appointed military commander of the fort at Good Hope?'

'*Ja*, that one.' Van de Velde reached for another sweetmeat. 'His rank will give him more standing when he presents your demand for my ransom to my father-in-law,' he pointed out.

Sir Francis studied the man's face as he chewed. He wondered why the Governor wanted to be rid of the colonel. He seemed a good man and resourceful; it would make more sense to keep him at hand. However, what van de Velde said of his status was true. And Sir Francis sensed that Colonel Schreuder might play the devil if he were kept captive aboard the galleon for any length of time. Much more trouble than he's worth, he thought, and said aloud, 'Very well, I will send him.'

The Governor's sugar-coated lips pouted with satisfaction. He was fully aware of his wife's interest in the dashing colonel. He had been married to her for only a few years, and yet he knew for a certainty that she had taken at least eighteen lovers in that time, some for only an hour or an evening.

Her maid, Zelda, was in the pay of van de Velde and reported to him each of her mistress's adventures, taking a deep vicarious pleasure in relating every salacious detail.

When van de Velde had first become aware of Katinka's carnal appetite, he had been outraged. However, his initial furious remonstrations had had no effect upon her and he learned swiftly that over her he had no control. He could neither protest too much nor send her away for on the one hand he was besotted by her, and on the other her father was too rich and powerful. The advancement of his own fortune and status depended almost entirely upon her. In the end his only course of action had been, as far as possible, to keep temptation and opportunity from her. During this voyage he had succeeded in keeping her a virtual prisoner in her quarters, and he was sure that, had he not done so, his wife would have already sampled the colonel's wares, which were ostentatiously on display. With him sent off the ship, her choice of diversion would be severely curtailed and, after a prolonged fast, she might even become amenable to his own sweaty advances.

'Very well,' Sir Francis agreed, 'I will send Colonel Schreuder as your emissary.' He turned the page of the almanac on the desk in front of him. 'With fair winds, and by the grace of Almighty God, the round trip from the Cape to Holland and back here to the rendezvous should not occupy more than eight months. We can hope that you might be free to take up your duties at the Cape by Christmas.'

'Where will you keep us until the ransom is received? My wife is a lady of quality and delicate disposition.'

'In a safe place, and in comfort. That I assure you, sir.'

'Where will you meet the ship returning with our ransom monies?'

'At thirty-three degrees south latitude and four degrees thirty minutes east.'

'Where, pray, might that be?'

'Why, Governor van de Velde, at the very spot upon the ocean where we are at this moment.' Sir Francis would not be tricked so readily into revealing the whereabouts of his base.

In a misty dawn the galleon dropped anchor in the gentler waters behind a rocky headland of the African coast. The wind had dropped and begun to veer. The end of the summer season was at hand; they were fast approaching the autumnal equinox. The *Lady Edwina*, her pumps pounding ceaselessly, came alongside and, with fenders of matted oakum between the hulls, she made fast to the larger vessel.

At once the work of clearing her out began. Blocks and tackle had already been rigged from the galleon's yards. They took out the guns first. The great bronze barrels on their trains were swayed aloft. Thirty seamen walked away with the tackle and then lowered each culverin to the galleon's deck. Once these guns were sited, the galleon would have the firepower of a ship of the line and would be able to attack any Company galleon on better than equal terms.

Watching the cannon come on board, Sir Francis realized that he now had the force to launch a raid on any of the Dutch trading harbours in the Indies. This capture of the *Standvastigheid* was only a beginning. From here he planned to become the terror of the Dutch in the Ocean of the Indies, just as Sir Francis Drake had scourged the Spanish on their own main in the previous century.

Now the powder kegs were lifted out of the caravel's magazine. Few remained filled after such a long cruise and the heavy actions she had fought. However, the galleon still carried almost two tons of excellent quality gunpowder, sufficient to fight a dozen battles, or to capture a rich Dutch entrepôt on the Trincomalee or Javanese coast.

When the furniture and stores had been brought across, water casks and weapons chests, brine barrels of pickled meats, bread bags and barrels of flour, the pinnaces were also hoisted aboard and broken down by the carpenters. They were stowed away in the galleon's main cargo hold on top of the stacks of rare oriental timbers. So bulky were they and so heavily laden with her own cargo was the galleon that to accommodate their bulk the hatch coamings had to be left off the main holds until the prize was taken into Sir Francis's secret base.

Stripped to her planks, the *Lady Edwina* rode high in the water when Colonel Schreuder and the released Dutch crew were ready to board her. Sir Francis summoned the colonel to the quarterdeck and handed him back his sword and the letter addressed to the Council of the Dutch East India Company in Amsterdam. It was stitched in a canvas cover, the seams sealed with red wax, and tied with ribbon. It made an impressive bundle, which Colonel Schreuder placed firmly under his arm.

'I hope we meet again, Mijnheer,' Schreuder said ominously to Sir Francis.

'In eight months from now I will be at the rendezvous,' Sir Francis assured. 'Then I shall be delighted to see you again, as long as you have the two hundred thousand gold guilders for me.'

'You miss my meaning,' said Cornelius Schreuder grimly.

'I assure you I do not,' responded Sir Francis quietly.

Then the colonel looked to the break in the poop where Katinka van de Velde stood at her husband's side. The deep bow that he made towards them and the look of longing in his eyes were not for the Governor alone. 'I shall return with all haste to end your suffering,' he told them.

'God be with you,' said the Governor. 'Our fate is in your hands.'

'You will be assured of my deepest gratitude on your return, my dear Colonel,' Katinka whispered, in a breathless little girl's voice, and the colonel shivered as though a bucket of icy water had been poured down his back. He drew himself to his full height, saluted her, then turned and strode to the galleon's rail.

Hal was waiting at the port with Aboli and Big Daniel. The colonel's eyes narrowed and he stopped in front of Hal and twirled his moustache. The ribbons on his coat fluttered in the breeze, and the sash of his rank shimmered as he touched the sword at his side.

'We were interrupted, boy,' he said softly, in good unaccented English. 'However, there will be a time and a place for me to finish the lesson.'

'Let us hope so, sir.' Hal was brave with Aboli at his side. 'I am always grateful for instruction.'

For a moment they held each other's eyes, and then Schreuder dropped over the galleon's side to the deck of the caravel. Immediately the lines were cast off and the Dutch crew set the sails. The *Lady Edwina* threw up her stern like a skittish colt and heeled to the press of her canvas. Lightly she turned away from the land to make her offing.

'We also will get under way, if you please, Master Ned!' Sir Francis said. 'Up with her anchor.'

The galleon bore away from the African coast, heading into the south. From the masthead where Hal crouched the *Lady Edwina* was still in plain view. The smaller vessel was standing out to clear the treacherous shoals of the Agulhas Cape, before coming around to run before the wind down to the Dutch fort below the great table-topped mountain that guarded the south-western extremity of the African continent.

As Hal watched, the silhouette of the caravel's sails altered drastically. He leaned out and shouted down, 'The *Lady Edwina* is altering course.'

'Where away?' his father yelled back.

'She's running free,' Hal told him. 'Her new course looks to be due west.'

She was doing precisely what they expected of her. With the sou'-easter well abaft her beam, she was now heading directly for Good Hope.

'Keep her under your eye.'

As Hal watched her, the caravel dwindled in size until her white sails merged with the tossing manes of the wind-driven white horses on the horizon.

'She's gone!' he shouted at the quarterdeck. 'Out of sight from here!'

Sir Francis had waited for this moment before he brought the galleon around onto her true heading. Now he gave the orders to the helm that brought her around towards the east, and she went back on a broad reach parallel with the African coast. 'This seems to be her best point of sailing,' he said to Hal, as his son came down to the deck after being relieved at the masthead. 'Even with her jury-rigging, she's showing a good turn of speed. We must get to know the whims and caprice of our new mistress. Make a cast of the log, please.'

With the glass in hand, Hal timed the wooden log on its reel, dropped from the bows on its journey back along the hull until it reached the stern. He made a quick calculation on the slate, and then looked up at his father. 'Six knots through the water.'

'With a new mainmast she will be good for ten. Ned Tyler has found a spar of good Norwegian pine stowed away in her hold. We will step it as soon as we get into port.' Sir Francis looked delighted: God was smiling upon them. 'Assemble the ship's company. We will ask God's blessing on her and rename her.'

They stood bare-headed in the wind, clutching their caps to their breasts, their expressions as pious as they could muster, anxious not to attract the disfavour of Sir Francis.

'We thank you, Almighty God, for the victory you have granted us over the heretic and the apostate, the benighted followers of the son of Satan, Martin Luther.'

'Amen!' they cried loudly. They were all good Anglicans, apart from the black tribesmen amongst them, but these Negroes cried, 'Amen!' with the rest. They had learned that word their first day aboard Sir Francis's ship.

'We thank you also for your timely and merciful intervention in the midst of the battle and your deliverance of us from certain defeat—'

Hal shuffled in disagreement, but without looking up. Some of the credit for the timely intervention was his, and his father had not acknowledged this as openly.

'We thank you and praise your name for placing in our hands this fine ship. We give you our solemn oath that we will use her to bring humiliation and punishment upon your enemies. We ask your blessing upon her. We beg you to look kindly upon her, and to sanction the new name which we now give her. From henceforth she will become the *Resolution*.'

His father had simply translated the galleon's Dutch name, and Hal was saddened that this ship would not bear his mother's name. He wondered if his father's memory of his mother was at last fading, or if he had some other reason for no longer perpetuating her memory. He knew, though, that he would never have the courage to ask, and he must simply accept this decision.

'We ask your continued help and intervention in our endless battle against the godless. We thank you humbly for the rewards you have so bountifully heaped upon us. And we trust that if we prove worthy you will reward our worship and sacrifice with further proof of the love you bear us.'

This was a perfectly reasonable sentiment, one with which every man on board, true Christian or pagan, could be in full accord. Every man devoted to God's work on earth was entitled to his rewards, and not only in the life to come. The treasures that filled the *Resolution*'s holds were proof and tangible evidence of his approval and consideration towards them.

'Now let's have a cheer for *Resolution* and all who sail in her.'

They cheered until they were hoarse, and Sir Francis silenced them at last. He replaced his broad-brimmed hat and gestured for them to cover their heads. His expression became stern and forbidding. 'There is one more task we have to perform now,' he told them, and looked at Big Daniel. 'Bring the prisoners on deck, Master Daniel.'

Sam Bowles was at the head of the forlorn file that came up from the hold, blinking in the sunlight. They were led aft and forced to kneel, facing the ship's company.

Sir Francis read their names from the sheet of parchment he held up. 'Samuel Bowles. Edward Broom. Peter Law. Peter Miller. John Tate. You kneel before your shipmates accused of cowardice and desertion in the face of the enemy, and dereliction of your duty.'

The other men growled and glared at them.

'How say you to these charges? Are you the cowards and traitors we accuse you of being?'

'Mercy, your grace. It was a madness of the moment. Truly we repent. Forgive us, we beg you for the sakes of our wives and the sweet babes we left at home,' Sam Bowles pleaded as their spokesman.

'The only wives you ever had were the trulls in the bawdy houses of Dock Street,' Big Daniel mocked him, and the crew roared.

'String them up at the yard-arm! Let's watch them dance a little jig to the devil.'

'Shame on you!' Sir Francis stopped them. 'What kind of English justice is this? Every man, no matter how base, is entitled to a fair trial.' They sobered and he went on. 'We will deal with this matter in proper order. Who brings these charges against them?'

'We do!' roared the crew in unison.

'Who are your witnesses?'

'We are!' they replied, with a single voice.

'Did you witness any act of treachery or cowardice? Did you see these foul creatures flee from the fight and leave their shipmates to their fate?'

'We did.'

'You have heard the testimony against you. Do you have aught to say in your defence?'

'Mercy!' whined Sam Bowles. The others were dumb.

Sir Francis turned back to the crew. 'And so what is your verdict?'

'Guilty!'

'Guilty as hell!' added Big Daniel, lest there be any lingering doubts.

'And your sentence?' Sir Francis asked, and immediately an uproar broke out.

'Hang 'em.'

'Hanging's too good for the swine. Keel haul 'em.'

'No! No! Draw and quarter 'em. Make them eat their own balls.'

'Let's fry some pork! Burn the bastards at the stake.'

Sir Francis silenced them again. 'I see we have some differences of opinion.' He gestured to Big Daniel. 'Take them down below and lock them up. Let them stew in their own stinking juices for a day or two. We will deal with them when we get into port. Until then there are more important matters to attend to.'

For the first time in his life aboard ship, Hal had a cabin of his own. He need no longer share every sleeping and waking moment of his life crammed in enforced intimacy with a horde of other humanity.

The galleon was spacious by comparison with the little caravel, and his father had found a place for him alongside his own magnificent quarters. It had been the cupboard of the Dutch captain's servant, and was a mere cubby-hole. 'You need a lighted place to continue your studies,' Sir Francis had justified this indulgence. 'You waste many hours each night sleeping when you could be working.' He ordered the ship's carpenter to knock together a bunk and a shelf on which Hal could lay out his books and papers.

An oil lamp swung above his head, blackening the deck overhead with its soot, but giving Hal just enough light to make out his lines and allow him to write the lessons his father set him. His eyes burned with fatigue and he had to stifle his yawns as he dipped his quill and peered at the sheet of parchment onto which he was copying the extract from the Dutch captain's sailing directions that his father had captured. Every navigator had his own personal manual of sailing directions, a priceless journal in which he kept details of oceans and seas, currents and coasts, landfalls and harbours; tables of the compass's changeable and mysterious deviations as a ship voyaged in foreign waters, and charts of the night sky, which altered with the latitudes. This was knowledge that each navigator painstakingly accumulated over his lifetime, from his own observations or gleaned from the experience and anecdotes of others. His father would expect him to complete this work before his watch at the masthead, which began at four in the morning.

A faint noise from behind the bulkhead distracted him, and he looked up with the quill still in his hand. It was a footfall so soft as to be almost inaudible and came from the luxurious quarters of the Governor's wife. He listened with every fibre of his being, trying to interpret each sound that reached him. His heart told him that it was the lovely Katinka, but he could not be certain of that. It might be her ugly old maid, or even the grotesque husband. He felt deprived and cheated at the thought.

However, he convinced himself that it was Katinka and her nearness thrilled him, even though the planking of the bulkhead separated them. He yearned so desperately for her that he could not concentrate on his task or even remain seated.

He stood, forced to stoop by the low deck above his head, and moved silently to the bulkhead. He leaned against it and listened. He heard a light scraping, the sound of a something being dragged across the deck, the rustle of cloth, some further sounds that he could not place, and then the purling sound of liquid flowing into a basin or bowl. With his ear against the panel, he visualized every movement beyond. He heard her dip water with her cupped hands and dash it into her face, heard her small gasps as the cold struck her cheeks, and then the drops splash back into the basin.

He looked down and saw that a faint ray of candlelight was shining through a crack in the panelling, a narrow sliver of yellow light that wavered in rhythm to the ship's motion. Without regard to the consequence of what he was doing, he sank to his knees and placed his eye to the crack. He could see little, for it was narrow, and the soft light of the candle was directly in his eye.

Then something passed between him and the candle, a swirl of silks and lace. He stared then gasped as he caught the pearly gleam of flawless white skin. It was merely a flash, so swift that he barely had time to make out the line of a naked back, luminous as mother-of-pearl in the yellow light.

He pressed his face closer to the panel, desperate for another glimpse of such beauty. He fancied that over the normal sound of the ship's timbers working in the seaway he could hear soft breathing, light as the whisper of a tropic zephyr. He held his own breath to listen until his lungs burned, and he felt light-headed with awe.

At that moment the candle in the other cabin was whisked away, the ray of light through the crack sped across his straining eye and was gone. He heard soft footfalls move away, and darkness and silence fell beyond the panelling.

He stayed kneeling for a long while, like a worshipper at a shrine, and then rose slowly and seated himself once more at his work shelf. He tried to force his tired brain to attend to the task his father had set him, but it kept breaking away like an unruly colt from the trainer's noose. The letters on the page before him dissolved in images of alabaster skin and golden hair. In his nostrils was a memory of that tantalizing odour he had smelt when first he burst into her cabin. He covered his eyes with one hand in an attempt to prevent the visions invading his aching brain.

It was to no avail: his mind was beyond his control. He reached for his Bible, which lay beside his journal, and opened the leather cover. Between the pages was a fine gold filigree, that single strand of hair that he had stolen from her comb.

He touched it to his lips, then gave a low moan: he fancied he could still detect a trace of her perfume on it, and he closed his eyes tightly.

It was some time before he became aware of the actions of his treacherous right hand. Like a thief it had crept under the skirts of the loose canvas petticoat that was his only garment in the hot, stuffy little cubby-hole. By the time he realized what he was doing it was too late to stop himself. He surrendered helplessly to the pumping and tugging of his own fingers. The sweat ran from his every pore and slicked down his hard young muscles. The rod he held between his fingers was hard as bone and endowed with a throbbing life of its own.

The scent of her filled his head. His hand beat fast but not as fast as his heart. He knew this was sin and folly. His father had warned him, but he could not stop. He writhed on his stool. He felt the ocean of his love for her pressing against the dyke of his restraint, like a high and irresistible tide. He gave a small cry and the tide burst from him. He felt the warm flood of it spray down his rigid straining thighs, heard it splatter the deck, and then its musky odour drove the sacred perfume of her hair from his nostrils.

He sat, sweating and panting softly, and let the waves of guilt and self-disgust overwhelm him. He had betrayed his father's trust, the promise he had made him, and with his profane lust, he had besmirched the pure and lovely image of a saint.

He could not remain in his cabin a moment longer. He flung on his canvas sea-jacket and fled up the ladder to the deck. He stood for a while at the rail breathing deeply. The raw salt air cleansed his guilt and self-disgust. He felt steadier, and looked about him to take stock of his surroundings.

The ship was still on the larboard tack, with the wind abeam. Her masts swung back and forth across the brilliant canopy of stars. He could just make out the lowering mass of the land down to leeward. The Great Bear stood a finger's breadth above the dark silhouette of the land. It was a nostalgic reminder of the land of his birth, and the childhood he had left behind.

To the south the sky was dazzling with the constellation of Centaurus standing above his right shoulder, and the mighty Southern Cross, burning in its heart. This was the symbol of this new world beyond the Line.

He looked to the helm and saw his father's pipe glow in a sheltered corner of the quarterdeck. He did not want to face him now, for he was certain that his guilt and depravity would still be so engraved on his features that his father would recognize it even in the gloom. Yet he knew that his father had seen him, and would count it as odd if he did not pay him respect. He went to him quickly. 'Your indulgence, please, Father. I came up for a breath of air to clear my head,' he mumbled, not able to meet Sir Francis's eyes.

'Don't idle up here too long,' his father cautioned him. 'I will want to see your task completed before you take your watch at the masthead.'

Hal hurried forward. This expansive deck was still unfamiliar. Much of the cargo and goods from the caravel could not fit into the galleon's already crammed holds and was lashed down on the deck. He picked his way among the casks and chests, and bronze culverins.

Hal was still so deep in remorse and guilt that he was aware of little around him, until he heard a soft, conspiratorial whispering near at hand. His wits returned to him with a rush, and he looked towards the bows.

A small group of figures was hiding in the shadows cast by the cargo stacked under the rise of the forecastle. Their furtive movements alerted him to something out of the ordinary.

After their trial by their peers, Sam Bowles and his men had been frogmarched down into the galleon's lower decks and thrown into a small compartment, which must have been the carpenter's store. There was no light and little air. The reek of pepper and bilges was stifling, and the space so confined that all five could not stretch out at the same time on the deck. They settled themselves as best they could into this hellhole, and lapsed into a forlorn, despairing silence.

'Whereabouts are we? Below the waterline, do you think?' Ed Broom asked miserably.

'None of us knows his way about this Dutch hulk,' Sam Bowles muttered.

'Do you reckon they're going to murder us?' Peter Law asked.

'You can be sure they ain't about to give us a hug and a kiss,' Sam grunted.

'Keel-hauling,' Ed whispered. 'I seen it done once. When they'd dragged the poor bastard under the ship and got him out t'other side he was drowned dead as a rat in a beer barrel. There weren't much meat on his carcass – it were all scraped off by the barnacles under the hull. You could see his bones sticking out all white, like.'

They thought about that for a while. Then Peter Law said, 'I saw 'em hang and draw the regicides at Tyburn back in 'fifty-nine. Them as murdered King Charlie, the Black Boy's father. They opened they bellies like fish, then they stuck in an iron hook and twisted it until they had caught up all they guts, and they pulled their intestines out of them like ropes. After that they hacked off their cocks and their balls—'

'Shut your mouth!' Sam snarled, and they lapsed into abject silence in the darkness.

An hour later Ed Broom murmured, 'There's air coming in here some place. I can feel it on my neck.'

After a moment Peter Law said, 'He's right, you know. I can feel it too.'

'What's behind this bulkhead?'

'Ain't nobody knows. Maybe the main cargo hold.'

There was a scrabbling sound, and Sam demanded, 'What you doing?'

'There's a gap in the planking here. That's where the air's coming in.'

'Let me see.' Sam crawled across and, after a few moments, agreed. 'You're right. I can get my fingers through the hole.'

'If we could open her up.'

'If Big Daniel catches you at it, you're in bad trouble.'

'What's he going to do? Draw and quarter us? He aims to do that already.'

Sam worked in the darkness for a while and then growled, 'If I had something to prise this planking open.'

'I'm sitting on some loose timber.'

'Let's have a piece of it here.'

They were all working together now, and at last they forced the end of a sturdy wooden strut through the gap in the bulkhead. Using it as a lever they threw their weight on it together. The wood tore with a crack and Sam thrust his arm into the opening. 'There's open space beyond. Could be a way out.'

They all pushed forward for a chance to tear at the edges of the opening, ripping out their fingernails and driving splinters into the palms of their hands in their haste.

'Back! Get back!' Sam told them, and wriggled head-first into the opening. As soon as they heard him crawling away on the far side they scrambled through after him.

Groping his way forward Sam choked as the fiery reek of pepper burned his throat. They were in the hold that contained the spice casks. There was a little more light in here: it came in through the gaps where the hatch coaming had not been secured.

They could hardly make out the huge casks, each taller than a man, stacked in ranks, and there was no room to crawl over the top, for the deck was too low. However, they could just squeeze between them, but it was a hazardous passage.

The heavy casks shifted slightly with the action of the ship. They scraped and thumped on the timbers of the deck and fretted against the ropes that restrained them. A man would be crushed like a cockroach if he were caught between them.

Sam Bowles was the smallest. He crawled ahead and the others followed. Suddenly a piercing scream rang through the hold and froze them all.

'Quiet, you stupid bastard!' Sam turned back in fury. 'You'll have 'em down on us.'

'My arm!' screamed Peter Law. 'Get it off me.'

One of the huge casks had lifted with the roll of the hull and then come down again, its full weight trapping the man's arm against the deck. It was still sliding and pounding down on his limb, and they could hear the bones in his forearm and elbow crushing like dry wheat between millstones. He was screeching in hysteria and there was no quieting him: pain had driven him beyond all reasoning.

Sam crawled back and reached his side. 'Shut your mouth!' He grabbed Peter's shoulder and heaved, trying to drag him clear. But the arm was jammed, and Peter screamed all the louder.

'Ain't nothing for it,' Sam growled, and from around his waist he pulled the length of rope that served him as a belt. He dropped a loop over the other man's head and drew the noose tight round his throat. He leaned back on it, anchoring both feet between his victim's shoulder blades, and pulled with all his strength. Abruptly Peter's wild screams were cut off. Sam kept the noose tight for some time after the struggles had ceased, then freed it and retied it about his waist. 'I had to do it,' he muttered to the others. 'Better one man dead than all of us.'

No one spoke, but they followed Sam as he crawled forward, leaving the strangled corpse to be crushed to mincemeat by the shifting casks.

'Give me a hand here,' Sam said and the others boosted him up onto one of the casks below the hatch.

'There's naught but a piece of canvas 'tween us and the deck now,' he whispered triumphantly, and reached up to touch the tightly stretched cover.

'Come on, let's get out of here,' Ed Broom whispered.

'Still broad day out there.' Sam held him as he tried to loosen the ropes that held the canvas cover in place. 'Wait for dark. Won't be long now.'

Gradually the light filtering down through the chinks around the canvas cover dulled and faded. They could hear the ship's bell tolling the watches.

'End of the last dog watch,' said Ed. 'Let's go now.'

'Give it a while more,' Sam urged. After another hour, he nodded. 'Loose those sheets.'

'What we going to do out there?' Now that it was time to move they were fearful. 'You'll not be thinking of trying to take the ship?'

'Nay, you donkey. I've had enough of your bloody Captain Franky. Find anything that floats and then it's over the side for me. The land's not far off.'

'What of the sharks?'

'Captain Franky bites worse than any sodding shark you'll meet out there.'

No one argued with that.

They freed a corner of the canvas, and Sam lifted the flap and peered out. 'All clear. There's some of the empty water casks at the foot of the foremast. They'll do us just Jack-a-dandy.'

He wriggled out from under the canvas and darted across the deck. The others followed, one at a time, and helped him tear at the lashing that held the empty casks in place. Within seconds they had two clear.

'Together now, lads,' Sam whispered, and they trundled the first across the deck. They heaved up the cask between them and flung it over the rail, ran back and grabbed a second.

'Hey! You men! What are you doing?' The challenge from close at hand shocked them all and they turned pale faces to look back. They all recognized Hal.

'It's Franky's whelp!' one cried, and they dropped the cask and scampered for the ship's side. Ed Broom was first over. He dived headlong, with Peter Miller and John Tate close behind him.

Hal took a moment to realize what they were up to, and then bounded forward to intercept Sam Bowles. He was the ringleader, the most guilty of the gang, and Hal tackled him as he reached the ship's rail.

'Father!' he shouted, loud enough for his voice to carry to every quarter of the deck. 'Father, help me!'

Locked chest to chest they struggled. Hal fastened a head-lock on him, but Sam threw back his head then butted forward in the hope of breaking Hal's nose. But Big Daniel had taught Hal his wrestling, and he had been ready: he dropped his chin on his chest so that his skull clashed with Sam's. Both men were half stunned by the impact, and broke from each other's grip.

Instantly Sam lurched for the rail but, on his knees, Hal grabbed at his legs. 'Father!' he screamed again. Sam tried to kick him off but Hal held on grimly. Then Sam looked up and saw Sir Francis Courtney charging down from the quarterdeck. His sword was out and the blade flashed in the starlight.

'Hold hard, Hal! I'm coming!'

There was no time for Sam to free the rope belt from around his middle, and drop the loop over Hal's head. Instead he reached down and locked both hands around his throat. He was a small man, but his fingers were work-toughened, hard as iron marlinspikes. He found Hal's windpipe and blocked it off ruthlessly.

The pain choked Hal, and his grip loosened on Sam's legs. He seized the man's wrists, trying to break his stranglehold, but Sam placed one foot on his chest, kicked him over backwards, then darted to the side of the ship. Sir Francis aimed a sword cut at him as he ran up, but Sam ducked under it and dived over the rail.

'The treacherous vermin will get clear away!' Sir Francis howled. 'Boatswain, call all hands to tack ship. We will go back to pick them up.'

Sam Bowles was driven deep by the force with which he hit the water, and the shock of the cold drove the wind from his lungs. He felt himself drowning, but fought and clawed his way up. At last his head broke the surface, he sucked in a lungful of air and felt the dizziness, and the weakness in his limbs, pass.

He looked up at the hull of the ship, trundling majestically past him, and then he was left in her wake, which glistened slick and oily in the starlight. That was the highway that would guide him back to the cask. He must follow it before the swells wiped it away and left him with no signpost in the darkness. His feet were bare and he wore only a ragged cotton shirt and his canvas petticoats, which would not encumber his movements. He struck out overarm for, unlike most of his fellows, he was a strong swimmer.

Within a dozen strokes he heard a voice in the darkness nearby. 'Help me, Sam Bowles!' He recognized Ed Broom's wild cries. 'Give me a hand, shipmate, or I'm done for.'

Sam stopped to tread water and, in the starlight, saw the splashes of Ed's struggles. Beyond him he saw something else lift on the crest of a dark swell, something black and round.

The cask!

But Ed was between him and this promise of survival. Sam started swimming again, but he sheered away from Ed Broom. It was dangerous to come too close to a drowning man, for he would always seize you and hang on with a death grip, until he had taken you down with him.

'Please, Sam! Don't leave me.' Ed's voice was growing fainter.

Sam reached the floating cask and got a handhold on the protruding spigot. He rested a while then roused himself as another head bobbed up beside him. 'Who's that?' he gasped.

'It's me, John Tate,' the swimmer blurted out, coughing up sea water as he tried to find a hold on the barrel.

Sam reached down and loosened the rope belt from around his waist. He used it to take a turn around the spigot and thrust his arm through the loop. John Tate grabbed at the loop too.

Sam tried to push him away. 'Leave it! It's mine.' But John's grip was desperate with panic and after a minute Sam let him be. He could not afford to squander his own strength in wrestling with a bigger man.

They hung together on the rope in a hostile truce. 'What happened to Peter Miller?' John Tate demanded.

'Bugger Peter Miller!' snarled Sam.

The water was cold and dark, and both men imagined what might be lurking beneath their feet. A pack of the monstrous tiger sharks always followed the ship in these latitudes, to pick up the offal and contents of the latrine buckets as they were emptied overboard. Sam had seen one of these fearsome creatures as long as the *Lady Edwina*'s pinnace and he thought about it now. He felt his lower body cringe and tremble with cold and the dread of those serried ranks of fangs closing over it to shear him in two, as he might bite into a ripe apple.

'Look!' John Tate choked as a wave hit him in the face and flooded his open mouth. Sam raised his head and saw a dark, mountainous shape loom out of the night close by.

'Bloody Franky come back to find us,' he growled, through chattering teeth. They watched in horror as the galleon bore down on them, growing larger with each second until she seemed to blot out all the stars and they could hear the voices of the men on her deck.

'Do you see anything there, Master Daniel?' That was Sir Francis's hail.

'Nothing, Captain,' Big Daniel's voice boomed from the bows. Looking down onto the black, turbulent water it would be nigh on impossible to make out the dark wood of the cask or the two heads bobbing beside it.

They were hit by the bow wave the galleon threw up as she passed and were left twisting and bobbing in her wake as her stern lantern receded into the darkness.

Twice more during the night they saw its glimmer, but each time the ship passed further from them. Many hours later, as the dawn light strengthened, they looked with trepidation for *Resolution*, but she was nowhere in sight. She must have given them up for drowned and headed off on her original course. Stupefied with cold and fatigue, they hung on to their precarious handhold.

'There's the land,' Sam whispered, as a swell lifted them high, and they could make out the dark shoreline of Africa. 'It's so close you could swim to it easy.'

John Tate made no reply but stared at him sullenly through eyes scalded red and swollen.

'It's your best chance. Strong young fellow like you. Don't worry about me.' Sam's voice was rough with salt.

'You'll not get rid of me that easy, Sam Bowles,' John grated, and Sam fell silent again, husbanding his strength, for the cold had sapped him almost to his limit. The sun rose higher and they felt it on their heads, first as a gentle warmth that gave them new strength and then like the flames of an open furnace that seared their skin and dazzled and blinded them with its reflection off the sea around them.

The sun climbed higher, but the land came no closer: the current bore them inexorably parallel to the rocky headlands and white beaches. Idly Sam noticed a patch of cloud shadow that passed close by them, moving darkly across the surface of the water. Then the shadow turned and came back, moving against the wind, and Sam stirred and lifted his head. There was no cloud in the aching blue vault of the sky to cast such a shadow. Sam looked down again and concentrated his full attention on that dark presence on the sea. A swell lifted the cask so high that he could look down upon it.

'Sweet Jesus!' he croaked, through cracked salt-seared lips. The water was as clear as a glass of gin, and he had seen a great dappled shape move beneath, the dark zebra stripes upon its back. He screamed.

John Tate lifted his head. 'What is it? The sun's got you, Sam Bowles.' He stared into Sam's wild eyes, then turned his head slowly to follow their gaze. Both men saw the massive forked tail swing ponderously from side to side, driving the long body forward. It was coming up towards the surface and the tip of the tall dorsal fin broke through, only to the length of a man's finger, the rest still hidden deep beneath.

'Shark!' John Tate hissed. 'Tiger!' He kicked frantically, trying to turn the cask to interpose Sam between himself and the creature.

'Stay still,' Sam snarled. 'He's like a cat. If you move he'll come for you.'

They could see its eye, small for such girth and length of body. It stared at them implacably as it began the next circle. Round it went, and round again, each circle narrower, with the cask at its centre.

'Bastard's hunting us like a stoat after a partridge.'

'Shut your mouth. Don't move,' Sam moaned, but he could no longer control his terror. His sphincter loosened, and he felt the fetid warm rush under his petticoats as involuntarily his bowels emptied. Immediately the creature's movements became more excited and its tail beat to a faster rhythm as it tasted his excrement. The dorsal fin rose to its full height above the surface, as long and curved as the blade of a harvester's scythe.

The shark's tail beat the surface white and foamy as it drove forward until its snout crashed into the side of the cask. Sam watched in terror as a miraculous transformation came over the sleek head. The upper lip bulged outwards as the wide jaws gaped. The ranks of fangs were thrust forward, fanning open, and clashed against the side of the wooden cask.

Both men panicked and scrabbled at their damaged raft, trying to lift their lower bodies clear of the water. They were screaming incoherently, clawing wildly at the barrel staves and at each other.

The shark backed off and started another of those terrible circles. Beneath the staring eye the mouth was a grinning crescent. Now the thrashing legs of the struggling men gave it a new focus, and it surged in again, its broad back thrusting aside the waters.

John Tate's shriek was cut off abruptly, but his mouth was still wide open, so that Sam looked down his pink gulping throat. No sound came from it but a soft hiss of expelled breath. Then he was jerked beneath the surface. His left wrist was still twisted into the loop of line and, as he was pulled under, the cask bobbed and ducked like a cork.

'Leave go!' Sam howled as he was thrown around, the rope biting deep into his own wrist. Suddenly the cask flew to the surface, John Tate's wrist still twisted into the bight of line. A dark roseate cloud spread to discolour the surface around them.

Then John's head broke out. He made a harsh, cawing sound, and his bloodstained spittle sprayed into Sam's eyes. His face was icy white as his life's blood drained from him. The shark came surging back and, beneath the surface, latched onto John's lower body, worrying and shaking him so that the damaged cask was again pulled under. As it shot once more to the surface, Sam sucked in a breath, and tugged at John's wrist. 'Get away!' he screamed at both man and shark. 'Get away from me.' With the strength of a madman, he pulled the loop free and he kicked at the other man's chest, pushing him clear, screaming all the while, 'Get away!'

John Tate did not resist. His eyes were still wide open but although his lips writhed, no sound came from them. Below the surface his body had been bitten away below the waist, and his blood turned the waters dark red. The shark seized him once again, then swam off, gulping down lumps of John Tate's flesh.

The damaged cask had taken in water and now floated low, but this gave it a stability it had lacked when it rode high and lightly. At the third attempt Sam dragged himself up onto it. He draped both arms and legs over it, straddling it. The cask's balance was precarious and he dared not lift even his head for fear of upsetting it and being rolled back into the sea. After a while he saw the great dorsal fin pass before his eyes as the creature came back once more to the cask. He dared not lift his head to follow the narrowing circles, so he closed his eyes and tried to shut his mind to the beast's presence.

Suddenly the cask lurched under him and his resolve was forgotten. His eyes flew wide and he shrieked. But after having bitten into the wood the shark was backing away. Twice more it returned, each time nudging the cask with its grotesque snout. However, each attempt was less determined, perhaps because it had assuaged its appetite on John Tate's carcass and was now discouraged by the taste and smell of the splinters of wood. Eventually Sam saw it turn and move away, its tall fin wagging from side to side as it swam up-current.

He lay unmoving, draped over the cask, riding the salty belly of the ocean, rising and falling to her thrusts like an exhausted lover. The night fell over him, and now he could not have moved even if he had wished to. He fell into delirium and bouts of oblivion.

He dreamed that it was morning again, that he had survived the night. He dreamed that he heard human voices near at hand. He dreamed that when he opened his eyes he saw a tall ship, hove to close alongside. He knew it was fantasy for, in a twelve-month span, fewer than two dozen ships rounded this remote cape at the end of the world. Yet, as he watched, a boat was lowered from the ship's side and rowed towards him. Only when he felt rough hands seize his legs did he realize dully that this was no dream.

The *Resolution* edged in towards the land with only a feather of canvas set and the crew standing ready for the order to whip it off and furl it on her masts.

Sir Francis's eyes darted from the sails to the land close ahead. He listened intently to the chant of the leadsman as he swung the line and let the weight drop ahead of their bows. As the ship passed over it, and the line came straight up and down, he read the sounding. 'By the deep twenty!'

'Top of the tide in an hour.' Hal looked up from the slate. 'And full moon in three days. She'll be making springs.'

'Thank you, pilot,' Sir Francis said, with a touch of sarcasm. Hal was only performing his duty, but the lad was not the only one aboard who had pored for hours over the almanac and the tables. Then Sir Francis relented. 'Get up to the masthead, lad. Keep your eyes wide open.'

He watched Hal race up the shrouds, then glanced at the helm and said quietly, 'Larboard a point, Master Ned.'

'A point to larboard it is, Captain.' With his teeth Ned moved the stem of his empty clay pipe from one corner of his mouth to the other. He, too, had seen the white surge of reef at the entrance to the channel.

The land was so close now that they could make out the individual branches of the trees that grew tall on the rocky heads that guarded the entrance. 'Steady as she goes,' Sir Francis said, as the *Resolution* crept forward between these towering cliffs of rock. He had never seen this entrance marked on any chart that he had either captured or purchased. This coast was depicted always as forbidding and dangerous, with few safe anchorages for a thousand miles north from Table Bay at Good Hope. Yet as the *Resolution* thrust deeper into the green water channel, a lovely broad lagoon opened ahead of her, surrounded on all sides by high hills, densely forested.

'Elephant Lagoon!' Hal exulted at the masthead. It was over two months since last they had sailed from this secret sallyport. As if to justify the name that Sir Francis had given this harbour, there came a clarion blast from the beach below the forest.

Hal laughed with pleasure as he picked out on the beach four huge grey shapes. They stood shoulder to shoulder in a solid rank, facing the ship, their ears spread wide. Their trunks were raised straight and high, the nostrils at the tips questing the air for the scent of this strange apparition they saw coming towards them. The bull elephant lifted his long yellow tusks and shook his head until his ears clapped like the tattered grey canvas of an unfurling main sail. He trumpeted again.

In the ship's bows, Aboli returned the greeting, raising his hand above his head in salute and calling out in the language that only Hal could understand, 'I see you, wise old man. Go in peace, for I am of your totem and I mean you no harm.'

At the sound of his voice the elephants backed away from the water's edge, then turned as one and headed back into the forest at a shambling run. Hal laughed again, at Aboli's words and to watch the great beasts go, trampling and shaking the forest with their might.

Then he concentrated once more on picking out the sandbanks and shoals, and in calling down directions to his father on the quarterdeck. The *Resolution* followed the meandering channel down the length of the lagoon until she came out into a wide green pool. The last scrap of her canvas was stripped and furled on her yards, and her anchor splashed into its depths. She swung round gently and snubbed at her anchor chain.

She lay only fifty yards off the beach, hidden behind a small island in the lagoon, so that she was concealed from the casual scrutiny of a passing ship looking in through the entrance between the heads. The way was scarcely off her before Sir Francis was shouting his orders. 'Carpenter! Get the pinnaces assembled and launched.'

Before noon the first was lowered from the deck to the water, and ten men went down into her with their ditty bags. Big Daniel took charge of the oarsmen, who rowed them down the lagoon and put them ashore at the foot of the rocky heads. Through his telescope Sir Francis watched them climb the steep elephant path to the summit. From there they would keep a lookout and warn him of the approach of any strange sail.

'On the morrow we will move the culverins to the entrance and set them up in stone emplacements to cover the channel,' he told Hal. 'Now, we will celebrate our arrival with fresh fish for our dinner. Get out the hooks and lines. Take Aboli and four men with you in the other pinnace. Dig some crabs from the beach and bring me back a load of fish for the ship's mess.'

Standing in the bows as the pinnace was rowed out into the channel, Hal peered down into the water. It was so clear that he could see the sandy bottom. The lagoon teemed with fish and shoal after shoal sped away before the boat. Many were as long as his arm, some as long as the spread of both arms.

When they anchored in the deepest part of the channel, Hal dropped a handline over the side, the hooks baited with crabs they had taken from their holes on the sandy beach. Before it touched the bottom, the bait was seized with such rude power that before he could check it the line scorched his fingers. Leaning back against the line he brought it in hand over hand, and swung a flapping, glistening body of purest silver over the gunwale.

While it still thumped upon the deck and Hal struggled to twist the barbed hook from its rubbery lip, Aboli shouted with excitement and heaved back on his own line. Before he could swing his fish over the side, all the other sailors were laughing and straining to pull heavy darting fish aboard.

Within the hour the deck was knee-deep in dead fish and they were all smeared to the eyebrows with slime and scales. Even the hard, rope-calloused hands of the seamen were bleeding from line burn and the prick of sharp fins. It was no longer sport but hard work to keep the inverted waterfall of living silver streaming over the side.

Just before sunset Hal called a halt, and they rowed back towards the anchored galleon. They were still a hundred yards from her when, on an impulse, Hal stood up in the stern and stripped off his stinking slime-coated clothes. Stark mother naked he balanced on the thwart, and called to Aboli, 'Take her alongside and unload the catch. I will swim from here.' He had not bathed in over two months, since last they had anchored in the lagoon, and he longed for the feel of cool clear water on his skin. He gathered himself and dived overboard. The men at the galleon's rail shouted ribald encouragement and even Sir Francis paused and watched him indulgently.

'Let him be, Captain. He's still a carefree boy,' said Ned Tyler. 'It's just that he's so big and tall that we sometimes forget that.' Ned had been with Sir Francis for so many years that he could be forgiven such familiarity.

'There's no place for a thoughtless boy in the *guerre de course*. This is man's work and it needs a hard head on even the most youthful shoulders or there'll be a Dutch noose for that thoughtless head.' But he made no effort to reprimand Hal as he watched his naked white body slide through the water, supple and agile as a dolphin.

Katinka heard the commotion on the deck above, and raised her eyes from the book she was reading. It was a copy of François Rabelais' *Gargantua and Pantagruel* which had been printed privately in Paris with beautifully detailed erotic illustrations, hand-coloured and lifelike. A young man she had known in Amsterdam before her hasty marriage had sent it to her. From close and intimate experience, he knew her tastes well. She glanced idly through the window and her interest quickened. She dropped the book and stood up for a better view.

'*Lieveling*, your husband,' Zelda warned her.

'The devil with my husband,' said Katinka, as she stepped out onto the stern gallery and shaded her eyes against the slanting rays of the setting sun.

The young Englishman who had captured her stood in the stern of a small boat, not far across the quiet lagoon waters. As she watched he stripped off his soiled and tattered clothing, until he stood naked and unashamed, balancing with easy grace on the gunwale.

As a young girl she had accompanied her father to Italy. There she had bribed Zelda to take her to see the collection of sculptures by Michelangelo, while her father was meeting with his Italian trading partners. She had spent almost an hour of that sultry afternoon standing before the statue of David. Its beauty had aroused in her a turmoil of emotion. It was the first depiction of masculine nudity she had ever looked upon, and it had changed her life.

Now she was looking at another David sculpture, but this one was not of cold marble. Of course, since their first encounter in her cabin she had seen the boy often. He dogged her footsteps like an over-affectionate puppy. Whenever she left her cabin he appeared miraculously, to moon at her from afar. His transparent adoration afforded her only the mildest amusement, for she was accustomed to no less from every man between the ages of fourteen and eighty. He had barely warranted more than a glance, this pretty boy, in baggy, filthy rags. After their first violent meeting, the stink of him had lingered in her cabin, so pungent that she had ordered Zelda to sprinkle perfume to dispel it. But, then, she knew from bitter experience that all sailors stank for there was no water on the ship other than for drinking, and little enough of that.

Now that the lad had shed his noisome clothing, he had become a thing of striking beauty. Though his arms and face were bronzed by the sun, his torso and legs were carved in pure unsullied white. The low sun gilded the curves and angles of his body and his dark hair tumbled down his back. His teeth were very white in the tanned face, and his laughter so musical and filled with such zest that it brought a smile to her own lips.

Then she looked down his body and her mouth opened. The violet eyes narrowed and became calculating. The sweet lines of his face were deceiving. He was a lad no longer. His belly was flat, ridged with fine young muscle like the sands of a wind-sculpted dune. At its base flared a dark bush of crisp curls, and his rosy genitals hung full and weighty, with an authority that those of Michelangelo's David had lacked.

When he dived into the lagoon, she could follow his every movement beneath the clear water. He came to the surface and, laughing, flung the sodden hair from his face with a toss of his head. The flying droplets sparkled like the sacred nimbus of light around the head of an angel.

He struck out towards where she stood, high in the stern, gliding through the water with a peculiar grace that she had not noticed he possessed when clothed in his canvas tatters. He passed almost directly under where she was but did not look up at her, unaware of her scrutiny. She could make out the knuckles of his spine flanked by ridges of hard muscle that ran down to merge with the deep crease between his lean, round buttocks, which tightened erotically with every kick of his legs, as though he were making love to the water as he passed through it.

She leaned out to follow him with her eyes, but he swam out of her view around the stern. Katinka pouted with frustration and went to retrieve her book. But the illustrations in it had lost their appeal, paling against the contrast of real flesh and glossy young skin.

She sat with it open on her lap and imagined that hard young body all white and glistening above her and those tight young buttocks bunching and changing shape as she dug her sharp fingernails into them. She knew instinctively that he was a virgin – she could almost smell the honey-sweet odour of chastity upon him and felt herself drawn to it, like a wasp to an overripe fruit. It would be her first time with a sexual innocent. The thought of it added spice to his natural beauty.

Her erotic daydreams were aggravated by the long period of her enforced abstinence and she lay back and pressed her thighs tightly together, beginning to rock gently back and forth in her chair, smiling secretly to herself.

Hal spent the next three nights camped on the beach below the heads. His father had placed him in charge of ferrying the cannon ashore and building the stone emplacements to house them, overlooking the narrow entrance to the lagoon.

Naturally Sir Francis had rowed across to approve the sites his son had chosen, but even he could find no fault with Hal's eye for a field of fire that would rake an enemy ship seeking to pass through the heads.

On the fourth day, when the work was done and Hal was rowed back down the lagoon, he saw from afar that the work of repairing the galleon was well in hand. The carpenter and his mates had built scaffolds over her stern, from which platform they were fitting new timbers to replace those damaged by gunfire, to the great discomfort of the guests aboard. The ungainly jurymast, raised by the Dutch captain to replace his gale-shattered main, had been taken down and the galleon's lines were awkward and unharmonious with one mast missing.

However, when Hal climbed up to the deck through the entryport, he saw that Ned Tyler and his work gang were swaying up the massive baulks of exotic timber that made up the heaviest part of the ship's cargo and lowering them into the lagoon to float across to the beach.

The spare mast was stowed at the bottom of the hold, where the sealed compartment contained the coin and ingots. The cargo had to be removed to reach them.

'Your father has sent for you,' Aboli greeted Hal, and Hal hurried aft.

'You have missed three days of your studies while you were ashore,' Sir Francis told him, without preamble.

'Yes, Father.' Hal knew that it was vain to point out that he had not deliberately evaded them. But, at least, I will not apologize for it, he determined silently, and met his father's gaze unflinchingly.

'After your supper this evening, I will rehearse you in the catechism of the Order. Come to my cabin at eight bells in the second dog watch.'

The catechism of initiation to the Order of St George and the Holy Grail had never been written down and for nearly four centuries the two hundred esoteric questions and answers had been passed on by word of mouth; master instructing novice in the Strict Observance.

Sitting beside Aboli on the foredeck, Hal wolfed hot biscuit, fried in dripping, and baked fresh fish. Now with an unlimited supply of firewood and fresh food on hand, the ship's meals were substantial, but Hal was silent as he ate. In his mind he went over his catechism, for his father would be strict in his judgement. Too soon the ship's bell struck and, as the last note faded, Hal tapped on the door to his father's cabin.

While his father sat at his desk Hal knelt on the bare planks of the deck. Sir Francis wore the cloak of his office over his shoulders, and on his breast sparkled the magnificent seal fashioned of gold, the insignia of a Nautonnier Knight who had passed through all the degrees of the Order. It depicted the lion rampant of England holding aloft the *croix patté* and, above it, the stars and crescent moon of the mother goddess. The lion's eyes were rubies and the stars were diamonds. On the second finger of his right hand he wore a narrow gold ring, engraved with a compass and a backstaff, the tools of the navigator, and above these a crowned lion. The ring was small and discreet, not as ostentatious as the seal.

His father conducted the catechism in Latin. The use of this language ensured that only literate, educated men could ever become members of the Order.

'Who are you?' Sir Francis asked the first question.

'Henry Courtney, son of Francis and Edwina.'

'What is your business here?'

'I come to present myself as an acolyte of the Order of St George and the Holy Grail.'

'Whence come you?'

'From the ocean sea, for that is my beginning and at my ending will be my shroud.' With this response Hal acknowledged the maritime roots of the Order. The next fifty questions examined the novice's understanding of the history of the Order.

'Who went before you?'

'The Poor Knights of Christ and of the Temple of Solomon.' The Knights of the Temple of the Order of St George and the Holy Grail were the successors to the extinct Order of the Knights Templar.

After that Sir Francis made Hal outline the history of the Order; how in the year 1312 the Knights Templar had been attacked and destroyed by the King of France, Philippe Le Bel, in connivance with his puppet Pope Clement V of Bordeaux. Their vast fortune in bullion and land was confiscated by the Crown, and most of them were tortured and burned at the stake. However, warned by their allies, the Templar mariners slipped their moorings in the French channel harbours and stood out to sea. They steered for England, and sought the protection of King Edward II. Since then, they had opened their lodges in Scotland and England under new names, but with the basic tenets of the Order intact.

Next Sir Francis made his son repeat the arcane words of recognition, and the grip of hands that identified the Knights to each other.

'*In Arcadia habito*. I dwell in Arcadia,' Sir Francis intoned, as he stooped over Hal to take his right hand in the double grip.

'*Flumen sacrum bene cognosco!* I know well the sacred river!' Hal replied reverently, interlocking his forefinger with his father's in the response.

'Explain the meaning of these words,' his father insisted.

'It is our covenant with God and each other. The Temple is Arcadia, and we are the river.'

The ship's bell twice sounded the passage of the hours before the two hundred questions were asked and answered, and Hal was allowed to rise stiffly from his knees.

When he reached his tiny cabin he was too weary even to light the oil lamp and dropped to his bunk fully clothed to lie there in a stupor of mental exhaustion. The questions and responses of the catechism echoed, an endless refrain, through his tired brain, until meaning and reality seemed to recede.

Then he heard faint sounds of movement from beyond the bulkhead and, miraculously, his fatigue cleared. He sat up, his senses tuned to the other cabin. He would not light the lamp for the sound of steel striking flint would carry through the panel. He rolled off his bunk and, in the darkness, moved on silent bare feet to the bulkhead.

He knelt and ran his fingers lightly along the joint in the woodwork until he found the plug he had left there. Quietly he removed it and placed his eye to the spyhole.

Each day his father allowed Katinka van de Velde and her maid, with Aboli to guard them, to go ashore and walk on the beach for an hour. That afternoon while the women had been away from the ship, Hal had found a moment to steal down to his cabin. He had used the point of his dirk to enlarge the crack in the bulkhead. Then he had whittled a plug of matching wood to close and conceal the opening.

Now he was filled with guilt, but he could not restrain himself. He placed his eye to the enlarged aperture. His view into the small cabin beyond was unimpeded. A tall Venetian mirror was fixed to the bulkhead opposite him and, in its reflection, he could see clearly even those areas of the cabin that otherwise would have been hidden from him. It was apparent that this smaller cabin was an annexe to the larger and more splendid main cabin. It seemed to serve as a dressing and retiring place where the Governor's wife could take her bath and attend to her private and intimate toilet. The bath was set up in the centre of the deck, a heavy ceramic hip bath in the Oriental style, the sides decorated with scenes of mountain landscapes and bamboo forests.

Katinka sat on a low stool across the cabin and her maid was tending her hair with one of the silver-backed brushes. It flowed down to her waist, and each stroke made it shimmer in the lamp-light. She wore a gown of brocade, stiff with gold embroidery, but Hal marvelled that her hair was more brilliant than the precious metal thread.

He gazed at her, entranced, trying to memorize each gesture of her white hands, and each delicate movement of her lovely head. The sound of her voice and her soft laughter were balm to his exhausted mind and body. The maid finished her task, and moved away. Katinka stood up from her stool and Hal's spirits plunged, for he expected her to take up the lamp and leave the cabin. But instead she came towards him. Though she passed out of his direct line of sight he could still see her reflection in the mirror. There was only the thickness of the panel between them now, and Hal was afraid she might become aware of his hoarse breathing.

He gazed at her reflection as she stooped and lifted the lid of the night cabinet that was affixed to the opposite side of the bulkhead against which Hal pressed. Suddenly, before he realized what she intended, she swept the skirts of her gown above her waist and, in the same movement, perched like a bird on the seat of the cabinet.

She continued to laugh and chat to her maid as her water purred into the chamber-pot beneath her. When she rose again Hal was given one more glimpse of her long pale legs before the skirts dropped over them and she swept gracefully from the cabin.

Hal lay on his hard bunk in the dark, his hands clasped across his chest, and tried to sleep. But the images of her beauty tormented him. His body burned and he rolled restlessly from side to side. 'I will be strong!' he whispered aloud, and clenched his fists until the knuckles cracked. He tried to drive the vision from his mind, but it buzzed in his brain like a swarm of angry bees. Once again he heard, in his imagination, her laughter mingle with the merry tinkle she made in her chamber-pot, and he could resist no longer. With a groan of guilt he capitulated and reached down with both hands to his swollen, throbbing loins.

Once the cargo of timber had been lifted out of the main hold, the spare mast could be raised to the deck. It was a labour that required half the ship's company. The massive spar was almost as long as the galleon and had to be carefully manoeuvred from its resting place in the bowels of the hold. It was floated across the channel and then dragged up the beach. There, in a clearing beneath the spreading forest canopy, the carpenters set it on trestles and began to trim and shape it, so that it could be stepped into the hull to replace the gale-shattered mast.

Only once the hold was emptied could Sir Francis call the entire ship's company to witness the opening of the treasure compartment that the Dutch authorities had deliberately covered with the heaviest cargo. It was the usual practice of the VOC to secure the most valuable items in this manner. Several hundred tons of heavy timber baulks stacked over the entrance to the strong room would deter even the most determined thief from tampering with its contents.

While the crew crowded the opening of the hatch above them Sir Francis and the boatswains went down, each carrying a lighted lantern, and knelt in the bottom of the hold to examine the seals that the Dutch Governor of Trincomalee had placed on the entrance.

'The seals are intact!' Sir Francis shouted, to reassure the watchers, and they cheered raucously.

'Break the hinges!' he ordered Big Daniel, and the boatswain went to it with a will.

Wood splintered and brass screws squealed as they were ripped from their seats. The interior of the strong room was lined with sheets of copper, but Big Daniel's iron bar ripped through the metal and a hum of delight went up from the spectators as the contents of the compartment were revealed.

The coin was sewn into thick canvas bags of which there were fifteen. Daniel dragged them out and stacked them into a cargo net to be hoisted to the deck. Next, the ingots of gold bullion were raised. They were packed ten at a time into chests of raw, unplaned wood on which the number and weight of the bars had been branded with a red-hot iron.

When Sir Francis climbed up out of the hold he ordered all but two of the sacks of coin, and all the chests of gold bars, to be carried down to his own cabin.

'We will divide only these two sacks of coin now,' Sir Francis told them. 'The rest of your share you will receive when we get home to dear old England.' He stooped over the two remaining canvas sacks of coin with a dagger in his hand and he slit the stitching. The men howled like a pack of wolves as a stream of glinting silver ten-guilder coins poured onto the planking.

'No need to count it. The cheese-heads have done that job for us.' Sir Francis pointed out the numbers stencilled on the sacks. 'Each man will come forward as his name is called,' he told them. With excited laughter and ribald repartee, the men formed lines. As each was called, he shuffled forward with his cap held out, and his share of silver guilders was doled out to him.

Hal was the only man aboard who drew no part of the booty. Although he was entitled to a midshipman's share, one two-hundredth part of the crew's portion, almost two hundred guilders, his father would take care of it for him. 'No fool like a boy with silver or gold in his purse,' he had explained reasonably to Hal. 'One day you'll thank me for saving it for you.' Then he turned with mock fury on his crew. 'Just because you're rich now, doesn't mean I have no more work for you,' he roared. 'The rest of the heavy cargo must go ashore before we can beach and careen her and clean her foul bottom and step the new mast and put the culverins into her. There's enough work in that to keep you busy for a month or two.'

No man was ever allowed to remain idle for long in one of Sir Francis's ships. Boredom was the most dangerous enemy he would ever encounter. While one of the watches went ahead with the work of unloading, he kept the off-duty watches busy. They must never be allowed to forget that this was a fighting ship and that they must be ready at any moment to face a desperate enemy.

With the hatches open and the huge casks of spice being lifted out, there was no space on the deck for weapons practice so Big Daniel took the off-duty men to the beach. Shoulder to shoulder, they formed ranks and worked through the manual of arms. Swinging the cutlass – cut to the left, thrust and recover, cut to the right, thrust and recover – until the sweat streamed from them and they gasped for breath.

'Enough of that!' Big Daniel told them at last, but they were not to be released yet.

'A bout or two of wrestling now, just to warm your blood,' he shouted, and strode amongst them matching man against man, seizing a pair by the scruff of their necks and thrusting them at each other, as though they were fighting-birds in the cockpit.

Soon the beach was covered with struggling, shouting pairs of men naked to the waist, heaving and spinning each other off their feet and rolling in the white sand.

Standing back among the first line of forest trees, Katinka and her maid watched with interest. Aboli stood a few paces behind them, leaning against the trunk of one of the giant forest yellow-woods.

Hal was matched against a seaman twenty years his elder. They were of the same height, but the other man was a stone heavier. Both struggled for a hold on each other's neck and shoulders as they danced in a circle, trying to force one another off balance or to hook a heel for a trip throw.

'Use your hip. Throw him over your hip!' Katinka whispered, as she watched Hal. She was so carried along by the spectacle that unconsciously she had clenched her fists and was beating them on her own thighs in excitement as she urged Hal on, her cheeks pinker than either the rouge pot or the heat had coloured them.

Katinka loved to watch men or animals pitted against each other. At every opportunity, her husband was made to accompany her to the bull-baiting and the cock-fights or the ratting contests with terriers.

'Whenever the red wine is poured, my lovely little darling is happy.' Van de Velde was proud of her unusual penchant for blood sport. She never missed a tournament of *épée*, and had even enjoyed the English sport of bare-fisted fighting. However, wrestling was one of her favourite diversions, and she knew all the holds and throws.

Now she was enchanted by the lad's graceful movements and impressed by his technique. She could tell that he had been well instructed, for although his opponent was heavier Hal was quicker and stronger. He used his opponent's weight against him, and the older man had to grunt and thrash around to recover himself as Hal tipped him to the edge of his balance. At his next lunge Hal offered no resistance but gave to his opponent's rush, and went over backwards, still maintaining his grip. As he struck the ground, he broke his own fall with an arch to his back, at the same time thrusting his heels into his opponent's belly to catapult him overhead. While the older man lay stunned, Hal whipped round to straddle his back and pin him face down. He grabbed the man's pigtail and forced his face into the fine white sand, until he slapped the earth with both hands to signal his surrender.

Hal released him and sprang to his feet with the agility of a cat. The seaman came to his knees gasping and spitting sand. Then, unexpectedly, he launched himself at Hal just as he was beginning to turn away. From the corner of his eye Hal spotted the swing of the bunched fist coming at his head and rolled away from the blow, but not quite quickly enough. It swiped across his face, bringing a flash of blood from one nostril. He seized the man's wrist as he reached the limit of his swing, twisting his arm and then lifting his wrist up between his shoulder-blades. The seaman squealed as he was forced him up on his toes.

'Mary's milk, Master John, but you must like the taste of sand.' Hal placed one bare foot on his backside and sent him sprawling head first on to the beach once more.

'You grow too clever and cocky, Master Hal!' Big Daniel strode up to him, frowning, and his voice was gruff as he tried to hide his delight at his pupil's performance. 'Next time I'll give you a harder match. And don't let the captain hear that milky blasphemy of yours or it's more than good clean beach sand you'll be tasting yourself.'

Still laughing, delighting in Daniel's ill-concealed approbation and in the hoots of encouragement from the other wrestlers, Hal swaggered to the lagoon's edge and scooped up a double handful of water to wash the blood from his upper lip.

'Joseph and Mary, but he loves to win.' Daniel grinned behind his back. 'Try as he will, Captain Franky will not break that one down. The old dog has sired a puppy of his own blood.'

'How old do you think he is?' Katinka asked her maid, in a reflective tone.

'I'm sure I don't know,' said Zelda primly. 'He's just a child.'

Katinka shook her head, smiling, remembering him standing naked in the stern of the pinnace. 'Ask our blackamoor watch-dog.'

Obediently Zelda looked back at Aboli, and asked in English, 'How old is the boy?'

'Old enough for what she wants from him,' Aboli grunted in his own language, a puzzled frown on his face as he pretended not to understand. These last few days, while he guarded her, he had studied this woman with sun-coloured hair. He had recognized the bright, predatory glimmer in the depths of those demure violet eyes. She watched a man the way a mongoose watches a plump chicken, and she carried her head in an affectation of innocence that was belied by the wanton swing of her hips beneath the layers of bright silks and gossamer lace. 'A whore is still a whore, whatever the colour of her hair and no matter if she lives in a beehive hut or a governor's palace.' The deep cadence of his voice was punctuated by the staccato clicks of his tribal speech.

Zelda turned away from him with a flounce. 'Stupid animal. He understands nothing.'

Hal left the water's edge and came up into the trees. He reached up to the branch on which hung his discarded shirt. His hair was still wet and his naked chest and shoulders were blotched red with the rough contact of the wrestling. A smear of blood was still streaked across his cheek.

His hand raised towards his shirt, he looked up. His eyes met Katinka's level violet regard. Until that moment he had been unaware of her presence. Instantly his arrogant swagger evaporated, and he stepped back as though she had slapped him unexpectedly. Now a dark blush spread over his face, obliterating the lighter blotches left by his opponent's blows.

Coolly Katinka looked down at his bare chest. He folded his arms across it, as if ashamed.

'You were right, Zelda,' she said, with a dismissive flick of her hand. 'Just a grubby child,' she added in Latin, to make certain that he understood. Hal stared after her miserably as she gathered her skirts and, followed by Aboli and her maid, sailed regally down the beach to the waiting pinnace.

That night, as he lay on the lumpy straw pallet on his narrow bunk, he heard movement, soft voices and laughter from the cabin next door. He propped himself up on one elbow. Then he recalled the insult she had thrown at him so disdainfully. 'I will not think of her ever again,' he promised himself, as he sank back onto the pallet and placed his hands over his ears to block out the lilting cadence of her voice. In an attempt to drive her from his mind, he repeated softly, '*In Arcadia habito.*' But it was long before weariness allowed him at last to fall into a deep black dreamless sleep.

At the head of the lagoon, almost two miles from where the *Resolution* lay at anchor, a stream of clear sweet water tumbled down through a narrow gorge to mingle with the brackish waters below.

As the two longboats moved slowly against the current into the mouth of the gorge, they startled the flocks of water birds from the shallows into the air. They rose in a cacophony of honks, quacks and cackles, twenty different varieties of ducks and geese unlike any they knew from the north. There were other species, too, with strangely shaped bills or disproportionately long legs trailing, and herons, curlews and egrets that were not quite the same as their English counterparts, bigger or brighter in plumage. The sky was darkened with their numbers, and the men rested for a minute upon their oars to gaze in astonishment at these multitudes.

'It's a land of marvels,' Sir Francis murmured, staring up at this wild display. 'Yet we have explored only a trivial part of it. What other wonders lie beyond this threshold, deep in the hinterland, that no man has ever laid eyes upon?'

His father's words excited Hal's imagination, and conjured up once more the images of dragons and monsters that decorated the charts he had studied.

'Heave away!' his father ordered, and they bent to the long sweeps again. The two were alone in the leading boat: Sir Francis pulled the starboard oar with a long powerful stroke that matched Hal's tirelessly. Between them stood the empty water casks, the refilling of which was the ostensible purpose of this expedition to the head of the lagoon. The real reason, however, lay on the floorboards at Sir Francis's feet. During the night Aboli and Big Daniel had carried the canvas sacks of coin and the chests of gold ingots down from the cabin and had hidden them under the tarpaulin in the bottom of the boat. In the bows they had stacked five kegs of powder and an array of weapons, captured along with the treasure from the galleon, cutlass, pistol and musket, and leather bags of lead shot.

Ned Tyler, Big Daniel and Aboli followed closely in the second boat, the three men in his crew whom Sir Francis trusted above all others. Their boat, too, was loaded with water casks.

Once they were well into the mouth of the stream, Sir Francis stopped rowing and leaned over the side to scoop a mugful of water and taste it. He nodded with satisfaction. 'Pure and sweet.' He called across to Ned Tyler, 'Do you begin to refill here. Hal and I will go on upstream.'

As Ned steered the boat in towards the riverbank, a wild, booming bark echoed down the gorge. They all looked up. 'What are those creatures? Are they men?' demanded Ned. 'Some kind of strange hairy dwarfs?' There was fear and awe in his voice, as he stared up at the ranks of human-like shapes that lined the edge of the precipice high above them.

'Apes.' Sir Francis called to him as he rested on his oar. 'Like those of the Barbary Coast.'

Aboli chuckled, then threw back his head and faithfully mimicked the challenge of the bull baboon that led the pack. Most of the younger animals leaped up and nervously skittered along the cliff at the sound.

The huge bull ape accepted the challenge. He stood on all fours at the edge of the precipice, and opened his mouth wide to display a set of terrible white fangs. Emboldened by this show, some of the younger animals returned and began to hurl small stones and debris down upon them. The men were forced to duck and dodge the missiles.

'Give them a shot to see them off,' Sir Francis ordered.

'It's a long one.' Daniel unslung his musket and blew on the burning tip of the slow-match as he raised the butt to his shoulder. The gorge echoed to the thunderous blast, and they all burst out laughing at the antics of the baboon pack, as it panicked at the shot. The ball knocked a chip off the lip of the ledge, and the youngsters of the troop somersaulted backwards with shock. The mothers seized their offspring, slung them under their bellies and scrambled up the sheer face, and even the brave bull abandoned his dignity and joined the rush for safety. Within seconds, the cliff was deserted and the sounds of the terror-stricken retreat dwindled.

Aboli jumped over the side, waist deep into the river, and dragged the boat onto the bank while Daniel and Ned unstoppered the water casks to refill them. In the other boat Sir Francis and Hal bent to the oars and rowed on upstream. After half a mile the river narrowed sharply, and the cliffs on both sides became steeper. Sir Francis paused to get his bearings and then turned the longboat in under the cliff and moored the bows to the stump of a dead tree that sprang from a crack in the rock. Leaving Hal in the boat he jumped out onto the narrow ledge below the cliff and began to climb upwards. There was no obvious path to follow but Sir Francis moved confidently from one handhold to another. Hal watched him with pride: in his eyes, his father was an old man – he must have long passed the venerable age of forty years – yet he climbed with strength and agility. Suddenly, fifty feet above the river, he reached a ledge invisible from below and shuffled a few paces along it. Then he knelt to examine the narrow cleft in the cliff face; the opening was blocked with neatly packed rocks. He smiled with relief when he saw that they were exactly as he had left them many months previously. Carefully he pulled them out of the cleft and laid them aside, until the opening was wide enough for him to crawl through.

The cave beyond was in darkness but Sir Francis stood up and reached to a stone shelf above his head where he groped for the flint and steel he had left there. He lit the candle he had brought with him, and then looked around the cave.

Nothing had been touched since his last visit. Five chests stood against the back wall. That was the booty from the *Heerlycke Nacht*, mostly silver plate and a hundred thousand guilders in coin that had been intended for payment of the Dutch garrison in Batavia. A pile of gear was stacked beside the entrance, and Sir Francis began work on this immediately. It took him almost half an hour to rig the heavy wooden beam as a gantry from the ledge outside the cave entrance, and then to lower the tackle to the boat moored below.

'Make the first chest fast!' he called down to Hal.

Hal tied it on and his father hauled it upwards, the sheave squeaking at each heave. The chest disappeared and a few minutes later the rope end dropped back and dangled where Hal could reach it. He tied on the next chest.

It took them well over an hour to hoist all the ingots and the sacks of coin and stack them in the back of the cave. Then they started work on the powder kegs and the bundles of weapons. The last item to go up was the smallest: a box into which Sir Francis had packed a compass and backstaff, a roll of charts taken from the *Standvastigheid*, flint and steel, a set of surgeon's instruments in a canvas roll, and a selection of other equipment that could make the difference between survival and a lingering death to a party stranded on this savage, unexplored coast.

'Come up, Hal,' Sir Francis called down at last, and Hal went up the cliff with the speed and ease of one of the young baboons.

When Hal reached him, his father was sitting comfortably on the narrow ledge, his legs dangling and his clay-stemmed pipe and tobacco pouch in his hands.

'Give me a hand here, lad.' He pointed with his empty pipe at the vertical crack in the face of the cliff. 'Close that up again.'

Hal spent another half-hour packing the loose rock back into the entrance, to conceal it and to discourage intruders. There was little chance of men finding the cache in this deserted gorge, but he and his father knew that the baboons would return. They were as curious and mischievous as any human.

When Hal would have started back down the cliff, Sir Francis stopped him with a hand on his shoulder. 'There is no hurry. The others will not have finished refilling the water casks.'

They sat in silence on the ledge while Sir Francis got his long-stemmed pipe to draw sweetly. Then he asked, through a cloud of blue smoke, 'What have I done here?'

'Cached our share of the treasure.'

'Not only our share alone, but that of the Crown and of every man aboard,' Sir Francis corrected him. 'But why have I done that?'

'Gold and silver is temptation even to an honest man.' Hal repeated the lore his father had drummed into his head so many times before.

'Should I not trust my own crew?' Sir Francis asked.

'If you trust no man, then no man will ever disappoint you.' Hal repeated the lesson.

'Do you believe that?' Sir Francis turned to watch his face as he replied, and Hal hesitated. 'Do you trust Aboli?'

'Yes, I trust him,' Hal admitted, reluctantly, as though it were a sin.

'Aboli is a good man, none better. But you see that I do not bring even him to this place.' He paused, then asked, 'Do you trust me, lad?'

'Of course.'

'Why? Surely I am but a man and I have told you to trust no man?'

'Because you are my father and I love you.'

Sir Francis's eyes clouded and he made as if to caress Hal's cheek. Then he sighed, dropped his hand and looked down at the river below.

Hal expected his father to censure his reply, but he did not. After a while Sir Francis asked another question. 'What of the other goods I have cached here? The powder and weapons and charts and the like. Why have I placed those here?'

'Against an uncertain future,' Hal replied confidently – he had heard the answer often enough before. 'A wise fox has many exits to his earth.'

Sir Francis nodded. 'All of us who sail in the *guerre de course* are always at risk. One day, those few chests may be worth our very lives.'

His father was silent again as he smoked the last few shreds of tobacco in the bowl of his pipe. Then he said softly, 'If God is merciful, the time will come, perhaps not too far in the future, when this war with the Dutch will end. Then we will return here and gather up our prize and sail home to Plymouth. It has long been my dream to own the manor of Gainesbury that runs alongside High Weald—' He broke off, as if not daring to tempt fate with such imagining. 'If harm should befall me, it is necessary that you should know and remember where I have stored our winnings. It will be my legacy to you.'

'No harm can ever come your way!' Hal exclaimed in agitation. It was more a plea than a statement of conviction. He could not imagine an existence without this towering presence at the centre of it.

'No man is immortal,' said Sir Francis softly. 'We all owe God a death.' This time he allowed his right hand to settle briefly on Hal's shoulder. 'Come, lad. We must still fill the water casks in our own boat before dark.'

As the longboats crept back down the edge of the darkening lagoon, Aboli had taken Sir Francis's place on the rowing thwart, and now Hal's father sat in the stern, wrapped in a dark woollen cloak against the evening chill. His expression was remote and sombre. Facing aft as he worked one of the long oars, Hal could study him surreptitiously. Their conversation at the mouth of the cave had left him troubled with a presentiment of ill-fortune ahead.

He guessed that since they had anchored in the lagoon his father had cast his own horoscope. He had seen the zodiacal chart covered with arcane notations lying open on his desk in his cabin. That would account for his withdrawn and introspective mood. As Aboli had said, the stars were his children and he knew their secrets.

Suddenly his father lifted his head and sniffed the cool evening air. Then his face changed as he studied the forest edge. No dark thoughts could absorb him to the point where he was unaware of his surroundings.

'Aboli, take us in to the bank, if you please.'

They turned the boat towards the narrow beach, and the second followed. After they had all jumped out onto the beach and moored both boats, Sir Francis gave a quiet order. 'Bring your arms. Follow me, but quietly.'

He led them into the forest, pushing stealthily through the undergrowth, until he stepped out suddenly onto a well-used path. He glanced back to make certain they were following him, then hurried along.

Hal was mystified by his father's actions until he smelt a trace of woodsmoke on the air and noticed for the first time the bluish haze along the tops of the dense forest trees. This must have been what had alerted his father.

Suddenly Sir Francis stepped out into a small clearing in the forest and stopped. The four men who were already there had not noticed him. Two lay like corpses on a battlefield, one still clutching a squat brown hand-blown bottle in his inert fingers, the other drooling strings of saliva from the corner of his mouth as he snored.

The second pair were wholly absorbed by the stacks of silver guilders and the ivory dice lying between them. One scooped up the dice and rattled them at his ear before rolling them across the patch of beaten bare earth. 'Mother of a pig!' he growled. 'This is not my lucky day.'

'You should not speak unkindly of the dam who gave birth to you,' said Sir Francis softly. 'But the rest of what you say is the truth. This is not your lucky day.'

They looked up at their captain in horrified disbelief, but made no attempt to resist or escape as Daniel and Aboli dragged them to their feet and roped them neck to neck in the manner used by the slavers.

Sir Francis walked over to inspect the still that stood at the far end of the clearing. They had used a black iron pot to boil the fermented mash of old biscuit and peelings, and copper tubing stolen from the ship's stores for the coil. He kicked it over and the colourless spirits flared in the flames of the charcoal brazier on which the pot stood. A row of filled bottles, stoppered with wads of leaves, was laid out beneath a yellowwood tree. He picked them up one at a time and hurled them against the tree-trunk. As they shattered the evaporating fumes were pungent enough to make his eyes water. Then he walked back to Daniel and Ned, who had kicked the drunks out of their stupor and had dragged them across the clearing to rope them to the other captives.

'We'll give them a day to sleep it off, Master Ned. Then tomorrow, at the beginning of the afternoon watch, have the ship's company assemble to witness their punishment.' He glanced at Big Daniel. 'I trust you can still make your cat whistle, Master Daniel.'

'Please, Captain, we meant no harm. Just a little fun.' They tried to crawl to where he stood, but Aboli dragged them back like dogs on the leash.

'I will not grudge you your fun,' said Sir Francis, 'if you do not grudge me mine.'

The carpenter had knocked up a row of four tripods on the quarterdeck, and the drunkards and gamblers were lashed to them by wrist and ankle. Big Daniel walked down the line and ripped their shirts open from collar to waist, so that their naked backs were exposed. They hung helplessly in their bonds like trussed pigs on the back of a market cart.

'Every man aboard knows full well that I will tolerate no drunkenness and no gaming, both of which are an offence and abomination in the eyes of the Lord.' Sir Francis addressed the company, assembled in solemn ranks in the ship's waist. 'Every man aboard knows the penalty. Fifty licks of the cat.' He watched their faces. Fifty strokes of the knotted leather thongs could cripple a man for life. A hundred strokes was a sentence of certain and horrible death. 'They have earned themselves the full fifty. However, I remember that these four fools fought well on this very deck when we captured this vessel. We still have some hard fighting ahead of us, and cripples are of no use to me when the culverins are smoking and the cutlasses are out.'

He paused to watch their faces, and saw the terror of the cat in their eyes, mixed with relief that it was not them bound to the tripods. Unlike the captains of many privateers, even some Knights of the Order, Sir Francis took no pleasure in this punishment. Yet he did not flinch from necessity. He commanded a ship full of tough, unruly men, whom he had handpicked for their ferocity and who would take any show of kindness as weakness.

'I am a merciful man,' he told them, and somebody in the rear ranks chuckled derisively. Sir Francis paused and, with a bleak eye, singled out the offender. When the culprit hung his head and shuffled his feet, he went on smoothly, 'But these rascals would test my mercy to its limits.'

He turned to Big Daniel, who stood beside the first tripod. He was stripped to the waist and his great muscles bulged in arms and shoulders. He had tied back his long greying hair with a strip of cloth, and from his scarred fist the lashes of the cat hung to the planks of the deck like the serpents of Medusa's head.

'Make it fifteen for each, Master Daniel,' Sir Francis ordered, 'but comb your cat well between the strokes.'

Unless Daniel's fingers separated the lashes of the cat after each stroke, the blood would matt them together and clot them into a single heavy instrument that would cut human flesh like a sword blade. Even fifteen with an uncombed cat would strip the meat off a man's back down to the vertebrae of his spine.

'Fifteen it is, Captain,' Daniel acknowledged, and shaking out the whip to separate the knotted thongs, stepped up to his first victim. The man twisted his head to watch him over his shoulder, his expression blanched with fear.

Daniel raised his arm high and let the lash stream out over his shoulder then, with a peculiar grace for such a big man, he swung forward. The lash whistled like the wind in the leaves of a tall tree and clapped loudly on bare skin.

'One!' chanted the crew in unison, as the victim shrieked on a high note of shock and agony. The lash left a grotesque pattern over his back, each red line studded with a row of brighter crimson stars where the knots had broken the skin. It looked like the sting from the venomous tendrils of a Portuguese man-of-war.

Daniel combed out the lash, and the fingers of his left hand were smeared with bright fresh blood.

'Two!' The watchers counted, and the man shrieked again and writhed in his bonds, his toes dancing a tattoo of pain on the deck timbers.

'Avast punishment!' Sir Francis called, as he heard a mild commotion at the head of the companionway leading down to the cabins in the stern. Obediently Daniel lowered the whip, and waited as Sir Francis strode to the ladder.

Governor van de Velde's plumed hat appeared above the coaming, followed by his fat flushed face. He stood wheezing in the sunlight, mopping his jowls with a silk handkerchief, and looked about him. His face brightened with interest as he saw the men hanging on the row of tripods. '*Ja! Goed!* I see we are not too late,' he said, with satisfaction.

Close behind him Katinka emerged from the hatch with a light, eager step, holding her skirts just high enough to reveal satin slippers embroidered with seed pearls.

'Good morrow, Mijnheer,' Sir Francis greeted the Governor with a perfunctory bow, 'there is punishment in progress. It is an unsuitable spectacle for a lady of your wife's delicate breeding to witness.'

'Truly, Captain,' Katinka laughed lightly as she intervened, 'I am not a child. Heaven knows, there is a great paucity of diversion aboard this ship. Just think, you would collect no ransom if I were to die of boredom.' She tapped Sir Francis's arm with her fan, but he pulled away from this condescending touch, and spoke again to her husband.

'Mijnheer, I think you should escort your wife to her quarters.'

Katinka stepped between them as though he had not spoken, and beckoned Zelda who followed her. 'Place my stool there in the shade.' She spread out her skirts as she settled herself on the stool and pouted prettily at Sir Francis. 'I will be so quiet that you will not even know that I am here.'

Sir Francis glared at the Governor, but van de Velde spread his pudgy hands in a theatrical gesture of helplessness. 'You know how it is, Mijnheer, when a beautiful woman sets her heart on something.' He moved up behind Katinka and placed a proud and indulgent hand on her shoulder.

'I cannot be responsible for your wife's sensibilities, if they should be offended by the spectacle,' Sir Francis warned grimly, relieved at least that his men could not understand this exchange in Dutch and be aware that he had bowed to pressure from his captives.

'I think you need not trouble yourself too deeply. My wife has a strong stomach,' van de Velde murmured. During their tour of duty in Kandy and Trincomalee his wife had never missed the executions that were carried out regularly on the parade ground of the fort. Depending on the nature of the offence these punishments had ranged from burning at the stake to branding, garrotting and beheading. Even on those days when she had been suffering the break-bone pains of dengue fever and, in accordance with her doctor's orders, should have remained in bed, her carriage had always been parked in its accustomed place overlooking the scaffold.

'Then it shall be at your own responsibility, Mijnheer.' Sir Francis nodded curtly, and turned back to Daniel.

'Proceed with the punishment, Master Daniel,' he ordered. Daniel threw back the whip, high behind his shoulder, and the coloured tattoos that decorated his great biceps rippled with a life of their own.

'Three!' yelled the crew, as the lash sang and snapped.

Katinka stiffened, and leaned forward slightly on her stool.

'Four!' She started at the crack of the cat and the high scream of pain that followed it. Slowly her face turned pale as candle tallow.

'Five!' Thin snakes of scarlet crawled down the man's back and soaked into the waistband of his canvas petticoat. Katinka let her long golden eyelashes droop half closed to hide the gleam in her violet eyes.

'Six!' Katinka felt a tiny drop of liquid strike her, like a single spot of warm tropical rain. She tore her eyes from the wriggling, moaning body on the tripod, and looked down at her graceful hand.

A drop of blood, flung from the sodden lash, had landed on her forefinger. Like a ruby set in a precious ring it sparkled against her white skin. She cupped her other hand over it, hiding it in her lap while she glanced around at the faces that surrounded her. Every eye was fixed in total fascination upon the gruesome spectacle in front of them. No one had seen the blood splash her. No one was watching her now.

She lifted her hand to her full soft lips as though in an involuntary gesture of dismay. The pink tip of her tongue darted out and dabbed away the droplet from her finger. She savoured its metallic salt taste. It reminded her of a lover's sperm, and she felt the viscous wetness welling up between her legs, so that when she rubbed her thighs together they slid against each other, slippery as mating eels.

There would be a need for lodgings on shore while the *Resolution* was careened on the beach, her hull cleaned of weed and examined for any sign of shipworm.

Sir Francis put Hal in charge of building the compound that was to accommodate their hostages. Hal took particular care over the hut that would house the Governor's wife, making it spacious and comfortable and siting it for privacy and security from wild animals. Then he had his men build a stockade of thorn branches around the entire prison compound.

When darkness brought the first day's work to a halt, he went down to the beach of the lagoon and soaked himself in the warm, brackish waters. Then he scrubbed his body with handfuls of wet sand until his skin tingled. Yet he still felt sullied by the memory of the floggings he had been forced to watch that morning. Only when he smelt the tantalizing odour of hot biscuit floating across the water from the ship's galley did his mood change, and he thrust his legs into his breeches and ran down the beach to scramble into the pinnace as it pulled away from the shore.

While he had been ashore his father had written on the slate a series of navigational problems for him to solve. He tucked it under his arm, grabbed a pewter mug of small beer, a bowl of fish stew and, holding a hot biscuit between his teeth, darted down the ladder to his cabin, the only place on the ship where he could be alone to concentrate on his task.

Suddenly he looked up as he heard water being poured in the cabin next door. He had noticed the buckets of fresh river water standing over the charcoal fire in the galley and laughed when the cook had complained bitterly that his fire was being used to heat water to bathe in. Now Hal knew for whom those steaming pails had been prepared. Zelda's guttural tones carried to him through the panel as she harangued Oliver, his father's servant. Oliver's reply was truculent. 'I don't understand a word you say, you grisly old bitch. But if you don't like it you can fill the sodding bath yerself.'

Hal grinned to himself, half with amusement and half in anticipation, as he blew out his lamp and knelt to remove the wooden plug from his peephole. He saw that the cabin was filled with clouds of steam, which frosted the mirror on the far bulkhead so that his view was restricted. Zelda was shooing Oliver from the cabin as Hal adjusted his eye to the aperture.

'All right, you old trull!' Oliver baited her, as he lugged the empty buckets from the cabin. 'There's nothing you've got that would keep me here a minute longer.'

When Oliver was gone, Zelda went through into the main cabin and Hal heard her speaking to her mistress. A minute later she ushered Katinka through the doorway. Katinka paused beside the steaming bath and dabbled her fingers in the water. She exclaimed sharply and jerked away her hand. Zelda hurried forward, apologizing, and poured cold water from the bucket that stood beside the bath. Katinka tested the temperature again. This time she nodded with satisfaction, and went to sit on the stool. Zelda came up behind her, lifted the splendid shimmering bundle of her hair with both hands to pile it on top of her head and pinned it there, like a sheaf of ripe wheat.

Katinka leaned forward and, with her fingertips, wiped a small clear window in the clouded surface of the mirror. She examined the vignette of herself in this clear spot. She thrust out her tongue to examine it for any trace of white coating. It was pink as a rose petal. Then she opened her eyes wide and peered into their depths, touching the skin beneath them with her fingertips. 'Look at these horrid wrinkles!' she lamented.

Zelda denied it vehemently. 'Not a single one!'

'I never want to grow old and ugly.' Katinka's expression was tragic.

'Then you had best die now!' said Zelda. 'That's the only way you'll avoid it.'

'What a terrible thing to say. You are so cruel to me,' Katinka complained.

Hal could not understand what they said but the tone of her voice touched him to the depths of his being.

'Come now,' Zelda chided her. 'You know you're beautiful.'

'Am I, Zelda? Do you really think so?'

'Yes. And so do you.' Zelda lifted her to her feet. 'But if you don't bathe now, you will stink just as beautifully.'

She unfastened her mistress's gown, then moved behind her, lifted the gown from her shoulders and Katinka stood naked before the mirror. Hal's involuntary gasp was muffled by the panel and the small sounds of the ship's hull.

From that slender neck down to her tiny ankles Katinka's body formed a line of heartbreaking purity. Her buttocks swelled out into two perfectly symmetrical orbs, like a pair of the ostrich eggs Hal had seen offered for sale in the markets of Zanzibar. But there were childish, vulnerable dimples at the back of her knees.

Katinka's own image in the clouded mirror was ethereal and could not hold her attention for long. She turned away from it and stood facing him. Hal's gaze flew to her breasts. They were large for her narrow shoulders. Each would have filled his cupped hands, yet they were not perfectly round as he had expected them to be.

Hal stared at them until his eye watered and he was forced at last to blink. Then he let his gaze sink down, over the slight but enthralling bulge of her belly, and onto the misty cloud of fine curls that nestled between her thighs. The lamp-light struck them and they sparked purest gold.

She stood a long time thus, longer than he had dared hope she might, staring down into the bath while Zelda poured perfumed oil from a crystal bottle into the water, and then knelt to stir it with her hand. Katinka continued to stand, her weight on one leg so that her pelvis was tilted at an enchanting angle, and there was a small sly smile on her lips as she reached up slowly and took one of her nipples between thumb and forefinger. For a moment Hal thought she stared directly at him, and he began to pull away guiltily from his peep-hole. Then he knew that it was an illusion for she dropped her eyes and looked down at the fat little berry that poked out rosily between her fingers.

She rolled it softly back and forth, and while Hal stared in amazement it changed colour and shape. It swelled and hardened and darkened. He had never imagined anything quite like this – a little miracle that should have filled him with reverence but instead tore at his loins with the claws of lust.

Zelda looked up from the bath she was mixing and, when she saw what her mistress was doing, snapped a prim reprimand. Katinka laughed and stuck out her tongue, but dropped her hand and stepped into the bath. With a luxurious sigh she sank into the hot, perfumed water, until only the thick coil of golden hair on top of her head showed above the rim of the bath.

Zelda fussed over her, lathering soap on a flannel, wiping and washing, murmuring endearments and cackling at her mistress's replies. Suddenly she rocked back on her heels and gave another instruction, in response to which Katinka stood up and the soapy water cascaded down her body. Her back was turned to Hal, and now the rounds of her bottom glowed pinkly from the hot water. At Zelda's instructions she moved compliantly to allow the old woman to soap down each leg in turn.

At last Zelda climbed stiffly to her feet and shuffled out of the cabin. As soon as she was gone Katinka, still standing in the bath, glanced over her shoulder. Again, Hal had the guilty illusion that she was looking directly into his own staring eye. It was only for a moment, then slowly and voluptuously she bent. Her buttocks changed shape at the movement. Katinka reached behind herself with both hands. She laid those small white hands on each of her glowing pink buttocks and drew them gently apart. This time Hal could not choke back the little abandoned cry that rose to his lips as the deep crease of her bottom opened to his feverish gaze.

Zelda bustled back into the cabin bearing an armful of towels. Katinka straightened and the enchanted crevice closed firmly, its secrets hidden once more from his eyes. She stepped from the bath and Zelda draped a towel over her shoulders that hung to her ankles. Zelda loosened the coil of her mistress's hair and brushed it out, and then braided it into a thick golden rope. She stood behind Katinka and held a gown for her to slip her arms into the sleeves, but Katinka shook her head and gave a peremptory order. Zelda protested but Katinka insisted and the maid threw the gown over the stool and left the cabin in an obvious pet.

When she was gone Katinka let the towel drop to the deck and, naked once more, crossed to the door and slid the locking bolt into place. Then she turned back and passed out of Hal's sight.

He saw a fuzzy pink blur of movement in the clouded mirror but could not be sure what she was doing until, abruptly and shockingly, her lips were an inch from the opposite side of his peep-hole and she hissed viciously at him, 'You filthy little pirate!' She spoke in Latin, and he recoiled as though she had flung a kettle of boiling water into his face.

Even in his confusion, though, the taunt had stung him to the quick, and he answered her, without thinking, 'I am not a pirate. My father carries Letters of Marque.'

'Don't you dare to contradict me.' Confusingly she was switching between Latin, Dutch and English. But her tone was sharp and stinging as a scourge.

Again he was stung into a reply. 'I did not mean to offend you.'

'When my noble husband finds out that you have been spying on me, he will go to your pirate father, and they will have you flogged on the tripod like those other men this morning.'

'I was not spying on you—'

'Liar!' She would not let him finish. 'You dirty lying pirate.' For a moment she had run out of breath and insults.

'I only wanted to—'

Her fury was recharged. 'I know what you wanted. You wanted to look at my *katjie* – ' he knew that was the Dutch word for kitten ' – and then you wanted to take your cock in your hand and pull it—'

'No!' Hal almost shouted. How had she known his shameful secret? He felt sick and mortified.

'Quiet! Zelda will hear you,' she hissed again. 'If they catch you it will be the lash.'

'Please!' he whispered back. 'I meant no harm. Please forgive me. I did not mean it.'

'Then show me. Prove your innocence. Show me your cock.'

'I can't.' His voice quivered with shame.

'Stand up! Put it here next to the hole so I can see if you are lying.'

'No. Please don't make me do that.'

'Quickly or I will scream for my husband to come.'

Slowly he came to his feet. The peep-hole was at almost exactly the same level as his aching crotch.

'Now, show me. Open your breeches,' her voice goaded him.

Slowly, consumed by shame and embarrassment he lifted the canvas skirt, and before it was fully raised his penis jumped out like the springy branch of a sapling. He knew she must be nauseated and speechless with disgust to see such a thing. After a minute of thick, charged silence that seemed the longest in his life, he began to lower his skirt over himself.

Instantly she stopped him in a voice that seemed to him to tremble with revulsion, so that he could hardly understand her distorted English words.

'No! Do not seek to cover your shame. This thing of yours condemns you. Do you still pretend you are guiltless?'

'No,' he admitted miserably.

'Then you must be punished,' she told him. 'I must tell your father.'

'Please don't do that,' he pleaded. 'He would kill me with his own hands.'

'Very well. I shall have to punish you myself. Bring your cock closer.'

Obediently he pushed his hips forward.

'Closer, so I can reach it. Closer.'

He felt the tip of his distended penis touch the rough wood that surrounded the peep-hole, and then shockingly cool soft fingers closed over the tip. He tried to pull away, but her grip tightened and her voice was sharp. 'Stay still!'

Katinka knelt at the bulkhead and threaded his glans through the opening, then eased it out into the lamp-light. It was so swollen that it could barely fit through the hole.

'No, do not pull away,' she told him, making her voice stern and angry, as she took a firmer grip upon him. Obediently he relaxed and gave himself over to the insistent pressure of her fingers, allowing her to draw his full length through the opening.

She gazed at it, fascinated. At his age she had not expected him to be so large. The engorged head was the glossy purple of a ripe plum. She drew the loose prepuce over it, like a monk's cowl, and then pulled back the skin again as far it would go. The head seemed to swell harder as though on the point of bursting, and she felt the shaft jump in her hands.

She repeated the movement, slowly forward and then back again, and heard him groan beyond the panel. It was strange but she had almost forgotten the boy. This mannikin she held in her hands had a life and existence of its own.

'This is your punishment, you dirty, shameless boy.'

She could hear his fingernails scratching at the wood, as her hand began to fly back and forth along the full length of him as though she were working the shuttle of a weaver's loom.

It happened sooner than she had expected. The hot glutinous spurting against her sensitive breasts was so powerful that it startled her, but she did not pull away.

After a time, she said, 'Do not think that I have forgiven you yet for what you have done to me. Your penitence has only just begun. Do you understand?'

'Yes.' His voice was ragged and hoarse.

'You must make a secret opening in this wall.' She tapped the bulkhead softly with her knuckle. 'Loosen this panel so that you can come through to me, and I can punish you more severely. Do you understand?'

'Yes,' he panted.

'You must conceal the opening. No one else must know.'

'It is my observation,' Sir Francis told Hal, 'that filth and sickness have a peculiar affinity, one for the other. I know not why this should be, but it is so.'

He was responding to his son's cautious enquiry as to why it was necessary to go through the onerous and odious business of fumigating the ship. With all the cargo out of her and most of the crew billeted ashore Sir Francis was determined to try to rid the hull of vermin. It seemed that every crack in the woodwork swarmed with lice, and the holds were overrun with rats. The galley was littered with the black pellets of their droppings, and Ned Tyler had reported finding some of the stinking bloated carcasses rotting in the water casks.

Since the day of their arrival in the lagoon a shore party had been burning cordwood and leaching the ashes to obtain the lye, and Sir Francis had sent Aboli into the forest to search for those special herbs that his tribe used to keep their huts clear of the loathsome vermin. Now a party of seamen waited on the foredeck, armed with buckets of the caustic substance.

'I want every crack and joint of the hull scrubbed out, but be careful,' Sir Francis warned them. 'The corrosive fluid will burn the skin from your hands—' He broke off abruptly. Every head on board turned towards the distant rocky heads, and every man upon the beach paused in what he was doing and cocked his head to listen.

The flat boom of a cannon shot echoed from the cliffs at the entrance to the lagoon and reverberated across the still waters of the wide bay.

''Tis the alarm signal from the lookout on the heads, Captain,' shouted Ned Tyler, and pointed across the water to where a puff of white gunsmoke still hung over one of the emplacements that guarded the entrance. As they stared, a tiny black ball soared to the top of the makeshift flag-pole on the crest of the western headland then unfurled into a red swallow-tail. It was the general alarm signal, and could only mean that a strange sail was in sight.

'Beat to quarters, Master Daniel!' Sir Francis ordered crisply. 'Unlock the weapons chests and arm the crew. I am going across to the entrance. Four men to row the longboat and the rest take up their battle stations ashore.'

Although his face remained expressionless, inwardly he was furious that he should have allowed himself to be surprised like this, with the masts unstepped and all the cannon out of the hull. He turned to Ned Tyler. 'I want the prisoners taken ashore and placed under your strictest guard, well away from the beach. If they learn that there is a strange ship off the coast, it might give them the notion to try to attract attention.'

Oliver rushed up the companionway with Sir Francis's cloak over his arm. While he spread it over his master's shoulders, Sir Francis finished issuing his orders. Then he turned and strode to the entryport where the longboat lay alongside and Hal was waiting, where his father could not ignore him, fretting that he might not be ordered to join him.

'Very well, then,' Sir Francis snapped. 'Come with me. I might have need of those eyes of yours.' And Hal slid down the mooring line ahead, and cast off the moment his father stepped into the boat.

'Pull till you burst your guts!' Sir Francis told the men at the oars and the boat skittered across the lagoon. Sir Francis sprang over the side and waded ashore below the cliff with the water slopping over the tops of his high boots. Hal had to run to catch up with him on the elephant path.

They came out on the top, three hundred feet above the lagoon, looking out over the ocean. Although the wind that buffeted them on the heights had kicked the sea into a welter of breaking waves, Hal's sharp eyes picked out the brighter flecks that persisted among the ephemeral whitecaps even before the lookout could point them out to him.

Sir Francis stared through his telescope. 'What do you make of her?' he demanded of Hal.

'There are two ships,' Hal told him.

'I see but one – no, wait! You are right. There is another, a little further to the east. Is she a frigate, do you think?'

'Three masts,' Hal shaded his eyes, 'and full rigged. Yes, I'd say she's a frigate. The other vessel is too far off. I cannot tell her type.' It pained Hal to admit it, and he strained his eyes for some other detail. 'Both ships are standing in directly towards us.'

'If they are intending to head for Good Hope, then they must go about very soon,' Sir Francis murmured, never lowering the telescope. They watched anxiously.

'They could be a pair of Dutch East Indiamen still making their westings,' Hal hazarded hopefully.

'Then why are they pushing so close into a lee shore?' Sir Francis asked. 'No, it looks very much as though they are headed straight for the entrance.' He snapped the telescope closed. 'Come along!' At a trot he led the way back down the path to where the longboat waited on the beach. 'Master Daniel, row across to the batteries on the far side. Take command there. Do not open fire until I do.'

They watched the longboat move swiftly over the lagoon and Daniel's men drag it into a narrow cove where it was concealed from view. Then Sir Francis strode along the gun emplacements in the cliff and gave a curt set of orders to the men who crouched over the culverins with the burning slow-match.

'At my command, fire on the leading ship. One salvo of round shot,' he told them. 'Aim at the waterline. Then load with chain shot and bring down their rigging. They'll not want to try manoeuvring in these confined channels with half their sails shot away.' He jumped up onto the parapet of the emplacement and stared out at the sea through the narrow entrance, but the approaching vessels were still hidden from view by the rocky cliffs.

Suddenly, from around the western point of the heads, a ship with all sail set drew into view. She was less than two miles offshore, and even as they watched in consternation she altered course, and trimmed her yards around, heading directly for the entrance.

'Their guns are run out, so it's a fight they're looking for,' said Sir Francis grimly, as he sprang down from the wall. 'And we shall give it to them, lads.'

'No, Father,' Hal cried. 'I know that ship.'

'Who—' Before Sir Francis could ask the question, he was given the answer. From the vessel's maintop a long swallow-tailed banner unfurled. Scarlet and snowy white, it whipped and snapped on the wind.

'The *croix patté*!' Hal called. 'It's the *Gull of Moray*. It's Lord Cumbrae, Father!'

'By God, so it is. How did that red-bearded butcher know we were here?'

Astern of the *Gull of Moray* the strange ship hove into view. It also trained its yards around, and in succession altered its heading, following the Buzzard as he stood in towards the entrance.

'I know that ship also,' Hal shouted, on the wind. 'There, now! I can even recognize her figurehead. She's the *Goddess*. I know of no other ship on this ocean with a naked Venus at her bowsprit.'

'Captain Richard Lister, it is,' Sir Francis agreed. 'I feel easier for having him here. He's good man – though, God knows, I trust neither of them all the way.'

As the Buzzard came sailing in down the channel past the gun emplacements, he must have picked out the bright spot of Sir Francis's cloak against the lichen-covered rocks, for he dipped his standard in salute.

Sir Francis lifted his hat in acknowledgement, but grated between his teeth, 'I'd rather salute you with a bouquet of grape, you Scottish bastard. You've smelt the spoils, have you? You're come to beg or steal, is that it? But how did you know?'

'Father!' Hal shouted again. 'Look there, in the futtock-shrouds! I'd know that grinning rogue anywhere. That's how they knew. He led them here.'

Sir Francis swivelled his glass. 'Sam Bowles. It seems that even the sharks could not stomach that piece of carrion. I should have let his shipmates deal with him while we had the chance.'

The *Gull* moved slowly past them, reducing sail progressively, as she threaded her way deeper into the lagoon. The *Goddess* followed her, at a cautious distance. She also flew the *croix patté* at her masthead, along with the cross of St George and the Union flag. Richard Lister was also a Knight of the Order. They picked out his diminutive figure on his quarterdeck as he came to the rail and shouted something across the water that was jumbled by the wind.

'You are keeping strange company, Richard.' Even though the Welshman could not hear him, Sir Francis waved his hat in reply. Lister had been with him when they captured the *Heerlycke Nacht*, they had shared the spoils amicably, and he counted him a friend. Lister should have been with them, Sir Francis and the Buzzard while they spent those dreary months on blockade off Cape Agulhas. However, he had missed the rendezvous in Port Louis on the island of Mauritius. After waiting a month for him to appear, Sir Francis had been obliged to accede to the Buzzard's demands, and they had sailed without him.

'Well, we'd best put on a brave face, and go to greet our uninvited guests,' Sir Francis told Hal, and went down to the beach as Daniel brought the longboat across the channel between the heads.

As they rowed back up the lagoon the two newly arrived vessels lay at anchor in the main channel. The *Gull of Moray* was only half a cable's length astern of the *Resolution*. Sir Francis ordered Daniel to steer directly to the *Goddess*. Richard Lister was at the entryport to greet him as he and Hal came aboard.

'Flames of hell, Franky. I heard the word that you had taken a great prize from the Dutch. Now I see her lying there at anchor.' Richard seized his hand. He did not quite stand as tall as Sir Francis's shoulder but his grip was powerful. He sniffed the air with the great florid bell of his nose, and went on, in his singing Celtic lilt, 'And is that not spice I smell on the air? I curse meself for not having found you at Port Louis.'

'Where were you, Richard? I waited thirty-two days for you to arrive.'

'It grieves me to have to admit it but I ran full tilt into a hurricane just south of Mauritius. Dismasted me and blew me clear across to the coast of St Lawrence Island.'

'That would be the same storm that dismasted the Dutchman.' Sir

Francis pointed across the channel at the galleon. 'She was under jury-rig when we captured her. But how did you fall in with the Buzzard?'

'I thought that as soon as the *Goddess* was fit for sea again I would look for you off Cape Agulhas, on the off-chance that you were still on station there. That's when I came across him. He led me here.'

'Well, it's good to see you, my old friend. But, tell me, do you have any news from home?' Sir Francis leaned forward eagerly. This was always one of the foremost questions men asked each other when they met out here beyond the Line. They might voyage to the furthest ends of the uncharted seas, but always their hearts yearned for home. Almost a year had passed since Sir Francis had received news from England.

At the question, Richard Lister's expression turned sombre. 'Five days after I sailed from Port Louis I fell in with *Windsong*, one of His Majesty's frigates. She was fifty-six days out from Plymouth, bound for the Coromandel coast.'

'So what news did she have?' Sir Francis interrupted impatiently.

'None good, as the Lord is my witness. They say that all of England was struck by the plague, and that men, women and children died in their thousands and tens of thousands, so they could not bury them fast enough and the bodies lay rotting and stinking in the streets.'

'The plague!' Sir Francis crossed himself in horror. 'The wrath of God.'

'Then while the plague still raged through every town and village, London was destroyed by a mighty fire. They say that the flames left hardly a house standing.'

Sir Francis stared at him in dismay. 'London burned? It cannot be! The King – is he safe? Was it the Dutch that put the torch to London? Tell me more, man, tell me more.'

'Yes, the Black Boy is safe. But no, this time it was not the Dutch to blame. The fire was started by a baker's oven in Pudding Lane and it burned for three days without check. St Paul's Cathedral is burned to the ground and the Guildhall, the Royal Exchange, one hundred parish churches and God alone knows what else besides. They say that the damage will exceed ten million pounds.'

'Ten millions!' Sir Francis stared at him aghast. 'Not even the richest monarch in the world could rise to such an amount. Why, Richard, the total Crown revenues for a year are less than one million! It must beggar the King and the nation.'

Richard Lister shook his head with gloomy relish. 'There's more bad news besides. The Dutch have given us a mighty pounding. That devil, de Ruyter, sailed right into the Medway and the Thames. We lost sixteen ships of the line to him, and he captured the *Royal Charles* at her moorings in Greenwich docks and towed her away to Amsterdam.'

'The flagship, the flower and pride of our fleet. Can England survive such a defeat, coming as it does so close upon the heels of the plague and the fire?'

Lister shook his head again. 'They say the King is suing for peace with the Dutch. The war might be over at this very moment. It may have ended months ago, for all we know.'

'Let us pray most fervently that is not so.' Sir Francis looked across at the *Resolution*. 'I took that prize barely three weeks past. If the war was over then, my commission from the Crown would have expired. My capture might be construed as an act of piracy.'

'The fortunes of war, Franky. You had no knowledge of the peace. There is none but the Dutch will blame you for that.' Richard Lister pointed with his inflamed trumpet of a nose across the channel at the *Gull of Moray*. 'It seems that my lord Cumbrae feels slighted at being excluded from this reunion. See, he comes to join us.'

The Buzzard had just launched a boat. It was being rowed down the channel now towards them, Cumbrae himself standing in the stern. The boat bumped against the *Goddess*'s side and the Buzzard came scrambling up the rope ladder onto her deck.

'Franky!' he greeted Sir Francis. 'Since we parted, I have not let a single day go past without a prayer for you.' He came striding across the deck, his plaid swinging. 'And my prayers were heard. That's a bonny wee galleon we have there, and filled to the gunwales with spice and silver, so I hear.'

'You should have waited a day or two longer, before you deserted your station. You might have had a share of her.'

The Buzzard spread his hands in amazement. 'But, my dear Franky, what's this you're telling me? I never left my station. I took a short swing into the east, to make certain the Dutchies weren't trying to give us the slip by standing further out to sea. I hurried back to you just as soon as I could. By then you were gone.'

'Let me remind you of your own words, sir. "I am completely out of patience. Sixty-five days are enough for me and my brave fellows?"'

'My words, Franky?' The Buzzard shook his head, 'Your ears must have played you false. The wind tricked you, you did not hear me fairly.'

Sir Francis laughed lightly. 'You waste your talent as Scotland's greatest liar. There is no one here for you to amaze. Both Richard and I know you too well.'

'Franky, I hope this does not mean you would try to cheat me out of my fair share of the spoils?' He contrived to look both sorrowful and incredulous. 'I agree that I was not in sight of the capture, and I would not expect a full half share. Give me a third and I will not quibble.'

'Take a deep breath, sir.' Sir Francis laid his hand casually on the hilt of his sword. 'That whiff of spice is all the share you'll get from me.'

The Buzzard cheered up miraculously and gave a huge, booming laugh. 'Franky, my old and dear comrade in arms. Come and dine on board my ship this evening, and we can discuss your lad's initiation into the Order over a dram of good Highland whisky.'

'So it's Hal's initiation that brings you back to see me, is it? Not the silver and spice?'

'I know how much the lad means to you, Franky – to us all. He's a great credit to you. We all want him to become a Knight of the Order. You have spoken of it often. Isn't that the truth?'

Sir Francis glanced at his son, and nodded almost imperceptibly.

'Well, then, you'll not get a chance like this again in many a year. Here we are, three Nautonnier Knights together. That's the least number it takes to admit an acolyte to the first degree. When will you find another three Knights to make up a Lodge, out here beyond the Line?'

'How thoughtful of you, sir. And, of course, this has no bearing on a share of my booty that you were claiming but a minute ago?' Sir Francis's tone dripped with irony.

'We'll not speak about that again. You're an honest man, Franky. Hard but fair. You'd never cheat a brother Knight, would you?'

Sir Francis returned long before the midnight watch from dining with Lord Cumbrae aboard the *Gull of Moray*. As soon as he was in his cabin he sent Oliver to summon Hal.

'On the coming Sunday. Three days from now. In the forest,' he told his son. 'It is arranged. We will open the Lodge at moonrise, a little after two bells in the second dog watch.'

'But the Buzzard,' Hal protested. 'You do not like or trust him. He let us down—'

'And yet Cumbrae was right. We might never have three knights gathered together again until we return to England. I must take this opportunity to see you safely ensconced within the Order. The good Lord knows there might not be another chance.'

'We will leave ourselves at his mercy while we are ashore,' Hal warned. 'He might play us foul.'

Sir Francis shook his head. 'We will never leave ourselves at the mercy of the Buzzard, have no fear of that.' He stood up and went to his sea-chest.

'I have prepared against the day of your initiation.' He lifted the lid. 'Here is your uniform.' He came across the cabin with a bundle in his hands and dropped it on his bunk. 'Put it on. We will make certain that it fits you.' He raised his voice and shouted, 'Oliver!'

His servant came at once with his housewife tucked under his arm. Hal stripped off his old worn canvas jacket and petticoats and, with Oliver's help, began to don the ceremonial uniform of the Order. He had never dreamed of owning such splendid clothing.

The stockings were of white silk and his breeches and doublet of midnight-blue satin, the sleeves slashed with gold. His shoes had buckles of heavy silver and the polished black leather matched that of his cross belt. Oliver combed out his thick tangled locks, then placed the Cavalier officer's hat on his head. He had picked the finest ostrich feathers in the market of Zanzibar to decorate the wide brim.

When he was dressed, Oliver circled Hal critically, his head on one side, 'Tight on the shoulders, Sir Francis. Master Hal grows wider each day. But it will take only a blink of your eye to fix that.'

Sir Francis nodded, and reached again into the chest. Hal's heart leaped as he saw the folded cloak in his father's hands. It was the symbol of the Knighthood he had studied so hard to attain. Sir Francis came to him and spread it over his shoulders, then fastened the clasp at his throat. The folds of white hung to his knees and the crimson cross bestrode his shoulders.

Sir Francis stood back and scrutinized Hal carefully. 'It lacks but one detail,' he grunted, and returned to the chest. From it he brought out a sword, but no ordinary sword. Hal knew it well. It was a Courtney family heirloom, but still its magnificence awed him. As his father brought it to where he stood, he recited to Hal its history and provenance one more time. 'This blade belonged to Charles Courtney, your great-grandfather. Eighty years ago, it was awarded to him by Sir Francis Drake himself for his part in the capture and sack of the port of Rancheria on the Spanish Main. This sword was surrendered to Drake by the Spanish governor, Don Francisco Manso.'

He held out the scabbard of chased gold and silver for Hal to examine. It was decorated with crowns and dolphins and sea sprites gathered around the heroic figure of Neptune enthroned. Sir Francis reversed the weapon and offered Hal the hilt. A large star sapphire was set in the pommel. Hal drew the blade and saw at once that this was not just the ornament of some Spanish fop. The blade was of the finest Toledo steel inlaid with gold. He flexed it between his fingers, and rejoiced in its spring and temper.

'Have a care,' his father warned him. 'You can shave with that edge.'

Hal returned it to its scabbard and his father slipped the sword into the leather bucket of Hal's cross belt, then stood back again to examine him critically. 'What do you think of him?' he asked Oliver.

'Just the shoulders.' Oliver ran his hands over the satin of the doublet. 'It's all that wrestling and sword-play that changes his shape. I shall have to resew the seams.'

'Then take him to his cabin and see to it.' Sir Francis dismissed them both and turned back to his desk. He sat and opened his leather-bound log-book.

Hal paused in the doorway. 'Thank you, Father. This sword—' He touched the sapphire pommel at his side, but could not find words to continue. Sir Francis grunted without looking up, dipped his quill and began to write on the parchment page. Hal lingered a little longer in the entrance until his father looked up again in irritation. He backed out and shut the door softly. As he turned into the passage, the door opposite opened and the Dutch Governor's wife came through it so swiftly, in a swirl of silks, that they almost collided.

Hal jumped aside and swept the plumed hat from his head. 'Forgive me, madam.'

Katinka stopped and faced him. She examined him slowly, from the gleaming silver buckles of his new shoes upwards. When she reached his eyes she stared into them coolly and said softly, 'A pirate whelp dressed like a great nobleman.' Then, suddenly, she leaned towards him until her face almost touched his and whispered, 'I have checked the panel. There is no opening. You have not performed the task I set you.'

'My duties have kept me ashore. I have had no chance.' He stammered as he found the Latin words.

'See to it this very night,' she ordered, and swept by him. Her perfume lingered and the velvet doublet seemed too hot and constricting. He felt sweat break out on his chest.

Oliver fussed over the fit of his doublet for what seemed to Hal half the rest of the night. He unpicked and resewed the shoulder seams twice before he was satisfied and Hal fumed with impatience.

When at last he left, taking all Hal's newly acquired finery with him, Hal could barely wait to set the locking bar across his door, and kneel at the bulkhead. He discovered that the panel was fixed to the oak framework by wooden dowels, driven flush with the woodwork.

One at a time, with the point of his dirk, he prised and whittled the dowels from their drilled seats. It was slow work and he dared make no noise. Any blow or rasp would reverberate through the ship.

It was almost dawn before he was able to remove the last peg and then to slip the blade of his dagger into the joint and lever open the panel. It came away suddenly, with a squeal of protesting wood against the oak frame that seemed to carry through the hull, and must surely alarm both his father and the Governor.

With bated breath he waited for terrible retribution to fall around his head, but the minutes slid by, and at last he could breathe again.

Gingerly he stuck his head and shoulders through the rectangular opening. Katinka's toilet cabin beyond was in darkness, but the odour of her perfume made his breath come short. He listened intently, but could hear nothing from the main cabin beyond. Then, faintly, the sound of the ship's bell reached him from the deck above and he realized with dismay that it was almost dawn and in half an hour his watch would begin.

He pulled his head out of the opening, and replaced the panel, securing it with the wooden dowels, but so lightly that they could be removed in seconds.

'Should you allow the Buzzard's men ashore?' Hal asked his father respectfully. 'Forgive me, Father, but can you trust him that far?'

'Can I stop him without provoking a fight?' Sir Francis answered with another question. 'He says he needs water and firewood, and we do not own this land or even this lagoon. How can I forbid it to him?'

Hal might have protested further, but his father silenced him with a quick frown, and turned to greet Lord Cumbrae as the keel of his longboat kissed the sands of the beach and he sprang ashore his legs beneath the plaid furred with wiry ginger hair like a bear's.

'All God's blessings upon you this lovely morning, Franky,' he shouted, as he came towards them. His pale blue eyes darted restlessly as minnows in a pool under his beetling red brows.

'He sees everything,' Hal murmured. 'He has come to find out where we have stored the spice.'

'We cannot hide the spice. There's a mountain of it,' Sir Francis told him. 'But we can make the thieving of it difficult for him.' Then he smiled bleakly at Cumbrae as he came up. 'I hope I see you in good health, and that the whisky did not trouble your sleep last night, sir.'

'The elixir of life, Franky. The blood in my veins.' His eyes were bloodshot as they darted about the encampment at the edge of the forest. 'I need to fill my water casks. There must be good sweet water hereabouts.'

'A mile up the lagoon. There's a stream comes in from the hills.'

'Plenty of fish.' The Buzzard gestured at the racks of poles set up in the clearing upon which the split carcasses were laid out over the slow smoking fires of green wood. 'I'll have my lads catch some for us also. But what about meat? Are there any deer or wild cattle in the forest?'

'There are elephants, and herds of wild buffalo. But all are fierce, and even a musket ball in the ribs does not bring them down. However, as soon as the ship is careened I intend sending a band of hunters inland, beyond the hills to see if they cannot find easier prey.'

It was apparent that Cumbrae had asked the question to give himself space, and he hardly bothered to listen to the reply. When his roving eyes gleamed, Hal followed their gaze. The Buzzard had discovered the row of thatched lean-to shelters a hundred paces back among the trees, under which the huge casks of spice stood in serried ranks.

'So you plan to beach and careen the galleon.' Cumbrae turned away from the spice store, and nodded across the water at the hull of the *Resolution*. 'A wise plan. If you need help, I have three first-rate carpenters.'

'You are amiable,' Sir Francis told him. 'I may call upon you.'

'Anything to help a fellow Knight. I know you would do the same for me.' The Buzzard clapped him warmly on the shoulder. 'Now, while my shore party goes to refill the water casks, you and I can look for a suitable place to set up our Lodge. We must do young Hal here proud. It's an important day for him.'

Sir Francis glanced at Hal. 'Aboli is waiting for you.' He nodded to where the big black man stood patiently a little further down the beach.

Hal watched his father walk away with Cumbrae and disappear down a footpath into the forest. Then he ran down to join Aboli. 'I am ready at last. Let us go.'

Aboli set off immediately, trotting along the beach towards the head of the lagoon. Hal fell in beside him. 'You have no sticks?'

'We will cut them from the forest.' Aboli tapped the shaft of the hand axe, the steel head of which was hooked over his shoulder, and turned off the beach as he spoke. He led Hal a mile or so inland until they reached a dense thicket. 'I marked these trees earlier. My tribe call them the *kweti*. From them we make the finest throwing sticks.'

As they pushed into the dense thicket, there was a explosion of flying leaves and crashing branches as some huge beast charged away ahead of them. They caught a glimpse of scabby black hide and the flash of great bossed horns.

'*Nyati!*' Aboli told Hal. 'The wild buffalo.'

'We should hunt him.' Hal unslung the musket from his shoulder, and reached eagerly for the flint and steel in his pouch to light his slow-match. 'Such a monster would give us beef for all the ship's company.'

Aboli grinned and shook his head. 'He would hunt you first. There is no fiercer beast in all the forest, not even the lion. He will laugh at your little lead musket balls as he splits your belly open with those mighty spears he carries atop his head.' He swung the axe from his shoulder. 'Leave old Nyati be, and we will find other meat to feed the crew.'

Aboli hacked at the base of one of the *kweti* saplings and, with a dozen strokes, exposed the bulbous root. After a few more strokes he lifted it out from the earth, with the stem attached to it.

'My tribe call this club an *iwisa*,' he told Hal, as he worked, 'and today I will show you how to use it.' With skilful cuts, he sized the length of the shaft and peeled away the bark. Then he trimmed the root into an iron-hard ball, like the head of a mace. When he was finished he hefted the club, testing its weight and balance. Then he set it aside and searched for another. 'We need two each.'

Hal squatted on his heels and watched the wood chips fly under the steel. 'How old were you when the slavers caught you, Aboli?' he asked, and the dextrous black hands paused in their task.

A shadow passed behind the dark eyes, but Aboli started working again before he replied, 'I do not know, only that I was very young.'

'Do you remember it, Aboli?'

'I remember that it was night when they came, men in white robes with long muskets. It was so long ago, but I remember the flames in the darkness as they surrounded our village.'

'Where did your people live?'

'Far to the north. On the shores of a great river. My father was a chief yet they dragged him from his hut and killed him like an animal. They killed all our warriors, and spared only the very young children and the women. They chained us together in lines, neck to neck, and made us march, many days, towards the rising of the sun, down to the coast.' Aboli stood up abruptly, and picked up the bundle of clubs he had finished. 'We talk like old women while we should be hunting.'

He started back through the trees the way they had come. When they reached the lagoon again, he looked back at Hal. 'Leave your musket and powder flask here. They will be no use to you in the water.'

As Hal hid his weapon in the undergrowth, Aboli selected a pair of the lightest and straightest of the *iwisa*. When Hal returned he handed him the clubs. 'Watch me. Do what I do,' he ordered, as he stripped off his clothing and waded out into the shallows of the lagoon. Hal followed him, naked, into the thickest stand of reeds.

Waist deep, Aboli stopped and pulled the stems of the tall reeds over his head plaiting them together to form a screen over himself. Then he sank down into the water, until only his head was exposed. Hal took up a position not far from him, and quickly built himself a similar roof of reeds. Faintly he could hear the voices of the watering party from the *Gull*, and the squeaking of their oars as they rowed back from the head of the lagoon where they had filled their casks from the sweet-water stream.

'Good!' Aboli called softly, 'Be ready now, Gundwane! They will put the birds into the air for us.'

Suddenly there was a roar of wings, and the sky was filled with the same vast cloud of birds they had watched before. A flight of ducks that looked like English mallard, except for their bright yellow bills, sped in a low V-formation towards where they were hidden.

'Here they come,' Aboli warned him, in a whisper, and Hal tensed, his face turned upwards to watch the old drake that led the flock. His wings were like knife blades as they stabbed the air with quick, sharp strokes.

'Now!' shouted Aboli, and sprang up to his full height, his right arm already cocked back with the *iwisa* in his fist. As he hurled it cartwheeling into the air, the line of wild duck flared in panic.

Aboli had anticipated this reaction and his spinning club caught the drake in the chest and stopped him dead. He fell in a tangle of wings and webbed feet, trailing feathers, but long before he struck the water Aboli had hurled his second club. It spun up to catch a younger bird, snapping her outstretched neck and dropping her close beside the floating carcass of the old drake.

Hal hurled his own sticks in quick succession, but both flew well wide of his mark and the splintered flock raced away low over the reed beds.

'You will soon learn, you were close with both your throws,' Aboli encouraged him, as he splashed through the reeds, first to pick up the dead birds, and then to recover his *iwisa*. He floated the two carcasses in a pool of open water in front of him, and within minutes they had decoyed in another whistling flock that dropped almost to the tops of the reeds before he threw at them.

'Good throw, Gundwane!' Aboli laughed at Hal as he waded out to pick up another two dead birds. 'You were closer then. Soon you may even hit one.'

Despite this prophecy, it was mid-morning before Hal brought down his first duck. Even then it was broken-winged, and he had to plunge and swim after it half-way down the lagoon before he could get a hand to it and wring its neck. In the middle of the day the birds stopped flighting and sat out in the deeper water where they could not be reached.

'It's enough!' Aboli put an end to the hunt, and gathered up his kill. From a tree at the water's edge he cut strips of bark and twisted these into strings to tie the dead ducks into bunches. They made up a load almost too heavy for even his broad shoulders to bear but Hal carried his own meagre bag without difficulty as they trudged back along the beach.

When they came round the point and could look into the bay where the three ships lay at anchor, Aboli dropped his burden of dead birds to the sand. 'We will rest here.' Hal sank down beside him, and for a while they sat in silence, until Aboli asked, 'Why has the Buzzard come here? What does your father say?'

'The Buzzard says he has come to make a Lodge for my initiation.'

Aboli nodded. 'In my own tribe the young warrior had to enter the circumcision lodge before he became a man.'

Hal shuddered and fingered his crotch as if to check that all was still in place. 'I am glad I will not have to give myself to the knife, as you did.'

'But that is not the true reason that the Buzzard has followed us here. He follows your father as the hyena follows the lion. The stink of treachery is strong upon him.'

'My father has smelt it also,' Hal assured him softly. 'But we are at his mercy, for the *Resolution* has no mainmast and the cannon are out of her.'

They both stared down the lagoon at the *Gull of Moray*, until Hal stirred uneasily. 'What is the Buzzard up to now?'

The longboat from the *Gull* was rowing out from her side to where her anchor cable dipped below the surface of the lagoon. They watched the crew of the small boat latch onto it and work there for several minutes.

'They are screened from the beach, so my father cannot see what they are up to.' Hal was thinking aloud. ''Tis a furtive air they have about them, and I like it not at all.'

As he spoke the men finished their secretive task and began to row back to the *Gull*'s side. Now Hal could make out that they were laying a second cable over their stern as they went. At that he sprang to his feet in agitation. 'They are setting a spring to their anchor!' he exclaimed.

'A spring?' Aboli looked at him. 'Why would they do that?'

'So that with a few turns of the capstan the Buzzard can swing his ship in any direction he chooses.'

Aboli stood up beside him, his expression grave. 'That way he can train his broadside of cannon on our helpless ship or sweep our encampment on the beach with grape shot,' he said. 'We must hurry back to warn the captain.'

'No, Aboli, do not hurry. We must not alert the Buzzard to the fact that we have spotted his trick.'

Sir Francis listened intently to what Hal was saying, and when his son had finished he stroked his chin reflectively. Then he sauntered to the rail of the *Resolution* and casually raised his telescope to his eye. He made a slow sweep of the wide expanse of the lagoon, barely pausing as his gaze passed over the *Gull* so that no one could mark his sudden interest in the Buzzard's ship. Then he closed the telescope and came back to where Hal waited. There was respect in Sir Francis's eyes as he said, 'Well done, my boy. The Buzzard is up to his usual tricks. You were right. I was on the beach and could not see him setting the spring. I might never have noticed it.'

'Are you going to order him to remove it, Father?'

Sir Francis smiled and shook his head. 'Better not to let him know we have tumbled to him.'

'But what can we do?'

'I already have the culverins on the beach trained on the *Gull*. Daniel and Ned have warned every man—'

'But, Father, is there no ruse we can prepare for the Buzzard to match the surprise he clearly plans for us?' In his agitation Hal found the temerity to interrupt, but his father frowned quickly and his reply was sharp.

'No doubt you have a suggestion, Master Henry.'

At this formal address Hal was warned of his father's rising anger, and he was immediately contrite. 'Forgive my presumption, Father, I meant no impertinence.'

'I am pleased to hear that.' Sir Francis began to turn away, his back still stiff.

'Was not my great-grandfather, Charles Courtney, with Drake at the battle of Gravelines?'

'He was, indeed.' Sir Francis looked round. 'But as you already know the answer well enough, is this not a strange question to put to me now?'

'So it may well have been Great-grandfather himself who proposed to Drake the use of devil ships against the Spanish Armada as it lay anchored in Calais Roads, may it not?'

Slowly Sir Francis turned his head and stared at his son. He began to smile, then to chuckle, and at last burst out laughing. 'Dear Lord, but the Courtney blood runs true! Come down to my cabin this instant and show me what it is you have in mind.'

Sir Francis stood at Hal's shoulder as he sketched a design on the slate. 'They need not be sturdily constructed, for they will not have far to sail, and will have no heavy seas to endure,' Hal explained deferentially.

'Yes, but once they are launched they should be able to hold a true course, and yet carry a goodly weight of cargo,' his father murmured, and took the chalk from his son. He drew a few quick lines on the slate. 'We might lash two hulls together. It would not do to have them capsize or expend themselves before they reach their destination.'

'The wind has been steady from the sou'-east ever since we have been anchored here,' said Hal. 'There is no sign of it dropping. So we must hold them up-wind. If we place them on the small island across the channel, then the wind will work for us when we launch them.'

'Very well.' Sir Francis nodded. 'How many do we need?' He could see how much pleasure he gave the lad by consulting him in this fashion.

'Drake sent in eight against the Spaniards, but we do not have the time to build so many. Five, perhaps?' He looked up at his father, and Sir Francis nodded again.

'Yes, five should do it. How many men will you need? Daniel must remain in command of the culverins on the beach. The Buzzard may spring his trap before we are ready. But I will send Ned Tyler and the carpenter to help you build them – and Aboli, of course.'

Hal stared at his father in awe. 'You will trust me to take charge of the building?' he asked.

'It is your plan so if it fails I must be able to lay full blame upon you,' his father replied, with only the faintest smile upon his lips. 'Take your men and go ashore at once to begin work. But be circumspect. Don't make it easy for the Buzzard.'

Hal's axemen cleared a small opening on the far side of the heavily forested island across the channel where they were hidden from the *Gull of Moray*. After a circuitous detour through the forest on the mainland, he was also able to ferry his men and material across to the island out of sight of the lookouts on the Buzzard's vessel.

That first night they worked by the wavering light of pitch-soaked torches until after midnight. All of them were aware of the urgency of their task, and when they were exhausted they simply threw themselves on the soft bed of leaf mould under the trees and slept until the dawn gave enough light to begin work again.

By noon of the following day all five of the strange craft were ready to be carried to their hiding place in the grove at the edge of the lagoon. At low tide, Sir Francis waded across from the mainland and made his way down the footpath through the dense forest that covered the island to inspect the work.

He nodded dubiously. 'I hope sincerely that they will float,' he mused, as he walked slowly round one of the ungainly vessels.

'We will only know that when we send them out for the first time.' Hal was tired, and his temper was short. 'Even to please you, Father, I cannot arrange a prior demonstration for the benefit of Lord Cumbrae.'

His father glanced at him, concealing his surprise. The puppy grows into a young dog and learns how to growl, he thought, with a twinge of paternal pride. He demands respect, and, truth to tell, he has earned it.

Aloud he said, 'You have done well in the time at your disposal,' which deftly turned aside Hal's anger. 'I will send fresh men to help you transport them, and place them in the grove.'

Hal was so tired that he could barely drag himself up the rope ladder to the entryport of the *Resolution*. But even though his task was complete, his father would not let him escape to his cabin.

'We are anchored directly behind the *Gull*.' He pointed across the moonlit channel at the dark shape of the other ship. 'Have you thought what might happen if one of your fiendish vessels drifts past the mark and comes down upon us here? Dismasted as we are, we cannot manoeuvre the ship.'

'Aboli has already cut long bamboo poles in the forest.' Hal's tone could not conceal that he was weary to his bones. 'We will use them to deflect any drifters from us and send them harmlessly up onto the beach over there.' He turned and pointed back towards where the fires of the encampment flickered among the trees. 'The Buzzard will be taken by surprise, and will not be equipped with bamboo poles.'

At last his father was satisfied. 'Go to your rest now. Tomorrow night we will open the Lodge, and you must be able to make your responses to the catechism.'

Hal came back reluctantly from the abyss of sleep into which he had sunk. For some moments he was not certain what had woken him. Then the soft scratching came again from the bulkhead.

Instantly he was fully awake, every vestige of fatigue forgotten. He rolled off his pallet, and knelt at the panel. The scratching was now impatient and demanding. He tapped a swift reply on the woodwork, then fumbled in the darkness to find the stopper of his peep-hole. The moment he removed it, a yellow ray of lamp-light shone through but was cut off as Katinka placed her lips to the opening on the far side and whispered angrily, 'Where were you last night?'

'I had duties ashore,' he whispered back.

'I do not believe you,' she told him. 'You try to escape your punishment. You deliberately disobey me.'

'No, no, I would not—'

'Open this panel at once.'

He groped for his dirk, which hung on his belt on the hook at the foot of his bunk, and prised out the dowels. The panel came away in his hands with only the faintest scraping sound. He set it aside, and a square of soft light fell through the hatch.

'Come!' her voice ordered, and he wriggled into the gap. It was a tight squeeze, but after a short struggle he found himself on his hands and knees on the deck of her cabin. He started to rise to his feet, but she stopped him.

'Stay down there.' He looked up at her as she stood over him. She was dressed in a flowing night-robe of some gossamer material. Her hair was loose and hung in splendour to her waist. The lamp-light shone through the cloth of her robe and silhouetted her body, the lustre of her skin gleaming through the transparent folds of silk.

'You have no shame,' she told him, as he knelt before her as though she were the sacred image of a saint. 'You come to me naked. You show me no respect.'

'I am sorry!' he gasped. In his anxiety to obey her he had forgotten his own nudity, and now he cupped his hands over his privy parts. 'I meant no disrespect.'

'No! Do not cover your shame.' She reached down and pulled away his hands. Both stared down at his groin. They watched him slowly stretch out and thicken, thrusting out towards her, his prepuce peeling back of its own accord.

'Is there nothing I can do to stop such revolting behaviour? Are you too far gone in Satan's ways?'

She seized a handful of his hair and dragged him to his feet and after her into the splendid cabin where first he had laid eyes on her beauty.

She dropped onto the quilted bed, and sat facing him. The white silk skirts parted and fell back on each side of her long slim thighs. She twisted the handful of his curls, and said, in a voice that was suddenly breathless, 'You must obey me in all things, you child of the dark pit.'

Her thighs fell apart, and she pulled his face down and pressed it hard at their apex against the impossibly soft and silky mound of golden curls.

He smelt the sea in her, brine and kelp, and the scent of the sparkling living things of the oceans, the warm soft odour of the islands, of salt surf breaking on a sun-baked beach. He drank it in through flaring nostrils, and then tracked down the source of this fabulous aroma with his lips.

She wriggled forward on the satin covers to meet his mouth, her thighs spread wider, and she tilted her hips forward to open herself to him. With a handful of his curls, she moved his head, guiding him to that tiny bud of pink, taut flesh that nestled in its hidden crevice. As he found it with the tip of his tongue she gasped and she began to move herself against his face as though she rode bareback upon a galloping stallion. She gave small incoherent contradictory cries. 'Oh, stop! Please stop! No! Never stop! Go on for ever!'

Then suddenly she wrenched his head out from between her straining thighs, and fell backwards upon the covers lifting him over her. He felt her hard little heels dig into the small of his back as she wrapped her legs around him, and her fingernails, like knives, cutting into the tensed muscles of his shoulders. Then the pain was lost in the sensation of slippery engulfing heat as he slid deeply into her, and he smothered his cries in the golden tangle of her hair.

The three Knights had set up the Lodge on the slope of the hills above the lagoon, at the foot of a small waterfall that dropped into a basin of dark water surrounded by tall trees hung with lichens and lianas.

The altar stood within the circle of stones, the fire burning before it. Thus all the ancient elements were represented. The moon was in its first quarter, signifying rebirth and resurrection.

Hal waited alone in the forest while the three Knights of the Order opened the Lodge in the first degree. Then his father, his bared sword in his hand, came striding through the darkness to fetch him, and led him back along the path.

The other two Knights were waiting beside the fire in the sacred circle. Their swords were drawn, the blades gleaming in the reflection of the flames. Lying upon the stone altar under a velvet cloth, he saw the shape of his great-grandfather's Neptune sword. They paused outside the circle of stones and Sir Francis begged entrance to the Lodge.

'In the name of the Father, the Son and the Holy Ghost!'

'Who would enter the Lodge of the Temple of the Order of St George and the Holy Grail?' Lord Cumbrae thundered, in a voice that rang against the hills, his long two-edged claymore glinting in his hairy red fist.

'A novice who presents himself for initiation into the mysteries of the Temple,' Hal replied.

'Enter on peril of your eternal life,' Cumbrae warned him, and Hal stepped into the circle. Suddenly the air seemed colder and he shivered, even as he knelt in the radiance of the watchfire.

'Who sponsors this novice?' the Buzzard demanded again.

'I do.' Sir Francis stepped forward and Cumbrae turned back to Hal.

'Who are you?'

'Henry Courtney, son of Francis and Edwina.' The long catechism began as the starry wheel of the firmament turned slowly overhead and the flames of the watchfire sank lower.

It was after midnight when, at last, Sir Francis lifted the velvet covering from the Neptune sword. The sapphire on the hilt reflected a pale blue beam of moonlight into Hal's eyes as his father placed the hilt in his hands.

'Upon this blade you will confirm the tenets of your faith.'

'These things I believe,' Hal began, 'and I will defend them with my life. I believe there is but one God in Trinity, the Father eternal, the Son eternal and the Holy Ghost eternal.'

'Amen!' chorused the three Nautonnier Knights.

'I believe in the communion of the Church of England, and the divine right of its representative on earth, Charles, King of England, Scotland, France and Ireland, Defender of the Faith.'

'Amen!'

Once Hal had recited his beliefs, Cumbrae called upon him to make his knightly vows.

'I will uphold the Church of England. I will confront the enemies of my sovereign lord, Charles.' Hal's voice quivered with conviction and sincerity. 'I renounce Satan and all his works. I eschew all false doctrines and heresies and schisms. I turn my face away from all other gods and their false prophets.'

'I will protect the weak. I will defend the pilgrim. I will succour the needy and those in need of justice. I will take up the sword against the tyrant and the oppressor.'

'I will defend the holy places. I will search out and protect the precious relics of Christ Jesus and his Saints. I will never cease my quest for the Holy Grail that contained his sacred blood.'

The Nautonnier Knights crossed themselves as he made this vow, for the Grail quest stood at the centre of their belief. It was the granite column that held aloft the roof of their Temple.

'I pledge myself to the Strict Observance. I will obey the code of my Knighthood. I will abstain from debauchery and fornication,' Hal's tongue tripped on the word, but he recovered swiftly, 'and I will honour my fellow Knights. Above all else, I will keep secret all the proceedings of my Lodge.'

'And may the Lord have mercy on your soul!' the three Nautonnier Knights intoned in unison. Then they stepped forward and formed a ring around the kneeling novice. Each laid one hand on his bowed head and the other on the hilt of his sword, their hands overlapping each other.

'Henry Courtney, we welcome you into the Grail company, and we accept you as brother Knight of the Temple of the Order of St George and the Holy Grail.'

Richard Lister spoke first, in his sonorous Welsh voice, almost singing his blessing. 'I welcome you into the Temple. May you always follow the Strict Observance.'

Cumbrae spoke next. 'I welcome you into the Temple. May the waters of far oceans open wide before the bows of your ship, and may the force of the wind drive you on.'

Then Sir Francis Courtney spoke with his hand firmly set on Hal's brow. 'I welcome you into the Temple. May you always be true to your vows, to your God and to yourself.'

Then between them the Nautonnier Knights lifted him to his feet and, one after another, embraced him. Lord Cumbrae's whiskers were stiff and pricking as a garland of thorns from the traitor's bush.

'I have a hold filled with my share of the spices that you and I took from *Heerlycke Nacht*, enough to buy me a castle and five thousand acres of the finest land in Wales,' said Richard Lister, as he clasped Sir Francis's right hand in his, using the secret grip of the Nautonniers. 'And I have a young wife and two stout sons upon whom I have not laid eyes for three years. A little rest in green and pleasant places with those I love, and then, I know, the wind will summon. Perhaps we will meet again on far waters, Francis.'

'Take the tide of your heart, then, Richard. I thank you for your friendship, and for what you have done for my son.' Sir Francis returned his grip. 'I hope one day to welcome both your boys into the Temple.'

Richard turned away towards his waiting longboat, but hesitated and came back. He placed one arm around Sir Francis's shoulders and his brow was grave, his voice low, as he said, 'Cumbrae had a proposition for me concerning you, but I liked it not at all and told him so to his face. Watch your back, Franky, and sleep with one eye open when he is around you.'

'You are a good friend,' Sir Francis said, and watched Richard walk to his longboat and cross to the *Goddess*. As soon as he went up the ladder to the quarterdeck his crew weighed the anchor. All her sails filled and she moved down the channel, dipping her pennant in farewell as she disappeared out through the heads into the open sea.

'Now we have only the Buzzard to keep us company.' Hal looked across at the *Gull of Moray* where she lay in the centre of the channel, her boats clustered around her discharging water casks, bundles of firewood and dried fish into her holds.

'Make your preparations to beach the ship, please, Mr Courtney,' Sir Francis replied, and Hal straightened his spine. He was unaccustomed to his father addressing him thus. It was strange to be treated as a Knight and a full officer, instead of as a lowly ensign. Even his mode of dress had changed with his new status. His father had provided the shirt of fine white Madras cotton on his back, as well as his new moleskin breeches, which felt soft as silk against his skin after the rags of rough canvas he had worn before today.

He was even more surprised when his father deigned to explain his order. 'We must go about our business as if we suspect no treachery. Besides which the *Resolution* will be safer upon the beach if it comes to a fight.'

'I understand, sir.' Hal looked up at the sun to judge the time. 'The tide will be fair for us to take her aground at two bells in tomorrow's morning watch. We will be prepared.'

All the rest of that morning the crew of the *Gull* behaved like that of any other ship preparing for sea, and though Daniel and his guncrews, with cannon loaded and aimed, and with slow-match burning, watched the *Gull* from their hidden emplacements dug into the sandy soil along the edge of the forest, she gave them no hint of treachery.

A little before noon Lord Cumbrae had himself rowed ashore and came to find Sir Francis where he stood by the fire upon which the cauldron of pitch was bubbling, ready to begin caulking the *Resolution*'s hull when she was careened.

'It's farewell, then.' He embraced Sir Francis, throwing a thick red arm around his shoulders. 'Richard was right. There's no prize to be won if we sit here upon the beach and scratch our backsides.'

'So you're ready to sail?' Sir Francis kept his tone level, not betraying his astonishment.

'With tomorrow morning's tide, I'll be away. But how I hate to leave you, Franky. Will you not take a last dram aboard the *Gull* with me now? I would fain discuss with you my share of the prize money from the *Standvastigheid*.'

'My lord, your share is nothing. That ends our discussion, and I wish you a fair wind.'

Cumbrae let fly a great blast of laughter. 'I've always loved your sense of fun, Franky. I know you only wish to spare me the labour of carrying that heavy cargo of spice back to the Firth of Forth.' He turned and pointed with his curling beard at the spice store under the forest trees. 'So I shall let you do it for me. But, in the meantime, I trust you to keep a fair accounting of my share, and to deliver it to me when next we meet – plus the usual interest, of course.'

'I trust you as dearly, my lord.' Sir Francis lifted his hat and swept the sand with the plume as he bowed.

Cumbrae returned the bow and, still rumbling with laughter, went down to the longboat and had himself rowed to the *Gull*.

During the course of the morning the Dutch hostages had been brought ashore and installed in their new lodgings, which Hal and his gang had built for them. These were set well back from the lagoon and separated from the compound in which the *Resolution*'s crew were housed.

Now the ship was empty and ready for beaching. As the tide pushed in through the heads the crew, under the direction of Ned Tyler and Hal, began warping it in towards the beach. They had secured the strongest sheaves and blocks to the largest of the trees. Heavy hawsers were fastened to the *Resolution*'s bows and stern, and with fifty men straining on the lines, the ship came in parallel to the beach.

When her bottom touched the white sand they secured her there. As the tide receded they hove her down with tackle attached to her mizzen and foremasts, which were still stepped. The ship heeled over steeply until her mastheads touched the tree-tops. The whole of the starboard side of her hull, down as far as the keel, was exposed, and Sir Francis and Hal waded out to inspect it. They were delighted to find little sign of shipworm infestation.

A few sections of planking had to be replaced and the work began immediately. When darkness fell the torches were lit, for the work on the hull would continue until the return of the tide put a halt to it. When this happened Sir Francis went off to dine in his new quarters, while Hal gave orders to secure the hull for the night. The torches were doused and Ned led away the men to find their own belated dinner.

Hal was not hungry for food. His appetites were of a different order, but it would be at least another hour before he could satisfy them. Left alone on the beach, he studied the *Gull* across the narrow strip of water. It seemed that she was settled in quietly enough for the night. Her small boats still lay alongside, but it would not take long to lift them on board and batten down her hatches ready for sea.

He turned away and moved back into the trees. He went down the line of gun emplacements, speaking softly to the men on watch behind the culverins. He checked once more the laying of each, making sure that they were truly aimed at the dark shape of the *Gull*, as she lay in a spangle of star reflections on the surface of the still, dark lagoon.

For a while he sat next to Big Daniel, dangling his legs into the gunpit.

'Don't worry, Mr Henry.' Even Daniel used the new and more respectful form of address naturally enough. 'We're keeping a weather eye on that red-bearded bastard. You can go off and get your supper.'

'When did you last sleep, Daniel?' Hal asked.

'Don't worry about me. The watch changes pretty soon now. I'll be handing over to Timothy.'

Outside his hut Hal found Aboli sitting as quietly as a shadow by the fire, waiting for him with a bowl that contained roasted duck and hunks of bread, and a jug of small beer.

'I'm not hungry, Aboli,' Hal protested.

'Eat.' Aboli thrust the bowl into his hands. 'You will need your strength for the task that lies ahead of you this night.'

Hal accepted the bowl, but he tried to determine Aboli's expression and to read from it the deeper meaning of his admonition. The firelight danced on his dark enigmatic features, like those of a pagan idol, highlighting the tattoos on his cheeks, but his eyes were inscrutable.

Hal used his dirk to split the carcass of the duck in half and offered one portion to Aboli. 'What task is this that I have to perform?' he asked carefully.

Aboli tore a piece off the duck's breast and shrugged as he chewed. 'You must be careful not to scratch the tenderest parts of yourself on a thorn as you go through the hole in the stockade to do your duty.'

Hal's jaw stopped moving and the duck in his mouth lost its taste. Aboli must have discovered the narrow passage through the thorn fence behind Katinka's hut that Hal had so secretly left open.

'How long have you known?' he asked, through his mouthful.

'Was I supposed not to know?' Aboli asked. 'Your eyes are like the full moon when you look in a certain direction, and I have heard your roars like those of a wounded buffalo coming from the stern at midnight.'

Hal was stunned. He had been so careful and cunning.

'Do you think my father knows?' he asked with trepidation.

'You are still alive,' Aboli pointed out. 'If he knew, that would not be so.'

'You would tell no one?' he whispered. 'Especially not him?'

'Especially not him,' Aboli agreed. 'But take a care that you do not dig your own grave with that spade between your legs.'

'I love her, Aboli,' Hal whispered. 'I cannot sleep for the thought of her.'

'I have heard you not sleeping. I thought you might wake the entire ship's company with your sleeplessness.'

'Do not mock me, Aboli. I will die for lack of her.'

'Then I must save your life by taking you to her.'

'You would come with me?' Hal was shocked by the offer.

'I will wait at your hole in the stockade. To guard you. You might need my help if the husband finds you where he would like to be.'

'That fat animal!' Hal said furiously, hating the man with all his heart.

'Fat, perhaps. Sly, almost certainly. Powerful, without doubt. Do not underrate him, Gundwane.' Aboli stood up. 'I will go first to make sure the way is clear.'

The two slipped quietly through the darkness, and paused at the rear of the stockade.

'You don't have to wait for me, Aboli,' Hal whispered, 'I might be a little while.'

'If you were not, I would be disappointed in you,' Aboli told Hal in his own language. 'Remember this advice always, Gundwane, for it will stand you in good stead all the days of your life. A man's passion is like a fire in tall, dry grass, hot and furious but soon spent. A woman is like a magician's cauldron that must simmer long upon the coals before it can bring forth its spell. Be swift in all things but love.'

Hal sighed in the darkness. 'Why must women be so different from us, Aboli?'

'Thank all your Gods, and mine also, that they are.' Aboli's teeth gleamed in the darkness as he grinned. He pushed Hal gently towards the opening. 'If you call I will be here.'

The lamp still burned in her hut. The slivers of yellow light shone through the weak places in the thatch. Hal listened softly at the wall, but heard no voices. He crept to the door, which stood open a crack. He peered through it, at the huge four-poster bed that his men had carried from her cabin in the *Resolution*. The curtains were closed to keep out the insects, so he could not be certain that there was only one person behind them.

Soundlessly he slipped through the door and crept to the bed. As he touched the curtains, a small white hand reached through the folds, seized his outstretched hand and dragged him in. 'Do not speak!' she hissed at him. 'Say not a word!' Her fingers flew nimbly down the buttons of his shirt front, opening it to the waist, then her nails dug painfully into his breast.

At the same time her mouth covered his. She had never kissed him before and the heat and softness of her lips astonished him. He tried to grasp her breasts but she seized his wrists and held them at his sides as her tongue slipped into his mouth and twined with his, slithering and twisting like a live eel, goading and teasing him slowly, higher than he had ever been before.

Then still holding his hands at his side she forced him over backwards. Her swift fingers opened the fastening of his moleskin breeches, and then in a flurry of silks and laces she bestrode his hips and pinned him to the satin coverlet. Without using her hands she searched with her pelvis until she found him and sucked him into her secret heat.

Much later, Hal fell into a sleep so deep that it was like a little death.

An insistent hand on his bare arm woke him, and he started up in alarm. 'What—' he began, but the hand whipped over his mouth and gagged his next word.

'Gundwane! Make no noise. Find your clothes and come with me. Quickly!'

Hal rolled gently off the bed, careful not to disturb the woman beside him, and found his breeches where she had thrown them.

Neither spoke again until they had crept out through the gap in the stockade. There, they paused as Hal glanced up at the sky and saw, by the angle of the great Southern Cross to the horizon, that it lacked only an hour or so till dawn. This was the witching hour when all human resources were at their lowest ebb. Hal peered back at Aboli's dark shape. 'What is it, Aboli?' Hal demanded. 'Why did you call me?'

'Listen!' Aboli laid a hand on his shoulder and Hal cocked his head.

'I hear nothing.'

'Wait!' Aboli squeezed his shoulder for silence.

Then Hal heard it, far off and faint, blanketed by the trees, a shout of uncontrolled laughter.

'Where . . . ?' Hal was puzzled.

'At the beach.'

'God's wounds!' Hal blurted. 'What devilry is this now?' He began to run, Aboli at his side, heading for the lagoon, stumbling in the darkness on the uneven forest floor with low branches whipping into their faces.

As they reached the first huts of the encampment, they heard more noise ahead, a snatch of slurred song and a hoot of crazed laughter.

'The gunpits,' Hal panted, and at that moment saw, in the last glimmer from the dying watchfire, a pale human shape ahead.

Then his father's voice challenged him. 'Who is that?'

''Tis Hal, Father.'

'What is happening?' It was clear that Sir Francis had only just awakened for he was in his shirt sleeves and his voice was groggy with sleep, but his sword was in his hand.

'I don't know,' Hal said. There was another roar of stupid laughter. 'It comes from the beach. The gunpits.'

Without another word, all three ran on, and came together to the first culverin. Here, at the edge of the lagoon, the canopy of leaves overhead was thinner, allowing the last rays of the moon to shine through, giving them enough light to see one of the guncrew draped over the long bronze barrel. When Sir Francis aimed an angry kick at him he collapsed in the sand.

It was then that Hal spotted the small keg standing on the lip of the pit. Oblivious to their arrival, one of the other gunners was on his hands and knees in front of it, like a dog, lapping up the liquid that dribbled from the spigot. Hal smelt the sugary aroma, heavy on the night air like the emanation of some poisonous flower. He jumped down into the pit and seized the gunner by his hair.

'Where did you get the rum?' he snarled. The man peered back at him blearily. Hal drew back his fist and struck him a blow that made his teeth clash together in his jaw. 'Damn you for a sot! Where did you get it?' Hal pricked him with the point of his dirk. 'Answer me or I'll split your windpipe.'

The pain and the threat rallied his victim. 'A parting gift from his lordship,' he gasped. 'He sent a keg across from the *Gull* for us to drink his health and wish him God speed.'

Hal flung the drunken creature from him and leapt onto the parapet. 'The other guncrews? Has the Buzzard sent gifts to all of them?'

They ran down the line of emplacements, and in each found sweetly reeking oaken kegs and inert bodies. Few of the crews were still on their feet, but even those who were, were staggering and slobbering in intoxication. Few English seamen could resist the ardent essence of the sugar cane.

Even Timothy Reilly, one of Sir Francis's trusted coxswains, had succumbed, and although he tried to answer Sir Francis's accusation, he reeled on his feet. Sir Francis struck him a blow with the hilt of his sword across the side of his head and the fellow collapsed in the sand.

At that moment, Big Daniel came running from the encampment. 'I heard the uproar, Captain. What has happened?'

'The Buzzard has plied the guncrews with liquor. They are all of them witless.' His voice shook with fury. 'It can only mean one thing. There is not a moment to lose. Rouse the camp. Stand the men to arms – but softly, mind!'

As Daniel raced away, Hal heard a faint sound from the dark ship across the still lagoon waters, a distant clank of ratchet and pawl, that sent tingling shocks up his spine.

'The capstan!' he exclaimed. 'The *Gull* is tightening up on her anchor spring.'

They stared across the channel, and in the moonlight saw the silhouette of the *Gull* begin to alter, as the hawser running from the anchor to her capstan pulled her stern round, and her full broadside was presented to the beach.

'Her guns are run out!' Sir Francis exclaimed, as the moonlight glinted on the barrels. Behind each they could now make out the faint glow of the burning slow-match in the hands of the *Gull*'s gunners.

'Satan's breath, they're going to fire on us! Down!' shouted Sir Francis. 'Get down!' Hal leapt over the parapet of the gunpit and flung himself flat on the sandy floor.

Suddenly the night was lit brightly, as if by a flash of lightning. An instant later the thunder smote their ear-drums and the tornado of shot swept across the beach and thrashed into the forest around them. The *Gull* had fired all her cannon into the encampment in a single devastating broadside.

The grape shot tore through the foliage above and branches, clusters of leaves and slabs of wet bark rained down upon them. The air was filled with a lethal swarm of splinters blasted from the tree-trunks.

The frail huts gave no protection to the men within. The broadside slashed through, sending poles flying and flattening the flimsy structures as though they had been hit by a tidal wave. They heard the terrified yells of men awakening into a nightmare, and the sobs, screams and groans of those cut down by the hail of shot or skewered by the sharp, ragged splinters.

The *Gull* had disappeared behind the pall of her own gunsmoke, but Sir Francis leapt to his feet and snatched the smouldering match from the senseless hand of the drunken gunner. He glanced over the sights of the culverin and saw that it was still aimed into the swirling smoke behind which the *Gull* lay. He pressed the match to the touch hole. The culverin bellowed out a long silver gush of smoke and bounded back against its tackle. He could not see the strike of his shot, but he roared an order to those gunners down the line still sober enough to obey. 'Fire! Open fire! Keep firing as fast as you can!'

He heard a ragged salvo but then saw many of the guncrews heave themselves up and stagger away drunkenly among the trees.

Hal jumped onto the lip of the emplacement, shouting for Aboli and Daniel. 'Come on! Each of you bring a match and follow me. We must get across to the island!'

Daniel was already helping Sir Francis reload the culverin, swabbing out the smoking barrel to douse the burning sparks.

'Avast that, Daniel. Leave that work to others. I need your help.'

As they started off together along the shore, the fog bank that covered the *Gull* drifted aside and she fired her next broadside. It had been but two minutes since the first. Her gunners were fast and well trained and they had the advantage of surprise. Again the storm of shot swept the beach and ploughed into the forest with deadly effect.

Hal saw one of their culverin struck squarely by a lead ball. The tackle snapped and it was hurled backwards off its train, so that its muzzle pointed to the stars.

The cries of the wounded and dying swelled in the pandemonium of despair as men deserted their posts and fled among the trees. The desultory return fire from the gunpits shrivelled until there was only an occasional bang and flash of cannon. Once the battery was silenced, the Buzzard turned his guns on the remaining huts and the clumps of bush in which the *Resolution*'s crew had taken shelter.

Hal could hear the crew of the *Gull* cheering wildly as they reloaded and fired. 'The *Gull* and Cumbrae!' they shouted.

There were no more broadsides, but a continuous stuttering roll of thunder as each gun fired as soon as it was ready. Their muzzle flashes flickered and flared within the sulphurous white smoke bank like the flames of hell.

As he ran Hal heard his father's voice behind him, fading with distance as he tried to rally his shattered, demoralized crew. Aboli ran at his shoulder and Big Daniel was a few paces further back, losing ground to the two swifter runners.

'We will need more men to launch,' Daniel panted. 'They're heavy.'

'You will not find them to help you now. They're all hog drunk or running for their very lives,' Hal grunted, but even as he spoke he saw Ned Tyler speed out of the forest just ahead, leading five of his seamen. All seemed sober enough.

'Good man, Ned!' Hal shouted. 'But we must hurry. The Buzzard will be sending his men onto the beach as soon as he has silenced our batteries.'

They charged in a group across the shallow channel between them and the island. The tide was low so at first they staggered through the glutinous mud-flat that sucked at their feet, then plunged into the open water. They waded, swam and dragged themselves across, the thunder of the *Gull*'s barrage spurring them onwards.

'There is only a breath of wind from the sou'-west,' Big Daniel gasped, as they staggered out, streaming water, onto the beach of the island. 'It will not be enough to serve us.'

Hal did not reply but broke off a dead branch and lit it from his slow-match. He held it high to give himself light to see the path and ran on into the forest. In minutes they had crossed the island and reached the beach on the far side. Here Hal paused and looked across at the *Gull* in the main channel.

The dawn was coming on apace, and the night fled before it. The light was turning grey and silvery, the lagoon gleaming softly as a sheet of polished pewter.

The Buzzard was training his guns back and forth, with the use of his anchor spring, swinging the *Gull* on her moorings so that he could pick out any target on the shore.

There was only the odd flash of answering fire from the gunpits on the beach, and the Buzzard responded immediately to these, swinging his ship and bringing to bear the full power of his broadside, snuffing them out with a whirlwind of grape, flying sand and falling trees.

All of Hal's party were blown by the hard run across the mud-flats and the plunge through the channel. 'No time to rest.' Hal's breath whistled in his throat. The devil ships were covered with mounds of cut branches and they dragged them clear. Then they formed a ring round the first of these vessels, and each took a handhold.

'Together now!' Hal exhorted them, and between them they just lifted the keels of the double-hulled vessel clear of the sand. It was heavy with its cargo, faggots of dried wood drenched with pitch to make it more flammable.

They staggered down the beach with it, and dropped it into the shallows, where it wallowed and rolled in the wavelets, the square of dirty canvas on the stubby mast stirring idly in the light puffs of wind coming down from the heads. Hal took a turn of the painter around his wrist to prevent it drifting away.

'Not enough wind!' Big Daniel lamented, looking to the sky. 'For the sweet love of God, send us a breeze.'

'Keep your prayers for later.' Hal secured the vessel, and led them back at a run into the trees. They carried, shoved and dragged two more of the boats down to the water's edge.

'Still not enough wind.' Daniel looked across at the *Gull*. In the short time it had taken them to launch, the morning light had strengthened, and now, as they paused for a moment to regain their breath, they saw the Buzzard's men leave their guns, and, cheering wildly, brandishing cutlass and pike, swarm down into the boats.

'Will you look at those swine! They reckon the fight's over,' grunted Ned Tyler. 'They're going in for the looting.'

Hal hesitated. Two more devil ships still lay at the edge of the forest, but to launch them would take too long. 'Then we must give them aught to change their opinion,' he said grimly, and gripped the burning match between his teeth. He waded out as deep as his armpits to where the first devil ship bobbed, just off the beach, and lobbed the slow-match onto the high pile of cordwood. It spluttered and flared, blue smoke poured from it and drifted away on the sluggish breeze as the pitch-soaked logs caught fire.

Hal grabbed the painter attached to the bows, and dragged her out into the channel. Within a dozen yards he was into deeper water and had lost the bottom. He swam round to the stern, and found a purchase on it, kicked out strongly with both legs and the boat moved away.

Aboli saw what he was doing and plunged headlong into the lagoon. With a few powerful strokes he reached Hal's side. With both of them swimming it out, the boat moved faster.

With one hand on the stern Hal lifted his head clear of the water to orientate himself and saw the flotilla of small boats from the *Gull* heading in towards the beach. They were crowded with wildly yelling seamen, their weapons glinting in the morning light. So certain was the Buzzard of his victory that he could have left only a few men aboard to guard the ship.

Hal glanced over his shoulder and saw that both Ned and Daniel had followed his example. They had led the rest of the gang into the water and were clinging to the sterns of two more craft, kicking the water to a white froth behind them as they pushed out into the channel. From all three boats rose tendrils of smoke as the flames took hold in the loads of pitch-soaked firewood.

Hal dropped back beside Aboli and set himself to work doggedly with both legs, pushing the boat ahead of him, down the channel to where the *Gull* lay at anchor. Then the incoming tide caught them firmly in its flood and, like a trio of crippled ducks, bore them along more swiftly.

As Hal's boat swung its bows around he had a better view of the beach. He recognized the flaming red head and beard of the Buzzard in the leading longboat heading into the attack on the encampment, and fancied that, even in the uproar, he heard peals of his laughter carrying over the water.

Then he had something else to think about for the fire in the cargo above him gained a firm hold and roared into boisterous life. The flames crackled and leapt high in columns of dense black smoke. They danced and swayed as their heat created its own draught, and the single sail filled with more determination.

'Keep her moving!' Hal panted to Aboli beside him. 'Steer her two points more to larboard.'

A gust of heat swept over him so fiercely that it seemed to suck the air from his lungs. He ducked his head beneath the surface and came up snorting, water cascading down his face from his sodden hair, but still kicking with all his strength. The *Gull* lay less than a cable's length dead ahead. Daniel and Ned followed close behind him, both their vessels wreathed in tarry black smoke and dark orange flame. The air over them quivered and throbbed with the heat like a desert mirage.

'Keep her going,' Hal blurted. His legs were beginning to ache unbearably, and he spoke more to himself than to Aboli. The painter tied to the bows of the devil ship trailed back, threatening to wrap around his legs, but he kicked it away – there was no time to loosen it.

He saw the first of the *Gull*'s longboats reach the beach and Cumbrae leap ashore, swinging his claymore in flashing circles around his head. As he landed on the sand he threw back his head, uttered a blood-curdling Gaelic war-cry, then went bounding up the steep beach. As he reached the trees he looked back to make certain his men were following him. There he paused with his sword held high, and stared back across the channel at the tiny squadron of devil ships, blooming with smoke and flame and bearing down steadily upon his anchored *Gull*.

'Nearly there!' Hal gasped, and the waves of heat that broke over his head seemed to fry his eyeballs in their sockets. He plunged his head underwater again to cool it, and this time when he came up he saw that the *Gull* lay only fifty yards ahead.

Even above the crackling roar of the flames he heard the Buzzard's roar: 'Back! Back to the *Gull*. The bastards are sending fireships at her.' The frigate was stuffed with the booty of a long, hard privateering cruise, and her crew sent up a wild chorus of outrage as they saw the fruits of three years so endangered. They raced back to their boats even faster than they had charged up the beach.

The Buzzard stood in the bows of his, prancing and gesticulating so that he threatened to upset her balance. 'Let me get my hands on the pox-ridden swine. I'll rip out their windpipes, I'll split their stinking—' At that moment he recognized Hal's head at the stern of the leading fire-ship, lit by the full glare of the swirling flames, and his voice rose a full octave. 'It's Franky's brat, by God! I'll have him! I'll roast his liver in his own fire!' he shrieked, then lapsed into crimson-faced, inarticulate rage and hacked at the air with his claymore to spur his crew to greater speed.

Hal was only a dozen yards now from the *Gull*'s tall side, and found fresh strength in his exhausted legs. Tirelessly Aboli swam on, using a powerful frog-kick that pushed back the water in a swirling wake behind him.

With the Buzzard's longboat bearing down swiftly upon them, they covered the last few yards and Hal felt the fireship's bows thump heavily into the *Gull*'s stern timbers. The push of the tide pinned her there, swinging her broadside so that the flames were fanned by the rising morning breeze to lick up along the *Gull*'s side, scorching and blackening the timbers.

'Latch onto her!' bellowed the Buzzard. 'Get a line on her and tow her off!' His oarsmen shot straight in towards the fireship but, as they felt the full heat blooming out to meet them, they quailed. In the bows the Buzzard threw up his hands to cover his face, and his red beard crisped and singed. 'Back off!' he roared. 'Or we'll fry.' He looked at his coxswain. 'Give me the anchor! I'll grapple her, and we'll tow her off.'

Hal was on the point of diving and swimming under water out of the circle of heat but he heard Cumbrae's order. The painter still trailed around his legs, and he groped beneath the surface for the end, clenching it between his feet. Then he sank below the water and swam under the fireship's hull, coming up in the narrow gap between it and the *Gull*.

The *Gull*'s rudder stock broke the surface and, spitting lagoon water from his mouth, Hal threw a loop of the painter around the pintle. His face felt as though it were blistering as the heat beat down upon his head with hammer strokes, but he hitched the flaming craft securely to the *Gull*'s stern.

Then he dived again and came up next to Aboli. 'To the beach!' he gasped. 'Before the fire reaches the *Gull*'s powder store.'

Both struck out overarm, and Hal saw the longboat, close by, almost close enough to touch, but the Buzzard had lost all interest in them. He was whirling the small anchor around his head, and as Hal watched he hurled it out over the burning vessel, hooking onto her.

'Lie back on your oars!' he shouted at his crew. 'Tow her off.' The boatmen went to it with all their strength, but immediately the fireship came up short on the mooring line Hal had tied, and their blades beat the water vainly. She would not tow, and now the planking of the *Gull*'s side was smouldering ominously.

Fire was the terror of all seamen. The ship was built of combustibles and stuffed with explosives, wood and pitch, canvas and hemp, tallow, spice barrels and gunpowder. The faces of the longboat's crew were contorted with terror. Even the Buzzard was wild-eyed in the firelight as he looked up and saw the other two fireships drifting remorselessly upon him. 'Stop those others!' he pointed with his claymore. 'Turn them away!' Then he turned his attention back to the burning vessel moored to the *Gull*.

By now Hal and Aboli were fifty yards away, swimming for the beach, but Hal rolled onto his back to watch and trod water. He saw at once that the Buzzard's efforts to tow away the fireship had failed.

Now he rowed around to the *Gull*'s bows and scrambled up onto her deck. As his crew followed him he roared, 'Buckets! Get a bucket chain going. Pumps! Ten men on the pumps. Spray the flames!' They scurried to obey, but the fire was spreading swiftly, eating into the stern and dancing along the gunwale, reaching up hungrily towards the furled sails on their outstretched yards.

One of the *Gull*'s longboats had grappled Ned's fireship and, with frantically beating oars, was dragging it clear. Another was trying to get a line on Big Daniel's fireship, but the flames forced them to keep their distance. Each time they succeeded in hooking on, Daniel swam round and cut the rope with a stroke of his knife. The men in the longboat who carried muskets and pistols were firing wildly at his bobbing head, but though the balls kicked up spray all around him, he seemed invulnerable.

Aboli had swum on ahead, and now Hal rolled onto his belly and followed him back to the beach. Together they raced up the white sand, and into the shot-shattered forest. Sir Francis was still in the gunpit where they had left him, but he had gathered around him a scratch crew of the *Resolution*'s survivors. They were reloading the big gun as Hal ran up to him and shouted, 'What do you want me to do?'

'Take Aboli with you to find some more of the men. Load another culverin. Bring the *Gull* under fire.' Sir Francis did not look up from the gun, and Hal ran back among the trees. He found half a dozen men, and he and Aboli kicked and dragged them out of the holes and bushes where they were cowering, and led them back to the silenced battery.

In the few short minutes it had taken him to gather the guncrew, the scene out on the lagoon had changed completely. Daniel had guided his fireship up to the *Gull*'s side and had secured her there. Her flames were adding to the confusion and panic on board the frigate. Now he was swimming back to the beach. He had seized two of his men, who could not swim, and was dragging them through the water.

The *Gull*'s crew had snared Ned's fireship – they had lines on it and were dragging it clear. Ned and his three fellows had abandoned it, and were also floundering back towards the shore. But, even as Hal watched, one gave up and slipped below the surface.

The sight of the drowning spurred Hal's anger: he poured a handful of powder into the culverin's touch hole as Aboli used an iron marlinspike to train the barrel around. It bellowed deafeningly, and Hal's men shouted with delight as the full charge of grape smashed into the longboat towing Ned's abandoned craft. It disintegrated at the blast, and the men packed into her were hurled into the lagoon. They splashed about, screaming for aid and trying to clamber into another longboat nearby, but it was already overcrowded and the men in her tried to beat off the frantic seamen with their oars. Some, though, managed to get a hold on the gunwale, and yelling and fighting among themselves, they caused the longboat to list heavily, until suddenly she capsized. The water around the burning hulks was filled with wreckage and the heads of struggling swimmers.

Hal was concentrating on reloading, and when he looked up again, he saw that some of the men in the water had reached the *Gull* and were climbing the rope ladders to the deck.

The Buzzard had at last got his pumps working. Twenty men were bobbing up and down like monks at prayer as they threw their weight on the handles, and white jets of water were spurting from the nozzles of the canvas hoses, aimed at the base of the flames, which were now spreading over the *Gull*'s stern.

Hal's next shot shattered the wooden rail on the *Gull*'s larboard side, and went on to sweep through the gang serving the bow pump. Four were snatched away, as though by an invisible set of claws, their blood splattering the others beside them on the handles. The jet of water from the hose shrivelled away.

'More men here!' Cumbrae's voice resounded across the lagoon, as he sent others to take the places of the dead. At once the jet of water was revived, but it made little impression on the leaping flames that now engulfed the *Gull*'s stern.

Big Daniel reached the shore, and dropped the two men he had rescued on the sand. He ran up into the trees, and Hal shouted, 'Take command of one of the guns. Load with grape and aim at her decks. Keep them from fighting the fire.'

Big Daniel grinned at Hal with black teeth and knuckled his forehead. 'We'll play his lordship a pretty tune to dance to,' he promised.

The crew of the *Resolution*, who had been demoralized by the *Gull*'s sneak attack, now began to take heart again at the swing in fortunes. One or two more emerged from where they had been skulking in the forest. Then, as the fire started to crash from the beach batteries and thump into the *Gull*'s hull, the others grew bold and rushed back to serve the guns.

Soon a sheet of flame and smoke was tearing from out of the trees across the water. Flames had reached the *Gull*'s mizzen-yards and were taking hold in the furled sails.

Hal saw the Buzzard striding through the smoke, lit by the flames of his burning ship, an axe in his hand. He stood over the anchor rope where it was drawn tightly through its fair lead and, with one gigantic swing he cut it free. Immediately the ship began to drift across the wind. He raised his head and bellowed an order to his seamen, who were clambering up the shrouds.

They shook out the main sail and the ship responded quickly. As she caught the rising breeze, the flames poured outwards, and the fire-fighters were able to run forward and direct the water from the hoses onto the base of the fire.

She towed the two fireships for a short distance, but when the lines that secured them burned through, the *Gull* left them as she headed slowly down the channel.

Along the beach the culverins continued to pour salvo after salvo into her but, as she drew out of range, the battery fell silent. Still streaming smoke and orange flame behind her, the *Gull* headed for the open sea. Then, as she entered the channel between the heads and looked to have sailed clear away, the batteries hidden in the cliffs opened up on her. Gunsmoke billowed out from among the grey rocks and cannonballs kicked up spouts of foam along the *Gull*'s waterline or punched holes in her sails.

Painfully she ran this gauntlet, and at last left the smoking batteries out of range.

'Mr Courtney!' Sir Francis shouted at Hal – even in the heat of the battle he had used the formal address. 'Take a boat and cross to the heads. Keep the *Gull* under observation.'

Hal and Aboli reached the far side of the bay, and climbed up to the high ground on top of the heads. The *Gull* was already a mile offshore, reaching across the wind with sail set on her two forward masts. Wisps of dark grey smoke trailed from her stern, and Hal could see that her mizzen sails and her spanker were blackened and still smouldering. Her decks seethed with the tiny figures of her crew as they snuffed out the last of the fire and laboured to get the ship under full control and sailing handily again.

'We have given his lordship a lesson he'll long remember,' Hal exulted. 'I doubt we'll be having any more trouble from him for a while.'

'The wounded lion is the most dangerous,' Aboli grunted. 'We have blunted his teeth, but he still has his claws.'

When Hal stepped out of the boat onto the beach below the encampment he found that his father already had a gang of men at work, repairing the damage to the battery of culverins along the shore. They were building up the parapets and levelling the two guns that had been shot off their mountings by the *Gull*'s broadsides.

Where she lay careened on the beach, the *Resolution* had been hit by shot. The *Gull*'s fire had knocked great raw wounds in the timbers. Grape shot had peppered her sides but had not penetrated her stout planks. The carpenter and his mates were already at work cutting out the damaged sections and checking the frames beneath them, preparatory to replacing them with new oak planking from the ship's stores. The pitch cauldrons were bubbling and smoking over the coals, and the rasping of saws and soughing of planes resounded through the camp.

Hal found his father further back among the trees, where the wounded had been laid out under a makeshift canvas shelter. He counted seventeen and, at a glance, could tell that at least three were unlikely to see tomorrow's dawn. Already the aura of death hung over them.

Ned Tyler doubled as the ship's surgeon – he had been trained for the role in the rough empirical school of the gundeck, and he wielded his instruments with the same rude abandon as the carpenters working on the *Resolution*'s punctured hull.

Hal saw that he was performing an amputation. One of the topmastmen had taken a blast of grape in his leg just below the knee and the limb hung by a tatter of flesh and exposed stringy white sinew from which protruded sharp white splinters of the shin bone. Two of Ned's mates were trying to hold down the patient on a sheet of blood-soaked canvas, as he bucked and writhed. They had thrust a doubled layer of leather belt between his teeth. The sailor bit down so hard upon it that the sinews in his neck stood out like hempen ropes. His eyes started out of his straining crimson face and his lips were drawn back in a terrifying rictus. Hal saw one of his rotten black teeth explode under the pressure of his bite.

He turned his eyes away and began his report to Sir Francis. 'The *Gull* was heading west the last I saw of her. The Buzzard seems to have the fire in hand, although she is still making a cloud of smoke—'

He was interrupted by screams as Ned laid aside his knife and took up the saw to trim off the shattered bone. Then, abruptly, the man lapsed into silence and slumped back in the grip of the men who held him. Ned stepped back and shook his head. 'Poor bastard's taken shore leave. Bring one of the others.' He wiped the sweat and smoke from his face with a blood-caked hand and left a red smear down his cheek.

Although Hal's stomach heaved, he kept his voice level as he went on with his report. 'Cumbrae was cracking on all the sail the *Gull* would carry.' He was determined not to show weakness in front of his men and his father, but his voice trailed off as near at hand Ned started to pluck a massive wood splinter from another seaman's back. Hal could not drag away his eyes.

Ned's two brawny assistants straddled the patient's body and held him down, while he got a grip on the protruding end of the splinter with a pair of blacksmith's tongs. He placed one foot on the man's back to give himself purchase and leaned back with all his weight. The raw splinter was as thick as his thumb, barbed like an arrowhead and relinquished its grip in the living flesh only with the greatest reluctance. The man's screams rang through the forest.

At that moment Governor van de Velde came waddling towards them through the trees. His wife was on his arm, weeping pitifully and barely able to support her own weight. Zelda followed her closely, attempting to thrust a green bottle of smelling-salts under her mistress's nose.

'Captain Courtney!' van de Velde said. 'I must protest in the strongest possible terms. You have placed us in the most dire danger. A ball passed through the roof of my abode. I might have been killed.' He mopped at his streaming jowls with his neckcloth.

At that moment the wretch who had been receiving Ned's ministrations let out a piercing shriek as one of the assistants poured hot pitch to staunch the bleeding into the deep wound in his back.

'You must keep these oafs of yours quiet.' Van de Velde waved disparagingly towards the severely wounded seaman. 'Their barnyard bleatings are frightening and offending my wife.'

With a last groan the patient sagged back limply into silence, killed by Ned's kindness. Sir Francis's expression was grim as he lifted his hat to Katinka. 'Mevrouw, you cannot doubt our consideration for your sensibilities. It seems that the rude fellow prefers to die rather than offend you further.' His expression was hard and unkind as he went on, 'Instead of caterwauling and indulging in the vapours, perhaps you might like to assist Master Ned with his work of tending the wounded?'

Van de Velde drew himself to his full height at the suggestion and glared at him. 'Mijnheer, you insult my wife. How dare you suggest that she might act as a servant to these coarse peasants?'

'I apologize to your lady, but I suggest that if she is to serve no other purpose here other than beautifying the landscape you take her back to her hut and keep her there. There will almost certainly be further unpleasant sights and sounds to test her forbearance.' Sir Francis nodded at Hal to follow him, and turned his back on the Governor. Side by side, he and his son strode towards the beach, past where the sailmakers were stitching the dead into their canvas shrouds and a gang was already digging their graves. In such heat they must be buried the same day. Hal counted the canvas-covered bundles.

'Only twelve are ours,' his father told him. 'The other seven are from the *Gull*, washed up on the beach. We have taken eight prisoners too. I'm going to deal with them now.'

The captives were under guard on the beach, sitting in a line with their hands clasped behind their heads. As they came up to them Sir Francis said, loudly enough for all to hear, 'Mr Courtney, have your men set eight nooses from that tree.' He pointed to the outspreading branches of a huge wild fig. 'We will hang some new fruit from them.' He gave a chuckle so macabre that Hal was startled.

The eight sent up a wail of protest. 'Don't hang us, sir. It were his lordship's orders. We only did as we was bade.'

Sir Francis ignored them. 'Get those ropes hung up, Mr Courtney.'

For a moment longer Hal hesitated. He was appalled at the prospect of having to carry out such a cold-blooded execution, but then he saw his father's expression and hurried to obey.

In short order ropes were thrown over the stout branches and the nooses were knotted at the hanging ends. A team of the *Resolution*'s sailors stood ready to heave their victims aloft.

One at a time the eight prisoners from the *Gull* were dragged to a rope's end, their hands bound behind their backs, their heads thrust through the waiting nooses. At his father's orders Hal went down the line and adjusted the knots under each victim's ears. Then he turned back to face his father, pale-faced and sick to the stomach. He touched his forehead. 'Ready to proceed with the execution, sir.'

Sir Francis's face was turned away from the condemned men and he spoke softly from the corner of his mouth. 'Plead for their lives.'

'Sir?' Hal looked bewildered.

'Damn you.' Sir Francis's voice cracked. 'Beg me to spare them.'

'Beg your pardon, sir, but will you not spare these men?' Hal said loudly.

'The blackguards deserve nothing but the rope's end,' Sir Francis snarled. 'I want to see them dance a jig to the devil.'

'They were only carrying out the orders of their captain.' Hal warmed to the role of advocate. 'Will you not give them a chance?'

The noosed heads of the eight men swung back and forth as they followed the argument. Their expressions were abject, but their eyes held a faint glimmer of hope.

Sir Francis fingered his chin. 'I don't know.' His face was still ferocious. 'What would we do with them? Turn them loose into the wilderness to serve as fodder for wild beasts and cannibals? It would be more merciful to string them up.'

'You could swear them in as crew to replace the men we have lost,' Hal pleaded.

Sir Francis looked still more dubious. 'They would not take an oath of allegiance, would they?' He glared at the condemned men who, had not the nooses restrained them, might have fallen to their knees.

'We will serve you truly, sir. The young gentleman is right. You'll not find better men nor more loyal than us.'

'Bring my Bible from my hut,' Sir Francis growled, and the eight seamen took their oath of service with the nooses round their necks.

Big Daniel freed them and led them away, and Sir Francis watched them go with satisfaction. 'Eight prime specimens to replace some of our losses,' he murmured. 'We'll need every hand we can find if we are to have the *Resolution* ready for sea before the end of this month.' He glanced across the lagoon at the entrance between the headlands. 'Only the good Lord knows who our next visitors might be if we linger here.'

He turned back to Hal. 'That leaves only the drunken sots who lapped up the Buzzard's rum. Do you fancy another flogging, Hal?'

'Is this the time to render half our crew useless with the cat, Father? If the Buzzard returns before we are fit for sea, then they'll fight no better with half the meat stripped off their backs.'

'So you say let them go scot free?' Sir Francis asked coldly, his face close to Hal's.

'Why not fine them their share of the spoils from the *Standvastigheid* and divide it among the others who fought sober?'

Sir Francis stared at him a moment longer, then smiled grimly. 'The judgement of Solomon! Their purses will give them more pain than their backs, and it will add a guilder or three to our own share of the prize.'

Angus Cochran, Earl of Cumbrae, stepped out on the saddle of the mountain pass at least a thousand feet above the beach where he had come ashore from the *Gull*. His boatswain and two seamen followed him. They all carried muskets and cutlasses. One of the men balanced a small keg of drinking water on his shoulder, for the African sun speedily sucks the moisture from a man's body.

It had taken half the morning of hard hiking, following the game trails along the steep and narrow ledges, to reach this lookout point, which Cumbrae knew well. He had used it more than once before. A Hottentot they had captured on the beach had first led him to it. Now as he settled comfortably on a rock that formed a throne-like seat, the Hottentot's white bones lay at his feet in the undergrowth. The skull gleamed like a pearl, for it had lain here three years and the ants and other insects had picked it clean. It would have been foolhardy of Cumbrae to allow the savage to carry tales of his arrival to the Dutch colony at Good Hope.

From his stone throne Cumbrae had a breathtaking panoramic view of two oceans and of rugged mountain scenery spread out all around him. When he looked back the way he had come he could see the *Gull of Moray* anchored not far off a tiny rind of beach that clung precariously to the foot of the soaring rocky cliffs where the mountains fell into the sea. There were twelve distinct peaks in this maritime range, marked on the Dutch charts he had captured as the Twelve Apostles.

He stared at the *Gull* through his telescope but could see little evidence of the fire damage she had suffered to her stern. He had been able to replace the mizzen yards, and furled new sails upon them. From this great height and distance she looked lovely as ever, tucked away from inquisitive eyes in the green water cove below the Apostles.

The longboat that had brought Cumbrae through the surf was still drawn up on the beach, ready for a swift departure if he should run into trouble ashore. However, he expected none. He might encounter a few Hottentots among the bushes but they were a harmless, half-naked tribe, a pastoral people with high cheekbones and slanted Asiatic eyes, who could be scattered willy-nilly by a musket shot over their heads.

Much more dangerous were the wild animals that abounded in this harsh, untamed land. The previous night, from the deck of the anchored *Gull*, they had heard terrifying, blood-chilling roars, rising and falling, then ending in a diminishing series of grunts and groans that sounded like the chorus of all the devils of hell.

'Lions!' the older hands who knew the coast had whispered to each other, and the ship's company had listened in awed silence. In the dawn they had seen one of the terrible yellow cats, the size of a pony, with a dense dark mane of hair covering its head and reaching back behind its shoulder, sauntering along the white beach sands with a regal indolence. After that it had taken the threat of the lash to force the boat crew to row Cumbrae and his party to the shore.

He reached into the leather pouch that hung in front of his plaid and brought out a pewter flask. He tipped its base to the sky and swallowed twice, then sighed with pleasure and screwed the stopper back into the neck. His boatswain and the two seamen watched him intently, but he grinned at them and shook his head. 'It would do you no good. Mark my words, whisky is the devil's own hot piss. If you have no pact with him, as I have, you should never let it past your lips.'

He slipped the flask back into the pouch, and lifted the telescope to his eye. On his left hand rose the sphinx-shaped mountain top that the earliest mariners had named Lion's Head, when viewing it from the sea. At his right hand stood the sheer cliff that towered up to the flat top of the mighty Table Mountain that dominated the horizon and gave its name to the bay that opened out beneath it.

Far below where he sat, Table Bay was a lovely sweep of open water, nursing a small island in its arms. The Dutch called it Robben Island, for that was their name for the thousands of seals that infested it.

Beyond that was the endless wind-flecked expanse of the south

Atlantic. Cumbrae scrutinized it for any sign of a strange sail, but when he could pick out nothing he transferred his attention below to the Dutch settlement of Good Hope.

There was little to make it stand out from the wild and rocky wilderness that surrounded it. The roofs of the few buildings were of thatch and blended into their surroundings. The Company gardens, which had been laid out to grow provisions for the VOC ships on their passage to the east, were the most obvious sign of man's intrusion. The regular rectangular fields were either bright green with crops or chocolate brown with new-turned earth.

Just above the beach was the Dutch fort. Even from this distance Cumbrae could see that it was unfinished. He had heard from other captains that since the outbreak of war with England the Dutch had tried to speed up the construction, but there were still raw gaps in the defensive outer walls, like missing teeth.

The fort, and its half-completed state, were of interest to Cumbrae only in as much as it could afford protection to the ships that lay at anchor in the bay, under its guns. At this moment three large vessels were there, and he fastened his attention on them.

One looked like a naval frigate. She flew the ensign of the Republic, orange, white and blue, from her masthead. Her hull was painted black, but the gunports were picked out in white. He counted sixteen on the side she presented to him. He judged that she would outgun the *Gull* if it ever came to a set-piece engagement with her. But that was not his intention. He wanted easier pickings, and that meant one of the other two vessels in the bay. Both were merchantmen, and both flew the Company ensign.

'Which one is it to be?' he mused, as he glassed them with the closest attention.

One looked familiar. She rode high in the water, and he reckoned that she was probably in ballast and on the eastern leg of her voyage, heading out to the Dutch possessions to take on valuable cargo.

'No, by God, I recognize the cut of her jib now,' he exclaimed aloud. 'She's the *Lady Edwina*, Franky's old ship. He told me he'd sent her back to the Cape with his ransom demand.' He studied her a while longer. 'She's been stripped bare – even the guns are out of her.'

Losing interest in her as a possible prize, Cumbrae turned his telescope on the second merchantman. This ship was slightly smaller than the *Lady Edwina* but she was heavy with her cargo, riding so low that her lower ports were almost awash. Clearly she was on her return voyage, and stuffed with the treasures of the Orient. What made her even more attractive was that she was anchored further off the beach than the other merchantman, at least two cables' length from the walls of the fort. Even under the best conditions that would be impossibly long cannon-shot for the Dutch gunners on the shore.

'A lovely sight.' The Buzzard grinned to himself. 'Fair makes one's mouth water to behold her.'

He spent another half-hour studying the bay, noting the lines of foam and spindrift that marked the flow of current along the beach and the set of the wind as it swirled down from the heights. He planned his entry into Table Bay. He knew that the Dutch had a small post on the slopes of Lion's Head whose lookouts would warn the settlement of the approach of a strange ship with a cannon-shot.

Even at midnight, with the present phase of the moon, they might be able to pick out the gleam of his sails while he was still well out at sea. He would have to make a wide circle, out below the horizon and then come in from the west, using the bulk of Robben Island as a stalking horse to creep in unobserved by even the sharpest lookout.

His crew were well versed in the art of cutting out a prize from under the shore batteries. It was a special English trick, one beloved of both Hawkins and Drake. Cumbrae had polished and refined it, and considered himself the master of either of those great Elizabethan pirates. The pleasure of plucking out a prize from under the enemy's nose rewarded him far beyond the spoils it yielded. 'Mounting the good wife while the husband snores in the bed beside her – so much sweeter than tipping up her skirts while he's off across the seas with no danger in it.' He chuckled, and swept the bay with his telescope, checking that nothing had changed since his last visit, that there were no lurking dangers such as newly emplaced cannon along the shore.

Even though the sun was past its noon and it was a long journey back to where the longboat waited on the beach, he spent a little longer studying the rigging of the prize through the glass. Once he had seized her, his men must be able to get her sails up speedily, and work her off the lee shore in the darkness.

It was after midnight when the Buzzard, using as his landmark the immense bulk of Table Mountain which blotted out half the southern sky, brought the *Gull* into the bay from the west. He was confident that, even on a clear starry night like this with half a moon shining, he was still well out of sight of the lookout on Lion's Head.

The dark whale shape of Robben Island rose with startling suddenness out of the gloom ahead. He knew there was no permanent settlement on this barren piece of rock so he was able to bring the *Gull* close into its lee, and drop his anchor in seven fathoms of protected water.

The longboat on deck was ready to launch. No sooner had the catted anchor splashed into the easy swells, than it was swung outboard and dropped to the surface. The Buzzard had already inspected the boarding-party. They were armed with pistol and cutlass and oak clubs, and their faces were darkened with lamp-black so that they looked like a party of wild savages with only their eyes and teeth gleaming. They were dressed in pitch-blackened sea-jackets, and two men had axes to cut the anchor cable of the prize.

The Buzzard was the last man down the ladder into the longboat, and as soon as he was aboard they pushed off. The oars were muffled, the rowlocks padded, and the only sound was the dip of the blades, but even this was lost in the breaking of the waves and the gentle sighing of the wind.

Almost immediately they crept out from behind the island they could see the lights on the mainland, two or three pinpricks from the watchfires on the walls of the fort, and lantern beams from the buildings outside the walls, spread out along the seafront.

The three vessels he had spotted from the saddle of the mountains were still anchored in the roads. Each showed a riding lantern at the masthead, and another at the stern. Cumbrae grinned in the darkness. 'Most obliging of the cheese-heads to put out a welcome for us. Don't they know there's a war a-raging?'

From this distance he was not yet able to distinguish one ship from the others, but his boat-crews pulled eagerly, the scent of the prize in their nostrils. Half an hour later, even though they were still well out in the bay, Cumbrae was able to pick out the *Lady Edwina*. He discarded her from his calculations and switched all his interest to the other vessel, which had not changed position and still lay furthest away from the batteries of the fort.

'Steer for the ship on the larboard side,' he ordered his boatswain in a whisper. The longboat altered a point, and the beat of the oars picked up. The second boat was close astern, like a hunting dog at heel, and Cumbrae peered back at its dark shape, grunting with approval. All the weapons were covered, there was no reflection of moonlight off a naked blade or pistol barrel to flash a warning to the watch on board the chase. Neither was there a lit match to send the reek of smoke down the wind, or a glow of light ahead of their arrival.

As they glided in towards the anchored vessel Cumbrae read her name from her transom, *De Swael*, the *Swallow*. He was alert for any sign of an anchor watch: this was a lee shore, with the sou'-easter swirling unpredictably around the mountain, but either the Dutch captain was remiss or the watch was asleep for there was no sign of life aboard the dark ship.

Two sailors stood ready to fend off from the side of the *Swallow* as they touched, and mats of knotted oakum hung over the longboat's side to soften the impact. A solid contact of timbers against hull would carry through the ship like the sounding body of a viol and wake every hand aboard.

They touched with the gentleness of a virgin's kiss, and one of the men, chosen for his simian climbing prowess, shot up the side and immediately made a line fast to the shackle of a gun train and dropped the coil back into the boat below.

Cumbrae paused long enough to lift the shutter of the storm lantern and light the slow-match from the flame, then seized the line and went up on bare feet hardened by hunting the stag without boots. In a silent rush the crews of both boats, also barefoot, followed him.

Cumbrae jerked the marlinspike from his belt and, his boatswain at his side, raced silently to the bows. The anchor watch was curled on the deck, out of the wind, sleeping like a hound in front of the hearth. The Buzzard stooped over him and clipped his skull with one sharp blow of the iron spike. The man sighed, uncurled his limbs and sagged into an even deeper state of unconsciousness.

His men were already at each of the *Swallow*'s hatches, leading to the lower decks, and as Cumbrae ran back towards the stern they were quietly closing the covers and battening them down, imprisoning the Dutch crew below decks.

'There'll no' be more than twenty of a crew on board her,' he muttered to himself. 'And, like as not, de Ruyter will have taken most of the prime seamen for the Navy. They'll be only boys and fat old fools on their last legs. I doubt they'll give us too much trouble.'

He looked up at the dark figures of his men silhouetted against the stars as they raced up the shrouds and danced out along the yards. As the sails unfurled, he heard from forward the soft clunk of an axe blow as the anchor cable was severed. Immediately the *Swallow* came alive and unfettered under his feet as she paid off before the wind. Already his boatswain was at the whipstaff.

'Take her straight out. Due west!' Cumbrae snapped, and the man put her head up into the wind as close as she would point.

Cumbrae saw at once that the heavily laden ship was surprisingly handy, and that they would be able to weather Robben Island on this tack. Ten armed men waited ready to follow him. Two carried shuttered storm lanterns, all had match burning for their pistols. Cumbrae seized one of the lanterns and led his men at a run down into the officers' quarters in the stern. He tried the door of the cabin that must open out onto the stern galleries and found it unlocked. He went through it swiftly and silently. When he flashed the lantern, a man in a tasselled night cap sat up in the bunk.

'*Wie is dit?*' he challenged sleepily. Cumbrae swept the bedclothes over his head to smother any further outcry, left his men to subdue and bind the captain, ran out into the passageway and burst into the next cabin. Here another Dutch officer was already awake. Plump and middle-aged, his greying hair tangled in his eyes, he was still staggering groggily with sleep as he groped for his sword where it hung in its scabbard at the foot of his bunk. Cumbrae shone the lantern in his eyes, and placed the sharp point of his claymore at the man's throat.

'Angus Cumbrae, at your service,' said the Buzzard. 'Yield, or I'll feed you to the gulls a wee bittie at a time.'

The Dutchman might not have understood the burred Scots accent, but Cumbrae's meaning was unmistakable. Gaping at him, he raised both hands above his head and the boarding-party swarmed over him and bore him to the deck, wrapping his bedclothes around his head.

Cumbrae ran on to the last cabin but, as he laid his hand on the door, it was flung open from inside with such force that he was thrown across the passage into the bulkhead. A huge figure charged out of the darkened doorway with a blood-curdling yell. He aimed a full overhead blow at the Buzzard, but in the narrow confines of the passageway the blade of his sword slashed into the door lintel, giving Cumbrae an instant to recover. Still bellowing with rage the stranger cut at him again. This time the Buzzard parried and the blade sped over his shoulder to shatter the panel behind him. The two big men raged down the passageway, fighting at close range, almost chest to chest. The Dutchman was shouting insults in a mixture of English and his own language, and Cumbrae answered him in full-blooded Scottish tones: 'You blethering cheese-headed nun-raper! I'll stuff your giblets down your ear-holes.' His men danced around them with clubs raised, waiting for an opportunity to cut down the Dutch officer, but Cumbrae shouted, 'Don't kill him! He's a dandy laddie, and he'll fetch a pretty price at ransom!'

Even in the uncertain lantern light, he had recognized his adversary's quality. Freshly roused from his bunk the Dutchman wore no wig on his shaven head but his fine pointed moustaches showed him to be a man of fashion. His embroidered linen nightshirt and the sword he wielded with the panache of a duelling master all proved that he was a gentleman, and no mistake.

The longer blade of the claymore was a disadvantage in the restricted space, and Cumbrae was forced to use the point rather than the double edges. The Dutchman thrust, then feinted low and slipped in under his guard. Cumbrae hissed with anger as the steel flew under his raised right arm, missing him by a finger's width and slashing a shower of splinters from the panel behind him.

Before his adversary could recover, the Buzzard whipped his left arm around the man's neck and enfolded him in a bear-hug. Locked together in the narrow passage, neither man could use his sword. They dropped them and wrestled from one end of the corridor to the other, snarling and snapping like a pair of fighting dogs, then grunting and howling with pain and outrage as first one then the other threw a telling fist to the head or smashed his elbow into the other's belly.

'Crack his skull,' Cumbrae gasped at his men. 'Knock the brute down.' He was unaccustomed to being bested in a straight trial of muscle, but the other was his match. His upthrust knee crashed into the Buzzard's crotch, and he howled again, 'Help me, damn your poxy yellow livers! Knock the rogue down!'

He managed to get one hand free and lock it round the man's waist then, bright crimson in the face with the effort, he lifted him and swung him round so that his back was presented to a seaman waiting with a raised oak club in his fist. It cracked down with a practised and controlled blow on the back of the shaven pate, not hard enough to shatter bone, but with just sufficient force to stun the Dutchman and turn his legs to jelly under him. He sagged in Cumbrae's arms.

Puffing, the Buzzard lowered him to the deck, and all four seamen bounced on him, pinning his limbs and straddling his back. 'Get a rope on this hellion,' he panted, 'afore he comes to and wrecks us and smashes up our prize.'

'Another filthy English pirate!' the Dutchman mouthed weakly, shaking his head to clear his wits and thrashing around on the deck as he tried to throw off his captors.

'I'll not put up with your foul insults,' Cumbrae told him genially, as he smoothed his ruffled red beard and retrieved his claymore. 'Call me a filthy pirate if you will, but I'm no Englishman and I'll thank you to remember it.'

'Pirates! All you scum are pirates.'

'And who are you to call me scum, you with your great hairy arse sticking in the air?' In the scuffle the Dutchman's night shirt had rucked up around his waist leaving him bare below. 'I'll not argue with a man in such indecent attire. Get your clothes on, sir, and then we will continue this discourse.'

Cumbrae ran up onto the deck, and found that they were already well out to sea. Muffled shouts and banging were coming from under the battened-down hatches, but his men had full control of the deck. 'Smartly done, you canty bunch of sea-rats. The easiest fifty guineas you'll ever put in your purses. Give yerselves a cheer, and cock a snook at the devil,' he roared so that even those up on the yards could hear him.

Robben Island was only a league dead ahead, and as the bay opened before them they could make out the *Gull* lying on the moonlit waters.

'Hoist a lantern to the masthead,' Cumbrae ordered, 'and we'll put a wee stretch of water between us before the cheese-heads in the fort rub the sleep out of their eyes.'

As the lantern went aloft, the *Gull* repeated the signal to acknowledge. Then she hoisted her anchor and followed the prize out to sea.

'There is bound to be a good breakfast in the galley,' Cumbrae told his men. 'The Dutchies know how to tend their bellies. Once you have them locked neatly in their own chains, you can try their fare. Boatswain, keep her steady as she goes. I'm going below to have a peep at the manifest, and to find what we've caught ourselves.'

The Dutch officers were trussed hand and foot, and laid out in a row on the deck of the main cabin. An armed seaman stood over each man. Cumbrae shone the lantern in their faces, and examined them in turn. The big warlike officer lifted his head and bellowed up at him, 'I pray God that I live to see you swinging on the rope's end, along with all the other devil-spawned English pirates who plague the oceans.' It was obvious that he had fully recovered from the blow to the back of his head.

'I must commend you on your command of the English language,' Cumbrae told him. 'Your choice of words is quite poetic. What is your name, sir?'

'I am Colonel Cornelius Schreuder in the service of the Dutch East India Company.'

'How do you do, sir? I am Angus Cochran, Earl of Cumbrae.'

'You, sir, are nothing but a vile pirate.'

'Colonel, your repetitions are becoming just a wee bit tiresome. I implore you not to spoil a most promising acquaintanceship in this manner. After all, you are to be my guest for some time until your ransom is paid. I am a privateer, sailing under the commission of His Majesty King Charles the Second. You, gentlemen, are prisoners of war.'

'There is no war!' Colonel Schreuder roared at him scornfully. 'We gave you Englishmen a good thrashing and the war is over. Peace was signed over two months ago.'

Cumbrae stared at him in horror, then found his voice again. 'I do not believe you, sir.' Suddenly he was subdued and shaken. He denied it more to give himself time to think than with any conviction. News of the English defeat at the Medway and the battle of the Thames had been some months old when Richard Lister had given it to him. He had also reported that the King was suing for peace with the Dutch Republic. Anything might have happened in the meantime.

'Order these villains of yours to release me, and I will prove it to you.' Colonel Schreuder was still in a towering rage, and Cumbrae hesitated before he nodded at his men.

'Let him up and untie him,' he ordered.

Colonel Schreuder sprang to his feet and smoothed his rumpled moustaches as he stormed off to his own cabin. There, he took down a silk robe from the head of his bunk. Tying the belt around his waist he went to his writing bureau and opened the drawer. With frosty dignity, he came back to Cumbrae and handed him a thick bundle of papers.

The Buzzard saw that most were official Dutch proclamations in both Dutch and English, but that one was an English news-sheet. He unfolded it with trepidation, and held it at arm's length. It was dated August 1667. The headline was in heavy black type two inches tall:

PEACE SIGNED WITH DUTCH REPUBLIC!

As his eye raced down the page, his mind tried to adjust to this disconcerting change in circumstances. He knew that with the signing of the peace treaty all Letters of Marque, issued by either side in the conflict, had become null and void. Even had there been any doubt about it, the third paragraph on the page confirmed it:

> All privateers of both combatant nations, sailing under commission and Letters of Marque, have been ordered to cease warlike expeditions forthwith and to return to their home ports to submit themselves to examination by the Admiralty assizes.

The Buzzard stared at the news-sheet without reading further, and pondered the various courses of action open to him. The *Swallow* was a rich prize, the Good Lord alone knew just how rich. Scratching his beard he toyed with the idea of flouting the orders of the Admiralty assizes, and hanging on to it at all costs. His great-grandfather had been a famous outlaw, astute enough to back the Earl of Moray and the other Scottish lords against Mary, Queen of Scots. After the battle of Carberry Hill they had forced Mary to abdicate and placed her infant son James upon the throne. For his part in the campaign his ancestor had received his earldom.

Before him all the Cochrans had been sheep thieves and border raiders, who had made their fortunes by murdering and robbing not only Englishmen but members of other Scottish clans as well. The Cochran blood ran true, so the consideration was not a matter of ethics. It was a calculation of his chances of getting away with this prize.

Cumbrae was proud of his lineage but also aware that his ancestors had come to prominence by adroitly avoiding the gibbet and the hangman's ministrations. During this last century, all the seafaring nations of the world had banded together to stamp out the scourge of the corsair and the pirate that, since the times of the pharaohs of ancient Egypt, had plagued the commerce of the oceans.

Ye'll not get away with it, laddie, he decided silently, and shook his head regretfully. He held up the news-sheet before the eyes of his sailors, none of whom was able to read. 'It seems the war is over, more's the pity of it. We will have to set these gentlemen free.'

'Captain, does this mean that we lose out on our prize money?' the coxswain asked plaintively.

'Unless you want to swing from the gallows at Greenwich dock for piracy, it surely does.'

Then he turned and bowed to Colonel Schreuder. 'Sir, it seems that I owe you an apology.' He smiled ingratiatingly. 'It was an honest mistake on my part, which I hope you will forgive. I have been without news of the outside world these past months.'

The Colonel returned his bow stiffly, and Cumbrae went on, 'It gives me pleasure to return your sword to you. You fought like a warrior and a true gentleman.' The Colonel bowed a little more graciously. 'I will give orders to have the crew of this ship released at once. You are, of course, free to return to Table Bay and to continue your voyage from there. Whither were you bound, sir?' he asked politely.

'We were on the point of sailing for Amsterdam before your intervention, sir. I was carrying letters of ransom to the council of the VOC on behalf of the Governor designate of the Cape of Good Hope who, together with his saintly wife, was captured by another English pirate, or rather,' he corrected himself, 'by another English privateer.'

Cumbrae stared at him. 'Was your Governor designate named Petrus van de Velde, and was he captured on board the company ship the *Standvastigheid*?' he asked. 'And was his captor an Englishman, Sir Francis Courtney?'

Colonel Schreuder looked startled. 'He was indeed, sir. But how do you know these details?'

'I will answer your question in due course, Colonel, but first I must know. Are you aware that the *Standvastigheid* was captured *after* the peace treaty was signed by our two countries?'

'My lord, I was a passenger on board the *Standvastigheid* when she was captured. Certainly I am aware that she was an illegal prize.'

'One last question, Colonel. Would not your reputation and professional standing be greatly enhanced if you were able to capture this pirate Courtney, to secure by force of arms the release of Governor van de Velde and his wife, and to return to the treasury of the Dutch East India Company the valuable cargo of the *Standvastigheid*?'

The Colonel was struck speechless by such a magnificent prospect. That image of violet-coloured eyes and hair like sunshine, which since he had last looked upon it had never been far from his mind, now returned to him in every vivid detail. The promise that those sweet red lips had made him outweighed even the treasure of spice and bullion that was at stake. How grateful the lady Katinka would be for her release, and her father also, who was president of the governing board of the VOC. This might be the most significant stroke of fortune that would ever come his way.

He was so moved that he could barely manage a stiff nod of agreement to the Buzzard's proposition.

'Then, sir, I do believe that you and I have matters to discuss that might redound to our mutual advantage,' said the Buzzard, with an expansive smile.

The following morning the *Gull* and the *Swallow* sailed in company back into Table Bay, and as soon as they had anchored under the guns of the fort the Colonel and Cumbrae went ashore. They landed through the surf, where a party of slaves and convicts waded out shoulder deep to drag their boat up the beach before the next wave could capsize it, and stepped out onto dry land without wetting their boots. As they strode together towards the gates of the fort they made a striking and unusual pair: Schreuder was in full uniform, his sashes, ribbons and the plumes in his hat fluttering in the sou'-easter. Cumbrae was resplendent in his plaid of red, russet, yellow and black. The population of this remote way-station had never seen a man dressed in such garb and crowded to the verge of the unpaved parade ground to gape at him.

Some of the doll-like Javanese slave girls caught Cumbrae's attention, for he had been at sea for months without the solace of feminine company. Their skin shone like polished ivory, and their dark eyes were languid. Many had been dolled up in European style by their owners, and their small, neat bosoms were jaunty under their lacy bodices.

Cumbrae acknowledged their admiration like royalty on a progress, lifting his beribboned bonnet to the youngest and prettiest of the girls, reducing them to titters and blushes with the bold stare of his blue eyes over the fiery bush of his whiskers.

The sentries at the gates of the fort saluted Schreuder, who was well known to them, and they went through into the interior courtyard. Cumbrae glanced around him with a penetrating eye, assessing the strength of the defences. It might be peace now, but who could tell what might transpire a few years from now? One day he might be leading a siege against these walls.

He saw that the fortifications were laid out in the shape of a five-pointed star. Clearly they had as their model the new fortress of Antwerp, which had been the first to adopt this innovative ground-plan. Each of the five points was crowned by a redoubt, the salient angles of which made it possible for the defenders to lay down a covering fire on the curtain walls of the fort, which before would have been dead ground, and indefensible. Once the massive outer walls of masonry were completed, the fort would be wellnigh impregnable to anything other than an elaborate siege. It might take many months to sap and mine the walls before they could be breached.

However, the work was far from finished. Gangs of hundreds of slaves and convicts were labouring in the moat and on top of the half-raised walls. Many of the cannon were stored in the courtyard and had not yet been sited in their redoubts atop the walls overlooking the bay.

'An opportunity lost!' the Buzzard wailed. This intelligence had come to him too late to be of profit. 'With another few Knights of the Order to help me – Richard Lister, and even Franky Courtney, before we fell out – I could have taken this fort and sacked the town. If we had combined our forces, the three of us could have sat here in comfort, commanding the entire southern Atlantic and snapping up every Dutch galleon that tried to round the Cape.'

As he looked around the courtyard, he saw that part of the fort was also used as a prison. A file of convicts and slaves in leg-irons was being led up from the dungeons under the northern wall. Barracks for the military garrison had been built above these foundations.

Although piles of masonry and scaffolding littered the courtyard, a company of musketeers in the green and gold doublets of the VOC was drilling in the only open space in front of the armoury.

Ox-drawn wagons, heavily laden with lumber and stone, rumbled in and out of the gates or cluttered the yard, and a coach, standing in splendid isolation, waited outside the entrance to the south wing of the building. The horses were a matching team of greys, groomed so that their hides gleamed in the sunlight. The coachman and footmen were in the green and gold Company livery.

'His excellency is in his office early this morning. Usually we don't see him before noon,' Schreuder grunted. 'News of your arrival must have reached the residence.'

They went up the staircase of the south wing and entered through teak doors with the Company crest carved into them. In the entrance lobby, with its polished yellow-wood floors, an aide-de-camp took their hats and swords, and led them through to the antechamber. 'I will tell his excellency that you are here,' he excused himself, as he backed out of the room. He returned in minutes. 'His excellency will see you now.'

The Governor's audience room overlooked the bay through narrow slit windows. It was furnished in a strange mixture of heavy Dutch furniture and Oriental artifacts. Flamboyant Chinese rugs covered the polished floors, and the glass-fronted cabinets displayed a collection of delicate ceramic ware in the distinctive and colourful glazes of the Ming dynasty.

Governor Kleinhans was a tall, dyspeptic man in late middle age, his skin yellowed by a life in the tropics and his features creased and wrinkled by the cares of his office. His frame was skeletal, his Adam's apple so prominent as to seem deformed, and his full wig too young in style for the withered features beneath it.

'Colonel Schreuder.' He greeted the officer stiffly, without taking his faded eyes, in their pouches of jaundiced skin, off the Buzzard. 'When I woke this morning and saw your ship was gone I thought you had sailed for home without my leave.'

'I beg your pardon, sir. I will give you a full explanation, but may I first introduce the Earl of Cumbrae, an English nobleman.'

'Scots, not English,' the Buzzard growled.

However, Governor Kleinhans was impressed by the title, and switched into good grammatical English, marred only slightly by his guttural accent. 'Ah, I bid you welcome to the Cape of Good Hope, my lord. Please be seated. May I offer you a light refreshment – a glass of Madeira, perhaps?'

With long-stemmed glasses of the amber wine in their hands, their high-backed chairs drawn up in a circle, the colonel leaned towards Kleinhans and murmured, 'Sir, what I have to tell you is a matter of the utmost delicacy,' and he glanced at the hovering servants and aide-de-camp. The Governor clapped his hands and they disappeared like smoke on the wind. Intrigued, he inclined his head towards Schreuder. 'Now, Colonel, what is this secret you have for me?'

Slowly, as Schreuder talked, the Governor's gloomy features lit with greed and anticipation, but, when Schreuder had finished his proposition he made a show of reluctance and scepticism. 'How do we know that this pirate, Courtney, will still be anchored where last you saw him?' he asked Cumbrae.

'As recently as twelve days ago the stolen galleon, the *Standvastigheid*, was careened upon the beach with all her cargo unloaded and her mainmast unstepped. I am a mariner, and I can assure you that Courtney could not have had her ready for sea again within thirty days. That means that we still have over two weeks in which to make our preparations and to launch our attack upon him,' the Buzzard explained.

Kleinhans nodded. 'So whereabouts is the anchorage in which this rascal is hiding?' The Governor tried to make the question casual, but his fever-yellowed eyes glinted.

'I can only assure you that he is well concealed.' The Buzzard side-stepped the question with a dry smile. 'Without my help your men will not be able to hunt him down.'

'I see.' With his bony forefinger the Governor picked at his nostril, then inspected the flake of dried snot he had retrieved. Without looking up, he went on, still casually, 'Naturally you would not require a reward for thus performing what is, after all, merely your bounden and moral duty, to root out this pirates' nest.'

'I would not ask for a reward, other than a modest amount to compensate me for my time and expenses,' Cumbrae agreed.

'One hundredth part of what we are able to recover of the galleon's cargo,' Kleinhans suggested.

'Not quite so modest,' Cumbrae demurred. 'I had in mind a half.'

'Half!' Governor Kleinhans sat bolt upright and his complexion turned the colour of old parchment. 'You are jesting, surely, sir.'

'I assure you, sir, that when it comes to money I seldom jest,' said the Buzzard. 'Have you considered how grateful the director-general of your company will be when you return his daughter to him unharmed, and without having to make the ransom payment? That alone would be a compelling factor in augmenting your pension, without even taking into account the value of the cargo of spice and bullion.'

While Governor Kleinhans considered this he began to excavate his other nostril, and remained silent.

Cumbrae went on persuasively, 'Of course, once van de Velde is released from the clutches of this villain and arrives here, you will be able to hand over your duties to him, and then you will be free to return home to Holland where the rewards of your long and loyal service await you.' Colonel Schreuder had remarked on how avidly the Governor was looking forward to his imminent retirement, after thirty years in the Company's service.

Kleinhans stirred at such an inviting prospect, but his voice was harsh. 'A tenth of the value of the recovered cargo, but not to include the value of any pirates captured and sold on the slave block. A tenth, and that is my final offer.'

Cumbrae looked tragic. 'I shall have to divide the reward with my crew. I could not consider a lesser figure than a quarter.'

'A fifth,' grated Kleinhans.

'I agree,' said Cumbrae, well content.

'And, of course, I will need the services of that fine naval frigate anchored in the bay, and three companies of your musketeers with Colonel Schreuder here to command them. And my own vessel needs to be replenished with powder and cartridge, not to mention water and other provisions.'

It had taken a prodigious effort by Colonel Schreuder, but by late afternoon the following day the three companies of infantry, each comprising ninety men, were drawn up on the parade ground outside the walls of the fort, ready to embark. The officers and non-commissioned officers were all Dutch, but the musketeers were a mixture of native troops, Malaccans from Malaysia, Hottentots recruited from the tribes of the Cape, and Sinhalese and Tamils from the Company's possessions in Ceylon. They were bowed like hunchbacks under their weapons and heavy back-packs but, incongruously, they were barefoot.

As Cumbrae watched them march out through the gates, in their flat black caps, green doublets and white cross belts, their muskets carried at the trail, he remarked sourly, 'I hope they fight as prettily as they march, but I think they may be in for a wee surprise when they meet Franky's sea-rats.'

He could carry only a single company with all its baggage on board the *Gull*. Even then her decks would be crowded and uncomfortable, especially if they ran into heavy weather on the way.

The other two companies of infantry went on board the naval frigate. They would have the easier passage, for *De Sonnevogel*, the *Sun Bird*, was a fast and commodious vessel. She had been captured from Oliver Cromwell's fleet by the Dutch Admiral de Ruyter during the battle of the Kentish Knock, and had been in de Ruyter's squadron during his raid up the Thames only months previously to her arrival off the Cape. She was sleek and lovely in her glossy black paint, and snowy-white trim. It was easy to see that her sails had been renewed before she sailed from Holland, and all her sheets and rigging were spanking new. Her crew were mostly veterans of the two recent wars with England, prime battle-hardened warriors.

Her commander, Captain Ryker, was also a tough, rugged deep-water mariner, wide in the shoulder and big in the gut. He made no attempt to hide his displeasure at finding himself under the direction of a man who, until recently, had been his enemy, an irregular whom he considered little short of a greedy pirate. His bearing towards Cumbrae was cold and hostile, his scorn barely concealed.

They had held a council of war aboard *De Sonnevogel* which had not gone smoothly, Cumbrae refusing to divulge their destination and Ryker making objection to every suggestion and arguing every proposal that he put to him. Only the arbitration of Colonel Schreuder had kept the expedition from breaking down irretrievably before they had even left the shelter of Table Bay.

It was with a profound feeling of relief that the Buzzard at last watched the frigate weigh anchor and, with almost two hundred musketeers lining her rail waving fond farewells to the throng of gaudily dressed or half-naked Hottentot women on the beach, follow the little *Gull* out towards the entrance to the bay.

The *Gull*'s own deck was crowded with infantrymen, who waved and jabbered and pointed out the landmarks on the mountain and on the beach to each other, and hampered the seamen as they worked the *Gull* off the lee shore.

As the ship rounded the point below Lion's Head and felt the first majestic thrust of the south Atlantic, a strange quiet fell over the noisy passengers, and as they tacked and went onto a broad easterly reach, the first of the musketeers rushed to the ship's side, and shot a long yellow spurt of vomit directly into the eye of the wind. A hoot of laughter went up from the crew as the wind sent it all back into the wretch's pallid face and splattered his green doublet with the bilious evidence of his last meal.

Within the hour most of the other soldiers had followed his example, and the decks were so slippery and treacherous with their offerings to Neptune that the Buzzard ordered the pumps to be manned and both decks and passengers to be sluiced down.

'It's going to be an interesting few days,' he told Colonel Schreuder. 'I hope these beauties will have the strength to carry themselves ashore when we reach our destination.'

Before they had half completed their journey, it became apparent that what he had said in jest was in fact dire reality. Most of the troops seemed moribund, laid out like corpses on the deck with nothing left in their bellies to bring up. A signal from Captain Ryker indicated that those aboard the *Sonnevogel* were in no better case.

'If we put these men straight from the deck into a fight, Franky's lads will eat them up without spitting out the bones. We'll have to change our plans,' the Buzzard told Schreuder, who sent a signal across to the *Sonnevogel*. While he hove to, Captain Ryker came across in his skiff with obvious bad grace to discuss the new plan of assault.

Cumbrae had drawn up a sketch map of the lagoon and the shoreline that lay on each side of the heads. The three officers pored over this in the tiny cabin of the *Gull*. Ryker's mood had been alleviated by the disclosure of their final destination, by the prospect of action and prize money, and by a dram of whisky that Cumbrae poured for him. For once he was disposed to agree with the plan with which Cumbrae presented him.

'There is a another headland here, about eight or nine leagues west of the entrance to the lagoon.' The Buzzard laid his hand on the map. 'With this wind there will be enough calm water in the lee to send the boats ashore and land Colonel Schreuder and his musketeers on the beach. Then he will begin his approach march.' He stabbed at the map with a forefinger bristling with ginger hair. 'The interlude on dry land and the exercise will give his men an opportunity to recover from their malaise. By the time they reach Courtney's lair they should have some fire in them again.'

'Have the pirates set up any defences at the entrance to the lagoon?' Ryker wanted to know.

'They have batteries here and here, covering the channel.' Cumbrae drew a series of crosses down each side of the entrance. 'They are so well protected as to be invulnerable to return fire delivered by a ship entering or leaving the anchorage.' He paused as he remembered the rousing send-off those culverins had given the *Gull* as she fled from the lagoon after his abortive attack on the encampment.

Ryker looked sober at the prospect of subjecting his ship to close-range salvoes from entrenched shore batteries.

'I will be able to deal with the batteries on the western approaches,' Schreuder promised them. 'I will send a small detachment to climb down the cliffs. They will not be expecting an attack from their rear. However, I will not be able to cross the channel and reach the guns on the eastern headland.'

'I will send in another raiding party to put those guns out of the game,' Ryker cut in. 'As long as we can devise a system of signals to co-ordinate our attacks.' They spent another hour working out a code with flag and smoke between the ships and the shore. By this time the blood of both Ryker and Schreuder was a-boil, and they were vying for the opportunity to win battle honours.

Why should I risk my own sailors when these heroes are eager to do the work for me? the Buzzard thought happily. Aloud he said, 'I commend you, gentlemen. That is excellent planning. I take it you will delay the attacks on the batteries at the entrance until Colonel Schreuder has brought up his main force of infantry through the forest and is in a position to launch the main assault on the rear of the pirate encampment.'

'Yes, quite so,' Schreuder agreed eagerly. 'But as soon as the batteries on the heads have been put out of action, your ships will provide the diversion by sailing in through them and bombarding the pirates' encampment. That will be the signal for me to launch my land attack into their rear.'

'We will give you our full support.' Cumbrae nodded, thinking comfortably to himself, How hungry he is for glory, and restrained an avuncular urge to pat him on the shoulder. The idiot is welcome to my share of the cannonballs, just as long as I can get my hands on the prize.

Then he looked speculatively at Captain Ryker. It only remained to arrange that the *Sonnevogel* lead the squadron through the heads into the lagoon, and in the process draw the main attentions of Franky's culverins along the edge of the forest. It might be to his advantage if she were to sustain heavy damage before Franky was overwhelmed. If the Buzzard were in command of the only seaworthy ship at the end of the battle, he would be able to dictate his own terms when it came to disposing of the spoils of war.

'Captain Ryker,' he said with an arrogant flourish, 'I claim the honour of leading the squadron into the lagoon in my gallant little *Gull*. My ruffians would not forgive me if I let you go ahead of us.'

Ryker's lips set stubbornly. 'Sir!' he said stiffly. 'The *Sonnevogel* is more heavily armed, and better able to resist the balls of the enemy. I must insist that you allow me to lead the entry into the lagoon.'

And that takes care of that, thought the Buzzard, as he bowed his head in reluctant acquiescence.

Three days later they put Colonel Schreuder and his three companies of seasick musketeers ashore on a deserted beach and watched them march away into the African wilderness in a long untidy column.

The African night was hushed but never silent. When Hal paused on the narrow path, his father's light footfalls dwindled ahead of him, and Hal could hear the soft sounds of myriad life that teemed in the forest around him: the warbling call of a night bird, more hauntingly beautiful than ever musician coaxed from stringed instrument; the scrabbling of rodents and other tiny mammals among the dead leaves and the sudden murderous cry of the small feline predators that hunted them; the singing and hum of the insects and the eternal soughing of the wind. All were part of the hidden choir in this temple of Pan.

The beam of the storm lantern disappeared ahead of him, and now he stepped out to catch up. When they had left the encampment, his father had ignored his question, but when at last they emerged from the forest at the foot of the hills, he knew where they were going. The stones that still marked the Lodge within which he had taken his vows formed a ghostly circle in the glow of the waning moon. At the entry to it Sir Francis went down on one knee and bowed his head in prayer. Hal knelt beside him.

'Lord God, make me worthy,' Hal prayed. 'Give me the strength to keep the vows I made here in your name.'

His father lifted his head at last. He stood up, took Hal's hand and raised him to his feet. Then, side by side, they stepped into the circle and approached the altar stone. '*In Arcadia habito!*' Sir Francis said, in his deep, lilting voice, and Hal gave the response.

'*Flumen sacrum bene cognosco!*'

Sir Francis set the lantern upon the tall stone and, in its yellow light, they knelt again. For a long while they prayed in silence, until Sir Francis looked up at the sky. 'The stars are the ciphers of the Lord. They light our comings and our goings. They guide us across uncharted oceans. They hold our destiny in their coils. They measure the number of our days.'

Hal's eyes went immediately to his own particular star, Regulus. Timeless and unchanging it sparkled in the sign of the Lion.

'Last night I cast your horoscope,' Sir Francis told him. 'There is much that I cannot reveal, but this I can tell you. The stars hold a singular destiny in store for you. I was not able to fathom its nature.'

There was a poignancy in his father's tone, and Hal looked at him. His features were haggard, the shadows beneath his eyes deep and dark. 'If the stars are so favourably inclined, what is it that troubles you, Father?'

'I have been harsh to you. I have driven you hard.'

Hal shook his head. 'Father—'

But Sir Francis quieted him with a hand on his arm. 'You must remember always why I did this to you. If I had loved you less, I would have been kinder to you.' His grip on Hal's arm tightened as he felt Hal draw breath to speak. 'I have tried to prepare you and give you the knowledge and strength to meet that particular destiny that the stars have in store for you. Do you understand that?'

'Yes. I have known this all along. Aboli explained it to me.'

'Aboli is wise. He will be with you when I have gone.'

'No, Father. Do not speak of that.'

'My son, look to the stars,' Sir Francis replied, and Hal hesitated, uncertain of his meaning. 'You know which is my own star. I have shown it to you a hundred times before. Look for it now in the sign of the Virgin.'

Hal raised his face to the heavens, and turned it to the east where Regulus still showed, bright and clear. His eyes ran on past it into the sign of the Virgin, which lay close beside the Lion, and he gasped, his breath hissing through his lips with superstitious dread.

His father's sign was slashed from one end to the other by a scimitar of flame. A fiery red feather, red as blood.

'A shooting star,' he whispered.

'A comet,' his father corrected him. 'God sends me a warning. My time here draws to its close. Even the Greeks and the Romans knew that the heavenly fire is the portent of disaster, of war and famine and plague, and the death of kings.'

'When?' Hal asked, his voice heavy with dread.

'Soon,' replied Sir Francis. 'It must be soon. Most certainly before the comet has completed its transit of my sign. This may be the last time that you and I will be alone like this.'

'Is there nothing that we can do to avert this misfortune? Can we not fly from it?'

'We do not know whence it comes,' Sir Francis said gravely. 'We cannot escape what has been decreed. If we run, then we will certainly run straight into its jaws.'

'We will stay to meet and fight it, then,' said Hal, with determination.

'Yes, we will fight,' his father agreed, 'even if the outcome has been ordained. But that was not why I brought you here. I want to hand over to you, this night, your inheritance, those legacies both corporal and spiritual which belong to you as my only son.' He took Hal's face between his hands and turned it to him so that he looked into his eyes.

'After my death, the rank and style of baronet, accorded to your great-grandfather, Charles Courtney, by good Queen Bess after the destruction of the Spanish Armada, falls upon you. You will become Sir Henry Courtney. You understand that?'

'Yes, Father.'

'Your pedigree has been registered at the College of Arms in England.' He paused as a savage cry echoed down the valley, the sawing of a leopard hunting along the cliffs in the moonlight. As the dreadful rasping roars died away Sir Francis went on quietly, 'It is my wish that you progress through the Order until you attain the rank of Nautonnier Knight.'

'I will strive towards that goal, Father.'

Sir Francis raised his right hand. The band of gold upon his second finger glinted in the lantern light. He twisted it off, and held it to catch the moonlight. 'This ring is part of the regalia of the office of Nautonnier.' He took Hal's right hand, and tried the ring on his second finger. It was too large, so he placed it on his son's forefinger. Then he opened the high collar of his cloak, and exposed the great seal of his office that lay against his breast. The tiny rubies in the eyes of the lion rampant of England, and the diamond stars above it, sparkled softly in the uncertain light. He lifted the chain of the seal from around his own neck, held it high over Hal's head and then lowered it onto his shoulders. 'This seal is the other part of the regalia. It is your key to the Temple.'

'I am honoured but humbled by the trust you place in me.'

'There is one other part to the spiritual legacy I leave for you,' Sir Francis said, as he reached into the folds of his cloak. 'It is the memory of your mother.' He opened his hand and in his palm lay a locket bearing a miniature of Edwina Courtney.

The light was not strong enough for Hal to make out the detail of the portrait, but her face was graven in his mind and in his heart. Wordlessly he placed it in the breast pocket of his doublet.

'We should pray together for the peace of her soul,' said Sir Francis quietly, and both bowed their heads. After many minutes Sir Francis again raised his head. 'Now, it remains only to discuss the earthly inheritance that I leave to you. There is firstly High Weald, our family manor in Devon. You know that your uncle Thomas administers the house and lands in my absence. The deeds of title are with my lawyer in Plymouth . . .' Sir Francis went on speaking for a long while, listing and detailing his possessions and estates in England. 'I have written all this in my journal for you, but that book may be lost or plundered before you can study it. Remember all that I have told you.'

'I will not forget any of it,' Hal assured him.

'Then there are the prizes we have taken on this cruise. You were with me when we cached the spoils from both the *Heerlycke Nacht* and from the *Standvastigheid*. When you return with that booty to England, be sure to pay over to each man of the crew the share he has earned.'

'I will do so without fail.'

'Pay also every penny of the Crown's share to the King's customs officers. Only a rogue would seek to cheat his sovereign.'

'I will not fail to render to my king.'

'I should never rest easy if I were to know that all the riches that I have won for you and my king were to be lost. I require you to make an oath on your honour as a Knight of the Order,' Sir Francis said. 'You must swear that you will never reveal the whereabouts of the spoils to any other person. In the difficult days that lie ahead of us, while the red comet rules my sign and dictates our affairs, there may be enemies who will try to force you to break this oath. You must bear always in the forefront of your mind the motto of our family. *Durabo!* I shall endure.'

'On my honour, and in God's name, I shall endure,' Hal promised. The words slipped lightly over his tongue. He could not know then that when they returned to him their weight would be grievous and heavy enough to crush his heart.

For his entire military career Colonel Cornelius Schreuder had campaigned with native troops rather than with men of his own race and country. He much preferred them, for they were inured to hardship and less likely to be affected by heat and sun, or by cold and wet. They were hardened against the fevers and plagues that struck down the white men who ventured into these tropical climes, and they survived on less food. They were able to live and fight on what frugal fare this savage and terrible land provided, whereas European troops would sicken and die if forced to undergo similar privations.

There was another reason for his preference. Whereas the lives of

Christian troops must be reckoned dear, these heathen could be expended without such consideration, just as cattle do not have the same value as men and can be sent to the slaughter without qualm. Of course, they were famous thieves and could not be trusted near women or liquor, and when forced to rely upon their own initiative they were as little children, but with good Dutch officers over them, their courage and fighting spirit outweighed these weaknesses.

Schreuder stood on a rise of ground and watched the long column of infantry file past him. It was remarkable how swiftly they had recovered from the terrible affliction of seasickness that only the previous day had prostrated most of them. A night's rest on the hard earth and a few handfuls of dried fish and cakes of sorghum meal baked over the coals, and this morning they were cheerful and strong as when they had embarked. They strode past him on bare feet, following their white petty-officers, moving easily under their burdens, chattering to each other in their own tongues.

Schreuder felt more confidence in them now than at any time since they had embarked in Table Bay. He lifted his hat and mopped at his brow. The sun was only just showing above the tree-tops but already it was hot as the blast from a baker's oven. He looked ahead at the hills and forest that awaited them. The map that the red-haired Scotsman had drawn for him was a rudimentary sketch that merely adumbrated the shoreline and gave no warning of this rugged terrain that they had encountered.

At first he had marched along the shore, but this proved heavy-going – under their packs the men sank ankle deep into sand at each pace. Also, the open beaches were interspersed with cliffs and rocky capes, which could cause further delay. So Schreuder had turned inland and sent his scouts ahead to find a way through the hills and forest.

At that moment there was a shout from up ahead. A runner was coming back down the line. Panting, the Hottentot drew himself up and saluted with a flourish. 'Colonel, there is a wide river ahead.' Like most of these troops he spoke good Dutch.

'Name of a dog!' Schreuder cursed. 'We will fall further behind and our rendezvous is only two days from now. Show me the way.' The scout led him towards the crest of the hill.

At the top of the slope a steep river valley opened beneath his feet. The sides were almost two hundred feet deep and densely covered with forest. At the bottom the estuary was broad and brown, racing out into the sea with the tide. He drew his telescope from its leather case and carefully scanned the valley where it cut deeply into the hills of the hinterland. 'There does not seem to be an easier way to cross and I cannot afford the time to search further.' He looked down at the drop. 'Fix ropes to those trees at the top to give the men purchase on the slope.'

It took them half the morning to get two hundred men down into the valley. At one stage a rope snapped under the weight of fifty men leaning on it to keep their footing as they descended. However, although most sustained grazes, cuts and sprains as they rolled down to the riverbank, there was one serious casualty. A young Sinhalese infantry-man's right leg caught in a tree root as he fell, and was fractured in a dozen places below the knee, the sharp splinters of bone sticking out of his shin.

'Well, we're down with only one man lost,' Schreuder told his lieutenant, with satisfaction. 'It could have been more costly. We might have spent days searching for another crossing.'

'I will have a litter made for the injured man,' Lieutenant Maatzuyker suggested.

'Are you soft in the head?' Schreuder snapped. 'He would hold up the march. Leave the clumsy fool here with a loaded pistol. When the hyena come for him he can make his own decision who to shoot, one of them or himself. Enough talk! Let's get on with the crossing.'

From the bank Schreuder looked across a hundred-yard sweep of river, the surface dimpled with small whirlpools as the outgoing tide spurred the muddy waters on their race for the sea.

'We will have to build rafts—' Lieutenant Maatzuyker ventured, but Schreuder snarled, 'Nor can I afford the time for that. Get a rope across to the other bank. I must see if this river is fordable.'

'The current is strong,' Maatzuyker pointed out tactfully.

'Even a simpleton can see that, Maatzuyker. Perhaps that is why you had no difficulty in making the observation,' said Schreuder ominously. 'Pick your strongest swimmer!'

Maatzuyker saluted and hurried down the ranks of troops. They guessed what was in store and every one found something of interest to study in sky or forest, rather than meeting Maatzuyker's eye.

'Ahmed!' he shouted at one of his corporals, grabbed his shoulder and pulled him out of the huddle of men where he was trying to make himself inconspicuous.

Resignedly Ahmed handed his musket to a man in his troop and began to strip. His naked body was hairless and yellow, sheathed in lithe, hard muscle.

Maatzuyker knotted the rope under his armpits and sent him into the water. As Ahmed edged out into the current it rose gradually to his waist. Schreuder's hopes for a swift, easy crossing rose with it. Ahmed's mates on the bank shouted encouragement as they paid out the line.

Then, when he was almost half-way across, Ahmed stumbled abruptly into the main channel of the river, and his head disappeared below the surface.

'Pull him back!' Schreuder ordered, and they hauled Ahmed back into the shallower water, where he struggled to regain his footing, snorting and coughing up the water he had swallowed.

Suddenly Schreuder shouted, with more urgency, 'Pull! Get him out of the water!'

Fifty yards upstream he had seen a mighty swirl on the surface of the opaque waters. Then a swift V-shaped wake sped down the channel to where the corporal was splashing about in the shallows. The team on the rope saw it then and, with yells of consternation, they hauled Ahmed in so vigorously that he was plucked over backwards and dragged thrashing and kicking towards the bank. However, the thing below the surface moved more swiftly still and arrowed in on the helpless man.

When it was only yards from him its deformed black snout, gnarled and scaled as a black log, thrust through the surface, and twenty feet behind the head a crested saurian tail exploded out. The hideous monster raced across the gap, and rose high out of the water, its jaws open to display the ragged files of yellow teeth.

Then Ahmed saw it, and shrieked wildly. With a crash like a falling portcullis the jaws closed over his lower body. Man and beast plunged below the surface in a whirlpool of creaming foam. The men on the line were jerked off their feet and dragged in a struggling heap down the bank.

Schreuder leapt after them and seized the rope's end. He took two turns around his wrist and flung his weight back on the line. Out in the brown tide-race there was another boiling explosion of foam as the huge crocodile, its fangs locked in Ahmed's belly, rolled over and over at dizzying speed. The other men on the line recovered their footing and hung on grimly. There was a sudden stain of red on the brown water as Ahmed was torn in half, the way a glutton might twist the leg off the carcass of a turkey.

The bloodstain was whipped away and dissipated downstream by the swift current, and the straining men fell back as the resistance at the other end of the rope gave way. Ahmed's upper torso was dragged ashore, arms jerking and mouth opening and shutting convulsively, like that of a dying fish.

Far out in the river the crocodile rose again, holding Ahmed's legs and lower torso crosswise in its jaws. It lifted its head to the sky and gulped and strained to swallow. As the dismembered carcass slid down into its maw, they saw it bulge the soft, pale scaly throat.

Schreuder was roaring with rage. 'This foul beast will delay us for days, if we allow it.' He rounded on the shaken musketeers who were dragging away Ahmed's sundered corpse. 'Bring that piece of meat back here!'

They dropped the corpse at his feet and watched in awe as he stripped off his own clothing, and stood naked before them, flat, hard muscle rippling his belly and his thick penis jutting out of the mat of dark hair at its base. At his impatient order they tied a rope under his armpits, then handed him a loaded musket with the match burning in the lock, which Schreuder shouldered. With his other hand he grabbed Ahmed's limp dead arm. An incredulous hum of amazement went up from the bank as Schreuder stepped into the river dragging the bleeding remnants with him. 'Come, then, filthy beast!' he bellowed angrily, as the water reached his knees and he kept going. 'You want to eat? Well, I have something for you to chew on.'

A moan of horror burst from every throat as, upstream from where Schreuder stood, with the water at his hips, there was another tremendous swirl and the crocodile rushed down-river towards him, leaving a long slick wake across the brown surface.

Schreuder braced himself and then, with a round-arm swing, hurled the upper half of Ahmed's dripping, dismembered corpse ahead of him into the path of the crocodile's flailing charge. 'Eat that!' he shouted, as he lifted the musket from his shoulder and levelled it at the human bait that bobbed only two arms' span ahead of him.

The monstrous head burst through the surface and the mouth opened wide enough to engulf Ahmed's pitifully shredded remains. Over the sights of the gun Schreuder looked down into its gaping jaws. He saw the ragged spikes of teeth, still festooned with shreds of human flesh, and beyond them the lining of the throat, which was a lovely buttercup yellow. As the jaws opened, a tough membrane automatically closed off the throat to prevent water rushing down it into the beast's lungs.

Schreuder aimed into the depths of the open throat and snapped the lock. The burning match dropped and there was an instant of delay as the powder flared in the pan. Then, as Schreuder held his aim unwaveringly, came a deafening roar and a long silver-blue spurt of smoke flew from the muzzle straight down the throat of the crocodile. Three ounces of antimony-hardened lead pellets drove through the membrane, tearing through windpipe, artery and flesh, lancing deep into the chest cavity, ripping through the cold reptilian heart and lungs.

Such a mighty convulsion racked the great lizard that fifteen feet of its length arched clear of the water and the grotesque head almost touched the crested tail before it fell back in a tall spout of foam. Then it rolled, dived and burst out again, swirling in leviathan contortions.

Schreuder did not pause to watch these hideous death throes, but dropped the smoking musket and dived head-first into the deepest part of the channel. Relying on the beast's frenzy to confuse and distract any other of the deadly reptiles, he lashed out towards the far bank with a full overarm stroke.

'Pay out the rope to him!' Maatzuyker yelled at the men who stood paralysed with shock, and they recovered their wits. Holding it high to keep it clear of the current they let it out as Schreuder clawed himself across the channel.

'Look out!' Maatzuyker shouted, as first one then another crocodile pushed through the surface. Their eyes were set on protuberant horny knuckles so they were able to watch the convulsions of their dying fellow without exposing the whole of their heads.

The softer splashes thrown up by Schreuder did not attract their attention until he was only a dozen strokes from the far bank, when one of the monsters sensed his presence. It turned and sped towards him, ripples spreading like a fan on each side of the twin lumps on its forehead.

'Faster!' Maatzuyker bellowed. 'He's after you!' Schreuder redoubled his stroke as the crocodile closed in swiftly upon him. Every man on the bank roared encouragement at him, but the crocodile was only a body length behind as Schreuder's feet touched the bottom. It raced in the last yard as Schreuder flung himself forward and the mighty jaws snapped closed only inches behind his feet.

Dragging the rope like a tail he staggered towards the tree-line – but still he was not clear of danger for the dragonlike creature raised itself on its stubby bowed legs as it came ashore, and waddled after him at a speed that the watchers could hardly credit. Schreuder reached the first tree of the forest only feet ahead of it and sprang for an overhanging branch. As the snaggle-toothed jaws clashed shut he was just able to lift his legs beyond their bite and, with the last of his strength, draw himself higher into the branches.

The frustrated reptile lurked below, circling the bole of the tree. Then, uttering a hissing roar, it retreated slowly down the bank. It carried high its long tail, crested like a gigantic cockscomb, but as it reached the river it lowered itself and slid back beneath the surface.

Even before it had disappeared, Schreuder shouted across the river, 'Make your end fast!'

He looped his own rope end around the thick trunk beside which he was perched, and knotted it. Then he yelled, 'Maatzuyker! Get those men busy building a raft. They can pull themselves over on the rope against the current.'

The hull of the *Resolution* had been cleaned of weed and barnacles, and as the crew paid off her hoving lines she righted herself slowly against the press of the incoming tide.

While she had been careened on the beach, the carpenters had finished shaping and dressing the new mainmast, and it was at last ready to step. It took every hand to carry the long, heavy spar down to the beach and lift the thick end over the gunwale. The tackle was made fast to her other two standing masts, and the slings were adjusted to raise the new spar.

With gangs heaving cautiously on the lines, and Big Daniel and Ned directing them, they raised the massive length of gleaming pine towards the vertical. Sir Francis trusted no one else to supervise the crucial business of fitting the heel of the mast through the hole in the main deck and then sliding its length down through the hull to the step on the keelson of the ship. It was a delicate operation that needed the strength of fifty men, and took most of that day.

'Well done, lads!' Sir Francis told them, when at last the massive spar slid home the last few inches and the heel clunked heavily into its prepared step. 'Slack off!' No longer supported by the ropes, the fifty-foot mast stood of its own accord.

Big Daniel shouted up to the deck from where he stood waist deep in the lagoon, 'Now woe betide those cheese-heads. Ten days from today, we'll sail her out through the heads, you mark my words.'

Sir Francis smiled down at him from the rail. 'Not before we get the shrouds on that mainmast. And that will not happen while you stand there with your mouth open and your tongue wagging.'

He was about to turn away when suddenly he frowned at the shore. The Governor's wife had come out of the trees, followed by her maid, and now she stood at the top of the beach, spinning the handle of her parasol between her long white fingers so it revolved over her head, a brightly coloured wheel that drew the eye of every man of his crew. Even Hal, who was overseeing the gang on the foredeck, had turned from his work to gawk at her like a ninny. Today she was dressed in a fetching new costume, cut so low in front that her bosom bulged out almost to her nipples.

'Mr Courtney,' Sir Francis called, loud enough to shame his son in front of his men, 'give a mind to your work. Where are the wedges to steady that spar?'

Hal started, and flushed darkly under his tan as he turned from the rail and seized the heavy mallet. 'You heard the captain,' he snapped at his gang.

'That strumpet is the Eve in this paradise,' Sir Francis dropped his voice, and spoke from the side of his mouth to Aboli at his shoulder. 'I have seen Hal mooning at her before and, sweet heavens, she looks back at him bold as a harlot with her dugs sticking out. He is only a boy.'

'You see him through a father's eyes.' Aboli smiled and shook his head. 'He is a boy no longer. He is a man. You told me once that your holy book speaks of an eagle in the sky and a serpent on a rock, and a man with a maid.'

Although Hal could steal little time from his duties, he responded to Katinka's summons like a salmon returning to its native river in the spawning season. When she called him, nothing could stop him answering. He ran up the path with his heart keeping time to his flying feet. It was almost a full day since last he had been alone with Katinka, which was much too long for his liking. Sometimes he was able to sneak away from the camp to meet her twice or even thrice in a single day. Often they could be together only for a few minutes, but that was time enough to get the business done. The two wasted little of their precious time together in ceremony or debate.

They had been forced to find a meeting place other than her hut. Hal's midnight visits to the hostage stockade had almost ended in disaster. Governor van de Velde could not have been sleeping as soundly as his snores suggested and they had grown careless and rowdy in their love play.

Roused by his wife's unrestrained cries and Hal's loud responses, Governor van de Velde seized the lantern and crept up on her hut. Aboli, on guard without, saw the glimmer of it in time to hiss a warning, giving Hal a space to snatch up his clothing and duck out of the hole in the stockade wall, just as van de Velde burst into the hut with the lantern in one hand and a naked sword in the other.

He had complained bitterly to Sir Francis the following morning. 'One of your thieving sailors,' he accused.

'Is there any item of value missing from your wife's hut?' Sir Francis wanted to know and, when van de Velde shook his head, he was heavy with innuendo. 'Perhaps your wife should not make such a show of her jewels for they excite avaricious thoughts. In future, sir, it might be prudent to take better care of *all* your possessions.'

Sir Francis questioned the off-duty watch, but as the Governor's wife could supply no description of the intruder – she had been fast asleep at the time – the matter was soon dropped. That had been the last nocturnal visit Hal dared risk to the stockade.

Instead they had found this secret place to meet. It was well hidden but situated close enough to the camp for Hal to be able respond to her summons and to reach it in just a few minutes. He paused briefly on the narrow terrace in front of the cave, breathing deeply in his haste and excitement. He and Aboli had discovered it as they returned from one of their hunting forays in the hills. It was not really a cave, but an overhang where the soft red sandstone had been eroded from the harder rock strata to form a deep veranda.

They were not the first men to have passed this way. There were old ashes in the stone hearth against the back wall of the shelter, and the low roof was soot-stained. Littering the floor were the bones of fish and small mammals, remnants of meals that had been prepared at the hearth. The bones were dry and picked clean, and the ashes were cold and scattered. The hearth was long disused.

However, these were not the only signs of human occupation. The rear wall was covered from floor to roof with a wild and exuberant cavalcade of paintings. Horned antelope and gazelle that Hal did not recognize streamed in great herds across the smooth rock face, hunted by stick-like human archers with swollen buttocks and incongruously erect sexual members. The paintings were childlike and colourful, the perspective and the relative size of men and beasts fantastical. Some human figures dwarfed the elephant they pursued, and eagles were twice the size of the herds of black buffalo beneath their outstretched wings. Yet Hal was enchanted by them. Often in the intervals of quiet between wild bouts of lovemaking, he would lie staring up at these strange little men as they hunted the game and fought battles with each other. At those times he felt a strange longing to know more about the artists, and these heroic little hunters and warriors they had depicted.

When he asked Aboli about them, the big black man shrugged disdainfuly. 'They are the San. Not really men, but little yellow apes. If you are ever unfortunate enough to meet one of them, a fate from which your three gods should protect you, you will find out more about their poison arrows than their paint pots.'

Today the paintings could hold his interest for only a moment, for the bed of grass that he had laid on the floor against the wall was empty. This was no surprise, for he was early to the tryst. Still, he wondered if she would come or if her summons had been capricious. Then, behind him, he heard the snap of a breaking twig from further down the slope.

He glanced around quickly for a place to hide. Down one side of the entrance trailed a curtain of vines, their dark green foliage starred with startlingly yellow blossoms, their light, sweet perfume wafting through the cave. Hal slipped behind it and shrank back against the rock wall.

A moment later Katinka sprang lightly onto the terrace outside the entrance and peered expectantly into the interior. When she realized it was empty, her frame stiffened with anger. She said one word in Dutch that, from her regular use of it, he had come to know well. It was obscene, and he felt his skin crawl with excitement at the delights presaged by that word.

Silently he slipped out from his hiding place and crept up behind her. He whipped one hand over her eyes and, with the other arm around her waist, lifted her off her feet and ran with her towards the bed of grass.

Much later Hal lay back on the grass mattress, his naked chest still heaving and running with sweat. She nibbled lightly at one of his nipples as though it were a raisin. Then she played with the golden medallion that hung from his neck.

'This is pretty,' she murmured. 'I like the red ruby eyes of the lion. What is it?' He did not understand this complex question in her language, and shrugged. She repeated it slowly and clearly.

'It is something given me by my father. It has great value to me,' he replied evasively.

'I want it,' she said. 'Will you give it to me?'

He smiled lazily. 'I could never do that.'

'Do you love me?' she pouted. 'Are you mad for me?'

'Yes, I love you madly,' he admitted, as with the back of his forearm he wiped the sweat out of his eyes.

'Then give me the medallion.'

He shook his head wordlessly and then, to avoid the looming argument, he asked, 'Do you love me as I love you?'

She gave a merry laugh. 'Don't be a silly goat! Of course I do not love you. Lord Cyclops is the only one I love.' She had nicknamed his sex after the one-eyed giant of the legend, and to affirm it she reached down to his groin. 'But even him I do not love when he is so soft and small.'

Her fingers were busy for a moment, and then she laughed again, this time throatily. 'There now, I love him better already. Ah, yes! Better still. The bigger he grows, the more I love him. I am going kiss him now to show him how much I love him.'

She slid the tip of her tongue down over his belly, but as she pushed her face into the dark bush of his pubic hair, a sound arrested her. It came rolling in across the lagoon below, and broke in a hundred booming echoes from the hills.

'Thunder!' Katinka cried, and sat up. 'I hate thunder. Ever since I was a little girl.'

'Not thunder!' Hal said, and pushed her away so roughly that she cried out again.

'Oh! You son of a pig, you have hurt me.'

But Hal took no heed of her complaint, and sprang to his feet. Naked, he rushed to the entrance of the cave and stared out. The entrance was situated high enough to enable him to see over the tops of the forest trees surrounding the lagoon. The bare masts of the *Resolution* towered into the blue noon sky. The air was filled with seabirds – the thunderous sound had startled them from the surface of the water and the sunlight sparkled on their wings so that circling high overhead they seemed to be creatures of ice and crystal.

A softly rolling bank of mist obscured half the lagoon. It blanketed the rocky cliffs of the heads in silvery-blue billows that were suddenly shot through with strange flickering lights. But this was not mist.

The thunder broke again, reaching Hal long after the flare of lights, the distant sound taking time to reach his ears. The swirling clouds thickened, spilling densely and heavily as oil across the lagoon waters. Above this cloud bank, the tall masts and sails of two great ships floated as though suspended above the waters. He stared at them, stupefied, as they sailed in serenely between the heads. Another broadside broke from the leading ship. He saw at once that she was a frigate, her black hull trimmed with white, her gunports gaping and the fire and smoke boiling out of her. High above the smoke banks the tricolour of the Dutch Republic rippled in the light noon breeze. In line behind her the *Gull of Moray* followed daintily, the colours of St George and St Andrew and the great red cross of the Temple bedecking her masts and rigging, her culverins bellowing out their warlike chorus.

'Merciful God!' Hal cried. 'Why do not the batteries at the entrance return their fire?'

Then with his naked eye he saw strange soldiers in green uniform overrunning the gun emplacements at the foot of the cliffs, their swords and the steel heads of their pikes flashing in the sunlight as they slaughtered the gunners, and flung their bodies over the parapets into the sea below.

'They have surprised our men in the forts. The Buzzard has led the Dutch to us, and shown them where our guns are placed.' His voice trembled with outrage. 'He will pay with his blood for this day, I swear it.'

Katinka sprang up from the grass mattress and ran to the entrance beside him. 'Look! It is a Dutch ship, come to rescue me from the den of your foul pirate father. I give thanks to God! Soon I will be away from this forsaken place and safe at Good Hope.' She danced with excitement. 'When they hang you and your father from the gibbet on the parade outside the fort, I shall be there to blow you one last kiss and to wave you farewell.' She laughed mockingly.

Hal ignored her. He ran back into the cave, pulled on his clothing hastily and belted on the Neptune sword.

'There will be fighting and great danger, but you will be safe if you stay here until it is over,' he told her, and started down.

'You cannot leave me alone here!' she screamed after him. 'Come back here, I command you!'

But he took no notice of her pleas and raced down the footpath through the trees. I should never have allowed her to tempt me from my father's side, he lamented silently as he ran. He warned me of the danger of the red comet. I deserve whatever cruel fate awaits me now.

He was in such distress that he was oblivious to all but the need to take up his neglected duties and almost ran full tilt into the lines of skirmishing soldiers moving through the trees ahead of him. Just in time, he smelt the smoke of their burning match and then picked out their green doublets and the white cross belts as they wove their way through the trees of the forest. He flung himself to the ground and rolled behind the trunk of a tall wild fig tree. He peered out from behind it, and saw that the strange green-clad ranks were moving away from him, advancing on the encampment, pikes and muskets at the ready, keeping good order under the direction of a white officer.

Hal heard the officer call softly in Dutch, 'Keep your spacing. Do not bunch up!' There could be no doubt now whose troops these were. The Dutchman's back was still turned, and Hal had a moment's respite to think. I must reach the camp to warn my father, but there is not enough time to find a way round. I will have to fight my way through the enemy ranks. He drew the sword from its scabbard and rose on one knee, then paused as a thought struck him with force. We are outnumbered on land and on the water. This time there are no fireships to drive off the Buzzard and the Dutch frigate. The battle may go hard for us.

Using the point of his sword, he scratched a hole in the soft, loamy soil at the base of the wild fig. Then he slipped the ring from his finger and the locket with the miniature of his mother from his pocket and dropped them into the hole. After that he lifted the seal of the Nautonnier from his neck and laid it on top of his other treasures. He swept the loose soil back over them, and tamped it down with the flat of his hand.

It had taken him only a minute but when he started to his feet the Dutch officer had disappeared into the forest ahead. Hal crept forward, guided to his quarry by the rustle and crackle of the undergrowth. Without their officers these men will not fight so well, he thought. If I can take this one I will quench some of the fire in their bellies. He slowed as he drew closer to the man he was stalking, and came up behind the Dutchman as he pushed his way through the undergrowth, the noise of his progress masking the fainter sounds of Hal's approach.

The Dutchman was sweating in dark wet patches down the back of his serge coat. By his epaulettes Hal realized that he was a lieutenant in the Company's army. He was thin and lanky, with angry red pustules studding the back of his scrawny neck. He carried his bared sword in his right hand. He had not bathed for many days and smelt like a wild boar.

'On guard, Mijnheer!' Hal challenged him in Dutch, for he could not run him through the back. The lieutenant spun round to face him, lifting his blade into the guard.

His eyes were pale blue, and they flew wide with shock and fright as he found Hal so close behind him. He was not much older than Hal, and his face blanched with terror, emphasizing the rash of purple acne that covered his chin.

Hal thrust and their blades rasped as they crossed. He recovered swiftly, but with that first light touch he had assessed his adversary. The Dutchman was slow and his wrist lacked the snap and power of a practised swordsman. His father's words rang in his ears. 'Fight from the first stroke. Do not wait until you are angry.' And he gave his heart over to a cold, murderous rage to kill. 'Ha!' he grunted, and feinted high, aiming the point at the Dutchman's eyes but balanced for his parry. The lieutenant was slow to counter, and Hal knew he could risk the flying attack that Daniel had taught him against such a foe. He could go for the quick kill.

His wrist tempered to steel by hours with Aboli on the practice deck, he caught up the Dutchman's blade, and whirled it with a stirring motion that threw the point off the line of defence. He had created an opening, but to exploit it with the flying attack he must open his own guard and place himself in full jeopardy of the Dutchman's natural riposte – suicide in the face of a skilled opponent.

He committed himself, throwing his weight forward over his left foot, and sped his point in through the other man's guard. The riposte came too late, and Hal's steel spiked through the sweat-stained serge cloth. It glanced off a rib and then found the gap between them. Despite the days he had spent with a sword in his hand this was Hal's first kill with the cold steel, and he was unprepared for the sensation of his blade running through human flesh.

It was a soggy, dead feeling, which smothered the speed of his thrust. Lieutenant Maatzuyker gasped and dropped his own sword as Hal's point stopped at last against his spine. He clutched at Hal's razor-sharp blade with bare hands. It slashed his palms to the bone, severing the sinews in a quick flush of bright blood. His fingers opened nervelessly, and he sank to his knees staring up into Hal's face with watery blue eyes, as though he were about to burst into tears.

Hal stood over him, and tugged at the sapphire pommel of the Neptune sword, but the Toledo blade clung fast in the wet flesh. Maatzuyker gasped in agony and held up his mutilated hands in appeal.

'I am sorry,' Hal whispered in horror, and heaved again on his sword hilt. This time Maatzuyker opened his mouth wide and whimpered. The blade had passed through his right lung, and a sudden gout of blood burst through his pale lips, poured down his coat front and splashed Hal's boots.

'Oh God!' Hal muttered, as Maatzuyker toppled backwards with the blade between his ribs. For a moment, he stood helplessly, watching the other man choke on and drown in his own blood. Then, close behind him, came a wild shout from the bushes.

A green-jacketed soldier had spotted him. A musket boomed, the pellets rattled into the foliage above Hal's head and sang off the tree trunk beside him. He was galvanized. All along he had known what he must do but, until that moment, he had not been able to bring himself to do it. Now he placed his booted heel firmly on Maatzuyker's heaving chest and leaned back against the resistance of the trapped blade. He tugged once and then again with all his weight behind it. Reluctantly the blade slid out until suddenly it came free and Hal reeled backwards.

Instantly he recovered his balance and leapt over Maatzuyker's body just as another musket shot crashed out and the pellets hissed past his head. The soldier who had fired was fumbling with his powder flask as he tried to reload and Hal ran straight at him. The musketeer looked up in fright, then dropped his empty weapon and turned his back to run.

Hal would not use the point again but slashed at the man's neck, just below his ear. The razor edge cut to the bone, and the side of his neck opened like a grinning red mouth. The man dropped without a sound. But all around him the bushes were alive with green-jacketed figures. Hal realized there must be hundreds of them. This was not a raiding party but a small army attacking the encampment.

He heard shouts of alarm and anger, and now a constant barrage of musket fire, much of it wild and undirected, but some slashing into the undergrowth close on either side of him as he ran with all his speed and strength. In the midst of the uproar Hal recognized, by its power and authority, one stentorian voice.

'Get that man!' it bellowed in Dutch. 'Don't let him get away! I want that one.' Hal glanced in the direction from which it was coming, and almost tripped with the shock of seeing Cornelius Schreuder racing through the trees to head him off. His hat and wig flew from his head, but the ribbons and sash of his rank were gold. His shaven head gleamed like an eggshell. His moustaches were scored heavily across his face. For such a big man, he was fast on his feet, but fear made Hal faster.

'I want you!' Schreuder yelled. 'This time you will not get away.'

Hal put on a burst of speed and, within thirty flying paces, had forged ahead to see the stockade of the encampment through the trees. It was deserted and he realized that his father and every other man would have been decoyed away to the lagoon's edge by the heavy fire of the two warships, and that they must be manning the culverins in the emplacements.

'To arms!' he screamed as he ran, with Schreuder pounding along only ten paces behind him. 'Rally to me, the *Resolution*. In your rear!'

As he burst into camp he saw, with huge relief, Big Daniel and a dozen seamen responding to his call, rushing back from the beach to support him. Immediately Hal rounded on the Dutchman.

'Come, then,' he said, and went on guard. But Schreuder came up short as he saw the *Resolution*'s men bearing down on him and realized that he had outrun his own troops, had left them without a leader, and was now outnumbered twelve to one.

'Again you are lucky, puppy,' he snarled at Hal. 'But before this day ends, you and I will speak again.'

Thirty paces behind Hal, Big Daniel pulled up short and lifted the musket he carried. He aimed at Schreuder but, as the lock snapped, the Colonel ducked and spun on his heels, the shot went wide and he bounded back into the forest, shouting to rally his attacking musketeers as they came swarming forward through the trees.

'Master Daniel,' Hal panted, 'the Dutchman leads a strong force. The forest is full of men.'

'How many?'

'A hundred or more. There!' He pointed as the first of the attackers came running and dodging towards them, stopping to fire and reload their muskets, then running forward again.

'What's worse, there are two warships in the bay,' Daniel told him. 'One is the *Gull* but the other is a Dutch frigate.'

'I saw them from the hill.' Hal had recovered his breath. 'We are outgunned in front and outnumbered in the rear. We cannot stand here. They will be on us in a minute. Back to the beach.'

The coloured troops behind them clamoured like a pack of hounds as Hal turned and led his men back at a run. Ball and shot thrummed and whistled around them, kicking up spurts of damp earth at their heels, speeding them on their way.

Through the trees he could see the piled earth of the gun emplacements and the drifting bank of gunsmoke. He could make out the heads of his own gunners as they reloaded the culverins. Out in the lagoon the stately Dutch frigate bore down on the shore, wreathed in her own powder smoke. As Hal watched, she put her helm over, bringing her broadside to bear, and again her gunports bloomed with great flashes of flame. Seconds later the thunder of the cannonade and the blast of howling grape shot swept over them.

Hal flinched in the turmoil of disrupted air, his eardrums singing. Whole trees crashed down, and branches and leaves rained upon them. Directly in front of him he saw one of the culverins hit squarely, and hurled off its train. The bodies of two of the *Resolution*'s sailors were sent spinning high into the air.

'Father, where are you?' Hal tried to make himself heard in the pandemonium but then, through it all, he heard Sir Francis's voice.

'Stand to your guns, lads. Aim at the Dutchmen's ports. Give those cheese-heads out there some of our good English cheer.'

Hal leapt down into the gunpit beside his father, seized his arm and shook it urgently.

'Where have you been, boy?' Sir Francis glanced at him, but when he saw the blood on his clothing he did not wait for an answer. Instead he grunted, 'Take command of the guns on the left flank. Direct your fire—'

Hal interrupted, in a breathless rush, 'The enemy ships are only creating a diversion, Father. The real danger is in our rear. The forest is full of Dutch soldiers, hundreds of them.' He pointed back with his blood-stained blade. 'They'll be on us in a minute.'

Sir Francis did not hesitate. 'Go down the line of guns. Order every second culverin to be swung round and loaded with grape. The front guns continue to engage the ships, but hold your fire with the back guns until the attack in our rear is point-blank. I will give the order to fire. Now, go!' As Hal scrambled out of the pit, Sir Francis turned to Big Daniel. 'Take these men of yours, and any other loafers you can find, go back and slow the enemy advance in our rear.'

Hal raced down the line, pausing beside each gunpit to shout his orders and then running on. The sound of the barrage and the answering fire from the beach was deafening and confusing. He reeled and almost went sprawling to the ground as another broadside from the black frigate swept over him like the devil-winds of a typhoon, smashing through the forest and ploughing the earth around him. He shook his head to clear it and ran on, hurdling a fallen tree-trunk.

As he passed each emplacement and alerted the gunners, they began to train the culverins around, aiming them back into the forest. Back there they could already hear musket fire and angry shouts as Big Daniel and his small band of seamen charged into the advancing hordes that poured from the forest.

Hal reached the gunpit at the end of the line and jumped down beside Aboli, who was captaining the team of gunners there. Aboli thrust his burning match into the touch hole. The culverin leapt and thundered. As the stinking smoke swirled back over them, Aboli grinned at Hal, his dark face stained even darker with soot and his eyes bloodshot with smoke. 'Ah! I thought you might never pull your root out of the sugar field in time to join the fight. I feared I might have to come up to the cave, and prise you loose with an iron bar.'

'You will grin less happily with a musket ball in your tail feathers,' Hal told him grimly. 'We are surrounded. The woods behind us are full of Dutchmen. Daniel is holding them, but not for much longer. There are hundreds of them. Train this piece around and load with grape.' While they reloaded, Hal went on giving his orders. 'We'll have time for only one shot, then we'll charge them in the smoke,' he said as he tamped down the charge with the long ramrod. As he pulled it out, a sailor lifted the heavy canvas bag filled with lead shot, and forced it down the muzzle. Hal drove it down to sit upon the powder charge. Then they ducked behind the parapet on both sides of the gun, keeping clear of the area where the train would recoil, and stared past the stockade into the forest beyond. They could hear the ring of steel on steel and the wild shouts as Daniel's men charged then fell back before the counter-charge of the green-jackets. Musket fire hammered steadily as Schreuder's men reloaded and ran forward to fire again.

Now they caught glimpses through the trees of their own seamen coming back. Daniel towered above the others: he was carrying a wounded man over one shoulder and swinging a cutlass in his other hand. The green-jackets were pressing him and his party hard.

'Ready now!' Hal grated at the seamen around him, and they crouched below the parapet and fingered their pikes and cutlasses. 'Aboli, don't fire until Daniel is out of the line.'

Suddenly Daniel threw down his burden, and turned back. He raced into the thick of the enemy, and scattered them with a great swipes of his cutlass. Then he ran to the wounded seaman, slung him over his shoulder and came on again towards where Hal crouched.

Hal glanced down the line of gunpits. Although the forward-pointing cannon were still banging away at the ships in the lagoon, every second culverin was directed into the forest, waiting for the moment to loose a storm of shot into the lines of attacking infantry.

'At such short range the shot will not spread, and they are keeping their spaces,' Aboli muttered.

'Schreuder has them well under control,' Hal agreed grimly. 'We can't hope to bring too many down with a single volley.'

'Schreuder!' Aboli's eyes narrowed. 'You did not tell me it was him.'

'There he is!' Hal pointed at the tall wigless figure striding towards them through the trees. His sash glittered and his moustache bristled as he urged his musketeers forward.

Aboli grunted, 'That one is the devil. We'll have trouble from him.' He thrust an iron bar under the culverin and turned it round a few degrees, trying to bring the sights to bear on the colonel.

'Stand still,' he urged, 'for just long enough to give me a shot.' But Schreuder was moving up and down the ranks of his men, waving them on. He was so close now that his voice carried to Hal as he snapped at his men, 'Keep your line! Keep the advance going. Steady now, hold your fire!'

His control over them was apparent in the determined but measured advance. They must have been aware of the line of waiting guns, but they came forward without wavering, holding their fire, not wasting the one fair shot they carried in their muskets.

They were close enough for Hal to make out their individual features. He knew that the Company recruited most of its troops in its eastern colonies, and this was apparent in the Asiatic faces of many of the advancing soldiers. Their eyes were dark and almond-shaped and their skins a deep amber.

Suddenly Hal realized that the broadsides from the two warships had ceased and snatched a glance over his shoulder. He saw that both the black frigate and the *Gull* had anchored a cable's length or so off the beach. Their guns were silent, and Hal realized that Cumbrae and the frigate captain must have arranged with Schreuder a code of signals. They had ceased firing for fear of hitting their own men.

That gives us a breathing space, he thought, and looked ahead again.

He saw that Daniel's band was much depleted: they had lost half their number, and the survivors were clearly exhausted by their foray and the fierce skirmishing. Their gait was erratic – many could barely drag themselves along. Their shirts were sodden with sweat and the blood from their wounds. One at a time they stumbled up and flopped over the parapet to lie panting in the bottom of the pit.

Daniel alone was indefatigable. He passed the wounded man over the parapet to the gunners and, so murderous was his mood, would have turned back and rushed at the enemy once more had not Hal stopped him. 'Get back here, you great ox! Let us soften them up with a little grape shot. Then you can have at them again.'

Aboli was still trying to line up the barrel on Schreuder's elusive shape. 'He is worth fifty of the others,' he muttered to himself, in his own language. Hal, though, was no longer paying him any heed, but trying anxiously to catch a glimpse of his father in the furthest emplacement, and take a lead from him.

'By God, he's letting them get too close!' he fretted. 'A longer shot would give the grape a chance to spread, but I'll not open fire before he gives the order.'

Then he heard Schreuder's voice again: 'Front rank! Prepare to fire!' Fifty men dropped obediently to their knees, right in front of the parapet, and grounded the butts of their muskets.

'Ready now, men!' Hal called softly to the sailors crowded around him. He had realized why his father had delayed the salvo of culverin until this moment: he had been waiting for the attackers to discharge their muskets, and then he would have them at a fleeting disadvantage as they tried to reload.

'Steady now!' Hal repeated. 'Wait for their volley!'

'Present your arms!' Schreuder's command rang out in the sudden silence. 'Take your aim!' The file of kneeling men lifted their muskets and aimed at the parapet. The blue smoke from the slow-match in the locks swirled about their heads, and they slitted their eyes to aim through it.

'Heads down!' Hal yelled.

The seamen in the gunpits ducked below the parapet, just as Schreuder roared, 'Fire!'

The long, ragged volley of musketry rattled down the file of kneeling men, and lead balls hissed over the heads of the gunners and thumped into the earth ramp. Hal leapt to his feet and looked down to the far end of the line of gunpits. He saw his father jump onto the parapet, brandishing his sword, and, although it was too far for his order to carry clearly, his gestures were unmistakable.

'Fire!' yelled Hal at the top of his lungs, and the line of guns erupted in a solid blast of smoke, flame and buzzing grape shot. It swept through the thin green line of Dutch infantry at point-blank range.

Directly in front of him Hal saw one of them hit by the full fury of the volley. He disintegrated in a burst of torn green serge and pink shredded flesh. His head spun high in the air, then fell back to earth and rolled like a child's ball. After that, all was obscured by the dense cloud of smoke, but though his ears still sang from the thunderous discharge, Hal could hear the screams and moans of the wounded resounding in the reeking blue fog.

'All together!' Hal shouted, as the smoke began to clear. 'Take the steel to them now, lads!'

After the mind-stopping blast of the guns their voices were thin and puny as they rose together from the gunpits. 'For Franky and King Charley!' they shouted, and the steel of cutlass and pike winked and twinkled as they jumped from the parapet and charged at the shattered rank of green uniforms.

Aboli was at Hal's left side and Daniel at his right as he led them into the mêlée. By unspoken agreement the two big men, one white the other black, placed protective wings over Hal but they had to run at their best speed to keep up with him.

Hal saw that his misgivings had been fully borne out. The volley of grape had not wrought the devastation among the Dutch infantry that they might have hoped for. The range had been too short: five hundred lead balls from each culverin had cut through them like a single charge of round shot. Men caught by the discharge had been obliterated, but for every one blown to nothingness, five others were unscathed.

These survivors were stunned and bewildered, their eyes dazed and their expressions blank. Most knelt blinking and shaking their heads, making no attempt to reload their empty muskets.

'Have at them, before they pull themselves together!' Hal screamed, and the seamen following him cheered again more lustily. In the face of the charge the musketeers started to recover. Some leapt to their feet, flung down their empty guns and drew their swords. One or two petty-officers had pistols tucked in their belts, which they drew and fired wildly at the seamen who rushed down on them. A few turned their backs and tried to flee back among the trees, but Schreuder was there to head them off. 'Back, you dogs and sons of dogs. Stand your ground like men!' They turned again, and formed up around him.

Every man of the *Resolution*'s crew who could still stand on his feet was in that charge – even the wounded hobbled along behind the rest, cheering as loudly as their comrades.

The two lines came together and immediately all was confusion. The solid rank of attackers split up into little groups of struggling men, mingled with the green serge coats of the Dutch. All around Hal fighting men were cursing, shouting and hacking at each other. His existence closed in, became a circle of angry, terrified faces and the clatter of steel weapons, most already dulled with new gore.

A green-jacket stabbed a long pike at Hal's face. He ducked under it and, with his left hand, seized the shaft just behind the spearhead. When the musketeer heaved back, Hal did not resist but used the impetus to launch his counter-attack, leading with the Neptune sword in his right hand. He aimed at the straining yellow throat above the high green collar, and his point slid in cleanly. As the man dropped the pike and fell back, Hal allowed the weight of his dropping body to pull him free of the blade.

Hal went smoothly back on guard, and glanced quickly around for his next opponent, but the charge of seamen had almost wiped out the file of musketeers. Few were left standing, and they were surrounded by clusters of attackers.

He felt his spirits soar. For the first time since he had seen those two ships sail into the lagoon, he felt that there was a chance that they might win this fight. In these last few minutes, they had broken up the main attack. Now they had only to deal with the sailors from the Dutch frigate and the *Gull* as they tried to come ashore.

'Well done, lads. We can do it! We can thrash them,' he shouted, and the seamen who heard him cheered again. Looking about him, he could see triumph on the face of every one of his men as they cut down the last of the green-jackets. Aboli was laughing and singing one of his pagan war-chants in a voice that carried over the din of the battle and inspired every man who heard it. They cheered him and themselves, rejoicing deliriously, in the ease of their victory.

Daniel's tall figure loomed at Hal's right side. His face and thick muscular arms were speckled with blood thrown from the wounds he had inflicted on his victims, and his mouth was wide open as he laughed ferociously, showing his carious teeth.

'Where is Schreuder?' Hal yelled, and Daniel sobered instantly. The laughter died as his mouth snapped shut and he glared around the quietening battlefield.

Then Hal's question was answered unequivocally by Schreuder himself. 'Second wave! Forward!' he bellowed lustily. He was standing on the edge of the forest, only a hundred paces from them. Hal, Aboli and Daniel started towards him, then came up short as another massed column of green-jackets poured out of the forest from behind where Schreuder stood.

'By God!' Hal breathed in despair. 'We haven't seen the half of them yet. The bastard has kept his main force in reserve.'

'There must be two hundred of the swine!' Daniel shook his head in disbelief.

'Quarter columns!' Schreuder shouted, and the advancing infantry changed their formation: they spread out behind him three deep in precisely spaced ranks. Schreuder led them forward at a trot, their ranks neatly dressed and their weapons advanced. Suddenly he held his sword high to halt them. 'First rank! Prepare to fire!' His men sank to their knees, while behind them the other two ranks stood steady.

'Present your arms!' A line of muskets was raised and levelled at the knots of dumbstruck seamen.

'Fire!' roared Schreuder.

The volley crashed out. From a distance of only fifty paces it swept through Hal's men, and almost every shot told. Men dropped and staggered as the heavy lead pellets struck. The line of Englishmen reeled and wavered. There was a chorus of yells – of pain and anger and fear.

'Charge!' Hal cried. 'Don't stand and let them shoot you down!' He lifted the Neptune sword high. 'Come on, lads. Have at them!'

On each side of him Aboli and Daniel started forward, but most of the others hung back. It was dawning on them that the fight was lost, and many looked back towards the safety of the gun emplacements. That was a dangerous signal. Once they glanced over their shoulders it was all up.

Second rank,' shouted Schreuder, 'prepare to fire!' Fifty more musketeers stepped forward, their weapons loaded and the matches burning. They walked through the gaps in the kneeling rank that had just fi ed, advanced another two paces in a brisk businesslike manner, then knelt.

'Present your arms!' Even Hal and the dauntless pair flanking him wavered as they gazed into the muzzles of fifty levelled muskets, while a moan of fear and horror went up from their men. They had never before faced such disciplined troops.

'Fire!' Schreuder dropped his sword, and the next volley slashed into the wavering seamen. Hal flinched as a ball passed his ear so closely that the wind of it flipped a curl of his hair into his eyes.

At his side Daniel gasped, 'I am struck!' jerked around like a marionette and sat down heavily. The volley had knocked over another dozen of the *Resolution*'s men and wounded as many more. Hal stooped to aid Daniel, but the big boatswain growled, 'Don't dither about here, you fool. Run! We're beaten, and there's another volley coming.'

As if to prove his words, Schreuder's next orders rang out close at hand. 'Third rank, present your arms!'

All around them the *Resolution*'s men who were still on their feet, broke and scattered in the face of the levelled muskets, running and staggering towards the gunpits.

'Help me, Aboli,' Hal shouted, and Aboli grabbed Daniel's other arm. Between them they hauled him to his feet and started back towards the beach.

'Fire!' Schreuder shouted, and at that instant, not waiting for a word from each other, Hal and Aboli flung themselves flat to earth, pulling Daniel down with them. The gunsmoke and the shot of the third volley crashed over their heads. Immediately they sprang up again and, dragging Daniel, ran for the shelter of the pits.

'Are you hit?' Aboli grunted at Hal, who shook his head, saving his breath. Few of his seamen were still on their feet. Only a handful had reached the line of gunpits and jumped into their shelter.

Half carrying Daniel, they staggered on, while behind them there were jubilant cheers, and the green-clad musketeers surged forward, brandishing their weapons. The three reached the gunpit and pulled Daniel down into it.

There was no need to ask of his wound for the whole of his left side ran red with blood. Aboli jerked the cloth from around his head, wadded it into a ball and stuffed it hurriedly into the front of Daniel's shirt.

'Hold that on the wound,' he told Daniel. 'Press as hard as you can.' He left him lying on the floor of the pit, and stood up beside Hal.

'Oh, sweet Mary!' Hal whispered. His sweat-streaked face was pale with horror and fury at what he beheld over the parapet. 'Look at those bloody butchers!'

As the green-jackets came clamouring forward, they paused only to stab the wounded seamen who lay in their path. Some of their victims rolled on their backs and lifted their bare hands to try to ward off the thrust, others screamed for mercy and tried to crawl away but, laughing and hooting, the musketeers ran after them, thrusting and hacking. This bloody work was quickly done, with Schreuder bellowing at them to close up and keep advancing.

In this moment of respite Sir Francis came dodging down the line and jumped into the pit beside his son.

'We are beaten, Father!' Hal said, dispiritedly, and they looked around at their dead and wounded. 'We have lost over half our men already.'

'Hal is right,' Aboli agreed. 'It is over. We must try to get away.'

'Where to?' Sir Francis asked, with a grim smile. 'That way?' He pointed through the trees towards the lagoon, where they saw boats speeding in towards the beach, driven by the oars of enemy sailors eager to join the fight.

Both the frigate and the *Gull* had lowered their boats which were crowded with men. Their cutlasses were drawn and the smoke of their matchlocks blued the air, trailing out across the surface of the water. They were shouting and cheering as wildly as the green-jackets in front.

As the first boats touched the beach the armed men spilled out of them and raced across the narrow strip of white sand. Howling with savage zeal, they stormed at the line of gunpits in which the empty culverins gaped silently, and the *Resolution*'s remaining crew cowered bewildered.

'We cannot hope for quarter, lads,' Sir Francis shouted. 'Look at what those bloodthirsty heathen do to those who try to yield to them.' With his sword he indicated the corpses of the murdered men that littered the ground in front of the guns. 'One more cheer for King Charley, and we'll go down fighting!'

The voices of his tiny band were small and hoarse with exhaustion as they dragged themselves over the parapet once more and sallied out to meet the charge of two hundred fresh and eager musketeers. Aboli was a dozen paces ahead, and hacked at the first green-jacket in his path. His victim went down under the blow but Aboli's blade snapped off at the hilt. He tossed it aside, stooped and picked up a pike from the dead hands of one of the fallen English seamen.

As Hal and Sir Francis ran up beside him, he hefted the long oak shaft and thrust at the belly of another musketeer who rushed at him with his sword held high. The pike-head caught him just under the ribs and transfixed him, standing out half an arm's length between his shoulder blades. The man struggled like a fish on a gaff, and the heavy shaft snapped off in Aboli's hands. He used the stub like a cudgel to strike down the third musketeer who rushed at him. Aboli looked around, grinning like a crazed gargoyle, his great eyes rolling in their sockets.

Sir Francis was engaged with a white Dutch sergeant, trading cut for thrust, their blades clanking and rasping against each other.

Hal killed a corporal with a single neat thrust into his throat, then glanced at Aboli. 'The men from the boats will be on us in an instant.'

They could hear wild cries in their rear as the enemy seamen swept over the gunpits, dealing out short shrift to the few men hiding there. Hal and Aboli did not need to look back – they both knew it was over.

'Farewell, old friend,' Aboli panted. 'They were good times. Would that they had lasted longer.'

Hal had no chance to reply, for at that moment a hoarse voice said in English, 'Hal Courtney, you bold puppy, your luck has just this moment ended.' Cornelius Schreuder pushed aside two of his own men and strode forward to face Hal.

'You and me!' he shouted and came in fast, leading with his right foot, taking the quick double paces of the master swordsman, recovering instantly from each of the swift series of thrusts with which he drove Hal backwards.

Hal was shocked anew at the power in those thrusts, and it taxed all his skill and strength to meet and parry them. The Toledo steel of his blade rang shrilly under the mighty blows and he felt despair as he realized that he could not hope to hold out against such magisterial force.

Schreuder's eyes were blue, cold and merciless. He anticipated each of Hal's moves, offering him a wall of glittering steel when once he attempted the riposte, beating his blade aside then coming on again remorselessly.

Close by, Sir Francis was absorbed in his own duel and had not seen Hal's deadly predicament. Aboli had only the stump of the pike-shaft in his hand – no weapon with which to take on a man like Cornelius Schreuder. He saw Hal, his immature strength already spent by his earlier exertions, wilting visibly before the overwhelming force of these attacks.

Aboli knew by Schreuder's expression when he judged his moment and gathered himself to make the kill. It was certain, inevitable, for Hal could never withstand the thunderbolt which was ready to loose itself upon him.

Aboli moved with the speed of a striking black cobra, faster even than Schreuder could send home his final thrust. He darted up behind Hal, and lifted the oak club. He struck Hal down with a crack over his ear, rapping him sharply across the temple.

Schreuder was amazed to have his victim drop to the ground, senseless, just as he was about to launch the death thrust. While he hesitated Aboli dropped the shattered pike-shaft and stood protectively over Hal's inert body.

'You cannot kill a fallen man, Colonel. Not on the honour of a Dutch officer.'

'You black Satan!' Schreuder roared with frustration. 'If I can't kill the puppy, at least I can kill you.'

Aboli showed him his empty hands, holding up his pale palms before Schreuder's eyes. 'I am unarmed,' he said softly.

'I would spare an unarmed Christian.' Schreuder glared. 'But you are a godless animal.' He drew back his blade and aimed the point at the centre of Aboli's chest, where the muscles glistened with sweat in the sunlight. Sir Francis Courtney stepped lightly in front of him, ignoring the colonel's blade.

'On the other hand, Colonel Schreuder, I am a Christian gentleman,' he said smoothly, 'and I yield myself and my men to your grace.' He reversed his own sword and proffered the hilt to Schreuder.

Schreuder glared at him, speechless with fury and frustration. He made no move to accept Sir Francis's sword, but placed the point of his weapon on the other man's throat and pricked him lightly. 'Stand aside, or by God I'll cut you down, Christian or heathen.' The knuckles of his right hand turned white on the hilt of his weapon as he prepared himself to make good the threat.

Another hail made him hesitate. 'Come now, Colonel, I am loath to interfere in a matter of honour. If you murder the brother of my bosom, Franky Courtney, then who will lead us to the treasure from your fine galleon the *Standvastigheid?*'

Schreuder's gaze flicked to the face of Cumbrae as he came striding up to them, the great blood-streaked claymore in his hand.

'The cargo?' Schreuder demanded. 'We have captured this pirate's nest. We will find the treasure is here.'

'Now don't you be so certain of that.' The Buzzard waggled his bushy red beard sadly. 'If I know my dear brother in Christ, Franky, he'll have squirrelled the best part of it away somewhere.' His eye glinted greedily from under his bonnet. 'No, Colonel, you are going to have to keep him alive, at least until we have been able to recompense ourselves with a handful of silver rix-dollars for doing God's work this day.'

When Hal recovered consciousness, he found his father kneeling over him. He whispered, 'What happened, Father? Did we win?' His father shook his head, without looking into his eyes, and made a fuss of wiping the sweat and soot from his son's face with a strip of grubby cloth torn from the hem of his own shirt.

'No, Hal. We did not win.' Hal looked beyond him, and it all came back. He saw that a pitiful few of the *Resolution*'s crew had survived. They were huddled together around where Hal lay, guarded by green-jackets with loaded muskets. The rest were scattered where they had fallen in front of the gunpits, or were draped in death upon the parapets.

He saw that Aboli was tending Daniel, binding up the wound in his chest with the red bandanna. Daniel was sitting up and seemed to have recovered somewhat, although clearly he had lost a great deal of blood. His face beneath the grime of battle was as white as the ashes of last night's camp-fire.

Hal turned his head and saw Lord Cumbrae and Colonel Schreuder standing nearby, in deep and earnest conversation. The Buzzard broke off at last and shouted an order to one of his men. 'Geordie, bring the slave chains from the *Gull*! We don't want Captain Courtney to leave us again.' The sailor hurried back to the beach, and the Buzzard and the colonel came to where the prisoners squatted under the muskets of their guards.

'Captain Courtney.' Schreuder addressed Sir Francis ominously. 'I am arresting you and your crew for piracy on the high seas. You will be taken to Good Hope to stand trial on those charges.'

'I protest, sir.' Sir Francis stood up with dignity. 'I demand that you treat my men with the consideration due to prisoners of war.'

'There is no war, Captain,' Schreuder told him icily. 'Hostilities between the Republic of Holland and England ceased under treaty some months ago.'

Sir Francis stared at him, aghast, while he recovered from the shock of this news. 'I was unaware that a peace had been concluded. I acted in good faith,' he said at last, 'but in any event I was sailing under a commission from His Majesty.'

'You spoke of this Letter of Marque during our previous meeting. Will you consider me presumptuous if I insist on having sight of the document?' Schreuder asked.

'My commission from His Majesty is in my sea-chest in my hut.' Sir Francis pointed into the stockade, where many of the huts had been destroyed by cannon fire. 'If you will allow me I will bring it to you.'

'Please don't discommode yourself, Franky my old friend.' The Buzzard clapped him on the shoulder. 'I'll fetch it for you.' He strode away and ducked into the low doorway of the hut that Sir Francis had indicated.

Schreuder rounded on him again. 'Where are you holding your hostages, sir? Governor van de Velde and his poor wife, where are they?'

'The Governor must still be in his stockade with the other hostages, his wife and the captain of the galleon. I have not seen them since the beginning of the fight.'

Hal stood up shakily, holding the cloth to his head. 'The Governor's wife has taken refuge from the fighting in a cave in the hillside, up there.'

'How do you know that?' Schreuder asked sharply.

'For her own safety, I led her there myself.' Hal spoke up boldly, avoiding his father's stern eye. 'I was returning from the cave when I ran into you in the forest, Colonel.'

Schreuder looked up the hill, torn by duty and the desire to rush to the aid of the woman whose rescue was, for him at least, the main object of this expedition. But at that moment the Buzzard swaggered out of the hut. He carried a roll of parchment tied with a scarlet ribbon. The royal seals of red wax dangled from it.

Sir Francis smiled with satisfaction and relief. 'There you have it, Colonel. I demand that you treat me and my crew as honourable prisoners, captured in a fair fight.'

Before he reached them, the Buzzard paused and unrolled the parchment. He held up the document at arm's length, and turned it so that all could see the curlicue script penned by some clerk of the Admiralty in black indian ink. At last, with a jerk of his head, he summoned one of his own seamen. He took the loaded pistol from the man's hand, and blew upon the burning match in the lock. Then he grinned at Sir Francis and applied the flame to the foot of the document in his hand.

Sir Francis stood appalled as the flame caught and the parchment began to curl and blacken as the pale yellow flame ran up it. 'By God, Cumbrae, you treacherous bastard!' He started forward, but the tip of Schreuder's blade lay on his chest.

'It would give me the greatest pleasure to thrust home,' he murmured. 'For your own sake, do not try my patience any further, sir.'

'That swine is burning my commission.'

'I can see nothing,' Schreuder told him, his back deliberately turned to the Buzzard. 'Nothing, except a notorious pirate standing before me with the blood of innocent men still warm and wet on his hands.'

Cumbrae watched the parchment burn, a great wide grin splitting his ginger whiskers. He passed the crackling sheet from hand to hand as the heat reached his fingertips, turning it to allow the flames to consume every scrap.

'I have heard you prate of your honour, sir,' Sir Francis flared at Schreuder. 'It seems that that is an illusory commodity.'

'Honour?' Schreuder smiled coldly. 'Do I hear a pirate speak to me of honour? It cannot be. Surely my ears play me false.'

Cumbrae allowed the flames to lick the tips of his fingers before he dropped the last blackened shred of the document to the earth and stamped on the ashes, crushing them to powder. Then he came up to Schreuder. 'I am afraid Franky's up to his tricks again. I can find no Letter of Marque signed by the royal hand.'

'I suspected as much.' Schreuder sheathed his sword. 'I place the prisoners in your charge, my lord Cumbrae. I must see to the welfare of the hostages.' He glanced at Hal. 'You will take me immediately to the place where you left the Governor's wife.' He looked round at his Dutch sergeant who stood attentively at his shoulder. 'Bind his hands behind his back and put a rope round his neck. Lead him on a leash like the mangy puppy he is.'

Colonel Schreuder delayed the rescue expedition while a search was conducted for his lost wig. His vanity would not allow him go to Katinka in a state of disarray. They found it lying in the forest through which he had chased Hal. It was covered with damp earth and dead leaves, but Schreuder beat it against his thigh then rearranged the curls carefully before placing it on his head. His beauty and dignity restored, he nodded at Hal. 'Show us the way!'

By the time they came out on the terrace in front of the cave Hal was a sorry object. Both hands were trussed behind his back and the sergeant had another rope round his neck. His face was blackened with dirt and gunsmoke and his clothing torn and smeared with blood diluted with his own sweat. Despite his exhaustion and distress, his concern was still for Katinka, and he felt a tremor of alarm as he went into the cave.

There was no sign of her. I cannot live if anything has happened to her, he thought, but aloud he told Schreuder, 'I left Mevrouw van de Velde here. No ill can have befallen her.'

'For your sake, you had better be correct in that.' The threat was more terrifying for having been uttered so softly. Then Schreuder raised his voice. 'Mevrouw van de Velde!' he called. 'Madam, you are safe. It is Colonel Schreuder, come to rescue you!'

The vines veiling the entrance to the cave rustled softly, and Katinka stepped out timidly from behind them. Her huge violet eyes were brimming with tears, and her face was pale and tragic, adding to her appeal. 'Oh!' she choked with emotion. Then, dramatically, she held out both hands towards Cornelius Schreuder. 'You came! You kept your promise!' She flew to him and stood on tiptoe to fling both her slim arms round his neck. 'I knew you would come! I knew you would never leave me to be humiliated and molested by these dreadful criminals.'

For one moment Schreuder was taken aback by her embrace, then he folded her in his arms, shielding and comforting her as she sobbed against the ribbons and sashes that covered his chest. 'If you have suffered the slightest affront, I swear I will avenge it a hundredfold.'

'My ordeal has been too terrible to relate,' she whimpered.

'This one?' Schreuder looked at Hal and demanded, 'Was he one of those who mistreated you?'

Katinka looked sideways at Hal, her cheek still pressed against Schreuder's chest. Her eyes narrowed viciously and a small sadistic smile twisted her luscious lips. 'He was the worst of all.' She sobbed. 'I cannot bring myself to tell you what disgusting things he said to me, or how he has harassed and humiliated me.' Her voice broke. 'I only thank God for the strength that he gave me to hold out against that man's importunity.'

Schreuder seemed to swell with the strength of his fury. Gently he set Katinka aside, then turned on Hal. He bunched his right fist and punched him hard in the side of his head. Hal was taken by surprise, and staggered back. Schreuder followed him swiftly, and his next punch caught Hal in the pit of his stomach, driving the wind from his lungs and doubling him over.

'How dare you insult and mistreat a high-born lady?' Schreuder was shaking with fury. He had lost all control of his temper.

Hal's forehead was almost touching his knees, as he gasped and wheezed to recover his breath. Schreuder aimed a kick at his face, but Hal saw it coming and jerked his head aside. The boot glanced off his shoulder, and sent him reeling backwards.

Schreuder's rage boiled over. 'You are not fit to lick the soles of this lady's slippers.' He braced himself to punch again, but Hal was too quick. Although his hands were tied behind his back he stepped forward to meet Schreuder and aimed a kick at his groin, but because he was hampered by his bonds the kick lacked power.

Schreuder was more startled than hurt. 'By God, puppy, you go too far!' Hal was still off-balance, and Schreuder's next blow knocked his legs out from under him. He collapsed and Schreuder set on him, using both feet, his boots thumping into Hal's curled-up body. Hal grunted and rolled over, trying desperately to avoid the barrage of kicks that slogged into him.

'Yes! Oh, yes!' Katinka trilled with excitement. 'Punish him for what he has done to me.' She goaded Schreuder, driving his violent temper to its limit. 'Make him suffer, as I was made to do.'

Hal knew in his heart that she was forced to reject him now in front of this man and even in his hurt he forgave her. He doubled over to protect his more vulnerable parts, taking most of the kicks on his shoulders and thighs, but he could not ride them all. One caught him in the side of the mouth and blood trickled down his chin.

Katinka squeaked and clapped her hands to see it flow. 'I hate him. Yes! Hurt him! Smash his pretty, insolent face!' But the blood seemed to bring Schreuder to his senses again. With an obvious effort, he curbed his wild temper and stepped back, breathing heavily and still trembling with rage. 'That is just a small taste of what is in store for him. Believe me, Mevrouw, he will be paid out in full when we reach Good Hope.' He turned back to Katinka and bowed. 'Please let me take you back to the safety of the ship that waits in the bay.'

Katinka gave a pathetic little cry, her fingers on her soft pink lips. 'Oh, Colonel, I fear I shall swoon.' She swayed on her feet, and Schreuder leapt forward to steady her. She leant against him. 'I do not think my legs can carry me.'

He swept her into his arms, and set off down the hill carrying her lightly. She clung to him as though she were a child being taken to her bed.

'Come along, gallows-bait!' The sergeant yanked Hal to his feet by the loop around his neck, and led him, still bleeding, down towards the camp. 'Better for you had the Colonel finished you off here and now. The executioner at Good Hope is famous. He's an artist, he is.' He tugged hard on the rope. 'He'll have some sport with you, I'll warrant.'

A pinnace brought the chains to the beach where the survivors of the *Resolution*'s crew, both wounded and unharmed, were squatting under guard in the blazing sun.

They carried the first set to Sir Francis. 'It's good to see you again, Captain.' The sailor with the irons in his hands stood over him. 'I have thought of you every day since last we met.'

'I, on the other hand, have never given you another thought, Sam Bowles.' Sir Francis barely glanced at him, but scorn was in his voice.

'It's Boatswain Sam Bowles, now. His lordship has promoted me,' said Sam, with an insolent grin.

'Then I wish the Buzzard joy of his new boatswain. 'Tis a marriage made in heaven.'

'Hold out your hands, Captain. Let's see how high and mighty you are with bracelets of iron on you,' Sam Bowles gloated. 'By Christ, you'll never know how much pleasure this gives me.' He snapped the shackles onto Sir Francis's wrists and ankles, and with the key screwed them so tight that they bit into his flesh. 'I hope that fits you as well as your fancy cloak ever did.' He stepped back and spat suddenly into Sir Francis's face, then burst out laughing. 'I give you my solemn promise that, the day they reef your top sails for you, I will be at the Parade at Good Hope to wish you Godspeed. I wonder what way they will send you. Do you think it will be the fire, or will they hang and draw you?' Sam chuckled again and went on to Hal. 'Good day to you, young Master Henry. It's your humble servant Boatswain Sam Bowles come to tend to your needs.'

'I did not get a glimpse of your yellow hide during the fighting,' Hal said quietly. 'Where were you hiding this time?' Sam flushed and swung the handful of heavy chains against Hal's head. Hal recovered and stared coldly into his eyes. Sam would have struck again, but a huge black hand reached up and seized his wrist. He looked down into the smoky eyes of Aboli, who crouched beside Hal. Aboli said not a word but Sam Bowles stayed the blow. He could not hold that murderous stare, and dropped his eyes, keeping them averted as he knelt hurriedly to clamp the chains on Hal's limbs.

He stood up and came to Aboli, who watched him with the same expressionless gaze as he hurriedly screwed the shackles onto him, then passed on to where Big Daniel lay. Daniel winced but uttered no sound as Sam Bowles tugged brutally at his arms. The bullet wound had stopped bleeding, but with this rough treatment it opened again and began to weep watery blood from under the red headcloth that Aboli had used to bandage it. The blood trickled over his chest and dripped into the sand.

When they were all shackled together they were ordered to their feet. Supporting him between them, Hal and Aboli half carried Daniel as they were led in a file to one of the larger trees. Again they were forced to sit while the end of the chain was passed around the trunk and made fast with two heavy iron padlocks.

There were only twenty-six survivors from the *Resolution*'s complement. Amongst these were four ex-slaves, of which Aboli was one. Nearly all were at least lightly wounded, but four, including Daniel, were gravely injured and must be in danger of their lives.

Ned Tyler had received a deep cutlass slash in his thigh. Hampered by their manacles, Hal and Aboli bound it up with another strip of cloth salvaged from the shirt of one of the dead men who littered the battlefield like flotsam on the windswept beach.

Parties of green-jacketed musketeers were working under their Dutch sergeants to gather up the corpses. Dragging them by the heels to a clearing among the trees, they stripped the bodies and searched them for the silver coins and other items of value that had been their share of the booty from the *Standvastigheid*.

A pair of petty-officers painstakingly searched through the discarded clothing, ripping out seams and tearing the soles off boots. Another team of three men, their sleeves rolled high and their fingers dipped in a pot of grease, probed the body orifices of the corpses, searching for any valuables that might be tucked away in these traditional hiding places.

The recovered booty was thrown into an empty water cask, over which a white sergeant stood with a loaded pistol as the keg filled slowly with a rich booty. When the ghoulish trio had finished with the naked corpses another gang dragged them away and threw them onto tall funeral pyres. Fuelled by dry logs the flames reached so high that they shrivelled the green leaves on the tall trees that surrounded the clearing. The smoke of charring flesh was sweet and nauseating, like burnt pork fat.

In the meantime, Schreuder and Cumbrae, assisted by Limberger, the captain of the galleon, were taking stock of the spice barrels. They were as officious as tax collectors, with their lists and books, checking the contents and weights of the recovered goods against the original ship's manifest, and marking the staves of the kegs with white chalk.

When they had made their tallies other gangs of seamen rolled the great barrels down to the beach and loaded them into the largest pinnace to be taken out to the galleon, which lay anchored out in the channel, under her new mainmast and rigging. The work went on all that night by the light of lantern and bonfire and the yellow flames of the cremation pyres.

As the hours passed Big Daniel became feverish. His skin was hot, and at times he raved. The bandage had at last staunched his wound, and under it a soft crusty scab had begun to form over the ugly puncture. But the skin around it was swollen and turning livid.

'The ball is still in there,' Hal whispered to Aboli. 'There is no wound in his back for it to have left his body.'

Aboli grunted, 'If we try to cut it out, we will kill him. From the angle which it entered, it must lie close to his heart and lungs.'

'I fear it will mortify.' Hal shook his head.

'He is strong as a bull.' Aboli shrugged. 'Perhaps strong enough to defeat the demons.' Aboli believed that all sickness was caused by demons that had invaded the blood. It was a groundless superstition, but Hal humoured him in his belief.

'We should cauterize the wounds of all the men with hot tar.' This was the sailor's cure-all and Hal pleaded in Dutch with the Hottentot guards to bring one of the pitch pots from the carpenter's shop in the stockade, but they ignored him.

It was after midnight before they saw Schreuder again. He strode out of the darkness and went directly to where Sir Francis lay chained to the others at the foot of the tree. Like the rest of his men, he was exhausted but able to snatch only brief moments of broken sleep, disturbed by the restless din and movements of the work gangs and the weak cries and groans of the wounded.

'Sir Francis.' Schreuder stooped and shook him fully awake. 'May I trouble you for a few minutes of your time?' From the tone of his voice, it seemed that his temper was on an even keel.

Sir Francis sat up. 'First, Colonel, may I trouble you for a little compassion? None of my men has had a drop of water since yesterday afternoon. As you can see, four are grievously wounded.'

Schreuder frowned, and Sir Francis guessed that he had not given orders for the prisoners to be deliberately mistreated. He himself had never thought that Schreuder was a brutal or sadistic man. His savage behaviour earlier had almost certainly been caused by his excitable nature, and by the strain and exigencies of battle. Now Schreuder turned to the guards and gave orders for water and food to be brought to the prisoners, and sent a sergeant to find the chest of medical supplies in Sir Francis's shattered hut.

While they waited for his orders to be carried out, Schreuder paced back and forth in the sand, his chin on his breast and his hands clasped behind his back. Hal suddenly sat up straighter.

'Aboli,' he whispered. 'The sword.'

Aboli grunted as he realized that on Schreuder's sword belt hung the inlaid and embossed Neptune sword of Hal's knighthood, that had once belonged to his grandfather. Aboli laid a calming hand on the young man's shoulder to prevent him accosting Schreuder, and said softly, 'The spoils of war, Gundwane. It is lost to you, but at least a real warrior still wears it.' Hal subsided, realizing the cruel logic of the other man's advice.

At last Schreuder turned back to Sir Francis. 'Captain Limberger and I have tallied the spice and timber cargo that you have stored in the godowns, and we find that most of it is accounted for and still intact. The shortfall would probably be due to seawater damage sustained during the taking of the galleon. I have been told that one of your culverin balls pierced the main hold, and part of the cargo was flooded.'

'I am pleased,' Sir Francis nodded with weary irony, 'that you have been able to recover all of your Company's property.'

'Alas, that is not the case, Sir Francis, as you are well aware. There is still a large part of the galleon's cargo missing.' He paused as the sergeant returned, and gave him an order. 'Take the chains off the black and the boy. Let them water the others.' Some men were following with a water cask, which they placed at the foot of the tree. Hal and Aboli immediately began to pour fresh water for their wounded, and all of them drank, gulping down the precious stuff with closed eyes and bobbing throats.

The sergeant reported to Colonel Schreuder, 'I have found the surgeon's instruments.' He displayed the canvas roll. 'But, Mijnheer, it contains sharp knives, which could be used as weapons, and the contents of the pitch pots could be used against my men.'

Schreuder looked down at Sir Francis where he squatted, haggard and dishevelled, beside the tree-trunk. 'Do I have your word as a gentleman not to use these medical supplies to harm my men?'

'You have my solemn word,' Sir Francis agreed.

Schreuder nodded at the sergeant. 'Give all of it into Sir Francis's charge,' he ordered, and the sergeant handed over the small chest of medical supplies, the tar pot and a bolt of clean cloth that could be used as bandages.

'Now, Captain,' Schreuder picked up the conversation where he had left off, 'we have retrieved the plundered spice and timber, but more than half the coin and all of the gold bullion that was in the hold of the *Standvastigheid* is still missing.'

'The spoils were distributed to my crew.' Sir Francis smiled humourlessly. 'I do not know what they have done with their share, and most are too dead to be able to enlighten us.'

'We have recovered what I calculate must be the greater part of your crew's share.' Schreuder gestured at the barrel containing the valuables collected in such macabre fashion from the battlefield casualties. It was being carried by a party of seamen down to a waiting pinnace and guarded by Dutch officers with drawn swords. 'My officers have searched the huts of your men in the stockade, but there is still no sign of the other half.'

'Much as I would like to be of service to you, I am unable to account to you for the missing portion,' Sir Francis told him quietly. At this denial, Hal looked up from ministering to the wounded men, but his father never glanced in his direction.

'Lord Cumbrae believes that you have cached the missing treasure,' Schreuder remarked. 'And I agree with him.'

'Lord Cumbrae is a famous liar and cheat,' Sir Francis said. 'And you, sir, are mistaken in your belief.'

'Lord Cumbrae is of the opinion that were he given the opportunity to question you in person he would be able to extract from you the whereabouts of the missing treasure. He is anxious to try to persuade you to reveal what you know. It is only with the greatest difficulty that I have been able to prevent him doing so.'

Sir Francis shrugged. 'You must do as you feel fit, Colonel, but unless I am a poor judge, the torture of captives is not something that a soldier like you would condone. I am grateful for the compassion that you have shown my wounded.'

Schreuder's reply was interrupted by an agonized scream from Ned Tyler as Aboli poured a ladleful of steaming tar into the sword gash in his thigh. As the scream subsided into sobbing, Schreuder went on smoothly. 'The tribunal that tries you for piracy at the fort at Good Hope will be headed by our new governor. I have serious doubts that Governor Petrus Jacobus van de Velde will feel himself so constrained to mercy as I am.' Schreuder paused and then went on, 'By the way, Sir Francis, I am reliably informed that the executioner employed by the Company at Good Hope prides himself on his skills.'

'I will have to give the Governor and his executioner the same answer I gave you, Colonel.'

Schreuder squatted on his heels and lowered his voice to a conspiratorial, almost friendly, tone. 'Sir Francis, in our short acquaintance I have formed a high regard for you as a warrior, a sailor and a gentleman. If I were to give evidence before the tribunal that your Letter of Marque existed, and that you were a legitimate privateer, the outcome of your trial might go differently.'

'You must have faith in Governor van de Velde that I lack,' Sir Francis replied. 'I wish I could further your career for you by producing the missing bullion, but I cannot help you, sir. I know nothing of its whereabouts.'

Schreuder's face stiffened as he stood up. 'I have tried to help you. I regret that you reject my offer. However, you are correct, sir. I do not have the stomach to have you put to the question under torture. What is more, I will prevent Lord Cumbrae from taking that task upon himself. I will simply do my duty and deliver you to the mercy of the tribunal at Good Hope. I beg you, sir, will you not reconsider?'

Sir Francis shook his head. 'I regret I cannot help you, sir.'

Schreuder sighed. 'Very well. You and your men will be taken aboard the *Gull of Moray* as soon as she is ready to sail tomorrow morning. The frigate *Sonnevogel* has other duties in the Indies and she will sail at the same time to go her separate way. The *Standvastigheid* will remain here under her true commander, Captain Limberger, to take on her cargo of spice and timber before she resumes her interrupted voyage to Amsterdam.'

He turned on his heel and disappeared back into the shadows, in the direction of the spice godown.

When they were aroused by their captors the following morning, four of the wounded, including Daniel and Ned Tyler, were unable to walk and their comrades were forced to carry them. The slave chains allowed little freedom of movement, and it was a clumsy line of men that shambled down to the beach. Each step was hampered by the clanking shackles, so that they could not lift their feet high enough to step over the gunwale of the pinnace, and had to be shoved in by their guards.

When the pinnace tied onto the foot of the rope ladder down the side of the *Gull*, the climb that faced the chained men to the deck was daunting and dangerous. Sam Bowles stood at the entryport above them. One of the guards in the pinnace shouted up to him, 'Can we loose the prisoners' chains, Boatswain?'

'Why do you want to do that?' Sam called down.

'The wounded can't help themselves. The others will not be able to hoist them. They'll not be able to make it up the ladder otherwise.'

'If they don't make it they're the ones that will be the poorer for it,' Sam answered. 'His lordship's orders. The manacles must stay on.'

Sir Francis led the climb, his every movement hampered by the string of men linked behind him. The four wounded men, moaning in their delirium, were dead weights that had to be dragged up by force. Big Daniel, in particular, tested all their strength. If they had allowed him to slip from their grasp, he would have plummeted into the pinnace and pulled the whole string of twenty-six men with him, almost certainly capsizing the small boat. Once in the lagoon, the weight of their heavy iron chains would have plucked them all to the bottom, four fathoms down.

If it had not been for the bull strength of Aboli, they would never have reached the deck of the *Gull*. Yet even he was completely played out when, at last, he heaved Daniel's inert form over the gunwale and collapsed beside him on the scrubbed white deck. They all lay there gasping and panting, to be roused at last by a tingling peal of laughter.

With an effort Hal raised his head. On the *Gull*'s quarterdeck, under a canvas awning, a breakfast table was laid. The glass was crystal and the silverware sparkled in the early sunlight. He smelt the heady aroma of bacon, fresh eggs and hot biscuit rising from the silver chafing dish.

At the head of the table sat the Buzzard. He raised his glass towards that sprawling heap of human bodies in the waist of his ship.

'Welcome aboard, gentlemen, and your astounding good health!' He drank the toast in whisky, then wiped his ginger whiskers with a damask napkin. 'The finest quarters on board have been prepared for you. I wish you a pleasant voyage.'

Katinka van de Velde laughed again, a musical sound. She sat at the Buzzard's left hand. Her head was bare, her golden curls piled high, her violet eyes wide and innocent in the flawless oval of her powdered face, and a beauty spot drawn carefully at the corner of her pretty, painted mouth.

The Governor sat opposite his wife. He stopped in the act of lifting a silver fork loaded with crisped bacon and cheese to his mouth, but continued to chew. A yellow drop of egg yolk escaped from between his pendulous lips and ran down his chin as he guffawed. 'Do not despair, Sir Francis. Remember your family motto. I am sure you will endure.' He stuffed the forkful into his mouth, and spoke through it. 'This is really excellent fare, fresh from Good Hope. What a pity you cannot join us.'

'How thoughtful of your lordship to provide us with entertainment. Will these troubadours sing for us, or will they amuse us with more acrobatics?' Katinka asked in Dutch, then made a pretty little *moue* and tapped Cumbrae's arm with her painted Chinese fan.

At that moment Big Daniel rolled his head from side to side, thumping it on the planks, and cried out in delirium. The Buzzard howled with laughter. 'As you see, they try their best, madam, but their repertoire does not suit every taste.' He nodded at Sam Bowles. 'Pray show them to their quarters, Master Samuel, and make sure they are well cared for.'

With a knotted rope end, Sam Bowles whipped the prisoners to their feet. They lifted their wounded and shambled down the companion ladder. In the depths of the hull, below the main hold, stretched the low slave deck. When Sam Bowles lifted the hatch that opened into it, the stench that rose to greet them made even him recoil. It was the essence of the suffering of hundreds of doomed souls who had languished here.

The headspace in this deck was no higher than a man's waist so they were forced to crawl down it and drag the wounded men with them. Iron rings were set into the bulkhead, bolted into the heavy oak beam that ran the length of the hold. Sam and his four mates crawled down after them and shackled their chains into the ringbolts. When they had finished, the captives were laid out like herrings in a barrel, side by side, secured at wrist and ankle, only just able to sit up, but unable to turn over or to move their limbs more than the few inches that their chains allowed.

Hal lay with his father on one side and the inert hulk of Big Daniel on the other. Aboli was on the far side of Daniel and Ned Tyler beyond him.

When the last man had been secured, Sam crawled back to the hatch and smirked down at them. 'Ten days to Good Hope with this wind. One pint of water a day for each man, and three ounces of biscuit, when I remember to bring it to you. You're free to shit and piss where you lie. See you at Good Hope, my lovelies.'

He slammed the hatch closed, and they heard him on the far side hammering the locking pins into their seats. When the mallet blows ceased, the sudden quiet was frightening. At first the darkness was complete, but then as their eyes adjusted they could just make out the dark forms of their mates packed around them.

Hal looked for the source of light and found a small iron grating set into the deck directly above his head. Even without the bars, it would not have been large enough to admit the head of a grown man, and he discounted it immediately as a possible escape route. At least it provided a whiff of fresh air.

The stench was hard to bear and they all gasped in the suffocating atmosphere. It smelt like a bear-pit. Big Daniel moaned, and the sound loosened their tongues. They started to talk all at once.

'Love of God, it smells like a shit-house in apricot season down here.'

'Do you think there's a chance of escaping from here, Captain?'

'Of course there is, my bully,' one of the men answered for Sir Francis. 'When we reach Good Hope.'

'I would give half my share of the richest prize that ever sailed the seven seas for five minutes alone with Sam Bowles.'

'All my share for the another five with that bloody Cumbrae.'

'Or that cheese-headed bastard, Schreuder.'

Suddenly Daniel gabbled, 'Oh, Mother, I see your lovely face. Come, kiss your little Danny.' The plaintive cry disheartened them, and the silence of despair fell over the dark, noisome slave deck. Gradually they sank into a torpor of despondency, broken occasionally by the groans of delirium and the clank of the links as they tried to find a more comfortable position.

Slowly, the passage of time lost all significance, and none were sure whether it was night or day when the sound of the anchor capstan from the upper deck reverberated through the hull and they heard the faint shouts of the petty-officers relaying the orders to get the *Gull* under way.

Hal tried to judge the ship's course and direction by the momentum and heel of the hull, but soon lost track. It was only when the *Gull* plunged suddenly and began to work with a light, frolicsome motion to the scend of the open sea that he knew they had left the lagoon and passed out through the heads.

For hour after hour the *Gull* battled with the sou'-easter to make good her offing. The motion threw them back and forth on the bare planks, sliding on their backs the few inches that their chains allowed before coming up hard on their manacles, and then sliding back the other way. It was a great relief when, at last, she settled into an easier reach.

'There now. That's a sight better.' Sir Francis spoke for them all. 'The Buzzard has made his offing. He has come about and we are running free with the sou'-easter abaft our beam, heading west for the Cape.'

As time passed, Hal made some estimate of the passage of the days by the intensity of light from the grating above his head. During the long nights there was a crushing blackness in the slave deck, like that at the bottom of a coal shaft. Then the softest light filtered down on him as the dawn broke, which grew in strength until he could make out the shape of Aboli's dark round head beyond the lighter face of Big Daniel.

However, even at noon the further reaches of the slave deck were hidden in darkness, from which the sighs and moans, and the occasional whispers of the other men echoed eerily between the oaken bulkheads. Then again the light faded away into that utter darkness to mark the passing of another day.

On the third morning a whispered message was passed from man to man. 'Timothy O'Reilly is dead.' He was one of the wounded: he had taken a sword thrust in his chest from one of the green-jackets.

'He was a good man.' Sir Francis voiced his epitaph. 'May God rest his soul. I would that we were able to afford him a Christian burial.' By the fifth morning, Timothy's corpse added to the miasma of decay and rot that permeated the slave deck and filled their lungs with each breath.

Often, as Hal lay in a stupor of despair, the scampering grey rats, big as rabbits, clambered over his body. Their sharp claws raised painful scratches across his bare skin. In the end he gave up the hopeless task of trying to drive them away by kicking and hitting out at them, and set himself to endure the discomfort. It was only when one sank its sharp, curved teeth into the back of his hand that he shouted and managed to seize it, squeaking shrilly, by the throat and throttle it with his bare hands.

When Daniel cried out in pain beside him, he realized then that the rats had found him also, and that he was unable to defend himself from their attacks. After that he and Aboli took turns at sitting up and trying to keep the voracious rodents away from the unconscious man.

Their fetters prevented them from squatting over the narrow gutter that ran along the foot of the bulkhead, designed to carry away their sewage. Every once in a while Hal heard the spluttering release as one of the men voided where he lay, and immediately afterwards came the fetid stench of fresh faeces in the confined and already musty spaces.

When Daniel emptied his bladder, the warm liquid spread to flood the planks under Hal and soaked into his shirt and breeches. There was nothing he could do to avoid it, except lift his head from the deck.

Most days, around what Hal judged to be noon, the locking pins on the hatch were suddenly driven out with thunderous mallet blows. When it was lifted the feeble light that flooded the hold almost blinded them, and they lifted their hands, heavy with chains, to shield their eyes.

'I have a special posset for you merry gentlemen today,' Sam Bowles's voice sang out. 'A mug of water from our oldest barrels, with a few little beasties swimming in it and just a drop of my spittle to give it flavour.' They heard him spit heartily, and then bray with laughter before he handed down the first pewter mug. Each mugful had to be passed along the deck, from hand to clumsy manacled hand, and when one was spilled there was none to replace it.

'One for each of our gentlemen. That's twenty-six mugs, and no more,' Sam Bowles told them cheerily.

Big Daniel was now too far gone to drink unaided, and Aboli had to lift his head while Hal dribbled water between his lips. The other sick men had to be treated in the same way. Much of the water was lost when it ran out of their slack mouths, and it was a long-drawn-out business. Sam Bowles lost patience before they were half through. 'None of you want any more? Well, I'll be off, then.' And he slammed the hatch closed and drove home the pins, leaving most of the captives pleading vainly, through parched throats and flaking lips for their share. But he was unrelenting, and they were forced to wait another day for their next ration.

After that Aboli filled his own mouth with water from the mug, placed his lips over Daniel's and forced it into the unconscious man's mouth. They did the same for the other wounded. This method was quick enough to satisfy even Sam Bowles, and less of the precious fluid was lost.

Sam Bowles chuckled when one of the men shouted up at him, 'For God's sweet sake, Boatswain, there's a dead man down here. Timothy O'Reilly is stinking to the high heavens. Can you not smell him?'

He answered, 'I'm glad you told me. That means he will not be using his water ration. It will be only twenty-five mugs I'll be serving from tomorrow.'

Daniel was dying. He no longer groaned or thrashed about in delirium. He lay like a corpse. Even his bladder had dried up and no longer emptied itself spontaneously on the reeking planks on which they lay. Hal held his head and whispered to him, trying to cajole him into staying alive. 'You can't give up now. Hold on just a while longer and we will be at the Cape before you know it. All the sweet fresh water you can drink, pretty slave girls to nurse you. Just think on that, Danny.'

At noon, on what he thought must be their sixth day at sea, Hal called across to Aboli, 'I have something to show you here. Give me your hand.' He took Aboli's fingers and guided them over Daniel's ribs. The skin was so hot that it was almost painful to the touch, and the flesh so wasted that the ribs stood out like barrel staves.

Hal rolled Daniel over as far as his chains would allow, and directed Aboli's fingers onto his shoulder blade. 'There. Can you feel that lump?'

Aboli grunted, 'I can feel it, but I cannot see.' He was so restricted by his chains that he could not look over the bulk of Daniel's inert body.

'I'm not sure, but I think I know what it is.' Hal put his face closer and strained his eyes in the dim light. 'There is a swelling the size of a walnut. It's black like a bruise.' He touched it gently, and even this light pressure made Daniel groan and fret against his bonds.

'It must be very tender.' Sir Francis had roused himself and leaned as close as he was able. 'I cannot see well. Where is it?'

'In the middle of his shoulder blade,' Hal answered. 'I believe that it is the musket ball. It has passed clean through his chest and is lying here under the skin.'

'Then that is what is killing him,' Sir Francis said. 'It is the seat and source of the mortification that is eating him up.'

'If we had a knife,' Hal murmured, 'we could try to cut it out. But Sam Bowles took the medical chest.'

Aboli said, 'Not before I hid one of the knives.' He searched in the waistband of his breeches and held up the thin blade. It glinted softly in the faint light from the grating above Hal's head. 'I was waiting for a chance to cut Sam's throat with it.'

'We must risk cutting,' Sir Francis told him. 'If it stays in his body the ball will kill him more certainly than the scalpel.'

'I cannot see to make the cut from where I lie,' Aboli said. 'You will have to do it.'

There was a scuffling and clinking of the chain links, then Sir Francis grunted, 'My chains are too short. I cannot lay a finger on him.'

They were all silent for a short while, then Sir Francis said, 'Hal.'

'Father,' Hal protested, 'I do not have the knowledge or the skill.'

'Then Daniel will die,' Aboli said flatly. 'You owe him a life, Gundwane. Here, take the knife.'

In Hal's hand the knife seemed heavy as a bar of lead. His mouth dry with dread, he tested the edge of the blade against the ball of his thumb and found it dulled by much use.

'It is blunt,' he protested.

'Aboli is right, my son.' Sir Francis laid a hand on Hal's shoulder and squeezed. 'You are Daniel's only chance.'

Slowly Hal reached out with his left hand, and felt the hard lump in Daniel's hot flesh. It moved under his fingers, and he felt it grate softly against the bone of the shoulder blade.

The pain roused Daniel, and he struggled against his chains. He shouted, 'Help me, Jesus. I have sinned against God and man. The devil comes for me. He is dark. Everything grows dark.'

'Hold him, Aboli,' Hal whispered. 'Hold him still.'

Aboli wrapped his arms around Daniel, like the coils of a great black python. 'Do it,' he said. 'Do it swiftly.'

Hal leaned in close to Daniel, as close as his chains would let him, his face a hand's breadth from the other man's back. Now he could see the swelling more clearly. The skin was stretched so tightly over it that it was glossy and purple as an overripe plum. He placed the fingers of his left hand on each side of it and spread the skin even tighter.

He took a deep breath, and placed the tip of the scalpel against the swelling. He steeled himself, counting silently to three, then pressed down with the strength of a trained sword arm. He felt the blade slide deep into Daniel's back, and then strike something hard and unyielding, metal on metal.

Daniel shrieked and then went slack in Aboli's enfolding arms. A spurt of purple and yellow pus erupted from the deep scalpel cut. Hot and thick as carpenter's glue, it struck Hal in the mouth and splattered across his chin. The smell was worse than all the other odours of the slave deck, and Hal's gorge rose to scald the back of his throat. He swallowed back his own vomit, and wiped the pus from his face with the back of his arm, before he could bring himself to peer gingerly once more at the wound.

Black pus still bubbled from it, but he saw extraneous matter caught in the mouth of the fresh cut. He dug at it with the tip of the scalpel, and freed a plug of dark and fibrous material, in which bone chips from the shattered scapula were mingled with jellied blood and pus.

'It's a piece of Danny's jacket,' he gasped. 'The ball must have pulled it into the wound.'

'Have you found the ball?' Sir Francis demanded.

'No, it must still be in there.'

He probed deeper into the wound. 'Yes. There it is.'

'Can you get it out?'

For a few minutes Hal worked in silence, thankful that Daniel was unconscious and did not have to suffer during this crude exploration. The flow of pus dwindled and now fresh clean blood oozed from the dark wound.

'I can't get it with the knife. It keeps slipping away,' he whispered. He put aside the blade and pushed his finger into Daniel's hot, living flesh. Breath rasping with horror, he worked in deeper and still deeper, until he could get his fingertip behind the lump of lead.

'There!' he exclaimed suddenly, as the musket ball popped out of the wound and dropped onto the planks with a thump. It was deformed by its violent contact with bone, and there was a mirror-bright smear in the soft lead. He stared at it in vast relief, then snatched his finger from the wound.

It was followed by another soft rush of pus and lumpy foreign matter. 'There is the musket wad.' He gagged. 'I think everything is out now.' He looked down at his besmeared hands. The stench from them struck him like a blow in the face.

For a while they were all silent. Then Sir Francis whispered, 'Well done, Hal!'

'I think he is dead,' Hal answered, in a small voice. 'He is so still.'

Aboli released Daniel from his grip, then groped down his naked chest. 'No, he is alive. I can feel his heart. Now, Gundwane, you must wash out the wound for him.'

Between them they dragged Daniel's inert body to the limit of his fetters and Hal half knelt above him. He opened his filthy breeches and dehydrated by the limited ration of water, strained to squirt a weak stream of urine into the wound. It was enough to wash out the last rotting shreds of wadding and corruption. Hal used the last few drops of his own water to cleanse some of the filth from his hands and then fell back, spent by the effort.

'Done like a man, Gundwane,' Aboli told him, and offered Hal the red headcloth, black and crackling with dried blood and pus. 'Use this to staunch the wound. It is all we have.'

While Hal bandaged the wound, Daniel lay like a corpse. He no longer groaned or fought against his chains.

Three days later, as Hal leaned over to give him water, Daniel suddenly reached up, pushed away his head and took the mug from Hal's hands. He drained it in three long swallows. Then he belched thunderously and said, in a weak but lucid voice, 'By God, that was good. I'll have a drop more of that.'

Hal was so delighted and relieved that he handed him his own ration and watched him drink it. By the following day, Daniel was able to sit up as much as his chains would allow.

'Your surgery would have killed a dozen ordinary mortals,' Sir Francis murmured, as he watched Big Daniel's recovery with amazement, 'but Daniel Fisher thrives upon it.'

On the ninth day of their voyage Sam Bowles opened the hatch and sang out cheerily, 'Good news for you, gentlemen. Wind has played us false these last fifty leagues. His lordship reckons it will be another five days before we round the Cape. So your pleasure cruise will last a little longer.'

Few had the strength or interest to rail at this dread news, but they reached up for the pewter water mug with frantic hands. When the daily ceremony of watering was done, this time Sam Bowles altered the routine. Instead of slamming the hatch closed for another day, he stuck his head down and called, 'Captain Courtney, sir, his lordship's compliments, and if you have no previous engagement, he would be obliged if you would take dinner with him.' He scrambled down into the slave deck and, with two of his mates to help him, unscrewed Sir Francis's shackles from his wrists and ankles, and withdrew them from the ringbolts in the bulkhead.

Even once Sir Francis was free, it took all three men to lift him to his feet. He was so weak and cramped that he swayed and staggered like a drunkard as they helped him climb painfully through the hatch. 'Begging your pardon, Captain,' Sam laughed in his face, 'you ain't exactly no bed of roses, you ain't. I've smelt pig-sties and cesspools a sight sweeter than you, that I have, Franky me lad.'

They dragged him up on deck, and stripped the stinking rags from his shrunken body. Then four seamen worked the handles of the deck pump while Sam turned the stream from the canvas hose full on him. The *Gull* had entered the tail end of the cold green Benguela current that sweeps down the west coast of the continent. The jet of icy seawater from the hose almost knocked Sir Francis from his feet, and he had to cling to the shrouds to keep his balance. Shivering and choking when Sam directed the hose full into his face, he was able yet to scrub most of the crusted filth from his hair and body. It was of no concern to him that Katinka van de Velde leaned on the rail of the poop deck and scrutinized his nudity without the least indication of modesty.

Only when the hose was turned off and he was left to stand in the wind to dry off did Sir Francis have a chance to look about him and form some estimate of the *Gull*'s position and condition. Although his emaciated body was blue with cold, he felt refreshed and strengthened by the dousing. His teeth chattered and his whole frame shuddered with involuntary spasms of cold as he looked overside, and he folded his arms over his chest to try to warm himself. The African mainland lay ten leagues or so to the north, and he recognized the cliffs and crags of the point that guarded the entrance to False Bay. They would have to weather that savage point before they could enter Table Bay on the far side of the peninsula.

The wind was almost dead calm, and the surface of the sea as slick as oil, with long, low swells rising and falling like the breathing of a sleeping monster. Sam Bowles was telling the truth: unless the wind picked up it would be many more days before they rounded the Cape and dropped anchor in Table Bay. He wondered how many more of his men would follow Timothy before they were released from the confines of the slave deck.

Sam Bowles threw a few pieces of threadbare but clean clothing on the deck at his feet. 'His lordship is expecting you. Don't keep him waiting now.'

'Franky!' Cumbrae rose to greet him as he stooped through the doorway into the *Gull*'s stern cabin. 'I am so pleased to see that you look none the worse for your little sojourn below decks.' Before Sir Francis could avoid it, Cumbrae seized him in a bear-hug. 'I must apologize deeply for your treatment but it was at the insistence of the Dutch Governor and his wife. I would never have treated a brother Knight in such a scurvy fashion.'

While he spoke the Buzzard ran his great hands quickly down Sir Francis's body, checking for a concealed knife or other weapon, then pushed him into the largest and most comfortable chair in the cabin.

'A glass of wine, my dear old friend?' He poured it with his own hand, then gestured for his steward to place a bowl of stew in front of Sir Francis. Though saliva flooded into his mouth at the aroma of the first hot food he had been offered in almost two weeks, Sir Francis made no move to touch the glass or the spoon beside the bowl of stew.

Cumbrae noticed his refusal and, although he raised one bushy ginger eyebrow, he did not urge him but seized his own spoon and slurped up a mouthful from his own bowl. He chewed with all the sounds of appetite and approval, then washed it down with a hearty swallow from his wine glass, and wiped his red whiskers with the back of his hand. 'No, Franky, left to my own choice I would never have treated you so shabbily. You and I have had our differences in the past, but it has always been in the spirit of gentlemanly sport and competition, has it not?'

'Such sport as firing your broadside into my camp without warning?' Sir Francis asked.

'Now, let us not waste time in idle recrimination.' The Buzzard waved away the remark. 'That would never have been necessary if only you had agreed to share the booty from the galleon with me. What I really mean was that you and I understand each other. At heart we are brothers.'

'I think that I understand you.' Sir Francis nodded.

'Then you will know that what gives you pain, pains me even more. I have suffered every minute of your incarceration with you.'

'I hate to see you suffer, my lord, so why not release me and my men?'

'That is my fervent wish and intention, I assure you. However, there remains one small impediment that prevents me doing so. I need from you a sign that my warm feelings towards you are reciprocated. I am still deeply hurt that you would not share with me, your old friend, what was rightly mine in the terms of our agreement.'

'I am certain that the Dutch have given you the share you lacked before. In fact I saw you loading what seemed to me a generous portion of the spice aboard this very ship. I wonder what the Lord High Admiral of England will make of such traffic with the enemy.'

'A few barrels of spice – barely worth the breath to mention it.' Cumbrae smiled. 'But there ain't nothing like silver and gold to rouse my fraternal instincts. Come, now, Franky, we have wasted enough time in the pleasantries. You and I know that you have the bullion from the galleon cached somewhere close by your encampment on Elephant Lagoon. I know I will find it if I search long enough, but by then you will be dead, sent messily on your way by the executioner at Good Hope.'

Sir Francis smiled and shook his head. 'I have cached no treasure. Search if you will, but there is nothing for you to find.'

'Think on it, Franky. You know what the Dutch did to the English merchants they captured on the isle of Bali? They crucified them and burnt off their hands and feet with sulphur flares. I want to save you from that.'

'If you have nothing further to discuss, I will return to my crew.' Sir Francis stood up. His legs were stronger now.

'Sit down!' the Buzzard snapped. 'Tell me where you hid it, man, and I will put you and your men ashore with no further harm done, I swear it on my honour.' Cumbrae wheedled and blustered for another hour. Then at last he sighed. 'You drive a hard bargain, Franky. I tell you what I'll do for you. I would do it for no one else, but I love you like a brother. If you take me back and lead me to the booty, I'll share it with you. Fifty-fifty, right down the middle. Now I can't be more fair than that, can I?'

Sir Francis met even this offer with a calm, detached smile, and Cumbrae could hide his fury no longer. He slapped the table so viciously with the palm of his hand, that the glasses overturned and the wine sprayed across the cabin. He bellowed furiously for Sam Bowles. 'Take this arrogant bastard away, and chain him up again.' As Sir Francis left the cabin he shouted after him, 'I will find where you hid it, Franky, I swear it to you. I know more than you think. Just as soon as I have seen you topped on the Parade at Good Hope, I will be going back to the lagoon, and I won't leave until I find it.'

One more of Sir Francis's seamen died in his chains before they anchored off the foreshore in Table Bay. The others were so stiff and weak that they were forced to crawl like animals up the ladder to the upper deck. They huddled there, their ragged clothing crusted with their own filth, gazing around them, blinking and trying to shield their eyes from the brilliant morning sunshine.

Hal had never been this close inshore of Good Hope. On the outward leg of their cruise, at the beginning of the war, they had stood well off and looked into the bay from a great distance. However, that brief glimpse had not prepared him for the splendour of this seascape, where the royal blue of the Atlantic, flecked with wind spume, washed up on beaches so dazzling they hurt his weakened eyes.

The fabled flat-topped mountain seemed to fill most of the blue African sky, a great cliff of yellow rock slashed by deep ravines choked with dense green forest. The top of the mountain was so geometrically level, and its proportions so pleasing, that it seemed to have been designed by a celestial architect. Over the top of this immense table-land spilled a standing wave of shimmering cloud, frothy as milk boiling over the rim of a pot. This silver cascade never reached the lower slopes of the mountain, but as it fell it evaporated in mid-flight with a magical suddenness, leaving the lower slopes resplendent in their cloaking of verdant natural forest.

The grandeur dwarfed and rendered inconsequential the buildings that spread like an irritating rash along the shore above the snowy beach, from which a fleet of small boats put out to meet the *Gull* as soon as she dropped her anchor.

Governor van de Velde refused to climb down the ladder, and was hoisted from the deck, swung outboard in a boatswain's chair, all the while shouting nervous instructions at the men on the ropes. 'Careful now, you clumsy oafs! Drop me and I will have the skin thrashed off your backs.'

He was lowered into the longboat at the *Gull*'s side, in which his wife already waited. Assisted by Colonel Cornelius Schreuder, her descent had been considerably more graceful than her husband's.

They were rowed to the foreshore, where five strong slaves lifted the new Governor from the boat that danced in the shore break of white foam at the edge of the beach. They waded ashore with him and deposited him on the sand.

As the Governor's feet touched African soil the first cannon shot of a salute of fourteen rang out. A long plume of silver gunsmoke shot from the embrasure on the top of the southern redoubt, and the thunderous report so startled the new representative of the Company that he leapt a foot in the air and almost lost his plumed hat to the sou'-easter.

Governor Kleinhans, overjoyed that his successor in office had at last arrived, was at the foreshore to meet him. The garrison commander, equally anxious to hand over to Colonel Schreuder and shake from his feet the rank African dust, was on the ramparts of the fortress, his telescope focused on the arriving dignitaries.

The state carriage was waiting above the beach, six beautiful greys in the traces. Governor Kleinhans dismounted from it to greet the new arrivals, clutching his hat in the wind. An honour guard from the garrison was drawn up around the carriage. Gathered along the waterfront were several hundred men, women and children. Every resident of the settlement who could walk or crawl had turned out to welcome Governor van de Velde as he struggled through the loose sand.

When at last he reached firm footing and had gathered his breath and dignity he accepted Governor Kleinhans' welcome. They shook hands to cheering and applause from the Company officials, free burghers and slaves gathered to watch. The military escort presented their arms, and the band launched into a spirited patriotic air. The music ended with a clash of cymbals and a roll of kettle drums. The two Governors spontaneously embraced each other, Kleinhans delighted to be free to return to Amsterdam, and van de Velde overjoyed at having escaped death by storm and piracy and to have Dutch soil under his feet once more.

While Sam Bowles and his mates were removing the corpses from the slave chains and tossing them overboard, Hal squatted in the rank of captives and watched from afar as Katinka was ushered into the carriage by Governor Kleinhans on one arm and Colonel Schreuder on the other.

He felt his heart tear with love for her, and he whispered to Daniel and Aboli, 'Is she not the most beautiful lady in the world? She will use her influence for us. Now that her husband has full powers, she will persuade him to treat us justly.' Neither of the two big men replied, but they exchanged a glance. Daniel grinned with broken teeth and Aboli rolled his eyes.

Once Katinka was settled on the leather seats, they boosted her husband aboard. The carriage swayed and rocked under his weight. As soon as he was safely installed beside his wife, the band struck up a lively march and the escort shouldered their muskets and stepped out, a stirring sight in their white cross belts and green jackets. The procession streamed across the open parade ground towards the fort, with the crowds running ahead of the carriage and lining both sides of the route.

'Farewell, gentlemen. It has been a pleasure and a privilege to have you aboard.' The Buzzard touched the brim of his hat in an ironic salute as Sir Francis shambled across the deck dragging his chains, and led the file of his crew down the ladder into the boat moored alongside. So many men in chains made a heavy load for it in this condition of swell. They were left with only a few inches of freeboard as they pushed off from the *Gull*'s side.

The oarsmen struggled to hold the longboat's stern into the breaking white waves as they approached the beach, but a taller swell got under her and threw her off line. She broached heavily, dug in her shoulder and rolled over in four feet of water. Crew and passengers were thrown into the white water, and the capsized boat was caught up in the wash.

Choking and coughing up seawater, the prisoners managed to drag each other from the surf by their chains. Miraculously none was drowned, but the effort taxed most to their limit. When the guards from the fortress hectored them to their feet and drove them with musket butt and curses up the beach, they were streaming water and coated with a sugaring of white sand.

Having seen the state carriage safely through the gates of the fort, the crowds poured back to the water-front to have a little sport with these wretched creatures. They studied them as though they were livestock at a market, and their laughter was unrestrained, their comments ribald.

'Look more like gypsies and beggars than English pirates to me.'

'I'm saving my guilders. I'll not be bidding when that lot go up on the slave block.'

'They don't sell pirates, they burn them.'

'They don't look much, but at least they'll give us all some sport. We haven't had a really good execution since the slave revolt.'

'There's Stadige Jan over there, come to look them over. I'll warrant he'll have a few lessons to teach these corsairs.'

Hal turned his head in the direction the speaker pointed to where a tall burgher in dark, drab clothing and a puritan hat stood a head above the crowd. He looked at Hal with pale expressionless yellow eyes.

'What do you think of these beauties, Stadige Jan? Will you be able to get them to sing a pretty tune for us?'

Hal sensed the repulsion and fascination this man held for those around him. None stood too close to him, and they looked at him in such a way that Hal instinctively knew that this was the executioner of whom they had been warned. He felt his flesh crawl as he looked into those faded eyes.

'Why do you think that they call him Slow John?' he asked Aboli, from the side of his mouth.

'Let us hope we never have to find out,' Aboli replied, as they passed where the tall, cadaverous figure stood.

Small boys, both brown and white, danced beside the column of chained men, jeering and pelting them with pebbles and filth from the open gutters that carried the sewage from the town down to the sea front. Encouraged by this example a pack of mongrel dogs snapped at their heels. The adults in the crowd were turned out in their best clothes for such an unusual occasion and laughed at the antics of the children. Some of the women held sachets of herbs to their noses when they smelt the bedraggled file of prisoners, shuddering in horrified fascination.

'Oh! What dreadful creatures!'

'Look at those cruel and savage faces.'

'I have heard that they feed those Negroes on human flesh.'

Aboli contorted his face and rolled his eyes at them. The tattoos on his cheeks stood proud, and his great white teeth were bared in a fearsome grin. The women squealed with delicious terror, and their little daughters hid their faces in their mothers' skirts as he passed.

At the rear of the crowd, hanging back from the company of their betters, taking no part in the sport of baiting the captives, were those men and women who, Hal guessed, must be the domestic slaves of the burghers. The slaves in the crowd ranged in colour from the anthracite black of Africa to the amber and gold skins of the Orient. Most were simply dressed in the cast-off clothing of their owners, although some of the prettier women wore the flamboyant finery that marked them as the favourite playthings of their masters.

They looked on quietly as the seamen trudged past in their clanking chains, and there was no sound of laughter among them. Rather, Hal sensed a certain empathy behind their closed impassive expressions for they were captives also. Just before they entered the gate to the fort, Hal noticed one girl in particular at the back of the crowd. She had climbed up on a pile of masonry blocks for a better view and stood higher than the intervening ranks of spectators. This was not the only reason why Hal had singled her out.

She was more beautiful than he had ever expected any woman to be. She was a flower of a girl, with thick glossy black hair and dark eyes that seemed too large for her delicate oval face. For one moment their eyes met over the heads of the crowd, and it seemed to Hal that she tried to pass him some message that he was unable to grasp. He knew only that she felt compassion for him, and that she shared in his suffering. Then he lost sight of her as they were marched through the gateway into the courtyard of the fort.

The image of her stayed with him over the dreadful days that followed. Gradually it began to supersede the memory of Katinka, and in the nights sometimes returned to give him the strength he needed to endure. He felt that if there were but one person of such loveliness and tenderness out there, beyond the gaunt stone walls, who cared for his abject condition, then it was worth fighting on.

In the courtyard of the fort, a military armourer struck off their shackles. A shore party under the command of Sam Bowles stood by to collect the discarded chains to take back aboard the *Gull*. 'I will miss you all, my shipmates.' Sam grinned. 'The lower decks of the old *Gull* will be empty and lonely without your smiling faces and your good cheer.' He gave them a salute from the gateway as he led his shore party away. 'I hope they look after you as well as your good friend Sam Bowles did. But, never fear, I'll be at the Parade when you give your last performance there.'

When Sam was gone, Hal looked around the courtyard. He saw that the fortress had been designed on a substantial scale. As part of his training his father had made him study the science of land fortifications, so he recognized the classical defensive layout of the stone walls and redoubts. He realized that once these works were completed, it would take an army equipped with a full siege train to reduce them.

However, the work was less than half finished, and on the landward side of the fort or, as their new gaolers referred to it, *het kasteel*, the castle, there were merely open foundations from which the massive stone walls would one day rise. Yet it was clear that the work was being hastened along. Almost certainly the two recent Anglo-Dutch wars had imparted this impetus. Both Oliver Cromwell, the Lord Protector of the Commonwealth of England, Scotland and Ireland, during the interregnum, and King Charles, son of the man he had beheaded, could claim some credit for the frenzy of construction that was going on around them. They had forcibly reminded the Dutch of the vulnerability of their far-flung colonies. The half-finished walls swarmed with hundreds of workmen, and the courtyard in which they stood was piled with building timber and blocks of dressed masonry hewn from the mountain that loomed over it all.

As dangerous captives they were kept apart from the other prisoners. They were marched from the courtyard down the short spiral staircase below the south wall of the fort. The stone blocks that lined floor, vaulted roof and walls glistened with moisture that had seeped in from the surrounding waterlogged soil. Even on such a sunny day in autumn the temperature in these dank forbidding surroundings made them shiver.

At the foot of the first flight of stairs Sir Francis Courtney was dragged out of the file by his gaolers and thrust into a small cell just large enough to hold one man. It was one in a row of half a dozen or so identical cells, whose doors were of solid timber studded with iron bolts and the tiny barred peep-hole in each was shuttered and closed. They had no sight of the other inmates. 'Special quarters for you, Sir Pirate,' the burly Dutch gaoler told him as he slammed the door on Sir Francis and turned the lock with a huge iron key from the bunch on his belt. 'We are putting you in the Skellum's Den, with all the really bad ones, the murderers and rebels and robbers. You will feel at home here, of that I'm sure.'

The rest of the prisoners were herded down to the next level of the dungeon. The sergeant gaoler unlocked the grille door at the end of the tunnel and they were shoved into a long narrow cell. Once the grille was locked behind them there was barely room for them all to stretch out on the thin layer of damp straw that covered the cobblestoned floor. A single latrine bucket stood in one corner, but murmurs of pleasure from all the men greeted the sight of the large water cistern beside the grille gate. At least this meant they were no longer on shipboard water rations.

There were four small windows set in the top of one wall and, once they had inspected their surroundings, Hal looked up at them. Aboli hoisted him onto his shoulders and he was able to reach one of these narrow openings. It was heavily barred, like the others, but Hal tried the gratings with his bare hands. They were set rock-firm, and he was forced to put out of his mind any notion of escaping this way.

Hanging on the grating, he drew himself up and peered through it. He found that his eyes were a foot or so above ground level, and from there he had a view of part of the interior courtyard of the castle. He could see the entrance gateway and the grand portals of what he guessed must be the Company offices and the Governor's suite. To one side, through the gap where the walls had not yet been raised, he could see a portion of the cliffs of the table-topped mountain, and above them the sky. Against the cloudless blue sailed a flock of white gulls.

Hal lowered himself and pushed his way through the throng of seamen, stepping over the bodies of the sick and wounded. When he reached the grille he looked up the staircase but could not see the door to his father's cell.

'Father!' he called tentatively, expecting a rebuke from one of the gaolers, but when there was no response he raised his voice and shouted again.

'I hear you, Hal,' his father called back.

'Do you have any orders for us, Father?'

'I expect they'll leave us in peace for a day or two, at least until they have convened a tribunal. We will have to wait it out. Tell the men to be of good heart.'

At that a strange voice intervened, speaking in English but with an unfamiliar accent. 'Are you the English pirates we have heard so much about?'

'We are honest sailors, falsely accused,' Sir Francis shouted back. 'Who and what are you?'

'I am your neighbour in the Skellum's Den, two cells down from you. I am condemned to die, as you are.'

'We are not yet condemned,' Sir Francis protested.

'It is only a matter of time. I hear from the gaolers that you soon will be.'

'What is your name?' Hal joined in the exchange. He was not interested in the stranger, but this conversation served to pass the time and divert them from their own predicament. 'What is your crime?'

'I am Althuda, and my crime is that I strive to be free and to set other men free.'

'Then we are brothers, Althuda, you and I and every man here. We all strive for freedom.'

There was a ragged chorus of assent, and when it subsided Althuda spoke again. 'I led a revolt of the Company slaves. Some were recaptured. Those Stadige Jan burned alive, but most of us escaped into the mountains. Many times they sent soldiers after us, but we fought and drove them off and they could not enslave us again.' His was a vital young voice, proud and strong, and even before Hal had seen his face he found himself drawn to this Althuda.

'Then if you escaped, how is it that you are back here in the Skellum's Den?' one of the English seamen wanted to know. They were all listening now. Althuda's story had moved even the most hardened of them.

'I came back to rescue somebody, another slave who was left behind,' Althuda told them. 'When I entered the colony again I was recognized and betrayed.'

They were all silent for a space.

'A woman?' a voice asked. 'You came back for a woman?'

'Yes,' said Althuda. 'A woman.'

'There is always an Eve in the midst of Eden to tempt us into folly,' one sang out and they all laughed.

Then somebody else asked, 'Was she your sweetheart?'

'No,' Althuda answered. 'I came back for my little sister.'

Thirty guests sat down to the banquet that Governor Kleinhans gave to welcome his successor. All the most important men in the administration of the colony, together with their wives, were seated around the long board.

From the place of honour Petrus van de Velde gazed with delighted anticipation down the length of the rosewood table above which hung massive chandeliers, each burning fifty perfumed candles. They lit the great hall as if it was day, and sparkled on the silverware and crystal glasses.

For months now, ever since sailing from the coast of Trincomalee, van de Velde had been forced to subsist on the swill and offal cooked on the galleon and then on the coarse fare that the English pirates had provided for him. Now his eyes shone and saliva flooded his mouth as he contemplated the culinary extravaganza spread before him. He reached for the tall glass in front of him, and took a mouthful of the rare wine from Champagne. The tiny seething bubbles tickled his palate and spurred his already unbridled appetite.

Van de Velde considered this a most fortunate posting, for which his wife's connection in the Council of Seventeen was to be thanked. Positioned here, at the tip of Africa, a constant procession of ships passed in both directions bringing the luxuries of Europe and the Orient into Table Bay. They would want for nothing.

Silently he cursed Kleinhans for his long-winded speech of welcome, of which he heard barely a word. All his attention was on the array of silver dishes and chargers that were laid before him, one after another.

There were little sucking pigs in crisp suits of golden crackling; barons of beef running with their own rich juices set around with steaming ramparts of roasted potatoes; heaps of tender young pullets and pigeons and ducks and fat geese; five different types of fresh fish from the Atlantic, cooked five different ways, fragrant with the curries and spices of Java and Kandy and Further India; tall pyramids of the huge clawless crimson lobsters that abounded in this southern ocean; a vast array of fruits and succulent vegetables from the Company gardens; and sherbets and custards and sugar dumplings and cakes and trifles and confitures and every sweet delight that the slave chefs in the kitchens could conceive. All this was backed by stalwart ranks of cheese brought by Company ships from Holland, and jars of pickled North-Sea herring, and smoked sides of wild boar and salmon.

In contrast to this superabundance, the service was all of delicate blue and white pattern. Behind each chair stood a house slave in the green uniform of the Company, ready to recharge glass and plate with nimble white-gloved hands. Would the man never stop talking and let them at the food, van de Velde wondered, and smiled and nodded at Kleinhans' inanities.

At last, with a bow to the new Governor and a much deeper one to his wife, Kleinhans sank back into his chair, and everyone looked expectantly at van de Velde. He gazed around at their asinine faces, and then with a sigh rose to his feet to reply. Two minutes will do it, he told himself, and gave them what they expected to hear, ending jovially, 'In conclusion, I want only to wish Governor Kleinhans a safe return to the old country, and a long and happy retirement.'

He sat down with alacrity and reached for his spoon. This was the first time the burghers had been privileged to witness the new Governor at table, and an amazed and respectful silence fell upon the company as they watched the level in his soup bowl fall like the outgoing tide across the mud-flats of the Zuider Zee. Then, suddenly realizing that when the guest of honour finished one course, the plates would be changed and the next course served, they fell to in a frenzied effort to catch up. There were many stout trenchermen amongst them, but none to match the Governor, especially when he had had a head start.

As his soup bowl emptied, every bowl was whisked away and replaced with a plate piled high with thick cuts of sucking pig. The first two courses were completed in virtual silence, broken only by slurping and gulping.

During the third course Kleinhans rallied and, as host, made a valiant attempt to revive the conversation. He leaned forward to distract van de Velde's attention from his plate. 'I expect that you will wish to deal with the matter of the English pirates before any other business,' he asked, and van de Velde nodded vigorously, although his mouth was too full of succulent lobster to permit a verbal reply.

'Have you decided yet how you will go about their trial and sentencing?' Kleinhans enquired lugubriously. Van de Velde swallowed noisily, before he replied, 'They will be executed, of course, but not before their captain, this notorious corsair Francis Courtney, reveals the hiding place of the missing Company cargo. I would like to convene a tribunal immediately for this purpose.'

Colonel Schreuder coughed politely, and van de Velde glanced at him impatiently. 'Yes? You wanted to say something? Out with it, then!'

'Today I had opportunity to inspect the work proceeding on the *kasteel* fortifications, sir. The good Lord alone knows when we will be at war with England again, but it may be soon. The English are thieves by nature, and pirates by vocation. It is for these reasons, sir, that the Seventeen in Amsterdam have placed the highest priority on the completion of our fortifications. That fact is spelt out very clearly in my orders and my letter of appointment to the command of the *kasteel*.'

Every man at the table looked grave and attentive at the mention of the sacred Seventeen, as though the name of a deity had been invoked. Schreuder let the silence run on for a while to make good his point, then said, 'The work is very much behind what their excellencies have decreed.'

Major Loten, the outgoing garrison commander, interjected, 'It is true that the work is somewhat behindhand, but there are good reasons for this.' The construction was his prime responsibility, and Governor van de Velde's eyes switched to his face. He placed another forkful of lobster in his mouth. The sauce was truly delicious, and he sighed with pleasure as he contemplated another five years of meals of this order. He must certainly buy the chef from Kleinhans before he sailed. He formed his features into a more solemn pattern as he listened to Loten making his excuses. 'I have been hampered by a shortage of labour. This most regrettable revolt among the slaves has left us severely undermanned,' he said lamely, and van de Velde frowned.

'Precisely the point I was about to make,' Schreuder picked up smoothly. 'If we are so short of men to meet the expectations of the Seventeen, would we be wise to execute twenty-four strong and able-bodied English pirates, instead of employing them in the workings?'

Every eye at the table turned to van de Velde to judge his reaction, waiting for him to give them a lead. The new Governor swallowed, then used his forefinger to free a shred of lobster leg caught in his back teeth before he spoke. 'Courtney cannot be spared,' he said at last. 'Not even to work on the fortifications. According to Lord Cumbrae, whose opinion I respect,' he gave the Buzzard a seated bow, 'the Englishman knows where the missing cargo is hidden, besides which my wife and I,' he nodded towards Katinka, who sat between Kleinhans and Schreuder, 'have been forced to suffer many indignities at his hands.'

'I quite agree,' said Schreuder. 'He must be made to tell all he knows of the missing bullion. But the others? Such a waste to execute them when they are needed on the walls, don't you think, sir. They are, after all, dull-witted cattle, with little understanding of the gravity of their offence but with strong backs to pay for it.'

Van de Velde grunted noncommittally. 'I would like to hear the opinion of Governor Kleinhans on this matter,' he said, and filled his mouth again, his head lowered on his shoulders and his small eyes focused on his predecessor. Sagely, he passed on the responsibility of making the decision. Later, if there were repercussions, he could always unload a share of the blame.

'Of course,' said Governor Kleinhans, with an airy wave of the hand, 'prime slaves are selling for almost a thousand guilders a head at the moment. Such a large addition to the Company purse would commend itself highly to their excellencies. The Seventeen are determined that the colony must pay for itself and not become a drain on the Company exchequer.'

All present gave this their solemn consideration. In the silence Katinka said, in ringing crystal tones, 'I, for one, will need slaves for my household. I would welcome the opportunity to acquire good workers even at those exorbitant prices.'

'By international accord and protocol it is forbidden to sell Christians into slavery,' Schreuder pointed out, as he saw the prospects of procuring labour for his fortifications beginning to recede. 'Even Englishmen.'

'Not all the captured pirates are Christians,' Kleinhans persisted. 'I saw a number of black faces amongst them. Negro slaves are much in demand in the colony. They are good workers and breeders. Would it not be a most desirable compromise to sell them for guilders to please the Seventeen? We could then condemn the English pirates to lifelong hard labour. They could be used to hasten the completion of the works, also to please the Seventeen.'

Van de Velde grunted again, and scraped his plate noisily to draw attention to the fact that he was ready to sample the beef. He pondered these conflicting arguments while a freshly loaded plate was placed in front of him. There was another consideration to take into account of which no one else was aware: his bitter hatred of Colonel Schreuder. He did not want to ease his lot in life and, truth to tell, he would be delighted if the Colonel failed dismally in his new command and was ordered home in disgrace – just as long as that failure did not redound to his own discredit.

He stared hard at Schreuder as he toyed with the idea of refusing him. He knew, all too well, what that one had in mind, and he turned his attention from the Colonel to his wife. Katinka looked radiant this evening. Within a few days of arriving at the Cape and moving into their temporary quarters in the castle, she was fully recovered from the long voyage and from the captivity forced upon them by Sir Francis Courtney. She was, of course, young and resilient, not yet twenty-four years of age, but that alone did not account for her gaiety and vivacity this evening. Whenever the bumptious Schreuder spoke, which was too often, she turned those huge, innocent eyes upon him, with full attention. When she spoke directly to him, which was also too often, she touched him, laying one of her delicate white hands on his sleeve, and once, to van de Velde's intense mortification, actually placing her fingers on Schreuder's bony paw, letting them linger there for all the company to see and smirk at.

It almost, but not quite, spoiled his appetite to have this blatant courtship ritual take place not only under his nose but under the collective noses of the entire colony. It would have been bad enough if, in private, he had been forced to face the fact that the valiant Colonel would soon be rummaging around under those rustling petticoats. It was insufferable that he must share this knowledge with all his underlings. How could he demand respect and sycophantic obedience from them while his wife was set on publicly placing horns upon his head? When I packed him off to Amsterdam to negotiate my ransom, I thought we had seen the last of Colonel Schreuder, he thought sullenly. It seems I will have to take sterner measures in the future. And as he ploughed his way through all sixteen courses, he turned over in his mind the various alternatives.

Van de Velde was so stuffed with good food that the short walk from the great hall of the castle to the council chamber was only accomplished with much heavy breathing and the occasional pause, ostensibly to admire the paintings and other works of art that decorated the walls, but in reality to recover his resources.

In the chamber he settled with a vast sigh into the cushions of one of the high-backed chairs, and accepted a glass of brandy and a pipe of tobacco.

'I will convene the court to try the pirates this coming week, that is immediately after I formally take over the governorship from Mijnheer Kleinhans,' he announced. 'No point in wasting any more time on this riff-raff. I appoint Colonel Schreuder to act as attorney-general and to prosecute the case. I will take on the duties of judge.' He looked across the table at his host. 'Will you have your officers make the necessary arrangements please, Mijnheer Kleinhans.'

'Certainly, Mijnheer van de Velde. Have you given any thought to appointing an advocate to defend the accused pirates?'

It was clear from van de Velde's expression that he had not, but now he waved a pudgy paw and said airily, 'See to that, will you? I am sure one of your clerks has sufficient knowledge of the law to perform the duty adequately. After all, what is there to defend?' he asked, and chuckled throatily.

'A name comes to mind.' Kleinhans nodded. 'I will appoint him and arrange for him to have access to the prisoners to receive their statements.'

'Dear God!' Van de Velde looked scandalized. 'Why would you do that? I don't want that English rogue Courtney putting all sorts of ideas into the man's head. I will set out the facts for him. He need only recite them to the court.'

'I understand,' Kleinhans agreed. 'It will all be ready to hand over to you before I step down next week.' He looked across at Katinka. 'My dear lady, you, of course, will wish to move out of your temporary quarters here in the castle, and into the much more commodious and comfortable Governor's residence as soon as possible. I thought that we could arrange an inspection of your new home after the church service on Sunday. I would be honoured to personally conduct you on a tour of the establishment.'

'That is kind, sir.' Katinka smiled at him, glad to be the focus of attention once more. For a moment Kleinhans basked in the warmth of her approval, then went on diffidently, 'As you can well imagine, I have acquired a considerable household during my term of office in the colony. Coincidentally, the cooks who prepared the humble little meal of which we partook this evening are part of my own span of slaves.' He glanced at van de Velde. 'I hope that their efforts met with your approval?' When the Governor nodded comfortably, he turned back to Katinka. ' As you know, very soon I shall return to the old country, and into retirement on my small country estate. Twenty slaves will be far in excess of my future requirements. You, Mevrouw, voiced your interest in purchasing quality slaves. I would like to take the opportunity of your visit to the residence to show you those creatures that I have for sale. They have all been hand-picked, and I think you will find it more convenient and cheaper to make a private acquisition than to bid at public auction. The trouble with buying slaves is that those who look good value on the auction block can have serious hidden defects. It is always comforting to know that the seller has sound and sufficient reasons for selling, is it not?'

Hal set a constant lookout at the high window of the cell. There was always one man standing on another's shoulders, clinging to the bars, to keep a watch on the castle courtyard. The lookout called down all sightings to Hal, who in turn relayed these up the stairwell to his father.

Within the first few days they were able to work out the timetable of the garrison, and to note the routine comings and goings of the Company officials, and of the free burghers who visited the castle regularly.

Hal called a description of each of these persons to the unseen leader of the slave rebellion in the Skellum's Den. Althuda knew the personal details of every person in the settlement and passed on all this accumulated knowledge, so that within the first few days Hal came to know not only the appearance but also the personality and character of each one.

He started a calendar, marking the passage of each day with a scratch on a slab of sandstone in one corner of the cell and registering the more important events beside it. He was not certain that anything was to be gained from these records, but at least it gave the men something to talk about, and fostered the illusion that he had a plan of action for their release or, failing that, for their escape.

'Governor's carriage at the staircase!' the lookout warned, and Hal jumped up from where he was sitting between Aboli and Daniel against the far wall.

'Come down,' he ordered. 'Let me up.'

Through the bars he saw the state carriage parked at the foot of the broad staircase that led up to the Company offices and the Governor's suite. The coachman's name was Fredricus, an elderly Javanese slave who belonged to Governor Kleinhans. According to Althuda, he was no friend. For thirty years he had been Kleinhans' dog, and he could not be trusted. Althuda suspected that he was the one who had betrayed him, and had reported his return from the mountains to Major Loten. 'We will probably be rid of him when Kleinhans leaves the colony. He is sure to take Fredricus back with him to Holland,' Althuda told them.

There was a sudden stir as a detachment of soldiers hurried across the courtyard from the armoury and formed up at the foot of the staircase.

'Kleinhans going out,' Hal called, recognizing these preparations, and as he spoke the double doors swung open and a small party emerged into the sunlight and descended towards the waiting carriage.

The tall, stooped figure of Kleinhans, with his sour dyspeptic face, contrasted sharply with the lovely young woman on his arm. Hal's heart tripped as he recognized Katinka but his feelings were no longer as intense as once they had been. Instead, his eyes narrowed as he saw that the Neptune sword hung in its chased and gold-encrusted scabbard at Schreuder's side as the colonel followed Katinka down the stairs. Each time he saw Schreuder wearing it his anger was rekindled.

Fredricus climbed stiffly from his high seat, folded down the steps, opened the carriage door, then stood aside to allow the two gentlemen to hand Katinka up and settle her comfortably.

'What is happening down there?' his father called and, with a guilty start, Hal realized that he had not spoken since he had laid eyes on the woman he loved. By now, though, she had been carried out of his sight. The carriage rolled out smoothly through the castle gates, and the sentries saluted as Fredricus shook the horses into a trot across the parade.

It was a sparkling autumn day, and the constant sou'-easter of summer had dropped. Katinka sat beside Governor Kleinhans, facing forward. Cornelius Schreuder sat opposite her. She had left her husband in his office in the castle, labouring over his reports for the Seventeen, and now she felt the devil in her. She flounced out her skirts and the rustling crinolines covered the Colonel's soft leather boots.

While still chatting animatedly to Kleinhans, she reached out one slippered foot under cover of her skirts and found Schreuder's toe. She pressed it coquettishly, and felt him start. She pressed again, and felt him respond sheepishly. Then she turned from Kleinhans and addressed Schreuder directly. 'Don't you agree, Colonel, that an avenue of oaks leading up to the residence would look splendid? I can imagine their thick hard trunks standing up vigorously. How beautiful that would be.' She opened her violet eyes wide to give the remark significance, and pressed his foot again.

'Indeed, Mevrouw.' Schreuder's voice was husky with double meaning. 'I agree with you entirely. In fact the image you paint is so vivid that you should be able to see the stem growing before your very eyes.'

At this invitation she glanced down at his lap and, to her amusement, saw the effect that she was having upon him. He is putting up a tent in his breeches for my sake!

Almost a mile beyond the forbidding pile of the castle, the Governor's residence stood at the mountain end of the Company gardens. It was a graceful building, with dark thatched roof and whitewashed walls, surrounded by wide shady verandas. Laid out in the shape of a cross, the gables at each of the four ends of the house were decorated with plaster friezes depicting the seasons. The gardens were well established; a succession of Company gardeners had lavished love and care upon them.

Even from a distance Katinka was delighted with her new home. She had dreaded being lodged in some ugly, bucolic hovel, but this far surpassed her most optimistic expectations. The entire domestic staff of the residence was drawn up on the wide front terrace to greet her.

The carriage rolled to a standstill and her two escorts hastened to help Katinka to earth. At a prearranged signal all the waiting manservants lifted their hats, and bowed so low as to sweep the ground before her with their headgear, while the females dropped into deep curtsies. Katinka acknowledged their greeting with a cool nod, and Kleinhans introduced each of them in turn to her. Most were merely brown or yellow faces that made no impression whatsoever on her, and she glanced vaguely in their direction then passed on, hurrying through this tedious little ritual as swiftly as she could.

However, one or two caught and held her attention for more than a few moments.

'This is the head gardener.' Kleinhans summoned the man with a snap of his fingers, and he stood bareheaded before her, holding over his chest the high-crowned Puritan hat with its silver buckled band and wide brim. 'He is a man of some importance in our community,' Kleinhans said. 'Not only is he responsible for these beautiful surroundings,' he indicated the wide green lawns and splendid flower beds, 'and for providing each Company ship that calls into Table Bay with fresh fruit and vegetables, but he is also the official executioner.'

Katinka had been on the point of passing on, but now, with a small thrill of excitement, she turned back to study this creature. He towered above her, and she looked up into his strange pale eyes, imagining what dread sights they had seen. Then she glanced down at his hands. They were farmer's hands, broad and strong and calloused, the backs covered with stiff bristles. She imagined them holding a spade or a branding iron, a pitchfork or the knotted coil of the strangling cord.

'They call you Stadige Jan?' She had heard the name spoken with fascination and revulsion, the way one speaks of a deadly, venomous snake.

'*Ja*, Mevrouw.' He nodded. 'That is what they call me.'

'A strange name. Why?' She found his level yellow stare disquieting, as though he was looking at something far behind her.

'Because I speak slowly. Because I never rush. Because I am thorough. Because plants grow slowly and fruitfully under my hands. Because men die slowly and painfully under these same hands.' He held up one for her to examine. His voice was sonorous yet melodious. She found herself swallowing hard with a strange, perverse arousal.

'We are soon to have a chance to watch you work, Stadige Jan.' She smiled slightly breathlessly. 'I believe that the dungeon of the castle is full of rogues awaiting your ministrations.' She had a sudden image of those broad strong hands working on Hal Courtney's slim straight body, the body she knew so well, changing it, gradually breaking it down. The muscles in her thighs and lower belly tightened at the thought. It would be the ultimate thrill to see the beautiful toy of which she had tired being maimed and disfigured, but slowly and slowly.

'We must talk again, Stadige Jan,' she said huskily. 'I am sure you have many amusing stories to tell me, about cabbages and other things.' He bowed again, replaced the hat on his shaven head and stepped back into the line of servants. Katinka passed on.

'This is my housekeeper,' Kleinhans said, but Katinka was so engrossed in her thoughts that, for several seconds, she gave no indication that she had heard him. Then she threw an idle glance at the female Kleinhans was presenting, and suddenly her eyes widened. She turned her full attention on the woman. 'Her name is Sukeena.' There was something in Kleinhans' tone that she could not immediately fathom.

'She is very young for such an important position,' Katinka said, to gain time in which to allow her instincts to have play. In an entirely different manner, she found this woman as enthralling as the executioner. She was so exquisitely small and dainty as to seem an artist's creation and not flesh and blood.

'It is a characteristic of her race to appear much younger than their years,' Kleinhans told her. 'They have such small childlike bodies – you will observe her tiny waist and her hands and feet, like those of a doll.'

He broke off abruptly, as he realized that he might have committed a solecism in discussing another woman's bodily parts.

Katinka's expression did not change to reveal the amusement she felt. The old goat lusts for her, she thought, and she studied the jewel-like qualities to which he had drawn her attention. The girl wore a high collar, but the stuff of her blouse was sheer and light as gossamer. Like the rest of her, her breasts were tiny but perfect. Katinka could see the shape and colour of her nipples through the silk: they were like a pair of imperial rubies wrapped in gossamer. That dress, although simple and of classical Eastern design, must have cost fifty guilders at the very least. Her sandals were gold-embroidered, rich raiment for a house slave. At her throat she wore an ornament of carved jade, a jewel fit for a mandarin's favourite. The girl must certainly be Kleinhans' pretty bauble, she decided.

Katinka's first carnal fulfilment had been at the age of thirteen, on the threshold of puberty. In the seclusion of the nursery, her nurse had introduced her to those forbidden delights. Occasionally, when her fancy dictated and opportunity presented, she still voyaged to the enchanted isles of Lesbos. Often she had found there enchantments that no man had been able to afford her. Now as she looked up from the childlike body to the dark eyes, she felt a tremor of desire run down her own belly and melt into her loins.

Sukeena's gaze smouldered like the lavas of the volcanoes of her native Bali. These were not the eyes of a subservient child slave but those of a proud, defiant woman. Katinka felt herself challenged and aroused. To subdue her, and have her, and then to break her. She felt her pulse quicken and her breath come short as she pictured it happening.

'Follow me, Sukeena,' she commanded. 'I want you to show me the house.'

'My lady.' Sukeena placed the palms of her hands together and touched her fingertips to her lips as she bowed, but her eyes held Katinka's with the same dark, furious expression. Was it hatred, Katinka wondered, and the idea increased her excitement.

Sukeena has intrigued her, as I knew she must. She will buy her from me, Kleinhans thought. I will be rid of the witch at last. He had been aware of that interplay of passions and emotions between the two women. Although he did not flatter himself that he could fathom the slave girl's oriental mind, she had been his chattel for almost five years and he had learned to recognize many of the nuances of her moods. The thought of parting with her filled him with dismay but for his own peace and sanity he knew he must do it. She was destroying him. He could not remember what it was to have a quiet mind, not to be plagued and tormented by passions and unfulfilled desires, not to be in the witch's thrall. Because of her he had lost his health. His stomach was being eaten away by the hot acids of dyspepsia, and he could not remember a night of unbroken sleep in all those long five years.

At least he was rid of her brother, who had been almost as great a torment to him. Now she, too, must go. He could no longer endure this blight on his existence.

Sukeena stepped out of the line of servants and fell in dutifully behind the three, her loathsome master, the boorish giant of a soldier and this beautiful cruel golden lady, who, she sensed somehow, already held her destiny in those slim white hands.

I will wrest it from her, Sukeena vowed. This vile old man could not own me, although for the last five years he has dreamed of nothing else. Neither will this golden tiger woman ever own me. I swear it on my father's sacred memory.

They passed in a group through the high airy rooms of the residence. Through the green-painted shutters spilled the mellow Cape sunshine, casting stark zebra shadows on the tiled floors. Katinka felt a lightness of the spirit in these sunny colonies. She felt a recklessness in herself, an eagerness for strange adventures and for unfathomed excitements.

In every room she encountered a subtle, delicate feminine influence. It was not only the lingering perfume of flowers and incense, but some other living presence that she knew could never have emanated from the sad and sick old man at her side. She did not have to glance behind her to be aware of the girl who had created this aura, her silk clothing whispering and the susurration of the golden sandals on her tiny feet, the scent of the jasmine blossom in her coal-dark hair and the sweet musk of her skin.

In counterpoint, there was the crisp staccato click of the Colonel's heels on the tiles, the creak of his leather and the clink of his scabbard as it swung at his side. His scent was more powerful than that of the girl. It was masculine and rank, sweat and leather and animal, like a stallion pushed hard, bounding between her thighs. In this emotional hothouse in which she found herself, every one of her senses was fully engaged.

At last Governor Kleinhans led them out of the house and across the lawns to where a small gazebo stood, secluded beneath the oaks. An alfresco repast had been laid for them, and Sukeena stood in close attendance, directing the service of the meal with a glance or a subtle, graceful gesture.

Katinka noticed that as each dish or bottle was presented Sukeena tasted a morsel or took a delicate sip, like a butterfly at an open orchid. Her silence was not self-effacing, for all three seated at the table were intensely aware of her presence.

Cornelius Schreuder sat so close to Katinka that his leg pressed against hers whenever he leaned close to speak to her. They looked down towards the bay, where the *Standvastigheid* lay at anchor, not far from the *Gull of Moray*. The galleon had come in during the night, fully laden with her cargo of recovered spices and timber. She would carry Kleinhans northwards on the next leg of her voyage, so he was in haste to settle his affairs here in the Cape. Katinka smiled sweetly at the old man over the rim of her wine glass, knowing that she had him at a disadvantage in the bargaining.

'I wish to sell fifteen of my slaves,' he told her, 'and I have prepared a list of them, setting out their personal details, their skills and training, their ages and the state of their health. Five of the females are pregnant, so already the buyer will be assured of an increase on his, or her, investment.'

Katinka glanced at the document he handed her, then dropped it on the table top. 'Tell me about Sukeena,' she commanded. 'Am I mistaken, or have I detected in her a drop of northern blood? Was her father Dutch?'

Although Sukeena stood close by, Katinka spoke about the girl as though she were an inanimate object, without hearing or human sensitivity, a pretty piece of jewellery or a miniature painting, perhaps.

'You are observant, Mevrouw.' Kleinhans inclined his head. 'But no, her father was not Dutch. He was an English trader and her mother was a Balinese but, nonetheless, a woman of high breeding. When I saw her she was in her middle age. However, I understand that in her youth she was a great beauty. Although she was merely his concubine, the English trader treated her like a wife.'

All three studied Sukeena's features openly. 'Yes, you can see the European blood. It is the tone of her skin, and the set and shape of her eyes,' said Katinka.

Sukeena kept her eyes lowered, and her expression did not change. Smoothly she continued with her duties.

'What do you think of her appearance, Colonel?' Katinka turned to Schreuder, and pressed her leg against his. 'I am always interested in what a man finds attractive. Do you not think her a delicious little creature?'

Schreuder flushed slightly, and moved his chair so that he was no longer looking directly at Sukeena.

'Mevrouw, I have never had a penchant for native girls, even if they are half-castes.' Sukeena's face remained impassive even though, at six feet from him, she had heard the derogatory description clearly. 'My tastes incline very much towards our lovely Dutch girls. I would not trade the dross for the pure gold.'

'Oh, Colonel, you are so gallant. I envy the pure golden Dutch girl who catches your fancy.' She laughed, and he gave her a look more eloquent than the words that rose to his lips, but perforce remained unspoken.

Katinka turned back to Kleinhans. 'So if her father was English, does she speak that language? That would be a useful accomplishment, would it not?'

'Indeed, she speaks it with great fluency, but that is not all. She has a way with guilders and runs the household with great economy and efficiency. The other slaves respect and obey her. She has intimate knowledge of Oriental medicines and remedies for all illness—'

'A paragon!' Katinka interrupted his recital. 'But what of her nature? Is she tractable, docile?'

'She is as she appears,' said Kleinhans, concealing the evasion with a ready reply and open face. 'I assure you, Mevrouw, that I have owned her for five years and have always found her completely compliant.'

Sukeena's face remained as if carved in jade, lovely and remote, but her soul seethed with outrage at the lie. For five years she had withstood him, and only on the few occasions when he had beaten her unconscious had he been able to invade her body. But that had been no victory for him, she knew, and took comfort from that knowledge. Twice she had recovered her senses while he was still grunting and straining over her like an animal, forcing himself into her dry, reluctant flesh. She did not count this as defeat, she did not even admit to herself that he had conquered her, for the moment that she regained consciousness she had begun to fight him again, with all the strength and determination of before.

'You are not a woman,' he had cried in despair, as she thrashed and kicked and wormed out from under him, 'you are a devil,' and, bleeding where she had bitten him and covered with deep gouges and scratches, he had slunk away, leaving her battered but triumphant. In the end he had given up any attempt at forcing her into submission, and instead had tried every other blandishment.

Once, weeping like an old woman, he had even offered her freedom and marriage, her deed of emancipation on the day that she married him. She spat like a cat at the thought.

Twice she had tried to kill him. Once with a dagger and once with poison. Now he made her taste every dish or bowl she served him, but the thought sustained her that one day she might succeed and watch his death throes.

'She does seem to have an angelic presence,' Katinka agreed, knowing instinctively that the description would enrage its subject. 'Come here, Sukeena,' she ordered, and the girl came to her moving like a reed in the wind.

'Kneel down!' said Katinka, and Sukeena knelt before her, her eyes modestly downcast. 'Look at me!' She raised her head.

Katinka studied her face, and spoke to Kleinhans without looking at him. 'You say she is healthy?'

'Young and healthy, never a day's illness in her life.'

'Is she pregnant?' Katinka asked, and ran her hand lightly over the girl's stomach. It was flat and hard.

'No! No!' Kleinhans exclaimed. 'She is a virgin.'

'There is never any guarantee of that state. The devil enters even the most heavily barred fortress.' Katinka smiled. 'But I will accept your word on it. I want to see her teeth. Open your mouth.' For a moment she thought Sukeena would refuse, but then her lips parted, and her small teeth sparkled in the sunlight, whiter than freshly carved ivory.

Katinka laid the tip of her finger on the girl's lower lip. It felt soft as a rose petal, and Katinka let the moment hang, drawing out the pleasure, prolonging Sukeena's humiliation. Then, slowly and voluptuously, she ran her finger between the girl's lips. The gesture was sexually fraught, a parody of the masculine penetration of the woman. As he watched, Kleinhans' hand began to tremble so violently that the sweet Constantia wine spilled over the rim of the glass he held. Cornelius Schreuder scowled and moved uneasily in his seat, crossing one leg over the other.

The inside of Sukeena's mouth was soft and moist. The two women stared at each other. Then Katinka began to move her finger slowly back and forth, exploring and probing while she asked Kleinhans, 'Her father, this Englishman, what happened to him? If he loved his concubine, as you say he did, why did he allow her children to be sold on the slave block?'

'He was one of the English bandits that were executed while I was Governor of Batavia. I am sure you are acquainted with the incident, are you not, Mevrouw?'

'Yes, I recall it well. The accused men were tortured by the Company executioner to ascertain the extent of their villainy,' Katinka said softly, still gazing into Sukeena's eyes. The extremity of the suffering she saw in them amazed and intrigued her. 'I did not know that you were the Governor at that time. The girl's father was executed at your orders, then?' Katinka asked, and Sukeena's lips quivered and closed softly around Katinka's long white finger.

'I have heard that they were crucified,' Katinka breathed huskily, and Sukeena's eyes filled with tears although her features remained serene. 'I have heard that burning sulphur flares were applied to their feet,' Katinka said, and felt the girl's tongue slide over her finger as she swallowed her grief. 'And then the flares were held under their hands.' Sukeena's sharp little teeth closed on her finger, not hard enough to be painful and certainly not hard enough to break or mark the white skin, but the threat was in her eyes, which were filled with hatred.

'I regret that it was necessary. The man's obstinacy was extraordinary. It must be a national trait of the English.' Kleinhans nodded. 'To endorse the punishment I ordered that the condemned man's concubine, her name was Ashreth, be made to watch the execution, she and the two children. Of course, at the time I knew nothing of Sukeena and her brother. It was not idle cruelty on my part but Company policy. These people do not respond to kindness, which they mistake for weakness.' Kleinhans gave a sigh of regret at such intransigence.

The tears were sliding silently down Sukeena's cheeks as Kleinhans went on, 'Once they had fully confessed their guilt, the criminals were burned. The flares were thrown onto the faggots of wood at their feet and the whole lot went up in the flames, which was a merciful release for all of us.'

With a small shudder Katinka withdrew her finger from between the girl's trembling lips. With the tenderness of a satisfied lover she stroked the satiny cheek, her finger still wet with the girl's saliva leaving damp streaks on the amber skin.

'What happened to the woman, the concubine? Was she also sold into slavery with the children?' Katinka asked, not taking her gaze from those grief-wet eyes in front of her.

'No,' Kleinhans said. 'That is the strange part of the story. Ashreth threw herself into the flames and perished on the same pyre as her English lover. There is no understanding the native mind, is there?'

There was a long silence, and when a cloud passed over the sun the day seemed suddenly dark and chill.

'I will take her,' Katinka said, so softly that Kleinhans cupped a hand to his ear.

'Please excuse me, Mevrouw, but I did not catch what you said.'

'I will take her,' Katinka repeated. 'This girl, Sukeena, I will buy her from you.'

'We have not yet agreed a price.' Kleinhans looked startled: he had not expected it to be so easy.

'I am certain your price will be reasonable – that is, if you also wish to sell me the other slaves in your span.'

'You are a lady of great compassion.' Kleinhans shook his head in admiration. 'I see that Sukeena's story has touched your heart and that you want to take her into your care. Thank you. I know you will treat her kindly.'

Hal hung on the grating of the cell window and called his sighting to Aboli, who held him on his shoulders.

'They have returned in the Governor's carriage. The three of them, Kleinhans, Schreuder and Governor van de Velde's wife. They are going back up the staircase—' He broke off and exclaimed, 'Wait! There is someone else alighting from the carriage. Someone I do not know. A woman.'

Daniel, who was standing at the grille gate, relayed this message up the staircase to the solitary cells at the top.

'Describe this strange woman,' Sir Francis called.

At that moment the woman turned to say something to Fredricus the driver and, with a start, Hal recognized her as the slave girl who had stood in the crowd while they were being marched across the parade.

'She is small and young, almost a child. Balinese, perhaps, or Malaccan, something about the look of her.' He hesitated. 'She is probably of mixed blood, and almost certainly a servant or a slave. Kleinhans and Schreuder walk ahead of her.'

Daniel passed this on, and suddenly Althuda's voice came back to them down the stairwell. 'Is she very pretty? Long dark hair twisted up on top of her head, with flowers in it. Does she wear a green jade ornament at her throat?'

'All those things,' Hal shouted back. 'Except that she is not pretty, she is lovely beyond the telling of it. Do you know her? Who is she?'

'Her name is Sukeena. She is the one for whom I came back from the mountains. She is my little sister.'

Hal watched Sukeena mount the stairs, moving with the lightness and alacrity of an autumn leaf in a gust of wind. Somehow, while he watched this girl, his thoughts of Katinka were not so all-consuming. When she disappeared from his sight, the light filtering into the dungeon seemed dimmer and the stone walls more damp and cold.

At first they had all been amazed by the treatment meted out to them in the castle dungeons. They were allowed to slop out the latrine bucket every morning, drawing lots for the privilege. At the end of the first week, a load of fresh straw was delivered by one of the Company field slaves, driving an oxcart, and they were allowed to throw out the verminous old straw that covered the floors. Through a copper pipe the water cistern was fed continuously from one of the streams that rushed down from the mountain, so they suffered no hardship from thirst. Each evening a loaf of coarse-grained bread, the size of a wagon wheel, and a great iron pot were sent down from the kitchens. The pot was filled with the peelings and offcuts of vegetables, boiled up with the meat of seals captured on Robben Island. This stew was more plentiful and tastier than much of the food they had eaten aboard ship.

Althuda laughed when he heard them discussing it. 'They also feed their oxen well. Dumb animals work better when they are strong.'

'We ain't doing much work here and now,' Daniel remarked comfortably, and patted his belly.

Althuda laughed again. 'Look out of the window,' he advised them. 'There is a fort to build. You will not be sitting down here much longer. Believe me when I say it.'

'Ahoy there, Althuda,' Daniel shouted, 'your sister isn't English, so it makes sense that you aren't an Englishman either. How is it that you speak like one?'

'My father was from Plymouth. I have never been there. Do you know the place?'

There was a roar of laughter and comment and clapping, and Hal spoke for them all. 'By God, except for Aboli and these other African knaves, we are all Devon men and true. You are one of us, then, Althuda!'

'You have never seen me. I must warn you that I don't look like you,' Althuda warned them.

'If you look half as good as your little sister, then you'll do well enough,' Hal replied, and the men hooted with laughter.

For the first week of their captivity, they saw the sergeant gaoler, named Manseer, only when the stew pot was brought in or when the bedding straw was changed. Then, suddenly, on the eighth morning, the iron door at the head of the stairs was thrown open with a crash and Manseer bellowed down the well, 'Two at a time, form up. We are taking you out to wash some of the stink off you, or the judge will suffocate before he has a chance to send you to Stadige Jan. Come on now, shake yourselves.'

With a dozen guards keeping watch over them they were taken out in pairs, made to strip naked and wash themselves and their clothing under the hand pump behind the stables.

The following morning they were turned out again with the dawn, and this time the castle armourer was waiting with his forge and anvil to shackle them together, not this time in one long ungainly file but into pairs.

When the iron-studded door to Sir Francis's cell was opened, and his father emerged with his hair hanging lankly to his shoulders and a grizzled beard covering his chin, Hal pushed himself forward so that they were shackled together.

'How are you, Father?' Hal asked with concern, for he had never seen his father looking so seedy.

Before Sir Francis could reply a bout of coughing overtook him. When it passed, he answered hoarsely, 'I prefer a good Channel gale to the air down here, but I am well enough for what has to be done.'

'I could not shout it to you, but Aboli and I have been working out a plan to escape,' Hal whispered to him. 'We have managed to lift one of the floor slabs in the back of the cell and we are going to dig a tunnel under the walls.'

'With your bare hands?' Sir Francis smiled at him.

'We need to find a tool,' Hal admitted, 'but when we do . . .'

He nodded with grim determination, and Sir Francis felt his heart might burst with love and pride. I have taught him to be a fighter, and to keep on fighting even when the battle is lost. Sweet God, I hope the Dutchies spare him the fate that they have in store for me.

In the middle of the morning they were marched from the courtyard up the staircase into the main hall of the castle, which had been converted into a courtroom. Shackled two by two, they were led to the four rows of low wooden benches in the centre of the floor and seated upon them, Sir Francis and Hal in the middle of the front row. Their guards, with drawn swords, lined up along the wall behind them.

A platform had been built against the wall before them and on it, facing the benches of the prisoners, was set a heavy table and a tall chair of dark teak. This was the judge's throne. At one end of the table was a stool, on which the court writer was already seated, scribbling busily in his journal. Below the platform was another pair of tables and chairs. At one of these sat someone Hal had seen many times before through the cell window. According to Althuda, he was a junior clerk in the Company administration. His name was Jacobus Hop and, after one nervous glance at the prisoners, he did not look at them again. He was rustling and scratching through a sheaf of documents, pausing from time to time to wipe his sweating face with a large white neckcloth.

At the second table sat Colonel Cornelius Schreuder. He was the romantic poet's image of the gallant and debonair soldier, all a-glitter with his medallions and stars and the wide sash across one shoulder. His wig was freshly washed, the curls hanging down to his shoulders. His legs were thrust out in front of him, his soft thigh-high boots crossed at the ankles. On the table top in front of him books and papers were scattered and laid carelessly upon them were his plumed hat and the Neptune sword. As he rocked backwards and forwards on his chair he stared relentlessly at Hal, and though Hal tried to match his gaze he was forced at last to drop his eyes.

There was a sudden uproar at the main doors, and when they swung open the crowds from the town burst in and scrambled to find seats on the benches down each side of the hall. As soon as the last seat was taken, the doors were forced closed again in the faces of those unfortunates at the rear. Now the hall was clamorous with excited comment and anticipation, as the lucky spectators studied the prisoners and loudly gave their opinions to each other.

To one side an area had been railed off, and two green-jackets with drawn swords stood guard over it. Behind the railing a row of comfortable cushioned chairs had been arranged. Now there was further hubbub, and the crowd's attention turned from the accused men to the dignitaries who filed out through the doors of the audience chamber. Governor Kleinhans led them, with Katinka van de Velde on his arm, followed by Lord Cumbrae and Captain Limberger, chatting casually together, ignoring the stir that their entrance was causing among the common folk.

Katinka took the chair in the centre of the row. Hal stared at her, willing her to look in his direction, to give him a sign of recognition and reassurance. He tried to sustain in himself the faith that she would never abandon him, and that she had already used her influence and had interceded with her husband for mercy, but she was deep in conversation with Governor Kleinhans and never as much as glanced at the ranks of English seamen. She does not want others to see her preference and concern for us, Hal consoled himself, but when the time comes for her to give her evidence she will surely speak out for us.

Colonel Schreuder clumped down his booted feet heavily and came to his feet. He stared around the crowded hall with huge disdain, and the female spectators gave little sighs and squeals of admiration.

'This tribunal is convened by virtue of the power conferred upon the honourable Dutch East India Company in the terms of the charter issued to the aforesaid Company by the government of the Republic of Holland and the Lowlands. Pray silence and stand for the president of the tribunal, His Excellency Governor Petrus van de Velde.'

The spectators came to their feet with a subdued murmur and stared in anticipation at the door behind the platform. Some of the prisoners struggled up, rattling their chains, but when they saw Sir Francis Courtney and Hal sit unmoving they subsided back onto the benches.

Through the far door appeared the president of the court. He mounted ponderously to the platform and glared down upon the seated rows of prisoners. 'Get those rogues on their feet!' he bellowed suddenly and the crowds quailed before his murderous expression.

In the stunned silence that followed this outburst, Sir Francis spoke out clearly in Dutch. 'Neither I nor any of my men recognize the authority of this assembly, nor do we accept the right of the self-appointed president to examine and sentence free-born Englishmen, subjects only of His Majesty King Charles the Second.'

Van de Velde seemed to swell like a great toad. His face turned a dark and furious shade of crimson, and he roared, 'You are a pirate and a murderer. By the sovereignty of the Republic and the charter of the Company, by the right of moral and international law, the authority is vested in me to conduct this trial.' He broke off to gasp for breath, then went on even louder than before. 'I find you guilty of gross and flagrant contempt of this court, and I sentence you to ten strokes of the cane to be administered forthwith.' He looked to the commander of the guard. 'Master of arms, take the prisoner into the courtyard and carry out the sentence at once.'

Four soldiers hurried forward from the back of the hall, and hauled Sir Francis to his feet. Hal, shackled to his father, was dragged with him to the main doors. Behind them, men and women leaped onto the benches and craned for a view, then rushed in a body to the doorway and the windows as Sir Francis and Hal were urged down the staircase into the yard.

Sir Francis kept silent, his head high and his back straight, as he was pushed to the hitching rail for officer's horses at the entrance of the armoury. At the shouted orders of the sergeant, he and Hal were placed on either side of the high rail, facing each other, their manacled wrists hooked into the iron rings.

Hal was powerless to intervene. The sergeant placed his forefinger in the back of the collar of Sir Francis's shirt and yanked down, splitting the cotton to the waist. Then he stepped back and swished his light malacca cane.

'You have made an oath on your Knighthood. Do you stand by it on your honour?' Sir Francis whispered to his son.

'I do, Father.'

The cane fluted and snapped on his bare flesh, and Sir Francis winced. 'This beating is but a little thing, the play of children compared to what must follow. Do you understand that?'

'I understand full well.'

The sergeant struck again. He was laying the stripes one on top of the other, the pain multiplying with each blow.

'No matter what you do or say, nothing and no one can change the flight of the red comet. The stars have laid out my destiny and you cannot intervene.'

The cane hummed and cracked, and Sir Francis's body stiffened, then relaxed.

'If you are strong and constant, you will endure. That will be my reward.'

This time he gave a small, hoarse gasp as the cane bit into the tautly stretched muscles of his back.

'You are my body and my blood. Through you I also will endure.'

The cane hummed and clapped, again and again.

'Swear it to me one last time. Reinforce your oath, that you will never reveal anything to these people in a futile attempt to save me.'

'Father, I swear it to you,' Hal whispered back, his face white as bleached bone, as the cane sang, a succession of cruel blows.

'I put all my faith and my trust in you,' said Sir Francis, and the soldiers lifted him down from the railing. As they marched back up the staircase, he leaned lightly on Hal's arm. When he stumbled Hal braced him, so that his head was still high and his bloody back straight as they entered the hall and marched together to their seats on the front bench.

Governor van de Velde was now seated on the dais. A silver tray was set at his elbow, loaded with small china bowls of appetizers and spiced savouries. He was munching contentedly on one of these and drinking from a pewter mug of small beer as he chatted to Colonel Schreuder at the table below him. As soon as Sir Francis and Hal were shoved by their guards onto the bench again his amiable expression changed dramatically. He raised his voice and an immediate, dense silence fell over the assembly. 'I trust that I have made it clear that I will brook no further hindrance to these proceedings.' He glowered at Sir Francis and then raised his eyes to sweep the hall. 'That goes for all persons gathered here. Anyone else who in any way attempts to make a mockery of this tribunal will receive the same treatment as the prisoner.' He looked down at Schreuder. 'Who appears for the prosecution?'

Schreuder stood up. 'Colonel Cornelius Schreuder, at your service, your excellency.'

'Who appears for the defence?' Van de Velde glowered at Jacobus Hop, and the clerk sprang to his feet, sending half the documents in front of him showering to the tiles.

'I do, your excellency.'

'State your name, man!' van de Velde roared at him, and Hop wriggled like a puppy.

He stammered, 'Jacobus Hop, clerk and writer to the Honourable Dutch East India Company.' This declaration took a long time to enunciate.

'In future speak out and speak clear,' van de Velde warned him, then turned back to Schreuder. 'You may proceed to present your case, Colonel.'

'This is a matter of piracy on the high seas, together with murder and abduction. The accused are twenty-four in number. With your indulgence, I will now read a list of their names. Each prisoner will stand when his name is read so that the court may recognize him.' From the sleeve of his tunic he drew a roll of parchment and held it at arm's length. 'The foremost accused person is Francis Courtney, captain of the pirate bark the *Lady Edwina*. Your excellency, he is the leader and instigator of all the criminal acts perpetrated by this pack of seawolves and corsairs.' Van de Velde nodded his understanding and Schreuder went on. 'Henry Courtney, officer and mate. Ned Tyler, boatswain. Daniel Fisher, boatswain . . .' He recited the name and rank of each man on the benches, and each stood briefly, some of them bobbing their heads and grinning ingratiatingly at van de Velde. The last four names on Schreuder's list were those of the black seamen.

'Matesi, a Negro slave.

'Jiri, a Negro slave.

'Kimatti, a Negro slave.

'Aboli, a Negro slave.

'The prosecution will prove that on the fourth day of September in the year of Our Lord sixteen sixty-seven, Francis Courtney, while commanding the caravel the *Lady Edwina*, of which the other prisoners were all crew members, did fall upon the galleon *De Standvastigheid*, Captain Limberger commanding . . .' Schreuder spoke without reference to notes or papers, and Hal felt a reluctant admiration for the thoroughness and lucidity of his accusations.

'And now, your excellency, if you please, I should like to call my first witness.' Van de Velde nodded, and Schreuder turned and looked across the floor. 'Call Captain Limberger.'

The captain of the galleon left his comfortable chair in the railed-off enclosure, crossed to the platform and stepped up onto it. The witness's chair stood beside the judge's table and Limberger seated himself.

'Do you understand the gravity of this matter and swear in the name of Almighty God to tell the truth before this court?' van de Velde asked him.

'I do, your excellency.'

'Very well, Colonel, you may question your witness.'

Swiftly Schreuder led Limberger through a recital of his name, rank and his duties for the Company. He then asked for a description of the *Standvastigheid*, her passengers and her cargo. Limberger read his replies from the list he had prepared. When he had finished Schreuder asked, 'Who was the owner of this ship and of the cargo she was carrying?'

'The honourable Dutch East India Company.'

'Now, Captain Limberger, on the fourth of September of this year was your ship voyaging in about latitude thirty-four degrees south and longitude four degrees east – that is approximately fifty leagues south of the Agulhas Cape?'

'It was.'

'That is some time after the cessation of hostilities between Holland and England?'

'Yes, it was.'

Schreuder picked up a leather-bound log-book from the table in front of him and passed it up to Limberger. 'Is this the log-book that you were keeping on board your ship during that voyage?'

Limberger examined it briefly, 'Yes, Colonel, this is my log.'

Schreuder looked at van de Velde. 'Your excellency, I think I should inform you that the log-book was found in the possession of the pirate Courtney after his capture by Company troops.' Van de Velde nodded, and Schreuder looked at Limberger. 'Will you please read to us the last entry in your log?'

Limberger turned the pages and then read aloud, '"Fourth September sixteen sixty-seven. Two bells in the morning watch. Position by dead reckoning four degrees twenty-three minutes south latitude thirty-four degrees, forty-five minutes east longitude. Strange sail in sight bearing south-south-east. Flying friendly colours."' Limberger closed the log and looked up. 'The entry ends there,' he said.

'Was that strange sail noted in your log the caravel the *Lady Edwina*, and was she flying the colours of the Republic and the Company?'

'Yes, to both questions.'

'Will you recount the events that took place after you sighted the *Lady Edwina*, please.'

Limberger gave a clear description of the capture of his ship, with Schreuder making him emphasize Sir Francis's use of false colours to get within striking distance. After Limberger had told of the boarding and fighting on board the galleon, Schreuder asked for a detailed account of the numbers of Dutch sailors wounded and killed. Limberger had a written list prepared and handed this to the court.

'Thank you, Captain. Can you tell us what happened to you, your crew and your passengers once the pirates had taken control of your ship?'

Limberger went on to describe how they had sailed east in company with the *Lady Edwina*, the transfer of cargo and gear from the caravel into the galleon, and the dispatch of the *Lady Edwina* in command of Schreuder to the Cape with letters of demand for ransom, the onward voyage aboard the captured galleon to Elephant Lagoon and the captivity of himself and his eminent passengers there until their salvation by the expeditionary force from the Cape, led by Schreuder and Lord Cumbrae.

When Schreuder had finished questioning him, van de Velde looked at Hop. 'Do you have any questions, Mijnheer?'

With both hands full of papers Hop stood up, blushed furiously, then took a deep, gulping breath and let out a long, unbroken stammer. Everybody in the hall watched his agony with interest, and at last van de Velde spoke. 'Captain Limberger intends sailing for Holland in two weeks' time. Do you think you will have asked your question by then, Hop?'

Hop shook his head. 'No questions,' he said at last, and sat down heavily.

'Who is your next witness, Colonel?' van de Velde asked, as soon as Limberger had left the witness chair and was seated back in the enclosure.

'I would like to call the Governor's wife, Mevrouw Katinka van de Velde. That is, if it does not inconvenience her.'

There was a masculine hum of approval as Katinka rustled her silk and her laces to the witness's chair. Sir Francis felt Hal stiffen beside him, but did not turn to look at his face. Only days before their capture, when Hal had been absent from the camp for long periods and had begun to neglect his duties, he had realized that his son had fallen into the golden whore's snare. By then it had been far too late to intervene, and in any case, he remembered what it was like to be young and in love, even with an utterly unsuitable woman, and had understood the futility of trying to prevent what had already happened. He had been waiting for the correct moment and the right means to end the liaison when Schreuder and the Buzzard had attacked the camp.

With great deference, Schreuder led Katinka gently through the recital of her name and position and then asked her to describe her voyage aboard the *Standvastigheid*, and how she had been taken prisoner. She answered in a sweet, clear voice that throbbed with emotion, and Schreuder went on, 'Please tell us, madam, how you were treated by your captors.'

Katinka began to sob softly. 'I have tried to put the memory from my mind, for it was too painful to bear thinking upon. But I will never be able to forget. I was treated like a caged animal, cursed and spat upon, kept locked up in a grass hut.' Even van de Velde looked amazed by the testimony, but realized that it would look impressive in the report that went to Amsterdam. After reading it Katinka's father and the other members of the Seventeen would have no other option but to approve even the harshest retribution visited on the prisoners.

Sir Francis was aware of the turmoil of emotion that Hal was suffering as he listened to the woman in whom he had placed so much trust pouring out her lies. He felt his son sag physically as she destroyed his faith in her.

'Be of good heart, my boy,' he said softly, from the corner of his mouth, and felt Hal sit up straighter on the hard bench.

'My dear lady, we know that you have suffered a terrible ordeal at the hands of these inhuman monsters.' By this time Schreuder was trembling with anger to hear of her ordeal. Katinka nodded and dabbed daintily at her eyes with a lace handkerchief. 'Do you believe that animals such as these should be shown mercy, or should they be subjected to the full force and majesty of the law?'

'Sweet Jesus knows that I am only a poor female, with a soft and loving heart for all God's creation.' Katinka's voice broke pitifully. 'But I know that everybody in this assembly will agree with me that a simple hanging is too good for these unspeakable wretches.' A murmur of agreement spread slowly along the benches of spectators, then turned into a deep growl. Like a pit full of bears at feeding time, they wanted blood.

'Burn them!' a woman screamed. 'They are not fit to be called men.'

Katinka lifted her head and, for the first time since entering the hall, she looked directly at Hal, staring through her tears straight into his eyes.

Hal lifted his chin and stared back. He felt the love and awe he had cherished for her withering, like a tender vine struck with the black mould. Sir Francis felt it too, and turned to look at him. He saw the ice in his son's eyes and could almost feel the heat of the flames in his heart.

'She was never worthy of you,' Sir Francis said softly. 'Now that you have renounced her, you have taken another mighty leap into manhood.'

Did his father really understand, Hal wondered. Did he know what had taken place? Did he know of Hal's feelings? If that were so, surely he would long ago have rejected him. He turned and looked into Sir Francis's eyes, fearing to see them filled with scorn and revulsion. But his father's gaze was mellow with understanding. Hal realized that he knew everything, and had probably known all along. Far from rejecting him, his father was offering him strength and redemption.

'I have committed adultery, and I have disgraced my Knighthood,' Hal whispered. 'I am no longer worthy to be called your son.'

The manacle on his wrist clinked as Sir Francis laid his hand on the boy's knee. ''Twas this harlot that led you astray. The blame is not yours. You will always be my son and I shall always be proud of you,' he whispered.

Van de Velde frowned down upon Sir Francis. 'Silence! No more of your muttering! Is it another touch of the cane you are seeking?' He turned back to his wife. 'Mevrouw, you have been very brave. I am sure Mijnheer Hop will not wish to trouble you further.' He transferred his gaze to the unfortunate clerk, who scrambled to his feet.

'Mevrouw!' The single word came out sharp and clear as a pistol shot, surprising Hop as much as everyone else in court. 'We thank you for your testimony, and we have no questions.' There was only one catch, on the word 'testimony', and Hop sat down again triumphantly.

'Well said, Hop.' Van de Velde beamed at him in avuncular fashion, and then turned a doting smile on his wife. 'You may return to your seat, Mevrouw.' There was a lust-laden hush and every man in the hall let his gaze drop as Katinka lifted her skirts just high enough to expose her perfect little ankles clad in white silk and stepped down from the platform.

As soon as she was seated, Schreuder said, 'Now, Lord Cumbrae, may we trouble you?'

In his full regalia the Buzzard mounted the platform, and as he took the oath placed one hand on the flashing yellow cairngorm in the hilt of his dagger. Once Schreuder had established who and what he was, he asked the Buzzard, 'Do you know the pirate captain, Courtney?'

'Like a brother.' Cumbrae smiled down on Sir Francis. 'Once we were close.'

'Not any more?' Schreuder asked sharply.

'Alas, it pains me but when my old friend began to change there was a parting of our ways, although I still feel great affection for him.'

'How did he change?'

'Well, he was always a braw laddie, was Franky. We sailed in company on many a day, through storm and the balmy days. There was no man I loved better, fair he was and honest, brave and generous to his friends—' Cumbrae broke off and an expression of deep sorrow knitted his brow.

'You speak in the past tense, my lord, what changed?'

''Twas Francis who changed. At first it was in little things – he was cruel to his captives and hard on his crew, flogging and hanging when it weren't called for. Then he changed towards his old friends, lying and cheating them out of their share of the prize. He became a hard man and bitter.'

'Thank you for this honesty,' Schreuder said, 'I can see it gives you no pleasure to reveal these truths.'

'No pleasure at all,' Cumbrae confirmed with sadness. 'I hate to see my old friend in chains, though God Almighty knows well he deserves no mercy for his murderous behaviour towards honest Dutch seamen, and innocent women.'

'When did you last sail in company with Courtney?'

'It was not too long ago, in April of this year. Our two ships were on patrol together off Agulhas, waiting to waylay the Company galleons as they rounded the Cape to call in here at Table Bay.' There was a murmur of patriotic anger from the spectators, which van de Velde ignored.

'Were you, then, also a corsair?' Schreuder glared at him. 'Were you also preying on Dutch shipping?'

'No, Colonel Schreuder, I was not a pirate or a corsair. During the recent war between our two countries, I was a commissioned privateer.'

'Pray, my lord, tell us the difference between a pirate and a privateer?'

''Tis simply that a privateer sails under Letters of Marque issued by his sovereign in times of war, and so is a legitimate man-of-war. A pirate is a robber and an outlaw, carrying out his depredations without any sanction, but that of the Lord of Darkness, Satan himself.'

'I see. So you had a Letter of Marque when you were raiding Dutch shipping?'

'Yes, Colonel. I did.'

'Are you able to show this document to us?'

'Naturally!' Cumbrae reached into his sleeve and drew out a roll of parchment. He leaned down and handed it to Schreuder.

'Thank you.' Schreuder unrolled it and held it up for all to see, heavy with scarlet ribbons and wax seals. He read aloud, 'Know you by these presents that our dearly beloved Angus Cochran, Earl of Cumbrae—'

'Very well, Colonel,' van de Velde interrupted testily. 'No need to read us the whole thing. Let me have it here, if you please.'

Schreuder bowed. 'As your excellency pleases.' He handed up the document. Van de Velde glanced at it then set it aside. 'Please go on with your questions.'

'My lord, did Courtney, the prisoner, also have one of these Letters of Marque?'

'Well, now, if he did I was not aware of it.' The Buzzard grinned openly at Sir Francis.

'Would you have expected to be aware of it, if the letter had, in fact, existed?'

'Sir Francis and I were very close. No secrets between us. Yes, he would have told me.'

'He never discussed the letter with you?' Schreuder looked annoyed, like a pedagogue whose pupil has forgotten his lines. 'Never?'

'Oh, yes. Now I do recall one occasion. I asked him if he had a royal commission.'

'And what was his reply?'

'He said, "It ain't nothing but a bit of paper anyway. I don't trouble meself with rubbish like that!"'

'So you knew he had no letter and yet you sailed in his company?'

Cumbrae shrugged. 'It was war-time, and it was none of my business.'

'So you were off Cape Agulhas with the prisoner after the peace had been signed, and you were still raiding Dutch shipping. Can you explain that to us?'

'It was simple, Colonel. We did not know about peace, that is until I fell in with a Portuguese caravel outward bound from Lisbon for Goa. I hailed her and her captain told me that peace had been signed.'

'What was the name of this Portuguese ship?'

'She was the *El Dragão*.'

'Was the prisoner Courtney present at this meeting with her?'

'No, his patrol station was north of mine. He was over the horizon and out of sight at the time.'

Schreuder nodded. 'Where is this ship now?'

'I have here a copy of a news-sheet from London, only three months old. It arrived three days ago on the Company ship lying in the bay at this moment.' The Buzzard produced the sheet from his sleeve with a magician's flourish. '*El Dragão* was lost with all hands in a storm in the Bay of Biscay while on her homeward voyage.'

'So, it would seem, then, that we will never have any way of disproving your meeting with her off Agulhas?'

'You'll just have to take my word for it, Colonel.' Cumbrae stroked his great red beard.

'What did you do when you heard of the peace between England and Holland?'

'As an honest man, there was only one thing I could do. I broke off my patrol, and went in search of the *Lady Edwina*.'

'To warn her that the war was over?' Schreuder suggested.

'Of course, and to tell Franky that my Letter of Marque was no longer valid and that I was going home.'

'Did you find Courtney? Did you give him that message?'

'I found him within a few hours' sailing. He was due north of my position, about twenty leagues distant.'

'What did he say when you told him the war was over?'

'He said, "It may be over for you, but it ain't over for me. Rain or shine, wind or calm, war or peace, I am going to catch myself a fat cheese-head."'

There was a ferocious clanking of chains and Big Daniel sprang to his feet, dragging the diminutive figure of Ned Tyler off the bench with him. 'There ain't a word of truth in it, you lying Scots bastard!' he thundered.

Van de Velde jumped up and wagged his finger at Daniel. 'Sit down, you English animal, or I'll have you thrashed, and not just with the light cane.'

Sir Francis turned and reached back to grab Daniel's arm. 'Calm yourself, Master Daniel,' he said quietly. 'Don't give the Buzzard the pleasure of watching us ache.' Big Daniel sank down, muttering furiously to himself, but he would not disobey his captain.

'I am sure Governor van de Velde will take notice of the unruly and desperate nature of these villains,' Schreuder said, then turned his attention back to the Buzzard. 'Did you ever see Courtney again before today?'

'Yes, I did. When I heard that, despite my warning, he had seized a Company galleon, I went to find him and remonstrate with him. To ask him to free the ship and its cargo, and to release the hostages he was holding to ransom.'

'How did he respond to your pleas?'

'He turned his guns upon my ship, killing twelve of my seamen, and he attacked me with fireships.' The Buzzard shook his head at the memory of this perfidious treatment by an old friend and shipmate. 'That was when I came here to Table Bay to inform Governor Kleinhans of the galleon's whereabouts and to offer to lead an expedition to recapture the ship and her cargo from the pirates.'

'As a soldier myself, I can only commend you, my lord, on your exemplary conduct. I have no further questions, your excellency.' Schreuder bowed at van de Velde.

'Hop, do you have any questions?' van de Velde demanded.

Hop looked confused, and glanced in appeal at Sir Francis.

'Your excellency,' he stuttered, 'might I speak to Sir Francis alone, if only for a minute?'

For a while it seemed that van de Velde might refuse the request, but he clasped his brow wearily. 'If you insist on holding up these proceedings all the time, Hop, we will be here all week. Very well, man, you may talk to the prisoner, but do try to be quick.'

Hop hurried across to Sir Francis and leaned close. He asked a question, and listened to the reply with an expression of dawning horror on his pale face. He nodded and kept nodding as Sir Francis whispered in his ear, then went back to his table.

He stared down at his papers, breathing like a pearl diver about to plunge out of his canoe into twenty fathoms of water. Finally he looked up and shouted at Cumbrae, 'The first you knew of the end of the war was when you tried to cut out the *Swallow* from under the fortress here in Table Bay and were told about it by Colonel Schreuder.'

It came out in a single rush, without check or pause, but it was a long speech and Hop reeled back, gasping from the exertion.

'Have you lost your wits, Hop?' van de Velde bellowed. 'Are you accusing a nobleman of lying, you little turd?'

Hop drew another full breath, took his fragile courage in both hands, and shouted again, 'You held Captain Courtney's Letter of Marque in your own two hands, then brandished it in his face while you burned it to ashes.' Again it came out fluently, but Hop was spent. He stood there gulping for air.

Van de Velde was on his feet now. 'If you are looking for advancement in the Company, Hop, you are going about it in a very strange way. You stand there hurling crazy accusations at a man of high rank. Don't you know your place, you worthless guttersnipe? How dare you behave like this? Sit down before I have you taken out and flogged.' Hop dropped into his seat as though he had received a musket ball in the head. Breathing heavily, van de Velde bowed towards the Buzzard. 'I must apologize, my lord. Every person here knows that you were instrumental in rescuing the hostages and saving the *Standvastigheid* from the clutches of these villains. Please ignore those insulting statements and return to your seat. We are grateful for your help in this matter.'

As Cumbrae crossed the floor, van de Velde suddenly became aware of the writer scribbling away busily beside him. 'Don't write that down, you fool. It was not part of the court proceedings. Here, let me see your journal.' He snatched it from the clerk, and as he read his face darkened. He leaned across and took the quill from the writer's hand. With a series of broad strokes he expurgated those parts of the text that offended him. Then he pushed the book back towards the writer. 'Use your intelligence. Paper is an expensive commodity. Don't waste it by writing down unimportant rubbish.' Then he transferred his attention to the two advocates. 'Gentlemen, I should like this matter settled today. I do not want to put the Company to unnecessary expense by wasting any more time. Colonel Schreuder, I think you have made a thoroughly convincing presentation of the case against the pirates. I hope that you do not intend to gild the lily by calling any more witnesses, do you?'

'As your excellency pleases. I had intended calling ten more—'

'Sweet heavens!' Van de Velde looked appalled. 'That will not be necessary at all.'

Schreuder bowed deeply and sat down. Van de Velde lowered his head like a bull about to charge and looked at the defence advocate. 'Hop!' he growled. 'You have just seen how reasonable Colonel Schreuder has been, and what an excellent example in the economy of words and time he has set for this court. What are your intentions?'

'May I call Sir Francis Courtney to give evidence?' Hop stuttered.

'I strongly advise against it,' van de Velde told him ominously. 'Certainly it will do your case little good.'

'I want to show that he did not know the war had ended and that he was sailing under a commission from the English King,' Hop ploughed on obstinately, and van de Velde flushed crimson.

'Damn you, Hop. Haven't you listened to a word I said? We know all about that line of defence, and I will take it into consideration when I ponder my verdict. You don't have to regurgitate those lies again.'

'I would like to have the prisoner say it, just for the court records.' Hop was close to tears, and his words limped painfully over his crippled tongue.

'You are trying my patience, Hop. Continue in this fashion, and you will be on the next ship back to Amsterdam. I cannot have a disloyal Company servant spreading dissension and sedition throughout the colony.'

Hop looked alarmed to hear himself described in such terms, and he capitulated with alacrity. 'I apologize for delaying the business of this honourable court. I rest the case for the defence.'

'Good man! You have done a fine job of work, Hop. I will make a notation to that effect in my next despatch to the Seventeen.' Van de

Velde's face resumed its natural colour and he beamed jovially about the hall. 'We will adjourn for the midday meal and for the court to consider its verdict. We will reconvene at four o'clock this afternoon. Take the prisoners back to the dungeons.'

To avoid having to remove their shackles Manseer, the gaoler, bundled Hal who was still chained to his father into the solitary cell near the top of the spiral staircase, while the rest went below.

Hal and Sir Francis sat side by side on the stone shelf that served as a bed. As soon as they were alone Hal blurted out, 'Father, I want to explain to you about Katinka – I mean about the Governor's wife.'

Sir Francis embraced him awkwardly, hampered by the chains. 'Unlikely as it now seems, I was young once. You do not have to speak about that harlot again. She is not worthy of your consideration.'

'I will never love another woman, not as long as I live,' Hal said bitterly.

'What you felt for that woman was not love, my son.' Sir Francis shook his head. 'Your love is a precious currency. Spend it only in the market where you will not be cheated again.'

At that there was a tapping on the iron bars of the next cell, and Althuda called, 'How goes the trial, Captain Courtney? Have they given you a good taste of Company justice?'

Sir Francis raised his voice to answer. 'It goes as you said it would, Althuda. It is obvious that you also have experienced it.'

'The Governor is the only god in this little heaven called Good Hope. Here, justice is that which pays a profit to the Dutch East India Company or a bribe to its servants. Has the judge pronounced your guilt yet?'

'Not yet. Van de Velde has gone to guzzle at his trough.'

'You must pray that he values labour for his walls more than revenge. That way you might still slip through Slow John's fingers. Is there anything you are hiding from them? Anything they want from you – to betray a comrade, perhaps?' Althuda asked. 'If there is not, then you might still escape the little room under the armoury where Slow John does his work.'

'We are hiding nothing,' Sir Francis said. 'Are we, Hal?'

'Nothing,' Hal agreed loyally.

'But,' Sir Francis went on, 'van de Velde believes that we are.'

'Then all I can say, my friend, is may Almighty Allah have pity on you.'

Those last hours together went too swiftly for Hal. He and his father spent the time talking softly together. Every so often Sir Francis broke off in a fit of coughing. His eyes glittered feverishly in the dim light, and when Hal touched his skin it was hot and clammy. Sir Francis spoke of High Weald like a man who knows he will never see his home again. When he described the river and the hill, Hal dimly remembered them and the salmon coming upstream in the spring and the stags roaring in the rut. When he spoke of his wife, Hal tried to recall his mother's face, but saw only the woman in the miniature painting he had left buried at Elephant Lagoon, and not the real live person.

'These last years she has faded in my own memory,' Sir Francis admitted. 'But now her face comes back to me vividly, as young and fresh and sweet as she ever was. I wonder, is it because soon we will be together again? Is she waiting for me?'

'I know she is, Father.' Hal gave him the reassurance he needed. 'But I need you most and I know that we will be together many more years before you go to my mother.'

Sir Francis smiled regretfully, and looked up at the tiny window set high in the stone wall. 'Last night I climbed up and looked through the bars, and the red comet was still in the sign of Virgo. It seemed closer and fiercer, for its fiery tail had altogether obliterated my star.'

They heard the tramp of the guards approaching and the clash of keys in the iron door. Sir Francis turned to Hal. 'For the last time let me kiss you, my son.'

His father's lips were dry and hot with the fever in his blood. The contact was brief, then the door to the cell was thrown open.

'Don't keep the Governor and Slow John waiting now,' said Sergeant Manseer jovially. 'Out with the pair of you.'

The atmosphere among the spectators in the court room was like that at the cockpit just before the spurred birds are released to tear into each other in a cloud of flying feathers.

Sir Francis and Hal led in the long file of prisoners and, before he could prevent himself, Hal looked quickly towards the railed-off area at the far end of the hall. Katinka sat in her place in the centre of the front row with Zelda directly behind her. The maid leered viciously at Hal, but there was a soft contented smile on Katinka's face, and her eyes sparkled with violet lights that seemed to light the dim recesses of the room.

Hal looked away quickly, startled by the sudden hot hatred that had replaced the adoration he had so recently felt for her. How could it have happened so quickly, he wondered, and knew that if he had a sword in his hand he would not hesitate to drive the point between the peaks of her soft white breasts.

As he sank into his seat he felt compelled to look up again into the pack of spectators. This time he went cold as he saw another pair of eyes, pale and watchful as those of a leopard, fastened on his father's face.

Slow John sat in the front row of the gallery. He looked like a preacher in his puritanical black suit, the wide-brimmed hat set squarely upon his head.

'Do not look at him,' Sir Francis said softly, and Hal realized that his father, too, was intensely aware of the scrutiny of those strange, faded eyes.

As soon as the hall had settled into an expectant silence, van de Velde appeared through the door of the audience chamber beyond. When he lowered himself into his seat his smile was expansive and his wig was just the slightest bit awry. He belched softly, for clearly he had eaten well. Then he looked down on the prisoners with such a benign expression that Hal felt an unwarranted surge of hope for the outcome.

'I have considered the evidence that has been laid before this court,' the Governor began, without preamble, 'and I want to say right at the outset that I was impressed with the manner in which both the advocates presented their cases. Colonel Schreuder was a paradigm of succinctness—' He stumbled over both of the longer words, then belched again. Hal fancied that he detected a whiff of cumin and garlic on the warm air that reached him a few seconds later.

Next van de Velde turned a paternal eye on Jacobus Hop. 'The advocate for the defence behaved admirably and made a good job of a hopeless case, and I shall make a note to that effect in his Company file.' Hop bobbed his head and coloured with gratification.

'However!' He now looked squarely at the benches of the prisoners. 'While considering the evidence, I have given much thought to the defence raised by Mijnheer Hop, namely that the pirates were operating under a Letter of Marque issued by the King of England, and that when they attacked the Company galleon, the *Standvastigheid*, they were unaware of the cessation of hostilities between the belligerents in the recent war. I have been forced by irrefutable evidence to the contrary to reject this line of defence in its entirety. Accordingly, I find all twenty-four of the accused persons guilty of piracy on the high seas, of robbery and abduction and murder.'

The seamen on the benches stared at him in pale silence.

'Is there anything you wish to say before I pass sentence upon you?' van de Velde asked, and opened his silver snuff box.

Sir Francis spoke out, in a voice that rang the length and breadth of the hall. 'We are prisoners of war. You do not have the right to chain us like slaves. Neither do you have the right to try us nor to pass sentence upon us.'

Van de Velde took a pinch of snuff up each nostril and then sneezed deliciously, spraying the court writer who sat beside him. The clerk closed the one eye nearest to the Governor but kept his quill flying across the page in an effort to keep up with the proceedings.

'I believe that you and I have discussed this opinion before.' Van de Velde nodded mockingly towards Sir Francis. 'I will now proceed to sentence these pirates. I will deal firstly with the four Negroes. Let the following persons stand forth. Aboli! Matesi! Jiri! Kimatti!'

The four were shackled in pairs, and now the guards prodded them to their feet. They shuffled forward and stood below the dais. Van de Velde regarded them sternly. 'I have taken into account that you are ignorant savages, and therefore cannot be expected to behave like decent Christians. Although your crimes reek to heaven and cry for retribution, I am inclined to mercy. I condemn you to lifelong slavery. You will be sold by the auctioneer of the Dutch East India Company to the highest bidder at auction, and the monies received from this sale will be paid into the Company treasury. Take them away, Sergeant!'

As they were led from the hall Aboli looked across at Sir Francis and Hal. His dark face was impassive behind the mask of tattoos, but his eyes sent them the message of his heart.

'Next I will deal with the white pirates,' van de Velde announced. 'Let the following prisoners stand forth.' He read from the list in his hand. 'Henry Courtney, officer and mate. Ned Tyler, boatswain. Daniel Fisher, boatswain. William Rogers, seaman . . .' He read out every name except that of Sir Francis Courtney. When Sir Francis rose beside his son, van de Velde stopped him. 'Not you! You are the captain and the instigator of this gang of rogues. I have other plans for you. Have the armourer separate him from the other prisoner.' The man hurried forward from the back of the court with the leather satchel containing his tools, and worked swiftly to knock the shackle out of the links that bound Hal to his father.

Sir Francis sat alone on the long bench as Hal left him and went forward to take his place at the head of the row of prisoners below the dais. Van de Velde studied their faces, beginning at one end of the line and moving his brooding gaze slowly along until he arrived at Hal. 'A more murderous bunch of cutthroats I have never laid eyes upon. No honest man or woman is safe when creatures like you are at large. You are fit only for the gibbet.'

As he stared at Hal, a sudden thought occurred to him, and he glanced away towards the Buzzard, who sat beside the lovely Katinka at the side of the hall. 'My lord!' he called. 'May I trouble you for a word in private?' Leaving the prisoners standing, van de Velde heaved his bulk onto his feet and waddled back through the doors in the audience chamber behind him. The Buzzard made an elaborate bow to Katinka and followed the Governor.

As he entered the chamber he found van de Velde selecting a morsel from the silver tray on the polished yellow-wood table. He turned to the Buzzard, his mouth already filled. 'A sudden thought occurred to me. If I am to send Francis Courtney to the executioner for questioning as to the whereabouts of the missing cargo, should not his son go also? Surely Courtney would have told his son or had him with him when he secreted the treasure. What do you think, my Lord?'

The Buzzard looked grave and tugged at his beard as he pretended to consider the question. He had wondered how long it would take this great hog to come round to this way of thinking, and he had long ago prepared his answer. He knew he could rely on the fact that Sir Francis Courtney would never reveal the whereabouts of his wealth, not even to the most cunning and persistent tormentor. He was just too stubborn and pigheaded unless – and here was the one possible case in which he might capitulate – if it were to save his only son. 'Your excellency, I think you need have no fear that any living person knows where the treasure is, apart from the pirate himself. He is much too avaricious and suspicious to trust another human being.'

Van de Velde looked dubious and helped himself to another curried samosa from the tray. While he munched, the Buzzard mulled over his best line of argument, should van de Velde choose to debate it further. There was no question in the Buzzard's mind but that Hal Courtney knew where the treasure from the *Standvastigheid* lay. What was more, he almost certainly knew where the other hoard from the *Heerlycke Nacht* was hidden. Unlike his father, the youngster would be unable to withstand the questioning by Slow John and, even if he proved tougher than the Buzzard believed, his father would certainly break down when he saw his son on the rack. One way or the other the two would lead the Dutch to the hoard, and that was the last thing on this earth that the Buzzard wanted to happen.

His grave expression almost cracked into a grin as he realized the irony of his being forced to save Henry Courtney from the attentions of Slow John. But if he wanted the treasure for himself, he must make sure that neither father nor son led the cheese-heads to it first. The best place for Sir Francis was the gallows, and the best place for his brat was the dungeon under the castle walls.

This time he could not prevent the grin reaching his lips as he thought that while Slow John was still cooling his branding irons in Sir Francis's blood, the *Gull* would be flying back to Elephant Lagoon to winkle out those sacks of guilders and those bars of gold from whatever nook or cranny Sir Francis had tucked them into.

He turned the grin now on van de Velde. 'No, your excellency, I give you my assurance that Francis Courtney is the only man alive who knows where it is. He may look hard and talk bravely, but Franky will roll over and spread his thighs like a whore offered a gold guinea just as soon as Slow John gets to work on him. My advice is that you send Henry Courtney to work on the castle, and rely on his father to lead you to the booty.'

'*Ja!*' Van de Velde nodded. 'That's what I thought myself. I just wanted you to confirm what I already knew.' He popped one last samosa into his mouth and spoke around it. 'Let's go back and get the business finished, then.'

The prisoners were still waiting in their chains below the dais, like oxen in the traces, as van de Velde settled himself into his chair again.

'The gibbet and the gallows, these are your natural homes, but they are too good for you. I sentence every last man of you to a lifetime of labour in the service of the Dutch East India Company, which you conspired to cheat and rob, and whose servants you abducted and maltreated. Do not think this is kindness on my part, or weakness. There will come a time when you will weep to the Almighty and beg him for the easy death that I denied you this day. Take them away and put them to work immediately. The sight of them offends my eyes, and those of all honest men.'

As they were herded from the hall, Katinka hissed with frustration and made a gesture of annoyance. Cumbrae leaned closer to her and asked, 'What is it that troubles you, madam?'

'I fear my husband has made a mistake. He should have sent them to the pyre on the parade.' Now she would be denied the thrill of watching Slow John work on the beautiful brat, and listening to his screams. It would have been a deeply satisfying conclusion to the affair. Her husband had promised it to her, and he had cheated her of the pleasure. She would make him suffer for that, she decided.

'Ah, madam, revenge is best savoured like a pipe of good Virginia tobacco. Not gobbled up in a rush. Any time in the future that the fancy takes you, you need only look up at the castle walls and there they will be, being worked slowly to death.'

Hal passed close by where Sir Francis sat on the long bench. His father looked forlorn and sick, with his hair and beard in lank ropes and black shadows beneath his eyes, in dreadful contrast with his pale skin. Hal could not bear it and suddenly he cried, 'Father!' and would have run to him, but Sergeant Manseer had anticipated him and stepped in front of him with the long cane in his right hand. Hal backed away.

His father did not look up, and Hal realized that he had taken his farewell and had moved on into the far territory where only Slow John would be able now to reach him.

When the file of convicts had left the hall and the doors had closed behind them, a hush fell and every eye rested on the lonely figure on the bench.

'Francis Courtney,' van de Velde said loudly. 'Stand forth!'

Sir Francis threw back his head, flicking the greying hair out of his eyes. He shrugged off the guards' hands and rose unaided to his feet. He held his head high as he marched to the dais, and his torn shirt flapped around his naked back. The cane stripes had begun to dry into crusted black scabs.

'Francis Courtney, it is not by chance, I am certain, that you bear the same Christian name as that most notorious of all pirates, the rogue Francis Drake.'

'I have the honour to be named for the famous seafarer,' said Sir Francis softly.

'Then I have the even greater honour of passing sentence upon you. I sentence you to death.' Van de Velde waited for Sir Francis to show some emotion, but he stared back without expression. At last the Governor was forced to continue. 'I repeat, your sentence is death, but the manner of your death will be of your own choosing.' Abruptly and unexpectedly, he let out a mellow guffaw. 'There are not many rogues of your calibre that are treated with such beneficence and condescension.'

'With your permission, I shall withhold any expression of gratitude until I hear the rest of your proposal,' Sir Francis murmured, and van de Velde stopped laughing.

'Not all the cargo from the *Standvastigheid* has been recovered. By far the most valuable portion is still missing, and there is no doubt in my mind that you were able to secrete this before you were captured by the troops of the honourable Company. Are you prepared to reveal the hiding place of the missing cargo to the officers of the Company? In that case, your execution will be by a swift and clean beheading.'

'I have nothing to tell you,' said Sir Francis, in a disinterested tone.

'Then, I fear, you will be asked the same question under extreme compulsion by the state executioner.' Van de Velde smacked his lips softly, as though the words tasted good on his tongue. 'Should you answer fully and without reservation the headsman's axe will put an end to your suffering. Should you remain obstinate, the questioning will continue. At all times the choice will remain yours.'

'Your excellency is a paragon of mercy,' Sir Francis bowed, 'but I cannot answer the question, for I know nothing of the cargo of which you speak.'

'Then Almighty God have mercy on your soul,' said van de Velde, and turned to Sergeant Manseer. 'Take the prisoner away and place him in the charge of the state executioner.'

Hal balanced high on the scaffolding on the unfinished wall of the eastern bastion of the castle. This was only the second day of the labours that were to last the rest of his natural life, and already the palms of his hands and both his shoulders were rubbed raw by the ropes and the rough, undressed stone blocks. One of his fingertips was crushed and the nail was the colour of a purple grape. Each masonry block weighed a ton or more and had to be manhandled up the rickety scaffolding of bamboo poles and planks.

In the gang of convicts working with him were Big Daniel and Ned Tyler, neither of whom was fully recovered from his wounds. Their injuries were plain to see for all were dressed only in petticoats of ragged canvas.

The musket ball had left a deep, dark purple crater in Daniel's chest and a lion's claw across his back, where Hal had cut him. The scabs over these wounds had burst open with his exertions and were weeping watery blood-tinged lymph.

The sword wound crawled like a raw red vine around Ned's thigh, and he limped heavily as he moved along the scaffold. After their privations in the slave deck of the *Gull* they were all honed clean of the last ounce of fat. They were lean as hunting dogs, and stringy muscle and bone stood out clearly beneath their sun-reddened skins.

Though the sun still shone brightly, the winter wind whistled in from the nor-'west and seemed to abrade their bodies like ground glass. In unison they hauled at the tail of the heavy manila rope and the sheaves screeched in their blocks as the great yellow lump of stone lifted from the truck of the wagon far below and began its perilous ascent up the high structure.

The previous day a scaffolding on the south bastion had collapsed under the weight of the stones and had hurled three of the convicts working upon it to their death on the cobbles far below. Hugo Barnard, the overseer, had muttered as he stood over their crushed corpses, 'Three birds with one stone. I'll have the next careless bastard that kills himself thrashed within an inch of his life,' and burst out laughing at his own gallows' humour.

Daniel took a turn of the rope end around his good shoulder and anchored it as the rest of the team reached out, seized the swinging block and hauled it onto the trestle. Between them they manhandled it into the gap at the top of the wall, with the Dutch stonemason in his leather apron shouting instructions at them.

They stood back panting after it had dropped into place, every muscle in their bodies aching and trembling from the effort, but there was no time to rest. From the courtyard below Hugo Barnard was already yelling, 'Get that cradle down here. Swiftly now or I'll come up and give you a touch of the persuader,' and he flicked out the knotted leather thongs of his whip.

Daniel peered over the edge of the scaffold. Suddenly he stiffened and glanced over his shoulder at Hal. 'There go Aboli and the other lads.'

Hal stepped up beside him and looked down. From the doorway to the dungeon a small procession emerged. The four black seamen were led out into the wintry sunshine. Once again, they were wearing light chains. 'Look at those lucky bastards,' Ned Tyler muttered. They had not been included in the labour teams, but had stayed in the dungeon, resting and being fed an extra meal each day to fatten them up while they waited to go on the auction block. This morning Manseer had ordered the four men to strip naked. Then Dr Saar, the Company surgeon, had come down to the cell and examined them, probing and peering into their ears and mouths to satisfy himself as to the state of their health. When the surgeon had left, Manseer ordered them to anoint themselves all over from a stone jar of oil. Now their skins shone in the sunlight like polished ebony. Though they were still lean and finely drawn from their stay aboard the *Gull*, the coating of oil made them appear sleek prime specimens of humanity. Now they were being led out through the gates of the castle onto the open Parade where already a crowd had gathered.

Before he passed through the gates Aboli raised his great round head and looked up at Hal on the scaffold, high above. For one moment their eyes met. There was no need for either to shout a message, chancing a cut of the cane from their keepers, and Aboli strode on without looking back.

The auction block was a temporary structure that at other times was used as a gibbet on which the corpses of executed criminals were placed on public view. The four men were lined up on the platform and Dr Saar mounted the platform with them and addressed the crowd. 'I have examined all of the four slaves being offered for sale today,' he stated, lowering his head to peer over the tops of his wire-framed eye-glasses. 'I can give the assurance that all of them are in good health. Their eyes and teeth are sound and they are hale in limb and body.'

The crowd was in a festive mood. They clapped at the doctor's announcement, and gave him an ironical cheer as he climbed down from the block and hurried back towards the castle gates. Jacobus Hop stepped forward and held up a hand for silence. Then he read from the proclamation of the sale, the crowd jeering and imitating him every time he stuttered. 'By order of His Excellency the Governor of this colony of the honourable Dutch East India Company, I am authorized to offer for sale, to the highest bidder, four Negro slaves—' He broke off and removed his hat respectfully as the Governor's open carriage came down the avenue from the residence, passing through the gardens and wheeling out onto the open Parade behind the six glossy greys. Lord Cumbrae and the Governor's wife sat side by side on the open leather seats facing forward, and Colonel Schreuder sat opposite them.

The crowd opened to let the carriage come to the foot of the block, where Fredricus, the coloured coachman, called the team to a halt and wound down the hand brake. None of the passengers dismounted. Katinka lolled elegantly on the leather seat, twirling her parasol, and chatting gaily to the two men.

On the platform Hop was thrown into confusion by the arrival of these exalted visitors, and stood flushing, stammering and blinking in the sunlight until Schreuder called out impatiently, 'Get on with it, fellow! We didn't come here to watch you goggle and gape.'

Hop replaced his hat and bowed first at Schreuder then at Katinka. He raised his voice. 'The first lot is the slave Aboli. He is about thirty years of age and is believed to be a member of the Qwanda tribe from the east coast of Africa. As you are aware, the Qwanda Negroes are much appreciated as field slaves and herdsmen. He could also be trained into an excellent wagon driver or coachman.' He paused to mop his sweaty face and gather his tripping tongue, then he went on, 'Aboli is said to be a skilled hunter and fisherman. He would bring in a good income to his owner from any of these occupations.'

'Mijnheer Hop, are you hiding anything from us?' Katinka called out, and Hop was once more thrown into disarray by the question. His stammer became so agonized that he could hardly get the words out.

'Revered lady, greatly esteemed lady,' he spread his hands helplessly, 'I assure you—'

'Would you offer for sale a bull wearing clothes?' Katinka demanded. 'Do you expect us to bid for something that we cannot see?'

As he caught her meaning, Hop's face cleared and he turned to Aboli.

'Disrobe!' he ordered loudly, to bolster his courage while facing this huge wild savage. For a moment Aboli stared at him unmoving then contemptuously slipped the knot of his loincloth and let it fall to the planks under his feet.

Naked and magnificent, he stared over their heads at the table-topped mountain. There was a hissing intake of breath from the crowd below. One of the women squealed and another giggled nervously, but none turned away their eyes.

'Hoots!' Cumbrae broke the pregnant pause with a chuckle. 'The buyer will be getting full measure. There is no makeweight in that load of blood-sausage. I'll start the bidding at five hundred guilders!'

'And a hundred more!' Katinka called out.

The Buzzard glanced at her and spoke softly from the corner of his mouth. 'I did not know you were intending to bid, madam.'

'I will have this one at any price, my lord,' she warned him sweetly, 'for he amuses me.'

'I would never stand in the way of a beautiful lady.' The Buzzard bowed. 'But you will not bid against me for the other three, will you?'

''Tis a bargain, my lord.' Katinka smiled. 'This one is mine, and you may have the others.'

Cumbrae folded his arms across his chest and shook his head when Hop looked to him to increase the bid. 'Too rich a price for my digestion,' he said, and Hop looked in vain for a buyer in the rest of the crowd. None was foolhardy enough to go up against the Governor's wife. Recently they had been given a glimpse of his excellency's temper in open court.

'The slave Aboli is sold to Mevrouw van de Velde for the sum of six hundred guilders!' Hop sang out, and bowed towards the carriage. 'Do you wish the chains struck off, Mevrouw?'

Katinka laughed. 'And have him bolt for the mountains? No, Mijnheer, these soldiers will escort him up to the slave quarters at the residence.' She glanced across at Schreuder who gave an order to a detachment of green-jackets waiting under their corporal at the edge of the crowd. They elbowed their way forward, dragged Aboli down from the block and led him away up the avenue towards the residence.

Katinka watched him go. Then she tapped the Buzzard on the shoulder with one finger. 'Thank you, my lord.'

'The next lot is the slave Jiri,' Hop told them, reading from his notes. 'He is, as you see, another fine strong specimen—'

'Five hundred guilders!' growled the Buzzard, and glared at the other buyers, as if daring them to bid at their peril. But without the Governor's wife to compete against, the burghers of the colony were bolder.

'And one hundred,' sang out a merchant of the town.

'And a hundred more!' called a wagoner in a jacket of leopardskins. The bidding went quickly to fifteen hundred guilders with only the wagoner and the Buzzard in the race.

'Damn and blast the clod!' Cumbrae muttered, and turned his head to catch the eye of his boatswain who, with three of his seamen, hovered beside the rear wheel of the carriage. Sam Bowles nodded and his eyes gleamed. With his men backing him he sidled through the press until he stood close behind the wagoner.

'Sixteen hundred guilders,' roared the Buzzard, 'and be damned to ye!'

The wagoner opened his mouth to push upwards and felt something prick him under the ribs. He glanced down at the knife in Sam Bowles's gnarled fist, closed his mouth and blanched white as baleen.

'The bid is against you, Mijnheer Tromp!' Hop called to him, but the wagoner scurried away across the Parade back towards the town.

Kimatti and Matesi were both knocked down to the Buzzard for well under a thousand guilders each. The other prospective buyers in the crowd had seen the little drama between Sam and the wagoner and none showed any further interest in bidding against Cumbrae.

All three slaves were dragged away by Sam Bowles's shore party towards the beach. When Matesi struggled to escape a shrewd crack over his scalp with a marlinspike quieted him and, with his mates, he was shoved into the longboat and rowed out to where the *Gull* lay anchored at the edge of the shoals.

'A successful expedition for both of us, my lord.' Katinka smiled at the Buzzard. 'To celebrate our acquisitions, I hope you will be able to dine with us at the residence this evening.'

'Nothing would have given me greater pleasure, but alas, madam, I was lingering only for the sale and the chance of picking up a few prime seamen. Now my ship lies ready in the bay, and the wind and the tide bid me away.'

'We shall miss you, my lord. Your company has been most diverting. I hope you will call on us and remain a while longer when next you round the Cape of Good Hope.'

'There is no power on this earth, no storm, ill wind or enemy which could prevent me doing so,' said Cumbrae and kissed her hand. Cornelius Schreuder glowered: he could not stand to see another man lay a finger on this woman who had come to rule his existence.

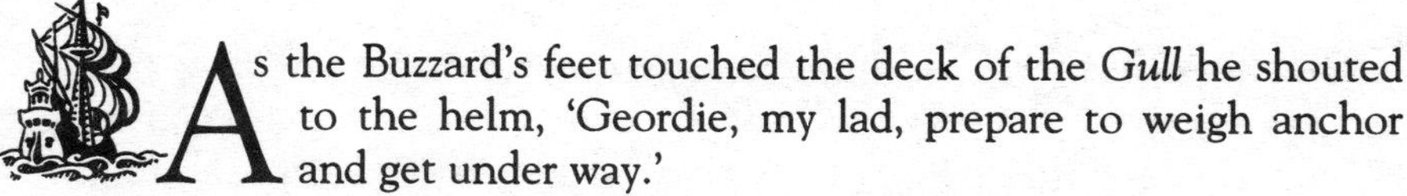

As the Buzzard's feet touched the deck of the *Gull* he shouted to the helm, 'Geordie, my lad, prepare to weigh anchor and get under way.'

Then he singled out Sam Bowles. 'I want the three Negroes on the quarterdeck, and swiftly.' As they were ranged before him, he looked them over carefully. 'Does any one of you three heathen beauties speak God's own language?' he asked, and they stared at him blankly. 'So it's only your benighted lingo, is it?' He shook his head sadly. 'That makes my life much harder.'

'Begging your pardon,' Sam Bowles tugged obsequiously at his Monmouth cap, 'I know them well, all three of them. We was shipmates together, we was. They're playing you for a patsy. They all three speak good English.'

Cumbrae grinned at them, with murder in his eyes. 'You belong to me now, my lovelies, from the tops of your woolly heads to the pink soles of your great flat feet. If you want to keep your black hides in one piece, you'll not play games with me again, do you hear me?' And with a swipe of his huge hairy fist he sent Jiri crashing to the deck. 'When I talk to you you'll answer clear and loud in sweet English words. We're going back to Elephant Lagoon and, for the sake of your health, you're going to show me where Captain Franky hid his treasure. Do you hear me?'

Jiri scrambled back onto his feet. 'Yes, Captain Lordy, sir! We hear you. You are our father.'

'I'd rather have lopped off my own spigot with a blunt spade than fathered the likes of one of you with it!' The Buzzard grinned at them. 'Now get ye up to the main yard to clap some canvas on her.' And he sent Jiri on his way with a flying kick in the backside.

Katinka sat in sunlight, in a protected corner of the terrace out of the wind, with Cornelius Schreuder beside her. At the serving table Sukeena poured the wine with her own hands, and carried the two glasses to the luncheon table with its decorations of fruit and flowers from Slow John's gardens. She placed a tall glass with a spiral stem in front of Katinka, who reached out and caressed her arm lightly.

'Have you sent for the new slave?' she asked with a purr in her voice.

'Aboli is being bathed and fitted with a uniform, as you ordered, mistress,' Sukeena answered softly, as if unaware of the other woman's touch. However, Schreuder had seen it, and it amused Katinka to watch him frown with jealousy.

She raised her glass to him and smiled over the rim. 'Shall we drink to a swift voyage for Lord Cumbrae?'

'Indeed.' He lifted his glass. 'A short swift voyage to the bottom of the ocean for him and all his countrymen.'

'My dear Colonel,' she smiled, 'how droll. But softly now, here comes my latest plaything.'

Two green-jackets from the castle escorted Aboli onto the terrace. He was dressed in a pair of tight-fitting black trousers and a white cotton shirt cut full to encompass his broad chest and massive arms. He stood silently before her.

Katinka switched into English. 'In future you will bow when you enter my presence and you will address me as mistress, and if you forget I will ask Slow John to remind you. Do you know who Slow John is?'

'Yes, mistress,' Aboli rumbled, without looking at her.

'Oh, good! I thought you might be tiresome, and that I would have to have you broken and tamed. This makes things easier for both of us.' She took a sip of the wine, then looked him over slowly with her head on one side. 'I bought you on a whim, and I have not decided what I shall do with you. However, Governor Kleinhans is taking his coachman home with him when he sails. I will need a new coachman.' She turned to Colonel Schreuder. 'I have heard these Negroes are good with animals. Is that your experience also, Colonel?'

'Indeed, Mevrouw. Being animals themselves they seem to have a rapport with all wild and domestic beasts.' Schreuder nodded, and studied Aboli unhurriedly. 'He is a fine physical specimen but, of course, one does not look for intelligence in them. I congratulate you on your purchase.'

'Later, I may breed him with Sukeena,' Katinka mused. The slave girl went still, but her back was turned so that they could not see her face. 'It might be diverting to see how the black blood mingles with the gold.'

'A most interesting mixture.' Schreuder nodded. 'But are you not worried that he may escape? I saw him fight on the deck of the *Standvastigheid* and he is a truculent savage. A leg iron might be suitable costume for him, at least until he has been broken in.'

'I do not think I need go to such pains,' Katinka said. 'I was able to observe him at length during my captivity. Like a faithful dog, he is devoted to the pirate Courtney and even more so to his brat. I believe he would never try to escape while either of them is alive in the castle dungeons. Of course, he will be locked in the slave quarters at night with the others, but during working hours he will be allowed to move around freely to attend to his duties.'

'I am sure you know best, Mevrouw. But I for one would never trust such a creature,' Schreuder warned her.

Katinka turned back to Sukeena. 'I have arranged with Governor Kleinhans that Fredricus is to teach Aboli his duties as coachman and driver. The *Standvastigheid* will not sail for another ten days. That should be ample time. See to it immediately.'

Sukeena made the gracious oriental obeisance. 'As Mistress commands,' she said, and beckoned for Aboli to follow her.

She walked ahead of him down the pathway to the stables where Fredricus had drawn up the coach and Aboli was reminded of the posture and carriage of the young virgins of his own tribe. As little girls they were trained by their mothers, carrying the water gourds balanced on their heads. Their backs grew straight and they seemed to glide over the ground, as this girl did.

'Your brother, Althuda, sends you his heart. He says that you are his tiger orchid still.'

Sukeena stopped so abruptly that, walking behind her, Aboli almost collided with her. She seemed like a startled sugarbird perched on a protea bloom on the point of flight. When she moved on again he saw that she was trembling.

'You have seen my brother?' she asked, without turning her head to look at him.

'I never saw his face, but we spoke through the door of his cell. He said that your mother's name was Ashreth and that the jade brooch you wear was given to your mother by your father on the day of your birth. He said that if I told you these things, you would know that I was his friend.'

'If he trusted you, then I also trust you. I, too, shall be your friend, Aboli,' she agreed.

'And I shall be yours,' Aboli said softly.

'Oh, do tell me, how is Althuda? Is he well?' she pleaded. 'Have they hurt him badly? Have they given him to Slow John?'

'Althuda is puzzled. They have not yet condemned him. He has been in the dungeon four long months and they have not hurt him.'

'I give all thanks to Allah!' Sukeena turned and smiled at him, her face lovely as the tiger orchid to which Althuda had likened her. 'I had some influence with Governor Kleinhans. I was able to persuade him to delay judgement on my brother. But now that he is going I do not know what will happen with the new one. My poor Althuda, so young and brave. If they give him to Slow John my heart will die with him, as slowly and as painfully.'

'There is one I love as you love your brother,' Aboli rumbled softly. 'The two share the same dungeon.'

'I think I know the one of whom you speak. Did I not see him on the day they brought all of you ashore in chains and marched you across the Parade? Is he straight and proud as a young prince?'

'That is the one. Like your brother, he deserves to be free.'

Again Sukeena's feet checked, but then she glided onwards. 'What are you saying, Aboli, my friend?'

'You and I together. We can work to set them free.'

'Is it possible?' she whispered.

'Althuda was free once. He broke his jesses and soared away like a falcon.' Aboli looked up at the aching blue African sky. 'With our help he could be free again, and Gundwane with him.'

They had come to the stableyard and Fredricus roused himself on the seat of the carriage. He looked down at Aboli and his lips curled back to show teeth discoloured brown by chewing tobacco. 'How can a black ape learn to drive my coach and my six darlings?' he asked the empty air.

'Fredricus is an enemy. Trust him not.' Sukeena's lips barely moved as she gave Aboli the warning. 'Trust nobody in this household until we can speak again.'

As well as the house slaves, and most of the furniture in the residence, Katinka had purchased from Kleinhans all the horses in his string and the contents of the tack room. She had written him an order on her bankers in Amsterdam. It was for a large sum, but she knew that her father would make good any shortfall.

The most beautiful of all the horses was a bay mare, a superb animal with strong graceful legs and a beautifully shaped head. Katinka was an expert horsewoman, but she had no feeling or love for the creature beneath her and her slim, pale hands were strong and cruel. She rode with a Spanish curb that bruised the mare's mouth savagely, and her use of the whip was wanton. When she had ruined a mount she could always sell it and buy another.

Despite these faults, she was fearless and had a dashing seat. When the mare danced under her and threw her head against the agony of the whip and the curb, Katinka sat easily and looked marvellously elegant. Now she was pushing the mare to the full extent of her pace and endurance, flying at the steep path, using the whip when she faltered or when it seemed as though she would refuse to jump a fallen tree that blocked the pathway.

The horse was lathered, soaked with sweat as though she had plunged through a river. The froth that streamed from her gaping mouth was tinged pink with blood from the edged steel of the curb. It splattered back onto Katinka's boots and skirt, and she laughed wildly with excitement as they galloped out onto the saddle of the mountain. She looked back over her shoulder. Schreuder was fifty lengths or more behind her: he had come by another route to meet her in secret. His black gelding was labouring heavily under his weight, and though Schreuder used the whip freely his mount could not hold the mare.

Katinka did not stop at the saddle but, with the whip and the tiny needle-sharp spur under her riding habit, goaded the mare onward and sent her plunging straight down the far slope. Here a fall would be disastrous, for the footing was treacherous and the mare was blown. The danger excited Katinka. She revelled in the feel of the powerful body beneath her, and of the saddle leather pounding against her sweating thighs and buttocks.

They came slithering off the scree slope and burst out into the open meadow beside the stream. She raced parallel with the stream for half a league, but when she reached a hidden grove of silverleaf trees she reined in the mare in a dozen lunges from full gallop to a wrenching halt.

She unhooked her leg from over the horn of the sidesaddle and in a swirl of skirts and laced underlinen dropped lightly to earth. She landed like a cat, and while the mare blew like the bellows of a smithy and reeled on her feet with exhaustion, Katinka stood, both fists clenched on her hips, and watched Schreuder come down the slope after her.

He reached the meadow and galloped to where she stood. There, he jumped from the gelding's back. His face was dark with rage. 'That was madness, Mevrouw,' he shouted. 'If you had fallen!'

'But I never fall, Colonel.' She laughed in his face. 'Not unless you can make me.' She reached up suddenly and threw both arms around his neck. Like a lamprey she fastened on his lips, sucking so powerfully that she drew his tongue into her own mouth. As his arms tightened around her she bit his lower lip hard enough to start his blood, and tasted the metallic salt on her own tongue. When he roared with pain, she broke from his embrace and, lifting the skirts of her habit, ran lightly along the bank of the stream.

'Sweet Mary, you'll pay dearly for that, you little devil!' He wiped his mouth, and when he saw the smear of blood on his palm, he raced after her.

These last days, Katinka had toyed with him, driving him to the frontiers of sanity, promising and then revoking, teasing and then dismissing, cold as the north wind one moment then hot as the tropical sun at noonday. He was dizzy and confused with lust and longing, but his desire had infected her. Tormenting him, she had driven herself as far and as hard. She wanted him now almost as much as he wanted her. She wanted to feel him deep inside her body, she had to have him quench the fires she had ignited in her womb. The time had come when she could delay no longer.

He caught up with her and she turned at bay. With her back against one of the silverleaf trees, she faced him like a hind cornered by the hounds. She saw the blind rage turn his eyes opaque as marble. His face was swollen and encarnadined, his lips drawn back to expose his clenched teeth.

With a thrill of real terror she realized that this rage into which she had driven him was a kind of madness over which he had no control. She knew that she was in danger of her life and, knowing that, her own lust broke its banks like a mighty river in full spate.

She threw herself at him and with both hands ripped at the fastenings of his breeches. 'You want to kill me, don't you?'

'You bitch,' he choked, and reached for her throat. 'You slut. I can stand no more. I will make you—'

She pulled him out through the opening in his clothes, hard and thick, swollen furious red and so hot he seemed to sear her fingers. 'Kill me with this, then. Thrust it into me so deeply that you pierce my heart.' She leaned back against the rough bark of the silverleaf and planted her feet wide apart. He swept her skirts up high, and with both hands she guided him into herself. As he lunged and bucked furiously against her, the tree against which she leaned shook as though a gale of wind had struck it. The silver leaves rained down over them glinting like newly minted coins as they spun and swirled in the sunlight. As she reached her climax Katinka screamed so that the echoes rang along the yellow cliffs high above them.

Katinka came down from the mountain like a fury, riding on the wings of the north-west gale that had sprung so suddenly out of the sunny winter sky. Her hair had broken free of her bonnet and streamed out like a brilliant banner, snapping and tangling in the wind. The mare ran as though pursued by lions. When she reached the upper vineyards, Katinka put her to the high stone wall, over which she soared like a falcon.

She galloped through the gardens down to the stableyard. Slow John turned to watch her go by. The green things he had nurtured were uprooted, torn and scattered beneath the mare's flying hoofs. When she had passed, Slow John stooped and picked up a shredded stem. He lifted it to his mouth and bit into it softly, tasting the sweet sap. He felt no resentment. The plants he grew were meant to be cut and destroyed, just as man is born to die. To Slow John, only the manner of the dying was significant.

He stared after the mare and her rider and felt the same reverence and awe that always overcame him at the moment when he released one of his little sparrows from this mortal existence. He thought of all the condemned souls who died under his hands as his little sparrows. The first time he had set his eyes on Katinka van de Velde he had fallen completely under her spell. He felt that he had waited all his life for this woman. He had recognized in her those mystical qualities that dictated his own existence but, compared to her, he knew that he was a thing crawling in primeval slime.

She was a cruel and untouchable goddess, and he worshipped her. It was as though these torn plants he held in his hands were a sacrifice to that goddess. As though he had laid them on her altar and she had accepted them. He was moved almost to the point of tears by her condescension. He blinked those strange yellow eyes and for once they mirrored his emotion. 'Command me,' he breathed. 'There is nothing that I would not do for you.'

Katinka spurred the mare at full gallop up the driveway to the front doors of the residence, and flung herself from its back before it had come fully to rest. She did not even glance at Aboli as he sprang down from the terrace, gathered up the reins and led the mare away to the stableyard.

He spoke gently to the horse in the language of the forests. 'She has made you bleed, little one, but Aboli will heal your hurt.' In the yard he unbuckled the girth and dried the mare's steaming sweat with the cloth, walking her in slow circles, then watering her before he led her to her stall.

'See where her whip and spurs have cut you. She is a witch,' he whispered, as he anointed the torn and bruised corners of the horse's mouth with salve. 'But Aboli is here now to protect and cherish you.'

Katinka strode through the rooms of the residence, singing softly to herself, her face lit with the afterglow of her loving. In her bedchamber she shouted for Zelda then, without waiting for the old woman to arrive, she stripped off her clothing and dropped it in a heap in the middle of the floor. The winter air through the shutters was cold on her body, which was damp with sweat and the juices of her passion. Her pale pink nipples rose in haloes of gooseflesh and she shouted again, 'Zelda, where are you?' When the maid came scurrying into the chamber she rounded on her, 'Sweet Jesus, where have you been, you lazy old baggage? Close those shutters! Is my bath ready, or have you been dozing off again in front of the fire?' But her words lacked their usual venom and when she lay back in the steaming, perfumed waters of her ceramic bathtub, which had been carted up from the cabin in the stern of the galleon, she was smiling warmly and secretly to herself.

Zelda hovered around the tub, lifting the thick strands of her mistress's hair out of the scented foam and pinning them atop her head, soaping her shoulders with a cloth.

'Don't fuss so! Leave me be for a while!' Katinka ordered imperiously. Zelda dropped the cloth and backed out of the bathroom.

Katinka lay for a while, humming softly to herself and lifting her feet one at a time above the foam to inspect her delicate ankles and pink toes. Then a movement in the steam-clouded mirror caught her attention and she sat up straight and stared incredulously. Quickly she stood up and stepped out of the tub, slipped a towel around her shoulders to soak up the drops of water that ran down her body and crept to the door of her bedroom.

What she had seen in the mirror was Zelda gathering up her soiled clothing from where she had dropped it on the tiles. The old woman stood now with Katinka's underlinen in her hands examining the stains upon it. As Katinka watched, she lifted the cloth to her face and sniffed at it like an old bitch scenting the entrance to a rabbit warren.

'You like the smell of a man's ripe cream, do you?' Katinka asked coldly.

At the sound of her voice Zelda spun about to face her. She hid the clothing behind her back and her cheeks went pale as ash as she stammered incoherently.

'You dried-up old cow, when did you last have a sniff of it?' Katinka asked.

She dropped the towel and glided across the floor, slim and sinuous as an erect female cobra and her gaze as icy and venomous. Her riding whip lay where she had dropped it and she scooped it up as she passed.

Zelda backed away in front of her. 'Mistress,' Zelda whined, 'I was worried only that your pretty things might be spoiled.'

'You were snuffling it up like a fat old sow with a truffle,' Katinka told her, and her whip arm flashed out. The lash caught Zelda in the mouth. She squealed and fell back on the bed.

Katinka stood over her, naked, and plied the whip across her back and arms and legs, swinging with all her strength, so that the layers of fat wobbled and shook on the maid's limbs as the lash bit into them. 'This is a pleasure too long denied,' Katinka screamed, her own fury increasing as the old woman howled and wriggled on the bed. 'I have grown weary of your thieving ways and your gluttony. Now you revolt me with this prurient trespass into intimate areas of my life, you sneaking, spying, whining old baggage.'

'Mistress, you are killing me.'

'Good so! But if you live you will be on board the *Standvastigheid* when she sails for Holland next week. I can abide you around me no longer. I will send you back in the meanest cabin without a penny of pension. You can eke out the rest of your days in the poorhouse.' Katinka was panting wildly now, raining her blows on Zelda's head and shoulders.

'Please, mistress, you would not be so cruel to your old Zelda, who wet-nursed you as a baby.'

'The thought of having sucked on those great fat tits makes me want to puke.' Katinka lashed out at them, and Zelda whimpered and covered her chest with both arms. 'When you leave I will have your baggage searched so that you take with you nothing that you have stolen from me. There will be not a single guilder in your purse, I shall see to that. You thieving, lying crone.'

The threat transformed Zelda from a pathetic wriggling fawning creature into a woman possessed. Her arm shot out and her plump fist seized Katinka's wrist as she was about to strike again. Zelda held onto her with a strength that shocked her mistress and she glared into Katinka's face with a terrible hatred.

'No!' she said. 'You will not take everything I have from me. You will not beggar me. I have served you twenty-four years and you will not cast me off now. I will sail on the galleon, yes, and nothing will give me greater joy than to see the last of your poisonous beauty. But when I go I will take with me all I own and on top of that I will have in my purse the thousand gold guilders you will give to me as my pension.'

Katinka was stunned out of her rage, and stared in disbelief at her.

'You rave like a lunatic. A thousand guilders? More likely a thousand cuts with the whip.'

She tried to pull her arm free, but Zelda hung on with a mad strength. 'A lunatic you say! But what will his excellency do when I bring him proof of how you have been rutting with the Colonel?'

Katinka froze at the threat then slowly lowered her whip arm. Her mind was racing, and a hundred mysteries unravelled as she stared into Zelda's eyes. She had trusted this old bitch without question, never doubting her complete loyalty, never even thinking about it. Now she knew how her husband always seemed to have intimate knowledge of her lovers and her behaviour that should have been secret.

She thought quickly now, her impassive expression masking the outrage she felt at this betrayal. It mattered little if her husband learned of this new adventure with Cornelius Schreuder. It would simply be an annoyance, for Katinka had not yet tired of the colonel. The consequences would, of course, be more serious for her new lover.

Looking back, she realized just how vindictive Petrus van de Velde had been: all her lovers had suffered some grievous harm once her husband knew about them. How he knew had always been a mystery to Katinka until this moment. She must have been naïve, but it had never occurred to her that Zelda had been the serpent in her bosom.

'Zelda, I have wronged you,' Katinka said softly. 'I should not have treated you so harshly.' She reached down and stroked the angry weal on the maid's chubby cheek. 'You have been kind and faithful to me all these years and it is time you went to a happy retirement. I spoke in anger. I would never dream of denying you that which you deserve. When you sail on the galleon you will have not a thousand but two thousand guilders in your purse, and my love and gratitude will go with you.'

Zelda licked her bruised lips and grinned with malicious triumph. 'You are so kind and good to me, my sweet mistress.'

'Of course, you will say nothing to my husband about my little indiscretions with Colonel Schreuder, will you?'

'I love you much too much ever to do you harm, and my heart will break on the day that I have to leave you.'

Slow John knelt in the flower bed at the end of the terrace, his pruning knife in his powerful hands. As a shadow fell over him, he looked up and rose to his feet. He lifted his hat and held it across his chest respectfully. 'Good morrow, mistress,' he said, in his deep melodious voice.

'Pray continue with your task. I love to watch you work.'

He sank to his knees again and the blade of the sharp little knife flickered in his hands. Katinka sat on a bench close at hand and watched him in silence for a while.

'I admire your skills,' she said at last, and though he did not raise his head he knew that she referred not only to his dexterity with the pruning knife. 'I have dire need of those skills, Slow John. There would be a purse of a hundred guilders as your reward. Will you do something for me?'

'Mevrouw, there is nothing I would not do for you.' He lifted his head at last and stared at her with those pale yellow eyes. 'I would not flinch from laying down my life if you asked it of me. I do not ask for payment. The knowledge that I do your bidding is all the reward I could ever want.'

The winter nights had turned cold and squalls of rain roared down off the mountain to batter the panes of the windows and howl like jackals around the eaves of the thatched roof.

Zelda pulled her nightdress over her ample frame. All the weight she had lost on the voyage from the east had come back to settle on her paunch and thighs. Since moving into the residence she had fed well at her corner in the kitchen, wolfing down the luscious scraps as they were carried through from the high table in the main dining hall, washing them down from her tankard filled with the dregs from the wine glasses of the gentry, Rhine and red wine mixed with gin and schnapps.

Her belly filled with good food and drink, she made ready for bed. First, she checked that the window casements in her small room were sealed against the draught. She stuffed wads of rags into the cracks and drew the curtains across them. She slid the copper warming pan under the covers of her bed and held it there until she smelt the linen begin to singe. Then she blew out the candle and crept under the thick woollen blankets.

Snuffling and sighing, she settled into the softness and warmth, and her last thoughts were of the purse of golden coins tucked under her mattress. She fell asleep, smiling.

An hour after midnight, when all the house was silent and sleeping, Slow John listened at the door of Zelda's room. When he heard her snores rattling louder than the wind at the casement, he eased open the door noiselessly and slipped through it the brazier of glowing charcoal. He listened for a minute, but the rhythm of the old woman's breathing was regular and unbroken. He closed the door softly and moved silently down the passage to the door at the end.

In the dawn Sukeena came to wake Katinka an hour before her appointed time. When she had helped her dress in a warm robe, she led her to the servants' quarters where a silent, frightened knot of slaves was gathered outside Zelda's door. They stood aside for Katinka to enter and Sukeena whispered, 'I know how much she meant to you, mistress. My heart breaks for you.'

'Thank you, Sukeena,' Katinka answered sadly, and glanced quickly around the tiny room. The brazier had been removed. Slow John had been thorough and reliable.

'She looks so peaceful and what a lovely colour she has.' Sukeena stood beside the bed. 'Almost as if she were alive still.'

Katinka came to stand beside her. The noxious fumes from the brazier had rouged the old woman's cheeks. In death she was more handsome than she had ever been in life. 'Leave me alone with her for a while, please, Sukeena,' she said quietly. 'I wish to say a prayer for her. She was so dear to me.'

As she knelt beside the bed Sukeena closed the door softly behind her. Katinka slid her hand under the mattress and drew out the purse. She could tell by its weight that none of the coins was missing. She slipped the purse into the pocket of her gown, clasped her hands in front of her and closed her eyes so tightly that the long golden lashes intermeshed.

'Go to hell, you old bitch,' she murmured.

Slow John came at last. Many long days and tormented nights they had waited for him, so long that Sir Francis Courtney had begun to imagine that he would never come.

Each evening, when darkness brought an end to the work on the castle walls, the prisoner teams came shuffling in, out of the night. Winter was tightening its grip on the Cape and they were often soaked by the driving rain and chilled to the bone.

Every evening, as he passed the iron-studded door of his father's cell, Hal called, 'What cheer, Father?'

The reply, in a voice hoarse and choked with the phlegm of his illness, was always the same. 'Better today, Hal. And with you?'

'The work was easy. We are all in good heart.'

Then Althuda would call from the next-door cell, 'The surgeon came this morning. He says that Sir Francis is well enough to be questioned by Slow John.' Or on another occasion, 'The fever is worse, Sir Francis has been coughing all day.'

As soon as the prisoners were locked into the lower dungeon they would gulp down their one meal of the day, scraping out the bowls with their fingers, and then drop like dead men on the damp straw.

In the darkness before dawn Manseer would rattle on the bars of the cell. 'Up! Up, you lazy bastards, before Barnard sends in his dogs to rouse you.'

They would struggle to their feet, and file out again into the rain and the wind. There, Barnard waited to greet them, with his two huge black boarhounds, growling and lunging against the leashes. Some of the seamen had found pieces of sacking or canvas with which to wrap their bare feet or cover their heads, but even these rags were still wet from the previous day. Most, though, were bare foot and half-naked in the winter gales.

Then Slow John came. He came at midday. The men on the high scaffolding fell silent and all work stopped. Even Hugo Barnard stood aside as he passed through the gates of the castle. In his sombre clothing, and with the wide-brimmed hat pulled low over his eyes, he looked like a preacher on his way to the pulpit.

Slow John stopped at the entrance to the dungeons, and Sergeant Manseer came running across the yard, jangling his keys. He opened the low door, stood aside for Slow John, then followed him through. The door closed behind the pair and the watchers roused themselves, as though they had awakened from a nightmare and resumed their tasks. But while Slow John was within a deep, brooding silence hung over the walls. No man cursed or spoke, even Hugo Barnard was subdued, and at every chance their heads turned to look down at the closed iron door.

Slow John went down the staircase, Manseer lighting the treads with a lantern, and stopped outside the door of Sir Francis's cell. The sergeant drew back the latch on the peep-hole and Slow John stepped up to it. There was a beam of light from the high window of the cell. Sir Francis sat on the stone shelf that served as his bunk, lifted his head and stared back into Slow John's yellow eyes.

Sir Francis's face was that of a sun-bleached skull, so pale as to seem luminous in the poor light, the long tresses of his hair dead black and his eyes dark cavities. 'I have been expecting you,' he said, and coughed until his mouth filled with phlegm. He spat it into the straw that covered the floor.

Slow John made no reply. His eyes, gleaming through the peep-hole, were fastened on Sir Francis's face. The minutes dragged by. Sir Francis was overwhelmed with a wild desire to scream at him, 'Do what you have to do. Say what you have to say. I am ready for you.' But he forced himself to remain silent and stared back at Slow John.

At last Slow John stepped away from the peep-hole and nodded at Manseer. He slammed the shutter closed and scurried back up the staircase to open the iron door for the executioner. Slow John crossed the courtyard with every eye upon him. When he went out through the gate men breathed again and there was once more the shouting of orders and the answering murmur of curse and complaint from the walls.

'Was that Slow John?' Althuda called softly from the cell alongside that of Sir Francis.

'He said nothing. He did nothing,' Sir Francis whispered hoarsely.

'It is the way he has,' Althuda said. 'I have been here long enough to see him play the same game many times. He will wear you down so that in the end you will want to tell him all he wants to know before he even touches you. That is why they named him Slow John.'

'Sweet Jesus, it half unmans me. Has he ever come to stare at you, Althuda?'

'Not yet.'

'How have you been so fortunate?'

'I know not. I know only that one day he will come for me also. Like you, I know how it feels to wait.'

Three days before the *Standvastigheid* was due to sail for Holland, Sukeena left the kitchens of the residence with her conical sunhat of woven grass on her dainty little head and her bag on her arm. Her departure caused no surprise among the other members of the household for it was her custom to go out several times a week along the slopes of the mountain to collect herbs and roots. Her skills and knowledge of the healing plants were famous throughout the colony.

From the veranda of the residence Kleinhans watched her go, and the knife blade of agony twisted in his guts. It felt as if an open wound were bleeding deep within him and often his stools were black with clotted blood. However, it was not only the dyspepsia that was devouring him. He knew that once the galleon sailed, with him aboard her, he would never again look upon Sukeena's beauty. Now that the time for this parting drew near he could not sleep at night, and even milk and bland boiled rice turned to acid in his stomach.

Mevrouw van de Velde, his hostess since she had taken over the residence, had been kind to him. She had even sent Sukeena out this morning to gather the special herbs that, when seeped and distilled with the slave girl's skills, were the only medicine that could alleviate his agony for even a short while – long enough at least to allow him to catch a few hours of fitful sleep. At Katinka's orders Sukeena would prepare enough of this brew to tide him over the long voyage northwards. He prayed that, once he reached Holland, the physicians there would be able to cure this dreadful affliction.

Sukeena moved quietly through the scrub that covered the slopes of the mountain. Once or twice she looked back but nobody had followed her. She went on, stopping only to cut a green twig from one of the flowering bushes. As she walked she stripped the leaves from it and, with her knife, trimmed the end into a fork.

All around her the wild blossom grew in splendid profusion; even now that winter was upon them, a hundred different species were on show. Some were as large as ripe artichoke heads, some as tiny as her little fingernail, all of them lovely beyond an artist's imagination or the powers of his palette to depict. She knew them all.

Meandering seemingly without direction, in reality she was moving gradually and circuitously towards a deep ravine that split the face of the table-topped mountain. With one more careful look around she darted suddenly down the steep, heavily bushed slope. There was a stream at the bottom, tumbling through a series of merry waterfalls and dreaming pools. As she approached one, she moved more slowly and softly. Tucked into a rocky crevice beside the dark waters was a small clay bowl. She had placed it there on her last visit. From the ledge above she looked down and saw that the milky white fluid, with which she had filled it, had been drunk. Only a few opalescent drops remained in the bottom.

Daintily she climbed cautiously into a position from which she could look deeper into the crack in the rock. Her breath caught as she saw in the shadows the soft gleam of ophidian scales. She opened the lid of the basket, took the forked stick in her right hand and moved closer. The serpent was coiled beside the bowl. It was not large, as slender as her forefinger. Its colour was a deep glowing bronze, each scale a tiny marvel. As she drew closer it raised its head an inch and watched her with black beady eyes. But it made no attempt to escape, sliding back into the depths of the crevice, as it had the first time she had discovered it.

It was lazy and somnolent, lulled by the milky concoction she had fed it. After a moment it lowered its head again and seemed to sleep. Sukeena was not tempted into any sudden or rash move. Well she knew that, from the bony needles in its upper jaw, the little reptile could dispense death in one of its most horrible and agonizing manifestations. She reached out gently with the twig and again the snake raised its head. She froze, the fork held only inches above its slim neck. Slowly the little reptile drooped back to earth and, as its head stretched out, Sukeena pinned it to the rock. It hissed softly and its body coiled and recoiled around the stick that held it.

Sukeena reached down and gripped it behind the head, with two fingers locked against the hard bones of the skull. It wrapped its long sinuous body around her wrist. She took hold of the tail and unwound it, then dropped the serpent into her basket. In the same movement she closed the lid upon it.

Retiring Governor Kleinhans went aboard the galleon on the evening before she sailed. Before the carriage took him down to the foreshore, all the household assembled on the front terrace of the residence to bid farewell to their former master. He moved slowly along the line with a word for each. When he reached Sukeena she made that graceful gesture, her fingertips together touching her lips, which made his heart ache with love and longing for her.

'Aboli has taken your luggage aboard the ship and placed all of it in your cabin,' she said softly. 'Your medicine chest is packed at the bottom of the largest trunk, but there is a full bottle in your small travelling case, which should last you several days.'

'I shall never forget you, Sukeena,' he said.

'And I shall never forget you, master,' she answered. For one mad moment he almost lost control of his emotions. He was on the point of embracing the slave girl, but then she looked up and he recoiled as he saw the undying hatred in her eyes.

When the galleon sailed in the morning with the dawn tide, Fredricus came to wake him and help him from his bunk. He wrapped the thick fur coat around his master's shoulders and Kleinhans went up on deck and stood at the stern rail as the ship caught the north-west wind and stood out into the Atlantic. He waited there until the great flat mountain sank away below the horizon and his vision was dimmed with tears.

Over the next four days the pain in his stomach was worse than he had ever known it. On the fifth night he woke after midnight, the acid scalding his intestines. He lit the lantern and reached for the brown bottle that would give him relief. When he shook it, it was already empty.

Doubled over with pain, he carried the lantern across the cabin and knelt before the largest of his trunks. He lifted the lid, and found the teak medicine chest where Sukeena had told him it was. He lifted it out and carried it to the table top against the further bulkhead, placing the lantern to light it so that he could fit the brass key into the lock.

He lifted the wooden lid and started. Laid carefully over the contents of the chest was a sheet of paper. He read the black print and, with amazement, realized that it was an ancient copy of the Company gazette. He read down the page and, as he recognized it, his stomach heaved with nausea. The proclamation was signed by himself. It was a death warrant. The warrant for the questioning and execution of one Robert David Renshaw. The Englishman who had been Sukeena's father.

'What devilry is this?' he blurted aloud. 'The little witch has placed it here to remind me of a deed committed long ago. Will she never relent? I thought she was out of my life for ever, but she makes me suffer still.'

He reached down to seize the paper and rip it to shreds but before his fingers touched it there was a soft, rustling sound beneath the sheet, and then a blur of movement.

Something struck him a light blow upon the wrist and a gleaming, sinuous body slid over the edge of the chest and dropped to the deck. He leapt back in alarm but the thing disappeared into the shadows and he stared after it in bewilderment. Slowly he became aware of a slight burning on his wrist and lifted it into the lamplight.

The veins on the inside of his wrist stood out like blue ropes under the pale skin blotched with old man's freckles. He looked closer at the seat of the burning sensation, and saw two tiny drops of blood gleaming in the lantern light like gemstones as they welled up from twin punctures.

He tottered backwards and sat on the edge of his bunk, gripping his wrist and staring at the ruby droplets.

Slowly, an image from long ago formed before his eyes. He saw two solemn little orphans standing hand in hand before the smoking ashes of a funeral pyre. Then the pain swelled within him until it filled his mind and his whole body.

There was only the pain now. It flowed through his veins like liquid fire and burrowed deep into his bones. It tore apart every ligament, sinew and nerve in his body. He began to scream and went on screaming until the end.

Sometimes twice a day Slow John came to the castle dungeon and stood at the peep-hole in the door of Sir Francis's cell. He never spoke. He stood there silently, with a reptilian stillness, sometimes for a few minutes and at others for an hour. In the end Sir Francis could not look at him. He turned his face to the stone wall, but still he could feel the yellow eyes boring into his back.

It was a Sunday, the Lord's day, when Manseer and four green-jacketed soldiers came for Sir Francis. They said nothing, but he could tell by their faces where they were taking him. They could not look into his eyes, and they wore the doleful expressions of a party of pall-bearers.

It was a cold, gusty day as Sir Francis stepped out into the courtyard. Although it was no longer raining, the clouds that hung low across the face of the mountain were an ominous blue grey, the colour of an old bruise. The cobbles beneath his feet were shining wetly with the rain squall that had just passed. He tried to stop himself shivering in the raw wind, lest his guards think it was for fear.

'God keep you safe!' A young clear voice carried to him above the wild wind, and he stopped and looked up. Hal stood high on the scaffold, his dark hair ruffled by the wind and his bare chest wet and shining with raindrops.

Sir Francis lifted his bound hands before him, and shouted back, '*In Arcadia habito!* Remember the oath!' Even from so far off, he could see his son's stricken face. Then his guards urged him on towards the low door that led down into the basement below the castle armoury. Manseer led him through the door and down the staircase. At the bottom he paused and knocked diffidently on the iron-bound door. Without waiting for a reply he pushed it open and led Sir Francis through.

The room beyond was well lit, a dozen wax candles flickering in their holders in the draught from the open door. To one side Jacobus Hop sat at a writing table. There was parchment and an inkpot in front of him, and a quill in his right hand. He looked up at Sir Francis with a pale terrified expression. An angry red carbuncle glowed on his cheek. Quickly he dropped his eyes, unable to look at the prisoner.

Along the far wall stood the rack. Its frame was of massive teak, the bed long enough to accommodate the tallest man with his limbs stretched out to their full extent. There were sturdy wheels at each end, with iron ratchets and slots into which the levers could be fitted. On the side wall opposite the recording clerk's desk, a brazier smouldered. On hooks set into the wall above it hung an array of strange and terrible tools. The fire radiated a soothing, welcoming warmth.

Slow John stood beside the rack. His coat and his hat hung from a peg behind him. He wore a leather blacksmith's apron.

A pulley wheel was bolted into the ceiling and a rope dangled from it with an iron hook at its end. Slow John said nothing while his guards led Sir Francis to the centre of the stone floor and passed the hook through the bonds that secured his wrists. Manseer tightened the rope through the sheave until Sir Francis's arms were drawn at full stretch above his head. Although both his feet were firmly on the floor he was helpless. Manseer saluted Slow John, then he and his men backed out of the room and closed the door behind them. The panels were of solid teak, thick enough to prevent any sound passing through.

In the silence, Hop cleared his throat noisily and read from the transcript of the judgement passed upon Sir Francis by the Company court. His stutter was painful, but at the end he laid down the document and burst out clearly, 'As God is my witness, Captain Courtney, I wish I were a hundred leagues from this place. This is not a duty I enjoy. I beg of you to co-operate with this inquiry.'

Sir Francis did not reply but looked back steadily into Slow John's yellow eyes. Hop took up the parchment once more, and his voice quavered and broke as he read from it. 'Question the first: is the prisoner, Francis Courtney, aware of the whereabouts of the cargo missing from the manifest of the Company ship, the *Standvastigheid*?'

'No,' replied Sir Francis, still looking into the yellow eyes before him. 'The prisoner has no knowledge of the cargo of which you speak.'

'I beg you to reconsider, sir,' Hop whispered hoarsely. 'I have a delicate disposition. I suffer with my stomach.'

For the men on the windswept scaffolding the hours passed with agonizing slowness. Their eyes kept turning back towards the small, insignificant door below the armoury steps. There was no sound or movement from there, until suddenly, in the middle of the cold rainswept morning, the door burst open and Jacobus Hop scuttled out into the courtyard. He tottered to the officers' hitching rail and hung onto one of the iron rings as though his legs could no longer support him. He seemed oblivious to everything around him as he stood gasping for breath like a man freshly rescued from drowning.

All work on the walls came to a halt. Even Hugo Barnard and his overseers stood silent and subdued, gazing down at the miserable little clerk. With every eye upon him, Hop suddenly doubled over and vomited over the cobbles. He wiped his mouth with the back of his hand, and looked around him wildly as though seeking an avenue of escape.

He lurched away from the hitching rail and set off at a run, across the yard and up the staircase into the Governor's quarters. One of the sentries at the top of the stairs tried to restrain him but Hop shouted, 'I have to speak to his excellency,' and brushed past him.

He burst unannounced into the Governor's audience chamber. Van de Velde sat at the head of the long, polished table. Four burghers from the town were seated below him, and he was laughing at something that had just been said.

The laughter died on his fat lips as Hop stood trembling at the threshold, his face deathly pale, his eyes filled with tears. His boots were flecked with vomit.

'How dare you, Hop?' van de Velde thundered, as he dragged his bulk out of the chair. 'How dare you burst in here like this?'

'Your excellency,' Hop stammered, 'I cannot do it. I cannot go back into that room. Please don't insist that I do it. Send somebody else.'

'Get back there immediately,' van de Velde ordered. 'This is your last chance, Hop. I warn you, you will do your duty like a man or suffer for it.'

'You don't understand.' Hop was blubbering openly now. 'I can't do it. You have no idea what is happening in there. I can't—'

'Go! Go immediately, or you will receive the same treatment.'

Hop backed out slowly and van de Velde shouted after him, 'Shut those doors behind you, worm.'

Hop staggered back across the silent courtyard like a blind man, his eyes filled again with tears. At the little door he stood and visibly braced himself. Then he flung himself through it and disappeared from the view of the silent watchers.

In the middle of the afternoon the door opened again and Slow John came out into the courtyard. As always he was dressed in the dark suit and tall hat. His face was serene and his gait slow and stately as he passed out through the castle gates and took the avenue up through his gardens towards the residence.

Minutes after he had gone, Hop rushed out of the armoury and across to the main block. He came back leading the Company surgeon, who carried his leather bag, and disappeared down the armoury stairs. A long time afterwards the surgeon emerged and spoke briefly to Manseer and his men, who were hovering at the door.

The sergeant saluted and he and his men went down the stairs. When they came out again Sir Francis was with them. He could not walk unaided, and his hands and feet were swaddled in bandages. Red stains had already soaked through the cloth.

'Oh, sweet Jesus, they have killed him,' Hal whispered as they dragged his father, legs dangling and head hanging, across the yard.

Almost as if he had heard the words, Sir Francis lifted his head and looked up at him. Then he called in a clear, high voice, 'Hal, remember your oath!'

'I love you, Father!' Hal shouted back, choking on the words with sorrow, and Barnard slashed his whip across his back.

'Get back to work, you bastard.'

That evening as the file of convicts shuffled down the staircase past the door of his father's cell, Hal paused and called softly, 'I pray God and all his saints to protect you, Father.'

He heard his father move on the rustling mattress of straw, and then, after a long moment, his voice. 'Thank you, my son. God grant us both the strength to endure the days ahead.'

From behind the shutters of her bedroom Katinka watched the tall figure of Slow John coming up the avenue from the Parade. He passed out of her sight behind the stone wall at the bottom of the lawns and she knew he was going directly to his cottage. She had been waiting half the day for his return, and she was impatient. She placed the bonnet on her head, inspected her image in the mirror and was not satisfied. She looped a coil of her hair, arranged it carefully over her shoulder, then smiled at her reflection and left the room through the small door out to the back veranda. She followed the paved path under the naked black vines that covered the pergola, stripped of their last russet leaves by the onset of the winter gales.

Slow John's cottage stood alone at the edge of the forest. There was no person in the colony, no matter how lowly his station, who would live with him as a neighbour. When she reached it Katinka found the front door open and she went in without a knock or hesitation. The single room was bare as a hermit's cell. The floors were coated with cow dung, and the air smelled of stale smoke and the cold ashes on the open hearth. A simple bed, a single table and chair were the only furniture.

As she paused in the centre of the room she heard water splashing in the back yard and she followed the sound. Slow John stood beside the water trough. He was naked to the waist, and he was scooping water from the trough with a leather bucket and pouring it over his head.

He looked up at her, with the water trickling from his sodden hair down his chest and arms. His limbs were covered with the hard flat muscle of a professional wrestler or, she thought whimsically, of a Roman gladiator.

'You are not surprised to see me here,' Katinka stated. It was not a question for she could see the answer in his flat gaze.

'I was expecting you. I was expecting the Goddess Kali. Nobody else would dare come here,' he said, and Katinka blinked at this unusual form of address.

She sat down on the low stone wall beside the pump, and was silent for a while. Then she asked, 'Why do you call me that?' The death of Zelda had forged a strange, mystic bond between them.

'In Trincomalee, on the beautiful island of Ceylon beside the sacred Elephant Pool, stands the temple of Kali. I went there every day that I was in the colony. Kali is the Hindu Goddess of death and destruction. I worship her.' She knew then that he was mad. The knowledge intrigued her, and made the fine, colourless hairs on her forearms stand erect.

She sat for a long time in silence and watched him complete his toilet. He squeezed the water from his hair with both hands, and then wiped down those lean, hard limbs with a square of cloth. He pulled on his undershirt, then picked up the dark coat from where it hung over the wall, shrugged into it and buttoned it to his chin.

At last he looked at her. 'You have come to hear about my little sparrow.' With that fine melodious voice he should have been a preacher or an operatic tenor, she thought.

'Yes,' she said. 'That is why I have come.'

It was as though he had read her thoughts. He knew exactly what she wanted and he began to speak without hesitation. He told her what had taken place that day in the room below the armoury. He omitted no detail. He almost sang the words, making the terrible acts he was describing sound as noble and inevitable as the lyrics from some Greek tragedy. He transported her, so that she hugged her own arms and began to rock slowly back and forth on the wall as she listened.

When he had finished speaking she sat for a long while with a rapturous expression on her lovely face. At last she shuddered softly and said, 'You may continue to call me Kali. But only when we are alone. No one else must ever hear you speak the name.'

'Thank you, Goddess.' His pale eyes glowed with an almost religious fervour as he watched her go to the gate in the wall.

There she paused and, without looking round at him, she asked, 'Why do you call him your little sparrow?'

Slow John shrugged. 'Because from this day onwards he belongs to me. They all belong to me and to the Goddess Kali, for ever.' Katinka gave a small ecstatic shiver at those words, then walked on down the path through the gardens towards the residence. Every step of the way she could feel his gaze upon her.

Sukeena was waiting for her when she returned to the residence. 'You sent for me, mistress.'

'Come with me, Sukeena.'

She led the girl to her closet, and seated herself on the chaise-longue in front of the shuttered window. She gestured for Sukeena to stand before her. 'Governor Kleinhans often discussed your skills as a physician,' Katinka said. 'Who taught you?'

'My mother was an adept. At a very young age I would go out with her to gather the plants and herbs. After her death I studied with my uncle.'

'Do you know the plants here? Are they not different from those of the land where you were born?'

'There are some that are the same, and the others I have taught myself.'

Katinka already knew all this from Kleinhans, but she enjoyed the music of the slave girl's voice. 'Sukeena, yesterday my mare stumbled and almost threw me. My leg was caught on the saddle horn, and I have an ugly mark. My skin bruises easily. Do you have in your chest of medicines one that will heal it for me?'

'Yes, mistress.'

'Here!' Katinka leaned back on the sofa, and drew her skirts high above her knees. Slowly and sensually she rolled down one of the white stockings. 'Look!' she ordered, and Sukeena sank gracefully to the silk carpet in front of her. Her touch was as soft upon the skin as a butterfly alighting on a flower, and Katinka sighed. 'I can feel that you have healing hands.'

Sukeena did not reply and a wave of her dark hair hid her eyes.

'How old are you?' Katinka asked.

Sukeena's fingers stopped for an instant and then moved on to explore the bruise that spread around the back of her mistress's knee. 'I was born in the year of the Tiger,' she said, 'so on my next birthday I will be eighteen years of age.'

'You are very beautiful, Sukeena. But, then, you know that, don't you?'

'I do not feel beautiful, mistress. I do not think a slave can ever feel beautiful.'

'What a droll notion.' Katinka did not hide her annoyance at this turn in the conversation. 'Tell me, is your brother as beautiful as you are?'

Again Sukeena's fingers trembled on her skin. Ah! That shaft went home. Katinka smiled softly in the silence, and then asked, 'Did you hear my question, Sukeena?'

'To me Althuda is the most beautiful man who has ever lived upon this earth,' Sukeena replied softly, and then regretted having said it. She knew instinctively that it was dangerous to allow this woman to discover those areas where she was most vulnerable, but she could not recall the words.

'How old is Althuda?'

'He is three years older than I am.' Sukeena kept her eyes downcast. 'I need to fetch my medicines, mistress.'

'I shall wait for you to return,' Katinka replied. 'Be quick.'

Katinka lay back against the cushions and smiled or frowned at the vivid procession of images and words that ran through her mind. She felt expectant and elated, and at the same time restless and dissatisfied. Slow John's words sounded in her head like cathedral bells. They disturbed her. She could not remain still a moment longer. She sprang to her feet and prowled around the closet like a hunting leopard. 'Where is that girl?' she demanded, and then she glimpsed her own reflection in the long mirror and turned back to consider it.

'Kali!' she whispered, and smiled. 'What a marvellous name. What a secret and splendid name.'

She saw Sukeena's image appear in the mirror behind her but she did not turn immediately. The girl's dark beauty was a perfect foil for her own. She considered their two faces together, and felt the excitement charge her nerves and sing through her veins.

'I have the salve for your injury, mistress.' Sukeena stood close behind her, but her eyes were fathomless.

'Thank you, my little sparrow,' Katinka whispered. I want you to belong to me for ever, she thought. I want you to belong to Kali.

She turned back to the sofa and Sukeena knelt before her again. At first the salve was cool on the skin of her leg, and then a warm glow spread from it. Sukeena's fingers were cunning and skilful.

'I hate to see something beautiful destroyed needlessly,' Katinka whispered. 'You say your brother is beautiful. Do you love him very much, Sukeena?'

When there was no reply Katinka reached down and cupped her hand under Sukeena's chin. She lifted her face so that she could look into her eyes. The agony she saw there made her pulse race.

'My poor little sparrow,' she said. I have touched the deepest place in her soul, she exulted. As she removed her hand she let her fingers trail across the girl's cheek.

'This hour I have come from Slow John,' she said, 'but you saw me on the path. You were watching me, were you not?'

'Yes, mistress.'

'Shall I repeat to you what Slow John told me? Shall I tell you about his special room at the castle, and what happens there?' Katinka did not wait for the girl to reply but went on speaking quietly. When Sukeena's fingers stilled she broke off her narrative to order, 'Do not stop what you are doing, Sukeena. You have a magical touch.'

When at last she finished speaking, Sukeena was weeping without a sound. Her tears were slow and viscous as drops of oil squeezed from the olive press. They glistened against the red gold of her cheeks. After a while Katinka asked, 'How long has your brother been in the castle? I have heard that it is four months since he came back from the mountains to fetch you. Such a long time, and he has not been tried, no sentence passed upon him.'

Katinka waited, letting the moments fall, a slow drop at a time, slow as the girl's tears. 'Governor Kleinhans was remiss, or was he persuaded by somebody, I wonder. But my husband is an energetic and dedicated man. He will not let justice be denied. No renegade can escape him long.'

Now Sukeena was no longer making any pretence; she stared at Katinka with stricken eyes as she went on, 'He will send Althuda to the secret room with Slow John. Althuda will be beautiful no longer. What a dreadful pity. What can we do to prevent that happening?'

'Mistress,' Sukeena whispered, 'your husband, he has the power. It is in his hands.'

'My husband is a servant of the Company, a loyal and unbending servant. He will not flinch from his duty.'

'Mistress, you are so beautiful. No man can deny you. You can persuade him.' Sukeena slowly lowered her head and placed it on Katinka's bare knee. 'With all my heart, with all my soul, I beg you, mistress.'

'What would you do to save your brother's life?' Katinka asked. 'What price would you pay, my little sparrow?'

'There is no price too high, no sacrifice from which I would turn aside. Everything and anything you ask of me, mistress.'

'We could never hope to set him free, Sukeena. You understand that, don't you?' Katinka asked gently. Nor would I ever wish that, she thought, for while the brother is in the castle the little sparrow is safely in my cage.

'I will not even let myself hope for that.'

Sukeena lifted her head and again Katinka cupped her chin, this time with both her hands, and she leaned forward slowly. 'Althuda shall not die. We will save him from Slow John, you and I,' she promised, and kissed Sukeena full on the mouth. The girl's lips were wet with her tears. They tasted hot and salty, almost like blood. Slowly Sukeena opened her lips, like the petals of an orchid opening to the sunbird's beak as it quests for nectar.

Althuda. Sukeena steeled herself with the thought of her brother, as without breaking the kiss Katinka took her hand and moved it slowly up under her skirts until it lay on her smooth white belly. Althuda, this is for you, and for you alone, Sukeena told herself silently, as she closed her eyes and her fingers crept timorously over the satiny belly, down into the nest of fine dense golden curls at the base.

The next day dawned in a cloudless sky. Although the air was chill the sun was brilliant and the wind had dropped. From the scaffold Hal watched the closed door to the dungeons. Daniel stayed close by his side; in taking Hal's share of the work on his broad shoulders he was shielding him from Barnard's lash.

When Slow John came through the gates and crossed the courtyard to the armoury, with his measured undertaker's tread, Hal stared down at him with stricken eyes. Suddenly, as he passed below the scaffold, Hal snatched up the heavy mason's hammer that lay on the planking at his feet and lifted it to hurl it down and crush the executioner's skull. But

Daniel's great fist closed around his wrist. He eased the hammer from Hal's grip, as though he were taking a toy from a child, and placed it on top of the wall beyond his reach.

'Why did you do that?' Hal protested. 'I could have killed the swine.'

'To no purpose,' Daniel told him, with compassion. 'You cannot save Sir Francis by killing an underling. You would sacrifice your own life and achieve nothing by it. They would simply send another to your father.'

Manseer brought Sir Francis up from the dungeons. He could not walk unaided on his broken bandaged feet, but his head was high as they dragged him across the courtyard.

'Father!' Hal screamed, in torment. 'I cannot let this happen.'

Sir Francis looked up at him, and called in a voice just loud enough to reach him on the high wall, 'Be strong, my son. For my sake, be strong.' Manseer forced him down the steps below the armoury.

The day was long, longer than any that Hal had ever lived through, and the north side of the courtyard was in deep shadow when at last Slow John re-emerged from below the armoury.

'This time I will kill the poisonous swine,' Hal blurted, but again Daniel held him in a grip that he could not shake off as the executioner walked slowly beneath the scaffold and out through the castle gates.

Hop came scampering into the courtyard, his face ghastly. He summoned the Company surgeon and the two men disappeared once more down the stairs. This time the soldiers brought out Sir Francis on a litter.

'Father!' Hal shouted down to him, but there was neither reply nor sign of life in response.

'I have warned you often enough,' Hugo Barnard bellowed at him. He strode out onto the boards and laid half a dozen whip strokes across his back. Hal made no attempt to avoid the blows, and Barnard stepped back astonished that he showed no pain. 'Any more of your imbecile chattering, and I will put the dogs onto you,' he promised, as he turned away. Meanwhile, in the courtyard, the Company surgeon watched gravely as the soldiers carried Sir Francis's unconscious form down to his cell. Then, accompanied by Hop, he set off for the Governor's suite on the south side of the courtyard.

Van de Velde looked up in irritation from the papers that littered his desk. 'Yes? What is it, Dr Saar? I am a busy man. I hope you have not come here to waste my time.'

'It is the prisoner, your excellency.' The surgeon looked flustered and apologetic at the same time. Van de Velde did not allow him to continue but turned on Hop, who stood nervously behind the doctor, twisting his hat in his fingers.

'Well, Hop, has the pirate succumbed yet? Has he told us what we want to know?' he shouted, and Hop retreated a pace.

'He is so stubborn. I would never have believed it possible, that any human being—' He broke off in a long, tormented stammer.

'I hold you responsible, Hop.' Van de Velde came menacingly from behind his desk. He was warming to this sport of baiting the miserable little clerk, but the surgeon intervened.

'Your excellency, I fear for the prisoner's life. Another day of questioning – he may not survive it.'

Van de Velde rounded on him now. 'That, doctor, is the main object of this whole business. Courtney is a man condemned to death. He will die, and you have my solemn word on that.' He went back to his desk and lowered himself into the soft chair. 'Don't come here to give me news of his imminent decease. All I want to know from you is whether or not he is still capable of feeling pain, and if he is capable of speaking or at least giving some sign of understanding the question. Well, is he, doctor?' Van de Velde glared.

'Your excellency,' the doctor removed his eye-glasses and polished the lenses vigorously as he composed a reply. He knew what van de Velde wanted to hear, and he knew also that it was not politic to deny him. 'At the moment the prisoner is not *compos mentis*.'

Van de Velde scowled and cut in, 'What of the executioner's vaunted skills? I thought he never lost a prisoner, not unintentionally anyway.'

'Sir, I am not disparaging the skills of the state executioner. I am sure that by tomorrow the prisoner will have recovered consciousness.'

'You mean that tomorrow he will be healthy enough to continue questioning?'

'Yes, your excellency. That is my opinion.'

'Well, Mijnheer, I will hold you to that. If the pirate dies before he can be formally executed in accordance with the judgement of the court, you will answer to me. The populace must see justice performed. It is no good the man passing peacefully away in a closed room below the walls. We want him out there on the Parade for all to see. I want an example made of him, do you understand?'

'Yes, your excellency.' The doctor backed towards the door.

'You too, Hop. Do you understand, dolt? I want to know where he has hidden the galleon's cargo, and then I want a good rousing execution. For your own good, you had better deliver both those things.'

'Yes, your excellency.'

'I want to speak to Slow John. Send him to me before he starts work tomorrow morning. I want to make certain that he fully understands his responsibilities.'

'I will bring the executioner to you myself,' Hop promised.

Once more it was dark when Hugo Barnard stopped work on the walls and ordered the lines of exhausted prisoners down into the courtyard. As Hal passed his father's cell on the way down the staircase, he called desperately to him, 'Father, can you hear me?'

When there was no reply, he hammered on the door with both his fists. 'Father, speak to me. In the name of God, speak to me!' For once Manseer was indulgent. He made no attempt to force Hal to move on down the staircase and Hal pleaded again, 'Please, Father. It's Hal, your son. Do you not know me?'

'Hal,' croaked a voice he did not recognize. 'Is that you, my boy?'

'Oh, God!' Hal sank to his knees and pressed his forehead to the panel. 'Yes, Father. It is me.'

'Be strong, my son. It will not be for much longer, but I charge you, if you love me, then keep the oath.'

'I cannot let you suffer. I cannot let this go on.'

'Hal!' His father's voice was suddenly powerful again. 'There is no more suffering. I have passed that point. They cannot hurt me now, except through you.'

'What can I do to ease you? Tell me, what can I do?' Hal pleaded.

'There is only one thing you can do now. Let me take with me the knowledge of your strength and your fortitude. If you fail me now, it will all have been in vain.'

Hal bit into the knuckles of his own clenched fist, drawing blood in the vain attempt to stifle his sobs. His father's voice came again. 'Daniel, are you there?'

'Yes, Captain.'

'Help him. Help my son to be a man.'

'I give you my promise, Captain.'

Hal raised his head, and his voice was stronger. 'I do not need anybody to help me. I will keep my faith with you, Father. I will not betray your trust.'

'Farewell, Hal.' Sir Francis's voice began to fade, as though he were falling into an infinite pit. 'You are my blood and my promise of eternal life. Goodbye, my life.'

The following morning when they carried Sir Francis up from the dungeon Hop and Dr Saar walked on either side of the litter. They were both worried men, for there was no sign of life in the broken figure that lay between them. Even when Hal defied Barnard's whip, and called down to him from the walls, Sir Francis did not raise his head. They took him down the stairs to where Slow John already waited, but within a few minutes all three came out into the sunlight, Saar, Hop and Slow John, and stood talking quietly for a short while. Then they walked together across to the Governor's suite and mounted the stairs.

Van de Velde was standing by the stained-glass window, peering out at the shipping that lay anchored off the foreshore. Late the previous evening, another Company galleon had come into Table Bay and he was expecting the ship's captain to call upon him to pay his respects and to present an order for provisions and stores. Van de Velde turned impatiently from the window to face the three men as they filed into his chamber.

'*Ja*, Hop?' He looked at his favourite victim. 'You have remembered my orders, for once, hey? You have brought the state executioner to speak to me.' He turned to Slow John. 'So, has the pirate told you where he has hidden the treasure? Come on, fellow, speak up.'

Slow John's expression did not change as he said softly, 'I have worked carefully not to damage the respondent beyond usefulness. But I am nearing the end. Soon he will no longer hear my voice, nor be sensible to any further persuasion.'

'You have failed?' van de Velde's voice trembled with anger.

'No, not yet,' said Slow John. 'He is strong. I would never have believed how strong. But there is still the rack. I do not believe that he will be able to withstand the rack. No man can weather the rack.'

'You have not used it yet?' van de Velde demanded. 'Why not?'

'To me it is the last resort. Once they have been racked, there is nothing left. It is the end.'

'Will it work with this one?' van de Velde wanted to know. 'What happens if he still resists?'

'Then there is only the scaffold and the gibbet,' said Slow John.

Slowly van de Velde turned to Dr Saar. 'What is your opinion, doctor?'

'Your excellency, if you require an execution then it should be carried out very soon after the man is racked.'

'How soon?' van de Velde demanded.

'Today. Before nightfall. After racking, he will not last the night.'

Van de Velde turned back to Slow John. 'You have disappointed me.

I am displeased.' Slow John did not seem to hear the rebuke. His eyes did not even flicker as he stared back at van de Velde. 'However, we must do what we can to make the best of this whole sorry business. I will order the execution for three o'clock this afternoon. In the meantime you are to go back and place the pirate on the rack.'

'I understand, your excellency,' said Slow John.

'You have failed me once. Do not do so again. He must be alive when he goes to the scaffold.' Van de Velde turned to the clerk. 'Hop, send messengers through the town. I am declaring the rest of today to be a holiday throughout the colony, except for the work on the castle walls, of course. Francis Courtney will be executed at three o'clock this afternoon. Every burgher in the colony must be there. I want all to see how we deal with a pirate. Oh, and by the way, make certain that Mevrouw van de Velde is informed. She will be very angry if she misses the sport.'

At two o'clock they brought Sir Francis Courtney on a litter from the cell below the armoury. They had not bothered to cover his naked body. Even from high up on the south wall of the castle, and with his vision blurred by his tears, Hal could see that his father's body had been grotesquely deformed by the rack. Every one of the great joints in his limbs and at his shoulders and pelvis were dislocated, swollen and bruised purple black.

An execution detail of green-jackets was drawn up in the courtyard. Led by an officer with a drawn sword, they fell in around the litter. Twenty men marched in front, and twenty followed behind, their muskets at the slope. The tap-tap tap-tap of the death drum set the pace. The procession snaked through the castle gates, out onto the Parade.

Daniel placed his arm around Hal's shoulder, as the boy watched, white-faced and shivering, in the icy wind. Hal made no move to pull away from him. Those seamen who had coverings for their heads removed them, unwinding the filthy rags and standing grim and silent as the bier passed beneath them.

'God bless you, Captain,' Ned Tyler called out. 'You were as good a man as ever hoisted sail!' There was a hoarse and ragged cheer from the others, and one of Hugo Barnard's huge black hounds bayed mournfully, a strangely harrowing sound.

Out on the parade the crowd waited around the gibbet in tense and expectant silence. Every living soul in the colony seemed to have answered the summons. Above their heads Slow John waited high on the platform. He wore his leather apron, and his head was covered with the mask of his office, the mask of death. His eyes and his mouth were all that showed through the slits in the black cloth.

Led by the drummer the procession marched with slow and measured tread towards him, and Slow John waited with his arms folded over his chest. Even he turned his head as the Governor's carriage came down the avenue through the gardens, and crossed the parade. Slow John bowed to the Governor and his wife as Aboli guided the six grey horses to the foot of the scaffold and bought the vehicle to a halt.

Slow John's yellow eyes met those of Katinka through the slits in his black headcloth. He bowed again, this time to her directly. She knew, without words being spoken, that he was dedicating the sacrifice to her, to his Goddess Kali.

'He has no reason to act so grand. The oaf has made a botch of the job so far,' van de Velde said grumpily. 'He has killed the man without getting a word out of him. I don't know what your father and the other members of the Seventeen are going to say when they hear that the cargo is lost. They are going to blame me, of course. They always do.'

'As always you will have me to protect you, my darling husband,' she said, and stood up in the carriage to have a better view. The escort stopped at the foot of the gallows and the litter with the still figure upon it was lifted high and placed at Slow John's feet. A low growl went up from the watchers as the executioner knelt beside it to begin his grisly task.

A little later when the crowd gave forth a lusty roar, made up of excitement and horror and obscene glee, the grey horses shied and fidgeted nervously in the traces at the sound and smell of fresh human blood. With an impassive face and gentle hands on the reins Aboli checked them and brought them back under control. Slowly he turned away his head from the dreadful spectacle taking place before his eyes and looked towards the unfinished walls of the castle.

He recognized the figure of Hal among the other convicts. He stood almost as tall as Big Daniel now, and he had the shape and set of a fully mature man. But he has a boy's heart still. He should not look upon this thing. No man or boy should ever have to watch his father die. Aboli's own great heart felt that it might burst in the barrel of his chest, but his face was still impassive beneath the cicatrice of tattoos. He looked back at the scaffold as Sir Francis Courtney's body rose slowly in the air and the crowd bellowed again. Slow John's pressure on the rope was gentle and sure as he lifted Sir Francis from the litter by his neck. It required a delicate touch not to snap the vertebrae, and end it all too soon. It was a matter of pride to him that the last spark of life must not be snuffed out of that broken husk until after the drawing out of the viscera.

Firmly Aboli turned away his eyes and looked again to the bereft and tragic figure of Hal Courtney on the castle walls. We should not mourn for him, Gundwane. He was a man and he lived the life of a man. He sailed every ocean, and fought as a warrior must fight. He knew the stars and the ways of men. He called no man master, and turned aside from no enemy. No, Gundwane, we should not mourn him, you and I. He will never die while he lives on in our hearts.

For four days Sir Francis Courtney's dismembered body remained on public display. Every morning as the light strengthened, Hal looked down from the walls and saw it still hanging there. The gulls came from the beach in a shrieking cloud of black and white wings and squabbled raucously over the feast. When they had gorged, they perched on the railing of the gibbet and whitewashed the planks with their liquid dung.

For once Hal hated the clarity of his own eyesight, that spared him no detail of the terrible transformation that was taking place as he watched. By the third day the birds had picked the flesh from his father's skull so that it grinned at the sky with empty eye-sockets. The burghers crossing the open parade on their way to the castle walked well downwind of the scaffold on which he hung, and the ladies held sachets of dried herbs to their faces as they passed.

However, on the dawning of the fifth day when Hal looked down upon it, the gibbet was empty. His father's pathetic remains no longer hung there, and the seagulls had gone back to the beach.

'Thank the merciful Lord,' Ned Tyler whispered to Daniel. 'Now young Hal can begin to heal.'

'Yet it is passing strange that they have taken the corpse away so soon.' Daniel was puzzled. 'I would not have thought that van de Velde could be so compassionate.'

Sukeena had shown him how to slip the grating on one of the small back windows of the slave quarters and squeeze his great body through. The night guard at the residence had become lax over the years, and Aboli had little difficulty in evading the watch. For three consecutive nights he escaped from the slave quarters. Sukeena had warned him that he must return at least two hours before dawn for at that hour the watch would rouse themselves and put on a show of vigilance to impress the awakening household.

Once he had escaped over the walls it took Aboli less than an hour to run through the darkness to the boundary of the colony, marked by a hedge of bitter almond bushes planted at the order of the Governor. Although the hedge was still scraggy and there were more gaps than barriers in its length, it was the line over which no burgher might pass without the Governor's permission. On the other hand, none of the scattered Hottentot tribes that inhabited the limitless wilderness of plain, mountain and forest beyond were allowed to cross the hedge and enter the colony. On the orders of the Company, they were to be shot or hanged if they transgressed the boundary. The VOC was no longer prepared to tolerate the savages' treachery, their sly thieving ways or their drunkenness when they were able to get their hands on spirits. The wanton whoring of their women, who would lift their short leather skirts for a handful of beads or a trifling trinket, was a threat to the morals of the God-fearing burghers of the colony. Selected tribesmen, who might be useful as soldiers and servants, were allowed to remain in the colony but the rest had been driven out into the wilderness where they belonged.

Each night Aboli crossed this makeshift boundary and ranged like a silent black ghost across the flat plain whose wide expanses cut off Table Mountain and its bastion of lesser hills from the main ranges of the African hinterland. The wild animals had not been driven off these plains, for few white hunters had been allowed to leave the confines of the colony to pursue them. Here, Aboli heard again the wild, heart-stopping chorus of a pride of hunting lions that he remembered from his childhood. The leopards sawed and coughed in the thickets, and often he startled unseen herds of antelope, whose hoofs drummed through the night.

Aboli needed a black bull. Twice he had been so close as to smell the buffalo herd in the thickets. The scent reminded him of his father's herds of cattle, which he had tended in his childhood, before his circumcision. He had heard the grunting of the great beasts and the lowing of the weaning calves, he had followed their deeply ploughed hoofmarks and seen splashes of their wet dung still steaming in the moonlight. But each time as he closed with the herd, the wind had tricked him. They had sensed him and gone crashing away through the brush, galloping on until the sound of their flight dwindled into silence. Aboli could not pursue them further, for it was past midnight and he was still hours away from the bitter almond hedge and from his cell in the slave quarters.

On the third night he took the chance of creeping out of the window of the slave quarters an hour earlier than Sukeena had warned him was wise. One of the hounds rushed at him, but before it could alarm the watch, Aboli calmed it with a soft whistle. The hound recognized him and snuffled his hand. He stroked its head and whispered softly to it in the language of the forests and left it whining softly and wagging its tail as he slipped over the wall like a dark moon shadow.

During his previous hunts, he had discovered that each night the buffalo herd left the fastness of the dense forest to drink at a waterhole a mile or so beyond the boundary hedge. He knew that if he crossed it before midnight he might be able to catch them while they were still at the water. It was his best chance of being able to pick out a bull and make his stalk.

From the hollow tree at the edge of the forest he retrieved the bow that he had cut and carved from a branch of wild olive. Sukeena had stolen the single iron arrowhead from the collection of weapons that Governor Kleinhans had assembled during his service in the Indies, which now hung on the walls of the residence. It was unlikely that it would be missed from among the dozens of swords, shields and knives that made up the display.

'I will return it to you,' he promised Sukeena. 'I would not have you suffer if it should be missed.'

'Your need of it is great than my risk,' she told him as she slipped the arrowhead, wrapped in a scrap of cloth, beneath the seat of the carriage. 'I also had a father who was denied a decent burial.'

Aboli had fitted the arrowhead to a reed shaft and bound it in place with twine and pitch. He had fletched it with the moulted feathers from the hunting falcons housed in the mews behind the stables. However, he did not have time to search for the insect grubs from which to brew poison for the barbs, and so he must rely on this single shaft flying true to the mark.

Now as Aboli hunted in the shadows, himself another silent gliding shadow, he found old forgotten skills returning to him, and recalled the instruction that he had undergone as a young boy from the elders of his tribe. He felt the night wind softly caress his bare chest and flanks and was aware of its direction at all times as he circled the waterhole until it blew straight into his face. It brought down to him the rich bovine stench of the prey he sought.

The wind was strong enough to shake the tall reeds and cover any sound he might make so he could move in swiftly over the last hundred paces. Above the soughing of the north wind and the rustle of the reeds he heard a coughing grunt. He froze and nocked his single arrow. Had the lions come to the water ahead of the herd, he wondered, for that had been a leonine sound. He stared ahead, and heard the sound of great hoofs plodding and sucking in the mud of the waterhole. Above the rippling heads of the reeds a dark shape moved, mountainous in the moonlight.

'A bull,' he breathed. 'A bull of a bull!'

The bull had finished drinking. The crafty old beast had come ahead of the cows and calves of the breeding herd. His back was coated with glistening wet mud from the wallow, and he plodded towards where Aboli crouched, his hoofs squelching in the mud.

Aboli lost sight of the prey as he sank down among the swaying stems and let him come on. But he could mark him by the sound of his heavy breathing, and by the rasping of the reeds dragging down his flanks. The bull was very close, but still out of Aboli's sight, when suddenly he shook his head as the reed stems tangled in his horns, and his ears flapped against his cheeks. If I reach out now I could touch his snout, Aboli thought. Every nerve in his body was drawn as tight as the bowstring in his fingers.

The reed bank parted in front of Aboli, and the massive head came through, the moonlight gleaming on the curved bosses of the horns. Abruptly the bull became aware of something amiss, of danger lurking close at hand, and he stopped and raised his huge black head. As he lifted his muzzle to test the air, his nose was wet and shining and water drooled from his mouth. He flared his nostrils into dark pits and snuffled the air. Aboli could feel his breath hot upon his naked chest and his face.

The bull turned his head, questing for the scent of man or cat, for the hidden hunter. Aboli stayed still as a tree-stump. He was holding the heavy bow at full draw. The power of the olive branch and the gut bowstring were so fierce that even the granite muscles in his arms and shoulder bulged and trembled with the effort. As the bull turned his head he revealed the notch behind his ear where the neck fused with the bone of his skull and the massive boss of his horns. Aboli held his aim for one heartbeat longer, then loosed the arrow. It flashed and whirred in the moonlight, leaping from his hand and burying half its length in the massive black neck.

The bull reeled back. If the arrowhead had found the gap between the vertebrae of the spine, as Aboli had hoped, he would have dropped where he stood but the iron point struck the spine and was deflected by bone. It glanced aside but sliced through the great artery behind the jawbone. As the bull bucked and kicked to the stinging impact of the steel, the severed artery erupted and a spout of blood flew high in the air, black as an ostrich feather in the light of the moon.

The bull dashed past Aboli, hooking wildly with those wide curved horns. If Aboli had not dropped his bow and hurled himself aside, the burnished point that hissed by, a finger's width from his navel, would have skewered him and ripped open his bowels.

The bull charged on and reached the hard dry ground. On his knees Aboli strained his ears to follow his quarry's crashing rush through the scrub. Abruptly it came up short. There was a long, fraught pause, in which he could hear the animal's laboured breathing and the patter of streaming blood falling on the leaves of the low bushes around it. Then he heard the bull stagger and stumble backwards, trying to remain on his feet while the strength flowed out of his huge body on that tide of dark blood. The beast fell heavily so that the earth trembled under Aboli's bare feet. A moment later came the rasping death bellow, and thereafter an aching quietness. Even the night birds and the bullfrogs of the swamp had been silenced by that dreadful sound. It was as though all the forest held its breath at the passing of such a mighty creature. Then, slowly, the night came alive once again, the frogs piped and croaked from the reedbeds, a nightjar screeched and from afar an eagle owl hooted mournfully.

Aboli skinned the bull with the knife that Sukeena had stolen for him from the residence kitchens. He folded the green skin and tied it with bark rope. It was heavy enough to tax even his strength. He staggered with the bundle until he could get under it and balance it on his head. He left the naked carcass for the packs of night-prowling hyena and the flocks of vultures, carnivorous storks, kites and crows that would find it with the first light of morning, and set off back towards the colony and the table-topped mountain, silhouetted against the stars. Even under his burden he moved at the ground-eating trot of the warriors of his tribe that was becoming so natural to him again after his confinement for two decades in a small ship upon the seas. He was remembering so much long-forgotten tribal lore and wisdom, relearning old skills, becoming once more a true son of this baked African earth.

He climbed to the lower slopes of the mountain and left the bundled skin in a narrow crevice in the rock cliff. He covered it with large boulders, for the hyenas roamed here also, attracted by the rubbish and wastes and sewage generated by the human settlement of the colony.

When he had placed the last boulder he looked up at the sky and saw that the curling scorpion was falling fast towards the dark horizon. Only then he realized how swiftly the night had sped, and went bounding back down the slope. He reached the edge of the Company gardens just as the first rooster crowed in the darkness.

Later that morning, as he waited on the bench with the other slaves outside the kitchens for his breakfast bowl of gruel and thick, curdled sour milk, Sukeena passed on her way to tend the affairs of the household. 'I heard you return last night. You were out too late,' she whispered, without turning her head on the orchid stem of her neck. 'If you are discovered, you will bring great hardship on all of us, and our plans will come to naught.'

'My task is almost finished,' he rumbled softly. 'Tonight will be the last time I need to go out.'

'Have a care, Aboli. There is much at risk,' she said and glided away. Despite her warning she had given him any help he had asked for, and without watching her go Aboli whispered to himself, 'That little one has the heart of a lioness.'

That night, when the house had settled down for the night, he slipped through the grating. Again the dogs were stilled by his quiet whistle, and he had lumps of dried sausage for each of them. When he reached the wall below the lawns, he looked to the stars and saw in the eastern sky the first soft luminescence of the moonrise. He vaulted over it and, keeping well clear of the road, guided himself by touch along the outside of the wall, towards the settlement.

No more than three or four dim lights were showing from the cottages and buildings of the village. The four ships at anchor in the bay were all burning lanterns at their mastheads. The castle was a dark brooding shape against the starlight.

He waited at the edge of the Parade and tuned his ears to the sounds of the night. Once, as he was about to set out across the open ground, he heard drunken laughter and snatches of singing as a party of soldiers from the castle returned from an evening of debauchery among the rude hovels on the waterfront, which passed as taverns in this remote station, selling the rough raw spirit the Hottentots called *dop*. One of the revellers carried a tar-dipped torch. The flames wove uncertainly as the man stopped before the gibbet in the middle of the Parade, and shouted an insult at the corpse that still hung upon it. His companions bellowed with drunken laughter at his humour, and then reeled on, supporting each other, towards the castle.

When they had disappeared through the gates, and when silence and darkness fell, Aboli moved out swiftly across the Parade. Though he could not see more than a few paces ahead, the smell of corruption guided him; only a dead lion smells as strongly as a rotting human corpse.

Sir Francis Courtney's body had been beheaded and neatly quartered. Slow John had used a butcher's cleaver to hack through the larger bones. Aboli brought down the head from the spike on which it had been impaled. He wrapped it in a clean white cloth and placed it in the saddle-bag he carried. Then he retrieved the other parts of the corpse. The dogs from the village had carried off some of the smaller bones, but even working in darkness Aboli was able to recover what remained. He closed and buckled the leather flap of the bag, slung it over his shoulder and set off again at a run towards the mountain.

Sukeena knew the mountain intimately, every ravine, cliff and crag. She had explained to him how to find the narrow concealed entrance to the cavern where, the previous night, he had left the raw buffalo skin. In the light of the rising moon, he returned unerringly to it. When he reached the entrance he stooped and swiftly removed the boulders that covered the buffalo skin. Then he crawled further into the crevice and drew aside the bushes that hung down from the cliff above to conceal the dark throat of the cavern.

He worked deftly, with flint and steel, to light one of the candles Sukeena had provided. Shielding the flame with cupped hands from any watcher below the mountain he went forward and crawled into the low natural tunnel on hands and knees, dragging the saddle-bag behind him. As Sukeena had told him, the tunnel opened suddenly into a cavern high enough for him to stand. He held the candle above his head and saw that the cavern would make a fitting burial place for a great chief. There was even a natural rock shelf at the far end. He left the saddle bag upon it and crawled back to retrieve the buffalo skin. Before he entered the tunnel again he looked back over his shoulder and reoriented himself in the direction of the moonrise.

'I shall turn his face to greet ten thousand moons and all the sunrises of eternity!' he said softly, and dragged the heavy skin into the cavern and spread it on the rock floor.

He placed the candle on the rock shelf and began to unpack the bag. First he set aside those small offerings and ceremonial items he had brought with him. Then he lifted out Sir Francis's covered head and laid it in the centre of the buffalo hide. He unwrapped it reverently, and showed no repugnance for the thick cloying odour of decay that slowly filled the cavern. He assembled all the other dismembered parts of the body and arranged them in their natural order, binding them in place with slim strands of bark rope, until Sir Francis lay on his side, his knees drawn up beneath his chin and his arms hugging his legs, the foetal position of the womb and of sleep. Then he folded the wet buffalo hide tightly around him so that only his ravaged face was still exposed. He stitched the folds of the hide around him so they would dry into an iron-hard sarcophagus. It was a long and meticulous task, and when the candle burnt down and guttered in a pool of its own liquid wax he lit another from the stump and worked on.

When he had finished, he took up the turtleshell comb, another of Sukeena's gifts, and combed out the tangled tresses that still adhered to Sir Francis's skull, and braided them neatly. At last he lifted the seated body and placed it on the stone shelf. He turned it carefully to face the east; to gaze for ever towards the moonrise and the dawn.

For a long while he squatted below the ledge and looked upon the ravaged head, seeing it in his mind's eye as it once was. The face of the vigorous young mariner who had rescued him from the slavers' hold two decades before.

At last he rose and began to gather up the grave-goods he had brought with him. He laid them one at a time on the ledge before the body of Sir Francis. The tiny model of a ship he had carved with his own hands. There had not been time to lavish care upon its construction, and it was crude and childlike. However, the three masts had sails set upon them, and the name carved into the stern was *Lady Edwina*.

'May this ship carry you over the dark oceans to the landfall where the woman whose name she bears awaits you,' Aboli whispered.

Next he placed the knife and the bow of olive wood beside the ship. 'I have no sword with which to arm you, but may these weapons be your defence in the dark places.'

Then he offered the food bowl and the water bottle. 'May you never again hunger or thirst.'

Lastly, the cross of wood that Aboli had fashioned and decorated with green abalone shell, white-carved bone and small bright stones from the river-bed. 'May the cross of your God which guided you in life, guide you still in death,' he said as he placed the cross before Sir Francis's empty eyes.

Kneeling on the cavern floor he built a small fire and lit it from the candle. 'May this fire warm you in the darkness of your long night.' Then, in his own language, he sang the funeral chant and the song of the traveller on a long journey, clapping his hands softly to keep the time, and to show respect. When the flames of the fire burned low he stood and moved to the entrance of the cavern.

'Farewell, my friend,' he said. 'Goodbye, my father.'

Governor van de Velde was a cautious man. At first, he had not allowed Aboli to drive him in the carriage. 'This is a whim of yours that I will not deny, my dear,' he told his wife, 'but the fellow is a black savage. What does he know of horses?'

'He is really very good, better by far than old Fredricus.' Katinka laughed. 'And he looks so splendid in the new livery I have designed for him.'

'His fancy maroon coat and breeches will be of little interest to me when he breaks my neck,' van de Velde said, but despite his misgivings he watched the way Aboli handled the team of greys.

The first morning that Aboli drove the Governor down from the residence to his suite in the castle, there was a stir and a murmur among the convicts working on the walls as the carriage crossed the Parade and approached the castle gates. They had recognized Aboli sitting high on the coachman's seat with the long whip in his white-gloved hands.

Hal was on the point of shouting a greeting to him, but checked himself in time. It was not the sting of Barnard's whip that dissuaded him, but he realized that it would be unwise to remind his captors that Aboli had been his shipmate. The Dutch would expect him to regard a black man as a slave and not as a companion.

'Nobody to greet Aboli,' he whispered urgently to Daniel, sweating beside him. 'Ignore him. Pass it on.' The order went swiftly down the ranks of men on the scaffold and then to those labouring in the courtyard. When the carriage came in through the gates to a turnout of the honour guard and the salutes of the garrison's officers, none of the convicts paid any attention. They devoted themselves to the heavy work with block and tackle and iron bar.

Aboli sat like a carved figurehead on the coachman's seat, staring directly ahead. His dark eyes did not even flicker in Hal's direction. He drew the team of greys to a halt at the foot of the staircase and sprang down to lower the folding steps and hand out the Governor. Once van de Velde had waddled up the stairs and disappeared into his suite, Aboli returned to his seat and sat upon it, unmoving, facing straight ahead. In a short time the gaolers and guards forgot his silent presence, turned their attention to their duties and the castle fell into its routine.

An hour passed and one of the horses threw its head and fidgeted. From the corner of his eye Hal had noticed Aboli touch the reins to agitate the animal slightly. Now he climbed unhurriedly down and went to its head. He held its leather cheek-strap and stroked its head and murmured endearments to it. The grey quietened immediately under his touch, and Aboli went down on one knee and lifted first one front foot and then the other, examining the hoofs for any injury.

Still on one knee and screened by the horse's body from the view of any of the guards or overseers, he looked up for the first time at Hal. Their gaze touched for an instant. Aboli nodded almost imperceptibly and opened his right fist to give Hal a glimpse of the tiny curl of white paper he had in his palm, then closed his fist and stood up. He walked down the team of horses examining each animal and making minute adjustments to the harness. At last he turned aside and leaned against the stone wall beside him, stooping to wipe the fine flouring of dust from his boots.

Hal watched him take the quill of paper and surreptitiously stuff it into a joint in the stonework of the wall. He straightened and returned to the coachman's seat to await the Governor's pleasure. Van de Velde never showed consideration for servant, slave or animal. All that morning the team of greys stood patiently in the traces with Aboli soothing them at intervals. A little before noon the Governor re-emerged from the Company offices and had himself driven back to the residence for the midday meal.

In the dusk, as the convicts wearily climbed down into the courtyard, Hal stumbled as he reached the ground and put out his hand to steady himself. Neatly he picked the scrap of folded paper from the joint in the stonework where Aboli had left it.

Once in the dungeon there was just sufficient light filtering down from the torch in its bracket at the top of the staircase for Hal to read the message. It was written in a fine neat hand that he did not recognize. Despite all his father's and Hal's own instruction, Aboli's handwriting had never been better than large, sprawling and malformed. It seemed that another scribe had framed these words. A tiny nub of charcoal was wrapped in the paper, placed there for Hal to write his reply on the reverse of the scrap.

'The Captain buried with honour.' Hal's heart leapt as he read that. So it was Aboli who had taken down his father's mutilated corpse from the gibbet. I should have known he would give my father that respect.

There was only one more word. 'Althuda?' Hal puzzled over this until he understood that Aboli, or the writer, must be asking after the welfare of the other prisoner.

'Althuda!' he called softly. 'Are you awake?'

'Greetings, Hal. What cheer?'

'Somebody outside asks after you.'

There was a long silence as Althuda considered this. 'Who asks?'

'I know not.' Hal could not explain for he was certain that the gaolers eavesdropped on these exchanges.

Another long silence. 'I can guess,' Althuda called. 'And so can you.

We have discussed her before. Can you send a reply? Tell her I am alive.'

Hal rubbed the charcoal on the wall to sharpen a point on it and wrote, 'Althuda well.' Even though his letters were small and cramped, there was space for no more on the paper.

The following morning, as they were led out to begin the day's work on the scaffold, Daniel screened Hal for the moment he needed to push the scrap of paper into the same crack from which he had retrieved it.

In the middle of the morning Aboli drove the Governor down from the residence and parked once more beneath the staircase. Long after van de Velde had disappeared into his sanctum, Aboli remained on the coachman's seat. At last he looked up casually at a flock of red-winged starlings that had come down from the cliffs to perch on the walls of the eastern bastion and give vent to their low, mournful whistles. From the birds his eye passed over Hal, who nodded. Once again Aboli dismounted and tended his horses, pausing beside the wall to adjust the straps on his boots and, with a magician's sleight-of-hand, to recover the message from the crack in the wall. Hal breathed easier when he saw it, for they had established their letterbox.

They did not make the mistake of trying to exchange messages every day. Sometimes a week or more might pass before Aboli nodded at Hal, and placed a note in the wall. If Hal had a message, he would give the same signal and Aboli would leave paper and charcoal for him.

The second message Hal received was in that artistic and delicate script: 'A. is safe. Orchid sends her heart.'

'Is the orchid the one we spoke of?' Hal called to Althuda that night. 'She sends you her heart, and says you are safe.'

'I do not know how she has achieved that, but I must believe it and be thankful to her in this as in so many things.' There was a lift of relief in Althuda's tone. Hal held the scrap of paper to his nose, and fancied that he detected the faintest perfume upon it. He huddled on his damp straw in a corner of the cell. He thought about Sukeena until sleep overcame him. The memory of her beauty was like a candle flame in the winter darkness of the dungeon.

Governor van de Velde was passing drunk. He had swilled the Rhenish with the soup and Madeira with the fish and the lobster. The red wines of Burgundy had accompanied the mutton stew and the pigeon pie. He had quaffed the claret with the beef, and interspersed each with draughts of good Dutch gin. When at last he rose from the board, he steadied himself as he wove to his seat by the fire with a hand on his wife's arm. She was not usually so attentive, but all this evening she had been in an affectionate and merry mood, laughing at his sallies which on other occasions she would have ignored, and refilling his glass with her own gracious hand before it was half emptied. Come to think of it, he could not remember when last they had dined alone, just the two of them, like a pair of lovers.

For once, he had not been forced to put up with the company of the rustic yokels from the settlement, or with the obsequious flattery of ambitious Company servants or, greatest blessing of all, without the posturing and boasting of that amorous prig Schreuder.

He fell back in the deep leather chair beside the fire and Sukeena brought him a box of good Dutch cigars to choose from. As she held the burning taper for him, he peered with a lascivious eye down the front of her costume. The soft swell of girlish breasts, between which nestled the exotic jade brooch, moved him so that he felt his groin swell and engorge pleasantly.

Katinka was kneeling at the open hearth, but she regarded him so slyly that he worried for a moment that she had seen him ogle the slave girl's bosom. But then she smiled and took up the poker that was heating in the fire and plunged its glowing tip into the stone jug of scented wine. It boiled and fumed, and she filled a bowl with it and brought it to him before it had time to cool.

'My beautiful wife!' He slurred a little. 'My little darling.' He toasted her with the steaming bowl. He was not yet so intoxicated or gullible that he did not realize there would be some price to pay for this unusual kindness. There always was.

Kneeling in front of him, Katinka looked up at Sukeena, who hovered close at hand. 'That is all for tonight, Sukeena. You may go.' She gave the slave girl a knowing smile.

'I wish you sweet sleep and dreams of paradise, master and mistress.' Sukeena gave that graceful genuflection, and glided from the room. She slid the carved oriental screen door closed behind her, and knelt there quietly with her face close to the panel. These were her mistress's orders. Katinka wanted Sukeena to witness what transpired between her and her husband. She knew that it would tighten the knot that bound the slave girl to her.

Now Katinka moved behind her husband's chair. 'You have had such a difficult week,' she said softly, 'what with the affair of the pirate's body being stolen from the scaffold, and now the new census and taxation ordinances from the Seventeen. My poor darling husband, let me massage your shoulders for you.'

She removed his wig and kissed the top of his head. The stubble prickled her lips, and she stood back and dug her thumbs into his heavy shoulders. Van de Velde sighed with pleasure, not only with the sensation of the knots being eased from his muscles but because he recognized this as the prelude to the infrequent dispensation of her sexual favours.

'How much do you love me?' she asked, and leaned over him to nibble at his ear.

'I adore you,' he blurted out. 'I worship you.'

'You are always so kind to me.' Her voice took on that husky quality that made his skin tingle. 'I want to be kind to you. I have written to my father. I have explained to him the circumstances of the pirate's demise and how it was not your fault that it happened. I shall give the letter to the captain of the homeward-bound galleon, which is anchored in the bay at the moment, to hand to Papa in person.'

'May I see the letter before you dispatch it?' he asked warily. 'It would carry much weight if it could accompany my own report to the Seventeen, which I shall send on the same ship.'

'Of course you may. I shall bring it to you before you leave for the castle in the morning.' She brushed the top of his head with her lips again, and slid her fingers from his shoulders down over his chest. She unhooked the buttons of his doublet and slipped both hands into the opening. She took a handful of each of his pendulous dugs and kneaded them as though they were lumps of soft bread dough.

'You are such a good little wife,' he said. 'I would like to give you a sign of my love. What do you lack? A jewel? A pet? A new slave? Tell your old Petrus.'

'I do have a little whimsy,' she admitted coyly. 'There is a man in the dungeons.'

'One of the pirates?' he hazarded.

'No, a slave named Althuda.'

'Ah, yes! I know about him. The rebel and runaway! I shall deal with him this coming week. His death warrant is already on my desk waiting for my signature. Shall I give him to Slow John? Would you like to watch? Is that it? You want to enjoy the sport? How can I deny you?'

She reached down and began to unlace the fastening of his breeches. He spread his legs and lay back comfortably in the chair to make the task easier for her.

'I want you to grant Althuda a reprieve,' she whispered in his ear.

He sat bolt upright. 'You are mad,' he gasped.

'You are so cruel to call me mad.' She pouted.

'But – but he is a runaway. He and his gang of thugs murdered twenty of the soldiers who were sent to recapture him. I could never free him.'

'I know you cannot release him. But I want you to keep him alive. You could set him to work on the walls of your castle.'

'I cannot do it.' He shook his shaven head. 'Not even for you.'

She came round from behind his chair and knelt in front of him. Her fingers began work again on the lacing of his breeches. He tried to sit up but she pushed him back and reached inside.

All the saints bear witness, the old sodomite makes it difficult for me. He is as soft and white as unrisen dough, she thought as she grasped him. 'Not even for your own loving wife?' she whispered, and looked up with swimming violet eyes, as she thought, That's a little better, I felt the drooping lily twitch.

'I mean, rather, that it would be difficult.' He was in a quandary.

'I understand,' she murmured. 'It was just as difficult for me to compose my letter to my father. I would hate to be forced to burn it.' She stood up and lifted her skirts as though she were about to climb over a stile. She was naked from the waist down and his eyes bulged like those of a cod hauled up abruptly from deep water. He struggled to sit up and at the same time tried to reach for her.

I'll not have you on top of me again, you great tub of pork lard, she thought as she smiled lovingly at him and held him down with both hands on his shoulders. Last time you nearly squashed the life out of me.

She straddled him as though she were mounting the mare. 'Oh, sweet Jesus, what a mighty man you are!' she cried, as she took him in. The only pleasure she received from it was the thought of Sukeena listening at the screen door. She closed her eyes and summoned up the image of the slave girl's slim thighs and the treasure that lay between them. The thought inflamed her, and she knew that her husband would feel her flowing response and think it was for him alone.

'Katinka,' he gurgled and snorted as though he was drowning, 'I love you.'

'The reprieve?' she asked.

'I cannot do it.'

'Then neither can I,' she said, and lifted herself onto her knees. She had to fight to keep herself from laughing aloud as she watched his face swell and his eyes bulge further out. He wriggled and heaved under her, thrusting vainly at the air.

'Please!' he whimpered. 'Please!'

'The reprieve?' she asked, keeping herself suspended tantalizingly above him.

'Yes,' he whinnied. 'Anything. I will give you anything you want.'

'I love you, my husband,' she whispered in his ear, and sank down like a bird settling on its nest.

Last time he lasted to a count of one hundred, she remembered. This time I shall try to bring him to the finishing line in under fifty. With rocking hips she set herself to better her own record.

Manseer opened the door of Althuda's cell and roared, 'Come out, you murderous dog. Governor's orders, you go to work on the wall.' Althuda stepped out through the iron door and Manseer glared at him. 'Seems you'll not be dancing a quadrille on the scaffold with Slow John, more's the pity. But don't crow too loud, you'll give us as much sport on the castle walls. Barnard and his hounds will see to that. You'll not last the winter out, I'll wager a hundred guilders on it.'

Hal led the file of convicts up from the lower cells, and paused on the stone step below Althuda. For a long moment they studied each other keenly. Both looked pleased at what they saw.

'If you give me a choice, then I think I prefer the cut of your sister's jib to yours.' Hal smiled. Althuda was smaller in stature than his voice had suggested and all the marks of his long captivity were plain to see: his skin was sallow and his hair matted and tangled. But the body that showed through the holes in his miserable rags was neat and strong and supple. His gaze was frank and his countenance comely and open. Although his eyes were almond-shaped and his hair straight and black, his English blood mingled well with that of his mother's people. There was a proud and stubborn set to his jaw.

'What cradle did you fall out of?' he asked Hal, with a grin. It was obvious that he was overjoyed to come out from the shadow of the gallows. 'I called for a man and they sent a boy.'

'Come on, you murdering renegade,' Barnard bellowed, as the gaoler handed over the convicts to his charge. 'You may have escaped the noose for the moment, but I have a few pleasures in store for you. You slit the throats of some of my comrades on the mountainside.' It was clear that all the garrison bitterly resented Althuda's reprieve. Then Barnard turned on Hal. 'As for you, you stinking pirate, your tongue is too loose by far. One word out of you today and I'll kick you off the wall, and feed the scraps to my dogs.'

Barnard separated the two of them: he sent Hal back onto the scaffold and set Althuda to work in the gangs of convicts down in the courtyard, unloading the masonry blocks from the ox-drawn wagons as they came down from the quarries.

However, that evening Althuda was herded into the general cell. Daniel and the rest crowded around him in the darkness to hear his story told in detail, and to ply him with all the questions that they had not been able to shout up the staircase. He was something new in the dreary, monotonous round of captivity and heart-breaking labour. Only when the kettle of stew was brought down from the kitchens and the men hurried to their frugal dinner did Hal have a chance to speak to him alone.

'If you escaped once before, Althuda, then there must be a chance we can do it again.'

'I was in a better state then. I had my own fishing boat. My master trusted me and I had the run of the colony. How can we escape from the walls that surround us? I fear it would be impossible.'

'You use the words fear and impossible. That is not a language that I understand. I thought perhaps I had met a man, not some faintheart.'

'Keep the harsh words for our enemies, my friend.' Althuda returned his hard stare. 'Instead of telling me what a hero you are, tell me instead now how you receive word from the outside.' Hal's stern expression cracked and he grinned at him. He liked the man's spirit, the way he could meet broadside with broadside. He moved closer and lowered his voice as he explained to Althuda how it was done. Then he handed him the latest message he had received. Althuda took it to the grille gate, and studied it in the torchlight that filtered down the staircase.

'Yes,' he said. 'That is my sister's hand. I know of no other who can pen her letters so prettily.'

That evening the two composed a message for Aboli to collect, to let him and Sukeena know that Althuda had been released from Skellum's Den.

However, it seemed that Sukeena already knew this, for the following day she accompanied her mistress on a visit to the castle. She rode beside Aboli on the driver's seat of the carriage. At the staircase she helped her mistress dismount. It was strange but Hal was by now so accustomed to Katinka's visits that he no longer felt angry and bitter when he looked upon her angelic face. She held his attention barely at all, and instead he watched the slave girl. Sukeena stood at the bottom of the staircase and darted quick birdlike glances in every direction as she searched for her brother's face among the gangs of convicts.

Althuda was working in the courtyard, chipping and chiselling the rough stone blocks into shape before they were swung up on the gantry to the top of the unfinished walls. His face and hair were powdered white as a miller's with the stone dust, and his hands were bleeding from the abrasion of tools and rough stone. At last Sukeena picked him out, and brother and sister stared at each other for one long ecstatic moment.

Sukeena's radiant expression was one of the most beautiful Hal had ever looked upon. But it was only for a fleeting instant, then Sukeena hurried up the stairs after her mistress.

A short time later they reappeared at the head of the staircase, but Governor van de Velde was with them. He had his wife on his arm and Sukeena followed then demurely. The slave girl seemed to be searching for someone other than her brother. When she mounted the driver's seat of the carriage, she murmured something to Aboli. In response, Aboli moved only his eyes, but she followed his gaze, up to the top of the scaffold where Hal was belaying a rope end.

Hal felt his pulse sprint as he realized that it was him she was seeking. They stared at each other solemnly and it seemed they were very close, for afterwards Hal could remember every angle and plane of her face and the graceful curve of her neck. At last she smiled, it was a brief, honeyed interlude, then dropped her eyes. That night in his cell he lay on the clammy straw and relived the moment.

Perhaps she will come again tomorrow, he thought, as sleep swept over him like a black wave. But she did not come again for many weeks.

They made a place on the straw for Althuda to sleep near Hal and Daniel so that they could talk quietly in the darkness.

'How many of your men are in the mountains?' Hal wanted to know.

'There were nineteen of us to begin with, but three were killed by the Dutch and five others died after we escaped. The mountains are cruel and there are many wild beasts.'

'What weapons do they have?' Hal asked.

'They have the muskets and the swords that we captured from the Dutch, but there is little powder, and by now it might all be used up. My companions have to hunt to live.'

'Surely they have made other weapons?' Hal enquired.

'They have fashioned bows and pikes, but they lack iron points for these weapons.'

'How secure are your hiding places in the wilderness?' Hal persisted.

'The mountains are endless. The gorges are a tangled labyrinth. The cliffs are harsh and there are no paths except those made by the baboons.'

'Do the Dutch soldiers venture into these mountains?'

'Never! They dare not scale even the first ravine.'

These discussions filled all their evenings, as the winter gales came ravening down from the mountain like a pride of lions roaring at the castle walls. The men in the dungeons lay shivering on the straw pallets. Sometimes it was only the talking and the hoping that kept them from succumbing to the cold. Even so, some of the older, weaker convicts sickened: their throats and chests filled with thick yellow phlegm, their bodies burned up with fever and they died, choking and coughing.

The flesh was burned off those who survived. Although they became thin, they were hardened by the cold and the labour. Hal reached his full growth and strength in those terrible months, until he could match Daniel at belaying a rope or hefting the heavy hods. His beard grew out dense and black and the thick pigtail of his hair hung down between his shoulder blades. The whip marks latticed his back and flanks, and his gaze was hard and relentless when he looked up at the mountain tops, blue in the distance.

'How far is it to the mountains?' he asked Althuda in the darkness of the cell.

'Ten leagues,' Althuda told him.

'So far!' Hal whispered. 'How did you ever reach them over such a distance, with the Dutch in pursuit?'

'I told you I was a fisherman,' Althuda said. 'I went out each day to kill seals to feed the other slaves. My boat was small and we were many. It barely served to carry us across False Bay to the foot of the mountains. My sister Sukeena does not swim. That is why I would not let her chance the crossing.'

'Where is that boat now?'

'The Dutch who pursued us found where we had hidden it. They burned it.' Each night these councils were shortlived, for they were all being driven to the limit of their strength and endurance. But, gradually, Hal was able to milk from Althuda every detail that might be of use.

'What is the spirit of the men you took with you to the mountains?'

'They are brave men – and women too, for there are three girls with the band. Had they been less brave they would never have left the safety of their captivity. But they are not warriors, except one.'

'Who is he, this one amongst them?'

'His name is Sabah. He was a soldier until the Dutch captured him. Now he is a soldier again.'

'Could we send word to him?'

Althuda laughed bitterly. 'We could shout from the top of the castle walls or rattle our chains. He might hear us on his mountain top.'

'If I had wanted a jester, I would have called on Daniel here to amuse me. His jokes would make a dog retch, but they are funnier than yours. Answer me now, Althuda. Is there no way to reach Sabah?'

Though his tone was light, it had an edge of steel to it, and Althuda thought a while before he replied. 'When I escaped I arranged with Sukeena a hiding place beyond the bitter-almond hedge of the colony, where we could leave messages for each other. Sabah knew of this post, for I showed it to him on the night I returned to fetch my sister. It is a long throw of the dice, but Sabah may still visit it to find a message from me.'

'I will think on these things you have told me,' Hal said, and Daniel, lying near him in the dark cell, heard the power and authority in his voice and shook his head.

'Tis the voice and the manner of Captain Franky he has now, Daniel marvelled. What the Dutchies are doing to him here might have put a lesser man up on the reef but, by God, all they have done to him is filled his main sail with a strong wind. Hal had taken over his father's role, and the crew who had survived recognized it. More and more they looked to him for leadership, to give them courage to go on and to counsel them, to settle the petty disputes that rose almost daily between men in such bitter straits, and to keep a spark of hope and courage burning in all their hearts.

The next evening Hal took up the council of war that exhaustion had interrupted the night before. 'So Sukeena knows where to leave a message for Sabah?'

'Naturally, she knows it well – the hollow tree on the banks of the Eerste River, the first river beyond the boundary hedge,' Althuda replied.

'Aboli must try to make contact with Sabah. Is there something that is known only to you and Sabah that will prove to him the message comes from you and is not a Dutch trap?'

Althuda thought about it. 'Just say 'tis the father of little Bobby,' he suggested at last. Hal waited in silence for Althuda to explain, and after a pause he went on, 'Robert is my son, born in the wilderness after we had escaped from the colony. This August he will be a year old. His mother is one of the girls I spoke of. In all but name she is my wife. Nobody inside the bitter-almond hedge but I could know the child's name.'

'So, you have as good a reason as any of us for wanting to fly over these walls,' Hal murmured.

The content of the messages that they were able to pass to Aboli was severely restricted by the size of the paper they could safely employ without alerting the gaolers or the sharp, hungry scrutiny of Hugo

Barnard. Hal and Althuda spent hours straining their eyes in the dim light and flogging their wits to compose the most succinct messages that would still be intelligible. The replies that returned to them were the voice of Sukeena speaking, little jewels of brevity that delighted them with occasional flashes of wit and humour.

Hal found himself thinking more and more of Sukeena, and when she came again to the castle, following behind her mistress, her eyes went first to the scaffold where he worked before going on to seek out her brother. Occasionally, when there was space in the letters that Aboli placed in the crack of the wall, she made little personal comments; a reference to his bushing black beard or the passing of his birthday. This startled Hal, and touched him deeply. He wondered for a while how she had known this intimate detail, until he guessed that Aboli had told her. He encouraged Althuda to talk about her in the darkness. He learned little things about her childhood, her fancies and her dislikes. As he lay and listened to Althuda, he began to fall in love with her.

Now when Hal looked to the mountains in the north they were covered by a mantle of snow that shone in the wintry sunlight. The wind came down from it like a lance and seemed to pierce his soul. 'Aboli has still not heard from Sabah.' After four months of waiting, Hal at last accepted that failure. 'We will have to cut him out of our plans.'

'He is my friend, but he must have given me up,' Althuda agreed. 'I grieve for my wife for she also must be mourning my death.'

'Let us move on, then, for it boots us not to wish for what is denied us,' Hal said firmly. 'It would be easier to escape from the quarry on the mountain than from the castle itself. It seems that Sukeena must have arranged for your reprieve. Perhaps in the same fashion she can have us sent to the quarry.'

They dispatched the message, and a week later the reply came back. Sukeena was unable to influence the choice of their workplace, and she cautioned that any attempt to do so would arouse immediate suspicion. 'Be patient, Gundwane,' she told him in a longer message than she had ever sent before. 'Those who love you are working for your salvation.' Hal read that message a hundred times then repeated it to himself as often. He was touched that she should use his nickname; Gundwane. Of course, Aboli had told her that also.

'Those who love you'? Does she mean Aboli alone, or does she use the plural intentionally? Is there another who loves me too? Does she mean me alone or does she include Althuda, her brother? He alternated between hope and dismay. How can she trouble my mind so, when I have never even heard her voice? How can she feel anything for me, when she sees nothing but a bearded scarecrow in a beggar's rags? But, then, perhaps Aboli has been my champion and told her I was not always thus.

Plan as they would, the days passed and hope grew threadbare. Six more of Hal's seamen died during the months of August and September: two fell from the scaffold, one was struck down by a falling block of masonry and two more succumbed to the cold and the damp. The sixth was Oliver, who had been Sir Francis's manservant. Early in their imprisonment his right foot had been crushed beneath the iron-shod wheel of one of the ox-wagons that brought the stone down from the quarry. Even though Dr Saar had placed a splint upon the shattered bone, the foot would not mend. It swelled up and burst out in suppurating ulcers that smelt like the flesh of a corpse. Hugo Barnard drove him back to work, even though he limped around the courtyard on a crude crutch.

Hal and Daniel tried to shield Oliver, but if they intervened too obviously Barnard became even more vindictive. All they could do was take as much of the work as they could on themselves and keep Oliver out of range of the overseer's whip. When the day came that Oliver was too weak to climb the ladder to the top of the south wall, Barnard sent him to work as a mason's boy, trimming and shaping the slabs of stone. In the courtyard he was right under Barnard's eye, and twice in the same morning Barnard laid into him with the whip.

The last was a casual blow, not nearly as vicious as many that had preceded it. Oliver was a tailor by trade, and by nature a timid and gentle creature, but, like a cur driven into an alley from which there was no escape, he turned and snapped. He swung the heavy wooden mallet in his right hand, and though Barnard sprang back he was not swift enough and it caught him across one shin. It was a glancing blow that did not break bone but it smeared the skin, and a flush of blood darkened Barnard's hose and seeped down into his shoe. Even from his perch on the scaffold Hal could see by his expression that Oliver was appalled and terrified by what he had done.

'Sir!' he cried, and fell to his knees. 'I did not mean it. Please, sir, forgive me.' He dropped the mallet and held up both hands to his face in the attitude of prayer.

Hugo Barnard staggered back, then stooped to examine his injury. He ignored Oliver's frantic pleas, and peeled back his hose to expose the long graze down his shin. Then still without looking at Oliver, he limped to the hitching rail on the far side of the courtyard where his pair of black boarhounds were tethered. He held them on the leashes and pointed them at where Oliver still knelt.

'Get him!' They hurled themselves against the leashes, baying and gaping with wide red mouths and long white fangs.

'Get him!' Barnard urged, and at the same time restrained them. The fury in his voice enraged the animals, and they leapt against the leashes so that Barnard was almost pulled off his feet.

'Please!' screamed Oliver, struggling to rise, toppling back, then crawling towards where his crutch was propped against the stone wall.

Barnard slipped the hounds. They bounded across the yard and Oliver had time only to lift his hands to cover his face before they were on him.

They bowled him over and sent him rolling over the cobbles, then slashed at him with snapping jaws. One went for his face, but he lifted his arm and it buried its fangs in his elbow. Oliver was shirtless and the other hound caught him in the belly. Both held on.

From high on the scaffold Hal was powerless to intervene. Gradually Oliver's screams grew weaker and his struggles ceased. Barnard and his hounds never let up: they went on worrying the body long after the last flutter of life had been extinguished. Then Barnard gave the mutilated body one last kick and stepped back. He was panting wildly and sweat slimed his face and dripped onto his shirtfront, but he lifted his head and grinned up at Hal. He left Oliver's body lying on the cobbles until the end of the work shift when he singled out Hal and Daniel. 'Throw that piece of offal on the dungheap behind the castle. He will be more use to the seagulls and crows than he ever was to me.' And he chuckled with glee when he saw the murder in Hal's eyes.

When spring came round again only eight were left. Yet the eight were tempered by these hardships. Every muscle and sinew stood proud beneath the tanned and weathered skin of Hal's chest and arms. The palms of his hands were tough as leather, and his fingers powerful as a blacksmith's tongs. When he broke up a fight a single blow from one of his scarred fists could drop a big man to the paving.

The first promise of spring dispersed the gale-driven clouds, and the sun had new fire in its rays. A restlessness took over from the resigned gloom that had possessed them all during winter. Tempers were short, fighting amongst them more frequent, and their eyes looked often to the far mountains, from which the snows had thawed or turned out across the blue Atlantic.

Then there came a message from Aboli in Sukeena's hand: 'Sabah sends greetings to A. Bobby and his mother pine for him.' It filled them all with a wild and joyous hope that, in truth, had no firm foundation for Sabah and his band could only help them once they had passed the bitter-almond hedge.

Another month passed, and the wild flame of hope that had lit their hearts sank to an ember. Spring came in its full glory, and turned the mountain into a prodigy of wild flowers whose colours stunned the eye, and whose perfume reached them even on the high scaffold. The wind came singing out of the south-east, and the sunbirds returned from they knew not where, setting the air afire with their sparkling plumage.

Then there was a laconic message from Sukeena and Aboli. 'It is time to go. How many are you?'

That night they discussed the message in whispers that shook with excitement. 'Aboli has a plan. But how can he get all of us away?'

'For me he is the only horse in the race,' Big Daniel growled. 'I'm laying every penny I have on him.'

'If only you had a penny to lay.' Ned chuckled. It was the first time Hal had heard him laugh since Oliver had been ripped to pieces by Barnard's dogs.

'How many are going?' Hal asked. 'Think on it a while, lads, before you give answer.' In the bad light he looked around the circle of heads, whose expressions turned grim. 'If you stay here you will go on living for a while at least, and no man will think the worse of you. If we go and we do not reach the mountains, then you all saw the way my father and Oliver died. 'Twas not a fitting death for an animal, let alone a man.'

Althuda spoke first. 'Even if it were not for Bobby and my woman, I would go.'

'Aye!' said Daniel, and 'Aye!' said Ned.

'That's three,' Hal murmured, 'What about you, William Rogers?'

'I'm with you, Sir Henry.'

'Don't test me, Billy. I have told you not to call me that.' Hal frowned. When they used his title he felt himself a fraud, for he was not worthy of the honour that his grandfather had won at the right hand of Drake. The title that his father had carried with such distinction. 'Your last chance, Master Billy. If your tongue trips again I'll kick some sense into the other end of you. Do you hear?'

'Aye, I hear you sweet and clear, Sir Henry.' Billy grinned at him, and the others roared with laughter as Hal caught him by the scruff of his neck and boxed his ears. They were all bubbling over with excitement – all, that was, but Dick Moss and Paul Hale.

'I've grown too old for a lark such as this, Sir Hal. My bones are so stiff I could not climb a pretty lad if you tied him over a barrel for me, let alone climb a mountain.' Dick Moss the old pederast grinned. 'Forgive me, Captain, but Paul and me have talked it over, and we'll stay on here where we'll get a bellyful of stew and a bundle of straw each night.'

'Perhaps you are wiser than the rest of us.' Hal nodded, and he was not saddened by the decision. Dicky was long past his glory days when he had been the man to beat to the masthead when they reefed sail in a full gale. This last winter had stiffened his limbs and greyed his hair. He would be non-paying cargo to carry on this voyage. Paul was Dicky's shipwife. They had been together for twenty years, and though Paul was still a fury with a cutlass in his hand he would stay with his ageing lover.

'Good luck to both of you. You're as good a pair as I ever sailed with,' Hal said, and looked at Wally Finch and Stan Sparrow. 'What about you two birds? Will you fly with us, lads?'

'As high and as far as you're going.' Wally spoke for both of them, and Hal clapped his shoulder.

'That makes six of us, eight with Aboli and Althuda, and it'll be high and far enough to suit all our tastes, I warrant you.'

There was a final exchange of messages as Aboli and Sukeena explained the plan they had worked out. Hal suggested refinements and drew up a list of items that Aboli and Sukeena must try to steal to make their existence in the wilderness more certain. Chief amongst these were a chart and compass, and a backstaff if they could find one.

Aboli and Sukeena made their final preparation without letting their trepidation or excitement become apparent to the rest of the household. Dark eyes were always watching everything that happened in the slave quarters, and they trusted nobody now that they were so close to the chosen day. Sukeena gradually assembled those items for which Hal had asked, and added a few of her own that she knew they would need.

The day before the planned escape, Sukeena summoned Aboli into the main living area of the residence where before he had never been allowed to enter. 'I need your strength to move the carved armoire in the banquet hall,' she told him, in front of the cook and two others of the kitchen staff. Aboli followed her submissively as a trained hound on a leash. Once they were alone, Aboli dropped the demeanour of the meek slave.

'Be quick!' Sukeena warned him. 'The mistress will return very soon. She is with Slow John at the bottom of the garden.' She moved swiftly to the shutter of the window that overlooked the lawns, and saw that the ill-assorted couple were still in earnest conversation under the oak trees.

'There is no limit to her depravity,' she whispered to herself, as she watched Katinka laugh at something the executioner had said. 'She would make love to a pig or a poisonous snake if the fancy came upon her.' Sukeena shuddered at the memory of that ophidian tongue exploring the secret recesses of her own body. It will never happen again, she promised herself, only four more days to endure before Althuda will be safe. If she calls me to her nest before then I will plead that my courses are flowing.

She heard something whirl in the air like a great bird in flight and glanced back over her shoulder to see that Aboli had taken one of the swords from the display of weapons in the hallway. He was testing its balance and temper, swinging it in singing circles around his head, so that the reflections of light off the blade danced on the white walls.

He set it aside and chose another, but liked it not at all and placed it back with a frown. 'Hurry!' she called softly to him. Within minutes he had picked out three blades, not for the jewels that decorated the hilts but for the litheness and temper of their blades. All three were curved scimitars made by the armourers of Shah Jahan at Agra on the Indian continent. 'They were made for a Mogul prince and sit ill in the hand of a rough sailor, but they will do until I can find a cutlass of good Sheffield steel to replace them.' Then he picked out a shorter blade, a *kukri* knife used by the hill people of Further India, and he shaved a patch of hair off his forearm. 'This will do for the close work I have in mind.' He grunted with satisfaction.

'I have marked well those you have chosen,' Sukeena told him. 'Now leave them on the rack or their empty slots will be noticed by the other house slaves. I will pass them to you on the evening before the day.'

That afternoon she took her basket and, the conical straw hat on her head, went up into the mountain. Although any watcher would not have understood her intent, she made certain that she was out of sight, hidden in the forest that filled the great ravine below the summit. There was a dead tree that she had noted on many previous outings. From the rotting pith sprouted a thicket of tiny purple toadstools. She pulled on a pair of gloves before she began to pick them. The gills beneath the parasol-shaped tops were of a pretty yellow colour. These fungi were toxic, but only if eaten in quantity would they be fatal. She had chosen them for this quality – she did not want the lives of innocent men and their families on her conscience. She placed them in the bottom of the basket and covered them with other roots and herbs before she descended the steep mountainside and walked sedately back through the vineyards to the residence.

That evening Governor van de Velde held a gala dinner in the great hall, and invited the notables from the settlement and all the Company dignitaries. These festivities continued late, and after the guests had left the household staff and slaves were exhausted. They left Sukeena to make her rounds and lock up the kitchens for the night.

Once she was alone she boiled the purple toadstools and reduced the essence to the consistency of new honey. She poured the liquid into one of the empty wine bottles from the feast. It had no odour and she did not have to sample it to know that it had only the faintest taste of the fungi. One of the women who worked in the kitchens at the castle barracks was in her debt: Sukeena's potions had saved her eldest son when he had been stricken by the smallpox. The next morning she left the bottle in a basket with remedies and potions in the carriage for Aboli to deliver to the woman.

When Aboli drove the Governor down to the castle, van de Velde was ashen-faced and grumpy with the effects of the previous night's debauchery. Aboli left a message in the slot in the wall that read, 'Eat nothing from the garrison kitchen on the last evening.'

That night Hal poured the contents of the stew kettle into the latrine bucket before any of the men were tempted to sample it. The steaming aroma filled the cell and to the starving seamen it smelled like the promise of eternal life. They groaned and gritted their teeth, and cursed Hal, their fates and themselves to see it wasted.

The next morning at the accustomed hour the dungeon began to stir with life. Long before dawn outlined the four small, barred windows, men groaned and coughed and then crept, one at a time to ease themselves, grunting and farting as they voided in the latrine bucket. Then, as the significance of the day dawned upon them, a steely, charged silence gripped them.

Slowly the light of day filtered down upon them from the windows and they looked at each other askance. They had never been left this late before. On every other morning they had been at work on the walls an hour earlier than this.

When at last Manseer's keys rattled in the lock, he looked pale and sickly. The two men with him were in no better case.

'What ails you, Manseer?' Hal asked. 'We thought you had changed your affections and that we would never see you again.' The gaoler was an honest simpleton, with little malice in him, and over the months Hal had cultivated a superficially amicable relationship with him.

'I spent the night sitting in the shithouse,' Manseer moaned. 'And I had company, for every man in the garrison was trying to get in there with me. Even at this hour half of them are still in their bunks—' He broke off as his belly rumbled like distant thunder, and a desperate expression came over his face. 'Here I go again! I swear I'll kill that poxy cook.' He started back up the stairs and left them waiting another half-hour before he returned to open the grille gate and lead them out into the courtyard.

Hugo Barnard was waiting to take over from him. He was in a foul mood. 'We have lost half a day's work,' he snarled at Manseer. 'Colonel Schreuder will blame me for this, and when he does I'll come back to you, Manseer!' He turned on the line of convicts. 'Don't you bastards stand there smirking! By God, you're going to give me a full day's work even if I have to keep you on the scaffold until midnight. Now leap to it, and quickly too!' Barnard was in fine fettle, his face ruddy and his temper already on the boil. It was clear that the colic and diarrhoea that afflicted the rest of the garrison had not touched him. Hal remembered Manseer remarking that Barnard lived with a Hottentot girl in the settlement down by the shore, and did not eat in the garrison mess.

He looked around quickly as he walked across the courtyard to the foot of the ladder. The sun was already well up and its rays lit the western redoubt of the castle. There were less than half the usual number of gaolers and guards: one sentry instead of four at the gates, none at the entrance to the armoury and only one more at the head of the staircase that led to the Company offices and the Governor's suite on the south side of the courtyard.

When he climbed the ladder and reached the top of the wall he looked across the parade to the avenue, and could just make out the roof of the Governor's residence among the trees.

'God speed, Aboli,' he whispered. 'We are ready for you.'

Aboli brought the carriage round to the front of the residence a few minutes earlier than the Governor's wife had ordered it, and pulled up the horses below the portico. Almost immediately Sukeena appeared in the doorway and called to him. 'Aboli! The mistress has some packages to take with us in the carriage.' Her tone was light and easy, with no hint of strain. 'Please come and carry them down.' This was for the benefit of the others whom she knew would be listening.

Obediently Aboli locked the brake on the carriage wheels and, with a quiet word to the horses, jumped down from the coachman's seat. He moved without haste and his expression was calm as he followed Sukeena into the house. He came out again a minute later carrying a rolled-up silk rug and a set of leather saddle-bags. He went to the back of the carriage and placed this luggage in the panniers, then closed the lid. There was no air of secrecy about his movements and no furtiveness to alert any of the other slaves. The two maids who were busy sweeping the front terrace did not even look up at him. He went back to his seat and picked up the reins, waiting with a slave's infinite patience.

Katinka was late, but that was not unusual. She came at last in a cloud of French perfume and rustling silks, sweeping down the stairs and scolding Sukeena for some fancied misdemeanour. Sukeena glided beside her on small, silent, slippered feet, contrite and smiling.

Katinka climbed up into the carriage like a queen on her way to her coronation, and imperiously ordered Sukeena, 'Come and sit here beside me!' Sukeena gave her a curtsy with her hands to her lips. She had hoped that Katinka would give her that command. When she was in the mood for physical intimacy, Katinka wanted her close enough to be able to stretch out her hand and touch her. At other times she was cold and aloof, but at all times unpredictable.

'Tis an omen for good that she does what I intended, Sukeena encouraged herself, as she took the seat opposite her mistress and smiled at her lovingly.

'Drive on, Aboli!' Katinka called and then, as the carriage pulled away, gave her attention to Sukeena. 'How does this colour suit me in the sunlight? Does it not make me seem pale and insipid?'

'It goes beautifully with your skin, mistress.' Sukeena told her what she wanted to hear. 'Even better than it does indoors. Also it brings out the violet lights in your eyes.'

'Should there not be a touch more lace in the collar, do you think?' Katinka tilted her head prettily.

Sukeena considered her reply. 'Your beauty does not rely on even the finest lace from Brussels,' she told her. 'It stands alone.'

'Do you think so, Sukeena? You are such a flatterer, but I must say you yourself are looking particularly fetching this morning.' She considered the girl thoughtfully. The carriage was now bowling down the avenue at a trot, the greys arching their necks and stepping out handsomely. 'There is colour in your cheeks and a twinkle in your eye. One might be forgiven for thinking that you were in love.'

Sukeena looked at her in a way that made Katinka's skin tingle. 'Oh, but I am in love with a special person,' she whispered.

'My naughty little darling,' Katinka purred.

The carriage came out into the parade and turned towards the castle. Katinka was so engrossed that for some while she did not realize where they were heading. Then a shadow of annoyance crossed her face and she called sharply, 'Aboli! What are you doing, idiot? Not the castle. We are going to Mevrouw de Waal.'

Aboli seemed not to have heard her. The greys trotted straight on towards the castle gates.

'Sukeena, tell the fool to turn round.'

Sukeena stood up quickly in the swaying carriage then sat down close beside Katinka and slipped her arm through that of her mistress, holding her firmly.

'What on earth are you doing, child? Not here. Have you lost your mind? Not in front of the whole colony.' She tried to pull away her arm, but Sukeena held it with a strength that shocked her.

'We are going into the castle,' Sukeena said quietly. 'And you are to do exactly what I tell you to do.'

'Aboli! Stop the carriage this instant!' Katinka raised her voice and made to stand up. But Sukeena jerked her down in her seat.

'Don't struggle,' Sukeena ordered, 'or I will cut you. I will cut your face first, so that you are no longer beautiful. Then if you still do not obey I will send this blade through your slimy, evil heart.'

Katinka looked down and, for the first time, saw the blade that Sukeena held to her side. That dagger had been a gift from one of Katinka's lovers and she knew just how sharp was its slender blade. Sukeena had stolen it from Katinka's closet.

'Are you mad?' Katinka blanched with terror, and tried to squirm away from the needle point.

'Yes. Mad enough to kill you and to enjoy doing it.' Sukeena pressed the dagger to her side and Katinka screamed. The horses pricked their ears. 'If you scream again I will draw your blood,' Sukeena warned. 'Now hold your tongue and listen while I tell you what you are to do.'

'I will give you to Slow John and laugh as he draws out your entrails,' Katinka blustered, but her voice shook and terror was in her eyes.

'You will never laugh again, not unless you obey me. This dagger will see to that,' and she pricked Katinka again, hard enough to pierce cloth and skin, so that a spot of blood the size of a silver guilder appeared on her bodice.

'Please!' Katinka whimpered. 'Please, Sukeena, I will do as you say. Please don't hurt me again. You said you loved me.'

'And I lied,' Sukeena hissed at her. 'I lied for my brother's sake. I hate you. You will never know the strength of my hatred. I loath the touch of your hands. I am revolted by every filthy, evil thing you forced me to do. So do not trade on any love from me. I will crush you with as little pity as I would rid my hair of lice.' Katinka saw death in her eyes, and she was afraid as she had seldom been in her life before.

'I will do as you tell me,' she whispered, and Sukeena instructed her in a flat, hard tone that was more threatening than any shouting or raging.

As Aboli drove the carriage through the castle gates, the usual stir of activity heralded its arrival. The single sentry came to attention and presented his musket. Aboli wheeled the team of greys and brought the carriage to a halt in front of the Company offices. The captain of the guard hurried from the armoury, hastily strapping on his sword-belt. He was a young subaltern, freshly out from Holland, and he had been taken by surprise by the unexpected arrival of the Governor's wife.

'The devil's horns!' he muttered to himself. 'Why does the bitch pick today to arrive when half my men are sick as dogs?' He looked anxiously at the single guard at the door to the Company offices, and saw that the man's face still had a pale greenish tinge. Then he realized that the Governor's wife was beckoning to him from her seat in the carriage. He broke into a run across the courtyard, straightening his cap and tightening the strap under his chin as he went. He reached the carriage and saluted Katinka. 'Good morning, Mevrouw. May I assist you to dismount?'

The Governor's wife had a strained, nervous look and her voice was high and breathless. The subaltern was instantly alarmed. 'Is something amiss, Mevrouw?'

'Yes, something is very much amiss. Call my husband!'

'Will you go to his office?'

'No. I will remain here in the carriage. Go to him this instant and tell him that I say he must come immediately. It is a matter of the utmost importance. Life and death! Go! Hurry!'

The subaltern looked startled and saluted quickly, then bounded up the steps two at a time and shot through the double doors into the offices. While he was gone Aboli dismounted, went to the panniers at the back of the carriage and opened the lid. Then he glanced around the courtyard.

There was one guard at the gates and another at the head of the stairs but, as usual, the slow-match in their muskets was unlit. There was no sentry posted at the doors to the armoury, but from where he stood he could see through the window that three men were in the guard room.

Each of the five overseers in the courtyard carried swords as well as their whips and canes. Hugo Barnard was at the far end of the yard and had both his hounds on the leash. He was haranguing the gang of common convicts laying the paving stones along the foot of the east wall. These other convicts, not part of the crew of the *Resolution*, might be a hazard when they made their attempt to escape. Nearly two hundred were working on the walls, the multi-hued dregs of humanity. They could easily hamper the rescue attempt by blocking the escape route or even by trying to join in with the *Resolution*'s crew and mobbing the carriage when they realized what was happening.

We will deal with that when it happens, he thought grimly, and turned his full attention to the armed guards and overseers who were the primary threat. With Barnard and his gang, there were ten armed men in sight but any outcry could bring another twenty or thirty soldiers hurrying out of the barracks and across the yard. The whole business could get out of hand quickly.

He looked up to find Hal and Big Daniel watching him from the scaffold. Hal already had the rope of the gantry in his hand, the tail looped around his wrist. Ned Tyler and Billy Rogers were on the lower tier, and the two birds, Finch and Sparrow, were working near Althuda in the courtyard. They were all pretending to carry on with their tasks, but were eyeing Aboli surreptitiously.

Aboli reached into the pannier and loosened the twine that secured the rolled silk carpet. He opened a flap of it and, without lifting them clear, revealed the three Mogul scimitars and the single *kukri* knife that he had chosen for himself. He knew that, from their vantage point, Hal and Big Daniel could see into the pannier. Then he stood immobile and expressionless at the back wheel of the carriage.

Suddenly the Governor burst hatless and in his shirt sleeves through the double doors at the head of the staircase and came down at an ungainly lurching run.

'What is it, Mevrouw?' he called urgently to his wife, when he was half-way down. 'They say you sent for me, and it's a matter of life and death.'

'Hurry!' Katinka cried plaintively. 'I am in the most terrible predicament.'

He arrived at the door of the carriage, panting wildly. 'Tell me what ails you, Mevrouw!' he gasped.

Aboli stepped up behind him and hooked one great arm around his neck, pinning him helplessly. Van de Velde began to struggle. For all his obesity he was a powerful man and even Aboli had difficulty in holding him.

'What in the devil's name are you doing?' he roared in outrage. Aboli placed the blade of the *kukri* at his throat. When van de Velde felt the cold touch of steel and the sting of the razor edge, his struggles ceased.

'I will slit your throat like the great hog you are,' Aboli whispered in his ear, 'and Sukeena has a dagger at your wife's heart. Tell your soldiers to stay where they are and throw down their arms.'

The subaltern had started forward at van de Velde's cry, and his sword was half-way out of its scabbard as he rushed down the stairs.

'Stop!' van de Velde shouted at him in terror. 'Don't move, you fool. You will have me killed.' The subaltern halted and dithered uncertainly.

Aboli tightened his lock around the Governor's throat. 'Tell him to throw down his sword.'

'Throw down your sword!' van de Velde whinnied. 'Do as he says. Can't you see he has a knife at my throat?' The subaltern dropped his sword, which clattered down the steps.

Fifty feet above the courtyard, Hal sprang out from the scaffold, hanging on the rope from the gantry, and Big Daniel belayed the other end, braking the speed of his fall. The sheave squealed as he plummeted down and landed in balance on the cobbles. He leaped to the rear of the carriage and seized one of the jewelled scimitars. With the next leap he was half-way up the steps where he stooped and swept up the subaltern's sword in his left hand. He placed the point under the officer's chin and said, 'Order your men to throw down their weapons!'

'Lay down your arms, all of you!' the subaltern yelled. 'If any man amongst you brings harm to the Governor or his lady, he will pay for it with his own life.' The sentries obeyed with alacrity, dropping their muskets and sidearms to the paving stones.

'You too!' van de Velde howled at the overseers, and with reluctance they obeyed. However, at that moment Hugo Barnard was screened by a pile of masonry blocks. He stepped quietly into the doorway to the kitchens, dragging his two hounds with him, and crouched there, waiting his opportunity.

Down from the scaffold scrambled the other seamen. Sparrow and Finch from the lower tier were first to reach the courtyard but Ned, Big Daniel and Billy Rogers were seconds behind them.

'Come on, Althuda!' Hal called, and Althuda dropped his mallet and chisel and ran to join him. 'Catch!' Hal lobbed the jewelled scimitar in a high, glinting parabola, and Althuda reached up and caught it by the hilt, plucking it neatly out of the air. Hal wondered what class of swordsman he was. As a fisherman it was unlikely that he would have had much practice.

I shall have to shield him if it comes to a fight, he thought, and looked around quickly. He saw Daniel pulling the other weapons out of the pannier at the back of the carriage. The twin scimitars looked like toys in his huge fist. He tossed one to Ned Tyler and kept the other for himself as he ran to join Hal.

Hal picked up a sword that a sentry had dropped and threw it to Big Daniel. 'This one is more your style, Master Danny,' he yelled, and Daniel grinned, showing his broken black teeth, as he caught the heavy infantry weapon and made it hiss in the air as he cut left and right.

'Sweet Jesus, it's good to have a real blade in my hand again!' he exulted, and tossed the light scimitar to Wally Finch. 'A tool for a man, but a toy for a boy.'

'Aboli, keep a firm hold on that great hog. Cut his ears off if he tries to be crafty,' Hal shouted. 'The rest of you follow me!' He dropped down the staircase and raced towards the doors of the armoury with Big Daniel and the others on his heels. Althuda began to follow him also, but Hal stopped him. 'Not you. You look after Sukeena!'

As Althuda turned back and they ran on across the courtyard, Hal snapped at Daniel, 'Where's Barnard?'

'The murdering bastard was here not a moment past, but I don't see him now.'

'Keep a good lookout for his top sails. We'll have trouble with that swine yet.'

Hal burst into the armoury. The three men in the guard room were slumped on the bench: two were asleep and the third scrambled to his feet in bewilderment. Before he could recover his wits, Hal's point was pressed to his chest. 'Stay where you are, or I'll look at the colour of your liver.' The man dropped back into his seat. 'Here, Ned!' Hal called to him as Ned rushed in. 'Play wet-nurse to these infants,' and left them in his charge as he ran after Daniel and the other seamen.

Daniel charged the heavy teak door at the end of the passage and it burst open before his rush. They had never before had a chance to look into the armoury, but now at a glance Hal saw that it was all laid out in a neat and orderly fashion. The weapons were in racks along the walls, and the powder kegs stacked to the ceiling at the far end.

'Pick your weapons and bring a keg of powder each,' he ordered, and they ran to the long racks of infantry swords, polished, gleaming and sharpened to a bright edge. Further back were the racks of muskets and pistols. Hal thrust a pair of pistols into the rope that served him as a belt. 'Remember, you'll have to carry everything you take with you up the mountains, so don't be greedy,' he warned them, and picked up a fifty-pound keg of gunpowder from the pyramid at the far end of the armoury, which he hoisted to his shoulder. Then he turned for the door. 'That's enough, lads. Get out! Daniel, lay a powder trail as you go!'

Daniel used the butt of a musket to stove in the bungs of two of the powder kegs. At the foot of the pyramid of barrels he poured a mound of black gunpowder. 'That lot will go off with an almighty bang!' He grinned, as he backed towards the door, the other keg under his arm spilling a long dark trail behind him.

Under their burdens they staggered out into the sunlight. Hal was the last to leave. 'Get out of here, Ned!' he ordered, and handed him the weapons he carried as Ned ran for the door. Then Hal turned on the three Dutch soldiers, who were cowering on the bench. Ned had disarmed them – their weapons were thrown in the corner of the guard room.

'I'm going to blow this place to hell,' he told them in Dutch. 'Run for the gates, and if you're wise you'll keep running without looking back. Go!' They sprang up and, in their haste to get clear, jammed in the doorway. They struggled and fought each other until they burst out into the courtyard and raced across it.

'Look out!' they yelled, as they sprinted for the gates. 'They're going to blow up the powder store!' The gaolers and the other common convicts who, until this point, had stood gaping at the carriage and the hostage Governor in Aboli's grip, now turned their heads towards the armoury and stared at it in stupid surprise.

Hal appeared in the armoury doorway with a sword in one hand and a burning torch that he had seized from its bracket in the other.

'I am counting to ten,' Hal shouted, 'and then I am lighting the powder train!' In his rags, and with his great bushy black beard and wild eyes, he looked like a maniac. A moan of horror and fear went up from every man in the yard. One of the convicts threw down his spade and followed the fleeing soldiers in a rush for the gate. Immediately pandemonium overwhelmed them all. Two hundred convicts and soldiers stormed the gates in a rush for safety.

Van de Velde struggled in Aboli's grip and screamed, 'Let me go! The idiot is going to blow us all to perdition. Let me go! Run! Run!' His shrieks added to the panic, and within the time it takes to draw and hold a long breath the courtyard was deserted except for the group of seamen around the carriage and Hal. Katinka was screaming and sobbing hysterically, but Sukeena slapped her hard across the face. 'Keep quiet, you simpering ninny, or I'll give you good reason to blubber,' and Katinka gulped back her distress.

'Aboli, get van de Velde into the carriage! He and his wife are coming with us,' Hal called, and Aboli lifted the Governor bodily and hurled him over the top of the door. He landed in an ungainly heap on the floorboards and struggled there, like an insect on a pin. 'Althuda, put your sword point to his heart and be ready to kill him when I give the word.'

'I look forward to it!' Althuda shouted, dragged van de Velde upright and thrust him into the seat facing his wife. 'Where should I give it to you?' he asked him. 'In your fat gut, perhaps?'

Van de Velde had lost his wig in the scuffle and his expression was abject, every inch of his huge frame seeming to quiver with despair. 'Don't kill me. I can protect you,' he pleaded, and Katinka started weeping and keening again. This time, Sukeena merely held her a little tighter, lifted the point of the dagger to her throat and whispered, 'We don't need you now we have the Governor. It won't matter at all if I kill you.' Katinka choked back the next sob.

'Daniel, load the powder and the spare weapons,' Hal ordered, and they piled them into the carriage. The elegant vehicle was no wagon, and the coachwork sagged under the load on its delicately sprung suspension.

'That's enough! It will take no more.' Aboli stopped them throwing the last few powder kegs on board.

'One man to each horse!' Hal commanded. 'Don't try to board them, lads. You're none of you riders. You'll fall off and break your necks, which won't matter much, but your weight will kill the poor beasts before we have gone a mile, and that will matter. Lay hold of their rigging and let them tow you along.' They ran to their places around the team of horses, and latched onto their harness. 'Leave space for me on the larboard bow, lads,' he called, and even in her excitement and agitation Sukeena laughed aloud at his use of the nautical terms. His men understood, though, and left the offside lead horse for him.

Aboli leaped to his place on the coachman's seat, while in the body of the carriage Althuda menaced van de Velde and Sukeena held her dagger to Katinka's white throat.

Aboli wheeled the team and shouted, 'Come on, Gundwane. It's time to go. The garrison will wake up at any moment now.' As he said it they heard the flat report of a pistol shot, and a garrison officer ran from the doorway of the barracks across the square waving his smoking pistol, shouting to his men to form up on him. 'Stand to arms! On me the First Company!'

Hal paused only a moment to light the slow-match of one of his pistols from the burning torch, then tossed the torch onto the powder train and waited to see it flare and catch. The smoking flame started snaking back through the doors of the armoury into the passageway that led to the main powder magazine. Then he sprang down the steps into the courtyard and raced to meet the overloaded carriage as Aboli drove the horses in a circle and lined up for the gates.

He was almost there, raising his hand to seize the bridle of the leading grey gelding, when suddenly Aboli shouted in agitation, 'Gundwane, behind you! Have a care!'

Hugo Barnard had appeared in the doorway where he and his hounds had taken shelter at the first sign of trouble. Now he slipped both dogs from the leash and with wild yells of encouragement sent them in pursuit of Hal. '*Vat hom!* Catch him!' he yelled and the animals raced towards him in a silent rush, running side by side, striding out and covering the length of the courtyard like a pair of whippets coursing a hare.

Aboli's warning had given Hal just time enough to turn to face them. The dogs worked as a team, and one leaped for his face while the other rushed for his legs. Hal lunged at the first while it was in the air and sent his point into the base of the black throat where it joined the shoulders. The flying weight of the hound's body drove the blade in full length, transfixing it cleanly through heart and lung and on into its guts. Even though it was dead, the momentum of its flight drove it on to crash into Hal's chest, and he staggered backwards.

The second hound snaked in low to the ground and, while Hal was still off balance, sank its fangs into his left shin just below the knee, jerking him over backwards. His shoulder crashed into the stone paving, but when he tried to rise the animal still had him in its grip and pulled back on all four braced legs, sending him sprawling again. Hal felt its teeth grate on the bone of his leg.

'My hounds!' Barnard yelled. 'You are hurting my darlings.' With his drawn sword in his hand he rushed to intervene. Again Hal tried to rise, and again the hound pulled him down. Barnard reached them and raised his sword to his full height above Hal's unprotected head. Hal saw the blow coming and rolled aside. The blade struck the flint cobbles beside his ear in a sheet of sparks.

'You bastard!' Barnard roared, and lifted the sword again. Aboli swerved the team of horses and drove them deliberately at Barnard. The overseer's back was turned to the approaching carriage, and he was so engrossed with Hal that he did not see it coming. As he was about to strike again at Hal's head, the rear wheel caught him a glancing blow on the hip and sent him staggering aside.

With a violent effort Hal hauled himself into a sitting position, and before the hound could drag him flat again, he stabbed it in the base of the neck, driving his blade at an angle back between its shoulder blades like the bull-fighter's coup, finding the heart. The beast let out an agonized howl and released its grip on his leg, staggered around in a circle then collapsed on the cobbles, kicking feebly.

Hal heaved himself to his feet just as Barnard rushed at him. 'You have killed my beauties!' He was maddened with grief, and hacked again at Hal, a wild uncontrolled blow. Hal turned it effortlessly aside and let it fly an inch past his head.

'You filthy pirate, I'll cut you down!' Barnard gathered himself and rushed in again. With the same apparent ease Hal deflected the next thrust, and said softly, 'Do you remember what you and your dogs did to Oliver?' He feinted high left, forcing Barnard to open his guard in the mid-line, and then, like a bolt of lightning, thrust home. The blade took Barnard just under the sternum, and sprang half its length out of his back. He dropped his sword and fell to his knees.

'The debt to Oliver is paid!' Hal said, placed his bare foot on Barnard's chest and, against its resistance, pulled his blade clear. Barnard toppled and lay beside the carcass of his dying hound.

'Come on, Gundwane!' Aboli was struggling to hold the team of greys, for the shouting and the smell of blood had panicked them. 'The magazine!' It was only seconds since Hal had lighted the powder train, but when he glanced in that direction he saw clouds of acrid blue smoke billowing from the doorway of the armoury.

'Hurry, Gundwane!' Sukeena called softly. 'Oh, please, hurry!' Her voice was so filled with concern for his safety that it spurred him. Even in these dire straits, Hal realized that it was the first time he had ever heard her speak his nickname. He started forward. The dog had bitten deeply into his leg, but its fangs could not have severed nerves or sinews for Hal found that, if he ignored the pain, he could still run on it. He leaped across the yard and grabbed hold of the leading horse's bridle. It tossed its head and rolled its eyes until the pink lining showed, but Hal hung on and Aboli gave the team its head.

The carriage went rocking and clattering under the archway of the gates, across the bridge, over the moat and out onto the open Parade. Suddenly from behind them came a shattering explosion, and a shock-wave of disrupted air swept over them like a tropical line squall. The horses reared and plunged in terror, and Hal was lifted off his feet. He clung desperately to the traces and looked back. A tower of dun-coloured smoke rose swiftly from the interior courtyard of the castle, spinning and revolving upon itself, shot through with dark flames and scraps of debris and wreckage. In the midst of this plume of destruction a single human body cartwheeled a hundred feet into the sky.

'For Sir Hal and King Charley!' Big Daniel roared, and the other seamen took up the cheering, beside themselves with excitement at their escape.

However, when Hal looked back again he could see that the massive outer walls of the castle were untouched by the detonation. The barracks had been built of the same heavy stonework, and almost certainly had withstood the blast. Two hundred men were housed in there, three companies of green-jackets, and even now they were probably recovering their wits after the explosion. Soon they would come pouring out through the castle gates in full pursuit – and where, he wondered, was Colonel Cornelius Schreuder?

The carriage was pounding across the parade at a gallop. Ahead ran a mob of escaped convicts. They were scattering in every direction, some leaping over the stone wall of the Company gardens and heading for the mountain, others running for the beach to find a boat in which to make good their flight. Out on the Parade were the few stunned burghers and house slaves who were abroad at this time of the forenoon. They gawked in amazement at the tide of fugitives, then at the rolling cloud of smoke that enveloped the castle and then at the even more extraordinary sight of the advancing Governor's carriage, festooned with a motley array of desperate tatterdemalion outlaws and pirates, screaming like madmen and brandishing their weapons. As the vehicle bore down on them they scattered frantically.

'The pirates have escaped from the castle. Run! Run!' At last they recovered and spread the alarm. The cry was taken up and shouted ahead of them through the huts and hovels of the settlement. Hal could see the burghers and their slaves hurrying to escape the bloodthirsty pirate crew. One or two of the braver souls had armed themselves, and there was a desultory popping of musket fire from some of the cottage windows, but the range was long, the aim hurried and poor. Hal did not even hear the flight of the balls and none of the men or horses were hit. The carriage swept on past the first buildings, following the only road that skirted the curving beach of Table Bay, and headed out into the unknown.

Hal looked back at Aboli. 'Slow down, damn you! You'll blow the horses before we've got past the town.' Aboli stood upright and pulled the horses back. 'Whoa, Royal! Slow down, Cloud!' But the team were bolting and had almost reached the outskirts of the settlement before Aboli was able to wrestle them to a trot. They were all sweating and snorting from the gallop, but were far from spent.

As soon as they were under control, Hal loosed his grip on the harness and turned back to jog beside the carriage. 'Althuda,' he called, 'instead of sitting up there like a gentleman on a Sunday picnic, make sure all the muskets are primed and loaded. Here!' He passed up the pistol with the burning match. 'Use this to light the match on all the weapons. They'll be after us soon enough.' Then he looked from Althuda to his sister.

'We have not been introduced. Your servant, Henry Courtney.' He grinned at her, and she laughed delightedly at his formal manner.

'Good morrow, Gundwane. I know you well. Aboli has warned me of what a fierce young pirate you are.' Then she turned serious. 'You are hurt. I should see to your leg.'

''Tis nothing that cannot wait until later,' he assured her.

'The bite of a dog will mortify swiftly if it is left untreated,' she told him.

'Later!' he repeated, and turned to Aboli.

'Aboli, are you acquainted with the road to the boundary of the colony?'

'There is only one road, Gundwane. We have to go straight through the village, skirt the marshland then head out across the sandy flatlands towards the mountains.' He pointed. 'The bitter-almond fence is five miles beyond the marsh.'

Looking beyond the settlement, Hal could already see marshland and the lagoon ahead, stands of reeds and open water, over which hovered flocks of water birds. He had heard that crocodiles and hippopotami lurked in the depths of the lagoon.

'Althuda, will there be any soldiers in our way?' Hal asked him.

'There are usually guards at the first bridge and there is always a patrol at the bitter-almond hedge to shoot any Hottentots who try to enter,' Althuda replied, without looking up from the musket he was loading.

Then Sukeena sang out, 'There will be no pickets or patrols today. From dawn I kept a watch on the crossroad. No soldiers went out to take up their posts. They are all too busy nursing their aching bellies.' She laughed gaily, as excited and wrought up as the rest of them. Suddenly she leaped up in the body of the carriage and called out in a ringing voice, 'Free! For the first time in my life I am free!' Her plait had tumbled down and come loose. Her hair streamed out behind her head. Her eyes sparkled, and she was so beautiful that she epitomized the dreams of every one of the ragged seamen.

Although they cheered her, 'You, and us also, darling!' it was Hal at whom she was looking with those laughing eyes.

As they passed the buildings of the settlement, the warning cries had been shouted ahead of them. 'Beware! The pirates have escaped. The pirates are on the rampage!' The good citizens of Good Hope scattered before them. Mothers rushed into the street to seize their offspring and drag them indoors, to throw the door-bolts and slam down the shutters.

'You are safe now. You have escaped clean away. Please will you not let me free, Sir Henry?' Katinka had recovered from her shock sufficiently to plead for her life. 'I swear I have never meant you harm. I saved you from the gallows. I saved Althuda also. I'll do anything you say, Sir Henry. Just please set me free,' she whimpered, clinging to the side of the carriage.

'You may call me sir now and make me those declarations of goodwill but they would have stood my father in better stead while he was on his way to the gallows.' Hal's expression was so cold and remorseless that Katinka recoiled and fell back in the seat beside Sukeena, sobbing as though her heart were breaking.

The seamen running with Hal shouted their scorn and hatred at her. 'You wanted to see us hanged, you painted doxy, and we're going to feed you to the lions out there in the wilderness,' gloated Billy Rogers.

Katinka sobbed afresh and covered her face with her hands. 'I never meant any of you harm. Please let me go.'

The carriage rolled steadily down the empty street, and the last few huts and hovels of the settlement were all that lay ahead when Althuda rose from his seat and pointed back down the gravel-surfaced road towards the distant parade. 'Horseman coming at a gallop!' he cried.

'So soon?' Big Daniel muttered, shading his eyes. 'I had not expected the pursuit yet. Do they have cavalry to send after us?'

'Have no fear of that, lads,' Aboli reassured them. 'There are no more than twenty horses in the whole colony, and we have six of those.'

'Aboli is right. 'Tis only one horseman!' shouted Wally Finch.

The rider was leaving a pale ribbon of dust in the air behind him, leaning forward over his mount's neck as he drove the animal to its top speed, using the whip in his right hand to flog it onwards mercilessly. He was still far off, but Hal recognized him from the sash that flowed out behind him with the speed of his gallop.

'Sweet Mary, it's Schreuder! I knew he would join us before too long.' His jaw clenched in anticipation. 'The hot-headed idiot comes alone to fight us. Brains he lacks, but he has a full cargo of guts.' Even from his seat Aboli could see what Hal intended by the narrowing of his eyes and the way he changed his grip on his sword.

'Don't think of going back to give him satisfaction, Gundwane!' Aboli called sternly. 'You will place every soul here at risk for any delay.'

'I know you think I'm no match for Schreuder but things have changed, Aboli. I can beat him now. I'm sure of it in my heart.' Aboli thought that he might well do so, for Hal was no longer a boy. The months on the walls had toughened him, and Aboli had seen him match strength with Big Daniel. 'Leave me here to see to this business, man to man, and I will follow you later,' Hal cried.

'No, Sir Hal!' shouted Big Daniel. 'Maybe you *could* best him but not with that leg bitten to the bone. Leave your feud with the Dutchman for another time. We need you with us. There will be a hundred green-jackets following close behind him.'

'No!' agreed Wally and Stan. 'Stay with us, Captain.'

'We've put our trust in you,' said Ned Tyler. 'We can never find our way through the wilderness without a navigator. You can't desert us now.'

Hal hesitated, still glaring back at the swiftly approaching rider. Then his eyes flicked to the face of the girl in the carriage. Sukeena stared at him, her huge dark eyes full of entreaty. 'You are sorely wounded. Look at your leg.' She leaned over the door of the carriage, so that she was very close, and spoke so softly that he could only just make out the words above the din of men and wheels and horses. 'Stay with us, Gundwane.'

He glanced down at the blood and pale lymph oozing from the deep puncture wounds. While he wavered Big Daniel ran back and jumped up onto the step of the carriage.

'I'll take care of this one,' he said, and lifted the loaded musket from Althuda's hands. Holding it, he dropped from the step into the dirt of the road and stood there checking the burning matchlock and the priming in the pan. He took his time as the carriage trotted away from him and Colonel Schreuder galloped down on him.

Despite all their pleas and warnings Hal started back to intervene. 'Daniel, don't kill the fool.' He wanted to explain that he and Schreuder had a destiny to work out together. It was a matter of chivalric honour in which no other should come between them, but there was no time to give voice to such a romantic notion.

Schreuder galloped to within earshot and stood in his stirrups. 'Katinka!' he shouted. 'Have no fear, I am come to save you, my darling. I will never let these villains take you.'

He plucked the bell-muzzled pistol from his sash and held the matchlock in the wind so that the smouldering match flared. Then he lay flat along his horse's neck with his pistol arm outstretched. 'Out of my way, oaf!' he roared at Daniel, and fired. His right arm was thrown high by the discharge and a wreath of blue smoke swirled around his head, but the ball flew wide, hitting the earth a foot from Daniel's bare right leg, showering him with gravel.

Schreuder threw aside the pistol and drew the Neptune sword from its scabbard at his side. The gold inlay on the blade glinted as he wielded it. 'I'll cleave your skull to the teeth!' Schreuder roared, and raised the blade high. Daniel dropped on one knee and let the Colonel's horse come on the last few strides.

Too close, Hal thought. Much too close. If the musket misfires Danny is a dead man. But Daniel held his aim steadily and snapped the lock. For an instant Hal thought his worst fear had been realized but then, with a sharp report, a spurt of flame and silver smoke, the musket discharged.

Perhaps Daniel had heeded Hal's shout, or perhaps the horse was a bigger and surer target than the rider upon its back, but he had aimed into the animal's wide, sweat-drenched chest and the heavy lead ball for once flew true. At full charge Schreuder's steed collapsed under him. He was thrown over its head, slamming face and shoulder into the ground.

The horse struggled and kicked, lying on its back, thrashing its head from side to side while its heart-blood pumped from the wound in its chest. Then its head fell back to earth with a thump and, with one last snorting breath, it lay still.

Schreuder lay motionless on the sun-baked road, and Hal felt a moment's fear that his neck was broken. He almost ran back to aid him, but Schreuder made a few disjointed movements, and Hal paused. The carriage was drawing away swiftly, and the others were shouting to him, 'Come back, Gundwane!'

'Leave the bastard, Sir Henry.'

Daniel sprang up, grabbed Hal's arm. 'He ain't dead, but we soon will be if we lie becalmed here much longer,' and dragged him away.

For the first few steps Hal resisted and tried to shake off Daniel's hand. 'It can't end like this. Don't you understand, Danny?'

'I understand well enough,' Big Daniel grunted, and at that Schreuder sat up groggily in the middle of the road. The gravel had torn the skin off one side of his face, but he was trying to get to his feet, lurching and falling, then trying again.

'He's all right,' said Hal, with a relief that almost surprised him, and allowed Daniel to pull him away.

'Aye!' said Daniel, as they caught up with the carriage. 'He's right enough to crop your acorns for you when next you meet. We'll not be rid of that one so easily.'

Aboli braked the carriage to allow them to catch up, and Hal grabbed the bridle of the leading horse and allowed it to lift him off his feet. He looked back to see Schreuder on his feet in the middle of the road, dusty, and bleeding. He staggered after the carriage like a man with a bottle of cheap gin in his belly, still brandishing the sword.

They pulled away from him at a brisk trot and Schreuder gave up the attempt to overhaul the departing carriage, instead screamed abuse after it: 'By God, Henry Courtney, I'm coming after you, even if I have to follow you to the very gates of hell. I have you in my eye, sir, I have you in my heart.'

'When you come, bring with you that sword you stole from me,' Hal shouted back. 'I'll spit you with it like a sucking pig for the devil to roast.' His seamen hooted with laughter and gave the colonel an assortment of obscene farewell gestures.

'Katinka! My darling!' Schreuder changed his tone. 'Do not despair. I will rescue you. I swear it on my father's grave. I love you with my very life.'

Throughout all the shouting and the musket fire, van de Velde had been crouching on the floor of the carriage but now he heaved himself back onto the seat and glared at the battered figure in the road. 'Is he raving mad? How dare he address my wife in such odious terms?' He rounded on Katinka with a red face and wobbling jowls. 'Mevrouw, I trust you have given the dolt of a soldier no cause for such licence.'

'I assure you, Mijnheer, his language and address come as more of a shock to me than they do to you. I take great offence, and I implore you to take him seriously to task at the first opportunity,' replied Katinka, clinging to the door of the carriage with one hand and to her bonnet with the other.

'I will do better than that, Mevrouw. He will be on the next ship back to Amsterdam. I cannot abide with such impertinence. Moreover, he is responsible for the predicament we are now in. As commander of the castle, the prisoners are his responsibility. Their escape is due to his incompetence and the dereliction of his duty. The dastard has no right to speak to you in such a fashion.'

'Oh, yes, he does,' said Sukeena sweetly. 'Colonel Schreuder has the right of conquest in his favour. Your wife has been lying under him often enough with her legs in the air for him to call her darling, or even to call her whore and slut if he chose to be more honest.'

'Quiet, Sukeena!' shrilled Katinka. 'Are you out of your mind? Remember your place. You are a slave.'

'No, Mevrouw. A slave no longer. A free woman now, and your captor,' Sukeena told her, 'so I can say to you anything I please, especially if it is the truth.' She turned to van de Velde. 'Your wife and the gallant colonel have been playing the beast with two backs so blatantly as to delight every tattle-tale in the colony. They have set a pair of horns on your head that are too large for even your grossly bloated body.'

'I will have you thrashed!' van de Velde gurgled apoplectically. 'You slave bitch!'

'No, you won't,' said Althuda, and placed the point of the jewelled scimitar against the Governor's pendulous belly. 'Rather, you will apologize for that insult to my sister.'

'Apologize to a slave? Never!' van de Velde began in a bellow, but this time Althuda pricked him with more intent and the bellow turned into a squeal, like air escaping from a pig's bladder.

'Apologize not to a slave, but to a freeborn Balinese princess,' Althuda corrected him. 'And swiftly.'

'I beg your pardon, madam,' van de Velde gritted through clenched teeth.

'You are gallant, sir.' Sukeena smiled at him. Van de Velde sank back in his seat and said no more, but he fixed his wife with a venomous stare.

Once they had left the settlement behind them, the surface of the road deteriorated. There were deep wheel ruts left by the Company wagons going out to fetch firewood, and the carriage rocked and lurched dangerously through them. Along the edge of the lagoon the water had seeped in to turn the tracks to mud and slush and, in many places, the seamen were forced to put their shoulders to the tall rear wheels to help the horses drag the vehicle through. It was late morning before they saw ahead the framework of the wooden bridge over the first river.

'Soldiers!' Aboli called. From his high seat he had picked out the glint of a bayonet and the shape of the tall helmets.

'Only four,' said Hal. His eyes were still the sharpest of all. 'They'll not be expecting trouble from this direction.' He was right. The corporal of the bridge guard came forward to meet them, puzzled but unalarmed, his sword sheathed and the match on his pistols unlit. Hal and his crew disarmed him and his men, stripped them to their breeches and sent them running back towards the colony with a discharge of muskets over their heads.

While Aboli walked the carriage over the bridge and took it on along the rudimentary track, Hal and Ned Tyler climbed beneath the wooden structure and roped a barrel of gunpowder under the heavy timber kingpost. When it was secure Hal used the butt of his pistol to drive in the bung of the barrel, thrust a short length of slow-match into it and lit it. He and Ned scrambled back onto the roadway and ran after the carriage.

Hal's leg was painful now. It was swelling and stiffening, but he was looking back over his shoulder as he hobbled along through the ankle-deep sand. The centre of the bridge suddenly erupted in a spout of mud, water, shattered planks and piers. The wreckage fell back into the river.

'That will not hold the good colonel long, but at least he will get his breeches wet,' Hal muttered, as they caught up with the carriage. Althuda jumped down and called to him, 'Take my place. You must favour that leg.'

'There is little wrong with my leg,' Hal protested.

'Other than that it can barely carry your weight,' said Sukeena sternly, leaning over the door. 'Come up here at once, Gundwane, or else you will do lasting damage to it.'

Meekly Hal climbed up into the coach and took the seat opposite Sukeena. Without looking at the pair, Aboli grinned to himself. Already she gives the orders and he obeys. It seems they have the tide and a fair wind behind them.

'Let me look at that leg,' Sukeena ordered, and Hal placed it on the seat between her and Katinka.

'Take care, clod!' Katinka snapped, and pulled away her skirts. 'You will bloody my dress.'

'If you do not have a care to your tongue, it will not be the only thing I will bloody,' Hal assured her, and scowled. She withdrew into the farthest corner of the seat.

Sukeena worked over the leg with swift, competent hands. 'I should lay a hot poultice on these bites, for they are deep and will certainly fester. But I need boiling water.' She looked up at Hal.

'You will have to wait for that until we reach the mountains,' he told her. Then, for a while, their conversation broke down and they gazed into each other's eyes bemusedly. This was as close as they had ever been and each found something in the other to amaze and delight them.

Then Sukeena roused herself. 'I have my medicines in the saddle-bags,' she said briskly, and climbed over the seat to reach the panniers on the back of the carriage. She hung there as she rummaged in the leather bags. The carriage jolted on over the rough track, and Hal looked with awe on her small rounded bottom, pointed skywards. Despite the ruffles and petticoats that shrouded it, he thought it almost as enchanting as her face.

She climbed back with cloths and a black bottle in her hand. 'I will swab out the wounds with this tincture and then bind them up,' she explained, without looking again into the distraction of his green eyes.

'Avast!' Hal gasped at the first touch of the tincture. 'That burns like the devil's breath.'

Sukeena scolded, 'You have endured whip and shot and sword and savaging by an animal. But the first touch of medicine and you cry like a baby. Now be still.'

Aboli's face creased into a bouquet of tattoos and merry laughter lines but, though his shoulders shook, he held his peace.

Hal sensed his amusement, and rounded on him. 'How far ahead is the bitter-almond hedge?'

'Another league.'

'Will Sabah meet us there?'

'That is what I believe, if the green-jackets don't catch up with us first.'

'Methinks we will have some respite. Schreuder made an error by rushing alone in pursuit of us. He should have mustered his troops and come after us in an orderly fashion. My guess is that most of the green-jackets will be chasing the other prisoners we turned free. They will concentrate on us only once Schreuder takes command.'

'And he has no horse,' Sukeena added. 'I think we will get clear away, and once we reach the mountains—' She broke off and lifted her eyes from Hal's leg. Both she and Hal looked ahead to the high blue rampart that filled the sky ahead.

Van de Velde had been avidly following this conversation, and now he broke in. 'The slave wench is right. You have succeeded in this underhand scheme of yours, more's the pity. However, I am a reasonable man, Henry Courtney. Set my wife and me free now. Give the carriage over to us and let us return to the colony. In exchange I will give you my solemn undertaking to call off the chase. I will order Colonel Schreuder to send his men back to their barracks.' He turned on Hal what he hoped was an open and guileless countenance. 'I offer you my word as a gentleman on it.'

Hal saw the cunning and malice in the Governor's eyes. 'Your excellency, I am uncertain of the validity of your claim to the title of gentleman, besides which I should hate to be deprived so soon of your charming company.'

At that moment one of the front wheels of the carriage crashed into a hole in the tracks. 'The aardvarks dig these burrows,' Althuda explained, as Hal clambered down from the lopsided vehicle.

'Pray, what manner of man or beast is that?'

'The earth pig, a beast with a long snout and a thick tail that digs up the burrows of ants with its powerful claws and devours them with its long sticky tongue,' Althuda told him.

Hal threw back his head and laughed. 'Of course, I believe that. I also believe that your earth pig flies, dances the hornpipe and tells fortunes by cards.'

'You have a few things yet to learn about the land that lies out there, my friend,' Althuda promised him.

Still chuckling, Hal turned from him. 'Come on, lads!' he called to his seamen. 'Let's get this ship off the reef and running before the wind again.'

He made van de Velde and Katinka get out and the rest of them strained with the horses to pull the carriage free. From here onwards, though, the track became barely passable, and the bush on either hand grew taller and more dense as they went on. Within the next mile they were stuck in holes twice more.

'It is almost time to get rid of the carriage. We can get on faster on our own shanks,' Hal told Aboli quietly. 'How much further to the hedge?'

'I thought we should have reached it by now,' Aboli replied, 'but it cannot be far.' They came to the boundary around the next kink in the narrow track. The famous bitter-almond hedge was a straggly and blighted excrescence, hardly shoulder high, but the road ended dramatically against it. There was also a rough hut, which served as a guard post to the border picket, and a notice in Dutch.

'WARNING!' the notice began, in vivid scarlet letters, and went on to forbid movement by any person beyond that point, with the penalty for infringement being imprisonment or the payment of a fine of a thousand guilders or both. The board had been erected in the name of the Governor of the Dutch East India Company.

Hal kicked open the door of the single room of the guard hut and found it deserted. The fire on the open hearth was cold and dead. A few articles of Company uniform hung on the wooden pegs in the wall, and a black kettle stood over the dead coals, with odd bowls, bottles and utensils lying on the rough wooden table or on shelves along the walls.

Big Daniel was about to put the slow-match to the thatch, but Hal stopped him. 'No point in giving Schreuder a smoke beacon to follow,' he said, 'and there's naught of value here. Leave it be,' and limped back to where the seamen were unloading the carriage.

Aboli was turning the horses out of the traces and Ned Tyler was helping him to improvise pack saddles for them, using the harness, leatherwork and canvas canopy from the carriage.

Katinka stood forlornly at her husband's side. 'What is to become of me, Sir Henry?' she whispered as he came up.

'Some of the men want to take you up into the mountains and feed you to the wild animals,' he replied. Her hand flew to her lips and she paled. 'Others want to cut your throat here and now for what you and your fat toad of a husband did to us.'

'You would never allow such a thing to happen,' van de Velde blustered. 'I only did what was my duty.'

'You're right,' Hal agreed. 'I think throat-cutting too good for you. I favour hanging and drawing, as you did to my father.' He glared at him coldly, and van de Velde quailed. 'However, I find myself sickened by you both. I want no further truck with either of you, and so I leave you and your lovely wife to the mercy of God, the devil and the amorous Colonel Schreuder.' He turned and strode away to where Aboli and Ned were checking and tightening the loads on the horses.

Three of the greys had kegs of gunpowder slung on each side of their backs, two carried bundles of weapons and the sixth horse was loaded with Sukeena's bulky saddle-bags.

'All shipshape, Captain.' Ned knuckled his forehead. 'We can up anchor and get under way at your command.'

'There's nothing to keep us here. The Princess Sukeena will ride on the lead horse.' He looked around for her. 'Where is she?'

'I am here, Gundwane.' Sukeena stepped out from behind the guard hut. 'And I need no mollycoddling. I will walk like the rest of you.'

Hal saw that she had shed her long skirts and that she now wore a pair of baggy Balinese breeches and a loose cotton shift that reached to her knees. She had tied a cotton headcloth over her hair, and on her feet were sturdy leather sandals that would be comfortable for walking. The men ogled the shape of her calves in the breeches, but she ignored their rude stares, took the lead rein of the nearest horse and led it towards the gap in the bitter-almond hedge.

'Sukeena!' Hal would have stopped her, but she recognized his censorious tone and ignored it. He realized the folly of persisting, and wisely tempered his next command. 'Althuda, you are the only one who knows the path from here. Go ahead with your sister.' Althuda ran to catch up with her, and brother and sister led them into the uncharted wilderness beyond the hedge.

Hal and Aboli brought up the rear of the column as it wound through the dense scrub and bush. No men had trodden this path recently. It had been made by wild animals: the marks of their hoofs and paws were plain to see in the soft sandy soil, and their dung littered the track.

Aboli could recognize each animal by these signs, and as they moved along at a forced pace, he pointed them out to Hal. 'That is leopard and there is the spoor of the antelope with the twisted horns we call kudu. At least we shall not starve,' he promised. 'There is a great plenty of game in this land.'

This was the first opportunity since the escape that they had had to talk, and Hal asked quietly, 'This Sabah, the friend of Althuda, what do you know of him?'

'Only the messages he sent.'

'Should he not have met us at the hedge?'

'He said only that he would lead us into the mountains. I expected him to be waiting at the hedge,' Aboli shrugged, 'but with Althuda to guide us we do not need him.'

They made good progress, the grey mare trotting easily with them hanging onto her traces and running beside her. Whenever they passed a tree that would bear Aboli's weight he shinned up it and looked back for signs of pursuit. Each time he came down and shook his head.

'Schreuder will come,' Hal told him. 'I have heard men say that those green-jackets of his can run down a mounted man. They will come.'

They moved on steadily across the plain, stopping only at the swampy waterholes they passed. Hal hung onto the horse to ease his injured leg and, as he limped along, Aboli recounted all that had happened in the months since they had last been together. Hal was silent as he described, in his own language, how he had retrieved Sir Francis's body from the gibbet and the funeral he had given him. 'It was the burial of a great chief. I dressed him in the hide of a black bull and placed his ship and his weapons within his reach. I left food and water for his journey, and before his eyes I set the cross of his God.' Hal's throat was too choked for him to thank Aboli for what he had done.

The day wore on, and their progress slowed as men and horses tired in the soft sandy footing. At the next marshy swamp where they stopped for a few minutes' rest, Hal took Sukeena aside.

'You have been strong and brave but your legs are not as long as ours, and I have watched you stumble with fatigue. From now on you must ride.' When she started to protest he stopped her firmly. 'I obeyed you in the matters of my wounds, but in all else I am captain and you must do as I say. From here on you will ride.'

Her eyes twinkled. She made a pretty little gesture of submission, placing her fingertips together and touching them to her lips, 'As you command, master,' and allowed him to boost her up on top of the saddle-bags on the leading grey.

They skirted the swamp and went on a little faster now. Twice more Aboli climbed a tree to look back and saw no sign of pursuit. Against his natural instincts Hal began to hope that they might have eluded their pursuers, that they might reach the mountains that loomed ever closer and taller without being further molested.

In the middle of the afternoon they crossed a broad open *vlei*, a meadow of short green grass where herds of wild antelope with scimitar-curved horns were grazing. They looked up at the approach of the caravan of horses and men, standing frozen in wide-eyed astonishment, their coats a metallic blue-grey hue in the afternoon sunlight.

'Even I have never seen beasts of that ilk,' Aboli admitted.

As the herds fled before them, wreathed in their own dust, Althuda called back, 'Those are the animals the Dutch call *blaauwbok*, the blue buck. I have seen great herds of them on the plains beyond the mountains.'

Beyond the *vlei* the ground began to rise in a series of undulating ridges towards the foothills of the range. They climbed towards the first ridge, with Hal toiling along at the rear of the column. By now he was moving heavily, in obvious pain. Aboli saw that his face was flushed with fever, and that blood and watery fluid had seeped through the bandage that Sukeena had placed on his leg.

At the top of the ridge Aboli forced a halt. They looked back at the great Table Mountain, which dominated the western horizon. To their left, the wide blue curve of False Bay opened. However, they were all too exhausted to spend long admiring their surroundings. The horses stood, heads hanging, and the men threw themselves down in any shade they could find. Sukeena slid off her mount and hurried to where Hal had slumped with his back to a small tree-trunk. She knelt in front of him, unwrapped the bandage from his leg and drew a sharp breath when she saw how swollen and inflamed it was. She leaned closer and sniffed the oozing punctures. When she spoke her voice was stern.

'You cannot walk further on this. You must ride as you force me to do.' Then she looked up at Aboli. 'Make a fire to boil water,' she ordered him.

'We have no time for such tomfoolery,' Hal murmured half-heartedly, but they ignored him. Aboli lit a small fire with a slow-match and placed over it a tin mug of water. As soon as it boiled, Sukeena prepared a paste with the herbs she had in her saddle-bag, and spread it on a folded cloth. While it still steamed with heat she clapped the cloth over Hal's wounds. He moaned and said, 'I swear I would rather Aboli pissed on my leg, than you burned it off with your devilish concoctions.'

Sukeena ignored his immodest language and went on with her task. She bound the poultice in place with a fresh cloth, then from her saddle-bags she fetched a loaf of bread and a dried sausage. She cut these into slices, folded bread and sausage together, and handed one to each of the men.

'Bless you, Princess.' Big Daniel knuckled his forehead, before taking his ration from her.

'God love you, Princess,' said Ned, and all the others adopted the name. From then on she was their princess, and the rough seamen looked upon her with increasing respect and burgeoning affection.

'You can eat on the march, lads.' Hal hauled himself to his feet. 'We have been lucky too long. Soon the devil will want his turn.' They groaned and muttered but followed his lead.

As Hal was helping Sukeena to mount, there was a warning shout from Daniel. 'There the bastards come at last.' He pointed back down at the open *vlei* at the bottom of the slope. Hal pushed Sukeena up between the saddle-bags and limped back to the rear of the column. He looked down the hillside and saw the long file of running men who had emerged from the edge of the scrub and were crossing the open ground. They were led by a single horseman who came on at a trot.

'It's Schreuder again. He has found another mount.' Even at that range there was no mistaking the Colonel. He sat tall and arrogant in the saddle, and there was a sense of deadly purpose about the set of his shoulders and the way he lifted his head to look up the slope towards them. It was obvious that he had not yet spotted them, hidden in the thick scrub.

'How many men with him?' Ned Tyler asked, and they all looked at Hal to count them. He slitted his eyes and watched them come out of the thick scrub. With their swinging trot they kept up easily with Schreuder's horse.

'Twenty,' Hal counted.

'Why so few?' Big Daniel demanded.

'Almost certainly Schreuder has chosen his fastest runners to press us hard. The rest will be following at their best speed.' Hal shaded his eyes. 'Yes, by God, there they are, a league behind the first platoon, but coming fast. I can see their dust and the shape of their helmets above the scrub. There must be a hundred or more in that second detachment.'

'Twenty we can deal with,' Big Daniel muttered, 'but a hundred of those murdering green-backs is more than I can eat for breakfast without belching. What orders, Captain?' Every man looked at Hal.

He paused before replying, carefully studying the lie and the grain of the land below before he said, 'Master Daniel, take the rest of the party on with Althuda to guide you. Aboli and I will stay here with one horse to slow down their advance.'

'We cannot outrun them. They've proved that to us, Captain,' Daniel protested. 'Would it not be better to fight them here?'

'You have your orders.' Hal turned a cold, steely eye upon him.

Daniel again knuckled his brow. 'Aye, Captain,' and he turned to the others. 'You heard the orders, lads.'

Hal limped back to where Sukeena sat on her horse, with Althuda holding the lead rein. 'You must go on, whatever happens. Do not turn back for any reason,' he told Althuda, and then he smiled up at Sukeena. 'Not even if her royal highness commands it.'

She did not return his smile but leaned down closer and whispered, 'I will wait for you on the mountain. Do not make me wait too long.'

Althuda led the column of horses forward again, and as they crossed the skyline there was a distant shout from the *vlei* below.

'So they have discovered us,' Aboli muttered.

Hal went to the single remaining horse, and loosened one of the fifty-pound kegs of gunpowder. He lowered it to the ground, and told Aboli, 'Take the horse on. Follow the others. Let Schreuder see you go. Tether it out of sight beyond the ridge and then come back to me.'

He rolled the keg to the nearest outcrop of rock and crouched beside it. With only the top of his head showing, he again studied the slope below him, then turned his full attention to Schreuder and his band of green-jackets. Already they were much closer, and he could see that two of the Hottentots ran ahead of Schreuder's horse. They watched the ground as they came on, following exactly the route that Hal's party had blazed.

They read our sign from the earth, like hounds after the stag, he thought. They will come up the same path we followed.

At that moment Aboli dropped back over the ridge and squatted beside him. 'The horse is tethered and the others go on apace. Now what is your plan, Gundwane?'

''Tis so simple, there is no need to explain it to you,' said Hal, as he prised the bung from the keg with the point of his sword. Then he unwound the length of the slow-match he had tied around his waist. 'This match is the devil. It either burns too fast or too slow. But I will take a chance on three fingers' length,' he muttered as he measured, then lopped off a length. He rolled it gently between the palms of his hands in an attempt to induce it to burn evenly, then threaded one end into the bunghole of the keg and secured it by driving back the wooden plug.

'You had best hurry, Gundwane. Your old fencing partner, Schreuder, is in great haste to meet you again.'

Hal glanced up from his task and saw that the pursuers had crossed the meadow and were already starting up the slope towards them. 'Keep out of sight,' Hal told him. 'I want to let them get very close.' The two lay flat on their bellies and peered down the hillside. Sitting high in the saddle, Schreuder was in full view, but the two trackers who led him were obscured by the scrub and flowering bushes from the waist down. As they came on Hal could make out the ugly gravel graze down Schreuder's face, the rents and dirt smears on his uniform. He wore neither hat nor wig, had probably lost them along the way, perhaps in his fall. Vain though he was, he had wasted no time in trying to regain them, so urgent was his haste.

The sun had already reddened his shaven pate and his horse was lathered. Perhaps he had not bothered to water it during the long chase. Closer still he came. His eyes were fastened on the ridge where he had seen the fugitives cross. His face was a stony mask, and Hal could see that he was a man driven by his volcanic temper, ready to take any risk or brave any danger.

On the steep slope even his indefatigable trackers began to flag. Hal could see the sweat streaming down their flat yellow Asiatic faces and hear their gasping breath.

'Come on, you rogues!' Schreuder goaded them. 'You will let them get clear away. Faster! Run faster.' They came scrambling and straining up the slope.

'Good!' Hal muttered. 'They are sticking in our tracks, as I hoped.' He whispered his final instructions to Aboli. 'But wait until I give you the word,' he cautioned him.

Closer they came until Hal could hear the Hottentots' bare feet slapping the ground, the squeak of Schreuder's tack and the jingle of his spurs. On he came, until Hal saw the individual beads of sweat that decorated the points of his moustache, and the little veins in his bulging blue eyes as he fixed his obsessed and furious stare on the skyline of the ridge, overlooking the enemy who lay hidden much closer at hand.

'Ready!' whispered Hal, and held the burning slow-match to the fuse of the powder keg. It flared, spluttered, caught, then burned up fiercely. The flame raced down the short length of fuse towards the bung hole.

'Now, Aboli!' he snapped. Aboli seized the keg and leapt to his feet, almost under the hoofs of Schreuder's horse. The two Hottentots yelled with shock and ducked off the path, while the horse shied and reared, throwing Schreuder forward onto its neck.

For a moment Aboli stood poised, holding the keg high above his head with both hands. The fuse sizzled and hissed like an angry puff-adder, and the powder smoke blew around his great tattooed head like a blue nimbus. Then he hurled the keg out over the hillside. It turned lazily in the air before striking the rocky ground and bounding away, bouncing and leaping as it gathered speed. It jumped up into the face of

Schreuder's horse, which reared away just as its rider had recovered his balance. Schreuder was thrown forward again onto its neck, lost one of his stirrups and hung awkwardly out of the saddle.

The horse spun and leaped back down the slope, almost into the platoon of infantry that was following close upon its heels. As both maddened horse and bouncing powder keg came hurtling back amongst them, the column of green-jackets sent up a howl of consternation. Every one recognized that the smoking fuse was the harbinger of a fearsome detonation only seconds away, and they broke ranks and scattered. Most turned instinctively downhill, rather than breaking out to the sides, and the keg overhauled them, bouncing along in their midst.

Schreuder's horse went down on its bunched hindquarters as it slipped and slid down the hillside. The reins snapped in one of its rider's hands while the other lost its precarious hold on the pommel of the saddle. Schreuder fell clear of his mount's driving hoofs, and as he hit the earth the keg exploded. The fall saved his life for he had tumbled into the lee of a low rock outcrop and the main force of the blast swept over him.

However, it ripped through the horde of routed soldiers. Those closest to it were hurled about and thrown upwards like burning leaves from a garden fire. Their clothing was stripped from their mangled bodies, and a disembodied arm was thrown high to fall back at Hal's feet. Both Aboli and Hal were knocked down by the force of the blast. Ears buzzing, Hal scrambled upright again and stared down in awe at the devastation they had created.

Not one of the enemy was still on his feet. 'By God, you killed them all!' Hal marvelled, but at once there were confused cries and shouts among the flattened bushes. First one and then more of the enemy soldiers staggered dazedly upright.

'Come away!' Aboli seized Hal's arm and dragged him to the top of the ridge. Before they dropped over the crest Hal glanced back and saw that Schreuder had hoisted himself upright. Swaying drunkenly he was standing over the mutilated carcass of his mount. He was still so dazed that, even as Hal watched, his legs folded under him and he sat down heavily among the broken branches and torn leaves, covering his face with his hands.

Aboli released Hal's arm, and changed his sword into his right hand. 'I can run back and finish him off,' he growled, but the suggestion stirred Hal from his own daze.

'Leave him be! It would not be honourable to kill him while he is unable to defend himself.'

'Then let us go, and fast.' Aboli growled. 'We may have put this band of Schreuder's men up on the reef but, look! The rest of his green-jackets are not far behind.'

Hal wiped the sweat and dust from his face and blinked to stop his eyes blurring. He saw that Aboli was right. The dustcloud from the second detachment of the enemy rose from the scrub of the flatlands on the far side of the *vlei*, but it was coming on swiftly.

'If we run hard now, we might be able to hold them off until nightfall and by then we should be into the mountains,' Aboli estimated.

Within a few paces, Hal stumbled and hopped as his injured leg gave way under him. Without a word Aboli gave him his arm to help him over the rough ground to where he had tethered the horse. This time Hal did not protest when Aboli boosted him up onto its back and took the lead rein.

'Which direction?' Hal demanded. As he looked ahead the mountain barrier was riven into a labyrinth of ravines and soaring rock buttresses, of cliffs and deep gorges in which grew dense strips of forest and tangled scrub. He could pick out no path nor pass through this confusion.

'Althuda knows the way, and he has left signs for us to follow.' The spoor of five horses and the band of fugitives was deeply trodden ahead of them, but to enhance it Althuda had blazed the bark from the trees along his route. They followed at the best of their speed, and from the next ridge saw the tiny shapes of the five grey horses crossing a stretch of open ground two or three miles ahead. Hal could even make out Sukeena's small figure perched on the back of the leading horse. The silver colour of the horses made them stand out like mirrors in the dark, surrounding bush, and he murmured, 'They are beautiful animals, but they draw the eye of an enemy.'

'In the traces of a gentleman's carriage there could be no finer,' Aboli agreed, 'but in the mountains they would flounder. We must abandon them when we reach the rough ground, or else they will break their lovely legs in the rocks and crevices.'

'Leave them for the Dutch?' Hal asked. 'Why not a musket ball to end their suffering?'

'Because they are beautiful, and because I love them like my children,' said Aboli softly, reaching up and patting the animal's neck. The grey mare rolled an eye at him and whickered softly, returning his affection.

Hal laughed, 'She loves you also, Aboli. For your sake we will spare them.'

They plunged down the next slope and struggled up the far side. The ground grew steeper at each pace and the mountain crests seemed to hang suspended above their heads. At the top they paused again to let the mare blow, and looked ahead.

'It seems Althuda is aiming for that dark gorge dead ahead.' Hal shaded his eyes. 'Can you see them?'

'No,' Aboli grunted. 'They are hidden by the folds of the foothills and the trees.' Then he looked back again. 'But look behind you, Gundwane!'

Hal turned and stared where he pointed, and exclaimed as though he were in pain. 'How can they have come so quickly? They are gaining on us as though we were standing still.'

The column of running green-jackets was swarming over the ridge behind them like soldier ants from a disturbed nest. Hal could count their numbers easily and pick out the white officers. The mid-afternoon sunlight flashed from their bayonets and Hal could hear their faint but jubilant cries as they viewed their quarry so close ahead.

'There is Schreuder!' Hal exclaimed bitterly. 'By God, that man is a monster. Is there no means of stopping him?' The dismounted colonel was trotting along near the rear of the long, spread-out column but, as Hal watched him, he passed the man ahead of him on the path. 'He runs faster than his own Hottentots. If we linger here another minute, he will be up to us before we reach the mouth of the dark gorge.'

The ground ahead rose up so steeply that the horse could not take it straight up, and the path began to zigzag across the slope. There was another joyous cry from below, like the halloo of the fox hunter, and they saw their pursuers strung out over a mile or more of the track. The leaders were much closer now.

'Long musket shot,' Hal hazarded, and as he said it one of the leading soldiers dropped to his knee behind a rock and took deliberate aim before he fired. They saw the puff of muzzle smoke long before they heard the dull pop of the shot. The ball struck a blue chip off a rock fifty feet below where they stood. 'Still too far. Let them waste their powder.'

The grey mare leaped upwards over the rocky steps in the path, much surer on her feet than Hal could have hoped. Then they reached the outer bend in the wide dog-leg and started back across the slope. Now they were approaching their pursuers at an oblique angle, and the gap between them narrowed even faster.

The men on the path below welcomed them with joyous shouts. They flung themselves down to rest, to steady their pounding hearts and shaking hands. Hal could see them checking the priming in the pans of their muskets and lighting their slow-match, preparing themselves to make the shot as the grey mare and her rider came within fair musket range.

'Satan's breath!' Hal muttered. 'This is like sailing into an enemy broadside!' But there was nowhere to run or hide, and they laboured on up the path.

Hal could see Schreuder now: he had worked his way steadily towards the head of the column and was staring up at them. Even at this range Hal could see that he had driven himself far beyond his natural strength: his face was drawn and haggard, his uniform torn, filthy, soaked with sweat, and blood from a dozen scratches and abrasions. He heaved and strained for breath, but his sunken eyes burned with malevolence. He did not have the strength to shout or to shake a weapon but he watched Hal implacably.

One of the green-jackets fired and they heard the ball hum close over their heads. Aboli was urging on the mare at her best pace over the steep, broken path, but they would be within musket range for many more minutes. Now a ripple of fire ran along the line of soldiers along the path below. Musket balls thudded among the rocks around them, some flattening into shiny discs where they struck. Others sprayed chips of stone down upon them, or whined away in ricochet across the valley.

Unscathed, the grey mare reached the outward leg of the path and started back. Now the range was longer and most of the Hottentot infantrymen jumped to their feet and took up the pursuit. One or two started directly up the slope, attempting to cut the corner, but the hillside proved too sheer for even their nimble feet. They gave up, slid back to the angled pathway and hurried after their companions along the gentler but longer route.

A few soldiers remained kneeling in the path, and reloaded, stabbing the ramrods frantically down the muzzles of their muskets, then pouring blackpowder into the pan. Schreuder had watched the fusillade, leaning heavily against a rock while his pounding heart and laboured breathing slowed. Now he pushed himself upright and seized a reloaded musket from one of his Hottentots, elbowing the other man aside.

'We are beyond musket shot!' Hal protested. 'Why does he persist?'

'Because he is mad with hatred for you,' Aboli replied. 'The devil gives him strength to carry on.'

Swiftly Schreuder stripped off his coat and bundled it over the rock, making a cushion on which to rest the forestock of the musket. He looked down the barrel and picked up the pip of the foresight in the notch of the backsight. He settled it for an instant on Hal's bobbing head, then lifted it until he had a slice of blue sky showing beneath it, compensating for the drop of the heavy lead ball when it reached the limit of its carry. In the same motion he swept the sight ahead of the grey's straining head.

'He can never hope for a hit from there!' Hal breathed, but at that instant he saw the silver smoke bloom like a noxious flower on the stem of the musket barrel. Then he felt a mallet blow as the ball ploughed into the ribs of the grey mare an inch from his knee. Hal heard the air driven from the horse's punctured lungs. The brave animal reeled backwards and went down on its haunches. It tried to recover its footing by rearing wildly, but instead threw itself off the edge of the narrow path. Just in time, Aboli grabbed Hal's injured leg and pulled him from its back.

Hal and Aboli sprawled together on the rocks and looked down. The horse rolled until it struck the bend in the pathway, where it came to rest in a slide of small stones, loose earth and dust. It lay with all four legs kicking weakly in the air. A resounding shout of triumph went up from the pursuing soldiers, whose cries rang along the cliffs and echoed through the gloomy depths of the dark gorge.

Hal crawled shakily to his feet, and quickly assessed their circumstances. Both he and Aboli still had their muskets slung over their shoulders and their swords in their scabbards. In addition they each had a pair of pistols, a small powder horn and a bag containing musket balls strapped around their waists. But they had lost all else.

Below them their pursuers had been given new heart by this reverse in their fortunes and were clamouring like a pack of hounds with the smell of the chase hot in their nostrils. They came scrambling upwards.

'Leave your pistols and musket,' Aboli ordered. 'Leave the powder horn and sword also, or their weight will wear you down.'

Hal shook his head. 'We will need them soon enough. Lead the way on.' Aboli did not argue and went away at full stride. Hal stayed close behind him, forcing his injured leg to serve his purpose through the pain and the quivering weakness that spread slowly up his thigh.

Aboli reached back to hand him up over the more formidable steps in the pathway, but the incline became sharper as they laboured upwards and began to work round the sheer buttress of rock that formed one of the portals of the dark gorge. Now, at every pace forward, they were forced to step up onto the next level, as though they were on a staircase, and were skirting the sheer wall that dropped into the valley far below. The pursuers, though still close, were out of sight around the buttress.

'Are we sure this is the right path?' Hal gasped, as they stopped for a few seconds' rest on a broader step.

'Althuda is leaving sign for us still,' Aboli assured him, and kicked over the cairn of three small pebbles balanced upon each other which had been erected prominently in the centre of the path. 'And so are my grey horses.' He smiled as he pointed out a pile of shining wet balls of dung a little further ahead. Then he cocked his head. 'Listen!'

Now Hal could hear the voices of Schreuder's men. They were closer than they had been when last they had stopped. They sounded as though they were just round the corner of the buttress behind them. Hal looked at Aboli with dismay, and tried to balance on his good leg to conceal the weakness of the other. They could hear the clink of sword on rock and the clatter of loose stones underfoot. The soldiers' voices were so clear and loud that Hal could distinguish their words, and Schreuder's voice relentlessly urging his troops onwards.

'Now you will obey me, Gundwane!' said Aboli, and he leaned across and snatched Hal's musket. 'You will go on at your best speed while I hold them here for a while.' Hal was about to argue but Aboli looked hard into his eyes. 'The longer you argue the more danger you place me in,' he said.

Hal nodded. 'See you at the top of the gorge.' He clasped Aboli's arm in a firm grip, then hobbled on alone. As the path turned into the main gorge, Hal looked back and saw that Aboli had taken shelter crouching in the bend of the path, and that he had laid the two muskets on the rock in front of him, close to his hand.

Hal turned the corner, looked up and saw the gorge open up above him like a great gloomy funnel. The sides were sheer rock walls and it was roofed over by trees with tall thin stems that reached up for the sunlight. They were draped and festooned with lichens. A small stream came leaping down, in a series of pools and waterfalls, and the path took to this stream bed and climbed up over water-worn boulders. Hal dropped to his knees, plunged his face into the first pool and sucked up water, choking and coughing in his greed. As the water distended his belly he felt strength flow back into his swollen, throbbing leg.

From the other side of the buttress behind him there came the thud of a musket shot, then the thump of a ball striking flesh, followed immediately by the scream of a man thrown into the abyss, a scream that dwindled and faded as he fell away. It was cut off abruptly as he struck the rocks far below. Aboli had made certain of his first shot, and the pursuers would be thrown back in disarray. It would take them time to regroup and come on more cautiously, so he had won precious minutes for Hal.

Hal scrambled to his feet, and launched himself up the stream bed. Each of the huge, smooth boulders tested his injured leg to its limit. He grunted, groaned and dragged himself upward, listening at the same time for the sounds of fighting behind him, but he heard nothing more until he reached the next pool where he stopped in surprise.

Althuda had left the five grey horses tethered to a dead tree at the water's edge. When he looked beyond them to the next giant step in the stream bed, Hal knew why they had been abandoned here. They could no longer follow this dizzy path. The gorge was constricted into a narrow throat high above his head – and his own courage faltered as he surveyed the perilous route that he had to follow. But there was no other way, for the gorge had turned into a trap from which there was no escape. While he wavered, he heard from far below another musket shot and a clamour of angry shouts.

'Aboli has taken another,' he said aloud, and his own voice echoed weirdly from the high walls of the gorge. 'Now both his muskets are empty and he will have to run.' But Aboli had won this reprieve for him, and he dared not squander it. He drove himself at the steep path, dragging his wounded leg over glassy, water-polished rock, which was slippery and treacherous with slimy green algae.

His heart pounding with exhaustion, and his fingernails ripped to the quick, he crawled the last few feet upwards and reached the ledge in the throat of the gorge. Here he dropped flat on his belly and looked back over the edge. He saw Aboli coming up, leaping from rock to rock without hesitation, a musket clutched in each hand, not even glancing down to judge his footing on the treacherous boulders.

Hal looked up at the sky through the narrow opening of the gorge high above his head, and saw that day was fading. It would be dark soon, and the tops of the trees were turning to gold in the last rays of sunlight.

'This way!' he shouted down to Aboli.

'Go on, Gundwane!' Aboli shouted back. 'Do not wait for me. They are close behind!'

Hal turned and looked up the steep stream bed behind him. For the next two hundred paces it was in full view: if he and Aboli tried to continue the climb, then Schreuder and his men would reach this vantage point while their backs were still exposed. Before they could reach the next shelter they would be shot down by short-range musket fire.

We will have to make our stand here, he decided. We must hold them until nightfall, then try to slip away in the dark. Quickly he gathered loose rocks from the choked watercourse in which he hid and stacked them along the lip of the ledge. When he looked down he saw that Aboli had reached the foot of the rock wall and was climbing rapidly up towards him.

When Aboli was half-way up, and fully exposed, there was a shout from further down the darkening gorge. Through the gloom Hal made out the shape of the first of their pursuers. There came the flash and bang of a musket shot, and Hal peered down anxiously but Aboli was uninjured and still climbing fast.

Now the bottom of the gorge was swarming with men, and a fusillade of shots set the echoes booming and crashing. Hal picked out Schreuder down there in the gloom: his white face stood out among the darker ones that surrounded him.

Aboli reached the top of the rock-wall, and Hal gave him a hand on to the ledge. 'Why have you not gone on, Gundwane?' he panted.

'No time for talking.' Hal snatched one of the muskets from him and began to reload it. 'We have to hold them here until dark. Reload!'

'Powder almost finished,' Aboli replied. 'Only enough for a few more shots.' As he spoke he was plying the ramrod.

'Then we must make every shot tell. After that we will beat them back with rocks.' Hal primed the pan of his musket. 'And when we have run out of rocks to throw, we will take the steel to them.'

Musket balls began to buzz and crack around their heads as the men below opened up a sustained rolling volley. Hal and Aboli were forced to lie below the lip, every few seconds popping up their heads to take a quick glance down the wall.

Schreuder was using most of his men to keep up the fusillade, controlling them so that weapons were always loaded and ready to fire at his command while others reloaded. It seemed that he had chosen a team of his strongest men to scale the wall, while his marksmen tried to keep Hal and Aboli from defending themselves.

This first wave of a dozen or more climbers carrying only their swords rushed forward and hurled themselves at the rock wall, scrambling upwards. Then, as soon as Hal and Aboli's heads appeared over the lip, there came a thunderous volley of musket fire and the muzzle flashes lit the gloom.

Hal ignored the balls that flew around and splashed against the rock below him. He thrust out the barrel of his musket and aimed down at the nearest climber. This was one of the white Dutch corporals, and the range was point-blank. Hal's ball struck him in the mouth, smashed in his teeth and shattered his jawbone. He lost his grip on the slippery face, and fell backwards. He crashed into the three men below him, knocking them loose, and all four plummeted down to shatter on the rocks below.

Aboli fired and sent another two green-jackets slithering downwards. Then both he and Hal snatched up their pistols and fired again, then again, clearing the wall of climbers, except for two men who clung helplessly to a crevice half-way up the polished rock face.

Hal dropped the empty pistols and seized one of the boulders he had placed at hand. It filled his fist, and he hurled it down at the man below him. The green-jacket saw it coming, but could not avoid it. He tried to tuck his head into his shoulders but the rock caught him on the temple, his fingers opened and he fell.

'Good throw, Gundwane!' Aboli applauded him. 'Your aim is improving.' He threw at the last man on the wall and hit him under the chin. He teetered for a moment, then lost his grip and plunged down.

'Reload!' Hal snapped, and as he poured in powder he glanced at the strip of sky above them. 'Will the night never come?' he lamented, and saw Schreuder send the next wave of climbers to rush the wall. Darkness would not save them for, before they had reloaded the muskets, the enemy soldiers were already half-way up.

They knelt on the lip and fired again, but this time their two shots brought down only one of the attackers and the rest came on steadily. Schreuder sent another wave of climbers to join them and the entire wall seethed with dark figures.

'We cannot beat them all back,' Hal said, with black despair in his heart. 'We must retreat back up the gorge.' But when he looked up at the steep, boulder-strewn climb, his spirits quailed.

He flung down his musket and, with Aboli at his side, went at the treacherous slope. The first climbers came over the lip of the wall and rushed, shouting, after them.

In the gathering darkness Hal and Aboli struggled upwards, turning when the pursuers pressed them too closely to take them on with their blades and drive them back just far enough to give them respite to go on upwards. But now more and still more green-jackets had reached the top of the wall, and it was only a matter of minutes before they would be overtaken and overwhelmed.

Just ahead, Hal noticed a deep crevice in the side wall of the gorge and thought that he and Aboli might take shelter in its darkness. He abandoned the idea, however, as he came level with it and saw how shallow it was. Schreuder would hunt them out of there like a ferret driving out a couple of rabbits from a warren.

'Hal Courtney!' a voice called from the dark crack in the rock. He peered into it and, in its depths, saw two men. One was Althuda, who had called him, and the other was a stranger, a bearded, older man dressed in animal skins. It was too dark to see his face clearly, but when both he and Althuda beckoned urgently neither Hal nor Aboli hesitated. They threw themselves at the narrow opening and squeezed in, between the two men already there.

'Get down!' the stranger shouted in Hal's ear, and stood up with a short-handled axe in his hand. A soldier appeared in the opening of the crevice and raised his sword to thrust at the four men crowded into it, but Althuda threw up the pistol in his hand and shot him at close range in the centre of his chest.

At the same time the bearded stranger raised the axe high then slashed down with a powerful stroke. Hal did not understand what he was doing, until he saw that the man had severed a rope of plaited bark, thick as a man's wrist and hairy. The axe bit cleanly through the taut rope, and as it parted the severed tail whipped away, as though impelled by some immense force. The end had been looped and knotted around a sturdy wooden peg, driven into a crack in the stone. The length of the rope ran round the corner of the crevice, then stretched upwards to some point lost in the gathering gloom higher up the steep gorge.

For a long minute nothing else happened, and Hal and Aboli stared at the other two in bewilderment. Then there was a creaking and a rustling from higher up the funnel of the gorge, a rumbling and a crackling as though a sleeping giant had stirred.

'Sabah has triggered the rockfall!' Althuda explained, and instantly Hal understood. He stared out into the gorge through the narrow entrance to the crevice. The rumbling became a gathering roar, and above it he could hear the wild, terrified screams of green-jackets caught full in the path of this avalanche. For them there was neither shelter nor escape. The gorge was a death trap into which Althuda and Sabah had lured them.

The roaring and grinding of rock rose to a deafening crescendo. The mountain seemed to tremble beneath them. The screams of the soldiers in its path were drowned, and suddenly a mighty river of racing boulders came sweeping past the entrance to the crevice. The light was blotted out, and the air was filled with dust and powdered rock so that the four men choked and gasped for breath. Blinded and suffocating, Hal lifted the tail of his ragged shirt and held it over his nose and mouth, trying to filter the air so that he could breathe in the tumultuous choking dust-storm thrown out by the tidal wave of rock and flying stone that poured past.

The avalanche went on for a long time but gradually the stream of moving rock dwindled to become a slow, intermittent slither and tumble of the last few fragments. At last silence, complete and oppressive, weighed down upon them, and the dust settled to reveal the outline of the opening to their shelter.

Aboli crawled out and balanced gingerly on the loose, unstable footing. Hal crept out beside him and both peered down the gloomy gorge. From wall to wall, it had been scoured clean by the avalanche. There was no sound or trace of their pursuers, not a last despairing cry or dying moan, not a shred of cloth or discarded weapon. It was as though they had never been.

Hal's injured leg could no longer bear his weight. He staggered and collapsed in the opening of the crevice. The fever in his blood from the festering wounds boiled up and filled his head with darkness and heat. He was aware of strong hands supporting him and then he lapsed into unconsciousness.

Colonel Cornelius Schreuder waited for an hour in the antechamber of the castle before Governor van de Velde condescended to see him. When, eventually, he was summoned by an aide-de-camp, he strode into the Governor's audience chamber, but still van de Velde declined to acknowledge his presence. He went on signing the documents and proclamations that Jacobus Hop laid before him, one at a time.

Schreuder was in full uniform, wearing all his decorations and stars. His wig was freshly curled and powdered, and his moustaches were dressed with beeswax into sharp spikes. Down one side of his face there were pink raw scars and scabs.

Van de Velde signed the last document and dismissed Hop with a wave of his hand. When the clerk had left and closed the doors behind him, van de Velde picked up Schreuder's written report from the desk in front of him as though it was a particularly revolting piece of excrement.

'So you lost almost forty men, Schreuder?' he asked heavily. 'Not to mention eight of the Company's finest horses.'

'Thirty-four men,' Schreuder corrected him, still standing stiffly to attention.

'Almost forty!' van de Velde repeated, with an expression of repugnance. 'And eight horses. The convicts and slaves you were pursuing got clean away from you. Hardly a famous victory, do you agree, Colonel?' Schreuder scowled furiously at the sculpted cornices on the ceiling above the Governor's head. 'The security of the castle is your responsibility, Schreuder. The minding of the prisoners is your responsibility. The safety of my person and that of my wife is also your responsibility. Do you agree, Schreuder?'

'Yes, your excellency.' A nerve beneath Schreuder's eye began to twitch.

'You allowed the prisoners to escape. You allowed them to plunder the Company's property. You allowed them to do grievous damage to this building with explosives. Look at my windows!' Van de Velde pointed at the empty casements from which the stained-glass panels had been blown. 'I have estimates from the Company surveyor that place the damage at over one hundred thousand guilders!' He was working himself steadily into a rage. 'A hundred thousand guilders! Then, on top of that, you allowed the prisoners to abduct my wife and myself and to place us in mortal danger—' He had to break off to get his temper under control. 'Then you allowed almost forty of the Company's servants to be murdered, including five white men! What do you imagine will be the reaction of the Council of Seventeen in Amsterdam when they receive my full report detailing the depths of the dereliction of your duties, hey? What do you think they will say? Answer me, you jumped-up popinjay! What do you think they will say?'

'They may be somewhat displeased,' Schreuder replied stiffly.

'Displeased? Somewhat displeased?' shrieked van de Velde, and fell back in his chair, gasping for breath like a stranded fish. When he had recovered, he went on, 'You will be the first to know whether or not they are somewhat displeased, Schreuder. I am sending you back to Amsterdam in the deepest disgrace. You will sail in three days' time aboard the *Weltevreden*, which is anchored in the bay at this moment.'

He pointed out through the empty windows at the cluster of ships lying at anchor beyond the surf line. 'My report on the affair will go to Amsterdam on the same ship, together with my condemnation of you in the strongest possible terms. You will stand before the Seventeen and make your excuses to them in person.' He leered at the colonel gloatingly. 'Your military career is destroyed, Schreuder. I suggest you consider taking up the calling of whoremaster, a vocation for which you have demonstrated considerable aptitude. Goodbye, Colonel Schreuder. I doubt I shall have the pleasure of your company ever again.'

Aching with the Governor's insults as though he had taken twenty lashes of the cat, Schreuder strode out to the head of the staircase. To give himself time in which to regain his composure and his temper, he paused to survey the damage that the explosion had inflicted on the buildings surrounding the courtyard. The armoury had been destroyed, blown into a rubble heap. The roof timbers of the north wing were shattered and blackened by the fire that had followed the blast, but the outer walls were intact and the other buildings only superficially damaged.

The sentries who once would have leapt to attention at his appearance now delayed rendering him his honours, and when finally they tossed him a lackadaisical salute, one accompanied it with an impudent grin. In the tiny community of the colony news spread swiftly, and clearly his dishonourable discharge from the Company's service was already known to the entire garrison. Jacobus Hop must have taken pleasure in spreading the news, Schreuder decided, and he rounded on the grinning sentry. 'Wipe that smirk off your ugly face or, by God, I will shave it off with my sword.' The man sobered instantly and stared rigidly ahead. However, as Schreuder crossed the courtyard, Manseer and the overseers whispered together and smiled behind their fists. Even some of the recaptured prisoners, now wearing chains, who were repairing the damage to the armoury stopped work to grin slyly at him.

Such humiliation was painfully hard for a man of his pride and temperament to bear, and he tried to imagine how much worse it would become when he returned to Holland and faced the Council of Seventeen. His shame would be shouted in every tavern and port, in every garrison and regiment, in the salons of all the great houses and mansions of Amsterdam. Van de Velde was correct: he would become a pariah.

He strode out through the gates and across the bridge of the moat. He did not know where he was going, but he turned down towards the foreshore and stood above the beach staring out to sea. Slowly he brought his turbulent emotions under some control, and began to look for some escape from the scorn and the ridicule that he could not bear.

I shall swallow the ball, he decided. It's the only way open to me. Then, almost instantly, his whole nature revolted against such a craven course of action. He remembered how he had despised one of his brother officers in Batavia who, over the matter of a woman, had placed the muzzle of a loaded pistol in his mouth and blown away the back of his skull. 'It is the coward's way!' Schreuder said aloud. 'And not for me.'

Yet he knew he could never obey van de Velde's orders to return home to Holland. But neither could he remain here at Good Hope, nor travel to any Dutch possession anywhere upon this globe. He was an outcast, and he must find some other land where his shame was unknown.

Now his gaze focused on the cluster of shipping anchored out in Table Bay. There was the *Weltevreden*, upon which van de Velde wished to send him back to face the Seventeen. His eye moved on over the three other Dutch vessels lying near it. He would not sail on a Dutch ship but there were only two foreign vessels. One was a Portuguese slaver, outward-bound for the markets of Zanzibar. Even the thought of sailing on a slaver was distasteful – he could smell her from where he stood above the beach. The other ship was an English frigate and, by the looks of her, newly launched and well found. Her rigging was fresh and her paintwork only lightly marred by the Atlantic gales. She had the look of a warship, but he had heard that she was privately owned and an armed trader. He could read her name on her transom: the *Golden Bough*. She had fifteen gunports down the side, which she presented to him as she rode lightly at anchor, but he did not know whence she had come nor whither she was bound. However, he knew exactly where to find this information so he settled his hat firmly over his wig and struck out along the shore, heading for the nearest of the insalubrious cluster of hovels that served as brothels and gin halls to the seafarers of the oceans.

Even at this hour of the morning the tavern was crowded, and the windowless interior was dark and rank with tobacco smoke and the fumes of cheap spirits and unwashed humanity. The whores were mostly Hottentots but there were one or two white women who had grown too old and pox-ridden to work in even the ports of Rotterdam or St Pauli. Somehow they had found ships to carry them southwards and had come ashore, like rats, to eke out their last days in these squalid surroundings before the French disease burned them out entirely.

His hand on the hilt of his sword, Schreuder cleared a small table for himself with a sharp word and haughty stare. Once he was seated he summoned one of the haggard serving wenches to bring him a tankard of small beer. 'Which are the sailors from the *Golden Bough?*' he asked, and tossed a silver rix-dollar onto the filthy table top. The trull snatched up this largesse and dropped it down the front of her grubby dress between her pendulous dugs before she jerked her head in the direction of three seamen at a table in the far corner of the room.

'Take each of those gentlemen another chamberpot filled with whatever foul piss you're serving them and tell them that I'm paying for it.'

When he left the tavern half an hour later Schreuder knew where the *Golden Bough* was heading, and the name and disposition of her captain. He sauntered down to the beach and hired a skiff to row him out to the frigate.

The anchor watch on board the *Golden Bough* spotted him as soon as he left the beach, and could tell by his dress and deportment that he was a man of consequence. When Schreuder hailed the deck of the frigate and asked for permission to come aboard, a stout, florid-faced Welsh petty-officer gave him a cautious greeting at the entryport, then led him down to the stern cabin where Captain Christopher Llewellyn rose to welcome him. Once he was seated, he offered Schreuder a pewter pot of porter. He was obviously relieved to find that Schreuder spoke good English. Llewellyn soon accepted him as a gentleman and an equal, relaxed and spoke easily and openly.

First they discussed the recent hostilities between their two countries, and expressed themselves pleased that a satisfactory peace had been concluded, then went on to speak about maritime trade in the eastern oceans and the temporal powers and politics that governed the regions of the East Indies and Further India. These were highly involved, and complicated by the rivalry between the European powers whose traders and naval vessels were entering the Oriental seas in ever greater numbers.

'There are also the religious conflicts that embroil the eastern lands,' Llewellyn remarked. 'My present voyage is in response to an appeal by the Christian King of Ethiopia, the Prester John, for military assistance in his war against the forces of Islam.'

At the mention of war in the East Schreuder sat up a little straighter in his chair. He was a warrior, at the moment an unemployed warrior, and war was his trade. 'I had not heard of this conflict. Please tell me more about it.'

'The great Mogul has sent his fleet and an army under the command of his younger brother, Sadiq Khan Jahan, to seize the countries that make up the seaboard of the Great Horn of Africa from the Christian king.' Llewellyn broke off his explanation to ask, 'Tell me, Colonel, do you know much about the Islamic religion?'

Schreuder nodded. 'Yes, of course. Many of the men I have commanded over the last thirty years have been Muslims. I speak Arabic and I have made a study of Islam.'

'You will know, then, that one of the precepts of this militant belief is the *hadj*, the pilgrimage to the birthplace of the prophet at Mecca, which is situated on the eastern shores of the Red Sea.'

'Ah!' Schreuder said. 'I can see where you are heading. Any pilgrim from the Great Mogul's realm in India would be forced to enter the Red Sea by passing around the Great Horn of Africa. This would bring the two religions into confrontation in the region, am I correct in my surmise?'

'Indeed, Colonel, I commend you on your grasp of the religious and political implications. That is precisely the excuse being used by the Great Mogul to attack the Prester John. Of course, the Arabs have been trading with Africa since before the birth of either our Saviour, Jesus Christ, or the prophet Muhammad. From a foothold on Zanzibar island they have been gradually extending their domination onto the mainland. Now they are intent on the conquest and subjugation of the heartland of Christian Ethiopia.'

'And where, may I be so bold to ask, is your place in this conflict?' Schreuder asked thoughtfully

'I belong to a naval chivalric order, the Knights of the Temple of the Order of St George and the Holy Grail, committed to defend the Christian faith and the holy places of Christendom. We are the successors to the Knights Templar.'

'I know of your order,' Schreuder said, 'and I am acquainted with several of your brother knights. The Earl of Cumbrae, for one.'

'Ah!' Llewellyn sniffed. 'He is not a prime example of our membership.'

'I have also met Sir Francis Courtney,' Schreuder went on.

Llewellyn's enthusiasm was unfeigned. 'I know him well,' he exclaimed. 'What a fine seaman and gentleman. Do you know, by any chance, where I might find Franky? This religious war in the Great Horn would draw him like a bee to honey. His ship joined with mine would make a formidable force.'

'I am afraid that Sir Francis was a casualty of the recent war between our two countries.' Schreuder phrased it diplomatically, and Llewellyn looked distraught.

'I am saddened by that news.' He was silent for a while then roused himself. 'To give you the answer to your question, Colonel Schreuder, I am on my way to the Great Horn in response to the Prester's call for assistance to repel the onslaught of Islam. I intend sailing with the tide this very evening.'

'No doubt the Prester will be in need of military as well as naval assistance?' Schreuder asked abruptly. He was trying to disguise the excitement he felt. This was a direct answer to his prayers, 'Would you look kindly upon my request for passage aboard your fine ship to the theatre of war? I, also, am determined to offer my services.'

Llewellyn looked startled. 'A sudden decision, sir. Do you not have duties and obligations ashore? Would it be possible for you to sail with me at such short notice?'

'Indeed, Captain, your presence here in Table Bay seems like a stroke of destiny. I have this very day freed myself from the obligations of which you speak. It is almost as though I had divine premonition of this call to duty. I stand ready to answer the call. I would be pleased to pay for my passage, and that of the lady who is to be my wife, in gold coin.'

Llewellyn looked doubtful, scratched his beard and studied Schreuder shrewdly. 'I have only one small cabin unoccupied, hardly fit accommodation for persons of quality.'

'I would pay ten English guineas for the privilege of sailing with you,' Schreuder said, and the captain's expression cleared.

'I should be honoured by your company, and that of your lady. However, I cannot delay my departure by a single hour. I must sail with the tide. I will have a boat take you ashore and wait for you on the beach.'

As Schreuder was rowed away he was seething with excitement. The service of an oriental potentate in a religious war would surely offer opportunities for martial glory and enrichment far beyond what he could ever have expected in the service of the Dutch East India Company. He had been offered an escape from the threat of disgrace and ignominy. After this war, he might still return to Holland laden with gold and glory. This was the tide of fortune he had waited for all his life and, with the woman he loved beyond everything else at his side, he would take that tide at the full.

As soon as the boat beached he sprang out and tossed a small silver coin to the boatswain, 'Wait for me!' and strode off towards the castle. His servant was waiting in his quarters, and Schreuder gave him instructions to pack all his possessions, have them carried down to the foreshore and placed upon the *Golden Bough*'s longboat. It seemed that the entire garrison must know already of his dismissal. Even his servant was not surprised by his orders, so none would think it odd that he was moving out.

He shouted for his groom and ordered him to saddle his single remaining horse. While he waited for the horse to be brought round from the stables, he stood before the small mirror in his dressing room and rearranged his uniform, brushed out his wig and reshaped his moustaches. He felt a glow of excitement and a sense of release. By the time that the Governor realized that he and Katinka were gone, the *Golden Bough* would be well out to sea and on course for the Orient.

He hurried down the stairs, out into the yard where the groom now held his horse, and sprang into the saddle. He was in great haste, anxious to be away, and he pushed his mount to a gallop along the avenues towards the Governor's residence. His haste was not so great, however, as to deprive him of all caution. He did not ride up the front drive through the lawns in front of the mansion, but took the side road through the oak grove which was used by slaves and the suppliers of firewood and provisions from the village. He reined his horse in as soon as he was close enough for its hoofbeats to be heard in the residence, and walked the animal sedately into the stableyard behind the kitchens. As he dismounted a startled groom hurried out to take the horse, and Schreuder skirted the kitchen wall, entering the gardens through the small gate in the corner.

He looked about carefully for the gardeners were often working in this part of the estate, but he saw no sign of them. He walked across the lawns, neither dawdling nor hurrying, and entered the residence through the double doors that led into the library. The long, book-lined room was deserted.

Schreuder was well acquainted with the layout of the residence. He had visited Katinka often enough while her husband was about his duties in the castle. He went first to her reading room, which overlooked the lawns and a distant vista of the bay and the blue Atlantic. It was

Katinka's favourite retreat, but this noon she was not there. A female slave was on her knees in front of the bookshelves, taking down each volume one at a time and polishing the leather bindings with a soft cloth. She looked up, startled, as Schreuder burst in upon her.

'Where is your mistress?' he demanded, and when she gawked dumbly at him he repeated, 'Where is Mevrouw van de Velde?'

The slave girl scrambled to her feet in confusion. 'The mistress is in her bedroom. But she is not to be disturbed. She is unwell. She left strict instructions.'

Schreuder spun on his heel and went down the corridor. Gently he tried the handle of the door at the end of the passage, but it was locked from within. He exclaimed with impatience. Time was wasting away, and he knew Llewellyn would not hesitate to make good his threat to sail without him when the tide turned. He hurried back along the corridor and stepped through the glazed doors out onto the long veranda. He went down to the windows that opened into the principal bedroom suite. The windows to Katinka's closet were shuttered, and he raised his fist to knock upon them but restrained himself. He did not want to alert the house slaves. Instead he drew his sword, slipped the blade through the gap in the shutters and lifted the latch on the inside. He eased open the shutter and stepped inside over the sill.

Katinka's perfume assailed his senses and, for an instant, he felt giddy with his love and longing for her. Then with a surge of joy, he remembered that she would soon be his alone, the two of them voyaging out, hand in hand, to make a new life and fortune together. He crossed the wooden floor, stepping lightly so as not to frighten her, and gently drew aside the curtains from the door into the main bedroom. Here, also, the shutters were closed and latched and the room was in semi-darkness. He paused to allow his eyes to adjust to the dim light and saw that the bed was in disarray.

Then, in the gloom, he made out the pearly sheen of her flawless white skin amongst the tumbled bedlinen. She was nude, her back turned to him, her silver-gold hair cascading down to the cleft of her perfect buttocks. He felt a surge of lust, his loins engorged, and he was so overcome with wanting her that for a moment he could not move, could not even breathe.

Then she turned her head and looked straight at him. Her eyes flew wide and all the colour drained from her face.

'You despicable swine!' she said softly. 'How dare you spy upon me?' Her voice was low but filled with scorn and fury. He recoiled in astonishment. She was his lover, and he could not understand that she would speak to him thus, nor that she should look upon him with such contempt and fury. Then he saw that her naked breasts shone with the soft dew of her own sweat, and that she was seated astride a supine masculine form. The man beneath her lay upon his back, and she was impaled upon him, in the act of passion, riding him like a steed.

The man's body was muscular, white and hard, the body of a gladiator. With one explosive movement Katinka sprang off him and spun to face Schreuder. As she stood beside the bed trembling with outrage her inner thighs glistened with the overflow of her venery.

'What are you doing in my bedroom?' she hissed at Schreuder.

Stupidly he answered, 'I came to take you away with me.' But his eyes went down to the man's body. His pubic hair was wet and matted and his sex thrust up towards the ceiling, thick and swollen and glistening, with a shiny, viscous coating. The man sat upright and looked straight at Schreuder, with a flat yellow gaze.

A wave of unspeakable horror and revulsion swept over Schreuder. Katinka, his love, had been rutting with Slow John, the executioner.

Katinka was speaking, but her words barely made sense to him. 'You came to take me away? What gave you the notion that I would go with you, the Company clown, the laughing stock of the colony? Get out of here, you fool. Go into obscurity and shame where you belong.'

Slow John stood up from the bed. 'You heard her. Get out or I shall throw you out.' It was not the words but the fact that Slow John's penis was still fully tumescent that turned Schreuder into a maniac. His temper which, until now, he had been able to keep under restraint boiled over and took control of him. To the humiliation, insults and rejection that had been heaped upon him all that day was added the black rage of his jealousy.

Slow John stooped to the pile of his discarded clothing, which lay upon the tiles beside the bed, and straightened up again with a pruning knife in his right hand. 'I warn you,' he said in that deep, melodious voice, 'leave now, at once.'

With one fluid movement the Neptune sword sprang from its scabbard as though it were a living thing. Slow John was no warrior. His victims were always delivered to him trussed and chained. He had never been matched against a man like Schreuder. He jumped forward, the knife held low in front of him, but Schreuder flicked his own blade across the inner side of Slow John's wrist, severing the sinews so that the man's fingers opened involuntarily and the knife dropped to the tiles.

Then Schreuder thrust for the heart. Slow John had neither time nor chance to evade the stroke. The point took him in the centre of his broad, hairless chest and the blade buried itself right up to the jewelled pommel. The two men stood, locked together by the weapon. Gradually

Slow John's sex wilted and hung white and flaccid. His eyes glazed over and turned opaque and sightless as yellow pebbles. As he sank to his knees, Katinka began to scream.

Schreuder plucked the blade from the executioner's chest. Its burnished length was dulled by his blood. Katinka screamed again as a feather of bright heart-blood stood out of the wound in Slow John's chest, and he toppled headlong to the tiles.

'Don't scream,' Schreuder snarled, with the black rage still upon him, and advanced upon her with the sword in his hand. 'You have played me false with this creature. You knew I loved you. I came to fetch you. I wanted you to come away with me.' She backed away before him, both fists clenched upon her cheeks, and screamed in high, ringing hysteria.

'Don't scream,' he shouted. 'Be quiet. I cannot bear it when you do that.' The dreadful sound echoed in his head and made it ache, but she retreated from him, her cries louder now, a terrible sound, and he had to make her stop.

'Don't do that!' He tried to catch hold of her wrist, but she was too swift for him. She twisted out of his grip. Her screams grew even louder, and his rage broke its bounds as though it were some terrible black animal over which he had no control. The sword in his hand flew without his brain or his hand commanding it, and he stabbed her satiny white belly, just above the golden nest of her *mons veneris*.

Her scream turned to a higher, agonized shriek and she clutched at the blade as he jerked it from her flesh. It cut her palms to the bone, and he thrust again to quieten her, twice more in the belly.

'Quiet!' he roared at her and she turned away and tried to run for the doors of her closet, but he stabbed her in the back just above her kidneys, pulled out the blade and thrust between her shoulders. She fell and rolled on her back, and he stood over her and stabbed and hacked and thrust at her. Each time the blade passed clean through her body and struck the tiles on which she squirmed.

'Keep quiet!' he yelled, and kept on stabbing until her screams and sobs died away. Even then he continued to thrust at her, standing in the spreading pool of her blood, his uniform drenched with gouts of scarlet, his face and arms splashed and speckled so that he looked like a plague victim covered with the rash of the disease.

Then, slowly, the black rage drained from his brain, and he staggered back against the wall, leaving daubs of her blood across the whitewash.

'Katinka!' he whispered. 'I did not mean to hurt you. I love you so.'

She lay in the wide deep pool of her own blood. The wounds were like a choir of red mouths on her white skin. The blood still trickled from each of them. He had not dreamed there could be so much blood in that slim white body. Her head lay in a scarlet puddle, and her hair was soaked red. Her face was daubed thickly with it. Her features were twisted into a rictus of terror and agony that was no longer lovely to look upon.

'Katinka, my darling. Please forgive me.' He started across the floor towards her, stepping through the river of her blood that spread across the tiles. Then he stopped with the sword in his hand as, in the mirror across the room, he glimpsed a wild blood-smeared apparition staring back at him.

'Oh, sweet Mary, what have I done?' He tore his eyes from the creature in the mirror, and knelt beside the body of the woman he loved. He tried to lift her, but she was limp and boneless. She slid out of his embrace, and flopped into the puddle of her own blood.

He stood again and backed away from her. 'I did not mean you to die. You made me angry. I loved you, but you were unfaithful.'

Again he saw his own reflection in the mirror, 'Oh sweet God, the blood. There is so much.' He wiped, with sticky hands, at the mess of crimson that covered his jacket, then at his face, spreading the blood into a scarlet carnival mask.

For the first time he thought of flight, of the boat waiting for him on the beach and the frigate lying out in the bay. 'I cannot ride through the colony like this! I cannot go aboard like this!'

He staggered across the room to the door of the Governor's dressing room. He stripped off his sodden jacket and threw it from him. A pitcher of water was standing in a basin on the cabinet and he plunged his gory hands into it and sloshed it over his face. He seized the washcloth from its hook and soaked it in the pink water, then scrubbed at his arms and the front of his breeches.

'So much blood!' he kept repeating, as he wiped then rinsed the cloth and wiped again. He found a pile of clean white shirts on one of the shelves, and pulled one on over his damp chest. Van de Velde was a big man, and it fitted him well enough. He looked down and saw that the bloodstains were not so obvious on the dark serge of his breeches. His wig was stained so he pulled it off and flung it against the far wall. He chose another from the row set on blocks along the back wall. He found a woollen cloak that covered him from shoulders to calves. He spent a minute cleaning the blade and the sapphire of the Neptune sword, then thrust it back into its scabbard. When he looked again in the mirror he saw that his appearance would no longer shock or alarm. Then a thought struck him. He picked up his soiled jacket and ripped the stars and decorations from the lapels. He wrapped them in a clean neckcloth he found on one of the shelves and stuffed them into the inner pocket of the woollen cloak.

He paused on the threshold of the Governor's dressing room and looked for the last time at the body of the woman he loved. Her blood was still moving softly across the tiles, like a fat, lazy adder. As he watched, it reached the edge of the smaller puddle in which Slow John lay. Their blood ran together, and Schreuder felt a deep sense of sacrilege that the pure should mingle thus with the base.

'I did not want this to happen,' he said hopelessly. 'I am so sorry, my darling. I wanted you to come with me.' He trod carefully over the rill of blood, went to the shuttered window and stepped out onto the veranda. He gathered the cloak around his shoulders and strode through the gardens to the small door in the stableyard where he shouted for the groom, who hurried up with his horse.

Schreuder rode down the avenue and crossed the Parade, looking straight ahead. The longboat was still on the beach and as he rode up the boatswain called to him, 'We was just about to give you up, Colonel. The *Golden Bough* is shortening her anchor cable and manning her yards.'

As he climbed to the deck of the frigate, Captain Llewellyn and his crew were so absorbed by the business of weighing anchor and getting the ship under sail that they paid him little heed. A midshipman showed him down to his small cabin, then hurried away leaving him alone. His travel chests had been brought aboard and were stowed under the narrow bunk. Schreuder stripped off all his soiled dress and found a clean uniform in one of his chests. Before donning it, he placed the stars and orders upon its lapels. His blood-smeared clothing he tied in a bundle, then looked around for something to weight it. Obviously the thin wooden bulkheads would be struck when the frigate was cleared for action, and his cabin would form part of the ship's gundeck. A culverin filled most of the available deck space. Beside the weapon was heaped a pyramid of iron cannonballs. He stuffed one into the bundle of blood-soaked clothing and waited until he felt the ship come on the wind and thrust out into the bay.

Then he opened the gunport a crack, and dropped the bundle through it into fifty fathoms of green water. When he went up on deck they were already a league offshore and running out strongly on the sou'easter to make their offing before coming about to round the cape.

Schreuder stared back at the land and made out the roof of the Governor's mansion among the trees at the base of the great mountain. He wondered if they had yet discovered Katinka's body, or whether she still lay joined in death to her base lover. He stood there at the stern rail until the great massif of Table Mountain was only a distant blue silhouette against the evening sky.

'Farewell, my darling,' he whispered.

It was only when he lay sleepless in his hard bunk at midnight that the enormity of his situation began to dawn upon him. His guilt was manifest. Every ship that left Table Bay would carry the tidings across the oceans and to every port in the civilized world. From this day forward he was a fugitive and an outlaw.

Hal woke to a sense of peace such as he had seldom known before. He lay with his eyes shut, too lazy and weak to open them. He realized that he was warm and dry and lying on a comfortable mattress. He expected the dungeon stench to assail him, the mouldy odour of damp, rotting straw, the latrine bucket and the smell of men who had not bathed for a twelve-month crowded together in a fetid hole in the earth. Instead he smelled fresh woodsmoke, perfumed and sweet, the scent of burning cedar faggots.

Suddenly the memories came flooding back, and, with a great lift of the spirits, he remembered their escape, that he was no longer a prisoner. He lay and savoured that knowledge. There were other smells and sounds. It amused him to try to recognize them without opening his eyes. There was the smell of the newly cut grass mattress on which he lay and the fur blanket that covered him, the aroma of meat grilling on the coals and another tantalizing fragrance that he could not place. It was a mingling of wild flowers and a warm kittenish musk that roused him strangely and added to his sense of well-being.

He opened his eyes slowly and cautiously, and was dazzled by the strong mountain light through the opening of the shelter in which he lay. He looked around and saw that it must have been built into the side of the mountain, for half the walls were of smooth rock and the sides nearest the opening were built of interwoven saplings daubed with red clay. The roof was thatch. Clay pots and crudely fashioned tools and implements were stacked against the inner wall. A bow and quiver hung from a peg near the door. Beside them hung his sword and pistols.

He lay and listened to the burble of a mountain stream, and then he heard a woman's laughter, merrier and more lovely than the tinkle of water. He raised himself slowly on one elbow, shocked by the effort it required, and tried to look through the doorway. The sound of an infant's laughter mingled with that of the woman. Through all his long captivity he had heard nothing to equal it, and he could not help but chuckle with delight.

The sound of feminine laughter ceased and there was a quick movement outside the hut. A lissom gamine figure appeared in the opening, backlit by the sunshine so that she was only a lovely silhouette. Though he could not see her face, he knew straight away who it was.

'Good morrow, Gundwane, you have slept long, but did you sleep well?' Sukeena asked shyly. She had the infant on her hip and her hair was loose, hanging in a dark veil to her waist. 'This is my nephew, Bobby.' She joggled the baby on her hip and he gurgled with delight.

'How long did I sleep?' Hal asked, beginning to rise, but she passed the baby to someone outside, and came quickly to kneel beside the mattress. She restrained him with a small warm hand on his naked chest.

'Gently, Gundwane. You have been in fever sleep for many days.'

'I am well again now,' he said, and then recognized the mysterious perfume he had noticed earlier. It was her woman smell, the flowers in her hair and the soft warmth of her skin.

'Not yet,' she contradicted him, and he let her ease his head back onto the mattress. He was staring at her and she smiled without embarrassment.

'I have never seen anything so beautiful as you,' he said, then reached up and touched his own cheek. 'My beard?'

'It is gone.' She laughed, sitting back with her legs curled under her. 'I stole a razor from the fat Governor especially for the task.' She cocked her head on one side and studied him. 'With the beard gone, you also are beautiful, Gundwane.'

She blushed slightly as she realized the import of her words, and Hal watched in delight as the red-gold suffused her cheeks. She turned her full attention to his injured leg, drew back the fur blanket to expose it and unwound the bandage.

'Ah!' she murmured, as she touched it lightly. 'It heals marvellously well with a little help from my medicines. You have been fortunate. The bite from the fangs of a hound is always poisonous, and then the abuse to which you put the limb during our flight might have killed you or crippled you for the rest of your life.'

Hal smiled at her strictures as he lay back comfortably and surrendered himself to her hands.

'Are you hungry?' she asked, as she retied the dressing over his wound. At that question Hal realized that he was ravenous. She brought him the carcass of a wild partridge, grilled on the coals, and sat opposite him, watching with a proprietary air as he ate and then sucked the bones clean.

'You will soon be strong again.' She smiled. 'You eat like a lion.' She gathered up the scraps of his meal, then stood up. 'Aboli and your other seamen have been pleading with me for a chance to come to you. I will call them now.'

'Wait!' He stopped her. He wished that this intimate time alone with her would not end so soon. She sank down beside him once more and watched his face expectantly.

'I have not thanked you,' he said lamely. 'Without your care, I would probably have died of the fever.'

She smiled softly and said, 'I have not thanked you either. Without you, I would still be a slave.' For a time they looked at each other without speaking, openly examining each other's face in detail.

Then Hal asked, 'Where are we, Sukeena?' He made a gesture that took in their surroundings. 'This hut?'

'It is Sabah's. He has lent it to us. To you and me, and he has gone to live with the others of his band.'

'So we are in the mountains at last?'

'Deep in the mountains.' She nodded. 'At a place that has no name. In a place where the Dutch can never find us.'

'I want to see,' he said. For a moment she looked dubious, then nodded. She helped him to stand and offered her shoulder to support him as he hopped to the opening in the thatched shelter.

He sank down and leaned against the doorpost of rough cedar wood. Sukeena sat close beside him as he gazed about. For a long time neither spoke. Hal breathed deeply of the crisp, high air that smelled and tasted of the wild flowers that grew in such profusion about them.

''Tis a vision of paradise,' he said at last. The peaks that surrounded them were wild and splendid. The cliffs and gorges were painted with lichens that were all the colours of the artist's palette. The late sunlight fell full upon the mountain tops across the deep valley and crowned them with a golden radiance. The long shadow thrown by the peak behind them was royal purple. The water of the stream below was clear as the air they breathed, and Hal could see the fish lying like long shadows on the yellow sandbanks, fanning their dark tails to keep their heads into the current.

'It is strange, I have never seen this place nor any like it, and yet I feel as though I know it well. I feel a sense of homecoming, as though I was waiting to return here.'

''Tis not strange, Henry Courtney. I also was waiting.' She turned her head and looked deep into his eyes. 'I was waiting for you. I knew you would come. The stars told me. That day I first saw you on the Parade outside the castle, I recognized you as the one.'

There was so much to ponder in that simple declaration that he was silent again for a long while, watching her face.

'My father was also an adept. He was able to read the stars,' he said.

'Aboli told me.'

'So you, too, can divine the future from the stars, Sukeena.'

She did not deny it. 'My mother taught me many skills. I was able to see you from afar.'

He accepted her statement without question. 'So you must know what is to become of us, you and me?'

She smiled, and there was a mischievous gleam in her eye. She slipped a slim arm through his. 'I would not have to be a great sage to know that, Gundwane. But there is much else that I am able to tell of what lies ahead.'

'Tell me, then,' he ordered, but she smiled again and shook her head. 'There will be time later. We will have much time to talk while your leg heals and you grow strong again.' She stood up. 'But now I will fetch the others, I cannot deny them any longer.'

They came immediately, but Aboli was the first to arrive. He greeted Hal in the language of the forests. 'I see you well, Gundwane. I thought you would sleep for ever.'

'Without your help, I might indeed have done so.'

Then Big Daniel and Ned and the others came to touch their foreheads and mumble their self-conscious greetings and squat in a semicircle in front of him. They were not much given to expressing their emotions in words, but what he saw in their eyes when they looked at him warmed and fortified him.

'This is Sabah, whom you already know.' Althuda led him forward.

'Well met, Sabah!' Hal seized his hand. 'I have never been happier to see another man than I was that night in the Gorge.'

'I would have liked to come to your aid much sooner,' Sabah replied in Dutch, 'but we are few and the enemy were as numerous as ticks on an antelope's belly in spring.' Sabah sat down in the ring of men and, with an apologetic air, began to explain. 'The fates have not been kind to us here in the mountains. We did not have the services of a physician such as Sukeena. We who were once nineteen are now only eight and two of those a woman and an infant. I knew we could not help you fight out in the open, for in hunting for food we have used up all our gunpowder. However, we knew Althuda would bring you up Dark Gorge. We built the rockfall knowing that the Dutch would follow you.'

'You did the brave and wise thing,' Hal said.

Althuda brought his woman out of the gathering darkness. She was a pretty girl, small and darker-skinned than he was, but Hal could not doubt that Althuda was the father of the boy on her hip.

'This is Zwaantie, my wife, and this is my son, Bobby.' Hal held out his hands and Zwaantie handed him the child. He held Bobby in his lap, and the little boy regarded him with huge solemn black eyes.

'He is a likely lad, and strong,' Hal said, and father and mother smiled proudly.

Zwaantie lifted the infant and strapped him on her back. Then she and Sukeena built up the fire and began to cook the evening meal of wild game and the fruits of the mountain forests, while the men talked quietly and seriously.

First Sabah explained their circumstances, addressing himself directly to Hal, enlarging on the brief report he had already given. Hal soon understood that, despite the beauty of their surroundings now in the summertime and the seeming abundance of the meal that the women were preparing, the mountains were not always as hospitable. During winter the snows lay thick even in the valleys and game was scarce. However, they dared not move down to lower altitudes where they would be seen by the Hottentot tribes and their whereabouts reported to the Dutch at Good Hope.

'The winters here are fierce,' Sabah summed up. 'If we stay here for another, then few of us will be left alive this time next year.' During their captivity Hal's seamen had garnered enough knowledge of the Dutch language to enable them to follow what Sabah had to say, and when he had finished speaking they were all silent and stared glumly into the fire, munching disconsolately on the food the women brought to them.

Then, one at a time, their heads turned towards Hal. Big Daniel spoke for them all when he asked, 'What are we going to do now, Sir Henry?'

'Are you seamen or mountaineers?' Hal answered his question with a question, and some of the men chuckled.

'We were born in Davey Jones's locker and we were all of us given salt water for blood,' Ned Tyler answered.

'Then I will have to take you down to the sea and find you a ship, won't I?' said Hal. They looked confused but some chuckled again, though half-heartedly.

'Master Daniel, I want a manifest of all the weapons, powder and other stores that we were able to bring with us,' Hal said briskly.

'There weren't much of anything, Captain. Once we left the horses we had just about enough strength left to get ourselves up the mountains.'

'Powder?' Hal demanded.

'Only what we had in our flasks.'

'When you went on ahead, you had two full kegs on the horses.'

'Those kegs weighed fifty pounds apiece.' Daniel looked ashamed. 'Too much cargo for us to haul.'

'I have seen you carry twice that weight.' Hal was angry and disappointed. Without a store of powder they were at the mercy of this wild terrain, and the beasts and tribes that infested it.

'Daniel carried my saddle-bags up Dark Gorge.' Sukeena intervened softly. 'No one else could do it.'

'I'm sorry, Captain,' Daniel muttered.

But Sukeena supported him fiercely. 'There is not a thing in my bags that we could do without. That includes the medicines that saved your leg and will save every one of us from the hurts and pestilences that we will meet here in the wilderness.'

'Thank you, Princess,' Daniel murmured, and looked at her like an affectionate hound. If he had possessed a tail Hal knew he would have wagged it.

Hal smiled and clapped Daniel's shoulder. 'I find no fault with what you did, Big Danny. There is no man alive who could have done better.'

They all relaxed and smiled. Then Ned asked, 'Were you serious when you promised us a ship, Captain?'

Sukeena stood up from the fire. 'That's enough for tonight. He must regain his strength before you plague him further. You must go now. You may come again tomorrow.'

One at a time they came to Hal, shook his hand and mumbled something incoherent, then wandered off through the darkness towards the other huts spread out along the valley floor. When the last had gone Sukeena threw another cedar log on the fire then came and sat close beside him. In a natural, possessive manner, Hal placed his arm around her shoulders. She leaned her slim body against him and fitted her head into the notch of his shoulder. She sighed, a sweet, contented sound, and neither spoke for a while.

'I want to stay here at your side like this for ever, but the stars may not allow it,' she whispered. 'The season of our love may be short as a winter day.'

'Don't say that,' Hal commanded. 'Never say that.'

They both looked up at the stars, and here, in the high thin air, they were so brilliant that they lit the heavens with the luminescence of the mother-of-pearl that lines the inside of an abalone shell taken fresh from the sea. Hal looked upon them with awe and considered what she had said. He felt a sense of hopelessness and sadness come upon him. He shivered.

Immediately she sat up straight and said softly, 'You grow cold. Come, Gundwane!'

She helped him to his feet and led him into the hut, to the mattress against the far wall. She laid him upon it and then lit the wick of the small clay oil lamp and placed it on a shelf in the rock wall. She went to the fire and lifted off the clay pot of water that stood on the edge of the coals. She poured steaming water into an empty dish and mixed in cold water from the pot beside the door until the temperature suited her.

Her movements were unhurried and calm. Propped on one elbow, Hal watched her. She placed the dish of warm water in the centre of the floor then poured a few drops from a glass vial into it and stirred it again with her hand. He smelt its light, subtle perfume on the waft of steam.

She rose, went to the doorway and closed the animal-skin curtain over the opening, then came back and stood beside the dish of scented water. She removed the wild flowers from her hair and tossed them onto the fur blanket at Hal's feet. Without looking at him, she let down the coils of her hair and combed them out until they shimmered like a wave of obsidian. She began to sing in her own language as she combed, a lullaby or a love song, Hal could not be certain. Her voice was mellifluous; it soothed and delighted him.

She laid aside her comb, and let the shift slip from her shoulders. Her skin gleamed in the yellow lamplight and her breasts were pert as small golden pears. When she turned her back to him Hal felt deprived that they were hidden from his sight. Her song changed now – it had a lilt of joy and excitement in it.

'What is it you sing?' Hal asked.

Sukeena smiled at him over her bare shoulder. 'It is the wedding song of my mother's people,' she answered. 'The bride is saying that she is happy and that she loves her husband with the eternal strength of the ocean, and the patience of the shining stars.'

'I have never heard anything so pleasing,' Hal whispered.

With slow voluptuous movements, she unwrapped the sarong from around her waist and threw it aside. Her buttocks were small and neat, the deep cleft dividing them into perfect ovals. She squatted down beside the dish to soak a small cloth in the scented water and began to bathe herself. She started at her shoulders and washed each arm down to her long tapered fingertips. There were silky clusters of black curls in her armpits.

Hal realized that it was a ritual bath she was performing, part of some ceremony she was enacting before him. He watched avidly each move she made, and every now and then she looked up and smiled at him shyly. The soft hairs behind her ears were damp from the cloth, and water droplets gleamed on her cheeks and upper lip.

She stood at last and turned slowly to face him. Once he had thought her body boyish, but now he saw that it was so feminine that his heart swelled hard with desire for her. Her belly was flat but smooth as butter, and at its base was a triangle of dark fur, soft as a sleeping kitten.

She stepped away from the dish and dried herself on the cotton shift she had discarded. Then she went to the oil lamp, cupped one hand around the wick and leaned towards it as if to snuff out the flame.

'No!' said Hal. 'Leave the light. I want to look at you.'

At last she came to him, gliding across the stone floor on small bare feet, crept onto the bed beside him, into his arms, and folded her body against his. She held her lips to his mouth. Hers were soft and wet and warm, and her breath mingled with his, and smelled of the wild flowers she had worn in her hair.

'I have waited all my life for you,' she whispered into his mouth.

He whispered back, 'It was too long to wait, but I am here at last.'

In the morning she proudly displayed the treasures she had brought for him in her saddle-bags. She had somehow procured everything he had asked for in the notes he had left for Aboli in the wall of the castle.

He snatched up the charts. 'Where did you get these from, Sukeena?' he demanded, and she was delighted to see how much value he placed upon them.

'I have many friends in the colony,' she explained. 'Even some of the whores from the taverns came to me to treat their ailments. Dr Saar kills more of his patients than he saves. Some of the tavern ladies go aboard the ships in the bay to do their business, and come back with divers things, not all of them gifts from the seamen.' She laughed merrily. 'If something is not bolted to the deck of the galleon they think it belongs to them. When I asked for charts these are what they brought me. Are they what you wanted, Gundwane?'

'These are more than I ever hoped for, Sukeena. This one is valuable and so is this.' The charts were obviously some navigator's treasures, highly detailed and covered with notations and observations in a well-formed, educated hand. They showed the coasts of southern Africa in wondrous detail, and from his own knowledge he could see how accurate they were. To his amazement the location of Elephant Lagoon was marked on one, the first time he had ever seen it shown on any chart other than his father's. The position was accurate to within a few minutes of angle, and in the margin there was a sketch of the landfall and seaward elevation of the heads, which he recognized instantly as having been drawn from observation.

Although the coast and the immediate littoral were accurately recorded, the interior, as usual, had been left blank or filled with conjecture, apocryphal lakes and mountains that no eye had ever beheld. The outline of the mountains in which they were now sequestered was sketched in, as though the cartographer had observed them from the colony of Good Hope or from sailing into False Bay and had guessed their shape and extent. Somewhere, somehow, Sukeena had found him a Dutch mariners' almanac to go with the charts. It had been published in Amsterdam and listed the movements of the heavenly bodies until the end of the decade.

Hal laid aside these precious documents and took up the backstaff Sukeena had found. It was a collapsible model whose separate parts fitted into a small leather case, the interior of which was lined with blue velvet. The instrument itself was of extraordinarily fine workmanship: the bronze quadrant, decorated with embodiments of the four winds, needles and screws were all engraved and worked in pleasing artistic shapes and classical figures. A tiny bronze plaque inside the lid of the case was engraved 'Cellini. Venezia'.

The compass she had brought was contained in a sturdy leather case; the body was brass and the magnetic needle was tipped with gold and ivory, so finely balanced that it swung unerringly into the north as he rotated the case slowly in his hand.

'These are worth twenty pounds at least!' Hal marvelled. 'You're a magician to have conjured them up.' He took her hand and led her outside, not limping as awkwardly as he had on the previous day. Seated side by side on the mountain slope he showed her how to observe the noon passage of the sun and to mark their position on one of the charts. She delighted in the pleasure she had given him, and impressed him with her immediate grasp of the esoteric arts of navigation. Then he remembered that she was an astrologer, and that she understood the heavens.

With these instruments in his hands, he could move with authority through this savage wilderness, and his dream of finding a ship began to seem less forlorn than it had only a day before. He drew her to his chest, kissed her, and she merged herself tenderly to him. 'That kiss is better reward than the twenty pounds of which you spoke, my captain.'

'If one kiss is worth twenty pounds, then I have aught for you that must be worth five hundred,' he said, laid her back in the grass and made love to her. A long time later she smiled up at him and whispered, 'That was worth all the gold in this world.'

When they returned to the encampment they found that Daniel had assembled all the weapons, and that Aboli was polishing the sword blades and sharpening the edges with a fine-grained stone he had picked from the stream bed.

Hal went carefully over the collection. There were cutlasses enough to arm every man, and pistols too. However, there were only five muskets, all standard Dutch military models, heavy and robust. Their lack was in powder, slow-match and lead ball. They could always use pebbles as missiles, but there was no substitute for blackpowder. They had less than five pounds weight of this precious substance in the flasks, not enough for twenty discharges.

'Without powder, we can no longer kill the larger game,' Sabah told Hal. 'We eat partridges and dassies.' He used the diminutive of the Dutch name for badger, *dasc*, to describe the fluffy, rabbity creatures that swarmed in the caves and crevices of every cliff. Hal thought he recognized them as the coneys of the Bible.

The urine from the dassie colonies poured down the cliff face so copiously that as it dried it covered the rock with a thick coating that shone in the sunlight like toffee but smelt less sweet. With care and skill, these rock-rabbits could be killed and trapped in such numbers as to provide the little band with a staple of survival. Their flesh was succulent and delicious as suckling pig.

Now that Sukeena was with them their diet was much expanded by her knowledge of edible roots and plants. Each day Hal went out with her to carry her basket as she foraged along the slopes. As his leg grew stronger they ventured further and stayed out in the wilderness a little longer each day.

The mountains seemed to enfold them in their grandeur and to provide the perfect setting for the bright jewel of their love. When Sukeena's foraging basket was filled to overflowing, they found hidden pools in the numerous streams in which to bathe naked together. Afterwards they lay side by side on the smooth, water-polished rocks and dried themselves in the sun. With tantalizing slowness they toyed with each other's bodies and at last made love. Then they talked and explored each other's minds as intimately as they had explored their bodies, and afterwards made love yet again. Their appetites for each other seemed insatiable.

'Oh! Where did you learn to please a girl so?' Sukeena asked breathlessly. 'Who taught you all these special things that you do to me?'

It was not a question he cared to answer, and he said, ''Tis simply that we fit together so perfectly. My special places were made to touch your special places. I seek pleasure in your pleasure. My pleasure is increased a hundredfold by yours.'

In the evenings when all the fugitives gathered around the cooking fire, they pressed Hal with questions about his plans for them, but he avoided these with an easy laugh or a shake of his head. A plan of action was indeed germinating in his mind but it was not yet ready to be disclosed, for there were still many obstacles he had to circumvent. Instead he questioned Sabah and the five escaped slaves, who with him had survived the mountain winter.

'How far to the east have you travelled across the range, Sabah?'

'In midwinter we travelled six days in that direction. We were trying to find food and a place where the cold was not so fierce.'

'What land lies to the east?'

'It is mountains such as these for many leagues, and then suddenly they fall away into plains of forest and rolling grassland, with glimpses of the sea on the right hand.' Sabah took up a twig and began to draw in the dust beside the fire. Hal memorized his descriptions, questioning him assiduously, urging him to recall every detail of what he had seen.

'Did you descend into these plains?'

'We went down a little way. We found strange creatures never before seen by the eyes of man – grey and enormous with long horns set upon their noses. One rushed upon us with terrible snorts and whistles. Though we fired our muskets at it, it came on and impaled the wife of Johannes upon its nose horn and killed her.'

They all looked at little one-eyed Johannes, one of Sabah's band of escaped slaves, who wept at the memory of his dead woman. It was strange to see tears squeezing out of his empty eye socket. They were all silent for a while, then Zwaantie took up the story. 'My little Bobby was only a month old, and I could not place him in such danger. Without powder for the muskets we could not go on. I prevailed on Sabah to turn back, and we returned to this place.'

'Why do you ask these questions? What is your plan, Captain?' Big Daniel wanted to know, but Hal shook his head.

'I'm not ready to explain it to you, but don't lose heart, lads. I have promised to find you a ship, have I not?' he said, with more confidence than he felt. In the morning, on the pretence of fishing, he led Aboli and Big Daniel up the stream to the next pool. When they were out of sight of the camp, they sat close together on the rocky bank.

'It is clear that unless we can better arm ourselves, we are trapped in these mountains. We will perish as slowly and despondently as most of Sabah's men already have. We must have powder for the muskets.'

'Where will we get that?' Daniel asked. 'What do you propose?'

'I have been thinking about the colony,' Hal told them.

Both men stared at him in disbelief. Aboli broke the silence. 'You plan to go back to Good Hope? Even there you will not be able to lay your hands on powder. Oh, perhaps you might steal a pound or two from the green-jackets at the bridge, or from a Company hunter, but that is not enough to see us on our journey.'

'I planned to break into the castle again,' Hal said.

Both men laughed bitterly. 'You lack not in enterprise or in heart, Captain,' Big Daniel said, 'but that is madness.'

Aboli agreed with him, and said, in his deep, thoughtful voice, 'If I thought there were even the poorest chance of success, I would gladly go alone. But think on it, Gundwane, I do not mean merely the impossibility of winning our way into the castle armoury. Say, even, that we succeeded in that, and that the store of powder we destroyed has since been replenished by shipments from Holland. Say that we were able to escape with some of it. How would we carry even a single keg back across the plains with Schreuder and his men pursuing us? This time we would not have the horses.'

In his heart Hal had known that it was madness, but he had hoped that even such a desperate and forlorn proposal might fire them to think of another plan.

At last, Aboli broke the silence. 'You spoke of a plan to find a ship. If you tell us that plan, Gundwane, then perhaps we can help you to bring it to pass.' Both men looked at him expectantly.

'Where do you suppose the Buzzard is at this very moment?' Hal asked.

Aboli and Big Daniel looked startled. 'If my prayers have prevailed he is roasting in hell,' Daniel replied bitterly.

Hal looked at Aboli. 'What do you think, Aboli? Where would you look for the Buzzard?'

'Somewhere out on the seven seas. Wherever he smells gold or the promise of easy pickings, like the carrion bird for which he is named.'

'Yes!' Hal clapped him on the shoulder. 'But where might the smell of gold be strongest? Why did the Buzzard buy Jiri and our other black shipmates at auction?'

Aboli stared blankly at him. Then a slow smile spread over his wide, dark face. 'Elephant Lagoon!' he exclaimed.

Big Daniel boomed with excited laughter. 'He scented the treasure from the Dutch galleons and he thought our Negro lads could lead him to it.'

'How far are we from Elephant Lagoon?' Aboli asked.

'By my reckoning, three hundred sea miles.' The immensity of the distance silenced them.

'It's a long tack,' said Daniel, 'without powder to defend ourselves on the way or with which to fight the Buzzard if we get there.'

Aboli did not reply, but looked at Hal. 'How long will the journey take us, Gundwane?'

'If we can make good ten miles a day, which I doubt, perhaps a little over a month.'

'Will the Buzzard still be there when we arrive, or will he have given up his search and sailed away?' Aboli thought aloud.

'Aye!' Daniel muttered. 'And if he has gone what will become of us then? We'd be marooned there for ever.'

'Do you prefer to be marooned here, Master Daniel? Do you want to die of cold and starvation on this God-forsaken mountain when winter comes round again?'

They were quiet again. Then Aboli said, 'I am ready to leave now. There is no other path open to us.'

'But what of Sir Henry's leg? Is it strong enough yet?'

'Give me another week, lads, and I'll walk the hind legs off all of you.'

'What do we do if we find the Buzzard still roosting at Elephant Lagoon?' Daniel was not ready to agree so easily. 'He has a crew of a hundred well-armed ruffians and, if all of us survive the journey, we will be a dozen armed with swords alone.'

'That's fine odds!' Hal laughed at him. 'I've seen you take on much worse. Powder or no powder, we're off to find the Buzzard. Are you with us or not, Master Daniel?'

'Of course, I'm with you, Captain.' Big Daniel was affronted. 'What made you think I was not?'

That night, around the council fire, Hal explained the plan to the others. When he had finished he looked at their sombre faces in the firelight. 'I will prevail on no man to come with us. Aboli, Daniel and I are determined to go, but if any amongst you wishes to remain here in the mountains we will leave half the store of weapons with you, including half the remaining gunpowder, and we will think no ill of you. Are there any of you who wish to speak?'

'Yes,' said Sukeena, without looking up from the food she was cooking. 'I go wherever you go.'

'Bravely spoken, Princess,' grinned Ned Tyler. 'And I go also.'

'Aye!' said the other seamen in unison. 'We are all with you.'

Hal nodded his thanks to them, and then looked at Althuda. 'You have a woman and your son to think of, Althuda. What say you?'

He could see the distress on the face of little Zwaantie as she suckled the baby at her breast. Her dark eyes were filled with doubts and misgivings. Althuda lifted her to her feet and led her away into the darkness.

When they were gone Sabah spoke for all his band. 'Althuda is our leader. He brought us out of captivity, and we cannot leave him and Zwaantie alone in the wilderness to perish with the baby of cold and hunger. If Althuda goes we go, but if he stays we must stay with him.'

'I admire your resolve and your loyalty, Sabah,' said Hal.

They waited in silence, hearing Zwaantie weeping with fear and indecision in the darkness. Then, after a long while, Althuda led her back to the fire, his arm around her shoulders, and they took their places in the circle.

'Zwaantie fears not for herself but for the baby,' he said. 'But she knows that our best chance will be with you, Sir Hal. We will come with you.'

'I would have mourned if your decision had been different, Althuda.' Hal smiled with genuine pleasure. 'Together our chances are much increased. Now we must make our preparations and agree on the time when we will set out.'

Sukeena came from the fire to sit beside Hal, and spoke out firmly: 'Your leg will not be healed for at least another five days. I will not allow you to march upon it before then.'

'When the Princess speaks,' Aboli declared, in his deep voice, 'only a foolish man does not listen.'

During those last days Hal and Sukeena foraged for the herbs and plants that she would use for medicine and food. The last of the infection in Hal's wounds yielded to her treatment, while climbing and descending the steep and rugged slopes of the mountains rapidly strengthened his injured limb.

On the day before the journey was due to commence, the two stopped at midday to bathe and rest and make love in the soft grass beside the stream. This was a branch of the river that they had not visited on their previous forays, and while Hal lay surfeited with passion in the warm sunlight, Sukeena stood up naked and moved away up the ravine a short distance to ease herself.

Hal watched her squat behind a patch of low bush, lay back and closed his eyes, drifting lazily to the edge of sleep. He was roused by the familiar sound of Sukeena's sharp pointed digging stick pounding into the earth. A few minutes later she returned, still naked, but with a crumbling lump of yellow earth in her hand.

'Flower crystals! The first I have found in these mountains.' She looked delighted with her discovery, and emptied some of the less valuable herbs from her basket to make place for the lumps of friable earth. 'Part of these mountains must once have been volcanoes for the flower crystals are spewed up from the earth in the lava.'

Hal watched her work, more interested in the way her naked body gleamed in the sunlight, like molten gold, and the way her small breasts changed shape as she wielded the stick vigorously, than in the crystalline lumps of yellow earth she was prising from the bank of the ravine.

'What do you use this earth for?' he asked, without rising from his grassy nest.

'It has many uses. It is a sovereign cure for headaches and colic. If I mix it with the juice of the verbena berry it will soothe palpitations of the heart and ease a woman's monthly courses . . .' She reeled off a list of the ailments that she could treat with it, but to Hal it did not seem to have any special virtue, and looked like any other clod of dry earth. The basket was so heavy by now that, on their return to camp, Hal had to take it from her.

That night while the band sat around the fire and held their final council before beginning the long journey east, Sukeena pounded the clods of earth in the crude stone mortar she had made and mixed the powder into a pot of water. She heated this over the fire, then came to sit beside Hal as he went over the order of march for the following day. He was allocating weapons and loads to the men. The weight and bulk of each load would be dictated by the age and strength of the man carrying it.

Suddenly Hal broke off and sniffed the air. 'Sweet heaven and all the apostles!' he cried. 'What have you in this pot, Sukeena?'

'I told you, Gundwane. 'Tis the yellow flowers.' She looked alarmed as he rushed back to her, picked her up in his arms, tossed her high in the air and caught her as she came down, skirts fluttering around her.

''Tis not any type of flower at all! I would know that smell in hell itself where it truly belongs!' He kissed her until she pushed his face away.

'Are you mad?' She laughed and gasped for breath.

'Mad with love for you!' he said, and turned her to face the men who had watched this display in amazement. 'Lads, the Princess has created the miracle which will save us all!'

'You speak in riddles!' said Aboli.

'Yes!' the others cried. 'Speak plain, Captain.'

'I'll speak plain enough so even the slowest-witted of you sea-rats will understand my words.' Hal laughed at their confusion. 'Her pot is filled with brimstone! Magical yellow brimstone!'

It was Ned Tyler who understood first, for he was the master gunner.

He also leaped to his feet, rushed to kneel over the pot and inhaled the fumes as though they were the smoke of an opium pipe.

'The captain's right, lads,' he howled with glee. 'It's brimstone sulphur, sure enough.'

Sukeena led a party, headed by Aboli and Big Daniel, back to the ravine in which she had discovered the sulphur deposit, and they returned to camp staggering under their loads of the yellow earth, packed into baskets or sewn into sacks made of animal skins.

While Sukeena supervised the boiling and leaching of the sulphur crystals from the ore, one-eyed Johannes and Zwaantie tended the slow fires, banked with earth, in which the baulks of cedarwood were being gradually reduced to pure black nuggets of charcoal.

Hal and Sabah's band climbed the steep mountainside above the camp to reach the cliffs in which the multitudes of rock rabbits had their colonies. Sabah's men clung to the precipice like flies to the wall as they scraped away the amber coloured crystals of dried urine. The little animals defecated in communal middens, and while the round pellets of dung rolled away, the urine dribbled down and soaked the rock face. They discovered that, in some places, this coating was several feet thick.

They lowered skin sacks of these odoriferous deposits to the foot of the cliff, then lugged them down to the camp. They worked in shifts to keep the fires burning all day and night under the clay pots, extracting the sulphur from the powdered earth and the saltpetre from the animal excreta.

Ned Tyler and Hal, the two gunners, hovered over these steaming pots like a pair of alchemists, straining the liquid and reducing it with heat. Finally they dried the thick residual pastes in the sun. From the first brewing of the stinking compounds they were left with a store of dried crystalline powders that filled three large pots.

When crushed the charcoal was a smooth black powder, while the saltpetre was pale brown and fine as sea salt. When Hal placed a small pinch of it on his tongue it was indeed as pungent and salty as the sea. The flowers of sulphur were daffodil yellow and almost odourless.

The entire band of fugitives gathered round to watch when, at last, Hal started to mix the three constituents in Sukeena's stone mortar. He measured the proportions and first ground together the charcoal and the sulphur, for without the final vital ingredient these were inert and harmless. Then he added the saltpetre and gingerly combined it with the dark grey primary powder until he had a flask filled with what looked and smelt like veritable gunpowder.

Aboli handed him one of the muskets and he measured a charge, dribbled it down the barrel, stuffed a wad of fibrous dried bark on top of it and rodded home a round pebble he had selected from the sandbank of the stream. He would not waste a lead ball in this experiment.

Meanwhile, Big Daniel had set up a wooden target on the opposite bank. While Hal squatted and took his aim the rest spread out on either side of him and plugged their ears with their fingers. An expectant silence fell as he took aim and pressed the trigger.

There was a thunderous report and a blinding cloud of smoke. The wooden target shattered and toppled down the bank into the water. An exultant cheer went up from everyone, and they pounded each other upon the back and danced delirious jigs of triumph in the sunlight.

'It's as fine a grade of powder as any you can find in the naval stores in Greenwich,' Ned Tyler opined, 'but it will have to be properly caked afore we can bag it and carry it away.'

To this end Hal ordered a large clay pot to be placed behind a grass screen at the edge of the camp, and all were strictly enjoined to make use of it on every possible occasion. Even the two women went behind the screen to make their demure contributions. Once the pot was filled, the gunpowder was moistened into paste with the urine, then formed into briquettes, which dried hard in the sun. These were packed into reed baskets for ease of transporting.

'We will grind the cakes as we need them,' Hal explained to Sukeena. 'Now we do not have to carry such a weight of dried fish and meat for we will hunt as we travel. If there is such an abundance of game, as Sabah tells us there is, we will not go short of fresh meat.'

Ten days later than they had first intended, the band was ready to set out into the east. Hal, as the navigator, and Sabah, who had travelled that route before, led the column; Althuda and the three musketeers were in the centre to guard the women and little Bobby, while Aboli and Big Daniel brought up the rear under their ponderous burdens.

They travelled with the grain and run of the range, not attempting to scale the high ground but following the valleys and crossing only through the passes between the high peaks. Hal estimated the distances travelled by eye and time, and the direction with the leather-cased compass. These he marked on his charts every evening before the light faded.

At night they camped in the open, for the weather was mild and they were too tired to build a shelter. When they woke each dawn, their skin blankets, that Sabah called karosses, were soaked with dew.

As Sabah had warned, it was six days of hard travel through the labyrinth of valleys before they reached the steep eastern escarpment and looked down from its crest on the lower ground.

Far out to their right they could make out the blue stain of the ocean merging with the paler heron's-egg blue of the sky, but below the land was not the true plains that Hal had expected but was broken up with hillocks, undulating grassy glades and streaks of dark green forest that seemed to follow the courses of the many small rivers that criss-crossed the littoral as they meandered down to the sea.

To their left, another range of jagged blue mountains marched parallel to the sea, forming a rampart that guarded the mysterious hinterland of the continent. Hal's sharp eyesight picked out the dark stains on the golden grassy plains, moving like cloud shadows when there were no clouds in the sky. He saw the haze of dust that followed the moving herds of wild game, and now and then he spotted the reflection of sunlight from tusks of ivory or from a polished horn.

'This land swarms with life,' he murmured to Sukeena, who stood at his shoulder. 'There may be strange beasts down there that man has never before laid eyes upon. Perhaps even fire-breathing dragons and unicorns and griffons.' Sukeena shivered and hugged her shoulders, even though the sun was high and warm.

'I saw such creatures drawn on the charts I brought for you,' she agreed.

There was a path before them, beaten by the great round pads of elephant and signposted by piles of their fibrous yellow dung, that wound down the slope, picking the most favourable gradient, skirting the deep ravines and dangerous gorges, and Hal followed it.

As they descended, the features of the landscape below became more apparent. Hal could even recognize some of the creatures that moved upon it. The black mass of bovine animals surmounted by a golden haze of dust and a cloud of hovering tick birds, sparkling white in the sunlight, must be the wild buffalo that Aboli had spoken of. *Nyati*, he had called them, when he had warned Hal of their ferocity. There must be several hundred of these beasts in each of the three separate herds that he had under his eye.

Beyond the nearest herd of buffalo was a small gathering of elephants. Hal remembered them well from his previous sightings long ago on the shores of the lagoon. But he had never before seen them in such numbers. At the very least there were twenty great grey cows each with a small calf, like a piglet, at her heels. Dotted upon the plain like hillocks of grey granite were three or four solitary bulls: he could barely credit the size of these patriarchs or the length and girth of their gleaming yellow ivory tusks.

There were other creatures, not as large as the elephant bulls, but massive and grey none the less, which at first he took for elephant also, but as they descended towards the low ground he was able to make out the black horns, some as long as a man is tall, that decorated their great creased grey snouts. He remembered then what Sabah had told him of these savage beasts, one of which had speared and killed Johannes' woman with its deadly horn. These 'rhenosters', which was Sabah's name for them, seemed solitary in nature for they stood apart from others of the same kind, each in the shade of its own tree.

As Hal strode along at the head of the tiny column, he heard the light tread of feet coming up behind him, footsteps that he had come to know and love so well. Sukeena had left her place at in the centre of the line, as she often did when she found some excuse to walk with him for a while.

She slipped her hand into his and kept pace with him. 'I did not want to go alone into this new land. I wanted to walk beside you,' she said softly, then looked up at the sky. 'See the way the wind veers into the south and the clouds crouch on the mountain tops like a pack of wild beasts in ambush? There is a storm coming.'

Her warning proved timely. Hal was able to lead them to a cave in the mountainside to shelter before the storm struck. They lay up there for three long days and nights while the storm raged without, but when they emerged at last, the land was washed clean and the sky was bright and burning blue.

Before the *Golden Bough* had made her offing from Good Hope and come onto her true course to round the Cape, Captain Christopher Llewellyn was already regretting having taken on board his paying passenger.

He had found out soon enough that Colonel Cornelius Schreuder was a difficult man to like, arrogant, outspoken and highly opinionated. He held firm and unwavering views on every subject that was raised, and was never diffident in giving expression to these. 'He picks up enemies as a dog picks up fleas,' Llewellyn told his mate.

The second day out from Table Bay, Llewellyn had invited Schreuder to dine with him and some of his officers in the stern cabin. He was a cultured man, and maintained a grand style even at sea. With the prize money that he had won in the recent Dutch war, he could afford to indulge his taste for fine things.

The *Golden Bough* had cost almost two thousand pounds to build and launch, but she was probably the finest vessel of her class and burden afloat. Her culverins were newly cast and her sails were of the finest canvas. The captain's quarters were fitted out with a taste and discrimination unparalleled in any navy, but her qualities as a fighting ship had not been sacrificed for luxury.

During the voyage down the Atlantic, Llewellyn had found, to his delight, that her sea-keeping qualities were all he had hoped. On a broad reach, with her sails full and the wind free, her hull sliced through the water like a blade, and she could point so high into the wind that it made his heart sing to feel her deck heel under his feet.

Most of his officers and petty-officers had served with him during the war and had proved their quality and courage, but he had on board one younger officer, the fourth son of George, Viscount Winterton.

Lord Winterton was the Master Navigator of the Order, one of the richest and most powerful men in England. He owned a fleet of privateers and trading ships. The Honourable Vincent Winterton was on his first privateering voyage, placed by his father under Llewellyn's tutelage. He was a comely youth, not yet twenty years of age but well educated, with a frank and winning manner that made him popular with both the seamen and his brother officers alike. He was one of the other guests at Llewellyn's dinner table that second night out from Good Hope.

The dinner started out gay and lively, for all the Englishmen were merry, with a fine ship under them and the promise of glory and gold ahead. Schreuder, however, was aloof and gloomy. With the second glass of wine warming them all, Llewellyn called across the cabin, 'Vincent, my lad, will you not give us a tune?'

'Could you bear to listen, yet again, to my caterwauling, sir?' The young man laughed modestly, but the rest of the company urged him on. 'Come on, Vinny! Sing for us, man!'

Vincent Winterton stood up and went to the small clavichord that was fastened with heavy brass screws to one of the main frames of the ship. He sat down, tossed back his long thick curling locks and struck a soft, silvery chord from the keyboard. 'What would you have me sing?'

'"Greensleeves"!' suggested someone, but Vincent pulled a face. 'You've heard that a hundred times and more since we sailed from home.'

'"Mother Mine"!' cried another. This time Vincent nodded, threw back his head and sang in a strong, true voice that transformed the mawkish lyrics and brought tears to the eyes of many of the company as they tapped their feet in time to the song.

Schreuder had taken an immediate and unreasoned dislike to the attractive youth, so comely and popular with his peers, so sure of himself and serene in his high rank and privileged birth. Schreuder, in comparison, felt himself ageing and overlooked. He had never attracted the natural admiration and affection of those about him, as this young man so obviously did.

He sat stiffly in a corner, ignored by these men who, not so long ago, had been his deadly enemies, and who, he knew, despised him as a dull foreigner and a foot soldier, not one of their élite brotherhood of the ocean. He found his dislike turning to active hatred of the young man, whose fine features were clear and unlined and whose voice had the timbre and tonal colour of a temple bell.

When the song ended, there was a moment of silence, attentive and awed. Then they all burst out clapping and applauding. 'Oh, well done, lad!' and 'Bravo, Vinny!' Schreuder felt his irritation become unbearable.

The applause went on too long for the liking of the singer, and Vincent rose from the clavichord with a deprecating wave of the hand that begged them to desist.

In the silence that followed, Schreuder said, softly but distinctly, 'Caterwauling? No, sir, that was an insult to the feline species.'

There was a shocked silence in the small cabin. The young man flushed and his hand dropped instinctively to the hilt of the short-bladed dirk that he wore at his jewelled belt, but Llewellyn said sharply, 'Vincent!' and shook his head. Reluctantly he dropped his hand from the weapon and forced himself to smile and bow slightly. 'You have a perceptive ear, sir. I commend your discerning taste.'

He resumed his seat at the board and turned away from Schreuder to engage his neighbour in light-hearted repartee. The awkward moment passed, and the other guests relaxed, smiled and joined in the conversation, which pointedly excluded the Colonel.

Llewellyn's cook had come with him from home, and the ship had been provisioned at Good Hope with fresh meat and vegetables. The meal was as good as any that might be served in the coffee shops and ale-houses of Fleet Street, the conversation as pleasing and the banter nimble and amusing, larded with clever puns, double meanings and fashionable slang. Most of this was above Schreuder's grasp of the language and his resentment built up like the brewing of a tropical typhoon.

He made one contribution to the conversation, a stinging reference to the Dutch victory in the Thames River and the capture of the *Royal Charles*, the pride of the English navy and the namesake of their beloved sovereign. The conversation froze into silence once more, and the company fixed him with chilly scrutiny, before continuing their conversation as though he had not spoken.

Schreuder consoled himself with the claret, and when the bottle in front of him was exhausted, he reached down the table for a flagon of brandy. His head for liquor was as adamantine as his pride, but today it seemed only to make him more truculent and angry. By the end of the meal he was spoiling for trouble, and prospecting for some way in which to ease the terrible sense of rejection and hopelessness that overpowered him.

At last Llewellyn stood up to propose the loyal toast. 'Here's health and a long life to the Black Boy!' Everyone rose enthusiastically to their feet, stooping under the low deck timbers overhead, but Schreuder stayed seated.

Llewellyn knocked on the table. 'If you please, Colonel, come to your feet. We are drinking the health of the King of England.'

'I am no longer thirsty, thank you, Captain.' Schreuder folded his arms.

The men growled, and one said loudly, 'Let me at him, Captain.'

'Colonel Schreuder is a guest aboard this ship,' Llewellyn said ominously, 'and none of you will offer him any discourtesy, no matter if he behaves like a pig himself and transgresses all the conventions of decent society.' Then he turned back to Schreuder. 'Colonel, I am asking you for the last time to join the loyal toast. If you do not, we are still within easy range of Good Hope. I will give the orders immediately for this ship to go about and sail back to Table Bay. There I will return your fare money to you, and have you deposited on the beach like a bucketful of kitchen slops.'

Schreuder sobered instantly. This was a threat he had not anticipated. He had hoped to provoke one of these English oafs into a duel. He would then have given them a display of swordsmanship that would have opened their cold-fish eyes and wiped those superior smirks from their faces, but the thought of being taken back to the scene of his crime and delivered into the vengeful hands of Governor van de Velde made his lips go numb and his fingers tingle with dread. He rose slowly to his feet with his glass in his hand. Llewellyn relaxed slightly, they all drank the toast and sat down again in a hubbub of laughter and talk.

'Does anybody fancy a few throws of the dice?' Vincent Winterton suggested, and there was general agreement.

'But not if you wish to play for shilling stakes again,' one of the older officers demurred. 'Last time I lost almost twenty pounds, all the prize money I won when we captured the *Buurman*.'

'Farthing stakes and a shilling limit,' another suggested, and they nodded and felt for their purses.

'Mr Winterton, sir,' Schreuder broke in, 'I will oblige you with whatever stakes your stomach will hold and not puke up again.' He was pale and sweat sheened his forehead, but that was the only visible effect the liquor had upon him.

Once again a silence fell on the table as Schreuder groped under his tunic and brought out a pigskin purse. He dropped it nonchalantly on the table and it clinked with the unmistakable music of gold. Every man at the table stiffened.

'We play in sport and in good fellowship here,' Llewellyn growled.

But Vincent Winterton said lightly, 'How much is in that purse, Colonel?'

Schreuder loosened the drawstring and, with a flourish, poured the coins into a heavy heap in the centre of the table where they sparkled in the lamplight. Triumphantly he looked around the circle of their faces.

They will not take me so lightly now! he thought, but aloud he said, 'Twenty thousand Dutch guilders. That is over two hundred of your English pounds.' It was his entire fortune, but there was a reckless, self-destructive pounding in his heart. He found himself driven on to folly as though he might wipe away the guilt of his terrible murder with gold.

The company was silenced by the size of his purse. It was an enormous sum, more than most of these officers might expect to accumulate in a lifetime of dangerous endeavour.

Vincent Winterton smiled graciously. 'I see you are indeed a sportsman, sir.'

'Ah! So!' Schreuder smiled coldly. 'The stakes are too high, are they?' And he swept the golden coins back into his purse and made as if to rise from the table.

'Hold hard, Colonel.' Vincent stopped him, and Schreuder sank back into his seat. 'I came unprepared, but if you will afford me a few minutes of your time?' He rose, bowed and left the cabin. They all sat in silence until he returned and placed a small teak chest in front of him on the table.

'Three hundred, was it?' He began to count out the coins from the chest. They made a splendid profusion in the centre of the table.

'Will you be kind enough to hold the stakes, Captain?' Vincent asked politely. 'That is, if the colonel agrees?'

'I have no objection.' Schreuder nodded stiffly and passed his purse to Llewellyn. Inwardly the first regrets were assailing him. He had not expected any of them to take up his challenge. A loss of such magnitude must beggar most men, as indeed it would beggar him.

Llewellyn received both purses, and placed them before him. Then Vincent took up the leather dice cup and passed it across to Schreuder.

'We usually play with these, sir,' Vincent said easily. 'Would you care to examine them? If they are not to your liking, perhaps we may be able to find others that suit you better.'

Schreuder shook the dice out of the cup and rolled them across the table. Then he picked up each ivory cube and held it to the lamplight. 'I can see no blemish,' he said, and replaced them in the cup. 'It remains only to agree on the game. Will it be Hazard?'

'English Hazard,' Vincent agreed. 'What else?'

'What limit on each coup?' Schreuder wanted to know. 'Will it be a pound or five?'

'A single coup only,' said Vincent. 'The shooter to be decided by high dice, and then two hundred pounds on his Hazard.'

Schreuder was stunned by the proposal. He had expected to make his wagers in small increments, which would allow him the possibility of withdrawing with some semblance of grace if the run of the dice turned against him. He had never heard of such an immense sum staked on a single throw of the dice.

One of Vincent's friends chortled delightedly. 'By God's truth, Vinny! That will show up the colour of the cheese-head's liver.'

Schreuder glared at him, but he knew he was trapped. For a moment longer he sought some escape, but Vincent murmured, 'I do hope I have not embarrassed you, Colonel. I mistook you for a sport. Would you rather call off the whole affair?'

'I assure you,' he said coldly, 'that it suits me very well. One hazard for two hundred pounds. I agree.'

Llewellyn placed one of the dice in the cup and passed it to Schreuder. 'One die to decide the shooter. High shoots. Is that your agreement, gentlemen?' Both men nodded.

Schreuder rolled the single die, 'Three!' said Llewellyn, and replaced it in the leather cup.

'Your throw, Mr Winterton.' He placed the cup in front of Vincent, who swept it up and threw in the same motion.

'Five!' said Llewellyn. 'Mr Winterton is the shooter at one coup of English Hazard for a purse of two hundred pounds.' This time he placed both dice in the cup. 'The shooter will throw to decide the main point. If you please, Mr Winterton.'

Vincent took up the cup and rolled it out. Llewellyn read the dice. 'The Main is seven.'

Schreuder's soul quailed. Seven was the easiest Main to duplicate. Many combinations of the dice would yield it. The odds had swung against him, and this realization was reflected on the gloating face of every one of the watchers. If Vincent threw another seven or an eleven he would win, which was likely. If he threw the 'crabs' one and one or one and two, or if he threw twelve then he lost. Any other number would become his Chance, and he would have to keep throwing until he repeated it or threw one of the losing combinations.

Schreuder leaned back and folded his arms as though to defend himself from a brutal attack. Vincent threw.

'Four!' said Llewellyn. 'The Chance is now four.' There was a simultaneous release of breath from every person at the table except Vincent. He had given himself the most difficult Main to achieve. The odds had swung back overwhelmingly in Schreuder's favour. Vincent must now throw a Chance four to win, or a Main seven to lose. Only two combinations could total four, whereas there were many others that would yield a losing seven.

'You have my sympathy, sir.' Schreuder smiled cruelly. 'Four is the devil's own number to make.'

'The angels favour the virtuous.' Vincent waved his hand lightly, and smiled. 'Would you care to increase your stake. I will give you even money for another hundred pounds?' It was a foolhardy offer, with the odds stacked heavily against him, but Schreuder had not another guilder to avail himself of it.

He shook his head curtly. 'I would not take advantage of a man who is on his knees.'

'How gallant you are, Colonel,' Vincent said, and threw again.

'Ten!' said Llewellyn. It was a neutral number.

Vincent picked up the dice and rattled them in the cup and threw again.

'Six!' Another neutral number and, though Schreuder sat still as a corpse, his colour was waxen and he could feel droplets of sweat crawling through his chest hairs like slimy garden slugs.

'This one is for all the pretty girls we left behind us,' said Vincent and the dice clattered on the walnut tabletop as he threw again. For a long terrible moment no man moved or spoke. Then a howl went up from every English throat that must have alarmed the watch on the deck above and reached to the lookout at the top of the mainmast.

'Mary and Joseph! Two pairs of titties! As sweet a little four as I have ever seen!'

'Mr Winterton has thrown his Chance,' intoned Llewellyn, and placed both heavy purses in front of him. 'Mr Winterton wins.' But his voice was almost drowned by the uproar of laughter and congratulation. It went on for several minutes while Schreuder sat immobile as a fallen forest log, his face grey and sweating.

At last Winterton waved away any further chaff and congratulation.

He stood up, leaned over the table towards Schreuder, and said seriously, 'I salute you, sir. You are a gentleman of iron nerve, and a sportsman of the first water. I offer you the hand of friendship.' He stretched out his right hand with the palm open. Schreuder looked at it disdainfully, still not moving, and the smiles faded away. Another charged silence fell over the little cabin.

Schreuder spoke out clearly: 'I should have examined those dice of *yours* more closely while I had the chance.' He placed a heavy emphasis on the possessive pronoun. 'I hope you will forgive me, sir, but I make it a rule never to shake hands with cheats.' Vincent recoiled sharply and stared at Schreuder in disbelief, while the others gasped and gaped.

It took Vincent a long moment to recover from the shock of the unexpected insult, and his handsome young face had paled under his sea- and salt-tanned skin as he replied, 'I would be deeply obliged if you could see fit to accord me satisfaction for that remark, Colonel Schreuder.'

'With the greatest of pleasure.' Schreuder rose to his feet, smiling with triumph. He had been challenged so the choice of weapons was his. There would be no aping about with pistols. It would be the steel and this English puppy would have the pleasure of a yard of the Neptune sword in his belly. Schreuder turned to Llewellyn. 'Would you do me the honour of acting as my second in this matter?' he asked.

'Not I!' Llewellyn shook his head firmly. 'I will not allow duelling on board any ship of mine. You will have to find yourself another person to act for you, and you will have to check your temper until we reach port. Then you can go ashore to settle this matter.'

Schreuder looked back at Vincent. 'I will inform you of the name of my second at the first opportunity,' he said. 'I promise you satisfaction as soon as we reach port.' He stood up and marched out of the cabin. He could hear their voices behind him, raised in comment and conjecture, but the brandy fumes rose to mingle with his rage until he feared the veins beating in his temples might burst with the strength of it.

The following day Schreuder kept to his own kennel of a cabin where a servant brought him his meals as he lay on his bunk like a battle casualty, nursing the terrible wounds to his pride and the unbearable pain caused by the loss of his entire worldly wealth. On the second day he came on deck while the *Golden Bough* was on a larboard tack and making good her course of west-north-west along the bulging coastline of southern Africa.

As soon as his head appeared above the coaming of the companionway, the officer of the watch turned away and busied himself with the pegs on the traverse board, while Captain Llewellyn raised his telescope and studied the blue mountains that loomed on the horizon to the north. Schreuder paced along the lee rail of the ship while the officers studiously ignored his presence. The servant who had waited at the Captain's dinner party had spread the news of the impending duel through all the ship, and the crew eyed him curiously and kept well out of his path.

After half an hour Schreuder stopped abruptly in front of the officer of the watch and, without preamble, asked, 'Mr Fowler, will you act as my second?'

'I beg your pardon, Colonel, Mr Winterton is a friend of mine. Will you excuse me, please?'

During the days that followed Schreuder approached every officer aboard to act for him, but in each case he was received with frigid refusals. Ostracized and humiliated, he prowled the open deck like a night-stalking leopard. His thoughts swung like a pendulum between remorse and agony over Katinka's death, and resentment of the treatment meted out to him by the captain and officers of the ship. His rage swelled until he could barely support it.

On the morning of the fifth day, as he paced the lee rail, a hail from the masthead aroused him from this black mist of suffering. When Captain Llewellyn strode to the windward rail and stared into the south-west, Schreuder followed him across the deck and stood at his shoulder.

For some moments he doubted his own eyesight as he stared at the mountainous range of menacing dark cloud that stretched from the horizon to the heavens and which bore down upon them with such speed that it made him think again of the avalanche sweeping down the dark gorge.

'You had best go below, Colonel,' Llewellyn warned him. 'We're in for a bit of a blow.'

Schreuder ignored the warning and stood by the rail, filled with awe as he watched the clouds roll down upon them. All around him the ship was in turmoil as the crew rushed to get the sails furled and to bring the bows around, so that the *Golden Bough* faced into the racing storm. The wind came on so swiftly that it caught her with her royals and jib still set and sheeted home.

The storm hurled itself upon the *Golden Bough*, howling with fury, and laid her over so that the lee rail went under and green water piled aboard to sweep the deck waist deep. Schreuder was borne away on this flood and might have been washed overboard had he not grabbed hold of the main shrouds.

The *Golden Bough*'s jib and royals burst as though they were wet parchment and for a long minute she wallowed half under as the gale pinned her down. The sea poured into her open hatches, and from below there was the crash and thunder as some of her bulkheads burst and her cargo shifted. Men screamed as they were crushed by a culverin that had broken its breeching tackle and was running amok on the gundeck. Other sailors cried like lost souls falling into the pit as they were carried over the side by the racing green waters. The air turned white with spray so that Schreuder felt himself drowning, even though his face was clear of the water, and the white fog blinded him.

Slowly the *Golden Bough* righted herself as her lead-weighted keel levered her upright, but her spars and rigging were in tatters, snapping and lashing in the gale. Some of her yards were broken away and they clattered, banged and battered the standing masts. Listing heavily with the seawater she had taken in the *Golden Bough* was driven out of control before the wind.

Gasping and choking, half-drowned and doused to the skin, Schreuder dragged himself across the deck to the shelter of the companionway. From there he watched in dread and fascination as the world around him dissolved in silver spray and maddened green waves streaked with long pathways of foam.

For two days the wind never ceased its assault upon them, and the seas grew taller and wilder with every hour until they seemed to tower higher than the mainmast as they rushed down upon them. Half-swamped, the *Golden Bough* was slow to lift to meet them, and as they struck her they burst into foam and tumbled green across her decks. Two helmsmen, lashed to the whipstaff, battled to keep her pointing with the gale, but each wave that came aboard burst over their heads. By the second day all aboard were exhausted and nearing the limits of their endurance. There was no chance of sleep and only hard biscuit to eat.

Llewellyn had lashed himself to the mainmast and from there he directed the efforts of his officers and men to keep the ship alive. No man could stand unsupported upon the open deck, so Llewellyn could not order them to man the main pumps, but on the gundeck teams of seamen worked in a frenzy at the auxiliary pumps to try to clear the six feet of water in her bilges. As fast as they pumped it out the sea poured back through the shattered gunports and the cracked hatch covers.

Always the land loomed closer in their lee as the storm drove them onwards under bare masts, and though the helmsmen strained muscle and heart to hold her off, the *Golden Bough* edged in towards the land. That night they heard the surf break and boom like a barrage of cannon out there in the darkness, growing every hour more tumultuous as they were driven towards the rocks.

When dawn broke on the third day they could see, through the fog and spume, the dark, threatening shape of the land, the cliffs and jagged headlands only a league away across the marching mountains of grey and furious waters.

Schreuder dragged himself across the deck, clinging to mast and shroud and backstay as each wave came aboard. Seawater streamed from his hair down his face, filling his mouth and nostrils, as he gasped at Llewellyn, 'I know this coast. I recognize that headland coming up ahead of us.'

'We'll need God's blessing to weather it on this course,' Llewellyn shouted. 'The wind has us in its teeth.'

'Then pray to the Almighty with all your heart, Captain, for our salvation lies not five leagues beyond,' Schreuder bellowed, blinking the salt water from his eyes.

'How can you be certain of that?'

'I have been ashore here and marched through the country. I know every wrinkle of the land. There is a bay beyond that cape, which we named Buffalo Bay. Once she is into it, the ship should be sheltered from the full force of the wind, and on the far side there stand a pair of rocky heads that guard the entrance to a wide and calm lagoon. In there we would be safe from even such a storm as this.'

'There is no lagoon marked on my charts.' Llewellyn's expression was riven with hope and doubt.

'Sweet Jesus, Captain, you must believe me!' Schreuder shouted. On the sea he was out of his natural element and for once even he was afraid.

'First we must weather those rocks, and after that we can prove the quality of your memory.'

Schreuder was silenced and clung desperately to the mast beside Llewellyn. He stared ahead in horror as he watched the sea open her snarling lips of white foam and bare fangs of black rock. The *Golden Bough* drove on helplessly into her jaws.

One of the helmsmen screamed, 'Oh, holy Mother of God, save our mortal souls! We're going to strike!'

'Hold your helm hard over!' Llewellyn roared at him. Close alongside, the sea opened viciously and the reef burst out like a blowing whale. Claws of stone seemed to reach out towards the frail planks of the little ship, and they were so near that Schreuder could see the masses of shellfish and weed that cloaked the rocks. Another wave, larger than the rest, lifted and flung them at the reef, but the rocks disappeared below the boiling surface and the *Golden Bough* rose up like a hunter at a fence and shot high over it.

Her keel touched the rock and she checked with such force that Schreuder's grip on the mast was broken and he was hurled to the deck, but the ship shook herself free, surged onwards, carried on the crest of that mighty wave, and slid off the reef into the deeper water beyond. She charged forward, the point of the headland dropping away behind her and the bay opening ahead. Schreuder dragged himself upright and felt at once that the dreadful might of the gale had been broken by the sprit of land. Though the ship still hurtled on wildly, she was coming back under control and Schreuder could feel her respond to the urging of her rudder.

'There!' he screamed in Llewellyn's ear. 'There! Dead ahead!'

'Sweet heaven! You were right.' Through the spume and seafret Llewellyn picked out the shape of the twin heads over the ship's bows. He rounded on his helmsmen. 'Let her fall off a point!' Though their terrified expressions showed how they hated to obey, they let her come down across the wind and point towards the next pier of black rock and surf.

'Hold her at that!' Llewellyn checked them, and the *Golden Bough* tore headlong across the bay.

'Mr Winterton!' he roared at Vincent, who crouched below the hatch-coaming close at hand with a half-dozen sailors sheltering on the companion behind him. 'We must shake out a reef on the main topgallant sail to give her steerage. Can you do it?'

He made the order a request, for it was the next thing to murder to send a man to the top of the mainmast in this gale. An officer must lead the way, and Vincent was the strongest and boldest amongst them.

'Come on, lads!' Vincent shouted at his men without hesitation. 'There's a golden guinea for any man who can beat me to the main topgallant yard.' He leapt to his feet and darted across the deck to the mainmast shrouds and went flying up them hand over hand with his men in pursuit.

The *Golden Bough* tore across Buffalo Bay like a runaway horse. Suddenly Schreuder shouted again, 'Look there!' and pointed to where the entrance to the lagoon began to open to their view between the heads that towered on either hand.

Llewellyn threw back his head and gazed up the mainmast at the tiny figures that spread out along the high yard and wrestled with the reefed canvas. He recognized Vincent easily by his lean athletic form and his dark hair whipping in the wind.

'Bravely done thus far,' Llewellyn whispered, 'but hurry, lad. Give me a scrap of canvas to steer her by.'

As he said it the studding-sail flew out and filled with a crack like a musket shot. For a dreadful moment Llewellyn thought the canvas might be shredded in the gale, but it filled and held and immediately he felt the ship's motion change.

'Sweet Mother Mary! We might make it yet!' he croaked, through a throat scoured and rough with salt. 'Hard over!' he called to the helm, and the *Golden Bough* answered willingly and put her bows across the wind.

Like an arrow from a longbow, she drove straight at the western headland as though to hurl herself ashore, but her hull slid away through the water and the angle of her bows altered. The passage opened full before her, and as she passed into the lee of the land she steadied, darted between the heads, caught the tide, which was at full flow, and sped upon it through the channel into the quiet lagoon where she was protected from the full force of the storm.

Llewellyn gazed at the green forested shores in wonder and relief. Then he started and pointed ahead. 'There's another ship at anchor here already!'

Beside him Schreuder shaded his eyes from the slashing gusts of wind that eddied around the cliffs.

'I know that vessel!' he cried. 'I know her well. 'Tis Lord Cumbrae's ship. 'Tis the *Gull of Moray*!'

'Eland!' whispered Althuda softly, and Hal recognized the Dutch name for elk, but these creatures were unlike any of the great red deer of the north that he had ever seen. They were enormous, larger even than the cattle that his uncle Thomas had raised on the High Weald estate.

The three of them, Hal, Althuda and Aboli, lay belly down in a small hollow filled with rank grass. The herd was strung out among the open grove of sweet-thorn trees ahead. Hal counted fifty-two bulls, cows and calves together. The bulls were ponderous and fat so that, as they walked, their dewlaps swung from side to side and the flesh on their bellies and quarters quivered like that of a jellyfish. At each pace there came a strange clicking sound like breaking twigs.

'It is their knees that make that noise,' Aboli explained in Hal's ear.

'The Nkulu Kulu, the great god of all things, punished them when they boasted of being the greatest of all the antelope. He gave them this affliction so that the hunter would always hear them from afar.'

Hal smiled at the quaint belief, but then Aboli told him something else that turned off that smile. 'I know these creatures, they were highly prized by the hunters of my tribe, for a bull such as that one at the front of the herd carries a mass of white fat around his heart that two men cannot carry.' For months now none of them had tasted fat, for all the game they had managed to kill was devoid of it. They all craved it, and Sukeena had warned Hal that for lack of it they must soon sicken and fall prey to disease.

Hal studied the herd bull as he browsed on one of the sweet-thorn trees, hooking down the higher branches with his massive spiralling horns. Unlike his cows, who were a soft and velvet brown, striped with white across their shoulders, the bull had turned grey-blue with age and there was a tuft of darker hair on his forehead between the bases of his great horns.

'Leave the bull,' Aboli told Hal. 'His flesh will be coarse and tough. See that cow behind him? She will be sweet and tender as a virgin, and her fat will turn to honey in your mouth.' Against Aboli's advice, which Hal knew was always the best available, he felt the urge of the hunter attract him to the great bull.

'If we are to cross the river safely, then we need as much meat as we can carry. Each of us will fire at his own animal,' he decided. 'I will take the bull, you and Althuda pick younger animals.' He began to snake forward on his belly, and the other two followed him.

In these last days since they had descended the escarpment they had found that the game upon these plains had little fear of man. It seemed that the dreaded upright bipod silhouette he presented had no especial terrors for them, and they allowed the hunters to approach within certain musket shot before moving away.

Thus it must have been in Eden before the Fall, Hal thought, as he closed with the herd bull. The soft breeze favoured him, and the tendrils of blue smoke from their slow-match drifted away from the herd.

He was so close now that he could make out the individual eyelashes that framed the huge liquid dark eyes of the bull, and the red and gold legs of the ticks that clung in bunches to the soft skin between his forelegs. The bull fed, delicately wiping the young green leaves from the twigs between the thorns with its blue tongue.

On each side of him two of his young cows fed from the same thorn tree. One had a calf at heel while the other was full-bellied and gravid. Hal turned his head slowly and looked at the men who lay beside him.

He indicated the cows to them with a slow movement of his eyes, and Aboli nodded and raised his musket.

Once more Hal concentrated all his attention on the great bull, and traced the line of the scapula beneath the skin that covered the shoulder, fixing a spot in all that broad expanse of smooth blue-grey hide at which to aim. He raised the musket and held the butt into the notch of his shoulder, sensing the men on either side of him do the same.

As the bull took another pace forward he held his fire. It stopped again and raised its head, on the thick dewlapped neck, to full stretch, laying the massive twisted horns across its back, reaching up over two fathoms high to the topmost sprigs of the thorn tree where the sweetest bunches of lacy green leaves grew.

Hal fired, and heard the detonation of the other muskets on either side of him blend with the concussion of his own weapon. A swirling screen of white gunsmoke blotted out his forward view. He let the musket drop, sprang to his feet and raced out to his side to get a clear view around the smoke bank. He saw that one of the cows was down, kicking and struggling as her lifeblood spurted from the wound in her throat, while the other was staggering away, her near front leg swinging loosely from the broken bone. Already Aboli was running after her, his drawn cutlass in his right hand.

The rest of the herd was rushing away in a tight brown mass down the valley, the calves falling behind their dams. However, the bull had left the herd, sure sign that the lead ball had struck him grievously. He was striding away up the gentle slope of the low, grass-covered hillock ahead. But his gait was short and hampered, and as he changed direction, exposing his great shoulder to Hal's view, the blood that poured down his flank was red as a banner in the sunlight and bubbling with the air from his punctured lungs.

Hal started to run, speeding away over the tussocked grass. The injury to his leg was by now only a perfectly healed scar, glossy blue and ridged. The long trek over the mountains and plains had strengthened that limb so that his stride was full and lithe. A cable's length or more ahead, the bull was drawing away from him, leaving a haze of fine red dust hanging in the air, but then its wound began to tell and the spilling blood painted a glistening trail on the silver grass to mark his passing.

Hal closed the gap until he was only a dozen strides behind the mountainous beast. It sensed his pursuit and turned at bay. Hal expected a furious charge, a lowering of the great tufted head and a levelling of those spiral horns. He came up short, facing the antelope, and whipped his cutlass from the scabbard, prepared to defend himself.

The bull looked at him with huge puzzled eyes, dark and swimming with the agony of its approaching death. Blood dripped from its nostrils and the soft blue tongue lolled from the side of its mouth. It made no move to attack him, or to defend itself, and Hal saw no malice or anger in its gaze.

'Forgive me,' he whispered, as he circled the beast, waiting for an opening, and felt the slow, sad waves of remorse break over his heart to watch the agony he had inflicted upon this magnificent animal. Suddenly he rushed forward and thrust with the steel. The stroke of the expert swordsman buried the blade full length in the bull's flesh, and it bucked and whirled away, snatching the hilt out of Hal's hand. But the steel had found the heart and, its legs folded gently under it, the bull sagged wearily onto its knees. With one low groan it toppled over onto its side and died.

Hal took hold of the cutlass hilt and withdrew the long, smeared blade, then chose a rock near the carcass and went to sit there. He felt sad yet strangely elated. He was puzzled and confused by these contrary emotions, and he dwelt on the beauty and majesty of the beast that he had reduced to this sad heap of dead flesh in the grass.

A hand was laid on his shoulder, and Aboli rumbled softly, 'Only the true hunter knows this anguish of the kill, Gundwane. That is why my tribe, who are hunters, sing and dance to give thanks to propitiate the spirits of the game they have slain.'

'Teach me to sing me this song and to dance this dance, Aboli,' Hal said, and Aboli began to chant in his deep and beautiful voice. When he had picked up the rhythm Hal joined in the repetitive chorus, praising the beauty and the grace of the prey and thanking it for dying so that the hunter and his tribe might live.

Aboli began to dance, shuffling, stamping and singing in a circle about the great carcass, and Hal danced with him. His chest was choked and his eyes were blurred when, at last, the song ended and they sat together in the slanting yellow sunlight to watch the tiny column of fugitives, led by Sukeena, coming towards them from far across the plain.

Before darkness fell Hal set them to building the stockade, and he checked carefully to make certain that the gaps in the breastwork were closed with branches of sweet-thorn.

They carried the quarters and shoulders of eland meat and stacked them in the stockade where scavengers could not plunder them. They left only the scraps and the offal, the severed hoofs and heads, the mounds of guts and intestines stuffed with the pulp of half-digested leaves and grass. As they moved away the vultures hopped in or sailed down on great pinions, and the hyena and jackal rushed forward to gobble and howl and squabble over this charnel array.

After they had all eaten their fill of succulent eland steaks, Hal allocated to Sukeena and himself the middle watch that started at midnight. Though it was the most onerous, for it was the time when man's vitality was at its lowest ebb, they loved to have the night to themselves.

While the rest of their band slept, they huddled at the entrance to the stockade under a single fur kaross, with a musket laid close to Hal's right hand. After they had made soft and silent love so as not to disturb the others, they watched the sky and spoke in whispers as the stars made their remote and ancient circuits high above.

'Tell me true, my love, what have you read in those stars? What lies ahead for you and me? How many sons will you bear me?' Her hand, cupped in his, lay still, and he felt her whole body stiffen. She did not reply and he had to ask her again. 'Why will you never tell me what you see in the future? I know you have drawn our horoscopes, for often when you thought I was sleeping I have seen you studying and writing in your little blue book.'

She laid her fingers on his lips. 'Be quiet, my lord. There are many things in this existence that are best hidden from us. For this night and tomorrow let us love each other with all our hearts and all our strength. Let us draw the most from every day that God grants us.'

'You trouble me, my sweet. Will there be no sons, then?'

She was silent again as they watched a shooting star leave its brief fiery trail though the heavens and at last perish before their eyes. Then she sighed, and whispered, 'Yes, I will give you a son but—' She bit off the other words that rose to her tongue.

'There is great sadness in your voice.' His tone was disquieted. 'And, yet, the thought that you will bear my son gives me joy.'

'The stars can be malevolent,' she whispered. 'Sometimes they fulfil their promises in a manner that we do not expect, or relish. Of one thing alone I am certain, that the fates have selected for you a labour of great consequence. It has been ordained thus from the day of your birth.'

'My father spoke to me of this same task.' Hal brooded on the old prophecy. 'I am willing to face my destiny, but I need you to help and sustain me as you have done so often already.'

She did not answer his plea, but said, 'The task they have set for you involves a vow and a talisman of mystery and power.'

'Will you be with me, you and our son?' he insisted.

'If I can guide you in the direction you must go, I will do so with all my heart and all my strength.'

'But will you come with me?' he pleaded.

'I will come with you as far as the stars will permit it,' she promised. 'More than that I do not know and cannot say.'

'But—' he started, but she reached up with her mouth and covered his lips with her own to stop him speaking.

'No more! You must ask no more,' she warned him. 'Now join your body with mine once again and leave the business of the stars to the stars alone.'

Towards the end of their watch, when the Seven Sisters had sunk below the hills and the Bull stood high and proud, they lay in each other's arms, still talking softly to fight off the drowsiness that crept upon them. They had become accustomed to the night sounds of the wilderness, from the liquid warble of night birds and the yapping, yodelling chorus of the little red jackals to the hideous shrieking and cackling of the hyena packs at the remains of the carcasses, but suddenly there came a sound that chilled them to the depths of their souls.

It was the sound of all the devils of hell, a monstrous roaring and grunting that stilled all lesser creation, rolled against the hills and came back to them in a hundred echoes. Involuntarily Sukeena clung to him and cried aloud, 'Oh, Gundwane, what terrible creature is that?'

She was not alone in her terror for all the camp was suddenly awake. Zwaantie screamed, and the baby echoed her terror. Even the men sprang to their feet and cried out to God.

Aboli appeared beside them like a dark moonshadow and calmed Sukeena with a hand on her trembling shoulder. 'It is no phantom, but a creature of this world,' he told them. 'They say that even the bravest hunter is frightened three times by the lion. Once when he sees its tracks, twice when he hears its voice, and the third time when he confronts the beast face to face.'

Hal sprang up, and called to the others, 'Throw fresh logs on the fire. Light the slow-match on all the muskets. Place the women and the child in the centre of the stockade.'

They crouched in a tight circle behind its flimsy walls, and for a while all was quiet, quieter than it had been all that night for now even the scavengers has been silenced by the mighty voice that had spoken from out of the darkness.

They waited, their weapons held ready, and stared out into the night where the yellow light of the flames could not reach. It seemed to Hal that the flickering firelight played tricks with his eyes, for all at once he thought he saw a ghostly shape glide silently through the shadows. Then Sukeena gripped his arm, digging her fingernails into his flesh, and he knew that she had seen it also.

Abruptly that gale of terrifying noise broke over them again, raising the hair on their scalps. The women shrieked and the men quaked and tightened their grip on the weapons that now seemed so frail and inadequate in their hands.

'There!' whispered Zwaantie, and this time there could be no doubt that what they saw was real. It was a monstrous feline shape that seemed as tall as a man's shoulder, which passed before their gaze on noiseless pads. The flames lit upon its brazen glossy hide, turning its eyes to glaring emeralds like those in the crown of Satan himself. Another came and then another, passing in swift and menacing parade before them, then disappearing into the night once more.

'They gather their courage and resolve,' Aboli said. 'They smell the blood and the dead flesh and they are hunting us.'

'Should we flee from the stockade, then?' Hal asked.

'No!' Aboli shook his head. 'The darkness is their domain. They are able to see when the night stops up our eyes. The darkness makes them bold. We must stay here where we can see them when they come.'

Then, from out of the night, came such a creature as to dwarf the others they had seen. He strode towards them with a majestic swinging gait, and a mane of black and golden hair covered his head and shoulders and made him seem as huge as a haystack. 'Shall I fire upon him?' Hal whispered to Aboli.

'A wound will madden him,' Aboli replied. 'Unless you can kill cleanly, do not fire.'

The lion stopped in the full glare of the firelight. He placed his forepaws apart and lowered his head. The dark hair of his mane came erect, swelling before their horrified gaze, seeming to double his bulk. He opened his jaws, and they saw the ivory fangs gleam, the red tongue curl out between them, and he roared again.

The sound struck them with a physical force, like a storm-driven wave. It stunned their ear-drums and startled their senses. The beast was so close that Hal could feel the breath from its mighty lungs blow into his face. It smelt of corpses and carrion long dead.

'Quietly now!' Hal urged them. 'Make no sound and do not move, lest you provoke him to attack.' Even the women and the child obeyed. They stifled their cries and sat rigid with the terror of it. It seemed an eternity that they remained thus, the lion eyeing them, until little one-eyed Johannes could bear it no longer. He screamed, flung up his musket and fired wildly.

In the instant before the gunsmoke blinded them Hal saw that the ball had missed the beast and had struck the dirt between its forelegs. Then the smoke billowed over them in a cloud, and from its depths came the grunts of the angry lion. Now both women screamed and the men barged into each other in their haste to run deeper into the stockade. Only Hal and Aboli stood their ground, muskets levelled, and aimed into the bank of smoke. Little Sukeena shrank against Hal's flank but did not run.

Then the lion burst in full charge out of the mist of gunsmoke. Hal pressed the trigger and his musket misfired. Aboli's weapon roared deafeningly, but the beast was a blur of movement so swift, in the smoke and the darkness, that it cheated the eye. Aboli's shot must have flown wide for it had no effect upon the lion, which swept into the stockade, roaring horribly. Hal flung himself down on Sukeena, covering her with his own body and the lion leapt over him.

It seemed to pick out Johannes from the huddle of terrified humanity. Its great jaws closed in the small of the man's back and it lifted him as a cat might carry a mouse. With one more bound it cleared the rear wall of the stockade and disappeared into the night.

They heard Johannes screaming in the darkness, but the lion did not carry him far. Just beyond the firelight it began to devour him while he still lived. They heard his bones crack as the beast bit into them, then the rending of his flesh as it tore out a mouthful. There was more roaring and growling as the lionesses rushed in to share the prey, and while Johannes still shrieked and sobbed they tore him to pieces. Gradually his cries became weaker until they faded away entirely and from the darkness there were only the grisly sounds of the feast.

The women were hysterical and Bobby wailed and beat his little fists in terror against Althuda's chest. Hal quieted Sukeena, who responded swiftly to the feel of his arm around her shoulder. 'Do not run. Move quietly. Sit in a circle. The women in the centre. Reload the muskets, but do not fire until I give the word.' Hal rallied them, then looked at Daniel and Aboli.

'It is our store of meat that draws them. When they have finished with Johannes they will charge the stockade again for more.'

'You are right, Gundwane.'

'Then we will give them eland meat to distract them from us,' Hal said. 'Help me.'

Between the three of them they seized one of the huge hindquarters of raw eland flesh and staggered with it to the edge of the firelight. They threw it down in the dust.

'Do not run,' Hal cautioned them again, 'for as the cat pursues the mouse, they will come after us if we do.' They backed into the stockade. Almost immediately a lioness rushed out, seized the bloody hindquarter and dragged it away into the night. They could hear the commotion as the others fought her for the prize, and then the sounds as they all settled down to feed, snarling and growling and spitting at each other.

That hunk of raw meat was sufficient to keep even that voracious pride of the great cats feeding and squabbling for an hour, but when once more they began to prowl at the edge of the firelight and make short mock charges at the huddle of terrified humans Hal said, 'We must feed them again.' It soon became clear that the lions would accept these offerings in preference to rushing the camp, for when the three men dragged out another hindquarter from the stockade, the beasts waited for them to retire before a lioness slunk out of the night to haul it away.

'Always it is the female who is boldest,' Hal said, to distract the others.

Aboli agreed with him. 'And the greediest!'

'It is not our fault that you males lack courage and the sense to help yourselves,' Sukeena told them tartly, and most of them laughed, but breathlessly and without conviction. Twice more during the night Hal had them carry out legs of eland meat to feed the pride. At last as the dawn started to define the tops of the thorn trees against the paling sky the lions seemed to have assuaged their appetites. They heard the roaring of the black-maned male fading with distance as he wandered away. He roared for the last time a league off, just as the sun pushed its flaming golden rim above the jagged tops of the mountain range that ran parallel with the route of their march.

Hal and Althuda went out to find what remained of poor Johannes. Strangely the lions had left his hands and his head untouched, but had consumed the rest of him. Hal closed the staring eyes and Sukeena wrapped these pathetic remnants in a scrap of cloth and prayed over the grave they dug. Hal placed slabs of rock over the fresh-turned earth to deter the hyenas from digging it up.

'We can spend no more time here.' He lifted Sukeena to her feet. 'We must start out immediately if we are to reach the river today. Fortunately, there is still enough meat left for our purpose.'

They slung the remaining legs of eland meat on carrying poles, and with a man at each end staggered with them over the rolling hills and grasslands. It was late afternoon when they reached the river and, from the high bluff, looked down onto its broad green expanse, which had already proved such a barrier to their march.

The *Golden Bough* dropped her anchor at the head of the channel in Elephant Lagoon, and at once Llewellyn set his crew to work, pumping out the bilges and repairing the storm damage to the hull and the rigging. A full gale still raged overhead, but though the surface of the lagoon was whipped into a froth of white wavelets the high ground of the heads broke its main force.

Cornelius Schreuder fretted to go ashore. He was desperate to get off the *Golden Bough* and rid himself of this company of Englishmen whom he had come to detest so bitterly. He looked upon Lord Cumbrae as a friend and an ally and was anxious to join him and ask him to act as his second in the affair of honour with Vincent Winterton. In his tiny cabin he packed his chests hurriedly and, when a man could not be spared to help him, lugged them up onto the deck himself. He stood with the pile of his possessions at the entryport, staring out across the lagoon to Cumbrae's shore base.

The Buzzard had set up his camp on the same site as Sir Francis Courtney's, which Schreuder had attacked with his green-jackets. A great deal of activity was taking place amongst the trees. It seemed to Schreuder that Cumbrae must be digging trenches and other fortifications and he was puzzled by this: he saw no sense in throwing up earthworks against an enemy that did not exist.

Llewellyn would not leave his ship until he was certain that the repairs to her were well afoot and that, in all other respects, she was snugged down and secure. Eventually he placed his first mate, Arnold Fowler, in charge of the deck and ordered one of his longboats made ready.

'Captain Llewellyn!' Schreuder accosted him, as he came to the ship's side. 'I have decided that, with Lord Cumbrae's agreement, I will leave your ship and transfer to the *Gull of Moray*.'

Llewellyn nodded. 'I understood that was your intention and, in all truth, Colonel, I doubt there will be many tears shed on board the *Golden Bough* when you depart. I am going ashore now to find where we can refill the water casks that have been contaminated with seawater during the gale. I will convey you and your possessions to Cumbrae's camp, and I have here the fare money which you paid to me for your passage. To save myself further unpleasantness and acrimonious argument, I am repaying this to you in full.'

Schreuder would have dearly loved to give himself the pleasure of disdainfully refusing the offer, but those few guineas were all his wealth in the world and he took the thin purse that Llewellyn handed him, and muttered reluctantly, 'In that, at least, you act like a gentleman, sir. I am indebted to you.'

They went down into the longboat, and Llewellyn sat in the stern sheets while Schreuder found a seat in the bows and ignored the grinning faces of the crew and the ironical salutes from the ship's officers on the quarterdeck as they pulled away. They were only half-way to the beach when a familiar figure wearing a plaid and a beribboned bonnet sauntered out from amongst the trees, his red beard and tangled locks blazing in the sunlight, and watched them approach with both hands on his hips.

'Colonel Schreuder, by the devil's steaming turds!' Cumbrae roared as he recognized him. 'It gladdens my heart to behold your smiling countenance.' As soon as the bows touched the beach Schreuder leapt ashore and seized the Buzzard's outthrust hand.

'I am surprised but overjoyed to find you here, my lord.'

The Buzzard looked over Schreuder's shoulder, and grinned widely. 'Och! And if it's not my beloved brother of the Temple, Christopher Llewellyn! Well met, cousin, and God's benevolence upon you.'

Llewellyn did not smile, and showed little eagerness to take the hand that Cumbrae thrust at him as soon as his feet touched the sand. 'How d'ye do, Cumbrae? Our last discourse in the Bay of Trincomalee was interrupted at a crucial point when you left in some disarray.'

'Ah, but that was in another land and long ago, cousin, and I'm sure we can both be magnanimous enough to forgive and forget such a trifling and silly matter.'

'Five hundred pounds and the lives of twenty of my men is not a trifling and silly matter in my counting house. And I'll remind you that I'm no cousin nor any kin of yours,' Llewellyn snapped, and his legs were stiff with the memory of his old outrage.

But Cumbrae placed one arm around his shoulder and said softly, '*In Arcadia habito*.'

Llewellyn was obviously struggling with himself, but he could not deny his knightly oath, and at last he gritted the response, '*Flumen sacrum bene cognosco*.'

'There you are.' The Buzzard boomed with laughter. 'That was not so bad, was it? If not cousins, then we are still brothers in Christ, are we not?'

'I would feel more brotherly towards you, sir, if I had my five hundred pounds back in my purse.'

'I could set off that debt against the grievous injury that you inflicted on my sweet *Gull* and my own person.' The Buzzard pulled back his cloak to display the bright scar across his upper arm. 'But I'm a forgiving man with a loving heart, Christopher, and so you shall have it. I give you my word on it. Every farthing of your five hundred pounds, and the interest to boot.'

Llewellyn smiled at him coldly. 'I will delay my thanks until I feel the weight of your purse in my hands.' Cumbrae saw the purpose in his level gaze and, without another look at the *Golden Bough*'s row of gunports and the handy businesslike lines of her hull, he knew that they were evenly matched and it would be hard pounding if it came to a fight between the two ships, just as it had been four years previously in the Bay of Trincomalee.

'I don't blame you for trusting no man in this naughty world of ours, but dine with me today, here ashore, and I will place the purse in your hands, I swear it to you.'

Llewellyn nodded grimly. 'Thank you for that offer of hospitality, sir, but I well remember the last time I availed myself of one of your invitations. I have a fine cook on board my own ship who can provide me with a meal more to my taste. However, I will return at dusk to fetch the purse you have promised me.' Llewellyn bowed and returned to his longboat.

The Buzzard watched him go, with a calculating look in his eyes. The longboat headed up the lagoon towards the stream of fresh water that flowed into its upper end. 'That dandy bastard has a nasty temper,' he growled and, beside him, Schreuder nodded.

'I have never been so pleased to be rid of somebody unpleasant and to be standing here on this beach and appealing to your friendship, as I am now.'

Cumbrae looked at him shrewdly. 'You have me at a disadvantage, sir,' he said. 'What indeed are you doing here, and what is it that I can do for you in good friendship?'

'Where can we talk?' Schreuder asked.

Cumbrae replied, 'This way, my old friend and companion in arms,' led Schreuder to his hut in the grove and poured him half a mug of whisky. 'Now, tell me. Why are you no longer in command of the garrison at Good Hope?'

'To be frank with you, my lord, I am in the devil's own fix. I stand accused by Governor van de Velde of a crime that I did not commit. You know well how bitterly he was obsessed by envy and ill-will towards me,' Schreuder explained, and Cumbrae nodded cautiously without committing himself.

'Please go on.'

'Ten days ago the Governor's wife was murdered in a fit of lust and bestial passion by the gardener and executioner of the Company.'

'Sweet heavens!' Cumbrae exclaimed. 'Slow John! I knew he was a madman. I could see it in his eyes. A blethering maniac! I am sorry to hear about the woman, though. She was a delicious little muffin. Fair put a bone in my breeches just to look at those titties of hers, she did.'

'Van de Velde has falsely accused me of this foul murder. I was forced to flee on the first available ship before he had me imprisoned and placed on the rack. Llewellyn offered me passage to the Orient where I had determined to enlist in the war that is afoot in the Horn of Africa between the Prester and the Great Mogul.'

Cumbrae's eyes lit up and he leaned forward on his stool at the mention of war, like a hyena scenting the blood of a battlefield. By this time he was heartily bored with digging for Franky Courtney's elusive treasure, and the promise of an easier way to fill his holds with riches had all of his attention. But he would not show this posturing braggart just how eager he was, so he left the subject for another time and said, with feeling and understanding, 'You have my deepest sympathy and my assurances of any aid I am able to render.' His mind was seething with ideas. He sensed that Schreuder was guilty of the murder he denied so vehemently but, guilty or not, he was now an outlaw and he was placing himself at Cumbrae's mercy.

The Buzzard had been given ample demonstration of Schreuder's qualities as a warrior. An excellent man to have serve under him, especially as he would be completely under Cumbrae's control by virtue of his guilt and the blood on his hands. As a fugitive and a murderer, the Dutchman could no longer afford to be too finicky in matters of morality.

Once a maid has lost her virginity she lifts her skirts and lies down in the hay with more alacrity the second time, the Buzzard told himself happily, but reached out and clasped Schreuder's arm with a firm and friendly grip. 'You can rely on me, my friend,' he said. 'How may I help you?'

'I wish to throw in my lot with you. I will become your man.'

'And heartily welcome you will be.' Cumbrae grinned through his red whiskers with unfeigned delight. He had just found himself a hunting hound, one perhaps not carrying a great cargo of intelligence but, none the less, fierce and totally without fear.

'I ask only one favour in return,' Schreuder said. The Buzzard let the friendly hand drop from his shoulder, and his eyes became guarded. He might have known that such a handsome gift would have a price written on the underside.

'A favour?' he asked.

'On board the *Golden Bough* I was treated in the most shabby and scurvy fashion. I was cheated out of a great deal of money at Hazard by one of the ship's officers, and insulted and reviled by Captain Llewellyn and his men. To cap it all, the person who cheated me challenged me to a duel. I could find no person on board willing to act as my second, and Llewellyn forbade this matter of honour to be pursued until we reached port.'

'Go on, please.' Cumbrae's suspicions were beginning to evaporate as he realized where the conversation was heading.

'I would be most grateful and honoured if you could consent to act as my second in this affair, my lord.'

'That is all you require of me?' He could hardly credit that it would be so easy. Already he could see the profits that might be reaped from this affair. He had promised Llewellyn his five hundred pounds, and he would give it to him, but only when he was certain that he would be able to get the money back from him, together with any other profit that he could lay hands upon.

He glanced out over the waters of the lagoon. There lay the *Golden Bough*, a powerful, warlike vessel. If he were able to add her to his flotilla, he would command a force in the oriental oceans that few could match. If he appeared off the Great Horn of Africa with these two vessels, in the midst of the war that Schreuder had assured him was raging, what spoils might there be for the picking?

'It will be my honour and my pleasure to act for you,' he told Schreuder. 'Give me the name of the dastard who has challenged you, and I will see to it that you obtain immediate satisfaction from him.'

When Llewellyn came ashore again for dinner, he was accompanied by two of his officers and a dozen of his seamen, carrying cutlass and pistols. Cumbrae was on the beach to welcome him. 'I have the purse I promised you, my dear Christopher. Come with me to my poor lodgings and take a dram with me for loving friendship and for the memory of convivial days we passed in former times in each other's company. But first will ye no' introduce me to these two fine gentlemen of yours?'

'Mr Arnold Fowler, first mate of my ship.' The two men nodded at each other. 'And this is my third officer, Vincent Winterton, son of my patron, Viscount Winterton.'

'Also, so I am informed, a paragon at Hazard, and a mean hand with the dice.' Cumbrae grinned at Vincent and the young man withdrew the hand he was on the point of proffering.

'I beg your pardon, sir, but what do you mean by that remark?' Vincent enquired stiffly.

'Only that Colonel Schreuder has asked me to act for him. Would you be good enough to inform me as to who is your own second?'

Llewellyn cut in quickly, 'I have the honour to act for Mr Winterton.'

'Indeed, then, we have much to discuss, my dear Christopher. Please follow me, but as it is Mr Winterton's affairs we will be discussing, it might be as well if he remained here on the beach.'

Llewellyn followed the Buzzard to his hut, and took the stool that he was offered. 'A dram of the water of life?'

Llewellyn shook his head. 'Thank you, no. Let us come to the matters at hand.'

'You were always impatient and headstrong.' The Buzzard filled his own mug and took a mouthful. He smacked his lips and wiped his whiskers on the back of his hand. 'You'll never know what you're missing. 'Tis the finest whisky in all the islands. But, here, this is for you.' He slid the heavy purse across the keg that served him for a table. Llewellyn picked it up and weighed it thoughtfully in his hand.

'Count it if you will,' the Buzzard invited him. 'I'll take no offence.' He sat back and watched with a grin on his face, sipping at his mug, while Llewellyn arranged the golden coins in neat stacks on the top of the keg.

'Five hundred it is, and fifty for the interest. I am obliged to you, sir.' Llewellyn's expression had softened.

'It's a small price to pay for your love and friendship, Christopher,' Cumbrae told him. 'But now to this other matter. As I told you, I act for Colonel Schreuder.'

'And I act for Mr Winterton.' Llewellyn nodded. 'My principal will be satisfied with an apology from Schreuder.'

'You know full well, Christopher, that my lad will no' give him one. I am afraid that the two young puppies will have to fight it out.'

'The choice of weapons lies with your side,' said Llewellyn. 'Shall we say pistols at twenty paces?'

'We will say no such thing. My man wants swords.'

'Then we must agree. What time and place will suit you?'

'I leave that decision to you.'

'I have repairs to make to my rigging and hull. Damage we sustained in the gale. I need Mr Winterton on board to help with these. May I suggest three days hence, on the beach at sunrise?'

The Buzzard tugged at his beard as he considered this proposal. He would need a few days to make the arrangements he had in mind. Three days' delay would suit him perfectly.

'Agreed!' he said, and Llewellyn rose to his feet immediately and placed the purse in the pocket of his tunic.

'Will you not take that dram I offered you now, Christopher?' Cumbrae suggested, but again Llewellyn declined.

'As I told you, sir, I have much to do on board my ship.'

The Buzzard watched him go down to the beach and step into his longboat. As they were rowed back to where the *Golden Bough* was anchored, Llewellyn and Winterton were in deep and earnest conversation.

'Young Winterton is in for a surprise. He can never have seen the Dutchman with a sword in his hand to have agreed so lightly to the choice of weapons.' He swigged back the few drops of whisky that remained in his mug, and grinned again. 'We shall see if we cannot arrange a little surprise for Christopher Llewellyn also.' He banged the mug onto the keg top, and bellowed, 'Send Mr Bowles to me, and be quick about it.'

Sam Bowles came smarming in, wriggling his whole body like a whipped dog to ingratiate himself with his captain. But his eyes were cold and shrewd.

'Sammy, me boy.' Cumbrae gave him a slap on the arm that stung like a wasp, but did not upset the smile on the man's lips. 'I have something for you, that should be much to your taste. Listen well.'

Sam Bowles sat opposite him and cocked his head so as not to miss a word of his instructions. Once or twice he asked a question or chortled with glee and admiration as Cumbrae unfolded his plans.

'You have always wanted the command of your own ship, Sammy me laddy. This is your chance. Serve me well, and you shall have it. Captain Samuel Bowles. How does that sound to you?'

'I like the sound of it powerful well, your grace!' Sam Bowles bobbed his head. 'And I'll not let you down.'

'That you won't!' Cumbrae agreed. 'Or not more than once, you won't. For if you do, you'll dance me a merry hornpipe while you dangle from the main yard of my *Gull*.'

The riverbanks were lined with wild willow and dark green acacia trees, which were covered with a mantle of yellow blossom. The river ran broad and deep, slow and green between its rocky piers. The sandbanks were exposed and, as they looked down upon them from the steep slopes of the valley, Sukeena shuddered and whispered, 'Oh, what foul and ugly creatures! Surely these are the very dragons we spoke of?'

'They are dragons indeed,' Hal agreed, as they gazed down on the crocodiles that lay sunning on the white beach. There were dozens of them, some not much larger than lizards and other brutes with the beam and length of a ship's boat, massive grey monsters, which surely could swallow a man whole. They had found out how ferocious these creatures were on their first attempt to ford the river, when Billy Rogers had been seized by one and dragged beneath the surface. They had not recovered any part of his body.

'I tremble at the thought of trying to cross again, with these creatures still guarding the river,' Sukeena whispered tremulously.

'Aboli knows them from his own land to the north, and his tribe have a way of dealing with them.'

On the rocky bluff, high above the river where the crocodiles could not reach, they stacked the piles of eland meat, which were already beginning to stink, in the hot sunlight. Then Hal sent some of the men to search the forest floor for dried logs that would float high in the water. Under Ned Tyler's instruction they shaped them with the cutlasses, although Hal hated to see the fine steel edges dulled and chipped. While this was being done Althuda, with Sukeena helping him, carefully slit the wet eland hides into long tough ropes as thick as her little finger.

Aboli sought out the species of tree he needed, and then chopped short supple stakes from its branches and carried bundles of these back to where the others were working. Big Daniel helped him to sharpen both ends of these short, resilient pieces of green wood into spear points, and harden them in the fire. Then, using a log of the correct circumference as a template, the two powerful men bent each stake around the log until it formed a circle, the sharpened points overlapping. While they held them in place, Hal lashed the ends together with strips of the raw eland hide. When they gingerly released the tension the coiled stakes were like the loaded steel springs of a musket lock, ready to fly open if the retaining strip of hide was severed. By sundown they had finished work on a pile of these snares.

They had learned from their encounter with the lion pride, and on this night they hoisted the legs of eland meat high into the top branches of one of the tallest trees that grew along the banks of the broad river. They built their stockade well downstream from this cache of meat, and made certain that the walls were of sturdy logs, and that the entrance was blocked with freshly cut thorn branches.

Though they slept little that night, lying and listening to the hyena and the jackal howling and gibbering below the tree where the meat hung, the lions did not trouble them again. In the dawn they left the stockade to begin work once more on their preparations for the river crossing.

Ned Tyler finished the construction of the raft by lashing the poles together with rawhide rope.

''Tis a rickety vessel.' Sukeena eyed it with obvious misgivings. 'One of those great river dragons could overturn it with a flick of its tail.'

'That is why Aboli has prepared his snares for them.'

They went back up the slope to where Althuda and Zwaantie were helping Aboli wrap the coiled green-wood circlets with a thick covering of half-putrid eland meat.

'The crocodile cannot chew his food,' Aboli explained to them as he worked. 'Each of these lumps of meat is the right size for one of the monsters to swallow whole.'

When all the baits had been prepared, they carried them down to the water's edge. As they approached the sandbank where the great saurians lay like stranded logs, they shouted clapped their hands and fired off the muskets, creating a commotion that alarmed even these huge beasts.

They raised their massive bulks on short stubby legs and lumbered to the shelter of their natural element, sliding into the deep green pools with mighty splashes and setting up waves that broke upon the far bank. As soon as the sandbank was clear, the men rushed out and placed the lumps of stinking meat along the water's edge. Then they hurried back and climbed up to where the women waited on the safety of the high bluff above the river.

After a while, the eye knuckles of the crocodiles began to pop up everywhere over the surface of the pool, and then to move in slowly towards the sandbank.

'They are cowardly, sneaking beasts,' Aboli said, with hatred in his tone and revulsion in his expression, 'but soon, when they smell the meat, their greed will overcome their fear.'

As he spoke one of the largest reptiles lifted itself out of the shallows at the edge and waddled cautiously out on to the sandbank, its massive crested tail ploughing a furrow behind it. Suddenly, with surprising speed and agility, it darted forward and seized one of the lumps of eland meat. It opened its jaws to their full stretch as it strained to swallow. From the bluff they watched in awe as the huge lump of meat slid down into its maw, bulging the soft white scales on the outside of its throat. It turned and rushed back into the pool, but immediately another of the scaly reptiles emerged and gobbled a bait. There followed a general mêlée of long slithering bodies, shining wet in the sunlight, that hissed and snapped and tumbled over each other as they fought for the meat.

Once every bait had been consumed, some crocodiles splashed back into the pool, but many settled down again in the sun-warmed sand from where they had been disturbed. Peace fell over the riverbank again, and the kingfishers darted and hovered over the green waters. A great grey hippopotamus thrust out his head on the far side of the pool and gave vent to a raucous grunt of laughter. His cows clustered around him, their backs like a pile of shiny black boulders.

'Your plan has not worked,' said Sabah in Dutch. 'The crocodiles are unharmed and still ready to fall upon any of us who goes near the water.'

'Be patient, Sabah,' Aboli told him. 'It will take a while for the juices of their stomach to eat through the rawhide. But when they do the sticks will spring open and the sharpened ends will pierce their guts and stab through their vitals.'

As he finished speaking, one of the largest reptiles, the first to take the bait, suddenly let out a thunderous roar and arched its back until the coxcombed tail flapped over its head. It roared again, and spun round to snap with mighty jaws at its own flank, its spiked yellow fangs tearing through the armoured scales, ripping out lumps of its own flesh.

'See there!' Aboli sprang to his feet and pointed. 'The sharp end of the stake has cut right through his belly.' Then they saw the fire-blackened point of sharpened green wood protruding a hand's breadth through the scaly hide. As the bull crocodile writhed and hissed in his hideous death throes, a second reptile began to thrash about in gargantuan convulsions, and then another and another, until the pool was turned to white foam, and their terrible stricken cries and roars echoed along the bluffs of the river, startling the eagles and vultures from their nesting platforms high on the cliffs.

'Bravely done, Aboli! You have cleared the way for us.' Hal leaped to his feet.

'Yes! We can cross now,' Aboli agreed. 'But be swift and do not linger in the water or near the edge for there may still be some of the *ngwenya* who have not felt the spikes in their bellies.'

They heeded his advice. Lifting the clumsy raft between them they rushed it down the bank, and as soon as it was afloat they flung aboard the baskets of provisions, the saddle-bags and the bags of gunpowder, then urged the two women and little Bobby onto the frail craft. The men were stripped to their petticoats, and swam the craft across the sluggish current. As soon as they reached the opposite bank they seized their possessions and scampered in haste up the rocky slope until they were well clear of the riverbank.

High above the water they could at last fall upon each other with laughter and congratulation. They camped there that night, and in the dawn Aboli asked Hal quietly, 'How far now to Elephant Lagoon?'

Hal unrolled his chart and pointed out his estimate of their position. 'Here, we are five leagues inland from the seashore and not more than fifty leagues from the lagoon. Unless there is another river as wide as this to bar our way, we should be there in five more days of hard marching.'

'Then let us march hard,' said Aboli, and roused the rest of the depleted band. At his urging, they took up their loads and, with the rays of the rising sun beating full into their faces, fell once more into the order of march that they had maintained through all the long journey.

The four longboats from the *Golden Bough* were crowded with seamen as they rowed ashore in that dark hour before the dawn. A sailor in the bow of each boat held high a lantern to light their way, and the reflections danced like fireflies on the calm black surface of the lagoon.

'Llewellyn is bringing half his crew ashore with him!' the Buzzard gloated, as he watched the little fleet head in towards the beach.

'He suspects treachery,' Sam Bowles laughed delightedly, 'so he comes in force.'

'What a churlish guest, to suspect us of villainy.' The Buzzard shook his head sadly. 'He deserves whatever Fate has in store for him.'

'He has split his force. There are at least fifty men in those boats,' Sam estimated. 'He makes it easier for us. From here it should all be plane sailing and a following wind.'

'Let us hope so, Mr Bowles,' the Buzzard grunted. 'I go now to meet our guests. Remember, the signal is a red Chinese rocket. Wait until you see it burn.'

'Aye, Captain!' Sam knuckled his forehead and slipped away into the shadows. Cumbrae strode down the sand to meet the leading boat. As it came in to the beach he could see in the lamplight that Llewellyn and Vincent Winterton were sitting together in the stern sheets. Vincent wore a dark woollen cloak against the dawn chill, but his head was bare. He had braided his hair into a thick pigtail down his back. He followed his captain ashore.

'Good morrow, gentlemen,' Cumbrae greeted them. 'I commend you for your punctuality.'

Llewellyn nodded a greeting. 'Mr Winterton is ready to begin.'

The Buzzard waggled his beard. 'Colonel Schreuder is waiting. This way, if you please.' They strode abreast along the beach, the seamen from the boats following in an orderly column. 'It is unusual to have such a crowd of ruffians to witness an affair of honour,' he remarked.

'There are but a few conventions out here beyond the Line,' Llewellyn retorted, 'but one is to keep your back well covered.'

'I take your point.' Cumbrae chuckled. 'But to demonstrate my good faith, I will not invite any of my own lads to join us. I am unarmed.' He showed his hands, then opened the front of his tunic to demonstrate the fact. Making a comforting lump in the small of his back, where it was tucked into his belt, was one of the new-fangled wheel-lock pistols, made by Fallon of Glasgow. It was a marvellous invention but prohibitively expensive, which was the main reason why it was not more widely employed. On pressing the trigger the spring-loaded wheel of the lock spun and the iron pyrites striker sent a shower of sparks into the pan to detonate the charge. The weapon had cost him well over twenty pounds but was worth the price for there was no burning match to betray its presence.

'To demonstrate your own good faith, my dear Christopher, will you kindly keep your men together at your side of the square and under your direct control?'

A short way down the beach, they came to the area where the sand had been levelled and a square roped off. A water cask had been set up at each of the four corners. 'Twenty paces each side,' Cumbrae told Llewellyn. 'Will that give your man enough searoom in which to work?'

Winterton surveyed the square then nodded briefly. 'It will suit us well enough.' Llewellyn spoke for him.

'We will have some time to wait for the light to strengthen,' Cumbrae said. 'My cook has prepared a breakfast of hot biscuit and spiced wine. Will you partake?'

'Thank you, my lord. A cup of wine would be welcome.' A steward brought the steaming cups to them, and Cumbrae said, 'If you will excuse me, I will attend my principal.' He bowed and went up the path into the trees, to return minutes later leading Colonel Schreuder.

They stood together at the far side of the roped square, talking quietly. At last Cumbrae looked up at the sky, said something to Schreuder, then nodded and came to where Llewellyn and Vincent waited. 'I think the light is good enough now. Do you gentlemen agree?'

'We can begin.' Llewellyn nodded stiffly.

'My principal offers his weapon for your examination,' Cumbrae said, and proffered the Neptune sword hilt first. Llewellyn took it and held the gold-inlaid blade up to the morning light.

'A fancy piece of work,' he murmured disparagingly. 'These naked females would not be out of place in a whorehouse.' He touched the gold engravings of sea nymphs. 'But at least the point is not poisoned and the length matches that of my principal's blade.' He held the two swords side by side to compare them, and then passed Vincent's sword to Cumbrae for inspection.

'A fair match,' he agreed, and passed it back.

'Five-minute rounds and first blood?' Llewellyn asked, drawing his gold timepiece from the pocket of his waistcoat.

'I am afraid we cannot agree to that.' Cumbrae shook his head. 'My man wishes to fight without pause until one of them cries for quarter or is dead.'

'By God, sir!' Llewellyn burst out. 'Those rules are murderous.'

'If your man pisses like a puppy, then he should not aspire to howl with the wolves.' Cumbrae shrugged.

'I agree!' Vincent interjected. 'We will fight to the death, if that's the way the Dutchman wants it.'

'That, sir, is exactly how he wants it,' Cumbrae assured him. 'We are ready to begin when you are. Will you give the signal, Captain Llewellyn?'

The Buzzard went back and, in a few terse sentences, explained the rules to Schreuder, who nodded and ducked under the rope of the barrier. He wore a thin shirt open at the throat so that it was clear that he wore no body armour beneath it. Traditionally, the brilliant white cotton would give his opponent a fair aiming mark, and show up the blood from a hit.

On the opposite side of the square Vincent loosened the clasp of his cloak and let it drop into the sand. He was dressed in a similar white shirt. With his sword in his hand, he vaulted lightly over the rope barrier and faced Schreuder across the swept beach sand. Both men began to limber up with a series of practice cuts and thrusts that made their blades sing and glitter in the early light.

'Are you ready, Colonel Schreuder?' After a few minutes, Llewellyn called from the side-line as he held on high a red silk scarf.

'Ready!'

'Are you ready, Mr Winterton?'

'Ready!'

Llewellyn let the scarf drop, and a growl went up from the *Gull*'s seamen at the far side of the square. The two swordsmen circled each other, closing in cautiously with their blades extended and their points circling and dipping. Suddenly Vincent sprang forward, and feinted for Schreuder's throat, but Schreuder met him easily and locked his blade. For a long moment they strained silently, staring into each other's eyes. Perhaps Vincent saw death in the other man's implacable gaze, and felt the steel in his wrist, for he broke first. As he recoiled Schreuder came after him with a series of lightning ripostes that made his blade glint and glitter like a sunbeam.

It was a dazzling display that drove Vincent, desperately parrying and retreating, against one of the water kegs that marked a corner of the square. Pinned there, he was at Schreuder's mercy. Abruptly Schreuder broke off the assault, turned his back contemptuously on the younger man and strode back into the centre. There, he took up his guard again and, blade poised, waited for Vincent to engage him once more.

All the watchers, except Cumbrae, were stunned by the Dutchman's virtuosity. Clearly Vincent Winterton was a swordsman of superior ability but he had been forced to call upon all his skill to survive that first blazing attack. In his heart Llewellyn knew that Vincent had survived not because of his skill but because Schreuder had wanted it that way. Already the young Englishman had been touched three times, two light cuts on the chest and another deeper wound on the upper left arm. His shirt was slashed in three irregular tears and was turning red and sodden as the wounds began to weep profusely.

Vincent glanced down at them, and his expression mirrored the despair he felt as he faced the knowledge that he was no match for the Dutchman. He lifted his head and looked across to where Schreuder waited for him, his stance classical and arrogant, his expression grave and intent as he studied his adversary over the weaving point of the Neptune sword.

Vincent straightened his spine and took his guard, trying to smile carelessly as he steeled himself to go forward to his certain death. The rough seamen who watched might have bayed and bellowed at the spectacle of a bull-baiting or a cockfight, but even they had fallen silent, awed by the terrible tragedy they saw unfolding. Llewellyn could not let it happen.

'Hold hard!' he cried, and vaulted over the rope. He strode between the two men, his right hand raised. 'Colonel Schreuder, sir. You have given us every reason to admire your swordsmanship. You have drawn first blood. Will you not give us good reason to respect you by declaring that your honour is satisfied?'

'Let the English coward apologize to me in front of all the present company, and then I will be satisfied,' said Schreuder, and Llewellyn turned to appeal to Vincent. 'Will you do what the colonel asks? Please, Vincent, for my sake and the trust I pledged to your father.'

Vincent's face was deathly pale but the blood that stained his shirt was bright crimson, as full blown June roses on the bush. 'Colonel Schreuder has this moment called me a coward. Forgive me, Captain, but you know I cannot accede to such conditions.'

Llewellyn looked sadly upon his young protégé. 'He intends to kill you, Vincent. It is such a shameful waste of a fine young life.'

'And I intend to kill him.' Vincent was able to smile now that it was decided. It was a gay, reckless smile. 'Please stand aside, Captain.' Hopelessly Llewellyn turned back to the sidelines.

'On guard, sir!' Vincent called, and charged with the white sand spurting from under his boots, thrust and parry for very life. The Neptune sword was an impenetrable wall of steel before him, meeting and turning his own blade with an ease that made all his bravest efforts seem those of a child. Schreuder's grave expression never faltered, and when at last Vincent fell back, panting and gasping, sweat diluting his streaming blood to pink, he was wounded twice more. There was black despair in his eyes.

Now, at last, the seamen from the *Golden Bough* had found their voices. 'Quarter! You bloody murdering cheese-head!' they howled, and 'Fair shakes, man. Let the lad live!'

'They'll get no mercy from Colonel Cornelius,' Cumbrae smiled grimly, 'but the din they're making will help Sam to do his job.' He glanced across the lagoon to where the *Golden Bough* lay in the channel. Every man still aboard her was crowded along the near rail, straining his eyes for a glimpse of the duel. Even the lookout at her main top had trained his telescope on the beach. Not one was aware of the boats that were speeding out from amongst the mangroves on the far shore. He recognized Sam Bowles in the leading boat, as it raced in under the *Golden Bough*'s tumble home and was hidden from his view by the ship's hull. Sweet Mary, Sam will take her without a shot fired! Cumbrae thought exultantly, and looked back at the arena.

'You have had your turn, sir,' said Schreuder quietly. 'Now it is mine. On guard, if you please.' With three swift strides he had covered the gap that separated them. The younger man met his first thrust, and then the second with a high parry and block, but the Neptune blade was swift and elusive as an enraged cobra. It seemed to mesmerize him with its deadly shining dance and, darting and striking, slowly forced him to yield ground. Each time he parried and retreated, he lost position and balance.

Then suddenly Schreuder executed a coup that few swordsmen would dare attempt outside the practice field. He caught up both blades in the classical prolonged engagement, swirling the two swords together so that the steel edges shrilled with a sound that grated across the nerve endings of the watchers. Once committed neither man dared break off the engagement, for to do so was to concede an opening. Around in a deadly glittering circle the two swords revolved. It became a trial of strength and endurance. Vincent's arm turned leaden and the sweat dripped from his chin. His eyes were desperate and his wrist began to tremble and bend under the strain.

Then Schreuder froze the fatal circle. He did not break away but simply clamped Vincent's sword in a vice of steel. It was a display of such strength and control that even Cumbrae gaped with amazement.

For a moment the duellists remained unmoving, then slowly Schreuder began to force both points upward, until they were aimed skywards at full stretch of their arms. Vincent was helpless. He tried to hold the other blade but his arm began to shudder and his muscles quivered. He bit down on his own tongue with the effort until a spot of blood appeared at the corner of his mouth.

It could not last longer, and Llewellyn cried out in despair as he saw that the young man had reached the furthest limits of his strength and endurance. 'Hold hard, Vincent!' It was in vain. Vincent broke. He disengaged with his right arm at full reach above his head, and his chest wide open.

'Ha!' shouted Schreuder, and his thrust was a blur, fast as the release of a bolt from a crossbow. He drove in his point an inch below Vincent's sternum, clear through his body and a foot out of his back. For a long moment Vincent froze like a figure carved from a block of marble. Then his legs melted under him and he toppled into the sand.

'Murder!' cried Llewellyn. He sprang into the square and knelt beside the dying youth. He took him in his arms, and looked up again at Schreuder. 'Bloody murder!' he cried again.

'I must take that as request.' Cumbrae smiled and came up behind the kneeling man. 'And I am happy to oblige you, cousin!' he said, and brought the wheel-lock pistol out from behind his back. He thrust the muzzle into the back of Llewellyn's head and pulled the trigger. There was a bright flare of sparks and then the pistol roared and leaped in the Buzzard's fist. At such close range the load of lead pellets drove clean through Llewellyn's skull and blew half of his face away in red tatters. He flopped forwards with Vincent's body still in his arms.

The Buzzard looked around quickly, and saw that from the dark grove the red rocket was already soaring upwards, leaving a parabola of silver smoke arched against the fragile blue of the early-morning sky, the signal to Sam Bowles and his boarding party to storm the decks of the *Golden Bough*.

Meanwhile, above the beach, the gunners hidden among the trees were dragging away the branches that covered their culverins. The Buzzard had sited the battery himself and laid them to cover all the far side of the square where the seamen from the *Golden Bough* stood in a row four deep. The culverins enfiladed the group, and each was loaded with a full charge of grape shot.

Even though they were unaware of the hidden battery, the seamen from the *Golden Bough* were swiftly recovering from the shock of seeing their officers slaughtered before their horrified gaze. A hum of fury and wild cries of outrage went up from their midst, but there was no officer to give the order, and though they drew their cutlasses, yet instinctively they hesitated and hung back.

The Buzzard seized Colonel Schreuder's free arm and grated in his ear. 'Come on! Hurry! Clear the range.' He dragged him from the roped ring.

'By God, sir, you have murdered Llewellyn!' Schreuder protested. He was stunned by the act. 'He was unarmed! Defenceless!'

'We will debate the niceties of it later,' Cumbrae promised, and stuck out one booted foot, hooking Schreuder's ankle at the same time shoving him forward. The two men sprawled headlong into the shallow trench in the sand that Cumbrae had dug specially for this purpose, just as the seamen from the *Golden Bough* burst through the ropes of the ring behind them.

'What are you doing?' Schreuder bellowed. 'Release me at once.'

'I am saving your life, you blethering idiot,' Cumbrae shouted in his ear, and held his head down below the lip of the trench as the first salvo of grape shot thundered from out of the grove and swept the beach.

The Buzzard had calculated the range with care so that the pattern of shot spread to its most deadly arc. It caught the phalanx of sailors squarely, raked the sand of the beach into a blinding white storm, and went on to tear across the surface of the quiet lagoon waters like a gale. Most of the *Golden Bough*'s men were struck down instantly, but a few stayed on their feet, bewildered and stunned, staggering like drunkards from their wounds and from the turmoil of grape shot and the blast of disrupted air.

Cumbrae seized his claymore from the bottom of the pit, where he had buried it under a light coating of sand, and leaped to his feet. He rushed on these few survivors, the great sword gripped in both hands. He struck the head clean from the torso of the first man in his path, just as his own sailors came charging out of the gunsmoke, yelling like demons and brandishing their cutlasses.

They fell upon the decimated shore party and hacked them down, even when Cumbrae bellowed, 'Enough! Give quarter to those who yield!' They took no heed of his order, and swung the cutlasses until the thrown blood drops wet them to the elbows and speckled their grinning faces. Cumbrae had to lay about him with his fists and the flat of his sword.

'Avast! We need men to sail the *Golden Bough*. Spare me a dozen, you bloody ruffians.' They gave him less than he demanded. When the carnage was over there were only nine, trussed ankle and wrist and lying belly down in the sand like porkers in the marketplace.

'This way!' the Buzzard bellowed again, and led his crew sprinting down the beach to where the longboats from the *Golden Bough* were drawn up. They piled into them and seized the oars. With Cumbrae roaring in the bows like a wounded animal they pulled for the *Golden Bough*, hooked onto her sides and went swarming up onto her deck with cutlass bared and pistols cocked.

There, help was not needed. Sam Bowles's men had taken the *Golden Bough* by surprise and storm. The deck was slippery with blood and corpses were strewn across it and huddled in the scuppers. Under the forecastle a small band of Llewellyn's men were hanging on desperately, surrounded by Sam's gang of boarders, but when they saw the Buzzard and his gang storm up onto the deck they threw down their cutlasses. Those few who could swim raced to the ship's side and dived into the lagoon while the others fell to their knees and pleaded for quarter.

'Spare them, Mr Bowles,' Cumbrae shouted. 'I need sailors!' He did not wait to see the order obeyed but snatched a musket from the hands of the man beside him and ran to the rail. The escaping sailors were splashing their way towards the mangrove trees. He took careful aim at the head of one, whose pink scalp showed through his wet grey hair. It was a lucky shot, and the man threw up both hands and sank, leaving a pink stain on the surface. The men around Cumbrae hooted with glee and joined in the sport, calling their targets and laying wagers on their marksmanship. 'Who'll give me fives in shillings on that rogue with the blond pigtail?' They shot the swimming men like wounded ducks.

Sam Bowles came grinning and bobbing to meet Cumbrae. 'The ship is yours, your grace.'

'Well done, Mr Bowles.' Cumbrae gave him such a hearty blow of commendation as to knock him almost off his feet. 'There will be some hiding below decks. Winkle them out! Try to take them alive. Put a boat in the water and drag those out also!' He pointed at the few survivors still splashing and swimming towards the mangroves. 'I am going down to Llewellyn's cabin to find the ship's papers. Call me when you have all the prisoners trussed up in the waist of the ship.'

He kicked open the locked door to Llewellyn's cabin, and paused to survey the interior. It was beautifully appointed, the furniture carved and polished and the drapery of fine velvet.

In the writing desk he found the keys to the iron strong-box that was bolted to the deck below the comfortable bunk. As soon as he opened it he recognized the purse he had given Llewellyn. 'I am much obliged to you, Christopher. You'll not be needing this where you're going,' he murmured as he slipped it into his pocket. Under it was a second purse, which he carried to the desk. He spilled the golden coins out onto the tabletop. 'Two hundred and sixteen pounds five shillings and twopence,' he counted. 'This will be the money for the running of the ship. Very parsimonious, but I am grateful for any contribution.'

Then his eyes lit on a small wooden chest in the bottom of the box. He lifted it out and inspected the name carved into the lid. 'The Hon. Vincent Winterton'. The chest was locked but it yielded readily to the blade of his dirk. He smiled as he saw what it contained, and let a handful of coins run through his fingers. 'No doubt the gambling losses of the good Colonel Schreuder are in here but he need never be tempted to wager them again. I will take care of them for him.'

He poured a mug of French brandy from the captain's stores and seated himself at the desk while he ran through the ship's books and documents. The log-book would make interesting reading at a later date. He set it aside. He glanced through a letter of partnership agreement with Lord Winterton who, it seemed, owned the *Golden Bough*. 'No longer, your lordship.' He grinned. 'I regret to inform you that she is all mine now.'

The cargo manifest was disappointing. The *Golden Bough* was carrying mostly cheap trade goods, knives and axes, cloth, beads and copper rings. However, there were also five hundred muskets and a goodly store of blackpowder in her holds.

'Och! So you were going to do a spot of gun smuggling. Shame on you, my dear Christopher.' He tutted disapprovingly. 'I'll have to find something better to fill her holds on the return voyage,' he promised himself, and took a pull at the brandy.

He went on sorting through the other documents. There was a second letter from Winterton, agreeing to the *Golden Bough*'s commission as a warship in the service of the Prester John, and a flowery letter of introduction to him signed by the Chancellor of England, the Earl of Clarendon, under the Great Seal, commending Christopher Llewellyn to the ruler of Ethiopia in the highest terms.

'Ah! That is of more value. With some small alteration to the name, even I would fall for that!' He folded it carefully and replaced the chest, the purses, the books and documents in the strong-box, and hung the key on a ribbon around his neck. While he finished the rest of the brandy he considered the courses of action that were now open to him.

This war in the Great Horn intrigued him. Soon the south-east trade winds would begin to blow across the Ocean of the Indies. On their benevolent wings the Great Mogul would be sending his dhows laden with troops and treasure from his empire on the mainland of India and Further India to his *entrepôts* on the African coast. There would also be the annual pilgrimage of the faithful of Islam taking advantage of the same fair wind to sail up the Arabian Sea on their journey to the birthplace of the Prophet of God. Potentates and princes, ministers of state and rich merchants from every corner of the Orient, they would carry with them such riches as he could only guess at, to lay as offerings in the holy mosques and temples of Mecca and Medina.

Cumbrae allowed himself a few minutes to dream of pigeon's-blood rubies and cornflower sapphires the size of his fist, and elephant-loads of silver and gold bullion. 'With the *Gull* and the *Golden Bough* sailing together, there ain't no black heathen prince who will be able to deny me. I will fill my holds with the best of it. Franky Courtney's miserly little treasure pales beside such abundance,' he consoled himself. It still rankled sorely that he had not been able to find Franky's hiding place, and he scowled. 'When I sail from this lagoon, I will leave the bones of Jiri and those other lying blackamoors as signposts to mark my passing,' he promised himself.

Sam Bowles interrupted his thoughts by sticking his head into the cabin. 'Begging your pardon, your grace, we've rounded up all the prisoners. It was a clean sweep. Not one of them got away.'

The Buzzard heaved himself to his feet, glad to have a distraction from these niggling regrets. 'Let's see what you've got for me, then.'

The prisoners were bound and squatting in three files in the ship's waist. 'Forty-two hardened salt-water men,' said Sam proudly, 'sound in wind and limb.'

'None of them wounded?' the Buzzard asked incredulously.

Sam answered in a whisper, 'I knew you wouldn't want to be bothered to play nursemaid to such. We held their heads under water to help them on their way into the bosom of Jesus. For most of them it was a mercy.'

'I'm amazed at your compassion, Mr Bowles,' Cumbrae grunted, 'but in future spare me such details. You know I'm a man of gentle persuasion.' He put that matter out of his mind and contemplated his prisoners. Despite Sam's assurance, many had been heavily beaten, their eyes were blackened and their lips cut and swollen. They hung their heads and none would look at him.

He walked slowly down the squatting ranks, now and then seizing a handful of hair and lifting the man's face to study it. When he reached the end of the line he came back and addressed them jovially: 'Hear me, my bully lads, I have a berth for all of you. Sail with me and you shall have a shilling a month and a fair share of the prize money and, as sure as my name is Angus Cochran, there'll be sackloads of gold and silver to share.'

None replied, and he frowned. 'Are you deaf or has the devil got your tongues? Who will sail with Cochran of Cumbrae?' The silence hung heavily over the deck. He strode forward and picked out one of the most intelligent-looking of his prisoners. 'What's your name, lad?'

'Davey Morgan.'

'Will you sail with me, Davey?'

Slowly the man lifted his head and stared at the Buzzard. 'I saw young Mr Winterton slaughtered and the captain shot down in cold blood on the beach. I'll not sail with any murdering pirate.'

'Pirate!' the Buzzard screamed. 'You dare to call me pirate, you lump of stinking offal? You were born to feed the seagulls, and that's what you shall do!' The great claymore rasped from its scabbard, and he swung it down to cleave Davey Morgan's head, through the teeth as far as his shoulders. With the bloody sword in his hand he strode down the line of prisoners.

'Is there another amongst you who would dare to call me pirate to my face?' No man spoke out, and at last Cumbrae rounded on Sam Bowles. 'Lock them all in the *Golden Bough*'s hold. Feed them on half a pint of water and a biscuit a day. Let them think about my offer more seriously. In a few days' time I'll speak to these lovelies again, and we shall see if they have better manners then.'

He took Sam aside and spoke in a quieter tone. 'There is still some storm damage that needs repair.' He pointed up at the rigging. 'She's your ship now, to sail and command. Make all good at once. I want to leave this godforsaken anchorage as soon as I can. Do you hear me, Captain Bowles?'

Sam Bowles's face lit with pleasure at the title. 'You can rely on me, your grace.'

Cumbrae strode to the entryport and slid down into one of the longboats. 'Take me back to the beach, varlets.' He jumped over the side before they touched the sand and waded knee-deep to the shore where Colonel Schreuder was waiting for him.

'My lord, I must speak to you,' he said, and the Buzzard smiled at him engagingly.

'Your discourse always gives me pleasure, sir. Come with me. We can talk while I go about my affairs.' He led the way across the beach, and into the grove.

'Captain Llewellyn was—' Schreuder began, but the Buzzard cut him off.

'Llewellyn was a bloody pirate. I was defending myself from his treachery.' He stopped abruptly and faced Schreuder, hauling up his sleeve to display the ridged purple scar that disfigured his shoulder. 'Do you see that? That's what I got for trusting Llewellyn once before. If I had not forestalled him, his desperadoes would have fallen on us and slaughtered us where we stood. I am sure that you understand and that you are grateful for my intervention. It could have been you going that way.'

He pointed at the group of his men who were staggering up from the beach, dragging the corpses of Llewellyn and Vincent Winterton by their legs. Llewellyn's shattered head left a red drag mark through the sand.

Schreuder stared aghast at the burial party. He recognized in Cumbrae's words both a warning and a threat. Beyond the first line of trees was a series of deep trenches that had been freshly dug all over the area where once Sir Francis Courtney's encampment had stood. His hut was gone but in its place was a pit twenty feet deep, its bottom filled with seepage of brackish lagoon water. There was another extensive excavation on the site of the old spice godown. It looked as though an army of miners had been at work amongst the trees. The Buzzard's men dragged the corpses to the nearest of these pits and dumped them unceremoniously into it. The bodies slid down the steep side and splashed into the puddle at the bottom.

Schreuder looked troubled and uncertain. 'I find it difficult to believe that Llewellyn was such a person.' But Cumbrae would not let him finish.

'By God, Schreuder, do you doubt my word? What of your assurance that you wanted to throw in your lot with me? If my actions offend you then it's better that we part now. I will give you one of the pinnaces from the *Golden Bough*, and a crew of Llewellyn's pirates to help you make your own way back to Good Hope. You can explain your fine scruples to Governor van de Velde. Is that more to your liking?'

'No, sir, it is not,' said Schreuder hurriedly. 'You know I cannot return to Good Hope.'

'Well, then, Colonel, are you still with me?'

Schreuder hesitated, watching the grisly labours of the burial teams. He knew that if he crossed Cumbrae he would probably end up in the pit with Llewellyn and the sailors from the *Golden Bough*. He was trapped.

'I am still with you,' he said at last.

The Buzzard nodded. 'Here's my hand on it, then.' He thrust out his huge freckled fist covered with wiry ginger hair. Slowly Schreuder reached out and took it. Cumbrae could see in his eyes the realization dawning that from now onwards he would be beyond the pale and was content that he could trust Schreuder at last. By accepting and condoning the massacre of the officers and crew of the *Golden Bough* he had made himself a pirate and an outlaw. He was, in every sense, the Buzzard's man.

'Come along with me, sir. Let me show you what we have done here.' Cumbrae changed the subject easily, and led Schreuder past the mass grave without another glance at the pile of corpses. 'You see, I knew Francis Courtney well – we were like brothers. I am still certain that his fortune is hidden hereabouts. He has what he took from the *Standvastigheid* and that from the *Heerlycke Nacht*. By the blood of all the saints, there must be twenty thousand pounds buried somewhere under these sands.'

At that they came to the long, deep trench where forty of Cumbrae's men were already back at work with spades. Amongst them were the three black seamen he had bought on the slave block at Good Hope.

'Jiri!' the Buzzard bellowed. 'Matesi! Kimatti!' The slaves jumped, threw down their spades and scrambled out of the ditch in trepidation to face their master.

'Look at these great beauties, sir. I paid five hundred florins for each. It was the worst bargain I ever struck. Here before your eyes you have living proof that there are only three things a blackamoor can do well. He can prevaricate, thieve and swive.' The Buzzard let fly a guffaw. 'Isn't that the truth, Jiri?'

'Yes, lordy.' Jiri grinned and agreed. 'It's God's own truth.'

The Buzzard stopped laughing as suddenly as he had begun. 'What do you know about God, you heathen?' he roared and, with a mighty swing of his fist, he knocked Jiri back into the ditch. 'Get back to work all three of you!'

They seized their spades and attacked the bottom of the ditch in a frenzy, sending earth flying over the parapet in a cloud. Cumbrae stood above them, his hands on his hips. 'Listen to me, you sons of midnight. You tell me that the treasure I seek is buried here. Well, then, find it for me or you won't be coming with me when I sail away. I'll bury all three of you in this grave that you're digging with your own sooty paws. Do you hear me?'

'We hear you, lordy,' they answered in chorus.

He took Schreuder's arm in a companionable grip and led him away. 'I have come to accept the sad fact that they never truly knew the whereabouts of Franky's hoard. They've been jollying me along all these months. My rascals and I have had just about a bellyful of playing at moles. Let me offer you the hospitality of my humble abode and a mug of whisky, and you can tell me all you know about this pretty little war that's a-going on between the great Mogul and the Prester. Methinks, you and I might well find better occupation and more profit elsewhere than here at Elephant Lagoon.'

In the firelight Hal studied his band as they ate, with ravenous appetite, their dinner of smoked meat. The hunting had been poor in these last days and most of them were tired. His own seamen had never been slaves. Their labour on the walls of the castle of Good Hope had not broken or cowed them. Rather it had hardened them, and now the long march had put a temper on them. He could want no more from them: they were tough and tried warriors. Althuda he liked and trusted, but he had been a slave from childhood and some of his men would never be fighters. Sabah was a disappointment. He had not fulfilled Hal's expectation of him. He had become sullen and obstructive. He shirked his duties and protested at the orders Hal gave him. His favourite cry had become, 'I am a slave no longer! No man has the right to command me!'

Sabah would not fare well if matched against the likes of the Buzzard's seamen, Hal thought, but he looked up and smiled as Sukeena came to sit beside him.

'Do not make an enemy of Sabah,' she whispered quietly.

'I do not wish that,' he replied, 'but every man amongst us must do his part.' He looked down at her tenderly. 'You are the worth of ten men like Sabah, but today I saw you stumble more than once and when you thought I was not watching you there was pain in your eyes. Are you sickening, my sweetheart? Am I truly setting too hard a pace?'

'You are too fond, Gundwane.' She smiled up at him. 'I will walk with you to the very gates of hell and not complain.'

'I know you would, and it worries me. If you do not complain, how will I ever know what ails you?'

'Nothing ails me,' she assured him.

'Swear it to me,' he insisted. 'You are not hiding any illness from me.'

'I swear it to you, with this kiss.' She gave him her lips. 'All is as well as God ever intended. And I will prove it to you.' She took his hand and led him to the dark corner of the stockade where she had laid out their bed.

Though her body melted into his as sweetly as before, there was a softness and languor in her loving that was strange and, though it delighted him while his passion was in white heat, afterwards it left him with a sense of disquiet and puzzlement. He was aware that something had changed but he was at a loss as to exactly what was different.

The next day he watched her carefully during the long march, and it seemed to him that on the steeper ground her step was not as spry as it had been. Then, when the heat was fiercest, she lost her place in the column and began to fall back. Zwaantie went to help her over a rough place in the elephant path that they were following but Sukeena said something sharply to her and thrust away her hand. Hal slowed the pace, almost imperceptibly, to give her respite, and called the midday halt earlier than he had on the preceding days.

Sukeena slept beside him that night with a deathlike stillness while Hal lay awake. By now he was convinced that she was not well, and that she was trying to hide her weakness from him. As she slept her breathing was so light that he had to place his ear to her lips to reassure himself. He held her close and her body seemed heated. Once, just before dawn, she groaned so pitifully that he felt his heart swell with love and concern for her. At last he also fell into a deep dreamless sleep. When he woke with a start and reached out for her, he found her gone.

He lifted himself on one elbow and looked around the stockade. The fire had died down to a puddle of embers, but the full moon, even though it was low in the west, threw enough light for him to see that she was not there. He could make out the dark shape of Aboli: the morning star was almost washed out by the more brilliant light of the moon, but it burned just above his head as he sat his watch at the entrance. Aboli was awake, for Hal heard him cough softly and then saw him draw his fur blanket closer around his shoulders.

Hal threw back his own kaross, and went to squat beside him. 'Where is Sukeena?' he whispered.

'She went out a short while ago.'

'Which way?'

'Down towards the stream.'

'You did not stop her?'

'She was going about her private business.' Aboli turned to look at him curiously. 'Why would I stop her?'

'I am sorry,' Hal whispered back. 'I meant no rebuke. She worries me. She is not well. Have you not noticed?'

Aboli hesitated. 'Perhaps.' He nodded. 'Women are children of the moon, which lacks but a few nights of full, so perhaps her courses are in flood.'

'I am going after her.' Hal stood up and went down the rough path towards the shallow pool where they had bathed the previous evening. He was about to call her name when he heard a sound that silenced and alarmed him. He stopped and listened anxiously. The sound came again, the sound of pain and distress. He started forward and saw her on the sandbank kneeling beside the pool. She had thrown aside her blanket, and the moonlight shone on her bare skin, imparting to it the patina of polished ivory. She was doubled up in a convulsion of pain and sickness. As he watched in distress, she retched and vomited into the sand.

He ran down to her and dropped on his knees beside her. She looked up at him in despair. 'You should not see me thus,' she whispered hoarsely, then turned her head away and vomited again. He put his arm around her bare shoulders. She was cold and shivering.

'You are sick,' he breathed. 'Oh, my love, why did you not answer me straight? Why did you try to hide it from me?'

She wiped her mouth with the back of her hand. 'You should not have followed,' she said. 'I did not want you to know.'

'If you are sick, then I must know. You should trust me enough to tell me.'

'I did not want to be a burden to you. I did not want you to delay the march because of me.'

He hugged her to him. 'You will never be a burden to me. You are the breath in my lungs and the blood in my veins. Tell me now truthfully what ails you, my darling.'

She sighed and shivered against him. 'Oh, Hal, forgive me. I did not want this to happen yet. I have taken all the medicines that I know of to prevent it.'

'What is it?' He was confused and dismayed. 'Please tell me.'

'I am carrying your child in my womb.' He stared at her in astonishment and could neither move nor speak. 'Why are you silent? Why do you look at me so? Please don't be angry with me.'

Suddenly he clasped her to his chest with all his strength. 'It is not anger that stops up my mouth. It is joy. Joy for our love. Joy for the son you promised me.'

That day Hal changed the order of march and took Sukeena to walk with him at the head of the column. Though she protested laughingly, he took her basket from her and added it to his own load. Thus relieved she was able to step out lightly and stay beside him without difficulty. Still he took her hand on the difficult places, and she did not demur when she saw what pleasure it gave him to protect and cherish her thus.

'You must not tell the others,' she murmured, 'else they will want to slow the march on my behalf.'

'You are as strong as Aboli and Big Daniel,' he assured her staunchly, 'but I will not tell them.'

So they kept their secret, walking hand in hand and smiling at each other in such obvious happiness that even if Zwaantie had not told

Althuda and he had not told Aboli, they must have guessed. Aboli grinned as if he were the father and showed Sukeena such special favour and attention that even Sabah, in the end, fathomed the reason for this new mood that had come over the band.

The land through which they were passing now became more heavily wooded. Some of the trees were monstrous and seemed, like great arrows, to pierce the very heavens. 'These must have been old when Christ the Saviour was born upon this earth!' Hal marvelled.

With Aboli's wise counsel and guidance they were coming to terms with this savage terrain, and the great animals that abounded in it. Fear was no longer their constant companion, and Hal and Sukeena had learned to take pleasure in the strangeness and beauty all around them. They would pause on a hilltop to watch an eagle sail on the high wind with motionless wings, or to take pleasure in a tiny gleaming metallic bird, no bigger than Sukeena's thumb, as it hung suspended from a flower while it sipped the nectar with a curved beak that seemed as long as its body.

The grassland teemed with a plethora of strange beasts that challenged their imagination. There were herds of the same blue buck that they had first encountered below the mountains, and wild horses barred with stark stripes of cream, russet and black. Often they saw ahead of them amongst the trees the dark mountainous shapes of the double-horned rhinoceros, but they had learned that this fearsome beast was almost blind and that they could avoid its wild, snorting charge by making a short detour from the path.

On the open lands, beyond the forest, there were flocks of small cinnamon-coloured gazelles, so numerous that they moved like smoke across the hills. Their flanks were slashed with a horizontal chocolate stripe, and lyre-shaped horns crowned their dainty heads. When alarmed by the sight of the human figures, they pranced with astonishing lightness of hoof, leaping high in the air and flashing a snowy plume upon their backs. Each ewe was followed by a tiny lamb, and Sukeena clapped her hands with delight and exclaimed to see the young animals nudging the udder or cavorting with their peers. Hal watched her fondly, knowing now that she also carried a child within her, sharing her joy in the young of another species and revelling with her in the secret they thought they had kept from the others.

He read the angle of the noon sun, and everyone in the band gathered around him to watch him mark their position on the chart. The string of dots on the heavy parchment sheet crept slowly towards the indentation on the coastline, which was marked on the Dutch chart as Buffels Baai or the Bay of the Buffaloes.

'We are not more than five leagues from the lagoon now.' Hal looked up from the chart.

Aboli agreed. 'While we were out hunting this morning I recognized the hills ahead. From the high ground I saw the line of low cloud that marks the coast. We are very close.'

Hal nodded. 'We must advance with caution. There is the danger that we might run into foraging parties from the *Gull*. This is a favourable place to set up a more permanent camp. There is an abundance of water and firewood and a good lookout from this hill. In the morning, Aboli and I will leave the rest of you here while we go on ahead to discover if the *Gull* is truly lying in Elephant Lagoon.'

An hour before dawn, Hal took Big Daniel aside and committed Sukeena to his care. 'Guard her well, Master Daniel. Never let her out of your sight.'

'Have no fear, Captain. She'll be safe with me.'

As soon as it was light enough to see the track that led eastwards Hal and Aboli left the camp, Sukeena walked a short distance with them.

'God speed, Aboli.' Sukeena embraced him. 'Watch over my man.'

'I will watch over him, even as you watch over his son.'

'You monstrous rogue, Aboli!' She struck him a playful blow on his great broad chest. 'How do you know everything? We were so sure we had kept it a secret even from you.' She turned laughing to Hal. 'He knows!'

'Then all is lost.' Hal shook his head. 'For on the day it is born this rascal will take it as his own, even as he did with me.'

She watched them climb the hill and wave from the crest. But as they disappeared the smile shrivelled on her lips and a single tear traced its way down her cheek. On her way back, she stopped beside the stream and washed it away. When she entered the camp again, Althuda looked up at her from the sword blade he was burnishing and smiled at her, unsuspecting of her distress. He marvelled at how beautiful and fresh she looked, even after all these months of hard travel in the wilderness.

When last they had been here, Hal and Aboli had hunted and explored these hills above the lagoon. They knew the run of the river, and they entered the deep gorge a mile above the lagoon, following an elephant path down to a shallow ford that they knew. They did not approach the lagoon from this direction. 'There may be watering parties from the *Gull*,' Aboli cautioned. Hal nodded and led them up the far side of the gorge and in a wide circuit around the back of the hills, out of sight of the lagoon.

They climbed the back slope of the hills until they were a few paces below the skyline. Hal knew that the cave of the ancient rock paintings, where he and Katinka had dallied, lay just over the crest in front of them, and that from the ridge there would be a panoramic view across the lagoon to the rocky heads and the ocean beyond.

'Use those trees to break your shape on the skyline,' Aboli told him quietly.

Hal smiled. 'You taught me well. I have not forgotten.' He inched his way up the last few yards, followed by Aboli, and, gradually, the view down the far side opened to his gaze. He had not had sight of the sea for weeks now, and he felt his heart leap and his spirits soar as he looked upon its serene blue expanse, flecked with the white horses that pranced before the south-easter. It was the element that ruled his life and he had missed it sorely.

'Oh, for a ship!' he whispered. 'Please, God, let there be a ship!'

As he moved up, there before his eyes appeared the great grey castles of the heads, the bastions that guarded the entrance to the lagoon. He paused before taking another step, steeling himself for the terrible disappointment of finding the anchorage deserted. Like a gambler at Hazard, he had staked his life on this coup of the dice of Fate. He forced himself to take another slow step up the slope, then gasped, seized Aboli's arm and dug his fingers into the knotted muscles.

'The *Gull*!' he muttered, as though it were a prayer of thanks. 'And not alone! There is another fine ship with her.'

For a long while neither spoke again, until Aboli said softly, 'You have found the ship you promised them. If you can seize it, you will be a captain at last, Gundwane.'

They crept forward and, on the crest of the hill, sank on their bellies and gazed down upon the wide lagoon below.

'What ship is that with the *Gull*?' Hal asked. 'I cannot make out her name from here.'

'She is an Englishman,' said Aboli, with certainty. 'No other would cross her mizzen topgallant yard in that fashion.'

'A Welshman, perhaps? She has a rake to her bows and a racy style to her sheer. They build them that way on the west coast.'

'It is possible, but whoever she is, she's a fighting ship. Look at those guns. There would be few to match her in her class,' Aboli murmured thoughtfully.

'Better than the *Gull*, even?' Hal looked at her with longing eyes.

Aboli shook his head. 'You dare not try to take her, Gundwane. Surely she belongs to an honest English sea captain. If you lay hands upon her you turn all of us into pirates. Better we try for the *Gull*.'

For another hour they lay on the hilltop, talking and planning quietly while they studied the two ships and the encampment amongst the trees on the near shore of the lagoon.

'By heavens!' Hal exclaimed abruptly. 'There is the Buzzard himself. I would know that bush of fiery hair anywhere.' His voice was sharp with hatred and anger. 'He is going out to the other ship. See him climb the ladder without a by-your-leave, as if he owns it.'

'Who is that greeting him at the companionway?' Aboli asked. 'I swear I know that walk, and the bald scalp shining in the sunlight.'

'It cannot be Sam Bowles aboard that frigate . . . but it is,' Hal marvelled. 'There is something very strange afoot here, Aboli. How may we find out what it is?'

While they watched the sun begin to slide down the western sky, Hal tried to keep his rage under control. Down there were the two men responsible for his father's terrible death. He relived every detail of his agony and he hated Sam Bowles and the Buzzard to the point where he knew that his emotions might override his reason. His strong instinct was to throw all else aside, go down to confront them and seek retribution for his father's agony and death.

I must not let it happen, he told himself. I must think first of Sukeena and the son that she carries for me.

Aboli touched his arm and pointed down the hill. The rays of the sinking sun had changed the angle of the shadows of the trees of the forest, so that they could see down more clearly through them into the encampment.

'The Buzzard is digging fortifications down there.' Aboli was puzzled. 'But there is no plan to them. His trenches are all higgledy-piggledy.'

'Yet all his men seem to be at work in the diggings. There must be some plan—' Hal broke off and laughed. 'Of course! This is why he came back to the lagoon! He is still searching for my father's hoard.'

'He is a long way off course.' Aboli chuckled. 'Perhaps Jiri and Matesi have deliberately misled him.'

'Sweet Mary, of course those rascals have played the fool with him. Cumbrae bought more than he bargained for in the slave market. They will tweak his nose while they pretend to grovel and call him Lordy.' He smiled at the thought, then became serious again. 'Do you think they may still be down there, or has the Buzzard murdered them already?'

'No, he will keep them alive as long as he thinks they are of value to him. He is digging, so he is still hoping. My guess is that they are still alive.'

'We must watch for them.' For another hour they lay on the hilltop in silence, then Hal said, 'The tide is turning. The strange frigate is swinging on her moorings.' They watched her bow and curtsy to the ebb with a stately grace, and then Hal spoke again. 'Now I can see the name on her transom, but it is difficult to read. Is it the *Golden Swan*? The *Golden Hart*? No, I think not. 'Tis the *Golden Bough*!'

'A fine name for a fine ship,' said Aboli, and then he started, and pointed excitedly down at the network of trenches and pits amongst the trees. 'There are black men coming out of that ditch, three of them. Is that Jiri? Your eyes are sharper than mine.'

'By heavens! So it is, and Matesi and Kimatti behind him.'

'They are taking them to a hut near the water's edge. That must be where they lock them up at night.'

'Aboli, we must speak to them. I will go down as soon as it's dark and try to reach their hut. What time will the moon rise?'

'An hour after midnight,' Aboli answered him. 'But I will not let you go. I made a promise to Sukeena. Besides your white skin shines like a mirror. I will go.'

Stripped naked, Aboli waded out from the far shore until the water reached his chin and struck out in a dog-paddle that made no splash and left only a silent oily wake behind his head. When he reached the far shore, he lay in the shallows until he was certain the beach was clear. Then he crawled swiftly across the open sand and huddled against the bole of the first tree.

One or two camp fires were burning in the grove, and from around them he heard the sound of men's voices and an occasional snatch of song or a shout of laughter. The flames gave him enough light to discern the hut where the slaves where imprisoned. Near the front of it he picked out the glow of a burning match on the lock of a musket, and from this he placed the single sentry, who sat with his back to a tree covering the door of the hut.

They are careless, he thought. Only one guard, and he seems to be asleep.

He crept forward on hands and knees, but before he reached the back wall of the hut he heard footsteps and moved quickly to the shelter of another tree-trunk and crouched there. Two of the Buzzard's sailors came sauntering through the grove towards him. They were arguing loudly.

'I'll no' sail with that little weasel,' one declared. 'He would cut a throat for the fun of it.'

'So would you, Willy MacGregor.'

'Aye, but I'd no' be using a pizened blade, like Sam Bowles would.'

'You'll sail with whoever the Buzzard says you will, and that's an end to your carping,' his mate announced and paused beside the tree where Aboli crouched. He lifted his petticoats and urinated noisily against the trunk. 'By the devil's nuggets, even with Sam Bowles as captain I'll be happy enough to get away from this place. I left bonnie Scotland to escape the coal pit, and here I am digging holes again.' He shook the droplets vigorously from himself and the two walked on.

Aboli waited until they were well clear, and then crawled to the rear wall of the hut. He found that it was plastered with unburnt clay, but that chunks of this were falling from the framework of woven branches beneath. He crawled slowly along the wall, gently probing each crack with a stalk of grass until he found a chink that went right through. He placed his lips to the opening and whispered softly, 'Jiri!'

He heard a startled movement on the far side of the wall, and a moment later a fearful whisper came back. 'Is that the voice of Aboli, or is it his ghost?'

'I am alive. Here feel the warmth of my finger – 'tis not the hand of a dead man.'

They whispered to each other for almost an hour before Aboli left the hut and crawled back down the beach. He slipped into the waters of the lagoon like an otter.

The dawn was painting the eastern sky the colours of lemons and ripe apricots when Aboli climbed the hill again to where he had left Hal. Hal was not in the cave, but when Aboli gave a soft warbling bird-call, he stepped out from behind the hanging vines that screened the entrance, his cutlass in his hand.

'I have news,' said Aboli. 'For once the gods have been kind.'

'Tell me!' Hal commanded eagerly, as he sheathed the blade. They sat side by side in the entrance to the cave from where they could keep the full sweep of the lagoon under their eyes, while Aboli related in detail everything that Jiri had been able to tell him.

Hal exclaimed when Aboli described the massacre of the captain and men of the *Golden Bough*, and the way in which Sam Bowles had drowned the wounded like unwanted kittens in the shallows of the lagoon. 'Even for the Buzzard that is a deed that reeks of hell itself.'

'Not all were killed,' Aboli told him. 'Jiri says that a large number of the survivors are locked up in the main hold of the *Golden Bough*.' Hal nodded thoughtfully. 'He says too that the Buzzard has given the command of the *Golden Bough* to Sam Bowles.'

'By heaven, that rogue has come up in the world,' Hal exclaimed. 'But all this could work to our advantage. The *Golden Bough* has become a pirate ship, and is now fair game for us. However, it will be a dangerous enterprise to hunt the Buzzard in his own nest.' He lapsed into a long silence, and Aboli did not disturb him.

At last Hal looked up and it was clear he had reached some decision. 'I swore an oath to my father never to reveal that which I am now to show you. But circumstances have changed. He would forgive me, I know. Come with me, Aboli.'

Hal led him down the back slope of the hill, and then turned towards the gorge of the river. They found a trail made by the baboons and scrambled down the steep side to the bottom. There Hal turned upstream, and the cliffs became higher and steeper as they went. At places they were forced to enter the water and wade alongside the cliff. Every few hundred yards Hal paused to take his bearings, until at last he grunted with satisfaction as he marked the dead tree. He waded along the lip of the bank until he reached it, then scrambled ashore and began to climb.

'Where are you going, Gundwane?' Aboli called after him.

'Follow me,' Hal answered, and Aboli shrugged and began to climb after him. He chuckled when Hal suddenly reached down and gave him a hand onto the narrow ledge that he had not been able to see from below. 'This has the smell of Captain Franky's lair to it,' he said. 'The Buzzard would have saved himself a lot of work by searching here instead of digging holes in the grove, am I right?'

'This way.' Hal shuffled along the ledge with his back to the cliff, and the hundred-foot drop that opened under his toes. When he reached the place where the ledge widened and the cleft split the face, he paused to examine the rocks that blocked the entrance.

'There have been no visitors, not even the apes,' he said, with relief, and began to move the rocks out of the opening. When there was space to pass he crept through and groped in the darkness for the flint and steel box and the candle that his father had placed on the ledge above head level. The tinder flared at the third stroke of the steel on the flint, and he lit the candle stub and held it high.

Aboli laughed in the yellow light as he looked upon the array of canvas sacks and chests. 'You are a rich man, Gundwane. But what use is all this gold and silver to you now? It will not buy you a mouthful of food or a ship to carry it all away.'

Hal crossed to the nearest chest and opened the lid. The gold bars glinted in the candle-light. 'My father died to leave me this legacy. I would rather have had him alive and me a beggar.' He slammed the lid, and looked back at Aboli. 'Despite what you may think, I did not come here for the gold,' he said. 'I came for this.' He kicked the powder keg beside him. 'And those!' He pointed to the piles of muskets and swords that were stacked against the far wall of the cave. 'And these also!' He crossed to where the sheaves and gantry were piled in a heap and picked up one of the coils of manila rope that he and his father had used. He tried the strength of the line by stretching a length of it over his back and straining to break it with his arms and shoulders.

'It is still strong, and has not rotted,' he dropped the coil, 'so we have all we need here.'

Aboli came to sit on the chest beside him. 'So you have a plan. Then share it with me, Gundwane.' He listened quietly as Hal laid it out for him, and once or twice he nodded or made a suggestion.

That same morning they set off for the base camp and by travelling fast, trotting and running most of the way, they reached it shortly after noon. Sukeena saw them climbing the hill and came running down to meet them. Hal seized her and swung her high in the air, then checked himself and set her down with great care as though she were woven of gossamer and might easily tear. 'Forgive me, I treat you roughly.'

'I am yours to treat as you will, and I will be happier for it.' She clung to him and kissed him. 'Tell me what you have found. Is there a ship in the lagoon?'

'A ship. A fine ship. A beautiful ship, but not half as lovely as you.'

With Hal urging them they broke the camp and moved out at once. He and Aboli scouted ahead to clear the path and to lead the band on towards the lagoon.

When they reached the river and climbed down the gorge Hal left Big Daniel there and all the other seamen but Ned Tyler. They were unaware that the treasure cave was only a cable's length upstream. 'Wait for me here, Master Daniel. I must take the others to a safe place. Hide yourselves well. I will return after dark.'

Aboli went with them, as Hal led the rest of the party up the far side of the gorge, then took them round the far side of the hills. They approached the sandbanks that separated the mainland from the island, on which they had built the fireships.

By this time it was late afternoon, and Hal allowed them to rest there until nightfall. As soon as it was dark they all waded across the shallows, Hal carrying Sukeena on his back. As soon as they reached the island they hurried deep into the thick bush, where they were safe from observation from the pirate encampment.

'No fires!' Hal cautioned them. 'Speak only in whispers. Zwaantie, keep little Bobby from crying. No one to wander away. Keep close. Ned is in command when I am not here. Obey him.'

Hal and Aboli went on across the island, through the bush to the beach facing the lagoon. In the area where they had built the fireships the undergrowth had sprung up again thickly. They groped and searched beneath it until they located the two abandoned double-hulled vessels that had not been used on the attack on the *Gull*, and dragged them closer to the beach.

'Will they still float?' Aboli asked dubiously.

'Ned made a good job of them, and they seem sturdy enough,' Hal told him. 'If we unload the combustibles, then they will float higher in the water.'

They stripped the ships of their cargo of dry tar-soaked wooden faggots. 'That's better,' Hal said, with satisfaction. 'They will be lighter and easier to handle now.' They concealed them again, covering them with branches.

'There is still much to do before daylight.' Hal led Aboli back to where most of Althuda's party were already asleep. 'Do not wake Sukeena,' he warned her brother. 'She is exhausted and must rest.'

'Where are you going?' Althuda asked.

'There is no time to explain. We will return before dawn.'

Hal and Aboli crossed the channel to the mainland and then hurried back through the forest in the darkness, but when they reached the line of hills Hal stopped and said, 'There is something I have to find.'

He turned back towards the flickering lights of the pirate camp, moving slowly and pausing often to get his bearings, until at last he stopped at the base of a tall tree.

'This is the one.' With the point of his cutlass he probed the soft loamy earth around the roots. He felt it strike metal, and fell to his knees. He dug with his bare hands, then lifted the golden chain and held it to catch the starlight.

''Tis your father's Nautonnier seal.' Aboli recognized it at once.

'The ring also. And the locket with its portrait of my mother.' Hal stood up and wiped the damp earth from the glass that had protected the miniature. 'With these in my hands, I feel a whole man again.' He dropped the treasures into his leather pouch.

'Let us go on, before we are discovered.'

It was after midnight when, once again, they scrambled down the side of the gorge and Big Daniel challenged them softly as they reached the riverbank.

''Tis me,' Hal reassured him, and the others emerged from where they were hidden.

'Stay here,' Hal ordered. 'Aboli and I will return shortly.'

The two set off upstream. Hal led the climb to the ledge and groped his way into the blackness of the cave. Working in the candle's feeble light, they tied the cutlasses into bundles of ten, then stacked them at the entrance. Hal emptied one of the chests of its precious contents, piling the gold bars disdainfully in a corner of the cave, and packed twenty pistols into the empty chest.

Then they rolled the kegs of gunpowder, with the slow-match, out onto the narrow ledge, and set up the gantry and sheave blocks with the rope rove through. Hal scrambled back down the cliff. When he reached the riverbank he whistled softly. Aboli lowered the bundles of weapons and the kegs down to him.

It was heavy work, but Aboli's great muscles made light of it. When they had finished Aboli climbed down to join Hal, and they began the weary porterage of the goods down to where Big Daniel and the other seamen waited.

'I recognize these,' Big Daniel chuckled, as he ran his hands over a bundle of cutlasses then examined them in the moonlight.

'Here is something else you will recognize,' Hal told him, and gave him two of the heavy powder kegs to carry.

All of them carrying as much as their backs would bear, they toiled up the side of the gorge, dumped their burdens and then scrambled down again to bring up the next load. At last fully laden they struck out through the forest. Hal made only one detour to cache the two kegs of powder, a bundle of slow-match, and three cutlasses in the cave of the rock paintings. Then they went on again.

It was almost morning when at last they joined Althuda and his band on the island. They ate the cold smoked venison that Sukeena and Zwaantie had ready for them. Then, when the others rolled in their karosses, Hal took Sukeena aside and showed her the great seal of the Nautonnier and the locket.

'Where did you find these, Gundwane?'

'I hid them in the forest on the day we were captured.'

'Who is the woman?' She studied the portrait.

'Edwina Courtney, my mother.'

'Oh, Hal, she is beautiful. You have her eyes.'

'Give my son those same eyes.'

'I will try. With all my heart I will try.'

In the late afternoon Hal roused the others and assigned their duties to them.

'Sabah, take the pistols out of the chest and draw the loads. Reload them, then pack them back into the chest to keep them dry.' The other man set to work at once.

'Big Daniel will help me load the boats. Ned, you take the women down to the beach and explain to them how to help you launch the second boat when the time comes. They must leave everything else behind. There will be neither space nor time to care for extra baggage.'

'Even my bags?' Sukeena asked.

Hal hesitated then nodded firmly. 'Even your bags,' he said, and she did not argue, merely gave him a demure look from under her lashes before she and Zwaantie, carrying Bobby strapped to her back, followed Ned away through the trees.

'Come with me, Aboli.' Hal took his arm and they moved silently to the top end of the island. Then they crept forward on hands and knees until they could lie and look across the open stretch of water at the beach where the boats from the *Gull* and the *Golden Bough* were drawn up below the encampment.

While they kept watch Hal explained the finer details and small modifications to his original plan. From time to time Aboli's tattooed head nodded. In the end he said, 'It is a good and simple plan, and if the gods are kind, it will work.'

In the sunset they studied the two ships anchored in the channel and watched the activity on the beach. As it grew darker, the teams of men who had worked all day, digging the Buzzard's trenches, were relieved. Some came down to bathe in the lagoon. Others rowed out to their berths on the *Gull*.

Smoke from their cooking fires spiralled up through the trees and spread in a pale blue haze across the waters. Hal and Aboli could smell grilling fish on the smoke. Sound carried clearly across the still water. They could hear men's voices and even make out something of what they were saying, a shouted oath or a boisterous argument. Twice Hal was sure that he recognized the Buzzard's voice but they had no further sight of him.

Just as darkness began to fall a longboat pulled away from the side of the *Golden Bough* and headed in towards the beach.

'That's Sam Bowles in the stern,' Hal said, and his voice was filled with loathing.

'Captain Bowles now, if what Jiri tells me is true,' Aboli corrected him.

'It is almost time to move,' Hal said, as the shapes of the anchored ships began to merge with the dark mass of the forest behind them. 'You know what to do, and God go with you, Aboli.' Hal gripped his arm briefly.

'And with you also, Gundwane.' Aboli rose to his feet and went down into the water. He made no noise as he swam across the channel, but he left a faint phosphorescent trail on the dark surface.

Hal found his way back through the bush to where the others waited by the ungainly shapes of the two fireships. He made them sit in a tight circle around him while he spoke to them softly. At the end he made each repeat his instructions, and corrected them when they erred.

'Now nothing remains but to wait until Aboli has done his work.'

Aboli reached the mainland and left the water quickly. He moved quietly through the forest, and the warm breeze had dried his body before he reached the cave of the paintings. He squatted beside the powder kegs and made his preparations as Hal had instructed him.

He cut two fuses from the slow-match. One was only a fathom in length, but the second was a coil thirty feet long. The time delay was an imprecise calculation and the first might burn for ten minutes, but the second for almost thrice as long.

He worked swiftly, and when both kegs were ready he tied the bundle of three cutlasses on his back, swung a powder keg up onto each shoulder and crept out of the cave. He remembered that the previous night when he had visited the hut in which Jiri and the other slaves were being held, he had observed that the Buzzard's men had become careless. The uneventful months they had been camped here had lulled them into a complacent mood. The sentries were no longer vigilant. Still he was not relying on their sloth.

Stealthily he moved closer to the camp, until he could clearly make out the features of the men sitting around the cooking fires. He recognized many, but there was no sign of either Cumbrae or Sam Bowles. He set up the first keg in a patch of scrub on the perimeter of the camp, as close as he dared approach, and then, without lighting the fuse, moved away until he reached one of the trenches where the Buzzard's men had been digging for treasure.

He placed the keg with the longest fuse on the lip of the trench and covered it with sand and debris from the excavation. Then he paid out the coiled fuse and took the end of it down into the trench. He crouched there and shielded the flint and steel with his body so the flare of sparks would not alert the men in the camp as he lit the slow-match. When it was glowing evenly he lit the fuse from it and watched it for a minute to make certain that it was also burning well. Then he climbed out of the trench and moved swiftly and silently back to the first keg. From the slow match in his hand he lit the shorter fuse.

'The first explosion will bring them running,' Hal had explained. 'Then the second keg will go off in their faces.'

Still carrying the bundle of cutlasses, Aboli moved away swiftly. There was always the danger that the flame of one of the fuses might jump ahead and set off the keg prematurely. Once he was clear, and moving with more caution, he found the path that ran down towards the beach. Twice he was forced to leave the path as other figures came towards him out of the darkness. Once he was not quick enough but he brazened it out, exchanging a gruff 'Good night!' with the pirate who brushed past him.

He picked out the mud hut against the glow of the campfires and crept up to the back wall. Jiri responded immediately to his whisper. 'We are ready, brother.' His tone was crisp and fierce, no longer the cringing whine of the slave.

Aboli laid down the bundle of weapons and, with his own cutlass, severed the twine that held them. 'Here!' he whispered, and Jiri's hand came out through the crack in the mud wall. Aboli passed the cutlasses through to him.

'Wait until the first keg blows,' he told him, through the hole in the wall.

'I hear you, Aboli.'

Aboli crept to the corner of the hut and glanced round it. The guard sat in his usual position in front of the door. Tonight he was awake, smoking a long-stemmed clay pipe. Aboli saw the burning tobacco glow in the bowl as he drew upon it. He squatted behind the corner of the wall and waited.

The time passed so slowly that he began to fear that the fuse on the first keg had been faulty and had burned out before reaching it. He decided that he would have to go back to check it, but as he began to rise to his feet the blast swept through the camp.

It tore branches from the trees and sent clouds of burning ash and sparks swirling from campfires. It struck the mud hut, knocking down half the front wall and ripping the thatch from the roof. It hit the guard by the front door and hurled him over backwards. He floundered about on his back, trying to sit up, but his big belly made him ungainly. While he struggled Aboli stood over him, placed one foot on his chest, pinning him to the earth, swung the cutlass and felt the hilt jar in his hand as the edge hacked into the man's neck. His whole body spasmed and then lay still. Aboli leaped away from him and grabbed the rope handle of the rough-hewn door to the hut. As he heaved at it the three men inside hurled their combined weight upon it from the far side, and it burst open.

'This way, brethren.' Aboli led them down towards the beach.

The camp was in uproar. The darkness was full of men blundering about, swearing, shouting orders and alarms.

'To arms! We are attacked.'

'Stand to here,' they heard the Buzzard roar. 'Have at them, lads!'

'Petey! Where are you, me darling boy?' a wounded man screamed for his shipwife. 'I am killed. Come to me, Petey.'

Burning brands from the campfires had been carried into the scrub and the flames were taking hold in the forest. They gave the scene a hellish illumination, and men's shadows made monsters of them as they rushed about, startling each other. Someone fired a musket, and immediately there was a wild fusillade as panic-stricken sailors fired at shadows and at one another. More screams and cries as the flying musket balls took their toll amongst the scurrying figures.

'The bastards are in the forest behind us!' It was the Buzzard's voice again. 'This way, my brave boys!' He was rallying them, and men came rushing up from the beach to join the defence. They ran full into the musket fire of their nervous fellows amongst the trees and fired back at them.

When Aboli reached the beach he found longboats drawn up, abandoned by their crews who had rushed away to answer the Buzzard's call to arms.

'Where do they keep their tools?' Aboli snapped at Jiri.

'There is a store over there.' Jiri led him to it at a run. The spades, axes and iron bars were stacked under an open lean-to shed. Aboli sheathed his cutlass and seized a heavy iron bar. The other three followed his example, then ran back to the beach, and fell upon the boats lying there.

With a few hefty blows they knocked in their bottom timbers, leaving only one unscathed.

'Come on! Waste no more time!' Aboli urged, and they threw down the tools and ran to the single undamaged boat. They thrust it out into the lagoon and tumbled aboard, grabbed an oar each and began to pull for the dark shape of the frigate, which was now emerging from the darkness as the flames of the burning forest lit her.

While they were still only a few oar strokes off the beach a mob of pirates poured out from the grove.

'Stop! Come back!' one shouted.

'It's those black apes. They're stealing one of the boats.'

'Don't let them get away!' A musket banged and a ball hummed over the heads of the men at the oars. They ducked and rowed the harder, putting all their weight into their strokes. Now all the pirates were firing and balls kicked spray off the water close at hand, or thumped into the timbers of the longboat.

Some of the pirates ran to the boats at the water's edge and swarmed into them. They pushed off in pursuit, but almost immediately there were howls of dismay as the water poured in through the shattered floorboards and the boats swamped and overturned. Few could swim, and the yells of rage turned to piteous cries for help as they splashed and floundered in the dark water.

At that moment the second explosion swept through the camp. It did even more damage than the first for, in response to his bellowed orders, the Buzzard's men were charging straight into the blast when it struck them.

'There's something to keep them busy for a while,' Aboli grunted. 'Pull for the frigate, lads, and leave the Buzzard to his kinsman the devil.'

Hal had not waited for the first explosion to shatter the night before he launched the fireship. With all the men in the party helping, they dragged the hull down the beach. Relieved of her cargo, she was a great deal lighter to handle. They piled into her the bundles of cutlasses and the chest filled with loaded pistols.

They left Sabah to hold her and ran back to fetch the second vessel. The women ran beside them as they dragged it down to the water's edge and scrambled on board. Big Daniel carried little Bobby and handed him to Zwaantie when she was safely seated on the floorboards. Hal lifted Sukeena in and placed her gently in the stern sheets. He gave her one last kiss.

'Keep out of danger until we have secured the ship. Listen to Ned. He knows what to do.'

He left her and ran back to take command of the first boat. Big Daniel and the two birds, Sparrow and Finch, were with him, as were Althuda and Sabah. They would need every fighting man on the deck of the frigate if they were to take her.

They pushed the boat out into the channel and as their feet lost the bottom they began to swim and steered her for the anchored frigate. The tide was at high slack: soon it would turn and give them its help as they ran the frigate for the deep channel between the heads.

But first we have to make her ours! Hal told himself as he kicked out strongly, clinging to the gunwale.

A cable's length from the *Golden Bough* Hal whispered, 'Avast, lads. We don't want to arrive before we're welcome.' They hung in the water as the boat drifted aimlessly in the slack of the tide.

The night was quiet, so quiet that they could hear the voices of the men on the beach and the tap and clatter of the frigate's rigging as she snubbed her anchor and her bare masts rolled, almost imperceptibly, against the blaze of the stars.

'Maybe Aboli has run into trouble,' Big Daniel muttered at last. 'We might have to board her without any diversion.'

'Wait!' Hal replied. 'Aboli will never let us down.'

They hung in the water, their nerves stretched to breaking point. Then came the sound of a soft splash behind them, and Hal turned his head. The shape of the second boat crept towards them from the island.

'Ned is over-eager,' Big Daniel said.

'He's only following my orders, but he must not get ahead of us.'

'How can we stop him?'

'I will swim across to speak to him,' Hal answered, and let go his hold on the gunwale. He struck out towards the other boat in a silent breaststroke that did not break the surface. Close alongside he trod water and called softly, 'Ned!'

'Aye, Captain!' Ned answered as softly.

'There is some delay. Wait here and do not get ahead of us. Wait until you hear the first explosion. Then take her in and latch on to the frigate's anchor cable.'

'Aye, Captain,' Ned replied, and looking up at the black hull Hal saw a head peering down at him over the side. The starlight glowed on Sukeena's honey-gold skin, and he knew he must not speak to her again or swim closer lest his concern for her affect his judgement – lest his love for her quench the fighting fire in his blood. He turned and swam back towards the other boat.

As he reached its side and lifted his hand to grip the gunwale, the quiet night was shattered by thunder and the echoes that burst against the hills swept over the lagoon. From the dark grove, flames shot up into the night sky and, for a brief moment, lit the scene like dawn. In that illumination Hal saw every sheet and spar of the frigate's rigging, but there was no sign of an anchor watch or other human presence aboard her.

'All together now, lads,' Hal said, and they struck out again with new heart. It took them only minutes to close the gap. But in that time the night was transformed. They could hear the shouting and musket fire from the beach and the flames of the burning forest danced and glimmered on the surface around them. Hal was afraid that they might be lit brightly enough to be spotted by a vigilant sentry on the frigate's deck.

With relief they swam the awkward craft into the shadow cast by the frigate's tall hull. He glanced back and saw Ned Tyler bringing the other boat close behind them. As Hal watched they reached the frigate's drooping anchor line and he saw Sukeena stand up in the bows and take hold of the cable. He felt a lift of relief. His orders to Ned were to keep the women safely out of the way until they had control of the frigate's deck.

He saw with satisfaction that a skiff was moored alongside the *Golden Bough*, a rope ladder dangling into her from the deck above. Even more fortunately, it was empty, and no heads showed above the frigate's rail. However, he could hear a babble of voices above. The crew must be lining the frigate's far rail facing the beach, staring across in alarm and consternation at the flames, watching the running figures and the flashes of musket fire in bewilderment.

They pushed the fireship the last few feet and bumped softly against the side of the empty skiff. Immediately Hal hauled himself out of the water over her side, leaving the others to secure her, and swarmed up the rope ladder to the deck.

As he had hoped, the skeleton crew of the frigate were all watching the disturbance, but he was dismayed at their numbers. There must be fifty of them at least. However, they were absorbed in what was happening ashore, and as Hal gathered himself to climb out onto the deck there was another mighty detonation from out of the forest.

'By God, will you no' look at that?' one of Sam Bowles's pirates shouted.

'There's a bloody great battle going on out there.'

'Our shipmates are in trouble. They need our help.'

'I owe no favours to any of them. They'll get no help from me.'

'Shamus is right. Let the Buzzard fight his own battles.'

Hal swung himself onto the deck and, with half a dozen quick steps, he had reached the shelter of the break in the forecastle. He crouched there and surveyed the deck. Jiri had told Aboli they were holding the frigate's loyal crew in the main hold. But the hatch was in full view of Sam Bowles's men at the far rail.

He glanced back, and saw Big Daniel's head appear at the entryport. He could not delay. He jumped up, ran out to the main hatch coaming and dropped on his knees behind it. There was a mallet lying beside the hatch, but he dared not use it to hammer out the wedges. The pirates would hear him and be upon him in an instant.

He knocked softly on the timbers with the hilt of his cutlass and spoke in a quiet voice. 'Ahoy there, *Golden Bough*. Do you hear me?'

A muffled voice from beneath the hatch cover answered immediately, in a lilting Celtic accent. 'We hear you. Who are you?'

'An honest Englishman, come to set you free. Will you fight with us against the Buzzard?'

'God love you, honest Englishman! We beg you for a taste of his mongrel blood.'

Hal glanced round. Big Daniel had brought up a bundle of cutlasses, and both Wally Finch and Stan Sparrow carried others. Althuda had the chest of loaded pistols. He lowered it to the deck and opened the lid. At first glance the weapons within seemed dry and ready to fire.

'We have weapons for you,' Hal whispered to the man under the hatch. 'Lend a hand to throw back the hatch when I knock out the wedges, then come out fighting like terriers but call your ship's name, so we will know you and you us.'

He nodded to Daniel and hefted the heavy mallet. Big Daniel seized the lip of the hatch and put all his weight under it. Hal swung the mallet, and with a resounding crack the first wedge flew across the deck. He leaped across the hatch and with another two more full-blooded swings of the mallet sent the remaining wedges clattering to the deck. With Big Daniel straining above and the trapped crew of the *Golden Bough* heaving underneath the coaming cover flew back with a crash and the prisoners came boiling out like angry wasps.

At this sudden uproar behind them, Sam Bowles's men turned and gaped. It took them a long moment to realize that they had been boarded and that their prisoners were free. But by that time Hal and Daniel faced them across the firelit deck, cutlass in hand.

Behind them Althuda was striking sparks from flint and steel as he hurried to light the slow-match on the locks of the pistols, and Wally and Stan were tossing cutlasses to the liberated seamen as they stormed out of the hold.

With a wild shout a pack of pirates led by Sam Bowles charged across the deck. They were twenty against two, and their first rush drove Daniel and Hal back, steel ringing and rasping against steel as they gave ground slowly. But the pair held them long enough for the seamen of the *Golden Bough* to dash into the fight.

Within minutes the deck was thronged with struggling men, and they were so mingled that only their shouted war-cries identified foe from new-made friend.

'Cochran of Cumbrae!' Sam Bowles howled, and Hal's men roared back, 'Sir Hal and the *Golden Bough*!'

The frigate's freed sailors were mad for vengeance – not merely for their own imprisonment but for the massacre of their officers and the drowning of their wounded mates. Hal and his men had a thousand better reasons for their rage, and they had waited infinitely longer to pay off this score.

Sam Bowles's crew were cornered animals. They knew they could expect no help from their fellows on the shore. Nor would they receive mercy or quarter from the avengers who confronted them.

The two sides were almost evenly matched in numbers, but perhaps the crew of the frigate had been weakened by their long confinement in the dark and airless hold. In the forefront of the fight Hal became aware that it was swinging against them. His men were being forced to yield more of the deck and retreat towards the bows.

From the corner of his eye he saw Sabah break and run, throwing aside his sword and scurrying for the hatch to hide below decks. Hal hated him for it. It takes but one coward to start a rout. But Sabah never reached the hatch. A tall black-bearded pirate sent a thrust through the small of his back that came out through his belly-button.

Another hour on the practice field might have saved him, Hal thought fleetingly, then concentrated all his mind and strength on the four men who crowded forward, yammering like hyenas around their bleeding prey, to engage him.

Hal killed one with a thrust under his raised arm into his heart and disarmed another with a neat slash across his wrist that severed his straining sinews. The sword dropped from the man's fingers and he ran screaming across the deck and threw himself, bleeding, overboard. Hal's other two attackers drew back in fear, and in the respite he looked around in the mêlée for Sam Bowles.

He saw him in the back of the horde, keeping carefully out of the worst of it, screaming orders and threats at his men, his ferrety features twisted with malice.

'Sam Bowles!' Hal shouted at him. 'I have you in my eye.' Over the heads of the men between them, Sam looked across at him and there was sudden terror in his pale, close-set eyes.

'I am coming for you now!' Hal roared, and bounded forward, but three men were in his way. In the seconds it took him to beat them aside and clear a path for himself, Sam had darted away and hidden himself in the throng.

Now the pirates clamoured about Hal like jackals around a lion. For a moment he fought side by side with Daniel and saw with amazement that the big man was wounded in a dozen places. Then he felt the hilt of the cutlass sticky in his hand as though he had scooped honey from a jar with his fingers. He realized that it was not honey but his own blood. He, too, was wounded, but in the heat of it all he felt no pain and fought on.

'Beware, Sir Hal!' Big Daniel roared, close beside him in the confusion. 'The stern!'

Hal jumped back, disengaging from the fight, and looked back. Daniel's warning had come just in time to save him.

Sam Bowles was at the rail of the stern overlooking the lower deck. There was a heavy bronze murderer in the slot of the rail and Sam had a lighted match in his hand as he swivelled and aimed the small hand cannon. He had picked out Hal from the press of fighting men and the murderer was aimed at him. Sam touched the match to the pan of the cannon.

In the instant before it fired Hal leaped forward, seized the pirate in front of him around his waist and lifted him off his feet. The man yelled with surprise as Hal held him like a shield, just as the murderer fired and a gale of lead shot swept the deck. Hal felt the body of the man in his arms jump as half a dozen heavy pellets smashed into him. He was dead even before Hal dropped him to the deck.

But the shot had done fearful slaughter amongst the crew of the *Golden Bough*, who were grouped close around where Hal stood. Three were down and kicking in their own blood while another two or three had been struck and were struggling to stay on their feet.

The pirates saw that this sudden onslaught had tipped the balance in their favour and surged forward in a pack, Sam urging them on with excited cries. Like a cracked dam Hal's men started to give way. They were seconds from total rout – when from over the rail behind the raging rabble of pirates rose a great black tattooed face.

Aboli let out a bellow that froze them all where they stood, and as he sprang over the rail he was followed closely by three other huge shapes, each with cutlass in hand. They had killed five men before the pirates had gathered themselves to face this fresh onslaught.

Those around Hal were given new heart: they rallied to Hal's hoarse shouts and, with Big Daniel leading them, rushed back into the fight. Caught between Aboli with his savages and the rejuvenated seamen, the pirates wailed with despair and fled. Those unable to swim scuttled down the hatchways into the bowels of the frigate while the others rushed to the rail and jumped overboard.

The fight was over and the frigate was theirs. 'Where is Sam Bowles?' Hal shouted across at Daniel.

'I saw him run below.'

Hal hesitated a moment, fighting the temptation to rush after him and have his revenge. Then, with an effort, he thrust it aside and turned to his duty.

'There will be time for him later.' He strode to the captain's place on the quarterdeck and surveyed his ship. Some of his men were firing their pistols over the side at the men splashing and swimming towards the beach. 'Avast that nonsense!' he shouted at them. 'Stand by to get the ship under way. The Buzzard will be upon us at any moment now.'

Even the strangers he had released from the hold rushed to obey his command, for they recognized the tone of authority.

Then Hal dropped his voice. 'Aboli and Master Daniel, get the women on board. As quick as you can.' While they ran to the entryport, he turned his full attention to the management of the frigate.

The topmast men were already half-way up the shrouds, and another gang was manning the capstan to weigh the anchor.

'No time for that,' Hal told them. 'Take an axe to the anchor cable and cut us free.' He heard the clunk of the axe into the timbers at the bows, and felt the ship pay off and swing to the ebb.

He glanced towards the entryport and saw Aboli lift Sukeena onto the deck. Big Daniel had little Bobby weeping on his chest and Zwaantie on his other arm.

The main sail blossomed out high above Hal's head, flapped lazily and filled with the gentle night breeze. Hal turned to the helm and felt another great lift of his heart as he saw that Ned Tyler was already at the whipstaff.

'Full and by, Mr Tyler,' he said.

'Full and by it is, Captain.'

'Steer for the main channel!'

'Aye, Captain!' Ned could not suppress his grin, and Hal grinned back at him.

'Will this ship do you, Mr Tyler?'

'It will do me well enough,' Ned said, and his eyes sparkled.

Hal seized the speaking trumpet from its peg and pointed to the sky as he called the order for the top sails to be set above the courses. He felt the ship start under his feet and begin to fly.

'Oh, sweet!' he whispered. 'She is a bird, and the wind is her lover.'

He strode across to where Sukeena was already kneeling beside one of the wounded seamen.

'I told you to leave those bags ashore, did I not?'

'Yes, my lord.' She smiled sweetly up at him. 'But I knew that you were jesting.' Then her expression changed to dismay. 'You are hurt!' She sprang to her feet. 'Let me attend to your injuries.'

'I am scratched, not hurt. This man needs your skills more than I do.' Hal turned from her, strode to the rail and looked across to the beach. The fire had taken fierce hold on the forest, and now the scene was lit like the dawn. He could clearly make out the features of the horde of men at the waterside. They were dancing with rage and frustration for they had realized at last that the frigate was being cut out under their noses.

Hal picked out the giant figure of Cumbrae in the front of the press of men. He was waving his claymore and his face was so swollen with rage that it seemed it might burst open like an overripe tomato. Hal laughed at him and the Buzzard's fury was magnified a hundredfold. His voice carried over the hubbub that his men were making. 'There is no ocean wide enough to hide you, Courtney. I will find you if it takes fifty years.'

Then Hal stopped laughing as he recognized the man who stood a little higher up the beach. At first he doubted his own eyesight, but the flames lit him so clearly that there could be no mistake. In contrast to the Buzzard's antics and transparent rage, Cornelius Schreuder stood, arms folded, staring across at Hal with a cold gaze that placed a sudden chill on Hal's heart. Their eyes locked, and it was as though they confronted each other upon the duelling field.

The *Golden Bough* heeled slightly as a stronger eddy of wind over the heads caught her, and the water began to gurgle under her forefoot like a happy infant. The deck trembled and she drew away from the beach. Hal gave all his attention to the con of the ship, lining her up for the run through the dangerous channel into the sea. It was long minutes before he could look back again towards the shore.

Only two figures remained on the beach. The two men whom Hal hated most in all the world, both his implacable enemies. The Buzzard had waded out waist-deep into the lagoon, as though to remain as close as he could. Schreuder still stood where Hal had last seen him. He had not moved and his reptilian stillness was every bit as chilling as Cumbrae's wild histrionics.

'The day will come when you will have to kill both of them,' said a deep voice beside him, and he glanced at Aboli.

'I dream of that day.'

Beneath his feet he felt the first thrust of the sea coming in through the heads. The flames had destroyed his night vision, and ahead lay utter darkness. He must grope his way through the treacherous channel like a blind man.

'Douse the lanterns!' he ordered. Their feeble light would not penetrate the darkness ahead and would serve only to dazzle him.

'Bring her up a point to larboard,' he ordered Ned Tyler quietly.

'A point to larboard!'

'Meet her!'

He felt rather than saw the loom of the cliff ahead, and heard the surge and break of the waves on the reef at the entrance. He judged his turn by the sounds of the sea, the feel of the wind on his chest and the deck beneath his feet.

After all the shouting and pistol fire, the ship was deathly quiet. Every seaman aboard her knew that Hal was leading them against an ancient enemy far more dangerous than the Buzzard or any man alive.

'Harden up your main and mizzen courses,' he called to the men on the sheets. 'Stand ready to let your topgallants fly.'

An almost palpable fear lay upon the *Golden Bough* for the ebb had her by the throat and there was no manner in which the crew could slow the ship's headlong rush towards the unseen cliffs in the aching blackness.

The moment came. Hal felt the back surge from the breaking reef push across the bows, and the puff of wind on his cheek coming from a new direction as the ship ran on into the maw of rock.

'Starboard your helm!' he said sharply. 'Hard over. Let your topgallants fly.'

The *Golden Bough* spun on her heel and her top sails flapped in the wind, like the wings of a vulture scenting death. The ship rushed on into the darkness and every man on the deck braced himself for the terrible crash as the belly was ripped out of her by the fangs of the reef.

Hal stepped to the rail and peered up into the sky. His eyes were adjusting to the darkness. He saw the line; high above, where the stars were extinguished by the loom of the rocky head.

'Midship your helm, Mr Tyler. Hold her at that.'

The ship steadied on her new course into the night, and Hal's heart beat fast to the echo of booming surf from the cliff close at hand. He clenched his fists at his sides in anticipation of the strike into the reef.

Instead he felt the scend of the open sea hump up under her, and the *Golden Bough* meet it with the passion thrust of a lover.

'Harden up your topgallants.' He raised his voice to carry on high. The flapping of sails ceased and he heard once again the thrumming of tight canvas.

The *Golden Bough* threw up her bows as the first ocean roller slid under her and for a moment no man dared believe that Hal had led them through the maelstrom to safety.

'Light the lanterns,' Hal said quietly. 'Mr Tyler, come around to due south. We will make a good offing.'

The silence persisted, then a voice from the main yard yelled down, 'Lord love you, Captain! We're through.' Then the cheering swept down the deck.

'For Sir Hal and the *Golden Bough*.' They cheered him until their throats ached, and Hal heard strange voices calling his name. The seamen he had released from the hold were cheering him as loudly as the others.

He felt a small warm hand creep into his and looked down to see Sukeena's sweet face glow in the lantern light beside the binnacle.

'Already they love you almost as much as I do.' She tugged softly on his hand. 'Will you not come away to where I can see to your wounds?'

But he did not want to leave his quarterdeck. He wanted to revel longer in the sounds and the feel of his new ship and the sea under her. So he kept Sukeena close beside him as the *Golden Bough* ran on into the night and the stars blazed down from above.

Big Daniel came to them at last, dragging with him an abject figure. For a moment Hal did not recognize the creature but then the whining voice made his skin crawl with loathing and the fine hairs at the back of his neck rise.

'Sweet Sir Henry, I pray you to have mercy on an old shipmate.'

'Sam Bowles.' Hal tried to keep his voice level. 'You have enough innocent blood on your conscience to float a frigate.'

'You do me injustice, good Sir Henry. I am a poor wretch driven by the storms and gales of life, noble Sir Henry. I never wanted to do no man harm.'

'I will deal with him in the morning. Chain him to the mainmast and put two good men to guard him,' Hal ordered Big Daniel. 'Make sure that this time he does not eel his way out of our hands and cheat us once again of the vengeance that we so richly deserve.'

He watched in the lantern light as they shackled Sam Bowles to the foot of the mainmast and two of the crew stood over him with drawn cutlasses.

'My little brother Peter was one of those you drowned,' the older of the two guards told Sam Bowles. 'I beg you for any excuse to stick this blade through your belly.'

Hal left Daniel in charge of the deck and, taking Sukeena with him, went below to the main cabin. She would not rest until she had bathed and bandaged his cuts and wounds, although none were serious enough to cause her alarm. When she had finished, Hal led her through into the small cabin next door. 'You will be able to rest here undisturbed,' he told her, lifted her onto the bunk and, though she protested, covered her with a woollen blanket.

'There are wounded men that need my help,' she said.

'Your unborn son and I need you more,' he told her firmly, and pushed her head down gently. She sighed and was almost immediately asleep.

He returned to the main cabin and sat down at Llewellyn's desk. In the centre of the mahogany top lay a great black leather-covered Bible. During all his captivity Hal had been denied access to the book. He opened the front cover, and read the inscription, written in a bold sloping hand: 'Christopher Llewellyn esq; Born 16th October in the year of grace 1621.'

Below it was another, fresher inscription: 'Consecrated as a Nautonnier Knight of the Temple of the Order of St George and the Holy Grail 2nd August 1643.'

Knowing that the man who had captained this ship before him was a brother Knight gave Hal a deep purpose and pleasure. For an hour he turned the pages of the Bible and reread the familiar and inspiring passages by which his father had taught him to steer his course through life. At last he closed it, stood up and began to search the cabin for the ship's books and documents. He soon discovered the iron strong-box below the bunk. When he could not find the key he called Aboli to help him. They forced open the lid and Hal sent Aboli away. He sat the rest of the night at Llewellyn's desk, studying the ship's books and papers in the lantern light. He was so absorbed by his reading that when Aboli came down to fetch him, an hour after the sun had risen, he looked up in surprise. 'What time is it, Aboli?'

'Two bells in the morning watch. The men are asking to see you, Captain.'

Hal stood up from the desk, stretching and rubbing his eyes, then crossed to the door of the cabin where Sukeena still slept.

'It would be best if you spoke to the new men as soon as you can, Gundwane,' Aboli said, behind him.

'Yes, you are right.' Hal turned back to him.

'Daniel and I have already told them who you are, but you must convince them now to sail under your command. If they refuse to accept you as their new captain, there is little we can do. There are thirty-four of them, and only six of us.'

Hal went to the small mirror on the bulkhead above the jug and basin of the toilet stand. When he saw his reflection he started with amazement. 'Sweet heavens, Aboli, I look such a pirate that I do not even trust myself.'

Sukeena must have been listening, for she appeared suddenly in the doorway with the blanket draped over her shoulders.

'Tell them we will come in a minute, Aboli, when I have made the best of his appearance,' she said.

When Hal and Sukeena stepped out onto the deck together, the men gathered in the ship's waist stared at them with astonishment. The transformation was extraordinary. Hal was freshly shaved and dressed in simple but clean clothing from Llewellyn's locker. Sukeena's hair was combed, oiled and plaited and she had fashioned a long skirt from one of the cabin's velvet drapes and wrapped it around her girlish waist and hips. They made an extraordinary couple, the tall young Englishman and the oriental beauty.

Hal left Sukeena at the companionway and strode out in front of the men. 'I am Henry Courtney. I am an Englishman, as you are. I am a sailor, as you are.'

'Aye, that you are, Captain,' one said loudly. 'We watched you take a strange ship out through the heads in darkness. You're enough sailor to fill my tankard and give me a warm feel in the guts.'

Another called out, 'I sailed with your father, Sir Francis, on the old *Lady Edwina*. He was a seaman and fighter, and an honest man to boot.'

Then another cried, 'Last night, by my count, you took down seven of the Buzzard's scum with your own blade. The pup is well bred from the old dog.'

They all began to cheer him so he could not speak for a long while, but at last he held up his hand. 'I tell you straight that I have read Captain Llewellyn's log. I have read the charter he had with the ship's owner, and I know whither the *Golden Bough* was bound and what was her purpose.' He paused, and looked at their honest, weather-beaten faces. 'We have a choice, you and I. We can say we were beaten by the Buzzard before we began and sail back home to England.'

They groaned and shouted protests until he held up his hand again. 'Or I can take over Captain Llewellyn's charter and his agreement with the owners of the *Golden Bough*. On your side, you can sign on with me on the same terms and with the same share of the prize you agreed before. Before you answer me, remember that if you come with me the chances are strong that we will run in with the Buzzard again, and you will have to fight him once more.'

'Lead us to him now, Captain,' one yelled. 'We'll fight him this very day.'

'Nay, lad. We're short-handed and I need to learn to con this ship before we meet the Buzzard again. We will fight the *Gull* on the day and at the place of my own choosing,' Hal told them grimly. 'On that day we will hoist the Buzzard's head to our masthead and divide up his booty.'

'I'm with you, Captain,' shouted a lanky fair-headed sailor. 'I cannot write my name, but bring me the book and I'll mark a cross so big and black it will fright the devil himself.' They all roared with fierce laughter.

'Bring the book and let us sign.'

'We're with you. My oath and my mark on it.'

Hal stopped them again. 'You will come one at a time to my cabin, so that I can learn each of your names and shake you by the hand.'

He turned to the rail and pointed back over their stern. 'We have made good our offing.' The African coast lay low and blue along the horizon. 'Get aloft now to make sail and bring the ship around onto her true course for the Great Horn of Africa.'

They swarmed up the shrouds and out along the yards and the canvas billowed out until it shone in the sunlight like a soaring thunderhead.

'What course, Captain?' Ned Tyler called from the helm.

'East by north, Mr Tyler,' Hal replied, and felt the ship surge forward under him, as he turned to watch the wake furrow the blue rollers with a line of flashing foam.

Whenever one of the crew passed the foot of the mainmast where Sam Bowles crouched, shackled at hand and foot like a captive ape, they paused to gather saliva and spit at him.

Aboli came to Hal in the forenoon watch. 'You must deal with Sam Bowles now. The men are becoming impatient. One of them is going to cheat the rope and stick a knife between his ribs.'

'That will save me a deal of bother.' Hal looked up from the bundle of charts and the book of sailing directions that he had found in Christopher Llewellyn's chest. He knew that his crew would demand a savage revenge on Sam Bowles, and he did not relish what had to be done.

'I will come on deck at once.' He sighed, surrendering at last to Aboli's ruthless persuasion. 'Have the men assembled in the waist.'

He had thought that Sukeena was still in the small cabin that adjoined the powder magazine, which she had turned into a sickbay and in which two of the wounded men still teetered on the edge of life. He hoped that she would stay there, but as he stepped out onto the deck she came to meet him.

'You should go below, Princess,' he told her softly. 'It will not be a sight fitting to your eyes.'

'What concerns you is my concern also. Your father was part of you, so his death touches upon me. I lost my own father in terrible circumstances, but I avenged him. I will stay to see that you avenge your father's death.'

'Very well.' Hal nodded, and called across the deck. 'Bring the prisoner!'

They were forced to drag Sam Bowles to face his accusers, for his legs could barely support him and his tears ran down to mingle with the spittle that the men had ejected into his face.

'I meant no ill,' he pleaded. 'Hear me, shipmates. 'Twas that devil Cumbrae that drove me to it.'

'You laughed as you held my brother's head under the waters of the lagoon,' shouted one of the seamen.

As they dragged him past where Aboli stood with his arms folded across his chest, he stared at Sam with eyes that glittered strangely.

'Remember Francis Courtney!' Aboli rumbled. 'Remember what you did to the finest man who ever sailed the oceans.'

Hal had prepared a list of the crimes for which Sam Bowles must answer. As he read aloud each charge, the men howled for vengeance.

Finally Hal came to the last item of the dreadful recital: 'That you, Samuel Bowles, in the sight of their comrades and shipmates, did murder the wounded seamen from the *Golden Bough*, who had survived your treacherous ambush, by causing them to be drowned.'

He folded the document, and demanded sternly, 'You have heard the charges against you, Samuel Bowles. What have you to say in your defence?'

'It was not my own fault! I swear I would not have done it but I was in terror of my life.'

The crew shouted him down, and it was some minutes until Hal could quieten them. Then he asked, 'So you do not deny the charges against you?'

'What use denying it?' one of the men shouted. 'We all saw it with our own eyes.'

Sam Bowles was weeping loudly now. 'For the love of sweet Jesus have mercy, Sir Henry. I know I have erred, but give me a chance and you will find no more trusty and loving creature to serve you all the days of your life.'

The sight of Bowles disgusted Hal so deeply that he wanted to wash the foul taste of it from his mouth. Suddenly an image appeared in the eye of his mind. It was of his father lying on the litter, being borne away to the scaffold, his body broken and twisted from the rack. He began to tremble.

Beside him, Sukeena sensed his distress. She laid her hand softly on his arm to steady him. He drew a deep, slow breath and fought back the black waves of sorrow that threatened to overwhelm him. 'Samuel Bowles, you have admitted your guilt to all the charges brought against you. Is there anything that you wish to say before I pronounce sentence upon you?' Grimly he stared into Sam's flooded eyes, and watched a strange transformation take place. He realized that the tears were a device that Sam could call upon at will. Something else burned out from a deep and hidden part of his soul, a nimbus so feral and evil that he doubted he still looked into the eyes of a human being and not those of a wild beast standing at bay.

'You think you hate me, Henry Courtney? You do not know what hatred truly is. I glory in the thought of your father screaming on the rack. Sam Bowles did that. Remember it every day you live. Sam Bowles might be dead but Sam Bowles did that!' His voice rose to a scream, and spittle foamed on his lips. His own evil overwhelmed him and his shrieks were barely coherent. 'This is my ship, my own ship. I would have been Captain Samuel Bowles, and you took it from me. May the devil drink your blood in hell. May he dance on your father's twisted and rotting corpse, Henry Courtney.'

Hal turned away from the revolting spectacle, trying to close his ears to the stream of invective.

'Mr Tyler.' He spoke loudly enough for all the crew to hear above Sam Bowles's screams. 'We will waste no more of the ship's time with this matter. The prisoner is to be hanged immediately. Reeve a rope to the main yard—'

'Gundwane!' Aboli roared a warning. 'Behind you!' And he started forward too late to intervene. Sam Bowles had reached under his petticoats. Strapped to the inside of his thigh was a leather sheath. He was as swift as a striking adder. In his hand the blade of the stiletto sparkled like a sliver of crystal, pretty as a maiden's bauble. He threw it with a snap of his wrist.

Hal had begun to turn to Aboli's warning, but Sam was swifter. The dagger flitted across the space that separated them, and Hal winced in anticipation of the sting of the razor-edged blade burying itself in his flesh. For an instant he doubted his own senses, for he felt no blow.

He looked down and saw that Sukeena had flung out one slim bare arm to block the throw. The silver blade had struck an inch below her elbow and buried itself to the haft.

'Sweet Jesus, shield her!' Hal blurted, seized her in his arms and hugged her to him. Both of them stared down at the hilt of the dagger protruding from her flesh.

Aboli reached Sam Bowles the instant after the stiletto had flown from his fingers and sent him crashing to the deck with a blow of his bunched fist. Ned Tyler and a dozen men leapt forward to seize him, and drag him to his feet. Sam shook his head blearily for Aboli's fist had stunned him. Blood dribbled from the side of his mouth.

'Reeve a rope through the main yard block,' Ned Tyler shouted, and a man raced up the shrouds to obey. He ran out along the main yard, and a minute later the rope fell down through the sheave and its tail flopped onto the deck.

'The blade has gone deep,' Hal whispered, as he held Sukeena against his chest and tenderly lifted her wounded arm.

'It is thin and sharp.' Sukeena smiled bravely up at him. 'So sharp I hardly felt it. Draw the blade swiftly, my darling, and it will heal cleanly.'

'Help me here! Hold her arm,' Hal called to Aboli, who sprang to his side, grasped the slim engraved hilt and, with one swift motion, plucked the blade from Sukeena's flesh. It came away with surprising ease.

She said softly, 'There is little harm done,' but her cheeks had paled and tears trembled on her lower eyelids. Hal lifted her in his arms and started towards the companionway of the stern. A wild scream stopped him.

Sam Bowles stood beneath the dangling rope. Ned Tyler was snugging the noose down under his ear. Four men waited ready with the tail of the rope in their hands.

'Your bitch is dead, Henry Courtney. She is dead just like your bastard sire. Sam Bowles killed both of them. Glory be, Captain Bloody Courtney, remember me in your prayers. I am the man you will never forget!'

''Tis a little cut. The Princess is a strong, brave girl. She will live on,' Ned muttered grimly in Sam Bowles's ear. 'You are the one who is dead, Sam Bowles.' He stepped back and nodded to the men on the rope's end, who walked away with it, slapping their bare feet on the deck timbers in unison.

The instant before the rope came up tight and stopped his breath,

Sam screamed again, 'Look well at the blade that cut your whore, Captain. Think on Sam Bowles when you try the point.' The rope bit into his throat and yanked him off his feet, throttling the next word before it reached his lips.

The crew howled with wolflike glee as Sam Bowles rose spiralling in the air, swinging on the rope's end as the *Golden Bough* rolled under him. His legs kicked and danced so that the chains on his ankles tinkled like sleigh bells.

He was still twitching and gurgling when his neck jammed up tight against the sheave block at the end of the main yard high above the deck.

'Let him hang there all night,' Ned Tyler ordered. 'We'll cut him down in the morning and throw him to the sharks.' Then he stooped and picked up the stiletto from the deck where Hal had flung it. He studied the blood-smeared blade and his tanned face turned yellow grey. 'Sweet Mary, let it not be so!' He looked up again at Sam Bowles's corpse swaying to the ship's motion high above him.

'Your death was too easy. If it were in my power, I would kill you a hundred times over, and each time more painfully than the last.'

Hal laid Sukeena on the bunk in the main cabin. 'I should cauterize the wound but the hot iron would leave a scar.' He knelt beside the bunk and examined it closely. 'It is deep but there is almost no bleeding.' He wrapped her arm in a fold of white linen that Aboli brought him from the sea-chest at the foot of the bunk.

'Bring me my bag,' Sukeena ordered, and Aboli went immediately.

As soon as they were alone, Hal bent over her and kissed her pale cheek. 'You took Sam's throw to save me,' he murmured, his face pressed to hers. 'You risked your own life and the life of the child in your womb for me. It was a bad bargain, my love.'

'I would strike the same bargain—' She broke off and he felt her stiffen in his arms and gasp.

'What is it that ails you, my sweetheart?' He drew back and stared into her face. Before his eyes, tiny beads of perspiration welled up out of the pores of her skin, like the dew on the petals of a yellow rose. 'You are in pain?'

'It burns,' she whispered. 'It burns worse than the hot iron you spoke of.'

Swiftly he unwrapped her arm and stared at the change in the wound that had taken place as they embraced. The arm was swelling before his eyes, like one of the Toby fish of the coral reef that could puff itself up to many times its original size when threatened by a predator.

Sukeena lifted the arm and nursed it to her bosom. She whimpered involuntarily as the pain flowed up from the wound to fill her chest like glowing molten lead.

'I do not understand what is happening.' She began to writhe upon the bunk. 'This is not natural. Look how it changes colour.'

Hal stared helplessly as the lovely limb slowly bloated and discoloured with lines of crimson and vivid purple, that ran up from the elbow to her shoulder. The wound began to weep a viscous yellow fluid.

'What can I do?' he blurted.

'I do not know,' she said desperately. 'This is something beyond my understanding.' A spasm of agony seized her in a vice, and her back arched. Then it passed and she pleaded, 'I must have my bag. I cannot endure this pain. I have a powder made from the opium poppy.'

Hal sprang to his feet and bounded across the cabin. 'Aboli, where are you?' he bellowed. 'Bring the bag, and swiftly!'

Ned Tyler stood upon the threshold of the door. He held something in his hand and there was a strange expression on his face. 'Captain, there is something I must show you.'

'Not now, man, not now.' Hal raised his voice again. 'Aboli, come quickly.'

Aboli came down the companionway in a rush, carrying the saddle-bags. 'What is it, Gundwane?'

'Sukeena! There is something happening to her. She needs the medicine—'

'Captain!' Ned Tyler forced his way past Aboli's bulk into the cabin and seized Hal's arm urgently. 'This cannot wait. Look at the dagger. Look at the point!' He held up the stiletto, and the others stared at it.

'In God's name!' Hal whispered. 'Let it not be so.'

A narrow groove down the length of the blade was filled with a black, tarry paste that had dried hard and shiny.

'It is an assassin's blade,' Ned said quietly. 'The groove is filled with poison.'

Hal felt the deck sway under his feet as though the *Golden Bough* had been struck by a tall wave. His vision went dark. 'It cannot be,' he said. 'Aboli, tell me it cannot be.'

'Be strong,' Aboli muttered. 'Be strong for her, Gundwane.' He gripped Hal's arm.

The hand steadied Hal and his vision brightened, but when he tried to draw breath the leaden hand of dread crushed in his ribs. 'I cannot live without her,' he said, like a confused child.

'Do not let her know,' Aboli said. 'Do not make the parting harder for her than it need be.'

Hal stared at him uncomprehendingly. Then he began to understand the finality, the significance of that tiny groove in the steel blade, and of the fatal threats that Sam Bowles had shouted at him with the hangman's noose around his neck.

'Sukeena is going to die,' he said, in a tone of bewilderment.

'This will be harder for you than any fight you have ever fought before, Gundwane.'

With an enormous effort Hal fought to regain control of himself. 'Do not show her the dagger,' he said to Ned Tyler. 'Go! Hurl the cursed thing overboard.'

When he got back to Sukeena he tried to conceal the black despair in his heart. 'Aboli has brought your bags.' He knelt beside her again. 'Tell me how to prepare the potion.'

'Oh, do it swiftly,' she pleaded as another spasm gripped her. 'The blue flask. Two measures in a mug of hot water. No more than that, for it is powerful.'

Her hand shook violently as she tried to take the mug from him. She had only the use of the one hand now: her wounded arm was swollen and purpled, the once dainty fingers so bloated that the skin threatened to burst open. She had difficulty holding the mug and Hal lifted it to her lips while she gulped down the potion with pathetic urgency.

She fell back with the effort and writhed on the bunk, drenching the bedclothes with the sweat of agony. Hal lay beside her and held her to his chest, trying to comfort her but knowing too well how futile were his efforts.

After a while the poppy flower seemed to have its effect. She clung to him and pressed her face into his neck. 'I am dying, Gundwane.'

'Do not say so,' he begged her.

'I have known it these many months. I saw it in the stars. That was why I could not answer your question.'

'Sukeena, my love, I will die with you.'

'No.' Her voice was a little stronger. 'You will go on. I have travelled with you as far as I am permitted. But for you the Fates have reserved a special destiny.' She rested a while, and he thought that she had fallen into a coma, but then she spoke again. 'You will live on. You will have many strong sons and their descendants will flourish in this land of Africa, and make it their own.'

'I want no son but yours,' he said. 'You promised me a son.'

'Hush, my love, for the son I give you will break your heart.' Another terrible convulsion took her, and she screamed in the agony of it. At last, when it seemed she could bear no more, she fell back trembling and wept. He held her and could find no words to tell her of his grief.

The hours passed, and twice he heard the ship's bell announce the watch changes. He felt her grow weaker and sink away from him. Then a series of powerful convulsions racked her body. When she fell back in his arms, she whispered, 'Your son, the son I promised you, has been born.' Her eyes were tightly closed, tears squeezing out between the lids.

For a long minute he did not understand her words. Then, fearfully, he drew back the blanket.

Between her bloody thighs lay a tiny pink mannikin, glistening wet and bound to her still by a tangle of fleshy cord. The little head was only half formed, the eyes would never open and the mouth would never take suck, nor cry, nor laugh. But he saw that it was, indeed, a boy.

He took her again in his arms and she opened her eyes and smiled softly. 'I am sorry, my love. I have to go now. If you forget all else, remember only this, that I loved you as no other woman will ever be able to love you.'

She closed her eyes and he felt the life go out of her, the great stillness descend.

He waited with them, his woman and his son, until midnight. Then Althuda brought down a bolt of canvas and sailmaker's needle, thread and palm. Hal placed the stillborn child in Sukeena's arms and bound him there with a linen winding sheet. Then he and Althuda sewed them into a shroud of bright new canvas, a cannonball at Sukeena's feet.

At midnight Hal carried the woman and child in his arms up onto the open deck. Under the bright African moon he gave them both up to the sea. They went below the dark surface and left barely a ripple in the ship's wake at their passing.

'Goodbye, my love,' he whispered. 'Goodbye, my two darlings.'

Then he went down to the cabin in the stern. He opened Llewellyn's Bible and looked for comfort and solace between its black-leather covers, but found none.

For six long days he sat alone by his cabin window. He ate none of the food that Aboli brought him. Sometimes he read from the Bible, but mostly he stared back along the ship's wake. He came up on deck at noon each day, gaunt and haggard, and sighted the sun. He made his calculations of the ship's position and gave his orders to the helm. Then he went back to be alone with his grief.

At dawn on the seventh day Aboli came to him. 'Grief is natural, Gundwane, but this is indulgence. You forsake your duty and those of us who have placed our trust in you. It is enough.'

'It will never be enough.' Hal looked at him. 'I will mourn her all the days of my life.' He stood up and the cabin swam around him, for he was weak with grief and lack of food. He waited for his head to steady and clear. 'You are right, Aboli. Bring me a bowl of food and a mug of small beer.'

After he had eaten, he felt stronger. He washed and shaved, changed his shirt and combed his hair back into a thick plait down his back. He saw that there were strands of pure white in the sable locks. When he looked in the mirror, he barely recognized the darkly tanned face that stared back at him, the nose as beaky as that of an eagle, and there was no spare flesh to cover the high-ridged cheek-bones or the unforgiving line of the jaw. His eyes were green as emeralds, and with that stone's adamantine glitter.

I am barely twenty years of age, he thought, with amazement, and yet I look twice that already.

He picked up his sword from the desk top and slipped it into the scabbard. 'Very well, Aboli. I am ready to take up my duty again,' he said, and Aboli followed him up onto the deck.

The boatswain at the helm knuckled his forehead, and the watch on deck nudged each other. Every man was intensely aware of his presence, but none looked in his direction. Hal stood for a while at the rail, his eyes darting keenly about the deck and rigging.

'Boatswain, hold your luff, damn your eyes!' he snapped at the helmsman.

The leech of the main sail was barely trembling as it spilled the wind, but Hal had noticed it and the watch, squatting at the foot of the mainmast, grinned at each other surreptitiously. The captain was in command again.

At first they did not understand what this presaged. However, they were soon to learn the breadth and extent of it. Hal started by speaking to every man of the crew alone in his cabin. After he had asked their names and the village or town of their birth, he questioned them shrewdly as to their service. Meanwhile he was studying each and assessing his worth.

Three stood out above the others; they had all been watchkeepers under Llewellyn's command. The boatswain, John Lovell, was the man who had served under Hal's father.

'You'll keep your old rating, boatswain,' Hal told him, and John grinned.

'It will be a pleasure to serve under you, Captain.'

'I hope you feel the same way in a month from now,' Hal replied grimly.

The other two were William Stanley and Robert Moone, both coxswains. Hal liked the look of them: Llewellyn had a good eye for judging men, he thought, and shook their hands.

Big Daniel was his other boatswain, and Ned Tyler, who could both read and write, was mate. Althuda, one of the few other literates aboard, became the ship's writer, in charge of all the documents and keeping them up to date. He was Hal's closest remaining link with Sukeena, and Hal felt the greatest affection for him and wished to keep him near at hand. They could share each other's grief.

John Lovell and Ned Tyler went through the ship's roster with Hal and helped him draw up the watch-bill, the nominal list by which every man knew to which watch he was quartered and his station for every purpose.

As soon as this was done Hal inspected the ship. He started on the main deck and then, with his two boatswains, opened every hatch. He climbed and sometimes crawled into every part of the hull, from her bilges to her maintop. In her magazine he opened three kegs, chosen at random, and assessed the quality of her gunpowder and slow-match.

He checked off her cargo against the manifest, and was surprised and pleased to find the amount of muskets and lead shot she carried, together with great quantities of trade goods.

Then he ordered the ship hove to, and a longboat lowered. He had himself rowed around the ship so he could judge her trim. He moved some of the culverins to gunports further aft, and ordered the cargo swung out on deck and repacked to establish the trim he favoured. Then he exercised the ship's company in sail setting and altering, sailing the *Golden Bough* through every point of the compass and at every attitude to the wind. This went on for almost a week, as he called out the watch below at noon or in the middle of the night to shorten or increase sail and push the ship to the limits of her speed.

Soon he knew the *Golden Bough* as intimately as a lover. He found out how close he could take her to the wind, and how she loved to run before it with all her canvas spread. He had a bucket crew wet down her sails so they would better hold the wind, and then, when she was in full flight, took her speed through the water with glass and log timed from bow to stern. He found out how to coax the last yard of speed out of her, and how to have her respond to the helm like a fine hunter to the reins.

The crew worked without complaint, and Aboli heard them talking amongst themselves in the forecastle. Far from complaining, they seemed to be enjoying the change from Llewellyn's more complacent command.

'The young 'un is a sailor. The ship loves him. He can drive the *Bough* to her limit, and make her fly through the water, he can.'

'He's happy to drive us to the limit, also,' another opined.

'Cheer up, all you lazy layabouts, I reckon there'll be prize money galore at the end of this voyage.'

Then Hal worked them at the guns, running them out then in again, until the men sweated, strained and grinned as they cursed him for a tyrant. Then he had the guncrews fire at a floating keg, and cheered with the best of them as the target shattered to the shot.

In between times, he exercised them with the cutlass and the pike, and he fought alongside them, stripped to the waist and matching himself against Aboli, Big Daniel or John Lovell, who was the best swordsman of the new crew.

The *Golden Bough* sailed on around the bulge of the southern African continent and Hal headed her up into the north. Now with every league they sailed the sea changed its character. The waters took on a vivid indigo hue that stained the sky the same colour. They were so clear that, leaning over the bows, Hal could see the pods of porpoises four fathoms down, racing ahead of the bows and frolicking like a pack of boisterous spaniels until they arched up to the surface. As they broke through it he could see the nostril on top of their head open to breathe, and they looked up at him with a merry eye and a knowing grin.

The flying fish were their outriders, sailing ahead of them on flashing silver wings, and the mountains of towering cumulus clouds were the beacons that beckoned them ever northwards.

When they sailed into the great calms he would not let his crew rest, but lowered the boats and raced watch against watch, the oars churning the water white. Then at the end of the course he had them board the *Golden Bough* as though she were an enemy, while he and Aboli and Big Daniel opposed them and made them fight for a footing on the deck.

In the windless heat of the tropics, while the *Bough* rolled gently on the sluggish swells and the empty sails slatted and lolled, he raced the hands in relay teams to the top of the mainmast and down, with an extra tot of rum as the prize.

Within weeks the men were fit and lean and bursting with high spirits, spoiling for a fight. Hal, however, was plagued by a nagging worry that he shared with nobody, not even Aboli. Night after night he sat at his desk in the main cabin, not daring to sleep, for he knew that the grief and the memories of the woman and the child he had lost would haunt his dreams, and he studied the charts and tried to puzzle out a solution.

He had barely forty men under his command, only just sufficient to work the ship, but too few by far to fight her. If they met again, the Buzzard would be able to send a hundred men onto the *Golden Bough*'s deck. If they were to be able to defend themselves, let alone seek employment in the service of the Prester, then Hal must find seamen.

When he perused the charts he could find few ports where he might enlist trained seamen. Most were under the control of the Portuguese and the Dutch, and they would not welcome an English frigate, especially one whose captain was intent on seducing their sailors into his service.

The English had not penetrated this far ocean in any force. A few traders had factories on the Indian continent, but they were under the thrall of the Great Mogul, and, besides, to reach them would mean a voyage of several thousand miles out of his intended course.

Hal knew that on the south-east shore of the long island of St Lawrence, which was also called Madagascar, the French Knights of the Order of the Holy Grail had a safe harbour which they called Fort Dauphin. If he called in there, as an English Knight of the Order he could expect a welcome but little else for his comfort, unless some rare circumstance such as a cyclone had caused a wreck and left sailors in the port without ship. However, he decided that he must take that chance and make Fort Dauphin his first call, and laid his course for the island.

As he sailed on northwards, with Madagascar as his goal, Africa was always there off the larboard beam. At times the land dreamed in the blue distance, and at other times it was so close that they could smell its peculiar aroma. It was the peppery scent of spice and the rich dark odour of the earth, like new-baked biscuit hot from the oven.

Often Jiri, Matesi and Kimatti clustered at the rail, pointing at the green hills and the lacy lines of surf, and talking together quietly in the language of the forests. When there was a quiet hour, Aboli would climb to the masthead and stare across at the land. When he descended his expression was sad and lonely.

Day after day they saw no sign of other men. There were no towns or ports along the shore that they could spy out, and no sail upon the sea, not even a canoe or coasting dhow.

It was not until they were less than a hundred leagues south of Cap St Marie, the southernmost point of the island, that they raised another sail. Hal stood the ship to quarters and had the culverin loaded with grape and the slow-match lit, for out here beyond the Line he dared take no ship on trust.

When they were almost within hail of the other ship, it broke out its colours. Hal was delighted to see the Union flag and the *croix patté* of the Order streaming from her masthead. He replied with the same show of cloth and both ships hove to within hail of each other.

'What ship?' Hal asked, and the reply came back across the blue swells, 'The *Rose of Durham*. Captain Welles.' She was an armed trader, a caravel with twelve guns a side.

Hal lowered a longboat and had himself rowed across. He was greeted at the entryport by a spry, elfin captain of middle years. '*In Arcadia habito*.'

'*Flumen sacrum bene cognosco*,' Hal replied, and they clasped hands in the recognition grip of the Temple.

Captain Welles invited Hal down to his cabin where they drank a tankard of cider together and exchanged news avidly. Welles had sailed four weeks previously from the English factory of St George near Madras on the east coast of Further India with a cargo of trade cloth. He intended to exchange this for slaves on the Gambian coast of West Africa, and then sail on across the Atlantic to the Caribbean where he would barter his slaves for sugar, and so back home to England.

Hal questioned him on the availability of seamen from the English factories on the Carnatic, that stretch of the shore of Further India from East Ghats down to the Coromandel coast, but Welles shook his head. 'You'll be wanting to give the whole of that coast a wide berth. When I left the cholera was raging in every village and factory. Any man you take aboard might bring death with him as a companion.'

Hal chilled at the thought of the havoc that this plague would wreak among his already depleted crew, should it take hold on the *Golden Bough*. He dared not risk a visit to those fever ports.

Over a second mug of cider, Welles gave Hal his first reliable account of the conflict raging in the Great Horn of Africa. 'The younger brother of the Great Mogul, Sadiq Khan Jahan, has arrived off the coast of the Horn with a great fleet. He has joined forces with Ahmed El Grang, who they call the Left-handed, the king of the Omani Arabs who holds sway over the lands bordering the Prester's empire. These two have declared *jihad*, holy war, and together they have swept down like a raging gale upon the Christians. They have taken by storm and sacked the ports and towns of the coast, burning the churches and despoiling the monasteries, massacring the monks and the holy men.'

'I intend sailing to offer my services to the Prester to help him resist the pagan,' Hal told him.

'It is another crusade, and yours is a noble inspiration,' Welles applauded him. 'Many of the most sacred relics of Christendom are held by the holy fathers in the Ethiopian city of Aksum and in the monasteries in secret places in the mountains. If they were to fall into the hands of the pagan, it would be a sad day for all Christendom.'

'If you cannot yourself go upon this sacred venture, will you not spare me a dozen of your men, for I am sore pressed for the lack of good sailors?' Hal asked.

Welles looked away. 'I have a long voyage ahead of me, and there are bound to be heavy losses amongst my crew when we visit the fever coast of the Gambia and make the middle passage of the Atlantic,' he mumbled.

'Think on your vows,' Hal urged him.

Welles hesitated, then shrugged. 'I will muster my crew, and you may appeal to them and call for volunteers to join your venture.'

Hal thanked him, knowing that Welles was on a certain wager. Few seamen at the end of a two-year voyage would forgo their share of profits and the prospect of a swift return home, in favour of a call to arms to aid a foreign potentate, even if he were a Christian. Only two men responded to Hal's appeal, and Welles looked relieved to be shot of them. Hal guessed that they were trouble-makers and malcontents, but he could not afford to be finicky.

Before they parted, Hal handed over to Welles two packets of letters, stitched in canvas covers with the address boldly written on each. One was addressed to Viscount Winterton, and in the long letter Hal had penned to him he set out the circumstances of Captain Llewellyn's murder, and his own acquisition of the *Golden Bough*. He gave an undertaking to sail the ship in accordance with the original charter.

The second letter was addressed to his uncle, Thomas Courtney, at High Weald, to inform him of the death of his father and his own inheritance of the title. He asked his uncle to continue to run the estate on his behalf.

When at last he took leave of Welles, the two seamen he had acquired went with him back to the *Golden Bough*. From his quarterdeck Hal watched the top sails of the *Rose of Durham* drop below the southern horizon, and days afterwards the hills of Madagascar rise before him out of the north.

That night Hal, as had become his wont, came up on deck at the end of the second dog watch to read the traverse board and speak to the helmsman. Three dark shadows waited for him at the foot of the mainmast.

'Jiri and the others wish to speak to you, Gundwane,' Aboli told him.

They clustered about him as he stood by the windward rail. Jiri spoke first in the language of the forests. 'I was a man when the slavers took me from my home,' he told Hal quietly. 'I was old enough to remember much more of the land of my birth than these others.' He indicated Aboli, Kimatti and Matesi, and all three nodded agreement.

'We were children,' said Aboli.

'In these last days,' Jiri went on, 'when I smelled the land and saw again the green hills, old memories long forgotten came back to me. I am sure now, in my deepest heart, that I can find my way back to the great river along the banks of which my tribe lived when I was a child.'

Hal was silent for a while, and then he asked, 'Why do you tell me these things, Jiri? Do you wish to return to your own people?'

Jiri hesitated. 'It was so long ago. My father and my mother are dead, killed by the slavers. My brothers and the friends of my childhood are gone also, taken away in the chains of the slavers.' He was silent awhile, but then he went on, 'No, Captain, I cannot return, for you are now my chief as your father was before you, and these are my brothers.' He indicated Aboli and the others who stood around him.

Aboli took up the tale. 'If Jiri can lead us back to the great river, if we can find our lost tribe, it may well be that we can find also a hundred warriors amongst them to fill the watch-bill of this ship.'

Hal stared at him in astonishment. 'A hundred men? Men who can fight like you four rascals? Then, indeed, the stars are smiling upon me again.'

He took all four down to the stern cabin, lit the lanterns and spread his charts upon the deck. They squatted around them in a circle, and the black men prodded the parchment sheets with their forefingers and argued softly in their sonorous voices, while Hal explained the lines on the charts to the three who, unlike Aboli, could not read.

When the ship's bell tolled the beginning of the morning watch, Hal went on deck and called Ned Tyler to him. 'New course, Mr Tyler. Due south. Mark it on the traverse board.'

Ned was clearly astounded at the order to turn back, but he asked no question. 'Due south it is.'

Hal took pity on him, for it was evident that curiosity itched him like a burr in his breeches. 'We're closing the African mainland again.'

They crossed the broad channel that separated Madagascar from the African continent. The mainland came up as a low blue smudge on the horizon and, at a good offing, they turned and sailed southwards once more along the coast.

Aboli and Jiri spent most of the hours of daylight at the masthead, peering at the land. Twice Jiri came down and asked Hal to stand inshore to investigate what appeared to be the mouth of a large river. Once it turned out to be a false channel and the second time Jiri did not recognize it when they anchored off the mouth. 'It is too small. The river I seek has four mouths.'

They weighed anchor and worked out to sea again, then went on southwards. Hal was beginning to doubt Jiri's memory but he persevered. Several days later he noticed the patent excitement of the two men at the masthead as they stared at the land and gesticulated to each other. Matesi and Kimatti, who as part of the off-duty watch had been lazing on the forecastle, scrambled to their feet and flew up the shrouds to hang in the rigging and stare avidly at the land.

Hal strode to the rail and raised Llewellyn's brass-bound telescope to his eye. He saw the delta of a great river spread before them. The waters that spilled out from the multiple mouths were discoloured and carried with them the detritus of the swamps and the unknown lands that must lie at the source of this mighty river. Squadrons of sharks were feeding on this waste, and their tall, triangular fins zigzagged across the current.

Hal called Jiri down to him and asked, 'What do your tribe call this river?'

'There are many names for it, for the one river comes to the sea as many rivers. They are called Muselo and Inhamessingo and Chinde. But the chief of them is Zambere.'

'They all have a noble ring to them,' Hal conceded. 'But are you certain this is the river serpent with four mouths?'

'On the head of my dead father I swear it is.'

Hal had two men in the bows taking soundings as he crept inshore, and as soon as the bottom began to shelve steeply he dropped anchor in twelve fathoms. He would not risk the ship in the narrow inland waters and the convoluted channels of the delta. But there was another risk he was unwilling to face.

He knew from his father that these tropical deltas were dangerous to the health of his crew. If they breathed the night airs of the swamp, they would soon fall prey to the deadly fevers that were borne upon them, aptly named the malaria, the bad airs.

Sukeena's saddle-bags, which with her mother's jade brooch were her only legacy to Hal, contained a goodly store of the Jesuit's powder, the extract of the bark of the Cinchona tree. He had also discovered a large jar of the same precious substance amongst Llewellyn's stores. It was the only remedy against the malaria, a disease that mariners encountered in every known area of the oceans, from the jungles of Batavia and Further India to the canals of Venice, the swamps of Virginia and the Caribbean in the New World.

Hal would not risk his entire crew to its ravages. He ordered the two pinnaces swung up from the hold and assembled. Then he chose the crews for these vessels, which naturally included the four Africans and Big Daniel. He placed a falconet in the bows of each and had a pair of murderers mounted in the sterns.

All the men in the expedition were heavily armed, and Hal placed three heavy chests of trade goods in each boat, knives and scissors and small hand mirrors, rolls of copper wire and Venetian glass beads.

He left Ned Tyler in charge of the *Golden Bough* with Althuda, and ordered them to remain anchored well offshore, and await his return. The distress signal would be a red Chinese rocket: only if he saw it was Ned to send the longboats in to find them.

'We may be many days, weeks even,' Hal warned. 'Do not lose patience. Stay on your station as long as you do not have word of us.'

Hal took command of the leading boat. He had Aboli and the other Africans in his crew. Big Daniel followed in the second.

Hal explored each of the four mouths. The water levels seemed low, and some of the entrances were almost sealed by their sand bars. He knew of the danger of crocodiles and would not risk sending men over the side to drag the boats over the bar. In the end he chose the river mouth with the greatest volume of water pouring through it. With the onshore morning breeze filling the lug sail and all hands at the oars they forced their way over the bar into the hot, hushed world of the swamps.

Tall papyrus plants and stands of mangroves formed a high wall down each side of the channel so that their vision was limited and the wind was blanketed from them. They rowed on steadily, following the twists of the channel. Each turn opened the same dreary view. Hal realized almost at once how easy it would be to lose his way in this maze and he marked each branch of the channel with strips of canvas tied to the top branches of mangrove.

For two days they groped their way westwards, guided only by the compass and the flow of the waters. In the pools wallowed herds of the great grey river-cows which opened cavernous pink jaws and honked at them with wild laughter as they approached. At first they steered well clear of them, but once they became more familiar with them Hal began to ignore their warning cries and displays of rage, and pushed on recklessly.

His bravado at first seemed justified and the animals submerged when he drove straight at them. Then they came round another bend into a large green pool. In the centre was a mud-bank, and on it stood a huge female hippopotamus and at her flank a new-born calf not much bigger than a pig. The cow bellowed at them threateningly as they rowed towards her, but the men laughed with derision and Hal shouted from the bows, 'Stand aside, old lady, we mean you no harm, but we intend to pass.'

The great beast lowered her head and, grunting belligerently, charged across the mud in a wild, ungainly gallop that hurled up clods of mud. As soon as he realized that the brute was in earnest Hal snatched up the slow-match from the tub at his feet. 'By heavens, she means to attack us.'

He grabbed the iron handle of the falconet and swung it to aim ahead, but the hippopotamus reached the water and plunged into it at full tilt, sending up a sheet of spray and disappearing beneath the surface. Hal swung the barrel of the falconet from side to side, seeking a chance to fire, but he saw only a ripple on the surface as the animal swam deep below it.

'It is coming straight for us!' Aboli shouted. 'Wait until you get a clear shot, Gundwane!'

Hal peered down, the burning match held ready, and through the clear green water he saw a remarkable sight. The hippo was moving along the bottom in a slow dreamlike gallop, clouds of mud boiling up under her hoofs with each stride. But she was still a fathom deep and his shot could never reach her.

'She has gone beneath us!' he shouted at Aboli.

'Get ready!' Aboli warned. 'This is how they destroy the canoes of my people.' The words had barely left his lips when beneath their feet came a resounding crack as the beast reared up under them, and the heavy boat with its full complement of ten rowers was lifted high out of the water.

They were hurled from their benches, and Hal might have been thrown overboard if he had not grabbed the thwart. The boat crashed back to the surface and Hal again seized the tail of the falconet.

The animal's charge would have stove in the hull of any lesser craft, and would certainly have splintered a native dugout canoe, but the pinnace was robustly constructed to withstand the ravages of the North Sea.

Close alongside, the huge grey head burst through the surface, and the mouth opened like a pink cavern lined with fangs of yellow ivory as long as a man's forearm. With a bellow that shocked the crew with its ferocity the hippopotamus rushed at them with gaping jaws to tear the timbers out of the boat's side.

Hal swung the falconet until it was almost touching the onrushing head. He fired. Smoke and flame shot straight down the gaping throat and the jaws clashed shut. The beast disappeared in a swirl, to surface seconds later half-way back to the mud-bank on which her calf stood, forlorn and bewildered.

The huge rotund body reared half out of the water in a gargantuan convulsion then collapsed back and sank away in death, leaving a long wake of crimson to mark the green waters with its passing.

The rowers wielded their oars with renewed vigour and the boat shot round the next bend, with Big Daniel's boat close astern. The hull of Hal's vessel was leaking fairly heavily, but with one man bailing they could keep her dry until they had an opportunity to beach her and turn her over to repair the damage. They pressed on up the channel.

Clouds of waterfowl rose from the dense stands of papyrus around them or perched in the branches of the mangroves. There were herons, duck and geese that they recognized, together with dozens of other birds that they had never seen before. Several times they caught glimpses of a strange antelope with a shaggy brown coat and spiral horns with pale tips, which seemed to make the deep swamps its home. At dusk they surprised one as it stood on the edge of the papyrus. With a long and lucky musket shot, Hal brought it down. They were astonished to find that its hoofs were deformed, enormously elongated. Such feet would act like the fins of a fish in the water, Hal reasoned, and give it purchase on the soft footing of mud and reeds. The antelope's flesh was sweet and tender and the men, long starved of fresh food, ate it with relish.

The nights, when they slept on the bare deck, were murmurous, troubled by great clouds of stinging insects, and in the dawn their faces were swollen and bloated with red lumps.

On the third day the papyrus began to give way to open flood plains. The breeze could reach them now, and blew away the clouds of insects and filled the lug sail they set. They went on at better speed and came to where the other branches of the river all joined up to form one great flow almost three cables' length in width.

The flood plains on each bank of this mighty river were verdant with a knee-high growth of rich grasses, grazed by huge herds of buffalo. Their numbers were uncountable, and they formed a moving carpet as far as

Hal could see, even when he shinned up the pinnace's mast. They stood so densely upon the plain that large areas of the grasslands were obscured by their multitudes. They were tarry lakes and running rivers of bovine flesh.

The outer fringes of these herds lined the banks of the river and stared across the water at them, their drooling muzzles lifted high and their bossed heads heavy with drooping horns. Hal steered the boat in closer and fired the falconet into the thick of them. With that single discharge he brought down two young cows. That night, for the first time, they camped ashore and feasted on buffalo steaks roasted on the coals.

For many days, they went on following the stately green flow, and the flood plains on either hand gradually gave way to forests and glades. The river narrowed, became deeper and stronger and their progress was slower against the current. On the eighth evening after leaving the ship, they went ashore to camp in a grove of tall wild fig trees.

Almost immediately they came upon signs of human habitation. It was a decaying stockade, built of heavy logs. Within its wooden walls were pens that Hal thought must have been for enclosing cattle or other beasts.

'Slavers!' said Aboli bitterly. 'This is where they have chained my people like animals. In one of these *bomas*, perhaps this very one, my mother died under the weight of her sorrow.'

The stockade had been long abandoned but Hal could not bring himself to camp on the site of so much human misery. They moved a league upstream and found a small island on which to bivouac. The next morning they went on along the river through forest and grassland innocent of any further evidence of man. 'The slavers have swept the wilderness with their net,' Aboli said sorrowfully. 'That is why they have abandoned their factory and sailed away. It seems that there are no men or women of our tribe who have survived their ravages. We must abandon the search, Gundwane, and turn back.'

'No, Aboli. We go on.'

'All around us is the ancient memory of despair and death,' Aboli pleaded. 'These forests are inhabited only by the ghosts of my people.'

'I will decide when we turn back, and that time is not yet come,' Hal told him, for in truth he was becoming fascinated by this strange new land and the plethora of wild creatures with which it abounded. He felt a powerful urge to travel on and on, to follow the great river to its source.

The next day, from the bows, Hal spied a range of low hillocks a short distance north of the river. He ordered them to beach the boats and left Big Daniel and his seamen to repair the leaks in the hull of the first caused by the hippopotamus attack. He took Aboli with him and they set off to climb the hills for a better view of the country ahead. They were further off than they had appeared to be, for distances are deceptive in the clear air and under the bright light of the African sun. It was late afternoon when they stepped out onto the crest and gazed down upon the limitless distances where forests and hills replicated themselves, rank upon rank and range upon range, like images of infinity in mirrors of shaded blue.

They sat in silence, awed by the immensity of this wild land. At last Hal stood up reluctantly. 'You are right, Aboli. There are no men here. We must return to the ship.'

Yet he felt deep within him a strange reluctance to turn his back upon this tremendous land. More than ever, he felt drawn to its mystery and the romance of its vast spaces.

'You will have many strong sons,' Sukeena had prophesied. 'Their descendants will flourish in this land of Africa and make it their own.'

He did not yet love this land. It was too strange and barbaric, too alien from all he had known in the gentler climes of the north, but deeply he felt the magic of it in his blood. The silence of dusk fell upon the hills, that moment when all creation held its breath before the insidious advance of the night. He took one last look, sweeping the horizon where, like monstrous chameleons, the hills changed colour. Before his eyes they turned sapphire, azure, and the blue of a kingfisher's back. Suddenly he stiffened.

He grasped Aboli's arm and pointed. 'Look!' he said softly. From the foot of the next range a single thin plume of smoke rose out of the forest and climbed up into the violet evening air.

'Men!' Aboli whispered. 'You were right not to turn back so soon, Gundwane.'

They went down the hill in darkness and moved through the forest like shadows. Hal guided them by the stars, fixing his eye upon the great shining Southern Cross that hung above the hill at the foot of which they had marked the column of smoke. After midnight, as they crept forward with increasing caution, Aboli stopped so abruptly that Hal almost ran into him in the darkness.

'Listen!' he said. They stood in silence for minute after minute.

Then Hal said, 'I hear nothing.'

'Wait!' Aboli insisted, and then Hal heard it. It was a sound once so commonplace, but one that he had not heard since he had left Good Hope. It was the mournful lowing of a cow.

'My people are herders,' Aboli whispered. 'Their cattle are their most treasured possessions.' He led Hal forward cautiously until they could smell the woodsmoke and the familiar bovine odour of the cattle pen. Hal picked out the puddle of faintly glowing ash that marked the campfire. Silhouetted against it was the outline of a sitting man, wrapped in a kaross.

They lay and waited for the dawn. However, long before first light the camp began to stir. The watchman stood up, stretched, coughed and spat in the dead coals. Then he threw fresh wood upon the fire, and knelt to blow it. The flames flared and, by their light, Hal saw that he was but a boy. Naked except for a loincloth, the lad left the fire and came close to where they were hidden. He lifted his loincloth and peed into the grass, playing games with his urine stream, aiming at fallen leaves and twigs and chuckling as he tried to drown a scurrying scarab beetle.

Then he went back to the fire and called out towards the lean-to of branches and thatch, 'The dawn comes. It is time to let out the herd.'

His voice was high and unbroken, but Hal was delighted to find that he understood every word the boy had said. It was the language of the forests that Aboli had taught him.

Two other lads of the same age crawled out of the hut, shivering, muttering and scratching, and all three went to the cattle pen. They spoke to the beasts as though they, too, were children, rubbed their heads and patted their flanks.

As the light strengthened Hal saw that these cattle were far different from those he had known on High Weald. They were taller and rangier, with huge humps over their shoulders, and the span of their horns was so wide as to appear grotesque, the weight almost too much for even their heavy frames to support.

The boys picked out a cow and pushed her calf away from the udder. Then one knelt under her belly and milked her, sending purring jets into a calabash gourd. Meanwhile, the other two seized a young bullock and passed a leather thong around its neck. They drew this tight and when the restricted blood vessels stood proud beneath the black skin, one pricked a vein with the sharp point of an arrow head. The first child came running with the gourd half-filled with milk and held the mouth of it under the stream of bright red blood that spurted from the punctured vein.

When the gourd was full, one staunched the small wound in the bullock's neck with a handful of dust, and turned it loose. The beast wandered away, none the worse for the bleeding. The boys shook the gourd vigorously, then passed it from one to the other, each drinking deeply from the mixture of milk and blood as his turn came, smacking his lips and sighing with pleasure.

So engrossed were they with their breakfast that none noticed Aboli or Hal until they were grabbed from behind and hoisted kicking and shrieking in the air.

'Be quiet, you little baboon,' Aboli ordered.

'Slavers!' wailed the eldest child, as he saw Hal's white face. 'We are taken by slavers!'

'They will eat us,' squeaked the youngest.

'We are not slavers!' Hal told them. 'And we will not harm you.'

This assurance merely sent the trio into fresh paroxysms of terror. 'He is a devil who can speak the language of heaven.'

'He understands all we say. He is an albino devil.'

'He will surely eat us as my mother warned me.'

Aboli held the eldest at arm's length and glared at him. 'What is your name, little monkey?'

'See his tattoos.' The boy howled in dread and confusion. 'He is tattooed like the Monomatapa, the chosen of heaven.'

'He is a great Mambo!'

'Or the ghost of the Monomatapa who died long ago.'

'I am indeed a great chief,' Aboli agreed. 'And you will tell me your name.'

'My name is Tweti – oh, Monomatapa, spare me for I am but little. I will be only a single mouthful for your mighty jaws.'

'Take me to your village, Tweti, and I will spare you and your brothers.'

After a while the children began to believe that they would neither be eaten nor turned into slaves, and they started to smile shyly at Hal's overtures. From there it was not long before they were giggling delightedly to have been chosen by the great tattooed chief and the strange albino to lead them to the village.

Driving the cattle herd before them, they took a track through the hills and came out suddenly in a small village surrounded by rudimentary fields of cultivation, in which a few straggling millet plants grew. The huts were shaped like bee-hives and beautifully thatched, but they were deserted. Clay pots stood on the cooking fires before each hut and there were calves in the pens and woven baskets, weapons and accoutrements scattered where they had been dropped when the villagers fled.

The three boys squeaked reassurances into the surrounding bush. 'Come out! Come and see! It is a great Mambo of our tribe come back from death to visit us!'

An old crone was the first to emerge timidly from a thicket of elephant grass. She wore only a greasy leather skirt, and her one eye socket was empty. She had but a single yellow tooth in the front of her mouth. Her dangling dugs flapped against her wrinkled belly, which was scarified with ritual tattoos.

She took one look at Aboli's face, then ran to prostrate herself before him. She lifted one of his feet and placed it on her head. 'Mighty Monomatapa,' she keened, 'you are the chosen of heaven. I am a useless insect, a dung beetle, before your glory.'

In singles and pairs, and then in greater numbers, the other villagers emerged from their hiding places and gathered before Aboli to kneel in obeisance and pour dust and ashes on their heads in reverence.

'Do not let this adulation turn your head, oh Chosen One,' Hal told him sourly in English.

'I give you royal dispensation,' Aboli replied, without smiling. 'You need not kneel in my presence, nor pour dust on your head.'

The villagers brought Aboli and Hal carved wooden stools to sit upon, and offered them gourds of soured milk mixed with fresh blood, porridge of millet, grilled wild birds, roasted termites and caterpillars seared on the coals so that their hairy coverings were burnt off.

'You must eat a little of everything they offer you,' Aboli warned Hal, 'or else you will give great offence.'

Hal gagged down a few mouthfuls of the blood and milk mixture, while Aboli swigged back a full gourd. Hal found the other delicacies a little more palatable, the caterpillars tasted like fresh grass juice and the termites were crisp and delicious as roasted chestnuts.

When they had eaten, the village headman came forward on hands and knees to answer Aboli's questions.

'Where is the town of the Monomatapa?'

'It is two days' march in the direction of the setting sun.'

'I need ten good men to guide me.'

'As you command, O Mambo.'

The ten men were ready within the hour, and little Tweti and his companions wept bitterly that they were not chosen for this honour but were instead sent back to the lowly task of cattle-herding.

The trail they followed towards the west led through open forests of tall, graceful trees interspersed with wide expanses of savannah grasslands. They began to encounter more herds of the humped cattle herded by small naked boys. The cattle grazed in close and unlikely truce with herds of wild antelope. Some of the game were almost equine, but with coats of strawberry roan or midnight sable, and horns that swept back like Oriental scimitars to touch their flanks.

Several times in the forests they saw elephants, small breeding herds of cows and calves. Once they passed within a cable's length of a gaunt bull standing under a flat-topped thorn tree in the middle of the open savannah. This patriarch showed little fear of them but spread his tattered ears like battle standards and raised his curved tusks high to peer at them with small eyes.

'It would take two strong men to carry one of those tusks,' Aboli said, 'and in the markets of Zanzibar they would fetch thirty English pounds apiece.'

They passed many small villages of thatched bee-hive huts, similar to the one in which Tweti lived. Obviously, the news of their arrival had gone ahead of them for the inhabitants came out to stare in awe at Aboli's tattoos and then to prostrate themselves before him and cover themselves with dust.

Each of the local chieftains pleaded with Aboli to honour his village by spending the night in the new hut his people had built especially for him as soon as they had heard of his coming. They offered food and drink, calabashes of the blood and milk mixture and bubbling clay pots of millet beer.

They presented gifts, iron spear- and axe-heads, a small elephant tusk, tanned leather cloaks and bags. Aboli touched each of these to signal his acceptance then returned them to the giver.

They brought him girls to choose from, pretty little nymphs with copper-wire bangles on their wrists and ankles, and tiny aprons of coloured trade beads that barely concealed their pudenda. The girls giggled and covered their mouths with dainty pink-palmed hands and ogled Aboli with huge dark eyes, liquid with awe. Their plump pubescent breasts were shining with cow fat and red clay, and their buttocks were bare and round and joggled with each disappointed pace as Aboli sent them away. They looked back at him over a bare shoulder with longing and reverence. What prestige they would have enjoyed if they had been chosen by the Monomatapa.

On the second day they approached another range of hills, but these were more rugged and their sides were sheer granite. As they drew closer they saw that the summit of each hill was fortified with stone walls.

'Yonder is the great town of the Monomatapa. It is built upon the hill tops to resist the attacks of the slavers, and his regiments of warriors are always at the ready to repel them.'

A throng of people came down to welcome them, hundreds of men and women wearing all their finery of beads and carved ivory jewellery. The elders wore head-dresses of ostrich feathers and skirts of cow tails. All the men were armed with spears, and war bows were slung upon their backs. They groaned with awe as they saw Aboli's face and flung themselves down before him so that he could tread upon their quivering bodies.

Borne along by this throng, they slowly ascended the pathway to the summit of the highest hill, passing through a series of gateways. At each gate part of the crowd about them fell back until, as they approached the final glacis before the fortress that crowned the summit, they were accompanied only by a handful of chieftains, warriors and councillors of the highest rank, wearing all the regalia and finery of their office.

Even these paused at the final gateway, and one noble ancient with silver hair and aquiline eye took Aboli by the hand and led him into the inner courtyard. Hal shrugged off the councillors who sought to restrain him and strode into the inner courtyard at Aboli's side.

The floor was of clay that had been mixed with blood and cow dung and then screeded until it dried like polished red marble. Huts surrounded this courtyard, but many times larger than Hal had seen before, and the thatching was of new golden grass, intricate and splendid. The doorway of each hut was decorated by what seemed, at first glance, to be orbs of ivory, and it was only when they were half-way across the courtyard that Hal realized they were human skulls, and that tall pyramids formed of hundreds stood at spaced intervals around the perimeter.

Beside each skull pyramid was planted a tall pole and on the sharpened point of these stakes a man or woman had been impaled through the anus. Most of these victims were long dead and stank, but one or two still twitched or groaned pitifully.

The old man stopped them in the centre of the courtyard. Hal and Aboli stood in silence for a while, until a weird cacophony of primitive musical instruments and discordant human voices issued from the largest and most imposing hut facing them. A procession of creatures came forth into the sunlight. They crawled and wriggled like insects on the polished clay surface, and their bodies and faces were daubed with coloured clay and painted in fantastic patterns. They were hung with charms, amulets and magical fetishes, skins of reptiles, bones and skulls of man and animal, and all the gruesome paraphernalia of the wizard and the witch. They whined and howled and gibbered, and rolled their eyes and chattered their teeth, and beat on drums and twanged single-stringed harps.

Two women followed them. Both were stark naked, the first a mature female with full and bountiful breast, her belly marked with the stria of childbearing. The other was a girl, slim and graceful with a sweet moon face and startlingly white teeth behind full lips. She was the loveliest of any that Hal had laid eyes upon since they had entered the land of the Monomatapa. Her waist was narrow and her hips full and her skin was like black satin. She knelt on hands and knees with her buttocks turned towards them. Hal shifted uneasily as the deepest folds of her privy parts were exposed to his gaze. Even in these circumstances of danger and uncertainty he found himself aroused by her nubility.

'Show no emotion,' Aboli warned him softly, without moving his lips. 'As you love life, remain unmoved.'

The wizards fell silent and for a space everyone was still. Then, out of the hut stooped a massively corpulent figure clad in a leopardskin cloak. Upon his head was a tall hat of the same dappled fur, which exaggerated his already magisterial height.

He paused in the doorway and glared at them. All the company of wizards and witches crouching at his feet moaned with amazement and covered their eyes, as if his beauty and majesty had blinded them.

Hal stared back at him. It was difficult to follow Aboli's advice to remain expressionless, for the features of the Monomatapa were tattooed in exactly the same pattern and style as the face he had known from childhood, the great round face of Aboli.

Aboli broke the silence. 'I see you, great Mambo. I see you, my brother. I see you, N'Pofho, son of my father.'

The Monomatapa's eyes narrowed slightly, but his patterned features remained as if carved in ebony. With slow and stately stride he crossed to where the naked girl knelt and seated himself upon her arched back as though she were a stool. He continued to glare at Aboli and Hal, and the silence drew out.

Suddenly he made an impatient gesture to the woman who stood beside him. She took one of her own breasts in her hand and, placing the engorged nipple between his thick lips, gave him suck. He drank from her, his throat bobbing, then pushed her away and wiped his mouth with the palm of his hand. Refreshed by this warm draught, he looked to his principal soothsayer. 'Speak to me of these strangers, Sweswe!' he commanded. 'Make me a prophecy, O beloved of the dark spirits!'

The oldest and ugliest of the wizards sprang to his feet and began a wild gyrating, whirling dance. He shrieked and leaped high in the air, shaking the rattle in his hand. 'Treason!' he screamed, and frothy spittle splattered from his lips. 'Sacrilege! Who dares claim blood ties with the Son of the Heavens?' He pranced in front of Aboli like a wizened ape on skinny shanks. 'I smell the stink of treachery!' He hurled his rattle at Aboli's feet and snatched a cow's-tail whisk from his belt. 'I smell sedition!' He brandished the whisk, and began to tremble in every muscle. 'What devil is this who dares to imitate the sacred Tattoo?' His eyes rolled back in his skull until only the whites showed. 'Beware! For the ghost of your father, the great Holomima, demands the blood sacrifice!' he shrieked, and gathered himself to spring full at Aboli's face to strike him with the magician's whisk.

Aboli was faster. The cutlass sprang from the scabbard on his belt as though it were a living thing. It flashed in the sunlight as he cut back-handed. The wizard's head was severed cleanly from his trunk and rolled down his back. It lay on the polished clay gazing with wide astonished eyes at the sky, and the lips writhing and twitching as they tried to utter the next wild denunciation.

The headless body stood, for a moment, on trembling legs. A fountain of blood from the severed neck spouted high in the air, the whisk fell from the hand and the body collapsed slowly on top of its own head.

'The ghost of our father Holomima demands the blood sacrifice,' said Aboli softly. 'And lo! I, Aboli his son, have given it to him.'

No person in the royal enclosure spoke or moved for what seemed half a lifetime to Hal. Then the Monomatapa began to shake all over. His belly began to wobble and his tattooed jowls danced and shook. His face contorted in what seemed a berserker's fury.

Hal placed his hand on the hilt of his cutlass. 'If he is truly your brother, then I will kill him for you,' he whispered to Aboli. 'You cover my back and we will fight our way out of here.'

But the Monomatapa opened his mouth wide and let fly a huge shout of laughter. 'The tattooed one has made the blood sacrifice that Sweswe demanded!' he bellowed. Then mirth overcame him and for a long while he could not speak again. He shook with laughter, gasped for breath, hugged himself then hooted again.

'Did you see him stand there with no head while his mouth tried still to speak?' he roared, and tears of laughter rolled down his cheeks.

The grovelling band of magicians burst out in squeaks and shrieks of sympathetic glee. 'The heavens laugh!' they whined. 'And all men are happy.'

Suddenly the Monomatapa stopped laughing. 'Bring me Sweswe's stupid head!' he commanded, and the councillor who had led them here bounded forward to obey. He retrieved it and knelt before the king to hand it to him.

The Monomatapa held the head by its matted plaits of kinky hair and stared into the wide blank eyes. He began to laugh again. 'What stupidity not to recognize the blood of kings. How could you not know my brother Aboli by his majestic bearing and the fury of his temper?'

He flung the dripping head at the other magicians, who scattered. 'Learn from the stupidity of Sweswe,' he admonished them. 'Make no more false prophecy! Tell me no more falsehoods! Begone, all of you! Or I will ask my brother to make another blood sacrifice.'

They fled in pandemonium, and the Monomatapa rose from his live throne and advanced upon Aboli, a huge and happy grin splitting his fat, tattooed face. 'Aboli,' he said, 'my brother who was long dead and who now lives!' and he embraced him.

One of the elaborately thatched huts on the perimeter of the courtyard was placed at their disposal, and a procession of maidens was sent to them, bearing clay pots of hot water balanced upon their heads for the two men to bathe. Still other girls carried trays on which was piled fine raiment to replace their travel-stained clothing, beaded loincloths of tanned leather and cloaks of fur and feathers.

When they had washed and changed into this finery, another file of girls came bearing gourds of beer, a type of mead fermented from wild honey, and the blended blood and milk. Others brought platters of hot food.

When they had eaten, the silver-headed councillor who had taken them into the presence of the Monomatapa came to them. With great civility and every mark of respect he squatted at Aboli's feet. 'Though you were far too young when last you saw me to remember me now, my name is Zama. I was the Induna of your father, the great Monomatapa Holomima.'

'It grieves me, Zama, but I remember almost nothing of those days. I remember my brother N'Pofho. I remember the pain of the tattoo knife and the cut of our circumcision that we underwent together. I remember that he squealed louder than I.'

Zama looked worried and shook his head as if to warn Aboli against such levity when speaking of the King, but his voice was level and calm. 'All this is true, except only that the Monomatapa never squealed. I was present at the ceremony of the knife, and it was I who held your head while the hot iron seared your cheeks and trimmed the hood from your penis.'

'Dimly now I think that I can remember your hands and your words of comfort. I thank you for them, Zama.'

'You and N'Pofho were twins, born in the same hour. Thus it was that your father commanded that both of you were to bear the royal tattoo. It was new to custom. Never before had two royal sons been tattooed in the same ceremony.'

'I remember little of my father, except how tall he was and strong. I remember how afraid I was at first of the tattoos on his face.'

'He was a mighty man and fearsome,' Zama agreed.

'I remember the night he died. I remember the shouting and the firing of muskets and the terrible flames in the night.'

'I was there when the slavemasters came with their chains of sorrow.' Tears filled the old man's eyes. 'You were so young, Aboli. I marvel that you remember these things.'

'Tell me about that night.'

'As was my custom and my duty, I slept at the portal of your father's hut. I was at his side when he was struck by a ball from the slavers' muskets.' Zama fell silent at the memory, and then he looked up again. 'As he lay dying he said to me, "Zama, leave me. Save my sons. Save the Monomatapa!" and I hurried to obey.'

'You came to save me?' Aboli asked.

'I ran to the hut where you and your brother slept with your mother. I tried to take you from her, but your mother would not hand you to me. "Take N'Pofho!" she commanded me, for you were always her favourite. So I seized your brother and we ran together into the night. Your mother and I were separated in the darkness. I heard her screams but I had the other child in my arms, and to turn back would have meant slavery for all of us and the extinction of the royal line. Forgive me now, Aboli, but I left you and your mother and I ran on, and with N'Pofho escaped into the hills.'

'There is no blame in what you did,' Aboli absolved him.

Zama looked around the hut carefully, and then his lips moved but he uttered no sound. 'It was the wrong choice. I should have taken you.' His expression changed, and he leaned closer to Aboli as if to say something more. Then he drew back reluctantly, as though he had not the courage to make some dangerous gamble.

He rose slowly to his feet. 'Forgive me, Aboli, son of Holomima, but I must leave you now.'

'I forgive you everything,' Aboli said softly. 'I know what is in your heart. Think on this, Zama. Another lion roars on the hill top that once might have been mine. My life now is linked to a new destiny.'

'You are right, Aboli, and I am an old man. I no longer have the strength or the desire to change what cannot be changed.' He drew himself up. 'The Monomatapa will grant you another audience tomorrow morning. I will come for you.' He lowered his voice slightly. 'Please do not try to leave the royal enclosure without the permission of the King.'

When he was gone, Aboli smiled. 'Zama has asked us not to leave. It would be difficult to do so. Have you seen the guards that have been placed at every entrance?'

'Yes, they are not easy to overlook.' Hal stood up from the carved ebony stool and crossed to the low doorway of the hut. He counted twenty men at the gate. They were all magnificent warriors, tall and well muscled, and each was armed with spear and war axe. They carried tall shields of dappled black and white ox hide, and their head-dresses were of cranes' feathers.

'It will be more difficult to leave this place than it was to enter,' Aboli said grimly.

At sunset there came another procession of young girls bearing the evening meal. 'I can see why your royal brother carries such a goodly cargo of fat,' Hal remarked, as he surveyed this superabundance of food.

Once they declared their hunger satisfied, the girls retired with the platters and pots, and Zama came back. This time he led two maidens, one by each hand. The girls knelt before Hal and Aboli. Hal recognized the prettiest and pertest of the two as the girl who had been the live throne of the Monomatapa.

'The Monomatapa sends these females to you to sweeten your dreams with the honey of their loins,' said Zama and retired.

In consternation Hal watched the pretty one raise her head and smile at him shyly. She had a calm sweet face with full lips and huge dark eyes. Her hair had been twisted and braided with beads so that the tresses hung to her shoulders. Her body was plump and glossy. Her breasts and buttocks were naked, only now she wore a tiny beaded apron in front.

'I see you, Great Lord,' she whispered, 'and my eyes are dimmed by the splendour of your presence.' She crept forward like a kitten and laid her head upon his lap.

'You cannot stay here.' Hal sprang to his feet. 'You must go away at once.'

The girl stared up at him in dismay, and tears filled her dark eyes. 'Do I not please you, Great One?' she murmured.

'You are very pretty,' Hal blurted, 'but—' How could he tell her that he was married to a golden memory?

'Let me stay with you, lord,' the girl pleaded pathetically. 'If you reject me, I will be sent to the executioner. I will die with the sharp stake thrust up through the secret opening of my body to pierce my bowels. Please let me live, O Great One. Have mercy on this unworthy female, O Glorious White Face.'

Hal turned to Aboli. 'What can I do?'

'Send her away.' Aboli shrugged. 'As she says, she is worthless. You can stop up your ears so that you do not have to listen to her screaming on the stake.'

'Do not mock me, Aboli. You know I cannot betray the memory of the woman I love.'

'Sukeena is dead, Gundwane. I also loved her, as a brother, but she is dead. This child is alive, but she will not be so by sunset tomorrow unless you take pity upon her. Your vow was not anything that Sukeena demanded of you.'

Aboli stooped over the other girl, took her hand and lifted her to her feet.

'I cannot give you any further help, Gundwane. You are a man and Sukeena knew that. Now that she has gone, she might deem it fitting that you live the rest of your life like one.'

He led his own girl to the rear of the hut, where a pile of soft karosses was laid and a pair of carved wooden head rests stood side by side. He laid her down and dropped the leather curtain that screened them.

'What is your name?' Hal asked the girl who crouched at his feet.

'My name is Inyosi, Honey-bee,' she answered. 'Please do not send me to die.' She crawled to him, clasped his legs and pressed her face to his lower body.

'I cannot,' he mumbled. 'I belong to another.' But he wore only the beaded loincloth and her breath was warm and soft on his belly and her hands stroked the backs of his legs.

'I cannot,' he repeated desperately, but one of Inyosi's little hands crept up under his loincloth.

'Your mouth tells me one thing, Mighty Lord,' she purred, 'but the great spear of your manhood tells me another.'

Hal let out a smothered groan, picked her up in his arms and ran with her across the floor to where his own pallet of furs had been laid out.

At first Inyosi was startled by the fury of his passion, but then she let out a joyous cry and matched him kiss for kiss and thrust for thrust.

In the dawn, as she prepared to leave him, she whispered, 'You have saved my worthless life. In return I must attempt to save your illustrious one.' She kissed him one last time, then murmured with her lips against his, 'I heard the Monomatapa speak to Zama while he bestrode my back. He believes that Aboli has returned to claim the Seat of Heaven from him. Tomorrow, during the audience to which he has commanded you and Aboli, he will give the order for his bodyguard to seize you and hurl you from the cliff top onto the rocks below, where the hyenas and the vultures wait to devour your corpses.' Inyosi snuggled against his chest. 'I do not want you to die, my lord. You are too beautiful.'

Then she rose from the pallet and slipped away silently into the darkness. Hal crossed to the hearth and threw a faggot of firewood upon it. The smoke rose up through the hole in the centre of the domed roof and the flames lit the interior with flickering yellow light.

'Aboli? Are you alone? We must talk at once,' he called, and Aboli came out from behind the curtain.

'The girl is asleep, but speak in English.'

'Your brother intends to have both of us killed during the audience.'

'The girl told you this?' Aboli asked, and Hal nodded guiltily at the mention of his infidelity.

Aboli smiled in sympathy. 'So the little Honey-bee saves your life. Sukeena would rejoice for that. You need feel no guilt.'

'If we attempt to escape, your brother would send an army to pursue us. We would never reach the river again.'

'So, do you have a plan, Gundwane?'

Zama came to lead them to the royal audience. They stepped out of the gloom of the great hut into the brilliant African sunlight, and Hal paused to gaze around the concourse of the Monomatapa.

He could only estimate their numbers, but a full regiment of the royal bodyguard ringed the open space, perhaps a thousand tall warriors with the high head-dresses of cranes' feathers turning each into a giant. The light morning breeze tossed and tumbled the feathers, and the sunlight glinted on their broad-bladed spears.

Beyond them the nobles of the tribe filled every space and lined the top of the wall of granite blocks that surrounded the citadel. A hundred royal wives clustered about the door to the King's hut. Some were so fat and loaded with bangles and ornaments that they could not walk unaided and leant heavily on their handmaidens. When they waddled along their buttocks rolled and undulated like soft bladders filled with lard.

Zama led Hal and Aboli to the centre of the courtyard and left them there. A heavy silence fell on the throng and no one moved, until suddenly the captain of the bodyguard blew a blast on a spiral kudu horn and the Monomatapa loomed in the doorway of his hut.

A moaning sigh swept through the gathering and, as one, they threw themselves full length to the earth and covered their faces. Only Hal and Aboli remained standing upright.

The Monomatapa strode to his living throne and sat upon Inyosi's naked back.

'Speak first!' Hal breathed from the side of his mouth. 'Don't let him give the order for our execution.'

'I see you, my brother!' Aboli greeted him, and the courtiers moaned with horror at this breach of protocol. 'I see you, Great Lord of the Heavens!'

The Monomatapa showed no sign of having heard.

'I bring you greetings from the ghost of our father, Holomima, who was the Monomatapa before you.'

Aboli's brother recoiled visibly, as though a cobra had reared up before his face. 'You speak with ghosts?' His voice trembled slightly.

'Our father came to me in the night. He was as tall as a great baobab tree, and his face was terrible with eyes of fire. His voice was as the thunder of the heavens. He came to me to issue a dire warning.' The congregation moaned with superstitious dread.

'What was this warning?' croaked the Monomatapa, staring at his brother with awe.

'Our father fears for our lives, yours and mine. Great danger threatens us both.' Some of the fat wives screamed, and one fell to the ground in a fit, frothing at the mouth.

'What danger is this, Aboli?' The King glanced around him fearfully, as if seeking an assassin amongst his courtiers.

'Our father warned me that you and I are joined in life as we were in birth. If one of us prospers, then so does the other.'

The Monomatapa nodded. 'What else did our father say?'

'He said that as we are joined in life, so we will be joined in death. He prophesied that we will die upon the very same day, but that that day is of our own choosing.'

The King's face turned a strange greyish tone and glistened with sweat. The elders shrieked and those nearest to where he sat drew small iron knives and slashed their own chests and arms, sprinkling their blood on the earth to protect him from witchcraft.

'I am deeply troubled by these words that our father uttered,' Aboli went on. 'I wish that I were able to abide with you here in the Land of Heaven, to protect you from this fate. But, alas, my father's shade warned me further that should I stay here another day then I will die and the Monomatapa with me. I must leave at once and never return. That is the only way in which we can both survive the curse.'

'So let it be.' The Monomatapa rose to his feet and pointed with a trembling finger. 'This very day you must be gone.'

'Alas, my beloved brother, I cannot leave here without that boon I came to seek from you.'

'Speak, Aboli! What is it that you lack?'

'I must have one hundred and fifty of your finest warriors to protect me, for a dreadful enemy lies in wait for me. Without these soldiers, then I go to certain death, and my death must portend the death of the Monomatapa.'

'Choose!' bellowed the Monomatapa. 'Choose of my finest Amadoda, and take them with you. They are your slaves, do with them as you wish. But then get you gone this very day, before the setting of the sun. Leave my land for ever.'

In the leading pinnace Hal shot the bar and rowed out through the Musela mouth of the delta into the open sea. Big Daniel followed closely, and there lay the *Golden Bough* at her anchor on the ten-fathom shoal where they had left her. Ned Tyler stood the ship to quarters and ran out his guns when he saw them approaching. The pinnaces were so packed with men that they had only an inch or two of freeboard. Riding so low in the water, from afar they resembled war canoes. The glinting spears and waving head-dresses of the Amadoda strengthened this impression and Ned gave the order to fire a warning shot across their bows. As the cannon boomed out and a tall plume of spray erupted from the water half a cable's length ahead of the leading boat, Hal stood up in the bows and waved the *croix patté*.

'Lord love us!' Ned gasped. ''Tis the Captain we're shooting at.'

'I'll not be in a hurry to forget that greeting you gave me, Mr Tyler,' Hal told him sternly, as he came in through the entryport. 'I rate a four-gun salute, not a single gun.'

'Bless you, Captain, I had no idea. I thought you was a bunch of heathen savages, begging your pardon, sir.'

'That we are, Mr Tyler. That we are!' And Hal grinned at Ned's confusion as a horde of magnificent warriors swarmed onto the *Golden Bough*'s deck. 'Think you'll be able to make seamen of them, Mr Tyler?'

As soon as he had made his offing, Hal turned the bows into the north once more and sailed up the inland channel between Madagascar and the mainland. He was heading for Zanzibar, the centre of all trade on this coast. There he hoped to have further news of the progress of the Holy War on the Horn and, if he were fortunate, to learn something of the movements of the *Gull of Moray*.

This was a settling-in time for the Amadoda. Everything aboard the *Golden Bough* was strange to them. None had ever seen the sea. They had believed the pinnaces to be the largest canoes ever conceived by man, and were overawed by the size of the ship, the height of her masts and the spread of her sails.

Most were immediately smitten by seasickness, and it took many days for them to find their sea-legs. Their bowels were in a turmoil induced by the diet of biscuit and pickled meat. They hungered for their pots of millet porridge and their gourds of blood and milk. They had never been confined in such a small space and they pined for the wide savannah.

They suffered from the cold, for even in this tropical sea the trade winds were cool and the warm Mozambique current many degrees below the temperature of the sun-scorched plains of the savannah. Hal ordered Althuda, who was in charge of the ship's stores, to issue bolts of sail canvas to them and Aboli showed them how to stitch petticoats and tarpaulin jackets for themselves.

They soon forgot these tribulations when Aboli ordered a platoon of men to follow Jiri and Matesi and Kimatti aloft to set and reef sail. A hundred dizzy feet above the deck and the rushing sea, swinging on the great pendulum of the mainmast, for the first time in their lives these warriors – who had each killed their lion – were overcome by terror.

Aboli climbed up to where they clung helplessly to the shrouds and mocked them: 'Look at these pretty virgins. I thought at first there might be a man among them, but I see they should all squat when they piss.' Then he stood upright on the swaying yard and laughed at them. He ran out to the end of it and there performed a stamping, leaping war dance. One of the Amadoda could abide his mockery no longer: he loosed his death grip on the rigging and shuffled out along the yard to where Aboli stood with hands on hips.

'One man amongst them!' Aboli laughed and embraced him. During the next week three of the Amadoda fell from the rigging while trying to emulate this feat. Two dropped into the sea but before Hal could wear the ship around and go back to pick them up the sharks had taken them. The third man struck the deck and his was the most merciful end. After that there were no more casualties, and the Amadoda, each one accustomed since boyhood to climbing the highest trees for honey and birds' eggs, swiftly became adept topmastmen.

When Hal ordered bundles of pikes to be brought up from the hold and issued to the Amadoda they howled and danced with delight, for they were spearmen born. They delighted in the heavy-shafted pikes with their deadly iron heads. Aboli adapted their tactics and fighting formation to the *Golden Bough*'s cramped deck spaces. He showed them how to form the classical Roman Testudo, their shields overlapping and locked like the scales of an armadillo. With this formation they could sweep the deck of an enemy ship irresistibly.

Hal ordered them to set up a heavy mat of oakum under the forecastle break to act as a butt. Once the Amadoda had learned the weight and balance of the heavy pikes they could hurl them the length of the ship to bury the iron heads full length in the mat of coarse fibres. They plunged into these exercises with such gusto that two of their number were speared to death before Aboli could impress upon them that these were mock battles and should not be fought to the death.

Then it was time to introduce them to the English longbow. Their own bows were short and puny in comparison and they looked askance at this six-foot weapon, dubiously tried the massive draw weight and shook their heads. Hal took the bow out of their hands and nocked an arrow. He looked up at the single black and white gull that floated high above the mainmast. 'If I bring down one of those birds will you eat it raw?' he asked, and they roared with laughter at the joke.

'I will eat the feathers as well!' shouted a big cocky one named Ingwe, the Leopard. In a fluid motion Hal drew and loosed. The arrow arced up, its flight curving across the wind, and they shouted with amazement as it pierced the gull's snowy bosom and the wide pinions folded. The bird tumbled down in a tangle of wings and webbed feet, and struck the deck at Hal's feet. An Amadoda snatched it up, and the transfixed carcass was passed from hand to hand amid astonished jabbering.

'Do not ruffle the feathers,' Hal cautioned them. 'You will spoil Ingwe's dinner for him.'

From that moment their love of the longbow was passionate and within days they had developed into archers of the first water. When Hal towed an empty water keg at a full cable's length behind the ship, the Amadoda shot at it, first individually then in massed divisions like English archers. When the keg was heaved back on deck it was bristling like a porcupine's back, and they retrieved seven out of every ten arrows that had been shot.

In one area alone the Amadoda showed no aptitude: at serving the great bronze culverins. Despite all the threats and mockery that Aboli with the scent of frangi-pani and yellow tamarind flowers. A tall figure, clad in flowing white robes and gold-corded Arabian head-dress, rose from the pile of silk carpets where he had been reclining.

'Indeed, I add a thousand welcomes to those of my children, my good Captain, and may Allah shower you with riches and blessing,' he said, in a familiar and comforting Yorkshire accent. 'I watched your fine ship anchor in the bay, and I knew you would soon call upon me.' He clapped his hands, and from the back of the house emerged a line of slaves each bearing trays that contained coloured glasses of sherbet and coconut milk and little bowls of sweetmeats and roasted nuts.

The consul sent Big Daniel and his seamen through to the servants' quarters at the rear of the house. 'They will be given refreshment,' he said.

Hal cast Big Daniel a significant look, which the boatswain interpreted accurately. There would be no liquor in this Islamic household, but there would be women and the seamen had to be protected from themselves. Hal kept Althuda beside him. There might be call for him to draw up documents or to take down notes.

The consul led them to a secluded corner of the courtyard. 'Now, let me introduce myself, I am William Grey, His Majesty's consul to the Sultanate of Zanzibar.'

'Henry Courtney, at your service, sir.'

'I knew a Sir Francis Courtney. Are you by chance related?'

'My father, sir.'

'Ah! An honourable man. Please give him my respects when next you meet.'

'Tragically he was killed in the Dutch war.'

'My condolences, Sir Henry. Please be seated.' A pile of beautifully patterned silk carpets had been set close at hand for Hal. The consul sat opposite him. Once he was comfortable, a slave brought Grey a water-pipe. 'A pipeful of *bhang* is a sovereign remedy for distempers of the liver and for the malaria which is a plague in these climes. Will you join me, sir?'

Hal refused this offer, for he knew of the tricks the Indian hemp flowers played upon the mind, and the dreams and trances with which it could ensnare the smoker.

While he puffed at his pipe, Grey questioned him cunningly as to his recent movements and his future plans, and Hal was polite but evasive. Like a pair of duellists, they sparred and waited for an opening. As the water bubbled in the tall glass bowl of the pipe and the fragrant smoke drifted across the courtyard Grey became more affable and expansive.

LISTING 11.1: Populating the ListBox Controls

```
Private Sub Form_Load()
DataEnvironment1.AllCategories
While Not DataEnvironment1.rsAllCategories.EOF
  List1.AddItem _
    DataEnvironment1.rsAllCategories._
    Fields("CategoryName")
  List1.ItemData(List1.NewIndex) = _
    DataEnvironment1.rsAllCategories._
    Fields("CategoryID")
  DataEnvironment1.rsAllCategories.MoveNext
Wend
DataEnvironment1.AllSuppliers
While Not DataEnvironment1.rsAllSuppliers.EOF
  List2.AddItem _
    DataEnvironment1.rsAllSuppliers._
    Fields("CompanyName")
  List2.ItemData(List2.NewIndex) = _
    DataEnvironment1.rsAllSuppliers._
    Fields("SupplierID")
  DataEnvironment1.rsAllSuppliers.MoveNext
Wend
End Sub
```

When the user selects one or more items in either list and clicks the corresponding button, the program builds an SQL statement to retrieve the products in the selected categories (or by the selected suppliers). This SQL statement is used to build the SelProducts Recordset, as shown in Listing 11.2. After the rsSelProducts Recordset has been created, it is used to populate the DataGrid control.

LISTING 11.2: Building an SQL Statement on the Fly

```
Private Sub bySupplier_Click()
If List2.SelCount = 0 Then
  MsgBox "Please select one or more" & _
    " suppliers first"
  Exit Sub
End If
For i = 0 To List2.ListCount - 1
  If List2.Selected(i) Then
    selSuppliers = selSuppliers & _
    List2.ItemData(i) & ", "
```

```
    End If
  Next i
  selSuppliers = Left(selSuppliers, _
    Len(selSuppliers) - 2)
  SQLcmd = "SELECT ProductName, UnitPrice, _
    QuantityPerUnit " & _
    "FROM Products " & _
    "WHERE SupplierID IN (" & selSuppliers & ")"
  DataEnvironment1.Commands(3).CommandText = _
    SQLcmd
  DataEnvironment1.Commands(3).CommandType = _
    adCmdText
  Set SelProducts = _
    DataEnvironment1.Commands(3).Execute
  PopulateDGrid
  End Sub
```

The PopulateGrid() subroutine populates the DataGrid control and sets the width of the various columns. You can open the project in the Visual Basic IDE and examine the code (it's worth taking a look at the code, which uses the Columns collection to access individual columns and set their properties).

ADO Error Handling

Error handling is one of the most important topics of any language, and I'm assuming you're familiar with Visual Basic's error handling capabilities (error trapping). ADO, however, is a database access component, and it sits between your application and a provider. The provider is a driver (a program); different databases come with different drivers. Each database has different capabilities, and ADO's role is to make all databases look the same to your application. This is especially difficult because each provider raises different errors. In addition to provider-specific errors, ADO itself can raise errors. This means that there are two types of errors you must handle: ADO errors and provider-specific errors. ADO errors are reported to Visual Basic and generate runtime errors, which you can trap in your VB code and handle as usual. Provider-specific errors are stored in the Errors collection of the Connection object. This means that as you code, you should know which operations cause ADO errors and which ones cause provider-specific errors. This is especially important, because not all provider-specific errors raise runtime errors in VB. Most provider-specific errors cause VB runtime errors, but the Err object contains information about the most recent error, whereas the Errors collection of the Connection object may contain multiple errors raised by the same operation. Most ADO errors are handled through Visual Basic's Err object and the error-trapping mechanism built into the language. In complicated situations you may have to examine the Errors collection to find out exactly what has happened.

Let's start with the ADO error codes and their descriptions. Table 11.1 summarizes the errors that ADO passes to Visual Basic. These are runtime errors, which you can trap from within your VB code, and you'll see how to handle them in the second half of this chapter.

TABLE 11.1: The ADO Error Codes and Descriptions

Constant	Error Number	Description
`adErrInvalidArgument`	3001	The application is using arguments that are of the wrong type, are out of acceptable range, or are in conflict with one another.
`adErrNoCurrentRecord`	3021	Either BOF or EOF is True; or the current record has been deleted; or the operation requested by the application requires a current record.
`adErrIllegalOperation`	3219	The operation requested by the application is not allowed in this context.
`adErrInTransaction`	3246	The application cannot explicitly close a Connection object while in the middle of a transaction.
`adErrFeatureNotAvailable`	3251	The operation requested by the application is not supported by the provider.
`adErrItemNotFound`	3265	ADO could not find the object in the collection corresponding to the name or ordinal reference requested by the application.
`adErrObjectInCollection`	3367	Can't append. The object is already in the collection.
`adErrObjectNotSet`	3420	The object referenced by the application no longer points to a valid object.

TABLE 11.1 continued: The ADO Error Codes and Descriptions

Constant	Error Number	Description
`adErrDataConversion`	3421	The application is using a value of the wrong type for the current operation.
`adErrObjectClosed`	3704	The operation requested by the application is not allowed if the object is closed.
`adErrObjectOpen`	3705	The operation requested by the application is not allowed if the object is open.
`adErrProviderNotFound`	3706	ADO could not find the specified provider.
`adErrBoundToCommand`	3707	The application cannot change the ActiveConnection property of a Recordset object with a Command object as its source.
`adErrInvalidParamInfo`	3708	The application has improperly defined a Parameter object.
`adErrInvalidConnection`	3709	The application requested an operation on an object with a reference to a closed or invalid Connection object.

The descriptions of the errors are quite thorough. The two errors you'll be getting most often are the errors `3704` and `3705`. `Error 3704` occurs when you attempt to access a recordset that hasn't been set yet. `Error 3705` occurs when you attempt to change the data source of a recordset. You must first close the recordset, then change its data source. To handle ADO errors, insert an `On Error Goto` statement to redirect program control to an error handler.

To handle provider-specific errors, use the `On Error Resume Next` statement and examine the Connection.Errors collection after each operation that could have raised a provider-specific error. The Errors collection is made up of Error objects, which display the properties listed in Table 11.2.

TABLE 11.2: The properties of the Error Object

PROPERTY	DESCRIPTION
Description	This property returns the description of the error and it's set either by ADO or a provider. Providers are responsible for passing specific error text to ADO. ADO adds an Error object to the Errors collection for each provider error or warning it receives.
HelpContext, HelpFile	Indicates the help file and topic associated with an Error object. HelpContextID returns a context ID, as a Long value, for a topic in a Help file. HelpFile is the path to a Help file.
NativeError	This property returns the provider-specific error's number. Consult the documentation of the provider for information on specific error codes.
Number	This is the provider-specific error number and you can use it in your error-handling routine to determine the error that has occurred.
Source	Indicates the name of the object or application that originally generated an error. Use the Source property on an Error object to determine the name of the object or application that originally generated an error. For ADO errors, this property value will be ADODB.ObjectName, where ObjectName is the name of the object that triggered the error.
SQLState	This property indicates the SQL state for a given Error object and it returns a five-character string that follows the ANSI SQL standard. Use the SQLState property to read the five-character error code that the provider returns when an error occurs during the processing of an SQL statement.

To find out all the errors in the Errors collection, use a loop like the following one:

```
For Each objError In CN.Errors
  Debug.Print "Number " & objError.Number
  Debug.Print "Decription " & _
    objError.Description
  Debug.Print "Source " & objError.Source
  Debug.Print "Native Error " & _
    objError.NativeError
  Debug.Print "SQLState " & objError.SQLState
Next
```

The Errors collection is cleared every time an operation causes a new provider-specific error. Operations that complete successfully do not clear the Errors collection.

Multiuser Considerations

In this section, you are going to explore the behavior of different types of cursors when you program them from within your VB application. Every cursor is updateable. It doesn't make any difference if it resides on the client or the server, or whether it's a dynamic, keyset, static, or forward-only cursor. If it's not a read-only cursor, it can be used to update the underlying tables.

Updating the underlying tables through a cursor is not trivial. When many users are accessing the same tables, any of the following may happen:

- One user edits a row and wants to commit the changes to the database. Does the application know that another user has already modified the same row since it was last read? And if the application detects it, what should it do? In most cases, we go ahead and overwrite other people's changes. But there are situations, as in reservation applications, where this is not an option. You should be able to find out whether someone else has touched the row we edited since we read it last. If another user has already changed the same row, the application should be able to warn the user and offer a few options.
- While one user is editing a row, another user might actually delete the very same row. This is an even more difficult situation, although quite rare. Why would a user edit a row in a table, when another user thinks that the row shouldn't even be there? Rare as this case is, your application should be able to handle this extreme situation. Ideally, you should offer users the option to add the row that was deleted by someone else. While a user thinks he's updating a row, your code is actually inserting a new one. At the very least, the application should let the user know what happened and cancel the operation.

Let's see how ADO updates tables through the various types of cursors. We are going to use the Customers application we developed in the Customers project of the last chapter. We'll simply change the type and location of the cursor, then see the error messages we get back from the server and the code to handle them. We'll use SQL Server in the examples of this chapter to see what happens in a real client/server environment.

Working with Client-Side Cursors

Let's start with an exploration of the various types of cursors. Open the Customers application (downloadable from the Sybex web site). Open the DataEnvironment Designer and right-click the AllCustomers object. Switch to the Advanced tab of its property pages and make sure the Cursor Location is set to client-side, and the Lock Type is set to Optimistic, as shown in Figure 11.2.

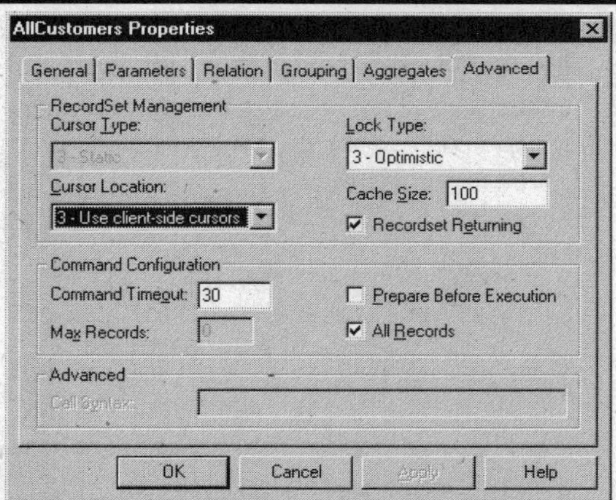

FIGURE 11.2: The CursorLocation and LockType properties are the two most important properties of a recordset.

Deleting Rows

Let's see how the basic operations are performed through this type of recordset. Run the application and delete a customer. Because customers can't be removed from the Customers table (they are linked to the Orders table), you'll get the following error message:

```
DELETE statement conflicted with COLUMN REFERENCE constraint
   'FK_Orders_Customers'. The conflict occurred in
   database 'Northwind', table 'Orders', column 'CustomerID'.
```

This error's number is 3604 (actually, it's a large negative value, from which you must subtract the constant `vbObjectError`). Your application should trap this error, display the appropriate message to the user, and abort the operation. To abort the operation, you must call the CancelUpdate method of the Recordset object. If you don't, the recordset's current row will be a deleted one, and you'll get the same error message as soon as you attempt to call one of the navigational methods. Listing 11.3 shows the code behind the Delete button.

LISTING 11.3: Deleting a Row in a Client-Side Cursor

```
Private Sub bttnDelete_Click()
  reply = MsgBox("Record will be" & _
    " deleted permanently. Proceed?", vbYesNo)
  If reply = vbYes Then
    On Error Resume Next
    DataEnvironment1.rsAllCustomers.Delete
    If Err.Number <> 0 Then
      MsgBox "Could not delete record" & _
        vbCrLf & "ERROR # " & _
        Err.Number - vbObjectError & _
        vbCrLf & Err.Description
      DataEnvironment1.rsAllCustomers._
        CancelUpdate
    End If
  End If
End Sub
```

Now, we'll examine what happens when you attempt to delete a row that has already been deleted by another user. Because all customers in this application are linked to one or more invoices, we must add a new customer that we can delete later. Add a new customer by clicking the Add Customer button. Specify a valid customer (a unique ID and a company name). Then switch to the SQL Enterprise Manager, open the Customers table (you may have to click Run to refresh the grid with the customers), and locate the new customer. Delete it by clicking Del; this action mimics deletion by another user. Click Run to make sure that the row is gone, and then return to the VB application. Clickthe Delete Customer button to delete the new customer, pretending we don't know it has already been deleted. After confirming your desire to delete the current customer, you will get the following runtime error:

```
The specified row could not be located for updating:
Some values may have been changed since it was last
read.
```

This is error number 3640. If you ignore this error, you won't be able to move to another row. You must call the CancelUpdate method to cancel the pending operation, as shown in the previous listing.

Add a few new customers and then delete them directly from your VB application (no need to experiment with the SQL Enterprise Manager any longer. The VB program can handle deletions on its own). If you attempt to navigate through the rows of the Customers table with the Next and Previous buttons, you'll realize that sometimes the navigational buttons don't take you to the previous/next row. This happens when the next and previous rows have been deleted. When you move to the next row, for example, and this row has been deleted, ADO "parks" on the current row. Actually, it moves to the deleted row, but it's smart enough not to bind the controls to the deleted row. Keep moving in the same direction. After you have gone through all the deleted rows in the direction of the navigation, you will see the fields of the first valid row it lands on.

The short version of the story is that rows are not actually removed from client-side cursors. They are marked as deleted so that you can no longer land on them, but they are still part of the cursors. (In case you're wondering, no, you can't restore the deleted rows from the cursor.)

Because you can't remove them from the cursors, there should be a way to skip them and land on the first valid row in the direction of the movement. The simplest method is to keep calling the same navigational method (MoveNext or MovePrevious) while the current row is deleted. To find out whether a row in a client-side cursor has been deleted, examine its Status property. If its value is adRecDBDeleted, it means the row is invalid. Listing 11.4 shows the revised code for the Next button.

LISTING 11.4: Skipping Deleted Rows during Navigation

```
Private Sub bttnNext_Click()
  DataEnvironment1.rsAllCustomers.MoveNext
  While _
    DataEnvironment1.rsAllCustomers._
      Status = adRecDBDeleted _
      And Not DataEnvironment1._
      rsAllCustomers.EOF
    DataEnvironment1.rsAllCustomers.MoveNext
  Wend
  If DataEnvironment1.rsAllCustomers.EOF Then
    DataEnvironment1.rsAllCustomers.MoveLast
  End If
End Sub
```

Updating Rows

If you edit a customer, then the changes will be committed to the database as soon as the Update method of the Recordset object is called. But let's interfere with the edit process. Click the Edit Customer button, change a field's value, and then switch to the SQL Enterprise Manager. Open the Customers table, locate the same row you're editing in your application, edit one of the fields you have already changed in the VB application, and move to another row. The changes have been committed to the database.

Now, switch back to the VB application and click OK. This time, you'll get the following error message:

```
The specified row could not be located for
updating: Some values may have been changed since
it was last read.
```

The error number is `3640 again`. Here's what happened. On the VB Form, you're editing the TextBoxes. Even though they are bound to the database, they do not reflect the actual values in the underlying table, because the cursor resides on the client. That's why you can't see the latest values of the fields on the form. What you see are the values of the fields when the cursor was read–which is when the form was loaded. Therefore, when ADO attempted to save the edited row, it found out that the original values of certain fields were no longer the same as they were when the row was read from the table. This caused it to generate the error message.

TIP

If you change some fields from within the VB application and different ones from within SQL Server's Enterprise Manager, then the update operation will not fail. SQL Server compares each field's original value to the value in the cursor to determine whether it can update it. If the two values match, it means that the field hasn't been changed. If not, then someone has changed the field since it was read into the cursor and it doesn't update it.

To commit the changes, you must call the Update method. If the update fails, then you must call the CancelUpdate method to abort the operation. Listing 11.5 shows the code behind the OK button.

LISTING 11.5: Updating a Row in a Client-Side Cursor

```
Private Sub bttnOK_Click()
  On Error Resume Next
```

```
    DataEnvironment1.rsAllCustomers.Update
    If Err.Number <> 0 Then
      If DataEnvironment1.rsAllCustomers._
        EditMode = adEditAdd Then
        MsgBox "Could not add record" & _
        vbCrLf & Err.Description
      Else
        MsgBox "Could not save changes." & _
          vbCrLf & Err.Description
      End If
      DataEnvironment1.rsAllCustomers.CancelUpdate
      DataEnvironment1.rsAllCustomers.Move 0
    Else
      DataEnvironment1.rsAllCustomers._
        Resync adAffectCurrent
    End If
    ShowButtons
  End Sub
```


In the previous listing, notice that the OK button is used to end both the addition of a new row and the editing of an existing one. The program simply displays a different message for each, but it handles both operations by calling the CancelUpdate method. To see why you must call the CancelUpdate method, comment it out temporarily (insert an apostrophe at the beginning of the line), as well as the following line that calls the Move method. Edit a record in the VB Form, then edit the same field(s) of the same row in SQL Server's Enterprise Manager. Then, return to the VB application. Click OK to commit the changes. ADO will generate an error message indicating that it couldn't update the row, but the application will not crash.

If you attempt to move to another row with the navigational keys, you'll get an error message again. An update operation hasn't completed successfully. Because of this pending operation on the current row, ADO refuses to move to another row. The line that cancels the operation is actually required. As you saw in the last chapter, the Data Form Wizard doesn't insert this line. It simply takes for granted the assumption of the optimistic locking mechanism—namely, that no two users will attempt to update the same row at the same time. This is a reasonable assumption, but it's only an assumption. The locking mechanism doesn't guarantee that two users will not attempt to update the database at once—it *assumes* that this will not happen. You must take action from within your code, or else a runtime error will be generated eventually.

If the Update method terminates successfully, the following line synchronizes the recordset with the underlying row:

```
DataEnvironment1.rsAllCustomers._
  Resync adAffectCurrent
```

Why do we need this line? Let's say you've changed one field in the table and another user has changed another field. Your update will not fail. Yet, the user will see the new values of the fields that were edited on the client, but the old values of the remaining fields. To make sure users view the latest version of the row after an update, call the Resync method for the specific row.

You will probably claim that this is a client-side cursor, and as such, we know that it won't always be up-to-date. Then again, when a row is modified, users expect to see the current field values, so it's not a bad idea to synchronize the row. Notice that we're not synchronizing the entire cursor, just a single line. This is what the adAffectCurrent argument does: it synchronizes the current row only. Had we synchronized the entire cursor, we would defeat the purpose of the client-side cursor.

Updating the Data-Bound Controls

You will probably be surprised to know that the controls on the form aren't updated at this point. The client-side cursor has been updated, but the data-bound control displays the old values. To see that this is true, let's print the values of the fields in the cursor so that we will have them in front of us to compare once we edit the rows. To do this, insert the following lines after the line that calls the Resync method:

```
For i = 0 To _
  DataEnvironment1.rsAllCustomers._
  Fields.Count - 1
  Debug.Print _
    DataEnvironment1.rsAllCustomers._
    Fields(i).Value
Next
```

Now, run the program again, edit the same row from within both the VB application and SQL Server's Enterprise Manager, then read the values of the fields both on the form's data-bound controls and on the Immediate window. They will be different, as shown in Figure 11.3. I've changed the Region field from "OR" to "OREGON" in the Enterprise Manager. The result is the annoying discrepancy shown in the figure.

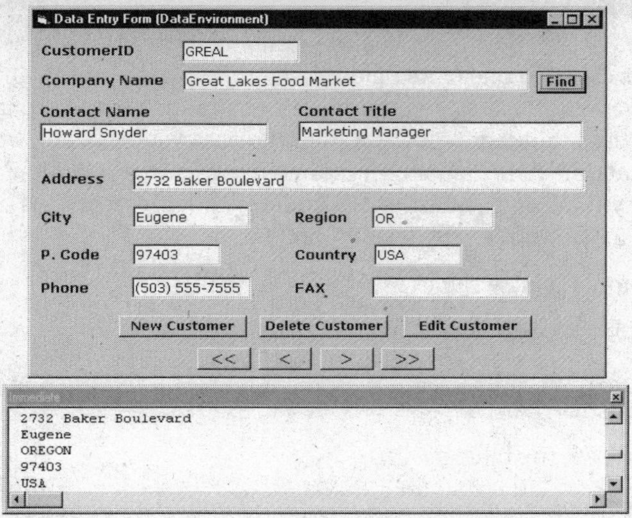

FIGURE 11.3: Data-bound controls are not refreshed automatically when you call the Recordset object's Resync method.

To force a data-bound control to read its value from the underlying cursor, you must set one of its data-binding properties. The following lines set the DataField property of the data-bound controls on the form:

```
txtCustID.DataField = "CustomerID"
txtCustName.DataField = "CompanyName"
txtContactName.DataField = "ContactName"
```

You should place these lines in a subroutine, say the ReBind() subroutine, and call it after each call to the Resync method. You can actually rebind the controls by setting their DataSource property too. There's a more elegant method to set the DataField property of all TextBox controls on the form, which is shown next:

```
Dim ctrl As Control
For Each ctrl In Me.Controls
  If ctrl.Tag = "TextBox" Then
    Set ctrl.DataSource = _
      DataEnvironment1.rsAllCustomers
  End If
Next
```

For this code to work, you must set the Tag property of each data-bound TextBox control to the string `TextBox` (or any other string that uniquely identifies the data-bound controls on the form).

Update Anyway!

What do you do when your application can't update a row because someone else has changed one of its fields already? If you attempt to update the table again, you'll keep getting the same error message. As long as the underlying field values are different than the ones you read, you won't be able to update the table. Most users would like to have the option "Update Anyway!" on their forms. To update the table regardless of the differences in the underlying fields, you must:

1. Store the new values into local variables.
2. Read the row again.
3. Move the values you have stored from the variables to the cursor.
4. Update the table again.

Fairly complicated, isn't it? ADO should provide a method to update a row unconditionally, but it doesn't. If it did, I bet it would be the most abused method. Still, you *can* use the Resync method to synchronize only the underlying values. The Resync method, whose syntax is shown next, accepts an argument that determines which values will be synchronized to the database fields:

```
ADODC1.Resync affectRecords, resyncValues
```

By default, the Resync method synchronizes the recordset's values with the actual field values in the database by reading the rows again from the database. The default value of the *resyncValues* argument is adResyncAllValues. The underlying values are also synchronized.

The other value of the *resyncValues* argument is adResyncUnderlyingValues. It causes the Resync method to synchronize only the UnderlyingValue properties of the recordset's rows. The practical value of this form of the Resync method is that you can make ADO think that your changes are the most recent ones, in which case they'll be committed to the database successfully.

Here's why this trick works. When you call the Update method, ADO compares the UnderlyingValue property of all the fields in the current row to the actual field values in the database. If they are the same, it means no other user has touched the row since your application read it and ADO can commit the changes. If they differ, it means that someone else has modified the row since your application read it, and ADO refuses to update the row. Actually, it generates the runtime error 3640, as you saw previously. By synchronizing the UnderlyingValue properties, you fool ADO into thinking that you have just read the row and edited it instantly. In most cases, your changes will be committed successfully to the database.

Adding Rows

Let's add a new row with the New Customer button. When this button is clicked, all data-bound controls on the form are cleared in preparation of the new customer's data. If you fail to specify a company name, you'll get the error message 3604:

```
Cannot insert the value NULL into column
'CompanyName', table 'Northwind.dbo.Customers';
column does not allow nulls. INSERT fails.
```

A similar error will be generated for all field values that violate a constraint. If you specify an ID that exists already, you'll get the same error number, but with the following description:

```
Violation of PRIMARY KEY constraint 'PK_Customers'.
Cannot insert duplicate key in object 'Customers'.
```

It's rather confusing to have to handle the same error number with different descriptions. You should simply display a message indicating that the operation can't be completed, followed by the message returned by ADO (the average user will not understand what this message says, so you may opt to display a custom message).

Both errors can be handled easily. The user must terminate the Add operation and return to the edit mode. The user can either change the value of the field that caused the problem and update the table again, or cancel the operation. Before you exit, though, you must call the Cancel-Update method to discard the new row that was created by the AddNew method (see the OK button's code in Listing 11.3).

Refreshing the Cursor

If your application is using a client-side cursor, you should probably provide a Refresh button. A user may keep the cursor open for editing for extended periods of time. In the meantime, the underlying data may undergo numerous changes. If the application has a Refresh button, the user can retrieve the most up-to-date values from the table.

You may be thinking, "Isn't this button going to confuse the users?" I will agree, users need not be concerned with cursor locations and cursor types; but sometimes you'll have to explain a few basic capabilities of your application.

To refresh the entire recordset, call the Resync method, specifying the `adAffectAll` argument, which causes ADO to refresh the entire recordset. The code behind the Refresh button is shown next:

```
Private Sub bttnRefresh_Click()
  DataEnvironment1.rsAllCustomers._
    Resync adAffectAll
End Sub
```

Working with Server-Side Cursors

Now, we'll explore the behavior of a server-side cursor under the same circumstances discussed in the preceding sections. As you should expect, server-side cursors behave differently because they reside on the same machine as the SQL Server and they can access the tables immediately.

Deleting Rows

Let's start with the deletion of a row that's linked to the Orders table and can't be removed from the table. If you attempt to remove a row from the Customers table, you'll get error 3617 with the following (hardly descriptive) message:

```
Errors occurred
```

You can cancel the deletion of a row that can't be removed, because it violates a primary/foreign key constraint using the CancelUpdate method. After canceling a deletion operation, you can use the navigational keys to move to another row. If you attempt to add a new row immediately after canceling the deletion of a row, you'll get the VB error message shown in Figure 11.4. This error message simply tells you that there's a row pending deletion. Unless this row is removed, you won't be able to add new row.

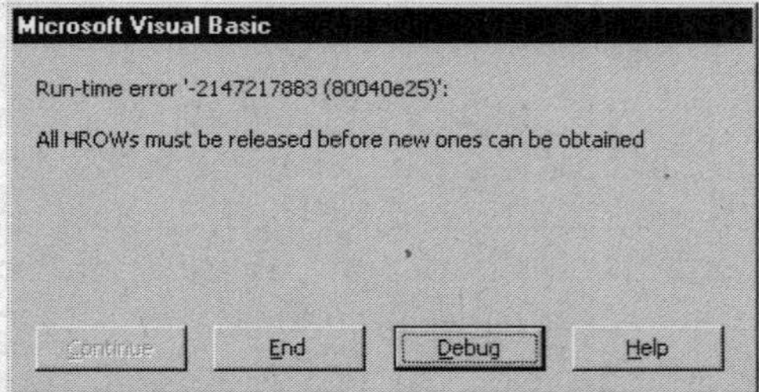

FIGURE 11.4: This error message will be generated if you don't call the CancelUpdate method after the unsuccessful deletion of a row.

If you delete a row from this recordset, it will be removed from the cursor too. Therefore, you need not insert the loop that skips the deleted records in the Next and Previous buttons. If the deletion fails, we must call the CancelUpdate method to restore the row that has been marked for deletion.

Updating Rows

Editing a row generally poses no problem. If the edit operation fails, however, it means someone else has edited the same row since you last read it. In this case, you should be able to retrieve the latest version of the row and display it on the form. Unfortunately, dynamic cursors don't support the Resync method. The Move 0 method will not force the row to be refreshed. The row will be read from the cache, and you'll get the values of the fields as they were before you started editing them, not the current values of the fields. You must try to move to the next or previous row and then back to the current one using the following syntax:

```
DataEnvironment1.rsAllCustomers.CancelUpdate
DataEnvironment1.rsAllCustomers.MoveNext
DataEnvironment1.rsAllCustomers.MovePrevious
```

This is a dynamic cursor, and it should fetch each row from the table. This looks like a neat trick, but it won't work. Can you guess why not? It won't work because the default cache size for the rsAllCustomers Recordset is 100 rows. Unless you're on the first row in the cache and you call the MovePrevious method (or you're on the last row and you call the MoveNext method), ADO isn't going to read rows from the actual table. The solution is to change the size of the cache. Open the DataEnvironment Designer's window, right-click the rsAllCustomers object and select Properties. In the Advanced tab of its property pages, set the cache size to 1 row. If you run the application again, it will work as intended. Every time an edit operation fails, it will display the row's current field values in the table. The complete listing of the OK button's Click event handler is shown next in Listing 11.6.

LISTING 11.6: Updating a Row in a Server-Side Cursor

```
Private Sub bttnOK_Click()
  On Error Resume Next
  DataEnvironment1.rsAllCustomers.Update
  If Err.Number <> 0 Then
    If DataEnvironment1.rsAllCustomers._
      EditMode = adEditAdd Then
      MsgBox "Could not add record" & _
        vbCrLf & Err.Description
```

Part ii

```
    Else
      MsgBox "Could not save changes." & _
        vbCrLf & Err.Description
    End If
    DataEnvironment1.rsAllCustomers.CancelUpdate
    DataEnvironment1.rsAllCustomers.MoveNext
    DataEnvironment1.rsAllCustomers.MovePrevious
  End If
  ShowButtons
  LockFields
End Sub
```

Specifying a cache size of 1 row defeats the purpose of the cache, right? The most efficient solution to the problem of updating server-side cursors is to use stored procedures, or execute an action query that inserts a new row directly against the database. If you want to use data-bound controls with a server-side cursor, you should set the cursor's cache size to 1.

Let's check out what happens when an edit operation fails because the current row has been removed from the table. Add a new customer, then edit it. Switch to the SQL Enterprise Manager and delete the new customer from the Customers table. Then switch back to the application and click OK to commit the changes. As expected, you'll get an error message. Then, the MoveNext/MovePrevious methods will be called. The MoveNext will take you to the next row momentarily. The MovePrevious method will return to the previous valid row, which obviously is not the one just deleted.

The MoveNext/MovePrevious combination may fail if you're on the last row. In this case you should call the two methods in reverse order. Insert the appropriate error-trapping code to make sure you always land on a valid row.

Adding Rows

Adding rows to a server-side cursor is fairly simple. The AddNew method creates an empty recordset in the table, and you edit it live. When the Update method is called, the new row is committed to the database. Only one of two things can go wrong at this point: Either one or more fields might be invalid (they violate a constraint, for example), or you might specify an invalid key. If your application generates primary keys, you will probably search the table for the new key and commit the new row only if this key does not already exist. Even then it is possible (although very unlikely) that another user will have added a row with the same key after you have verified that your key is not being used, and before you call the

Update method. The only approach that will work in all cases is to call the Update method anyway and see whether ADO returns an error message about duplicate keys. If it does, the primary key you've chosen already exists in the database.

This will not happen if you let the DBMS generate keys for you (an Identity field in SQL Server, or an AutoNumber field in Access). These keys, which are called *surrogate keys*, are totally meaningless, but they are very convenient. Primary keys are used to link tables, and we're never interested in their actual values. Sometimes the entity stored in a table may have a primary key of its own. Books, for example, have ISBNs, which are unique by definition. Of course users make mistakes, and the "unique" value may already have been used. So, to make your application totally fail-safe, you must still verify that an ISBN value has not already been used by mistake with another book.

As with client-side cursors, a new row is automatically committed to the database as soon as the application moves to another row (by calling a navigational method, or the Find method, for example). It is strongly suggested that you disable the navigational keys while a row is being added or edited.

How About the ADO Data Control?

The application we used in this section is based on the DataEnvironment objects. Most developers will use the Connection and Command objects of the DataEnvironment object to build database applications. If you want to use the ADO Data Control instead, the same techniques will work as described. You can place an ADO Data Control on the form, set it up to see the Customers table in the Northwind database, and then replace all the instances of:

```
DataEnvironment1.rsAllCustomers
```

in the code with the following expression:

```
ADODC1.Recordset
```

This is the only change required, and the new project that's based on the ADO Data Control will work as before. The two expressions evaluate to a Recordset object, and they support the same properties and methods. There is one difference I should mention, however. Remember the loop that skips the deleted rows in the navigational buttons? This loop is not needed when you use the ADO Data Control. The control will skip the deleted rows automatically, and it will land on the first valid row in the direction of navigation in the recordset.

You may choose to use the ADO Data Control to simplify the testing of an application, but manipulate the recordset via VB code. In the production version of the application, you should hide the Data controls by setting their Visible property to False.

ADO Events

It is also possible to program the ADO objects and the ADO Data Control using events. Both objects support several events with which you can simplify certain programming tasks. Like the properties and methods, the ADO objects and ADO Data Control share the same events, which are discussed here. These events can be categorized according to the object that fires them:

- The *Connection object events*, which are fired when you establish asynchronous connections, or execute commands asynchronously
- The *Recordset object events*, which are fired when the current row changes (because a Move method has been called, for example), or when the underlying Recordset is about to be updated

NOTE

The Command object does not raise any events. To execute commands asynchronously, use the Connection object's Execute method.

You will find the complete list of events later in this section, but the Connection object and Recordset object events have common characteristics that I will discuss first. Many of the ADO events are paired. One of the events in the pair is fired right before an action takes place, and the other event is fired when the action has completed. The events fired prior to the action begin with the prefix "Will," and the events fired upon completion end with the suffix "Complete." The events WillChangeRecord and RecordChangeComplete are an example.

Another common characteristic of the ADO events is that they accept a large number of arguments, which complicate their coding a little (and sometimes considerably). If you have programmed the ADO Data Control's events, you know that the ADO objects support the same events. They are also equivalent to the DAO (the older Data Access Objects component) events—only ADO recognizes more events and offers finer control over the actions it performs on the database.

To take advantage of the ADO events in your code, you must declare variables that represent the Recordset and Connection events with the WithEvents keywords. If the following declaration appears in the form's declarations section, then its name will appear in the Code window's Object list and you can select the event you want to program in the window's Events list, as shown in Figure 11.5.

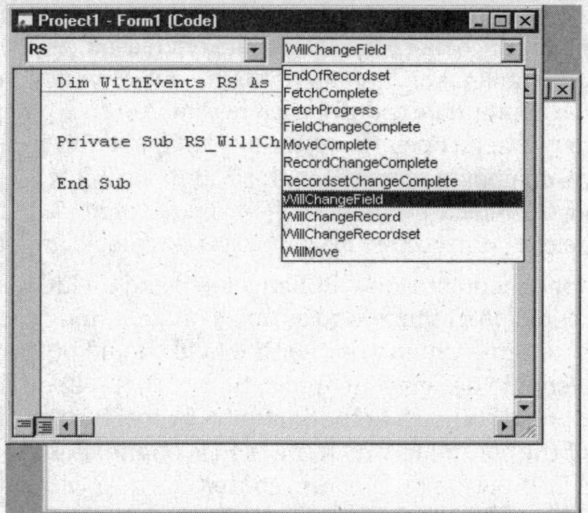

FIGURE 11.5: The ADO Recordset object's events

USING ADO EVENTS

ADO events are available to be used in programming your applications, but most developers don't use them extensively. As I explained already, there's no reason to code the WillChangeField or WillChangeRecordset event to validate the data. Validate your data with your own subroutine, when the user clicks OK to commit the changes. If you're using the ADO Data Control and allow users to add new records by setting the EOFAction property to adDoAddNew, then you must use the Will events to find out when certain actions will take place. Other than monitoring the progress of asynchronous operations, the ADO events are not used extensively in database programming, especially if you consider that databases are usually updated through stored procedures.

The Will and Complete Events

In general, the Will events let you examine what's about to happen and, optionally, cancel the operation from within the event's handler. The Complete events notify your application that the operation completed, and you can examine the error code returned by the event (if any).

The most confusing aspect of the Will and Complete events is that the same events may be fired more than once for the same operation. Each time this happens, they are being called for a different reason, which means you must examine the `adReason` argument to find out why they were called and insert the appropriate code for each reason. Another potentially confusing situation is that an operation you cancel may still fire events. If you decide to cancel an update from within the WillChangeField event handler, the FieldChangeComplete event will still be fired to indicate that the operation has completed (unsuccessfully, but it has completed anyway).

Let's consider for a moment the WillChangeField and FieldChangeComplete events. Some programmers go as far as programming the WillChangeField event to examine whether the field should be changed or not. I think you should design your application so that it knows when a field can change or not. When a field shouldn't change, turn on the Locked property of the control to which the field is bound. For example, you should use an Edit button on the form so that the user will signal his intention to start editing a record. If a field's value depends on the contents of other controls on the form, use its Change or LostFocus events to determine whether the user can change its value. The benefit of this approach is that you can take immediate action, instead of deferring all validation until the moment when the user is ready to commit the changes to the database.

Some Common Event Arguments

In this section, we are going to discuss some arguments that are used by a number of different events. These arguments apply to many operations and we can discuss them before we look at each event's description.

The adStatus Argument

When the event handler routine is called, the *adStatus* parameter is set to one of the informational values presented in Table 11.3.

TABLE 11.3: Values of the adStatus Argument on Input

CONSTANT	DESCRIPTION
adStatusOK	This value indicates that the operation that caused the event completed successfully.
adStatusErrorsOccurred	This value indicates that the operation that caused the event did not complete successfully, or the operation was cancelled from within a Will event's code.
adStatusCantDeny	A Will event cannot request cancellation of the operation about to occur.

The *adStatus* parameter can also be set from within the event handler to pass information to back to the ADO. You can set the *adStatus* parameter to one of the values presented in Table 11.4.

TABLE 11.4: Values of the adStatus Argument on Output

CONSTANT	DESCRIPTION
adStatusUnwantedEvent	Requests that this event handler will receive no further notifications.
adStatusCancel	Requests cancellation of the operation that is about to occur.

The pError Argument

The *pError* argument is a reference to an ADO Error object containing details about why the operation failed if the status parameter equals adStatusErrorsOccurred. If an operation has completed successfully, the *pError* argument is not set and you should not access it from within your code. If you do, you'll get a runtime VB error because you've attempted to access an object that hasn't been set.

```
If status = adStatusErrorsOccurred Then
  {process pError}
End If
```

The Object Argument

This argument is an object variable representing the Connection or Recordset object to which the operation applies. Use this parameter to identify the specific object that raised the event, in case multiple objects fire the same event. If you have initiated two asynchronous connections, for example, you will receive two ConnectComplete events, one for each object. Use the event's object parameter to find out which connections has been established.

The adReason Argument

A number of actions can fire the same event. The WillChangeRecord event, for example, is fired when the current record is edited, as well as when it's deleted. To find out why an event was fired, use the *adReason* argument. Notice that events with an *adReason* parameter may be called several times for the same operation, but for a different reason each time.

The WillChangeRecord event handler, for instance, is called for operations that are about to do or undo the insertion, deletion, or modification of a record. Use the *adReason* argument to find out the operation that fired the event. You must return `adStatusUnwantedEvent` in the *adStatus* argument to request that an event handler without an *adReason* argument stop receiving event notifications. However, an event handler with an *adReason* argument may receive several notifications, each for a different reason. Therefore, you must return `adStatusUnwantedEvent` for each notification caused by a different reason.

For example, assume you have a WillChangeRecord event handler in your code. If you don't want to receive any further notifications whatsoever, simply code the following:

```
Set adStatus = adStatusUnwantedEvent
```

However, if you want to process events where the row is about to be deleted, but cancel notifications for all other reasons, then code the following:

```
if (adReason = adRsnDelete)
' Process an event for this reason.
...
else
' Stop receiving events for any other reason.
Set adStatus = adStatusUnwantedEvent
```

Table 11.5 summarizes the values of the *adReason* argument.

TABLE 11.5: The adReason Argument's Values

Constant	Description
adRsnAddNew	The AddNew method was called.
adRsnClose	The Close method was called.
adRsnDelete	The Delete method was called.
adRsnFirstChange	The current row was changes for the first time.
adRsnMove	The Move method was called.
adRsnMoveFirst	The MoveFirst method was called.
adRsnMoveLast	The MoveLast method was called.
adRsnMoveNext	The MoveNext method was called.
adRsnMovePrevious	The MovePrevious method was called.
adRsnRequery	The Requery method was called.
adRsnResync	The Resync method was called.
adRsnUndoAddNew	The Cancel method was called after a call to the AddNew method.
adRsnUndoDelete	The Delete method was called, and then cancelled with a call to the CancelUpdate or CancelBatch method.
adRsnUndoUpdate	An Update method was called, and then cancelled with a call to the CancelUpdate or CancelBatch method.
adRsnUpdate	The Update method was called.

You may be wondering when you will receive an event notification with a parameter of adRsnUndoDelete or adRsnUndoAddNew. You may call the AddNew to add a new row. To commit the new record to the database, you must call the Update method. This method will fire a WillChangeRecordset event. Even though you have issued the Update method, the information passed back by the arguments of the WillChangeRecordset event handler may necessitate the abortion of the AddNew operation. Even so late in the process, you can abort the operation by calling the CancelUpdate method. If you do so, the RecordsetChangeComplete event will be fired, to notify your application that the original operation was cancelled. The *adReason* argument's value will be adRsnUndoAddNew.

Now we can examine the individual ADO events and their arguments in detail. In the following sections the events are grouped according to the operation that fires them.

Transaction Events

The following events are fired when you implement multiple actions as a transaction:

```
BeginTransComplete(TransactionLevel As Long, _
  pError As Error, adStatus As _
  EventStatusEnum, pConnection As Connection)
```

This event is fired to indicate that the BeginTransaction method has completed (in effect ADO started processing the transaction). *pConnection* is a reference to the Connection object that initiated the transaction. The *pError* and *adStatus* arguments were discussed earlier. The *TransactionLevel* argument, finally, indicates the transaction's depth when multiple transactions are nested.

```
CommitTransComplete(pError As Error, _
  adStatus As EventStatusEnum, _
  pConnection As Connection)
```

This event simply notifies your application that the transaction you initiated on the `pConnection` object was committed. The *adStatus* argument tells you whether the transaction was committed successfully and, if not, the *pError* Error object gives more information about the error.

You probably want to know how it's possible for a transaction to be committed unsuccessfully. The CommitTransComplete event simply tells your application that SQL Server has processed the transaction; even though the transaction itself may have failed. The CommitTransComplete event is raised in response to the CommitTrans method, which signals your intention to commit the transaction. The transaction may fail because it violates a constraint in one of the tables involved. SQL Server will not process the transaction before you call the CommitTransaction method. The CommitTransComplete event notifies your code that the CommitTransaction method has been processed, and it reports whether the transaction was successful or not.

```
RollbackTransComplete(pError As Error, _
  adStatus As EventStatusEnum, pConnection _
  As Connection)
```

The RollbackTransComplete event is analogous to the CommitTransComplete event, but it's fired when a transaction is rolled back. Its arguments are the same as with the CommitTransComplete event.

Connection Events

The events of this section are fired when you establish and abort connections through the Connection object, or when you execute a command through the same object.

```
WillConnect(ConnectionString As String, _
  UserID As String, Password As String, _
  Options As Long, adStatus As _
  EventStatusEnum, pConnection As Connection)
```

This event is fired in response to the Connect method and notifies your application that a new connection is about to be established. The *ConnectionString*, *UserID*, and *Password* arguments contain all the information required to establish the connection, and *pConnection* is a reference to the Connection object whose Connect method you have called. This event isn't programmed frequently.

```
ConnectComplete(pError As Error, _
  adStatus As EventStatusEnum, _
  pConnection As Connection)
```

The ConnectComplete event is used in establishing asynchronous connections. It notifies your code that a connection attempt has completed. Use the *adStatus* argument to find out whether the connection attempt was successful or not. If ADO wasn't able to connect successfully, you will find more information about the error in the `pError` argument.

```
Event Disconnect(adStatus As EventStatusEnum, _
  pConnection As Connection)
```

The Disconnect event is fired when a connection is closed with the Close method. The *pConnection* argument is a reference to the corresponding Connection object, and *adStatus* reports the success or failure of the Close method.

```
WillExecute(Source As String, CursorType _
  As CursorTypeEnum, LockType As _
  LockTypeEnum, Options As Long, _
  adStatus As EventStatusEnum, pCommand _
  As Command, pRecordset As Recordset, _
  pConnection As Connection)
```

The WillExecute method is fired before a Command object is executed. The ExecuteComplete event is fired when the command's execution completes and is used in executing commands asynchronously.

The WillExecute event recognizes a number of arguments. The *CursorType* and *LockType* arguments are the values of the Recordset's CursorType and LockType properties. *pCommand* is a reference to the Command object on which you will execute the command; *pConnection* is a reference to the Connection object that's used for the execution of the command; and pRecordset is a Recordset object where the results of a query will be stored.

The *Source* argument is an SQL statement that is the name of a stored procedure or table. It specifies how the command will act on the database. Finally, *adStatus* returns information about the success or failure of the operation.

Recordset Events

The following events are fired while you're editing the fields of the current row in a Recordset object. The first group of recordset events are the navigational events that are fired in response to Move methods, as well as when the end of the recordset is reached. The second group of recordset events is fired in response to operations that update the tables.

```
WillMove(adReason As EventReasonEnum, _
  adStatus As EventStatusEnum, _
  pRecordset As Recordset)
```

The *adReason* and *adStatus* arguments were explained earlier. The *pRecordset* is a reference to the Recordset object that fired the event.

```
MoveComplete(adReason As EventReasonEnum, _
  pError As Error, adStatus As _
  EventStatusEnum, pRecordset As Recordset)
```

A WillMove or MoveComplete event is not fired only when you call one of the Recordset object's Move methods. It may also be fired by the following methods: Open, Bookmark, AddNew, and Requery. Setting any of the following properties will also fire these events, because they may cause the current row to change: Filter, Index, AbsolutePage, and AbsolutePosition.

```
EndOfRecordset(fMoreData As Boolean, _
  adStatus As EventStatusEnum, _
  pRecordset As Recordset)
```

The EndOfRecordset event is fired when the end of the recordset identified by the last argument has been reached. The *adStatus* event indicates whether the operation that fired the event completed successfully. The first argument emulates the behavior of the ADO Data Control's EOFAction property. Set the *fMoreData* argument to True to append a new empty row to the end of the Recordset (in effect, you'll move the end of the Recordset by one row).

A number of events are fired in pairs and are related to Field, Record, and Recordset changes. The WillChangeField and ChangeFieldComplete events are fired before and after ADO changes a field's value.

```
WillChangeField(cFields As Long, Fields, _
  adStatus As EventStatusEnum, pRecordset _
  As Recordset)
FieldChangeComplete(cFields As Long, _
  Fields, pError As Error, _
  adStatus As EventStatusEnum, _
  pRecordset As Recordset)
```

In the previous event, *cFields* represents the number of fields that will change value (or the number of fields that changed value in the Field-ChangeComplete event). ADO raises a single event, regardless of how many fields you change in the current row. If you're changing multiple rows, then a pair of WillChangeField and FieldChangeComplete events will be fired for each row.

Likewise, the WillChangeRecord and RecordChangeComplete events are fired before and after one or more rows in the Recordset are changed. The WillChangeRecordset event is fired after the FieldChangeComplete event. If no field has been changed by the operation (an Update operation, for example), then the WillChangeRecord and RecordChange-Complete events are not fired.

```
WillChangeRecord(adReason As EventReasonEnum, _
  cRecords As Long, adStatus As _
  EventStatusEnum, pRecordset As Recordset)
RecordChangeComplete(adReason As _
  EventReasonEnum, cRecords As Long, _
  pError As Error, adStatus As _
  EventStatusEnum, pRecordset As Recordset)
```

The *adReason* argument indicates what action caused the row change. *cRecords* is the number of records that will change (or the number of records that were changed in the RecordChangeComplete event).

The WillChangeRecordset and RecordsetChangeComplete events are fired when the recordset changes. (A recordset can change when new rows are added to it or deleted, not when individual rows are changed.) When you Refresh a Recordset object, for example, these two events should be fired once. If the ecordset's size exceeds the size specified with the CacheSize property, then these events will be fired each time a new group of rows is read from the cache. The smaller the CacheSize property, the more often these events are fired.

```
WillChangeRecordset(adReason As _
```

```
    EventReasonEnum, adStatus As _
    EventStatusEnum, pRecordset As Recordset)
  RecordsetChangeComplete(adReason As _
    EventReasonEnum, pError As Error, _
    adStatus As EventStatusEnum, _
    pRecordset As Recordset)
```

The *adReason* argument specified the action that caused the recordset to be changed and can have one of the following values: *adRsnRequery*, *adRsnResync*, *adRsnClose*, and *adRsnOpen*.

Asynchronous Operations' Events

The following events are fired by asynchronous operations, and you can use them to monitor the progress of the operations.

```
  Event FetchProgress(Progress As Long, _
    MaxProgress As Long, adStatus _
    As EventStatusEnum, pRecordset As _
    Recordset)
```

The Event FetchProgress is fired periodically during a lengthy asynchronous operation to report how many more rows have been retrieved so far into the Recordset represented by the *pRecordset* parameter. The number of rows is given by the *Progress* argument, and the (anticipated) total number of rows in the Recordset is *MaxProgress*. You can express the progress of the operation with the fraction `Progress / MaxProgress`, as long as *MaxProgress* is not zero. The *adStatus* argument should be `adStatusFetching`.

```
  Event FetchComplete(pError As Error, _
    adStatus As EventStatusEnum, pRecordset _
    As Recordset)
```

This Event FetchComplete event is fired when an asynchronous operation completes. The *pError* argument indicates a possible error, and you should examine it only if the *adStatus* argument is adStatusErrorsOccurred.

Summary

This chapter covered more of the advanced aspects of ADO, including cursors, error handling, and events. Now that you understand some of the potential ADO has to offer your VB applications, it's time to delve deeper into the process of integrating the two. In the next chapter, you'll learn more about the Connection, Command and Recordset objects and how to use them to work directly with your data through Visual Basic code.

Chapter 12

Fine-Tuning ADO through Visual Basic Code

As you've seen, Visual Basic 6.0 empowers you to use ADO in many ways without writing much code. You can explore data sources with the Data View, create data entry and inquiry forms using bound controls, and connect to complex hierarchies of data using the Data Environment. You can even present information in a form suitable for printing by using the Data Report. But at some point, you'll find that you've exhausted the built-in user interface resources and you'll need to roll up your figurative sleeves and start writing code. In this chapter, you'll learn how to perform some of the most essential data-related tasks using ADO from Visual Basic code.

Adapted from *Visual Basic® Developer's Guide to ADO*, by Mike Gunderloy

ISBN 0-7821-2556-5 480 pages $ 39.99

Basic Operations

Any data access library needs to support some basic operations. Of course, ADO easily allows you to perform all these operations, including:

- Connecting to a data source
- Running a stored procedure
- Creating a recordset
- Sorting and finding information in a recordset
- Adding, deleting, and updating records

In this section, you'll learn to perform these basic operations using ADO from your Visual Basic applications. For the most part, ADO makes these operations simple and straightforward, but there are some pitfalls that you need to watch out for.

Connecting to Data Sources

Not surprisingly, you use the Connection object to connect to a data source. After all, that's what a Connection object represents: a connection to a single data source. All data operations in ADO involve instantiating a Connection object, either explicitly or implicitly. When you create a Connection object and later associate that object with a recordset, you're using an *explicit* connection. When you simply open a recordset, supplying a connection string when you do so, you're using an *implicit* connection. ADO still creates a Connection object in the latter case, but it's strictly internal to ADO's own workings.

You can control the behavior of the Connection object to some extent by setting properties before you call the object's `Open` method. The properties of interest are:

- ConnectionString
- ConnectionTimeout
- Mode
- CursorLocation
- DefaultDatabase

- IsolationLevel
- Provider

The `ConnectionString` property can be used to specify a data source or to supply other information making up an ADO connection string. I'll discuss the format used for connection strings in the next section of this chapter. Although you can specify the `ConnectionString` property before calling the `Open` method, it's usually just as convenient to supply it as an argument to that method. If you're working as part of a development team, consider setting the properties explicitly to make the code more maintainable.

The `ConnectionTimeout` property tells ADO how many seconds it should wait for a data source to respond. By default, this is set to 15. If you're connecting across a busy network or the Internet, you may need to increase this timeout value. You can only change the value of this property before you've called the `Open` method on the Connection object.

You can use the `Mode` property to ask for particular permissions when you open a connection. If the requested permissions can't be set, you'll get an error when you call the `Open` method. By default, the Mode of a Connection object is adModeUnknown. Usually it makes more sense to set this property on a Record or a Stream object, rather than on a connection as a whole, to preserve flexibility in your code.

The `CursorLocation` property can be set to adUseServer to use the cursors supplied by the OLE DB provider for the connection, or to adUseClient to use the client-side cursor library. For advanced functionality you may need to use the client-side library, although this will add additional overhead.

You can use the `DefaultDatabase` property to specify which database on a server a particular Connection should use for data operations. Alternatively, you can specify this as a part of the connection string. For example, if you're using the SQL Server provider, you can either set the `DefaultDatabase` property or put the name of the default database in as the Initial Catalog argument in the connection string. The advantage of using the `DefaultDatabase` property is that it's provider-independent. Any objects that use this Connection object will inherit its default database.

The `IsolationLevel` property controls the effect that one transaction has on other transactions. Table 12.1 shows the possible settings for this property. You normally won't need to alter this property.

TABLE 12.1: *IsolationLevel* Property Values

Constant	Effect
adXactUnspecified	Value returned when the provider is unable to determine the current isolation level.
adXactChaos	Prohibits overwriting pending changes from more highly isolated transactions. This is the default setting.
adXactBrowse	Allows you to view, but not change, uncommitted changes from other transactions.
adXactReadUncommitted	Same as adXactBrowse.
adXactCursorStability	Allows you to view changes from other transactions only after they've been committed.
adXactReadCommitted	Same as adXactCursorStability.
adXactRepeatableRead	Allows requerying a recordset to include changes pending from other transactions.
adXactIsolated	Forces all transactions to be isolated from other transactions. You should choose this value for the strictest transactional processing.
adXactSerializable	Same as adXactIsolated.

The `Provider` property allows you to specify an OLE DB Provider before opening the connection. It's usually more convenient to include this as the Provider argument in the connection string.

I discussed using the Connection object's `Open` method in Chapter 9. Now it's time to dig in a little further. The syntax of the `Open` method is as follows:

```
Connection.Open ConnectionString, UserID, Password, Options
```

Depending on how you write your code, you might supply all, some, or none of the four arguments to the method. One way or another, you must supply a connection string, either by filling in the ConnectionString argument in the `Open` method or by setting the connection's `ConnectionString` property before calling the `Open` method.

Usually, you'll supply the UserID and Password as part of the connection string. However, in cases where that information is supplied by the user, you might find it more convenient to use the arguments to the `Open` method. For example, you'll find this code in frmOpen in the ADOCode sample project:

```
Private Sub cmdConnect_Click()
```

```
    ' Connect using ID and password supplied
    ' by the user interface
    Dim cnn As ADODB.Connection

    On Error GoTo HandleErr

    Set cnn = New ADODB.Connection
    cnn.Open "Provider=SQLOLEDB.1;" & _
      "Server=(local);Initial Catalog=pubs", _
      txtUserID, txtPassword

    MsgBox "Connection Succeeded"
    cnn.Close

ExitHere:
    Exit Sub

HandleErr:
    MsgBox "Error " & Err.Number & ": " & _
      Err.Description
    Resume ExitHere
End Sub
```

As you can see, by using the UserID and Password arguments, you can avoid either hard-coding security information or manipulating the connection string to insert these values. If you specify UserID and Password both in the connection string and as separate arguments, the arguments override any values set in the connection string.

The last argument to the Open method specifies whether the connection should be opened synchronously. You can use the constants adConnectUnspecified for a synchronous connection (the default, so you needn't bother to specify a value at all in this case) or adAsyncConnect for an asynchronous connection. Chapter 9 shows how to use ADO events to monitor the progress of an asynchronous connection.

You should also be familiar with the `Close` method of the Connection object. This method disconnects the Connection object from the data source without destroying the object itself. While the object is in this state, you can change the connection string or other properties, and then execute the Open method again to reconnect with new information. When you're completely done with a Connection object, you can either set it equal to Nothing or just let it go out of scope to reclaim the memory it's using.

Connection Strings

You'll recall from Chapter 9 that an OLE DB connection string has this format:

```
Provider=value;File Name=value;Remote Provider=value; Remote
   Server=value; URL=value;
```

- The Provider argument specifies the name of the OLE DB provider to use. Table 12.2 shows the possible values that this argument can have for the providers that are shipped with the Microsoft Data Access Components.
- The File Name value specifies a file containing connection information—for example, an ODBC file data source. If you use the File Name argument, you must omit the Provider argument.
- The Remote Provider value specifies the name of a provider to use on the server when opening a client-side connection. This option applies to Remote Data Service (RDS) connections only.
- The Remote Server value specifies the name of a server to retrieve data from when using RDS.
- The URL value specifies the connection string as a URL rather than as an ODBC-style string.

All these arguments are optional. You can include additional arguments in the `ConnectionString` A property, in which case they are passed to the OLE DB provider without any alteration by ADO.

NOTE

You can specify a provider by a name with or without a version number. For example, SQLOLEDB.1 refers to a particular release of the SQL Server provider, whereas SQLOLEDB refers to the most recent release of the driver installed on the computer where the code is running. If you use versioned names, you don't have to worry about retesting your code when a provider is updated (though you also can't take advantage of any of the new features of the provider).

TABLE 12.2: OLE DB Provider Names

Provider	Value
Microsoft.Jet.OLEDB.3.51	Microsoft Jet 3.51 OLE DB Provider
Microsoft.Jet.OLEDB.4	Microsoft Jet 4 OLE DB Provider

TABLE 12.2 continued: OLE DB Provider Names

Provider	Value
DTSPackageDSO.1	Microsoft OLE DB Provider for DTS Packages
MSDAIPP.DSO	Microsoft OLE DB Provider for Internet Publishing
MSDASQL.1	Microsoft OLE DB Provider for ODBC Drivers
MSOLAP.1	Microsoft OLE DB Provider for OLAP Services
MSDAORA.1	Microsoft OLE DB Provider for Oracle
SQLOLEDB.1	Microsoft OLE DB Provider for SQL Server
MS Remote.1	MS Remote
MSDataShape.1	MSDataShape
MSIDX	Microsoft OLE DB Provider for Microsoft Indexing Services
ADSDSOObject	Microsoft OLE DB Provider for Microsoft Active Directory Service
MSPersist	Microsoft OLE DB Persistence Provider

Although you normally can connect to a data source using just the provider name, User ID, and password, if you examine connection strings built using the Data Link Properties dialog box, you'll find that they're usually much more complex. This is because any argument that's not understood by ADO itself is automatically passed to the underlying OLE DB driver for interpretation, and most OLE DB drivers understand a wide variety of arguments.

For an exhaustive listing of the arguments understood by any given provider, consult that provider's documentation. For the providers supplied by Microsoft, you'll find that documentation in the Platform SDK, available as part of the Microsoft Developer Network Library. Table 12.3 lists some of the most common and useful arguments for the Jet, SQL Server, and Oracle providers.

TABLE 12.3: Sample Connection String Arguments

Provider	Argument	Description
Jet	Data Source	Name of the Jet database to connect to
Jet	Jet OLEDB:System Database	Name of the system database to use when verifying username and password

TABLE 12.3 continued: Sample Connection String Arguments

Provider	Argument	Description
SQL Server	Integrated Security	Set to the literal value "SSPI" to use Windows NT login security
SQL Server	Data Source	Name of the SQL Server to connect to
SQL Server	Server	Name of the SQL Server to connect to
SQL Server	Initial Catalog	Name of the SQL Server database to connect to
Oracle	Data Source	Name of the Oracle server to connect to

Running Stored Procedures

As you saw in Chapter 9, you can use the Command object to execute statements on a connection. In this section, you'll learn how to use a Command object to execute a stored procedure in a SQL Server database.

Stored procedures are collections of SQL statements that are saved in a database. Some databases also precompile these statements for faster execution. These procedures can take input parameters and return output parameters. For example, in the Northwind SQL Server database, there's a stored procedure named SalesByCategory. Here's the SQL that creates that stored procedure:

```
CREATE PROCEDURE SalesByCategory
  @CategoryName nvarchar(15),
  @OrdYear nvarchar(4) = '1998'
AS
IF @OrdYear != '1996'
  AND @OrdYear != '1997'
  AND @OrdYear != '1998'
BEGIN
  SELECT @OrdYear = '1998'
END
SELECT ProductName,
  TotalPurchase =
  ROUND(SUM(CONVERT(decimal(14,2),
  OD.Quantity * (1-OD.Discount) *
  OD.UnitPrice)), 0)
FROM [Order Details] OD, Orders O,
  Products P, Categories C
WHERE OD.OrderID = O.OrderID
```

```
  AND OD.ProductID = P.ProductID
  AND P.CategoryID = C.CategoryID
  AND C.CategoryName = @CategoryName
  AND SUBSTRING(CONVERT(
  nvarchar(22), O.OrderDate, 111), 1, 4) =
  @OrdYear
GROUP BY ProductName
ORDER BY ProductName
```

Here, @CategoryName and @OrdYear are a pair of input parameters to the stored procedure, both defined as being of the nvarchar datatype. The stored procedure uses these parameters to filter a recordset of order information. The recordset becomes the return value of the stored procedure.

Retrieving a recordset from a stored procedure is a three-step process:

1. Create a command object and connect it to a data source.
2. Supply values for any input parameters.
3. Use the command object's Execute method to retrieve the data.

As an example, consider this code from frmStoredProcedure in the ADOCode sample project:

```
Private Sub cmdGo_Click()
  ' Fill a listbox with the results
  ' of a stored procedure

  Dim cnn As New ADODB.Connection
  Dim cmd As New ADODB.Command
  Dim prm As ADODB.Parameter
  Dim rst As ADODB.Recordset
  Dim fld As ADODB.Field

  Dim strTemp As String

  ' Connect to the data source and the SP
  cnn.Open "Provider=SQLOLEDB.1;" & _
    "Data Source=(local);Initial Catalog=" & _
    "Northwind;Integrated Security=SSPI"
  With cmd
    .ActiveConnection = cnn
    .CommandText = "SalesByCategory"
    .CommandType = adCmdStoredProc
    .Parameters.Refresh
  End With
```

Part ii

```
    ' Now walk through the Parameters, filling
    ' in the input parameters
    For Each prm In cmd.Parameters
      If (prm.Direction = adParamInput) Or _
        (prm.Direction = adParamInputOutput) Then
        prm.Value = InputBox(prm.Name, _
          "Enter parameter value")
      End If
    Next prm

    ' Retrieve and display the records
    Set rst = cmd.Execute
    For Each fld In rst.Fields
      strTemp = strTemp & fld.Name & vbTab
    Next fld
    lboResults.AddItem strTemp
    Do Until rst.EOF
      strTemp = ""
      For Each fld In rst.Fields
        strTemp = strTemp & fld.Value & vbTab
      Next fld
      lboResults.AddItem strTemp
      rst.MoveNext
    Loop

  End Sub
```

This code starts by connecting to the Northwind database on the local SQL Server, using Windows NT security. (As always, if your environment is different, you may have to modify the connection string.) Then, it creates a Command object and loads it with the alesByCategory stored procedure. Setting theCommandType property of the Command object to adCmdStored-Proc is optional, but the code will execute faster if you tell ADO that this is a stored procedure, rather than make ADO figure that out by itself.

The call to the Refresh method of the Command object's Parameters collection tells ADO to query the data source and find out what parameters are required by this stored procedure. Once the Parameters collection is populated, the code walks through it one parameter at a time and prompts the user for values for all input parameters.

Finally, the Execute method of the Command object is used to send the parameter values to the data source and fill in the recordset with the returned data.

Although this method works, it's not the most efficient way to execute a stored procedure. The bottleneck is the Refresh method of the Parameters collection, which can require multiple round trips of information between the client and the server to do its job. If you already know the details of the stored procedure, you can avoid using the Refresh method by creating your own parameters. This method is also demonstrated in frmStoredProcedure in the ADOCode sample project:

```
Private Sub cmdCreateParameters_Click()
  ' Fill a listbox with the results
  ' of a stored procedure. Create all
  ' necessary parameters on the client.

  Dim cnn As New ADODB.Connection
  Dim cmd As New ADODB.Command
  Dim prm As ADODB.Parameter
  Dim rst As ADODB.Recordset
  Dim fld As ADODB.Field

  Dim strTemp As String

  ' Connect to the data source and the SP
  cnn.Open "Provider=SQLOLEDB.1;" & _
    "Data Source=(local);Initial Catalog=" & _
    "Northwind;Integrated Security=SSPI"
  With cmd
    .ActiveConnection = cnn
    .CommandText = "SalesByCategory"
    .CommandType = adCmdStoredProc
  End With

  ' Create the necessary parameters, using
  ' the values supplied through the UI
  Set prm = cmd.CreateParameter( _
    "@CategoryName", _
    adVarWChar, adParamInput, 15, _
    txtCategoryName.Text)
  cmd.Parameters.Append prm
  Set prm = cmd.CreateParameter( _
    "@OrdYear", _
    adVarWChar, adParamInput, 4, _
    txtOrdYear.Text)
  cmd.Parameters.Append prm

  ' Retrieve and display the records
  Set rst = cmd.Execute
  For Each fld In rst.Fields
    strTemp = strTemp & fld.Name & vbTab
```

```
    Next fld
    lboResults2.AddItem strTemp
    Do Until rst.EOF
      strTemp = ""
      For Each fld In rst.Fields
        strTemp = strTemp & fld.Value & vbTab
      Next fld
      lboResults2.AddItem strTemp
      rst.MoveNext
    Loop

End Sub
```

The difference between this and the previous procedure is in the method used to populate the Parameters collection of the Command object. This procedure uses the CreateParameter method of the Command object:

```
Command.CreateParameter Name, Type, Direction, Size, Value
```

- The Name argument must match the name that the underlying data source is expecting for the parameter.
- The Type argument specifies a datatype for the parameter. These datatypes are expressed by constants supplied by ADO. Because ADO uses a single set of constants for all data sources, you might have trouble determining the appropriate constant to use in some cases. The simplest solution to this problem is to first use the Parameters.Refresh method to get the parameter from the server and then examine the Type property of the returned parameter. Once you know what this type is, you can create your own matching parameter in the future.
- The Direction argument is a constant that tells ADO whether this is an input or an output parameter (or both).
- The Size argument specifies the size of the parameter. You do not need to specify a Size for fixed-length datatypes such as integer or datetime. On the other hand, with some datatypes you might need to set additional properties. For floating-point parameters, for example, you need to explicitly set the Precision and NumericScale properties.
- The Value argument specifies the actual value to use for the parameter. Make sure to specify Null for the value if there's a chance you won't be passing a value to the stored procedure; otherwise

the stored procedure will "think" there's no data for the parameter and raise an error.

All these arguments are optional when you're calling the CreateParameter method. You can create parameters and then set the properties afterwards if you prefer not to do the entire operation in one line of code.

WARNING

Note that newly created Parameter objects are not appended to the Parameters collection by default. You must remember to call the Command object's Parameters collection's Append method, or your newly created Parameter won't be attached to the Command. ADO is deliberately designed this way to allow you to create additional provider-specific properties before appending the Parameter, if that's ever necessary.

In general, if you're writing code that will always call the same stored procedure, it's worth your while to explicitly code the parameters using the CreateParameter method. You should save the Parameters.Refresh method for situations where you don't know in advance what the Parameters collection should contain.

Retrieving Data

To retrieve data in ADO, use the Recordset object (or, sometimes, the Record or Stream objects). I covered the basics of the Recordset's Open method in Chapter 9. To refresh your memory, the syntax of this method is:

```
Recordset.Open Source, ActiveConnection, CursorType,
   LockType, Options
```

All these arguments are optional, because they can all be supplied by setting properties of the Recordset object before calling the Open method. For example, you can omit the LockType argument here if you have already set the LockType property of the Recordset object, or if you're happy with the default read-only locking.

The Source argument specifies where the records should be retrieved from. Because Providers are so flexible, there are a lot of possibilities for the Source argument. It can be

- A Command object that returns records
- An SQL statement
- A table name

- A stored procedure name
- The name of a file containing a persisted recordset
- The name of a Stream object containing a persisted recordset
- A URL that specifies a file or other location with data

Not all these options, of course, are valid for all providers.

The ActiveConnection argument specifies the ADO connection to use. This can be either a Connection object that you've already opened or a connection string. In the latter case, ADO creates a connection "behind the scenes" specifically for this recordset to use.

The CursorType and LockType arguments correspond to the cursor type and lock type parameters discussed in the previous section.

The Options argument supplies additional information to the provider. Generally, you can omit this argument, but some Open methods may be faster if you include it. Valid Options include:

- adCmdUnknown, which is the default and supplies no additional information to the provider.
- adCmdText, which tells the provider that the CommandText property is a textual definition of a stored procedure.
- adCmdTable, which tells the provider that the CommandText property is the name of a table.
- adCmdStoredProc, which tells the provider that the CommandText property is the name of a stored procedure.
- adCmdFile, which tells the provider that the CommandText property is the name of a file.
- adCmdTableDirect, which tells the provider that the CommandText property is the name of a table that should be opened using low-level calls. Most providers don't support this.
- adCmdURLBind, which tells the provider that the CommandText is a URL.
- adAsyncExecute, which tells the provider that the command should be executed asynchronously.
- adAsyncFetch, which tells the provider that the cache should be filled synchronously, and then additional rows fetched asynchronously.

- adAsyncFetchNonBlocking, which tells the provider to fetch records asynchronously if it can be done without blocking the main thread of execution.

For examples of recordset operations, see the frmRecordset form in the ADOCode sample project. Perhaps the simplest way to open a recordset is to just supply the name of a table in the data source as the source of the recordset:

```
Private Sub cmdTable_Click()
  ' Open a recordset based on a table
  Dim rst As New ADODB.Recordset
  Screen.MousePointer = vbHourglass
  rst.Open "Customers", _
    "Provider=Microsoft.Jet.OLEDB.4.0;" & _
    "Data Source=C:\Program Files\" & _
    "Microsoft Visual Studio\VB98\Nwind.mdb", _
    adOpenKeyset, adLockOptimistic
  Screen.MousePointer = vbDefault
  MsgBox rst.RecordCount & " records retrieved"
End Sub
```


In this case, the entire table is opened as a recordset. If you're using ADO to retrieve data in a client-server or three-tier setting, this probably isn't the best thing to do. A general rule of client-server processing is to retrieve only the data that you actually need at the moment. You can do this by supplying a SQL statement to be resolved by the data source. In this case, only the requested records will be returned:

```
Private Sub cmdStatement_Click()
  ' Open a recordset based on a SQL statement
  Dim rst As New ADODB.Recordset
  Screen.MousePointer = vbHourglass
  rst.Open "SELECT * FROM authors " & _
   "WHERE au_lname = 'Ringer'", _
    "Provider=SQLOLEDB.1;" & _
    "Data Source=(local);" & _
    "Initial Catalog=pubs;" & _
    "User ID=sa", _
    adOpenStatic, adLockPessimistic
  Screen.MousePointer = vbDefault
  MsgBox rst.RecordCount & " records retrieved"
End Sub
```

Alternatively, you can open a recordset on a view instead of a table. This allows you to define a persistent set of joins and restrictions directly on the server:

```
Private Sub cmdView_Click()
  ' Open a recordset based on a View
  Dim rst As New ADODB.Recordset
  Dim intRecords As Integer
  Screen.MousePointer = vbHourglass
  rst.Open "SALES", _
    "Provider=MSDAORA.1;" & _
    "Data Source=CASTOR;" & _
    "User ID=DEMO;" & _
    "Password=DEMO"
  Do Until rst.EOF
    intRecords = intRecords + 1
    rst.MoveNext
  Loop
  Screen.MousePointer = vbDefault
  MsgBox intRecords & " records retrieved" & _
    "; RecordCount is " & rst.RecordCount
End Sub
```

Note the loop used in this example to count the records returned. That's because the RecordCount property isn't always accurate. You'll find that:

- If the provider doesn't support counting records, the RecordCount property will be equal to −1.
- If the provider supports approximate positioning or bookmarks, the RecordCount will be accurate.
- If the provider (or cursor type) doesn't support approximate positioning or bookmarks, the RecordCount won't be accurate until you've retrieved every record in the recordset.
- Forward-only cursors will always return −1 for the RecordCount, even after all the records have been retrieved.

Finding and Sorting Data

Given a set of records, there are some common tasks. For example, you might want to find a particular record, or the first record meeting some criterion. Or, you might want to sort the recordset. In this section, I'll review the basics of finding and sorting data in ADO recordsets.

How you find a record depends on the type of recordset. A few OLE DB providers (notably the Microsoft Jet Provider) support a special type of recordset, the *direct table recordset*. Such recordsets (opened with the adCmdTableDirect option) can use an indexed search to find data. Other recordsets must use a slower sequential search.

Finding Data in a Direct Table Recordset

If you've created a direct table access Recordset object, some providers allow you to use the fast Seek method to locate specific rows. (Attempting to use the Seek method with any other recordset results in a runtime error.) Take two specific steps to use the Seek method to find data:

1. Set the recordset's Index property to the name of an index on the underlying table. This tells ADO which index you'd like it to search through. If you want to use the primary key for searching, you must know the name of the primary key. (It's usually PrimaryKey, unless your application has changed it.)
2. Use the Seek method to find the value you want. The Seek method works from a search operator and one or more values to search for. The search operator must be one of the intrinsic constants shown in Table 12.4. If the index is on a single column, you supply a value to search for in that column. If the index is on multiple columns, you should supply one search value for each column, using the Visual Basic Array() function to create an array from these values.

WARNING

Currently, the only provider shipped as part of MDAC that supports Index and Seek is the Jet provider.

TABLE 12.4: Seek Options

Seek Option	Meaning
adSeekAfterEQ	Seek the key equal to the value supplied, or, if there is no such key, the first key after the point where the match would have occurred.
adSeekAfter	Seek the first key after the point where a match occurs or would occur.

Part ii

TABLE 12.4 continued: Seek Options

Seek Option	Meaning
adSeekBeforeEQ	Seek the key equal to the value supplied, or, if there is no such key, the first key before the point where the match would have occurred.
adSeekBefore	Seek the first key before the point where a match occurs or would occur.
adSeekFirstEQ	Seek the first key equal to the value supplied.
AdSeekAfterEQ	Seek the last key equal to the value supplied.

You'll find an example of using the Seek method in the frmRecordset form in the ADOCode sample project:

```
Private Sub cmdSeek_Click()
  ' Find a record using the Seek method
  ' This requires a direct table recordset
  Dim rst As New ADODB.Recordset
  Dim strSeek As String

  Screen.MousePointer = vbHourglass
  rst.Open "Customers", _
    "Provider=Microsoft.Jet.OLEDB.4.0;" & _
    "Data Source=" & App.Path & _
    "\ADOCode.MDB", _
    adOpenDynamic, adLockOptimistic, _
    adCmdTableDirect
  Screen.MousePointer = vbDefault

  ' Now set the index we want to seek on
  rst.Index = "PrimaryKey"
  ' Get a value to seek for
  strSeek = InputBox("Customer ID to Find:", _
    "Seek input", "FOLKO")

  ' Seek the record and report results
  rst.Seek strSeek, adSeekAfterEQ
  If rst.EOF Then
    MsgBox "No matching record found"
  Else
    MsgBox "Found customer " & _
      rst("CompanyName")
  End If
End Sub
```

Note that the procedure checks the EOF property of the recordset after invoking the Seek method. If the Seek fails, EOF will be set to True. This is the only way to tell whether the Seek method found a matching record.

WARNING

With the Jet 4 OLE DB provider, the Seek method only works on recordsets created from Jet 4 databases (for example, databases created with Microsoft Access 2000). When in doubt, you can use the Supports method, discussed later in this chapter, to determine whether the Seek method will work at all.

Finding Data Using the Find Method

Most recordsets cannot use the Seek method for finding data. Fortunately, ADO provides a second method for finding records that's universally supported. This is the Find method of the recordset, which is implemented with a great deal of flexibility. It allows you to optimize the search so it has to look through the smallest number of rows to find the data it needs. Because you can use Find to continue searching with the next record, you won't need to start back at the beginning of the recordset to find subsequent matches. In addition, you can use loops to walk your way through the records, because you can restart the search without going back to the first row. The biggest disadvantage to the Find method is that you can only search on a single criterion. For multiple criteria, you can use the Filter property instead.

The syntax for the Find method is:

```
Recordset.Find Criteria, SkipRows, SearchDirection, Start
```

- All but the first parameter are optional.
- `Criteria` is a WHERE clause formatted as though in a SQL expression, without the word *WHERE*.
- `SkipRows` specifies the offset from the current row where the search should begin. It defaults to starting with the current row.
- `SearchDirection` can be adSearchForward (the default) or adSearchBackward.
- `Start` is an optional bookmark where the search should begin. The default is to begin with the current row.

Part ii

For an example of the Find method, see the frmRecordset form in the ADOCode sample project:

```
Private Sub cmdFind_Click()
  ' Use the Find method to locate records
  Dim rst As New ADODB.Recordset
  Dim strCriteria As String

  Screen.MousePointer = vbHourglass
  rst.Open "SELECT * FROM authors", _
    "Provider=SQLOLEDB.1;" & _
    "Data Source=(local);" & _
    "Initial Catalog=pubs;" & _
    "User ID=sa", _
    adOpenStatic, adLockPessimistic
  Screen.MousePointer = vbDefault

  ' Find all the authors in California
  strCriteria = "State = 'CA'
  With rst
    .Find strCriteria
    Do While Not .EOF
      lboFound.AddItem rst("au_lname")
      ' Continue with the next record
      .Find strCriteria, 1
    Loop
  End With
End Sub
```

Just as with the Find method, you must follow every call to a Find method with a check of the recordset's EOF property (or BOF property, if SearchDirection is adSearchBackward). If that property is True, there is no current row, and the Find method failed to find any matching records.

Note also the use of the SkipRows argument in the second call to the Find method in the sample code. By skipping a single row with each call, you can continue to find records starting at the point where the last search left off.

WARNING

Find criteria treat null values differently from the way that some database engines (such as Jet) do. Because the ADO Find method does not understand the IsNull() or similar functions, the correct way to search for a Null using the Find method is with an expression such as "FieldName = Null" or "FieldName < > Null."

Sorting Recordsets

Unless you specify a sorting order for a recordset, the rows for that recordset might show up in any order. The order could depend on data from more than one table, and on the OLE DB provider that's supplying the original data. In any case, if you need a specific ordering, you must set up that ordering yourself. You can do this either with a SQL statement or with the Recordset object's Sort property.

Using a SQL ORDER BY Clause

You can create a Recordset object using a SQL statement including an ORDER BY clause. To do so, specify the SQL expression as the row source for the Recordset's Open method. For example, you could use this code fragment to create a recordset based on the Customers table, ordered by Company Name:

```
Dim rst As New ADODB.Recordset
  Screen.MousePointer = vbHourglass
  rst.Open "SELECT * FROM Customers " & _
    "ORDER BY CompanyName", _
    "Provider=Microsoft.Jet.OLEDB.4.0;" & _
    "Data Source=C:\Program Files\" & _
    "Microsoft Visual Studio\VB98\Nwind.mdb", _
    adOpenKeyset, adLockOptimistic
```

Using the *Sort* Property

You can also set the Sort property of a recordset to change its sort order. The Sort property must be a string, in the same style as the ORDER BY clause of a SQL expression (that is, it's a comma-separated list of field names, optionally with ASC or DESC to indicate ascending or descending sorts).

Some OLE DB providers don't implement the necessary interfaces to allow sorting. If you're using a recordset from such a provider, you can still use the Sort method, but only if you've created a client-side cursor.

For example, this code from the frmRecordset form in the ADOCode sample demonstrates how to change the sort order of a recordset from the Jet provider, even though the Jet provider itself doesn't support sorting:

```
Private Sub cmdSort_Click()
  ' Sort a recordset in descending order
  Dim rst As New ADODB.Recordset
  ' Fetch a recordset in native order
  Screen.MousePointer = vbHourglass
  rst.CursorLocation = adUseClient
```

Part ii

```
  rst.Open "Customers", _
    "Provider=Microsoft.Jet.OLEDB.4.0;" & _
    "Data Source=C:\Program Files\" & _
    "Microsoft Visual Studio\VB98\Nwind.mdb", _
    adOpenKeyset, adLockOptimistic
  Screen.MousePointer = vbDefault
  lboFound.Clear
  Do Until rst.EOF
    lboFound.AddItem rst.Fields("CompanyName")
    rst.MoveNext
  Loop
  ' Now sort it on the CompanyName field
  MsgBox "Click OK to sort descending"
  rst.Sort = "CompanyName DESC"
  lboFound.Clear
  Do Until rst.EOF
    lboFound.AddItem rst.Fields("CompanyName")
    rst.MoveNext
  Loop
End Sub
```

Note the use of the SQL DESC keyword to force a descending sort. The new sort takes effect as soon as the Sort property is set. In some cases, you may find that it's faster to simply open a new recordset based on a SQL statement with an ORDER BY clause than it is to use the Sort property.

Updating, Adding, and Deleting Data

Almost any database application needs to be able to update, add, and delete data. ADO provides methods for accomplishing each of these tasks. The next few sections discuss the various data-manipulation methods that ADO supports. Of course, all these methods work on the Recordset object.

Changing Data in a Recordset

Changing data in a recordset is a three-step process:

1. Move to the row of the recordset containing the data.
2. Set new values for the fields that you want to change.
3. Use the Recordset object's Update method to save the new values.

You must explicitly call the Update method before you move to another row of the recordset, unless you're performing batch updates (see the next section for more information on batch updates). If you don't explicitly call the Update method, ADO calls it automatically when you move off a row and saves any pending changes to the record. You can also explicitly discard changes by calling the recordset's CancelUpdate method.

Batch Updates

If you use the client-side cursor library with a keyset or static cursor, you can also take advantage of ADO's ability to perform batch updates. That is, you can edit multiple records in a database, and then send all the updates to the underlying OLE DB provider to be stored in a single operation.

To use batch updates, simply change as many records as you please, and then call the UpdateBatch method. If you've used a client-side cursor, your changes will be cached on the client until you call the UpdateBatch method. At that time, all the changes will be sent to the server as a single operation.

If any of your changes can't be saved (for example, because another user has deleted the record), a runtime error occurs. In this case, you can use the Filter property with the adFilterAffectedRecords constant to filter the recordset down to only those records that had problems.

Adding New Rows to a Recordset

Adding new rows to a recordset is also a three-step process:

1. Call the AddNew method of the Recordset object to create a new row.
2. Fill in the Value property of any field you wish to assign a non-default value to.
3. Call the Update method to save the new row to the data source.

If you move off the row without calling Update, ADO helpfully calls the Update method for you (unless you've opened the recordset for batch updating). When you use the AddNew method, the new record becomes the current row as soon as you call the Update method.

Deleting Data from a Recordset

Deleting a record from a recordset is simple. You just move to the desired row and call the Delete method of the Recordset object.

You don't need to use the Update methods when deleting a row, unlike the case of adding a row. Once you delete it, it's gone—unless, of course, you wrapped the entire thing in a transaction. In that case, you can roll back the transaction to retrieve the deleted row.

After you delete a record, it is still the current record. The previous row is still the previous row, and the next row is still the next row. Use MoveNext to move to the next row, if that's where you'd like to be.

Data Manipulation Example

To see the Update, UpdateBatch, AddNew, and Delete methods in action, you can examine the frmRecordsetChanges form in the ADOCode sample project. This form, shown in Figure 12.1, allows you to invoke each of these four methods on a form-level Recordset object opened with a client-side cursor.

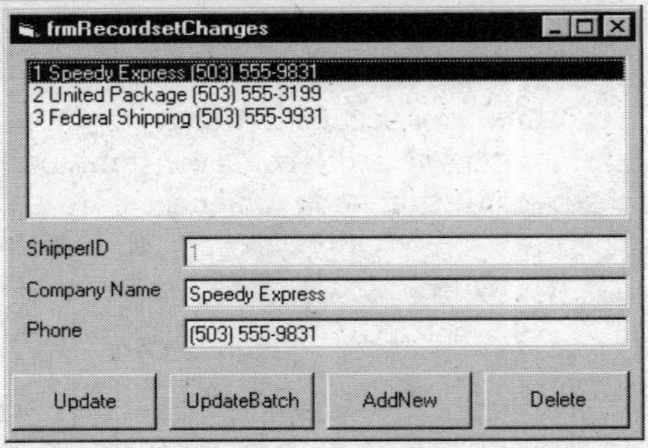

FIGURE 12.1: The frmRecordsetChanges sample form

The form starts by opening a recordset as soon as the form itself is loaded:

```
Private Sub Form_Load()
   ' Initialize the recordset
   GetRecordset
End Sub

Private Sub GetRecordset()
   ' Get the current records from the server
   gfLoading = True
   ' If the recordset is open, close it.
   ' Otherwise, create it.
   If Not grst Is Nothing Then
      grst.Close
   Else
      Set grst = New ADODB.Recordset
```

```
    End If
    ' Use a client cursor to support
    ' batch updates
    grst.CursorLocation = adUseClient
    grst.Open "Shippers", _
      "Provider=SQLOLEDB.1;Server=(local);" & _
      "Initial Catalog=Northwind;User ID=sa", _
      adOpenDynamic, adLockOptimistic
    lboShippers.Clear
    ' Walk the recordset, displaying each record
    Do Until grst.EOF
      lboShippers.AddItem grst(0) & " " & _
        grst(1) & " " & grst(2)
      grst.MoveNext
    Loop
    gfLoading = False
    ' Highlight the first record
    lboShippers.ListIndex = 0
  End Sub
```

Once the recordset is loaded, this code moves through each record, concatenating all the fields and placing the concatenated strings in a list box. Note that the CursorLocation property of the recordset is set to adUseClient to support batch updating.

When a record is selected in the list box, the code uses the recordset's Find method to display the details of the appropriate record in the text boxes on the form:

```
  Private Sub lboShippers_Click()
    ' Find the record that's been selected and
    ' move its data to the textboxes
    Dim strCriteria As String

    strCriteria = "ShipperID = " & _
      Left(lboShippers.Text, 1)
    grst.MoveFirst
    grst.Find strCriteria
    If Not grst.EOF Then
      txtShipperID = grst.Fields("ShipperID")
      txtCompanyName = grst.Fields("CompanyName")
      txtPhone = grst.Fields("Phone")
    End If
  End Sub
```

Because the ShipperID field is an identity field, it can't be edited by the user. For this reason, the Enabled property of the txtShipperID text box is set to False. The other two text boxes have code attached to their

Change events to push any changes from the user interface back to the recordset:

```
Private Sub txtCompanyName_Change()
  ' Save changes back to the recordset
  If Not gfLoading Then
    grst.Fields("CompanyName") = _
      txtCompanyName.Text
  End If
End Sub

Private Sub txtPhone_Change()
  ' Save changes back to the recordset
  If Not gfLoading Then
    grst.Fields("Phone") = _
      txtPhone.Text
  End If
End Sub
```

The command buttons on the form simply call the corresponding recordset methods:

```
Private Sub cmdAddnew_Click()
  ' Add a new record and clear the
  ' textboxes to accept the details
  grst.AddNew
  txtShipperID = ""
  txtCompanyName = ""
  txtPhone = ""
End Sub

Private Sub cmdDelete_Click()
  ' Delete the current record
  grst.Delete
  GetRecordset
End Sub

Private Sub cmdUpdate_Click()
  ' Update the current record
  grst.Update
  GetRecordset
End Sub

Private Sub cmdUpdateBatch_Click()
  ' Update all cached records
  grst.UpdateBatch
  GetRecordset
End Sub
```

The Supports Method

As you've seen throughout this chapter, not all recordsets are created equal. When you take into account the different ways that you can open recordsets, the various permutations of the CursorLocation, CursorType, LockType, and Options properties, and the different potential OLE DB providers that can be supplying the data, it can be difficult to be sure just which methods will work on which recordsets. Fortunately, ADO provides the Supports method, which allows you to query a recordset as to the functionality that it supports.

The Supports method returns True or False for specific options:

```
fReturn = rst.Supports(Option)
```

where `Option` is one of the intrinsic constants shown in Table 12.5.

TABLE 12.5: Constants for the Supports Method

Option	Returns True if...
adAddNew	You can use the AddNew method to add records to this recordset.
adApproxPosition	You can use the AbsolutePosition and AbsolutePage properties with this recordset.
adBookmark	You can use the Bookmark property with this recordset.
adDelete	You can use the Delete method to delete records from this recordset.
adFind	You can use the Find method to find records in this recordset.
adHoldRecords	You can change the recordset position without committing changes to the current record. This is necessary for batch updates.
adIndex	You can use the Index property to set an index for this recordset.
adMovePrevious	You can use MoveFirst and MovePrevious, or the Move method, to move backwards in this recordset.
adNotify	This recordset supports events.
adResync	You can use the Resync method to resynchronize this recordset with the underlying data.
adSeek	You can use the Seek method to find records in this recordset.
adUpdate	You can use the Update method to modify records in this recordset.
adUpdateBatch	You can use the UpdateBatch and CancelBatch methods on this recordset.

Working with Persisted Recordsets

If you're familiar with DAO or RDO, you might think of recordsets as entities that exist only in memory during the course of an application. ADO adds the ability to persist a recordset to a file on disk or to a Stream object. In fact, you can persist a recordset, later reopen it, edit it, reconnect it to the original data source, and save changes.

Saving a Recordset

To persist a recordset to disk for later use, call its Save method:

```
rst.Save Destination, PersistFormat
```

The Destination parameter is the full path and filename to the file that you wish to use to hold the contents of this recordset. The PersistFormat parameter is one of two intrinsic constants:

- adPersistADTG is the default. This saves the recordset in the Microsoft proprietary Advanced Data Tablegram format.
- adPersistXML can be specified to save the recordset as XML. If you save the recordset in XML format, you can open it directly in an advanced Web browser, such as Internet Explorer 5.

ADTG files are smaller than XML files, so unless you need the advanced browser connection, stick to ADTG.

For an example of saving a recordset, see the frmPersist form in the ADOCode sample project. This procedure opens a recordset on the authors table from the SQL Server pubs database and saves it to an XML file:

```
Private Sub cmdSaveRecordset_Click()
  ' Save a recordset to disk
  Dim rst As New ADODB.Recordset
  Dim strFile As String
  ' Open the recordset from the database
  rst.CursorLocation = adUseClient
  rst.Open "SELECT * FROM authors", _
    "Provider=SQLOLEDB.1;" & _
    "Data Source=(local);" & _
    "Initial Catalog=pubs;" & _
    "User ID=sa", _
    adOpenStatic, adLockPessimistic
  ' Construct a file name
```

```
    strFile = App.Path & "\authors.xml"
    ' Destroy any existing file
    On Error Resume Next
    Kill strFile
    On Error GoTo 0
    ' Now save the recordset to disk
    rst.Save strFile, adPersistXML
    ' And remove it from memory
    rst.Close
    Set rst = Nothing
End Sub
```

Figure 12.2 shows the resulting XML file open in Internet Explorer 5. While XML is beyond the scope of this book, you can see that the XML encoding includes both schema and data information for the recordset.

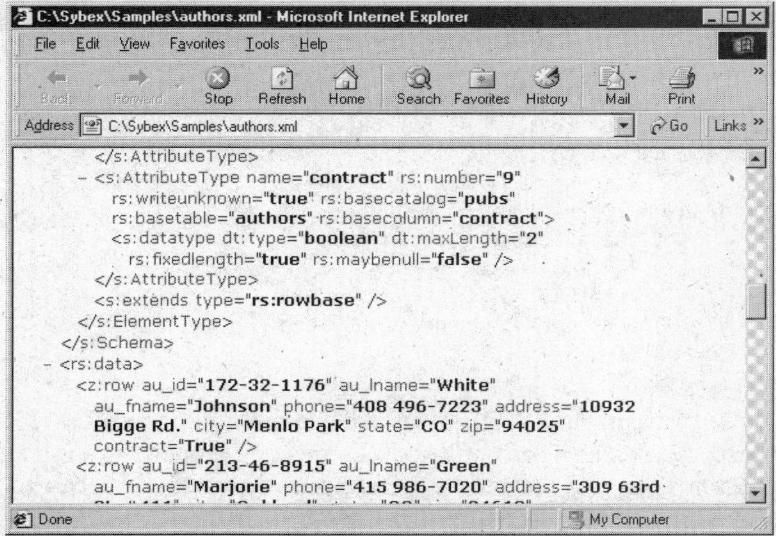

FIGURE 12.2: Authors table saved to XML

If you save a recordset and continue to work with it, updating records, your changes are written to the disk file whenever you call the Update method, until you call the recordset's Close method. When the Save method is invoked, the current record is reset to the first record in the recordset.

Some providers don't support the functionality necessary to save a recordset. If you have this problem, you can always set the CursorLocation property to adUseClient to create a client-side cursor.

Loading a Saved Recordset

To retrieve a saved recordset, you use the Open method of the recordset object. As the Source parameter, you supply the name of the disk file that contains the previously saved recordset. You don't have to create a Connection object when you reopen the recordset. Here's an example from the frmPersist form in the ADOCode sample database:

```
Private Sub cmdLoadRecordset_Click()
  ' Load a previously-saved recordset
  Dim rst As New ADODB.Recordset
  Dim cnn As New ADODB.Connection
  Dim strFile As String
  ' Construct a file name
  strFile = App.Path & "\authors.xml"
  ' Make sure the file exists
  If Len(Dir(strFile)) > 0 Then
    ' Open the recordset from the file
    rst.Open strFile, , adOpenStatic, _
      adLockPessimistic
    ' Show that we've got data
    MsgBox rst.RecordCount & " records found"
    ' Reconnect it to the database
    cnn.Open "Provider=SQLOLEDB.1;" & _
      "Data Source=(local);" & _
      "Initial Catalog=pubs;" & _
      "User ID=sa"
    Set rst.ActiveConnection = cnn
  End If
End Sub
```

As you can see in the previous code, to reconnect a recordset to a database, you set the recordset's ActiveConnection property to a valid Connection object for the database. Once you've done this, you can update the recordset just like any other recordset.

WARNING

Cursor options are not persisted as part of a saved recordset. Be sure to specify the cursor type and locking type when you reopen a saved recordset. Otherwise, you'll get a default forward-only, read-only recordset.

ADVANCED OPERATIONS

ADO includes a number of methods to perform more complex data operations than those that you've already seen in this chapter. In the remainder of the chapter, you'll learn about two of these capabilities. First, I'll take a look at the use of asynchronous operations to avoid blocking program execution on slow connections. Next, I'll cover the use of batch updating, with emphasis on the things that you can do to deal with conflicts between client-side and server-side changes to your data.

Asynchronous Operations and ADO Events

With the rise of two-tier, three-tier, and intranet/Internet database applications, it's a fact of life that retrieving data can be a relatively slow operation. Fortunately, the designers of ADO recognized this fact and have implemented asynchronous operations to help out. Dealing with data asynchronously doesn't get the data back any faster, but it does mean that your entire application doesn't lock up during the time that ADO is performing an operation. In this section, I'll show you the three things you can do asynchronously in ADO:

- Make a connection.
- Execute a command.
- Retrieve a recordset.

To perform any of these options asynchronously, you must be able to monitor the events of the associated object. That means that you'll need to declare your object with the Visual Basic WithEvents keyword, which in turn, means that the object must be declared with module-level scope.

To perform an asynchronous connection, you must use the adAsyncConnect option when you execute the Connection object's Open method. For example, here's some code from the frmAsynchronous form in the ADOCode sample application:

```
Private WithEvents mcnn As ADODB.Connection

Private Sub Form_Load()
  txtConnectionString.Text = _
    "Provider=SQLOLEDB.1;" & _
    "Data Source=BIGREDBARN;" & _
    "Initial Catalog=Northwind;" & _
    "User ID=sa"
```

```
End Sub

Private Sub cmdConnect_Click()
  Set mcnn = New ADODB.Connection
  mcnn.ConnectionString = _
    txtConnectionString.Text
  mcnn.Open , , , adAsyncConnect
End Sub

Private Sub mcnn_ConnectComplete( _
  ByVal pError As ADODB.Error, _
  adStatus As ADODB.EventStatusEnum, _
  ByVal pConnection As ADODB.Connection)
  If adStatus = adStatusOK Then
    MsgBox "Connection is complete"
  Else
    MsgBox "Connection error: " & _
      pError.Description
  End If
End Sub

Private Sub mcnn_InfoMessage( _
  ByVal pError As ADODB.Error, _
  adStatus As ADODB.EventStatusEnum, _
  ByVal pConnection As ADODB.Connection)
  txtInfoMessage.Text = _
    pError.Description
End Sub
```

When you open the form, a text box on the user interface is filled in with a sample connection string (you'll need to modify this unless your SQL Server just happens to be named BIGREDBARN). Clicking the Connect button tells ADO to open a connection, using whatever string is currently displayed, and to make the connection asynchronously. If you like, you could perform other operations in code in this same procedure; they would not be blocked while waiting for the Open method to complete.

When the connection is made, or when ADO gives up trying to make the connection, the connection's ConnectComplete event is fired. Note that the name is somewhat misleading: this event will occur even if the connection is never completed, as soon as ADO decides there is a problem (try using the name of a nonexistent server or nonexistent database in your connection string to see this).

There's also an InfoMessage event, which is specified to occur if the OLE DB provider emits a warning during the connection operation. You'll seldom see this event with the Microsoft providers.

Both of these events supply the same three parameters: an Error object containing information on any error that occurred during the operation, a status value that contains further information on the events, and a pointer to the Connection object firing the event. The adStatus parameter can have five possible values in these and other events (not all of these values are sensible for all events):

- adStatusOK indicates that the operation was successful.
- adStatusErrorsOccurred indicates that the operation failed. In this case, you should examine the pError object or the pConnection.Errors collection for further information.
- adStatusCantDeny indicates that you tried to cancel an event that can't be cancelled. This value might be set by ADO after you've set the adStatus parameter in a previous occurrence of the event to adStatusCancel.
- adStatusCancel is a value that you can set within the event procedure. If you set the adStatus parameter to adStatusCancel, the event tells ADO to cancel the operation that caused the event in the first place.
- adStatusUnwantedEvent is another value that you can set within your event procedure code. By returning this value to ADO, you notify ADO that you don't want this event to continue firing for the duration of this operation.

To execute a command asynchronously, simply execute it on a connection that's already been opened asynchronously. Here's an example from the frmAsynchronous form in the ADOCode sample project:

```
Private Sub cmdExecute_Click()
  ' Execute a command asynchronously
  Dim cmd As New ADODB.Command
  Dim rst As ADODB.Recordset
  cmd.CommandText = _
    txtCommandText.Text
  Set cmd.ActiveConnection = mcnn
  Set rst = cmd.Execute()
End Sub
```

```
Private Sub mcnn_WillExecute(Source As _
  String, CursorType As ADODB.CursorTypeEnum, _
  LockType As ADODB.LockTypeEnum, _
  Options As Long, _
  adStatus As ADODB.EventStatusEnum, _
  ByVal pCommand As ADODB.Command, _
  ByVal pRecordset As ADODB.Recordset, _
  ByVal pConnection As ADODB.Connection)
  MsgBox "About to execute " & Source
End Sub

Private Sub mcnn_ExecuteComplete( _
  ByVal RecordsAffected As Long, _
  ByVal pError As ADODB.Error, _
  adStatus As ADODB.EventStatusEnum, _
  ByVal pCommand As ADODB.Command, _
  ByVal pRecordset As ADODB.Recordset, _
  ByVal pConnection As ADODB.Connection)
  If adStatus = adStatusOK Then
    MsgBox "Command Executed"
  Else
    MsgBox "Command execution error: " & _
      pError.Description
  End If
End Sub
```

Once again, there are two events of interest here. The WillExecute event fires every time you try to execute a command on the connection whose events are being trapped. This is especially useful in situations where the user can submit ad hoc commands that you might want to examine before allowing. If you set the adStatus parameter in this event to adStatusCancel, the command won't be sent to the data source.

The ExecuteComplete event fires when the command is completed, either successfully or unsuccessfully. Again, you need to check the adStatus parameter to determine why the event was fired.

To open a recordset asynchronously, specify the adAsyncFetch constant when you call the Recordset object's Open method. Here's an example from frmAsynchronous in the ADOCode sample project. It assumes you've already opened the connection to the database:

```
Private WithEvents mrst As ADODB.Recordset

Private Sub cmdOpen_Click()
  ' Open a recordset asynchronously
  Set mrst = New ADODB.Recordset
```

```
    mrst.ActiveConnection = mcnn
    mrst.CursorLocation = adUseClient
    mrst.CacheSize = 10
    mrst.Open txtSource.Text, , adOpenKeyset, , _
      adAsyncFetch
  End Sub

  Private Sub mrst_FetchComplete( _
    ByVal pError As ADODB.Error, _
    adStatus As ADODB.EventStatusEnum, _
    ByVal pRecordset As ADODB.Recordset)
    If adStatus = adStatusOK Then
      MsgBox "Fetch is complete"
    Else
      MsgBox "Recordset error: " & _
        pError.Description
    End If
  End Sub

  Private Sub mrst_FetchProgress( _
    ByVal Progress As Long, _
    ByVal MaxProgress As Long, _
    adStatus As ADODB.EventStatusEnum, _
    ByVal pRecordset As ADODB.Recordset)
    txtProgress = "Fetched " & Progress & _
      " of " & MaxProgress
  End Sub
```

For an asynchronous fetch, you should use client-side cursors. You may also want to set the CacheSize property, as shown here, to specify the number of records to be retrieved at a time. The FetchProgress event will be fired as the records are being retrieved, and the FetchComplete event will be fired when all the records are retrieved.

The ADO documentation states that you must be using Visual Basic 6.0 or higher for FetchProgress and FetchComplete to fire. However, I've found that FetchProgress is unreliable, even with Visual Basic 6.0.

Batch Updates and Conflicts

Batch updating, like most other programming techniques, has its good side and its bad side. On the good side, you can cache multiple changes on the client until you're ready to submit them to the server, and so cut down on potentially slow and expensive client-server round trips. On the bad side, in a multiuser environment (which most multiple-tier environments are), the longer you cache changes, the more chance that someone else will have changed a record that you were both working with.

ADO provides two methods to deal with record conflicts while batch updating. You can use the Resync method of the Recordset object to investigate changes on the server before submitting your changes. Alternatively, you can use the Filter method to determine which (if any) changes failed after calling the BatchUpdate method. I'll work through both of these methods in the remainder of this chapter.

Using Resync to Detect Potential Conflicts

As you might guess, the Resync method is used to resynchronize client and server recordsets. The syntax is:

```
Recordset.Resync AffectRecords, ResyncValues
```

The AffectRecords argument takes one of four values:

- adAffectCurrent to resynchronize only the current record
- adAffectGroup to resynchronize all records matching the current Filter setting
- adAffectAll to resynchronize the entire recordset
- adAffectAllChapters to resynchronize multiple recordsets in a hierarchical recordset

The ResyncValues can be either adResyncAllValues (the default) or adResyncUnderlyingValues. If you choose adResyncAllValues, the client recordset is made to match the server recordset, and any pending updates are cancelled. This isn't what you'd want to do when checking the potential of update conflicts, of course. The alternative, adResyncUnderlyingValues, retrieves data from the server, but stores it in the UnderlyingValue property instead of the Value property.

An example from the frmConflict form in the ADOCode sample project will help make this clear:

```
Private Sub cmdResync_Click()
    ' Open two recordsets, change both, and
    ' demonstrate the Resync method
    Dim rst1 As New ADODB.Recordset
    Dim rst2 As New ADODB.Recordset

    lboResults.Clear
```

```
    ' Retrieve the records on one connection
    rst1.CursorLocation = adUseClient
    rst1.Open "Customers", _
      "Provider=SQLOLEDB.1;Server=(local);" & _
      "Initial Catalog=Northwind;User ID=sa", _
      adOpenDynamic, adLockBatchOptimistic
    rst1.MoveFirst

    ' And on another connection
    rst2.CursorLocation = adUseClient
    rst2.Open "Customers", _
      "Provider=SQLOLEDB.1;Server=(local);" & _
      "Initial Catalog=Northwind;User ID=sa", _
      adOpenDynamic, adLockBatchOptimistic
    rst2.MoveFirst

    ' Change and commit from the first recordset
    rst1.Fields("ContactTitle") = "SalesRep"
    rst1.UpdateBatch
    lboResults.AddItem _
      "Title changed to SalesRep on server"

    ' Now change the second recordset
    rst2.Fields("ContactTitle") = _
      "Representative"
    lboResults.AddItem _
      "Title changed to Representative on client"

    ' Resync the changes
    rst2.Resync adAffectAll, _
      adResyncUnderlyingValues

    ' And show the results
    lboResults.AddItem _
      "Value = " & _
      rst2.Fields("ContactTitle").Value
    lboResults.AddItem _
      "Original Value = " & _
      rst2.Fields("ContactTitle").OriginalValue
    lboResults.AddItem _
      "Underlying Value = " & _
      rst2.Fields("ContactTitle").UnderlyingValue

End Sub
```

This procedure starts by opening two recordsets on the same data. Because these recordsets are using implicit connections, they each get their own connection to the database, and it's perfectly possible to make independent changes on each recordset. Both recordsets are opened on the client with batch-optimistic locking, to enable batch updating.

First, the code makes a change to the first record in rst1 and uses the UpdateBatch method to save this change back to the server. Then it makes a conflicting change to the same record in rst2. Rather than call the UpdateBatch method, though, the code calls the Resync method to investigate the properties of this field. If you run the code, you'll see results similar to these:

```
Value = Representative
Original Value = Sales Representative
Underlying Value = SalesRep
```

This tells you that, although the original value on the server was "Sales Representative," it's now "SalesRep," indicating that another user changed the record during the course of your edits. How you'd respond to this in code, of course, depends on the business logic that you're trying to implement. You might want to save your updates anyhow, or you might want to warn the user that there had been a change and perform a full Resync operation to reset to the values currently on the server.

Using Filter to Detect Actual Conflicts

As an alternative, you might just go ahead and call the UpdateBatch method after making whatever changes are necessary to your copy of the recordset. In this case, if there are any conflicts (records that have already been changed by another user), ADO will ignore those records in your changes, although it will save all the other changes. ADO will also raise an error for your Visual Basic code to intercept.

But then what? The best answer is to use the Filter property of the Recordset object to see exactly what records failed to update. To see this technique, you can examine frmConflict in the ADOCode sample project:

```
Private Sub cmdFilter_Click()
  ' Open two recordsets, change both, and
  ' demonstrate the Filter method
  Dim rst1 As New ADODB.Recordset
  Dim rst2 As New ADODB.Recordset

  On Error GoTo HandleErr

  lboResults.Clear
```

```
    ' Retrieve the records on one connection
    rst1.CursorLocation = adUseClient
    rst1.Open "Customers", _
      "Provider=SQLOLEDB.1;Server=(local);" & _
      "Initial Catalog=Northwind;User ID=sa", _
      adOpenDynamic, adLockBatchOptimistic
    rst1.MoveFirst

    ' And on another connection
    rst2.CursorLocation = adUseClient
    rst2.Open "Customers", _
      "Provider=SQLOLEDB.1;Server=(local);" & _
      "Initial Catalog=Northwind;User ID=sa", _
      adOpenDynamic, adLockBatchOptimistic
    rst2.MoveFirst

    ' Change and commit from the first recordset
    rst1.Fields("ContactTitle") = "SalesCritter"
    rst1.UpdateBatch
    lboResults.AddItem _
      "Title changed to SalesCritter on server"

    ' Now change the second recordset
    rst2.Fields("ContactTitle") = "New Rep"
    lboResults.AddItem _
      "Title changed to New Rep on client"

    ' Update the changes to the server
    rst2.UpdateBatch

  ExitHere:
    Exit Sub

  HandleErr:
    rst2.Filter = adFilterConflictingRecords
    lboResults.AddItem _
      "In error handler, " & rst2.RecordCount & _
      " record(s) conflicting"
    Resume ExitHere
  End Sub
```

This code performs the same operations as the previous example, up to the point where the second recordset is changed. Then, instead of checking to see whether the changes can be saved, it simply calls the UpdateBatch method to try to save them. This will cause a runtime error, which will be thrown into the error-handling routine.

This routine sets the Filter property of the recordset in question to adFilterConflictingRecords. This tells ADO to rework the recordset, keeping only the records that didn't update successfully. You could then take necessary action, such as prompting the user or resyncing and then resaving changes.

The Filter property is designed for flexibility. Table 12.6 shows the possible values that you can set for this property.

TABLE 12.6: *Filter* Property Values

VALUE	MEANING
Criterion string (such as "LastName = 'Butler'")	Filters the recordset to include only records matching the specified criterion.
Array of Bookmarks	Filters the recordset to include only records matching the supplied bookmarks.
"" (Zero-length string)	Removes any filters and returns all records to the recordset.
adFilterNone	Removes any filters and returns all records to the recordset.
adFilterPendingRecords	Filters the recordset to hold only records with changes that have not yet been sent to the server.
adFilterAffectedRecords	Filters the recordset to hold only records that were changed by the last call to the Delete, Resync, UpdateBatch, or CancelBatch method.
adFilterFetchedRecords	Filters the recordset to hold only the most recent records placed in the record cache.
adFilterConflictingRecords	Filters the recordset to hold only the records that failed to update in an UpdateBatch operation.

SUMMARY

This chapter demonstrated how to create and work with ADO objects in your Visual Basic code. This is the most important step towards mastering ADO. But if you're designing web sites, it's only the first step. Adding database calls to web pages, or more specifically Active Server Pages using VBScript, requires a few special considerations because of the stateless nature of the web. The next few chapters cover some of the basics of building a web page and how ADO technology can play a major role in your site.

PART iii

WEB AND XML DATABASE PROGRAMMING

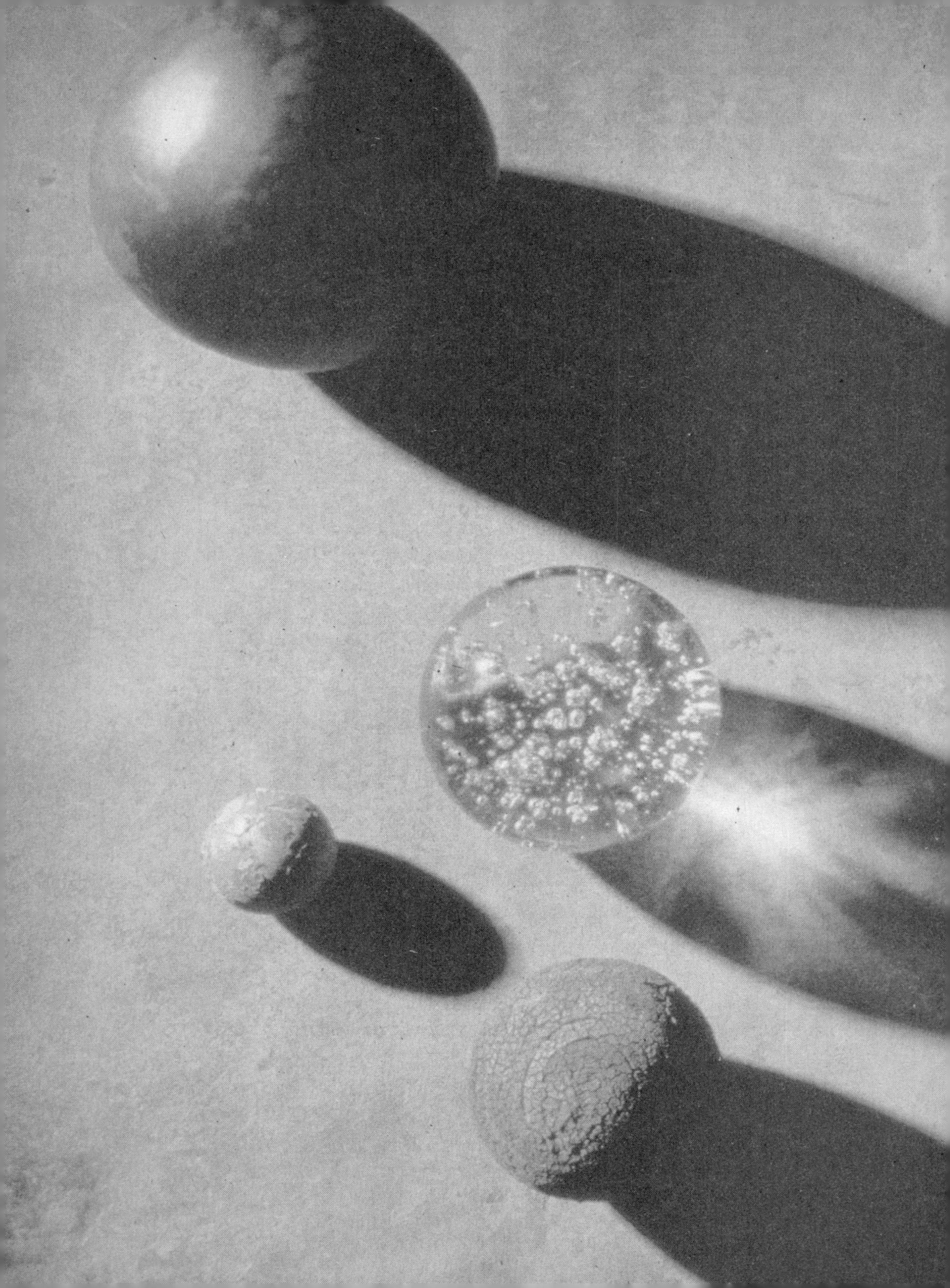

Chapter 13

Accessing Databases over the Web

In this chapter, you will find all the information you need to access your database over the Web. You will learn how to create web pages that can query and/or update a database, request registration information from viewers, accept orders through a website, and perform related operations. This chapter shows you how to apply your knowledge of Visual Basic and the ADO components to build web applications.

The Web is by its nature a client-server environment. The browser is the client whose task is to present the information, and the web server's task is to provide the documents requested by the client. Elaborate websites use multiple tiers as well. The web server is the first tier on the server's side, and it provides the HTML documents to the client. If a page requires data that resides on a database, as is the case with online stores, there's

Adapted from *Mastering™ Database Programming with Visual Basic® 6* by Evangelos Petroutsos

ISBN 0-7821-2598-1 896 pages $39.99

an additional tier: the database server. As you will see, the web server can't access databases directly. It uses ADO to access the database server. If the site incorporates business rules, it may require a third tier, which provides the ActiveX components that implement these rules.

The various tiers of the server may be running on the same or different machines. The tiers are distinguished according to the functionality they provide, not the machine they run on. You can start with a single machine that runs both Internet Information Server (IIS) and SQL Server. When the number of visitors outgrows your web server, you can move the SQL Server to a different machine. You may also develop ActiveX components that can be called by the web server, but reside on a third machine. A bank's site, for example, may use a single machine to verify the user, but retrieve the customer's data from a different server (depending on the customer's branch or state).

The picture of the Web as a three-tier environment is depicted in Figure 13.1. The principles behind the operation of the Web are quite simple. In order to build web applications, however, you must understand how these tiers are implemented. If browsers could execute VB code, building web applications would be very simple. Unfortunately, browsers can't handle anything but HTML and JavaScript. (Sure, Internet Explorer can execute VBScript code too, but Netscape can't.) At this point, web applications rely heavily on the server, rather than the client, and you must learn how to write applications that access databases on one end and interact with the client on the other end.

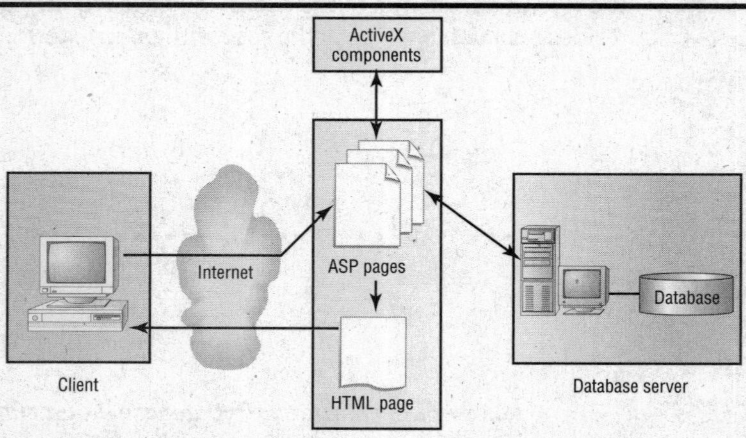

FIGURE 13.1: The tiers of the Web

WEB APPLICATIONS

This chapter is about web applications. I do not intend to show you how to write HTML pages or how to download ActiveX components or Java classes to the client, where they can be executed. No, web applications are not games you play over the Internet. They are plain old HTML pages that interact with the server.

Web pages are by definition interactive. Clients make requests and servers respond by providing the requested documents. Although this model of interaction has proved to be so functional and so efficient that it took the world by storm, it doesn't take into consideration the need for the client to pass any significant amount of information to the server. The Web was based on the premise that clients request new documents from the server. This was a reasonable assumption for the early days of the Internet, but the unexpected adoption of this technology led very quickly to the need for a more elaborate scheme of information flow between clients and servers.

People are no longer interested in simply requesting documents from a server; they need up-to-date, live information. That type of information can't be stored in HTML documents; instead, it must be retrieved from a database the moment it's requested. In effect, you would like to be able to interact with the servers through an interface comprising cute boxes, buttons, and any of the controls we use in building Windows applications. It's too late for that, however. The web interface was adopted because it was simple, and it was implemented on just about every operating system. If it weren't for its simplicity, it's doubtful that the Web would have grown as rapidly. Some companies have actually tried to make web pages look more like forms, but these attempts have failed.

To allow for better two-way communication between clients and servers, the HTML standard was enhanced with forms and controls. A *form* is a section of a page into which users can enter information (enter text in Text controls, select an option from a drop-down list, or check a radio button). The *controls* are the items that present or accept information on the form. The values of the controls are sent to the server by the browser and processed there. HTML forms and controls are quite rudimentary when compared to VB forms and controls, but they are the only means of interaction between clients and servers (excluding the click of the mouse on a hyperlink).

Therefore, if you want to build a web application, you must limit yourself to these controls. Your page may not look quite like a VB form, but this is something you must live with until the development tools become more sophisticated. Yet, these controls coupled with hyperlinks are adequate for building applications that run over the Internet.

NOTE

Technically, you're not limited to the standard HTML controls. You can create custom ActiveX controls to use on your HTML pages. However, these custom controls must first be downloaded and installed on the client computer before your pages can use them. Most users wouldn't allow third-party controls to be installed on their systems, so using ActiveX controls means your page won't look as intended and won't even function as designed. That's why very few sites ask you to download custom ActiveX controls. If you develop web applications to be used on an intranet in which IE has been adopted as the standard browser, however, you can use any ActiveX control on your pages.

Another limitation had to be overcome. Browsers are designed to communicate with web servers in a very simple manner. They request documents by submitting a string known as a *Uniform Resource Locator* (*URL*). URLs are the addresses of HTML documents on the Web. The URL of the desired document is usually the destination of a hyperlink in the document itself. The browser knows how to extract the destination of the selected hyperlink and request the document. Alternatively, you can specify the URL of the desired document by entering its name in the browser's address box.

To interact with the server, browsers should be able to pass more than a document's URL to the server. Sometimes, they have to pass a lot of information back to the server, such as query criteria, registration information, and so on. This problem was solved by allowing the client to attach all the information that must be passed to the server along with the destination's URL. The destination need not be an HTML document. It can be the name of an application that runs on the server and knows how to process the parameter values passed by the browser.

Figure 13.2 shows what happens when you use the AltaVista search engine to locate articles on database programming. The search argument is "+database +programming", and the browser passes the following URL to the server:

```
http://www.altavista.com/cgi-
bin/query?pg=q&kl=XX&q=%2Bdatabase+%2Bprogramming
```

This is not a common URL. The first part is the URL of an application that runs on the server. It's the query application in the `cgi-bin` folder under the web server's root folder. The question mark separates the name of the application from its arguments. The query application accepts three arguments: *pg*, *kl*, and *q*. The first two arguments are of no interest to you. The last argument is the search string. The symbol "+" was replaced by the string `%2B` (the hexadecimal representation of the plus character). The query application will read the information passed by the client, query the database with the specified keywords, and return another HTML document with the results of the query. The question mark in this URL separates the name of the application from the arguments. The ampersand symbol separates multiple arguments.

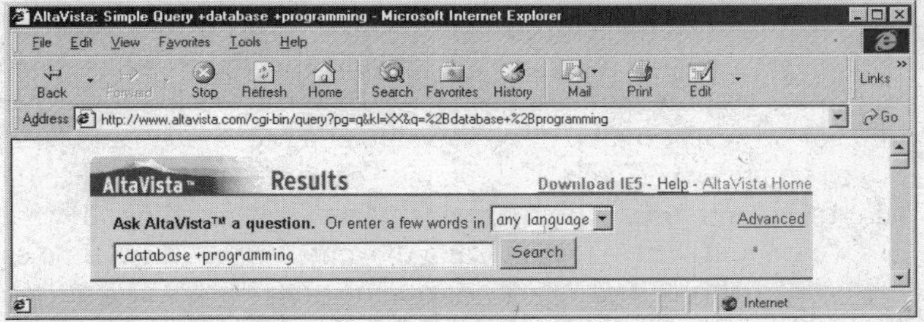

FIGURE 13.2: Invoking a server application and passing arguments to it from within the browser

In effect, we fool the browser into thinking that the destination document has a really long URL. The web server will figure out what the browser is about to do and it will invoke the query application and pass the specified parameters to it.

A *web application* is a site with multiple HTML pages and server programs that interact with each other. HTML pages call server applications and pass parameters to them. These applications, which are called *scripts*, are executed on the server, process the values submitted by the client, format the results as HTML documents, and send them to the client. In all honesty, web applications shouldn't even be called applications, but we shouldn't be so critical. Just think of the fact that a single machine can serve thousands of clients, make sales for your company, and allow people to interact with their company's database across the country or across the globe.

Typical Web Applications

Let's look at a few typical web applications and analyze their requirements. Most corporations have a website already for "a presence on the Web," as they claim. A simple website with static pages is of no interest to you (but it's the starting point for any corporation ready to do business on the Web).

The most common web applications are online stores. An online store uses an intuitive interface that allows users to browse through products, locate and select the ones they're interested in, and order them. Even companies that do not sell online, like automobile companies, have set up online stores where users can compare prices, customize a car, and then look up dealer names in their area.

Of all types of online stores, bookstores are one of the most common and most popular ones. Every major bookstore is also selling through the Web, not to mention a few bookstores that operate exclusively through the Web. Computer manufacturers also have a dynamic presence on the Web. Nearly every mail-order company selling computers and peripherals is also selling on the Web. The common characteristic of all these stores is that they don't focus on intensive searches. Instead, they allow you to build a custom system (by selecting the amount of RAM, hard disk size, and other options) and then calculate the price of your dream machine. I could go on and on, but I will end this list with a third form of online store, one that sells through bids. These stores advertise new or used products, accept bids, and sell to the highest bidder(s). Bids take place in real time, usually in a very short period. Airlines will frequently offer tickets at reduced prices through a bidding process. You can see the bids as other viewers place them and either continue or give up.

The information presented in this chapter applies to all types of websites, but I will focus on the components of accessing databases over the Web. After all, a database can be found behind every application. An online store has two basic requirements:

- Its products database is accessed through the controls on a form. A component on the server must read the data entered by the user on the form, select the appropriate rows from the database, and format them as an HTML document that can be displayed on the client.
- It accepts orders. To accept an order, the online store must read user-supplied information (including sensitive information, such as credit card numbers), validate it, and store it in a database. This information will be used later to materialize the order.

A site that's used for user registration and online support has similar requirements. This type of web application is used to provide support to registered users. The first time you connect to a site like this, you provide some data, and you specify a username and password. After that, you can connect to the site, visit areas that are limited to registered users, and browse the site as usual. In most cases, you are allowed to search a database with keywords and related articles of interest.

For the purposes of this chapter, I assume that you are familiar with HTML. The examples in this section do not use elaborate web pages, just text, hyperlinks, and tables. And HTML controls, of course. The HTML controls are stripped-down versions of the intrinsic Visual Basic controls and are discussed in the section "HTML Forms and Controls." You'll start by exploring the structure of a web application and its special requirements. An overview of VBScript and HTML controls follows. The majority of the chapter discusses the objects of the Active Server Pages, and especially how to use the ADO components to access databases from within server scripts.

The Structure of Web Applications

Web applications have a special requirement. The various forms of an application are mapped to HTML pages. In a VB application, there are many options for its forms to communicate with one another. They can use public variables, they can read directly the values of the controls on any page, and they can set each other's properties. The situation is different on the Web. Each page is a separate entity, and it can't interact directly with another page of the same site–not to mention the fact that users can bookmark any page and jump to it directly.

A web application is a site that works like a VB application. You enter information on a form, this information is transmitted to the server, and the result of the processing returns to the client as another document. The processing that takes place on the server is (in 99% of the cases) a database search. The results of the search are then furnished back to the client in the form of another HTML page.

Here's the first main difference between a VB interactive application and a web application: The forms of the VB application can remain open on the desktop, and users can switch from one to the other with a mouse-click. This is not true with a web application; it can display only one form (page) at a time. In order to switch to another page, you must either select a link on the current page, or click Back to view a page you already visited.

How about running multiple instances of Internet Explorer, so that you can view multiple pages of the same site at once? That's the worst thing you can do. It will confuse the server, which in turn will confuse you.

Let's say you're looking for VB titles on the Sybex site. Imagine that you opened two windows of IE: one with the search form and another one with the results. If this were a VB application, every time you changed the search criteria on the first page and clicked a button, the second form would be populated with the results. This isn't going to happen on the Web. The server doesn't keep track of how many and which pages you have opened on your computer. As far as the server is concerned, you are viewing a single page at a time.

HTML pages cannot easily communicate with one another like VB forms. When a form's controls are submitted to the server, the script running on the server must store all the parameter values to local variables and use them to prepare the next page. After the page has been prepared and transmitted to the client, the information is lost forever–unless the server stores it into a local file or database, or on the client computer as a cookie.

HTML Forms and Controls

To interact with the viewer, besides the ubiquitous hyperlinks, HTML recognizes a few special tags that insert controls on a form. HTML controls are stripped-down versions of common controls from Windows that you're used to using in VB. You can use controls to collect information from the user for registration purposes, take orders over the Internet, or let the user specify selection criteria for record retrieval from databases. HTML provides the controls seen in Table 13.1.

TABLE 13.1: The HTML Controls

Control Name	Description
CheckBox	A box that can be checked or cleared to indicate that an option is selected.
RadioButton	A circular button that can be checked or cleared to indicate one of multiple options. This control is similar to Visual Basic's Option control.
Text	A box that accepts a single line of text, similar to Visual Basic's default TextBox control.
Password	A text control that doesn't display the characters as they are typed; it displays a * instead.

TABLE 13.1 continued: The HTML Controls

Control Name	Description
TextArea	A box that accepts multiple lines of text, similar to a TextBox control with its MultiLine property set to True.
Selection	A list of options from which the user can select one or more, similar to Visual Basic's ListBox or combo box controls.
Button	A usual button that can trigger various actions, similar to Visual Basic's CommandButton control.

Before you place any controls on a page, you must create a form with the <FORM> tag. All controls must appear within a pair of <FORM> tags (you can place the controls anywhere in the HTML file, but the simplest method of transmitting the values entered by the viewer on the controls is to place all controls in a Form section):

```
<FORM NAME = "myForm">
{your Controls go here}
</FORM>
```

The NAME attribute is optional, but it's a good practice to name forms. Beyond the NAME attribute, the <FORM> tag accepts two more attributes, METHOD and ACTION, which determine how the data will be submitted to the server and how it will be processed there. The METHOD attribute can have one of two values, POST and GET. These two attributes are discussed in detail in the section "The GET and POST Methods" later in this chapter.

The <FORM> tag recognizes the ID attribute as well. The ID is similar to the NAME attribute, but it can be used in programming the form from within a client-side script. This is also true for the controls. If you want to be able to program the controls on the form from within a script on the client, use the ID attribute with various control tags, which are discussed in the following sections.

The CheckBox Control

The *CheckBox control* is a little square with an optional check mark. Figure 13.3 shows a typical situation that calls for CheckBox controls. The check mark is a toggle that turns on and off every time the user clicks on the control. It is used to present a list of options, from which the user can select none, one, or more. When the check mark is turned on, the CheckBox is said to be *checked*; when it's turned off, the control is said to be *cleared*. The user may check any number of options, from none to all.

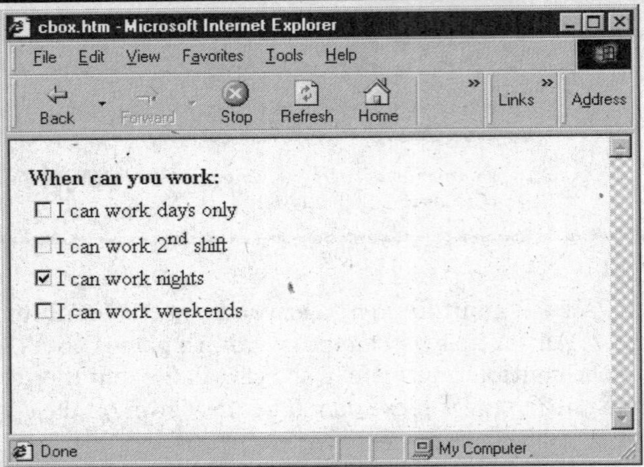

FIGURE 13.3: CheckBox controls are used to present to users a list of options, from which they can check none, one, or more.

The CheckBox control can be inserted in a document with the following tag:

```
<INPUT TYPE = CHECKBOX NAME = "Check1">
```

where *Check1* is the control's name. You'll use it later to find out whether the control is marked or not, for instance. By default, a check box is cleared. To make a check box checked initially, you use the CHECKED option in its <INPUT> tag:

```
<INPUT TYPE = CHECKBOX NAME = "Check1" CHECKED>
```

The RadioButton Control

The *RadioButton control* is similar to the CheckBox control, except that it's round and, instead of a check mark, a solid round mark appears in the center of a checked radio button. RadioButton controls are used to present a list of options, similar to a group of CheckBox controls, but only one option can be selected in a group of radio buttons. Figure 13.4 shows a typical arrangement of several radio buttons. Notice that the options are mutually exclusive and only one of them can be checked. Not only that, but the responsibility of clearing the previously checked button lies on the control itself; there's nothing you must do in your code to clear the checked button every time the user makes a new selection.

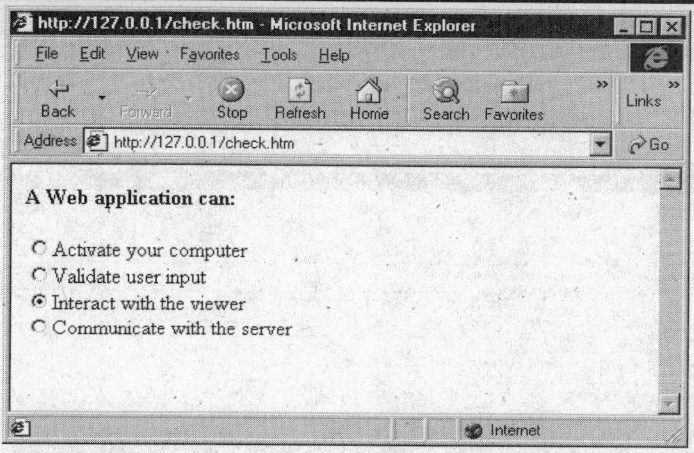

FIGURE 13.4: Radio buttons are used to display mutually exclusive options, and only one of them can be active.

To insert a radio button in a document, use a line similar to the one for the check box, only this time enter the type of the Control as RADIO:

```
<INPUT TYPE = RADIO NAME = "Radio1">
```

Although each check box on a form has its own name, you can have several radio buttons with the same name. All radio buttons with the same name form a group and only one member of the group can be checked at a time. Every time the user clicks on a radio button to check it, the previously checked one is cleared automatically. To initially check a radio button, use the CHECKED attribute, which works similarly to the attribute with the same name of the CheckBox control.

Because several RadioButton controls may belong to the same group but only one of them can be checked, they must also share the same name. The group of RadioButton controls on the page in Figure 13.4 was created with the following lines:

```
<B>A Web application can:</B>
<P>
<INPUT TYPE=RADIO NAME="Q"
    VALUE=1>Activate your computer<BR>
<INPUT TYPE=RADIO NAME="Q"
    VALUE=2>Validate user input<BR>
<INPUT TYPE=RADIO NAME="Q"
    VALUE=3>Interact with the viewer<BR>
<INPUT TYPE=RADIO NAME="Q"
    VALUE=4>Communicate with the server<BR>
```

The Text Control

The *Text control* is a box that can accept user input. It is used for entering items such as names, addresses, and any form of free text. Figure 13.5 is a form that contains several Text controls.

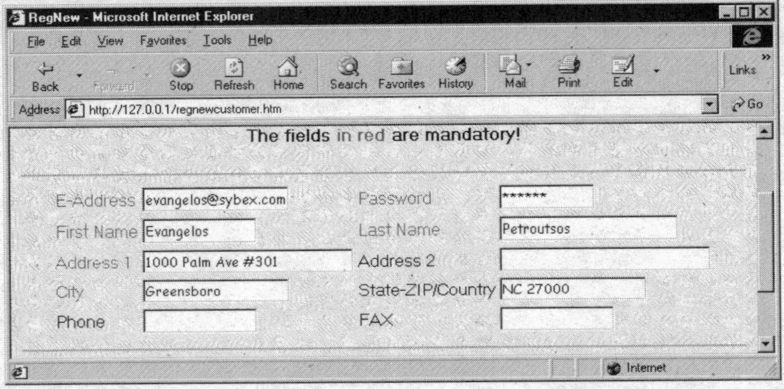

FIGURE 13.5: The Text control accepts user input on a single line.

To insert a Text control on a page, use the <INPUT> tag and set the TYPE attribute to TEXT. The line will display a Text control on the page, with the string "Sybex" in it:

```
<INPUT TYPE = TEXT NAME = "Publisher" VALUE = "Sybex">
```

The viewer can enter any string by overwriting the existing one or appending more text at its end. The usual text editing and navigational keys (Home key, arrow keys, the Del and Ins keys) will work with the Text control. However, you can't format the text in a Text control by using different fonts, or even font attributes such as bold and italic.

Finally, you can specify the size of the control on the page with the SIZE attribute, and you can specify the maximum amount of text it can accept with the MAXLENGTH attribute. For example, the Text control defined as the following can accept user input up to 100 characters, whereas its length on the page corresponds to the average length of 40 characters in the current font:

```
<INPUT TYPE = TEXT NAME = "Publisher" SIZE = 40
    MAXLENGTH = 100 VALUE = "Sybex">
```

The Password Control

The *Password control* is a variation on the Text control. Its behavior is identical to that of the Text control, but the characters entered are not displayed.

In their places, the user sees asterisks instead. It's meant for input that should be kept private. To create a Password control, you use an input tag similar to that for a Text control, but specify the PASSWORD type:

```
<INPUT TYPE = PASSWORD NAME = "Secret Box"
     SIZE = 20 MAXLENGTH = 20>
```

Other than a different TYPE attribute, Password controls are identical to Text controls.

The TextArea Control

You can also provide your users with a control that accepts multiple lines of text. The operation of the *TextArea control* is similar to that of a Visual Basic TextBox control that has its MultiLine property set to True (this handles the carriage-return character and causes it to add a new line). All navigational and editing keys will work with the TextArea control as well. To place a TextArea control on a form, use the <TEXTAREA> tag:

```
<TEXTAREA NAME = COMMENTS ROWS = 10 COLS = 50></TEXTAREA>
```

This tag creates a box on the page, whose dimensions are 10 rows of text with 50 characters per line. The ROWS and COLS tags specify the dimensions of the control on the page (in units of the current font).

Besides its attributes, another difference between the TextArea control and the other controls you've seen so far is that the TextArea control must end with the </TEXTAREA> tag. The reason for this is that the TextArea control can contain a lengthy, multiple-line default text that must be enclosed between the two tags and can't be assigned to an attribute:

```
<TEXTAREA NAME = COMMENTS ROWS = 10 COLS = 50>
This is the greatest Web site I've seen in years!
Congratulations!!!
</TEXTAREA>
```

The text between the two <TEXTAREA> tags is displayed initially in the box. A user who is less than excited about your pages could overwrite your initial comments. Notice that all line breaks in the text will be preserved. There's no need to use paragraph or line break tags to format the initial text of a TextArea control. (If you do include HTML tags in the text, they will be displayed in the text box as you typed them.) If the text can't fit in the space provided, the appropriate scrollbars will automatically be added to the control.

Figure 13.6 shows a form with two TextArea controls of different sizes. The first TextArea control and its contents were defined with the following lines. Notice the lack of any HTML formatting tags in the text. The line breaks are preserved, but the control isn't going to process any HTML tags:

```
<TEXTAREA NAME=INGREDIENTS ROWS = 10 COLS = 40
    MAXLENGTH = 2000>
2  pounds lamb, no bones
1  lt white wine
4  large white onions
12 teaspoons curry
1  tablespoons cooking oil
2  large bananas
1  fresh pineapple
</TEXTAREA>
```

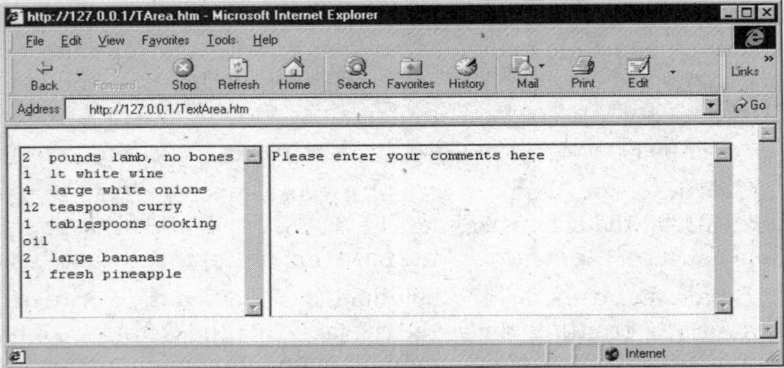

FIGURE 13.6: A form with two TextArea controls, one that displays information and one that allows new information to be entered

The second TextArea control was defined and filled with text with a similar pair of tags. Remember that the TextArea control doesn't insert line breaks on its own, so you must try not to exceed the maximum line length (as defined with the ROW attribute) if you want the contents of the control to be entirely visible along each line.

The Selection Control

The *Selection control* is a control that presents a list of options to the viewer, and lets him or her select none, one, or more of them. The tag for the Selection control is <SELECT>, and it must be followed by a matching </SELECT> tag. The attributes that can appear in a <SELECT> tag are NAME (the control's name), SIZE (which specifies how many options will be visible), and MULTIPLE (which specifies whether the user may chose multiple items or not). To place a Selection control on your form, use the following tag:

```
<SELECT NAME = "UserOptions" SIZE = 4 MULTIPLE = MULTIPLE>
</SELECT>
```

Between the two <SELECT> tags, you can place the options that make up the list, each one in a pair of <OPTION> tags:

```
<SELECT NAME = "UserOptions" SIZE = 6 MULTIPLE = MULTIPLE>
<OPTION>Computer</OPTION>
<OPTION>Monitor</OPTION>
<OPTION>Printer</OPTION>
<OPTION>Modem</OPTION>
<OPTION>Speakers</OPTION>
<OPTION>Microphone</OPTION>
<OPTION>Mouse</OPTION>
</SELECT>
```

This Selection control is shown in Figure 13.7, along with two more lists. Although the control contains seven options, only six of them are visible. The SIZE attribute will help you save space on your pages when you have a long list of options to present to the user. The user can also select multiple options (with the Shift and Control keys), even if some of them are not visible. To disable multiple selections, omit the MULTIPLE attribute.

To minimize the Selection control's size on the form, omit the MULTIPLE attribute (if possible), and don't specify how many items will be visible. The result will be a list with just one visible element. If the user clicks on the arrow, the list will expand and all its elements will become visible until the user makes a selection. Then, the list collapses back to a single item.

The <OPTION> tag has a VALUE attribute, too. This attribute specifies the string(s) that will be sent back to the server when the user submits the form with that option selected. In other words, it is possible to display one string in the list, but send another value to the server. Here's a modified version of the previous list:

```
<SELECT NAME = "UserOptions" SIZE = 6 MULTIPLE = MULTIPLE>
<OPTION VALUE=1>Computer</OPTION>
<OPTION VALUE=2>Monitor</OPTION>
<OPTION VALUE=3>Printer</OPTION>
<OPTION VALUE=4>Modem</OPTION>
<OPTION VALUE=5>Speakers</OPTION>
<OPTION VALUE=6>Microphone</OPTION>
<OPTION VALUE=7>Mouse</OPTION>
</SELECT>
```

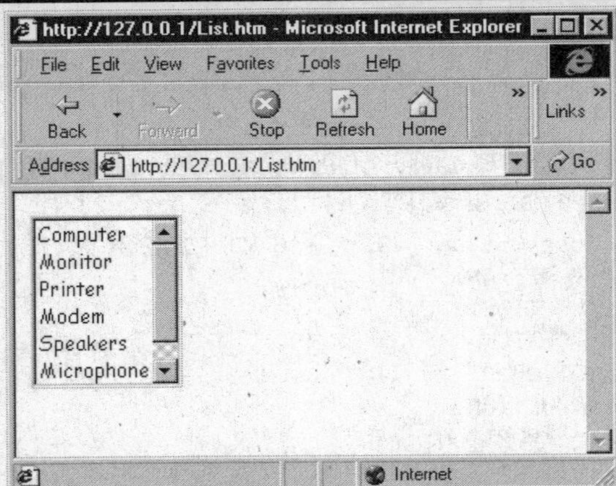

FIGURE 13.7: The Selection control lets you present lists of options, from which viewers can select one or more.

When the selection on this list is submitted to the server, instead of the actual string, the server sees a number, which corresponds to the viewer's selection.

The Button Control

The *Button* is a control that can be clicked to trigger certain actions. Buttons are used to trigger two actions: Submit the data to the server, or reset all controls on the form to their original values. With VBScript, buttons can be used to trigger any actions you can program in your pages with VBScript statements that are executed on the client. However, I am not going to discuss client-side scripting in this book (not all browsers support VBScript).

You can place two types of buttons on a form. The most important one is the SUBMIT Button; it transmits the contents of all controls on the form to the server. The RESET Button clears the controls on the form (or resets them to their initial values) and doesn't submit anything.

These two types of Buttons can be placed on a form with the following <INPUT> tags:

```
<INPUT TYPE = SUBMIT VALUE = "Send Data">
<INPUT TYPE = RESET VALUE = "Reset Values">
```

where VALUE is the caption that appears on the button. Each form should contain at least a SUBMIT Button to transmit the information entered by the user to the server. (If the page contains a script, then you can submit the data to the server via the script and you don't have to include a SUBMIT Button.)

VBScript

VBScript is a scripting language that is based, obviously, on Visual Basic. The first application of VBScript was to program web pages and activate the client. Microsoft pushed VBScript as the language of the Web, but other browsers didn't follow. Today, only Internet Explorer supports VBScript natively, and JavaScript has become the de facto standard of client languages. The situation is quite different on the server, however.

Microsoft moved VBScript from the client to the server. Whereas older web servers used Perl or other peculiar languages to interact with the client, Microsoft added support for VBScript in its IIS, and simplified the development of server-side scripts. Today, VBScript is used as a general scripting language by applications such as Outlook, and it can be easily incorporated into VB applications with the Scripting control. VBScript may not have activated the Web as Microsoft promised, but it's a major scripting language.

I will not spend any time discussing VBScript. It's a core language without a user interface, which manipulates objects exposed by the web server. The structure of the language is identical to that of Visual Basic: It supports all the math, string, date, and time functions; it supports the same flow-control statements; and it recognizes the same data types as Visual Basic. VBScript, however, is a type-less language. Its variables are variants, and you don't have the option to declare variables of any other type. However, you can cast variants to specific data types with the type-conversion functions.

The great benefit of VBScript is its simplicity. In addition to support for VBScript, Microsoft designed several components for handling client requests on the web server. These components, along with server-side VBScript, are known as *Active Server Pages* (*ASPs*). An Active Server Page is a script on the server that corresponds to an HTML page. Traditionally, web pages contained text, images, and hyperlinks to other HTML documents. Every time a hyperlink in a web document is activated, a request for a new HTML document is made. ASP documents are HTML documents, interspersed with VBScript statements. An HTML document can contain any number of VBScript statements, anywhere. The only requirement is that they are enclosed in a pair of <% and %>

tags. Everything that appears between these two tags is treated as VBScript code and executed on the server. The output it produces replaces the original VBScript code.

Instead of a trivial example, let me start with one of the examples that I'll use later in this chapter. The following is a script that displays the customers of the Northwind database. It's a mixture of HTML and VBScript statements (the VBScript statements are enclosed by the <% %> tags):

LISTING 13.1: The AllCustomers.asp Script

```
<HTML>
<H1>Query Results</H1>
<TABLE>
<%
Set DBObj = Server.CreateObject("ADODB.Connection")
DBObj.Open "NWindDB"
SQLQuery = "SELECT Country, CompanyName, ContactName,
            ContactTitle FROM Customers ORDER BY Country"
Set RSCustomers = DBObj.Execute(SQLQuery)
Do While Not RSCustomers.EOF
%>
  <TR>
    <TD> <FONT FACE="Verdana" SIZE=2>
    <% = RSCustomers.Fields("Country") %>
    </FONT></TD>
    <TD> <FONT FACE="Verdana" SIZE=2>
     <% = RSCustomers.Fields("ContactName") & " (" &
           RSCustomers.Fields("ContactTitle") & ")"  %>
    </FONT></TD>
    <TD><FONT FACE="Verdana" SIZE=2>
      <% = RSCustomers.Fields("CompanyName") %>
    </FONT></TD>
  </TR>
<%
RSCustomers.MoveNext
Loop
%>
</HTML>
```

The first three lines are plain HTML tags that start a new page and open a table. Then comes some VBScript code that sets up a connection to the Northwind database and opens the RSCustomers recordset, which holds all the rows of the Customers table. The last statement in this first group of VBScript statements starts a loop that iterates through the rows of the RSCustomers recordset. Notice that the groups of VBScript statements is delimited with the tags <% and %>.

The script starts with a few plain HTML tags (they add a new row to the table). The loop's body consists mostly of HTML tags with a few embedded VBScript statements. The following statement returns the value of the Country field of the current row in the recordset:

```
<% = RSCustomers.Fields("Country") %>
```

When this script is processed on the server, the above expression will be replaced by the actual field value. A few more VBScript statements at the end of the script terminate the loop and close the HTML document.

To test this script, store it in a text file with extension ASP (it's the `AllCustomers.asp` file in this chapter's folder on the Sybex website). Place the file in the web server's root folder (or a virtual folder). Then connect to your website and open it. If the web server is running on the same machine that you're using to test the projects, use the address

```
http://127.0.0.1/allcustomers.asp
```

You can test ASP files with both IIS and the Personal Web Server. You will see a page like the one shown in Figure 13.8.

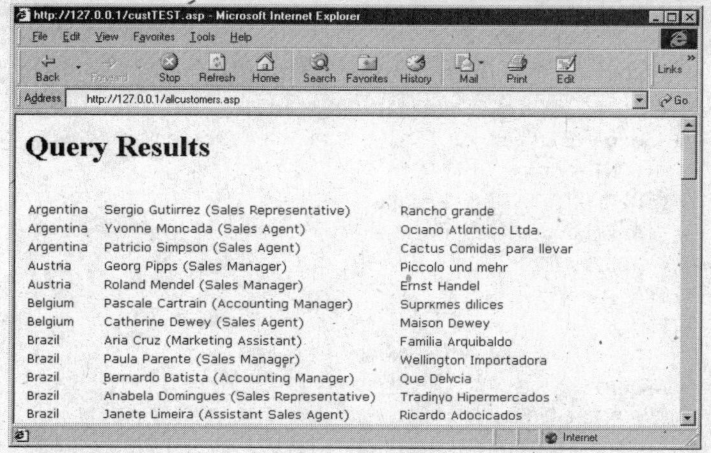

FIGURE 13.8: The output of the AllCustomers.asp script

If you double-click the ASP file's icon, you will not see the page in Figure 13.8. The ASP file must be processed by the server. Only then will the VBScript statements be replaced by the output they produce. The web server executes the script as follows:

- Text outside the special tags <% and %> is sent to the client as is (it's considered to be HTML code that will be processed by the client).
- VBScript statements are executed and replaced by the output they produce. Some statements, such as the While and Wend statements, do not produce any output at all. They are needed to control the flow of the script. To understand how ASP scripts are executed on the server, open the `AllCustomers.asp` file with a text editor and then view the document's source code with the browser's View ➢ Source command, which is shown below. As you can see, the document sent to the client doesn't contain a single VBScript statement, only HTML code.

LISTING 13.2: The Output Produced by the AllCustomers.asp Script

```
<HTML>
<H1>Query Results</H1>
<TABLE>
  <TR>
    <TD> <FONT FACE="Verdana" SIZE=2>
    Argentina
    </FONT></TD>
    <TD> <FONT FACE="Verdana" SIZE=2>
     Sergio Gutiérrez (Sales Representative)
    </FONT></TD>
    <TD><FONT FACE="Verdana" SIZE=2>
      Rancho grande
    </FONT></TD>
  </TR>
  <TR>
    <TD> <FONT FACE="Verdana" SIZE=2>
    Argentina
    </FONT></TD>
    <TD> <FONT FACE="Verdana" SIZE=2>
     Yvonne Moncada (Sales Agent)
    </FONT></TD>
    <TD><FONT FACE="Verdana" SIZE=2>
      Océano Atlántico Ltda.
    </FONT></TD>
```

```
    </TR>
    <TR>
      <TD> <FONT FACE="Verdana" SIZE=2>
      Argentina
      </FONT></TD>
      <TD> <FONT FACE="Verdana" SIZE=2>
       Patricio Simpson (Sales Agent)
      </FONT></TD>
      <TD><FONT FACE="Verdana" SIZE=2>
        Cactus Comidas para llevar
      </FONT></TD>
    </TR>
  {more lines with the same structure follow}
```

The ASP Object Model

Server-side VBScript and Active Server Pages support several built-in objects, which I will discuss here and demonstrate with examples. I'll start by listing these objects and their descriptions. In the following sections, you will see examples that demonstrate how to use these objects in ASP scripts to accomplish practical and useful tasks.

As always, it's quite easy to understand and use the objects exposed by a component, if you understand what the component was designed to do. ASP was designed to simplify the development of web server applications: programs that run on the server and interact with the client. Therefore, ASP should provide the following functionality:

- Prepare output to be downloaded to the client. This is done with the Response object, which represents the output stream that will be transmitted to the client. The Response object's Write method, for example, sends a string to the client and the Response.Cookie() method sends a cookie to the client computer.
- Accept the parameter values submitted to the server by the client. This is done with the Request object. The Request.Cookie() method, for example, returns the value of a cookie on the client computer.
- Access other components on the server. VBScript is the core of a programming language. On its own, it can do very little. The Server object allows VBScript to contact COM components on the server. With the Server object, VBScript can create ADO objects and view databases. Most scripts retrieve information from a database with

the help of the Server object, encode it in HTML format, and return it to the client with the Response object.

- Maintain information about each client on the server via server-side scripts. When a user logs into a site with a user name and password, ASP should keep this information on the server so that the user won't have to submit it every time he or she jumps to another page of the same site. This is done with the Session object.
- Maintain information about the state of the current website, such as the number of hits it has taken. This is done with the Application object.

The Response, Request, Server, Session, and Application objects are the five basic objects that nearly every web application uses. There are other optional components, but they are not discussed in this book. You'll use these five objects to write server applications that interact with the clients and focus on applications that access databases over the Web.

I will start with a discussion of these objects, and then move on to show you how to access databases from within your server-side scripts. The ASP objects covered in this chapter are not nearly as complicated as the ADO object.

The Application Object

This object represents an ASP application, which is the collection of all ASP files in the virtual folder and its subfolders. You can use the *Application object* to share information among all users of an ASP application. The Application object has two methods, which are the Lock and Unlock methods. The Lock method prevents other clients from modifying any of the Application object's properties. The Unlock method allows other clients to modify these properties.

The Application object also supports two events: the Application_onStart event, which is triggered when the application starts; and the Application_onEnd event, which is triggered when the application ends. Use these events to execute initialization code or cleanup code, respectively.

The purpose of the Application object is to store values that can be shared among the clients. This is especially useful in intranet environments, in which the users of the ASP application have a common goal. You can also use the Application object on pages that are posted on the

Internet. To create a new variable or change the value of an existing variable in the Application object, use statements like the following ones:

```
<%
   Application("WelcomeMessage") = "Happy Valentine's Day!"
   Application("MaxScore") = 254000
%>
```

WelcomeMessage is a string variable; and *MaxScore* is a numeric one. Of course, *WelcomeMessage* must be changed on February 14. To make sure that no other client is attempting to set (or read) the same variable at the time the scripts accesses it, first lock the Application object, then change the variable, and finally unlock the object, as shown here:

```
<%
    Application.Lock
    Application("WelcomeMessage") = "Happy Valentine's Day!"
    Application("MaxScore") = 254000
    Application.Unlock
%>
```

You can use the Application object to build a simple visitor counter, by keeping track of a variable:

```
<%
    Application.Lock
    Application("Visitors") = Application("Visitors") + 1
    Application.Unlock
%>
```

These commands must be executed in the home page of your site, which is displayed the first time a user connects to your site. You can then display the value of the *Visitors* variable on your web page with a line like the following one:

```
You are visitor # <% = Application("Visitors") %>
```

To make sure that this variable maintains its value, you must save it in a local file and retrieve it, update it, and save it again. See the description of the TextStream object later in this chapter for a discussion on how to access files on the server through the server-side script. The *Visitors* variable must be initialized when the home page of the application is first loaded, an action that is signaled by the Application_onStart event. As long as the server is up and running, the application maintains the values of its variables.

The Session Object

This object represents an ASP session. Each time a new user connects to the site by opening its main page, a new *Session object* is created for that viewer. You can use the Session object to store information that's specific to the viewer. Like the Application object, the Session object supports two events: the Session_onStart event, which is triggered when the session starts; and the Session_onEnd event, which is triggered when the session ends. The following statement stores a variable in the Session object:

```
Session("ViewerName") = "Charles Brannon"
```

This variable will live for the duration of the current session and will automatically be released when the session ends. The next time the same user connects to the same site, a new Session object will be created and the previous statement must be executed again (you'll probably prompt the user for his or her name).

Use the Session object to store information you want to share among the application's pages. HTTP is a stateless protocol, and maintaining state between the pages of the application is something you can't take for granted. You can use the Session object to store "global" variables (variables that can be shared by all the pages of the site). However, you should not store object variables in the Session object. This is just about the worst thing you can do for your web application.

If you want to store information that persists between sessions, you can't store them in the Session object. Use cookies instead. Cookies are stored on the client computer and your application can read them again when the same client connects to the site. This is how shopping baskets work with most sites. Some sites store the orders in the database and don't use cookies (some viewers may turn off cookies), but this requires that viewers identify themselves every time they connect to the site.

The Request Object

The *Request object* retrieves the values (query parameters) that the client passes to the server during an HTTP request, the values of the cookies stored on the client computer through the Response object, and server variables. The Request object exposes the collections shown in Table 13.2:

TABLE 13.2: The Collections Exposed by the Request Object

COLLECTION NAME	DESCRIPTION
ClientCertificate	The values of fields stored in the client certificate that is sent in the HTTP request
Cookies	The values of cookies sent in the HTTP request
Form	The values of form elements in the HTTP request body
QueryString	The values of variables in the HTTP query string
ServerVariables	The values of predetermined environment variables

The QueryString collection is the most important one because it retrieves the values of the parameters in the HTTP query string, that is, the values encoded after the question mark in the HTTP request. These are the values of the form's elements passed by the client using the GET method. You can also pass parameter values to the web server by creating a URL from within a client script. The syntax of the QueryString collection is

```
Request.QueryString(variable)
```

where *variable* is the name of the variable in the HTTP query string to retrieve. If a client calls the `TestPage.asp` file as

```
/ASPages/TestPage.asp?Name=Joe+Doe&EMail=JDoe@local.net
```

the query string is

```
Name=Joe+Doe&EMail=JDoe@local.net
```

Name and *EMail* are the names of two controls where the viewer has entered some information. To retrieve the values of the two parameters, use the statements

```
Request.QueryString("Name")
```

which will return the string "Joe Doe," and

```
Request.QueryString("EMail")
```

which will return the string "Jdoe@local.net."

If you retrieve the value of the property Request.QueryString without any parameters, it will return the entire query string. See the section "Making Queries with ASP Files" later in this chapter for examples on the Request method. The section "Using Cookies" shows how to retrieve the cookies stored on the client computer through the Request.Cookies collection.

The Response Object

The *Response object* represents the output stream that's sent to the client. All the information you want to send to the client must be submitted through the Response object's Write method. In addition to textual information, which can be sent to the client with the Response object's Write method, you can also send cookie values to the client with the Cookies collection of the Response object.

The Cookies collection of the Response object contains all the cookies stored on the client computer by your site, and their values. You can create new cookies by adding more members to the collection, or read the values of existing ones. The syntax of the Cookies collection of the Response object is

```
Response.Cookies(cookie)(key).attribute = value
```

where *cookie* is the name of the cookie. To specify a simple cookie and its value, use a statement like the following one:

```
Response.Cookies("ServerName")="www.myserver.com"
```

key is an optional argument indicating that the cookie is a dictionary (an array of name value pairs). To read the value of the ServerName cookie, use the following expression:

```
SNname = Response.Cookies("ServerName")
```

To create a cookie with a key, use statements such as the following:

```
<%
Response.Cookies("Preferences")("ForeColor") = "Blue"
Response.Cookies("Preferences")("BackColor") = "lightyellow"
%>
```

The ForeColor and BackColor cookies are attributes of the Preferences key. When you request the value of a cookie from within a script on the server (this is done through the Response object's properties), you can determine whether a cookie has keys with the following statement:

```
<%= Response.Cookies("Preferences").HasKeys %>
```

If Preferences is a cookie dictionary, the preceding expression evaluates to True. Otherwise, it evaluates to False. The following statements create a cookie on the client and set various attributes:

```
<%
Response.Cookies("Favorites") = "Century"
Response.Cookies("Favorites").Expires = "December 31, 2000"
Response.Cookies("Favorites").Domain = "myserver.com"
Response.Cookies("Favorites").Path = "/Dates"
```

```
Response.Cookies("Favorites").Secure = FALSE
%>
```

The first line sets the Favorites cookie value to "Century." The remaining lines set the various attributes of the cookie. The cookie expires at the end of the millennium, is not secure, and is sent to the virtual folder `Dates` only. Scripts that are executed from within another virtual folder on the server can't access this cookie.

The *attribute* argument specifies information about the cookie itself and can have one of the following values, shown in Table 13.3.

All arguments are write-only, except for the *HasKeys* argument, which is read-only.

Finally, the *value* argument specifies the value to be assigned to the key or an attribute.

TABLE 13.3: Cookie Attributes and Their Meaning

Attribute	Description
Expires	The date on which the cookie expires.
Domain	If specified, the cookie is sent only to requests to this domain.
Path	If specified, the cookie is sent only to requests to this path, and not to every page in the virtual folder.
Secure	Specifies whether the cookie is secure.
HasKeys	Specifies whether the cookie contains keys (in other words, it's a dictionary).

If you have placed orders online, you already know that the IDs of the products you select are stored on the client computer (your computer) as cookies. They remain in your basket until you either order them or empty the basket. Shopping baskets are usually implemented as cookies. There are other methods for implementing a shopping basket, but cookies are the simplest and most convenient.

Let's say you want to implement an online bookstore, and you decide to store the IDs (ISBNs) of the books chosen by the user on the client computer, in the form of cookies. Instead of using cookie names such as "0-310-943917," you can create a directory of cookies and access them with an index value:

```
Response.Cookies("ISBN")(1)
Response.Cookies("ISBN")(2)
```

The name of the first cookie in this collection is the ISBN of the first book (0-310-943917, for example), and its value is the number of copies ordered. The following few sections discuss the Response object's methods: the Write, Clear, and End methods.

The Write Method

The Write method writes a string to the current HTTP output. Its syntax is

```
<% Response.Write string %>
```

where *string* is the data to write. This argument is a variant; it can contain text, numeric values, or dates. However, it can't contain the combination "%>". To display the delimiter, use the escape sequence "%\>".

TIP

The longest string you can you can pass to the Response.Write method with a literal argument can't exceed 1,022 characters (VBScript limits static strings to 1,022 bytes). If the string is stored in a variable, you can specify longer strings.

The Write method of the Response object is used to create any output you want to send to the client. The following statement will cause the value of the Address field of the current row of the Recordset object to be sent to the client:

```
<% Response.Write RS.Fields("Address") %>
```

The following example sends a customer name, but formats it as a hyperlink:

```
<% Response.Write "<A HREF=ShowCustomer.asp?ID='>" &
     RS.Fields("CustomerID") & "'>" &
     RS.Fields("CompanyName") &  "</A>" %>
```

This statement displays the company name as a hyperlink to the `ShowCustomer.asp` script on the server and passes the company's ID as a parameter. This technique is used in the AllCountries example, later in this chapter.

You will use the Response object in several examples in later sections of this chapter. The advantage of using the Write method over mixing HTML tags and VBScript commands is that scripts that use the Write method don't contain too many delimiters and the resulting server-side script is easier to read.

The Clear Method

The Clear method erases any buffered HTML output. You can use this method before sending output to the client with the Write method, or to handle errors. The Clear method will work only if the Response.Buffer property has been set to False; its syntax is

```
Response.Clear
```

Let's say you're creating an HTML table and populating it with field values read from a recordset. If an error occurs in the process, you can clear any information you have written to the output stream by calling the Response object's Clear method. As you may have guessed, the Buffer property prevents the server from sending any information to the client before the End method is called. Normally, the server doesn't wait for the script to close the Response object before it transmits the information to the client. Whatever information you wrote to the output stream through the Response object can be sent to the client at any time. To change this default behavior, set the Buffer property to False.

The Flush Method

The output generated by the Write method is stored in a buffer, and the web server transmits it to the client when it gets a chance. That's why you don't have to wait for the entire page to arrive when you connect to a URL. You can force the buffer to be transmitted to the client by calling the Flush method. If the script takes a long time to execute, you can flush the output every now and then, so that the viewer won't think that the web server is not responding. To use the Flush method, you must first set the Response object's Buffer property to True, as shown in the following code segment:

```
Response.Buffer = True
{ Response.Write <text>
  Response.Write <text> }
Response.Flush
```

When buffering is on, the web server doesn't send any output to the client, unless you call the Flush method.

The End Method

The End method causes the web server to stop processing the script and return the current result. The remaining contents of the file are not processed and its syntax is

```
Response.End
```

The Server Object

The *Server object* provides access to methods and properties on the server. It has a single property, the ScriptTimeOut property, which sets a time limit for a script's execution, and several methods.

The ScriptTimeOut Property

The ScriptTimeout property specifies the maximum amount of time a script can run before it is terminated. Its default value is 90 seconds. The timeout will not take effect while a server component is processing (for example, an operation on a database that takes awhile to complete won't be timed out).

The MapPath Method

The *MapPath method* maps a specified relative or virtual path to the corresponding physical directory on the server. It must be used when opening files for input or output with the TextStream object, discussed later in the chapter. Its syntax is

```
Server.MapPath( path )
```

where *path* is the relative or virtual path to be mapped to a physical directory. If path starts with either a backward or forward slash (either / or \), the MapPath method assumes that the path argument is a virtual path. If path doesn't start with a slash, the MapPath method assumes that the path is relative to the directory of the asp file being processed.

Normally, your script shouldn't care about the actual value returned by the MapPath method, because it's passed as argument to another method, usually the CreateTextFile or OpenTextFile method, which creates or opens a file, respectively. These methods are discussed in the section "The File Access Component" later in the chapter.

The CreateObject Method

The *CreateObject method* creates an instance of a server component, similar to the CreateObject() function of Visual Basic. A server component is an application on the server computer that can be contacted through the methods and properties it exposes. After a server component is created, you can call its methods and properties from within a server-side script. A typical example of a server component that can be called from within a script is the ADO component, which you can use to access databases on the server.

There are also a few components, installed along with the Active Server Pages, which can be accessed through the CreateObject method. The server components that you will explore in this chapter are the ActiveX Data Objects component (ADO), which allows your script to access databases on the server; the FileSystem component, which allows your script to access files on the server; and the Browser Capabilities component, which lets your script know the capabilities of the browser used to view a page.

The syntax of the CreateObject method is

```
Server.CreateObject( progID )
```

where *progID* is the type of object to create. The value of the progID argument for any given server can be found in the Registry or in Visual Basic's Object Browser. This method returns an object variable, through which you can access the server component's methods and properties, just as you do with Visual Basic.

The URLEncode Method

The *URLEncode method* applies URL encoding rules to a string. Its syntax is

```
Server.URLEncode(text)
```

where *text* is the string to be URL encoded. Use this method to prepare URLs with parameters. The statement

```
<%= Server.URLEncode("Function name 4-cos(X/3)") %>
```

will pass the client the following string:

```
Function name 4%252Dcos(X%252F3)
```

All characters that are not letters or numeric digits are replaced with their hexadecimal values, prefixed with the % symbol.

The HTMLEncode Method

The *HTMLEncode method* applies HTML encoding to a string. Its syntax is

```
Server.HTMLEncode(text)
```

where *text* is the string to be HTML-encoded. Use this method to place HTML listings on the page. The statement below will display the following string on the browser's window:

```
<%= Server.HTMLEncode("The <IMG> tag doesn't
                       have a matching </IMG> tag") %>

The &lt;IMG&gt; tag doesn't have a matching &lt;/IMG&gt; tag
```

Part iii

Using Cookies

A *cookie* is a fancy term for a value that's sent by the HTTP server to the client. The browser extracts this value from the HTML file's header and stores it on the local computer. Cookies are binary values that are stored by the browser into a special folder—this means they can't harm your computer. If you want to see the cookie values left by the various HTTP servers on your computer, open the `Cookies` folder under the Windows directory or under the Profiles directory in Windows NT. You'll probably find quite a few cookies there.

As you already know, the HTTP protocol is stateless. In other words, the web server doesn't remember what computers have connected to it. Every time a client requests a document, the server establishes a connection, furnishes the document, and closes the connection. As a result, it's not easy to maintain state between sessions. When you select a few items in an online store, they are placed in a basket. How does the server know the items selected by each client? The answer is that it doesn't! The IDs of the selected products are stored on the client computer, and the server reads them from the client when it needs them.

The ISBNCookies Example

This is a slightly more complicated example, which stores a directory of cookies on the client. Let's say you're building an online store (as you will do in Chapter 16), and you decide to store the shopping basket's contents on the client computer in the form of cookies. (This approach assumes that the client hasn't disabled cookies on the client computer, but most people don't. That's why some of the most popular electronic stores leave cookies on the client.)

The other alternative is to store the basket's contents on the server. This means additional storage requirements, more work for the server, and less convenience for the viewer. Some sites require that you place an order before you abandon the current session. If you leave the store, your basket is empty the next time you connect. Even if the basket isn't emptied between sessions, you must identify yourself in order to view your basket. This process isn't repeated every time you open the basket, only the first time in each session. Even so, it's not the ultimate in user-friendliness.

Maintaining state between sessions is a sore point in web applications. If every user had a unique IP address, similar to one's electronic address (or phone number, for that matter), things would be significantly simpler. Unfortunately, IP addresses are typically assigned to users as they connect to the Internet, and you can't assume that a user's current IP will belong to the same user in another session.

For each order, you want to store the book's ID (its ISBN) and the corresponding quantity on the client computer. Because you don't know how many books a user may select, it's best to create an array of ISBN and quantity cookies. Every time the user selects a new title, you must search for the specific ISBN in the cookies collection. If the ISBN has been ordered already, you will increase the quantity by one (and notify users that they have selected this title already). If it has not been selected already, then a new cookie must be added to the cookies collection of your website to the client.

One of the sample documents for this chapter on the Sybex website is the `ISBNCOOKIES.HTM` document. Place this document in your web server's root folder and open it with your browser. In the browser's Address box, enter

```
http://127.0.0.1/ISBNCOOKIES.HTM
```

If the web server is running, you will see the page shown in Figure 13.9. This is a very simple document that contains two hyperlinks to the `SAVECOOKIES.ASP` and `READCOOKIES ASP` files. The `SAVECOOKIES.ASP` file creates three cookies on the client computer: they are three ISBNs, and their values are integers (number of items).

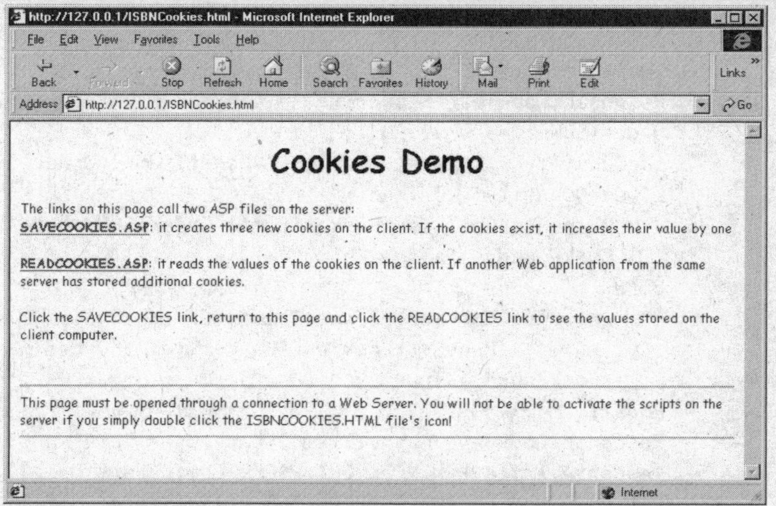

FIGURE 13.9: The ISBNCOOKIES.HTM page

The SAVECOOKIES.ASP script is shown in Listing 13.3.

LISTING 13.3: The SAVECOOKIES.ASP Script

```
<%
    OrderISBN="0-300-999991"
    CurQuantity = Request.Cookies("BasketItem")(OrderISBN)
    If CurQuantity = 0 Then
        Response.Cookies("BasketItem")(OrderISBN) = "1"
        BookFound = False
    Else
        Response.Cookies("BasketItem")(OrderISBN) =
                 Request.Cookies("BasketItem")(OrderISBN)+1
        BookFound = True
    End If
    Response.Cookies("BasketItem").Expires = Date + 365

    OrderISBN="0-300-999992"
    CurQuantity = Request.Cookies("BasketItem")(OrderISBN)
    If CurQuantity = 0 Then
        Response.Cookies("BasketItem")(OrderISBN) = "1"
        BookFound = False
    Else
        Response.Cookies("BasketItem")(OrderISBN) =
                 Request.Cookies("BasketItem")(OrderISBN)+1
    BookFound = True
    End If
    Response.Cookies("BasketItem").Expires = Date + 365
    OrderISBN="0-300-999993"
    CurQuantity = Request.Cookies("BasketItem")(OrderISBN)
    If CurQuantity = 0 Then
        Response.Cookies("BasketItem")(OrderISBN) = "1"
        BookFound = False
    Else
        Response.Cookies("BasketItem")(OrderISBN) =
                 Request.Cookies("BasketItem")(OrderISBN)+1
         BookFound = True
    End If
    Response.Cookies("BasketItem").Expires = Date + 365
    Response.Write "<HTML><FONT FACE='Comic Sans MS'>"
    Response.Write "<H3>SAVECOOKIES Script</H3>"
```

```
    Response.Write "This script increased the values of the
                    following product IDs (ISBNs)"
    Response.Write
        "<BR>0-300-999991, 0-300-999992, 0-300-999993"
%>
```

This script reads the first cookie's value in the *BasketItem* collection with the following expression:

```
Request.Cookies("BasketItem")(OrderISBN)
```

If the cookie exists, the script increases its value by one and then writes it back to the client:

```
Response.Cookies("BasketItem")(OrderISBN) =
    Request.Cookies("BasketItem")(OrderISBN)+1
```

If the cookie does not exist, the value 1 is written to the client with a similar expression. The same process is repeated for the other two cookies (ISBNs). The output of the script is shown in Figure 13.10.

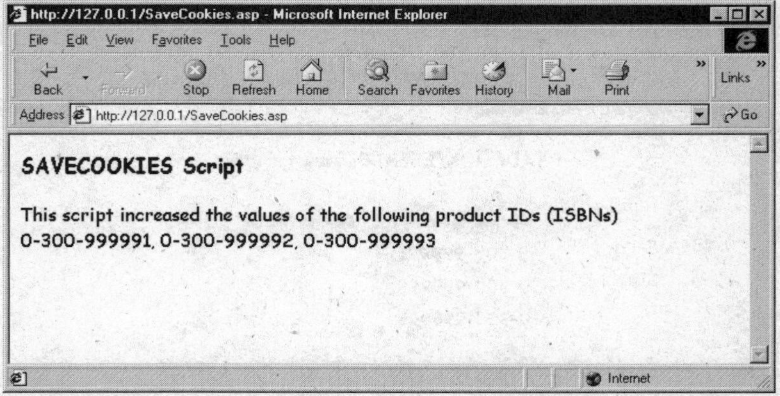

FIGURE 13.10: The output produced by the SAVECOOKIES.ASP script

The READCOOKIES.ASP script (Listing 13.4) reads the three cookies from the client computer and displays their names (ISBN numbers) and values (quantities) on a new page, which is shown in Figure 13.11. This script uses a For ... Next loop to scan the members of the BasketItem cookie:

LISTING 13.4: The READCOOKIES.ASP Script

```
<%
    Response.Write "<HTML><FONT FACE='Comic Sans MS'>"
    Response.Write "<CENTER>"
```

```
        Response.Write "<H3>READCOOKIES.ASP Script
            Output<BR><BR>"
        Response.Write "<TABLE BORDER=ALL>"
        Response.Write "<TR><TD><B>Cookie Name</B>"
        Response.Write "<TD><B>Cookie Value</B>"
        For Each cookie in Request.Cookies("BasketItem")
            Response.Write "<TR>"
            Response.Write "<TD ALIGN=CENTER>" & cookie &
                           "     " &
                           " "
            Response.Write "<TD ALIGN=CENTER> "
            Response.Write Request.Cookies("BasketItem")(cookie)
        Next
        Response.Write "</TABLE>"
        Response.Write "</HTML>"
    %>
```

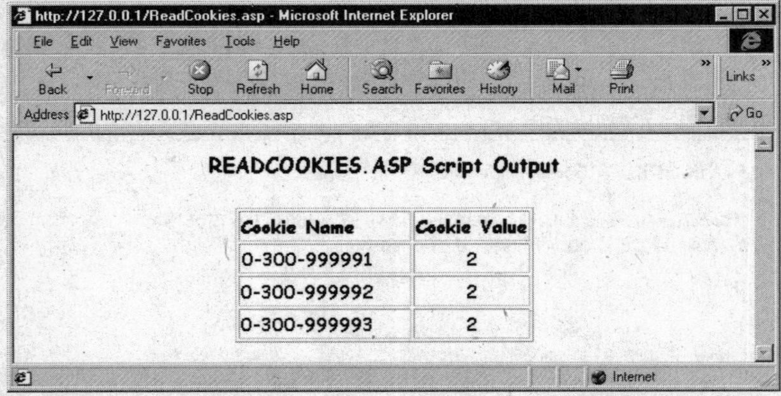

FIGURE 13.11: The output produced by the READCOOKIES.ASP script

MAKING QUERIES WITH ASP FILES

ASP scripts accept query parameters from the client computer and process them. Before you can process the values submitted by the client, however, you must read them. In the early days of the Web, the process of extracting the values submitted from the client was difficult, and web developers were using languages such as Perl to write server scripts. VBScript changed all that. As you recall from the discussion of the <FORM> tag, there are two methods of submitting parameter values to the server: the GET and the POST methods. They are both specified with the METHOD attributes of the <FORM> tag.

The GET and POST Methods

The main difference between the two methods is the way data is sent to the server. The GET method appends all parameter values to the URL of the client script, producing a very long URL. In addition, there's a limit of 2Kb on the number of characters that can be returned to the server, and all the information is visible to the user in the Address box of the browser. The POST method can transmit longer parameter strings, and it doesn't display them on the browser's Address box along with the URL of the script. The POST method, however, can return values that have been entered on a form's controls to the server.

The two methods are handled differently on the server, too. To extract the values submitted with the POST method, you must use the Form collection of the Request object. To extract the values submitted with the GET method, you must use the QueryString collection of the Request object. The following two examples demonstrate the two methods for submitting parameter values to the server.

The Form Collection (Use with POST Method)

The Form collection contains a member for each control on the form. The value of the first control on the form is the following:

```
Request.Form(0).Value
```

To access all the control values, you can use a loop like the following one:

```
For Each ctrl In Request.Form
    {process value Request.Form(ctrl)}
Next
```

If you use the previous structure to access the parameters, keep in mind that *ctrl* is the name of the parameter and *Request.Form(ctrl)* is the parameter's value.

If the script knows the name of the control, you can access a value by name. If the form contains a control named *Email*, you can read this control's value with this statement:

```
CustEmail = Request.Form("Email")
```

- To retrieve the entire string submitted to the server, use the Form property of the Request object without an index:

```
Request.Form
```

The QueryString Collection (Use with GET Method)

The QueryString collection contains a member for each parameter passed to the server in the URL. To access the first parameter in the collection use the following expression:

```
Request.QueryString(0)
```

If you know the name of the parameter, you can access it by name:

```
Request.QueryString("Email")
```

The Request object also exposes a QueryString property, which contains the entire string returned by the client.

The *BOXESGET* and *BOXESPOST* Pages

The BOXESGET.HTM and BOXESPOST.HTM pages demonstrate the GET and POST methods. The pages are identical when viewed with a browser (see Figure 13.12). The page displays a form with six Text controls on it. You could use this arrangement to accept product codes and quantities, for example. The three long Text controls are members of the BOX array, and the other three Text controls are members of the QTY array. Both pages use identical statements to display the form:

```
<INPUT TYPE=TEXT SIZE=40 NAME=Box><INPUT TYPE=TEXT
    SIZE=5 NAME=QTY>
<BR>
<INPUT TYPE=TEXT SIZE=40 NAME=Box><INPUT TYPE=TEXT
    SIZE=5 NAME=QTY>
<BR>
<INPUT TYPE=TEXT SIZE=40 NAME=Box><INPUT TYPE=TEXT
    SIZE=5 NAME=QTY>
<INPUT TYPE=SUBMIT>
```

The data supplied by the user is submitted to the server with the GET and POST methods, respectively. Here are the <FORM> tags for both files:

BoxesGET.HTM

```
<FORM ACTION=ReadGET.asp METHOD=GET>
```

BoxesPOST.HTM

```
<FORM ACTION=ReadPOST.asp METHOD=POST>
```

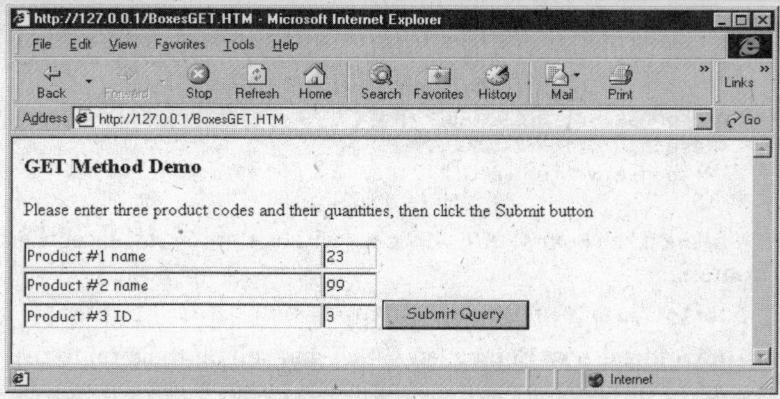

FIGURE 13.12: The BoxesGET.HTM and BoxesPOST.HTM pages display the same form, but they use different methods to submit the parameter values to the server.

To open the `Boxesget.ASP` page with your browser, enter the address

```
http://127.0.0.1/Boxesget.HTM
```

in the Address box. Enter a few values and submit the form to the web server by clicking the Submit button. The page will call the `ReadGET.asp` script on the server with the following URL:

```
http://127.0.0.1/ReadGET.asp?
    Box=Box1&QTY=Q1&Box=Box2&QTY=Q2&Box=Box3&QTY=Q3
```

The GET method passes the parameter values to the server along with the URL of the script. To process the parameter values on the server, the `ReadGET.asp` script uses the QueryString property of the Request object. The `ReadGET.asp` script displays the entire string passed by the client, as well as the values of the individual fields. Here's the script's listing:

```
<%
Response.Write "<HTML>"
Response.Write "<BODY BGCOLOR=#F0F0F0>"
Response.Write "<H2>Passing Parameters with the GET
    Method</H2>"
Response.Write "<FONT SIZE=+1>"
Response.write "The following parameter string was passed
    to the server: "
Response.Write "<BR><KBD>" & request.QueryString & "</KBD>"
Response.Write "<BR><BR>"
Response.Write "The individual field names and values are: "
Response.Write "<TABLE BORDER>"
Response.Write "<TR><TD>" & UCase(request.QueryString("Box")
    (1)) "<TD>" & Request.QueryString("QTY")(1)
```

```
Response.Write "<TR><TD>" & UCase(request.QueryString("Box")
    (2)) "<TD>" & Request.QueryString("QTY")(2)
Response.Write "<TR><TD>" & UCase(request.QueryString("Box")
    (3)) "<TD>" & Request.QueryString("QTY")(3)
Response.Write "</TABLE>"
Response.Write "</BODY>"
Response.write "</HTML>"
%>
```

To open the BoxesPOST.ASP page with your browser, enter the address

```
http://127.0.0.1/BoxesPOST.HTM
```

in the Address box. Enter a few values and submit the form to the web server by clicking the Submit button. The page will call the readPOST.asp script on the server with the URL

```
http://127.0.0.1/readPOST.asp
```

The POST method doesn't pass the parameter values to the server along with the URL of the script. The first advantage of this method is that viewers don't see what information you pass from the client to the server.

To process the parameter values on the server, the readPOST.asp script uses the Form property of the Request object. The readPOST.asp script displays the entire string passed by the client, as well as the values of the individual fields. Here's the script's listing:

```
<%
Response.Write "<HTML>"
Response.Write "<BODY BGCOLOR=#F0F0F0>"
Response.Write "<H2>Passing Parameters with the POST
    Method</H2>"
Response.Write "<FONT SIZE=+1>"
Response.write "The following parameter string was passed
               to the server: "
Response.Write "<BR><KBD>" & request.Form & "</KBD>"
Response.Write "<BR><BR>"
Response.Write "The individual field names and values are:"
Response.Write "<TABLE BORDER>"
Response.Write "<TR><TD>" & UCase(request.Form("Box")(1)) &
    "<TD>"  Request.Form("QTY")(1)
Response.Write "<TR><TD>" & UCase(request.Form("Box")(2)) &
    "<TD>"  Request.Form("QTY")(2)
Response.Write "<TR><TD>" & UCase(request.Form("Box")(3)) &
    "<TD>"  Request.Form("QTY")(3)
Response.Write "</TABLE>"
Response.Write "</BODY>"
```

```
Response.write "</HTML>"
%>
```

Figure 13.13 shows how the two pages call the appropriate script on the server.

The Apply.asp Example

The next example uses an actual form to submit its contents to the server with the form's Submit method. The page with the form is shown in Figure 13.14. In this section, you will submit the form to the server, where an ASP page will process it (it will actually display its values). After you extract the values of the parameters, you can process them any way you like—Save them to a database, create a report, and so on.

A

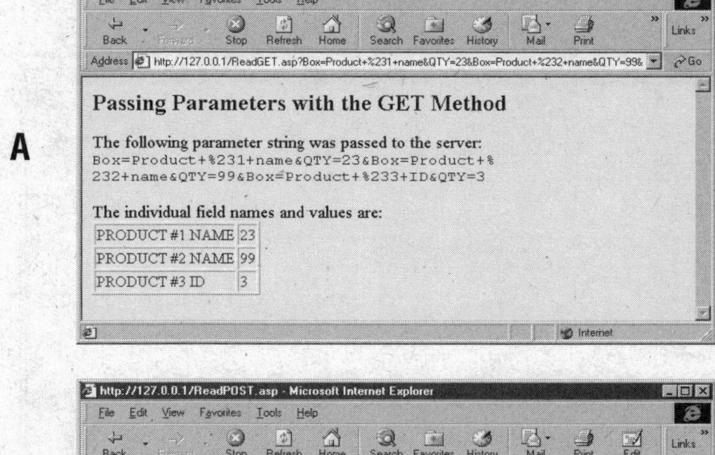

B

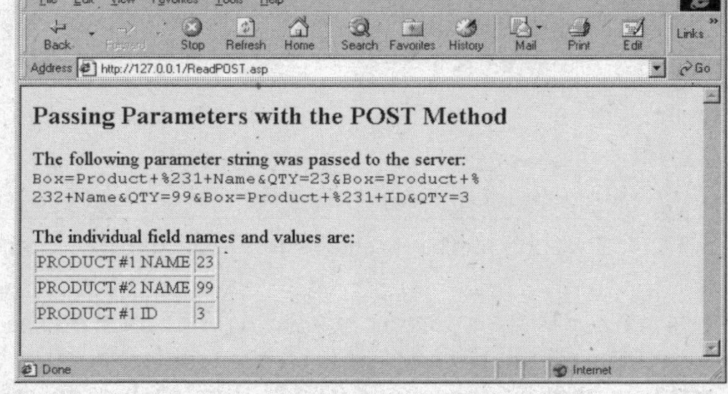

FIGURE 13.13: Passing the same parameter values with the (a) GET and (b) POST methods

The page with the form shown in Figure 13.14 is called `Apply.htm`. It contains the following controls:

- A SELECT control (POSITION), where the user selects the desired position
- Five TEXT controls (LNAME, FNAME, ADDRESS, TEL, FAX), where the user enters first and last name, address, and phone and fax numbers
- A group of three RADIO controls (DGREE1, DGREE2, DGREE3), used to specify the applicant's education
- A group of CHECKBOX controls (DAYS, NIGHTS, SHIFT, WEEKEND), used to specify when the applicant can work
- Another group of CHECKBOX controls (MARRIED, MINORITY, CITIZEN), used to specify the applicant's status

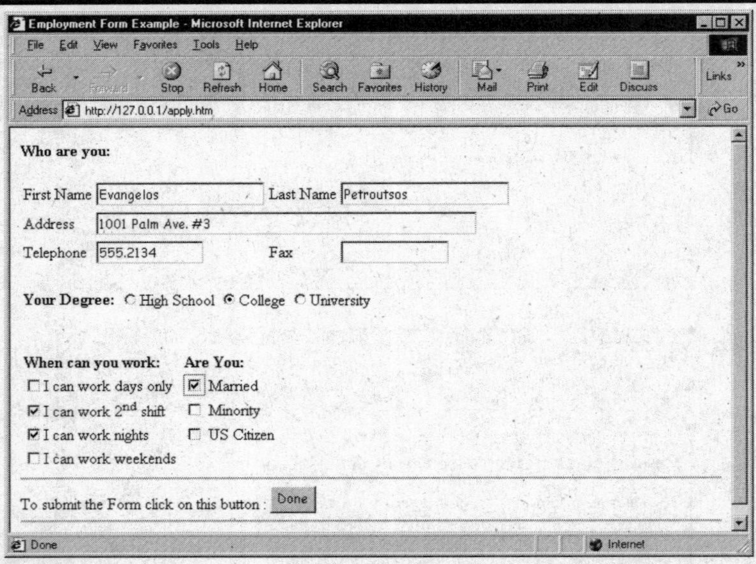

FIGURE 13.14: The apply.htm page contains a form with the HTML intrinsic controls.

Here's the `apply.htm` document's listing. The form on the Apply page contains all the HTML controls you can use to interact with the viewers from within your web applications. The ASP script that processes this page demonstrates how to read the values of all the controls on the web server.

LISTING 13.5: The apply.htm Page

```
<HTML>
<HEAD>
<TITLE>Employment Form Example</TITLE>
</HEAD>
<BODY>
<FORM name=APPFORM ACTION=APPLY.ASP METHOD=GET>
<P><B>Who are you:</B>
<P>
<TABLE>
  <TBODY>
  <TR>
    <TD>First Name</TD>
    <TD><INPUT maxLength=25 name=FNAME size=25> </TD>
    <TD>Last Name</TD>
    <TD><INPUT maxLength=25 name=LNAME size=25> </TD></TR>
  <TR>
    <TD>Address</TD>
    <TD colSpan=3><INPUT maxLength=60 name=ADDRESS size=60>
        </TD></TR>
  <TR>
    <TD>Telephone</TD>
    <TD><INPUT maxLength=15 name=TEL size=15> </TD>
    <TD>Fax</TD>
    <TD><INPUT maxLength=15 name=FAX size=15>
    </TD></TR></TBODY></TABLE>
<P>
<P>
<TABLE>
  <TBODY>
  <TR>
    <TD><B>Your Degree:</B></TD>
    <TD><INPUT name=DGREE1 type=radio
        value=HighSchool>High School</TD>
    <TD><INPUT name=DGREE2 type=radio
        value=College>College</TD>
    <TD><INPUT name=DGREE3 type=radio
        value=University>University</TD>
    </TR></TBODY></TABLE>
<P><BR>
<P>
<TABLE>
```

```
<TBODY>
<TR>
  <TD><B>When can you work:</B></TD>
  <TD></TD>
  <TD><B>Are You:</B></TD>
<TR>
  <TD><INPUT name=DAYS type=checkbox>
      I can work days only</TD>
  <TD></TD>
  <TD><INPUT name=MARRIED type=checkbox value=MARRIED>
      Married </TD>
<TR>
  <TD><INPUT name=SHIFT type=checkbox>I can work 2
      <SUP>nd</SUP>
      shift</TD>
  <TD></TD>
  <TD><INPUT name=MINORITY type=checkbox value=MINORITY>
      Minority</TD>
<TR>
  <TD><INPUT name=NIGHTS type=checkbox>I can work nights
      </TD>
  <TD></TD>
  <TD><INPUT name=CITIZEN type=checkbox value=CITIZEN>
      US Citizen</TD>
<TR>
  <TD><INPUT name=WEEKEND type=checkbox>
      I can work weekends</TD>
  <TD></TD>
  <TD></TD></TR></TBODY></TABLE>
<HR>
To submit the Form click on this button :
  <INPUT type=SUBMIT     value=Done>
<HR>
</FORM>
</BODY>
</HTML>
```

Notice that the RADIO controls aren't called DEGREE1, DEGREE2, and DEGREE3. There is an interesting HTML-related problem here, which you will discover only by testing the page. Because the various parameters in the query string are separated by the ampersand character, somewhere the following character combination will appear:

```
&DEGREE=some+value
```

To HTML, &DEG is the symbol for degrees (a small, raised circle) and the name of this parameter on the server will no longer be DEGREE. The characters &DEG will be substituted with the symbols for degrees. They will create serious problems when parsing the string at the server. The & symbol will disappear, joining the name of the control with the name of the previous control in the string.

The control's contents are submitted to the server with the form's Submit button. The <FORM> tag contains the name of the application on the server that will handle this request:

```
<FORM NAME=APPFORM ACTION="/ASPages/Apply.asp" METHOD=GET>
```

The `Apply.asp` page on the server uses the Request.QueryString property to display the entire query string. Then, it uses the same property with the names of the various controls as indexes to extract the individual values of the controls and display them. Notice that only the checked CHECKBOX and RADIO controls are transmitted. That's why the script on the server examines all possible values. If a given CHECKBOX or RADIO control's value is empty, it means that the control hasn't been checked (or selected). The output produced by the `Apply.asp` page for the document from Figure 13.14 is shown in Figure 13.15.

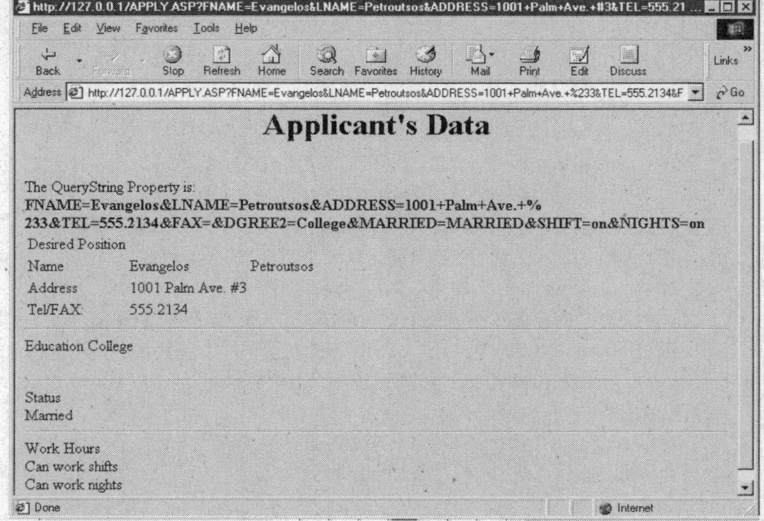

FIGURE 13.15: The output of the Apply.asp page for the data submitted with the form of the Apply.htm page shown in Figure 13.14

The `Apply.asp` file used to produce the response shown in Figure 13.14 is detailed in Listing 13.6.

LISTING 13.6: The Apply.asp Script

```
<HTML>
<BODY BGCOLOR=silver>
<FONT FACE=Verdana SIZE=2>
<CENTER>
<H1>Applicant's Data</H1>
</CENTER>
<BR>
<BR>
<SCRIPT LANGUAGE=VBScript RUNAT=Server>
   Response.write "The QueryString Property is: <BR>"
   Response.write "<B>" & Request.QueryString & "</B>"
   Response.write "<TABLE>"
   Response.write "<TD> Desired Position <TD>" & _
       Request.QueryString("POSITION")
   Response.write "<TR>"
   Response.write "<TD>Name <TD>" &
       Request.QueryString("FNAME")
   Response.write "<TD>" & Request.QueryString("LNAME")
   Response.write "<TR>"
   Response.write "<TD> Address <TD>" &
       Request.QueryString("ADDRESS")
   Response.write "<TR>"
   Response.write "<TD> Tel/FAX: <TD>" &
       Request.QueryString("TEL")
   Response.write "<TD>" & Request.QueryString("FAX")
   Response.write "</TABLE>"
   Response.write "<HR>Education"
'  NOW EXAMINE EACH DEGREE RADIO BUTTON'S VALUE
   If Request.QueryString("DGREE1") <>"" Then
      Response.Write "High School<P>"
   End If
   If Request.QueryString("DGREE2") <>"" Then
      Response.Write "College<P>"
   End If
   If Request.QueryString("DGREE3") <>"" Then
      Response.Write "University<P>"
   End If
'  NOW EXAMINE THE MARRIED CHECKBOX
```

```
    Response.write "<HR>Status"
    If Request.QueryString("MARRIED") <>"" Then
       Response.Write "<BR>Married"
    End If
'   NOW EXAMINE THE MINORITY CHECKBOX
    If Request.QueryString("MINORITY") <>"" Then
       Response.Write "<BR>Minority"
    End If
'   NOW EXAMINE THE CITIZEN CHECKBOX
    If Request.QueryString("CITIZEN") <>"" Then
       Response.Write "<BR>US Citizen"
    End If
'   NOW EXAMINE THE LAST GROUP OF CHECKBOXES ON THE FORM
    Response.write "<HR>Work Hours"
    If Request.QueryString("DAYS") <>"" Then
       Response.Write "<BR>Can work days"
    End If
    If Request.QueryString("SHIFT") <>"" Then
       Response.Write "<BR>Can work shifts"
    End If
    If Request.QueryString("NIGHTS") <>"" Then
       Response.Write "<BR>Can work nights"
    End If
    If Request.QueryString("WEEKEND") <>"" Then
          Response.Write "<BR>Can work weekends"
    End If

   Response.Write "</CENTER>"
   Response.End
</SCRIPT>
</BODY>
</HTML>
```

To test the `Apply.asp` example, copy the `Apply.*` files from the code on the Sybex website into the web server's root folder. Then, start Internet Explorer, connect to the local HTTP server, and invoke the file `apply.htm` by entering the following URL in the Address box:

```
http://127.0.0.1/apply.htm
```

Notice the RUNAT attribute of the <SCRIPT> tag. This is an alternative to the <% and %> tags; it instructs the web server to treat the entire script as a server-side script.

Part iii

Accessing Databases with ASP

The most important applications you will build with ASP are applications that extract data from databases on the server, format them with HTML tags, and return them as new HTML pages to the client. With Active Server Pages, you can use ADO to access the database, possibly process the data, and then format it as HTML tables. ADO uses the ODBC drivers and can access all databases supported by ODBC.

To use ADO, you can create a Data Source Name (DSN) for the database you want to access, or specify the connection string in the script. In this chapter's examples, we are going to use the Northwind database, which comes with Visual Basic. I'm assuming you have set up a DSN for the Northwind database, and you've named it NWINDDB. You can use either the SQL Server or the Access version of the database. To use an ADO object, you must create an object variable with the CreateObject method, whose syntax is

```
<%
Set DBObj = Server.CreateObject("ADODB.Connection")
%>
```

The *DBObj* object variable is your gateway to the ODBC databases installed on the server. To actually open a database, call the Open method of the *DBObj* object variable, as shown here:

```
<%
DBObj.Open "NWINDDB"
%>
```

NWindDB is the name I used as the System Data Source for the Northwind database on my system. You may have to change the name of the database accordingly on your system. For the examples in this book, I set up two DSNs: the NWINDDB DSN for the Northwind database and the BIBLIO DSN for the Biblio database.

Querying Databases

After connecting to the database, you can use the Execute method of the *DBObj* object to execute SQL commands and retrieve records from the database represented by the DSN. Let's say you want to create a Recordset variable with the names of all customers in the Northwind database.

First, create a string variable with the SQL statement:

```
SQLQuery = "SELECT Country, CompanyName, ContactName, "
SQLQuery = SQLQuery & " ContactTitle FROM Customers "
SQLQuery = SQLQuery & " ORDER BY Country"
```

This SQL statement retrieves a few fields of all the rows from the Customers table and sorts them according to the Country field. To actually create the recordset with the customers, call the Execute method of the *DBObj* object and pass the *SQLQuery* string as parameter:

```
Set RSCustomers = DBObj.Execute(SQLQuery)
```

RSCustomers is the name of a Recordset variable, which you can manipulate through your code. When the recordset is first created, the pointer is located at the first record, and you can read the field values with the Fields collection. To display the company name of the first record on the page, use the following statement:

```
<% = RSCustomers.Fields("CompanyName") %>
```

To scan the entire recordset, use a Do loop to examine the recordset's EOF property. While it's not True, it moves to the next record with the MoveNext method. Here's the structure of a loop that scans the entire recordset:

```
<% Do While Not RSCustomers.EOF %>
    { statements to process the current record }
<% RSCustomers.MoveNext
Loop %>
```

The AllCustomers.asp Example

Let's look at an example that uses the methods and properties of the ADO objects to retrieve all the customers in the Northwind database and display them on a web page. The `AllCustomers.asp` page uses ADO to open the Northwind database and create a recordset with the SQL statement presented earlier. Then, it scans all the rows of the recordset and displays them in HTML format. Here's the complete listing of the `AllCustomers.asp` page:

Part iii

LISTING 13.7: The AllCustomers.asp Page

```
<HTML>
<%
Set DBObj = Server.CreateObject("ADODB.Connection")
DBObj.Open "NWindDB"
SQLQuery = "SELECT Country, CompanyName, ContactName, "
SQLQuery = SQLQuery & "ContactTitle FROM Customers "
SQLQuery = SQLQuery & "ORDER BY Country"
Set RSCustomers = DBObj.Execute(SQLQuery)
%>
```

```
<H1>Query Results</H1>
<% Do While Not RSCustomers.EOF %>
  <TR>
    <TD> <FONT FACE="Verdana" SIZE=2>
    <% = RSCustomers("Country") %>
    </FONT></TD>
    <TD> <FONT FACE="Verdana" SIZE=2>
      <% = RSCustomers("ContactName") & " (" %>
      <% = RSCustomers("ContactTitle") & ")" %>
    </FONT></TD>
    <TD><FONT FACE="Verdana" SIZE=2>
      <% = RSCustomers("CompanyName") %>
    </FONT></TD>
  </TR>
<%
RSCustomers.MoveNext
Loop
%>
</HTML>
```

The `AllCustomers.asp` file's code is straightforward. It extracts the values of the fields using the Fields collection of a Recordset variable (*RSCustomers*). The output of the `AllCustomers.asp` page is shown in Figure 13.16. There's an even simpler method to produce an HTML page based on a recordset; the GetString method of the Recordset object can retrieve and then format the recordset using the delimiter you supply to this method as an argument.

The AllCountries Example

In the next example, you will use a more complicated SQL statement to allow the user to select a country and then display the customers from the selected country. Although you could prompt the user to enter the country name, you will do something more interesting and user-friendly. You'll create a page with all country names, making each country name a hyperlink. When a hyperlink is clicked, you will call an ASP page on the server, passing the hyperlink's name as parameter.

To test the project, open the `AllCountries.asp` file and click a country name. Each country name is a hyperlink to another ASP file that displays the names of the companies (and their contact) of the selected country on a new page. The `AllCountries.asp` page displays the names of the countries, as shown in Figure 13.17.

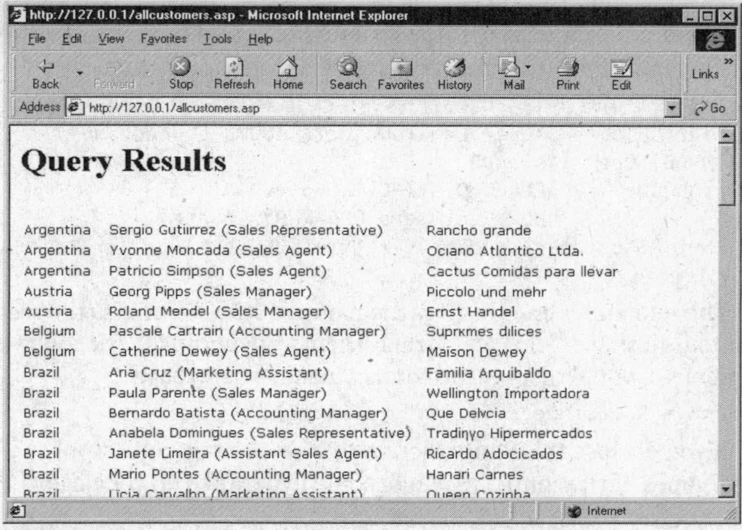

FIGURE 13.16: The output of the AllCustomers.asp page

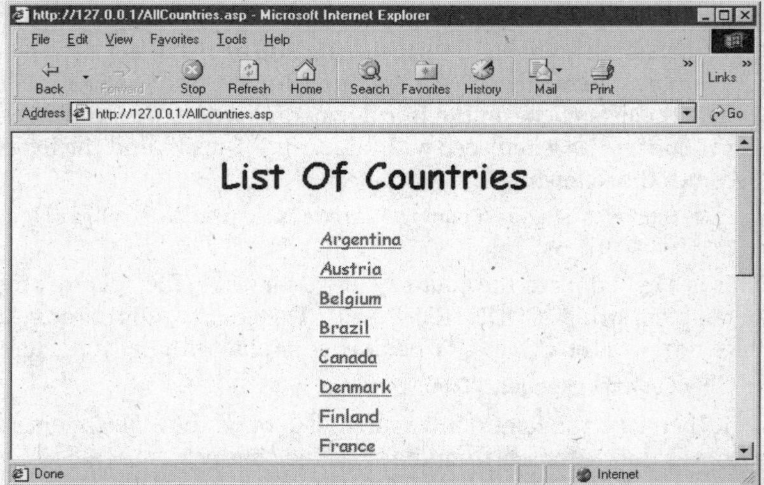

FIGURE 13.17: The AllCountries.asp file displays the names of the countries in the Customers table as hyperlinks. Clicking a country name displays the customers from the selected country.

The AllCountries.asp page is quite similar to the AllCustomers.asp page, but it uses a different SQL statement. The following statements open the database and create the recordset with the country names:

```
<%
Set DBObj = Server.CreateObject("ADODB.Connection")
DBObj.Open "NWindDB"
SQLQuery = "SELECT DISTINCT country
            FROM Customers ORDER BY Country"
Set RSCustomers = DBObj.Execute(SQLQuery)
%>
```

The remaining lines display the names of the countries (the recordset contains a single field) and format them as hyperlinks. The following statement would display the country name on the page:

```
<% = RSCustomers.Fields("Country") %>
```

If you enclose this expression in pair of <A> tags and supply a URL, the names of the countries can become hyperlinks on the page:

```
<A HREF="/ASPages/CountryCustomersH.asp?COUNTRY=
<% = RSCustomers.Fields("Country") %> ">
<% = RSCustomers.Fields("Country") %> </A>
```

The hyperlink's destination is the CountryCustomers.asp file, which is similar to the AllCustomers.asp page. Instead of displaying all the customers in the database, the CountryCustomers.asp page uses a different SQL statement, which extracts customers from a specific country only. If the user clicks on the Brazil hyperlink, the expression <% = CustCountry %> is replaced with the string "Brazil", and the hyperlink becomes the following:

```
<A HREF="/ASPages/CountryCustomers.asp?COUNTRY=Brazil">
    Brazil</A>
```

This is a hyperlink to the CountryCustomers.asp file, followed by the parameters string "COUNTRY=Brazil". The CountryCustomers.asp page retrieves the COUNTRY parameter's value with the statement:

```
ReqCountry=Request.QueryString("COUNTRY")
```

It then uses the ReqCountry variable to build the SQL statement that retrieves the customers from the specified country:

```
SQLQuery = "SELECT CompanyName, ContactName, " & _
           "ContactTitle FROM Customers " & _
           "WHERE Country = '" & _
           ReqCountry & "' ORDER BY ContactName"
Set RSCustomers = DBObj.Execute(SQLQuery)
```

Then, the program proceeds to display the customers from the specified country with the following loop:

```
<% Do While Not RSCustomers.EOF %>
  <TR>
  <TD> <FONT FACE="Verdana" SIZE=2>
  <% =RSCustomers("ContactName")&" (" &
      RSCustomers("ContactTitle") & ")"  %>
      </FONT>
  </TD>
  <TD><FONT FACE="Verdana" SIZE=2>
  <% = RSCustomers("CompanyName") %>
      </FONT>
  </TD>
  </TR>
<%
RSCustomers.MoveNext
Loop
%>
```

Let's revise the `CountryCustomers.asp` script, so that instead of simply displaying the company names as text, it formats them as hyperlinks, as shown in Figure 13.18. The destination of each hyperlink will be the `Customer.asp` script, which will display all the information about a customer on a new page.

The revised script is different only in the segment that displays the customers. The script creates hyperlinks using the CustomerID field as parameter:

```
<A HREF= /AXPages/Customer.asp?CUSTOMERID=
        <% =RSCustomers("CustomerID") %> </A>
        <% =RSCustomers("CompanyName") %>
```

Notice that the code is using the CustomerID field as parameter because this field is an index field and the SQL engine will locate the desired customer more quickly. The CustomerID field is retrieved from the database by the `CountryCustomers.asp` script, but it's not displayed anywhere. It's passed as a parameter to the `Customer.asp` script.

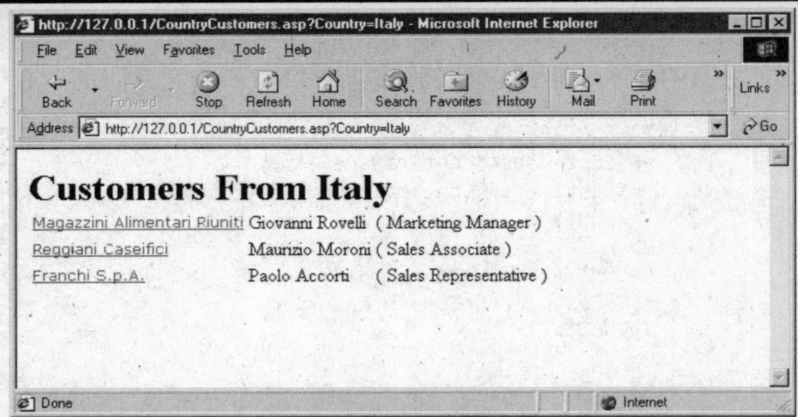

FIGURE 13.18: The output of the CountryCustomers.asp page

The `Customer.asp` page uses the value of the query parameter to locate a specific customer and then displays the customer's complete data. The code of the `Customer.asp` file is shown next.

LISTING 13.8: The Customer.asp Script

```
<HTML>
<%
ReqCustomer=Request.QueryString("CUSTOMERID")
Set DBObj = Server.CreateObject("ADODB.Connection")
DBObj.Open "NWindDB"
SQLQuery = "SELECT * FROM Customers WHERE CustomerID = '" &
           ReqCustomer & "'"
Set RSCustomers = DBObj.Execute(SQLQuery)
%>
<CENTER>
<H1>Query Results</H1>
<H3>Customer Data (CustomerID = <% = ReqCustomer %>)</H3>
</CENTER>
<FONT FACE="Verdana">
<CENTER>
<TABLE>
<TR>
<TD><B>Company Name <TD> <% = RSCustomers("CompanyName") %>
<TR>
<TD><B>Contact Name <TD> <% = RSCustomers("ContactName") %>, _
<% = RSCustomers("ContactTitle") %>
```

```
<TR>
<TD><B>Address <TD> <% = RSCustomers("Address") %>
<TR>
<TD><B>City <TD> <% = RSCustomers("City") %>
<TR>
<TD><B>Region <TD> <% = RSCustomers("Region") %>
<TR>
<TD><B>Postal Code <TD> <% = RSCustomers("PostalCode") %>
<TR>
<TD><B>Country <TD> <% = RSCustomers("Country") %>
<TR>
<TD><B>Phone <TD> <% = RSCustomers("Phone") %>
<TR>
<TD><B>Fax <TD> <% = RSCustomers("Fax") %>
</TABLE>
</CENTER>
</HTML>
```

Taking an Order

The last example in this section demonstrates how to build a web application for entering order data and how to read and validate the values entered by the user with a server-side script. The Place Order page, shown in Figure 13.19, allows the user to enter a series of Product IDs and quantities (to a maximum of 20 lines per order). The Order page contains a form with 40 text box controls: 20 for entering product codes and 20 more for entering quantities. This is not the most user-friendly interface for placing orders, but it's intended for business-to-business orders. When you visit an online store on the Web, you spend your time browsing and occasionally placing an order. Businesses know what they need (often their inventory applications generate lists of purchases), and they don't need to browse the products, just order them. A form with a TextArea control in which users could paste a list of product IDs and quantities, with one pair of items per line, might work even better.

The controls you see on the form of Figure 13.19 were not placed there by 40 <INPUT> tags. The page was generated by the following server-side script:

```
<%
For i=1 to 10
   Response.Write "<TR><TD><INPUT TYPE=TEXT SIZE=10 _
             NAME=ProdID><TD><INPUT TYPE=TEXT SIZE=5
➥NAME=QTY>"
   Response.Write "<TD><TD><INPUT TYPE=TEXT SIZE=10 _
```

Part iii

```
                NAME=ProdID><TD><INPUT TYPE=TEXT SIZE=5
➥NAME=QTY>"
Next
%>
```

(The underscore characters used here to break the long lines are not valid in HTML and ASP files. They are used here to indicate that multiple text lines should be entered as a single line.)

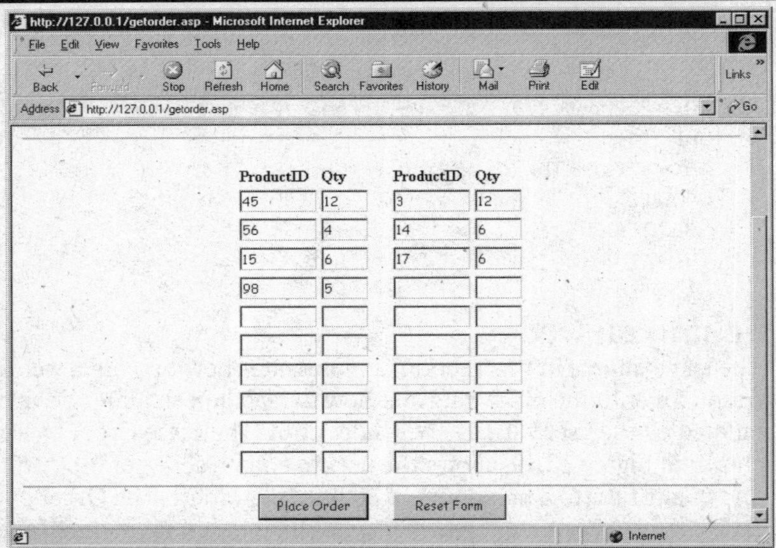

FIGURE 13.19: The GetOrder.asp page

Notice that all the controls for entering product IDs are named *ProdID*, and all the controls for entering quantities are named *QTY*. By using the same name for a group of controls, you automatically create an array of controls. Individual controls can be accessed by an index value.

The <FORM> tag's ACTION attribute specifies the name of the script on the server, the `ConfirmOrder.asp` script, which will process the order placed by the user. This script reads the product IDs and the quantities entered by the client, looks them up in the Products table of the Northwind database, and displays a confirmation page (shown in Figure 13.20). In this section, you'll build a simple script that displays the product names, quantities, and subtotals.

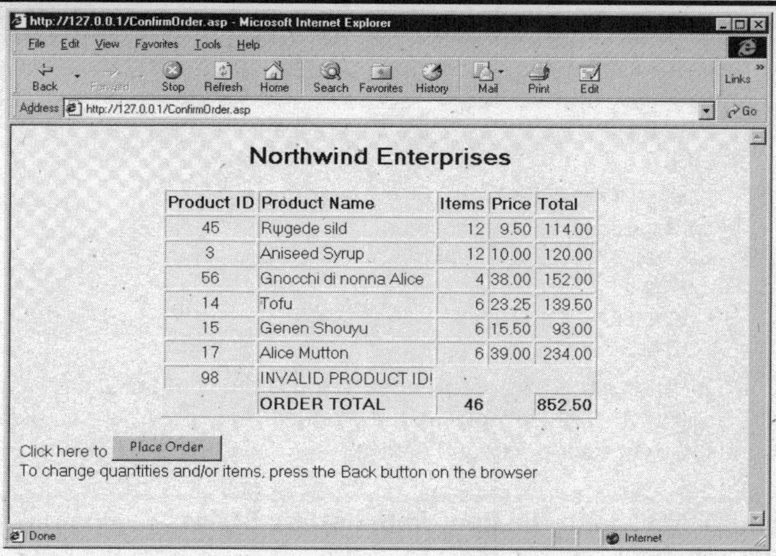

FIGURE 13.20: The ConfirmOrder.asp script confirms the order placed through the GetOrder.asp page.

Here's the listing of the `GetOrder.asp` script:

LISTING 13.9: The GetOrder.asp Script

```
<HTML>
<CENTER>
<H1>Northwind Enterprises</H1>
<H2>Web Order Form</H2>
<HR>
<FORM ACTION="ConfirmOrder.asp" METHOD=POST>
<TABLE>
<TR>
<TD><B>ProductID</B>
<TD><B>Qty</B>
<TD>    
<TD><B>ProductID</B>
<TD><B>Qty</B>
<%
For i=1 to 10
   Response.Write "<TR><TD><INPUT TYPE=TEXT SIZE=10 _
           NAME=ProdID><TD><INPUT TYPE=TEXT SIZE=5 NAME=QTY>"
```

```
        Response.Write "<TD><TD><INPUT TYPE=TEXT SIZE=10 _
                NAME=ProdID><TD><INPUT TYPE=TEXT SIZE=5 NAME=QTY>"
    Next
    %>
    </TABLE>
    <HR>
    <INPUT TYPE=SUBMIT VALUE="Place Order">
        
    <INPUT TYPE=RESET  VALUE=" Reset Form ">
    </FORM>
    </CENTER>
    </HTML>
```

The interesting part of this application is the `ConfirmOrder.asp` script (Listing 13.10), which looks up the product IDs in the Northwind database and retrieves their prices and names.

LISTING 13.10: The ConfirmOrder.asp Script

```
<%
    AllProducts = Request.Form
    ProductList = "(" & Request.Form("ProdID")(1)
    For i=2 to 20
        currID = Trim(Request.Form("ProdID")(i))
        If Len(currID) > 0 And IsNumeric(currID) Then
            ProductList = ProductList & ", " & _
                          Request.Form("ProdID")(i)
        End IF
    Next
    ProductList=ProductList & ")"
    Set DBConnection=Server.CreateObject("ADODB.Connection")
    DBConnection.Open "NWINDDB"
    SQLArgument = "SELECT ProductID, ProductName, UnitPrice "
    SQLArgument = SQLArgument & "FROM Products WHERE
➥ProductID "
    SQLArgument = SQLArgument & "IN " & ProductList
    Set SelProducts = Server.CreateObject("ADODB.Recordset")
    SelProducts.Open SQLArgument, DBConnection, 2
    HTMLOut = "<BODY BGCOLOR=lightyellow>"
    HTMLOut = HTMLOut & "<FONT FACE='MS Sans Serif'>"
    HTMLOut = HTMLOut & "<CENTER>"
    HTMLOut = HTMLOut & "<H2>Northwind Enterprises</H2>"
```

```
    HTMLOut = HTMLOut & "<TABLE BORDER=FRAME BGCOLOR=light
➥cyan>"
    HTMLOut = HTMLOut & "<TR><TD><B>Product ID</B>"
    HTMLOut = HTMLOut & "<TD><B>Product Name</B>"
    HTMLOut = HTMLOut & "<TD><B>Items</B><TD><B>Price</B>"
    HTMLOut = HTMLOut & "<TD><B>Total</B>"
    HTMLOut = HTMLOut & "<TR>"
    iProd=1
    HLine=""
    For iProd=1 to 20
        ProdID=Request.Form("ProdID")(iProd)
        Items=Request.Form("QTY")(iProd)
        SelProducts.MoveFirst
        If IsNumeric(ProdID) And Len(ProdID) > 0 _
                             And IsNumeric(Items) Then
            If Items > 0 Then
                SelProducts.Find "ProductID=" & ProdID
                Cells=Cells+1
                If SelProducts.EOF Then
                    HTMLOut = HTMLOut & "<TD ALIGN=CENTER>" &
➥_
                    ProdID & "<TD> INVALID PRODUCT
➥ID!<TD><TD>"
                Else
                    Price=SelProducts.Fields("UnitPrice")
                    HTMLOut = HTMLOut & "<TD ALIGN=CENTER>" &
➥_
                    SelProducts.Fields("ProductID") & "   " &
➥_
                    "<TD>" & SelProducts.Fields("ProductName")
➥& _
                    "   " & "<TD ALIGN=RIGHT>" & Items & _
                    "<TD ALIGN=RIGHT>" & _
                     FormatNumber(Price, 2) &  _
                    "<TD ALIGN=RIGHT>" & _
                    FormatNumber(Price * Items, 2)
                    HLine=HLine & ProdID & Space(6-
➥Len(ProdID))
                    HLine=HLine & Price & Space(6-Len(Price))
                    HLine=HLine & Items & Space(6-Len(Items))
```

Part iii

```
                    OrderTotal = OrderTotal + Price * Items
                    OrderItems = OrderItems + CInt(Items)
                End If
                HTMLOut = HTMLOut & "<TR>"
            End If
        End If
    Next
    HTMLOut = HTMLOut & "<TD><TD><B>ORDER TOTAL</B>"
    HTMLOut = HTMLOut & "<TD ALIGN=RIGHT><B>" & OrderItems
    HTMLOut = HTMLOut & "</B><TD><TD ALIGN=RIGHT><B>"
    HTMLOut = HTMLOut & "FormatNumber(OrderTotal, 2) & "</B>"
    HTMLOut = HTMLOut & "</TABLE>"
    HTMLOut = HTMLOut & "</CENTER>"
    HTMLOut = HTMLOut & "<FORM ACTION='AcceptOrder.asp' _
                         METHOD='POST'>"
    HTMLOut = HTMLOut & "<INPUT TYPE=HIDDEN NAME=All VALUE="
➥& _
                        Server.URLEncode(HLine) & ">"
    HTMLOut = HTMLOut & "Click here to "
    HTMLOut = HTMLOut & _
             "<INPUT TYPE=SUBMIT VALUE='Place Order'><BR>"
    HTMLOut = HTMLOut & "To change quantities and/or items, _
              press the Back button on the browser"
    HTMLOut = HTMLOut & "</FORM>"
    Response.Write HTMLOut
%>
```

This script doesn't iterate through the product IDs and look up each one. To avoid the execution of many commands against the database, it generates a comma-separated list of Product IDs and then uses this list with the IN clause of a SELECT statement. The recordset returned by this statement contains the names and the prices of all the products specified on the form of the `GetOrder.asp` page. Product IDs without quantities are ignored. The script can then process the recordset locally, without any additional database queries.

The ConfirmOrder script doesn't place orders; it simply confirms them. A viewer who wants to change the products and/or quantities must click the Back button to return to the GetOrder page. To actually place the order, the user must click the Place Order button at the bottom of the form. This button calls the AcceptOrder script on the server (you'll see how this script handles the order later in the chapter). The ConfirmOrder script must also pass the list of Product IDs and quantities to the AcceptOrder script by building a long string with the Product IDs, prices, and quantities, and placing it on a Hidden control. The user never sees this control (and can't change it, of course). When the Place Order button is clicked, the control's contents are submitted to the server.

Each order line has a length of 18 characters and contains three fields of six characters: one each for the product's ID, the price, and the quantity of the specific product. This technique enables you to add rows to multiple tables of the Northwind database with a single command. You'll see how the order will be added to the database later in this chapter.

The form with the Hidden control and the button is inserted at the bottom of the ConfirmOrder script with a <FORM> tag. Here are the statements that insert the <FORM> tag:

```
HTMLOut = HTMLOut & "<FORM ACTION='AcceptOrder.asp' _
                     METHOD='POST'>"
HTMLOut = HTMLOut & "<INPUT TYPE=HIDDEN NAME=All VALUE=" & _
                    Server.URLEncode(HLine) & ">"
HTMLOut = HTMLOut & "Click here to "
HTMLOut = HTMLOut & _
         "<INPUT TYPE=SUBMIT VALUE='Place Order'><BR>"
HTMLOut = HTMLOut & "To change quantities and/or items, _
          press the Back button on the browser"
HTMLOut = HTMLOut & "</FORM>"
```

To place the long string with the order's information on the Hidden control, the script encodes it as a URL string with the URLEncode method, so that it can be transmitted to the server with the POST method. Here's what the <FORM> tags look like on the client:

```
<FORM ACTION='AcceptOrder.asp' METHOD='POST'>
<INPUT TYPE=HIDDEN NAME=All
VALUE=45++++9%2E5+++12++++3+++++10++++12++++56++++38
++++4+++++14++++23%2E25+6+++++15++++15%2E5++6+++++17
++++39++++6+++++>
Click here to <INPUT TYPE=SUBMIT VALUE='Place Order'>
<BR>
To change quantities and/or items, press the Back
    button on the browser
</FORM>
```

The `AcceptOrder.asp` script can be found on the sample code from the Sybex website. This script retrieves the single parameter value and replaces the plus signs with spaces before processing it. Notice that the decimal point is encoded as %2E. The script must also replace all instances of the string %2E with a period before breaking up the string into its components, and then process the order. Of course, you don't need to confirm the order. You could retrieve the order's details from within the ConfirmOrder.asp script. It's actually simpler to do so, but I've chosen to include the AcceptOrder.asp script to show you how to pass information to a server-side script from within a page's code, without user interaction.

Updating a Database

The second basic requirement of an online store is to store orders to a database. To update a database from within an ASP file, you can use ADO, just as you would do from within your VB applications. The simpler method is to call the AddNew method and then use the Recordset object's Fields collection to assign the values passed by the browser to the appropriate fields. You can also create an INSERT statement with the appropriate arguments from within the ASP script and execute it against the database with the Command object.

As usual, you must validate the data supplied by the client. First, you should make sure that the non-nullable fields have valid values. If they don't, you must display another page, prompting the user to correct any errors and resubmit the page. To view the form, the user must click the browser's Back button. After the initial validation, you must make sure that the new record will not be rejected by the database. The usual approach is to attempt to locate the record with same key field(s). If such a record exists, you must prompt the user again. If everything goes well, you can add the new record with the AddNew method, assign values to the fields, and finally commit the new record with the Update method. Let's look at an example of adding new records to the database. The example of this section allows users to register through the Web.

A Customer Registration Form

The form shown in Figure 13.21 allows the viewer to enter information for the purposes of an online registration. If you open the RegNewCustomer.htm page with your browser, you will see that the mandatory fields are displayed in red. After entering the required data on the form's controls, the user can submit the form to the server by clicking the Submit button.

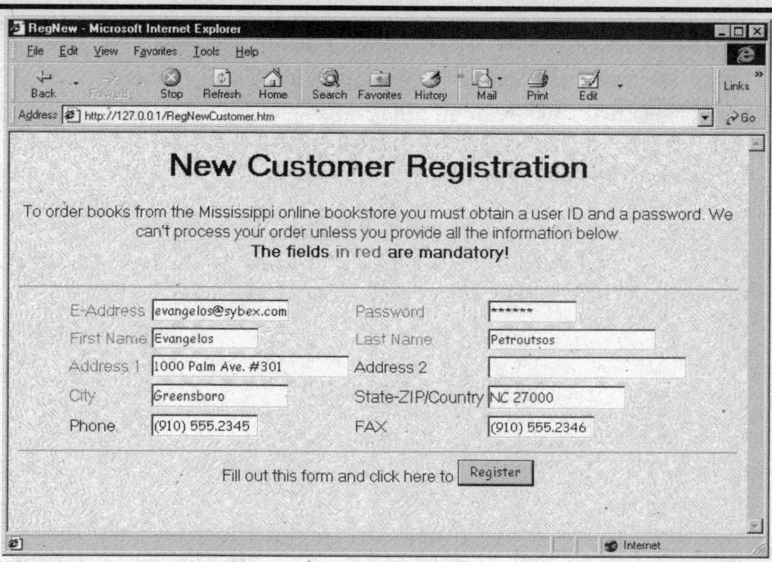

FIGURE 13.21: The RegNewCustomer.htm page accepts registration information from the viewer and submits it to the server.

The HTML source of the RegNewCustomer.htm page is shown next. The form on this page submits the control values to the RegisterNew .asp script using the GET method.

LISTING 13.11: The RegNewCustomer.htm Page

```
<HTML><FONT FACE='MS Sans Serif'>
<HEAD>
<meta http-equiv="Content-Type"
content="text/html">
<TITLE>RegNew</TITLE>
</HEAD>
<BODY BGCOLOR=#F0F0B0>
<CENTER>
<FONT SIZE="6"><B>New Customer Registration</B></FONT>
<P>To order books from the Mississippi online bookstore
you must obtain a user ID and a password.
We can't process your order unless you provide all the
information below.
<BR>
<B>The fields <FONT COLOR=red>in red</FONT> are mandatory!
```

```
</B>
<P>
<FORM NAME=RegNew ACTION=/ASPages/RegisterNew.ASP
    METHOD="GET">
<HR>
<TABLE BORDER="0">
    <TR>
        <TD><FONT COLOR=red>E-Address
        <TD><input type="text" size="20" name="EMail">
        <TD><FONT COLOR=red>Password
        <TD><input type="text" size="12" name="Password">
    <TR>
        <TD><FONT COLOR=red>First Name
        <TD><input type="text" size="15" name="FName">
        <TD><FONT COLOR=red>Last Name
        <TD><input type="text" size="25" name="LName">
    <TR>
        <TD><FONT COLOR=red>Address 1
        <TD><input type="text" size="30" name="Address1">
        <TD>Address 2
        <TD><input type="text" size="30" name="Address2">
    <TR>
        <TD><FONT COLOR=red>City
        <TD><input type="text" size="20" name="City">
        <TD>State-ZIP/Country
        <TD><input type="text" size="20" name="ZIP">
    <TR>
        <TD><FONT>Phone
        <TD><INPUT TYPE="text" size="15" name="Phone">
        <TD>FAX
        <TD><input type="text" size="15" name="FAX">
    <TR>
</TABLE>
<HR>
Fill out this form and click here to <INPUT TYPE=SUBMIT
VALUE="Register">
</FORM>
</BODY>
</HTML>
```

To test this page, you need a database with a table in which new registrations will be entered. I have created a new database with a single table, the RegCustomers table. In Chapter 16, where you'll build an online bookstore, you'll be asked to add this table to the Biblio database, so you might as well do it now. Here are the fields of the RegCustomers table:

EMail	char(20)
Password	char(12)
FName	char(15)
LName	char(25)
Address1	char(30)
Address2	char(30)
City	char(20)
StateZip	char(20)
Phone	char(15)

The ASP script assumes that the DSN for the database with the RegCustomers table is WEBOrders. If you use a different name, modify the `RegisterNew.asp` script accordingly. Let's look at the script that processes the registration data. The `RegisterNew.asp` script extracts the parameter values submitted to the server through the Request.QueryString object. First, it validates the data; in the case of an error, it redirects the viewer to an `InvalidRegData.htm` page with the following statements:

```
If CustEmail = "" Or CustPassword = "" Or _
   CustFName = "" Or  CustLName = "" Then
      Response.Redirect "InvalidRegData.htm"
      Response.End
End If
```

The `InvalidRegData.htm` file should contain a message indicating that all required data was not supplied and should prompt the user to click the Back button to return to the previous page.

Then, it displays the data on a new page (this is a debugging aid so you don't really need to display the control values). Before committing any data to the database, the script attempts to locate a record with the same e-mail and password. If such a record doesn't exist, this is a first-time customer who is then registered. If the record exists, the script welcomes the user. This application is not very elaborate. It requires that the e-mail and password combination be unique. Usually, each customer is identified by a single field. If the e-mail field exists in the database, but the password is incorrect, the script should not register the user. Most likely, the user has mistyped the password and the script should not register a customer with the same e-mail twice.

Here's the listing of the ASP script that processes the registration data on the server:

LISTING 13.12: The RegisterNew.asp Script

```
<%
   CustEMail = Request.QueryString("EMail")
   CustPassword = Request.QueryString("Password")
   CustFName = Request.QueryString("FName")
   CustLName = Request.QueryString("LName")
   CustAddr1 = Request.QueryString("Address1")
   CustAddr2 = Request.QueryString("Address2")
   CustCity = Request.QueryString("City")
   CustZIP = Request.QueryString("ZIP")
   CustPhone = Request.QueryString("Phone")
   CustFAX = Request.QueryString("FAX")
   CustMyAddress = Request.QueryString("MyAddress")
   CustMailPromo = Request.QueryString("MailPromo")
   If CustEmail = "" Or CustPassword = "" Or
      CustFName = "" Or    CustLName = "" Then
      Response.Redirect "InvalidRegData.htm"
      Response.End
   End If
   Response.Write "<HTML><FONT FACE='MS Sans Serif'>"
   Response.Write "<BODY BGCOLOR=#F0F0B0>"
   Response.Write "<HR>"
   Response.Write CustEMail & "   
                                 "
   Response.Write CustPassword & "<BR>"
   Response.Write CustLName & ", "
   Response.Write CustFName & "<BR>"
   Response.Write CustAddr1 & "<BR>"
   Response.Write CustAddr2 & "<BR>"
   Response.Write CustCity & "   
                                "
   Response.Write CustZIP & "<BR>"
   Response.Write CustPhone & "   
                                 "
   Response.Write CustFAX & "<BR>"
   Response.Write "<HR>"
```

```
    SQLArgument = "SELECT * FROM RegCustomers WHERE " &
        EMail='" UCase(CustEMail) & "'" & " AND  &
        Password='" & CustPassword & "'"
    connectString="DSN=WEBOrders;User ID=sa;password="
    adOpenKeyset = 1
    adUseServer = 2
    adLockOptimistic=3
    Set SelTitles=Server.CreateObject("ADODB.Recordset")
    SelTitles.CursorLocation=adUseServer
    SelTitles.Open SQLArgument, connectString,
       adOpenDynamic, adLockOptimistic
    If SelTitles.EOF Then
       SelTitles.AddNew
       SelTitles.Fields("EMail")=CustEMail
       SelTitles.Fields("Password")=CustPassword
       SelTitles.Fields("LName")=CustLName
       SelTitles.Fields("FName")=CustFName
       SelTitles.Fields("Address1")=CustAddr1
       SelTitles.Fields("Address2")=CustAddr2
       SelTitles.Fields("City")=CustCity
       SelTitles.Fields("StateZIP")=CustZIP
       SelTitles.Fields("Phone")=CustPhone
       SelTitles.Fields("FAX")=CustFAX
       SelTitles.Update
       Response.Write "<FONT SIZE=+2>You were successfully
registered!</FONT>"
    Else
       SelTitles.MoveFirst
       Response.Write "<FONT SIZE=+2>Welcome back " &
           CustFName & CustLName & "</FONT>"
    End If
    SelTitles.Close
    Set SelTitles=Nothing
%>
```

You can explore this project on your own and modify the script so that it registers users by their e-mail address only. If an existing address is specified with a different password, the script should display a page, explaining that the e-mail address is already assigned and giving the user a chance to correct the password and try again. As you understand, I'm using the e-mail address as user ID because this is a unique string and people don't forget it.

The File Access Component

The *File Access component* consists of two objects that give your scripts access to text files: the FileSystemObject object and the TextStream object, which were introduced with VBScript 2.0. The FileSystemObject object gives your script access to the server computer's file system, and the TextStream object lets your script open, read from, and write to text files. These objects can't be used with binary files, because this would make VBScript unsafe even on the server.

The FileSystemObject Object

The *FileSystemObject object* gives your script access to the server computer's file system and is available only with the server-side VBScript. To gain access to server's file system, you must create a FileSystemObject variable with the CreateObject method:

```
Set fs = CreateObject("Scripting.FileSystemObject")
```

The *fs* variable represents the file system. You can use the FileSystemObject object to access text files on the server computer's disk with the methods described next.

CreateTextFile Method

The first method of the FileSystemObject object creates a text file that returns a TextStream object that can be used to read from or write to the file. The syntax of the CreateTextFile method is

```
fs.CreateTextFile(filename, overwrite, unicode)
```

The *filename* argument specifies the name of the file to be created and is the only required argument. *overwrite* is a Boolean value that indicates whether you can overwrite an existing file (if True) or not (if False). If the overwrite argument is omitted, existing files are not overwritten. The last argument, *unicode*, indicates whether the file is created as a Unicode or ASCII file. If the *unicode* argument is True, the new file will be created as a Unicode file; otherwise, it will be created as an ASCII file. If omitted, an ASCII file is assumed.

To create a new text file, you must first create a FileSystemObject object variable and then call its CreateTextFile method as follows:

```
Set fs = CreateObject("Scripting.FileSystemObject")
Set TStream = fs.CreateTextFile("c:\testfile.txt", True)
```

The *TStream* variable represents a TextStream object, whose methods allow you to write to or read from the specified file.

OpenTextFile Method

In addition to creating a new text file, you can open an existing file with the OpenTextFile method, whose syntax is

```
Set TStream = fs.OpenTextFile(filename, iomode, create, format)
```

The OpenTextFile method opens the specified file and returns a TextStream object that can be used to read from or write to the file.

The *filename* argument is the only required one. Of the remaining optional arguments, *iomode* can be one of the constants:

ForReading The file is opened for reading data.

ForAppending The file is opened for appending data.

The *create* optional argument is a Boolean value that indicates whether a new file can be created if the specified filename doesn't exist. The last argument, *format*, is also optional. It can have one of the following values, which indicate the format of the opened file. If the format argument is True, the file is opened in Unicode mode; if it's False, the file is opened in ASCII mode. If omitted, the file is opened using the system default (ASCII).

To open a TextStream object for reading, use the following statements:

```
Set fs = CreateObject("Scripting.FileSystemObject")
Set TStream = fs.OpenTextFile("c:\testfile.txt", ForReading)
```

Like the CreateTextFile method, the OpenTextFile method returns a TextStream object, whose methods allow you to write to or read from the specified file.

The TextStream Object's Methods

After a TextStream object is created with the CreateTextFile or the OpenTextFile method, you can use the following methods to read from and write to the file:

Read The Read method reads a specified number of characters from a TextStream object. Its syntax is

```
TStream.Read(characters)
```

where *characters* is the number of characters to be read from.

ReadAll The ReadAll method reads an entire TextStream (text file) and returns the resulting string. Its syntax is simply the following:

```
TStream.ReadAll
```

ReadLine The ReadLine method reads one line of text at a time (up to, but not including, the new-line character) from a TextStream file and returns the resulting string. Its syntax is

```
TStream.ReadLine
```

Skip Method The Skip method skips a specified number of characters when reading a TextStream file. Its syntax is

```
TStream.Skip(characters)
```

where *characters* is the number of characters to be skipped.

SkipLine The SkipLine method skips the next line when reading from a TextStream and its syntax is

```
TStream.SkipLine
```

The characters of the skipped lines are discarded, up to and including the next new-line character.

Write The Write method writes the specified string to a TextStream file. Its syntax is

```
TStream.Write(string)
```

where `string` is the string (literal or variable) to be written to the file. Strings are written to the file with no intervening spaces or characters between each string. Use the WriteLine method to write a new-line character or a string that ends with a new-line character.

WriteLine The WriteLine method writes the specified string followed by a new-line character to the file. Its syntax is

```
TStream.WriteLine(string)
```

where *string* is the text you want to write to the file. If you call the WriteLine method without an argument, a new-line character is written to the file.

WriteBlankLines The WriteBlankLines method writes a specified number of blank lines (new-line characters) to the file. Its syntax is

```
TStream.WriteBlankLines(lines)
```

where *lines* is the number of blank lines to be inserted in the file.

The TextStream Object's Properties

The *TextStream object* provides several properties that allow your code to know where the pointer is in the current TextStream. These properties are:

AtEndOfLine This is a read-only property that returns True if the file pointer is at the end of a line in the TextStream object; otherwise, it returns False. The AtEndOfLine property applies to files that are open for reading. You can use this property to read a line of characters, one at a time, with a loop similar to the following one:

```
Do While TSream.AtEndOfLine =False
    newChar = TStream.Read(1)
    {process character}
Loop
```

AtEndOfStream This is another read-only property that returns True if the file pointer is at the end of the TextStream object. The AtEndOfStream property applies only to TextStream files that are open for reading. You can use this property to read an entire file, one line at a time, with a loop like the following one:

```
Do While TStream.AtEndOfStream = False
    newChar = TStream.ReadLine
    {process line}
Loop
```

Column This is another read-only property that returns the column number of the current character in a TextStream line. The first character in a line is in column 1. Use this property to read data arranged in columns, without tab or other delimiters between them.

Line This is a read-only property that returns the current line number in the TextStream. The Line property of the first line in a TextStream object is 1.

Using the TextStream Object

The `TextFile.asp` page demonstrates several of the TextStream object's methods. When this file is called, it creates a text file on the server computer and writes a few lines in it. Then, it opens the file, reads its lines, and displays them on an HTML page (shown in Figure 13.22), which is returned to the client computer. As you will see, it uses the Write method of the Response object to send its output to the client.

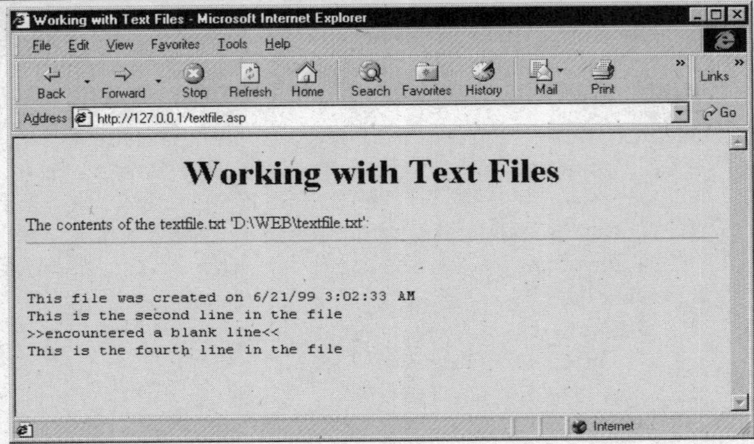

FIGURE 13.22: The output of the TextFile.asp page, which reads the lines of a text file on the server and displays them on the browser's window on the client.

LISTING 13.13: The TextFile.asp Script

```
<HTML>
<HEAD>
<TITLE>Working with Text Files</TITLE>
</HEAD>
<BODY BGCOLOR=#E0E0E0>
<CENTER>
<H1>Working with Text Files</H1>
</CENTER>
<%
  Set FileObj = Server.CreateObject
    ("Scripting.FileSystemObject")
  TestFile = Server.MapPath ("/ASPages/textfile.txt")
  Set OutStream= FileObj.CreateTextFile
    (TestFile, True, False)
  str1 = "This file was created on " & Now()
  OutStream.WriteLine Str1
  OutStream.WriteLine "This is the second line in the file"
  OutStream.WriteBlankLines(1)
  OutStream.WriteLine "This is the fourth line in the file"
  Set OutStream = Nothing
  Response.Write "The contents of the textfile.txt '" & _
                TestFile & "':<BR>"
```

```
   Response.Write "<HR>"
   Set InStream= FileObj.OpenTextFile _
                 (TestFile, 1, False, False)
%>
   <PRE>
<%
   Response.Write Instream.Readline & "<BR>"
   While InStream.AtEndOfStream = False
    TLine = Instream.ReadLine
    If Trim(TLine) <> "" Then
            Response.Write TLine & "<BR>"
         Else
            Response.Write ">>encountered a blank line<<" &
               "<BR>"
         End If
   Wend
   Set Instream=Nothing
%>
</PRE>
</BODY>
</HTML>
```

The Server object's CreateObject method is used to create a FileSystemObject object, through which the script can access the server's hard disk. Then, it calls the MapPath method, to map a virtual folder to the actual folder name and specify a full path name. OutStream is a TextStream object, whose Write method you use to write to the file. After the desired lines are written to the file, you set the TextStream object variable to Nothing to release the resources it occupied.

In the second half of the script, you create another TextStream object to read the lines of the same file. The file's lines are read with a While ... Wend loop, which examines the value of the TextStream object's AtEndOfStream property to find out how many lines to read from the file:

```
While InStream.AtEndOfStream = False
   TLine = Instream.ReadLine
   {process Tline text line}
Wend
```

The output is formatted with the <CODE> tag to display them as a listing. Notice that the use of the Response object minimized the need for <% and %> delimiter tags.

SUMMARY

In this chapter, you've learned the structure of web applications, how to build server-side scripts that use the ASP objects, and how to maintain state among the various pages of a website. The tool we used to build the examples is the simplest one there is: NotePad. You won't find many developers building websites from scratch. There are many tools that automate the design and programming of a site, one of them being Microsoft's Visual InterDev. Before you can use any tool to design a web application, however, you must understand the ASP objects and server-side scripting. Now that you can write server-side scripts with NotePad, things can only get easier.

Now that we've covered how to connect to and work with databases over the Web, we're ready to tackle more complex data access issues. Therefore, next chapter will cover handling transactions over the Web.

Chapter 14

Controlling Transactions in ASP

In the previous chapter, we looked at how to access databases from ASP pages using various technologies, including VBScript and ADO. We used the ADO Connection and Recordset objects to both retrieve and update data. However, the updates were fairly simple, typically involving a single record. In more complex applications, you may need to perform a sequence of updates as a single unit; this is called a *transaction*.

A transaction is a unit of work that must either succeed completely or fail completely. A transaction is a *failure* if any of the actions taken during the transaction fail. In other words, all actions in a transaction must succeed for the transaction to be successful, but only one action must fail for the entire transaction to fail. Transactions can be managed directly in SQL Server, but that's not the only way to manage transactions in

Adapted from *Mastering™ Active Server Pages 3* by A. Russell Jones

ISBN 0-7821-2619-1 928 pages $49.99

ASP. An ASP page itself can manage transactions where the work for the transaction occurs in external components and in SQL Server. All of this happens through Microsoft Transaction Server (MTS) or COM+ services in Windows 2000.

NOTE

For brevity, I'm going to use the term MTS/COM+ in this book. Those of you running Windows NT 4 should think MTS and ignore the COM+ terminology. Those of you running Windows 2000 should think COM+ Application whenever you see the term MTS.

In this chapter, we'll cover how MTS/COM+ handles transactions. We'll look at an example of how to implement transactions directly in your ASP code. You're most likely using components to handle database interaction in your ASP pages, so this chapter also covers how MTS/COM+ handles transactions in your components. You'll also find out how to create packages for your components in both MTS and COM+.

Introduction to MTS/COM+ Applications

MTS/COM+ serves two purposes. First, as its name implies, it manages transactions. Second, it provides a memory space in which to run and manage component instances. In Windows NT, you manage MTS with a Microsoft Management Control (MMC) application called *Transaction Server Explorer*. MTS doesn't appear as a separate item in Windows 2000; you access it through the Component Services administrative application under the name COM+ Applications. Nevertheless, the functionality and much of the administrative interface and procedures are similar between the two server versions. You've already seen some components that you instantiated with ASP, but you may not know that those components are already running in MTS/COM+. Yes, that's right, all IIS applications, including the root Web, pooled IIS applications, and IIS applications that run in their own memory space, run in MTS/COM+.

MTS/COM+ manages components by intercepting the `Server.CreateObject` call. When you create an object, MTS/COM+ intercepts the call, creates the object within MTS/COM+, and passes back an object reference that points to the MTS/COM+ instance of that object. Your code uses the object normally. When the page ends or you destroy the object explicitly,

MTS/COM+ doesn't actually destroy the object. The object remains instantiated and ready for another call to one of its methods or properties.

The end result is that MTS/COM+ lets you avoid much of the overhead of object creation and destruction by maintaining a pool of live objects in memory. Because IIS applications run inside MTS/COM+, your websites can take advantage of MTS/COM+ transactions with a few simple commands.

MTS/COM+ is completely integrated with SQL Server via the Distributed Transaction Coordinator (DTC). The DTC acts as a transaction manager and coordinates transactions in a distributed environment. When you create transactional ASP pages, you don't need to test the transaction results yourself; instead, MTS/COM+ raises events that let you know whether the transaction succeeded or failed. MTS/COM+ considers all calls to transactionally aware components and database calls that occur within the transactional page to be part of the transaction.

MTS/COM+ raises events through the ObjectContext object, which is ASP's connection to MTS/COM+.

The ObjectContext Object

The ObjectContext object appeared with IIS 4 and does not work with IIS 3.0. I haven't introduced it before now, because you don't need it until you're either writing transactional pages or writing components for use with ASP.

The ObjectContext object has two purposes. First, it gives other components access to the same transactional context as your ASP page, which means those other components use the ObjectContext object to gain references to the other ASP intrinsic objects, such as the Request and Response objects. It also manages transactions, ensuring that all components created on a page are within the context of the transaction for that page. Like the other ASP intrinsic objects, your pages have access to the ObjectContext object automatically—you don't have to create one with the `Server.CreateObject` method. The object has two methods, as shown in Table 14.1.

TABLE 14.1: ObjectContext Object Methods

METHOD	DESCRIPTION
`SetComplete`	Completes a portion of a transaction. Each component involved in the transaction must also call the `SetComplete` method. When all components in the transaction have called `SetComplete`, the transaction will complete.

TABLE 14.1 continued: ObjectContext Object Methods

METHOD	DESCRIPTION
`SetAbort`	Rolls back a transaction. The `SetAbort` method prevents the components involved in the transaction from updating any resources, leaving the resources in the same state they were in prior to the beginning of the transaction.

The ObjectContext object also raises two events, as shown in Table 14.2.

TABLE 14.2: ObjectContext Object Events

EVENT	DESCRIPTION
`OnTransactionCommit`	This event fires when the transactional script and all the components involved in the transaction have called the `SetComplete` method.
`OnTransactionAbort`	This event fires if any of the components involved in the transaction call the `SetAbort` method.

Before you can use these methods and events in an ASP script, you must declare your script as a transactional script. In the next section, you'll see how to do that.

ASP AND TRANSACTIONS

The first step in an ASP transaction is to create a *transactional script*. To do that, place the `@TRANSACTION=<transactionMode>` directive at the top of the page. The `transactionMode` constant can take one of the values shown in Table 14.3.

TABLE 14.3: *ASP transactionMode* Constants

VALUE	DESCRIPTION
`REQUIRES NEW`	Starts a new transaction.
`REQUIRED`	Starts a new transaction.
`SUPPORTED`	Does not start a transaction.
`NOT_SUPPORTED`	Does not start a transaction.

Although you can use any of the four values in an ASP script, only the first two begin a transaction. There are four values, so that you can have components participate in a transaction, but not actually start a transaction. You must place the `@Transaction` directive on the first line in the script, otherwise ASP raises an error. You can combine directives on the same line, but you cannot enter both the `@LANGUAGE` and `@TRANSACTION` directives on separate lines. For example:

```
<%@ Language=VBScript @TRANSACTION=REQUIRED %>
```

The directive begins a transaction. When the transaction succeeds or fails, the ObjectContext object raises either the `OnTransactionCommit` or `OnTransactionAbort` event. You can define subroutines to handle these events by naming the subroutines with the name of the event. For example:

```
<%
Sub onTransactionCommit()
    Response.Write "<br>Transaction Committed<Br>"
End Sub
Sub onTransactionAbort()
    Response.Write "<br>Transaction Aborted<br>"
End Sub
%>
```

If the transaction succeeds, the `onTransactionCommit` subroutine executes. If the transaction fails, the `onTransactionAbort` subroutine executes. In neither case can you reverse the outcome of the transaction. For example, you can't successfully use the `onTransactionCommit` routine to call the `ObjectContext.SetAbort` method, because the transaction has already committed by the time the `onTransactionCommit` routine begins executing.

Listing 14.1 contains all the necessary parts for a transaction. It begins a transaction, uses a SQL statement to update a table row, then explicitly calls the `SetAbort` method to roll back the result. Note that the script does not use SQL Server's `BEGIN TRAN` or `ROLLBACK TRAN` methods to create or control a transaction. MTS/COM+ automatically begins and rolls back the SQL Server transaction for you.

Listing 14.1: Sample Transactional Script

```
<%@ Language=VBScript @TRANSACTION=REQUIRED %>
<%
Sub onTransactionCommit()
    Response.Write "<br>Transaction Committed<Br>"
End Sub
```

```
Sub onTransactionAbort()
    Response.Write "<br>Transaction Aborted<br>"
End Sub
%>

<HTML>
<HEAD>
</HEAD>
<BODY>
<%
Dim conn
Dim SQL
Dim aConnectionString
aConnectionString = "Provider=SQLOLEDB;Data " _
   & "Source=(local);Database=ClassRecords;" _
   & "UID=sa;PWD=;"
Set conn = Server.CreateObject("ADODB.Connection")
conn.Mode = adModeRead
conn.ConnectionString = aConnectionString
conn.CursorLocation = adUseClient
conn.open
SQL = "Update Students SET Grade = 4 WHERE LastName='Chen'"
conn.Execute SQL
ObjectContext.SetAbort
%>
</BODY>
</HTML>
```

To prove to yourself that the SQL statement actually executed properly, you can add two SELECT statements surrounding the UPDATE statement. Listing 14.2 shows the script.

Listing 14.2: SetAbort Method Rolls Back SQL Server Transaction

```
<%@ Language=VBScript @TRANSACTION=REQUIRED %>
<%
Sub onTransactionCommit()
    Dim conn
    Dim SQL
    Dim aConnectionString
    aConnectionString = "Provider=SQLOLEDB;Data " _
       & "Source=(local);Database=ClassRecords;" _
       & "UID=sa;PWD=;"
```

```
    Set conn = Server.CreateObject("ADODB.Connection")
    conn.Mode = adModeRead
    conn.ConnectionString = aConnectionString
    conn.CursorLocation = adUseClient
    conn.open
    SQL = "SELECT Grade FROM Students WHERE LastName='Chen'"
    Set R = conn.execute(SQL, , adCmdText)
    Response.Write "After commit, grade = " &
        R("Grade").Value & "<br>"
    R.Close
    Response.Write "<br>Transaction Committed<Br>"
End Sub
Sub onTransactionAbort()
    Dim conn
    Dim SQL
    Dim aConnectionString
    aConnectionString = "Provider=SQLOLEDB;Data " _
       & "Source=(local);Database=ClassRecords;" _
       & "UID=sa;PWD=;"
    Set conn = Server.CreateObject("ADODB.Connection")
    conn.Mode = adModeRead
    conn.ConnectionString = aConnectionString
    conn.CursorLocation = adUseClient
    conn.open
    SQL = "SELECT Grade FROM Students WHERE LastName='Chen'"
    Set R = conn.execute(SQL, , adCmdText)
    Response.Write "After abort, grade = " &
        R("Grade").Value & "<br>"
    R.Close
    Response.Write "<br>Transaction Aborted<br>"
End Sub
%>
<html>
<head>
</head>
<body>
<%
Dim conn
Dim SQL
Dim aConnectionString
aConnectionString = "Provider=SQLOLEDB;Data " _
   & "Source=(local);Database=ClassRecords;" _
```

Part iii

```
    & "UID=sa;PWD=;"
Set conn = Server.CreateObject("ADODB.Connection")
conn.Mode = adModeRead
conn.ConnectionString = aConnectionString
conn.CursorLocation = adUseClient
conn.open
SQL = "SELECT Grade FROM Students WHERE LastName='Chen'"
Set R = conn.execute(SQL, , adCmdText)
Response.Write "Before update, grade = " &
    R("Grade").Value & "<br>"
R.Close
SQL = "Update Students SET Grade = 4 WHERE LastName='Chen'"
conn.execute SQL, , adCmdText
SQL = "SELECT Grade FROM Students WHERE LastName='Chen'"
Set R = conn.execute(SQL, , adCmdText)
Response.Write "After update, Grade = " &
    R("Grade").Value & "<br>"
R.Close
ObjectContext.SetAbort
Set conn = Nothing
%>
</body>
</html>
```

When you run this script, it looks like Figure 14.1.

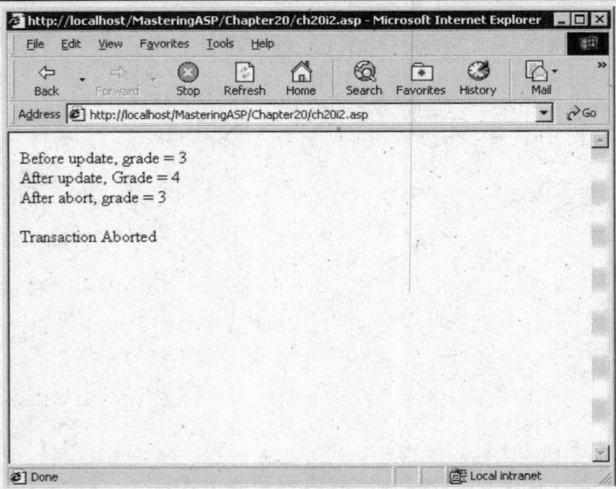

FIGURE 14.1: Transactional script (ch20i2.asp)

COMPONENTS AND MTS/COM+ TRANSACTIONS

The examples in the previous section were simplistic. You can control more than SQL Server with MTS/COM+ transactions; you can control components as well. You haven't seen how to create components yet, but to illustrate the point, I've included a small component in the sample code as a VB-generated DLL called `UpdateStudent.dll`. This DLL changes a student's last name, first name, or grade.

The component works in concert with two HTML forms. You alter the information in the form. First, select a student from the list and click Details (see Figure 14.2).

The application then displays the details for that student. You can change the contents of any field or fields and click Save to save your changes. You've seen forms similar to this already; the difference is that this form submits its information to a page that requires a transaction. When you submit this form, it creates a `ClassRecords.CStudent` component to update the `Students` table. The component participates in the update by checking each submitted value to see if it meets certain requirements. If so, the component updates the row, then calls the `SetComplete` method; otherwise, it calls `SetAbort`, which cancels the transaction. Figure 14.3 shows the student detail form.

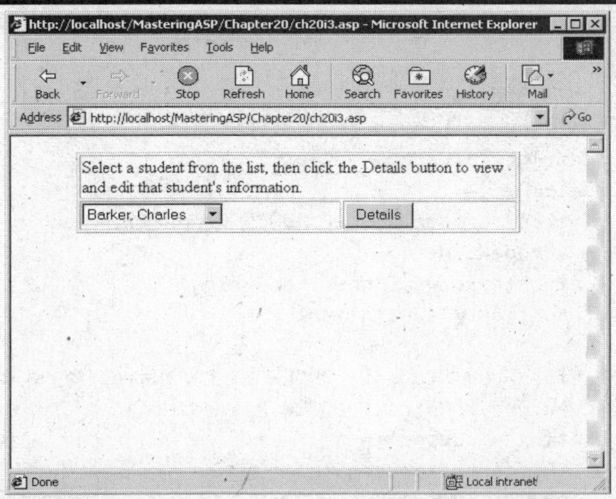

FIGURE 14.2: Student selection form (`ch20i3.asp`)

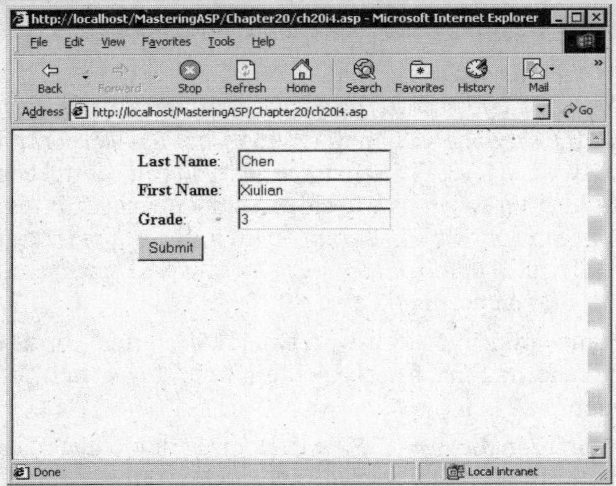

FIGURE 14.3: Student Detail Form (`ch20i4.asp`)

Listing 14.3 contains the code for the student selection form.

Listing 14.3: Student Selection Form

```
<%@ Language=VBScript %>
<% Option Explicit %>
<%
Dim conn
Dim SQL
Dim R
Dim aConnectionString
aConnectionString = "Provider=SQLOLEDB;Data " _
   & "Source=(local);Database=ClassRecords;" _
   & "UID=sa;PWD=;"
Set conn = Server.CreateObject("ADODB.Connection")
conn.Mode = adModeRead
conn.ConnectionString = aConnectionString
conn.CursorLocation = aduseclient
conn.Open
SQL = "SELECT * FROM Students ORDER BY LastName, FirstName"
Set R = Server.CreateObject("ADODB.Recordset")
R.CursorLocation = aduseclient
Call R.Open(SQL, conn, adOpenStatic, _
   adLockReadOnly, adcmdtext)
```

```
Set R.ActiveConnection = Nothing
conn.Close
Set conn = Nothing
%>
<html>
<head>
</head>
<body>
<form name="frmSelectStudent" method="post" _
   action="ch20i4.asp">
<table align="center" width="80%" border="1">
   <tr>
      <td colspan="2">
         Select a student from the list, then click
         the Details button to view and edit that
         student's information.
      </td>
   </tr>
      <td valign="top" width="60%">
         <select name="StudentID">
            <%
            While Not R.EOF
               Response.Write "<option value='" & _
               R("StudentID").Value & "'>" & _
               R("LastName").Value & ", " & _
               R("Firstname").Value & "</option>"
               R.movenext
            Wend
            R.Close
            Set R = Nothing
            %>
         </select>
      </td>
      <td valign="top">
         <input type="Submit" value="Details"
          name="Details">
      </td>
   </tr>
</table>
</form>
</body>
</html>
```

Listing 14.4 contains the ASP script for the detail form.

Listing 14.4: Student Detail Form

```
<%@ Language=VBScript %>
<% Option Explicit %>
<% Response.Buffer=True %>
<%
Dim oStudent
Dim StudentID
Dim LastName
Dim FirstName
Dim Grade
Dim conn
Dim SQL
Dim R
Dim aConnectionString
StudentID = Request("StudentID")
If StudentID = "" Then
   Response.redirect "ch20i3.asp"
End If
aConnectionString = "Provider=SQLOLEDB;Data " _
   & "Source=(local);Database=ClassRecords;" _
   & "UID=sa;PWD=;"
Set conn = Server.CreateObject("ADODB.Connection")
conn.Mode = adModeRead
conn.ConnectionString = aConnectionString
conn.CursorLocation = adUseClient
conn.open
SQL = "SELECT * FROM Students WHERE StudentID=" & StudentID
Set R = conn.execute(SQL, , adcmdtext)
LastName = R("LastName").Value
FirstName = R("FirstName").Value
Grade = R("Grade").Value
conn.Close
Set conn = Nothing
%>
<html>
<head>
</head>
<body>
<form name="frmSelectStudent" method="post"
    action="ch20i5.asp">
```

```
<input type="hidden" name="StudentID"
    value="<%=StudentID%>">
<table align=center width="60%">
   <tr>
      <td width="30%">
         <b>Last Name</b>:
      </td>
      <td width="*">
         <input type="text" name="LastName"
          value="<%=LastName%>">
      </td>
   </tr>
   <tr>
      <td width="30%">
         <b>First Name</b>:
      </td>
      <td width="*">
         <input type="text" name="FirstName"
          value="<%=FirstName%>">
      </td>
   </tr>
   <tr>
      <td width="30%">
         <b>Grade</b>:
      </td>
      <td width="*">
         <input type="text" name="Grade"
          value="<%=Grade%>">
      </td>
   </tr>
   <tr>
      <td colspan="2">
         <input type="Submit" name="Submit"
            value="Submit">
      </td>
   </tr>
</table>
</form>
</body>
</html>
```

Listing 14.5 contains the transactional ASP script to update the row.

Listing 14.5: Transactional Script to Update Student Information

```
<%@ Language=VBScript @TRANSACTION=REQUIRED%>
<%
Dim oStudent
Dim StudentID
Dim LastName
Dim FirstName
Dim Grade
Sub onTransactionCommit()
   Response.Write "The record has been updated.<br>"
   Response.Write "Click <a href='ch20i3.asp'>here</a>
       to return to the list."
   Response.end
End Sub
Sub onTransactionAbort()
   Response.Write "Some of the information you " _
      & "entered is not valid.<br>"
   Response.Write "Error Description: " & _
      Err.Description & "<br>"
   Response.Write "Click <a href='ch20i4.asp?StudentID=" _
      & StudentID & "'>here</a> to update the information."
   Response.end
End Sub
Set oStudent = server.CreateObject("ClassRecords.CStudent")
StudentID = Request("StudentID")
LastName = Request("LastName")
FirstName = Request("FirstName")
Grade = Request("Grade")
On Error Resume Next
Call oStudent.UpdateStudent(StudentID, LastName, _
   FirstName, Grade)
If Err.Number <> 0 Then
   objectContext.setAbort
Else
   objectContext.SetComplete
End If
%>
```

Finally, Listing 14.6 contains the code for the `ClassRecords.Cstudent` class that updates the row.

Listing 14.6: `ClassRecords.CStudent` Class – `UpdateStudent` Method

```
Option Explicit
Implements ObjectControl
Private Const Classname = "ADCTResponses"
Private oc As ObjectContext
Public Enum CStudentErrorEnum
    ERR_BAD_STUDENTID = vbObjectError + 1500
    ERR_BAD_LASTNAME
    ERR_BAD_FIRSTNAME
    ERR_BAD_GRADE
End Enum

Public Sub UpdateStudent(StudentID As Variant,
    LastName As Variant, FirstName As Variant,
    Grade As Variant)
    On Error GoTo ErrUpdateStudent
    If Val(StudentID) <= 0 Then
        Err.Raise ERR_BAD_STUDENTID, "UpdateStudent",
            "Invalid StudentID"
    End If
    If VarType(LastName) <> vbString Then
        Err.Raise ERR_BAD_LASTNAME, "UpdateStudent",
            "Last name must be a string."
    End If
    If Len(LastName) < 2 Or Len(LastName) > 20 Then
        Err.Raise ERR_BAD_LASTNAME, "UpdateStudent",
            "The last name must be between 2 and 20
            characters in length."
    End If
    If containsNumbers(CStr(LastName)) Then
        Err.Raise ERR_BAD_LASTNAME, "UpdateStudent",
            "The last name may not contain numbers."
    End If
    If VarType(FirstName) <> vbString Then
        Err.Raise ERR_BAD_FIRSTNAME, "UpdateStudent",
            "Last name must be a string."
    End If
    If Len(FirstName) < 2 Or Len(FirstName) > 20 Then
        Err.Raise ERR_BAD_FIRSTNAME, "UpdateStudent",
        "The last name must be between 2 and 20
        characters in length."
```

```
    End If
    If containsNumbers(CStr(FirstName)) Then
        Err.Raise ERR_BAD_FIRSTNAME, "UpdateStudent",
            "The last name may not contain numbers."
    End If
    If Not containsNumbers(CStr(Grade)) Then
        Err.Raise ERR_BAD_GRADE, "UpdateStudent",
            "Invalid grade."
    End If
    If Grade <= 0 Or Grade >= 9 Then
        Err.Raise ERR_BAD_GRADE, "UpdateStudent",
            "The grade must be between 1 and 8."
    End If
    Dim conn
    Dim SQL
    Dim aConnectionString
    aConnectionString = "Provider=SQLOLEDB;Data " _
       & "Source=(local);Database=ClassRecords;" _
       & "UID=sa;PWD=;"
    Set conn = CreateObject("ADODB.Connection")
    conn.Mode = adModeReadWrite
    conn.ConnectionString = aConnectionString
    conn.CursorLocation = adUseClient
    conn.Open
    SQL = "UPDATE Students SET LastName='" & LastName & "',
FirstName='" & FirstName & "',Grade=" & Grade &
       " WHERE StudentID=" & StudentID
    conn.Execute SQL, , adCmdText
    conn.Close
    Set conn = Nothing
ExitUpdateStudent:
    Exit Sub
ErrUpdateStudent:
    Call setAbort
    Err.Raise Err.Number, Err.Source, Err.Description
    Resume ExitUpdateStudent
End Sub
Private Sub setComplete()
    If Not oc Is Nothing Then
        oc.setComplete
    End If
End Sub
```

```
Private Sub setAbort()
    If Not oc Is Nothing Then
        oc.setAbort
    End If
End Sub
Private Function containsNumbers(s As String)
    Dim i As Integer
    Const numbers = "0123456789"
    For i = 1 To Len(s)
        If InStr(numbers, Mid$(s, i, 1)) > 0 Then
            containsNumbers = True
            Exit Function
        End If
    Next
End Function
Private Sub ObjectControl_Activate()
    On Error GoTo ErrObjectControl_Activate
    Dim methodname As String
    methodname = Classname & ".ObjectControl_Activate"
    Set oc = GetObjectContext
ExitObjectControl_Activate:
    Exit Sub
ErrObjectControl_Activate:
    Err.Raise Err.Number, methodname, Err.Description &
        vbCrLf & "Unable to acquire a reference to the
        ObjectContext object."
    Resume ExitObjectControl_Activate
End Sub

Private Function ObjectControl_CanBePooled() As Boolean
    ObjectControl_CanBePooled = False
End Function

Private Sub ObjectControl_Deactivate()
    On Error GoTo ErrObjectControl_Deactivate
    Dim methodname As String
    methodname = Classname & ".ObjectControl_Deactivate"
    Set oc = Nothing
ExitObjectControl_Deactivate:
    Exit Sub
ErrObjectControl_Deactivate:
    Err.Raise Err.Number, methodname, Err.Description &
```

```
            vbCrLf & "Unable to release the reference to the
            ObjectContext object."
        Resume ExitObjectControl_Deactivate
    End Sub
```

You don't need to worry about the code in this listing at the moment—I've included it for informational purposes only so the curious can see how it works internally. The component participates in a transaction by implementing the `ObjectControl` interface, using the command:

```
Implements ObjectControl
```

The `ObjectControl` interface provides access to the ObjectContext object, defined in the class as the oc variable. When MTS/COM+ receives the `CreateObject` call, it fires an event called `ObjectControl_Activate`. The component sets the oc variable to the object context for the calling code. When the client releases the CStudent object (in this case, when the calling ASP page ends) MTS/COM+ fires the `ObjectControl_Deactivate` event, which releases the ObjectContext object.

The only public method in the class is `UpdateStudent`, which accepts `StudentID`, `LastName`, `FirstName`, and `Grade` as arguments, checks the arguments, opens a connection, and updates the row values. The component raises a specific error from the list of public `CStudentErrorEnum` values, as well as raising any other error back to the calling code.

I've written this component so it can run both inside and outside MTS/COM+. If the component runs outside of MTS/COM+, the `ObjectControl_Activate` event code never executes; therefore, the oc `ObjectContext` variable has the default value of `Nothing`. The calls in the `setAbort` and `setComplete` subroutines first check to see if the oc variable is `Nothing`. If so, the code doesn't try to set any properties, thus avoiding errors if the object is not running in MTS/COM+.

Creating the component is relatively simple, but setting it up to run in MTS/COM+ involves a slightly more complicated set of steps—and the steps are different for NT 4 and Windows 2000. I've included both procedures in following sections. Follow the procedure for your server to register the component with MTS/COM+.

NT 4 MTS Package Creation and Component Registration

Perform this procedure on your server, either physically or remotely, using the MMC application Transaction Server Explorer.

1. **Install the Component**: The `ClassRecords.DLL` resides in the `MasteringASP\VBCode\Chapter20` directory. There's a `Setup.exe` file in that directory. Run the installation program to install the component. If you already have the Visual Basic 6 runtime files installed on your computer, you can ignore the setup program and just register the component by clicking Start, Run, and typing the following line into the Run field (ignore any line breaks that appear in the text of this book; enter the information on a single line):

NOTE

The following paths work on my server, but you may need to adjust the paths for your server.

```
c:\winnt\system32\regsvr32.exe
   "c:\inetpub\wwwroot\MasteringASP\VBCode\Chapter20\
   ClassRecords.dll"
```

2. **Create a MasteringASP Package in MTS**: Open the Microsoft Transaction Server Explorer applet. Click Start, Programs, Windows NT 4.0 Option Pack, Microsoft Transaction Server, Transaction Server Explorer. Expand the items in the left-hand pane under Computers by clicking the + signs until you see the Packages Installed item. Right-click that item and select New, then click Package. From the dialog that appears, click Create an Empty Package. Enter **`MasteringASP`** as the title of the package, then click Next. You'll see the Set Package Identity screen. Accept the default, which is Interactive User, then click Finish. MTS creates your new package.

3. **Set Package Properties**: Find your new package by clicking the + sign next to the Packages Installed item. Right-click on the MasteringASP package and select Properties. Click the Security tab and check the Enable Authorization Checking checkbox. Click OK to save your changes.

4. **Add Roles**: Click the + sign next to the MasteringASP package. Select and then right-click the Roles item and select New, then Role, from the context menu. Enter **`MasteringASPUser`** into the name field, then click OK. MTS creates the new Role. Click the + sign until you see the new entry in the list.

5. **Add Users to Role**: Click the + sign next to the MasteringASPUser entry. Right-click on the Users entry and select New, then User, from the context menu. You'll see a standard NT user/group dialog. Click Show Users to list the users. Select the IUSR_MACHINENAME account. Remember, the MACHINENAME corresponds to your server's machine name so you won't actually see `MACHINENAME`. IIS impersonates this account for anonymous requests. You need this account to have permission to launch your component. Click OK to add the account to the list of Users for this role.
6. **Add Components**: Scroll the list until you can see the MasteringASP\Components entry. Right-click the Components entry and select New, then Component, from the context menu. Click Install New Component(s). From the Install Components dialog, click Add Files and navigate to the directory that contains the `ClassRecords.dll` file you registered in Step 1. Double-click that file. MTS adds the filename and the list of public components contained in the class to the Install Components dialog. Click Finish to close the dialog. MTS adds the new component to the Components item.
7. **Assign Role**: You want the `CStudent` component to run in the MasteringASP role you created in Steps 4 and 5. To assign that role, click the + sign next to the `ClassRecords.CStudent` item, then right-click the Role Membership item. Select New, then Role, from the context menu. Select the MasteringASPUser role from the list, then click OK to add the role. An icon for the new role appears in the right-hand pane of the Transaction Explorer.

Windows 2000 COM+ Package Creation and Component Registration

This procedure must be performed on your server, either physically or remotely, using the Component Services application.

1. **Install the Component**: The `ClassRecords.DLL` resides in the `MasteringASP\VBCode\Chapter20` directory. There's a `Setup.exe` file in that directory. Run the installation program to install the component. If you already have the Visual Basic 6 runtime files installed on your computer, you can ignore the setup program and just register the component by

clicking Start, Run, and typing the following line into the Run field (ignore any line breaks that appear in the text of this book; enter the information on a single line):

NOTE

The following paths work on my server, but you may need to adjust the paths for your server.

```
c:\winnt\system32\regsvr32.exe
   "c:\inetpub\wwwroot\MasteringASP\VBCode\Chapter20\
   ClassRecords.dll"
```

2. **Create a MasteringASP COM+ Application**: Open the Component Services application. Click Start, Programs, Administrative Tools, Component Services. Expand the items under the Component Services item by clicking the + signs until you see the COM+ Applications item. Select the COM+ Applications item, then right-click it and select New, then click Application. You'll see the COM Application Install Wizard. Click Next once, then click Create an Empty Application. Enter **`MasteringASP`** as the name of the application and select the Server Application radio button, then click Next. You'll see the Set Application Identity screen. Accept the default, which is Interactive User. Click Next, then Finish to create the application.
3. **Set Application Properties**: Find your new application in the list of applications under the COM+ Applications item. Select the MasteringASP application, then right-click it and select Properties. Click the Security tab and check the Enforce access checks for this application check box. Leave all other options set to the defaults. Click OK to save your changes.
4. **Add Roles**: Click the + sign next to the MasteringASP package. Select and then right-click the Roles item and select New, then Role, from the context menu. Enter **`MasteringASPUser`** into the name field, then click OK. Click the + sign next to Roles to see the new entry in the list.
5. **Add Users to Role**: Click the + sign next to the MasteringASPUser role item. Select the Users entry, then right-click it and select New, then User, from the context menu. Select the IUSR_MACHINENAME account. Remember, the MACHINENAME corresponds to your server's machine

name so you won't actually see MACHINENAME. IIS impersonates this account for anonymous requests. You want this account to have permission to launch your component. Click OK to add the account to the list of Users for this role.

6. **Add Components**: Scroll the list until you can see the MasteringASP\Components entry. Select the Components entry, then right-click it and select New, then Component, from the context menu. You'll see the COM Component Install Wizard. Click Next, then click Install New Component(s). From the Select Files to Install dialog, navigate to the directory that contains the `ClassRecords.dll` file you registered in Step 1. Double-click that file. The COM Component Install Wizard adds the filename and the list of public components contained in the class. Click Next, then Finish, to close the dialog. Component Services adds the new component to the Components item.

7. **Assign Role**: You want the `CStudent` component to run in the MasteringASP role you created in Steps 4 and 5. To assign that role, select the `ClassRecords.CStudent` item, then right-click it and select Properties from the context menu. Click the Security Tab, then select the MasteringASPUser role from the list. Click OK to add the role.

The steps in the previous procedure (although not the individual names and selections) are generic; you can create a new package and assign roles using these steps. Registering and updating components in MTS/COM+ can be a painful process; follow the procedure exactly, or you may need to reboot your server to get things working again.

The point of this exercise is to create a component that can participate in transactions. Unless the component runs inside MTS/COM+, it cannot either initiate a transaction or inherit the context of its instantiator, hence it will not be able to participate in a transaction. You can use the component outside of MTS/COM+, so you can run the code even if you don't have access to a server with MTS/COM+ installed, although it will not run correctly.

You won't see anything except the messages in the browser, so it's enlightening to watch the transactions in the Microsoft Transaction Explorer (Windows NT 4) applet or Component Services (Windows 2000) application. Resize your browser so you can see both the browser window and the appropriate application/applet for your server.

Select, then right-click the Components entry under the Mastering-ASP package or application title (see Figure 14.4), then select `View\Status View` from the context menu. Now select a student and submit the Details form (you don't have to change any data to watch the transaction occur). You will see numbers (zeroes) appear in the Status View pane (NT 4 only). You may even briefly see one of the zeroes change to a one, signifying that the object was active. Depending on your server, this may happen too fast to see with a single client.

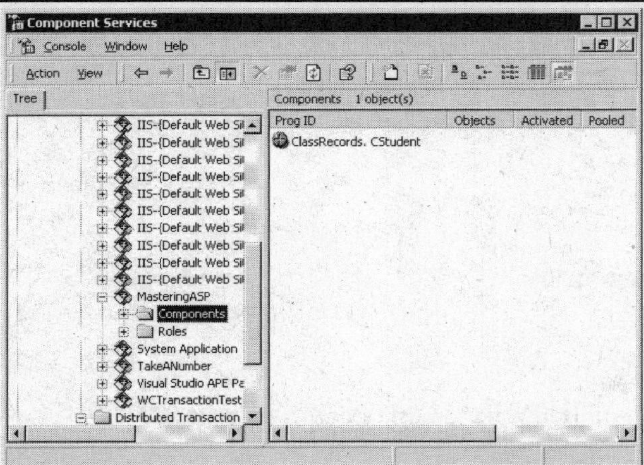

FIGURE 14.4: MTE status view

What you're seeing is a display showing the count of objects instantiated, activated, or actually performing work at the point in time the display was last refreshed. You can repeat the transaction many times by pressing F5 from the informational screen that appears after you click Submit from the Student Details screen. (You will get a dialog that asks if you want to resubmit the information. That's okay; click Retry to resubmit the form). If you do this many times in rapid succession, you'll see the ball icon next to the `CStudent` component item begin to spin, showing you that the component is currently in use.

NOTE

The ball icon doesn't spin in Windows 2000 in this view.

You can also view transaction statistics showing how many transactions are in progress, have completed, aborted, or are still in doubt, as well as transaction totals since MS DTC was last started on the server. In NT 4, the Transaction Statistics item is the last entry under the My Computer item in the left-hand pane. Click it to change to the Transaction Statistics view. In Windows 2000, scroll to the bottom of the COM+ Applications list and select the Transaction Statistics item under the Distributed Transaction Coordinator entry (see Figure 14.5).

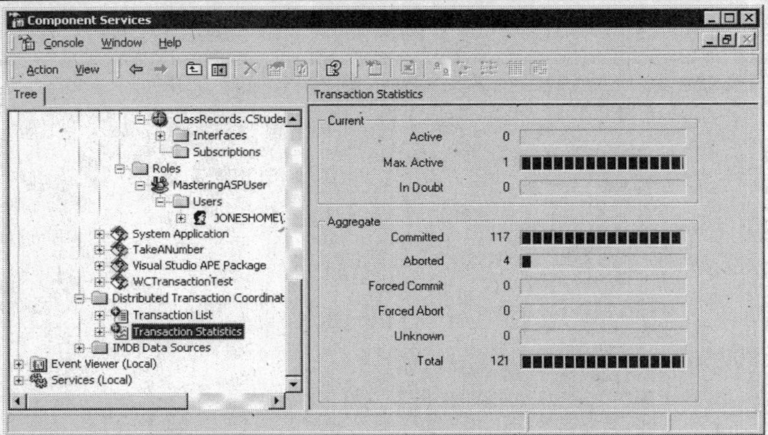

FIGURE 14.5: MTE Transaction Statistics view in Windows 2000

In this chapter, you've seen how to create transactional ASP pages that control transactions using both SQL Server through ADO code within the ASP pages themselves and with external components running in MTS/COM+. At this level of complexity, you're beginning to move away from websites into the realm of ASP applications. The next two chapters will take you through the intricacies of XML and on to implementing what you've learned by building an online store.

SUMMARY

In this chapter, you've seen how to create transactional ASP pages that control transactions using both SQL Server through ADO code within the ASP pages themselves and with external components running in MTS/COM+. At this level of complexity, you're beginning to move away from websites into the realm of ASP applications. The next two chapters will take you through the intricacies of XML and on to implementing what you've learned by building an online store.

Chapter 15

XML AND MS DATABASES

In previous chapters we looked at how to connect web pages to databases using VBScript and ADO. We also covered a variety of methods for handling transactions in web applications. Extensible Markup Language (XML) is the latest standard for cross-application and cross-component communication, and as such, is an integral part of Microsoft's development platforms, including .NET.

XML is a language for representing structured information, and as such, it's an ideal mechanism for exchanging information between different database management systems, or for building front ends for database applications that run on thin clients. Internet Explorer 5 supports XML, and Microsoft is adding XML support to its databases. In fact, SQL Server 2000 supports XML natively. ActiveX Data Objects (ADO), Microsoft's data access technology, supports XML already.

Adapted from *XML Developer's Handbook™* by Kurt Cagle
ISBN 0-7821-2704-1 640 pages $49.99

In addition to adding XML features to its databases, Microsoft is enhancing XML support in Internet Explorer. As you probably know, any features added to Internet Explorer are also available to any language, like VBScript or Visual Basic. At this point, there are many XML tools, both on the database side and on the client side, but these tools are still rough around the edges. For one thing, you must write programs (or scripts, in the case of Internet Explorer) to parse XML documents. Eventually, XML must become transparent to developers so that you won't have to write code to manipulate the XML document itself. At this point, you must not only write code to process XML data, you must use JavaScript to make sure your client applications will run in both browsers.

In this chapter, you'll learn how to retrieve XML-formatted data from a database, pass it to the client, and bind the data to HTML controls. In the first part of the chapter, I discuss the Remote Data Services (RDS) and data-binding techniques. Once you learn how data binding works and you can bind a recordset to the HTML controls on a web page, you'll be able to apply the same techniques to XML recordsets as well. You'll also learn how to use the XML Data Control and how to create data islands.

In the second half of the chapter, you'll learn how to use ADO's methods to persist recordsets in XML format and how to update the tables in the database through an XML recordset. You'll see the syntax used to mark changes in a recordset and how the modified recordset is submitted to the database and committed there. In the last section of the chapter, you'll learn about the new XML features of SQL Server 2000. You'll see how you can query SQL Server remotely through an HTTP connection and how to execute stored procedures against a SQL Server database remotely. As you will see, it is possible to directly access and manipulate SQL Server databases from within your browser.

RDS and Data Binding

Before examining the specifics of ADO's XML support, it is important to understand the basics of data binding. *Data binding* is the process of associating a control to a data field. When the underlying field changes value, the control is updated automatically. Likewise, when the viewer edits the control, the underlying field is updated automatically. The recordset whose fields are bound to the controls of a Form on a web page is a *disconnected recordset*, and the changes are not immediately reflected to the database. The disconnected recordset is one of the most prominent features of ADO 2.1 and later versions; unlike the regular recordset we've been using for years, a disconnected recordset does not maintain an open connection to the database. It's populated through an open connection, but it maintains its data even after the connection to the database has been closed. Disconnected recordsets are updateable. You can edit their rows, and the changes can be committed to the database after the connection to the database has been established again. In this section, you'll see how to move a disconnected recordset to the client and display its fields on HTML controls.

HTML is nothing more than a language for formatting text to be displayed on a browser. Yet, modern web applications do not rely on static content that can be stored in HTML pages and transmitted to the client. For example, you want to be able to display field values on certain controls, but the exact fields that will be displayed on the controls are not known ahead of time. Thus, you need a technique to bind the fields of a database to elements of a page, so that when you connect to the database, the elements will be populated automatically.

Visual Basic programmers have been doing this for years, but they can have a quick link to the database. However, web applications can't assume that they have immediate access to a database. Despite this, it is possible for a web page to "see" the fields of a database through the *RDS Data Control*. The control connects to a database server, such as SQL Server, and retrieves the data from tables. The viewer can then edit the data and update the database en masse.

If you're familiar with database programming, you already see the similarities between the usual Data Controls used in building database front ends with VB or other high-level languages (the DAO and ADO Data Controls) and the RDS Data Control. The main difference is that the RDS Data Control connects to the database over the HTTP protocol. Because dial-up connections are not fast enough for database operations, the RDS Data Control maintains the data in a disconnected recordset and updates the database only when requested. This happens at the end of a session. Now you'll see how to bind the fields of the recordset to HTML elements.

Binding Fields to HTML Elements

The RDS Data Control can bind HTML elements to database fields, but it can also bind them to XML data. The following lines insert an RDS Data Control onto a page and specify the database it connects to, as well as a query to retrieve the desired data:

```
<OBJECT
    CLASSID="clsid:BD96C556-65A3-11D0-983A-00C04FC29E33"
```

```
    ID="Products" WIDTH = 0 HEIGHT = 0>
    <PARAM NAME="Connect" VALUE="DSN=NWindDB">
    <PARAM NAME="Server" VALUE = "PROTO">
    <PARAM NAME="SQL" VALUE="SELECT * FROM Products">
</OBJECT>
```

This <OBJECT> tag tells the RDS Data Control to connect to a local database—the Northwind database—and retrieve all the rows from the Products table. PROTO is the name of the machine on which SQL Server is running, and DSN is a Data Source Name that points to the Northwind database.

NOTE

To set up a DSN, use the ODBC Data Source tool in the Control Panel (if you're using Windows 98 or Windows NT) or in the Administrative Tools (if you're using Windows 2000).

Instead of connecting directly to a database, you can specify the name of a script with the URL attribute. The script will retrieve the data from the database server and return it to the client as a recordset. Here's the alternate <OBJECT> tag that uses the URL of a script to get the data:

```
<OBJECT
    CLASSID="clsid:BD96C556-65A3-11D0-983A-00C04FC29E33"
    ID="Products" WIDTH = 0 HEIGHT = 0>
    <PARAM NAME="URL" VALUE="GetProducts.asp">
</OBJECT>
```

Both tags create a recordset—the Products recordset—on the client. By definition, this is a disconnected recordset, and you can bind its fields to HTML elements on the page (discussed in the next section). As you navigate through the rows of the recordset with its navigational methods, the values of the bound HTML controls are updated. If you edit a field (provided that the control allows editing), the new value is committed to the local recordset as soon as you move to another row. The changes are not sent to the server.

To update the underlying tables, you must call the disconnected recordset's SubmitChanges method. Another method, Refresh, discards the changes and reloads the recordset from the database.

Data Binding Properties

To bind an HTML element to the RDS Data Control, you must use the following two properties.

DATASRC This is the name of the RDS Data Control that contains the data. You must prefix the name of the data source with the pound sign (#) to indicate that the data source is local to the client.

DATAFLD This is the name of the field in the control to which the element is bound.

Table 15.1 lists the HTML elements that support data binding, as well as the name of the properties you bind to the data fields.

TABLE 15.1: The Data-Bound HTML Elements

HTML Element	Bound Property
A	HREF
BUTTON	innerText and innerHTML
DIV	innerText and innerHTML
FRAME	SRC
IFRAME	SRC
IMG	SRC
INPUT TYPE=CHECKBOX	CHECKED
INPUT TYPE=HIDDEN	VALUE
INPUT TYPE=PASSWORD	VALUE
INPUT TYPE=RADIO	CHECKED
INPUT TYPE=TEXT	VALUE
SELECT	<OPTION>
SPAN	innerText and InnerHTML
TEXTAREA	VALUE
TABLE	<TD>

To display a field on the page, use the SPAN tag as follows:

```
ProductID   <SPAN DATASRC="#Products"
             DATAFLD="ProductID">
            </SPAN>
ProductName <SPAN DATASRC="#Products"
             DATAFLD="ProductName">
            </SPAN>
```

```
Description <SPAN DATASRC="#Products"
             DATAFLD="Description">
            </SPAN>
```

The following statements display the entire recordset on a table:

```
<TABLE DATASRC="#Products">
<TR><TD>ProductID</TD>
    <TD><SPAN DATAFLD="ProductID"></SPAN>
    </TD>
    <TD>ProductName</TD>
    <TD><SPAN DATAFLD="ProductName"></SPAN>
    </TD>
    <TD>Description</TD>
    <TD><SPAN DATAFLD="Description">
        </SPAN>
    </TD>
</TR>
</TABLE>
```

As you can see, you don't have to specify more than a single row of the table. Because the data-bound element is a table, the browser knows that it must iterate through the entire recordset and create a new table row for each row in the recordset.

When you bind a table to a recordset, the DATASRC attribute is specified in the <TABLE> tag, so that you won't have to repeat it in every <TD> cell. The DATASRC attribute's value doesn't change from row to row.

The <TABLE> tag supports yet another attribute, DATAPAGESIZE, which specifies how many rows will be displayed on the table. The following tag creates a table with the first 20 products:

```
<TABLE ID="ProdTable"
       DATASRC="#Products" DATAPAGESIZE="20">
```

In this example, you've specified an ID for the table, because you want to be able to move to any group of 20 products. To do so, you must provide scripts for two buttons that take the viewer to the previous group and the next group, respectively. These buttons must call the control's PreviousPage and NextPage methods. The following statements insert two buttons after the table that implement the table's navigational methods:

```
<INPUT TYPE=Button VALUE="PREVIOUS"
    onClick="ProdTable.PreviousPage()"/>

<INPUT TYPE=Button VALUE="NEXT"
    onClick="ProdTable.NextPage()"/>
```

The `ProductsTable.htm` page in the accompanying sample code retrieves product information from the Northwind database and displays it in tabular format on the browser. Before you open the document, change the following two lines in the definition of the RDS Data Control:

```
<PARAM NAME="Connect" VALUE="DSN=NWindDB">
<PARAM NAME="Server" VALUE = "PROTO">
```

The `Connect` attribute should be the name of a DSN on your computer, and the `Server` attribute should be the name of the computer on which SQL Server is running. Figure 15.1 shows a small section of the Products table with the product data.

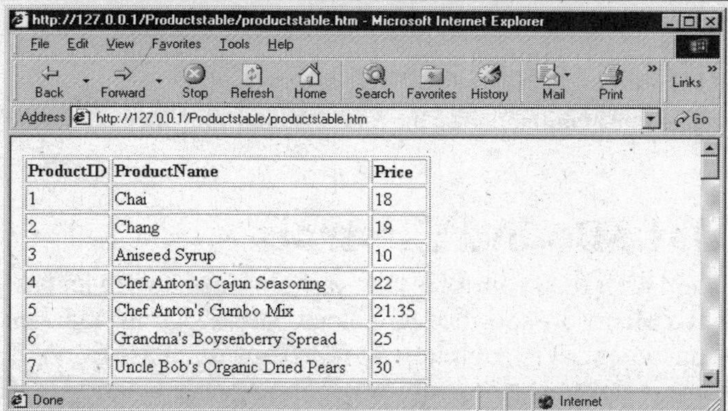

FIGURE 15.1: Binding a table to a disconnected recordset

NOTE

If you only have Access on your system, set up a DSN for the Northwind database and omit the `Server` parameter.

Retrieving Data with ASP Files

If you want to use an ASP file on the server to retrieve the data, open the `ProductsTableScript.htm` file. You must copy the file to the root folder of the web server, start your browser, and connect to the address `127.0.0.1/ProductsTableScript.asp`. The RDS Data Control will invoke the `GetProducts.asp` script (Listing 15.1), which will furnish the rows of the Products table.

Listing 15.1: The *GetProducts.asp* Script

```
<%
Set RS = Server.CreateObject("ADODB.Recordset")
RS.Open "Products", "DSN=NWINDDB"
RS.Save Response, adPersistXML
RS.Close
Set RS=Nothing
%>
```

The Save method places the recordset's rows directly in the Response stream. The adPersistXML argument tells ADO to save the recordset in XML format.

NOTE

There is more information on the Save method later in this chapter.

Editing Data-Bound Controls

The problem with RDS control is that you can't use it with just any browser; it's Microsoft-specific technology. XML is a universal language that has the potential to communicate with any database (if not now, hopefully someday in the near future). By being able to bind HTML elements to the fields of an XML data island, you can develop web pages that allow viewers to edit the fields and update the database. The HTML elements that can be bound to fields (either database fields or XML fields) support the DATASRC and DATAFLD properties. DATASRC is the name of the database, or the name of an XML data island, in our case. DATAFLD is the name of the field we want to bind to the element.

If you want viewers to be able to edit the fields of the recordset, you must place a Text control in every cell of the table. Here are the statements of the previous table, only this time each cell is a Text control, so that you can edit the fields. You'll see later how to commit the changes to the database.

```
<TABLE DATASRC="#Products">
<TR><TD>ProductID</TD>
    <TD><INPUT TYPE=Text DATAFLD="ProductID"/></TD>
    <TD>ProductName</TD>
    <TD><INPUT TYPE=Text DATAFLD="ProductName"/></TD>
```

```
        <TD>Description</TD>
        <TD><INPUT TYPE=Text DATAFLD="Description"/></TD>
    </TR>
    </TABLE>
```

These revised pages have two drawbacks: too many rows to edit at once, and no mechanism to submit the changes to the database. We'll revise this page as we go along in the chapter. Also in upcoming sections of this chapter, you will learn how to display a single row and allow the user to navigate through the recordset, as well as how to submit the changes to the database.

The XML Data Control

The previous section showed you how to connect an RDS Data Control to an XML recordset: You specify the URL of a script that returns a disconnected recordset. In this section, you'll learn how to do the same with the XML Data Control. In essence, the <XML> tag is the XML Data Control. The following statements create an XML Data Control, name it Prod, and populate it with XML data:

```
<XML ID="Prod">
<Products>
  <Product>
    <ProductID>1</ProductID>
    <ProductName>ProductName1/ProductName>
    <UnitPrice>1.11</UnitPrice>
  </Product>
  <Product>
    <ProductID>2</ProductID>
    <ProductName>ProductName2/ProductName>
    <UnitPrice>2.22</UnitPrice>
  </Product>
{ XML statements for the remaining products }
</Products>
</XML>
```

The XML Data Control supports the same navigational methods as the RDS Data Control, and all the changes are maintained in a local XML recordset. After the viewer has edited the fields, your page should be able to transmit the modified rows to another script on the web server that will update the database. This takes more than a call to the `SubmitChanges` method; you'll see later in this chapter how to commit the changes to the database.

XML Data Islands

A recordset that's transmitted to the client as part of the HTML document is called a *data island*. The data island's fields can be bound to any of the HTML controls listed in Table 15.1, shown earlier. An advantage of the XML Data Control is that, technically, it's not an ActiveX control. This means that you don't have to use the `<OBJECT>` tag to insert it on a page, and it can be used with any browser that supports XML.

The problem with XML data islands is how they're created. Coding XML data islands by hand is obviously out of the question. Luckily, the major data access mechanism, ADO, supports XML, which means that the databases themselves don't have to support XML natively. In the following section, you'll see how to retrieve recordsets in XML format from Access and SQL Server. First, we'll look at ADO support for XML.

ADO Support for XML

ActiveX Data Objects is a key technology and one of the cornerstones of the Windows data access technologies. Though ADO has limited support for XML right now, future versions will provide more elaborate XML support.

One of the most important features of ADO is its ability to retrieve recordsets in XML format. ADO 2.5 (and subsequent versions) can format recordsets as XML documents and save them in a file or in a `Stream` object. The web server's response to the client is such a stream, and ADO can save a recordset in XML format directly to the `Response` object. The data is then sent to the client, where a client-side script can traverse the XML data and display, or otherwise manipulate, the rows.

The XML format contains information about the structure of the data, so the XML recordset carries with it a description of its structure, as well as the data itself. Because XML is an open standard, you should be able to use XML recordsets to exchange structured data between any two machines. This is the promise of XML, but we aren't quite there yet. There are no tools that would allow you to store the structure of an Access database as an XML document and use it to create a DB2 database populated with the Access data. This situation may change, as Microsoft is pushing this technology and wants to incorporate it into flagship products like SQL Server.

NOTE

Because ADO is not database specific, the XML techniques discussed in this chapter apply to Access, SQL Server, and every other DBMS that has support for ADO.

Web developers who are not into database programming can also use an XML-formatted recordset. So long as they're familiar with XML and the Document Object Model (DOM), they can work with this document without having to understand how the data is stored in the database, or even how to query the database.

In this section of the chapter, you'll explore how to use ADO to extract information from databases, format the recordset as an XML document, and display it on the client computer. You'll also see how to write a front end for the browser to edit the data and submit the changes back to the server in XML format.

Persisting Recordsets in XML Format

The ADO recordset object supports the `Save` method, which stores the rows of the recordset to a file or a `Stream` object. In ADO jargon, saving the data to a file or `Stream` object is called *persisting the recordset*. The `Save` method can store the data in a proprietary binary format, in the Advanced Data Table Gram (ADTG) format, or in XML format. To store the recordset represented by the `RS` object variable to a file in XML format, use the following statement:

```
RS.Save fileName, adPersist
```

where *`fileName`* is the name of the file and *`adPersist`* is a constant that determines the structure of the file, and its value can be one of two constants: `adPersistADTG` or `adPersistXML`.

Assuming that you have Access installed on your system and you have created a Data Source Name for the Northwind database, you can use the following VB statements to create a file with the rows of the Categories table in XML format. Just start a new VB project and enter the following lines in a button's Click event handler:

```
Dim RS As New ADODB.Recordset
FName = "C:\Temp\Categories.xml"
RS.Open "SELECT CategoryID, CategoryName, " & _
        "Description FROM Categories", "DSN=NWIND"
If Dir$(FName) <> "" Then Kill FName
RS.Save FName, adPersistXML
```

NOTE

If the file created by the previous code exists already, the Save method won't overwrite it. Instead, it will cause a runtime error. That's why you must either delete the file or prompt the user for a different filename.

The first few rows of the RS recordset in XML format are shown in Figure 15.2.

If you want to access the database and produce XML output from within a server-side script, you can use the equivalent VBScript statements. With a server-side script, you need not save the XML-formatted recordset to a database. You can send it directly to the client by writing the output to the Response stream, as shown here:

```
Set RS = Server.CreateObject("ADODB.Recordset")
RS.Open "SELECT CategoryID, CategoryName, " & _
        "Description FROM Categories", "DSN=NWIND"
RS.Save Response, adPersistXML
```

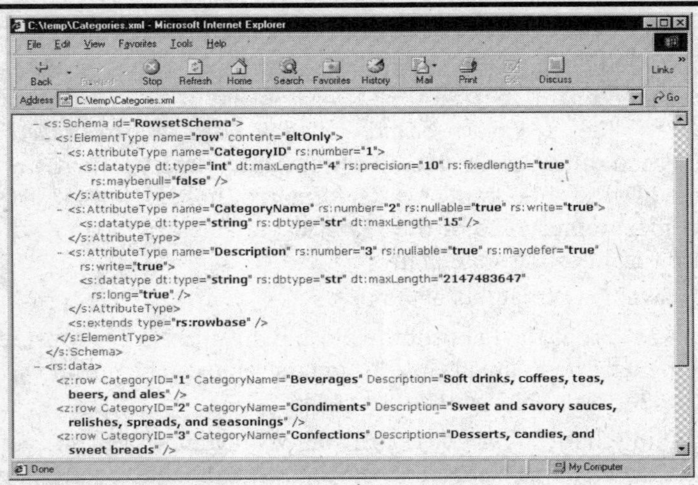

FIGURE 15.2: Persisting a table in XML format

TIP

You should probably insert a few HTML statements above and below the XML data island, telling the client what to do with the XML data. Use the Response.Write method to send additional output to the client.

Though the XML document produced by the `Save` method (shown in Figure 15.2, displayed in Internet Explorer) looks quite elementary, let's take a close look at it. The appearance of the document called `categories.xml` may be of interest to developers, but it's not what a typical viewer would like to see on their browser. The simplest method to format the XML is to write an Extensible Stylesheet Language (XSL) file. Yet, because this book is addressed to developers, I'm assuming you'll find it easier to write scripts rather than XSL files, so I won't discuss XSL files in this chapter.

Namespace Prefixes

The XML format used by ADO contains up to four sections, which in XML jargon are called *namespaces*. These sections are distinguished by a unique prefix, as shown in Table 15.2.

TABLE 15.2: XML Namespace Prefixes

Prefix	Description
`s`	Marks the beginning of the recordset's schema
`dt`	Marks the beginning of each row's data type
`rs`	Marks the beginning of the data section
`z`	Marks the beginning of each data row

The following rows in the `categories.xml` file in Figure 15.2, shown earlier, use three of the four available prefixes:

```
<s:AttributeType name="CategoryID" rs:number="1">
<s:datatype dt:type="int" dt:maxLength="4"
   rs:precision="10" rs:fixedlength="true"
   rs:maybenull="false" />
</s:AttributeType>
```

This section specifies the structure of a column. It's very unlikely that you will use this information on the client, but it's needed by ADO if you use the XML document to update a database.

The `dt` prefix appears in front of the row's data type attributes. Different data types have different attributes, of course. The *string* data type, for instance, doesn't have a precision attribute.

Later in the `categories.xml` file, you'll find the actual data. Each row in this section is identified with the z prefix:

```
<z:row CategoryID="2" CategoryName="Condiments"
```

```
Description="Sweet and savory sauces, relishes,
             spreads, and seasonings" >
```

(The `Description` line was broken to fit on the page.) If you select all the fields in the table, you'll see that the data section of the XML file contains a very long field, which is an image encoded as a sequence of characters. The image is not rendered on the client, because the content type of the file is text/html.

Although it is possible to include a textual representation of binary data in an XML-formatted recordset, it is not possible to directly bind the binary data to an <IMG> tag. To display a picture on a page with data-bound fields, use the <IMG> tag along with a URL, as shown here:

```
<IMG SRC="CategoryPicture.asp?CategoryID=XX">
```

The `CategoryPicture.asp` script reads the Picture column of the row in the Categories table that matched the specified Category ID. Most developers don't even store binary information in the database; they prefer to create image files in a specific folder and name them according to a key field in the database. This way they can easily match a row in the table to the corresponding file. For the Categories table, you should store each category's image to a file named `xx.gif`, where *xx* is the ID of the category.

The `s:datatype` attribute specifies the data type of each field, as well as other field attributes (whether the field can have a null value, for example). The data types that may appear in an XML file are shown in Table 15.3.

TABLE 15.3: XML Data Types

Type	Description
`bin.base64`	A binary object.
`bin.hex`	Binary values in hex format.
`Boolean`	A True/False value.
`Char`	A string that contains a single character.
`Date`	A date value in the format *yyyy-mm-dd.*
`DateTime`	A date and time value in the format *yyyy-mm-ddThh:mm:ss*. The time value is optional; if omitted, it's assumed to be 00:00:00.
`DateTime.tz`	A date and time value that includes time zone information in the format *yyyy-mm-ddThh:mm:ss-hh:mm*. The time zone information is expressed in hours and minutes ahead or behind GMT.
`fixed.14.4`	A fixed floating-point value with up to 14 integer digits and up to four fractional digits.

TABLE 15.3 continued: XML Data Types

Type	Description
`Float`	A floating-point value.
`Int`	An integer value.
`Number`	A floating-point value.
`Time`	A time value in the format *hh:mm:ss.*
`Time.tz`	A time value that includes time zone information in the format *hh:mm:ss-hh:mm*. The time zone information is expressed in hours and minutes ahead or behind GMT.
`i1`	A single-byte integer value.
`i2`	A two-byte integer value.
`i4`	A four-byte integer value.
`r4`	A four-byte fractional value.
`r8`	An eight-byte fractional value.
`ui1`	A single-byte, unsigned integer value.
`ui2`	A two-byte, unsigned integer value.
`ui4`	A four-byte, unsigned integer value.
`Uri`	A Universal Resource Indicator.
`Uuid`	A universally unique ID made up of hex digits.

The first thing to keep in mind when you work with XML recordsets generated by ADO (or SQL Server's native XML format, for that matter) is that the XML recordsets contain a description of the schema of the data. Moreover, each row contains all the column values in a single tag, the `<z:row>` tag. As you will see later in the chapter, it takes some extra coding to get rid of the schema information. As far as the structure of the tags goes, Microsoft designers opted for a less verbose XML format: All the columns in a row are listed in the same `<z:row>` tag. For example, the line

```
<z:row CategoryID="2" CategoryName="Condiments"
Description="Sweet and savory sauces,
            relishes, spreads, and seasonings" >
```

corresponds to the following lines of straight XML code:

```
<Category>
<CategoryID>2</CategoryID>
<CategoryName>Condiments<CategoryName/>
```

```
<Description>Sweet and savory sauces, relishes,
            spreads, and seasonings<Description/>
</Category>
```

Updating XML Recordsets

The XML format used by ADO can also handle updates by storing edits, insertions, and deletions in the XML document itself. This is a very interesting feature, because it will eventually allow you to read data from any data source, edit it, and then post the changes to the original database. The software you use need not be aware of the capabilities of the database from where the data came. This is not the case right now, however. The various vendors are just beginning to add XML features to their databases, but it won't be long before XML becomes a standard feature for exchanging data between databases. But, let's start by looking at the tags for updating recordsets.

Editing Rows

An edited row is specified with the `<rs:update>` and `<rs:original>` tags. The `<rs:update>` tag signifies the changes, and `<rs:original>` signifies the original row. Here's a typical example. The following lines correspond to the first row of the Customer table of the Northwind database, after we have changed the CompanyName column from `BLAUER SEE DELIKATESSEN` to `BLAUER SEE DELIKATESSEN1` and set the `Region` field to `REGION`:

```
- <rs:update>
- <rs:original>
  <z:row CustomerID="ALFKI"
         CompanyName="BLAUER SEE DELIKATESSEN"
         ContactName="MARIA ANDERS"
         ContactTitle="Sales Representative"
         Address="Obere Str. 577" City="Berlin"
         Region="REGION" PostalCode="12209"
         Country="GERMANY"
         Phone="030-0074321" Fax="030-0076545" />
  </rs:original>
  <z:row CompanyName="BLAUER SEE DELIKATESSEN1" />
  </rs:update>
```

Notice that all the columns appear in the `<rs:update>` tag, even though only one of them was changed.

You may be wondering why ADO keeps track of the original values. ADO won't post any updates to the database if a row has been changed since it was read. If another user has already modified the same line after your application has read it, ADO generates a runtime error and won't overwrite the edited columns. When the updates take place through a disconnected recordset, ADO needs to know what the values of the columns in the recordset were before it can commit any changes to the database.

Inserting Rows

Inserted rows appear at the end of the document in an `<rs:insert>` tag. The following lines add a new customer to the XML document:

```
<rs:insert>
  <z:row CustomerID="TEST" />
  <z:row CustomerID="TEST"
         CompanyName="TEST-CompanyName"
         ContactName="TEST-ContactName"
         ContactTitle="TEST-ContactTitle" />
</rs:insert>
```

To summarize, you must follow these steps to persist a recordset to an XML document and to edit the persisted rows:

1. Create a disconnected recordset by setting its `LockType` property to `adLockBatchOptimistic`. You can persist all types of recordsets, but ADO won't reflect the changes in the recordset to the XML document representing the recordset. Other types of recordsets update the database as soon as a row is changed. Only disconnected recordsets maintain a list of changes and submit all the changes to the database at once.
2. Persist the recordset to an XML file. Do so by calling the recordset's `Save` method with the `adPersistXML` argument. ADO will convert the current recordset into an XML document and save it to disk. The disk file is a static image of the recordset the moment you saved it (in XML format, of course).
3. Edit the recordset and resave it as an XML file. ADO maintains internally all the changes made to the recordset. (It's actually the Cursor service that maintains the changes, in addition to the original data.) This is the information that will be stored to the database.
4. If you update the recordset by calling its `UpdateBatch` method, the changes will be committed to the database. An updated disconnected recordset doesn't contain any `<rs:update>` tags.

NOTE

If the Cursor engine can't commit the changes to the database, a runtime error will occur.

Deleting Rows

Deleted rows appear at the end of the document in an `<rs:delete>` tag. As an example, if you remove the customer with key ANTON from the Customers table of the Northwind database, the following lines will be appended to the `<rs:data>` section of the XML file:

```
<rs:delete>
  <z:row CustomerID="ANTON"
         CompanyName="Antonio Moreno Taquer a"
         ContactName="Antonio Moreno"
         ContactTitle="Owner"
         Address="Mataderos 23129"
         City="M xico D.F." PostalCode="05023"
         Country="Mexico" Phone="(5) 555-3932" />
</rs:delete>
```

As you can see, the entire row, not just the primary key of the row, appears in the XML document.

Editing Disconnected Recordsets: An Example

Let's look at an example of editing disconnected recordsets persisted in XML format. This is a Visual Basic project, but you don't really need to understand Visual Basic. Because the code is quite simple, you can understand what's happening, even if you're not familiar with the data-access features of Visual Basic. The project is called `DisconnectedRS`, and you will find it in a folder called DisconnectedRS in the accompanying sample code.

To begin, start a new project and add a reference to the Microsoft Active Data Object 2.5 Library to the project. Then, place a Command button on the form and enter the following code in the button's Click event handler:

```
Private Sub Command1_Click()
Dim RS As New ADODB.Recordset
    RS.CursorLocation = adUseClient
    RS.LockType = adLockBatchOptimistic
    RS.Open "C:\Customers.xml"
    RS.Fields(1) = RS.Fields(1) & "1"
```

```
    RS.MoveNext
    RS.Delete
    Kill "C:\Customers.xml"
    RS.Save "C:\Customers.xml", adPersistXML
End Sub
```

The code is quite simple—a real recordset-editing application would be too complicated. But, if you're familiar with ADO's basic features, you can easily develop a user interface for an application that allows users to edit any row.

When the Save method is called to persist the recordset to a local XML file, the updates are saved along with the original data. If you call the UpdateBatch method, however, the changes are committed to the XML representation of the recordset. The UpdateBatch method makes changes in the <rs:data> section of the XML document.

The code shown above edits the first row (by appending a single character to the CompanyName field value) and then deletes the next row. To add a new row, insert the following statements:

```
RS.AddNew
RS.Fields(0)="TEST"
RS.Fields(1)="TEST-CompanyName"
RS.Fields(2)="TEST-ContactName"
RS.Fields(3)="TEST-ContactTitle"
RS.Update
```

If you persist the recordset to an XML file, the following lines will be appended to the <rs:data> section:

```
<rs:insert>
  <z:row CustomerID="TEST"
         CompanyName="TEST-CompanyName"
         ContactName="TEST-ContactName"
         ContactTitle="TEST-ContactTitle" />
</rs:insert>
```

Multiple inserts appear together in a single <rs:insert> section, but each row has its own <z:row> element.

This example uses the XML representation of a recordset, but there are no advantages to using XML with a desktop application. In the next section, you'll see how to pass the XML representation of a recordset to the client and how to get back the same recordset in XML format to update the database.

Part iii

Passing XML Data to the Client

In addition to files, ADO recordsets can be persisted in `Stream` objects, which represent streams of data. The most common `Stream` object is the ASP `Response` object, which represents the stream of data from the web server to the client. For more about ASP objects, see Chapter 13, "Accessing Databases Over the Web." If you have ASP 3.0 installed on your server (ASP 3.0 comes with Windows 2000, and so does ADO 2.5), you can persist a recordset directly to the `Response` object. Use the following statement:

```
RS.Save Response, 1
```

where the second argument is the value of the constant `adPersistXML`. (ASP doesn't consult type libraries to resolve constant names.)

WARNING

If you use constant names in your code, as you should, make sure you have declared them or have included the appropriate INC file. If not, VBScript will assume it's a variable and will initialize it to zero.

NOTE

If you're using VB to create the recordset, you don't have to declare the constants.

The previous statement creates a recordset and sends it to the client. The browser sees an XML document and displays the raw data. Normally, you don't want to display raw data to the client; therefore, you add a client-side script, or an XSL file, to display the data in a more appropriate format. The XML data that is part of an HTML page forms a *data island*. The viewer sees what you display on the browser from within your script, not the raw XML data.

Now that you have seen how to create disconnected recordsets and how you can XML format the rows of a disconnected recordset, let's switch our attention to the client and see how to bind the XML-formatted data to HTML elements.

Creating and Using Data Islands

A section of XML data enclosed in a pair of XML tags forms a data island. You can create data islands by simply retrieving the desired data from the database and sending it directly to the client by persisting the recordset to the `Response` object.

First, create the `Products.xml` file by persisting the recordset with the rows of the Products table in the Northwind database. Then, create a file with the XML data to the client with the following script:

```
<%
Const adPersistXML = 1
Set RS = Server.CreateObject("ADODB.Recordset")
RS.Open "Products", "DSN=NWINDDB"
RS.Save "C:\Products.xml", adPersistXML
%>
```

This short script generates a typical XML output. The XML output produced by the Save method is not really an XML island; it contains an <XML>, but this tag doesn't have an ID attribute. Thus, you must surround the entire file by the following pair of <XML> tags:

```
<XML ID="Products">

</XML>
```

However, there is a problem with this solution: You can't have nested <XML> tags in an XML document. The correct solution is to rename the <XML> tags in the XML document generated by the Save method to something else and then embed the entire document in a new pair of <XML> tags. You can rename the existing <XML> tags into anything; (I used the tag <ADOXML> in testing the scripts). Here are the first two and last two lines of the revised XML file:

```
<XML ID="XMLProducts">
<ADOXML    xmlns:s=

</ADOXML>
</XML>
```

Don't be concerned that if you open the edited file with Internet Explorer, you won't see anything. There's nothing wrong with the file; the XML document sent to the client has become a data island. The data is available to the client, but there's no script to tell the browser what to do with the data.

To turn the data island into an HTML page that can be displayed on the browser, add a few HTML statements to the XML file by adding the following HTML elements and binding them to the fields of the recordset:

```
<HTML>
<TABLE DATASRC="#XMLProducts">
<TR><TD>
<TABLE DATASRC="#XMLProducts" DATAFLD="rs:data">
<TR><TD>
<TABLE DATASRC="#XMLProducts" DATAFLD="z:row" >
<TR>
<TD><SPAN DATAFLD="ProductID"></SPAN></TD>
<TD><SPAN DATAFLD="ProductName"></SPAN></TD>
<TD><SPAN DATAFLD="UnitPrice"></SPAN></TD>
</TR>
</TABLE>
</TD></TR>
</TABLE>
</TD></TR>
</TABLE>
</HTML>
```

If you want to be able to edit the table, replace the table's cells with Text controls. Figure 15.3 shows a section of the page with the Northwind products displayed on a table. You will find the XML data island and the HTML code for binding the fields to a table's cells in the `ProductsXML.htm` file in the sample code. To create this file, I generated the recordset with the recordset's `Save` method and then edited it a little.

I must explain the statements that bind the table to the data islands. They're rather different from the binding statements you've seen so far. The fields to bind to the table are the ones prefixed by the `<z:row>` tag, but these tags appear under the `<rs:data>` tag. So, to skip the `<rs:data>` section, bind the fields in the `<rs:data>` tag to a table that has no rows of its own. Then, within this table, nest another table whose cells are bound to the fields in the `<z:row>` tag. You'll have to use this simple trick with all the data islands you create with ADO's `Recordset.Save` method. The alternative is to include an XSL file or a client-side script to exploit the XML document's DOM.

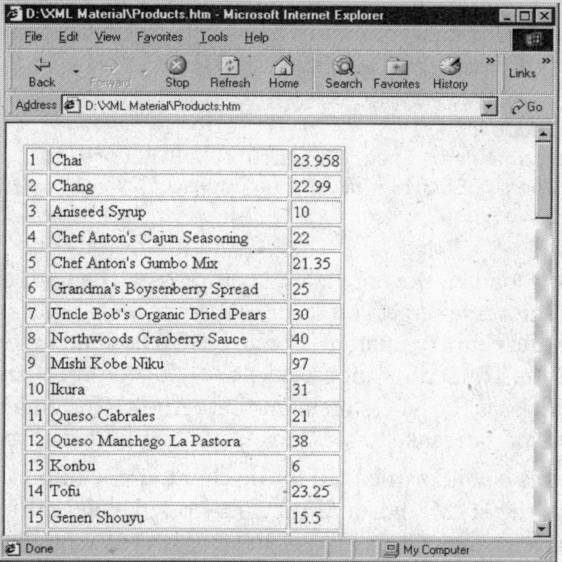

FIGURE 15.3: Displaying a data island on a table

Creating Data Islands on the Fly

The example in the previous section demonstrates how to create XML data islands and process them on the client. As you have probably noticed, we had to edit the XML recordset. We persisted the recordset to an XML file, then edited it to convert the file into a form suitable for use as a data island on the client. To make this technique more useful, you should be able to edit the XML data from within your server-side script. This would allow you to create XML data islands on the fly, without user intervention.

To do so, first insert an RDS Data Control that provides the data. The following <OBJECT> tag places an RDS Data Control on the page, which calls a script on the server to retrieve the data:

```
<OBJECT
   CLASSID="clsid:bd96c556-65a3-11d0-983a-00c04fc29e33"
   ID="DSOCustomers" WIDTH="0" HEIGHT="0">
<PARAM NAME= "URL" VALUE="GetCustomersXML.asp">
</OBJECT>
```

The name of the script is `GetCustomersXML.asp`, and here's what it does. First, it creates a local recordset (on the web server) with the desired data. Then, it saves the data on the `Response` stream:

```
<%
CN = "DSN=NWINDDB
Set RSCustomers=Server.CreateObject("ADODB.Recordset")
RSCustomers.Open "SELECT * FROM Customers", CN
RSCustomers.Save Response, 1
%>
```

When the page is loaded, the data island contains all the rows of the Customers table. The same script could accept a parameter to select customers from a specific country, customers who have placed an order in the last month, and so on. The script that provides the data doesn't change; the only thing that changes is the SQL statement that retrieves the data to populate the recordset. You can make this statement as complicated as you wish.

Once the data has been downloaded to the client, it's bound to the HTML elements of the HTML Form. If the data-bound elements allow editing of their content, the viewer can modify the recordset on the client. Of course, you should also be able to return the edited recordset to the server, where it will be used to update the database. You'll see how to post the data to the server shortly. But first, let's look at the code for editing the recordset on the client.

Navigational and Editing Operations

The code for binding the XML recordset's fields to Text controls on the Form is fairly simple, and you've seen it before. This time, we'll use the following statements to bind one row at a time to a few Text controls:

```
Company Name
<INPUT TYPE=TEXT DATASRC="#DSOCustomers"
                 DATAFLD="CompanyName" SIZE="40">
</INPUT>
<BR>
Contact Name
<INPUT TYPE=TEXT DATASRC="#DSOCustomers"
                 DATAFLD="ContactName" SIZE="30">
</INPUT>
Contact Title
<INPUT TYPE=TEXT DATASRC="#DSOCustomers"
                 DATAFLD="ContactTitle" SIZE="25">
</INPUT>
```

This code binds the CompanyName, ContactName, and ContactTitles fields to three Text controls. You can add the statements to bind the remaining fields, as well. When the page is loaded, you'll see the fields of the first row, as shown in Figure 15.4.

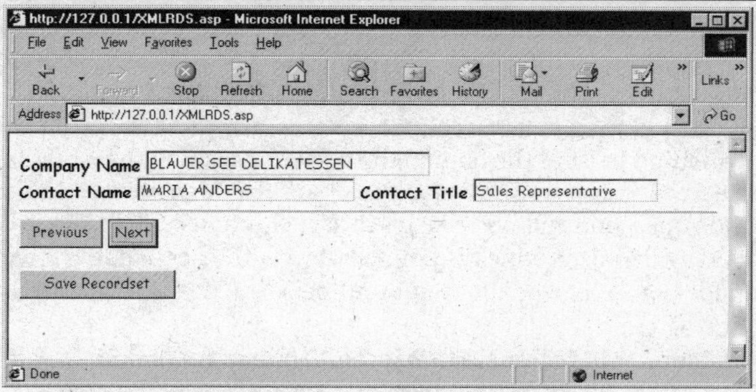

FIGURE 15.4: Editing an XML recordset on the client

You must also add a few buttons (shown in Figure 15.4) to allow the viewer to navigate through the recordset. Add the Previous and Next buttons with the following statements:

```
<INPUT TYPE=button VALUE="Previous" ONCLICK="PrevRec">
<INPUT TYPE=button VALUE="Next" ONCLICK="NextRec">
```

You must also provide the code for the PrevRec and NextRec buttons (seen as Previous and Next). This code must simply call the MovePrevious and MoveNext methods of the RDS Data Control:

```
Sub NextRec
    If Not DSOCustomers.Recordset.EOF Then
        DSOCustomers.Recordset.MoveNext
    End If
End Sub

Sub PrevRec
    If Not DSOCustomers.Recordset.BOF Then
       DSOCustomers.Recordset.MovePrevious
    End If
End Sub
```

Notice that the code examines the BOF and EOF properties to make sure that the script doesn't attempt to move before the first row or beyond the last row in the recordset.

Finally, add a button for submitting the changes to the server. The definition of this button, Save Recordset, is shown here:

```
<INPUT TYPE=button VALUE="Save Recordset"
       ONCLICK="PostData">
```

The PostData subroutine, which posts the modified recordset to the server, is the most interesting part of the page. The code uses the XML-HTTP object, which uses the HTTP protocol to pass XML-encoded data to the server. This script uses two of the XMLHTTP object's methods: the Open method to establish a connection to a script on the server, and the Send method to send the data to the server by reading the XML data from a Stream object. The last argument of the Open method indicates that the operation will not take place asynchronously. This object is an ADO Stream object, which is populated with the Recordset.Save method. Here's the PostData subroutine:

```
Sub PostData()
   Set XMLHTTP = CreateObject("Microsoft.XMLHTTP")
   Set StrData = CreateObject("ADODB.Stream")
   DSOCustomers.Recordset.Save StrData, 1
   XMLHTTP.Open "POST", "GetXMLData.asp", False
   XMLHTTP.Send STRDATA.ReadText()
End Sub
```

You may have noticed that this technique requires the presence of two objects on the client: the XMLHTTP and ADO objects. XMLHTTP comes with Internet Explorer, and ADO 2.5 (the ADO version that supports the Stream object) is also installed along with Windows 2000. The bottom line is that this technique works with Internet Explorer only. For the time being, Microsoft is ahead of Netscape in using XML as a universal data exchange protocol, but it's too early to say which methods will be adopted by the industry for exchanging XML data between servers and clients, especially for posting data to the server.

Listing 15.2 shows the entire document that allows editing of recordsets on the client.

Listing 15.2: Editing Recordsets on the Client (*XMLRDS.asp*)

```
<HTML>
<OBJECT CLASSID="clsid:bd96c556-65a3-11d0-983a-00c04fc29e33"
   ID="DSOCustomers" WIDTH="0" HEIGHT="0">
<PARAM NAME= "URL" VALUE="Customers.xml">
</OBJECT>
```

```
<SCRIPT LANGUAGE=VBScript>
Sub PostData()
   Set XMLHTTP = CreateObject("Microsoft.XMLHTTP")
   Set StrData = CreateObject("ADODB.Stream")
   DSOCustomers.Recordset.Save StrData, 1
   XMLHTTP.open "POST", "GetXMLData.asp", False
   XMLHTTP.Send STRDATA.ReadText()
End Sub

Sub NextRec
    If Not DSOCustomers.Recordset.EOF Then
        DSOCustomers.Recordset.MoveNext
    End If
End Sub

Sub PrevRec
    If Not DSOCustomers.Recordset.BOF Then
       DSOCustomers.Recordset.MovePrevious
    End If
End Sub

</SCRIPT>
<FONT FACE="Comic Sans MS" SIZE=3>
Company Name <INPUT TYPE=TEXT DATASRC="#DSOCustomers"
              DATAFLD="CompanyName" SIZE="40"></INPUT>
<BR>
Contact Name <INPUT TYPE=TEXT
              DATASRC="#DSOCustomers"
              DATAFLD="ContactName" SIZE="30">
</INPUT>
Contact Title
<INPUT TYPE=TEXT DATASRC="#DSOCustomers"
       DATAFLD="ContactTitle" SIZE="25"></INPUT>
<HR>
<INPUT TYPE=button VALUE="Previous" ONCLICK="PrevRec">
<INPUT TYPE=button VALUE="Next" ONCLICK="NextRec">
<P>
<INPUT TYPE=button VALUE="Save Recordset"
       ONCLICK="PostData">
</FONT>
</HTML>
```

Reading XML Data on the Server

Now you need a method to read the edited recordset on the server. The client-side script transmitted the data with the POST method, so you must use the Request object on the server to read the data. To read the data, use the recordset object's Open method, specifying that it should read from a file:

```
NewRS = Server.CreateObject("ADODB.Recordset")
NewRS.Open Request, , , , adCmdFile
```

Notice that no connection information is specified in the Open method. This technique will work only if:

- The recordset sent to the client is opened as a disconnected recordset. Only a disconnected recordset maintains the changes to the data, and not just the new values of the fields.
- The recordset is mapped to an RDS Data Control on the client, and not to an XML Data Control.
- The recordset that receives the XML data on the server is also opened as a disconnected recordset, so that you can call its UpdateBatch method to commit the changes.

Once the remote XML recordset is read into a local recordset on the server, you can call the UpdateBatch method to commit the changes to the database. The following script accepts the edited XML recordset on the server and posts the changes to the database:

```
<%
NewRS = Server.CreateObject("ADODB.Recordset")
NewRS.CursorLocation = adUseClient
NewRS.Open Request, ,adOpenKeyset , _
          adLockBatchOptimistic , adCmdFile
NewRS.ActiveConnection = "DSN=NWIND"
NewRS.UpdateBatch
NewRS.Close
Set NewRS = Nothing
%>
```

This script reads the data posted by the client. The NewRS recordset variable is opened with the adLockBatchOptimistic option, because it's a disconnected recordset. Then, it connects the disconnected recordset to the database and calls the UpdateBatch method to update the database. This is the GetXMLData.asp script, which you will find in the accompanying sample code.

Hierarchical Recordsets

The recordsets used so far are uniform—each row contains the same number of columns. These recordsets are very similar to tables, although they may contain rows from multiple tables.

Another type of recordset contains not only rows from multiple tables, but the relationship between the tables they're based on. These are called *hierarchical*, or *shaped*, recordsets. They're made up of different sections, and each section has a different structure. Let's say you want a list of all customers in a city, their orders, and the items of each order. A hierarchical recordset with this information contains a row for each customer. Under each customer, there's another recordset with the customer's orders.

In this table, the customer rows have a different structure from the order rows, and the order rows have a different structure from the item rows. Thus, the recordset carries with it information about the structure of the entities it includes, as shown in this example:

```
Customer 1
  Order 1
    Item 1
    Item 2
    Item 3
  Order 2
    Item1
    Item2
Customer 2
  Order 1
    Item 1
    Item 2
    Item 3
    Item 4
  Order 2
    Item 1
    Item 2
  Order 3
    Item 1
    Item 2
```

Each customer has one or more orders, and all the orders belonging to the same customer appear under the customer's name. Likewise, each order has one or more items, and all the items (detail lines) belonging to the same order appear under the order's ID.

Hierarchical recordsets are structured, and they lend themselves to XML descriptions. You can use ADO to produce hierarchical recordsets, but these recordsets are pretty useless outside ADO. You just can't process a hierarchical recordset on a computer that doesn't support ADO. However, if you translate a hierarchical recordset to an XML document, you can process it on every computer that supports XML.

The SHAPE Language

To create hierarchical recordsets, a special language is used, the *SHAPE language*, which supports all of the SQL statements, plus a few more keywords, to specify the relationships between the different recordsets. Following is the SHAPE statement that produces a hierarchical recordset with the customers, their orders, and the details of each order:

```
SHAPE {SELECT * FROM Customers}  AS
Command1 APPEND (( SHAPE {SELECT * FROM Orders}
AS  & Command2 APPEND ({SELECT * " & _
    " FROM [Order Details]}  AS Command3 RELATE 'OrderID'
```

Fortunately, you don't have to learn the SHAPE language to create hierarchical recordsets. The simplest method to define a hierarchical recordset is to use the Visual Database Tools that come with Visual Studio. You can also write the statement yourself; conceptually, it's a little more complicated than straight SQL.

Building Hierarchical Recordsets with VB

Let's build a shaped recordset with VB. To do so, start a new VB project and enter the following statements in a button's Click event handler:

```
Private Sub Command1_Click()
Dim RS As New Recordset
ShapedCommand =
    " SHAPE {SELECT * FROM Customers}  AS " & _
    " Command1 APPEND (( SHAPE {SELECT * FROM Orders}" & _
    " AS " & Command2 APPEND ({SELECT * " & _
    " FROM [Order Details]}  AS Command3 RELATE " & _
    " 'OrderID' TO 'OrderID') AS Command3) " & _
    " AS Command2 RELATE 'CustomerID' TO" & _
    " 'CustomerID') AS Command2"
RS.Open ShapedCommand, CN
RS.Save "C:\Temp\Sales.xml", adPersistXML
```

You must set the CN Connection object to point to the Northwind database on your system. If you run the program and click the button, a recordset will be created and saved to a disk file as `Sales.xml`, which is shown in Listing 15.3.

Listing 15.3: The *Sales.xml* File

```
- <xml xmlns:s="uuid:BDC6E3F0-6DA3-11d1-A2A3-00AA00C14882"
      xmlns:dt="uuid:C2F41010-65B3-11d1-A29F-00AA00C14882"
      xmlns:rs="urn:schemas-microsoft-com:rowset"
      xmlns:z="#RowsetSchema">
- <s:Schema id="RowsetSchema">
  - <s:ElementType name="row" content="eltOnly"
            rs:CommandTimeout="30"
rs:ReshapeName="Command1">
  - <s:AttributeType name="CustomerID" rs:number="1"
            rs:writeunknown="true">
    <s:datatype dt:type="string" dt:maxLength="5"
            rs:fixedlength="true" rs:maybenull="false" />
    </s:AttributeType>
  - <s:AttributeType name="CompanyName"
            rs:number="2" rs:writeunknown="true">
    <s:datatype dt:type="string" dt:maxLength="40"
            rs:maybenull="false" />
    </s:AttributeType>
  - <s:AttributeType name="ContactName"
            rs:number="3" rs:nullable="true"
            rs:writeunknown="true">
    <s:datatype dt:type="string" dt:maxLength="30" />
    </s:AttributeType>
    - <s:ElementType name="Command2" content="eltOnly"
            rs:CommandTimeout="30"
            rs:ReshapeName="Command2"
            rs:relation="010000000200000000000000">
    - <s:AttributeType name="OrderID" rs:number="1">
      <s:datatype dt:type="int" dt:maxLength="4"
            rs:precision="10" rs:fixedlength="true"
            rs:maybenull="false" />
      </s:AttributeType>
    - <s:AttributeType name="CustomerID" rs:number="2"
            rs:nullable="true" rs:writeunknown="true">
      <s:datatype dt:type="string" dt:maxLength="5"
            rs:fixedlength="true" />
      </s:AttributeType>
    - <s:AttributeType name="EmployeeID" rs:number="3"
            rs:nullable="true" rs:writeunknown="true">
      <s:datatype dt:type="int" dt:maxLength="4"
            rs:precision="10" rs:fixedlength="true" />
```

```
        </s:AttributeType>
      - <s:AttributeType name="OrderDate"
              rs:number="4" rs:nullable="true"
              rs:writeunknown="true">
        <s:datatype dt:type="dateTime" rs:dbtype="timestamp"
              dt:maxLength="16" rs:scale="3"
              rs:precision="23" rs:fixedlength="true" />
        </s:AttributeType>
        - <s:ElementType name="Command3" content="eltOnly"
              rs:CommandTimeout="30"
rs:ReshapeName="Command3"
              rs:relation="010000000100000000000000">
        - <s:AttributeType name="OrderID"
              rs:number="1" rs:writeunknown="true">
          <s:datatype dt:type="int" dt:maxLength="4"
              rs:precision="10" rs:fixedlength="true"
              rs:maybenull="false" />
          </s:AttributeType>
        - <s:AttributeType name="ProductID"
              rs:number="2" rs:writeunknown="true">
          <s:datatype dt:type="int" dt:maxLength="4"
              rs:precision="10" rs:fixedlength="true"
              rs:maybenull="false" />
          </s:AttributeType>
        - <s:AttributeType name="UnitPrice"
              rs:number="3" rs:writeunknown="true">
          <s:datatype dt:type="i8" rs:dbtype="currency"
              dt:maxLength="8" rs:precision="19"
              rs:fixedlength="true" rs:maybenull="false" />
          </s:AttributeType>
          </s:ElementType>
          </s:Schema>
```

To explore the structure of this script, I'll use one of the sample pages at the Microsoft XML site. If you connect to `msdn.microsoft.com/xml/general`, you will find a list of interesting samples. Connect to this URL, click the Sync TOC button, and when the frames with the TOC appear, click the Samples and Downloads link. Select the XML Data Source Object, and download it to your computer. After you have saved all the necessary files in a folder on your system, double-click the `dsoMap.htm` file's icon, and you will see the page shown in Figure 15.5.

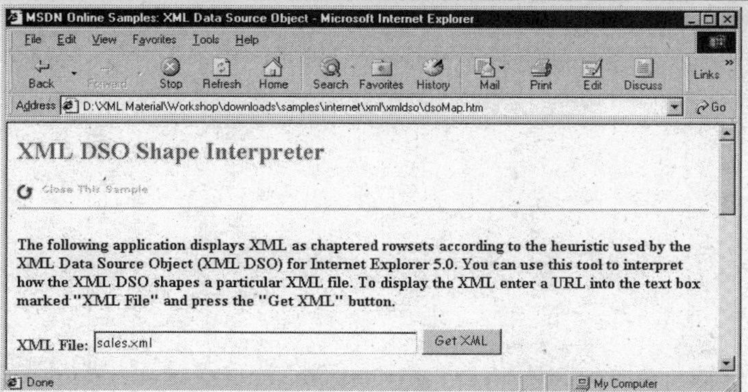

FIGURE 15.5: On this page, select the XML file to map.

Enter **Sales.xml** in the XML File textbox, and click the Get XML button. Scroll to the bottom of the XML DSO Shape Interpreter page, and you'll see the two sections in the file: the schema section and the data section. Both items are hyperlinks, and you can click the `<rs:data>` hyperlink to see the data of the hierarchical recordset. This section is made up of `<z:row>` tags.

When you click the `<rs:data>` hyperlink, you'll see another table that contains the `<z:row>` hyperlink. Click this hyperlink and you will see the nodes of the parent recordset, which contains all the customers in the database, as shown in Figure 15.6. For each customer, you see the number of orders placed by the customer (in the TotInvoices column) as well as the total revenue for the specific customer (in the CustomerTotal column).

In each customer's Orders column is another hyperlink, leading to the child recordset that corresponds to each customer and contains all of their orders. For example, if you click the Orders hyperlink for the customer ANTON, you'll see all of Anton's orders, as shown in Figure 15.7.

This recordset contains each order's ID (in the OrderID column), as well as its total (in the OrderTotal column). The order's total is not stored along with each order; it's a calculated field. Each row in the Orders recordset has its own child recordset, which contains the order's detail lines. Click an order's `Details` hyperlink to see the order's details.

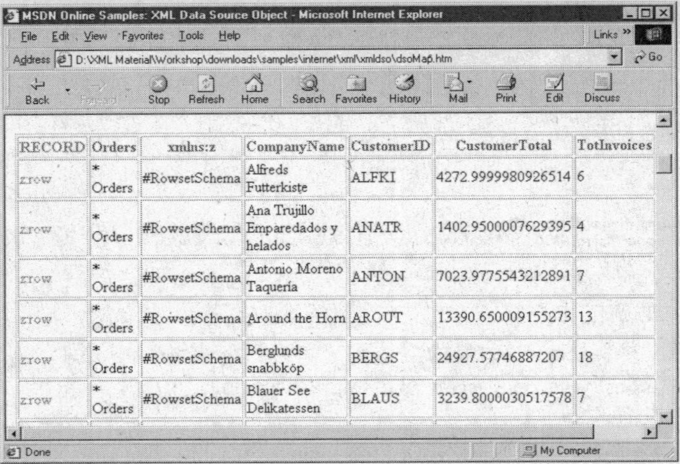

RECORD	Orders	xmlns:z	CompanyName	CustomerID	CustomerTotal	TotInvoices
zrow	* Orders	#RowsetSchema	Alfreds Futterkiste	ALFKI	4272.9999980926514	6
zrow	* Orders	#RowsetSchema	Ana Trujillo Emparedados y helados	ANATR	1402.9500007629395	4
zrow	* Orders	#RowsetSchema	Antonio Moreno Taquería	ANTON	7023.9775543212891	7
zrow	* Orders	#RowsetSchema	Around the Horn	AROUT	13390.650009155273	13
zrow	* Orders	#RowsetSchema	Berglunds snabbköp	BERGS	24927.57746887207	18
zrow	* Orders	#RowsetSchema	Blauer See Delikatessen	BLAUS	3239.8000030517578	7

FIGURE 15.6: Viewing the customers in the Sales.xml recordset

RECORD	Details	CustomerID	OrderID	OrderTotal	$Text
Orders	* Details	ANTON	10365	403.20001220703125	
Orders	* Details	ANTON	10507	749.0625	
Orders	* Details	ANTON	10535	1940.8499908447266	
Orders	* Details	ANTON	10573	2082	
Orders	* Details	ANTON	10677	813.36505126953125	
Orders	* Details	ANTON	10682	375.5	
Orders	* Details	ANTON	10856	660	

Press the "Back" button to navigate back up the tree.

Back

FIGURE 15.7: Viewing a customer's orders

While you're exploring hierarchical recordsets with the `DSOMap.htm` page, you can view the XML recordset by clicking the View XML button at the bottom of the page. This appends the entire XML recordset to the current page.

The Shape Interpreter page is an interesting example of a client-side script that handles complicated recordsets. However, developers shouldn't have to write complicated scripts to handle hierarchical recordsets (and

DSOMap.htm deploys a complicated script on the client). The promise of XML is to make data exchange between different systems a reality. This can't happen by placing the burden on the programmer. We need tools that will allow us to display hierarchical recordsets easily and even manipulate them from within scripts with a few statements. It won't be long before you see numerous tools for interpreting and manipulating complicated recordsets.

You will also notice that it takes Internet Explorer a while to load the XML document and bind its fields to the nested tables. Scripting languages are interpreted, not compiled, and they're not as fast as a compiled VB application.

DSOMap.htm is a helpful tool, because it allows you to visualize both the structure of a hierarchical recordset, as well as the data. However, this is not how you would display a hierarchical recordset on a page. A page made up by nested tables, like the one shown in Figure 15.8 in the next section, is more appropriate. Let's see how to create nested tables by binding a hierarchical recordset to a table.

Binding Hierarchical Recordsets

Again, let's assume that the XML recordset was generated by ADO. The first step in creating nested tables with hierarchical recordsets is to bind the <rs:data> section to a table with no rows. Then we can bind the <x:row> section to a nested table. This is what we did with flat recordsets earlier in the chapter. A hierarchical recordset's <z:row> section, however, contains rows from multiple tables. We must be able to separate each child recordset's rows and display them in their own table.

To begin, the outermost table must be bound to the section <rs:data>, as usual:

```
<TABLE BORDER="1" DATASRC="#Sales" DATAFLD="rs:data">
```

The first nested table corresponds to the customers, and it must be bound to the section <z:row>:

```
<TABLE BORDER="1" DATASRC="#Sales" DATAFLD="z:row">
```

Then, the cells of this table must be bound to the columns of the Customers child recordset:

```
<TD VALIGN=top><B>
    <SPAN DATAFLD="CompanyName"></B></SPAN></TD>
<TD>
```

To bind the next nested section in the recordset to an HTML table, use the following value of the DATAFLD attribute:

```
<TABLE BORDER="1" DATASRC="#Sales"
                  DATAFLD="rs:data.z:row.Orders">
```

This table's cells must be bound to the fields of the Orders child recordset:

```
<TD VALIGN=top><SPAN DATAFLD="OrderID"></SPAN></TD>
<TD VALIGN=top><SPAN DATAFLD="OrderTotal"></SPAN></TD>
```

The details are a child recordset of the Orders recordset. Their table must be bound to the following field:

```
<TABLE BORDER="1" DATASRC="#Sales"
                  DATAFLD="rs:data.z:row.Orders.Details">
```

The Details recordset, which is a child of the Orders recordset, is in turn, a child of the Customers recordset.

Now let's look at Listing 15.4, the complete `Sales.htm` file. The file is fairly lengthy, but not difficult to understand.

Listing 15.4: Binding Hierarchies to an HTML Table (*Sales.htm*)

```
<TABLE DATASRC="#Sales">
<TR>
  <TD>
    <TABLE BORDER="1" DATASRC="#Sales" DATAFLD="rs:data">
    <TR>
      <TD>
        <TABLE BORDER="1" DATASRC="#Sales" DATAFLD="z:row">
        <TR>
          <TD VALIGN=top><B>
               <SPAN DATAFLD="CompanyName"></B></SPAN></TD>
          <TD>
          <TABLE BORDER="1" DATASRC="#Sales"
                 DATAFLD="rs:data.z:row.Orders">
          <THEAD>
          <TR>
          <TD><B>OrderID</B></TD>
          <TD><B>Total</B></TD>
          </TR>
          </THEAD>
          <TBODY>
          <TR>
            <TD VALIGN=top>
```

```
                <SPAN DATAFLD="OrderID"></SPAN></TD>
            <TD VALIGN=top>
                <SPAN DATAFLD="OrderTotal"></SPAN></TD>
            <TD>
            <TABLE DATASRC="#Sales"
                   DATAFLD="rs:data.z:row.Orders.Details">
            <THEAD>
            <TR>
              <TD><B>ID</B></TD>
              <TD><B>Price</B></TD>
              <TD><B>Qty</B></TD>
              <TD><B>SubTotal</TD>
            </TR>
            </THEAD>
            <TBODY>
            <TR>
              <TD><SPAN DATAFLD="ProductID"></SPAN></TD>
              <TD><SPAN DATAFLD="UnitPrice"></SPAN></TD>
              <TD><SPAN DATAFLD="Quantity"></SPAN></TD>
              <TD><SPAN DATAFLD="LineTotal"></SPAN></TD>
            </TR>
            </TBODY>
            </TD>
          </TR>
          </TBODY>
          </TABLE>
          </TD>
        </TR>
        </TABLE>
      </TD>
    </TR>
    </TABLE>
  </TD>
</TR>
</TABLE>
```

Part iii

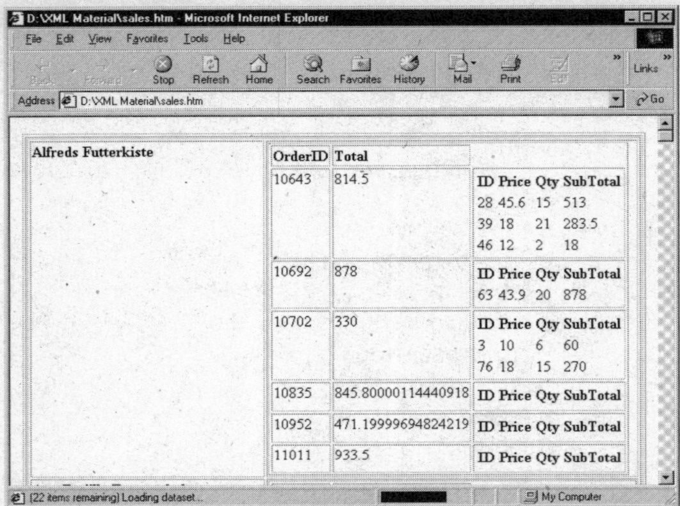

FIGURE 15.8: Binding a hierarchical recordset to nested tables on an HTML page

Viewing Reduced Recordsets

One of the most common and most useful applications of XML recordsets is to reduce the information displayed on the client. Let's say you want to display a hierarchical recordset with sales information. If you download a data island with the orders of a few customers, you are defeating the purpose of the data island. Clearly, you must download all the information in a single data island.

If you download all the information at once and display all the rows of the recordset on the same page, this page will be too long to be practical. The solution is to hide the child recordsets and let the user expand (and collapse) them as needed. This way, the viewer can quickly locate and view the desired information. When they're done with a child recordset (a customer's orders, or an orders' lines), they can simply hide it and move to another one.

To collapse and expand sections of the table, you must insert a script that reacts to the click of the mouse over a customer's name or an order ID. Assuming that the cells with the customers are named Orders and the nested tables with the orders are named OrdersTable, Listing 15.5 (`SalesTree.htm`) can be used to display and hide each customer's orders.

Listing 15.5: The Mouse Event Handlers for the Bound Recordset (*SalesTree.htm*)

```
<SCRIPT LANGUAGE=JavaScript FOR=Orders EVENT=onclick>
  rowID = this.recordNumber - 1;
  if (OrdersTable[rowID].style.display == "none")
  {
    OrdersTable[rowID].style.display = "inline";
  }
  else
  {
    OrdersTable[rowID].style.display = "none";
  }
  window.event.cancelBubble = true;
</SCRIPT>

<SCRIPT LANGUAGE=JavaScript FOR=Details EVENT=onclick>
  rowID = this.recordNumber - 1;
  if (DetailsTable[rowID].style.display == "none")
  {
    DetailsTable[rowID].style.display = "inline";
  }
  else
  {
    DetailsTable[rowID].style.display = "none";
  }
  window.event.cancelBubble = true;
</SCRIPT>
```

This file is identical to the `Sales.htm` page we saw earlier, except that some of the HTML elements have different names and styles. Also, there is some added script that expands/collapses the orders and details for each customer.

The SalesTree page is shown in Figure 15.9. As you can see, the page lets you select a customer and view their orders and order details.

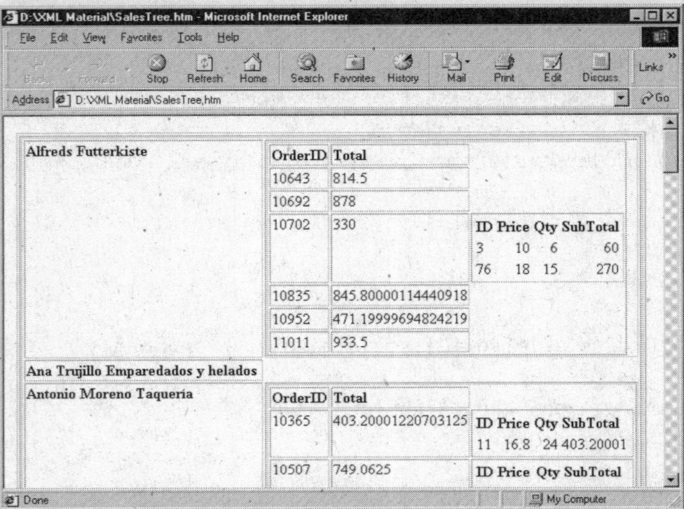

FIGURE 15.9: The SalesTree page

XML AND SQL SERVER 2000

Everything we discussed in the earlier section, "ADO Support for XML," applies to SQL Server as well, but SQL Server 2000 provides native support for XML. What this means is that SQL Server can produce XML-formatted cursors and transmit them directly to the client. The XML support for SQL Server is provided in the form of DLLs that sit between the DBMS and the web server. These DLLs convert the cursors, returned by SQL Server in response to a query to XML data.

Let me start by showing you how easy it is to execute a SQL statement against a SQL Server database and retrieve a cursor in XML format. As you recall, a data island need not be included as is in an ASP file. You can use the SRC attribute of the <XML> tag to specify the URL of the XML file, or the URL of an ASP script that will return the desired data. The following lines can be entered in the browser's Address box to contact the SQL Server running on the same machine and execute a SQL statement against the Northwind database:

```
http://127.0.0.1/NorthWind?sql=SELECT+
CategoryName,+Description+FROM+Categories
FOR+XML+RAW
```

NOTE

This long line was broken to fit on the book page. Don't worry about this—you can't break lines in the browser's Address box anyway.

Any string entered in the browser's Address box must not contain any special characters. These characters must be replaced by their URL-encoded equivalents, which are shown in Table 15.4.

TABLE 15.4: The URL Encoding of Special Characters

SPECIAL CHARACTER	URL ENCODING
Space	+
+	%2B
/	%2F
?	%3F
%	%25
#	%23
&	%26

Once you enter the appropriate information into the browser's Address box, SQL Server 2000 will execute the query and return the names and descriptions of the categories in the Northwind database, as shown here:

```
<?xml version="1.0" encoding="UTF-8" ?>
<root>
<row CategoryName="Beverages"
     Description="Soft drinks  "/>
<row CategoryName="Condiments"
     Description="Sweet and Savory "/>
<row CategoryName="Confections"
     Description="Desserts, "/>
<row CategoryName="Dairy Products"
     Description="Cheeses"/>
<row CategoryName="Grains/Cereals"
     Description="Breads, crackers "/>
<row CategoryName="Meat/Poultry"
     Description="Prepared meats "/>
<row CategoryName="Produce"
     Description="Dried fruit  "/>
```

```
<row CategoryName="Seafood"
     Description="Seaweed and fish"/>
</root>
</xml>
```

Figure 15.10 shows how this file is rendered on your browser's window. This is an XML data island, and it contains row data, but no information about the structure of the data in the cursor.

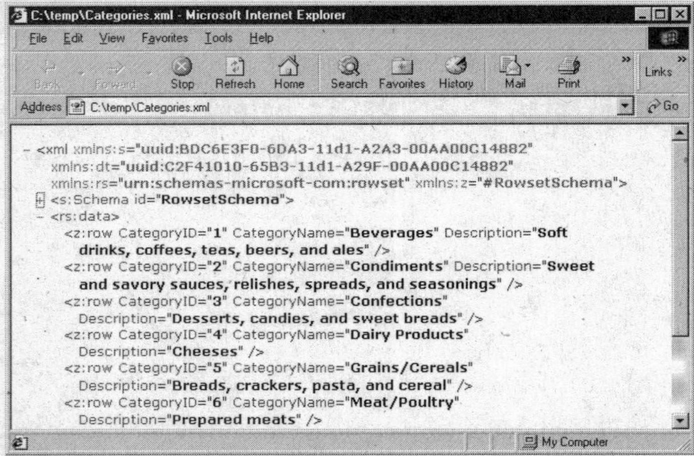

FIGURE 15.10: The XML-formatted cursor produced by SQL Server in response to a simple query

Being able to extract XML-formatted data directly from SQL Server is a very powerful feature, but you must still format the data as an HTML document. As you know very well by now, the simplest method to convert XML data to HTML documents is to use an XSL file. It should reside on the server, and you can include it in the response by simply adding its name to the previous URL:

```
http://127.0.0.1/NorthWind?sql=SELECT+
CategoryName,+Description+FROM+Categories
FOR+XML+RAW
&xsl=http://127.0.0.1/categories.xsl
```

The `categories.xsl` file must reside in the server's virtual folder.

Before you can contact SQL Server through the HTTP protocol, you must configure it accordingly with the `regxmlss` utility, which is described in the next section.

MICROSOFT'S TECHNOLOGY PREVIEW

You don't need SQL Server 2000 to test drive the product's new features. If you're not running SQL Server 200, you can download the XML Technology Preview from Microsoft's website and use it with SQL Server 7.5. Connect to the site `msdn.microsoft.com/SQLServer`, and select the SQL Server XML Technology Preview hyperlink. The most prominent feature of the XML Technology Preview is that you can contact SQL Server directly from a client through the HTTP protocol and execute SQL statements directly against the database. The results are returned to the client in the form of XML documents. As you can imagine, this raises some security issues, but more on this later.

The *regxmlss* Utility

The `regxmlss` utility defines a virtual folder, which is the root folder of the SQL Server server. SQL Server will service requests made to this folder only, and this is where SQL Server expects to find all auxiliary files (like XSL or template files). Of course, this virtual root folder can have subfolders, just like the web server's root folder.

The SQL Server's virtual root folder is different from the web server's home page, so that the functionality of the two components is separated. I'm sure you don't want to place all the template files for accessing a database in the web's root folder. Their place is the virtual folder of SQL Server. You can define an alias for the virtual root of SQL Server and map it to the web server's physical root folder.

To specify the SQL Server's virtual root folder, follow these steps:

1. Open the SQL Server's menu and select the Configure IIS option to see the Register XML SQL Server Extensions dialog box (see Figure 15.11).

2. In the Internet Information Server section of the dialog box, specify the names of the IIS server (in the Site text box), the virtual root, and the physical folder (in the Directory text box) that will be mapped to the virtual root folder.

3. In the SQL Server section of the dialog box, set the name of the server and the name of the database. Note that all

requests apply to this database, and you can't specify that a query be applied to a different database via the URL.

4. In the Connection Settings section of the dialog box, specify the type of authorization to be used.

5. To enable viewers to execute queries against a database through the HTTP protocol, select the Allow URL Queries check box at the bottom of the dialog box. To enable viewers to use templates for their queries, select the Allow Template Queries check box. (A *template* is a query that can be called by name, and it accepts parameters, just like stored procedures. Using templates and stored procedures is discussed later in this chapter.

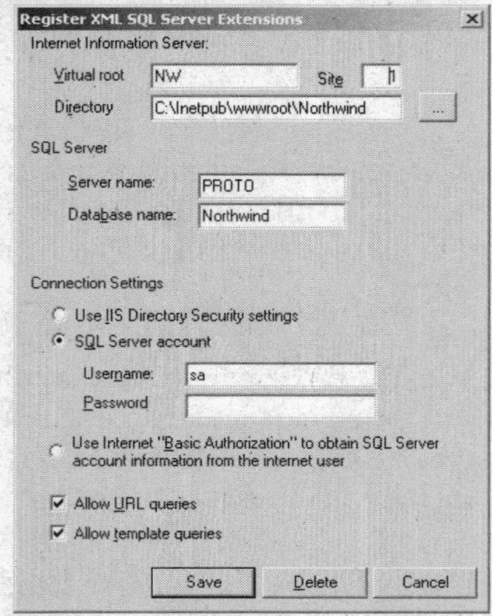

FIGURE 15.11: The Register XML SQL Server Extensions dialog box

SQL Server's XML Modes

The XML returned by SQL Server in response to a query over the Web can be in one of three different flavors. These flavors are called *XML modes*, and they are `RAW`, `AUTO`, and `EXPLICIT`.

RAW

RAW mode converts each row into a single XML element, using the generic tag <row>. For example, the statement:

```
SELECT ProductName, CategoryName
FROM Products, Categories
WHERE Products.CategoryID=Categories.CategoryID
FOR XML ROW
```

produces the following output (only the first few lines are shown):

```
<row ProductName="Chai" CategoryName="Beverages"/>
<row ProductName="Chang" CategoryName="Beverages"/>
<row ProductName="Aniseed Syrup"
          CategoryName="Condiments"/>
<row ProductName="Chef Anton&apos;s Cajun Seasoning"
     CategoryName="Condiments"/>
<row ProductName="Ikura" CategoryName="Seafood"/>
```

AUTO

AUTO mode returns a nested XML tree. Each table in the FROM clause is represented by an XML element, and the names of the fields become attributes. The same statement we used in the example of RAW mode will return the following rows, if you replace RAW with AUTO:

```
<Categories CategoryName="Beverages">
<Products ProductName="Chai"/>
<Products ProductName="Chang"/>
</Categories>
<Categories CategoryName="Condiments">
<Products ProductName="Aniseed Syrup"/>
<Products ProductName="Chef Anton&apos;s Cajun Seasoning"/>
<Products ProductName="Chef Anton&apos;s Gumbo Mix"/>
<Products ProductName="Grandma&apos;s Boysenberry Spread"/>
</Categories><Categories CategoryName="Produce">
<Products ProductName="Uncle Bob&apos;s Dried Pears"/>
</Categories>
```

As you can see, SQL Server is intelligent enough to consider the structure of the data and put together a hierarchical recordset, because this is exactly what you get in the AUTO mode. Each category section contains all the products in the category.

EXPLICIT

EXPLICIT mode allows you to define the exact shape of the XML tree. In effect, you must visualize the XML tree and write your query following specific rules. These rules are described in SQL Server's documentation, so I will not discuss them here. Since the RAW and AUTO modes are simpler, I'll use them in the following section's examples.

TIP

You can use the Query Analyzer to experiment with the various XML modes and see the output they produce. However, you can't direct the XML output produced by a query in the Results Pane of the Query Analyzer to a client.

The *FOR* Clause

Here is the complete syntax of the FOR option:

```
FOR [mode][, schema][, ELEMENTS]
```

Notice that all arguments are optional. As you learned in the previous sections, the *mode* argument can be RAW, AUTO, or EXPLICIT. The *schema* argument specifies whether the recordset will contain schema information, and it can have the value DTD (Document Type Definition) or XMLDATA. The statement

```
SELECT ProductName, CategoryName
FROM Products, Categories
WHERE Products.CategoryID=Categories.CategoryID
FOR XML AUTO, DTD
```

inserts the following schema information at the beginning of the document:

```
<!DOCTYPE root
[<!ELEMENT root (Categories)*>
<!ELEMENT Products EMPTY>
<!ATTLIST Products ProductName CDATA #IMPLIED>
<!ELEMENT Categories (Products)*>
<!ATTLIST Categories CategoryName CDATA #IMPLIED>]>
<root>
```

The DTD option inserts the <root> element, and all data rows follow this tag. If you executed the same statement with the XMLDATA option, the following schema information will be inserted at the beginning of the document (the last four lines correspond to the first category):

```
<Schema xmlns="urn:schemas-microsoft-com:xml-data"
    xmlns:dt="urn:schemas-microsoft-com:datatypes">
<ElementType name="Products"
             content="textOnly" model="closed">
    <AttributeType name="ProductName" dt:type="string"/>
    <attribute type="ProductName" required="no"/>
</ElementType>
```

```
<ElementType name="Categories"
             content="mixed" model="closed">
<element type="Products"/>
    <AttributeType name="CategoryName" dt:type="string"/>
    <attribute type="CategoryName" required="no"/>
</ElementType>
</Schema>
<Categories CategoryName="Beverages">
<Products ProductName="Chai"/>
<Products ProductName="Chang"/>
</Categories>
```

NOTE

If you omit the schema option, no schema information will be prepended to the document.

The ELEMENTS argument specifies that the columns will be returned as subelements. ELEMENTS can be used with AUTO mode only, and it produces straight XML code, which can be used as is in a data island. Let's try our sample statement with the ELEMENTS option:

```
SELECT ProductName, CategoryName
FROM Products, Categories
WHERE Products.CategoryID=Categories.CategoryID
FOR XML AUTO, ELEMENTS
```

The first few lines of the output produced by the preceding statement are shown here:

```
<Categories>
<CategoryName>Beverages</CategoryName>
<Products>
<ProductName>Chai</ProductName>
</Products>
<Products>
<ProductName>Chang</ProductName>
</Products>
</Categories>
<Categories>
<CategoryName>Condiments</CategoryName>
<Products>
<ProductName>Aniseed Syrup</ProductName>
</Products>
<Products>
<ProductName>Chef Anton&apos;s Cajun
             Seasoning</ProductName>
</Products>
```

Okay, there's a catch here. The output produced by SQL Server doesn't contain an <XML> or <ROOT> tag, and it doesn't encode the text for transmission over the HTTP protocol.

Executing Stored Procedures

Stored procedures can be executed via a URL as easily as SQL statements. Actually, it's simpler to execute stored procedures, because the URL is simpler—it contains only the stored procedure's name and, optionally, one or more parameters. To call the `Ten Most Expensive Products` stored procedure of the Northwind database, use the following URL:

```
http://127.0.0.1/NW?sql=execute+
[Ten+Most+Expensive+Products]
```

The square brackets are needed because the procedure's name contains spaces. This syntax uses the `execute` reserved keyword, followed by the name of the stored procedure.

If the stored procedure accepts parameters, you must supply their values either by ordinal position or by name. The `Sales by Year` stored procedure, also of the Northwind database, expects two arguments: the beginning and ending dates, in this order. The names of the parameters are `@BeginningDate` and `@EndingDate`, respectively. Here's the definition of the Sales by Year stored procedure:

```
create procedure "Sales by Year"
   @Beginning_Date DateTime, @Ending_Date DateTime AS
SELECT Orders.ShippedDate, Orders.OrderID, "Order
   Subtotals".Subtotal, DATENAME(yy,ShippedDate) AS Year
FROM Orders INNER JOIN "Order Subtotals" ON Orders.OrderID
   = "Order Subtotals".OrderID
WHERE Orders.ShippedDate Between @Beginning_Date And
   @Ending_Date
```

To execute this stored procedure with the arguments 1/1/1998 and 12/31/1998, you can use either of the following two URLs:

```
http://127.0.0.1/NW?sql=execute+
[Sales by Year]+1/1/1998+12/31/1998
```

or

```
http://127.0.0.1/NW?sql=execute+
[Sales by Year]+@EndingDate=1/1/1998+
@BeginningDate=12/31/1998
```

Using the first form, you can specify the values of the parameters, as expected by the stored procedure. You don't have to know the names of the parameters, but you must know their order. With the second form, you use named parameters. You must know the names of the parameters, but you can specify them in any order, as you can see in the example.

Using Templates

In addition to XSL files, you can use templates to automate the process. Although it's possible to pass any statement as a URL, this requires a lot of typing, not to mention that you won't get the statement right the first time. As mentioned earlier in the chapter, it is possible to create template files with queries you want to execute against the database and call these template files by names, instead of supplying the actual SQL statement. The scripts need not be aware of the structure of the database. The database can prompt viewers for the values of some parameters and pass them as arguments to the template.

Another good reason for using template files is security. By placing a template file in the virtual root directory, you can enforce security by removing the URL query processing service on the virtual root. SQL Server will invoke the XML ISAPI to process the template file.

Finally, templates may contain other statements you want to include in your output. For example, you can insert the <XML> tags around the output, which are not produced automatically when you use the ELEMENTS argument in the FOR clause.

So, what exactly is a template file? A *template* is an XML file that contains SQL statements and parameters definitions like this:

```
<ROOT xmlns:sql="urn:schemas-microsoft-com:xml-sql">
<SQL:query">
enter your SQL statements here
</SQL:query>
</ROOT>
```

The first and last lines are always the same; only the SQL statements change from template to template.

Let's create a template for retrieving product categories. To begin, enter the following code in a text file and store it in the SQL Server's XML-enabled root folder:

```
<ROOT xmlns:sql="urn:schemas-microsoft-com:xml-sql">
<SQL:query">
SELECT CategoryID, CategoryName, Description
FROM Categories
FOR XML AUTO
```

```
</SQL:query>
</ROOT>
```

Assuming that the name of the template file is `AllCategories.xml`, you can execute this query against SQL Server by entering the following URL in your browser's Address Box:

```
http://127.0.0.1/NW/AllCategories.xml
```

If the template accepts parameters (and most templates do), use the following syntax:

```
<ROOT xmlns:sql="urn:schemas-microsoft-com:xml-sql">
<SQL:query
 name1='value1' name2='value2'>
{ enter your SQL statement(s) here }
</SQL:query>
</ROOT>
```

Replace the strings *name1* and *name2* with the names of the parameters. *value1* and *value2* are the default values of the parameters, and they'll be used only if no values are specified in the URL.

The following template file will select the products of a specific category. Its name is `ProdByCategory.xml`, and it must be stored in SQL Server's root folder:

```
<ROOT xmlns:sql="urn:schemas-microsoft-com:xml-sql">
<SQL:query
 SelCategory='3'>
 SELECT * FROM Products
 WHERE CategoryID = ?
</SQL:query>
</ROOT>
```

This template will select all the files in the category specified by the request. If no Category ID is specified, it will return the products belonging to the category with an ID of 3. To call this template passing the Category ID 4 as the parameter, connect to the following URL:

```
http://127.0.0.1/NW/ProdsByCategory.xml?SelCategory=4
```

Using Update Grams

In the section "Updating XML Recordsets" earlier in this chapter, you saw how to post updates to a database using XML. SQL Server supports XML-based insert, update, and delete operations with a similar syntax. The statements for updating the database are called *grams*, and they can be used to post new rows and to edit or delete existing ones.

The syntax of an update gram is:

```
<sql:sync xmlns:sql="urn:schemas-microsoft-com:xml-sql">
   <sql:before>
      <TABLENAME [sql:id="value"]
                 col1="value1"
                 col2="value2"/>
   </sql:before>
   <sql:after>
      <TABLENAME [sql:id="value"]
                 [sql:at-identity="value"]
                 col1="value1"
                 col2="value2"/>
   </sql:after>
</sql:sync>
```

The words before and after are keywords that specify field values before and after the update. The sync keyword delimits the operation, and everything between a pair of <sync> and </sync> tags is treated as a transaction. In other words, SQL Server will not update only a few of the fields if an error occurs. If one of the specified values is incompatible with the definition of the column, then the entire operation will be aborted.

In the `<before>` section, you specify the field values of an existing row. In the `<after>` section, you specify the new values for one or more fields. You must provide as many `column="value"` pairs as there are fields to be changed.

The `<before>` and `<after>` sections are optional. If the `<before>` section is missing, then it's assumed that you're inserting a new row to the database. The new row's fields must be specified in an `<after>` section. If the `<after>` section is missing, then the row identified by the field values in the `<before>` section is removed from the table.

It is possible to specify multiple updates in a single gram. If the `<after>` section contains rows with no matching entry in the `<before>` section, then these are new rows. The rows in the `<after>` section with a matching row in the `<before>` section are updated. Rows that appear only in the `<before>` section are deleted.

Inserting Rows

Following is an update gram that inserts a new row to the Customers table:

```
<ROOT xmlns:sql="urn:schemas-microsoft-com:xml-sql">
    <sql:sync>
      <sql:after>
         <Customers CustomerID="NEW"
```

```
                              CompanyName="New Company"
                              ContactName="New Contact"
                              ContactTitle="New Owner/>
      </sql:after>
    </sql:sync>
  </ROOT>
```

This is quite a URL, if you're thinking about submitting it to the server.

The information you retrieve from SQL Server via a URL is not a disconnected recordset. As a result, any changes you make are not going to be embedded in the recordset. The easiest approach is to create the update grams from within a client-side script and submit them to the server, just as you would submit a normal query via URL. Alternatively, you can call a template file and pass the values of the fields as arguments.

Most applications don't add rows to unrelated tables. A practical example is the insertion of a new order to the Northwind database. To add an order, you must add a new row to the Orders table. SQL Server will automatically assign a new ID to the order. Then, you must use this ID to insert one or more rows to the Order Details table. Each item has its own row in the Order Details table, and all the rows that belong to the same order must have the same OrderID. The following statement adds a new row to the Orders table:

```
<sql:sync>
  <sql:after>
    <Orders sql:at-identity='newID' CustomerID='ALFKI'/>
  </sql:after>
</sql:sync>
```

newID is a variable name that will be assigned the ID of the new order. The OrderID field in the Order table is an AutoNumber field, so SQL Server knows which value to assign to the *newID* variable.

Now, you can use this variable to add the order's details. For each detail, add a new row to the Order Details table and set the OrderID field to the value of the *newID* variable. The following statements add a single detail for the new order:

```
<sql:sync>
   <sql:after>
   <OrderDetails OrderID='newID'
                 ProductID='11'
                 Quantity='10'/>
   </sql:after>
</sql:sync>
```

Listing 15.6 is a page that adds a new order for the customer ALFKI. The order contains three items, for the products with ID of 11, 12, and 13. To add the new order, the HTML page uses the AddOrder() function, which builds a template file. The contents of the template file are transmitted to the server by redirecting the script to the new URL.

Listing 15.6: The AddOrder Script

```
<HTML>
<SCRIPT>
  function AddOrder()
  {
    NewOrderXML = "http://127.0.0.1/NW/?template=
    <ROOT xmlns:sql='urn:schemas-microsoft-com:xml-sql'>
       <sql:sync>
          <sql:after>
          <Orders sql:at-identity='newID'
                      CustomerID='ALFKI'/>
          <OrderDetails OrderID='newID'
                        ProductID='11'
                        Quantity='10'/>
          <OrderDetails OrderID='newID'
                        ProductID='12'
                        Quantity='20'/>
          <OrderDetails OrderID='newID'
                        ProductID='13'
                        Quantity='30'/>
          </sql:after>
      </sql:sync>
   </ROOT>
     document.location.href = newOrderXML;
  }
</SCRIPT>
<BODY>
Click here to
<INPUT type="button" value="ADD ORDER"
      OnClick="AddOrder();">
</BODY>
</HTML>
```

You can modify this script so that it reads the values of the various fields from controls and builds the appropriate template file. This file isn't stored on the server. SQL Server simply executes it, and nothing is saved on the root folder.

An even better method to update the database is to write a stored procedure that accepts the same information we pass to the template file with the AddOrder() function and updates the database by adding new rows to the appropriate tables. The stored procedure should also be able to handle errors and return a True/False value indicating whether or not the operation was successful. It should also perform all the updates in the context of a transaction. The template file is also executed as a transaction, so that if a single insertion fails, the entire transaction is aborted.

Deleting Rows

To delete one or more rows in a table, specify the <before> section of the update gram and omit the <after> section. The sure method to delete the desired row is to supply its primary key. For example, the following statements remove the customers with ID TEST1 and TEST2 from the Customers table in the Northwind database:

```
<ROOT xmlns:sql='urn:schemas-microsoft-com:xml-sql'>
  <sql:sync>
    <sql:before>
      <Customers  CustomerID="TEST1"/>
      <Customers  CustomerID="TEST2"/>
    </sql:before>
  </sql:sync>
</ROOT>
```

If the primary key of the row to be deleted is not known, supply as much information as possible to uniquely identify the row you want to remove. The following statements attempt to locate a row in the Customers table with ContactName="Joe Doe" and City="NY":

```
<ROOT xmlns:sql='urn:schemas-microsoft-com:xml-sql'>
  <sql:sync>
    <sql:before>
      <Customers  ContactName="Joe Doe" City="NY"/>
    </sql:before>
  </sql:sync>
</ROOT>
```

If such a customer exists, it will be removed from the database. If two or more rows meet the specified criteria, only the first row will be removed from the table. As you can understand, deleting rows with criteria other than the primary key is tricky, and you can't be sure that the deleted row was the one you intended. For instance, to remove an order, you must first delete the details from the Order Details table. These are the lines whose `OrderID` field matches the ID of the order you want to remove. For example, the following statement will not remove all the rows whose `OrderID` field is 9840. Instead, it will remove only the first row that matches the criteria:

```
<ROOT xmlns:sql='urn:schemas-microsoft-com:xml-sql'>
  <sql:sync>
    <sql:before>
      <[Order Details] OrderID="9840"/>
    </sql:before>
  </sql:sync>
</ROOT>
```

To remove multiple rows from a table with a single statement, you must repeat the statement as many times as there are rows to be removed, or execute an action query against the database. The following statements will remove all the detail lines of the order with `ID=9840`:

```
<ROOT xmlns:sql="urn:schemas-microsoft-com:xml-sql">
<SQL:query
 DELETE FROM [Order Details]
 WHERE OrderID = 9840
</SQL:query>
</ROOT>
```

As you may have guessed, the best method to remove an order is to write a stored procedure that accepts the ID of the order to be removed as an argument and that performs all the deletions as a single transaction. For example, you can define the following stored procedure that deletes the detail lines of an order:

```
USE NORTHWIND
CREATE PROCEDURE DeleteDetails
@OrderID int
AS
DELETE FROM [Order Details]
WHERE [Order Details].OrderID = @OrderID
```

You can call the `DeleteDetails` stored procedure to delete the detail lines of an order and pass the ID of the order whose details you want to delete as an argument:

```
http://127.0.0.1/NW?sql=execute+
DeleteDetails+19088
```

Templates Versus Stored Procedures

It seems that templates are nearly identical to stored procedures, and you can write a stored procedure instead of a template. Although this is true in most situations, template files can be used to execute multiple SQL statements. In fact, you can use template files that call stored procedures themselves.

Another good use of templates is to define update and delete grams. As you recall from our earlier discussion, the syntax of grams is a bit peculiar, and it takes a bit of effort to implement the gram from within a client script. You can insert all the tags of the gram in a template file and pass the necessary values as parameters.

Summary

This fairly lengthy chapter introduced the basic concepts of using XML with Microsoft databases. You learned how to retrieve data from databases in XML format and how to bind individual fields to HTML controls on a web page. You also learned how to create XML data islands and pass a lot of information to the client with a single trip to the server. (Once the information is on the client, you can control how it will be displayed with a client-side script.)

There are two methods to create XML data islands: You can either use ADO's `Recordset.Save` method or use the native XML support of SQL Server 2000. The advantage of the first method is that the DBMS need not support XML, and it works with any database that can be accessed through ADO. SQL Server's native XML support allows you to query databases through the HTTP protocol.

XML is an emerging standard, and ADO 2.5/2.6 provides rather limited support for XML-formatted data. Recently, Microsoft announced ADO.NET, which will provide better XML support, so you should check the Microsoft MSDN site (`msdn.microsoft.com`) for more information on this technology. According to recent announcements by Microsoft, XML will be one of the cornerstones of products ranging from databases to future versions of the Windows operating system.

Chapter 16

Building an Online Store

In the previous chapters in this section, we've covered how to access databases over the Web using ASP. We'll implement these techniques in this chapter by creating a web application, an online bookstore. It uses the titles stored in the Biblio database that ships with Visual Basic, so you have a wealth of data to test your site. The Biblio database doesn't contain any tables for storing customer and order information, so you must edit the database a little and add two tables for storing the orders.

The Online Bookstore sample application is stored in the ONLINE folder in the sample code which can be found on the Sybex website (`www.sybex.com`). You must copy the entire folder as is onto your computer's hard disk and clear the read-only attribute of all the files (so that you can edit the files later). Then, you must make the ONLINE folder the root folder of your

Adapted from *Mastering™ Database Programming with Visual Basic® 6* by Evangelos Petroutsos

ISBN 0-7821-2598-1 896 pages $39.99

website. This step is required, because the site uses a GLOBAL.ASA file, which is activated when the application starts. The GLOBAL.ASA file holds a "global" variable: the maximum number of rows that can be retrieved by any SQL statement in the application's scripts. In addition, when the application starts, two session variables are created; these hold the login information for a generic user. The first time a user logs in with a real user ID and password, these values replace the generic ones. Here's the application's GLOBAL.ASA file:

```
<SCRIPT LANGUAGE = VBScript RUNAT = Server>
Sub Application_OnStart
   Application("maxRecordsAllowed") = 500
End Sub
Sub Session_OnStart
   Session("UserID") = "GUEST"
   Session("Password") = "anonymous"
End Sub
</SCRIPT>
```

As you can understand, the application should not allow any user to register with the GUEST/anonymous combination. You must insert the corresponding validation code in the script that registers new users and records the information to the database.

REVISING THE BIBLIO DATABASE

First, you must add two tables in the Biblio database, where customer and order information will be stored. They are the Customers and Orders tables:

Table Customers

Field Name	**Field Type**
EMail	Text (25)
Password	Text (15)
FirstName	Text (25)
LastName	Text (25)
Address1	Text (50)
Address2	Text (50)
City	Text (15)
Phone	Text (12)
FAX	Text (15)

Table Orders

Field Name	**Field Type**
UserID	Text (25)
OrderDate	Date/Time (short date format)
BookISBN	Text (12)
BookQTY	Integer

Customers are identified by their e-mail addresses so they won't have to memorize user IDs. You can apply some rules to the password, such as minimum length, one or more special characters required, and so on. There's no credit card information in the table, so all orders will ship COD. You can accept credit card information over the Web, as long as you use a secure web server. You can use IIS, as long as you specify the HTTPS protocol. The address prefix `https://` tells the browser to encrypt the information before sending it to the server. The viewer will see the usual message box, informing them that they're about to switch to a secure connection. You can expect that they'll click the OK button and proceed.

I've modified the Titles table a little. I've changed the name of the Description column to Price, because if you look at the values stored in this column, you'll realize that they are prices. I also added a new column, Discount, that stores discount information. The following query was used to populate this column with random discounts between 10 percent and 40 percent. The discount is stored as a real value between 0 and 1:

```
UPDATE Titles SET Discount = 0.1 + Int(Rnd(Price)*30)/100;
```

Make a copy of the Biblio database, implement the changes, and then create a Data Source Name (DSN) for the new database. I've named this DSN BIBLIO2000 on my system. That's because I've converted the database to Access 2000 format; the original database that comes with VB will work just as well.

NOTE

To set up a DSN, use the ODBC Data Source tool in the Control Panel (if you're using Windows 98 or Windows NT) or in the Administrative Tools, Data Sources (if you're using Windows 2000).

Part iii

THE WEB APPLICATION

The main page of the online bookstore is shown in Figure 16.1. The hyperlinks don't lead anywhere, except for the My Basket link. On this page, you can specify a part of the title and click the Now button to retrieve selected titles. The search capabilities of this page are limited; you can't specify isolated keywords to select titles. You can use the Titles component to perform more complicated searches—or build your own SQL statement that retrieves titles based on multiple keywords.

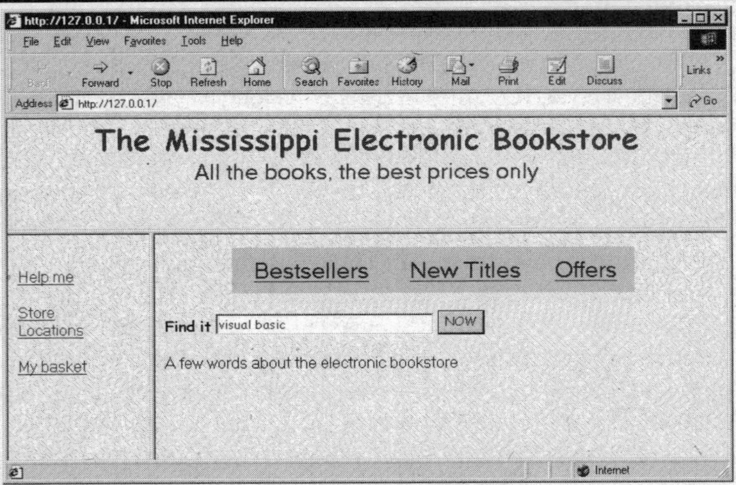

FIGURE 16.1: The main page of the online bookstore

Clicking the Now button calls SRCHTITLES.ASP on the server, which processes the user-supplied string. Here's the FORM tag of the main page:

```
<FORM ACTION="SRCHTITLES.ASP" METHOD="POST" NAME="SRCHFORM">
```

This page is responsible for extracting and displaying the titles that match the user-supplied criteria. It extracts the string entered by the user on the main page and builds a SELECT statement, which it executes against the database with the following statements:

```
ReqTitle = Request.QueryString("SRCHARG")
SQLArgument = "SELECT Titles.ISBN, Title, Price, Author "
SQLArgument = SQLArgument & "FROM Titles, Authors,
              [Title Author] "
SQLArgument = SQLArgument &
              "WHERE Titles.Title LIKE '%" &
```

```
                UCase(ReqTitle) & "%' AND "
    SQLArgument = SQLArgument &
                "Titles.ISBN=[Title Author].ISBN AND [Title
Author].Au_ID=Authors.Au_ID"
    connectString="DSN=BIBLIO2000"
    Set SelTitles=Server.CreateObject("adodb.Recordset")
```

The script retrieves the titles that contain the user-supplied string. You can modify the script so that it uses the TITLES component to retrieve titles by keywords and/or author names.

The selected titles are displayed (Figure 16.2) on a new page with 20 titles per page. The page allows the viewer to select any page with a group of 20 books. This arrangement is most useful when the titles are sorted. Titles can be sorted either by title or by selling order (start with the best-selling titles in the first page and proceed to the less-successful ones). This information does not exist in the Biblio database, but you can easily keep track of this information in a database with sales data.

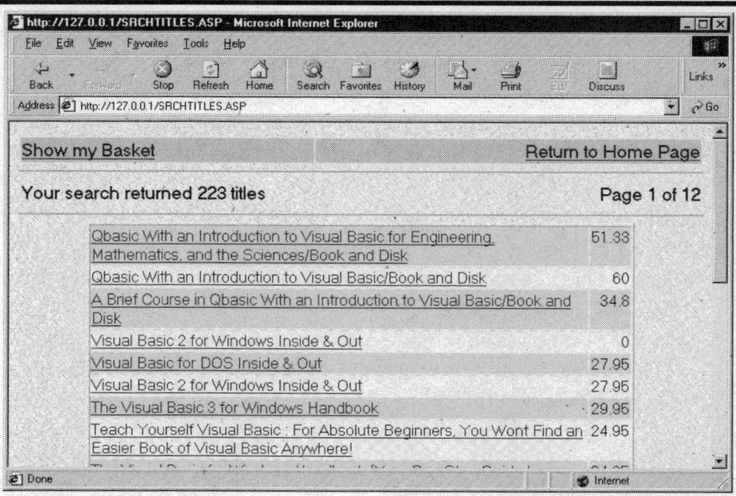

FIGURE 16.2: The titles on this page are hyperlinks to each individual title's page.

The trick to breaking a large page into smaller ones and creating paged output is to manipulate the PageSize and AbsolutePage properties of a client-side recordset. The code of the `SRCHTITLES.ASP` follows.

LISTING 16.1: The SRCHTITLES.ASP Server-Side Script

```
<HTML><FONT FACE='MS Sans Serif'>
<body BGCOLOR="#F0F0B0">
<%
   currentPage=Request.QueryString("whichpage")
   If currentPage="" Then
      currentPage=1
   End If
   pageSize=Request.QueryString("pagesize")
   If pageSize="" Then
      pageSize=20
   End If
   ReqTitle = Request.QueryString("SRCHARG")
   SQLArgument = "SELECT Titles.ISBN, Title, Price, Author "
   SQLArgument = SQLArgument &
                 "FROM Titles, Authors, [Title Author] "
   SQLArgument = SQLArgument &
                 "WHERE Titles.Title LIKE '%" &
                  UCase(ReqTitle) & "%' AND "
   SQLArgument = SQLArgument &
                 "Titles.ISBN=[Title Author].ISBN AND
                  [Title Author].Au_ID=Authors.Au_ID"
   connectString="DSN=BIBLIO2000"
   adOpenStatic = 3
   adUseClient = 3
   Set SelTitles=Server.CreateObject("adodb.Recordset")
   SelTitles.CacheSize=5
   SelTitles.MaxRecords=Application("maxRecordsAllowed")
   SelTitles.Open SQLArgument, connectString, adOpenStatic
   If SelTitles.EOF Then
      Response.Write "Sorry, no title matches your search
                     criteria (" & ReqTitle & ")"
      Response.Write "<BR>"
      Response.Write "Please press Back to return to
                     the main page"
      Response.End
   End If
   SelTitles.MoveFirst
   SelTitles.PageSize=pageSize
   PageCount = CInt(SelTitles.PageCount)
   If PageCount > CInt(Application("maxRecordsAllowed") /
          PageSize) Then
```

```
        maxCount = CInt(Application("maxRecordsAllowed") /
                   PageSize)
    Else
        maxCount = PageCount
    End If
    SelTitles.AbsolutePage=currentPage
    totRecords=0
    BooksTotal=SelTitles.RecordCount
'   BASKET ICONS HERE ..........................................
    Response.Write "<TABLE WIDTH=100% BORDERCOLOR=cyan><TR>"
    Response.Write "<TD ALIGN=LEFT BGCOLOR=cyan><FONT
                   SIZE=+1><A HREF=BASKET.ASP" &
                   ">Show my Basket</A></FONT>"
    Response.Write "<TD ALIGN=RIGHT BGCOLOR=cyan>
                   <FONT SIZE=+1><A HREF=DEFAULT.HTM>
                   Return to Home Page</A></FONT></TABLE>"
    Response.Write "<HR>"
'   ............................................................
    Response.Write "<TABLE WIDTH=100% ><TR><TD ALIGN=LEFT>"
    Response.Write "<FONT SIZE=4>Your search returned " &
                   booksTotal & " titles</FONT>"
    Response.Write "<TD ALIGN=RIGHT>"
    Response.Write "<FONT SIZE=4> Page " & currentPage &
                   " of " & maxcount & "<br>"
    Response.Write "</TABLE>"
    Response.Write "<HR>"
%>
<CENTER>
<TABLE RULES=none WIDTH=80%>
<%
    BooksFound = False
    bcolor = "lightyellow"
    Do While Not SelTitles.EOF And totRecords <
        SelTitles.PageSize
      If bcolor = "lightyellow" Then
          bcolor = "lightgrey"
       Else
          bcolor = "lightyellow"
       End If
%>
<TR BGCOLOR = <% =bcolor %>>
<TD> <A HREF="BookISBN.asp?ISBN=<% =SelTitles("ISBN") %>">
<%
```

```
            =SelTitles("Title") %></A>
<%
    currentISBN=SelTitles.Fields("ISBN")
    currentPrice=SelTitles.Fields("Price")
    BookISBN=SelTitles.Fields("ISBN")
    Authors=""
    Do
        If Not IsNull(SelTitles.Fields("Author")) Then
             Authors=Authors & SelTitles.Fields("Author") &
             ", "
        SelTitles.MoveNext
        If SelTitles.EOF Then
            currentISBN=""
        Else
            currentISBN = SelTitles.Fields("ISBN")
        End If
    Loop While currentISBN = BookISBN
    Authors = Left(Authors, Len(Authors)-2)
%>
<BR> <% =Authors %>
<TD ALIGN=RIGHT VALIGN=TOP> <% =currentPrice %>
<%
      BooksFound = True
      If Not SelTitles.EOF Then SelTitles.MoveNext
      totRecords = totRecords + 1
   Loop
%>
</TABLE>
<%
   If BooksFound=False Then
      Response.Write "No books were found"
   End If
   Set SelTitles = Nothing
%>
<P>
<%
   pad = "0"
   Scriptname = Request.ServerVariables("script_name")
   For pgCounter=1 to maxcount
      If pgCounter>=10 then pad=""
      ref="<a href='" & Scriptname & "?whichpage=" &
          pgCounter
      ref=ref & "&SRCHARG=" & ReqTitle & "&pagesize=" &
```

```
            pageSize & "'>" & pad & pgcounter &
            "</a>  "
        response.write ref & " "
    Next
    If PageCount > CInt(Application("maxRecordsAllowed") /
            PageSize) Then
        Response.Write "<HR>"
        Response.Write "<FONT SIZE=3>Your search for [" &
            ReqTitle & "] at the Mississippi
                bookstore returned "
            & booksTotal & " titles, "
        Response.Write "but you will see only the first " &
            Application("maxRecordsAllowed") & " of them. "
        Response.Write "Please specify better the titles
            you're interested in. </FONT>"
        Response.Write "<HR>"
    End If
%>
</HTML>
```

The script formats each title as a hyperlink. The destination of all hyperlinks is the BookISBN.asp script on the server. This script accepts the book's ISBN as a parameter, extract the book's complete information from the database, and displays it on a separate page. When a title is clicked, the book's details are displayed on a new page, which is shown in Figure 16.3. Here's the BookISBN.asp script:

LISTING 16.2: The BookISBN.asp Server-Side Script

```
<HTML><FONT FACE='MS Sans Serif'>
<%
    Set FSys=Server.CreateObject(
        "Scripting.FileSystemObject")
    ReqISBN = Request.QueryString("ISBN")

'   BASKET ICON HERE
    Response.Write "<HTML>"
    Response.Write "<body BGCOLOR=#F0F0B0>"
    Response.Write "<TABLE WIDTH=100% BORDERCOLOR=cyan><TR>"
    Response.Write "<TD ALIGN=LEFT BGCOLOR=cyan><FONT
                   SIZE=+0>
                   <A HREF=BASKET.ASP" & "> _
                   Show my Basket</A></FONT>"
    Response.Write "<TD ALIGN=RIGHT BGCOLOR=cyan>
                   <FONT SIZE=+0>
```

Part iii

```
                 <A HREF=DEFAULT.HTM> _
                 Home Page</A></FONT></TABLE>"
    Response.Write "<HR>"
''''''''''''''''''''''''''''''''''''''''''''''''''''''''''''''''''''''''''''''''''
    FName1="Images\" & ReqISBN & "S.GIF"
    FName2="Images\" & ReqISBN & "L.GIF"
    If Not FSys.FileExists(FName) Then
       FName1 = "Images\LOGOSMALL.JPG"
    End If
    Set DBConnection=Server.CreateObject("ADODB.Connection")
    DBConnection.Open "DSN=BIBLIO2000"
    SQLArgument = "SELECT Title, Notes, Price, Discount, _
                  [Company Name] FROM (Titles INNER JOIN _
                  Publishers ON Titles.PubID = _
                  Publishers.PubID)
                  WHERE Titles.ISBN='" & ReqISBN & "'"
    Set SelTitle = DBConnection.Execute(SQLArgument)
    Response.write "<TABLE>"
    Response.Write "<TR ALIGN=center VALIGN=center><TD>"
    If FName1 = "Images\LOGOSMALL.JPG" Then
       Response.Write "<IMG SRC = " & chr(34) & _
              FName1 & chr(34) & " BORDER = 2 ALT =
              'Book cover'>"
    Else
       Response.Write "<A HREF = " & chr(34) & FName2 &
              chr(34) & "><IMG SRC = " & chr(34) & FName1 & _
              " BORDER =2 ALT = 'Book cover'>"
    End If
    Response.Write "<TD ALIGN=left><H2>"
    Response.Write SelTitle.Fields("Title")
    ReqTitle = SelTitle.Fields("Title")
    Response.Write "</H2>"
    Response.Write "<TABLE><TR>"
    If Not IsNull(SelTitle.Fields("Company Name")) Then
                 Response.Write "<TD ALIGN=left> _
                 Published by <TD ALIGN=left>" & _
                 SelTitle.Fields("Company Name") & "<BR>"
    Response.write "<TR><TD ALIGN=left>Publisher's Price
                 <TD ALIGN=left>" & _
                 SelTitle.Fields("Price") & "<BR>"
    Response.write "<TR><TD ALIGN=left><FONT COLOR=red> _
                  Sale Price <TD ALIGN=left> _
                  <FONT COLOR=red>" & _
```

```
                    FormatNumber((1 - _
                       CDbl(SelTitle.Fields("Discount"))) * _ _
                       SelTitle.Fields("Price"), 2) & _
                       "</FONT><BR>"
    Response.Write "</TABLE>"
    Response.Write "<TR><TD>"
    Response.Write "<FORM ACTION=ISBNOrder.ASP METHOD=POST>"
    Response.Write "<INPUT TYPE=HIDDEN NAME=ISBN VALUE='" & _
                     ReqISBN & "'>"
    Response.Write "<INPUT TYPE=HIDDEN NAME=TITLE VALUE='" _
                    & ReqTitle & "'>"
    Response.Write "<INPUT TYPE=Submit NAME=Order _
                     VALUE='Order this Title'>"
    Response.Write "</FORM>"
    Response.Write "<BR>"
    Response.Write "</TABLE>"
    Response.Write "<HR>"
    Response.Write SelTitle.Fields("Notes")
    Response.write "<HR>"
    Set DBConnection=Nothing
%>
</HTML>
```

The script assumes that the thumbnails of the book covers are stored in the folder IMAGES and their names are each book's ISBN with the character "S" (for small) or "L" (for large) appended. If the book's cover picture is missing, then the `LOGOSMALL.JPG` image is displayed.

The most interesting part of this script is the code that sets up the Order button. This is the usual Submit button, but it passes the ISBN of the selected books to the `ISBNOrder.ASP` script through a hidden control. This trick allows you to pass information to a script with the POST method (so the values of the parameters won't appear along with the script's URL in the Address box). The POST method works with controls, but there are no controls on this form. You can't just redesign the page so that it uses controls. The hidden box control solves the problem by allowing the script to retrieve the ISBN with the Request.Form collection. Notice that this page passes the selected book's title along with its ISBN (you'll see why shortly). The listing of the `ISBNOrder.ASP` script is shown on the next page.

Part iii

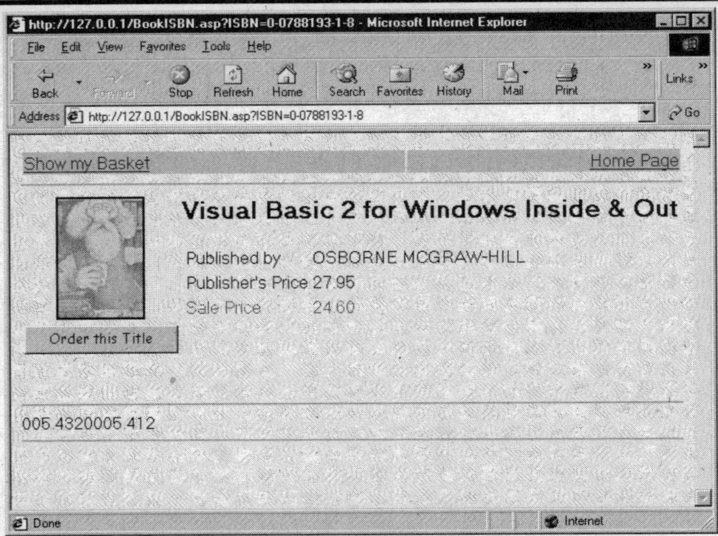

FIGURE 16.3: A book's page

LISTING 16.3: The ISBNOrder.ASP Server-Side Script

```
<%
    OrderISBN=Request.Form("ISBN")
    OrderTitle=Request.Form("Title")
    CurQuantity = Request.Cookies("BasketItem")(OrderISBN)
    If CurQuantity = 0 Then
        Response.Cookies("BasketItem")(OrderISBN) = "1"
        BookFound = False
    Else
        BookFound = True
    End If
    Response.Cookies("BasketItem").Expires = Date + 365
    Response.Write "<HTML><FONT FACE='MS Sans Serif'>"
    Response.Write "<TABLE WIDTH=100% BORDERCOLOR=cyan><TR>"
    Response.Write "<TD ALIGN=LEFT BGCOLOR=cyan>
                    <FONT FACE='MS Sans Serif'>
                    <A HREF=BASKET.ASP" & ">
                    Show my Basket</A></FONT>"
    Response.Write "<TD ALIGN=RIGHT BGCOLOR=cyan>
                    <FONT FACE='MS Sans Serif'>
                    <A HREF=DEFAULT.HTM>
                    Home Page</A></FONT></TABLE>"
```

```
%>
<P>
<CENTER><B>Title Order</B></CENTER>
</FONT>
<BR>
<FONT SIZE=4>
<% If BookFound = False Then %>
The book <I> <% =OrderTitle %> </I> was added to your
    basket.<BR>
Use the Back button to return to the book's page.
You can always remove this title from your <A
HREF=BASKET.ASP>basket</A>.
<P>
<% Else %>
The title <I> <% =OrderTitle %> </I> has been selected
    already.<BR>
View your <A HREF=BASKET.ASP>basket</A> and change the
quantity, or the BACK button to return to this book's page.
You can always cancel this title from your basket.
<P>
<% End If %>
<H1>The titles you have chosen so far</H1>
<%
For Each cookie in Request.Cookies("BasketItem")
    Response.Write "ISBN=" & cookie &
                   "      "
    Response.Write "QUANTITY= " &
                    Request.Cookies("BasketItem")(cookie)
    Response.Write "<BR>"
Next
%>
```

This page retrieves the selected book's ISBN and title through the Request.Form collection. The script doesn't access the database, but it needs to display the book's title. To avoid an unnecessary trip to the server, the script passes the title along with its ISBN to the server.

The ISBNOrder script reads the values of the cookies sent by the client. The online bookstore stores the ordered items in the BasketItem array. This is an array of cookies that stores two pieces of information for each title ordered: its ISBN and its quantity. The script attempts to locate an existing cookie for the selected title. If one exists, the script doesn't change its quantity. It simply prompts the user (via the window shown in Figure 16.4) to visit the basket's page and change the quantity there.

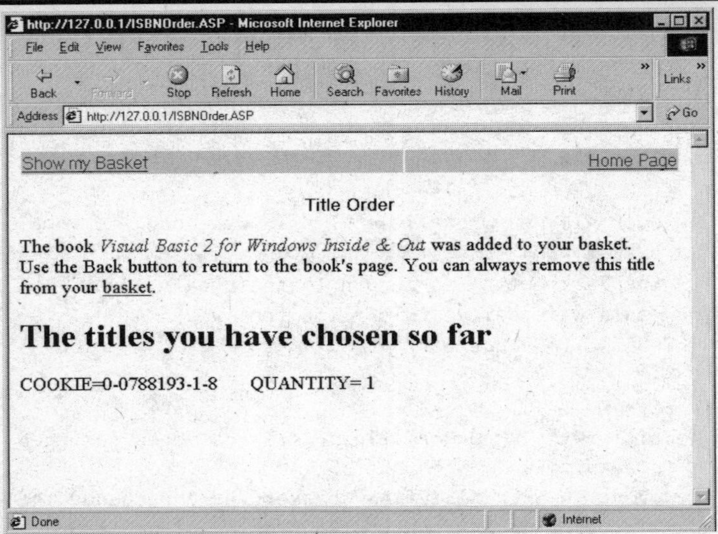

FIGURE 16.4: The order's confirmation page

Finally, the script iterates through the site's cookies and displays them on the page. This segment of the script isn't required; it was inserted as a debugging aid, and you must redesign this page after testing your site. This script should update the cookies silently, as it does now, and then simply display a confirmation page.

This page contains two hyperlinks, which allow the viewer to jump to the site's main page or view the page with the basket's cookies—the page that displays all the titles ordered so far (Figure 16.5) and allows the viewer to change their quantities. This page doesn't contain a client-side script to process the quantities. If the customer changes a quantity, they must click Recalculate at the bottom of the page to update the total.

This is an interesting page. Each time the shopper clicks Recalculate, the same page must be displayed again, only this time with the new total. The statements that insert the buttons at the bottom of the form are shown next:

```
<INPUT TYPE=SUBMIT NAME=RecalcBttn VALUE='Recalculate'>
<INPUT TYPE=SUBMIT NAME=RecalcBttn VALUE='Empty Basket'>
<INPUT TYPE=SUBMIT NAME=RecalcBttn VALUE='Place Order'>
```

All buttons call the same page, `Recalc.asp`, which examines the value of the button pressed to take the appropriate action. Listing 16.4 shows the `Recalc.asp` page.

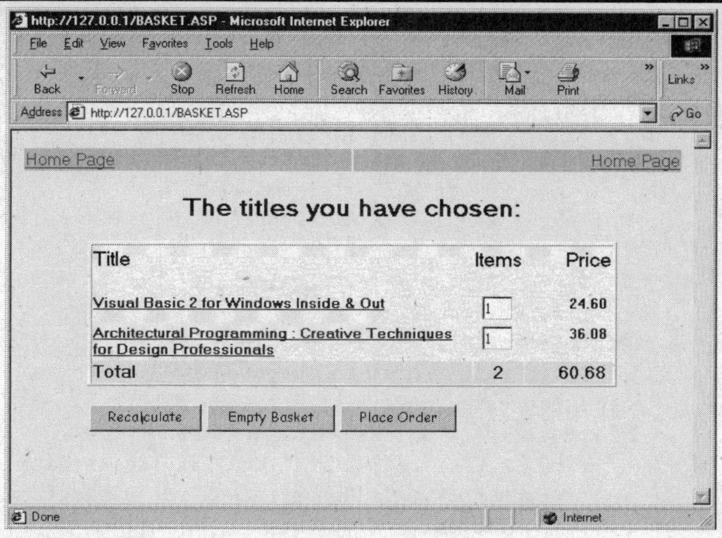

FIGURE 16.5: The viewer's basket page

LISTING 16.4: The Recalc.asp Server-Side Script

```
<%
        HTMLText = "<HTML><FONT FACE='MS Sans Serif'>"
        HTMLText = HTMLText & "<HEAD>"
        HTMLText = HTMLText & "<META HTTP-EQUIV='Expires'
                   CONTENT='0'>"
        HTMLText = HTMLText & "</HEAD>"
        HTMLText = HTMLText & "<BODY BGCOLOR=F0F0F0>"
        HTMLText = HTMLText & "<TABLE WIDTH=100%
                   BORDERCOLOR=cyan><TR>"
        HTMLText = HTMLText & "<TD ALIGN=LEFT BGCOLOR=cyan>
                   <FONT SIZE=+0><A HREF=DEFAULT.HTM>
                   Home Page</A></FONT>"
        HTMLText = HTMLText & "<TD ALIGN=RIGHT BGCOLOR=cyan>
                   <FONT SIZE=+0><A HREF=DEFAULT.HTM>
                   Home Page</A></FONT></TABLE>"
        HTMLText = HTMLText & "</TABLE>"
        HTMLText = HTMLText & "<CENTER>"
        HTMLText = HTMLText & "<FORM NAME=AllOrders
                   ACTION='ReCalc.asp' METHOD='POST'>"
        HTMLText = HTMLText & "<H2>The titles you have chosen:
```

Part iii

```
                </H2>"
        HTMLText = HTMLText & "<TABLE BGCOLOR=lightyellow
                WIDTH=80% RULES=none>"
        HTMLText = HTMLText & "<TR><TD VALIGN=top>
                <FONT SIZE=+1>Title</FONT>"
        HTMLText = HTMLText & "<TD VALIGN=top ALIGN=center>
                <FONT SIZE=+1>Items</FONT>"
        HTMLText = HTMLText & "<TD VALIGN=top ALIGN=right>
                <FONT SIZE=+1>Price</FONT>"
        Set DBConnection=Server.CreateObject
            ("ADODB.Connection")
        DBConnection.Open "DSN=Biblio2000"
'   DELETE ALL COOKIES, will be resent
        RequestedAction = Request.Form("RecalcBttn")
        If RequestedAction="Recalculate" Then
           Response.Cookies("BasketItem").Expires = Date-1
           For Each cookie in Request.Cookies("BasketItem")
               HTMLText = HTMLText & "<TR>"
               ISBN = cookie
               QTY=Request.Form("Q" & ISBN)
' RETRIEVE TITLE, PRICE AND PROCESS WITH NEW QUANTITY
               If QTY > 0 Then
                  SQLArgument = "SELECT Title, Price,
                                 Discount FROM Titles
                                 WHERE Titles.ISBN='" &
                                 ISBN & "'"
                  Set SelTitle = DBConnection.Execute
                      (SQLArgument)
                  BookTitle = SelTitle.Fields("Title")
                  HTMLText = HTMLText & "<TD VALIGN=top>
                             <FONT SIZE=-1><B>" &
                             "<A HREF=BookISBN.asp?ISBN=" &
                              ISBN & ">" & BookTitle &
                             "</A>" &
                             & "     &
                             </B>"
                  HTMLText = HTMLText & "<TD VALIGN=top
                  ALIGN=center><FONT SIZE=-1>
                  <INPUT TYPE=TEXT SIZE=2 MAXSIZE=3
                  NAME='Q" & ISBN & "'"
                  HTMLText = HTMLText &
```

```
                "VALUE = " & QTY & ">"
                HTMLText = HTMLText &
                "<TD ALIGN=right VALIGN=top>
                <FONT SIZE=-1><B>" &
                FormatNumber((1-SelTitle.Fields
                    ("Discount")) *
                SelTitle.Fields("Price"), 2) & " 
                    </B>"
                Cost = Cost + (1-SelTitle.Fields
                    ("Discount")) *
                       SelTitle.Fields("Price") * QTY
                Items = Items + CInt(QTY)
                Response.Cookies("BasketItem")(ISBN) =
                    CStr(QTY)
                Response.Cookies("BasketItem").Expires =
                       Date + 365
             End If
       Next
' NOW PRINT BASKET'S CONTENTS
    HTMLText = HTMLText & "<TR><TD BGCOLOR=yellow>
               <FONT COLOR=black><B>Total</B></FONT>
               <TD BGCOLOR=yellow ALIGN=center>
               <FONT COLOR=black><B>" & Items &
               "</B></FONT>
                <TD BGCOLOR = yellow ALIGN=right>
                <FONT COLOR=black><B>   
                     "
               & FormatNumber(Cost, 2, , -1) &
               " </B></FONT>"
    HTMLText = HTMLText &  "</TABLE>"
    Response.Write HTMLText
    DBConnection.Close
    Set DBConnection = Nothing
    Set SelTitle = Nothing
  %>
  <TABLE WIDTH=80%>
  <TR><TD>
  <FONT SIZE=+1>
  <INPUT TYPE=SUBMIT NAME=RecalcBttn VALUE='Recalculate'>
  <INPUT TYPE=SUBMIT NAME=RecalcBttn VALUE='Empty Basket'>
  <INPUT TYPE=SUBMIT NAME=RecalcBttn VALUE='Place Order'>
```

Part iii

```
</FONT>
</TABLE>
</FORM>
</HTML>
<%
   Else
      If RequestedAction="Empty Basket" Then
         For Each ctrl in Request.Form
            If ctrl <> "RecalcBttn" Then
               ISBN = ctrl
               Response.Cookies("BasketItem")(ISBN) = "0"
               Response.Cookies("BasketItem").Expires =
                                     Date - 365
            End If
         Next
         HTMLText = "<HTML>"
         HTMLText = HTMLText & "<HEAD>"
         HTMLText = HTMLText &
                   "<META HTTP-EQUIV='Expires'
                   CONTENT='0'>"
         HTMLText = HTMLText & "</HEAD>"
         HTMLText = HTMLText & "<BODY BGCOLOR=F0F0F0
                    FONT=>"
         HTMLText = HTMLText &
                   "<TABLE WIDTH=100% BORDERCOLOR=cyan>
                   <TR>"
         HTMLText = HTMLText &
                   "<TD ALIGN=LEFT BGCOLOR=cyan>
                    <FONT SIZE=+1><A HREF=DEFAULT.HTM>
                     Home Page</A></FONT>"
         HTMLText = HTMLText &
                   "<TD ALIGN=RIGHT BGCOLOR=cyan>
                    <FONT SIZE=+1><A HREF=DEFAULT.HTM>
                     Home Page</A></FONT></TABLE>"
         HTMLText = HTMLText & "</TABLE>"
         Response.Write HTMLText
         Response.Write "<BR><BR><BR>"
         Response.Write "<CENTER><H1>
              Your basket has been emptied</H1></CENTER>"
      Else
         ' The following statements
```

```
                ' process the order. The matching
                ' End If statement
                ' appears at the end of the script
%>
<HTML>
<HEAD>
<meta http-equiv="Content-Type"
content="text/html">
<TITLE>RegNew</TITLE>
</HEAD>
<BODY bgcolor="#FFFFFF">
<FONT SIZE=+1><H1>Place an order</H1>
<p>Please enter your ID and password in the boxes below.
   If this is the first time you're ordering, write down
   your ID and password for future use and make sure you
   don't share this information with anyone else.
<P>
Your ID must be your e-mail address and it will be used
to confirm your order.
<P>
<FORM NAME=GetCustomer ACTION="GetCustomer.ASP" METHOD=
    "POST">
<HR>
<table border="0">
    <tr>
        <td>User ID (your e-mail address)
        <td><input type="text" size="20" maxsize=30
            name="UserID">
        <td>Password
        <td><input type="password" size="15" maxsize=20
             name="Password">
</table>
<HR>
If you already have an ID and password, enter them and
click here to
<INPUT TYPE=SUBMIT VALUE="Place Order">.
<BR>
If not, click here to see the <A HREF="RegNewCustomer.htm">
New Customer</A> page to request your personal ID and
password.
</FORM>
```

```
</body>
</html>
<%
        End If
    End If
%>
```

When the customer decides to actually order the items in the basket, they must provide information that will enable us to charge them and deliver the items ordered. The application displays a login screen (Figure 16.6) where return customers must enter their e-mail address and password (the e-mail address is used as a UserID to identify the customer). New customers must follow the link to the New Customer Registration page, where they can enter all the information needed to process and deliver the order. This information is entered once and stored in the Customers table. For the next order, the customer need enter only an e-mail address and password.

The page shown in Figure 16.7 is an HTML file. The New Customer Registration page displays a form with the controls you see, and its Submit button calls the `RegNewCustomer.htm` (Listing 16.5), which stores the information entered by the viewer in the Customers table.

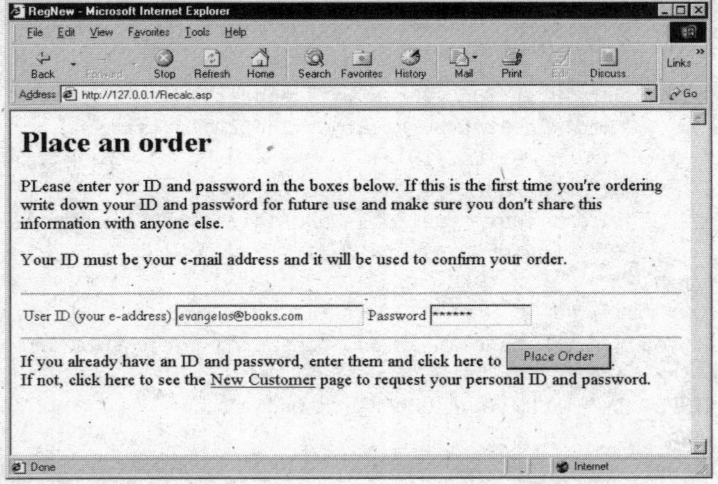

FIGURE 16.6: The bookstore's login screen

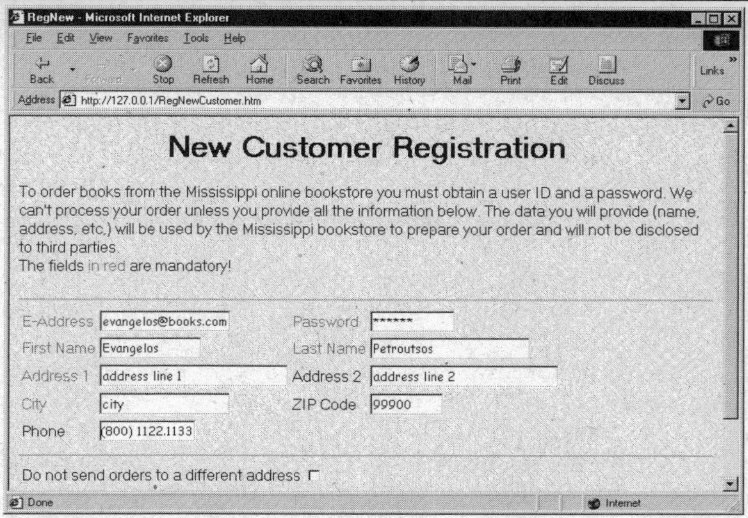

FIGURE 16.7: The New Customer Registration page

LISTING 16.5: The RegNewCustomer.htm Page

```
<HTML><FONT FACE='MS Sans Serif'>
<HEAD>
<meta http-equiv="Content-Type"
content="text/html">
<TITLE>RegNew</TITLE>
</HEAD>
<body BGCOLOR=#F0F0B0>
<p align="center"><font size="6"><strong>New Customer
Registration</strong></font></p>
<p>To order books from the Mississippi online bookstore
you must obtain a user ID and a password.
We can't process your order unless you provide all the
information below.
The data you will provide (name, address, etc,) will be
used by the Mississippi bookstore
to prepare your order and will not be disclosed to third
parties.
<BR>
The fields <FONT COLOR=red>in red</FONT> are mandatory!
<P>
```

```
<FORM NAME=RegNew ACTION=RegisterNew.ASP METHOD="POST">
<HR>
<table border="0">
    <tr>
        <td><FONT COLOR=red>E-Mail Address
        <td><input type="text" size="20" name="EAddress">
        <td><FONT COLOR=red>Password
        <td><input type="text" size="12" name="Password">
    <tr>
        <td><FONT COLOR=red>First Name
        <td><input type="text" size="15" name="FName">
        <td><FONT COLOR=red>Last Name
        <td><input type="text" size="25" name="LName">
    <tr>
        <td><FONT COLOR=red>Address 1
        <td><input type="text" size="30" name="Address1">
        <td>Address 2
        <td><input type="text" size="30" name="Address2">
    <tr>
        <td><FONT COLOR=red>City
        <td><input type="text" size="20" name="City">
        <td>ZIP Code
        <td><input type="text" size="10" name="ZIP">
    <tr>
        <td>Phone
        <td><input type="text" size="14" name="Tel">
    <tr>
</table>
<HR>
<table border="0">
    <tr>
        <td>Do not send orders to a different address
        <td><input type="checkbox" VALUE=ON
            name="MyAddress">
    <tr>
        <td>Do not mail promotional material
        <td><input type="checkbox" VALUE=ON
            name="MailPromo">
</table>
<P>
Fill out this form and click here to <INPUT TYPE=SUBMIT
VALUE="Register">
```

```
</FORM>
</body>
</html>
```

Once the customer logs in, a new page with the order is displayed (Figure 16.8). This is the customer's last chance to cancel the order. This is a plain HTML page and need not be listed here.

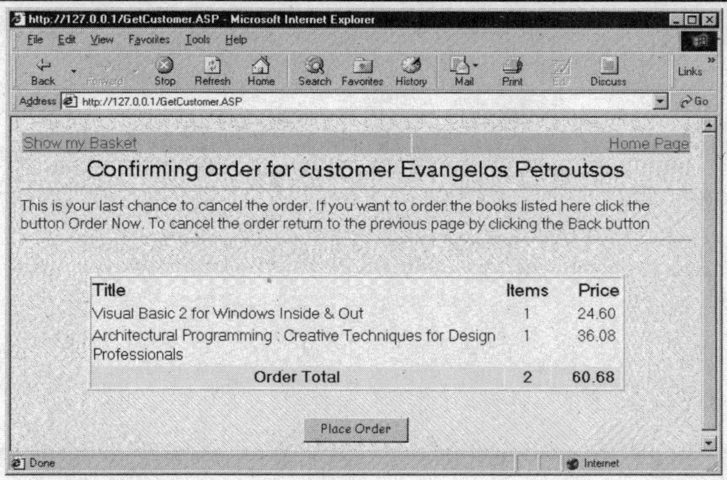

FIGURE 16.8: The final order confirmation page

If the Place Order button is clicked, the application stores the order in the Orders table and displays the thank-you message seen in Figure 16.9. You can read the orders placed by a customer (they all have the same customer ID and date) and process the order. The database isn't nearly as complicated as the Northwind database, but you can add more features to the store. For example, you can create an Orders and an Order Details table and store the exact same information as we did with the Northwind database. You can also use similar classes (or stored procedures, if you'd rather work with SQL Server) to enter new orders. By the way, if you port the Biblio database to SQL Server with the Data Transformation Wizard (the DTS Wizard discussed in Chapter 20) and then add the new tables as discussed in the first section of this tutorial, the same web application will also work with the SQL Server database (that's because we use a DSN and ADO to access the database).

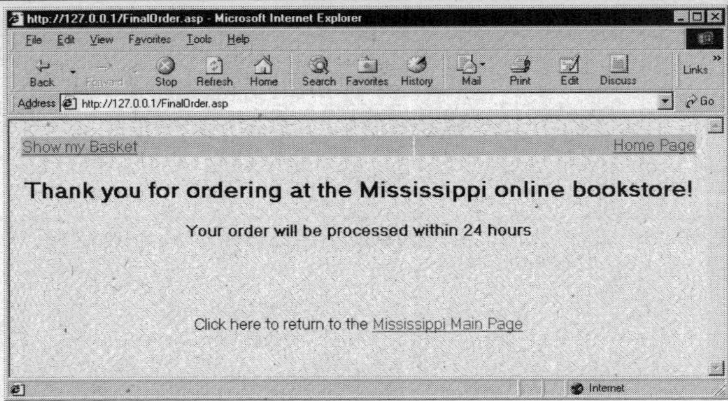

FIGURE 16.9: The order has been accepted.

The last page of the application informs the user that the order has been accepted and the books are practically on their way.

SUMMARY

This sample application concludes the Web and XML Database Programming section.

PART IV
SQL Server Programming with Visual Basic

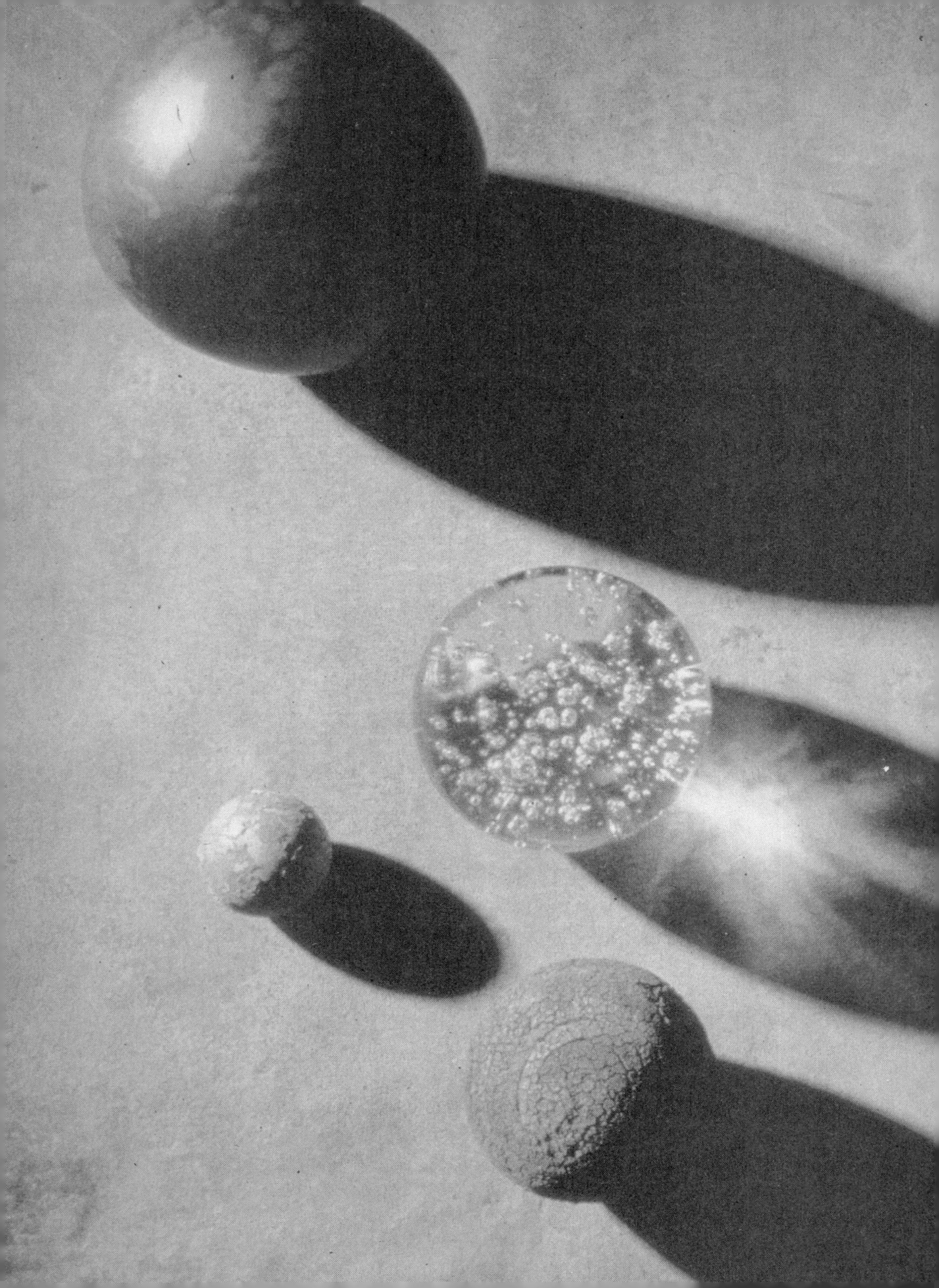

Chapter 17

Overview of Visual Basic and SQL Server

In the next four chapters, we'll take a look at SQL Server and Visual Basic. Specifically, we'll cover the various options developers have for using Visual Basic to work with SQL Server. Both Visual Basic and SQL Server have gone through a number of versions to evolve into the stable products they are today. Of course, no development software is perfect and they each have their quirks. In spite of this, Visual Basic has continued to be Microsoft's premier RAD (rapid application development) tool for developing client applications. By the same token, SQL Server is their primary back-end database product. Luckily, each new version has brought new features and better integration for Visual Basic developers using SQL Server.

This book is designed to help Visual Basic programmers work with SQL Server. In this chapter, we'll take a look at how both of

Adapted from *Visual Basic® Developer's Guide to SQL Server™* by Dianne Siebold

ISBN 0-7821-2679-1 480 pages $39.99

these tools have evolved. In particular, each successive version has provided new and different ways that developers can access SQL Server from Visual Basic. This chapter will introduce you to Visual Basic and SQL Server and give you some background on both. Finally, it will give you an overview of the technologies that enable integration with SQL Server in Visual Basic development.

Brief History of Visual Basic

Visual Basic has gone through a number of versions and barely resembles the original product. With each new version, it has evolved to keep pace with software development technologies. Microsoft software benefits from the company's emphasis on the integration of their products, which has also improved with each new release.

Visual Basic 1.0 was released in mid-1991. It evolved from the DOS-based QuickBasic, Microsoft's version of the BASIC programming language. Visual Basic was designed to be easy to use and to enable a new generation of programmers to create applications for the Windows operating system. The first bare-bones version was essentially a graphical version of Quick-Basic and included tools for creating user interface elements like text boxes, a programming syntax, and custom controls.

In early 1992, the *Visual Basic Professional Toolkit* was released. This update was a packaged set of additional custom controls created by Microsoft and other companies. At this time, object orientation and reusability were becoming important concepts in software development. Although Visual Basic itself was far from being an object-oriented language, its support of *custom controls* was a step in the right direction. Custom controls were a real plus for developers. They could use them to standardize pieces of code in reusable parts that performed a particular function, and to create complex functionality that would otherwise be time-consuming to code and test themselves. This capability was one of the primary reasons that Visual Basic became so popular in its early days.

Visual Basic 2.0 was released in 1992 and included the variant data type, predefined True and False constants, and object variables. *Object variables* took Visual Basic one step further in object orientation by providing the ability to declare and reference objects (much like pointers in C).

At this point, VBSQL and the ODBC API were the only available data access methods that Visual Basic developers could use. Both methods provided 16-bit access, and *VBSQL* holds the dubious honor of being the first VB-native interface to SQL Server. The *ODBC API* is a complex low-level database interface with a steep learning curve.

In 1993, Visual Basic 3.0 was released and included the *standard data control*. This custom control provided database access in applications with minimal coding. This version also supported VBX (16-bit) custom controls.

This version of Visual Basic was delivered containing version 1.1 of the Jet database engine. Jet was used for database connectivity through Data Access Objects (DAO) or the data control. Although Jet continues to this day with version 4.0, ActiveX Data Objects (ADO) is the most recent and preferred data access method, because it's one of the primary components in Microsoft's Universal Data Access strategy.

Visual Basic 4.0 was delivered in 1995 and was a significant rewrite of the previous versions. It kept pace with software development advances by incorporating OLE technology and the ability to create objects. This version also supported 32-bit custom controls called *OCXs*. At this time, changes were being made to other applications like Word and Excel so that they could be accessed from within Visual Basic applications using Visual Basic for Applications (VBA).

On the data access front, this version of Visual Basic shipped with *Remote Data Objects* (RDO) and the *RemoteData Control*. RDO was a data access method designed from the bottom up to replace DAO. This 32-bit ActiveX library was faster and smaller than DAO and was designed with an object hierarchy similar to the ODBC API. Unfortunately the RemoteData Control was plagued with problems and never really caught on.

In 1997, Visual Basic 5.0 was released. It supported the Microsoft COM standard and allowed the creation of *ActiveX controls*. This version was a real breakthrough, because now developers could create their own custom controls and DLLs using Visual Basic, which had not been previously possible.

Visual Basic 6.0 was released in 1998. Because of developer demand, this version of Visual Basic had a host of new and enhanced methods for interacting with SQL Server. This included improved data access, new tools and controls for working with databases (like the ADO Data Control), improved Internet features (like Web Classes), and a number of new wizards.

ADO 2.0, the latest and greatest data access model at the time, shipped with Visual Basic 6.0. This interface to OLE DB is similar to RDO, but with a smaller and less hierarchical structure. ADO was designed for performance in enterprise and Internet apps and is one of the primary components in Microsoft's Universal Data Access (UDA). The most recent version of ADO ships with Windows 2000 or can be downloaded from the Microsoft website. Microsoft has continued the data access role of ADO by releasing ADO.NET as the data access mechanism for its .NET platform.

Visual Basic is part of Microsoft's suite of development tools called *Visual Studio*, which also includes Visual C++, Visual FoxPro, Visual InterDev, Visual J++, and Visual SourceSafe. When you purchase Visual Basic, you'll find that it comes in three editions; each edition has successively more features and functionality than the previous.

The Learning Edition Is a scaled-down version and contains the basic development environment and controls. In addition, it comes with a multimedia CD for learning Visual Basic.

The Professional Edition Has all the features of the Learning Edition, plus additional ActiveX controls, the Visual Database Tools, the Data Environment Designer, and the DHTML Page Designer. This more full-featured version provides Internet development functionality and has more tools for working with databases.

The Enterprise Edition Includes all the features of the previous editions plus Back Office tools like SQL Server, Microsoft Transaction Server, IIS, and Visual SourceSafe. This version is designed for developing enterprise-wide distributed applications and provides all the tools for full integration with SQL Server.

Brief History of SQL Server

SQL Server has also been around for a while and new features have continually been added and others enhanced. SQL Server is part of Microsoft's BackOffice suite of products, which also includes BackOffice Server, Exchange Server, Proxy Server, Site Server, Small Business Server, SNA Server, and System Management Server.

SQL Server had its humble beginnings in a joint partnership between Microsoft and Sybase. At the time, Microsoft was partnering with IBM on a new operating system called *OS/2*. They wanted a database that would run under OS/2, so they partnered with Sybase to port their existing UNIX-based DataServer product to OS/2. In order to gain credibility and market share, Microsoft also teamed up with Ashton-Tate, who had the majority of the database market with their dBase product.

In 1988, a beta version of Ashton-Tate/Microsoft SQL Server that ran on OS/2 shipped. From a technology standpoint, this database was a joint development effort with Sybase. In 1989, version 1.0 shipped and subsequently the agreement between Microsoft and Ashton-Tate was terminated.

In 1990, the newly named Microsoft SQL Server version 1.1 shipped. This version ran under OS/2 and contained bug fixes to version 1.0. The most important feature of this version was its support for a new client platform called *Windows 3.0*. This version also included utilities, programming libraries, and administration tools.

In 1991, Microsoft SQL Server version 1.11 maintenance release was released. At this time, Microsoft ended its joint development of OS/2 with IBM to pursue development of its own multi-user operating system, *Windows NT*.

In early 1992, Microsoft SQL Server version 4.2 was released and included a Windows-based GUI database administration tool. Microsoft continued to work in parallel development with Sybase to keep Microsoft's version of SQL Server that ran under OS/2 in sync with the Sybase version, which ran under UNIX.

Late 1992 brought the release of a version of Microsoft SQL Server that ran under their new Windows NT operating system. At this point, Microsoft made a business decision to continue development for Windows NT only. This version of SQL Server supported the 32-bit architecture and was a complete rewrite from the ground up.

In 1994, Microsoft ended its joint development effort with Sybase and assumed full responsibility for the SQL Server code.

In mid-1995, SQL Server 6.0 shipped with some much-requested features like replication, scrollable cursors, and a host of new management tools that included the first version of Enterprise Manager. This release positioned SQL Server as a serious competitor to Sybase, Informix, and Oracle databases.

Early 1996 brought the release of Microsoft SQL Server version 6.5. This version includes conformance to the ANSI SQL standard and improved data warehousing capabilities.

In 1999, version 7.0 of Microsoft SQL Server was released. This version had a completely re-architected database engine, full row-level locking, and a new query processor. It also included upgraded administration utilities and a host of new wizards. This version responded to demands of scalability, going from desktop to enterprise to Internet. SQL Server is now a database platform contender for enterprise-wide and data warehousing applications with technologies like Online Analytical Processing (OLAP).

The latest and greatest version, *SQL Server 2000*, was released in mid-2000. This version sports improved hardware scalability and supports devices ranging from Windows CE handhelds to eight-way multiprocessor cluster servers. This version also includes native support for XML, 4-node failover support, cascading updates and deletes, improved full text search, and the ability to run multiple instances on a single server.

Like Visual Basic, SQL Server also comes in three editions: Small Business Server (SBS) edition, Standard edition, and Enterprise edition. All editions contain the core database engine and tools. The SBS edition is the most limited; for example, it only supports a database size of 10 GB and does not support SQL Server's data warehousing OLAP services. The Standard and Enterprise editions are each successively more full-featured. Table 17.1 illustrates the differences between the SQL Server editions.

TABLE 17.1: Feature Comparison for SQL Server Editions

Feature	SBS Edition	Standard Edition	Enterprise Edition
Runs on Microsoft BackOffice Small Business Server	Yes	Yes	No
Runs on Microsoft Windows NT Server	No	Yes	No
Runs on Microsoft Windows NT Server Enterprise edition	No	Yes	Yes
Max database size	10GB	Unlimited	Unlimited
Number of SMP CPUs	4	4	32
Extended memory support	No	No	Yes
Failover support	No	No	Yes
Supports full-text catalogs and full-text indexes	Yes	Yes	Yes
Supports SQL Server OLAP services	No	Yes	Yes

One of the primary differences among these editions is the operating system that each runs on. Regardless of which edition you choose, each has a standard installation and a desktop installation. The standard installation is the full database server and runs only on Windows NT Server. SQL Server Desktop, on the other hand, is designed for local database storage requirements. For example, if you have a remote application that is not always connected to a network, this installation allows you to have a complete version of the SQL Server database that runs locally. SQL Server Desktop runs under Windows 95, Windows 98, Windows NT Workstation, Windows NT Server, or Windows NT Server Enterprise.

There are three other versions that are available with SQL Server 2000: the Developer Edition, the Windows CE Edition and the Evaluation Edition. The Developer Edition is functionally the same as the Enterprise Edition, but is only for use by developers that need the database to write and test applications. This version cannot be used as a production server. The Windows CE Edition provides a database on any device running Windows CE which can be synchronized with other SQL Server databases. The Evaluation Edition is a 120-day trial version of SQL Server to be used for evaluating the database. You can download this version from Microsoft at `http://www.microsoft.com/sql/evaluation/trial/2000/default.asp`.

One final database that deserves mention here is the *Microsoft Data Engine* (*MSDE*). MSDE is essentially a scaled-down version of SQL Server that ships with Microsoft Office and Visual Studio. It has a 2GB size limit and is recommended for applications with no more than five concurrent users. It's royalty-free and distributable, so developers can provide a database with their applications at no extra charge. MSDE can be used with Access or Visual Basic client applications. The biggest advantage to MSDE over the Jet engine is that it's fully compatible with SQL Server and provides an easy upgrade path.

INTEGRATION WITH SQL SERVER

With each new version, Visual Basic has provided developers with new and better ways to work with SQL Server. This has produced a number of APIs, tools, and components. Some of these methods include client-side object models that access SQL Server, like SQL-DMO or ADO. Others are server-side utilities, like the SQL Server Query Analyzer or Data Transformation Services. Figure 17.1 shows the tools that are available to developers and how they fit into the big picture of software development.

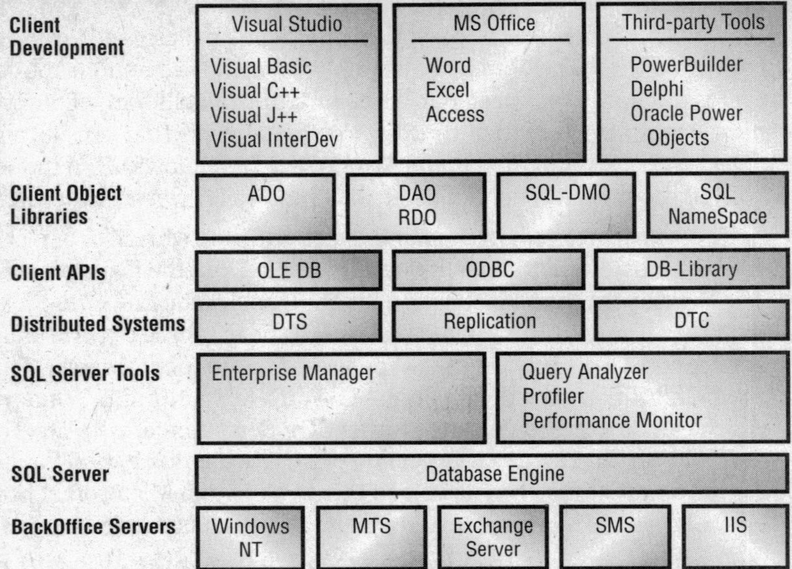

FIGURE 17.1: The big picture of development with SQL Server

Visual Basic Tools

A number of tools and object models are available that access SQL Server from within the Visual Basic IDE. Although each of these tools has a different purpose and implementation, the common thread they share is that they are used to access and interact with SQL Server databases. These include, but are not limited to, Visual Database Tools, the Data Environment Designer, SQL-DMO, ADO, and the T-SQL Debugger. Some client-side tools use SQL Server as their data store, like the Microsoft Repository and Visual Modeler.

Visual Database Tools

The *Visual Database Tools* are new to Visual Basic 6.0 and are included with the Enterprise Edition. They are available as an add-in for Visual Basic 5.0. The Visual Database Tools are actually a suite of four tools that includes:

- Data View Window
- Database Designer

- Query Designer
- Source Code Editor

One of the shortcomings of the Visual Basic IDE has always been its lack of database integration. Up until version 6.0, you always had to switch between the Visual Basic IDE for coding and SQL Server's Enterprise Manager for database tasks. Version 4.0 attempted to build in the ability to access the database by providing the VisData sample application, but it was cumbersome and didn't provide all the functionality needed to work with a database. With the Visual Database Tools, developers now have a full-featured set of tools for working with database schemas and data.

The aptly named *Data View Window* gives you a view of your database objects based on an open connection to a database. You can create database connections (called *Data Links*) graphically in the Data View Window by selecting a data provider and providing the necessary connection information, like database server name, username, and password. However, it actually uses ADO under the covers to create the connection. Once you have established a connection, you can open, create, and modify database objects. The Data View Window is the gateway to working with the Database Designer, the Query Designer, and the Source Code Editor.

Some tasks that you can perform in the Data View Window are:

- Create, modify, and view database diagrams
- Create, modify, and view tables
- Create, modify, and view views
- Create, modify, and view stored procedures
- Create, modify, and view triggers

After connecting to a database, you're presented with a tree view representation of your database. In the Data View Window, you can navigate through the database objects, as shown in Figure 17.2.

NOTE

The type of objects that you see in the Data View Window is dependent on the database you're connected to. For example, if you connect to a SQL Server database, you can view and modify database diagrams. However, these are not available when you connect to an Access database, because it does not have any equivalent objects.

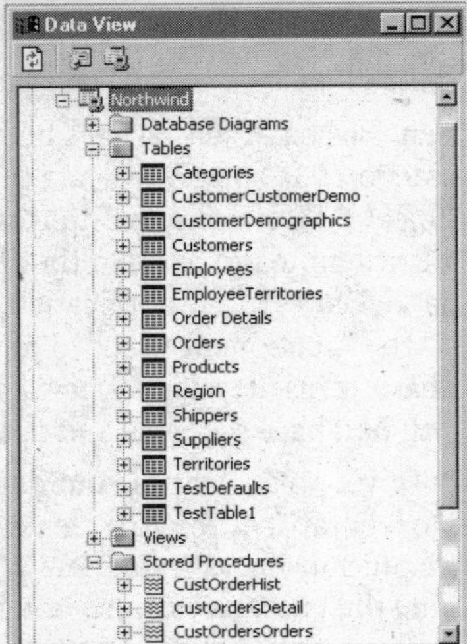

FIGURE 17.2: The Data View Window

The Database Designer provides a graphical interface for creating, modifying, viewing, or deleting database objects for databases to which you're connected. You can access the Database Designer through the Data View Window by right-clicking and opening a database diagram or table.

Database diagrams provide a visual representation of the tables in your database and their relationships. A database diagram shows all the details of tables, like table names, column names, and primary keys. The lines in the diagram represent foreign key relationships between tables. You can use a database diagram to modify your database, because any changes made to the tables or relationships can be saved back to the database.

The *Query Designer* is a tool that lets you design and run queries using a graphical interface. The Query Designer has four panes, as shown in Figure 17.3.

The Diagram Pane Displays the tables and fields used as sources of data for your query. You can modify or remove the table joins and select columns to be included in your query.

The Grid Pane Provides another method for selecting columns. You can also define column aliases, selection criteria (WHERE clauses), sorting and grouping.

The SQL Pane Displays the SQL statements generated from your query or you can enter the SQL in here directly.

The Results Pane Shows you the data returned as a result of running your query.

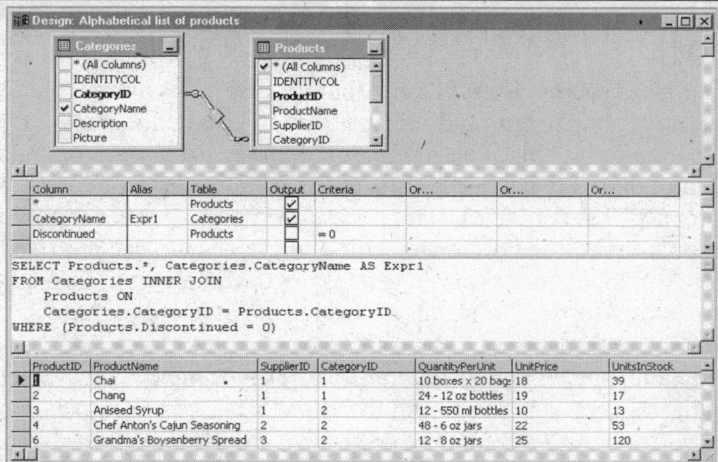

FIGURE 17.3: The Query Designer

The Query Designer keeps the panes synchronized, so that as you modify your query, the data in each of the panes is updated. Access the Query Designer through the View object in the Data View Window.

The *Source Code Editor* is the edit window where you create and modify stored procedures and triggers. This window displays the Transact-SQL statements in a color-coded format. You can debug stored procedures from the Source Code Editor, but you must have this capability set up to do so. You can get to the Source Code Editor from the Data View Window by modifying or creating a stored procedure or trigger.

Data Environment Designer

The *Data Environment Designer* is a graphical interface that is used to create DataEnvironment objects. A *DataEnvironment object* contains ADO connections and commands and can be created at design time to provide runtime data access. It can contain multiple connections and commands that can be programmed to connect to SQL Server, and call stored procedures, or issue SQL queries and return recordsets.

DataEnvironments simplify data access in applications and can be bound to forms. You can also drag and drop DataEnvironment connections and commands onto forms or reports. The Data Environment Designer replaces the limited UserConnection Designer that was based on RDO and supported only a single connection.

ADO

ADO is a data access object model that provides the communication between your application and the database. ADO is an interface to OLE DB and the means by which you connect to, retrieve, manipulate, or update data from SQL Server. ADO is one of the primary components in Microsoft's UDA (Universal Data Access) strategy. The theory behind this strategy is to provide developers with a single, easy-to-use interface for accessing data, regardless of where it resides or whether it's in a relational or non-relational form. This means access to data in relational databases, file directories, spreadsheets, XML, or even e-mail. This object model is similar to RDO, but smaller and less hierarchical. For example, when you create a Recordset object, you don't need to explicitly create a Connection object; when you open the recordset, it creates a connection behind the scenes. ADO ships with Visual Basic or can be downloaded from the Microsoft Universal Data Access website at `http://www.microsoft.com/data`.

T-SQL Debugger

The *T-SQL Debugger* enables you to debug SQL Server stored procedures. You can access the T-SQL Debugger from within the Data View Window or as a Visual Basic add-in. This tool provides many of the standard debugging features, like the ability to set breakpoints, step through the stored procedure code, and modify local variables (see Figure 17.4). The T-SQL Debugger can be very valuable when working with stored procedures in Visual Basic, but you must have it set up correctly on both the client and server.

NOTE

Debugging stored procedures is covered in depth in Chapter 8 of *Visual Basic® Developer's Guide to SQL Server™* by Dianne Siebold (Sybex, 2000).

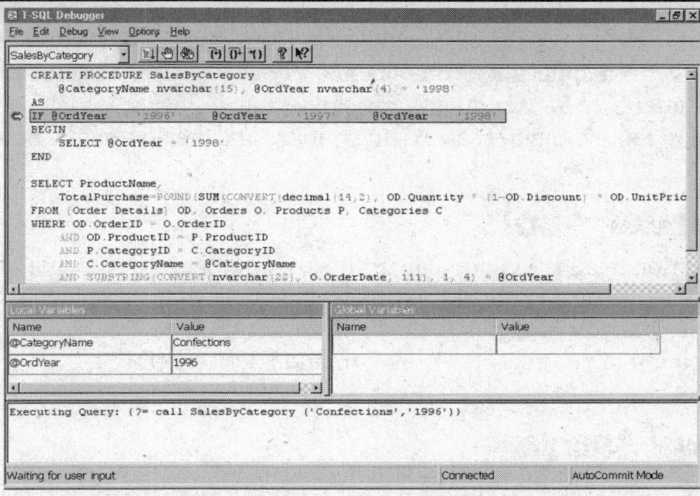

FIGURE 17.4: Debugging a stored procedure in the T-SQL Debugger

Other Tools

The Microsoft Repository, Visual Component Manager, and Visual Modeler are all tools that are included in the Visual Studio Enterprise Edition to address the need for software development process tools. Basically, these applications help developers manage the development process. This means they can design and model the application architecture of a project before any coding is done. From this design, the actual software components can be created, stored, and reused in other projects. The ability to reuse software components is the basis of component-based software development.

Microsoft Repository provides a common location to store information about objects and their relationships. It uses SQL Server as its database to store this component information. In the Repository, information is exposed as COM objects so it can be accessed by any other language that supports COM. The Repository is not used by itself, but is the foundation for other tools that manage the software development process. These could be Microsoft applications like Visual Component Manager or other third-party tools.

The *Visual Component Manager* is a front end to the Repository. This graphical interface lets you publish, share, and reuse software components in a central location. For example, Visual Component Manager can be used to publish models created in Visual Modeler for use by other developers.

Visual Modeler is a tool for modeling your application. It organizes objects based on the three-tier model: user, business, or data services. After modeling your application components, Visual Modeler will generate the object interfaces for you. Another useful feature in Visual Modeler is the ability to reverse engineer an existing project and create a model from it.

SQL Server Tools

In addition to all the client-side utilities, a number of server-side tools are available to Visual Basic developers who work with SQL Server. These include Query Analyzer, SQL Server Profiler, SQL-DMO, SQL Namespace, Replication tools, and Data Transformation Services (DTS).

Query Analyzer

Query Analyzer comes with SQL Server and replaces iSQL. This tool lets you execute Transact-SQL statements and scripts interactively. Query Analyzer does more than just show you the results of your query; for example, you can also view the execution plan for a query. The execution plan shows you graphically exactly what steps SQL Server will follow to perform your query and the percentage of time each step takes. With this information, you can tune your queries for optimal performance. For example, if you have a query that accesses a table without an index, you can implement various indexes and use the Query Analyzer to find out if those indexes will increase the query performance. Another useful optimization feature in Query Analyzer is the Index Tuning Wizard, which suggests what table indexes to create based on a particular query.

SQL Server Profiler

SQL Server Profiler is the latest incarnation of SQL Trace. This much improved utility lets you monitor the activity between a client and a SQL Server database (see Figure 17.5). Once a SQL query or command is issued, it's difficult to know exactly what is received by the database. This utility lets you see what commands and parameter values were received at the server. You can create a trace based on criteria, trace particular events, and even save your trace definition for use later. Data gathered from a trace can be saved to a file or table for analysis.

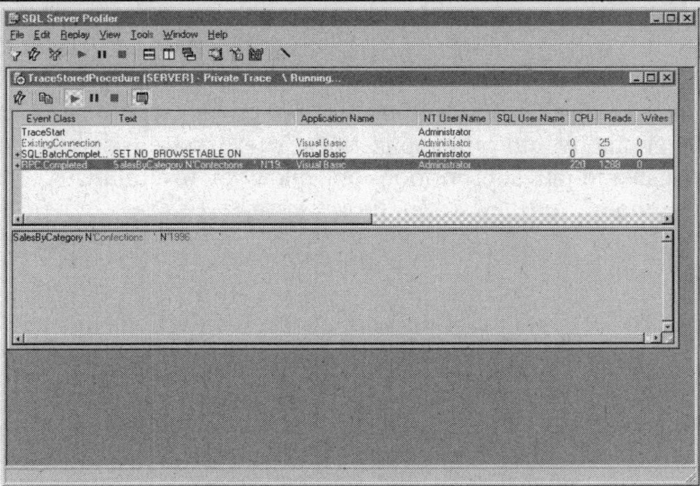

FIGURE 17.5: Trace activity with SQL Server Profiler

SQL-DMO

SQL-DMO is a COM-based object library that represents all the objects in a SQL Server database. This version replaces the previous SQL OLE library. It lets you perform database administration tasks programmatically from inside your Visual Basic applications. The SQL-DMO objects can be used for administrative tasks like starting and stopping a server, modifying space usage, accessing SQL Server agents, and monitoring database backups and restores. SQL-DMO is also ideal for modifying database structures. For example, the Database object can be used to modify database security, add or drop tables, columns, and constraints, and so on.

SQL Namespace

SQL Namespace was first released in SQL Server 7.0 and is a set of COM interfaces that represents the objects that make up the SQL Server Enterprise Manager interface. It lets you build elements of the Enterprise Manager user interface, like dialog boxes and wizards into Visual Basic applications. SQL Namespace is used in conjunction with SQL-DMO; SQL Namespace handles the user interface aspects of SQL Server and SQL-DMO handles connecting to SQL Server and working with its objects.

Replication Controls

Distributing and synchronizing SQL Server data from various locations is known as *replication*. The SQL Distribution Control and the SQL Merge Control are ActiveX controls that allow you to embed SQL Server replication functionality into your applications. These controls support anonymous push-and-pull subscriptions and allow you to administer subscriptions.

DTS

The *Data Transformation Services* (*DTS*) object model includes objects that can be used to copy or transform data from one SQL Server to another. This utility also allows you to import and export data to and from a variety of data sources such as spreadsheets, text files, Access databases and ISAM databases. This is done using object interfaces that create and run DTS packages and tasks.

SUMMARY

So far we've looked at the evolution of Visual Basic and SQL Server and seen what tools are available for each of these products. Now we'll get into how you can work with SQL Server from within Visual Basic.

Chapter 18

SQL Distributed Management Objects

We've seen some background on both Visual Basic and SQL Server. Now, let's take a look at some of the tools available for working with SQL Server. Enterprise Manager is the application that comes with SQL Server and provides the capability for managing databases. If you write applications that connect to a SQL Server database, chances are you're already familiar with this utility. But if you need to perform any database administration tasks programmatically, SQL-DMF is the framework that provides the tools. *SQL Distributed Management Framework* (SQL-DMF) is a set of integrated APIs and services that are used to manage SQL Server. SQL-DMO is just one of the components in SQL-DMF.

In this chapter, we'll review all the services available to programmers in the SQL-DMF framework. In particular, we'll cover the SQL-DMO object model in depth. One of the most powerful

Adapted from *Visual Basic® Developer's Guide to SQL Server™* by Dianne Siebold

ISBN 0-7821-2679-1 480 pages $39.99

features of SQL-DMO is the ability to integrate both database and server administration functions into applications. We'll first take a look at how SQL-DMO is used to create databases, tables, columns, and other data definition language (DDL) functions. To use SQL-DMO it must be properly installed, so we'll review the files you'll need and how to access its objects in your Visual Basic code. We'll then take a tour of the sample application that accompanies this chapter. This application uses SQL-DMO to compare the tables in two databases and reports any differences.

SQL-DMF

SQL-DMF is the set of tools that Microsoft provides for accessing SQL Server outside of the utilities that come with the database engine (Query Analyzer, for example). This framework consists of APIs and services that allow you to access all of the objects inside SQL Server. With SQL-DMF, you can manage servers and databases, perform backups, trigger alerts, and raise events. Figure 18.1 illustrates the components that make up SQL-DMF, and the various methods for accessing them. The functionality of SQL-DMF is exposed by three APIs:

- SQL Namespace (SQL-NS)
- SQL Distributed Management Objects (SQL-DMO)
- Data Transformation Services (DTS)

All of the elements in this framework represent objects in SQL Server. Use these components to perform these tasks:

- Define SQL Server objects and permissions.
- Integrate database administration tasks into applications.
- Integrate server administration functions into applications.
- Programmatically perform repetitive tasks or tasks that must be performed at intervals.
- Integrate Enterprise Manager user interface (UI) elements into your client applications.
- Access DTS services to transfer and transform data from within your client applications.

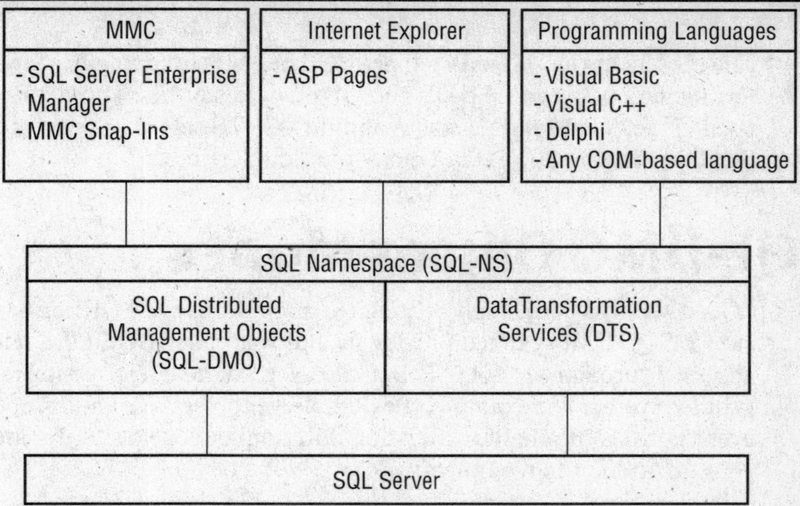

FIGURE 18.1: The SQL-DMF framework enables you to programmatically manage SQL Server objects.

SQL-NS

The SQL-NS object model contains COM objects that expose the user interface elements of Enterprise Manager. These objects are used to implement the screens that you see in Enterprise Manager within Visual Basic applications. SQL-NS provides UI functionality only and uses SQL-DMO to access SQL Server objects. SQL-NS is covered in depth in Chapter 19, "SQL Namespace."

SQL-DMO

SQL-DMO is a COM-based object library that exposes interfaces to any objects in SQL Server. Any COM-compliant language, such as Visual Basic, can be used to access objects such as servers, databases, tables, columns, stored procedures, permissions, and so on. This API enables you to embed administrative functionality in your programs. For example, you can programmatically create tables in a database or perform a database backup and restore.

DTS

The objects in the DTS API expose SQL Server's functionality for transferring data between OLE DB and ODBC data sources. These objects are used to create and run packages and tasks. DTS services are covered in detail in Chapter 20, "Data Transformation Services."

SQL-DMO Object Model

SQL-DMO was completely redesigned and released in SQL Server version 7. SQL-DMO existed previously, but was called *SQL OLE* and accessed through the `SQLOLE.DLL` file. New to the latest version is support for events. For example, the SQL Server object's `ConnectionBroken` event notifies the client application if its connection was terminated and you can attempt to reconnect.

SQL-DMO uses ODBC to communicate with SQL Server, so you must have the latest ODBC SQL Server driver. However, it uses ODBC directly, so you don't need to create a DSN. The SQL-DMO object model is full-featured, and anything you can accomplish in Enterprise Manager can be done in your Visual Basic applications. In fact, Enterprise Manager uses SQL-DMO in the background. Each object in the SQL-DMO object model represents an object found in SQL Server. These objects can be administrative in nature, like BackupDevices or Logins. All of the database objects, such as databases, tables, indexes, and stored procedures, are also represented in SQL-DMO.

Unlike ADO, the SQL-DMO object model is hierarchical in nature. For example, you must create the SQLServer object and connect to SQL Server before you can access the Databases collection. Like all other objects, each object in the SQL-DMO model has methods, properties, and collections. The Database object contains a Tables collection, the Table object contains a Columns collection, and so on.

At the heart of the SQL-DMO object model is the *SQLServer object*. Through this object, you can access all the other collections and objects on a single server (see Figure 18.2), including BackupDevices, Configuration, Databases, FullTextService, IntegratedSecurity, JobServer, Languages, LinkedServer, Logins, Registry, RemoteServers, Replication, and ServerRoles.

From the root SQLServer object, there are three main branches.

- *Database Administration objects* allow you to create, modify, and delete databases, tables, indexes, triggers, or any object found in a database. These objects are accessed through the Databases collection, as shown in Figure 18.3.

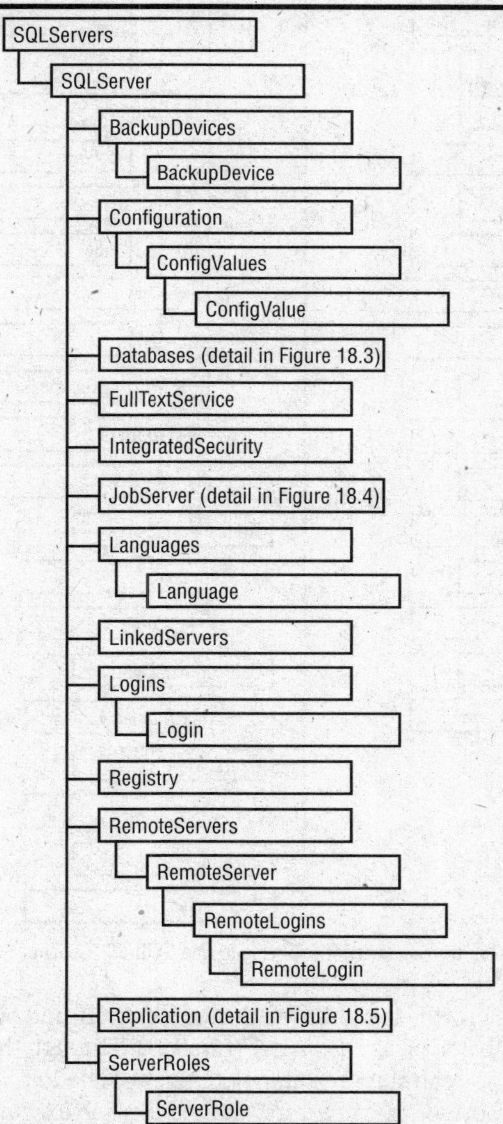

FIGURE 18.2: The SQLServer object

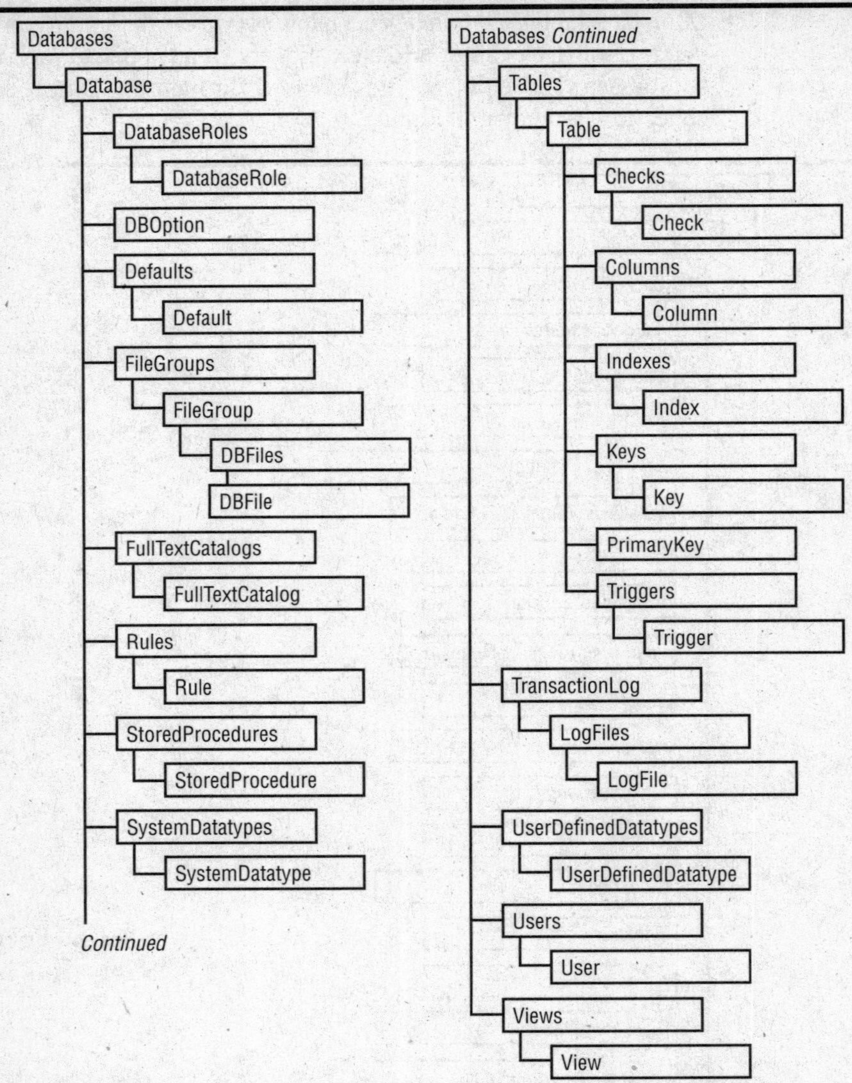

FIGURE 18.3: The database administration objects in the SQL-DMO object model

- *JobServer objects* provide the ability to access alert, job, and operator objects in SQL Server, as shown in Figure 18.4. Through these object interfaces, you can start and stop SQL Agent, schedule jobs, create alerts to report any server errors, and manage job execution on other servers.

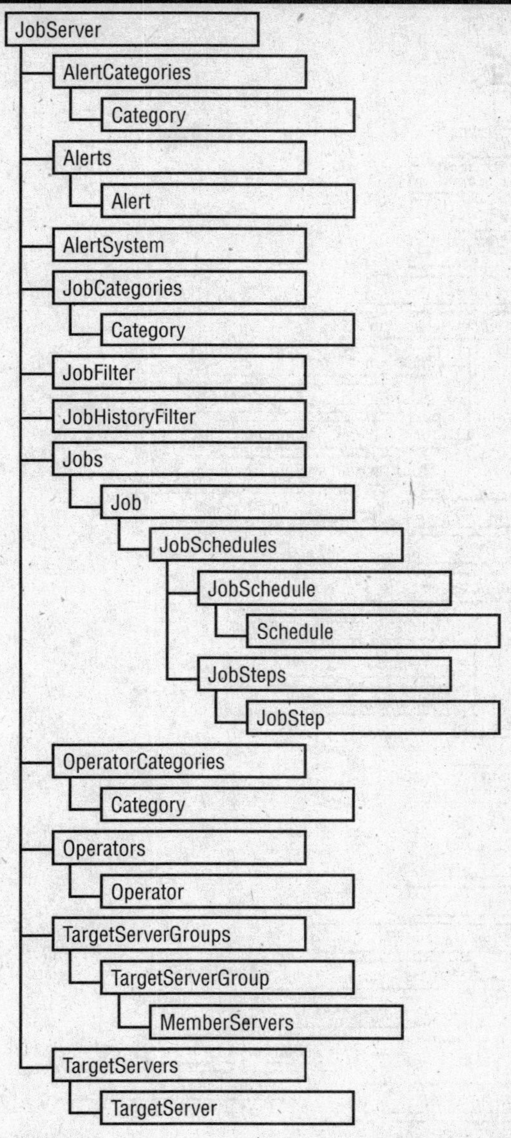

FIGURE 18.4: The JobServer objects in the SQL-DMO object model

- *Replication objects* expose SQL Server replication functionality, as shown in Figure 18.5, and allow you to create and manage replication publications and subscriptions.

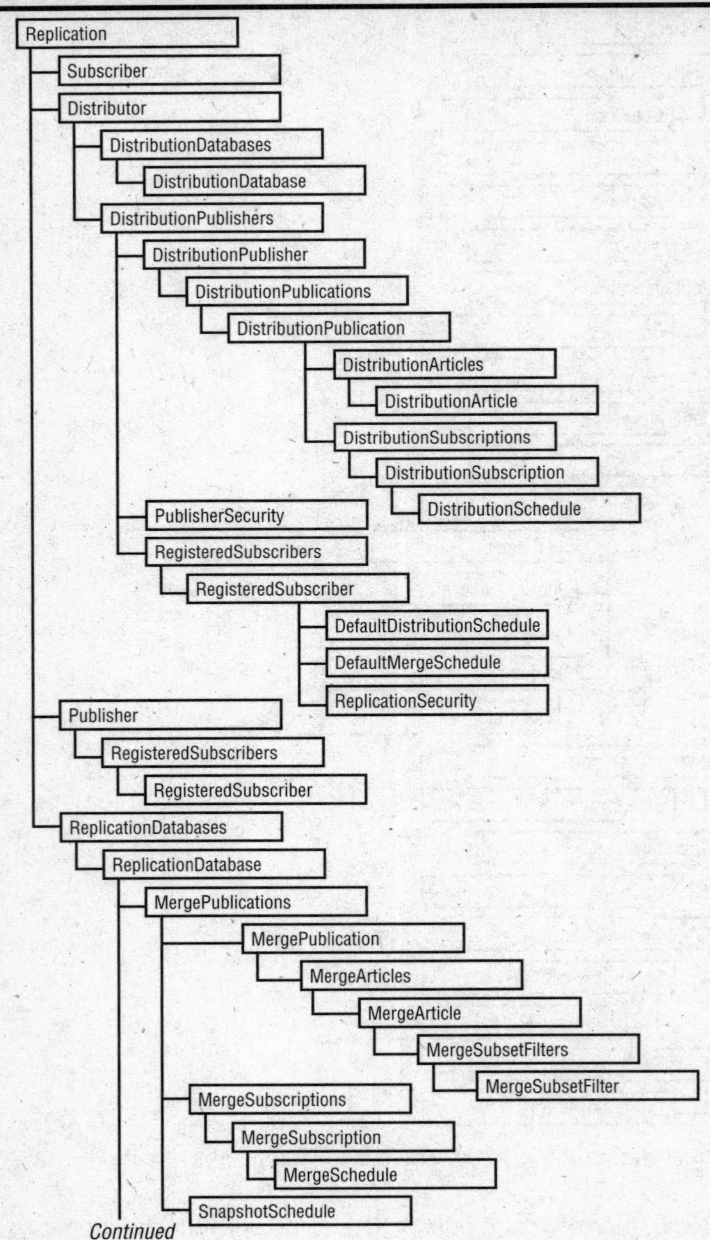

FIGURE 18.5: The Replication objects in the SQL-DMO object model

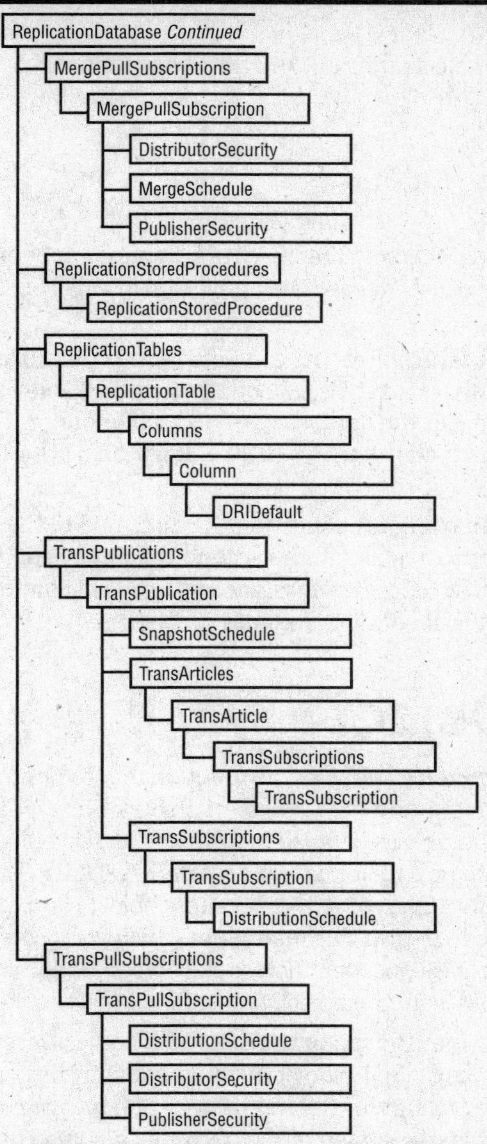

FIGURE 18.5 continued: The Replication objects in the SQL-DMO object model

Object Types

There are three types of objects in the SQL-DMO object model:

- Objects
- Collections
- Lists

An *object* in the SQL-DMO model represents a single component in SQL Server. For example, the Database object refers to a single SQL Server database.

A SQL-DMO *collection* is an object that contains other objects of a single type. For example, a database's Tables collection contains Table objects that each represent a table in the database. As with a standard collection, you can enumerate through all the tables in a database using the Tables collection.

The *list* type object is a read-only collection. It's returned to the client as a SQLObjectList object. To query all the accounts that have particular permissions, call the ListDatabasePermissions method. This method returns a SQLObjectList that contains Permission objects.

SQLServer Object

The SQL-DMO object interfaces provide the functionality to perform any server or database administration task necessary in SQL Server. The objects exposed by the Databases collection represent all the objects in a SQL Server database and are a major component of SQL-DMO. The complete object model is quite large, so we'll cover these objects and collections and how they work in depth. The manner in which you access and use the SQL-DMO objects is consistent across the object model, so the points made in here apply to all the objects and collections.

The SQLServer object is at the top of the SQL-DMO object model. This object represents a single SQL Server installation. Only by connecting to a SQL Server server using this object can you then navigate to its databases and other objects, as shown in Figure 18.6. To connect to a server you must:

- Create a SQLServer object.

- Call the Connect method and pass it a valid server name, user name, and password.

```
Dim MyServer As New SQLDMO.SQLServer

MyServer.Connect "Dev1", "sa", ""
Debug.Print MyServer.Databases.Count
MyServer.DisConnect
```

TIP

The username and password parameters of the Connect method are required for SQL Server authentication. If you want to use NT authentication, set the LoginSecure property to true and the Connect method will use the currently logged in user and ignore the user name and password parameter values.

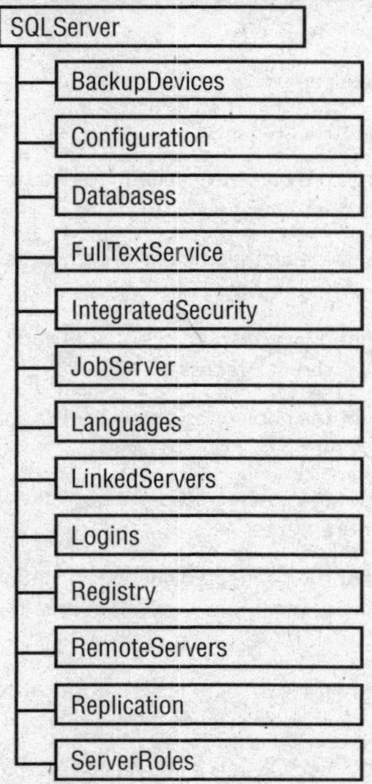

FIGURE 18.6: Collections and objects available from the SQLServer object

Once you have connected using the SQLServer object, you can access all its properties, methods, and events. The SQLServer object's properties are detailed in Table 18.1.

TABLE 18.1: SQLServer Object Properties

PROPERTY	DESCRIPTION
AnsiNulls	When set to true, table columns are Null by default if no value is supplied. Affects null handling for the current connection only.
ApplicationName	Provides the name of the client application to SQL Server.
AutoReConnect	When set to true, the SQLServer object attempts to reconnect if the current connection is broken.
BlockingTimeout	The time in milliseconds that a blocked resource request will wait before timing out.
CodePage	Returns the character set used by the current server.
CommandTerminator	Specifies the delimiter used in T-SQL batch statements. The default delimiter is GO.
ConnectionID	The unique identifier for a SQLServer object's connection to a valid server.
EnableBcp	Enables the use of bulk copy objects.
HostName	The machine name of the client application.
Isdbcreator	Returns whether or not the connected client application has permissions to create and modify databases.
Isdiskadmin	Returns whether or not the connected client application can perform disk administration tasks.
Isprocessadmin	Returns whether or not the connected client application has permissions to execute server processes.
Issecurityadmin	Returns whether or not the connected client application has permissions to create, modify, or delete users.
Isserveradmin	Returns whether or not the connected client application has permissions to configure the server.
Issetupadmin	Returns whether or not the connected client application has permissions to install and configure replication or extended stored procedures.
Issysadmin	Returns whether or not the connected client application has system administrator (sa) permissions on the server.
Language	The language used by the SQL Server server to return error messages and warnings and to format dates.
Login	The SQL Server user name used to connect to the server.
LoginSecure	If true, the connection to SQL Server uses Windows NT authentication.
LoginTimeout	The number of seconds a connection attempt waits until timing out. If set to 0, the connection will wait indefinitely.

TABLE 18.1 continued: SQLServer Object Properties

PROPERTY	DESCRIPTION
MaxNumericPrecision	The greatest number of decimals allowed for numeric data types.
Name	The server name.
NetName	The machine name of the SQL Server server to which the client application is connected.
NetPacketSize	Specifies the packet size for data transfer between the client application and the server. The default is 4096 bytes.
ODBCPrefix	If set to true, any ODBC errors are prefaced by the error source.
Password	The password used to connect to a server using SQL Server authentication.
ProcessID	Returns the process ID for the current connection.
ProcessInputBuffer	Returns the value in memory used for input by a SQL Server process.
ProcessOutputBuffer	Returns the value in memory used for output by a SQL Server process.
QueryTimeout	The number of seconds before a statement issued against SQL Server will time out.
QuotedIdentifier	When set to true, identifiers are delimited with double quotes and character literal values are delimited by single quotes. If false, identifiers are not quoted and character literal values can be enclosed in single or double quotes.
RegionalSetting	Specifies the regional settings for the ODBC driver during a connection. If true, the driver uses the local settings of the client when converting date, time, and currency data.
SaLogin	Returns true if the login used to create the current connection has system administrator privileges on the server.
Status	Identifies the status of component execution on the server, such as paused, running, stopped, or in transition.
StatusInfoRefetchInterval	The frequency with which server status information is retrieved. By default it's every 30 seconds. This property can be used to verify that a connection hasn't been broken, to check for available database space, or check the status of a database.
TranslateChar	Defines the ODBC driver's translation setting for a single connection. If true, the ODBC driver translates character data exchanged between the client and server.
TrueLogin	Returns the SQL Server login used by the connection even if it differs from the login provided to the Connect method. Useful if NT to SQL Server user name mapping is used.

TABLE 18.1 continued: SQLServer Object Properties

PROPERTY	DESCRIPTION
TrueName	Returns the value of the *@@SERVERNAME* global variable for the currently connected server (may differ from the machine name).
UserProfile	Returns the permissions of the user that created the current connection. Identifies if a user has the ability to create a database and load or unload extended stored procedures, and whether the user is a member of sysadmin role or has no privileges.
VersionMajor	The part of the SQL Server version number to the left of the first decimal point.
VersionMinor	The part of the SQL Server version number to the right of the first decimal point.
VersionString	Returns the value from the *@@VERSION* function reporting the full version number, copyright, and OS information for the server.

The SQLServer object also has events that are raised by the occurrence of particular operations. In order to use events, the SQLServer object must be declared at the module level using the `WithEvents` keyword: `Private WithEvents mSQLServer As SQLDMO.SQLServer`. The SQLServer object's events are listed in Table 18.2.

TABLE 18.2: SQLServer Object Events

EVENT	DESCRIPTION
CommandSent	Occurs when one or more T-SQL commands are submitted to SQL Server.
ConnectionBroken	Occurs when the SQLServer object loses its connection to the server. This event is raised only when the AutoReConnect property is false.
QueryTimeout	The execution of a batch of T-SQL statements has timed out.
RemoteLoginFailed	A remote login to another SQL Server has failed. This event also returns the severity, error number, state, and error message text.
ServerMessage	Occurs when a success-with-information message is returned from an action that occurred on SQL Server.

The methods associated with the SQLServer object are detailed in Table 18.3.

TABLE 18.3: SQLServer Object Methods

Method	Description
AddStartParameter	Adds a startup option to the SQLServer object. These options take effect after the SQLServer object starts the SQLServer service on the target server. For example, you can start SQL Server in single-user mode or with minimal configuration.
AttachDb	Enables a database to be visible to SQL Server. The connected user must have membership in the sysadmin role.
AttachDbWithSingleFile	Makes a database visible to SQL Server when the database is contained in a single operating system file.
BeginTransaction	Starts a transaction. For use when submitting batch T-SQL commands to the server.
Close	Disconnects the SQLServer object and removes it from the SQLServers collection.
CommandShellImmediate	Executes an external operating system command on the server.
CommandShellWithResults	Executes an external operating system command on the server and returns a QueryResults object. The resultset from the command is contained in QueryResults.
CommitTransaction	Commits any changes made after the BeginTransaction method was called.
Connect	Establishes a connection to SQL Server. Takes optional server name, user name, and password parameters.
Continue	Restarts a paused SQL Server service.
DetachDB	Makes a database invisible to allow reallocation of storage and moving of database files.
DisConnect	Terminates the connection to SQL Server.
EnumAccountInfo	Returns a QueryResults object with account name, type, privilege, mapped login name, and permission path for each account on the server.
EnumAvailableMedia	Returns a QueryResults object containing entries for the media available on the server. This includes CD-ROM drives, disk drives, floppy drives, and tape drives.
EnumDirectories	Returns a QueryResults object with all the subdirectories for the specified path.
EnumErrorLogs	Returns a QueryResults object containing the log number and the date last updated for all the error logs on a server.
EnumLocks	Returns a QueryResults object with the process ID, lock type, table name, index name, database name, and status for all the locks on a server.

TABLE 18.3 continued: SQLServer Object Methods

METHOD	DESCRIPTION
EnumLoginMappings	Returns a QueryResults object containing SQL Server logins and their mapped database user names.
EnumNTDomainGroups	Returns a QueryResults object with all group account information for a specified domain.
EnumProcesses	Returns a QueryResults object listing information for all the processes running on a server
EnumServerAttributes	Returns a QueryResults object containing all the properties for a server.
EnumVersionInfo	Returns a QueryResults object containing the server's version information.
ExecuteImmediate	Submits batch T-SQL commands to a server and executes them.
ExecuteWithResults	Submits batch T-SQL commands to a server, executes them, and returns the resultset in a QueryResults object.
ExecuteWithResults-AndMessages	Submits batch T-SQL commands to a server, executes them, and returns the resultset in a QueryResults object. Any messages generated by the execution are also returned to the client application.
IsLogin	Returns whether or not the specified login name is valid on the current server.
IsNTGroupMember	Returns whether or not the specified user is a member of the specified NT group.
IsOS	Returns whether or not the server is running under the specified operating system.
IsPackage	Identifies the edition of SQL Server running on the current server. Can be unknown, Desktop, MSDE, Standard, or Enterprise.
KillDatabase	Forces a drop of the specified database.
KillProcess	Forces the termination of the specified process.
ListMembers	Returns a NameList object with all the roles in which the current login has membership.
ListStartupProcedures	Returns a SQLObjectList object with all the stored procedures that execute automatically when the server is started.
Pause	Temporarily stops the SQL Server service. Use the Continue method to restart the service.
PingSQLServerVersion	Returns the SQL Server version of the specified server. Recognizes versions pre-6.0, 6.0, 6.5, and 7.0. This method connects and disconnects from the server it's querying.

TABLE 18.3 continued: SQLServer Object Methods

METHOD	DESCRIPTION
ReadBackupHeader	Returns a QueryResults object with the contents of the backup media.
ReadErrorLog	Returns a QueryResults object containing the specified error log.
ReConnect	Reestablishes a connection to SQL Server.
RollbackTransaction	Discards any changes made since the BeginTransaction method was called.
SaveTransaction	Creates a transaction *midpoint* so that changes can be rolled back to this point.
Shutdown	Stops the SQL Server service.
Start	Starts the SQL Server service. If the login and password parameters are provided, the method will connect the SQLServer object after starting the service.
Stop	Stops the SQL Server service.
UnloadODSDLL	Unloads the specified DLL from memory on the server.
VerifyConnection	Tests the connection to the server and returns true or false.

DATABASE OBJECT

After connecting a SQLServer object to an existing server, you have access to all its collections. You can enumerate through all the databases on a server using the Databases collection. Figure 18.7 illustrates the Database object hierarchy and the objects available to you. To access all the objects within a single database, create a Database object and set it to a specific database. You can then access all the properties, methods, and collections for that database. This code lists all the tables within the Northwind database and the space used by each table (in kilobytes).

```
Dim i As Long
Dim MyServer As New SQLDMO.SQLServer
Dim MyDatabase As New SQLDMO.Database

MyServer.Connect "Mercury", "sa", ""
Set MyDatabase = MyServer.Databases("Northwind")

For i = 1 To MyDatabase.Tables.Count
```

```
        Debug.Print MyDatabase.Tables.Item(i).Name
        Debug.Print MyDatabase.Tables.Item(i).DataSpaceUsed
    Next i

    MyServer.DisConnect
```

Just as with all other Visual Basic collections, you can reference objects either by name or ordinal position. Other functions you can accomplish with the Database object include:

- Create a new database and specify the size, file group, and transaction log file name.
- Create, modify, or delete database objects such as rules, stored procedures, tables, views, and data types.
- Modify the disk storage resources for a database.
- Back up and restore a database and its transaction log.
- Create a batch SQL file to re-create the database schema.
- Update the statistics on all tables in a database.

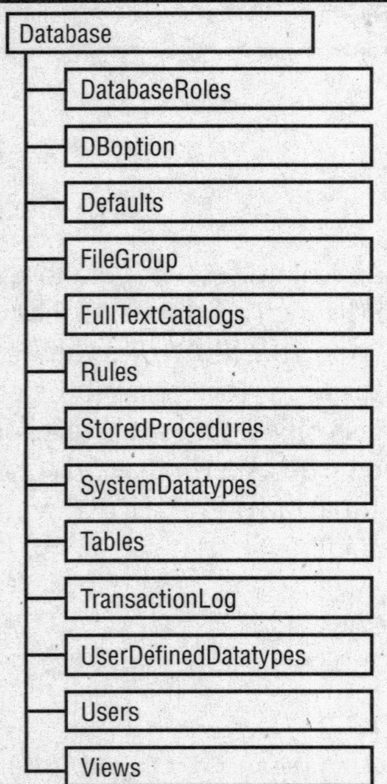

FIGURE 18.7: Collections and objects available from the Database object

Creating any objects in SQL Server using SQL-DMO involves three steps: declaring the object, setting the properties, and adding it to the necessary collection. For example, to create a database in SQL Server, you need to connect to the server, set the properties of the database, set the properties of the database file, set the properties of the transaction log, and then add it to the Databases collection:

```
Dim MyServer As New SQLDMO.SQLServer
Dim MyDatabase As New SQLDMO.Database
Dim DatabaseFile As New SQLDMO.DBFile
Dim TransactionLog As New SQLDMO.LogFile

'Connect to the server
MyServer.Connect "techmedia", "sa", ""

'Name the database
MyDatabase.Name = "TestDB"

'Create the physical file and set the growth
DatabaseFile.Name = "TestDBData"
DatabaseFile.PhysicalName = "c:\program
files\mssql7\data\TestDB.mdf"
DatabaseFile.PrimaryFile = True
DatabaseFile.FileGrowthType = SQLDMOGrowth_MB
DatabaseFile.FileGrowth = 1

'Add the Database file to the database
MyDatabase.FileGroups("PRIMARY").DBFiles.Add
    DatabaseFile

'Create the transaction log
TransactionLog.Name = "TestDBLog"
TransactionLog.PhysicalName = "c:\program
files\mssql7\data\TestDB.ldf"
'Add the transaction log to the database
MyDatabase.TransactionLog.LogFiles.Add TransactionLog

'Add the database to the Databases collection
MyServer.Databases.Add MyDatabase

MyServer.DisConnect
```

SQL-DMO can be particularly useful for applications that require the creation of database objects dynamically. For example, if you have a requirement to create a table temporarily from a client application, you can easily create the table, add it to a database, and then drop it when the application is done with it. However, the appropriate error handling must be in place to ensure that the table doesn't already exist. In addition, if the application experiences an error and the table is never deleted, there will be unused objects taking up space in the database. The drawback with this overall approach is that database objects are created and appear in the database as a result of client code and not stored procedures or other database objects, making troubleshooting and maintenance more difficult.

Once you have a reference to a SQL Server database with the Database object, you can access its properties and methods, as defined in Tables 18.4 and 18.5. The Database object has no events.

TABLE 18.4: Database Object Properties

PROPERTY	DESCRIPTION
CompatabilityLevel	Sets the behavior of the SQL Server to that of version 6.0, 6.5, or 7.0.
CreateDate	Returns the date that the database was created.
CreateForAttach	If true, the database is created from files specified in the File-Groups and LogFiles collections.
DataSpaceUsage	Returns the actual space used by the current database in megabytes.
DboLogin	If true, the current logged-in user has database ownership privileges.
ID	The identifier of the database in the SQL Server system tables.
IndexSpaceUsage	The disk space in kilobytes used for index storage.
Isdb_accessadmin	If true, the current user is a member of the db_accessadmin role and can create, modify, and delete database users.
Isdb_backupoperator	If true, the current user is a member of the db_backupoperator role and can back up and restore databases.
Isdb_datareader	If true, the current user is a member of the db_datareader role and can see data from any table in the database.
Isdb_datawriter	If true, the current user is a member of the db_datawriter role and can add, modify, or delete data in any table in the database.
Isdb_ddladmin	If true, the current user is a member of the db_ddladmin role and can add, modify, or delete database objects such as tables or stored procedures.
Isdb_denydatareader	If true, the current user is a member of the db_denydatareader-role and cannot see data from any table in the database.
Isdb_denydatawriter	If true, the current user is a member of the db_denydatawriter role and cannot add, modify, or delete data in any table in the databas

TABLE 18.4 continued: Database Object Properties

PROPERTY	DESCRIPTION
Isdb_owner	If true, the current user is a member of the db_owner role and has full database ownership permissions.
Isdb_securityadmin	If true, the current user is a member of the db_securityadmin role and can modify role membership and user permissions in the database.
IsFullTextEnabled	Specifies whether or not the database can be searched using full-text queries.
Name	The database name.
Owner	Returns the owner of the current database.
Permissions	Returns the database permissions for the connected user. Identifies if the user can create a database, create a default, create a stored procedure, create a rule, create a table, create a view, back up a database, or back up the transaction log.
PrimaryFilePath	Identifies the path and directory where the primary file for the current database is located.
Size	The total size of the database in megabytes.
SpaceAvailable	The amount of space in kilobytes that is unused by the database.
SpaceAvailableInMB	The amount of space in megabytes that is unused by the database.
Status	The status of a database. Identifies if the database is in emergency mode, inaccessible, loading, normal, offline, recovering, standby, or suspect.
SystemObject	Returns true if the specified object is a system object. Returns false if the specified object was created and owned by a user.
UserName	Returns the name of the current database user.
UserProfile	Returns the roles for the current database user.
Version	Returns the version of SQL Server used to create the database.

TABLE 18.5: The Database Object Methods

METHOD	DESCRIPTION
CheckAllocations	Tests the pages of the specified database to ensure data integrity and repairs them.
CheckAllocationsDataOnly	Same as CheckAllocations.
CheckCatalog	Tests the integrity of the current database catalog.

TABLE 18.5 continued: The Database Object Methods

METHOD	DESCRIPTION
CheckIdentityValues	Verifies that the next identity value for a particular column is less than the maximum value in the column for all the tables in the database.
Checkpoint	Forces the *write* of all database pages that have not been saved.
CheckTables	Verifies the integrity of all database pages used to store tables and indexes and repairs them if necessary.
CheckTablesDataOnly	Checks the integrity of all database pages used to store tables and indexes by calling the DBCC CHECKTABLE command. Returns the output from this command.
Deny	Denies database permissions granted to the specified users.
DisableFullTextCatalogs	Removes full-text catalogs from the database.
EnableFullTextCatalogs	Enables full-text indexing for a database.
EnumCandidateKeys	Returns a QueryResults object listing the tables in a database and the unique or primary key constraints on those tables that could be used for a primary key.
EnumDependencies	Returns a QueryResults object listing database objects and their dependencies.
EnumFileGroups	Returns a QueryResults object listing the file groups for a database.
EnumFiles	Returns a QueryResults object listing all the files used to store a database.
EnumLocks	Returns a QueryResults object listing all the locks for a server or a single process.
EnumLoginMappings	Returns a QueryResults object with SQL Server logins and the database users to which they are mapped.
EnumMatchingSPs	Returns a QueryResults object listing the stored procedures that contain the specified text.
EnumNTGroups	Returns a QueryResults object with the NT user names that have permissions in the current database.
EnumUsers	Returns a QueryResults object containing the users defined in a database and their roles.
ExecuteImmediate	Submits batch T-SQL commands and executes them.
ExecuteWithResults	Submits batch T-SQL commands, executes them, and returns the results in a QueryResults object.
ExecuteWithResults-AndMessages	Submits batch T-SQL commands to a server, executes them, and returns the resultset in a QueryResults object. Any messages generated by the execution are also returned to the client application.

TABLE 18.5 continued: The Database Object Methods

METHOD	DESCRIPTION
FullTextIndexScript	Returns T-SQL commands to the client application than can enable full-text indexing.
GenerateSQL	Returns T-SQL commands to the client application that can be used to re-create the current database.
GetDatatypeByName	Returns an object reference to the specified data type.
GetMemoryUsage	For backward compatibility only.
GetObjectByName	Returns an object reference to the specified database object.
Grant	Assigns database permissions to a user. You can grant all permissions or the ability to create a database, create a default, create a stored procedure, create a table, create a rule, create a view, back up a database, or back up the transaction log.
IsUser	If true, the specified user is defined in the database.
IsValidKeyDatatype	Returns whether or not a column of the specified data type can be used as a primary or foreign key.
ListDatabasePermissions	Returns a list object with the permissions for the current database.
ListObjectPermissions	Returns a list object with the accounts that have explicit permissions. For example, this method can identify all users that have INSERT privileges.
ListObjects	Returns a list object containing all the system and user-defined objects in a database.
RecalcSpaceUsage	Updates space usage statistics for the current database.
RemoveFullTextCatalogs	Deletes all the catalogs that enable full-text searching on a database.
Revoke	Rolls back the *grant* or *deny* of the specified database permission for the specified users.
Script	Creates the T-SQL commands that can be used to re-create the database.
ScriptTransfer	Creates the T-SQL commands that can be used to create the database. These commands can be used in other processes such as a scheduled transfer.
SetOwner	Reassigns ownership of the current database.
Shrink	Reduces the current database space usage to its smallest size or to the percentage specified.
Transfer	Copies the schema and data from one database to another.
UpdateIndexStatistics	Updates the index statistics on all tables in a database.

QueryResults Object

The *QueryResults object* is a read-only tabular object that returns data to the client application. Data returned as the result of SQL statement execution on the server is returned as a QueryResults object. Or, if you call one of the methods like EnumCandidateKeys, it returns a QueryResults object listing each table in the database and the unique or primary key constraints that could define primary or foreign key candidates.

The number of columns and rows in each QueryResults object varies depending on the data it returns. The following code calls the EnumCandidateKeys method and loops through each column and row to retrieve the data. Each column in the QueryResults object may also be a different data type, so you may want to use the ColumnType property to identify which methods to call to get the column data.

```
Dim i As Long
Dim x As Long
Dim SQLServer As New SQLDMO.SQLServer
Dim SQLDatabase As New SQLDMO.Database
Dim Results As QueryResults

SQLServer.Connect "TECHMEDIA", "sa", ""
Set SQLDatabase = SQLServer.Databases("Northwind")

Set Results = SQLDatabase.EnumCandidateKeys

For i = 1 To Results.Rows
    For x = 1 To Results.Columns
        Debug.Print Results.GetColumnString(i, x)
    Next x
Next i
```

The output from this code lists each table and the constraints on that table that could be used for a primary key like this:

```
[dbo].[Categories]
PK_Categories
[dbo].[CustomerCustomerDemo]
PK_CustomerCustomerDemo
[dbo].[CustomerDemographics]
PK_CustomerDemographics
[dbo].[Customers]
PK_Customers
[dbo].[dtproperties]
PK_dtproperties
[dbo].[Employees]
```

```
PK_Employees
[dbo].[EmployeeTerritories]
PK_EmployeeTerritories
[dbo].[Order Details]
PK_Order_Details
[dbo].[Orders]
PK_Orders
[dbo].[Products]
PK_Products
[dbo].[Region]
PK_Region
[dbo].[Shippers]
PK_Shippers
[dbo].[Suppliers]
PK_Suppliers
[dbo].[Territories]
PK_Territories
```

The properties of the QueryResults object are listed in Table 18.6.

TABLE 18.6: QueryResults Object Properties

Property	Description
ColumnMaxLength	Maximum number of characters that can be stored in the column.
ColumnName	The name of the column.
Columns	The total number of columns in the QueryResults object.
ColumnType	The base data type of the column.
CurrentResultSet	The current resultset. The QueryResults object can contain multiple resultsets of data. For example, each batch statement returns a resultset to the client.
ResultSets	The total number of resultsets.
Rows	The total number of rows returned.

The methods of the QueryResults object are detailed in Table 18.7.

TABLE 18.7: QueryResults Object Methods

Method	Description
GetColumnBinary	Returns a memory pointer to the binary data for the specified row and column.
GetColumnBinaryLength	Returns the number of bytes in a binary column.

TABLE 18.7 continued: QueryResults Object Methods

Method	Description
GetColumnBool	Returns the Boolean value for the specified row and column.
GetColumnDate	Returns the date value for the specified row and column.
GetColumDouble	Returns the double value for the specified row and column.
GetColumnFloat	Returns the float value for the specified row and column.
GetColumnGUID	Returns a memory pointer to the GUID value for the specified row and column.
GetColumnLong	Returns the long value for the specified row and column.
GetColumnString	Returns the string value for the specified row and column.
GetRangeString	Returns the entire QueryResults object data in a string.

SQL-DMO Files

SQL-DMO ships with SQL Server, and all the necessary components are installed when you install the server or client. The files used to implement SQL-DMO applications can be found in Table 18.8.

TABLE 18.8: SQL-DMO Files

File	Directory	Description
`sqldmo.dll`	`\Mssql7\Binn or \Program Files\ Microsoft SQL Server\ 75\Tools\ Binn`	The DLL used to implement SQL-DMO in client applications. In order to create SQL-DMO objects, you must first add a reference to this file.
`sqldmo.rll`	`\Mssql7\Resources\ 1033 or\ Program Files\ Microsoft SQL Server\ 75\Tools\Binn\ Resources\1033`	SQL-DMO resource file.
`sqldmo.hlp`	`\Mssql7\Binn or \Program Files\ Microsoft SQL Server\ 75\Tools\ Binn`	SQL-DMO help file.

TABLE 18.8 continued: SQL-DMO Files

File	Directory	Description
sqldmo.h	\Mssql7\Devtools\Include	C header file.
sqldmoid.h	\Mssql7\Devtools\Include	C header file containing interface and class identifiers.
sqldmo.sql	Mssql7\Install	T-SQL script that will re-create SQL-DMO stored procedures on the server.
Client application samples	\Mssql7\Devtools\Samples\ Sqldmo	implementing SQL-DMO. Samples are provided for C, C++, and Visual Basic.

WARNING

After installing SQL Server and selecting all the components, you may find that the SQL-DMO samples are still not installed. They can be found on the SQL Server CD under the `devtools\samples\sqldmo\vb\` directory.

SQL-DMO Sample Applications

SQL Server comes with two sample client applications that show SQL-DMO in action. These applications, in addition to the SQL-DMO sample application for this chapter, are excellent references on how to use this library.

Explorer

The Explore.mak sample shows you how to connect to a server and explore all the objects that reside on that server. In the first combo box, as shown in Figure 18.8, you can see all the collections that are children of the SQLServer object. As you select objects, their child collections are displayed to the right. The properties for each selected object are displayed in the box below. This application was written in a previous version of Visual Basic, so you'll have to open Visual Basic and explicitly open the project file.

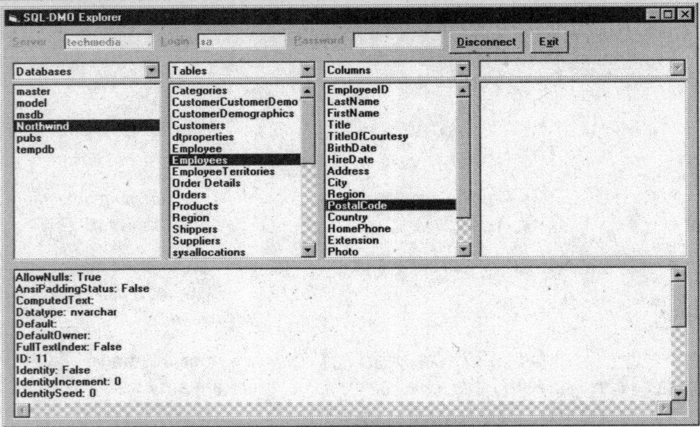

FIGURE 18.8: The Explorer sample application that comes with SQL Server

Index Test

The IdxTest.vbp sample application connects to a database and lets you test stored procedure performance. You can run a stored procedure and then test its performance after the addition of various indexes on the tables it references. This application was also written in a previous version of Visual Basic and still has a few bugs in it. For example, it fails if you try to test a stored procedure that has a name containing spaces in it. Figure 18.9 illustrates using IdxTest to test stored procedure performance before and after the implementation of indexes.

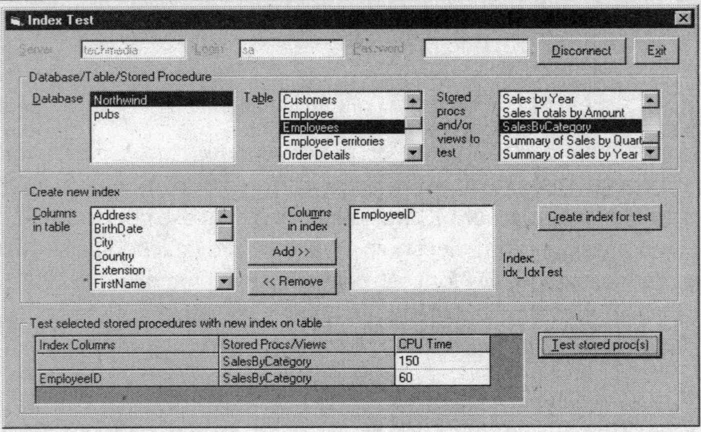

FIGURE 18.9: The Index Test sample application that comes with SQL Server

SAMPLE APPLICATION TOUR

To get an idea of what you can do with SQL-DMO, let's take a look at the sample application for this chapter, CompDb (Compare Databases). In many development environments, there is a development database where new changes are implemented and code is tested against these tables. There may also be a database used by the QA testers for testing new code. In a perfect world, these databases should always be synchronized. However, ensuring that changes to tables, constraints, stored procedures, indexes, etc., on one database are also implemented on another can be quite a chore. The CompDb application compares the tables in two existing databases and identifies if any new tables have been added to either database.

Automating these types of tasks can save a lot of time, because no longer do changes in one database need to be tracked down and implemented manually. Using SQL-DMO is also much more accurate, because it queries the database directly for changes instead of depending on people to record and notify each other when database changes occur.

The first thing you'll need to do when using SQL-DMO in your own applications is add a reference to the appropriate library, as shown in Figure 18.10. This application uses ADO 2.5, so if you don't have this version, go to the references and add a reference to the version of ADO that you have installed.

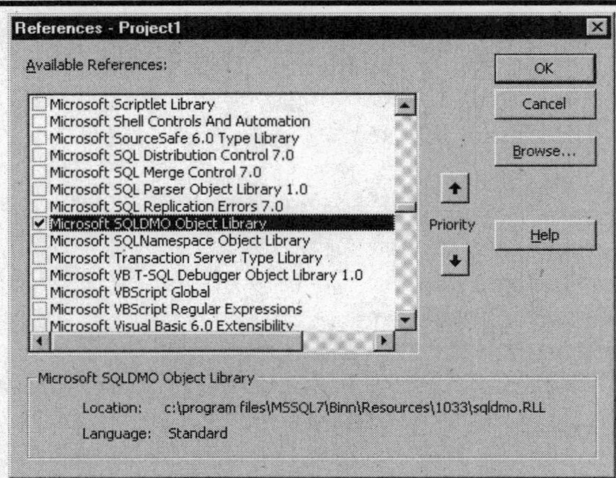

FIGURE 18.10: Adding a reference to SQL-DMO

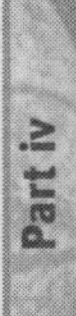

When you start the CompDb application, the first thing it does is attempt to connect to the server with the SQLServer object. It uses the server name, user name, and password that you provide, as shown in Figure 18.11.

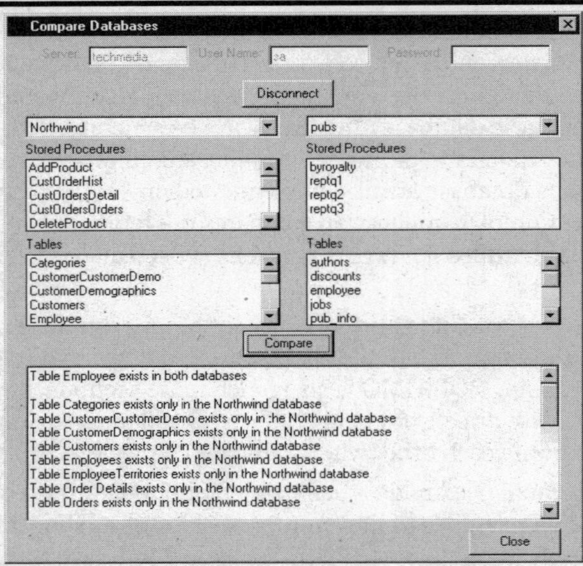

FIGURE 18.11: The CompDb (Compare Databases) sample application uses SQL-DMO to compare the tables in two databases.

Once connected, the application enumerates through the Databases collection for the specified server and populates two combo boxes with all the databases, as shown in the following code.

```
Private Sub cmdConnect_Click()

    On Error GoTo ErrorHandler

    Dim i As Integer

    If mConnected = True Then
        mSQLServer.DisConnect
        mConnected = False

        cmdConnect.Caption = "Connect"

        lblServer.Enabled = True
        txtServer.Enabled = True
```

```
        lblUserName.Enabled = True
        txtUserName.Enabled = True
        lblPassword.Enabled = True
        txtPassword.Enabled = True

        cboDatabase1.Clear
        cboDatabase2.Clear
        lstProcs1.Clear
        lstProcs2.Clear
        lstTables1.Clear
        lstTables2.Clear
        txtTableComp.Text = ""
    Else
        Screen.MousePointer = vbHourglass

        mSQLServer.ApplicationName = "CompDb"
        If txtServer.Text = "" Then
            MsgBox "You must supply a valid server name"
            Screen.MousePointer = vbDefault
            Exit Sub
        End If

        If txtUserName = "" Then
            MsgBox "You must supply a valid user name"
            Screen.MousePointer = vbDefault
            Exit Sub
        End If

        Screen.MousePointer = vbHourglass

        With mSQLServer
            'Connect to the SQL Server - no DSN required
            .Connect txtServer.Text, txtUserName.Text,
                txtPassword.Text
            mConnected = True
            cmdConnect.Caption = "Disconnect"
            lblServer.Enabled = False
            txtServer.Enabled = False
            lblUserName.Enabled = False
            txtUserName.Enabled = False
            lblPassword.Enabled = False
            txtPassword.Enabled = False

            'Load all the database names in the combo boxes
            If .Databases.Count > 0 Then
                cboDatabase1.Enabled = True
```

```
                cboDatabase2.Enabled = True
                For i = 1 To .Databases.Count
                    cboDatabase1.AddItem .Databases(i).Name
                    cboDatabase2.AddItem .Databases(i).Name
                Next i
            Else
                cboDatabase1.Enabled = False
                cboDatabase2.Enabled = False
            End If
        End With
    End If

    Screen.MousePointer = vbDefault

    Exit Sub
ErrorHandler:
    MsgBox Err.Description & "(" & Err.Source & ")",
        vbCritical, "Error - frmCompDb::Form_Load"
    Screen.MousePointer = vbDefault

End Sub
```

When you select a database from the combo box, a reference to that database is created with the Database object. The code enumerates through both the Tables collection and the StoredProcedures collection for the selected database and lists the tables and stored procedures, as shown in the following code:

```
Private Sub cboDatabase1_Click()

    On Error GoTo ErrorHandler

    Dim i As Integer
    Dim Database As New SQLDMO.Database

    Screen.MousePointer = vbHourglass

    If cboDatabase1.ListIndex > -1 Then
        lstTables1.Clear
        lstTables1.Enabled = True
        lstProcs1.Clear
        lstProcs1.Enabled = True

        'Set the database to the user selected db
        Set Database = mSQLServer.Databases
            (cboDatabase1.ListIndex + 1)
```

```
        'Loop thru and list all the tables in the database
        For i = 1 To Database.Tables.Count
            If Database.Tables(i).SystemObject = False Then
                lstTables1.AddItem Database.Tables(i).Name
            End If
        Next i

        'Loop thru and list all the stored procedures
        'in the database
        For i = 1 To Database.StoredProcedures.Count
            If Database.StoredProcedures(i).SystemObject =
                False Then
                lstProcs1.AddItem
                    Database.StoredProcedures(i).Name
            End If
        Next i
    End If

    Screen.MousePointer = vbDefault

    Exit Sub
ErrorHandler:
    MsgBox Err.Description & "(" & Err.Source & ")",
        vbCritical, "Error - frmCompDb::cboDatabase1_Click"
    Screen.MousePointer = vbDefault

End Sub
```

After the tables are retrieved for each database, the Compare button puts the names in an ADO recordset along with the database name and a flag as to whether the table exists in that database. This recordset is then used to compare the flag values and identify if each table exists in one of the databases and not the other or in both databases.

```
Private Sub cmdCompare_Click()

    Dim i As Integer

    If Not (lstTables1.ListCount > 0 And _
            lstTables2.ListCount > 0) Then
        MsgBox "You must have tables in both " & _
                "databases to do a Compare"
        Exit Sub
    Else
        txtTableComp.Enabled = True
        txtTableComp.Text = ""
```

Part iv

```
'Gets all the tables from the first database
'and puts them in the rs
For i = 1 To lstTables1.ListCount
    With mTablesRS
        .AddNew
        .Fields("Db1Name").Value = cboDatabase1.Text
        .Fields("Db1Contains").Value = "Y"
        .Fields("TableName").Value =
            lstTables1.List(i - 1)
        .Update
    End With
Next i

'Compares the tables in the second database
'to those in the first
For i = 1 To lstTables2.ListCount
    With mTablesRS
        .Filter = "TableName = '" & _
            lstTables2.List(i - 1) & "'"
        If .RecordCount > 0 Then
            .Fields("Db2Name").Value =
                cboDatabase2.Text
            .Fields("Db2Contains").Value = "Y"
        Else
            .AddNew
            .Fields("Db2Name").Value =
                cboDatabase2.Text
            .Fields("Db2Contains").Value = "Y"
            .Fields("TableName").Value =
                lstTables2.List(i - 1)
            .Update
        End If
        .Filter = ""
    End With
Next i

'Show the results in the bottom listbox
With mTablesRS
    .MoveFirst
    .Filter =
        "Db1Contains = 'Y' and Db2Contains = 'Y'"
    If .RecordCount > 0 Then
        While (Not .EOF) And (Not .BOF)
            txtTableComp.Text =
                txtTableComp.Text & "Table " & _
                .Fields("TableName").Value & _
```

```
                        " exists in both databases" & _
                        vbCrLf
                .MoveNext
            Wend
            txtTableComp.Text = txtTableComp.Text & _
                vbCrLf
        End If

        .Filter = ""
        .Filter = "Db1Contains = 'Y' and " & _
                  "Db2Contains = Null"
        If .RecordCount > 0 Then
            While (Not .EOF) And (Not .BOF)
                txtTableComp.Text =
                    txtTableComp.Text & "Table "  & _
                    .Fields("TableName") & _
                        " exists only in the "  & _
                        .Fields("Db1Name") & _
                        " database" & vbCrLf
                .MoveNext
            Wend
            txtTableComp.Text = txtTableComp.Text & _
                vbCrLf
        End If

        .Filter = ""
        .Filter =
            "Db1Contains = Null and Db2Contains = 'Y'"
        If .RecordCount > 0 Then
            While (Not .EOF) And (Not .BOF)
                txtTableComp.Text =
                    txtTableComp.Text & "Table " & _
                    .Fields("TableName") & _
                        " exists only in the " & _
                        .Fields("Db2Name") & _
                        " database" & vbCrLf
                .MoveNext
            Wend
        End If

    End With

End If

End Sub
```

Part iv

As you can see, using SQL-DMO can add powerful functionality to your Visual Basic applications. This sample assumes that the two databases being compared are on a single server. However, the code could easily be modified to allow for the selection of SQL Servers and comparison of databases on separate servers.

Summary

In this chapter, you read about the SQL-DMO object model, which allows you to workwith database object programmatically. The next chapter discusses SQL Namespace (SQL-NS), one of the component APIs in the SQL DMF (Distributed Management Framework). This is a collection of object models that provides the interfaces needed to programmatically integrate any server administration functions in client applications.

Chapter 19

SQL Namespace

Along with SQL-DMO and the DTS API, *SQL Namespace* (*SQL-NS*) is one of the component APIs in the SQL Distributed Management Framework (DMF). This collection of object models provides the interfaces necessary to programmatically integrate any server administration functions in client applications.

In the previous chapter, we covered SQL-DMO, the object model that allows you to work with database objects programmatically. SQL-NS is a COM-based object library that is used to incorporate user interface elements of SQL Server's Enterprise Manager into applications. Any COM-compliant language can use this object model. The components you can build into your applications include:

- Dialogs
- Property pages
- Wizards

Adapted from *Visual Basic® Developer's Guide to SQL Server™* by Dianne Siebold

ISBN 0-7821-2679-1 480 pages $39.99

Enterprise Manager uses the same SQL-NS library to display its windows, so these objects provide the ability to integrate the same user interface elements in your Visual Basic applications without having to code them yourself. The SQL-NS library itself doesn't contain many objects, but there are many screens you can access with it.

We'll start by taking a look at the objects that make up SQL-NS and its object hierarchy. We'll also cover what user interface elements are available in the SQL-NS library. We'll use the SQL-NS sample project that comes with SQL Server, which provides an excellent example of how to initialize the SQLNamespace object, connect to SQL Server, and traverse the namespace hierarchy. Once you drill down to a SQL Server object, you can display dialogs or property pages and make changes to these objects. We'll also cover how you can use SQL-NS to invoke the SQL Server wizards. This functionality is demonstrated in the `WizardBrowser.vbp` sample application that's included with the code samples for this book. We'll wrap up with a look at SQL-NS errors and how to handle them.

SQL-NS Object Model

The SQL-NS object model is deceptively simple and consists of only four objects: the SQLNamespace object, the SQLNamespaceObject object, the SQLNamespaceCommands collection, and the SQLNamespaceCommand object. (See Figure 19.1.)

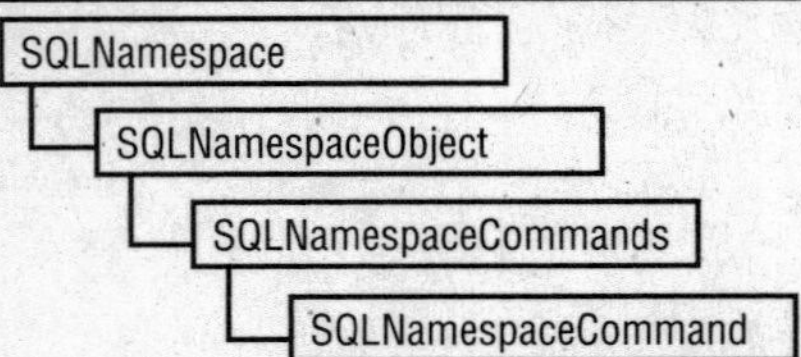

FIGURE 19.1: The SQL-NS object model has only four objects.

SQL-NS is unlike many other object models we've looked at so far. It has only four objects, but can represent over a hundred different objects. For example, the SQLNamespaceObject object can represent a database, a table, a SQL Server Agent, or even a login. The SQL-NS object model is also hierarchical. This means that the SQLNamespace object must be instantiated and initialized before the SQLNamespaceObject object, and so on down the object tree.

Essentially, any screen in Enterprise Manager can be accessed through SQL-NS. The four objects in SQL-NS all work together to allow you to traverse the SQL Server namespace:

- The *SQLNamespace object* is the top-level object in the SQL-NS library. After this object is initialized, you can then create the associated SQLNamespaceObject objects.
- The *SQLNamespaceObject object* represents different objects within the SQL Server namespace, based on the object type specified. Different commands are available from this object, depending on the type of object that's created.
- The *SQLNamespaceCommands object* is a collection containing SQLNamespaceCommand objects. This collection is available from the SQLNamespaceObject object and you can enumerate through the collection to identify the available commands for the current SQLNamespaceObject object.
- The *SQLNamespaceCommand object* represents a single command that displays the specified dialog or property page. This is done by setting the SQLNamespaceCommand object to one of the objects from the collection and calling its Execute method.

SQLNamespaceObject

The SQLNamespace object is the top-level object in the hierarchy and must be initialized before you can work with any other SQL-NS objects. The SQLNamespace object can be initialized at one of four different levels that are associated with the Enterprise Manager tree structure, as shown in Figure 19.2.

When we talk about the term *namespace*, we refer to the object tree that you see in Enterprise Manager. The level at which you initialize the SQLNamespace object defines the entry point of SQL-NS. Any child objects in the namespace below that entry point are available. For example, if you want to work with a single database, you can initialize the SQL-Namespace at the database level. Then, all the database objects in the namespace for that database will be available to you. If you need to see all the databases on a single server, initialize the SQLNamespace object at the server level.

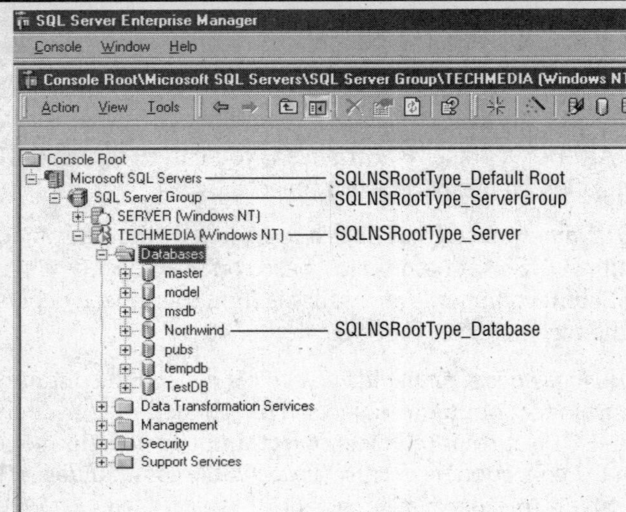

FIGURE 19.2: The SQLNamespace object can be initialized at one of four different starting points.

WARNING

Using the DefaultRoot and ServerGroup as starting points is risky because both use the connection information from the current installation of Enterprise Manager and therefore depend on a particular Enterprise Manager configuration. Instead, use the Server or Database levels and provide the database connection information.

Initialize the SQLNamespace Object

The level at which you initialize the SQLNamespace object is called the *root type* and can be one of the four values shown in Table 19.1.

TABLE 19.1: The SQLNSRootType Constants

Level	Constant	Value
All SQL Servers	SQLNSRootType_DefaultRoot	0
Server Group	SQLNSRootType _ServerGroup	1
Server	SQLNSRootType_Server	2
Database	SQLNSRootType_Database	3

The root type constants are found in the SQLNSRootType enum. To initialize the SQLNamespace object, you must first declare the object and then call the Initialize method. The Initialize method takes four parameters: application name, root type, connection string, and window handle. Only the application name parameter is required The following code initializes the SQLNamespace object at the database level, pointing to the Northwind database:

```
Dim SQLNS As SQLNS.SQLNamespace
Set SQLNS = New SQLNamespace

SQLNS.Initialize "Test Application", _
    SQLNSRootType_Database, _
    "Server=DSIEBOLD;UID=sa;PWD=;Database=Northwind;", _
    hWnd
```

Application Name This argument is of type string and specifies the name of the client application initializing the SQLNamespace object.

Root Type The root type parameter is a long value and one of the SQLNSRootType constants. This value specifies the level at which the SQLNamespace object is initialized.

Connection String This argument provides the database connection information required to connect to the server. The parameter type is variant pointer so you can pass either a literal string or use the CStr function with a string variable. You'll receive an error if you attempt to pass a standard string variable to the Initialize method.

hWnd The hWnd argument specifies the location of the window requesting initialization. The hWnd property in Visual Basic provides the window handle of the current form. This variable is defined with a datatype of Long.

Connection String Options The connection string you create and pass to the Initialize method is similar to an ODBC connection string and can have the following values:

- Server
- SrvGrp
- UID
- PWD

- Trusted_Connection
- Database

The connection string requires different values, depending on the root type that's used to initialize the SQLNamespace object. Each of the connection string values is separated by a semicolon. For example, if you're connecting using the SQLNSRootType_DefaultRoot, you don't need to provide a connection string—all of the connection details are retrieved from the local Enterprise Manager configuration in the Registry.

To initialize the SQLNamespace object using the SQLNSRootType_ServerGroup root type, you must provide the server group name to which you wish to connect. The rest of the connection information is retrieved from the configuration of the local Enterprise Manager. The syntax for initializing the SQLNamespace object at the server group level is

```
SrvGrp=SQL Server Group;
```

As you get more specific in the root type, you must provide more detailed connection information. Here's the syntax to connect at the server level:

```
Server=DEV1;UID=sa;PWD=;
```

To initialize the SQLNamespace object with a root type of SQLNS-RootType_ Database, you need to provide the database information in the connection string like this:

```
Server=DEV1;UID=sa;PWD=;Database=Northwind;
```

SQLNamespace Object Methods

The SQLNamespace object has 13 methods, as detailed in Table 19.2, and no properties or events. The methods are used primarily for navigating the namespace and initializing the object. We'll look at using these methods in code later on in this chapter.

TABLE 19.2: SQLNamespace Object Methods

Method	Description
GetChildrenCount	The number of children items associated with the current object.
GetFirstChildItem	Returns the first child object of the specified type or name.
GetName	Takes a handle as an argument and returns the name of the item.
GetNextSiblingItem	Retrieves the next sibling item as specified by the item type or name.

TABLE 19.2 continued: SQLNamespace Object Methods

METHOD	DESCRIPTION
GetParentItem	Returns the parent object of the current object.
GetPreviousSiblingItem	Retrieves the sibling item before the current object as specified by the item type or name.
GetRootItem	Returns a handle to the root item as defined by the SQLNamespace.Initialize method.
GetSQLDMOObject	Returns a SQL-DMO Server or Database object (if there is one) associated with the current object.
GetSQLNamespaceObject	Returns the SQL-NS interface for the current object. Used to set an object reference to the current object.
GetType	Returns the object type of an item as defined in the SQLNSObjectType enum.
Initialize	Initializes the SQLNamespace object with the specified application name, root type, connection string, and window handle.
Refresh	Refreshes the console tree under the specified node.
SetLCID	Sets the locale ID value for SQL-NS.

Namespace Browser

The *Namespace Browser* is a sample application that demonstrates how to use SQL-NS in your own applications. This application lets you step through the namespace, as shown in Figure 19.3. For each object in the namespace, this application displays any sibling or children items. As you select items on the left side of the screen, the commands available from that object are displayed on the right side. These commands are used to invoke the dialogs and property pages by calling the Execute method.

According to Microsoft documentation, this application should be installed on the hard drive when you install SQL Server and select to install the samples. However, I found that many of the sample applications did not install from the CD. The Namespace Browser project is called *browse.vbp* and should be located in the `Mssql7\devtools\samples\Sqlns\vb\browse` directory. If you can't find this project on your hard drive, just copy it from the `devtools\samples\Sqlns\ vb\browse` directory on the SQL Server CD.

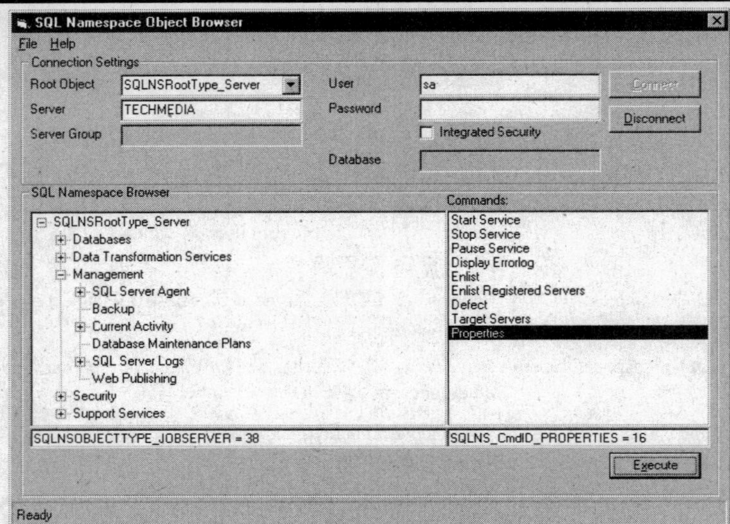

FIGURE 19.3: The Namespace Browser sample application illustrates how to use SQL-NS.

The Namespace Browser is an excellent way to see SQL-NS in action. Because there are so many user interface elements that can be accessed through SQL-NS, this tool is also useful for navigating to all the available namespace objects and identifying the types of screens you can use in your applications. We'll go though this application in more detail as we look at the other namespace objects but here are the steps to using it to display the property pages of a table:

1. Enter the root type—in this case, SQLNSRootType_Database—and the server name (it will default to the local machine name).
2. Specify a username, password, and the Northwind database name.
3. Click the Connect button.
4. Expand the SQLNSRootType_Database node in the tree on the left side.
5. Drill down to the Categories table in the Northwind database. The commands available for that table are listed in the listbox on the right.

6. Click Properties and then click Execute. This displays the Table Properties dialog for that table and should resemble Figure 19.4.

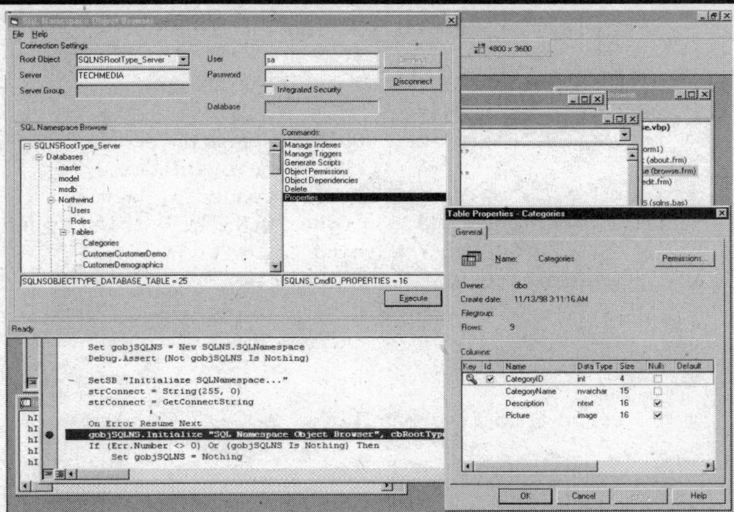

FIGURE 19.4: Use the Namespace Browser to find out what screens you can access.

Now, let's look at how the Namespace Browser uses the SQL-NS objects. After you select the root type, provide the connection information, and click Connect, the first thing the Namespace Browser does is to create the connection string and initialize the SQLNamespace object. This is shown in the following abbreviated listing:

```
Private Sub cmdConnect_Click()

    Dim objNode As ComctlLib.Node
    Dim hItem As Long
    Dim strConnect As String

    If Not gobjSQLNSObj Is Nothing Then
        Set gobjSQLNSObj = Nothing
    End If

    If Not gobjSQLNS Is Nothing Then
        Set gobjSQLNS = Nothing
    End If

    'Set the SQLNamespace object to new
```

```
        Set gobjSQLNS = New SQLNS.SQLNamespace

        'Build the connection string from the form fields
        SetSB "Initialiaze SQLNamespace..."
        strConnect = String(255, 0)
        strConnect = GetConnectString

        'Initialize the SQLNamespace object
        On Error Resume Next
        gobjSQLNS.Initialize "SQL Namespace Object Browser", _
                              cbRootType.ListIndex, _
                              CStr(strConnect), hWnd
        If (Err.Number <> 0) Or (gobjSQLNS Is Nothing) Then
            Set gobjSQLNS = Nothing
            MsgBox "SQLNamespace could not be initiated", _
                   vbOKOnly, "Error"
            Exit Sub
        End If

        On Error GoTo ErrorHandler

        . . .

    End Sub
```

This code uses the value selected in the Root Object combo box to initialize the SQLNamespace. By default the application uses the server root type and provides the name of the local machine.

GetRootItem Method

One of the differences between SQL-NS and other object libraries is SQL-NS's use of handles. A *handle* identifies the internal memory location of a particular object. The handle value is stored in a long variable. Once you retrieve the handle of a SQL-NS object, you can use that handle to retrieve the handles of other related objects or create a reference to an object. These objects can be children, siblings, or parents of the current object.

In the Namespace Browser, the handle to the top-level SQLNamespace object is retrieved into a module-level variable by calling the GetRootItem method, as follows:

```
hItem = gobjSQLNS.GetRootItem
```

This handle is required to navigate to other items in the namespace hierarchy.

TIP

When retrieving a handle, you should always be sure the value is a number other than zero. It's a good idea to check for a zero value and handle the error right after getting a handle. Otherwise, you'll receive a SQLNS_E_InvalidObjectHandle error when you attempt to use the handle later on.

GetChildrenCount Method

This method takes the handle of the SQLNamespace object and is used to find out if the current object has any children before enumerating through them.

```
Dim lChildCount As Long
lChildCount = pNS.GetChildrenCount(hItem)
```

GetFirstChildItem Method

The GetFirstChildItem method returns the handle of the first child item relative to the current SQLNamespace object. If the SQLNamespace object represents a single SQL Server, the first child item will probably be Databases. If the SQLNamespace object represents a single database, then the first child item will most likely be Users or Tables in that database (see Figure 19.5).

Once you retrieve the handle to the first child item, you can retrieve its sibling objects with the GetNextSiblingItem method. This method takes the handle of the child and returns the handle of the next item on the same level. The Namespace Browser uses this logic to retrieve all the children of the SQLNamespace object and populate the treeview control using this code:

```
If (i = 1) Then
    hChild = pNS.GetFirstChildItem(hItem, -
             SQLNSOBJECTTYPE_EMPTY, vbNullString)
Else
    hChild = pNS.GetNextSiblingItem(hChild, _
             SQLNSOBJECTTYPE_EMPTY, vbNullString)
End If
```

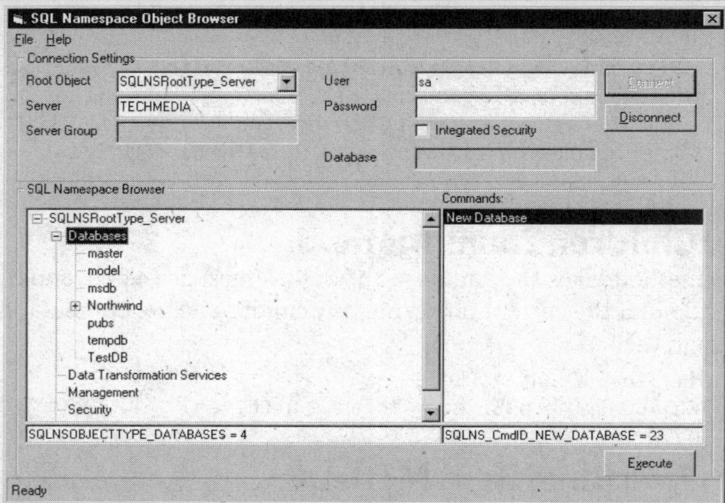

FIGURE 19.5: The children objects in the namespace

SQLNamespaceObject Object

After navigating to the desired item, you have its handle but not an actual reference to that object. This where the SQLNamespaceObject object is used. To get an actual reference to an object in the namespace, call the GetSQLNamespaceObject method and pass it the handle for the object you wish to instantiate.

The following code is an example of connecting to SQL-NS at the Northwind database level and getting a reference to the Categories table. Once you have a reference to the object with the SQLNamespaceObject object, you can execute commands to actually bring up Enterprise Manager screens.

```
Dim hTbs As Long
Dim hTb
Dim hDb As Long
Dim SQLNS As SQLNS.SQLNamespace
Dim tblCategories As SQLNS.SQLNamespaceObject

Set SQLNS = New SQLNamespace

SQLNS.Initialize "Categories App", _
                 SQLNSRootType_Database, _
                 "UID=sa;PWD=;SERVER=TECHMEDIA; _
                 DATABASE=Northwind", hWnd
```

```
hDb = SQLNS.GetRootItem
hTbs = SQLNS.GetFirstChildItem(hDb, _
            SQLNSOBJECTTYPE_DATABASE_TABLES)
hTb = SQLNS.GetFirstChildItem(hTbs, _
            SQLNSOBJECTTYPE_DATABASE_TABLE, _
            "Categories")

Set tblCategories = SQLNS.GetSQLNamespaceObject(hTb)
```

Methods and Properties

The SQLNamespaceObject object has only two methods for executing commands, as shown in Table 19.3.

TABLE 19.3: SQLNamespaceObject Methods

METHOD	DESCRIPTION
ExecuteCommandByID	Executes a command as specified by the Command ID parameter.
ExecuteCommandByName	Executes a command as specified by the Command Name parameter.

Table 19.4 details the properties available from the SQLNamespace-Object object.

TABLE 19.4: SQLNamespaceObject Properties

PROPERTY	DESCRIPTION
Commands	Returns a collection of commands associated with an object. Executing a command displays the specified namespace screen.
Handle	Returns a handle to the current SQLNamespaceObject object.
Name	Returns the name of the current object as found in SQL Server.
Type	The type of object that the current SQLNamespaceObject object represents. Specified by one of the SQLNSObjectType enum constants.

The SQLNSObjectType enum contains the values for all the different object types. The SQLNamespaceObject can be set to any one of these object types. There are about 100 different object types, including backup devices, database objects, security objects, DTS packages, error logs, replication objects, server objects, and so on. You can locate all the possible object types by using the Visual Basic object browser or referencing them in the SQL Server BOL (books online).

SQLNameSpaceCommand Object

The SQLNamespaceCommand object represents a single command associated with a SQLNamespaceObject object. For example, in the previous code we created an object reference to the Categories table. That object has an associated SQLNamespaceCommands collection that contains SQLNamespaceCommand objects. Each of the objects represents a single dialog or property pages screen.

After getting a reference to the Categories table, you can enumerate through all the possible commands like this:

```
    Dim hTbs As Long
    Dim hTb
    Dim hDb As Long
    Dim SQLNS As SQLNS.SQLNamespace
    Dim tblCategories As SQLNS.SQLNamespaceObject

    Set SQLNS = New SQLNamespace

    SQLNS.Initialize "Categories App", _
                     SQLNSRootType_Database, _
                     "UID=sa;PWD=;SERVER=TECHMEDIA; _
                     DATABASE=Northwind", hWnd

hDb = SQLNS.GetRootItem
    hTbs = SQLNS.GetFirstChildItem(hDb, _
                 SQLNSOBJECTTYPE_DATABASE_TABLES)
    hTb = SQLNS.GetFirstChildItem(hTbs, _
                 SQLNSOBJECTTYPE_DATABASE_TABLE, _
                 "Categories")

    Set tblCategories = SQLNS.GetSQLNamespaceObject(hTb)

    Dim i As Long
    For i = 1 To tblCategories.Commands.Count
        Debug.Print tblCategories.Commands.Item(i).Name & _
            " " & tblCategories.Commands.Item(i).HelpString
    Next i
```

The output from this code displays all the possible screens you can call from this object and looks something like this:

```
Manage Indexes Manage indexes for a table
```

```
Manage Triggers Manage triggers for a table
Generate Scripts Generate Scripts for an object
Object Permissions Display object Permissions
Object Dependencies Display object Dependencies
Delete Delete Object
Properties Properties of the object
```

There are about 80 command IDs that each bring up a different dialog or wizard window. You can reference the exact ID values and their associated windows through the Visual Basic Object Browser or the SQL Server BOL.

Methods and Properties

The SQLNamespaceCommand object has only one method: Execute. This method executes the command to display a screen. More on executing commands will follow. The properties of the SQLNamespaceCommand object are listed in Table 19.5.

TABLE 19.5: SQLNamespaceCommand Properties

Property	Description
CommandGroup	The ID of the command group to which the current command belongs.
CommandID	The actual ID of the command to be executed. This value is one of the SQLNSCommandID enum constants.
HelpString	Description of the current command's function.
Name	Returns the command name.

Executing a Command

The SQLNamespaceCommand object is used to acquire a reference to a particular command. If you want to display the screen to manage the indexes for the Categories table, you must first get an object reference to the Manage Indexes command and then call the Execute method to issue the command.

The Execute method takes two optional parameters: the window handle where the dialog should be displayed, and modality. The syntax looks like this:

```
SQLNSCmd.Execute hWnd, Modality
```

The Modality argument specifies the modality of the screen displayed by the Execute method. These values can be found in the SQLNSModality-Enum and are detailed in Table 19.6. If a window must be displayed with a particular modality, the window will override the settings you provide. For example, the wizard dialogs are always displayed modally regardless of the Modality argument.

TABLE 19.6: The Modality Values Define How a Dialog Is Displayed.

CONSTANT	DESCRIPTION
SQLNamespace_DontCare	The window displays according to the default window behavior.
SQLNamespace_PreferModal	Display the window modally if possible. In this mode the user must close the window before accessing any other windows.
SQLNamespace_PreferModeless	Display the window modeless. Other windows are accessible while the dialog is open.

Building on our previous example, the following code displays the screen to manage the indexes on the Categories table. Although an object reference to the command is retrieved, you could also call the Execute method from the collection with the syntax `tblCategories.Commands.Item("Manage Indexes").Execute`.

Here's the code that uses the SQLNamespaceCommand object to call the Execute method:

```
Dim hTbs As Long
Dim hTb
Dim hDb As Long
Dim SQLNS As SQLNS.SQLNamespace
Dim tblCategories As SQLNS.SQLNamespaceObject

Set SQLNS = New SQLNamespace

SQLNS.Initialize "Categories App", _
                 SQLNSRootType_Database, _
                 "UID=sa;PWD=;SERVER=TECHMEDIA; _
                 DATABASE=Northwind", hWnd


hDb = SQLNS.GetRootItem
hTbs = SQLNS.GetFirstChildItem(hDb, _
             SQLNSOBJECTTYPE_DATABASE_TABLES)
hTb = SQLNS.GetFirstChildItem(hTbs, _
             SQLNSOBJECTTYPE_DATABASE_TABLE, _
```

```
                    "Categories")

        Set tblCategories = SQLNS.GetSQLNamespaceObject(hTb)

        Dim i As Long
        For i = 1 To tblCategories.Commands.Count
            Debug.Print tblCategories.Commands.Item(i).Name
        Next i

        Dim MngIndexes As SQLNamespaceCommand

        Set MngIndexes = tblCategories.Commands.Item
                        ("Manage Indexes")
        MngIndexes.Execute , SQLNamespace_PreferModal
```

After calling the Execute method, the dialog for working with the indexes on the Categories table appears as shown in Figure 19.6.

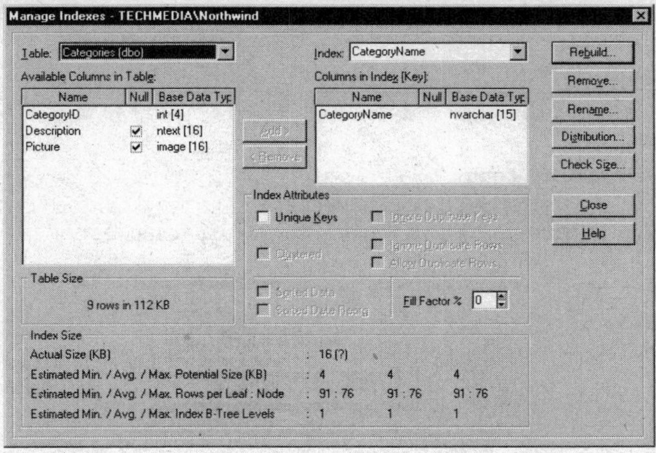

FIGURE 19.6: The resulting dialog after calling the Execute method

If you don't use the SQLNamespaceCommand object, commands can still be executed from the SQLNamespaceObject object by using one of these methods:

- ExecuteCommandByID
- ExecuteCommandByName

The ExecuteCommandByID method executes the command specified by the Command ID parameter. The ExecuteCommandByID method takes three arguments: SQLCommandID, hWnd, and Modality.

SQLCommandID Is one of the constants found in the SQLNSCommandID enum. For example, to invoke the dialog to create a new database, use the SQLNS_CmdID_NEW_DATABASE command ID.

hWnd Is an optional parameter and specifies where the dialog or window should appear.

Modality Is an optional parameter and defines whether the window should be displayed according to the default behavior of the window, modally, or modeless. This value is defined by the SQLNSModality enum we saw earlier.

To use our previous example, the Manage Indexes dialog can be called from the SQLNamespaceObject object by specifying the appropriate command ID instead of creating a SQLNamespaceCommand object. The code would look like this:

```
Dim hTbs As Long
Dim hTb
Dim hDb As Long
Dim SQLNS As SQLNS.SQLNamespace
Dim tblCategories As SQLNS.SQLNamespaceObject

Set SQLNS = New SQLNamespace

SQLNS.Initialize "Categories App", _
                 SQLNSRootType_Database, _
                 "UID=sa;PWD=;SERVER=TECHMEDIA; _
                 DATABASE=Northwind", hWnd

hDb = SQLNS.GetRootItem
hTbs = SQLNS.GetFirstChildItem(hDb, _
             SQLNSOBJECTTYPE_DATABASE_TABLES)
hTb = SQLNS.GetFirstChildItem(hTbs, _
             SQLNSOBJECTTYPE_DATABASE_TABLE, _
             "Categories")

Set tblCategories = SQLNS.GetSQLNamespaceObject(hTb)

Dim i As Long
For i = 1 To tblCategories.Commands.Count
    Debug.Print tblCategories.Commands.Item(i).Name
```

```
Next i

tblCategories.ExecuteCommandByID
    SQLNS_CmdID_TABLE_INDEXES
```

The ExecuteCommandByName method is also used to invoke screens but does so by the use of the command name. This method also takes three parameters: Command Name, hWnd, and Modality. The Command Name argument specifies the name of the command instead of its ID. Using the Command ID references the enum value and is probably a better idea in case any of the command names change in future versions of SQL Server. If we use our previous example and execute the command with this method, the syntax would look like this:

```
Dim hTbs As Long
Dim hTb
Dim hDb As Long
Dim SQLNS As SQLNS.SQLNamespace
Dim tblCategories As SQLNS.SQLNamespaceObject

Set SQLNS = New SQLNamespace

SQLNS.Initialize "Categories App", _
                 SQLNSRootType_Database, _
                 "UID=sa;PWD=;SERVER=TECHMEDIA; _
                 DATABASE=Northwind", hWnd

hDb = SQLNS.GetRootItem
hTbs = SQLNS.GetFirstChildItem(hDb, _
             SQLNSOBJECTTYPE_DATABASE_TABLES)
hTb = SQLNS.GetFirstChildItem(hTbs, _
             SQLNSOBJECTTYPE_DATABASE_TABLE, _
             "Categories")

Set tblCategories = SQLNS.GetSQLNamespaceObject(hTb)

Dim i As Long
For i = 1 To tblCategories.Commands.Count
    Debug.Print tblCategories.Commands.Item(i).Name
Next i

tblCategories.ExecuteCommandByName "Manage Indexes"
```

What You Need

The SQL-NS libraries are installed when you run the client or server setup for SQL Server. There are a few requirements to keep in mind when developing and running SQL-NS applications:

- SQL-NS client applications require the use of SQL Server Enterprise Manager, so this utility must be installed on any client that accesses the SQL-NS library. For example, in some cases the SQLNamespace object retrieves connection information from the Enterprise Manager configuration in the registry.
- In order to access the SQL-NS objects when developing Visual Basic applications, you must first add a reference to the `Microsoft SQLNamespace Object Library`, as shown in Figure 19.7. Although SQL-NS uses SQL-DMO, it does so behind the scenes, and a reference to SQL-DMO is not required.

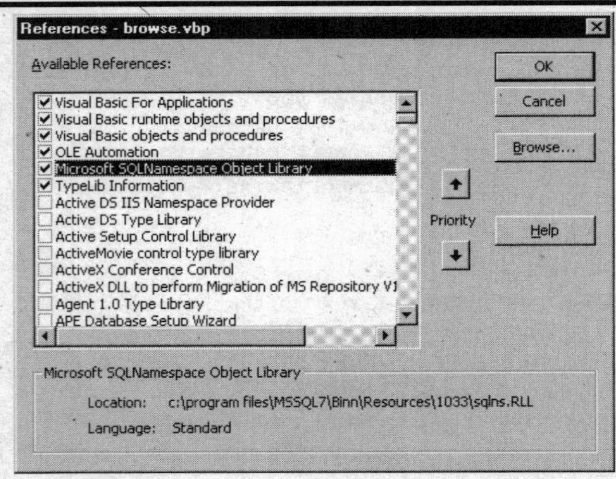

FIGURE 19.7: Add a reference to SQL-NS in Visual Basic

- SQL-NS is one of the component APIs in SQL-DMF. This library is tightly integrated with Enterprise Manager, which was completely redesigned in SQL Server 7. For this reason, SQL-NS works only with servers running SQL Server version 7 or greater. You'll receive an error if you attempt to run SQL-NS with earlier versions of SQL Server.

Using SQL-NS to Invoke Wizards

As we've seen, SQL-NS can be used to bring up any dialogs or property pages you see in Enterprise Manager. SQL-NS can also be used to launch any of the SQL Server wizards from a Visual Basic application. There are 15 wizards that can be accessed from SQL-NS:

- Wizards (you can run all the other wizards from here)
- Create Database Wizard
- Create Index Wizard
- Data Import Wizard
- Data Export Wizard
- Create Job Wizard
- Security Wizard
- Create Stored Procedure Wizard
- Create View Wizard
- Index Tuning Wizard
- Create Alert Wizard
- Database Maintenance Plan Wizard
- Web Assistant Wizard
- Backup Wizard
- Create Trace Wizard

Invoking a wizard is functionally the same as accessing a dialog. You call the SQLNamespaceCommand.Execute method and pass the Command ID. The Command ID values for the wizards are also found in the SQLNSCommandID enum. However, the SQLNamespaceObject must initialized at the server level.

To demonstrate how to access the wizards, I have included the WizardBrowser sample application. This application connects to the specified server and presents a list of all the available wizards (see Figure 19.8). You can run a particular wizard by double-clicking it.

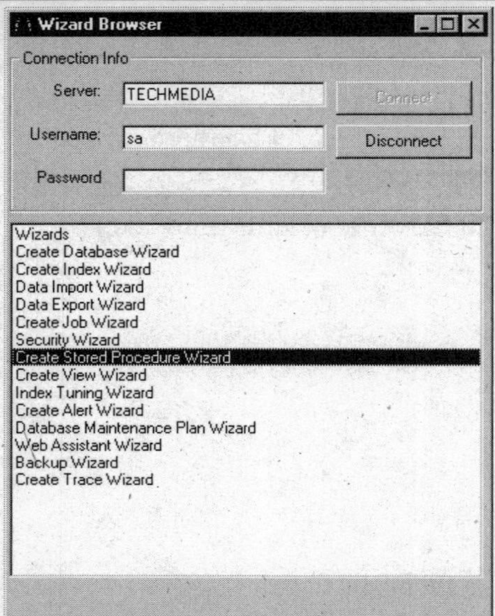

FIGURE 19.8: With SQL-NS you can invoke the SQL Server wizards

The first thing the WizardBrowser does when you click the Connect button is create the connection string and initialize the SQLNamespace object at the server level.

```
If Not mNS Is Nothing Then Set mNS = Nothing
If Not mNSObject Is Nothing Then Set mNSObject = Nothing

If Len(txtServer.Text) = 0 Then
    MsgBox "You must enter a server to connect to"
    Exit Sub
End If

If Len(txtUsername.Text) = 0 Then
    MsgBox "You must enter a username"
    Exit Sub
End If

Set mNS = New sqlns.SQLNamespace

mConnect = String(255, 0)
mConnect = "SERVER=" & txtServer.Text & ";UID=" &
           txtUsername.Text & ";PWD=" &
           txtPassword.Text & ";"
```

```
On Error Resume Next
mNS.Initialize "Wizard Browser", 2, CStr(mConnect), hWnd

If (Err.Number <> 0) Or (mNS Is Nothing) Then
    Set mNS = Nothing
    MsgBox "SQLNamespace could not be initialized",
        vbCritical + vbOKOnly, "Error"
    Exit Sub
End If
```

After the SQLNamespace object successfully initializes, the handle to it is retrieved. Commands are executed from the SQLNamespaceObject object, so this handle is used to set the SQLNamespaceObject to that server. Then the code enumerates through the commands collection and displays only the wizard command names in the list box. Here's the code:

```
hServer = mNS.GetRootItem
If hServer <> 0 Then
    Set mNSObject = mNS.GetSQLNamespaceObject(hServer)
    For i = 1 To mNSObject.Commands.Count
        If InStr(LCase(mNSObject.Commands(i).Name),
            "wizard") > 0 Then
            lstWizards.AddItem
                mNSObject.Commands.Item(i).Name
        End If
    Next i
End If
```

When you double-click a wizard name in the list box, a SQLNSCommand object is created. It is then set to reference the SQLNSCommand object of the selected wizard and the Execute method is called. The code is only three lines:

```
Private Sub lstWizards_DblClick()

    Dim NSCommand As SQLNS.SQLNamespaceCommand
    Set NSCommand = mNSObject.Commands(lstWizards.Text)

    NSCommand.Execute

End Sub
```

SQL-NS Errors

Errors raised by SQL-NS are found in the SQLNSErrors enum. You can trap these errors when they are raised and either continue or exit based on the type of error you encounter, as shown in the following listing. SQL-NS errors are accessed through the standard Visual Basic Err object.

```
On Error GoTo HandleError
. . .
HandleError:
    Select Case Err.Number
        Case SQLNS_E_InvalidDBName
            Msgbox "Invalid database name specified"
            Exit Sub
        Case SQLNS_E_InvalidServerVersion"
            Msgbox "You must be using SQL Server version
                "7.0 or greater"
            Exit Sub
    End Select
```

The details of SQL-NS–specific errors are detailed in Table 19.7.

TABLE 19.7: SQL-NS Errors

Enum Constant	Value	Description
SQLNS_E_Already_Initialized	1005	The Initialize method on the current SQLNamespace object was already called.
SQLNS_E_DatabaseNotFound	1019	The database specified in the connection string could not be found.
SQLNS_E_ExternalError	1100	An error external to SQL-NS occurred.
SQLNS_E_InvalidCommandID	1011	The command specified in an ExecuteCommandByID method call is invalid.
SQLNS_E_InvalidCommandName	1010	The command name specified in an ExecuteCommandByName method call is invalid.
SQLNS_E_InvalidConnectString	1016	The connection string specified is invalid.
SQLNS_E_InvalidDBName	1015	The specified database name is invalid.
SQLNS_E_InvalidLoginInfo	1014	The login information specified is invalid.
SQLNS_E_InvalidObjectHandle	1008	The object handle is invalid.
SQLNS_E_InvalidRootInfo	1012	The connection string doesn't match the specified root object.
SQLNS_E_InvalidRootType	1006	The item specified doesn't match the current root type.
SQLNS_E_InvalidServerName	1013	An invalid server name was specified.
SQLNS_E_InvalidServerVersion	1020	The specified server isn't running SQL Server version 7.0 or greater.

TABLE 19.7 continued: SQL-NS Errors

Enum Constant	Value	Description
SQLNS_E_NameDup	1004	Reserved.
SQLNS_E_NameNotFound	1003	The command name specified in an Execute-CommandByName method call wasn't found.
SQLNS_E_NoDMOObject	1009	No underlying SQL-DMO object exists.
SQLNS_E_NotImplemented	1001	The SQLNamespace object isn't implemented.
SQLNS_E_OrdOutOfRange	1002	A call was made into a DLL and the ordinal value doesn't exist.
SQLNS_E_RequireAppName	1007	The client application name is required when the Initialize method is called.
SQLNS_E_ServerNotFound	1018	The specified server was not found when initializing with the SQLNSRootType_Server root type.
SQLNS_E_SrvGrpNotFound	1017	The specified server group was not found when initializing with the SQLNSRootType_Server-Group root type.

SUMMARY

In this chapter, we discussed the objects that compose SQL-NS and its object hierarchy, as well as the user interface elements available in the SQL-NS library. We also looked at the SQL-NS sample project, the SQL Server wizards, and SQL-NS error handling. In the next chapter, we'll cover the DTS object model, which lets you import and export SQL Server data programmatically.

Chapter 20

Data Transformation Services

In previous chapters, we've seen the object models that allow Visual Basic developers to work with SQL Server databases, as well as integrate user interface elements in Visual Basic programs. The final technology we'll cover in this section is the DTS object model, which provides the ability to work with SQL Server data programmatically.

Data Transformation Services (*DTS*) was first released as part of SQL Server 7 and is a utility used for moving data between OLE DB data sources. You can optionally transform or reformat the data and perform data validation before you transfer it.

We'll start this chapter with an overview of what DTS is and what you can do with it. If you're not familiar with using DTS, you can step through using the DTS Wizard to transfer data.

Adapted from *Visual Basic® Developer's Guide to SQL Server™* by Dianne Siebold

ISBN 0-7821-2679-1 480 pages $39.99

This wizard is accessed through SQL Server. If you've already used DTS and are familiar with how it works, you can jump right into the following section in this chapter on the DTS API. The DTS objects allow you to build DTS functionality into Visual Basic applications. First, we'll look at the objects that make up the DTS object model. Then, we'll step through using them to transform and transfer data. You can create this application as we go or download it with the samples for this book.

DTS

DTS is a utility that installs as part of SQL Server and provides the ability to import, export, and transform data. Data sources and destinations can be any OLE DB data source. In fact DTS itself is a data consumer–it consumes data from data providers. So, it doesn't require SQL Server. DTS supports transferring relational data like SQL Server data with the native OLE DB SQL Server driver. DTS also supports non-relational data sources, such as text files or ISAM databases, like FoxPro or Paradox.

Although it ships with SQL Server, DTS doesn't require it to create or run packages (we'll cover more on packages later). Although the graphical tools to design packages are part of Enterprise Manager, SQL Server isn't required to use DTS. The file `dtswiz.exe` starts the DTS Wizard from the command line to create packages. The `dtsrun.exe` executable runs a package from the command line.

DTS differs significantly from the tools previously available to import and export data, such as `bcp` (bulk copy) and replication. Some of these differences include:

- DTS can create the destination tables or files before transferring data.
- Unlike other data transfer tools, DTS allows data to be validated, transformed, or summarized before reaching its target. This is possible because DTS supports the use of scripts. With DTS, you can copy columns directly to the destination data source. Or, you could combine two source columns into a single destination column.
- Data transformation is a part of the entire DTS process, thus eliminating much of the complexity when importing and exporting data. This tool eliminates the need for interim tables and complex data manipulation queries required when using `bcp` or replication.

DTS Files

The DTS files are installed on your hard drive when you install the SQL Server client or server. If you plan to run DTS independently of SQL Server, you'll find the necessary files on the SQL Server CD under the `x86\Binn` directory. The files required by DTS are listed in Table 20.1. These files are located in the Microsoft SQL Server `\75\Tools\Binn` directory or in the `Mssql7\Binn` directory for SQL Server 7.

TABLE 20.1: DTS Files

File Name	Description
`Axscplist.fll`	Data pump interface for scripting languages used by ActiveX script transformations
`Dtsffile.dll`	OLE DB text file provider used by the DTS Designer and DTS Wizard
`Dtspckg.dll`	Interface that implements a DTS package
`Dtspump.dll`	Interface that defines ActiveX script task constants
`Dtsrun.exe`	Command line executable used to run packages
`dtswiz.exe`	Command line executable that runs the DTS Wizard
`Sqldts.hlp`	DTS programming help file
`Sqldts.cnt`	DTS programming help contents file
`Datapump.h`	Header file that implements a DTS custom transformation used in C/C++

Packages

The DTS package is the primary unit in DTS. A package contains all the steps involved in a single import or export process. A DTS package can contain connections, tasks, precedence constraints, and transformations.

Connections

One or more connections, each defining a source or destination data source. A data source can be a relational database like SQL Server or Oracle, Access databases, an ODBC data source, or a text file.

Tasks

A package can contain one or more tasks that each define a single operation to take place during the import or export process. A task can be:

- An execution of one or more SQL statements. These can be data definition language (DDL) statements like the drop or creation of a table. Or, they can be data SELECT, INSERT, UPDATE, or DELETE statements.
- An execution of an ActiveX script. The ability to use a scripting language, such as VBScript or JScript, enables the use of complex logic in DTS tasks.
- A package that can execute a process that allows you to invoke an external executable or batch file.
- A bulk insert task, which allows you to insert data in SQL Server tables from text files. This is one of the fastest methods of importing data. However, you don't have the option of validating or transforming the data in a bulk insert.
- A SendMail task, which lets you send an e-mail message, perhaps to report on the status of the package execution.
- A Data Driven Query task, which allows the creation of a query to perform data transformations.
- A Transfer SQL Server Objects task, which allows you to transfer database objects, such as tables, views, stored procedures, constraints, rules, and user-defined data types between two servers. You also have the option to transfer existing data.

Precedence Constraints

All the tasks in a package occur in a particular order. This order is controlled through precedence constraints. The task precedence can be:

On Success The next task in the sequence executes only if the previous task executes successfully.

On Failure The next task executes only if the previous task fails.

On Completion The next task executes as soon as the previous task completes, whether or not it's successful.

Saving and Executing Packages

Once you have created a package with all the necessary tasks, you can save it to one of four locations:

- Packages can be saved to SQL Server, which saves the package to the current server. The details about the package and any information about when it's scheduled to run are stored in the `msdb` system database. Packages can be opened or executed from the Data Transformation Services folder in Enterprise Manager (see Figure 20.1).
- Packages can be saved to the Repository if you have implemented object tracking and sharing. If you save a package to the Repository, you can track versions of the same package and maintain a version history. Saving a package to the Repository also saves package metadata.
- Packages can be saved to a file located on a hard drive. These files have a `.dts` extension and are saved in a compiled format.
- A package can be saved to a Visual Basic `.bas` file. This re-creates the entire package in Visual Basic code using the DTS objects. This can be useful for finding out how the objects can be used to create packages.

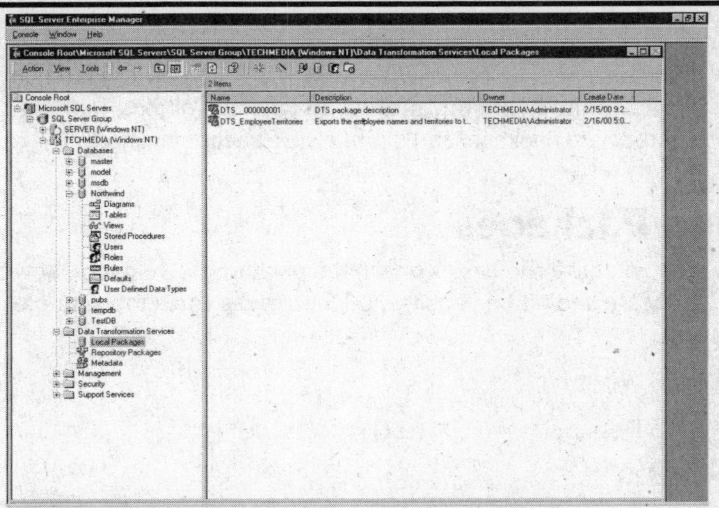

FIGURE 20.1: DTS packages saved to SQL Server can be found in the Data Transformation Services folder

Part iv

There are also a number of options for executing a saved package:

- A package can be run from the command line with the `dtsrun.exe` utility. The parameters of this executable include the server name, user name, password, and package name. Packages saved in SQL Server, the Repository, or to a file, can be executed with this utility. The syntax `dtsrun?` lists all the possible command switches.
- You can execute a package from within Enterprise Manager. Packages saved in SQL Server or in the Repository are executed by first navigating to the Local Packages or Repository Packages icons in the Data Transformation Services folder. Right-click the package and select Execute Package. A package saved to a file can't be executed directly from inside Enterprise Manager.
- Any package can be run through the DTS Designer. To get to this utility, right-click a package under the Repository or Local Packages icons in Enterprise Manager and select Design Package. Or, you can right-click the Data Transformation Services icon and select All Tasks ➢ Open Package. Once the package is open in the DTS Designer, you can run it by selecting Package ➢ Execute or selecting the Execute toolbar button.
- A package can be scheduled for execution by setting up a SQL Server Agent job.
- A package can be run in Visual Basic by using the DTS objects. This is done by instantiating the Package object, loading the appropriate package, and calling the Execute method.

Creating Packages

Now that you have the basics on what a package is, we'll look at what you need to create and edit a package. DTS provides three tools for creating packages:

- DTS Wizard
- DTS Designer
- DTS API

DTS Wizard

The DTS Wizards include both an Import and an Export Wizard although they both launch the same wizard. This tool steps you through the process of creating a package, including creating connections, creating queries, mapping data, and editing scripts. The DTS Wizard allows you to save the package, run it, or schedule it for execution at another time.

Essentially, the DTS Wizard creates all the items you would see in the package if you opened it in the DTS Designer. However, you can only create and run packages with this utility; you can't open existing packages.

The DTS Wizard may be able to handle your data transformation requirements, but like most wizards, it has some limitations. Using the wizard is a good way to get started with DTS, because you can create packages and then add more complex logic or tasks to them in the DTS Designer.

To start the DTS Wizard, open Enterprise Manager and select Tools ➢ Data Transformation Services ➢ Import Data (or Export Data). You can also select Tools ➢ Wizards and launch the Select Wizard dialog, as shown in Figure 20.2. You can then launch the appropriate wizard from there. If you need to launch the DTS Wizard from the command line, use the `dtswiz.exe` file. We'll step through creating a package with this wizard later on in this chapter.

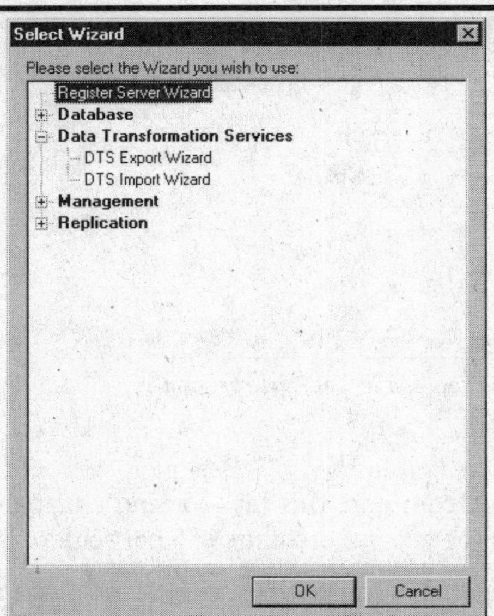

FIGURE 20.2: Launch the DTS Wizard from the Select Wizard dialog

DTS Designer

The *DTS Designer* is a graphical tool for editing DTS packages. Using this designer you can create and modify any of the connections, tasks, or precedence constraints in a package. The DTS Designer is used to open existing packages that were created using this designer or the DTS Wizard. Each component in a package is represented graphically, as shown in Figure 20.3.

The DTS Designer has more features and lets you do more with packages than the DTS Wizard. Some of the differences between these two tools are:

- The DTS Designer lets you open an already existing package. The package can be saved in SQL Server, in the Repository, or to a file.
- The DTS Designer allows you to create multiple connections to data sources of different types.
- Complex transformations can be created using the DTS Designer and ActiveX scripts written in VBScript or JScript.

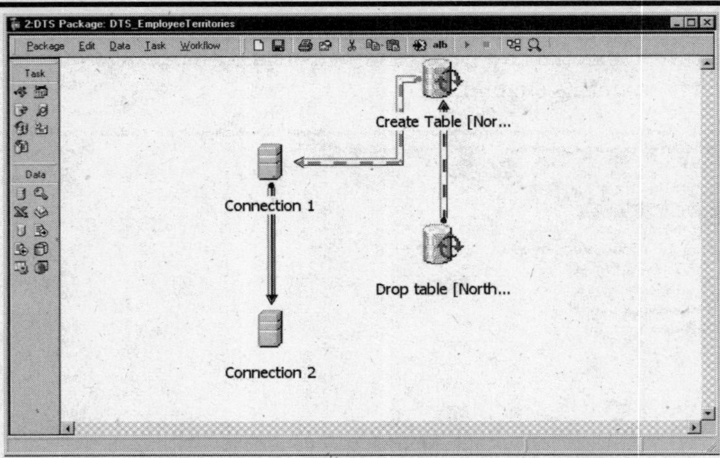

FIGURE 20.3: The DTS Designer represents packages graphically

- Specific tasks can be created in the DTS Designer, such as the SendMail task. You can configure this task to send e-mail and attachments based on the success or failure of a particular task.
- The precedence of the tasks in a package can be defined and changed in the DTS Designer.

DTS API

The DTS object model is one of the components in the SQL Distributed Management Framework (SQL-DMF), along with SQL-DMO and SQL-NS. The components in the DTS object model can be used to create and run packages programmatically. This library is found in the `dtspckg.dll`, which exposes COM interfaces that can be used by any COM-based programming language. In fact, DTS can be used completely independently of SQL Server with these objects.

Now that we've covered the basics of DTS, packages, and the utilities to create them, let's take a look at the DTS Wizard.

USING THE DTS WIZARD

The DTS Wizard steps you through the process of creating a package to import or export data. To get familiar with DTS before delving into the DTS object model, let's take a look at using this tool to create a package.

The first thing you'll need to do is create a table in the Northwind database with a name of EmpTerritory and the properties as shown in Figure 20.4. You can run the CreateEmpTerritoryTable.sql script from the code samples on the web to create this table.

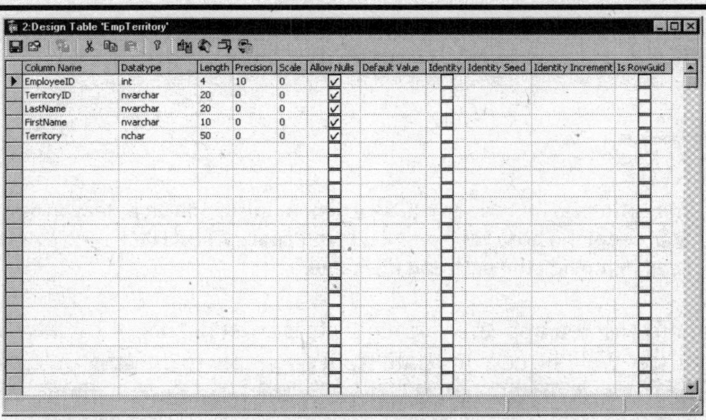

2:Design Table 'EmpTerritory'

Column Name	Datatype	Length	Precision	Scale	Allow Nulls	Default Value	Identity	Identity Seed	Identity Increment	Is RowGuid
EmployeeID	int	4	10	0	✓					
TerritoryID	nvarchar	20	0	0	✓					
LastName	nvarchar	20	0	0	✓					
FirstName	nvarchar	10	0	0	✓					
Territory	nchar	50	0	0	✓					

FIGURE 20.4: The EmpTerritory table

Once you have this table created, go to the Start menu and select Programs ➢ Microsoft SQL Server 7.5 ➢ Import and Export data. This launches the DTS Wizard and the initial screen appears. Click Next to bring up the screen to select the data source (see Figure 20.5).

By default the SQL Server data provider is selected with the `(local)` server. Windows NT authentication is used unless the server isn't running on Windows NT. In that case you can enter a user name and password to connect to the data source. Select the Northwind database in the Database combo box and click Next.

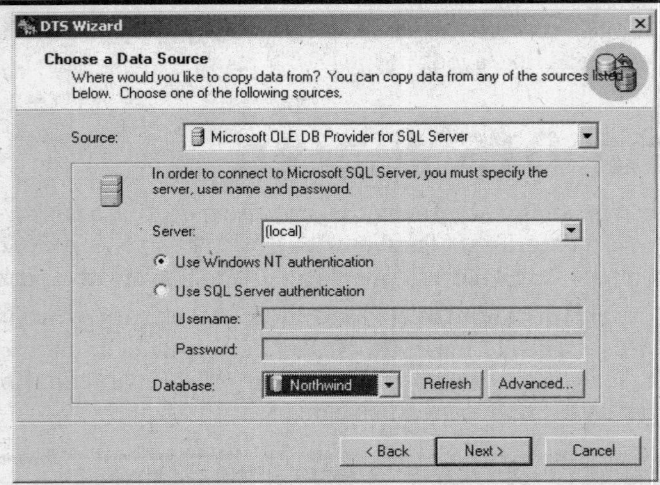

FIGURE 20.5: Select a data source in the Data Source dialog

NOTE

The options in this screen will vary depending on the provider you select in the Source combo box. For example, if you specify Text File as the source, you'll need to provide the path and file name.

The next screen appears and requests the details about the destination data source. We'll be copying data from one table to another in the Northwind database, so it will look the same as the Data Source dialog we just saw (see Figure 20.6). Click Next to continue.

The next screen is where you specify whether the data to be copied will come directly from a table in the database or from a query (see Figure 20.7). If you choose a table, the following screen allows you to enter the details about the source and destination columns. If you select to transfer objects and data, the DTS Wizard does a direct copy of all the specified objects between two databases, like the standard SQL Server object transfer. For this example select the Use Query option.

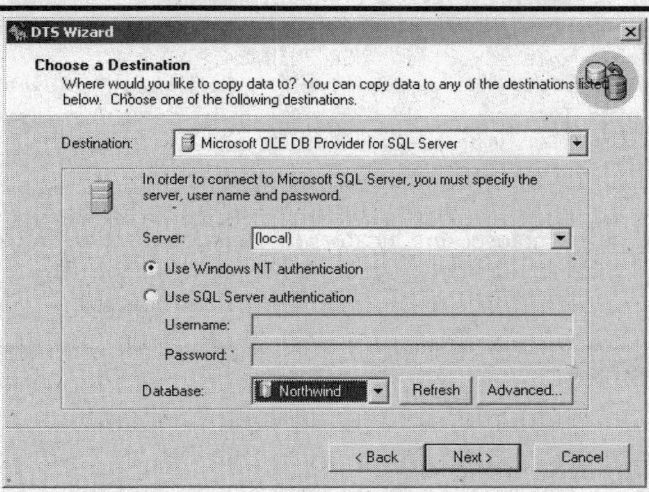

FIGURE 20.6: Select the destination data source

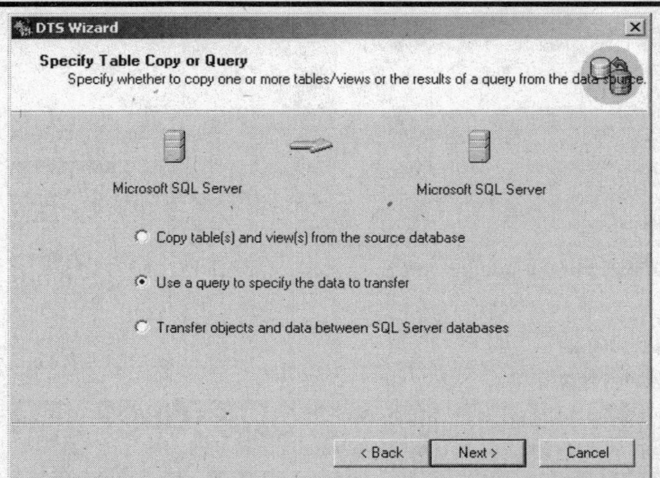

FIGURE 20.7: Specify what to export: a table, query, or object transfer

Because we selected to use a query as the basis for this export, the next screen prompts you for the SQL query (see Figure 20.8). Enter this query:

```
SELECT EmployeeTerritories.EmployeeID,
    EmployeeTerritories.TerritoryID, Employees.LastName,
    Employees.FirstName, Territories.TerritoryDescription
FROM EmployeeTerritories INNER JOIN Employees ON
    EmployeeTerritories.EmployeeID = Employees.EmployeeID
INNER JOIN Territories ON
    EmployeeTerritories.TerritoryID =
    Territories.TerritoryID
```

This query joins the Employee, Territories, and EmployeeTerritories tables to retrieve employee and territory information. In this screen the Parse button checks the query to ensure that it's valid. You can also use the Query Builder to create the query. Click the Next button.

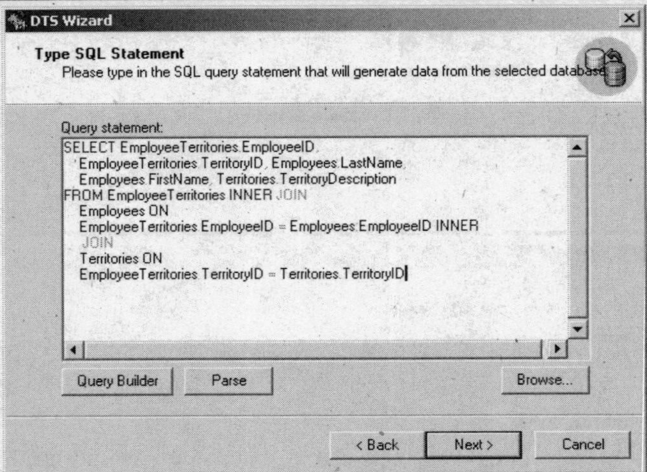

FIGURE 20.8: Enter the query that's the source of the data

WARNING

The Query Builder available in the DTS Wizard isn't the same as the Query Designer from the Visual Database Tools and it isn't very full featured. If you're going to create a query as the basis of a package, it's a good idea to use the Query Designer in Visual Basic to graphically create the query. You can then cut and paste the SQL code into the DTS Wizard.

The next screen allows you to specify the source and destination tables (see Figure 20.9). In this case, the source table is the query we just created. Select the EmpTerritory table that we created earlier as the Destination Table. Then click the Transform button in the last column.

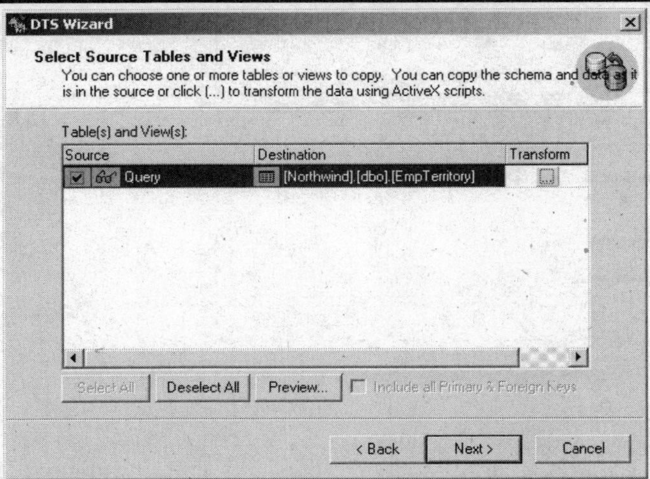

FIGURE 20.9: Select the source and destination tables

This brings up the Column Mappings and Transformations dialog. The columns in the source table are shown in the first column. The destination columns in the EmpTerritory table are displayed in the second column. Column mappings are done by selecting the matching source column for the destination column. The columns in this case are mapped as follows:

- EmployeeID to EmployeeID
- TerritoryID to TerritoryID
- LastName to LastName
- FirstName to FirstName
- TerritoryDescription to TerritoryDescription

Select the Create Destination Table option. Check the Drop and re-create destination table to ensure that the table is dropped and re-created every time the package is run (see Figure 20.10).

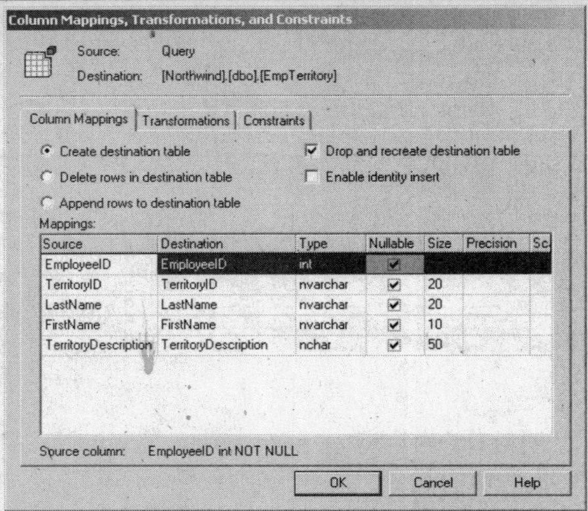

FIGURE 20.10: The Column Mappings tab

If you click on the Transformations tab, you can view and edit the transformation script. This script can be modified in a scripting language like VBScript (see Figure 20.11). In our case, keep the default to copy the source columns directly to the destination columns. Click OK and then Next.

The next screen brings up the options for running and saving the package. You can run the package immediately or schedule it for execution later. If you schedule the package for execution, SQL Server will create a SQL Agent job with the parameters you specify. You can also save the package for replication, allowing the package to be replicated to other servers (see Figure 20.12).

WARNING

If you want to schedule a package for future execution, the SQL Agent service must be running on the server.

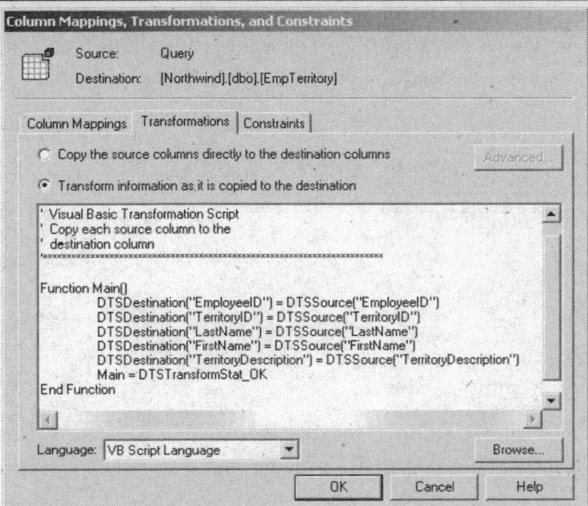

FIGURE 20.11: The transformation script

You can save the package to one of four locations: SQL Server, the Repository, a DTS file, or a Visual Basic file. If you want to keep the package on the server, you can choose to save it. If you need to distribute the package, you can save it to a DTS file. You can also save the package to the Repository if you want to track versions of the package or if you have implemented saving and sharing of objects in the Repository. If you select to save the package to a Visual Basic file, it saves the package as a `.bas` file that you can add to your projects. Click Next.

If you choose to save the package, a dialog appears requesting the package name, description, and passwords. If you choose to save the package to a server, you must also provide the server name and authentication information (see Figure 20.13). Click Next.

A summary of all the options specified appears on the next screen. Click Finish. A package execution progress screen appears detailing each step and whether or not it completed successfully, as shown in Figure 20.14. If a task fails, the wizard attempts to continue with the next task.

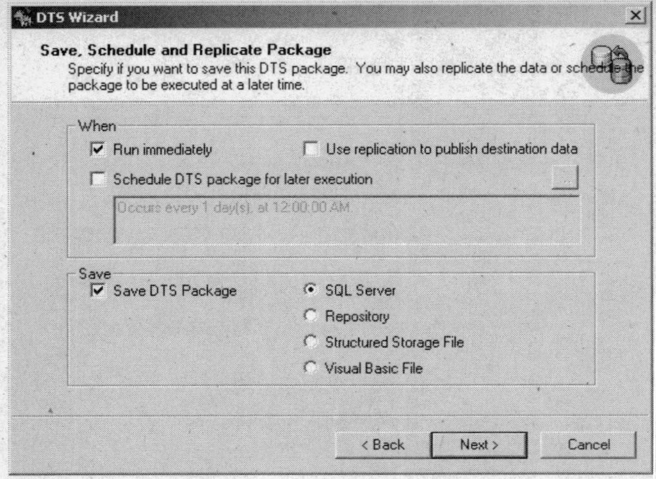

FIGURE 20.12: Select the options to run and save the package.

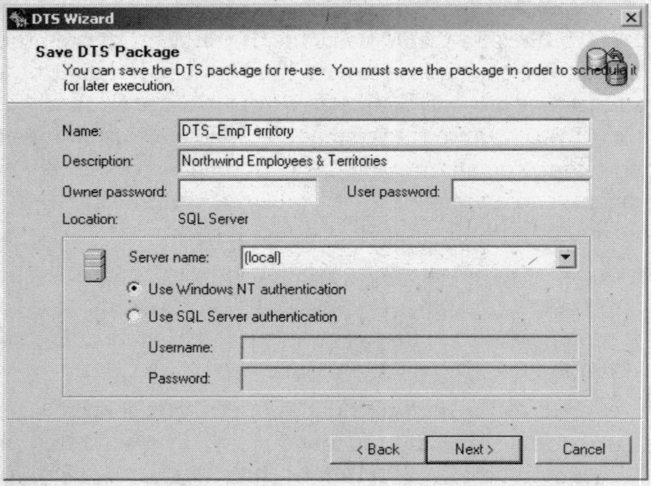

FIGURE 20.13: Provide a name and description to save the package.

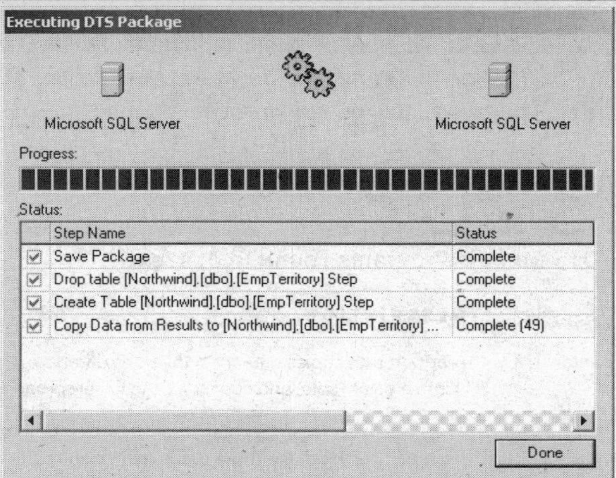

FIGURE 20.14: The status of each step is displayed.

This package now appears in SQL Server under the Local Packages within the Data Transformation Services folder. To edit this package or view it, just right-click it and select Design Package. This launches the DTS Designer. The DTS Designer is the tool to use for editing packages. This utility allows you to add precedence constraints, define additional tasks, and make other changes to the package.

DTS SAMPLE APPLICATIONS

There are a number of sample applications that come with SQL Server and provide examples of how to use DTS in various scenarios. These applications are a good way to learn about DTS and find out how it can be used. The samples include:

- Sample programs that demonstrate how to use DTS programmatically with Visual Basic or C++.
- Sample DTS packages that show you how to create packages, from a simple table copy to using DTS in complex data warehousing scenarios.
- Sample DTS ActiveX scripts that illustrate how ActiveX scripts can be used to transform data, invoke ADO, and perform database lookups.

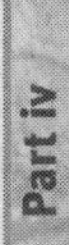

Like many of the SQL Server samples, these applications may not end up on your hard drive, even if you specify to install them. These files can be copied from the SQL Server CD and are found in the `Devtools\samples\DTS` folder. The two files that contain the samples are `dts.exe` and `dtsdemo.exe`. The `dts.exe` file is a self-extracting executable that decompresses the sample programs listed in Table 20.2.

TABLE 20.2: DTS Sample Programs Found in `dts.exe`

Project	Description
Cptaxdll.vbp and Dtsexmp1.vbp	Program that copies data from the Pubs database, transforms it into a pivot table, and copies it to an Excel spreadsheet.
Dtsexmp1.vbp	This code uses the DTS objects to perform a simple copy from a Pubs database table to a destination table. You must run the `Creattbl.sql` file to create the sample table called authorname.
Dtsqry.vbp	A project that lets you create a package from a SQL statement or ActiveX script. This package can have multiple data sources and destinations.

The `dtsdemo.exe` file is also a self-extracting executable, which creates a directory called `Designer`. In this directory are some sample packages that demonstrate different methods for using DTS. You can open these sample packages in Enterprise Manager by right-clicking the Data Transformation Services folder and selecting All Tasks ➢ Open Package.

The packages in `dtsdemo.exe` are detailed in Table 20.3. Also included is a Visual Basic application called ScriptPckg.vbp. This application reads an existing package from the local server and creates a script. This script can be loaded into Visual Basic and used to execute the package.

TABLE 20.3: Sample Packages in `dtsdemo.exe`

Package	Description
DTS—Execute SQL DDL and DML.dts	Executes SQL DDL to create new databases, tables, and indexes.
DTS—Transfer Database and Objects.dts	Transfers the Northwind database to `tempdb`.
DTS—Transform Customers.dts	Demonstrates the use of ActiveX scripts to transform and copy the Customers table to `tempdb`.

TABLE 20.3: continued: Sample Packages in dtsdemo.exe

PACKAGE	DESCRIPTION
DTS—Workflow Example.dts	This package demonstrates the use of precedence constraints.
OLTP to Star Schema Sample Package.dts	Provides an example of using DTS in a data-warehousing scenario. This package transforms OLTP data to a star schema.

DTS OBJECT MODEL

So far, we've seen how you can create and run packages with the utilities provided with SQL Server: the DTS Wizard and the DTS Designer. In this section, we'll cover how to create and execute a package using the DTS objects. The DTS object model is a set of COM interfaces that can be used to programmatically create and execute DTS packages. Like all COM objects, the DTS components can be used by a COM-compliant language such as Visual Basic or C++. In fact, the SQL Server utilities use the DTS object model as well.

The files required to use the DTS components are installed automatically when you install the SQL Server server or client. These files are detailed in Table 20.4. DTS uses OLE DB to connect to data sources so be sure to have the latest version of MDAC installed.

TABLE 20.4: The Files Containing the DTS Objects

OBJECT	FILE
DTS Package Objects	`\Mssql7\Binn\Dtspkg.dll` or Microsoft SQL Server `\75\Tools\Dtspkg.dll`
DTS Scripting Objects	`\Mssql7\Binn\Dtspump.dll` or Microsoft SQL Server `\75\Tools\Dtspump.dll`
Data Pump Headers	`Mssql7\Devtools\Include\Dtspump.h` or Microsoft SQL Server `\75\Devtools\ Include\Dtspump.h`

The DTS object model contains all the necessary objects for performing any DTS operation. The complete object model is shown in Figure 20.15.

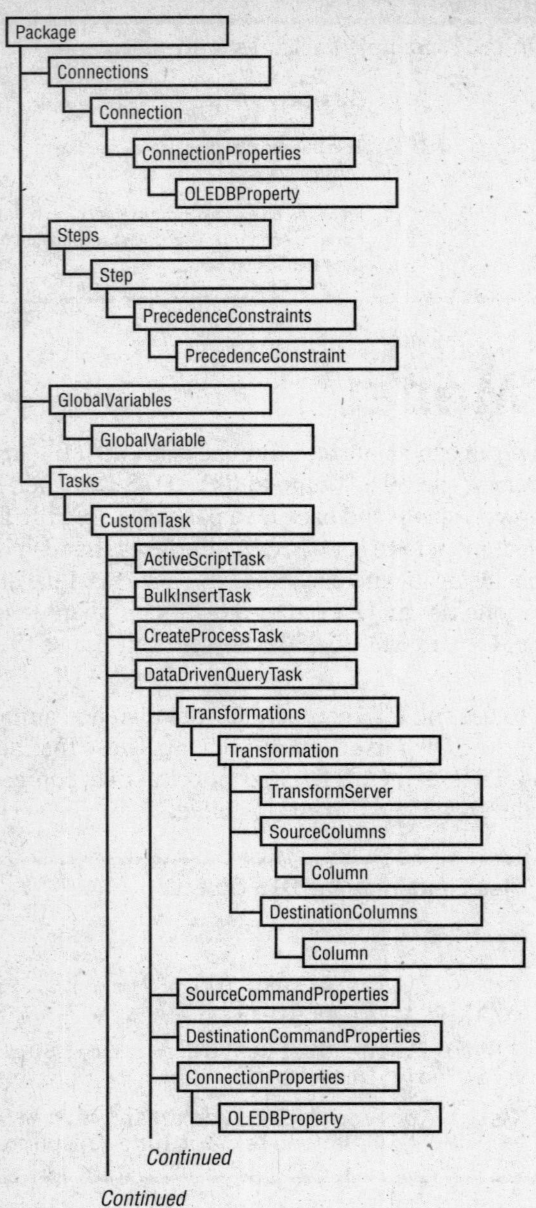

FIGURE 20.15: The DTS object model

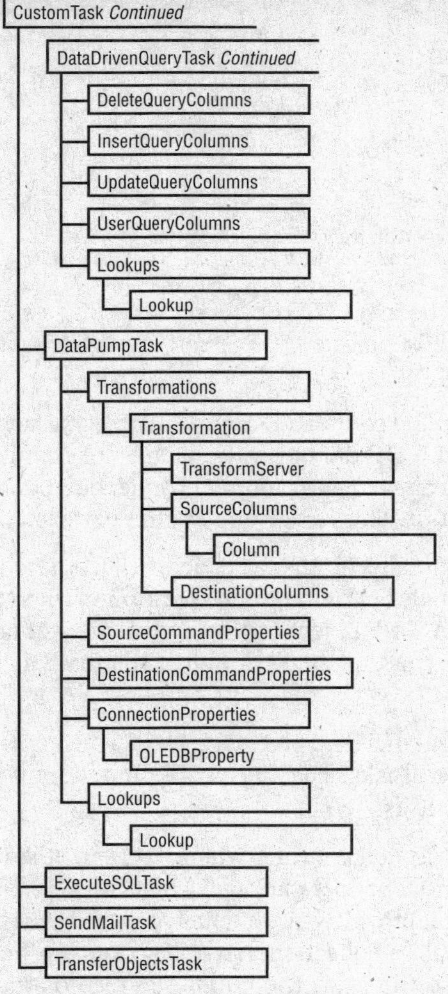

FIGURE 20.15 continued: The DTS object model

There are many DTS objects, but the primary objects are the Package object, the Connections collection, the Tasks collection, the Steps collection, and the GlobalVariables collection (see Figure 20.16).

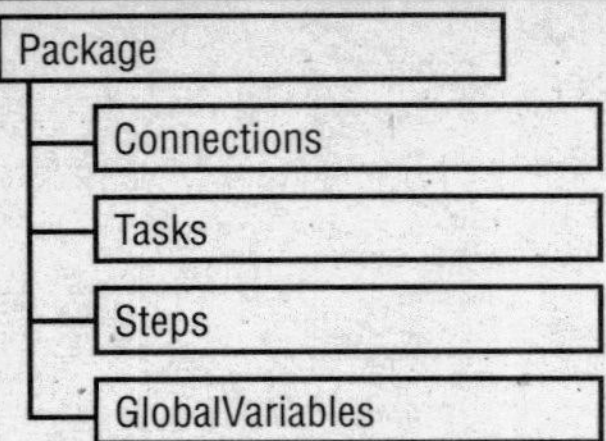

FIGURE 20.16: The primary objects in the DTS object model

- The *Package object* is the main DTS object representing a single package. All the other DTS objects are accessed through the package object.
- The *Connections collection* contains Connection objects, each of which contains the OLE DB data provider details for that connection. Connections can be reused through connection pooling if the provider supports it. This can give you better performance.
- The *Tasks collection* contains all the tasks defined in a package. The Task object is a single operation that is performed when the package is executed. A Task object can be one of the standard tasks, or you can use the CustomTask object to create a customized task.
- The *Steps collection* contains Step objects, each of which is associated with one or more Tasks. The Steps collection defines the flow and execution of tasks.
- The *GlobalVariables collection* is an area where data can be stored and accessed by other steps in a package. The GlobalVariable objects in this collection provide variant data types. You can pass data in the GlobalVariables collection between scripts in a package; for example, you could track the number of records transformed by a script.

The Package Object

The *Package object* is the primary object is the DTS model. All the other objects and collections are accessible from the Package object. We won't cover every method and property of each object, but we'll look at the methods and properties of this object. The collections available from the Package object are detailed in Table 20.5.

TABLE 20.5: Package Object Collections

COLLECTION	DESCRIPTION
Connections	Contains Connection objects that contain the OLE DB data source details. Connection pooling enables the reuse of database connections.
GlobalVariables	Contains GlobalVariable objects that allow data to be shared across steps in a package. These objects are of variant data type.
Steps	A collection of Step objects that contain information about the flow and execution of tasks in a package. A task must have at least one step.
Tasks	Contains Task objects, each of which defines a unit of work. All the tasks that occur in a package are contained in this collection.

The methods available from the Package object are listed in Table 20.6 and the Package properties are listed in Table 20.7.

TABLE 20.6: Package Object Methods

METHOD	DESCRIPTION
Execute	Runs the package.
GetDTSVersionInfo	Returns the package version information.
GetLastExecutionLineage	Returns the lineage information stored in the Repository after a package is executed.
GetSavedPackageInfos	Returns a list of package versions.
LoadFromRepository	Loads the specified package that has been saved to the Repository.
LoadFromSQLServer	Loads the specified package from SQL Server.
LoadFromStorageFile	Loads the specified package that has been saved to a file.
RemoveFromRepository	Deletes a package from the Repository.
RemoveFromSQLServer	Deletes a package saved in SQL Server.
SaveAs method	Saves the package with a new ID and name.
SaveToRepository	Saves the package to the Repository.
SaveToSQLServer	Saves the package to SQL Server.
SaveToStorageFile	Saves the package to a file on the hard drive.
Uninitialize	Releases all related objects and clears any state information in the package. This allows the package to be reused.

TABLE 20.7: Package Object Properties

PROPERTY	DESCRIPTION
AutoCommitTransaction	Defines whether an active transaction should be automatically committed when execution is completed.
CreationDate	Returns the date the package was created.
CreatorComputerName	The name of the computer that created the package.
CreatorName	Returns the username of the package creator.
Description	Returns a string with the textual description of the package.
FailOnError	Specifies whether package execution stops if an error occurs in any step.
LineageOptions	Set to one of the DTSLineageOptions values that specify how the package execution lineage is recorded and presented.
LogFileName	Specifies the path and file name of the log file to which package execution status information and any errors are written.
MaxConcurrentSteps	The maximum number of steps that can execute concurrently on separate threads.
Name	The package name.
PackageID	Returns a string representing the package unique identifier (GUID).
PackagePriorityClass	The thread priority class of the package process.
Parent	Returns the parent of the current object. The parent of a package is itself.
PrecedenceBasis	Defines whether to use the current status of a Step or the execution results to determine if its precedence constraint has been satisfied.
TransactionIsolationLevel	Set to one of the DTSIsolationLevel values, this property specifies the isolation level of a package transaction (if the UseTransaction property is true).
UseOLEDBServiceComponents	Specifies whether to use the OLE DB service components when initializing a data source.
UseTransaction	Specifies whether the tasks in a package should execute in a transaction.
VersionID	Specifies the unique identifier (GUID) of a package version.
WriteCompletionStatusToNTEventLog	Specifies whether the completion status is written to the application log in Windows NT.

The Package object also supports events if it's declared using the `WithEvents` keyword. The events available from the Package object are listed in Table 20.8.

TABLE 20.8: Package Object Events

EVENT	DESCRIPTION
OnError	This event is raised when an error occurs executing a task or step. Event arguments ErrorSource and ErrorCode provide details about the error. Set the Cancel argument to true to stop execution of the package. If Cancel is not set to true, the package attempts to execute the next task.
OnFinish	Occurs when task or step execution is completed. The EventSource argument specifies the name of the task or step that completed.
OnProgress	Reports the progress of a task as specified in the EventSource argument. The PercentComplete argument returns the percentage complete of the executing task.
OnQueryCancel	Terminates the execution of a task. If the Cancel argument is true the execution will fail with an error.
OnStart	Raised when the execution of a task or step is started.

Executing a Package

Now that we've seen the DTS object model and some of its key components, let's take a look at using them to create and run packages from within Visual Basic. The first step required to use DTS is to add a reference to it. This is done by selecting Project ➢ References and selecting the `Microsoft DTSPackage Object Library`, as shown in Figure 20.17.

If you have an existing package created with the DTS Wizard or the DTS Designer, you can execute it using the Package objects. First, you must load the package and then call the Package object's Execute method. You can load packages saved to a file, to SQL Server, or to the Repository, by calling one of these methods:

- LoadFromStorageFile
- LoadFromSQLServer
- LoadFromRepository

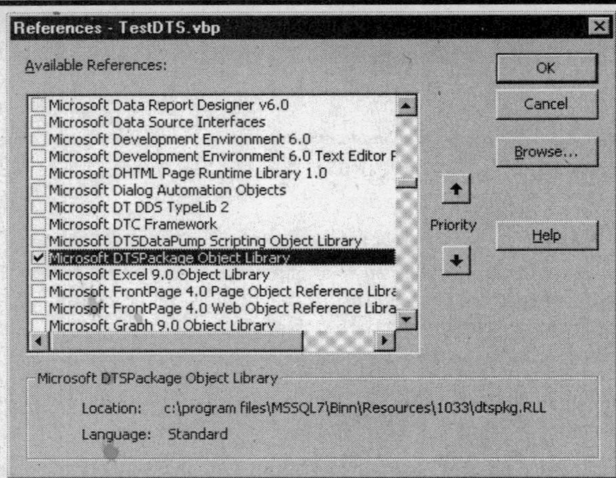

FIGURE 20.17: Add a reference to DTS inside Visual Basic

To run the `DTS_EmpTerritory.dts` package that we created earlier, just instantiate the Package object, load the package, and call the Execute method, as in the following code. The LoadFromSQLServer and LoadFromRepository methods allow you to access packages from SQL Server or the Repository, respectively.

```
Dim Package As New DTS.Package

Package.LoadFromStorageFile App.Path & _
    "\DTS_EmpTerritory.dts", ""
Package.Execute
```

Creating a Package

If you want to put the entire process of creating and executing a package in code, you can do it with the DTS components. This section uses the `TestDTS.vbp` project. This project creates and runs a package that creates a table and copies data into it based on a query. In this example, we're creating a package in code that models the one we created in the DTS Wizard. Figure 20.18 illustrates the tasks in this package.

Each component of the `DTS_EmpTerritory` package must be represented using objects. If we break this package down to its individual elements, they are:

- An ExecuteSQL task that drops the EmpTerritory table
- An ExecuteSQL task that creates the EmpTerritory table

- A connection to the source of the data
- A connection to the destination data source
- A data transformation that executes a query and copies the query results to the EmpTerritory table

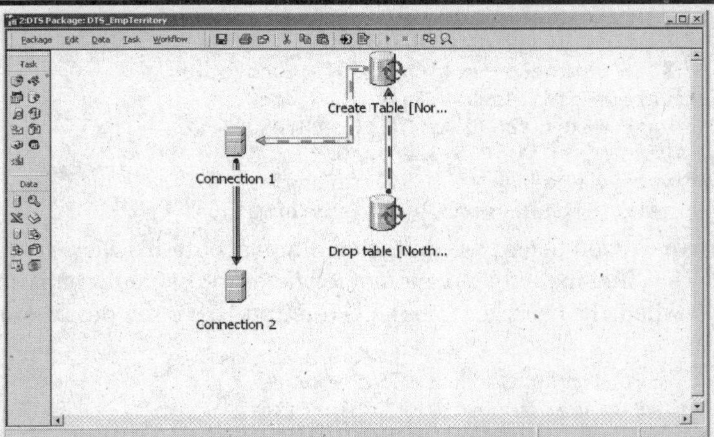

FIGURE 20.18: The data transformation package can also be created in code.

Now let's look at how to create and run this package in code. Open the `TestDTS` project and you'll see a form with a grid and command button (see Figure 20.19).

Create & Run DTS Packages

Provider=SQLOLEDB;Data Source=TECHMEDIA;Initial Catalog=Northwind;User ID=sa;Password=;

EmpTerritory Table

	EmployeeID	TerritoryID	LastName	FirstName	TerritoryDescription
	1	06897	Davolio	Nancy	Wilton
	1	19713	Davolio	Nancy	Neward
	2	01581	Fuller	Andrew	Westboro
	2	01730	Fuller	Andrew	Bedford
	2	01833	Fuller	Andrew	Georgetow
	2	02116	Fuller	Andrew	Boston
	2	02139	Fuller	Andrew	Cambridge
	2	02184	Fuller	Andrew	Braintree
	2	40222	Fuller	Andrew	Louisville
	3	30346	Leverling	Janet	Atlanta
	3	31406	Leverling	Janet	Savannah
	3	32859	Leverling	Janet	Orlando
	3	33607	Leverling	Janet	Tampa

Import Data

FIGURE 20.19: The TestDTS project

The command button creates and runs the package and then displays the results in the grid. The connection information in the text box is not used by DTS, but is used to retrieve the recordset displayed in the grid. To run this application, make sure the connection string points to a valid database. In the Declarations all the necessary objects are created:

```
Option Explicit

Private mPackage As DTS.Package
Private mNwindConnection As DTS.Connection
Private mTask  As DTS.Task
Private mExecuteSQL As DTS.ExecuteSQLTask
Private mStep As DTS.Step
Private mDataPump As DTS.DataPumpTask
Private mTransform As DTS.Transformation
```

All the action takes place in the cmdImport button's click event. The package is first instantiated and named here. You can optionally specify a log file where the package status and any errors that occur during execution are saved.

```
    Set mPackage = New DTS.Package
    mPackage.Name = "DTS_EmpTerritory"
    mPackage.LogFileName = _
        "D:\Temp\DTS_EmpTerritoryLog.txt"
```

After the package is created, the source data source and the destination data source connections are defined. You must specify the connection details, such as the server name, database name, user name, and password. Then the connections are added to the Package object's Connections collection.

```
    'Setup the first connection
    Set mNwindConnection = _
        mPackage.Connections.New("SQLOLEDB.1")
    mNwindConnection.DataSource = "(local)"
    mNwindConnection.UserID = "sa"
    mNwindConnection.Password = ""
    mNwindConnection.Catalog = "Northwind"
    mNwindConnection.ID = 1

    'Add the connection to the package
    mPackage.Connections.Add mNwindConnection

    'Setup the second connection
    Set mNwindConnection = _
        mPackage.Connections.New("SQLOLEDB.1")
    mNwindConnection.DataSource = "(local)"
```

```
mNwindConnection.UserID = "sa"
mNwindConnection.Password = ""
mNwindConnection.Catalog = "Northwind"
mNwindConnection.ID = 2

'Add the connection to the package
mPackage.Connections.Add mNwindConnection
```

Now we're ready to define the first task. As we saw in the package we created in the DTS Wizard, the first thing to occur is the EmpTerritory table is dropped. This is done using a SQL statement, so the task is created as a DTSExecuteSQL task, as shown in this code:

```
'Create the task to drop the EmpTerritory table
Set mTask = mPackage.Tasks.New("DTSExecuteSQLTask")
mTask.Description = "Drop the EmpTerritory table"
mTask.Name = "DropEmpTerritory"

Set mExecuteSQL = mTask.CustomTask
mExecuteSQL.ConnectionID = 1
mExecuteSQL.SQLStatement = "IF EXISTS (SELECT * " & _
    "FROM sysobjects WHERE NAME = 'EmpTerritory' " & _
    "AND TYPE = 'U') DROP TABLE " & _
    "[Northwind].[dbo].[EmpTerritory]"

'Add the task to the package
mPackage.Tasks.Add mTask

Set mStep = mPackage.Steps.New
mStep.Name = "Step1"
mStep.TaskName = "DropEmpTerritory"

'Add the step to the package
mPackage.Steps.Add mStep
```

In the previous code, a step is also created and associated with the task. The step is also added to the package's Steps collection. Each task must have at least one step.

The next task creates the EmpTerritory table. This is also an ExecuteSQL task and is defined in the same way as the previous task.

```
'Create the task to create the EmpTerritory table
Set mTask = mPackage.Tasks.New("DTSExecuteSQLTask")
mTask.Description = "Create the EmpTerritory table"
mTask.Name = "CreateEmpTerritory"

Set mExecuteSQL = mTask.CustomTask
mExecuteSQL.ConnectionID = 1
```

```
    mExecuteSQL.SQLStatement = "CREATE TABLE "  & _
        " [Northwind].[dbo].[EmpTerritory] (" & _
        "[EmployeeID] int NULL, " & _
        "[TerritoryID] nvarchar (50) NULL, " & _
        "[LastName] nvarchar (20) NULL, " & _
        "[FirstName] nvarchar (10) NULL, " & _
        "[TerritoryDescription] nchar (50) NULL )"

    'Add the task to the package
    mPackage.Tasks.Add mTask

    Set mStep = mPackage.Steps.New
    mStep.Name = "Step2"
    mStep.TaskName = "CreateEmpTerritory"

    'Add the step to the package
    mPackage.Steps.Add mStep
```

The next task defined handles the job of transferring the data between the source and destination data sources and is created as a DTSDataPumpTask. The query that is the source of the data transfer is specified in this task. The source and destination connections that we created earlier are also used in the data pump task.

```
Set mTask = mPackage.Tasks.New("DTSDataPumpTask")
    mTask.Name = "CopyRecords"
    Set mDataPump = mTask.CustomTask
    mDataPump.SourceConnectionID = 1
    mDataPump.SourceSQLStatement = "SELECT " & _
        "EmployeeTerritories.EmployeeID, " & _
        "EmployeeTerritories.TerritoryID, " & _
        "Employees.LastName, Employees.FirstName, " & _
        "Territories.TerritoryDescription FROM " & _
        "EmployeeTerritories INNER JOIN Employees ON " & _
        "EmployeeTerritories.EmployeeID = " & _
        "Employees.EmployeeID " & _
        "INNER Join Territories ON " & _
        "EmployeeTerritories.TerritoryID = " & _
        "Territories.TerritoryID"
    mDataPump.DestinationConnectionID = 2
    mDataPump.DestinationObjectName = "EmpTerritory"
```

A Transformation object is also created and specifies that data is going to be copied from the source to the destination. Because the columns returned from the query match those in the destination table, we only have to create and name the Transformation object. If the source and destination columns didn't match, then the specified columns would have to be created and added to the SourceColumns and DestinationColumns collections in the Transformation object.

```
    Set mTransform = mDataPump.Transformations.New
("DTS.DataPumpTransformCopy")
    mTransform.Name = "CopyResults"

    mDataPump.Transformations.Add mTransform
    mPackage.Tasks.Add mTask

    Set mStep = mPackage.Steps.New
    mStep.Name = "Step3"
    mStep.TaskName = "CopyRecords"
    mPackage.Steps.Add mStep
```

Now, all that's left to do is run the package. This is done by calling the Execute method. After running the package, the code handles any errors by checking the ExecutionResult of each Step. This property can be one of two values in the DTSStepExecResult enum: DTSStepExecResult_Failure or DTSStepExecResult_Success.

```
'Execute the task
    mPackage.Execute

    With mPackage
        For i = 1 To .Steps.Count
            If .Steps(i).ExecutionResult = _
                DTSStepExecResult_Failure Then
                MsgBox "Step " & .Steps.Item(i).Name &
                    " failed"
                StepError = True
                Exit For
            End If
        Next i
    End With
```

After the code ends, the only thing left to do is set the objects to Nothing. DTS is a powerful and flexible tool for transferring data. You can transfer data between various data sources, including non-relational data sources. In addition, DTS provides the ability to transform the data before it's copied. Complex logic can be integrated into packages with the use of scripts. Packages can not only be defined in the utilities provided, but also created programmatically.

Summary

In this chapter, you learned how to work with DTS from inside Visual Basic. First, we looked at how to create a package using the wizard that comes with SQL Server. This chapter also covered the DTS object model and how to use these objects to create and run packages. This is the final chapter in this section on programming SQL Server with Visual Basic. The next section delves into OLAP and working with multidimensional data.

PART V
OLAP AND ANALYSIS SERVICES

Chapter 21

OLAP and Data Mining Concepts

In this chapter, we'll take a look at what online analytical processing (usually referred to simply as *OLAP*) means and how it can help you in your own projects. We'll discuss some of the business problems that many organizations face relating to information management and explain how OLAP helps solve such problems. We'll then proceed to describe the basic database concepts that underpin "analytical" or multidimensional databases, and how OLAP can help your organization get the most out of the information it stores. This chapter will help you answer these questions:

- What does OLAP mean?
- What relevance does it have to my organization?
- What are the differences between relational and multidimensional databases?
- What are the differences between "data warehouse," "data mart," and "data mining"?

Adapted from *SQL Server™ Developer's Guide to OLAP with Analysis Services* by Mike Gunderloy and Tim Sneath

ISBN 0-7821-2957-1 480 pages $49.99

NOTE

SQL Server 7.0 introduced OLAP capabilities in a component named *OLAP Services*. In SQL Server 2000, this component has been renamed *Analysis Services*, to reflect its extension beyond simple OLAP into the realm of data mining.

TURNING DATA INTO INFORMATION

We live in a data-rich world. Organizations across the globe have vast database systems containing all kinds of data related to their business operations.

Make a mental estimate of the number of different IDs, account numbers, and other references you have been allocated by the various institutions you regularly deal with: It's likely that an awful lot of companies have your details on file. Now multiply that number by the number of customers each of those organizations has worldwide, and you just begin to get a sense of the sheer quantity of customer-specific data that's available to these organizations. But how do they manage that data? In particular, how does such an organization bracket their customers for marketing purposes?

The problem with data is that, by itself, it doesn't mean anything. For example, a single field in a database might contain the value "345". Without knowing whether that's a customer ID, a price, or an item number, you can't extract any information from the data. Data itself, without interpretation, is largely meaningless. Data plus interpretation and analysis adds up to information, a much more valuable commodity than raw data. Sometimes information is distributed across multiple pieces of data. For example, no single entry in a sales database will identify frequent buyers of a particular product. The information as to which customers are frequent buyers is spread across multiple pieces of data. Extracting this sort of information from a mass of data is one of the most challenging aspects of database analysis.

Most organizations these days rely on database systems to keep their businesses running. From payroll to stock control, from the help desk to the sales executive, databases keep track of the operations of an organization. With the recent Y2K issues just behind us, companies are freshly aware of the importance that their IT systems have in keeping businesses alive. The new "Internet economy" is increasing still further the need for organizations to have information resources that enable them both to handle customers more effectively and to identify changing trends and new market opportunities.

The key to companies understanding their business is, therefore, better analysis of the information they possess on their customers, operations, staff, and processes. Without knowing their own strengths and weaknesses, a company can do little in the face of a rapidly changing marketplace.

As an example of the problem, imagine that you are a store manager for a nationwide chain of retail supermarkets. Suppose for a moment that you are given a large box containing all the paper cash register receipts for the last week's transactions. It'll no doubt be a big box containing thousands of receipts and tens of thousands of individual sale items. Now your boss calls you, wanting to know some information about the performance of your store over this time period:

- What was the most popular item your store sold over the last week?
- What was the *least* popular item?
- Which department took the most money for sale items?
- Which checkout operator was the most efficient, and which was the least efficient?
- What was the overall average value of a customer's shopping basket?

Well, you've got all the information at your fingertips: Every sale is recorded on a receipt, and all the data necessary to answer each of the above questions is at hand. But how do you go about getting the answers when you've got to sort through all those receipts manually? Answering these kinds of questions would be an almost impossible challenge using purely paper-based means. Yet not only are the questions relevant; in fact, the answers are absolutely central knowledge for the business to understand how it is operating, where it can improve its efficiency, and how to maximize profits and revenue.

If you had enough time to analyze all the receipts, there's no reason why it would not be possible to answer the questions. You'd have to sort through the receipts one by one, tallying up the individual product sales until you got to a total figure, then sorting those figures by department and checkout operator, as well as calculating averages to enable you to answer the last question asked. But it would be a very repetitive task. Of course, repetitive tasks are *exactly* the kinds of things computers are well suited for.

The sad thing is that even with the incredible amount of computing power that most organizations possess, answering these kinds of questions is still tough for a lot of companies. Many business managers are still frustrated by the lack of access they have to the information they need. Getting management reports in some organizations still takes weeks or even months—if the desired information is even available at all.

Fortunately, there is an answer to this problem. What's needed is a different type of database system than the traditional relational database. Such a system needs to be able to take extracts of data from an operational system, to summarize the data into working totals, and to present that data to the end users of the system intuitively. This is the realm of OLAP, or *online analytical processing*.

Traditional Database Systems

Although much data is stored in databases, those databases are rarely optimized for the kinds of analysis discussed in the previous section. Most database information is stored in OLTP systems. *OLTP* stands for *online transaction processing* and describes a distributed or centralized system that is typically designed to handle a large number of concurrent database connections, with each either inserting, updating, or querying a small number of records. Examples of the kinds of transactions that might involve an OLTP system include the following:

- Insert a record into the sales database for customer 325903, showing a purchase of a number of items.
- Show all purchases made by customer 583472 that have not yet been invoiced.
- Update the details for supplier 1032 to show a change of company address.

These transactions share a couple of attributes in common:

- They operate on a very small number of discrete rows of data at a particular time.
- The context of each operation requires that the data is as up to date as possible with the real-world environment to which the data maps.
- They need an almost instantaneous response if the users of the system are to be satisfied with the performance of the application.

The above examples are not unusual. Other systems that share these characteristics include stock control systems, billing systems, customer management systems, and help desk systems, among many others. Generally, OLTP applications allow their users to manipulate individual (or at least a small quantity of) data records at any one time.

To achieve this, modern database systems are usually *relational* and *highly normalized.* A relational database holds its information in several individual linked tables. Each table contains data on a particular entity (for example, customers, sales, products, stores, etc.). Where there is a semantic link between two tables, those tables are joined together by means of a *relationship*. Relationships are created by one or more fields in a table acting as a pointer to matching records in another table. For example, a table of orders will often contain a field that holds a customer number that matches the customer number in a table of customers.

The secret to a database system being optimized for OLTP usage is *normalization*. Normalization is a process of removing redundancy from database structures. Wherever a table contains information duplicated across multiple rows for an individual entity, that information can be split off into a separate table.

As an example, consider a database that might handle payroll information for a company. This database will likely need to store information concerning individual employees and their job positions. Table 21.1 is an example of the type of information that could be stored in this environment.

TABLE 21.1: Sample Payroll Table

Surname	Forename	Payroll #	Job Position	Grade
Smith	Harry	384192	Developer	F
O'Connell	Julia	349283	Senior Developer	G
Ahmed	Aleena	321458	Senior Developer	G
Matthews	Gloria	358299	Project Manager	H

Note the duplication of Job Position and Grade data in the second and third rows of the table. In a normalized relational database, we want to have a table containing information on individual employees, as well as a separate table that stores information on positions within the company. By giving each position a unique reference (or ID), we can connect the

Employees table to the Positions table. Tables 21.2 and 21.3 demonstrate how this relationship might be implemented in the database.

TABLE 21.2: Sample Employees Table

SURNAME	FORENAME	PAYROLL #	POSITION ID
Smith	Harry	384192	1
O'Connell	Julia	349283	2
Ahmed	Aleena	321458	2
Matthews	Gloria	358299	3

TABLE 21.3: Sample Positions Table

POSITION ID	JOB POSITION	GRADE
1	Developer	F
2	Senior Developer	G
3	Project Manager	H

A relational structure works well for OLTP databases. Columns within tables can be indexed to ensure that individual records can be quickly retrieved or filtered. Normalizing data removes (or at least greatly reduces) data redundancy, ensuring that changes to data get reflected across all affected rows and minimizing the chances of inconsistencies across the database.

Unfortunately, the structures that work so well for day-to-day operational use of such a database do not work as well for answering the kinds of questions we asked our beleaguered store manager earlier. OLTP systems are designed for very high levels of data throughput; they may well contain many millions of rows of data per table, but because the operations they handle typically involve just a few specific rows at a time, they deliver great performance levels.

OLTP databases are almost always *transactional* as well. A transactional database is one that helps ensure that updates to multiple tables are performed consistently. Transactional features add overhead to a database, but they're essential for a database where data is changed frequently.

TIP

For a more detailed introduction to normalization and transactions, see Mike Gunderloy and Joseph L. Jorden's book, *Mastering™ SQL Server™ 2000* (Sybex, 2000).

Now, take a very real business-oriented question such as, "Which product has lost the largest percentage of market share over time?" Ask those same database systems to categorize and summarize those millions of rows of data to answer such an analytical query, and they choke.

DATA ANALYSIS WITH OLAP

Fundamentally, the analytical or querying tasks that we want to use for a large amount of data require a very different kind of database design, tuned for handling more general, exploratory queries. Such a design is often classified as an *OLAP database*. An OLAP database, as distinct from a relational database, is designed primarily for handling exploratory queries rather than updates. By storing the data in a structure that is optimized for analytical purposes, OLAP solutions provide faster and more intuitive analysis capabilities than traditional environments. In addition, OLAP databases dispense with some of the features of OLTP databases (such as transactional processing), because they typically contain data that is never edited, only added to.

OLAP databases are focused specifically on the problem of data analysis. They give rapid responses to complex queries involving large amounts of data because of two distinct attributes:

- Rather than storing data in a purely relational database format, OLAP databases are normally stored in a "multidimensional" data structure. (In fact, this is a slightly simplistic statement compared to the real world, as we shall see in later chapters, but it is at least true that the optimum structure for the information we are storing is multidimensional.)
- They perform some of the summary calculations before the user requests them. By providing general information on the structure of the underlying data, an OLAP environment can pre-calculate totals and averages that enable the system to respond quickly to a user, even if their query requires analysis of thousands or millions of rows of data to answer.

These two concepts are crucial to the performance of OLAP and, more important, in terms of its underlying architecture.

NOTE

Several (more or less) synonymous terms are used within the computing industry to describe "analytical" databases as discussed within this book. In particular, you will sometimes hear the term "decision support" used in place of OLAP. The older term "executive information system (EIS)" has fallen out of fashion.

Comparing OLTP and OLAP Databases

The design of OLAP systems is fundamentally different from the design of OLTP systems. Many of the overriding principles of traditional, relational database designs are even the opposite of the best practices in OLAP multidimensional database designs.

For example, relational database designers strive to minimize or eliminate data redundancy within their schemas. Instead of having information duplicated across multiple rows of data, relational databases use normalization techniques to store pointers to duplicated information. So a database containing books and their authors would separate book information from author information into tables to ensure that if, for example, an author changed their address details, the change would only need to be made in one location (specifically, the Authors table). Conversely, in an OLAP database design, redundancy is not only acceptable, it is positively encouraged! By reducing normalization and keeping multiple copies of information, the query processor can go to a single part of the database to obtain all relevant information, thus improving performance. Of course, there are trade-offs for this performance improvement. In particular, storing redundant data increases the size of an OLAP database compared to the corresponding OLTP database.

Table 21.4 compares and contrasts the requirements of each of the different forms of database design, based on the nature of tasks each performs.

TABLE 21.4: OLTP and OLAP Database Design Requirements

Transactional Database (OLTP)	Analytical Database (OLAP)
Deals with *specific* items.	Interested in *general* trends.
High throughput (often millions of transactions per day).	Low throughput (tens or hundreds of transactions per day).

TABLE 21.4 continued: OLTP and OLAP Database Design Requirements

TRANSACTIONAL DATABASE (OLTP)	ANALYTICAL DATABASE (OLAP)
Operations make changes.	Operations answer questions.
Queries typically involve a few records only.	Queries often span the whole database.
Many operations update the source data.	Operations are generally read-only in nature.
Supports transactions.	Does not support transactions.
Needs to be completely up to date.	Often updated on a batch basis (e.g., at night or on weekends).
Reflects new data immediately.	Reflects new data eventually.

Let's look at a practical example of the differences between relational and multidimensional databases in a real-world situation. Imagine a sales manager who wishes to explore a product sales database to identify trends in marketing activities. The sales manager might be interested in viewing sales categorized by product, by time period, by sales executive, by region, by customer.

Now, let's think about how we might store such information in a relational database format. The most obvious solution is to create a table for each major entity within the database. Figure 21.1 shows an example relationship diagram that implements this arrangement.

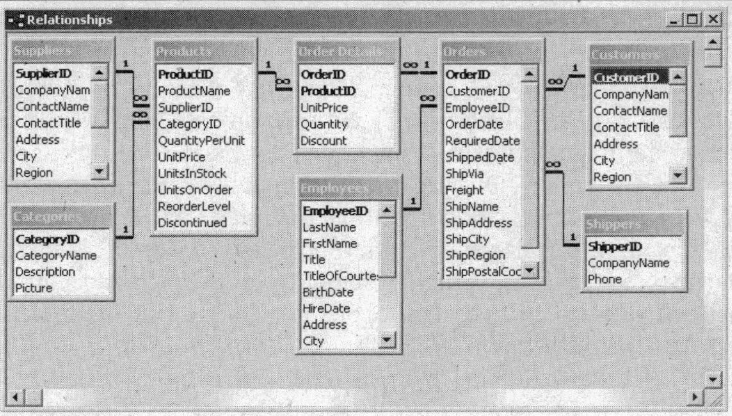

FIGURE 21.1: Sales relationship diagram

NOTE

The database used to generate this relationship diagram is the Northwind product database, which ships as a sample database for several Microsoft applications, including SQL Server 2000, Access, and Visual Studio.

This structure is optimized for data storage and manipulation: It minimizes redundancy by splitting each entity into a separate table. Making a change to a supplier's address only needs to be done once (in the Suppliers table), rather than amending the Products table for each item supplied by the company. However, it is hard to perform complex queries against this table structure.

Suppose we want to see the year-by-year changes in the sales of beverages made by particular suppliers. It's certainly true that all the data needed to answer this question is stored within the database. However, such a query would not be easy to write: We'd need to join five tables (Suppliers, Categories, Products, Order Details, and Orders), filter the data by category (Beverages), and then perform a SELECT operation on the suppliers, showing the total sales for each year together with the percentage difference between each.

Such a query is certainly beyond the capabilities of a novice or intermediate system user, yet queries just like this are commonly asked by anyone who wants to get an overview of the information held within their organization. By creating an OLAP database that stores this information in a multidimensional format, you can use a client tool to drag and drop the required information onto your desktop. The OLAP engine automatically joins the required tables and returns data in the relevant format without your having to specify this information yourself.

Let's examine a couple further examples of the kinds of queries people might ask and how OLAP-based solutions can help. Most organizations have accounting applications that store information on every aspect of their financial affairs. Once again, those organizations can use OLAP software to identify trends within their data that may improve their financial efficiency. They may want to view invoices by customer, department, date invoiced, payment period, payment type. "Slicing and dicing" the resultant data according to a range of criteria is the kind of problem that OLAP is ideal at tackling.

For another example that isn't specific to a particular industry, imagine a time sheet application that allows employees to record their working activities over a weekly period. Their managers will want to compare different employees' work patterns by project, client, week, and activity type. Similarly, the finance staff will want to know which clients are the most (or least) profitable, this time viewing income or profit by client, project manager, time period, and service type. Once again, OLAP solutions provide an effective mechanism for users to browse through this information, without necessarily understanding the underlying systems or the SQL syntax they would need to interrogate the database manually.

We've focused here on the structures and mechanisms of OLAP; later we'll explain what software you can use to analyze the information once it is stored in an OLAP environment.

DATA WAREHOUSES AND DATA MARTS

The terms *data warehouse* and *data mart* are often used to describe corporate stores for data gleaned from production systems. There are almost as many definitions of these two terms as there are people talking about them! By and large, the difference is a matter of scale, with data warehouses being centralized systems containing all relevant data across the business processes of the whole organization and data marts being departmental-based subsets of the entire organization's data.

When building OLAP solutions, you might start by extracting data directly from a production system. This does not require the use of a data warehouse or data mart.

An alternative approach is to build a data mart or data warehouse containing extracts from one or more production systems. The data can then be cleaned up (cleansed) in this intermediate environment before you take it into the OLAP environment. This latter approach is often suitable where you wish to first restructure the data or add additional information from other databases (such as a market research database).

Applying OLAP in Your Organization

There are almost certainly hundreds of potential applications for OLAP solutions within your own organization: Wherever you have a reasonable quantity of related data, you can probably get some benefit from applying OLAP techniques and technologies for reporting and summary purposes.

Until fairly recently, OLAP was a horribly expensive technology for companies to adopt. The software available for use typically cost a four-figure sum *per desktop*, which meant that you had to get very significant business benefit out of its use to make it financially viable. This limited the use of such technology to high-end, typically financial or marketing applications.

In particular, many people have had bad experiences with data warehouse systems falling short on the promises they originally made. By attempting to act as the central repository for all data analysis, data warehousing projects have often failed due to issues such as poor data reconciliation, errors in the original data, and slow updates.

One reason for the failure of many data warehousing projects has been an attempt to solve all an organization's data storage and reconciliation issues in one go. Some multimillion-dollar projects never achieve any business benefit as a result. One benefit of using a product such as Analysis Services within SQL Server 2000 is that you can start with a cheap and easily implemented solution that works on a small part of the problem, then evolve the implementation to take on larger quantities of data and business analysis activity as the success of the initial solution is demonstrated.

Such a "bottom up" design approach allows analytical databases to be built in a modular fashion across a distributed environment and later joined as necessary without drastically impacting the performance of the end solution.

The good news, however, is that OLAP is now a mass-market technology that can deliver real bottom-line benefits for everyone. Most important, the price point has changed dramatically since the launch of SQL Server 7.0, the first version of Microsoft SQL Server with OLAP capabilities. SQL Server Analysis Services is included at no extra licensing costs as part of SQL Server, meaning that any database system based on SQL Server can add analytical functionality for little or no cost beyond the original database system.

Limitations of OLAP Solutions

Although OLAP solutions can be helpful in the business environment for reporting and analysis purposes, they are *not* a replacement for the traditional relational and flat-file database models. The idea behind OLAP is to supplement existing databases and allow for resource-intensive queries to be offloaded to a secondary machine. The transactional updates and queries that are always required in a production database remain in the existing environment.

OLAP is largely a read-only solution, rather than a read-write solution. Because we're dealing with a snapshot of a live environment, writing back to that snapshot would not impact the original database anyway, even if there were a good reason for doing so. On the other hand, there is a case for doing "what if" types of analysis (for example, "What would happen if production costs were raised by 10 percent?"). Analysis Services therefore provides a limited set of facilities for writing back such values to a separate partition within the OLAP database. However, if you are doing such activities on a regular basis, you might want to take some OLAP data back into a traditional relational database for ease of access.

The release of Analysis Services extends the scalability of OLAP solutions on the Microsoft platform considerably. The analysis of multiple terabytes of data is well within the capabilities of Analysis Services. With sufficient processing power, memory, and hard disk capacity, Analysis Services can handle the majority of business requirements.

Summary

In this chapter, you've seen that OLAP solutions provide a valuable and necessary addition to the armory of tools that should be available to any database designer. Relational databases are great for many tasks, but reporting and analysis activities can be both complex and resource intensive as the number of related tables and the quantity of data stored increase.

In the next three chapters, we'll look further at the terminology and architecture of OLAP solutions, as well as examine in greater depth the facilities provided in SQL Server 2000 for data analysis.

Chapter 22

Analysis Services Architecture

In the last chapter, we described the difference between transactional, relational (OLTP) databases and analytical, multidimensional (OLAP) databases. We looked at the kinds of tasks that might be put to OLTP systems (specific tasks such as "update invoice #33864 to include product #138204") and contrasted them with the kinds of queries that might be asked of OLAP systems (general purpose queries, such as "How many insurance policies were sold last year?").

In this chapter, we'll develop this further by covering some of the central concepts and terms used in Microsoft SQL Server 2000 Analysis Services. We'll define terms such as cubes, dimensions, and measures, and give examples of how those elements are applied to real-world situations. The chapter will then go on to describe SQL Server 2000 and the key features within the product, before concluding with a discussion of Microsoft's Data Warehousing Framework and a brief description of some third-party products that support the use of Analysis Services for decision support systems.

Adapted from *SQL Server™ Developer's Guide to OLAP with Analysis Services* by Mike Gunderloy and Tim Sneath

ISBN 0-7821-2957-1 480 pages $49.99

If you're unfamiliar with the terminology used in the OLAP world or have no direct experience with Microsoft Analysis Services, this chapter is worth careful reading. The concepts we define here are going to crop up regularly in later chapters. Even if you've worked with another OLAP product, the chapter is worth carefully reading to understand how Microsoft uses the key terms in its product.

KEY CONCEPTS

The human brain is an amazing organ. Our brains are designed to assimilate and store huge quantities of information for long periods of time. Our brains are more powerful than any computer, with greater storage than the most impressive database system, and we can but hope to duplicate in software the feats that our brains can already perform.

We're still a long way from fully understanding the workings of the brain, and we certainly know that it operates in a very different manner from the computer. So we can only get glimpses of its operation by understanding the way we do things. We do know that human beings have always categorized and ordered the world around us. By sorting the information we have in such a way, we can more readily remember facts and put new memories into a context. Psychologists believe that one of the most important purposes of dreaming is to "reshuffle" our brains, arranging different pieces of information accordingly to better facilitate recollection at a future date.

To come back to the subject matter of the book, one of the best ways to quickly comprehend a large body of information (particularly computer-based data) is to organize it in such a way that we can identify broad trends and anomalies. This process is a specialist task, which we shall spend time looking at; for now, we'll identify a couple of concepts that will help us in our discussion.

Analyzing Sales with Analysis Services

Let's go back to the example we discussed at the beginning of Chapter 21, that of our beleaguered store manager in a chain of retail supermarkets. If we were to ask what types of information the store managers found difficult to access, they might say something along the lines of "I want to know *what* we're selling, *when*, and *for how much*." We'll develop this picture a little further by generalizing it to the overall operations of a supermarket, thinking about the kinds of information a supermarket receives, and suggesting ways in which it could be used.

First, the supermarket has *products*. Each product comes from a manufacturer and is typically stored in a warehouse before being displayed on the shelves. As the supermarket receives new products at its warehouse, their personnel will enter a record for each product SKU onto the warehouse computer. At a minimum, this record will contain information on the product, its type, its location in the warehouse, its receipt date, and its sell-by date.

TIP

SKU stands for *Stock Keeping Unit*. It is an alphanumeric value that uniquely identifies a particular product in a salable quantity and type (e.g., Brand X Diet Cola 6 × 12-ounce cans).

Meanwhile, each individual supermarket itself stocks the products as individual items on its shelves. It has its own stock records, containing information on how many products of each type are left on the shelves. Some of the most critical tasks for the store manager to perform are predicting the demand for each product over a period of time and ensuring that sufficient quantities either are in the store or can be ordered from the warehouse. To do that, the manager needs a clear understanding of sale trends.

NOTE

This is not as simple a process as it might at first appear. Fixed calendar events, such as Easter and Christmas, as well as sporting events, will cause a surge in demand for certain products and a drop for others. People may be more likely to buy certain products on weekends; a sudden change of weather will have a significant impact. Special offers or deals will increase the popularity of one product while diminishing others. Add to the above the powerful effect of TV commercials and recommendations (one UK store had a rush for wild boar steak after it was featured in a cooking show!), and the underlying patterns can be very difficult to extract.

Assuming that the store has the right products in the right places at the right time, it will then also want to track purchases at the other end of the chain: the checkout. A large retail store uses a barcode scanner to identify products purchased, and the data scanned is generally saved to a central database of sales. The database contains information on the name of the product as displayed on the cash register receipt, together with its price, and any special offers on the product. Having scanned all the products, the store produces a receipt and saves the sales data back to the database, so that the supermarket can track stock levels.

It becomes more interesting if the store offers a loyalty reward program. In such a case, the supermarket chain may already have information on you from the loyalty program application form; this probably includes the area you live in, the size of your family, your age, your salary bracket and/or occupation, and perhaps even your interests.

Match this personal information with your purchasing history, and the store has a marketing database of immense potential, *if* it can successfully analyze and use that information in an intelligent way. Here are a couple of examples:

- The store has information on products that other people similar to you are buying (based on age, family size, etc.). By knowing the kinds of product you are likely to buy, it can entice you to make purchases from the store that you were perhaps making elsewhere.
- If you switch stores for some or all purchases, the change in purchasing profile can be identified. Perhaps you weren't happy with something in the store: The supermarket might send a customer satisfaction survey, together with some coupons to encourage you back.
- Perhaps you've started (or stopped) buying something significant that gives away a change in your lifestyle. If you're suddenly buying diapers for the first time, chances are you've had a baby! The supermarket will no doubt then want to send information on special offers relating to other baby products.

Because the supermarket concept is such an easy one to relate to, we'll be using it throughout the book. In fact, Microsoft includes a sample database that is based on exactly this business context as part of Analysis Services. Among others, we'll be using this database, *Foodmart,* extensively in the remainder of this section on OLAP to demonstrate specific examples of how to use Analysis Services to its fullest, along with a couple of other examples that we'll develop along the way.

NOTE

It's important to make clear that although Foodmart is a good sample for demonstrating concepts, it is based on fictional data in a fictional supermarket. The best way to see how this operates in practice is to take a sample of your own data and modify the included samples to work in your own business context. In this way, you can start getting real benefits immediately from this technology.

To turn these real-world scenarios into a structure that can be used, we need to build some structure into the information we have to make it easier to store and analyze.

In Microsoft Analysis Services, pretty much all data can be classified into one of three types: *measures*, *dimensions*, and *cubes*. These terms will be used throughout the book, so take careful heed of the information here if you are not already familiar with this terminology.

Measures

In any database, we are ultimately storing some kind of information about the entities within that database. Usually the pieces of data that are most likely to be summarized are stored as values of some description, either as a currency, as integers, or as floating point numbers. A database of a company's business customers may hold information on the number of employees in their target customer, their annual turnover and profit, the number of products purchased, the discount level applied, and the total revenue returned from that customer. These values form the *measures* used within an Analysis Services database.

Back to our supermarket example and the marketing information they have stored on product sales: They will have data on the number of products sold, the cost of those products (to the supermarket), the price of those products (in terms of the cost to the customer), and so on. We call the values that are of interest to us as parts of aggregates or summaries *measures.*

If we wanted to get an idea of the success (or otherwise) of a particular store, we could check all of the individual cash register receipts to see how often the product was sold and in what quantities. Alternatively, we could add up this information once and store a figure for each product to identify the performance of that product.

WARNING

If we want to choose how we view these measures at a later stage rather than producing static tables, we need to store these measures against the lowest practical element of information within our database. We might choose to either make this an individual sale item or a cash register receipt as a whole. We'll discuss the general choice in design terms later on.

A measure is a numeric piece of information we are interested in analyzing. Some pieces of data that are likely to be measures include the following:

- Quantity

- Cost
- Profit
- Score
- Value

Note that when we aggregate a measure across a number of dimensions (e.g., showing a value for electrical products in the northern region in 2000), the value may not necessarily be a total produced by summing. The revenue across the dimensions above will certainly be calculated by adding up the revenue for individual sales of all matching products; however, what about the profit on all such products? We might calculate this by taking the cost to the store of a product, subtracted from its sale price; in other words,

```
Profit = Sales Price - Cost to Store
```

Alternatively, we might even calculate the profit margin, thus,

```
Profit Margin = (Sales Price - Cost to Store)/Cost to Store
```

Profit and *profit margin* are examples of *calculated measures*.

We can use multiple columns of source data to derive a calculated measure. For that reason, we can classify the source values into two types:

Additive Values that can be summed together to give a meaningful result in aggregation (e.g., price).

Non-additive Values that, summed together, make no meaningful sense (e.g., account numbers).

Non-additive values are themselves not suitable as measures, but they can be combined with other data to produce a calculated measure. We'll discuss calculated measures in more detail over the next few chapters.

Dimensions

Being able to produce a single value representing the total quantity of sales across all stores is not spectacularly useful in its own right. Most people want to see the information broken down in categories, rather than the absolute top-line figure or the individual cell-level data.

Within the supermarket sales scenario, it might be relevant to see sales figures broken down by store, by time period, by department, by product, by customer age, and by customer gender. In OLAP terminology, each of these different categories represents a single *dimension*.

For instance, Table 22.1 isn't necessarily helpful for understanding sales patterns, because it simply shows the overall sales figure without any breakdown of how that number is reached by product.

TABLE 22.1: Total aggregate sales

SALES PRICE	ALL TIME PERIODS
All products	$151,482,232.48

On the other hand, although Table 22.2 shows detailed information on each item, it is *too* detailed to be valuable for establishing overall business trends. Here we can see the individual line items, but we have no concept of which category each products fits into.

TABLE 22.2: Individual item sales

PRODUCT SKU	STORE COST	SALES PRICE	QUANTITY	CUSTOMER ID
48312KS	$2.87	$4.99	2	19238490
14839TT	$14.53	$20.00	8	19238490
49231FX	$0.37	$0.70	20	19548392

Table 22.3 offers far more useful management information than either of the previous two tables, because it breaks down the overall sales figure to intermediate categories from the time and product dimensions. Here we can immediately see how sales vary by product and time. For example, we can see that 1998 was a generally weak year for sales of non-electrical products.

TABLE 22.3: Sales aggregated by time and product category

	YTD 1997	YTD 1998	YTD 1999	YTD 2000
Kitchenware	$1,385,482.88	$1,281,110.38	$1,493,104.20	$804,319.22
Clothing	$4,239,145.67	$3,850,139.68	$4,280,254.72	$2,691,582.44
Foods	$3,001,403.13	$2,789,104.58	$3,505,937.43	$1,864,302.68
Electrical	$5,194,493.93	$6,231,454.99	$5,739,002.42	$3,132,394.13

Each way of breaking down the overall figure (or aggregating the individual pieces of data) constitutes a different dimension. Common types of dimension include the following:

- Products
- Organizational structures
- Time
- Geography
- Customers
- Promotions
- Discount ratios
- Channels of sale (e.g., direct, reseller, Internet, etc.)

For a different example, let's imagine a busy customer call center or help desk. Here, the measures might be number of calls taken, number of calls resolved, satisfaction level of caller, length of call, and so on. We might be interested in breaking this information down by time, by call center representative, by problem type, by caller, by training pattern, and so on. These categories would then be the dimensions.

TIP

In general, if you can describe your problem in terms of, "I need to see *x, y,* and *z* pieces of information broken down by *a*, by *b*, by *c*...," the x, y, and z will represent measures and the a, b, and c will represent dimensions.

Levels

Dimensions alone aren't always sufficient to break down the information to a manageable or interesting form. A large supermarket may have as many as 100,000 product lines available at any one time. It would be frustrating if we could only see measures for all products or individual ones. We therefore usually break down our dimensions into a hierarchical structure. Each member of the hierarchy is called a *level*.

Looking at products, for example, we might break them down as shown in Figure 22.1.

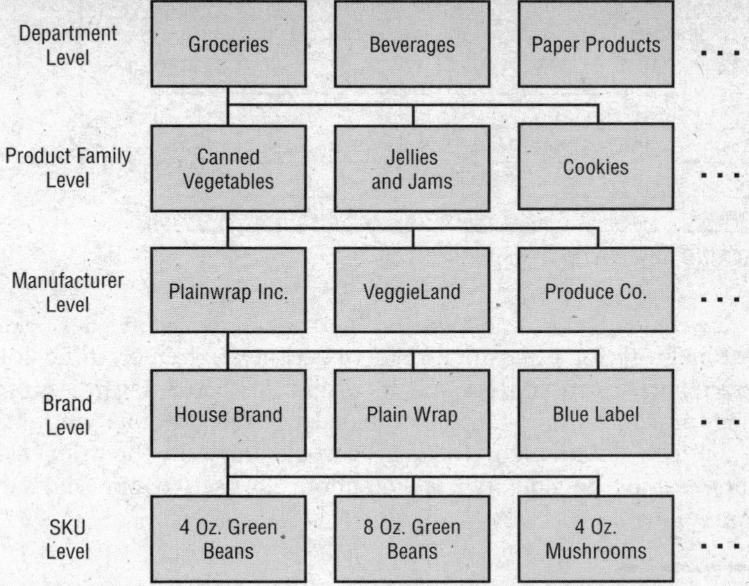

FIGURE 22.1: Dividing a product's dimension into multiple levels

The "product" dimension in this case would therefore have five levels; an OLAP tool should allow us to navigate through each of these levels, showing the measures against each of the level information.

Cubes

In OLAP terms, the basic unit of analysis is the *cube*. A cube represents a particular domain of inquiry, such as "sales data" or "help desk statistics." A cube is a storage unit that combines a number of dimensions and the measures they contain into one whole.

We've used the term "dimension" to indicate a category by which the data will be analyzed. If we only wished to store measures indexed by two dimensions (sales by product by time), we could have a two-dimensional table, as shown, for example, in Table 22.3. Now, let's imagine that we want to add a third dimension: that is, to analyze sales by product by time by region. To draw a picture of all this information, we would need a three-dimensional cube, as shown in Figure 22.2.

	YTD 1997	YTD 1998	YTD 1999	YTD 2000
Kitchenware	$461,827.62	$400,346.99	$514,863.52	$259,457.82
Clothing	$1,695,658.26	$1,283,379.89	$1,455,868.95	$961,279.44
Foods	$1,111,630.79	$996,108.78	$1,168,645.81	$582,594.59
Electrical	$1,675,643.11	$2,023,199.67	$2,125,556.45	$1,030,392.81

FIGURE 22.2: A three-dimensional cube

If we added a fourth dimension (perhaps to represent sales by product by time by region by customer age), it becomes extremely difficult to represent such a structure graphically within this book! Regardless of how many dimensions are actually contained, however, we still term the storage unit a "cube." Although a literal cube would only store three dimensions of information, the same term is metaphorically used to represent *n* dimensions of data.

NOTE

The term "cube" can sometimes be confusing, as it implies both a number of dimensions and, worse, an underlying structure for the data storage. As described above, cubes can contain three dimensions, but can also contain more. In the absence of a more general term and given the widespread usage of the word "cube" within Analysis Services, the term will continue to be used within this book, however.

The process we describe in this book is therefore one of *multidimensional data analysis*; in other words, extracting useful knowledge from an *n*-dimensional structure and representing it in such a form as to be easily understood.

Figure 22.3 shows an actual cube from the Foodmart 2000 sample application (which is installed when you install Analysis Services). In this example,

- Product and Education are dimensions.
- Product Family, Product Department, and Product Category are levels.
- The sales for each combination (in the unshaded cells) are a measure.
- All of these together make up one view of a cube.

			Education Level		
- Product Family	- Product Department	+ Product Category	All Education Level	Bachelors Degree	Graduate Degree
All Products	All Products Total		266,773.00	68,839.00	15,570.00
- Drink	Drink Total		24,597.00	6,423.00	1,325.00
	+ Alcoholic Beverages	Alcoholic Beverages Total	6,838.00	1,763.00	352.00
	- Beverages	Beverages Total	13,573.00	3,591.00	730.00
		+ Carbonated Beverages	3,407.00	917.00	188.00
		+ Drinks	2,469.00	631.00	141.00
		+ Hot Beverages	4,301.00	1,090.00	256.00
		+ Pure Juice Beverages	3,396.00	953.00	145.00
	+ Dairy	Dairy Total	4,186.00	1,069.00	243.00
+ Food	Food Total		191,940.00	49,365.00	11,255.00
+ Non-Consumable	Non-Consumable Total		50,236.00	13,051.00	2,990.00

FIGURE 22.3: Cubes, dimensions, levels and measures

OLAP Storage Choices

Once we've worked out what kinds of information we want to access, designed our cube, and chosen the relevant dimensions and measures, we need to go ahead and physically create the structure. In the last chapter, we described the benefits that Analysis Services provides by storing data in a multidimensional structure. In fact, it's *slightly* more complicated than that: as an OLAP designer, you have several choices as to how the data, coupled with the aggregations, is stored. Analysis Services can store data in two locations:

- In the relational database that contains the source data
- In a special repository optimized for cube storage

Certain elements of information are always stored by Analysis Services in its own repository format, regardless of the storage design chosen. Examples of this include dimensional metadata, processing instructions, and data transformation options. Other parts can either be stored in multidimensional format or as part of the source tables. To understand the different choices for storing data, let's consider the problem of precalculated aggregations.

Aggregations and Exponential Growth

It would be perfect if we could store ahead of time all the measures against each level of every combination of dimensions. That way, any time a query was put to Analysis Services, it could get the value directly using these previously calculated *aggregations*, without having to sum up any source data while the user waits.

Unfortunately, this is just not possible in practice. To explain why, let's imagine the number of aggregations one would need for cubes of various sizes. In a simple cube with three dimensions (products, regions, and time) and just one level, you would simply need to store three aggregations. As you increase the number of dimensions, and particularly the number of levels per dimension, the number of aggregations rises exponentially as

```
a = ld
```

where d is the number of dimensions and l is the number of levels. Table 22.4 will give you some sense of how quickly the number of aggregations can grow.

TABLE 22.4: Number of aggregations by dimensions and levels

DIMENSIONS \ LEVELS	2	3	4	5
2	4	9	16	25
3	8	27	64	125
4	16	81	256	625
5	32	243	1,024	3,125
6	64	729	4,096	15,625
7	128	2,187	16,384	78,125
8	256	6,561	65,536	390,625

Many real-world cubes may have twenty or more dimensions, perhaps with an average of three levels per dimension. That would leave us requiring 3,486,784,401 aggregations! Although in theory we could precalculate 3 billion aggregations, in practice this would take an immense amount of time and storage space. In fact, it makes little sense to calculate many of the lower-level aggregations, because they are often only summing up a few rows of source data.

For that reason, the pragmatic solution to the problem of "exploding aggregations" is to precalculate those aggregations that either will be frequently accessed or that involve many thousands of rows of the source data.

This means that OLAP databases must store (or have access to) two kinds of data:

- Source data, i.e., the individual rows of data that are used to build aggregations
- Aggregations themselves, i.e., the measures combined across a dimensional level

As we mentioned previously, both types of information can be stored either in a multidimensional structure or in a relational database. The storage choices are abbreviated MOLAP, ROLAP, and HOLAP.

MOLAP The *M* in *MOLAP* stands for *Multidimensional*. In MOLAP, *both* the source data *and* the aggregations are stored in a multidimensional format. MOLAP is almost always the fastest option for data retrieval; however, it often requires the most disk space.

ROLAP In the *ROLAP* (or *Relational OLAP*) approach, all data, including aggregations, is stored within the source relational database structure. ROLAP is always the slowest option for data retrieval. Whether an aggregation exists or not, a ROLAP database must access the database itself.

HOLAP *HOLAP* (or *Hybrid OLAP)* is an attempt to get the best of both worlds. A HOLAP database stores the aggregations that exist within a multidimensional structure, leaving the cell-level data itself in a relational form. Where the data is preaggregated, HOLAP offers the performance of MOLAP; where the data must be fetched from tables, HOLAP is as slow as ROLAP.

We'll go into the various choices in more detail in Chapter 23, "Using Analysis Services." Figure 22.4 shows the differences between these choices schematically.

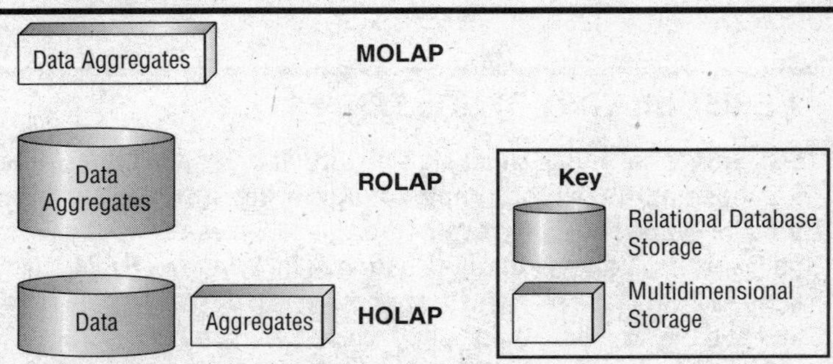

FIGURE 22.4: MOLAP, ROLAP, and HOLAP

MICROSOFT SQL SERVER 2000

Microsoft SQL Server 2000 is a large and complex piece of software. At its heart resides a powerful relational database engine, but a broad range of associated services, tools, and development technologies are also available for installation. We will be using many of these features throughout the course of this book to build our OLAP solutions. In this section, we'll take a look at what SQL Server provides for data mart developers. Figure 22.5 shows the major SQL Server components that we'll be discussing, together with their relationships.

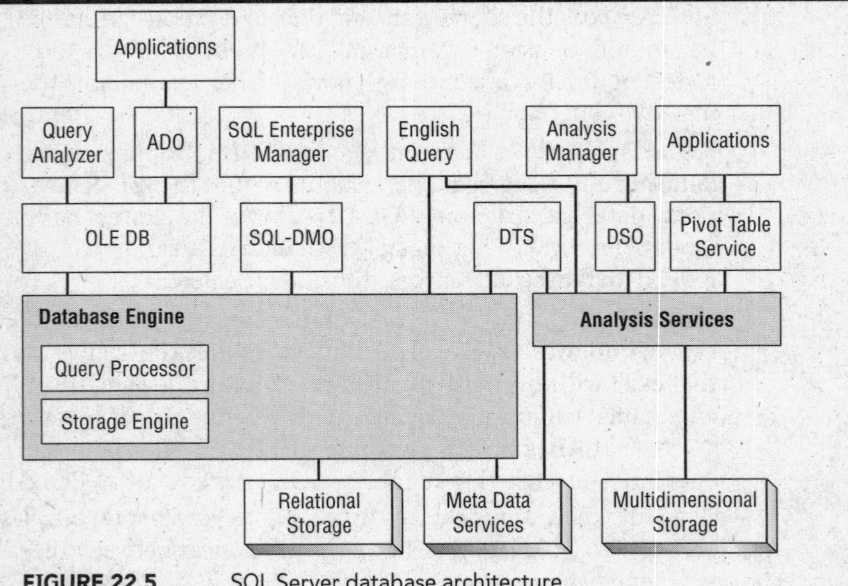

FIGURE 22.5 SQL Server database architecture

A BRIEF HISTORY OF SQL SERVER

SQL Server has had a checkered history: It originally began life as a Sybase database for a range of operating systems, including VAX/VMS and UNIX. Microsoft co-licensed Sybase's product, originally for LAN Manager on OS/2 and then for Windows NT. Microsoft needed a database platform to support their own strategic direction, and Sybase was more than happy to see their database product

CONTINUED →

extended to different operating platforms. Eventually Microsoft and Sybase went their separate ways, leading to Microsoft SQL Server 6.0 as the first release produced entirely by Microsoft without coding from Sybase.

Microsoft SQL Server 6.0 (and the 6.5 update) still greatly reflected its origins, however. The original code base from Sybase was designed to be portable across various operating systems. Although Microsoft had updated significant portions of the code, much of the architecture remained from the original releases.

Since all serious commercial database systems are written to protect the integrity of their underlying data files at all costs (including operating system crashes), most systems effectively reimplement significant portions of the underlying operating system, including locking and caching mechanisms, file storage, and write access. Whereas this insulates the database from changes between different platforms, it also adds a significant performance and administrative overhead. In SQL Server 6.*x*, this was visible in several ways, including the use of "devices" as files on which databases could be stored. Even though Microsoft was only supporting one operating system, this portable code was still present in its database system. Added to this, other parts of the architecture were starting to become obsolete or inconsistent with the rest of the product, and vendors were publicly humiliating Microsoft for the lack of support for features that were by then considered essential by most relational database administrators (for example, row-level locking).

In early January 1999, Microsoft released SQL Server 7, a major revision of the product. SQL Server 7 introduced a new engine that for the first time was fully integrated into the operating system, as well as a redesigned query processor and administrative facilities. In addition, SQL Server 7 added some important new features, including support for OLAP Services and Data Transformation Services. SQL Server 7 was a major step forward, yet in many ways it was almost like version 1.0 of a new product. OLAP Services provided a great set of features, and yet somehow omitted several crucial features, including a robust security model.

SQL Server 2000 builds further on the architecture introduced with SQL Server 7. It adds some much-needed features in both the core database engine and the supporting products (including

CONTINUED ➞

an updated version of OLAP Services, now with a change of name to Analysis Services) and is a worthwhile upgrade. The marketplace continues to evolve, however, and other vendors themselves offer increasingly competitive features integrating the core database platform with comparatively new applications, such as *Enterprise Resource Planning* (*ERP*) and *Customer Relationship Management* (*CRM*). Time will tell whether Microsoft can continue to evolve its product at a sufficient pace to stay competitive.

SQL Server Database Engine

SQL Server 2000 would be nothing without the core database engine. The new database engine provided in SQL Server 7 and later is a world away from the rather slow and dated engine in previous versions. Many of the new features, such as row-level locking, multiple instances (new in SQL Server 2000), automated consistency checks, and transactional replication, make it feasible to now use SQL Server for highly intensive transactional environments, where the database provides mission-critical services to an organization.

NOTE

The SQL Server database engine comes in several versions, including desktop and enterprise versions, as well as a version called Microsoft Database Engine (MSDE) that is bundled with other products, such as Microsoft Office 2000.

The SQL Server database engine itself contains two major components: the *query processor* and the *storage engine*. The query processor takes SQL statements and breaks them down into a number of constituent atomic steps that can be processed sequentially or in parallel. It then selects an execution plan from a range of choices, choosing to use indexes as appropriate. The storage engine itself is responsible for performing those operations against the physical database itself: It manages the database file structure and handles all tasks that directly interact with the data on disk.

The two components of the database engine are accessed from other applications by using an interface called *OLE DB*. OLE DB is a database-independent communication layer (much like the older Open Database

Connectivity, or ODBC standard) that allows SQL statements to execute against any compliant database. The advantage of this is that you can link different databases into SQL Server (see "Linked Servers" in the SQL Server Books Online), allowing one SQL statement or query to operate against multiple databases at once.

TIP

The SQL Server query processor is a *cost-based* rather than *syntax-based* processor. Syntax-based processors simply look at the SQL statement itself, picking an execution plan based purely on the various keywords of the statement itself. Cost-based processors also take into account the size of the tables that are used within the expression, any indexes, and other factors calculating a "cost" for each element of the execution plan. This takes account of the fact that what works well for a ten-row table may work very poorly for a million-row table.

Most people access a SQL Server database using an application, rather than writing queries directly against the database itself. Such access is these days typically provided through *ActiveX Data Objects* (ADO). ADO provides an object-oriented interface atop OLE DB. Alternatively, you can use the *SQL Server Query Analyzer*, a tool that allows you to enter and execute SQL statements. Query Analyzer is particularly useful when you want to see how a SQL statement will be executed. You can ask it to show the execution plan for a query that has been or will be executed, and Query Analyzer displays graphically the different steps it will take, along with the time and processor cost for each part of the operation.

SQL Server is typically administered through a Microsoft Management Console (MMC) snap-in, called the *SQL Enterprise Manager* (SQL/EM). This provides the ability to create and modify databases, tables, indexes, replication, triggers, etc., as well as set security and run other tools and wizards. SQL/EM does not interact directly with the database engine; instead, it communicates with a compiled COM library called *SQL Distributed Management Objects* (*SQL-DMO*). The DMO interface is well documented, making it possible to write management applications that do any or all of what the Enterprise Manager does, coupled with custom actions.

Data Transformation Services

Data Transformation Services (*DTS*) comes in really useful for shifting data around. It effectively acts like a pump: It sucks in data from one or more data sources and puts that data back into another database. But it's more than just a kind of bulk copier:

- DTS supports *any* OLE DB or ODBC data source or destination, neither of which needs to be SQL Server (or for that matter, even a Microsoft product). That means you can use it, for example, to transfer data from Oracle to DB2.
- DTS provides a rich script-based programming interface that allows you to manipulate the data on the way through the pump. You can write VBScript or JavaScript code to "cleanse" your data, split or merge different fields between source and destination, and even create new fields by performing calculations or string operations on existing fields. If scripting languages don't deliver sufficient power, you can go still further and call out to external COM components to deliver the functionality you need.
- DTS includes a workflow editor that allows you to string together several steps into a single process. Perhaps you want to transfer some data from one location to another, then run a stored procedure on the target, and finally e-mail the database administrator to let them know when the tasks are complete and if any errors occurred. You can even build in "success/failure" paths so that you can trigger remedial action if one task fails, or only continue with further tasks if the previous one succeeds.

DTS is fast: On an old Pentium II/450MHz with 256MHz RAM and Windows 2000, it copies multiple tables with a sustained rate of well over 50,000 rows of data per minute. You can also use it in combination with the SQL Server Agent to automate the transfer of data (for example, as a batched, nightly process).

SQL Server 2000 increases the significance of DTS for OLAP applications. One of the major new features is that DTS is now directly integrated with the Analysis Services tasks, meaning that you can load some data from multiple separate source databases, cleansing that data as it is loaded. On the successful completion of that task, you can automatically start processing an OLAP cube based on those databases to produce a cube with refreshed data.

TIP

Some fairly large commercial organizations have bought a copy of SQL Server for no other purpose than because DTS is better than anything available separately. They effectively "throw away" the SQL database engine and simply use DTS itself for their own data integration/migration needs across other database systems!

Analysis Services

The software that became SQL Server OLAP Services was originally available as part of a software suite from Panorama, a small Israeli software firm specializing in data analysis software. Microsoft bought the rights from Panorama and developed it further to fit better into the SQL Server 7 architecture and to add supporting features. Now renamed *Analysis Services*, the product can exist independently of SQL Server on a machine. It provides a fully functional OLAP environment—that is, it contains the following:

- A multidimensional database engine that can store and access data through read-only and read-write interfaces using *Multidimensional Expressions* (*MDX*), a query language similar to SQL
- An extensible management tool, *Analysis Manager*, which provides an MMC-based user interface for carrying out administrative functions, including creating and editing cubes, dimensions, and measures
- A COM library called *Decision Support Objects* (*DSO* for short), which provides programmatic access to the administrative layers exposed in the user interface (and slightly more beyond)
- A PivotTable service that allows other applications supporting OLE DB for OLAP to store and access locally cached copies of an OLAP cube

Analysis Services is not a unique product: other offerings are available as part of database suites from Oracle and IBM, for example, as well as dedicated OLAP or decision support packages from companies such as Cognos, Business Objects, and Hyperion. Each has its strengths and weaknesses. Some of the major strengths of Microsoft SQL Server Analysis Services are the following:

- Price per seat: Any client machine with a SQL Server Client Access License (CAL) can freely use Analysis Services. This compares with other OLAP software suites, some of which can cost upward of $1000 per seat.

- Automatic dimension design/usage-based optimization: Analysis Services can automatically assess which aggregations will offer the most significant performance improvement and create those, rather than a database administrator having to manually design aggregations for each dimension. It then logs the *actual* usage profile, to identify whether this affects the optimal arrangement of aggregations, and can modify the processing accordingly.
- OLE DB for OLAP architecture: Analysis Services integrates well with a range of third-party analytical tools, including Cognos PowerPlay, Knosys ProClarity, and Hungry Dog Software's IntelliBrowser, allowing freedom of choice in terms of the client front-end tools. Analysis Services also supports Excel PivotTables to allow dimensional analysis from within a spreadsheet environment.

In SQL Server 2000, Analysis Services adds several new features that were sorely lacking in the original version, including parent-child dimensions, ragged dimensions, and cell-level security.

Probably the biggest new feature in Analysis Services, which reflects the name change from the previous OLAP Services, is the introduction of *data mining* capabilities within the core product. Data mining provides a way to understand the cause-and-effect relationships between the dimensions within a cube and the resulting values within the measures. Data mining technologies allow you to predict outcomes for new data based on historical data and to discover patterns within the data in your cube.

English Query

One of the frustrating things about database systems is that seemingly simple English questions can turn into spaghetti SQL code when translated into the database's native language. A query phrased in English, such as "Show me all products sold by John Bradley," may require the use of several tables, with corresponding database joins and filters, to give a correct set of answers. In addition, such a question masks much underlying contextual information. For example, who is John Bradley? Is he a salesperson, a customer, or a supplier? And for that matter, how do we know that John Bradley is a person in the first place?

These difficulties occur even before we address the issue that human languages are by nature vague and flexible. One of the key differences between machine-based languages (such as SQL) and human languages (such as English) is how specific the languages are. A SQL statement will always mean exactly the same thing, no matter how often executed or by which computer. English phrases are, by contrast, highly subjective and can be misinterpreted (or at least, differently interpreted) by different listeners.

Microsoft English Query, first shipped with SQL Server 6.5 Enterprise Edition, is an attempt to try to bridge these difficulties by providing a machine-based interpreter for database queries phrased in English rather than SQL. It uses two different elements to understand and break down a query:

- First, it has a natural language interpreter that parses English sentences, removing redundant words that play no part in giving the sentence meaning and identifying words as grammatical elements within a sentence.
- Second, English Query draws on stored contextual information about the various database entities. For example, it knows that "salespeople sell products" and that "sold by" is an English construct drawn from the verb "to sell." Using this information, it can map words onto the underlying databases, even if a synonym is used rather than the specific word chosen by the database designer for an entity.

Using the information provided, English Query can continue to produce a SQL statement that (hopefully) matches the intent of the original English question or statement. If necessary, English Query can prompt for further clarification, if there is not sufficient information within the question for the parser to link the relevant database entities together.

English Query has shown increasing promise but, until SQL Server 2000, was only able to query against the central database engine itself using SQL. Given that the vast majority of uses for English Query reside within the analytical domain, it has been a notable omission that the product provided no support for queries against Analysis Services in the native language, MDX. SQL Server 2000 fulfills that promise by allowing English queries to be parsed into MDX. Thus, English Query can now be used to perform queries directly against cubes stored by Analysis Services. Among other new features in SQL Server 2000, English Query now uses Visual Studio as its development environment and provides a graphical designer for building the contextual information around the database, as well as providing a usable client for entering and displaying queries written in English.

Meta Data Services

Microsoft Meta Data Services is one of the aspects of the product that's hardest to fully describe. The purpose of Meta Data Services is basically to provide an "information store" into which developers can put almost anything they want. For example, Meta Data Services can be used as a library for shared COM components, so that developers can build up a toolbox that contains groups of COM components together with their source code and documentation. The structure and presentation of the store is up to you: What you get out of the box is the Meta Data Services engine itself and a series of COM interfaces that expose the functionality of the engine.

TIP

Meta Data Services **is new name for Microsoft Repository, which shipped with SQL Server 7 and Visual Studio 6. It is a direct upgrade for the previous version, containing all the old features as well as several new ones.**

The product is often used as a repository for *metadata*; that is, data *about* data. While a traditional database is good at storing structured information itself, it is often less good at holding information about the nature of the data, such as its origin, the underlying meaning of the data, and the purpose of the data.

TIP

Visual Basic includes a version of the original Repository engine as part of its Enterprise Edition. The Repository comes with add-ins for Visual Basic that allow you to store and manage COM components. In fact, the VB6 version includes a sample component library that can be used as a starting point for your own component-based projects.

Within the OLAP context, Meta Data Services is frequently used to store information on *data lineage*; that is, where the data has come from originally. This is particularly helpful when working with multiple source databases because it can otherwise be hard to keep track of which data comes from each source.

Meta Data Services is also used by Analysis Services in SQL Server 2000 to store much of the cube and database metadata, including the data sources, structure and properties of cubes, and so on. In Analysis Services, the metadata can be stored either separately in an Access database called msmdrep.mdb or within a SQL Server database itself. For more details, see the SQL Server Books Online documentation.

Data Access Components 2000

Microsoft has provided a fairly rich architecture that makes it easy for developers to directly access the database structure itself and get at the various components necessary to do their work (see Figure 22.6). The examples in this section use Visual Basic to demonstrate how to access the Analysis Services engine programmatically.

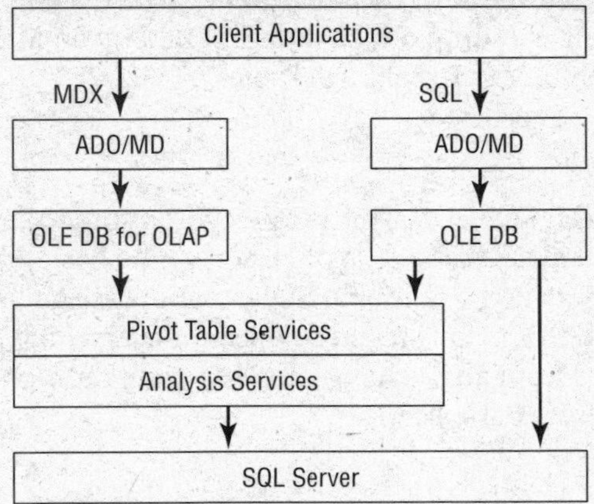

FIGURE 22.6: Tiers of the Microsoft data access component architecture related to OLAP

Read on for a brief overview of the role each of these architectural layers plays in promoting connectivity to OLAP cubes.

SQL

SQL, of course, stands for *Structured Query Language*. This is a standard, implemented by a wide variety of products, for retrieving information from a database. The problem with SQL, from our point of view, is that it is optimized for non-aggregated individual rows of data (found in relational databases). Although the dialect of SQL implemented by Microsoft SQL Server contains some multidimensional features (such as support for the CUBE and ROLLUP operators), it does not have any easy way to refer to the structure of a cube.

MDX

MDX stands for *Multidimensional Expressions*. MDX is a language, based on SQL, that is designed specifically for retrieving multidimensional information. Thus, it's optimized to gather the sort of information that one might like to retrieve from an Analysis Services cube.

MDX is at the heart of programmatic access to Analysis Services. Using MDX, you can produce pretty much any view of a cube, showing aggregations, comparisons between measures within a dimension, calculated measures, and so on. You can change the structure of a cube in terms of its presentation and even write back updated values into the cube or dimension you are viewing. SQL Server 2000 includes *MDX Builder*, a graphical tool that allows you to drag and drop dimensions to build up an MDX statement (in a similar manner to Excel PivotTables).

ADO

ADO stands for *ActiveX Data Objects*. This is Microsoft's core technology for providing object-oriented access to data of all sorts. The basic ADO library is optimized for executing traditional SQL statements against relational databases, but with extensions it can be used for everything from retrieving e-mail messages from an Exchange mailbox to updating the design of a table in an Access database.

TIP

For more information on ADO and ADO MD, see *Visual Basic Developer's Guide to ADO* by Mike Gunderloy (Sybex, 1999).

ADO MD

ADO MD is a set of extensions to ADO that allow COM-based applications to operate against a multidimensional source via the OLE DB for OLAP interfaces. ADO MD uses some of the existing ADO objects and collections but extends them with some additional new objects that you can use to query specific elements of the multidimensional structures.

Here's an example:

```
Dim cnn As New ADODB.Connection
Dim cat As New ADLMD.Catalog
DIM cub As ADOMD.CubeDef
DIM dmn As ADOMD.Dimension
```

```
cnn.Open "Provider=MSOLAP;Data Source=localhost;" & _
    "Initial Catalog=Foodmart 2000"
Set cat.ActiveConnection = cnn
Set cub = cat.CubeDefs("Sales")

For Each dmn In cub.Dimensions
    Debug.Print dmn.Name
Next dmn
```

NOTE

To run this code, you'll need to set references to the Microsoft ActiveX Data Objects 2.6 Library and the Microsoft ActiveX Data Objects (MultiDimensional) 2.5 Library within your Visual Basic project. The sample also assumes that you're running Visual Basic on the computer that also runs Analysis Services. If that's not the case, you'll need to change the name of the data source in the Open statement from "localhost" to the actual name of the computer that runs Analysis Services. This sample, like all the other code in the book, is available on the Sybex web site, `www.sybex.com`.

In this example, the code makes a connection to the Analysis Services database using an ADO connection object. Once the connection is activated, you can drill down into the cubes and dimensions using the relevant ADO MD objects. In this example, we simply print the names of each dimension, but we could do much more, as you'll see in Chapter 24.

Of course, you can also use ADO MD to execute MDX statements against Analysis Services. Rather than using an ADO recordset object, the ADO MD cellset object provides much better access to the potentially *n*-dimensional structure that could be returned as the result of a query. Here's an example:

```
Dim cst As New ADOMD.Cellset
Dim axs As ADOMD.Axis
Dim intI As Integer

With cst
    .ActiveConnection = "Provider=MSOLAP;" & _
     "Data Source=localhost;" & _
     "Initial Catalog=Foodmart 2000"
    .Source = "SELECT " & _
     "{[Measures].[Units Shipped]} ON COLUMNS," & _
     "NON EMPTY {[Store].[Store Name].MEMBERS} ON ROWS " & _
     "FROM Warehouse"
    .Open
End With
```

```
Set axs = cst.Axes(1)
For intI = 0 To axs.Positions.Count - 1
   Debug.Print axs.Positions(intI).Members(0).Caption & _
      " " & vbTab & cst(0, intI).Value
Next
```

This example opens a cellset that includes the total units shipped for each store in a cube named `Warehouse`. It then prints the results by iterating through the cellset. We'll discuss ADO MD in greater depth in Chapter 24, "Using ADO MD to Summarize Data."

OLE DB

OLE DB is a set of COM interfaces that sit underneath ADO. ADO translates the object-oriented syntax that it presents to client applications into procedural calls to the OLE DB interfaces. By using different software drivers, OLE DB can use identical interfaces for a wide variety of database and other data storage systems. When you're writing code in Visual Basic, you won't be working directly with OLE DB, but it's always there, translating your code so that it works with the ultimate data source.

OLE DB for OLAP

OLE DB for OLAP provides the extensions to OLE DB that are necessary for client applications to use the Analysis Services engine. OLE DB for OLAP provides a series of COM interfaces that can be utilized from within a separate component or application. Although it is possible to write applications that directly implement the OLE DB for OLAP interfaces, this interface is too low-level for any but the most sophisticated uses. Unless you're an Independent Software Vendor (ISV) writing a complex data mining tool that transfers large quantities of data in and out of the Analysis Services engine, you're better off using the object-oriented view of the data provided by ADO MD.

OLAP Support for SQL/ADO

Despite the fact that MDX, coupled with the multidimensional extensions to ADO, provides a querying language optimized for OLAP-based activities, it is still possible to use "traditional" techniques based around ADO. That's why Figure 22.6 shows a connection directly from OLE DB to the PivotTable service. In most cases, you'll be better off using ADO MD and MDX instead of ADO and SQL when working with multidimensional data, but you may occasionally want to use an ADO recordset to retrieve a single-dimensional view of OLAP data.

Using Analysis Services with Non-Microsoft Databases

Despite Microsoft's own aspirations, the vast majority of corporate data is not stored in SQL Server. There is a general perception within many companies (although this attitude is changing) that SQL Server is not capable of storing the volumes of data or handling the high levels of transaction throughput required. In the longer term, and as a result of recent substantive improvements to the engine and administrative tools, SQL Server may gain greater acceptance within the corporate world, but here and now data is stored on a broad mix of environments and databases.

Much of the data you might want to use as source material for your own OLAP solution may therefore reside in a completely different environment. Does that mean that the OLAP capabilities built into SQL Server are not sufficient for your OLAP tasks? By no means!

First, Analysis Services does not require SQL Server as its host database: It can also use Microsoft Access or Oracle (7.3.3 or later) to store multidimensional data. In fact, the demonstration database, Foodmart 2000, included with Analysis Services is stored in the Access format.

Second, it's rare to see a tool such as Analysis Services used directly against a production database system, even if the data is held in a separate database. More common is to create a separate environment for Analysis Services purposes and transfer the data from the production environment using a data extraction/transformation tool such as DTS. An obvious candidate database for this would be SQL Server since buying a license for Analysis Services entitles you to also use the parent database engine. So, it's possible to transfer your heterogeneous data to a single SQL Server database before analyzing it.

Finally, SQL Server 2000 itself includes connectivity to other databases. By using linked servers, you can cause data in other database systems to appear as native SQL Server data to other tools such as Analysis Services. So using the combination of SQL Server and Analysis Services allows you to build multidimensional cubes based on heterogeneous data.

Either way, Analysis Services operates well in a heterogeneous environment and is suitable for any environment where Windows client software can be used.

Summary

In this chapter, we've concentrated on describing the key concepts that prevail in Analysis Services:

- Measures, the values we want to be able to "slice and dice"
- Dimensions, the categories under which we wish to view our measures
- Levels, the hierarchy for an individual dimension
- Cubes, the domain of interest for a particular set of analysis

Additionally, we've learned about the various storage options that exist, including MOLAP, ROLAP, and HOLAP.

This chapter also introduced the basic building blocks of OLAP solutions in SQL Server 2000, including the various services and drivers that we'll use in the rest of the book.

Chapter 23

Using Analysis Services

Now that you've had the 30,000-foot view of Analysis Services and have probably started thinking about how to use it in your own organization, it's time to come down to earth. In this chapter, we'll open up the Analysis Services interface and see how to build a new cube and how to view the results. When you finish this chapter, you'll be prepared to build your own cubes and start performing multidimensional analysis. You'll also have seen the first of many ways in which Visual Basic can interact with Analysis Services.

Adapted from *SQL Server™ Developer's Guide to OLAP with Analysis Services* by Mike Gunderloy and Tim Sneath

ISBN 0-7821-2957-1 480 pages $49.99

CREATING AND CONNECTING A DATABASE

The first step in using Analysis Services is to launch the Analysis Manager (Start ➢ Programs ➢ Microsoft SQL Server ➢ Analysis Services ➢ Analysis Manager). *Analysis Manager* is a Microsoft Management Console (MMC) snap-in, just like SQL Server Enterprise Manager. Figure 23.1 shows the default Analysis Manager interface, with the treeview on the left expanded to show some of the objects that Analysis Services installs as sample data.

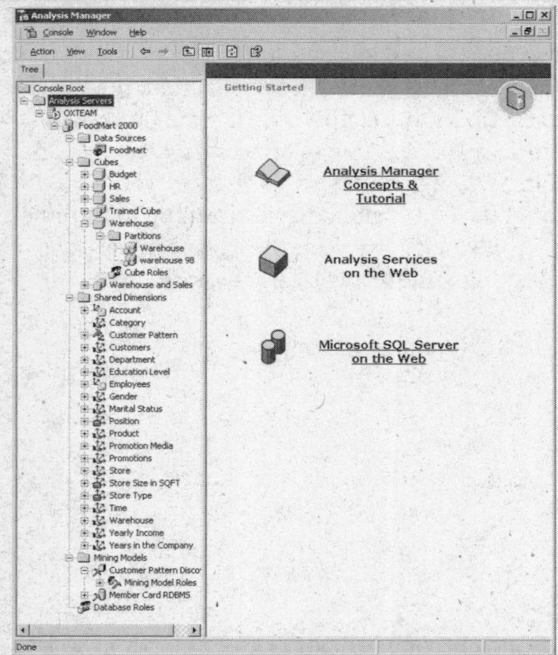

FIGURE 23.1: Analysis Manager

The next step is to create an Analysis Manager database and tell Analysis Services where the data in that database should come from. Don't confuse an Analysis Services database with a SQL Server database. Even if the data you want to analyze is stored in SQL Server, you still need to create a separate Analysis Services database to hold the metadata and aggregations that are specific to Analysis Services.

NOTE

For the examples in the first part of this chapter, we'll be using some sample website traffic log data, rather than the FoodMart 2000 data that ships with Analysis Services. That's because FoodMart 2000 is already installed, and we want to show you the full process. The traffic log data is included in the companion code, together with instructions on loading it to your own SQL Server if you'd like to follow the examples in this chapter.

To create a new Analysis Services database, follow these steps:

1. Launch Analysis Manager and expand the treeview to show the server where you want the database to reside.
2. Right-click the server node and choose New Database. You'll be prompted for a database name and (optional) database description. We'll call our database for this chapter BookSamples.
3. Click OK. Analysis Services will create the new database.

After you've created a new database, you'll need to tell Analysis Services where to find the data for that database. To do that, follow these steps:

1. Expand the BookSamples database in the Analysis Manager treeview to show its child nodes.
2. Right-click the Data Sources folder and choose New Data Source. This will open the Data Link Properties dialog box.
3. Select an appropriate OLE DB provider and fill in the required data. For our sample SQL Server database, we've used the Microsoft OLE DB Provider for SQL Server. For the sample data, you'll need to enter the server name, BookSamples as the database name, and your username and password if you're not using Windows Integrated authentication.
3. Click OK to use the specified database as the data source for this Analysis Services database.

If you expand the Data Sources folder in Analysis Manager, you can click the data source and see the metadata information that Analysis Services has stored for the server, as shown in Figure 23.2 (here, OXTEAM is the name of our test server).

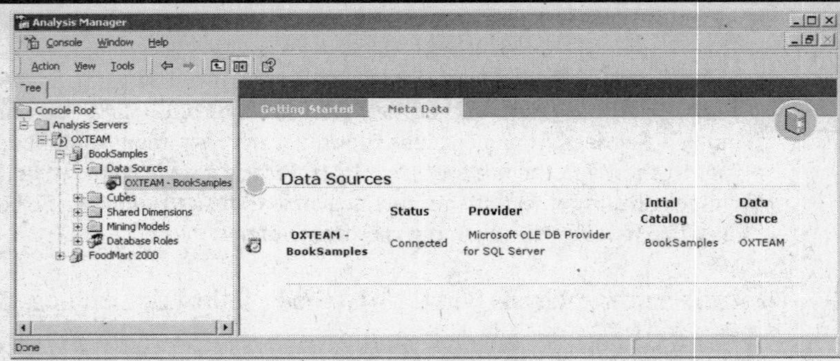

FIGURE 23.2: Data Sources in Analysis Manager

TIP

You can add multiple data sources to a single Analysis Services database. However, a single cube can only have one data source. The exception is a cube that's split over multiple partitions. In that case, each partition can have a different data source, as long as each data source contains fact and dimension tables with the same structure.

Although the Data Link Properties dialog box will show you all of the OLE DB drivers on your computer, Analysis Services is limited to using only a few source database types:

- SQL Server 6.5 or later
- Microsoft Access 97 or later
- Oracle 7.3 or 8.0

If you try to use another OLE DB provider, Analysis Services will let you link to the data, but it will give you an error message when you try to actually build a cube. To use a different data source, you should use Data Transformation Services to first migrate the data into a SQL Server Data Mart.

CREATING A CUBE

Once you've created your Analysis Services database and connected it to a data source, you're ready to begin creating cubes. In this section, we'll demonstrate the Cube Wizard, which walks you through the cube creation process step-by-step. There's also a Cube Editor, which allows you to build cubes without using the wizard and to modify existing cubes.

Figure 23.3 shows the schema of the tables that we'll be using in this section. As you can see, this database is set up with a relatively small star schema. There is a single fact table (tblWeblog) and three dimension tables (tblClientIP, tblUserAgent, and tblURL).

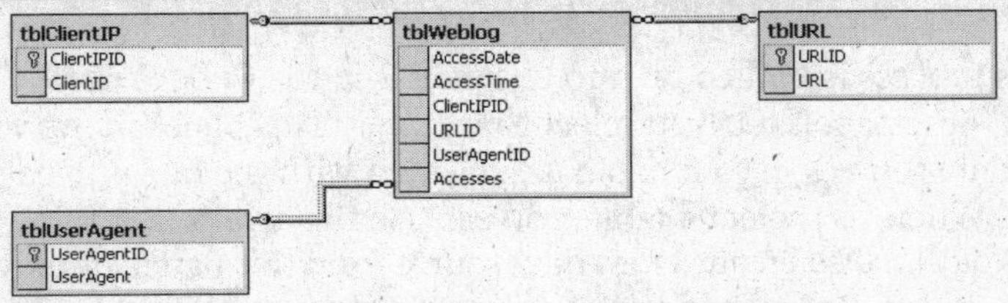

FIGURE 23.3: The Weblog tables in the sample database

To begin the process of creating a cube with the wizard, right-click the Cubes folder in the Analysis Services database and choose New Cube ➢ Wizard. This will launch the Cube Wizard, shown in Figure 23.4. Like most wizards, the Cube Wizard starts with a panel that explains the purpose of the wizard, together with a check box to suppress this panel in the future.

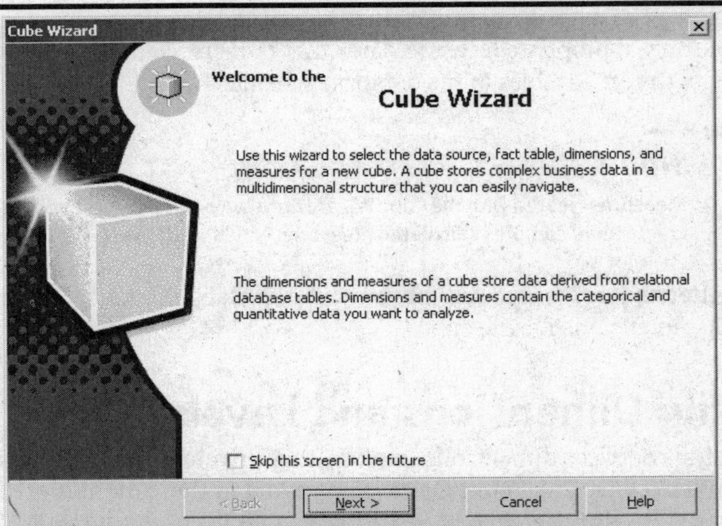

FIGURE 23.4: Introductory panel of the Cube Wizard

Click Next on this panel to proceed with creating measures for your cube.

Creating Measures

Creating measures for a cube is a two-step process:

1. Select the fact table for the cube.
2. Select the columns that define the measures.

This process is broken up into two panels in the Cube Wizard. The first of these panels lets you select a fact table. This panel shows you all of the data sources in your database, together with the tables in each data source. When you select a table, you can see the columns within that table. You can also create a new data source from this panel, or browse the data in a table. Browsing the data will show you up to 1000 rows from the table so you can determine whether it's an appropriate table to use as a fact table.

In our sample cube, we want to use tblWeblog as the fact table. It's easy to see this from the database diagram in Figure 23.3; the fact table is nearly always the central table in a star schema.

After you select a table and click Next, the Cube Wizard presents a panel to allow you to choose the measures in your cube. This panel shows you all of the numeric columns in the selected fact table and lets you choose one or more of them to be measures. In our sample data, the Accesses column is the only appropriate measure. The other numeric columns are foreign keys to the other tables in the database schema.

TIP

Measures created with the Cube Wizard are always simple additive measures. To create more complex calculated measures, you'll need to use the Cube Editor.

After choosing measures for your cube, click Next to proceed with creating dimensions for the cube.

Creating Dimensions and Levels

Analysis Services dimensions can be either private to a cube or shared between cubes. The Select Dimensions panel in the Cube Wizard thus opens with a list of shared dimensions within the current Analysis Services database. You can select any or all of these to be dimensions in the new cube that you're creating.

Of course, the first time you create a cube in a particular database, there won't be any shared dimensions for you to choose. In this case, your only option is to click New Dimension to launch the Dimension Wizard.

The Dimension Wizard includes these panels:

Introductory panel This panel explains the use of the wizard. You can choose to suppress this panel on subsequent uses of the wizard.

Dimension Type panel In this chapter, we'll limit our cube to using star schema dimensions. There are four other choices (Snowflake Schema, Parent-Child, Virtual Dimension, and Mining Model).

In some cases, each dimension table is not related to the fact table, so you would use the snowflake schema instead. A snowflake schema allows you to select a set of tables that together contain the information for a single dimension.

Parent-Child dimensions are used to capture data that's hierarchical in nature. Typically, this type of data can be represented in a relational database with a self-join. A table of employees, for example, might include a field for the employee ID of the employee's boss, which would relate back to a different record in the same employees table. In this schema, instead of storing each path separately, the paths are stored in a hierarchy.

A *virtual dimension* is a dimension that's based on a member property in a shared dimension.

A mining model dimension is created from a column of a mining model. In Analysis Services, data mining is based around a *data mining model*, which, conceptually, is very similar to a cube: It is a persistent data structure that Analysis Services constructs based on low-level data. Like a cube, a data mining model can be browsed to see the data and relationships that it contains.

Select Dimension Table panel If you've chosen a star schema dimension, you can only select a single table here. For example, in the sample database, we'll select the tblClientIP table. When you select a table, the wizard shows you the columns in this table. You can also browse up to a thousand rows of data in each table from this panel.

Select Levels panel In the case of the tblClientIP table, there's only a single level, represented in the ClientIP column. In some cases, you'll want to choose multiple levels here. For example, a denormalized Address table might contain columns for Country, Region, and Postal Code, which would lead to a hierarchy of three levels on this panel.

Specify Member Key Column panel In most cases, you can leave the columns you selected as levels to be the member keys. However, if the data in those columns is not unique, you'll need to provide an alternate key column on this panel.

Select Advanced Options panel We'll discuss these options in the next chapter. For now, you can just leave them untouched.

Finish Panel This panel, shown in Figure 23.5, lets you assign a name to the dimension, preview the data in the dimension, and decide whether the dimension should be shared with other cubes.

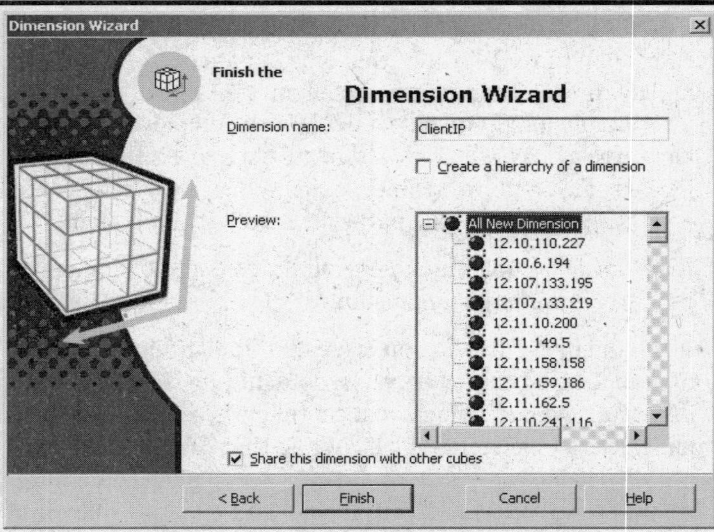

FIGURE 23.5: Finish panel of the Dimension Wizard

When you've clicked Finish in the Dimension Wizard, you'll be returned to the Cube Wizard. Here, you can create more dimensions or proceed. For our example, we'll start by creating three dimensions, one for each of the dimension tables in the star schema:

- ClientIP, from tblClientIP

- URL, from tblURL
- UserAgent, from tblUserAgent

You might think that exhausts the possibilities for dimensions in this case, because we've used up all of the dimension tables. However, if you look back at Figure 23.3, you'll see that the fact table itself contains two fields that are useful as dimensions: AccessDate and AccessTime. It's not unusual to find dimensions, particularly date and time dimensions, stored in the fact table. This is often the case where there are not many duplicate values in the dimension, as typically happens with time columns. In such a case there's nothing to be gained from splitting the dimension off to a separate table.

Having a dimension stored in the fact table is not a problem for Analysis Services. Simply create a new dimension and select the fact table as the dimension table. If you do this with tblWeblog in the sample database, you'll find that you get an extra panel in the wizard after choosing the dimension table. Figure 23.6 shows the Select Dimension Type panel. The wizard will present this panel whenever it detects any date or time columns in the selected dimension table.

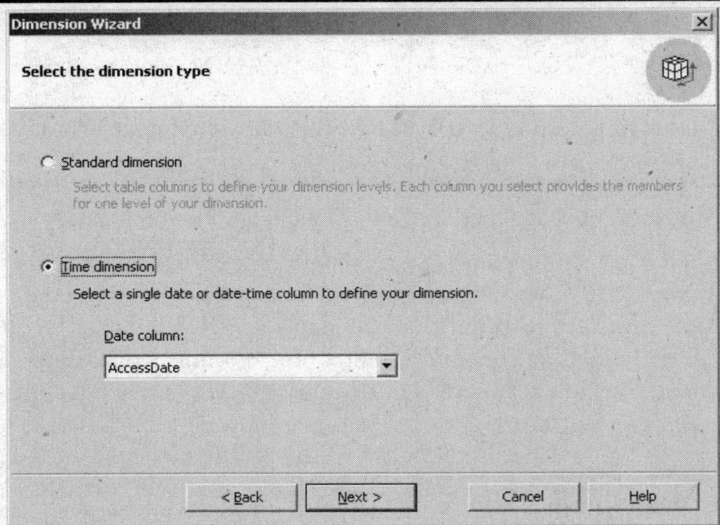

FIGURE 23.6: Select Dimension Type panel of the Dimension Wizard

If you select a datetime field as a dimension, the next panel you see will be the Create Time Dimension Levels panel, shown in Figure 23.7.

Often, what you'll want to do with a datetime column is sort records into groups based on natural units of time (weeks, months, years, and so on). Analysis Services is smart enough to do this sorting for you, as long as you decide what levels you want to use for grouping.

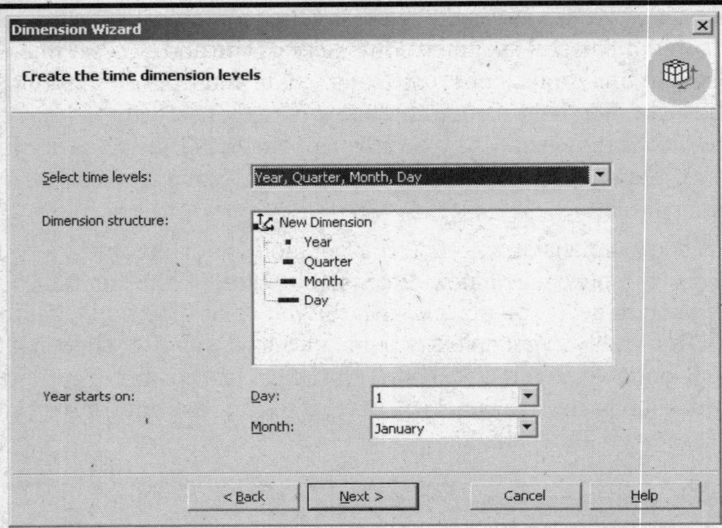

FIGURE 23.7: Create Time Dimension Levels panel of the Dimension Wizard

For our sample cube, we'll create two time dimensions:

- AccessDate, grouped by Year, Quarter, Month, Day
- AccessTime, grouped by Year, Month, Day, Hour, Minute

When you're done creating dimensions, click Next to move to the Finish panel of the Cube Wizard. Analysis Manager will offer to count the fact table rows at this point; you can skip this if you'd rather postpone that potentially time-consuming step until the cube is processed. Assign a name to the cube (we named our sample Weblog) and click Finish to exit the Cube Wizard.

WARNING

If you do skip the row-counting step, you need to open the cube in the Cube Editor and resave it before processing. Otherwise, you'll get an error telling you that the object structure is not valid when you attempt to process the cube.

Setting Storage Options

When you exit the Cube Wizard, Analysis Services will automatically load your new cube into the Cube Editor. This allows you to fine-tune any of the choices you made in the Cube Wizard. For now, you might just like to note that the fact and dimension tables are automatically joined according to the relationships that were present in the source database.

To proceed with this initial cube, close the Cube Editor (either with the Close button or with the File ➢ Exit menu item). This will bring up a dialog box with the prompt, "You must design storage options and process the cube to query it. Do you want to set the data storage options now?" You can postpone setting data storage options, but you must do this before you can use the cube. So generally, it's a good idea to answer "Yes" to this prompt, which will open the Storage Design Wizard.

After the introductory panel, the Storage Design Wizard will prompt you to select the type of data storage. Here's a brief review of the possible choices:

- MOLAP stores both the data and the aggregations in the multidimensional Analysis Services database. This choice takes the most disk space, but will also give the best performance for browsing the cube.
- ROLAP stores the data and the aggregations in the relational database that is the source of the cube. ROLAP takes less space than MOLAP, but may result in performance degradation. If you're using a SQL Server 2000 data source, you can also enable real-time updates for a ROLAP cube, which allows the cube to present up-to-date information without reprocessing.
- HOLAP stores the data in the relational database and the aggregations in the multidimensional database. HOLAP represents a compromise between MOLAP and ROLAP for both storage space and performance.

After you select a storage type (we chose MOLAP storage for the sample, because there is so little data that disk space really isn't a consideration here), the Storage Design Wizard will move to the Set aggregation options panel, shown in Figure 23.8. As you can see in the figure, the Next button on this panel is initially disabled. That's because you must tell the wizard what aggregation options to use before proceeding.

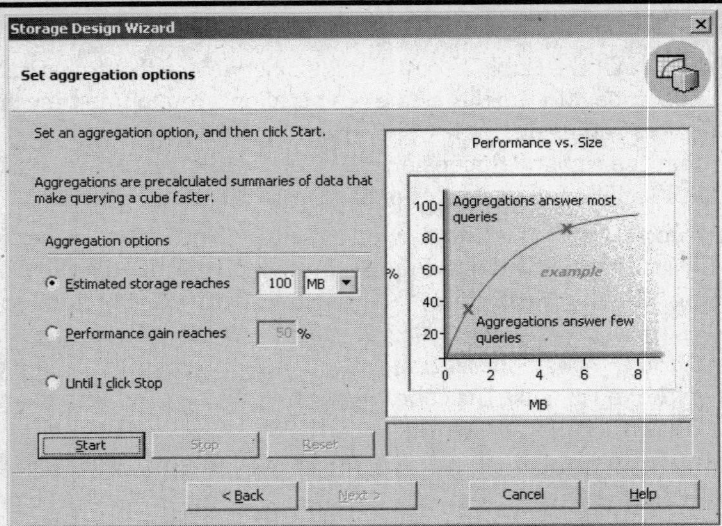

FIGURE 23.8: Setting aggregation options in the Storage Design Wizard

Choosing aggregation options offers you another tradeoff between storage space and processing speed. Suppose you have a cube that includes several dimensions. If Analysis Services were to calculate the totals for every combination of those dimensions when you created the cube, then it could answer any query almost instantly. On the other hand, the storage space to store all those precalculated aggregations might be immense. So the goal is to figure out how many aggregations to calculate in advance to be able to answer queries quickly without taking up too much storage space.

Rather than making you make decisions about individual aggregations, Analysis Services offers three ways for you to tell it when to stop calculating:

- You can select a maximum amount of storage to use for the aggregations.
- You can specify the percentage of performance improvement that you want the aggregations to provide.
- You can watch the graph on this page and click the Stop button when you're satisfied with the combination of storage space and performance improvement that it shows.

When you've selected one of these options, click Start. When the Storage Design Wizard is done determining which aggregations it should create, you'll be able to click Next to move to the final panel of the Storage Design Wizard.

Processing the Cube

The final step in creating a cube is to process the cube. Processing is the time that Analysis Services uses to create the precalculated aggregations. Because this can take a long while to finish, the final panel of the Storage Design Wizard offers you the choice between processing the new cube immediately and saving it to process later.

TIP

If you choose to save a cube without processing it, you can process it later by right-clicking the cube in the Analysis Manager interface and choosing Process.

When Analysis Services processes a cube, it will continually update a dialog box showing its progress. Figure 23.9 shows this dialog box for our sample Weblog cube.

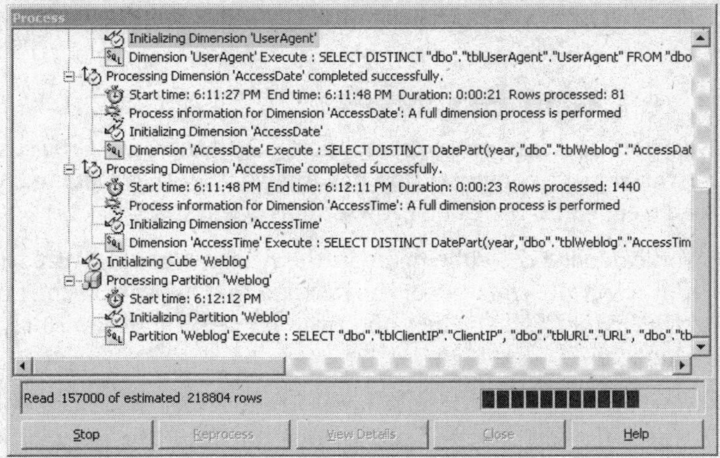

FIGURE 23.9: Processing a cube

BROWSING A CUBE

After you've created a cube, you can use its data. In the next chapter, you'll see how to interact programmatically with Analysis Services. For now, though, we'd like to show you a few ways to manually view data from an Analysis Services cube:

- Using the Cube Browser

- Using Excel
- Using Visual Basic
- Using a web browser
- Using Knosys ProClarity
- Using Hungry Dog IntelliBrowser
- Using Cognos PowerPlay

In this section, we'll use the FoodMart 2000 sample data to demonstrate the various browsing alternatives. That way, you can follow along even if you didn't create the new Weblog cube from the first part of this chapter.

PowerPlay, ProClarity, and IntelliBrowser are examples of third-party OLAP clients. Because the Analysis Services API is well-documented, it's possible for anyone to write an application that displays Analysis Services data. We've chosen these three applications as a representative sample of the many that are on the market.

Using the Cube Browser

Analysis Services ships with a component called the *Cube Browser*. If you're working at a computer that has Analysis Services installed, you can load a cube into the Cube Browser in two ways:

- You can click the cube name in the Analysis Manager treeview and select the Data tab of the taskpad that appears in the main MMC panel to host the Cube Browser directly in the Analysis Manager.
- You can right-click the cube name in the Analysis Manager treeview and select Browse Data to open the Cube Browser in a separate window.

Figure 23.10 shows the default view of the Sales cube from the FoodMart 2000 sample database in a stand-alone Cube Browser window.

The Cube Browser interface displays quite a bit of information. (That's because a cube is a complex structure.) Microsoft's designers have done an excellent job of allowing the user to manipulate a cube within the constraints of a two-dimensional interface.

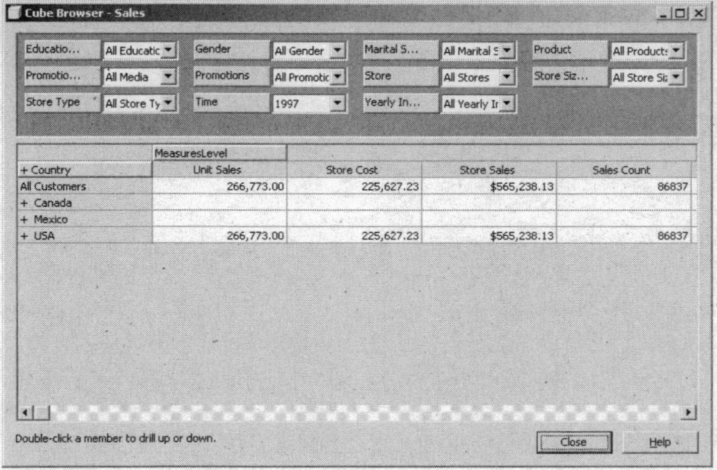

FIGURE 23.10: The Cube Browser

Turn your attention first to the grid in the lower part of the Cube Browser. This is where you can see dimensions and measures that you are actively working with. In the default view of the Sales cube shown in Figure 23.10, only one dimension is displayed: the Country dimension, which occupies the leftmost column of the grid. The other columns of the grid are taken up with the measures in this cube: Unit Sales, Store Cost, and so on. The result is a grid that shows all of the measures broken down by the top level in the Country dimension. For example, the Store Sales for all records from stores in the USA totals $565,238.13.

You can expand and contract the levels within a dimension by double-clicking them. For example, you can expand the Country dimension to the StateProvince level for all measures and then suppress the StateProvince breakdown for Mexico by following these two steps:

1. Double-click the `+ Country` label to expand all of the countries to show the StateProvince column.
2. Double-click the `– Mexico` cell to collapse the StateProvince detail for Mexico to a single `Mexico Total` row.

Figure 23.11 shows the results of these actions. The Cube Browser still shows all the measures broken down by various elements in the Country dimension.

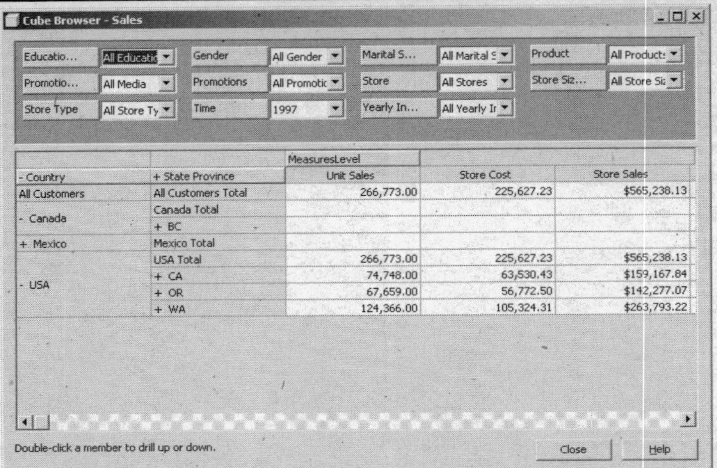

FIGURE 23.11: Modifying the display of a dimension in the Cube Browser

The Sales cube in the FoodMart 2000 sample database has a dozen dimensions: the eleven dimensions that are displayed above the grid, plus the Customers dimension, which supplies the grid rows. The Cube Browser wouldn't be very useful if you could only view the data broken down by a single dimension. Fortunately, the Cube Browser allows you to choose dimensions in a flexible manner. It's easy to add a new dimension to the grid, or to replace an existing dimension with a new one.

For example, to see a count of sales broken down by education, gender, and marital status, follow these steps (starting with the Cube Browser as shown in Figure 23.11):

1. Drag the button (not the combo box) for the Education dimension from the upper part of the Cube Browser to the lower part and drop it directly on top of the `- Country` button to replace the Country dimension with the Education dimension. You'll know you're in the right place to drop the dimension when the cursor shows a picture containing a two-headed arrow.

2. Drag the button (not the combo box) for the Gender dimension from the upper part of the Cube Browser to the lower part and drop it directly on top of the `MeasuresLevel` button to replace the Measures with the Gender dimension.

3. Drag the button (not the combo box) for the Marital Status dimension from the upper part of the Cube Browser to the lower part and drop it beside the `Gender` button. You'll know you're in the right place when the cursor does not show a two-headed arrow.

4. Select Sales Count in the Measures combo box in the upper part of the Cube Browser.

The result of following these steps is shown in Figure 23.12. Note that we've used the horizontal scroll bar to move sideways in the grid. The rows of the grid show the various education levels in the data; the columns are broken down first by gender and then by marital status; and the numbers in the white portion of the grid are the Sales Count measure values. For example, single females with a bachelor's degree were responsible for 5,418 sales.

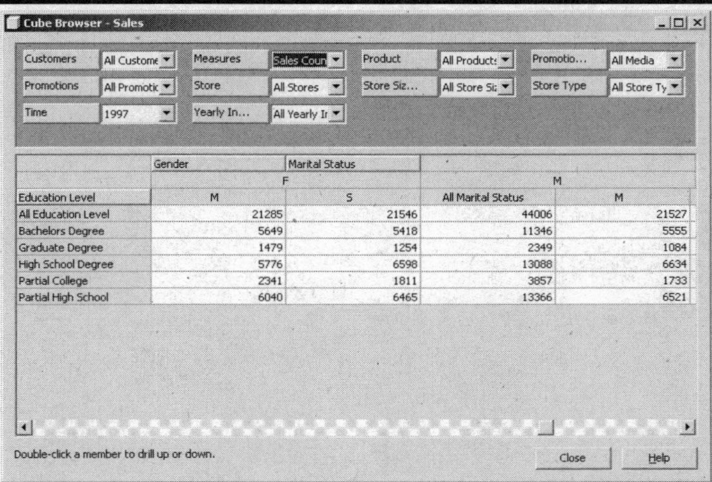

	Gender	Marital Status		
	F		M	
Education Level	M	S	All Marital Status	M
All Education Level	21285	21546	44006	21527
Bachelors Degree	5649	5418	11346	5555
Graduate Degree	1479	1254	2349	1084
High School Degree	5776	6598	13088	6634
Partial College	2341	1811	3857	1733
Partial High School	6040	6465	13366	6521

FIGURE 23.12: The Sales cube sliced by a different set of dimensions

The activities we've performed on the Sales cube thus far (choosing different combinations of dimensions and measures) are sometimes referred to as "slicing," because each combination represents a different slice through the *n*-dimensional data in the cube. You can also use the Cube Browser to perform "dicing," that is, selecting a filtered subset of the data.

Suppose, for example, you want to see what the buying patterns look like only in the data for California. To filter the existing Cube Browser view to show only the totals for California, follow these steps:

1. Click the drop-down arrow for the Store dimension in the upper part of the Cube Browser.
2. Click the + sign next to `All Stores` to expand the list of countries.
3. Click the + sign next to `USA` to expand the list of states.
4. Click `CA` to filter the records to include only records for California.

Figure 23.13 shows the process of choosing to filter data in the Cube Browser. When you complete the operation, the combo box for Store will show CA, the value that's being used for filtering.

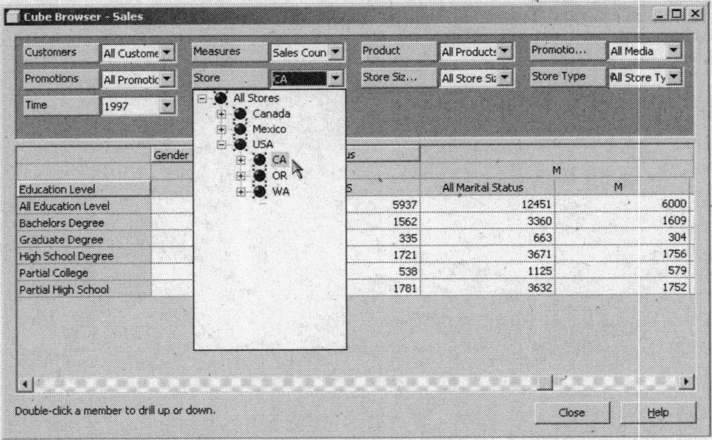

FIGURE 23.13: Filtering records in the Cube Browser

Finally, if a cube supports drillthrough, you can use the Cube Browser to view the original source data behind an aggregation. *Drillthrough* is a process in which Analysis Services retrieves the source data that was used to produce an aggregation from the cube's data source. The data is joined according to the joins in the cube's schema and presented as a simple recordset. To drillthrough in the Cube Browser, right-click any white cell and choose Drillthrough. Figure 23.14 shows some drillthrough data from the Sales cube.

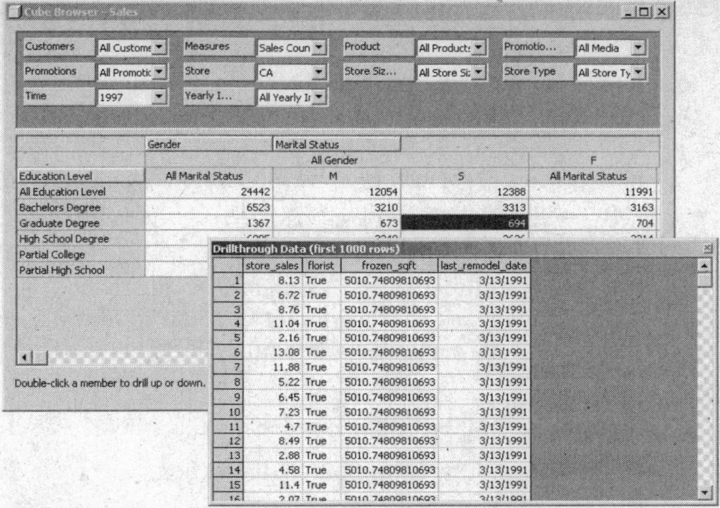

FIGURE 23.14: Cube with drillthrough data

Using Excel

Of course, the Cube Browser is not the only application that can display data from an Analysis Services cube. (That's a good thing, because the Cube Browser only works on computers where you've installed Analysis Services.) Perhaps the easiest client in widespread use is Microsoft Excel. You can connect Excel 2000 directly to cube data by using an Excel PivotTable.

To display the FoodMart 2000 Sales cube as an Excel PivotTable, follow these steps:

1. Launch Excel 2000 and open a new worksheet.
2. Select Data ➢ PivotTable and PivotChart Report from the Excel menus.
3. In the first step of the PivotTable and PivotChart Wizard, choose External Data Source as the source of your data, and PivotTable as the type of report that you wish to create. Click Next.
4. In the second step of the PivotTable and PivotChart Wizard, click Get Data. This will open the Choose Data Source dialog box.

5. Click the OLAP Cubes tab of the Choose Data Source dialog box. Select <New Data Source> and click OK.
6. In the Create New Data Source dialog box, enter a name for your data source and choose Microsoft OLE DB Provider for Olap Services 8.0 as the OLAP provider to use. Click the Connect button. Depending on the software that's installed on your computer, you may also see a driver for an older version of the Olap OLE DB provider.
7. In the Multidimensional Connection dialog box, select Analysis Server as the location of the data source and enter the name of the computer where Analysis Services is running. Click Next.
8. Select the FoodMart 2000 database. Click Finish.
9. In the Create New Data Source dialog box, select the Sales cube. Click OK.
10. In the Choose Data Source dialog box, select the data source that you just created (the one that you named in step 6). Click OK.
11. In the PivotTable and PivotChart Wizard, click Next.
12. In step 3 of the PivotTable and PivotChart Wizard, choose whether you would like the PivotTable in a new worksheet or an existing worksheet, and click Finish.

Figure 23.15 shows the results of following these steps: a blank PivotTable. Although this doesn't look like much, you've now made all the connections necessary to work with the Sales cube data from within Excel.

To fill in the skeleton of an Excel 2000 PivotTable, drag fields from the list at the bottom of the PivotTable toolbar (this area is sometimes called "*the well*") and drop them at the indicated spots in the skeleton of the PivotTable. Although the terminology is different from that of the Cube Browser, the idea is the same:

- You can drag dimensions to the Drop Row Fields Here and Drop Column Fields Here areas. These become the basis for the slice of the cube to be displayed.
- You can also drag dimensions to the Drop Page Fields Here area. Dimensions in this area provide a drop-down interface to filter the displayed data.

- You can drag measures to the Drop Data Items Here area. If you're in doubt as to whether something is a dimension or a measure, you can look at the little icon to the left side of the well. It will show you the areas where you can drop this field.

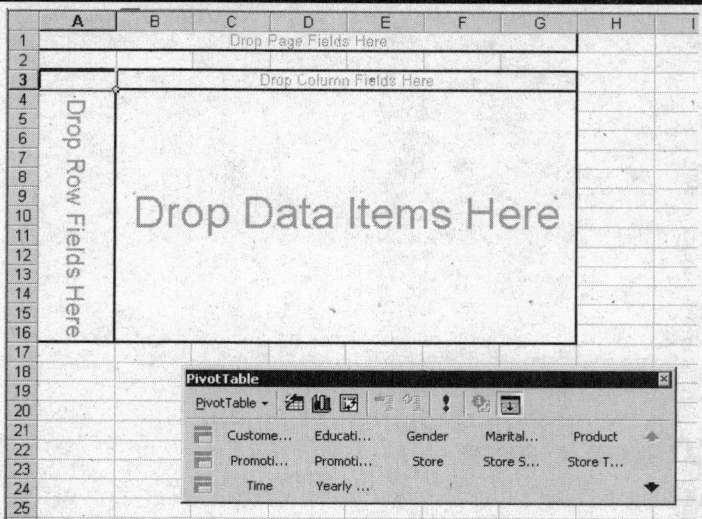

FIGURE 23.15: Blank Excel 2000 PivotTable connected to an Analysis Services cube

Excel will let you drag fields back and forth and rearrange them, so you get the same sort of interactive analysis that you can achieve with the Cube Browser. You can also right-click the PivotTable and choose PivotChart to create a bar graph from the data. Figure 23.16 shows a PivotChart of Store Cost and Profit, sliced by education, gender, and marital status, for stores in California.

TIP

Excel PivotCharts and PivotTables can display data from multiple measures at the same time, even when you're slicing by more than one dimension, unlike the Cube Browser.

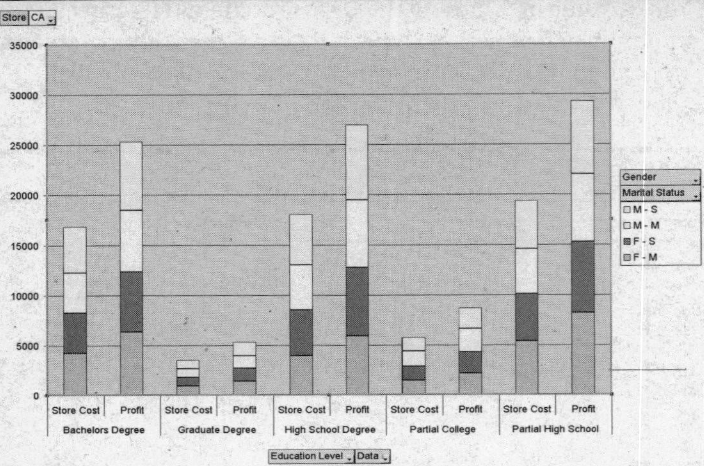

FIGURE 23.16: An Excel PivotChart based on an Analysis Services cube

Using Visual Basic

Visual Basic 6.0 does not display the same tight integration with Analysis Services that Excel 2000 displays. That's because Visual Basic 6.0 came out well before SQL Server 2000 did. Nevertheless, if you just want a quick look at Analysis Services data on a Visual Basic form, it's pretty easy. Follow these steps for an example:

1. Launch Visual Basic and create a new standard EXE project.
2. Use Ctrl+T to open the Components dialog and add the Microsoft ADO Data Control 6.0 and Microsoft DataGrid Control 6.0 to the project.
3. Add an ADO Data Control and a DataGrid Control to the default form in the project.
4. Set the ADO Data Control's ConnectionString property to

   ```
   Provider=MSOLAP;Integrated Security=SSPI;
   ➥Data Source=localhost;Initial Catalog=FoodMart 2000
   ```

   If your Analysis Server is on a different computer than the one where you're running the Visual Basic project, change localhost to the name of that computer.

5. Set the ADO Data Control's RecordSource property to

```
SELECT
[Education Level].MEMBERS ON ROWS,
{[Measures].[Unit Sales]} ON COLUMNS
FROM Sales
```

6. Set the DataGrid control's DataSource property to the name of the ADO Data Control (by default, Adodc1).

7. Run the project.

Figure 23.17 shows the result of running this simple Visual Basic project.

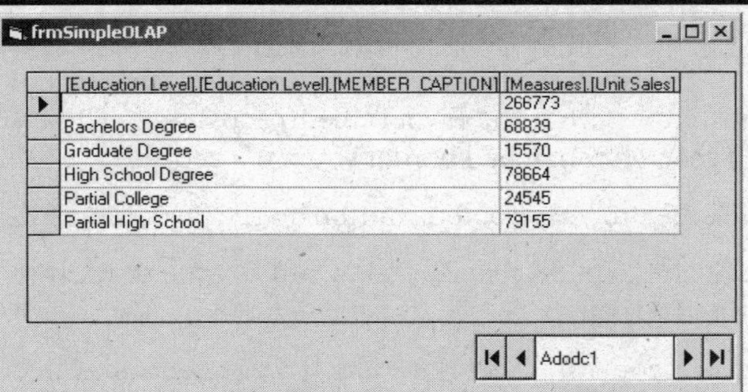

frmSimpleOLAP
[Education Level].[Education Level].[MEMBER_CAPTION]
[Measures].[Unit Sales]
266773
Bachelors Degree
68839
Graduate Degree
15570
High School Degree
78664
Partial College
24545
Partial High School
79155
Adodc1

FIGURE 23.17: Analysis Services data in Visual Basic

The RecordSource property that you entered in step 4 is an example of a *Multidimensional Expression* (*MDX*), Analysis Server's extension to SQL to allow access to multidimensional data.

NOTE

This example shows how easy it is to establish a connection between Visual Basic and Analysis Services. You may also want to investigate the SimpleOLAP sample that installs as part of Analysis Services. You'll find it in the `Program Files\Microsoft Analysis Services\Samples\VbAdoSimple` folder on your hard drive.

Using a Web Browser

Of course, these days the user interface of choice for many organizations is the web browser. You can display Analysis Services data directly in a web browser if you choose. The main problem is that there's no good cross-browser way to do this. However, if you're working in a Microsoft-centric organization, the Office Web Components offer a PivotTable control that can display data from an Analysis Services cube. As you'll see, this control is reminiscent of the Excel PivotTable, although there are some differences.

We'll demonstrate the creation of a web page using the PivotTable control with Microsoft FrontPage 2000. To display Analysis Services data in your web browser, follow these steps:

1. Open FrontPage and create a new web page.
2. Select Insert ➢ Component ➢ Office PivotTable from the FrontPage menus. This will place a blank PivotTable on your web page.
3. Click once within the PivotTable to activate it. The control will get a crosshatched border when it's activated.
4. Click the Property Toolbox button on the PivotTable toolbar.
5. Click the expand icon for the Data Source section in the Property Toolbox.
6. Set the control to get data using a connection. Click the Connection Editor button to open the Data Link Properties dialog box.
7. On the Provider tab of the Data Link Properties dialog box, choose the Microsoft OLE DB Provider for OLAP Services.
8. On the Connection tab of the Data Link Properties dialog box, enter the name of your Analysis Server as the Location of the data, and enter appropriate security information. Select FoodMart 2000 as the initial catalog to use. Click OK to dismiss the Data Link Properties dialog box.
9. Select Sales as the Data Member in the PivotTable Property Toolbox.
10. Click the Field List toolbar button in the PivotTable control. This will open a list of all the measures and dimensions in the Sales cube. Figure 23.18 shows this stage in the design process.

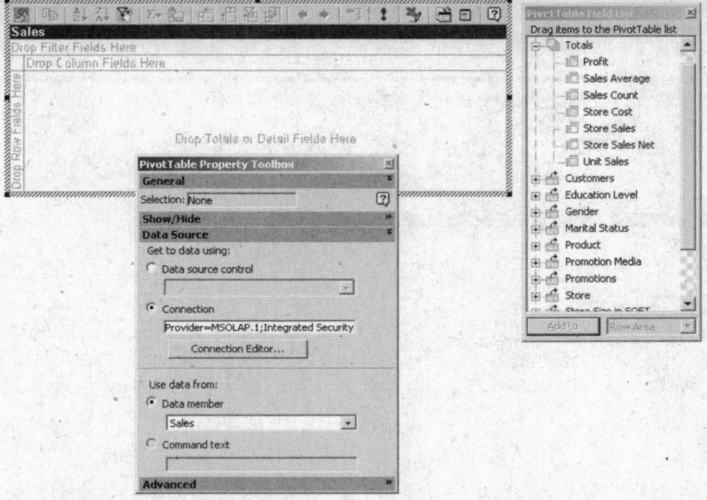

FIGURE 23.18: Designing a web page using the PivotTable control

11. You can drag and drop fields from the PivotTable Field List to the PivotTable control, just as you can drag and drop fields from the well to the PivotTable in Excel. Drag the Sales Count field to the data area.

12. Drag the Education Level dimension to the Row Fields area.

13. Drag the Gender dimension to the Column Fields area.

14. Drag the Product dimension to the Filter Fields area.

15. Save the web page and open it in a web browser.

Figure 23.19 shows the completed page open in Internet Explorer. Note that the web page is interactive. Internet Explorer automatically displays the Field List, and the user can drag and drop, rearrange fields, and filter the data, just as they could in Excel 2000.

Although the completed web page is flexible and easy to use for anyone with Excel experience, this is probably only a solution for users on an intranet, rather than on the wider Internet. There are two problems with using the Office Web Controls to display data. The first is that they won't work in all browsers, so if you're not in control of the browser version, you can't guarantee that the viewer of the page will actually see the data. The second problem is licensing. To use the Office Web Controls, you must have a valid Office 2000 license on the viewing computer. There is currently no supported, legal way to redistribute these controls.

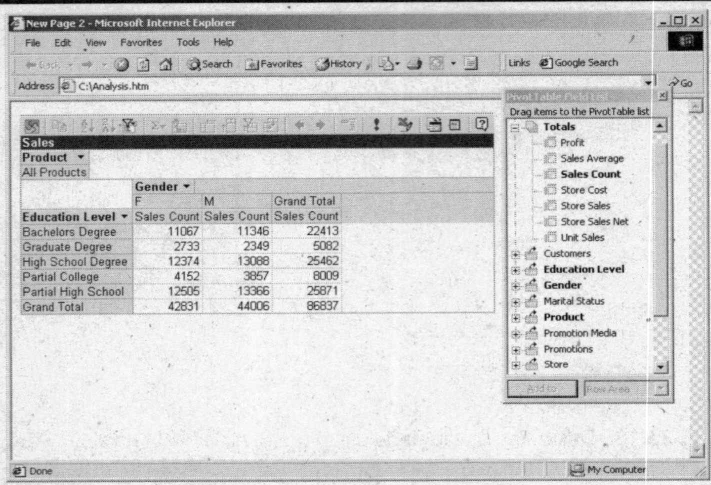

FIGURE 23.19: Data from Analysis Services in a web browser

PARTITIONED CUBES, LINKED CUBES, AND VIRTUAL CUBES

So far, we've only used what are sometimes called regular cubes. Analysis Services supports other varieties of cubes. In particular, you should be familiar with these three types of cubes:

Partitioned cubes Use different storage modes for subsets of data within a single cube.

Linked cubes Are based on data stored on a different Analysis Services server.

Virtual cubes Are combinations of regular cubes in a larger logical cube.

In this section, you'll learn the basics of creating and working with these types of cubes.

NOTE

In addition to regular, partitioned, linked, and virtual cubes, you'll also run across references to local cubes, real-time cubes, and write-enabled cubes. *Local cubes* are disk files created and maintained by Microsoft Excel that can be used as the basis for PivotTables; we won't cover them in this book. *Real-time cubes* provide an up-to-date view of the source data. A real-time cube uses ROLAP storage, and whenever the data in the underlying relational database changes, the aggregates are updated without forcing the cube to be placed offline for processing. *Write-enabled cubes* allow you to write data back to the cube. Changes can be written to the cube's data—but the original fact table is never modified. Rather, the changes are stored in a separate table defined by the cube's developer.

Partitioned Cubes

Cubes are stored by Analysis Services in units called *partitions*. When you create a new cube, Analysis Services automatically creates a default partition for the cube and stores the data for the cube in this partition. You can see the partition structure of any cube by expanding that cube in the Analysis Manager treeview and inspecting the contents of its Partitions folder.

If you're running the Enterprise Edition of Analysis Services, you can distribute the data in a single cube over multiple partitions. Multiple partitions give you finer control over the storage of the cube's data than a single partition allows. For example,

- You can store part of the data on the same Analysis Server that stores the cube (a *local partition*) or on another Analysis Server (a *remote partition*).
- You can choose between MOLAP, ROLAP, and HOLAP storage on a partition-by-partition basis.
- You can devote more or less space to aggregations on a partition-by-partition basis

All of these decisions are completely transparent to the end user who is browsing the data stored in a cube. The cube always appears as one large dataset, no matter how many partitions it uses.

The sample Sales cube that ships as part of the FoodMart 2000 database contains only sales data for 1997. If you open the underlying Access 2000 database, you'll discover that the database also includes data for 1998 sales. This data is in a second fact table that has the same structure as the 1997 fact table.

Suppose you were responsible for this cube and had just gotten the 1998 data to update the cube. You might want to add the 1998 data, while at the same time minimizing the space occupied by the 1997 data. To do this, you can adjust the storage options for the 1997 data and then add the 1998 data as an additional partition. To perform these tasks, follow these steps:

WARNING

You can only follow this entire sequence of steps if you have installed the Enterprise Edition of Analysis Services.

1. Expand the treeview of the Sales cube until you can see the default Sales partition. This is where the 1997 data is stored.
2. Right-click the Sales partition and choose Design Storage. This will open the Storage Design Wizard. Click Next to skip past the introductory panel if it's displayed.
3. Inspect the aggregations that already exist for this partition, select Replace the Existing Aggregations, and click Next.
4. Select HOLAP as the data storage type and click Next.
5. Select Performance Gain Reaches 10% and click Start. Click Next when the wizard has finished designing aggregations.
6. Choose to process the aggregations and click Finish to exit the Storage Design Wizard. When Analysis Services has finished processing the partition, click Close to dismiss the dialog box.
7. Right-click the Partitions folder and select New Partition to launch the Partition Wizard.
8. Click Next to skip the introductory panel of the Partition Wizard.
9. The Specify Data Source and Fact Table will default to showing the data source and fact table that are used by the default partition of the cube. We'll use a different fact table from the same data source for the second partition of the cube. Click Change and select `sales_fact_1998` as the fact table for this partition. Click Next.
10. You can optionally select to store just part of a cube on a partition. We're going to store all of the dimensions on the new partition, so just click Next to move on.

11. The next panel will give you the choice of creating a local or remote partition. If you have a second Analysis Server on your network, you can choose to create a remote partition here. Whether the partition is local or remote will not affect the behavior of the cube. Click Next after you've made your selection.
12. Name the new partition `Sales 1998`, choose to design the partitions now, and click Finish. This will launch the Storage Design Wizard. Click Next to skip the introductory panel for the Storage Design Wizard if it's displayed.
13. Select MOLAP as the type of the new partition.
14. Choose to create aggregations until the performance gain reaches 50 percent. Click Start to create the aggregations. Note that these aggregations will take much more space than those you created for the existing partition.
15. Click Next, choose to process the cube immediately, and click Finish.

Figure 23.20 shows the resulting partition information within Analysis Manager. The green color for the Sales partition indicates that it is the default partition for this cube. If you browse the data for the full Sales cube, you'll find that it's impossible to tell from the user interface which partition is responsible for a particular aggregation.

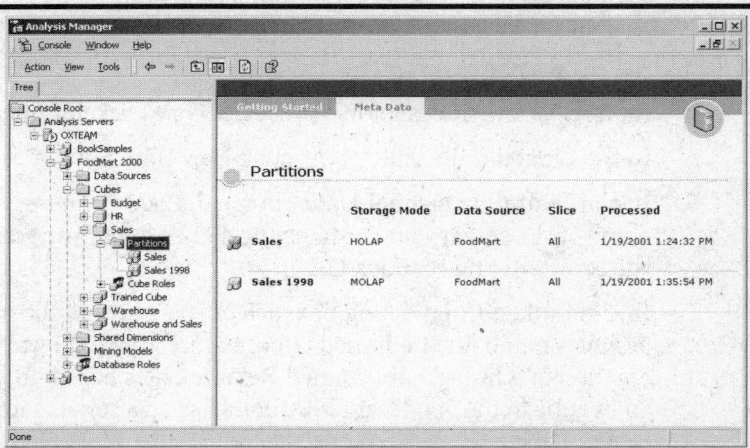

FIGURE 23.20: Partition information for the Sales cube

Linked Cubes

It's possible for a cube to get all of its data from a cube stored on a different Analysis Server. This is referred to as a *linked cube*. In other words, the cube named Sales on Server1 might actually be stored as a cube named SalesCurrent on Server2.

NOTE

Linked cubes are only available in the Enterprise Edition of Analysis Services.

Why might you want to create a linked cube? Here are some reasons:

- The cube can be more easily available to users who log on to different servers, without the overhead of storing the data on all the servers.
- Security can be implemented so that the source data of the cube is protected but the aggregations are available more widely.
- A cube can be maintained and updated by a single group in your company and made widely available to users who can't modify it, even by accident.

If you happen to have multiple installations of Analysis Server available, creating linked cubes is simple. Follow these steps:

1. In Analysis Manager, navigate to the Cubes folder of the database where you wish to create the linked cube. This is the database where the new linked cube will be available, not the database containing the existing cube.
2. Right-click the Cubes folder and select New Linked Cube.
3. In the Linked Cube dialog box, click New Data Source.
4. In the Multidimensional Data Source dialog box, enter the name of the server that contains the source cube, and select the source database. Click OK.
5. In the Linked Cube dialog box, select the source cube and assign a name for the linked cube. Figure 23.21 shows the creation of a linked cube named Remote Sales based on the Sales cube in the FoodMart 2000 database on a server named STALLION.

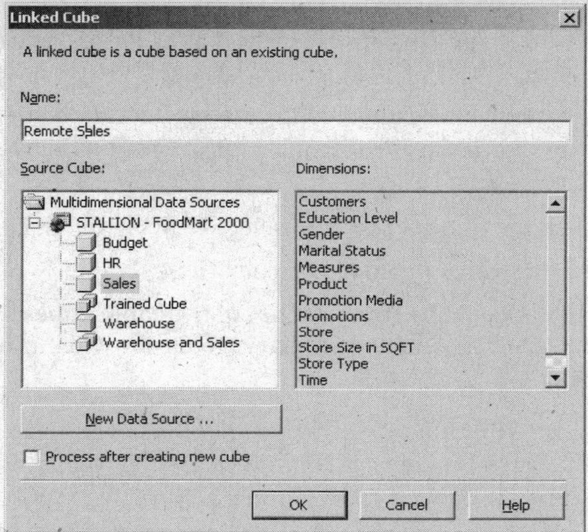

FIGURE 23.21: Creating a linked cube

6. Click OK to create the linked cube.
7. In the Analysis Manager treeview, right-click the new linked cube and select Process.
8. In the Process a Cube dialog box, select Full Process and click OK.
9. Close the Process dialog box when Analysis Services has finished processing the cube.

You'll find that you can now browse the data in the linked cube just as if it were located on the server where you created the link.

Virtual Cubes

A *virtual cube* consists of one or more measures and one or more dimensions from one or more regular or linked cubes. There are generally two reasons why you might want to create a virtual cube. The first is to combine the data from several cubes into a set of data that can be browsed all at once. For example, if you had separate cubes for 1997 sales, 1998 sales, and 1999 sales, you could use a virtual cube to represent all of the data on sales from 1997 through 1999. Second, a virtual cube can hide excess detail from some users. For example, you might have a cube with eight dimensions of which only three interest the bulk of your users. You could create a virtual cube that uses only those three dimensions.

Virtual cubes do not store their own data, so there is very little overhead to creating a virtual cube compared to creating another regular cube to display the same data. To create a virtual cube in the FoodMart 2000 database, follow these steps:

1. Right-click the Cubes folder and select New Virtual Cube.
2. Read the introductory panel and click Next.
3. Select the Sales cube from the list of available cubes and move it to the list of cubes that the virtual cube will include. Click Next.
4. Select the Store Sales measure and click Next.
5. Select the Store, Product, and Store Size in SQFT dimensions and click Next.
6. Name the virtual cube MiniSales. Select Process Now and click Finish.
7. When Analysis Manager is done processing the cube, close the Process dialog box. Processing the cube should be very fast because Analysis Manager can extract all of the necessary information from the existing Sales cube.

Figure 23.22 shows the MiniSales cube in the Cube Browser. Note how much less confusing this virtual cube is compared to the full Sales cube.

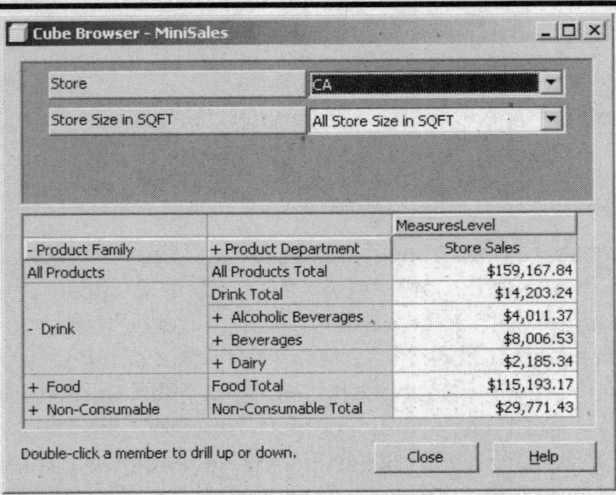

FIGURE 23.22: Browsing a virtual cube

Updating a Cube

One of the problems that any Analysis Services administrator faces is that of keeping cubes up-to-date when their source data changes. From the user interface, it's as simple as right-clicking the cube, choosing Process, and selecting the type of processing to do:

- The *Incremental Update* option adds any new data from the data source to the cube and recalculates the affected aggregations.
- The *Refresh Data* option clears and reloads all of the data in the cube and then recalculates the aggregations.
- The *Full Process* option completely rebuilds the entire cube, just as if you had deleted and recreated it from scratch.

Manually processing a cube, though, is not an attractive option for routine use. More typically an administrator will want to reprocess a cube on a regular basis as a scheduled job. You can use SQL Server 2000 Data Transformation Services (DTS) to accomplish this.

To create a DTS job to process an Analysis Services cube, follow these steps:

1. Launch SQL Server 2000 Enterprise Manager.
2. Navigate to the Data Transformation Services folder of the server that hosts your Analysis Server.
3. Right-click the Data Transformation Services folder and select New Package.
4. From the DTS Package menu, choose Task ➢ Analysis Services Processing Task.
5. Expand the treeview to show the cube you wish to process.
6. Select the type of processing to perform. Figure 23.23 shows the Sales cube being selected for Refresh Data processing.
7. Assign a name and description to the task and click OK to add it to the DTS package.
8. Save the DTS package to the local SQL Server.
9. Close the DTS package and navigate to the Local Packages node of the SQL Server Enterprise Manager treeview.

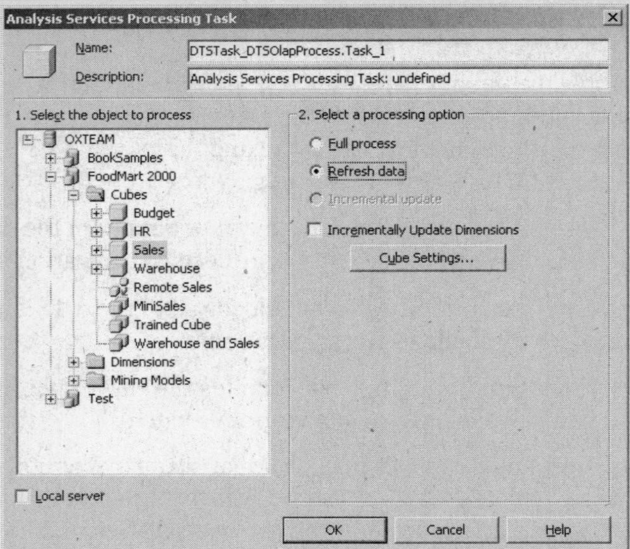

FIGURE 23.23: Creating a DTS task to process an Analysis Services cube

10. Right-click the DTS package and choose Schedule Package. This will open the SQL Server recurring job schedule dialog box, which offers flexible options for executing the package on a regular basis.

In most cases you would create the Analysis Services Processing Task as part of a larger DTS package that actually collects new source data. For example, a DTS package might use a Transform Data task to move data from an OLTP database to a data warehouse, followed by one or more Analysis Services Processing Tasks to update the cubes that depend on that data.

SUMMARY

In this chapter, you've learned the basic skills that you'll need to deal with Analysis Services from the Analysis Manager user interface. You now know how to create cubes and how to browse cubes. We also discussed some varieties of cubes other than regular cubes and showed how you can use Data Transformation Services to keep a cube up-to-date.

In the next chapter, we'll dig into the data by using ADO to retrieve and work with the OLAP data you've built.

Chapter 24

Using ADO MD to Summarize Data

As you learned in earlier chapters, ADO is the set of COM objects used to work with data from within applications. ADO is designed to be extensible—that is, you can load multiple libraries, each of which adds some objects designed to work with the core ADO objects. This chapter covers one of those libraries, the *ActiveX Data Objects (Multidimensional)*, or *ADO MD*, library.

This library provides objects that are designed to help you work with both the schema and data provided by multidimensional data sources. In this chapter, I'll dig into the basics of multidimensional data, especially as provided by the new Microsoft OLAP Server, and then show how you can use the ADO MD objects to work with this data.

Adapted from *Visual Basic® Developer's Guide to ADO*
by Mike Gunderloy
ISBN 0-7821-2556-5 480 pages $39.99

NOTE

This chapter was written for SQL Server 7.0. In SQL Server 2000, OLAP Server is replaced by Analysis Services. Any of the code for this chapter will work in both versions.

Basics of Multidimensional Data

Here, I'll explore the basics of multidimensional data. First, I'll take a quick look at the basic concept and explain what distinguishes multidimensional data from the relational data you're probably more familiar with. Then, I'll introduce Microsoft OLAP Server (formerly code-named "Plato") and show you how it helps slice and dice your data. Finally, I'll review the basic objects in the ADO MD object model. If you're anxious to work with ADO MD in Visual Basic code and are already familiar with multidimensional data, you might want to skip ahead to the next section.

NOTE

For more about multidimensional data and OLAP vs. OLTP, refer to Chapter 21, "OLAP and Data Mining Concepts."

Understanding Multidimensional Data

So what's this "multidimensional" thing all about, anyhow? It's about summarizing masses of data in a way that makes sense to human beings. Given, say, 500,000 individual sales receipts, how do you find patterns in them? Normally, the answer is that you summarize the data by looking for similarities and counting noses. Each way of summarizing the data amounts to a *dimension*.

Grouping queries give you a means to summarize along a single dimension. For example, you might use a GROUP BY clause in a query to determine what proportion of the sales for the last year were from stores in the US, as opposed to stores in Canada or Mexico. In this case, "location" would be the dimension of interest and the field to group by.

If you're familiar with Microsoft Access, you know about crosstab queries, which let you summarize data along two dimensions at once. For example, you could use a crosstab to answer the question "What were the sales in stores in the US, Canada, and Mexico during 1997 and 1998?" The crosstab query takes two dimensions (location and time, in this case) and populates a grid with some summary measure for all combinations of those dimensions.

What multidimensional data does is extend this concept to more than two dimensions. For example, you might define dimensions of Yearly Income, Marital Status, and Education Level, and ask what sales came from low-income families where the buyer was married and had a high school degree—as opposed to all other combinations of those three factors. Figure 24.1 shows an application (the Cube Browser that ships with Microsoft OLAP Server) displaying the results of just such a multidimensional query.

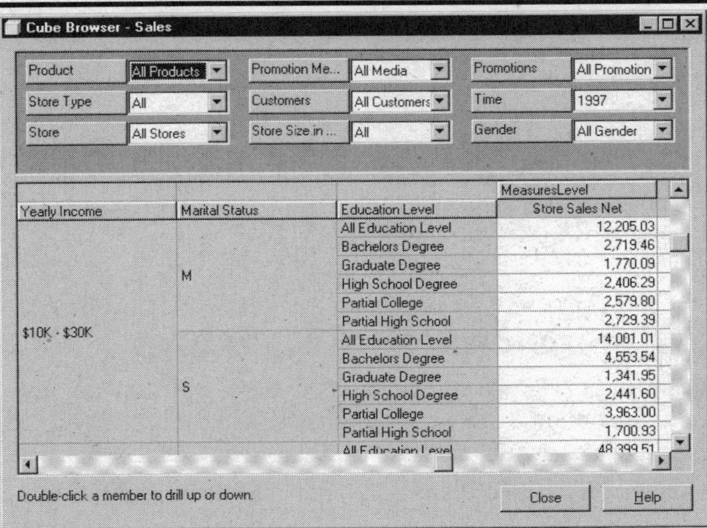

FIGURE 24.1: Multidimensional data

Introduction to Microsoft OLAP Server

Although there are many sources of multidimensional data available, the examples in this chapter work with Microsoft OLAP Server. This server ships with SQL Server, although you need to run a separate installation program to get it up and running on your system. The sample project for this chapter is configured to assume that you've got Microsoft OLAP Server running on the same computer as both SQL Server and Visual Basic. As always, you may need to modify the connection strings in the samples if your configuration is different.

WARNING

In the samples, the server name is BEAVER. Although the Microsoft SQL Server OLE DB provider recognizes "(local)" as a valid name for the SQL Server running on the local machine, the Microsoft OLAP Server OLE DB provider does not.

To get started, I'll review the basic terminology and concepts used by Microsoft OLAP Server. I'll also briefly discuss the Microsoft OLAP Manager, which is a Microsoft Management Console (MMC) application that provides access to data from Microsoft OLAP Server.

NOTE

ADO MD is based on the OLE DB for OLAP specification, which Microsoft is developing as a somewhat open standard. For information on other companies supporting this standard, see `http://www.microsoft.com/data/oledb/olap/indsupp.htm`.

Cubes, Dimensions, and Measures

The basic unit of storage and analysis in Microsoft OLAP Services is the *cube*. Cubes contain dimensions and measures. Dimensions come from dimension tables, while measures come from fact tables.

A dimension table contains relational data that you'd like to summarize by. For example, you might have a clients table, which you could group by Country, State, and City, or an inventory table, where you might want to group detail information by Year, Month, Week, and Day of sale.

A single cube can have multiple dimensions, each based on one or more dimension tables. A dimension represents a category for analyzing business data: geographical region or time in the previous examples. Typically, a dimension has a natural hierarchy so that lower results can be "rolled up" into higher results: cities aggregated into states, or state totals into country totals. Each type of summary that can be retrieved from a single dimension is called a *level*, so you speak of a city level or a state level in a geographic dimension.

A fact table contains the basic information that you wish to summarize. This might be order detail information, payroll records, stock prices, or anything else that's amenable to summing and averaging. Any table that has supplied a field to a Sum or Avg function in a totals query is a good candidate for a fact table.

A cube must contain at least one measure, based on a column in a fact table (or a calculated expression), that you'd like to analyze. Cubes can also contain multiple measures. For example, a cube containing stock price information might use high, low, and close as measures. This cube could let you look at, say, the average closing price for three stocks over five years.

Of course, fact tables and dimension tables must be related—hardly surprising, given that you use the dimension tables to group information from the fact table. There are two basic OLAP schemas for relating these tables. In a *star schema*, every dimension table is related directly to the fact table. In a *snowflake schema*, some dimension tables are related indirectly to the fact table. For example, if your cube includes tblOrderDetails as a fact table, with tblCustomers and tblOrders as dimension tables, and tblCustomers is related to tblOrders, which in turn is related to tblOrderDetails, then you're dealing with a snowflake schema.

Microsoft OLAP Manager

Installing Microsoft OLAP Server also installs Microsoft OLAP Manager. Just like SQL Enterprise Manager (and the Windows 2000 administrative tools), this application runs within the confines of the MMC, a plug-in-oriented application that uses a TreeView to represent and manage hierarchical objects. Figure 24.2 shows Microsoft OLAP Manager at work. In this case, I've drilled down to the Sales cube in the FoodMart sample database that ships as part of Microsoft OLAP Server.

Explaining the Microsoft OLAP Manager in-depth is beyond the scope of this chapter. Fortunately, the designers did an excellent job of making it nearly intuitive to use. When you first launch the Manager, it displays a hyperlinked "Getting Started" page that will walk you through a basic tutorial. And, although it includes an editor for complex operations, you'll find that the built-in wizards will do almost any task for you. If you right-click the Cubes folder beneath a database name and choose New Cube ➢ Wizard, it will walk you through the process of using a series of wizards to build, store, and process your data:

- Cube Wizard

- Dimension Wizard
- Storage Design Wizard

You can also right-click a cube and choose "Browse Data" to see the information stored in the cube. This will open the Cube Browser application that you saw in Figure 24.1.

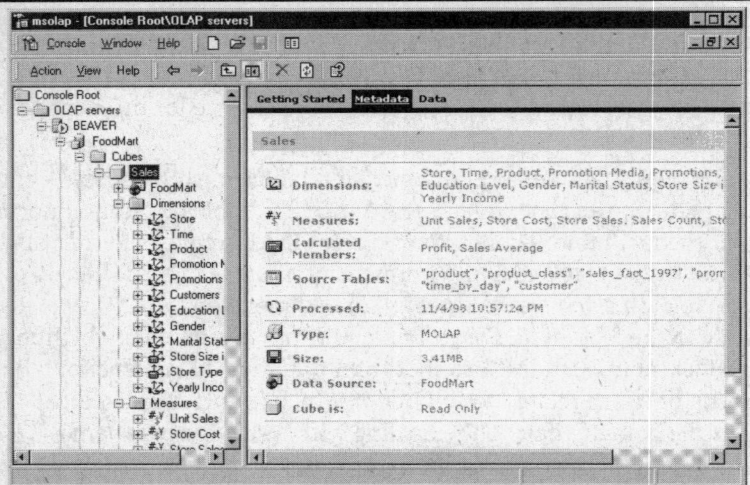

FIGURE 24.2: Microsoft OLAP Manager

NOTE

In SQL Server 2000, the OLAP Manager tool is known as *Analysis Manager*.

ADO MD Objects

Although ADO MD is an extension to regular ADO, it actually defines more objects than ADO itself does! That's because it includes objects to model both the schema and the data of multidimensional data sources. Figure 24.3 shows the ADO MD object model.

Here, I'll examine each object briefly, describe its relation to what you can see in the Microsoft OLAP Manager (the sample multidimensional provider I'm using), and show you its use in Visual Basic code. This isn't meant to be an exhaustive reference. If you want to see all the methods and properties of the ADO MD objects, refer to the Microsoft ADO MD Programmer's Reference, part of the Platform SDK.

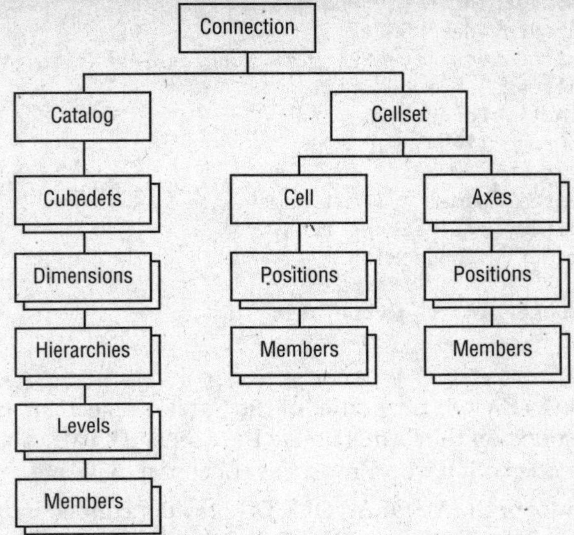

FIGURE 24.3: ADO MD object model

Schema Objects

The *schema objects* in the ADO MD object model are used for retrieving design information about the particular multidimensional data source you're retrieving data from. You can't get to any of the actual data from these objects. You also can't create any new objects by manipulating the ADO MD schema objects. These objects are limited strictly to retrieving information on existing objects.

Catalog

The *Catalog object* represents schema information for a single multidimensional database. This object isn't very interesting, but it's necessary as the way to get to all the other schema objects. You can experiment with the Catalog object by clicking the Catalog button on the frmObjects form in the ADOMDSamples sample project. This runs the following code:

```
Private Sub cmdCatalog_Click()

    Dim cnn As New ADODB.Connection
    Dim cat As New ADOMD.Catalog
    Dim prp As ADODB.Property
```

```
        Screen.MousePointer = vbHourglass
        cnn.Open "Provider=MSOLAP.1; " & _
         "Integrated Security=SSPI;Data Source=BEAVER;" & _
         "Initial Catalog=FoodMart;"
        Set cat.ActiveConnection = cnn
        With lboProperties
            .Clear
            .AddItem "Name: " & cat.Name
            .AddItem "ActiveConnection: " & _
             cat.ActiveConnection
        End With
        Screen.MousePointer = vbDefault

    End Sub
```

This code retrieves the two properties of the Catalog object and displays them in a list box on the form. (Unlike the other ADO MD objects, the Catalog object does not have a Properties collection to iterate.)

Note the similarity of the MSOLAP OLE DB provider connection string to the string used by the SQL Server OLE DB provider. Here, the Data Source parameter names the OLAP server to use and the Initial Catalog parameter names the database to investigate.

You'll see also that this code sets the mouse pointer to the hourglass while the connection is being made. Retrieving schema information from the Microsoft OLAP Server via ADO MD is quite slow.

If you like, you can connect to an OLAP catalog without explicitly using an ADO Connection object:

```
    cat.ActiveConnecton = "Provider=MSOLAP.1; " & _
         "Integrated Security=SSPI;Data Source=BEAVER;" & _
         "Initial Catalog=FoodMart;"
```

CubeDef

The *CubeDef object* represents a single cube from a multidimensional data source. The Catalog object contains a collection of CubeDef objects that you can iterate using For Next or For Each syntax. When you retrieve an individual CubeDef, you can inspect its properties, as in this sample code from the frmObjects form in the ADOMDSamples project:

```
    Private Sub cmdCubeDef_Click()

        Dim cat As New ADOMD.Catalog
        Dim cdf As ADOMD.CubeDef
        Dim prp As ADODB.Property
```

```
        Screen.MousePointer = vbHourglass
        cat.ActiveConnection = "Provider=MSOLAP.1; " & _
         "Integrated Security=SSPI;Data Source=BEAVER;" & _
         "Initial Catalog=FoodMart;"
        Set cdf = cat.CubeDefs(0)
        With lboProperties
            .Clear
            .AddItem "Name: " & cdf.Name
            .AddItem "Description: " & cdf.Description
            For Each prp In cdf.Properties
                .AddItem prp.Name & ": " & prp.Value
            Next prp
        End With
        Screen.MousePointer = vbDefault

    End Sub
```

Table 24.1 lists some of the properties of the CubeDef object. The properties are all provider-supplied properties from the MSOLAP provider; that is, they might or might not be present, depending on the OLE DB provider used to initialize the cube. As you can see in the previous source code, there are also some properties (Name and Description) that are intrinsic to the object and are not included in the Properties collection.

TABLE 24.1: CubeDef Properties from the MSOLAP Provider

Property	Description
CATALOG_NAME	Name of the parent Catalog object. Note that this substitutes for a more standard Parent property.
LAST_SCHEMA_UPDATE	Date and time of the last design change to this cube.
LAST_DATA_UPDATE	Date and time of the last data change to this cube.
CUBE_NAME	Name of the cube.
DESCRIPTION	Readable description of the cube.

The CubeDef object provides two intrinsic properties regardless of the provider used: Name and Description. These will not necessarily match the provider-supplied properties. For instance, with the MSOLAP provider, `CubeDef.Properties("DESCRIPTION")` may return Null while `CubeDef.Description` returns an empty string.

The CubeDef object has no methods.

Dimension

The *Dimension object* represents a dimension within a cube. A dimension is a single way of summarizing data—for example, by geographic location. The Dimension button on the frmObjects form in the ADOMDSamples project calls code that instantiates a Dimension object and then retrieves its properties:

```
Private Sub cmdDimension_Click()

    Dim cat As New ADOMD.Catalog
    Dim dmn As ADOMD.Dimension
    Dim prp As ADODB.Property

    Screen.MousePointer = vbHourglass
    cat.ActiveConnection = "Provider=MSOLAP.1; " & _
     "Integrated Security=SSPI;Data Source=BEAVER;" & _
     "Initial Catalog=FoodMart;"
    Set dmn = cat.CubeDefs(0).Dimensions(0)
    With lboProperties
        .Clear
        .AddItem "Name: " & dmn.Name
        .AddItem "UniqueName: " & dmn.UniqueName
        .AddItem "Description: " & dmn.Description
        For Each prp In dmn.Properties
            .AddItem prp.Name & ": " & prp.Value
        Next prp
    End With
    Screen.MousePointer = vbDefault

End Sub
```

As with the other ADO MD objects, the Dimension object has both intrinsic properties (supplied by ADO MD itself) and provider-supplied properties (supplied, in this case, by the MSOLAP provider). Table 24.2 shows some of the properties for a Dimension object. The Type column in this table contains "I" for intrinsic properties and "P" for provider-supplied properties. Note that the intrinsic properties do *not* show up when you iterate through the Properties collection; you must retrieve them specifically by name.

TABLE 24.2: Selected Properties of the Dimension Object

Property	Type	Description
Name	I	Name of the dimension.
Description	I	Description of this dimension (can be empty).

TABLE 24.2 continued: Selected Properties of the Dimension Object

PROPERTY	TYPE	DESCRIPTION
UniqueName	I	Unambiguous name for the dimension. Since you can have, for example, a Dimension and a Level with the same name, this property provides a way to disambiguate the two in code.
CATALOG_NAME	P	Name of the owning Catalog object.
CUBE_NAME	P	Name of the parent CubeDef object.
DIMENSION_CAPTION	P	Value to be used to identify this dimension to human beings.
DIMENSION_ORDINAL	P	Number of this dimension among all the dimensions in the cube. Note that this will not necessarily be its place in the Dimensions collection.
DIMENSION_CARDINALITY	P	Number of unique values at the most detailed level of drilldown in this dimension.

Hierarchy

The *Hierarchy object* represents a way in which a dimension can be summarized or "rolled up." Each Dimension object has a collection of Hierarchy objects (the Hierarchies collection), one of which is identified as being the highest level of rollup. You can retrieve the properties of a Hierarchy object with code similar to this code from behind the Hierarchy button on the frmObjects form in the ADOMDSamples project:

```
Private Sub cmdHierarchy_Click()

    Dim cat As New ADOMD.Catalog
    Dim hrc As ADOMD.Hierarchy
    Dim prp As ADODB.Property

    Screen.MousePointer = vbHourglass
    cat.ActiveConnection = "Provider=MSOLAP.1; " & _
     "Integrated Security=SSPI;Data Source=BEAVER;" & _
     "Initial Catalog=FoodMart;"
    Set hrc = cat.CubeDefs(0).Dimensions(0).Hierarchies(0)
    With lboProperties
        .Clear
        .AddItem "Name: " & hrc.Name
        .AddItem "UniqueName: " & hrc.UniqueName
        .AddItem "Description: " & hrc.Description
        For Each prp In hrc.Properties
```

```
            .AddItem prp.Name & ": " & prp.Value
        Next prp
    End With
    Screen.MousePointer = vbDefault

End Sub
```

Table 24.3 lists some of the properties of a Hierarchy object supplied by the MSOLAP provider. Once again, the properties are identified as to whether they are intrinsic or provider supplied.

TABLE 24.3: Selected Properties of the Hierarchy Object

Property	Type	Description
Name	I	Name of the hierarchy.
Description	I	Description of this hierarchy (can be empty).
UniqueName	I	Unambiguous name for the hierarchy.
CATALOG_NAME	P	Name of the owning Catalog object.
CUBE_NAME	P	Name of the parent CubeDef object.
HIERARCHY_CARDINALITY	P	Number of unique values in the bottom level of the hierarchy.
ALL_MEMBER	P	Name of the Hierarchy Member that includes the entire hierarchy in rolled-up fashion.

Level

The *Level object* represents a single part of a hierarchy—for example, the city information in a geographic level. By this time, the code for retrieving the properties of a Level object should come as no surprise. Note that ADO MD lends itself to long strings of nested hierarchical objects, unlike regular ADO:

```
Private Sub cmdLevel_Click()

    Dim cat As New ADOMD.Catalog
    Dim lvl As ADOMD.Level
    Dim prp As ADODB.Property

    Screen.MousePointer = vbHourglass
    cat.ActiveConnection = "Provider=MSOLAP.1; " & _
     "Integrated Security=SSPI;Data Source=BEAVER;" & _
     "Initial Catalog=FoodMart;"
    Set lvl = cat.CubeDefs(0).Dimensions(0). _
```

```
        Hierarchies(0).Levels(1)
    With lboProperties
        .Clear
        .AddItem "Caption: " & lvl.Caption
        .AddItem "Depth: " & lvl.Depth
        .AddItem "Name: " & lvl.Name
        .AddItem "UniqueName: " & lvl.UniqueName
        .AddItem "Description: " & lvl.Description
        For Each prp In lvl.Properties
            .AddItem prp.Name & ": " & prp.Value
        Next prp
    End With
    Screen.MousePointer = vbDefault

End Sub
```

Levels have more of the intrinsic type of properties than the other schema objects above them in the object model. Table 24.4 shows some of the properties of the Level object (when MSOLAP is used as the provider).

TABLE 24.4: Selected Properties of the Level Object

Property	Type	Description
Name	I	Name of the level.
Description	I	Description of the level (can be empty).
UniqueName	I	Unambiguous name for the level.
Caption	I	Label to use for this level.
Depth	I	Number of levels between this level and the top of the hierarchy.
CATALOG_NAME	P	Name of the owning Catalog object.
CUBE_NAME	P	Name of the parent CubeDef object.
LEVEL_CARDINALITY	P	Number of unique values in this level.

Member

The *Member object* represents the basic unit of information that's summarized in a particular data cube. To make matters somewhat confusing, there's only one Member object in the type library, but it's used in several different ways. Here it's a child of the Level object; in a few pages you'll meet it again as a child of the Position object.

You can think of a Member as the building block of a cube. Members in a Level are the different values that that particular level can take on. To retrieve the information on a member, just retrieve it from the Level's Members collection, as in this code from the Member button of the frmObjects sample in the ADOMDSamples project:

```
Private Sub cmdMember_Click()

    Dim cat As New ADOMD.Catalog
    Dim mbr As ADOMD.Member
    Dim prp As ADODB.Property

    Screen.MousePointer = vbHourglass
    cat.ActiveConnection = "Provider=MSOLAP.1; " & _
     "Integrated Security=SSPI;Data Source=BEAVER;" & _
     "Initial Catalog=FoodMart;"
    Set mbr = cat.CubeDefs(0).Dimensions(0). _
     Hierarchies(0).Levels(1).Members(0)
    With lboProperties
        .Clear
        .AddItem "Caption: " & mbr.Caption
        .AddItem "ChildCount: " & mbr.ChildCount
        .AddItem "Description: " & mbr.Description
        .AddItem "LevelDepth: " & mbr.LevelDepth
        .AddItem "LevelName: " & mbr.LevelName
        .AddItem "Name: " & mbr.Name
        .AddItem "Type: " & mbr.Type
        .AddItem "UniqueName: " & mbr.UniqueName
        For Each prp In mbr.Properties
            .AddItem mbr.Name & ": " & prp.Value
        Next prp
    End With
    Screen.MousePointer = vbDefault

End Sub
```

The MSOLAP provider doesn't add any provider-specific properties to a Member object in a Level. Table 24.5 lists the intrinsic properties for such a Member object.

TABLE 24.5: Properties of a Member in a Level

Property	Type	Description
Caption	I	Label to use for the member.
ChildCount	I	Number of child members of this member.

TABLE 24.5 continued: Properties of a Member in a Level

PROPERTY	TYPE	DESCRIPTION
Description	I	Description of the member.
LevelDepth	I	Number of levels between the parent Level of this member and the top of the hierarchy.
LevelName	I	Parent Level of this member.
Name	I	Name of the member.
Type	I	Type of this member. Possible values are adMemberRegular (for an instance of a business entity), adMemberMeasure (for a summarized value), adMemberFormula (for a calculated member), adMemberAll (for the "All" member of a Hierarchy), and adMemberUnknown.
UniqueName	I	Unambiguous name for the member.

Members in Levels are recursive. That is, a Member returns a ChildCount property, and if that count is greater than zero, it has a Children collection of Member objects of its own. This is the information that's used in progressive drilldown and filtering of a Dimension. The children of a Member of a Level are those Members of the next Level in the Hierarchy whose parent in the original data is the parent Member. If you think this is confusing, you're right. Figure 24.4 may make this a bit clearer. Note that all the children of the members in the level "Store Country" are themselves members in the level "Store State."

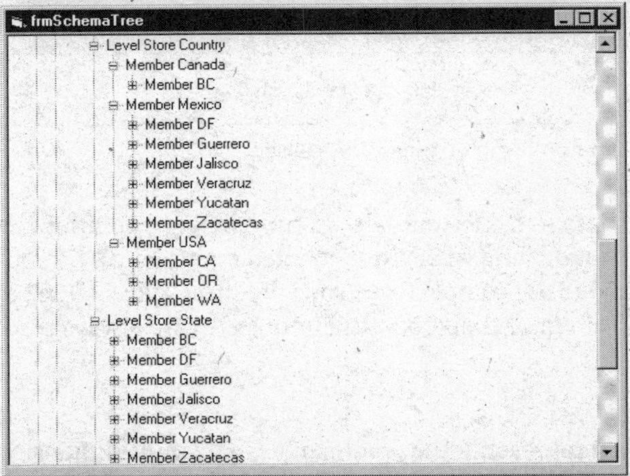

FIGURE 24.4: A portion of the object hierarchy of the Sales cube

NOTE

Figure 24.4 is drawn from the frmSchemaTree sample form in the ADOMDSamples project. Just about all the code behind this form, which allows you to see graphically the relation between the ADO MD schema objects, is TreeView bookkeeping code that won't be reviewed here.

Data Objects

In addition to the schema objects, ADO MD defines a selection of objects that you can use to return the data from a Cube. Just as a relational database gives rise to recordsets, a multidimensional database gives rise to cellsets. ADO MD defines a set of objects that you can use to create and explore these cellsets. Figure 24.5 displays some of the data from the sample Sales cube on a Hierarchical FlexGrid on a Visual Basic form (this is frmCellset from the ADOMDSamples project).

frmCellset

```
SELECT NEST([Promotion Media].MEMBERS,
[Gender].MEMBERS) ON ROWS,
NEST([Education Level].MEMBERS,
[Marital Status].MEMBERS) ON COLUMNS
FROM Sales
```

Populate Grid

		All Education Level			Bachelors Degree			Graduate Degree		
		All Marital St	M	S	All Marital St	M	S	All Marital St	M	S
All Media	All Gender	266,773.00	135,032.00	131,741.00	68,186.00	34,667.00	33,519.00	35,248.00	17,622.00	17,
	F	131,558.00	67,942.00	63,616.00	34,637.00	18,208.00	16,429.00	16,718.00	9,276.00	7,
	M	135,215.00	67,090.00	68,125.00	33,549.00	16,459.00	17,090.00	18,530.00	8,346.00	10,
Bulk Mail	All Gender	4,320.00	2,049.00	2,271.00	959.00	397.00	562.00	620.00	328.00	
	F	2,111.00	1,016.00	1,095.00	527.00	234.00	293.00	196.00	111.00	
	M	2,209.00	1,033.00	1,176.00	432.00	163.00	269.00	424.00	217.00	
Cash Regist	All Gender	6,697.00	3,130.00	3,567.00	1,847.00	813.00	1,034.00	762.00	318.00	
	F	3,266.00	1,570.00	1,696.00	956.00	461.00	495.00	363.00	155.00	
	M	3,431.00	1,560.00	1,871.00	891.00	352.00	539.00	399.00	163.00	
Daily Paper	All Gender	7,738.00	4,179.00	3,559.00	2,091.00	1,293.00	798.00	1,053.00	596.00	
	F	3,687.00	2,097.00	1,590.00	1,060.00	714.00	346.00	390.00	214.00	
	M	4,051.00	2,082.00	1,969.00	1,031.00	579.00	452.00	663.00	382.00	
Daily Paper,	All Gender	6,891.00	3,319.00	3,572.00	1,772.00	904.00	868.00	831.00	418.00	
	F	3,374.00	1,623.00	1,751.00	834.00	419.00	415.00	358.00	224.00	
	M	3,517.00	1,696.00	1,821.00	938.00	485.00	453.00	473.00	194.00	

FIGURE 24.5: Data from a multidimensional cellset

Because the data in a cube consists of summary information, it's never editable (we're not dealing with write-enabled cubes here). So you don't have to worry about the complexities you sometimes face when editing recordsets. Cellsets (and their constituent objects) are always read-only.

Cellset

The *Cellset object* represents the results of a single multidimensional query. It's analogous to a Recordset object in regular ADO. A cellset has a source, just as a recordset does. However, where the source of a recordset is a SQL statement, the source of a cellset is a Multidimensional Expression (MDX) statement. MDX is a set of extensions to SQL designed to capture the selection, drilldown, and filtering qualities of multidimensional data manipulation. The basic idea is that an MDX statement specifies a series of axes and a cube to select them from. For instance, the MDX statement that led to the information in Figure 24.5 is:

```
SELECT
NEST([Promotion Media].MEMBERS,
[Gender].MEMBERS) ON ROWS,
NEST([Education Level].MEMBERS,
[Marital Status].MEMBERS) ON COLUMNS
FROM Sales
```

This statement specifies a cellset where rows are aggregated first on the Promotion Media dimension and then on the Gender dimension, columns are aggregated first on the Education Level dimension and then on the Marital Status dimension, and all the data is drawn from the cube named Sales.

The frmCellset form in the ADOMDSamples project first opens a cellset and then modifies a Hierarchical FlexGrid to display the contents of the cellset. You can't bind a cellset directly to any other control, because a cellset isn't a recordset (but see the discussion of opening a recordset from a cellset later in this chapter). Instead, data is copied piece by piece from the cellset to the Hierarchical FlexGrid control.

Once you've created a valid MDX statement, opening a cellset is simple:

```
Dim cat As New ADOMD.Catalog
Dim cst As New ADOMD.Cellset

txtSource.Text = "SELECT NEST([Promotion Media].
                  MEMBERS, " & _
 vbCrLf & "[Gender].MEMBERS) ON ROWS, " & _
 vbCrLf & "NEST([Education Level].MEMBERS, " & _
 vbCrLf & "[Marital Status].MEMBERS) ON COLUMNS" & _
 vbCrLf & "FROM Sales"
' Get the data into the cellset
cat.ActiveConnection = "Provider=MSOLAP.1; " & _
 "Integrated Security=SSPI;Data Source=BEAVER;" & _
 "Initial Catalog=FoodMart;"
cst.Source = txtSource.Text
Set cst.ActiveConnection = cat.ActiveConnection
cst.Open
```

Although the Cellset does not have a default collection, it's most easily thought of as a collection of cells—and, in fact, the Item method of the Cellset returns a Cell object. A cellset can have more than two axes. The Item method takes as many arguments as the number of axes contained in the cellset. So, in the case of the sample shown here, you need to provide two arguments (row and column) to retrieve a cell from a cellset.

NOTE

For the formal syntax of MDX statements, refer to the ADO MD documentation in the MDAC SDK.

Cell

The *Cell object* represents one piece of information from a single multidimensional query. It's analogous to a Field object in regular ADO. However, there's a major difference due to the fact that cellsets can have multiple axes and have no concept of "current record." In a recordset, you first navigate to the record of interest by (for example) a series of calls to MoveNext, and then retrieve the Field of interest. In a cellset, you navigate directly to the cell of interest by specifying its position along all the axes in the cellset.

In the frmCellset form of the ADOMDSamples project, a two-dimensional loop transfers cell values directly from the cellset to the Hierarchical FlexGrid control:

```
' Now iterate through the cellset and transfer it
' to the grid
For intCol = 0 To cst.Axes(0).Positions.Count - 1
    For intRow = 0 To cst.Axes(1).Positions.Count - 1
        With fgResults
            .Col = intCol + .FixedCols
            .Row = intRow + .FixedRows
            .Text = cst(intCol, intRow).FormattedValue
        End With
    Next intRow
Next intCol
```

This code relies on the cellset having only two axes and retrieves cells by calling the (default) Item method of the cellset object. If there were three axes, the line setting properties would perhaps read:

```
.Text = cst(intPage, intCol, intRow).FormattedValue
```

The Cell object has three properties of interest:

- Value holds the value of the summary for the cell in question.

- FormattedValue holds the value with server-side formatting.
- Ordinal holds a number uniquely identifying the cell within the cellset.

Different data providers may also add properties of their own to the Cell object.

Axis

The *Axis object* represents one of the dimensions that you've actually chosen in constructing a Cellset. For example, consider the sample MDX statement we used a few pages ago:

```
SELECT
NEST([Promotion Media].MEMBERS,
[Gender].MEMBERS) ON ROWS,
NEST([Education Level].MEMBERS,
[Marital Status].MEMBERS) ON COLUMNS
FROM Sales
```

This statement gives rise to two Axis objects (the collection is named Axes), one to represent the rows and one to represent the columns. Axis(0) includes the column information (Education Level and Marital Status) while Axis(1) holds the row information (Promotion Media and Gender). In the frmCellset sample, the DimensionCount property of the Axis object is used to determine how many non-scrollable rows the grid will contain:

```
.FixedCols = cst.Axes(1).DimensionCount
For intCol = 0 To .FixedCols - 1
    .MergeCol(intCol) = True
Next intCol
.FixedRows = cst.Axes(0).DimensionCount
For intRow = 0 To .FixedRows - 1
    .MergeRow(intRow) = True
Next intRow
```

Name and DimensionCount are the only two intrinsic properties of the Axis object. However, the Axis object is also the parent of the Positions collection, which is an important part of properly labeling your multidimensional data.

Position and Member

The *Position object* provides information about one of the values along an Axis. You'll seldom do anything directly with the Position object. However, Position objects each have a Members collection that contains information on which exact values make up that point on the Axis. For example, in an axis consisting of Promotion Media and Gender, one of the Position objects would contain two Member objects, Bulk Mail and All Gender, representing the values of the particular dimensions making up that position.

In the frmCellset sample in the ADOMDSamples project, these Members (which should not be confused with the Member objects found when iterating through the schema, as discussed earlier) are used to fill in the information in the fixed cells of the Hierarchical FlexGrid:

```
With fgResults
    For intRow = 0 To cst.Axes(1).Positions.Count - 1
        For intCol = 0 To .FixedCols - 1
            .Row = intRow + .FixedRows
            .Col = intCol
            .Text = cst.Axes(1).Positions(intRow). _
             Members(intCol).Caption
        Next intCol
    Next intRow
    For intCol = 0 To cst.Axes(0).Positions.Count - 1
        For intRow = 0 To .FixedRows - 1
            .Row = intRow
            .Col = intCol + .FixedCols
            .Text = cst.Axes(0).Positions(intCol). _
             Members(intRow).Caption
        Next intRow
    Next intCol
End With
```

Additional ADO MD Techniques

ADO MD, of course, is not a completely independent object model. It's integrated with the ADO object model. There are two ways in which you can use ADO and ADO MD together. First, it's possible to get schema information from a multidimensional data source into a recordset, rather than examining it hierarchically. Second, you can "flatten" a cellset into a recordset and use it like any other read-only ADO recordset.

WARNING

The integration, alas, isn't perfect. While you can create a Data Environment or a Data Link based on the MSOLAP OLE DB provider, you won't find any useful information in either one. Data Environments and Data Links are unable to retrieve MSOLAP information.

Using OpenSchema to List Objects

You saw earlier in this chapter how to use the ADO MD object model to drill down into schema information. The ADO Connection object includes an OpenSchema method to retrieve generalized schema information. ADO MD extends this OpenSchema method by providing six additional constants:

- adSchemaCubes
- adSchemaDimensions
- adSchemaHierarchies
- adSchemaLevels
- adSchemaMeasures
- adSchemeMembers

Figure 24.6 shows the frmSchema form from the ADOMDSamples project. In this particular case, it's displaying the contents of a recordset containing all the Dimensions to be found on a particular server.

The code that generated this particular recordset is:

```
Private Sub cmdDimensions_Click()

    Dim cnn As New ADODB.Connection
    Dim rst As ADODB.Recordset

    Screen.MousePointer = vbHourglass
    fgResults.Clear
    cnn.Open "Provider=MSOLAP.1; " & _
     "Integrated Security=SSPI;Data Source=BEAVER;" & _
     "Initial Catalog=FoodMart;"
    Set rst = cnn.OpenSchema(adSchemaDimensions)
    Set fgResults.DataSource = rst
    fgResults.Refresh
    Screen.MousePointer = vbDefault

End Sub
```

As you can see, the only multidimensional elements to this code snippet are the connection string used (via the MSOLAP provider) and the adSchemaDimensions constant that tells the OpenSchema method how to populate its recordset.

frmSchema

Cubes | Dimensions | Hierarchies | Levels | Measures | Members

DIMENSION_CAPT	ORDINAL	TYPE	CARDINALITY	DEFAULT_HIERARCHY	DESCRIPTION
Customers	6	3	10407	[Customers]	
Education Level	7	3	6	[Education Level]	
Gender	8	3	3	[Gender]	
Marital Status	9	3	3	[Marital Status]	
Measures	0	2	5	[Measures]	
Product	3	3	2256	[Product]	
Promotion Media	4	3	15	[Promotion Media]	
Promotions	5	3	52	[Promotions]	
Store	1	3	61	[Store]	
Store Size in SQFT	10	3	1	[Store Size in SQFT]	
Store Type	11	3	1	[Store Type]	
Time	2	1	34	[Time]	
Yearly Income	12	3	9	[Yearly Income]	
Measures	0	2	7	[Measures]	
Product	3	3	2256	[Product]	
Store	1	3	61	[Store]	
Store Size in SQFT	4	3	1	[Store Size in SQFT]	
Store Type	5	3	1	[Store Type]	

FIGURE 24.6: Recordset with Dimension information

The OpenSchema method is most useful when you want to get an overall view of the contents of an entire server, because it lists all the objects regardless of which cube they belong to. If you're trying to determine information about a particular cube, you're probably better off drilling down through the ADO MD object hierarchy.

WARNING

Because the OpenSchema recordsets contain information on all the cubes on a server, they can grow quite large. In particular, opening a recordset of all Member information on a server with many cubes is likely to be a very slow operation.

Opening a Recordset from a Cellset

If you like, you can "flatten" a cellset into a recordset. You do so by creating a Recordset object, but using a multidimensional connection string and an MDX statement as the source, rather than using a SQL statement. You can see an example of this technique in frmRecordset in the ADOMDSamples project, shown in Figure 24.7.

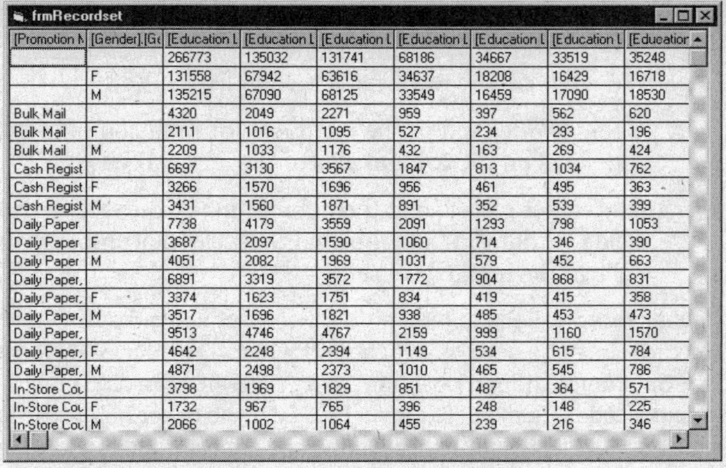

frmRecordset

[Promotion M	[Gender].[Ge	[Education L	[Education L	[Education L	[Education L	[Education L	[Education L	[Educatior
		266773	135032	131741	68186	34667	33519	35248
	F	131558	67942	63616	34637	18208	16429	16718
	M	135215	67090	68125	33549	16459	17090	18530
Bulk Mail		4320	2049	2271	959	397	562	620
Bulk Mail	F	2111	1016	1095	527	234	293	196
Bulk Mail	M	2209	1033	1176	432	163	269	424
Cash Regist		6697	3130	3567	1847	813	1034	762
Cash Regist	F	3266	1570	1696	956	461	495	363
Cash Regist	M	3431	1560	1871	891	352	539	399
Daily Paper		7738	4179	3559	2091	1293	798	1053
Daily Paper	F	3687	2097	1590	1060	714	346	390
Daily Paper	M	4051	2082	1969	1031	579	452	663
Daily Paper,		6891	3319	3572	1772	904	868	831
Daily Paper,	F	3374	1623	1751	834	419	415	358
Daily Paper,	M	3517	1696	1821	938	485	453	473
Daily Paper,		9513	4746	4767	2159	999	1160	1570
Daily Paper,	F	4642	2248	2394	1149	534	615	784
Daily Paper,	M	4871	2498	2373	1010	465	545	786
In-Store Cou		3798	1969	1829	851	487	364	571
In-Store Cou	F	1732	967	765	396	248	148	225
In-Store Cou	M	2066	1002	1064	455	239	216	346

FIGURE 24.7: Recordset based on multidimensional data

The code that generated this recordset is simple and doesn't explicitly use any ADO MD objects. Instead, it takes direct advantage of the MSOLAP provider to return the recordset of interest:

```
Private Sub Form_Load()

    Dim cnn As New ADODB.Connection
    Dim rst As New ADODB.Recordset

    Screen.MousePointer = vbHourglass
    fgResults.Clear
    cnn.Open "Provider=MSOLAP.1; " & _
     "Integrated Security=SSPI;Data Source=BEAVER;" & _
     "Initial Catalog=FoodMart;"
    rst.Source = "SELECT NEST([Promotion Media].
                 MEMBERS, " & _
     vbCrLf & "[Gender].MEMBERS) ON ROWS, " & _
     vbCrLf & "NEST([Education Level].MEMBERS, " & _
     vbCrLf & "[Marital Status].MEMBERS) ON COLUMNS" & _
     vbCrLf & "FROM Sales"
    rst.ActiveConnection = cnn
    rst.Open
    Set fgResults.DataSource = rst
    fgResults.Refresh
    Screen.MousePointer = vbDefault

End Sub
```

The provider follows three rules in creating the recordset:

1. There is one row in the recordset for each combination of members on the row axis of the implied cellset.

2. There is one field in the recordset for each combination of members on the column axis of the implied cellset.

3. The values returned at the intersection of these records and fields are derived from the unformatted Value property of the cells in the implied cellset.

The major advantage to returning a recordset instead of a cellset is that the recordset can be used in any context where a regular ADO recordset is valid. For example, it can be bound to a grid control (as in this example) or even passed back over HTTP via RDS. On the other hand, the formatting of the recordset is uninspiring, and the concatenated field names can be difficult to work with. If you're developing an interface that allows people to work with multidimensional data interactively, you're almost certainly better off using cellsets rather than recordsets.

Summary

This concludes our coverage of OLAP. In this chapter, we covered the ADO MD object model whose objects are used to work with both the schema and data of a multidimensional data source. We also looked at how to use these objects to access multidimensional data from within Visual Basic.

This final chapter also concludes this book in which we have attempted to provide Visual Basic developers with the information they need to work with SQL Server. We started out with the database basics and how to use SQL. We then looked at ADO and how to access data from within Visual Basic. Web applications are standard now, so we covered how to access databases from the Web and showed you how to implement the techniques from this section to build an online store. We also covered the SQL-DMO, SQL-NS, and DTS object models to show you how to work with SQL Server data and objects from Visual Basic. The final section gave you the concepts behind OLAP and made the jump to working with multidimensional data.

INDEX

Note to the reader: Bolded page references indicate definitions and main discussions of a topic. *Italicized* page references indicate illustrations.

NUMBERS AND SYMBOLS

A

B

D

E

F

G

H

I

J

K

L

M

N

O

P

Q

S

T

U

V

W

X

Y

Z